The Inheritance

Awakening

Lenore Kieseling

ISBN: 0692340424
ISBN 13: 9780692340424
Library of Congress Control Number: 2014921311
Bluelight Books, Summerville SC

For my father, my teacher.
An inspiration in individuality.
An artist, an astronomer, a scientist.
A thinker.
My link to my Celtic heritage.
A man who, in another time, may have been
A Druid scholar.
And in this lifetime, was simply
The smartest man I know.

For my Patty with her loving eyes, easy smile and generous heart.

And for my Ryan who taught me important things.

My loves, I feel the hollow space in my life where you used to be but my heart is filled when you visit me in my dreams.

I know I'll see you all again.

Preface

This book is completed with help and support from a generous many and with serendipitous moments that solidified my belief that I was meant to write this tale. I give abundant thanks to my family members and friends without whom there would be no story: First, to my husband Walter, who took on the family financial responsibility for more than a few years so I could focus wholly on research and writing and who celebrated every minor success with me along the way. To my sister Nancy, who traveled to Ireland with me, gave me unlimited information on astrology and the Tarot and also tolerated getting me through the first rough and scratchy chapters until I believed I could actually do this. To my son Lucas who, bless his generous heart, called me an author from the very first day I sat at my computer to write. Profound thanks to my father Patrick, who gave to me my love for words and to my mother Barbara who rescued me by gifting me a new PC that was actually manufactured in this century when my old laptop decided to hold the first fourteen chapters hostage. To Patty and Julie who sprinkled confidence when I needed it, let me cry when I needed it, made me laugh when I needed it and kept me sane, (sort of). Thanks to Liane for her help in all things technical but mostly for her unflagging faith in me. And thanks to Eric, the Norwegian, who taught me how to make mead. I must also give thanks to all those nameless people along the way who were kind enough to answer my endless questions on just about everything. It's been a journey in finding myself and my spiritual place in this world.

While embarking on the adventures of novel writing, I made discoveries along the way I hadn't anticipated. I discovered days and sometimes weeks of mental dry spells. Every dry spell marked with self-doubt and dotted with temptation to go get a "paying job" eventually came to an end. Conversely, there were periods of gold rushes of research information and inspiration so vast that I boggled myself as to how I could bend and twist my story to fit all the interesting and juicy nuggets into the story of one family. Sadly, I discovered that not every fact could go into the tale.

I identified with the main character, Lee, who sat for hours in the back of a book store, so totally absorbed in her research that she lost all track of time. My struggle was to end the research at some point and begin to weave the material into a feasible tale. The hard thing was to make the story mesh with actual facts and history. What made that infinitely easier is that with magic, anything is possible.

This book can't be strictly classified as historical fiction, fantasy, or auto-biographical, but much of the tale is based on actual personal experiences, family facts, names, history and dates. Some minor details have been changed to suit the purposes of the novel but the family history is largely written in truth and the fictional tale is woven, to incorporate it as such. For example, my father's birthday is February 1st, not the typical date of Imbolc, February 2nd just as my mother's birthday is March 19th, rather than of the Spring Equinox on March 20th, however if one contemplates that all Celtic festivals were celebrated on the eve of the festival, the night before, as the sun sets, the dates fit quite well. Lucas, my son was not actually born in the year 2000, but his birth time was at exactly 9:25 pm, the precise time between Gemini and Cancer in the year 2000; minor but important changes.

Cath's story of the porcelain china pattern dishes is actually that of my parents. My father gave the set to my mother as a wedding gift, and I now enjoy the very dishes as my own. My paternal grandfather actually was from County Cork and did speak with the Irish accent and kept the burning barrel with holes poked in it, but I never knew my paternal grandmother who died before my birth. In truth, her character was based on an amalgam of my father's three sisters, my aunts, Mae, Peg and Celia who always had a kind word, a smile and some tasty tid-bit when I visited their house, right next door just as it is described early in the story. Grandma's character was developed through my father's recounting of stories about when my grandmother would tell tales of the "wee folk" and seeing bonfires of the "old ways" on the countryside when she was a girl in County Kerry. On the other side of the family, my maternal grandmother's name was Sigrid Hook and she always brought with her the mystery of the Yule Tomtien (Swedish Santa) during the holidays.

The imaginative magical parts of my childhood were about as close to truth as I remember them: elf hunting with my sister, the mirror world, and magical paper key. So, to my family, if your character in print seems to deviate in some way from how you know yourself to be, I claim artistic license to suit the story and mean neither harm nor insult. And to the readers, in case you're wondering, some names have been changed to protect anyone from that which they feel they may need protecting.

The weaving of this tale incorporated scads of research information regarding the Iron Age, mining and smelting, smith craft, Astrology, The Tarot, Pagan religions, spell work, Irish Celtic and Nordic mythology, Christian history, Druids, Gnosticism, the Bible, fairytales, cartography and archaeology of Ireland and Western Europe, actual occurrences of lunar and solar eclipses, the meaning of names based on country of origin, basics of multiple languages including Irish

Gaelic, Italian, Swedish, and German, growing plants and healing plants of Ireland, early Celtic construction and dress, fabric weaving, history of ring stones and lay lines, bog men and women, the works of Edgar Allen Poe and extensive research on the Gundestrup cauldron to name just a few. If there is one immutable fact about this work, despite all the actual details, real-life characters and historical and geographical foundation, it is that the work is fiction. I have taken actual archaeological sites and artifacts and taken liberty with their dates of origin to suit the timeline of the story. For example, the bog man found in 2003 near Croghan Hill, Ireland, upon whom I based the mythological character Briciu's death, was in reality carbon dated to have died between 363 and 175 B.C.; the oldest of the dates, 363 B.C., being right on the cusp of the Iron Age following the Bronze Age might suit the story which is set during the time of the Iron age, however, The Tuatha de Danann, the clan of the Goddess Danu, were said to have come to Lough Corrib, Galway during the Bronze Age as early as 2000 B.C. Flawed though some of the facts or timelines may be, I hope the flaws are minor enough that they will be forgiven.

At first, I tried to write the book purely without any religious point of view or perspective but found myself consistently coming to the same position over and again so I gave up the struggle and allowed myself to follow my heart. Simply put, I think religion, or in search of a better word, spirituality is a personal journey, which cannot be directed or dictated by any other than the self. But, each individual must sincerely quest for their own true faith and once they've found it, only he or she can determine how they choose to manifest their process or journey.

So whether you are a lover of magic, on a spiritual journey, or simply seeking entertainment in a densely woven tale, I truly hope you are rewarded.

Table of Contents

Introduction
The Awakening

There are over 35 million people in the United States alone whose heritage, at least in part, is of Irish decent. This is almost nine times the population of Ireland itself. The greatest percentage of the millions who now live in America is in some way due to the flight of their ancestors to America to escape the English tyranny in the 1700's and the famine during the mid to late 1800's and then for a generation or two after to escape abject poverty.

The first generation of famine refugees to arrive here on the eastern shores of America in New York, Boston and Salem, MA, Newport, RI, Philadelphia, PA, Savannah, GA, were embroiled in the struggle for survival.

There was no looking back with a sense of loss for the old ways at that time, there was a forward rush toward a new beginning with a tenacity that has insured the survival of the Irish through many adaptations. Throughout history, it appeared that the Irish people had been slowly losing their sense of self through invasions from many lands, the influence of Rome, the coming of a new religion, and under the tyranny of foreign rule for centuries.

By the 19th century, the Irish Celtic identity had been squelched in all aspects of what made them who they were. The language they spoke, the way they worshiped, the music they played, and the songs they sang were all outlawed at one time or another. The very land on which they lived, Irish land, was not their own. But what could not be wholly governed was this resilient people.

So when they arrived on American shores they strove to feed their families, find work, and forge a better life for the next generation. During this period, there was no time for mourning for the loss of heritage. There was no conscious keeping of the old ways or a thought or reverence for the generations before.

Gone was the time when the Irish, the Celts, would have looked to their honored and revered ancestors for the guidance as to how to survive and take back their own lands; and again rule through king and clan. The immigrants knew turmoil, but also relief for an opportunity to be established away from starvation, poverty and tyranny. So they did not look to their ancestors and the old ways, strength and magic, buried and long forgotten...sleeping. They did not feel the force of their history riding on the tides with them as they sailed toward their future. They did not remember the tales of the Keeper for the Tuatha De Danann who journeyed as the first sacred traveler. They had no recollection of the hero Laoghaire, whose fierceness of determination, once harnessed in his blood, brought forward the magic of the days of old. They did not recall the stories carefully recounted of the dousing of the fire that kindled the magic and how its ember of the knowing was secreted underground.

But now comes the time for a harkening to a calling that reaches from far back beyond the reign of the English, the Christians and even the Romans and the Mils. When a soul tenses to the call from the time of auld that strums a familiar chord within. It calls first to the few, like a distant melody that dances illusively in the back of one's head just out of reach. Theirs is a frustration that one should know the song, be able to sing it loud and well, but can't quite grasp the familiar tune. It is from whence that call comes, the very brink of time and history that the ember is stoked and the fire grows. It is the time of the awakening.

I am born of those immigrants. I am of the clan of Laoghaire. I am captured by my heritage and am set once again to travel the road. My ear is tuned to the song of history. I am beckoned, at last, and called to tell my tale.

Part I: The Prophecy

1

The Cottage

Half-opened eyes scanned the unfamiliar room. Linen sheets crackled over the sturdy mattress as I rolled. I had just been somewhere but now I couldn't quite remember. Surfacing, I struggled to reach the top of consciousness. *Where the hell am I?*

"Dreaming." I mumbled into the pillow and wiped the drool from the corner of my mouth. After a few blinks, "Ireland." I mumbled again and dropped my lazy head back on the pillow. *The light is wrong. What time is it?* I gave a one-eyed glance at the clock. "You've got to be kidding me! It can't be after 11:00 o'clock!" Inwardly I cursed. *Can't get past this jet lag. Three days and I still can't wake up even to the alarm.* I rolled onto my back and stretched from fingertip to toes thinking it felt so good not to have to get up for kids or classes or anything involving duty. "I could sleep all day." I managed to say through the stretch. *I'll probably sleep my whole vacation away at this rate.* This last thought got me moving.

The cozy, homey scent of the peat fire drifted through the cottage we'd rented for the month. Moving toward the edge of the bed with a groan I thought, *I want to go back.* I was tempted to roll over to drift off again. *Back where?* I was dreaming about being somewhere. Such strange dreams I have in this place. So strong, vivid, urgent but I can't seem to remember any of them. The smell of the peat always put me in mind of the dreams I couldn't quite recall.

Zombie-like sluggishness was only one of the changes I'd notice in myself since we arrived in Ireland. I heaved my body upright in the warm cocoon. "All right then O'Leary, up and out." *O'Leary*: my maiden name. I haven't thought of myself that way since I was married over 15 years ago. My sister, Nora, has been married some 20 odd years with a Scottish name by marriage. But since we arrived here, people refer to us using our maiden names as if it were a title, *The O'Leary Sisters*. Must be an Irish thing. So I guess it's only natural to think of ourselves this way again too.

I flung my feet over the side of the solid double bed, pulled on some socks to protect my feet from the cold slate floor and followed the kitchen noises to find Nora perched at the sensible kitchen table having tea and toast with jam and fruit. She looked at me with a 'well it's about time' look, but I could tell she hadn't been up very long herself, still in her cotton nightgown, fluffy robe and wearing glasses rather than her contacts. She had faithfully prepared some breakfast for me too, trusting that I'd wake sometime before the day was totally behind us.

"At this rate," I grumbled at Nora, "I'll be lucky to go back home with any memories of Ireland at all, never mind enough information to write a decent paper."

The peat fire was smoldering in the iron stove that had been added to the oversized hearth in the renovated, 200-year old cottage. We had been fortunate to find such a rental in the height of Ireland's tourist season but as many things happened for us regarding this trip, it just happened! Like a circumstance with a will of its own, as soon as we'd decided to make the trip to Ireland, schedules cleared, money appeared, and for me, the dreaded child-care was miraculously a non-issue so that nothing stood in our way.

I came to Ireland to do research for a dissertation I'd been constructing on ancient Celtic customs, traditions and rituals based on belief in gods and magic as preserved in the lore that had been passed down through hundreds of generations by word of mouth from as early as the Bronze Age; sort of a pre-Christian verbal bible that survived to current day society.

Nora, a knowledgeable astrologer and consultant had her own research to do on this trip. For us, this was to be a working vacation, involving exploration and discovery. I plan to do research and conduct interviews with local people on their knowledge of customs and traditions, myths and legends connected with ancient archeological sites. My goal was to document the historical basis and chronology of how the ancient ways are still active in modern society. But even more daunting, I aimed to connect these customs masquerading as Christian traditions, with some of the folklore and myths of Ireland and Western Europe. I hoped to prove that there is some factual basis for the myths and legends and that they are, as part of the oral traditions, metaphors of a sort that teach actual history with lessons hidden beneath the mythological tales.

Sligo, a town about 100 miles north of where we're staying in County Clare, is reputed to be rich with the ancient history I sought. A coastal community on the northwestern shore of Ireland, the area is seemingly untouched by the modern changes taking place in the country. As with some of the islands off the coast, the old language is still the primary one spoken there, as if the essence of the ancient archaeological sites in Sligo have captured and hidden the Old Ways, preserving them like a secret, but as the force of the ancient knowledge seeps out of the stones, sea and sky, evidence of its existence is proofed in the ancient tongue of the people.

"How'd you sleep?" Nora asked in a half sarcastic tone as she eyed me over the kettle, pouring me a cup of tea.

She looked different to me somehow. Maybe it was the jet lag, or too much sleep but my perception of things had taken on a surreal quality since I'd come to Ireland. She was probably just as tired as I was, and that could have been the reason, but it seemed that her hair, normally shiny chestnut brown, waist length, and very curly, was a bit dull, almost gray. For a moment I thought she looked very much like our maternal grandmother, a woman who, when she died, was 51 years older than Nora is now. I rubbed the sleep from my eyes and looked again. Nope, just Nora. Her eyes the same as ever were bright, deep blue orbs that hearkened back to some Celtic warrior or queen in times long past. These were eyes that could catch one in an unwavering stare and strip them naked of all defenses just as a hawk calculates its prey, yet at the same time they are exactly the smiling Irish eyes that the song speaks of, ever youthful and kind.

"Like the dead." I answered. "I thought we were getting up early to take the ride to Sligo today." I half-heartedly tried to sound accusatory, needing to blame someone for not getting me up earlier and not wanting it to be myself. I was a bit preoccupied with trying to recapture my dream that seemed to be about something important but it was like chasing a firefly: now you see it, now you don't. "It's too late to start out to Sligo now." I said, sipping my tea.

Back in America, a 100-mile trip would not seem impossible given a mid-day starting point but we weren't in America. One thing we had not anticipated about Ireland is that everything moves at a much slower pace, travel-time included. It's not that there is excessive traffic, quite the contrary. The roads are almost deserted at times. It just seems that the roads are so narrow that one has to drive more cautiously to maneuver without running off into a ditch. But that's really not the complete story. It seems, when traveling in Ireland, that the roads are designed to confound a traveler rather than get them from point A to point B. The maps we had, were often missing roads necessary to travel from one point to another. And the roads that actually did exist on the map, when found in reality, were labeled with anywhere from 10 to 20 signs on the signpost, so we had to stop the car to refer to directions and see if any of the street or town names on the signpost matched where we were supposed to be heading. Not only were the maps and roads difficult, when we stopped to ask directions the language barrier became a comical but frustrating issue. Although both parties were speaking the English language, it was near impossible to decipher what the natives were saying as they spoke with the country-side Irish accent and us with our clipped, high speed, Boston accent, missing any evidence of the letter "r," roadside instructions could only be counted on to get us hopelessly lost rather than just lost.

Since I was doing the driving, I contemplated the possibility that we'd actually make it to Sligo, then calculated the 'When in Ireland Rule:' Figure however long you think it's going to take and double it. I came to an executive decision as I raised my steaming cup.

"Let's do that another day. Why don't we just get in the car and see what's around locally."

Content to have what at least passed for a plan, I hoped Nora was satisfied to let me enjoy my breakfast for a bit before we had to get moving.

Ugh! I thought. *Tea. Who the hell drinks tea?*

"What's the matter?" Nora asked. She'd picked up on my distaste for the tea. I tried to be grateful for the drink and not to let my true feelings show on my face.

"Nothing. Tea's hot. Just needs a little milk...and sugar." *And coffee grounds*. I thought to myself. This entire part of the world is obsessed with tea. It was one of the things about Ireland that I just couldn't get used to. I want my coffee. I want it strong, and I want it now. Tea is just too timid a drink for me. I would pay a fortune for just one cup of real coffee but I couldn't seem to get a decent cup anywhere, one that was actually brewed a deep rich brown, with an aroma to match. Not the fake, freeze-dried, amber colored water that passed for coffee around here. No wonder I can't wake up. I feel like I'm sleep walking half the time . . . *and sleeping the other half!* Resigned, for now, I drank my tea with a sigh. It was probably the only dose of caffeine I was guaranteed today. If I was going to be awake enough to hunt down the local magic and myth, I needed to be on my toes.

———

Due to the nature of my family, and my upbringing, since I was a young girl I have felt secure in the knowledge that not only does magic exist, but that I play a part in the world of magic. I think this is so because I lived my childhood in a family that did not dismiss or disregard magical happenings and circumstance as just coincidence. We accepted and allowed magic into our lives and perhaps saw the magical possibilities within the mundane: a budding tree, a gust of wind, light dancing on a lake or blazing stars the night sky. I was drawn to magical stories, movies, and books. Tales of the fairy, and fantasy never waned in my fascination with them even into my adulthood. All of the books I recall reading as a girl had some element of magic from my first library book entitled, 'Which Witch is Which?' to my choice of movies and books in adulthood. The standard fairytales were always a point of fascination for me and it was this lifelong fascination that brought me to do research on their origins. This opened up a world that was like a coming home for me because so many of those fairytales were similar to the mythic stories told by my father and grandparents. I began the process of earning a philosophy degree in Celtic Studies, a field of investigation that had ultimately brought me to Ireland in search of its magical history and my part in its legacy of magic, myth and lore.

As children, my sister Nora and I would spend hours upon hours in the local woods or at the pond hunting for elves. Though we never actually saw any, it seemed as if time stood still for us when we created these games. And truly, those woods were magical forests for us. Whether spawned of our imagination or created by the sheer force of belief, in those moments, we could feel the power of magic within us and around us and since that time we discovered that we could make *things* happen. We created a bond in childhood that would keep us connected in a way that we find natural, but others find a bit disturbing in that we have a kind of telepathy as sisters or twins sometimes do. But for us, it's more intensified. We pick up on each other's thoughts and moods to the degree that we often answer questions not actually asked out loud. Some would call this phenomenon psychic ability; we just call it magic. There was no doubt that, when I planned to go on a quest to find the magical history of the ancients, I would choose to once again, go in search of elves, fairies and magic with my sister Nora, one of my three sisters but one closest to me in age and of philosophy.

———

I did not have to search for the uncommon in Ireland; it found me but not in the academic way I'd been anticipating. The time gobbling roads of Ireland and the peculiar taste for tea were only mild inconveniences in the way of unusual occurrences. But since our arrival in Ireland, some deeply strange events had shaken me. Not those coincidental sort of things one sees and says, "Huh! That was weird." But the kind that shocks one to saying, "Did you see that? What the hell was that?" These vivid visions or apparitions came through in Technicolor rather than the comparatively pale feelings or sensations I was used to receiving back home in America. Our cozy cottage was one of the many things that fell into place for us upon coming to Ireland but it was also the scene of the first of some incredible occurrences that had happened since we'd come here.

After a grueling, overnight trans-Atlantic flight beside a fellow who nervously whistled through the entire trip, a four-hour wait for our rental car, and a fun adventure in 'Which road is the right road,' when we finally found our cottage I was struck with a very powerful sense of déjà vu. As we drove the rental car up the long path-like road to our temporary home, we happened upon a scene right off a painting or picture book of Ireland. It was gently raining a mist that put a soft focus on everything. The green of the farmland that surrounded the cottage was the fresh, clean green we only see in early spring back in Massachusetts. The hillside was dotted with livestock and the air even smelt green. The thought occurred to me that I was experiencing some kind of highway hypnosis after flying all night and driving all morning. In that moment, all my senses were standing at attention. Skin raised with the sensation of the sultry mist grazing over it, my nose awoke with the scent of air so clean and wet, my ears registered the sounds of country life absent of mechanical clatter, and the sight of the cottage caused my skin to pucker into little white goose bumps. As we parked the car next to the small home, I knew, I just *knew* where all the rooms in the cottage were situated before I ever entered the cheery front door. I never doubted the knowledge. It was just there in my head as if I'd been here before and was casually returning after a period of absence. But there was nothing casual about the vibrating sense of anticipation I had as I walked toward the vibrant blue door of the cottage.

Just beyond the entrance alcove, the front door opened up to the main living room with open interior rafters and a large stone hearth. I thought to myself, *this used to be the kitchen.* The door immediately off to our left led to a modest bedroom. *There's the mother's room,* my mind said. An infrequent occurrence, but not entirely new to me that I was able to, in addition to sharing thoughts with Nora, mentally pick up tidbits of information, unimportant pieces of cosmic flotsam, or bits and pieces of other peoples' thoughts. This time though, it was not the small, fuzzy transmission I was accustomed to and often ignored until sometime later when the thought made sense having some connection with circumstance. This felt as if someone were standing next to me whispering directly into my head; only it wasn't like they were talking to me, it was as if I just had the knowing of something right there in my brain. I had a strange feeling of vertigo.

Bridey Flynn was a most welcoming, warm-hearted hostess. She stood about 5 feet tall and could have been anywhere between 60 and 75 years old. She was a round, white haired, tiny woman barely five feet tall but one would make no mistake, Bridey ruled the roost. She sized us up with one sweep of her penetrating blue eyes and she told us what was what. The cottage rental business was her livelihood and there'd be no fooling about on her watch. She told us she'd already warned the three brothers, living in another cottage a ways back down the long driveway that we were two American girls and we wouldn't want to be bothered with the likes of them! This was said, I think, as much as a warning to us as it was to them. No fooling around! She took us under her wing and was very protective of us "girls" traveling "alone." I think she was initially a bit suspicious of two women traveling without benefit of our husbands' company. Likely she wanted to make sure our virtue or at least the reputation of her business remained intact.

Once we told her that part of our plans was to visit distant relatives we have in Ireland by the names of O'Leary, Finnegan, and McGillicutty she lost the suspicious veneer and spoke to us in conspiratorial tones about other guests who'd stayed in the cottage and the "goings on" of those "outside the Irish". Once she heard that we were just "foreign born" Irish, she was the first to nominate us as the "O'Leary girls."

Through my sensation of vertigo, I tried to follow the conversation as our hostess told us the history of the cottage.

"The cottage and land has been in me family for many generations." The lilt of her accent had made me warm to her immediately. "'Tis the original cottage for the farm." She pronounced this as fhaarrm. "But we've done it over now, for the visitors. The roof was the thatched kind but due to the insurance on the cottage with the stove, you know, we had to go with the regular roof kind now." She nodded her head toward the stove that contained a snappy fire to greet and warm us after traveling in the constant misty rain for which Ireland is famous.

The cottage had been tastefully renovated to include all the modern conveniences but the renovations had been done to preserve the original quaintness of the countryside cottage. As I observed the room, the smoke started to thicken and Bridey's voice took on an echo like quality and sounded thin and far away.

The room took on a different appearance before my eyes. The lovely renovated cottage with the kitchen addition off the main room and the updated modern bathroom faded as though someone had lowered the lighting to about 20 watts, dimmed, but not completely from view. A much older, smaller, darker room appeared before me. The walls on the hearthside of the room were painted with smoke stains all the way up and onto the ceiling. I could see cast iron pans piled by the giant hearth where there was a large arm over the hearth, which bore the weight of a great rounded, black pot. In the large room by the window with a deep sill overlooking the front pastures was a wood table, covered with a mix of wooden bowls and crock-ware and what appeared to be pewter or tin cups. The modern kitchen was not there at all but replaced with a wall harboring a thin wooden door.

It was as if the old were superimposed upon the new; I could still see the rental cottage but it didn't seem to me that I was actually in the rental cottage, nor was I actually in the old style cottage, but in both at the same time peering into the other. I felt as though I was looking at the same room, from two different points of view but removed from both. One in the present and one as it must have looked many years in the past.

Often when I would be assaulted with uninvited thoughts or information I would feel as if my head were encased in a bubble. Disconnected from the world momentarily, in order that I might receive what I thought of as a 'transmission'. That's what it was usually like for me. Picking up a feeble flash of a transmission on a frequency that was available to me briefly and only occasionally.

This time however, I was shaken because the episode was much more vivid and seemed to last what felt like a full five or six minutes. My head was abuzz with echoes of distant voices and I felt if I moved, I would fall into the abyss of a time that no longer existed.

"...room for you Lee?" Nora was asking.

"Hmm? Sorry. What did you say?" My head hurt.

"Do you have a preference for any one of the rooms?" She asked again.

"Oh, I'll take the room down the hall on the left. The one with the bathroom suite, if you don't mind." How long had I been like that I wondered? No one seemed to notice, but I did get a strange look from Nora. She knew something was up. The way we had always been connected, of course she would know something was going on. But she didn't ask just then. Not with Bridey's inquisitive blue eyes trying to penetrate our silent communication.

"O.K. with me." She said, and gave me another queer look as she headed down the hall with our hostess toward the bedrooms we had chosen to make our home for the next month. Neither of us had chosen the room off to the left of the main room, 'the mother's room' as it had been revealed to me. We never again entered the room for the duration of our stay. It was as though the cheerfully decorated, lavender room did not exist in the cottage. It had a forbidding and strange off limits feel to it, which we respected. *'Stay clear.'* So we did.

2

The Circle

The night began, as any other except there was no moon. As the sun surrendered to the full dark of the night, Faidhe faced west for her ritual in the Circle. Opening with a prayer of petition for the spirits to be in attendance she stood, as always, alone at the altar stone and dropped grasses, bits of plants, and stones into the large cauldron bubbling over the fire at her feet. Each item she added to the mixture engaged the energy that infused the specific plant or stone to raise it in petition and thanks. Faidhe croaked in her voice grown parched from lack of use and raised her arms in a welcoming gesture.

"A sprig of pine brings new life and renewal. An acorn to infuse great strength. Stones, picked from the earth to invoke the energy of the Earth Mother."

Her voice gained force with the rhythm of her task. The contents of the cauldron hissed with the energy of the words as the old woman fairly cackled and released the items into the great bowl. The exacting energies of the tokens she tossed were woven into a binding union with her prayer and the energy was cast as sacred words were uttered.

Thanks were given for the mild winter and the advent of spring. It was a time for new things to be planned and spring crops to be planted. Her ritual was routine in her petition for the clan to be watchful and aware as new signs were given for the most fruitful planting days and successful hunt or for warnings of any encroaching danger.

Although it was past the longest dark night of the winter and past even the time when the ewes in the field came to milking, the warm days had not yet taken sway. The shadowless night of each moon cycle when nothing but the stars hung in the sky was a reminder to Faidhe and her clan to prepare, even in spring, for the harshness of dark winter.

Satisfied that about half the water in the cauldron boiled into the air, Faidhe spilled the other half upon the ground blowing her long graying hair back with a powerful updraft. She commanded to be heard.

"I spill these waters upon the earth and as the steam arises, I give thanks and respect to the three spirits: water, earth and air. Hear my praise and petitions. Release the magical blend from within the cauldron. Arise Mother Earth! Arise Goddess water! Arise, and take union with the air, the very breath of my words. Release the energy summoned and stored in the sacred bowl to do its work."

Upon the close of the ritual, Faidhe again gave thanks for a mild winter and a healthy stock of new lambs for the rich warm wool, milk and meat they would provide for her clan's survival. To repeat the prayers and petitions three times, Faidhe knew would create the most potent magic possible; it was also a sign of reverence to offer praise and prayer in threes.

Having said the closing prayer, Faidhe, banked the ritual fire, but did not douse it. The magic she had just released to do its work would be all the more potent if the fire were allowed to burn itself out. At the conclusion of the ceremony Faidhe looked up at the spring sky from the center of the Stone Circle where she had performed these sacred rituals for nearly her whole life. In a moment of satisfaction Faidhe inhaled the salty air with pleasure. She always felt the sense of contentment having communed between the worlds with the Goddess and the spirits in a place where there is no time or distance between her world and the place of Gods and spirits. The wise woman left the Circle in the direction of her hut to prepare for her rest.

She lived in a hut that was built to specifications that originated and were passed down from generations long since gone to the spirits. Two circular rooms served as her shelter. The roof was thickly thatched with a smoke-hole at the peak to allow egress for the interior stone hearth. The smaller circular room was for the keeping of ritual accoutrements and sacred implements so Faidhe did her daily living in the large part of the hut if the weather was foul, but in mild weather, chose to do all but sleep outside under the sky in the company of the spirits of the trees, sky and stones.

All was well and routine when she slipped under the skins on her sleeping platform, comforted by the scent and crackle of fresh straw and sweet herbs, grateful for the comforts she enjoyed as the Keeper of the Circle. Hers was a solitary life but it was the small pleasures she enjoyed and she was humbly grateful for the sweet scent as she closed her eyes.

Faidhe worked hard and long, planting and gathering, drying, mixing, and storing magic and medicine plants and tending her ritual duties as the Keeper of the Circle. She worked diligently, early to late and when it came time to close her eyes she luxuriated in sinking into a deep, restful sleep. So she closed her eyes with a sense of wellbeing after completion of the ritual for the dark of the moon, warmed by a cheery hearth-fire, feeling the rising current of spring pulsing through her veins and the scent of the thawing earth in each breath she took.

———

I'm dying. She thought as a surge of alarm spewed through her midsection, terror woke her. The dread in her body was matched by the discomfort from the piercing noise that threatened to split her head apart. The earsplitting shriek echoed up from the depths of the earth beneath the Great Stones.

There had been no apparition to warn her of the coming of ill spirits, no twinge of knowing that harm approached or any of the usual forewarnings of the coming of the Power. It was perhaps the unexpectedness of the situation that panicked her most. As a Seer and Magic Woman, she was accustomed to seeing the unusual but she could make no sense of what was happening to her now.

Faidhe found herself outside the safety of her hut in the center of the giant Circle of Stones that had been home to her since she was a small girl. But now, she was prostrate, naked and cold as if the Stones themselves had summoned her into their midst. A place of worship and reverence, these Stones welcomed each day, each moon cycle, and each revolution of the sun for centuries with benevolent openness. Now they loomed like jagged teeth jutting up from the earth all around as if about to devour her.

Losing the battle to stay calm Faidhe frantically tried to rationalize what was happening. She knew she was not dreaming and the day's events were routine as any other. *What has happened? What ill winds blow with the screaming of the Earth?* Though it was something she'd never heard before, she thought: *That's what the Earth would sound like if she screamed.* It was not the sound of a singular voice, not a voice at all but the declaration of what might be all souls wailing at once with an ominous violent vibration that threatened destruction.

Faidhe became aware of the stinging burn on her palms and knees and knew they had been stripped of some skin. With this she knew that she'd somehow been thrown into the midst of the Great Circle of Stones but she could neither explain why nor how. Forcing herself through the raging noise to become aware of her surroundings, she felt the cold earth under her naked skin. As she looked above, the ominous Circle appeared to be domed in a pulsating blue light that crackled bolt-like energy akin to summer lightening from stone to enormous stone. *How is it that I am here again between the Stones?*

Amidst the turbulence Faidhe found herself surprised by an unbidden memory, percolating through her panic, when as a small girl she had secretly slipped into the sacred spring to see if she could find the water sprites said to live at the bottom.

She swam to the depths of the spring and watched the bubbles rise as she let all the air out of her lungs in order to stay submerged. *I'll wait*, she decided, *at the bottom until I can see the sprites.* As she sat on the sandy bottom, feeling warm and cold water currents of the spring slip past her, gently pushing at her, she looked up toward the water's surface and saw the sunlight and the water dancing together creating the most beautifully gentle designs that neither the sun nor the water could have made alone. It was then that Faidhe realized, *Oh, there! I see them! I see the water spirit and the sun spirit dancing.* These were not just rays and waves, Faidhe caught a rare glimpse of the God and Goddess cavorting together as she'd only heard about. In that instant, as if a veil had been lifted from her consciousness she saw all around her, sprites, fairies, and strange, lovely water creatures. At the age of five seasons, Faidhe had her first experience as one who Sees and was elated to be a part of this special, secret world. She gave over to the sensation of being with the *others.* As she tried to swim with and touch them she could hear what they were thinking. Faidhe was euphoric in her newfound glimpse into the world of hidden knowledge...and she was drowning.

Since that time in her childhood, Faidhe had come to trust the Power and she'd always been shown its purpose but in its time, not her own. With that thought Faidhe was determined to quell her terror. *I have always been in service of the Goddess and the spirits. If they call me in such a way...I will be calm!* She reminded herself. *They will reveal what is happening in their own time. Question not!* Faidhe chastised herself.

In response to her efforts to be calm, feeling like an insignificant scrap being tossed about, she realized that her body, hands and feet no longer touched the earth below her. Slowly being lifted up away from the earth she lost the battle to be calm, Faidhe wretched and she voided in response to her terror.

The pitch of the piercing earth-scream heightened still as Faidhe grew closer to arcs of blue light, being tossed from stone to stone like giants playing a game of toss with lightening now just an arm's length over her head. The arcs illuminated the Stones a radiant blue but Faidhe felt no heat, only the searing sound that felt as though it would pull her mind apart. The closer to the light she was lifted an increasing pressure pushed at the back of her eyeballs and produced the sensation of too much blood in her veins. A sudden warm rush of blood burst from her nose but she was powerless to put an instinctual hand to her face. Rising from the earth, higher still until she was at the very center of the arcs of light. Faidhe was in dread fear of touching the light knowing it would be the end of her as the energy of light and sound would rip her apart. Helpless to move as her feet dangled, toes stretched earthward, and head convulsed skyward, arms rigid at her sides.

Inching upward, first the crown of her head, then her forehead was absorbed into the light and Faidhe became the eye of the storm. There was silence that in the absence of sound, echoed paradoxically loud after only moments ago, being cast about in an unbridled tempest of sound. She was aware that the storm still raged around her but she experienced only silence and with it, came her calm. The strain in her body was suddenly gone. She felt as though she were floating, oddly reminiscent of her childhood experience in the sacred spring. She was surprised at her amusement as she realized she *was* floating! Faidhe's muscles relaxed so that as she brought her head to a normal position, the light formed an eerie blue crown extending from around the apex of her head out to the giant standing Stones of the Circle. She wondered again for a brief moment if she were dreaming...or dying. Then out of the silence, it was made clear to her why she had been summoned. She heard and knew and could not ever go back to not knowing. The news brought by the sound energy was of such magnitude, she thought she could not stay alive with the knowing. She absorbed understanding with a complexity that was not humanly possible. Faidhe acknowledged that all her dealings, as an accomplished Magic Woman, Seer and Keeper of the Circle with vision and premonition, prior to this was but a grain of sand in comparison to all of the beach. She was experiencing the voice of everything. The message was not in any spoken language, but the language of immediate understanding, a knowing in the mind and spirit and soul. The flood of knowledge washed through her, in her, over her, on her, around her. All parts of her spirit, her soul: Faidhe of now, and of the past, and the Faidhe who had not yet become, the Faidhe of the Tuatha De Danann, clan daughter of Dagda, and Danu, blood descendant to Lugh; Seer, Keeper of the Circle, maid, mother and wise woman, simultaneously absorbed the unrelenting knowledge of the Power of the Universe...and understood.

With glimpses of everything she took in the tidal wave of prophecy. She felt her very being expand with the urgency of knowledge as if she alone was not vessel enough to capture and contain the knowledge. She wept and bled, she keened and rejoiced, she cursed the future and the past, and she saw the images as they flooded her existence and for the first time in her years as a Seer, asked not to be the one who sees. At last, she relented and surrendered knowing that there was naught else she could do. She had been summoned. Her path in this life and every other had been altered.

She knew she would no longer be alone in what she must now do, but she knew with bitterness, that she would not give up her position as the Keeper to return to the bosom of her family as she had always anticipated. She must now journey at her advanced age. The task at hand would cause dissention, upheaval, and great strife. There are those who will not understand. She would be doubted or accused of being addled by her solitary time on the Hill. She feared she would not be able to accomplish all that she recognized would be needed. The complexity of her fears was so overwhelming yet she pleaded in one last vain attempt to relinquish this task. She felt immeasurably small and insufficient and the protest she could muster was evidence of her emotions. "I am not enough." Faidhe managed in barely a whisper. With the wan small voice she heard from herself, other emotions started to roil.

Resentment welled with-in her as to why the task was not assigned when she was young and vibrant and could perhaps have used her physical strength, or feminine gifts of beauty and fertility to help exact loyalty from her Tuath and those beyond. How would she succeed as her fertile years waned and was left with only half an arsenal of magic? At the base of all the self-doubt, she feared for much more beyond her own pride, self-worth and clan, she feared for the earth and its people. If she failed in this newly bestowed task, it would not be just her legacy that would suffer. She saw and felt a deep unyielding sorrow for the understanding of what was truly at stake and the magnitude of the great shift in the eart-tide and spirit that was ahead. She lamented what will come and what needed to be done to preserve all that is sacred.

Her final surrender cowed her completely to her task. She knew and told herself, *I have no choice. I must prepare my Tuath and myself. I must bring the news.* She must translate this new knowledge she absorbed in such an unearthly way into terms that will be humanly understood. There was need to plant the seed of change, nurture the roots to grow strong and deep into the collective spirit, then cultivate the inevitable change that is coming as one prunes a vine to grow in the direction of her choosing, to suit her new purpose.

I must petition the Gods to be my strength before they have none of their own and are no longer able to help. I have much to do. Then with a pang of foreboding, I must sew these seeds deep and smartly for it will be a great long time before they will bear a fruitful harvest.

3

A Birth

Faidhe was strong. She had spent 35 sun seasons in service of the Goddess, Gods and her people. Many clanswomen didn't live that long but she had been respected and treated well. Her strength was drawn from the Universe, she knew how to call upon its Power and it energized her, preserved her. But now, she knew that the reason she had been born into the Universal Power was fast upon her. All her life and experience as the Keeper of the Circle, all her sacrifice and loneliness, her ability as a conduit for the Power, the unions of the blood of her ancestors to bring her to be birthed at this time in history, everything up until now was designed to bring her to this one moment, this one task.

After the light and noise of the Circle episode had fulfilled its purpose, it had subsided and Faidhe was thrown down to the earth in a crumpled mass on the Circle floor. Even still, the blue light that rendered her eyes useless during the maelstrom blinded her. She had no need of them. The visions she had experienced were not ones that she actually saw, but rather had the knowing of them behind her eyes.

Faidhe reached to her head, irrationally afraid that it had exploded with either the sound, or the message that came through the giant Stones. She tasted coppery salt in her mouth and knew it was blood. *At least, if I taste blood, I know my head is still there and I'm alive.* Her ears still ringing, she tried to sit up and found herself completely disoriented. She struggled for minutes, naked and cold, to bring herself back into the world. And with that thought, Faidhe mused that she *was* experiencing a birth of sorts. She was being born through the great womb of the Stones into this new world. One that will never be the same for the knowing of what must now take place. Born into a turbulence that will last into future times unfathomable. And like the newborn babe, she drew in her breath and began to wail. She cried for the death of a people, she cried for the loss of her hope, she wept over the inevitability of useless wars; she lamented the imminent, profane defamation of the Goddess and disappearance of the lesser Gods. She grieved for a world unable to draw upon the Universal Power to manifest magic. She could not imagine a world where earth's children were lost to their gifts of communion with the Spirits and Gods. And worse, those who were not lost to their gifts would be condemned for them. She cried.

———

Only women born into the Power were chosen to be the Keeper of the Circle. This was the way of it for centuries upon centuries. And after a lifetime of service, Faidhe felt the ebb and flow of Power in her subtly changing. She'd seen the omens of the coming of the end of her time on the Hill, with the slowing of her moon blood, her body had already begun its transition to her cycle of wisdom, nearing the time when she could no longer bear children. She knew her time was closing and patiently awaited when she would return to her people and what was left of her family. She had served as the Keeper of the Circle since she was 10 seasons old. This was a great honor and also a most consuming responsibility. Faidhe had spent her life preparing the Circle for gatherings and rituals for her people and had presided over the festival rituals at each honored point throughout the sacred calendar. Dutifully, she had taken the offerings brought by the clans and washed them in the sacred waters then heated the stones to cook for the sacred meal. She had tended and collected the medicinal herbs to aid with care of the sick. She had fasted and allowed the Universal Power to course through her, she had honed her magical skills of vision, played the role of the Goddess with those who had come to her wearing the face of the God in the great marriage ritual, she had brought news of her visions to her clan and saved them more than once from being taken unaware in a slave raid or from starvation. She was revered, honored, Powerful... and she was lonely.

Faidhe had not relinquished her seat as the Keeper to a younger woman of a more youthful childbearing age because there were none who called upon and held the Power as deftly as she. Many who have held this seat would have borne children of the Circle ceremonies during the festivals and sent them to fosterage with the clan until such time when another was recognized as better suited to the seat. Or as sometimes happened, when the Keeper's health or mental ability began to show signs of strain from performing the duties of the Circle, another took the seat for an interim period until one with true, unwavering power was brought up to the Hill-site as Keeper of the Circle. At that time, upon relinquishing her duties as Keeper, the Seer would rejoin the clan and instruct others in their craft and raise her own children. Some performed the duties of the Keeper for only a sun season, from harvest to harvest, while for others, as many as ten cycles were served. Faidhe had diligently performed her duties for 35 sacred annual harvests. She held the title as being both the youngest, and the oldest of Keepers. She had extraordinary strength of Power, and could see and summon the Gods and the earth's Power more prodigiously than any other Keeper within memory. She was both humble and regal in her position as she conducted herself flawlessly in all her years as Keeper.

And now, she wept most bitterly for the loss of any hope of rejoining her clan in any customary way. She longed for nearly 30 sun seasons to forge a bond with her own daughters, both children of the Circle, conceived during the festival celebrations when Faidhe played the role of the Goddess and lay with a clansman chosen to play the God's role in ritual celebration. Having come to the position as Keeper at such a young age, she had not time to develop relationships with her own siblings that would withstand the test of years apart and she missed her parents greatly in the beginning of her time on the Hill. She did have the wise women to guide and teach her the ways of the Circle but they were only distant kin within the clan and when her training was finished and she came to childbearing age, these women returned to the clan down below or to the outer reaches of the tribe from whence they came. Through her long years, she glimpsed visions of her daughters as they grew, but longed for more intimate knowledge of who they are and how they fared. Faidhe knew she had to resist using magic to learn of her daughters or communicate with them. She understood that to use the Universal Power for her own purposes was unwise in her powerful position. Magic has a way of taking on its own direction despite the original intent of the practitioner. Once unleashed, the energy of magic may achieve the petitioner's goal in ways most unexpected. If she received unbidden visions of her girls, then so be it, but to initiate contact and communication or even just to observe the girls by making their images appear in the sacred spring could cause a disruption in the natural flow of energy by changing the course of circumstance and may cause unknown effects in the lives of the girls and those around them. Many times Faidhe, in her loneliness, found herself in the Circle standing by the sacred Cauldron staring into its blackened depths, thinking of her children and wrestling in her heart whether to call the magic to reach out to them. Each time she summoned her strength and resisted.

"Not today." She'd whisper and resolutely go about her duties ignoring the temptation of her lonely existence.

The Circle itself stood proudly on the Hill's top with the sacred Stones jutting up about the height of three men from the earth. Eighteen stones in all with the Keystone at the east side of the ring and an altar stone set upon two foundation stones that created a Dolmen for the ancestors gone beneath, but also the place that serves as a focal point of ritual and worship. From the Keystone at the east side of the Circle, across the middle of the Circle to the footstone at the west measures 54 tri-paces. The earth in the Circle is compact and hard almost as if a slab of stone itself. Scarcely anything grows within the circle other than the most tenacious of weeds. The grayish blue ocean can be seen from the Circle down miles of rolling hills and grassland. The open sky above gives ample opportunity for observing the progress of the moon, stars and sun as they make their way across the Circle. Because of the sacred spring within the Circle, the unique site brings all three elements, water, earth and air together in one magical place. For this reason, this Circle is particularly powerful and active, as all the spirits of each element can speak and be petitioned more plainly through the Circle. It has been known forever to Faidhe and her people that places such as these, built by generations of the clan back beyond memory, are to be cared for, revered, honored and respected, for they are a place between two worlds, a portal, and they hold great Power of both the Gods and ancestors.

She crawled, this night, before the altar stone of the Circle unleashing finally all of her regret for having served at this alter for so long. Lamenting the void in her heart that would have been filled by being a mother to her own daughters, rather than a mother to the clan as the Keeper of the Circle. The Keeper could not be distracted from the responsibilities of her exalted position. Faidhe's daughters had never been hers to train, to hold, or to pass on the secrets of the Power. That time had come and gone. Her girls, Colm and Lon Dubh, both products of the Sacred Union in the Circle during a festival of fertility; Colm at a spring festival, the second planting of wheat, and Lon Dubh, at the cattle slaughter at the end of the warm days, both have strong potential for magic but have long since moved past the traditional age of fostering the magic for the purpose of training as the Keeper. They both have strong magic in varying areas: Colm has alchemical abilities to create potent medicines and can create varying, purposeful states of mind with potions, plants, oils and tinctures while Lon Dubh, her younger sister, had shown promise in the gift of vision and the ability to communicate directly with the Gods and Spirits. Both daughters had strong potential for a magical life but Faidhe's own extended tenure as the Keeper had precluded her daughters and many other daughters of the tribe from even the possibility of taking the seat as the Keeper of the Circle. She knew they had missed their opportunity due to her lengthy term as the Keeper and now, how would they receive her? How would they take delivery of her news? How much would they resent her? Would they see her return as an intrusion on their lives after so long having abandoned her position as their mother?

Faidhe knew Lon Dubh thought she was justified to begrudge her mother's extensive stay as the Keeper and she felt she should have long since taken the position herself. Instead she was discontented and had not married in the hopes that someday, before she grew too old herself, her mother would step down. Now that Faidhe must come down from the Hill, she suspected that Lon Dubh would be equally discontent in what was now necessarily planned for her. Perhaps, she thought, Colm will content herself with what lay ahead and maybe her children . . . but due to what she'd been shown in the prophesy, she knew there would be no time for personal hopes or sorrows now. Still physically exhausted, having been thrown down in front of the altar stone, Faidhe fought to gain control of her mind as it struggled to fit back into human parameters after such a consuming union with the Universe. She struggled to quell the racing thoughts caused by the blue electric current that even in its remnants still brought forth images of a world so far beyond the one in which Faidhe lived and was familiar. At the same time she tried to capture the fleeting glimpses flashing behind her eyes in order that she retain all that was shown to her so that she might carry out her mission spotlessly in service of the Power of the Universe.

Faidhe committed to her memory: *This Power encompasses all. It is the well-spring of all life-energy. It is the past, present and future. It contains all the potential courses of choices made and opportunities surrendered. It is the wisdom of the heart, mind and soul of each living thing. It is the constantly available help, hope and love readily drawn upon only for the asking. It is the authority that meters out universal justice. It is all that was, is and will be. It is the beginning and the end. It is the She and the He. It is the collective spirit. It was this that spoke to Faidhe and gave her vision. Being touched by such Power, one must obey, of course, but one would understandably, never be the same for having been touched so.*

Always supported by the Power, Faidhe now felt surprisingly used up by what had always given her strength. She was bone weary but had to ignore her personal grief, shock and discomfort to try to bring her racing heart under control. For ahead of her loomed an overwhelming duty. She could feel the tremendous energy of the Universe and even as it ebbed from her body she was frightened at the magnitude of its strength as it vibrated within her but was even more horrified at the enormity of the changes that must take place, and the sacrifices that must be made beginning with her clan and her own daughters.

This was her last thought before her mind and body gave up the battle to give forth any further effort and her world went black.

4

Suffer the Children

We were different than the rest of the world, my parents, my grandparents, my aunts, cousins and my sisters but especially Nora and I. The youngest two of four sisters, we knew, even at a very young age that our family did not fit in. We stood out in a melting pot neighborhood as a large group of Irish who shared two triple-decker houses side by side; my grandparents, cousins and aunts lived in the #11 house, and we, my parents, all my sisters and I, in the #13 house. There was power in our numbers, I felt, and we "owned" we didn't rent as many other families in the neighborhood did so there was a bit of pride in that. In that respect, my family could have been considered better off than many other families in the working class district, but as far as the neighbors were concerned, we were different in other ways. There was always a bit of the unexplained in how we went about things.

As many families did, we kept a giant old, rusty trash barrel with holes poked in its sides in the backyard for burning leaves or trash. But our neighbors saw us outside, quite a bit more often than was usual, in the yard with our entire family, grandparents, sisters, cousins, all gathered round to "burn leaves." And they may have caught a Gaelic phrase or two float their way on a smoky breeze, chanted for a blessing, good luck or health, by one of my grandparents, aunts or my own father as we watched the flames lick up the inside of the barrel.

I knew to duck when I saw ol' Mrs. Givanello, in her monochromatic, uniform of black dress, thick black stockings, sturdy black shoes with the clumpy heals, nondescript black cardigan sweater wrapped closed by a long black purse strap draped across her southward breasts, topped with the triangular black kerchief. She'd mumble unfriendly sounding words in Italian and poke her first and pinky fingers in the direction of our houses as she came home from her daily grocery, trailing her two-wheeled shopping cart behind her. If an adult from our family happened to catch her walking by, her face would screw up into a toothless grin as she'd wave her hand spastically up and down trying to look her neighborly best, as she hurried as fast as a thousand year old, *or so I thought,* woman could, to be out of the vicinity of our houses. But if any of the kids from our family were unfortunate enough to meet her on the street without benefit of adults, she'd stamp her feet and hiss curses at us in rapid fire Italian to send us scattering. Superstition, others may have called it, but we came from a home where the unusual was usual and Mrs. Givanello wasn't alone in recognizing us as being different.

My paternal grandparents were right off the boat from Ireland and with them came myth and lore of leprechauns, fairies, Fomorii, Fenians and Fionn MacCumal. As my Grandma told the tales, I tried to speak the names in her musical accent and sounded just like her in my head, when I spoke the words though, my imitation always sounded flat and Anglicized: 'Fenyinz' and 'Finn Mcoool.' From Eire, they brought these strange and wonderful stories and old traditions too. Odd little ceremonies when we gathered for special occasions and family birthdays throughout the year to throw some salt, burn different herbs and spices, light a candle, or chant a poem. I never fully understood the importance of the ceremonies at the time but eagerly looked forward to the gatherings that would surely be followed by a story session or "seisiun" as my folks called it. I so enjoyed getting together with the entire family, aunts, uncles, cousins, grandparents, all of us, for the feasting and storytelling that inevitably followed the outside burnings. Inciting pictures in my mind of a magical past was somehow better for the recitation rather than reading from a book. When Grandma told the tales, each time could be a bit different, spun from a different perspective, once with humor, another time with heart wrenching emotions. Her stories became three dimensional after having heard them so many times in such diversity. It was not difficult to imagine that the Gods she mentioned or the heroes and heroines in the stories were friends of my grandparents or that if we traveled back to Ireland, someday, we would meet these magical characters, for the way the stories were told, there was no more magical a place than Ireland and no thought in my mind that the stories were anything other than absolutely true. My grandfather, father or aunts, not to be outdone in the theatrics of the telling would interject with bits of the story Grandma had supposedly forgotten. Or Grandma would turn to my father and inquire, "What was it he was sayin' now Patrick?" As if to verify her recollection and obtain validation that the story was nothing other than the utter truth.

My father would respond with something like, "He said 'No,' to making weapons, Ma. He swore that after he took to the road that he'd craft only a bowl of the finest silver." And they would carry on discussions for the sake of our entertainment as to whether this one was still asleep under the earth or that one might return as promised and when that might be.

In this family microcosm, especially when we were all gathered, it was not unusual for us, particularly us kids, to frequently say the same thing at the same time and jab each other in gales of laughter shouting "Coke me!" which meant the person who'd stolen the thought must then buy the victim a Coke in payment of the theft. Sometimes, some of us would dream the same dream, only to see a day or week later, that the dream had come true. There was much talk about things we'd see that we knew the outside world did not: a gray orb gliding across the room or an unexplained shadow passing through our home. In fact it was not unusual to hear one of my sisters, aunts or cousins say they'd seen a deceased relative as casually as saying they'd run into a neighbor at the supermarket. A statement like "I saw Uncle Tom yesterday in the front hall." was greeted with comments like, "Did you now? And how did he look?" These were common responses despite the fact that Uncle Tom had been long in the ground. Being a part of this unit was a wonderful place to be a child where imaginations were fertilized and despite our odd reputation in the neighborhood, it was a safe and nurturing place to belong.

We went to the local church as Catholics, most of us. We were baptized and received First Holy Communion and were enlisted as "Soldiers of God" at our respective Confirmation ceremonies. My sister Patrice was even chosen to play the prestigious role of Mary whose title was pronounced as one word 'HolyMarymotherofGod,' during the annual May procession. To the outside eye, much the way my mother would have it, we were a virtuous Catholic family of the Church. But at home, we learned to light the fires and tell stories on special days, and leave out a bit of bread or milk for the wee folk. Our ritual days often fell on the same day as a family birthday or near the Catholic holy days so it made for an extra festive time for us. But we kept these traditions to ourselves. The way it was explained to me was, the people at the church would not understand our ways, the "Old Ways" nor would any of our non-Irish neighbors so we didn't speak of them outside our home.

Then came the time when, after the passing of my grandmother, it was as if there was no longer any glue to hold our family together. My father's brother, Uncle Joe and his wife moved with their three kids, my cousins, to the western part of the state. My grandfather and his three daughters, Celia, Peg and Mae, my father's sisters, and all the rest of my cousins moved out of the triple-decker house beside us, and away to a shorefront community north of Boston. Ipswich would be the place that my cousins, Sheila, Mike, Maureen and Pegie grew up. The ocean front neighborhood was a reminder of home for my grandfather, a reminder for him of Ireland, the place where he'd met and fallen in love with my grandmother.

I felt a profound loss at this time in my life. I lost my Grandma who, for me, was the embodiment of mystery and magic, humor and kindness. Always ready to offer warm welcome, a word of comfort with a treat from the breadbox. She smelt of flour, as she'd wrap me in a giant hug or dab a bit of dirt from my face with a corner of the apron that was her uniform for my entire life of six years.

She used to say with an air of satisfaction as she looked over our gatherings "Ni neart go cur le cheile," *togetherness is strength*. But then, my Grandma was gone, and with her went the center of our family and a big part of Grandpa was gone too. Grandpa without Grandma was like having a home without a kitchen, or a body without a heart, he was there, but not there. The magical stories were gone, my aunts, my uncles, my cousins, and our secret world of celebrations; all gone. The protection of the family against being the misfits, the outsiders, was no longer there. Our strength in togetherness, power in numbers was gone.

Their house was a vacant gaping void for me where once there had been safety, warmth, welcome, traditions, similarities and protection. I guess my parents were affected in much the same way, because the decision was made and, like a wave that sucked me under and tumbled me without any sense of direction or control, everything changed when I heard the announcement that we would move too.

My family no longer resided in a melting pot neighborhood with names like Givenello, Litchenberg, Bowman, Dugnazzi and LaLiberty posted on the brass mailbox with the doorbell at the bottom that was found at the front door of every triple-decker in the neighborhood. Our new neighbors bore names such as Monahan, Doherty, Shea, Wilson, Fitzgerald, Ramsey, Laffin and Donnelley displayed on tidy mailboxes in front of single-family homes. We were surrounded by what should have been our own people, with similar customs and traditions but once again, we were different.

I thought coming into an Irish neighborhood meant that everyone would have the same background, stories and magical instincts as we did. I thought everyone would leave bread for the wee folk and light the fires at special times. I thought there would be friends that could name the stars and who would share where they went when they dreamed. I thought, these folks of Irish blood will know their clans and from which county they hailed. But I was wrong.

A predominantly Irish-Catholic neighborhood, where everyone went to Saint Gregory's School and attended Saint Gregory's Church was as foreign to me and as torturous psychologically as it could have been. Ours was a family of all girls. We came from a family of mostly women, Grandma, aunts and mostly female cousins. Strong women, all partners to their men or choosing a career path rather than traditional marriage. But in this new parish, the expectation that we, as girls were supposed to behave as a subordinate rather than partner to men and boys was contrary to everything I'd been exposed to in my family up until that time. I was both overwhelmed and confused. Where was the respect for the Old Ways? How could they not understand the importance of the female role in keeping the traditions alive? Equally as horrifying, how could they forsake their magical power? It was a disappointing realization for me that these new Irish people didn't know anything of the Old Ways or the old stories. They didn't know about that stuff because

I finally realized that *we* were the different ones. We had always been different, not because we were the only Irish people in the old neighborhood, but we were different even in a neighborhood of all Irish people. When I asked my parents about it, they had no answers for me. My mother even tried to suggest that maybe it was time that we tried to behave as the others now, to try to fit in.

At the age of seven years old, I understood all too well that our family held something different and unique, powerful and wonderful but also dangerous in the sight of others. I was no longer encapsulated in a cocoon safe environment of a large family, free to ask questions or talk about anything within that shelter. The many families of the O'Leary clan living as a group gave me the illusion that we were not alone in our traditions and beliefs. I knew there must be others out there like us, because there were so many of us in our family unit. We just needed to find other Irish, I thought, and we'd find more of our kind in magic and tradition.

When I found out the truth after we'd moved, I didn't question why our family had these unique abilities and ways of seeing things while the other Irish, *The New Irish* as I'd come to think of them, didn't. I had been awakened to the fact that being different may not be the best way to pave a path to new friendships in a new neighborhood.

As other families prepared for Saint's Days or Holy Days of obligation, the extra celebrations we held at home were a private matter. Since the death of my grandmother and the separation of our family, I understood our magical life was not something to be shared with those who neither welcomed it nor understood it. Gradually, our story sessions became more like lessons at the table or philosophical discussions. Our father's talents and interests were in knowing things that other people didn't. Sports did not interest him but the names of all the trees in the local arboretum did. He might not have been able to identify what type of car, but he could name the stars in any night sky. Those were the things that were taught to us around the dinner table just as they were taught to my father by his parents. We learned odd sounding Latin words for trees and plants; we memorized their uses, and recited names of the stars as though it were a game. Eager to learn and please, Nora and I learned well what would turn out to be age-old information.

The traditional rituals were carried on but over the years were minimized and eventually overtaken by the Christian hubbub about the holidays at school and in the neighborhood much like a giant wave will bury shells and rocks in the sand on the beach, unseen but still there. So I held it within me, this secret life, never talking about it, using it or revealing it with anyone beyond Nora.

It is because of this protective mode with my magic, that in our childhood years, I believed, I was almost dependent on Nora in order to access and utilize my abilities. She was a conduit of sorts for me to tap into the psychic side of myself. I "plugged in" to her in order to see clearly "that way." It's a way of turning up the volume or clarifying the picture of psychic transmissions. When we combine our strength, the picture becomes clearer for me.

We have the gift of making each other laugh uproariously and this seems to strengthen the magical bond between us. At times, the laughter will make me almost drunk. Perhaps it is the altered state, the uncluttered euphoria of laughter that allows the psychic energy to flow freely without filtering through the murk of consciousness or logic. Whatever it is that promotes the magic, laughter is a mind-altering intoxicant for us.

As kids, Nora was the other half of myself. We filled in personality gaps for each other. She helped me with school subjects I just couldn't seem to grasp and I was the sensitive one that could cry for both of us. At a young age, Nora created armor around her heart that few were allowed to penetrate. She knew of course that our family was different but decided to wrap herself in the glory of being different. She had the ability to have people admire the difference in her and created an air of being in an elite club and no one would dare mock her for it, at least not to her face. Social pressures did not hinder her; no amount of teasing, cajoling, or bribery, would incite her to do what she did not want to do. I knew this strength and self-containment was burdensome for Nora despite the fact that she was able to make friends in the new neighborhood and in school. But I did not have the ability to forge friendships so for me, the loneliness was devastating.

"How do you do it Nora?" I asked in frustration one day after being teased and taunted by neighborhood boys who knew just how to push my buttons.

"Do what?"

The tear at the lip of my eye was quivering as much as my chin. "How do you make friends? With them, I mean. They make fun of me. I try to make them like me but they're just mean. Sometimes, if it's just one of them alone, they act nice to me but as soon as someone else comes out to play, then they don't like me anymore."

"Put on the mask." She said, as naturally as if I should have known just what that meant.

"What do you mean? What mask?"

She took in a breath to assemble her thoughts eyeing me speculating as to whether I was ready to hear what she was going to tell me. "The mask, the mask. It's well, if I try hard enough, I know I can make people see me the way I want them to see me." She studied me to see if I was getting it. My face told her I wasn't. She tried again. I do good in school, right?"

"Yeah."

"Do you think I'm smart?"

"Nora had always brought home the grades in school, another thing in which I was not particularly adept." "Well duh! 'Course."

"It's not that I don't study or do my homework, 'cause I do, but...well sometimes when I'm in class I concentrate on the nuns *seeing* me as really smart. If they call on me, I tell them my opinion, even if it might not be exactly the right answer and I see them get sort of nervous and they say, 'Yeah, good answer.' or something like that and they just think I'm smart and sometimes I just *know* they think I'm smarter than them so they move on to someone else!"

"Wait a minute! So what does that mean, about people not being mean to me?" I knew she was getting to something but I wasn't quite catching on just yet.

"So I do the same thing with the other kids around the neighborhood only I make them see me as someone they'd like to be like. I make them think that what I say is really cool and important and so they like me."

"How do you do it?"

"I don't know for sure, I just really think it *hard*, whatever I want them to see, and then I can almost see it work in their eyes. Like it registers there and their faces change or something."

"Do it to me." I said, fascinated.

"Well, you know I'm doing it so I don't know if it will work."

"Just try. C'mon."

"Okay, Watch." Nora looked directly at me and I saw her as always. Long, brown curly hair with blondish highlights and big, round, blue eyes that carried a hint of a possible secret in them all the time. She was a about an inch taller than I was and a bit rounder in the body. She had a round, pleasant face that to me would always mean home. Then for just a flash, I saw Nora look large and looming. I wasn't sure if what I saw was just because I was expecting something to happen or whether it actually did happen. A flash, so fast that had I blinked, I'd have missed it, then nothing...just Nora.

I asked, "What did you do? What were you trying to look like?"

"I don't try to look like anything, I concentrate on them seeing me a certain way." I really don't know what they see. What did you see?"

"Well, you just looked, not bigger but um... more there. I guess." Knowing my description was inadequate for what I thought I'd seen, I asked, "How did you want me to see you?"

Nora looked like she was contemplating on that and said, "I tried to look older to you. I want to get a job to make some money but no one will hire me to work at 12 years old. I didn't look older?"

"No you still looked like you but sort of, um, with a magnifying glass. And just for a second. Then it was gone."

"Maybe it doesn't work with you." She said. "Or maybe it didn't work because you knew what I was doing."

"Maybe it didn't work because I *know* who you are." I said. And that made perfect sense to both of us because of everyone in the world, we two, did know all of each other. We sensed each other's feelings, we picked up each other's thoughts, and we shared discoveries in our abilities such as these. We were satisfied that this 'mask' thing would work on other people but that we would remain untainted to knowing each other. We grew excited that we could share the discovery and we practiced to see if I had the same ability.

———

I found it difficult to reconcile my home life, that offered knowledge of nature and learning of natural tides of the seasons, the meaning behind the movement of the stars, and the urges that come naturally to us as beings of the earth, with the outside the home, Catholic life. The inside life made perfect sense to me. It came with common sense and trusted cycles; it was a world of balance where I was allowed to be myself. To leave this type of background, and to try to survive in a world that had no understanding or tolerance for all that I understood to be good, wholesome and true, was nearly the ruin of my self-esteem. I was a failure at being a *young lady*. It seemed that the outside world had the expectation that girls should behave a certain way. They do not run filthy through the woods playfully chanting rhymes and make-believe spells. They do not light fires and spin furiously, allowing the intoxication of the earth-power to overtake them as they spin. They do not speak unknown languages while in a daydream. They do not succumb to the pubescent urges of coming womanhood. Apparently what is expected is that they should feel shame of the body and be submissive. I struggled, caught between two ways of being reverent: the Old Ways and the Catholic way and was stymied in both.

Catholic girls, the good ones anyway, are to deny the power that is gifted to them. They are to bury this Universal Power deep down and pray to another distant power that they may be granted favor. They are to do these things unquestioningly and they are to ignore their natural intuition should it flare up or to recognize it as some kind of innate evil because after all, being a girl, any *natural* instinct had to be wrong. Through the ages, it had been generally accepted by the Catholics and other Christians, that Eve was the first sinner and being a girl, it was best that I do what I was told rather than what I felt in order not to regress to my natural Eve-like tendency; to be evil and a sinner.

Bury the Power, ignore the intuition and pray that, as a female, I can resist my natural proclivity to be evil? That made no sense to me, as I became a young woman. Why am I evil, a sinner or less than, just because I am female? And why would I give up my Power that is a natural gift only to petition in prayer to have someone or thing hand a teeny piece of it back to me? I am of the Universe and am grateful for my place in that Universe, and so I share in its Power. I did not understand this Catholic way of thinking. I just knew it felt as though the religion was designed to make me doubt my abilities and my proper place as a strong and valued member of the human race. As I was instructed to pray for things I thought: *Why would I mail away a letter asking someone, unknown to me, to give me a bite of what is already in my own cupboard?* No, we were taught, within my family that as a part of the Universe, take what is needed and make useful what is taken. This idea that I had to go to a Priest or some middle person in order to be heard by God smacked of deception to me. I needed to know more. I wanted explanation. I wanted proof!

Naturally, I was regarded as a nuisance in school because my true self eked through all the Catholic education and I committed the audacious crime of asking questions during religion class in an effort to truly understand it rather than the more acceptable display of silent reflection on the "Mysteries of Faith." Hence, the Sisters of Notre Dame were not kind to me.

One day during a lesson on the sinfulness of women, I couldn't take being maligned anymore just for being born a girl. I raised my hand and didn't wait to be called on. I just asked, "Why was Eve the big sinner if Adam bit the apple too? Aren't we supposed to be responsible for our own actions? And don't you always say that if someone is trying to get you to do something you know is wrong then you're more at fault if you do it 'cause you knew it was wrong? And you said that Adam is the man and he's supposed to be the boss of her and he should have told her it was wrong so if all that is true, then isn't the original sin on him more than her? How come it's Eve's fault about the whole apple thing?"

The class took on the hush of spectatorship in anticipation of the impending meltdown our religion teacher was famous for. "Miss O'Leary!" Sister Gertrude Elizabeth thundered at me in a voice that oozed with venom and sarcasm. "Your questions are too close to impertinence. Part of having faith is obedience. And children should keep their questions to themselves instead of interrupting my lessons; so do as you're told and keep *silent* and pay attention. Keep a humble heart and support the church for any hope of getting your lazy, foolish soul into heaven." She was on the verge of a right rant at this point and after a snapshot glimpse into her emotions, I knew the reason for this was that she didn't have a valid or logical answer to my question.

"Doesn't it say somewhere that Jesus loves the voices of children?" I responded in a moment of insanity when my tongue forgot to listen to my brain and keep still. I knew trouble was coming when I saw the vein stand out on Gertie's forehead. But it was too late. I'd opened the lid to her wrath and I knew if I was going to get it, I might as well make it worth my while. "Let the children come to me."

I quoted. "'And do not hinder them. For the kingdom of God belongs to such as these. I tell you the truth.' Jesus said. 'Anyone who will not receive the kingdom of God like a child will never enter it.' So wouldn't that mean that we're supposed to try to find out the answers we have about all this stuff?" I had hope for a fleeting moment when she sat in her chair with her mouth hanging open that I might have impressed her with my knowledge of the verses. But then, her solid 5' tall and 4' wide frame led by her formidable bust came streaking down the aisle faster than anyone might imagine she could move. Looming over me, her threat was palpable as her spit flew from her bared teeth as she tried to regain control of her classroom by sheer domination. I guessed our discussion was over.

My mother, who for reasons of her own, wanted us to keep appearances as a good and devout Catholic family, urged me to make a greater effort to do better at school as I asked her to sign the scathing, two-page note from Gertie explaining why I had earned detention for a month and lost recess indefinitely. I did not see the benefit of trying to fit in and do better but it was expected of me so I was sent to school each day without the advantage of having yet completely mastered the mask ability to any helpful degree with anyone except the family dog, and so I tried my hand at being invisible to try to go unnoticed but after the bible quoting incident, that didn't work too well either.

This label of being different is handled better by some of us than others. Myself, I continued to be a lonely child. The effects of being apart from the rest left me with few friends but not for lack of trying. I was a sensitive child understood by very few except for Nora. Being accustomed to a thing doesn't make it any easier to endure.

5

She Wakes

When she awoke, it was well past sunrise. It took some time for Faidhe to bring herself up to the edge of awareness. She watched, in her mind's eye, as remnants of the prophecy skittered past her consciousness. A vague sense of where she was began to occur to her as the pulse of wakefulness began to rise within her. Realizing that for the first time in 35 years, she had missed the ritual of the coming of the sun, as he outshined the stars and sent the moon to her rest. She felt a gnawing sense of sorrow and loss for the traditions that had already begun to crumble. Great walls, she ruminated feeling desolate, begin to fall with the first crack. That she had been unable to initiate this ancient daily ritual of reverence would be only one break, the first of many, in age-old traditions. She grimaced at the thought.

The morning was filled with all the usual sounds; the distant call of the ocean, birds a twitter in the trees, the rustle of the dry grass as a breeze frolicked through its blades. There was the briny smell wafting in from the ocean on moist, unseen droplets of air. The musky smell of a far off skunk marking his territory whispered its way into her awareness. The perfume of cold ashes from a defunct fire was nearby mingled with something less pleasant. As Faidhe lay on the earth, she allowed herself to come to full consciousness with amazement that the world should smell and sound the same after what had taken place, how long ago? She thought. Only half a night? She was not sure how long she'd been lying unconscious and exposed in the Circle.

She tried to open her eyes against their resistance. They were sealed shut with dirt, salt, dried tears and refused to open as if they didn't want to acknowledge the possibility they may not still function. Faidhe remembered being blinded by the light and a bolt of fear went through her solar plexus at the prospect of having to be a Seer without eyes. As the panic threatened to well up in her again, she calmed herself as she began to notice that she could see the redness of the sunlight painting flowerlike swirls on the inside of her thin eyelids. If she could see the light... *All right then*, she tried to reign in her mind, and reminded herself to breathe in and breathe out. *Feel the Earth Power, and be part of its tide. Trust what has come to pass and allow its full meaning to be revealed to you. Trust Faidhe. Breathe in...breathe out.*

It took her a moment to work up some moisture in her mouth and wet her fingers with her tongue. Clearing away the crust from her eyes, she opened them to the brilliance of the day. Faidhe took in what could be seen of the hilltop from her prone perspective; things she had seen every day of her life at the Circle for the last 35 years. She was awed by the clarity of everything in her field of vision. As she worked to open her eyes from a squint she saw tiny purple and yellow crocuses that had begun to peek up out of the soft grass as droplets of color sparkling in the early green grass growing just outside of the Circle. Closer still, she noticed the soft yellow-green color of the new shoots of grass that made a bed for the crocuses. The wide-open sky was a vibrant blue, punctuated by the most magnificent white clouds taking shape and continuously reforming as if to speak to her through illustration. The earth under her head could be seen in the minutest detail as her eyes observed individual grains of dirt and pebbles, each offering their own shape and color to play their part in the mosaic that makes the soil across which her own hair was splayed. Faidhe lay in wonderment at how she could have lived here almost her entire lifetime without ever noticing the infinitesimal and enormous beauty of everything around her. She was familiar with the stories of those who had come close to death having painted a description of their view of the world in just this way. Having come close to death, made the living so much more, *alive.* She wondered: *Did I actually come so close to death? Of course*, she thought, *and on many levels: a physical death, a spiritual death, death of all that I have known until now. All necessary for a renewal,* she thought.

She looked back again at the little faces of the crocuses and at the grass as it waved at her in the breeze. The earth itself stirred under her breath as she exhaled and as she reveled in the wonderment of all this life surrounding her, she began to actually see something face-like in the flowers. The grains of dirt were collecting themselves together into something that had the essence of life, right in front of her eyes! Faidhe looked all around her and began to recognize that she was not just seeing nature in its resplendence, but that she was able to see the actual spirit of each individual thing about her.

Of course she had seen sprites before but only during her childhood and from then much less as time marched farther and farther away from the incident in the sacred spring. As she grew older she had honed her skills in medicine, ritual and magic however as she became more attentive to the steps of the medicine making or ritual, she moved away from her actual ability to be a part of the magic and was left with the practice of just conjuring the magic. Subsequently, she'd weakened the connection to the spirit of magic by merely performing it. Even still, Faidhe was considered a supreme Seer and magic woman due to the fact that her ability was so much stronger than others in her position. But the fact was, the magical energy and its spirits were ebbing on the earth. She knew this now.

Faidhe had many times called the spirits of the Mother and the Father as she'd performed the rituals in the Circle and felt them greatly as they made their presence known to her. But this profound awakening for Faidhe enabled her to see the life spark in everything as an entity equal to herself. She always knew she was of the Universe and that brought her closer to her Mother the Earth but she now saw that all that was here and of the Earth were her family in some distant way, all being of the same life spark, all of the same Mother. Faidhe's eyes were more than just open; she now knew what it truly meant to be a Seer of long ago, during the time when magic was strong on the Earth. Before even the Circle had newly been erected and before all the years had passed with humans in service of the will and thirst for power that would dilute the magical potency. Before the profane abused the gift that was theirs, in the advancement of war or in the quest for land or power, that diminished all the potential in the gift that was magic. She knew now of a time when all the tribes shared the earth as proof of the kindred spirit, teeming with thriving life rather than the few scattered remnants of the 'others' that remained still on the earth: the giants, elves, dwarves, humans, fairies, magicians, centaurs, dragons, merfolk, and Gods all but a smattering of what once was. She saw now, how such a great many of them had slipped the shackles of earth to live within the realm of the spirits.

Abruptly stopped by pain as she began to move, though she was a strong woman, particularly for her age, she was no longer young and her body had so recently been tossed about and stretched to its limits; she was forced to move in slow and precise measurements. Her bones took some convincing to do as she commanded and her muscles raucously resisted any attempt to put them to work. Slowly, and not without resolute determination, she worked into a sitting position. The cold morning air was now beginning to bite at her skin and pitilessly raise the flesh into protesting bumps. She decided to be invigorated rather than irritated by the cold air and once again began to take in deep gulps of it to fill her lungs and feed her blood. She fought past the throb in her head as she controlled the rhythm of her breathing. She allowed a recollection of what had taken place to wash over her and through her, with each breath, she relived the visions she'd seen the night before and attempted to begin to put the prophecy into words that could be humanly understood. The coming of the end for the ways of magic. The birth of a new religion that will have no reverence for the Goddess. The silencing of the maternal voice and the oppression of anyone who would practice the reverence of the Earth, respect for the water, and veneration of the air. Obliteration of the sacred ways, and symbols. Her people would be impugned and reviled for participating in their most sacred practices. With a calm she would not have thought possible, she knew what she had to do, at least for now, and began to formulate a plan.

———

When she was able to stand erect and move without too much discomfort, Faidhe went to the sacred spring and filled several turnip shells with water. She returned to the center of the Circle and rinsed clean where her body had involuntarily emptied during the force of the prophecy. She then returned to the spring and washed with all the pomp and care as if she were about to perform a Circle ritual for one of the high sun days or cross moon days. She called upon the sprites, and deities alike from the water as she'd done many times before but now she could actually see them as they came to help cleanse her of anything but the highest of thoughts, unhampered by her personal wants or needs. "How fitting," She spoke to them, "That you are here for me today on my last day here, as you were here for me on the day that started my time with you back these 35 sun seasons."

She carefully washed away the dried blood from her face, breasts and hair that had gushed from her nose, careful not to allow the tainted water to run back into the spring. The ritual cleansing allowed her to slough off any doubt about what had to be done. She symbolically rinsed away her laments and sorrows for the rituals, traditions and ways of life that would be affected by the coming changes and realized that she could actually see the filmy little bits of energy she was purging as she washed them away. She had cleansed away the filth and blood of her symbolic birth and only then, submerged her whole self into the sacred waters warmed by a spring far beneath the surface. She emerged from the Earth's waters renewed, freshly cleaned and invigorated with the prospect of being a proponent of the Circle in order that the ways and traditions of her people, their lives and legacy would be preserved.

Faidhe parted her hair into two halves and began to finger out the tangles as she dried in the sun. It had been too long since she'd tended to herself in this way. She took her time as the mid-morning sun warmed her skin and dried her hair. She chewed on the gritty plant that was bitter but had a refreshing quality as it cleaned her mouth. Her heightened senses accentuated the song of the Earth as it hummed all around her. The dove's wings that emitted a squeaking sound as it took flight kept time with the distant droning of the early bees in the nearby woods as they ventured out to greet the sun after a long slumber. The flying dove's partner cooed its protest at being left behind. Faidhe was awed as she recognized that she even sensed the worms just now waking underground as the earth softened to the spring. The golden morning sun ripened as the shushing of the grass added to the music. Faidhe played her own notes and became part of the music with the rhythm of her chewing and combing out her hair. When she finished grooming her tresses, she rinsed her mouth and twisted her hair into a knot then secured it out of her way with a horse bone so that she could attend her injuries by dressing the wounds on her knees and palms with a soothing balm made of common speedwell, a flowering plant that grows wild in the lowland meadows, some ground ivy and a tuft of star moss that Faidhe harvested from the forest a few miles beyond the Ring Hill. These with a bit of honey stored from last season served to alleviate her discomfort and help to heal her raw skin.

A careful selection of the most necessary and powerful medicines, magical items and dried herbs from her hut was made along with items of more mundane use: some flints, bone hooks, and a knife. After taking careful inventory of the items, she stored them in a sealskin satchel to be tied about her waist. Just before she pulled the sinew strap to draw the pouch closed, Faidhe impulsively pulled three feathers from those she had hanging on the rafters of her hut and put them in the satchel: one white, one red and the other black.

She chose her most regal ritual clothing to wear on her new quest, an ankle-length tunic of fine woven linen made from the golden hillside flax. Over the tunic, she pulled on a beautifully tanned doeskin, scraped and brushed to a comfortable suppleness, as were her buckskin slippers, stuffed with insulating straw. The seal-skin pouch was tied about her waist and it gathered the doeskin to her body about her middle. She finally wrapped her finest woolen cloak, made for her of the fur of the dark sheep in the clan's flock, about her shoulders and bound it at her shoulder with a bronze brooch fashioned in the shape of a Circle.

The Circle to Faidhe's people is a symbol in representation of all things sacred and involved in creation or propagation of life: the cycle of the year, the moon, the sun, the womb and birth canal through which all life is delivered, the egg, the seed. But in her case, the circle that formed the brooch is also a symbol that Faidhe is a Keeper of the Circle of Stones. In relief at the center of the circle lay a triangle built of stones to represent the indestructible sacred three. In Faidhe's tribe, the Tuatha De Danann, all things sacred were represented by the constancy of three: the feminine triad, Maid, Mother and Wise Woman, the sacred givers of life, earth, water, air, as well as the life cycle, birth, life, death, and in representation of all the miracles of the cycle of three within her religion. Displayed at the very center of the brooch is a single opened eye that signifies the bearer of the brooch is an exalted soul who has sacrificed much in service of the tribe as a Seer.

There are some who wear the Circle as members of the Council. There are others who bear the triangle as with the celebrants of the sacred ways such as the Wise Women. And there are those who bear the eye as Seers for their clan or the larger Tuath. There are a few in the Tuatha De Danann who wear two of the symbols, but Faidhe is one of the extreme minority who have ever held the honor to combine all three symbols in service of the Goddess, God, lesser Gods, the Circle, and the Tuath. Hers is a powerful symbol that heralds the personification of the sacred three. It will serve as a talisman that will aid her in her current quest to bring the news of the prophecy to her people.

Faidhe not only wanted to muster all the dignity that came with her position, she wanted to insure that her appearance would carry the weight of the prophecy she was about to proclaim. She drew upon the earth, air and water to fill her with the energy and power to make her appearance overwhelming and forceful. She drew herself up tall and majestic as she reached up and pulled the bone from her hair to allow her black tresses, streaked with bolts of silver, to cascade down to her knees.

The hair, unbound, more than anything else she'd done to command attention for the news she was bringing, was a signal to the others that she brought them words of prophecy. As she'd performed her rituals at the great Circle gatherings in the past, drawing upon the Power of the Universe to generate great magic, she came to the Circle unbound by clothing, brooches or anything that would tether her in any way; her hair too, was unbound and flowing. That she would come down from the Hill unannounced would draw the clan's attention quickly, but her unbound hair would bring the news much more quickly to the surrounding camps and villages as a symbol that she carries with her the authority of the Universal Power even outside of the great Circle.

She brought with her one other item of symbolic importance. The sacred cauldron she used in the Circle rituals was one of the vivid images that had come to her in the prophecy storm. This is a central symbol, for her own clan and that of countless others, of the creation and sustaining of life. The vessel, that is simultaneously symbolic of the cauldron of Ceridwen, the Goddess whose vessel offers inspiration and knowledge of all things together with the cauldron of the Great Dagda, chief of the Tuatha de Danann, renewing life, giving forth of all the needs of the living providing for both spiritual and physical.

Faidhe attached a strong staff-like hook made of sturdy, oiled ash to the cauldron's handle. The staff was designed so that just one person could bear the weight of the heavy cauldron. She turned around and crouched down with the indent on the shaft of the staff designed for the comfort of the carrier, resting on her shoulder. She used her shoulder as a fulcrum and lifted the cauldron as she stood.

The large vessel is heavy, designed of strong metal that is used to make tools and implements. It is festooned with many pictures and sacred symbols created artfully through years of magical workmanship; each symbol carrying and emanating a particular magical force, each image, depicting great feats or abilities of various Gods or tribe's people. The Dagda himself is depicted on the massive tribal basin giving of the renewing qualities of his own cauldron. The staff used to shift and move the great cup is also artfully adorned with hundreds of symbols imbuing it too with magical traits and sacred energy.

Faidhe winced as she adjusted the staff on her shoulder and gritted her teeth at the fact that she literally carried the weight of the world on her shoulder. This was the last selfish thought she allowed herself to have as she walked away from the only home she'd known for most of her life. She looked back and understood that she was not leaving her beloved and revered Circle but was in a way, taking it with her. The vessel was all that the Circle would ever be; a tool to create a sacred space by combining water within the vessel, earth represented by the material of the vessel itself and air, the variable element using steaming water or aromatics. It, as well as she is a sacred conduit for the Universal Power. And as this realization dawned, the weight of the cauldron and staff had significantly eased. She spied the luminescence of many earth, plant and water sprites perched along the staff and filling the cauldron, somehow helping her bear the weighty burden. Their light caused the items, upon which they sat, both cauldron and staff, to appear as though they were made of millions of fireflies, twinkling and buzzing with life. Faidhe no longer simply called the spirits; she truly walked with the spirits now.

As she turned to go, something amiss caught Faidhe's attention. She turned back and recognized what she had not noticed before. The Keystone of the Circle, the tallest of them all, a solid stone for millennia, had split in two. The monolith was rent and the pieces listed, one to the north and the other to the south so that the blue sky could be seen through the score in the V-shape of a drinking vessel. Upon one half of the stone was perched the ring dove she'd heard earlier or one of its kin, and upon the other half of the stone was perched a great raven, a sentinel cawing for its own clan as if to tell the news of the great rending that had happened here. And whether it was another omen or just a trick of the eye, it was the time of day that the sun, being guided by the avian sentries, had begun to hang higher in the sky and from Faidhe's perspective it looked as if the dual stone was cradling the sun in the crux of its new opening.

6

Wonderful Things

Nora and I had reserved a luxury vehicle for us to travel in style to various places around Ireland visiting, to conduct research, pub hop and so on. Our idea of luxury was quite different from what we found after a considerable wait at the airport when we'd landed at Shannon. The trunk was barely big enough to fit our carry-on bags, never mind two ridiculously huge rolling bureaus we'd packed.

We were going away for a month after all. And one never knows when one might be invited to a ball or to find oneself attending a formal countryside shindig requiring four-inch heels and sequin bags. We packed for all contingencies.

After a late breakfast we were driving our teeny car to the town nearest where our cottage was located, having determined that the luxury label we were assured it bore must be due to the car being an automatic rather than a standard transmission. The town was the epitome of the word quaint, with lovely window boxes hovering outside every window and cascading flowering plants that hung from every local bridge. There were sidewalk cafes and small corner pubs with weathered signs proudly declaring the names of the establishments, "Helen Calnan's" or "Liam Fitzpatrick, Proprietor," which gave the impression that everyone who lived or worked there knew each other. There was a simple, 1950's feel to the town.

Until now, the only adventures in driving we'd experienced were the drive home from the airport, to the store for supplies, and to the local, Fanny O'Dea's for an evening meal. As the designated driver, because Nora determined that we'd, "without a doubt be killed" if she got behind the wheel to drive "on the wrong side of the road." I was relearning how to drive as I mastered the lingo and backward arrangements of the roads in Ireland. "Accident Black Spot" was to our chagrin posted all over the country roads that had been designated so, due to multiple auto fatalities at that particular location. It's a wonder we left the cottage at all but we made it to town and as I searched for a parking space I managed to achieve the impossible. I was driving our tiny car on town roads that actually seemed smaller than the car I was driving. I found in a moment of relief that car manufacturers for vehicles in this part of the world built cars specifically for these road conditions or built them with road hog American drivers in mind whose concept of a luxury car is a small living room on wheels. In the next moment, I was grateful that our luxury car was, by American standards, a compact.

First, a nasty sounding thump then, "Oh crap. I just smashed mirrors with that car." I looked into the interior rear-view to see the mirror on the car I'd just hit, flattened against its driver's side door. "Ahhh!" I said. "Shit! Let me go around again to leave a note." My mind started its internal conversation, thinking about, how much is this going to cost us in time, paperwork and insurance bullshit? I drove around the block and came back to the spot where I'd hit the car, to witness a young woman walk over to the damaged vehicle.

"Did she see us hit her?" Nora asked when she saw the young woman.

"I guess." I paused to think for a second. "Okay." I said and began rummaging in my bag for my license. "She's right here so at least we'll get this over-with now. You got the rental car paperwork over there?"

"Hold on." Nora said as she thumbed through papers and maps in the glove compartment. As we got closer to the victim, she poked a cigarette into her mouth, lighted it, stretched her hand out to the damaged mirror and yanked it back into position.

Then the unexpected happened and the woman hopped into her car, butt hanging from her mouth, and with smooth acceleration drove away leaving me with a perfectly timed entrance into her parking space. "Do you think they make them that way on purpose?" I hand-cranked my luxury car window down with the luxury handle and shoved the unbroken mirror on our car back into position. Immediately brightened at the circumstance I chirped "All right then. Dodged that bullet and found a parking space to boot."

Nora got out and came around the car to check. "Are you sure?"

"Yeah. Look." As I waggled the mirror back and forth we could hear the click, click, click of the several positions it could bend to in order to accommodate this type of situation. "Must be the luck o' the Irish" I said in a mock accent.

"Shh!" Nora hissed, as she guiltily checked around to make sure I hadn't embarrassed myself. "People will be insulted if they hear you do that!"

"How will they know I'm not from here?"

"Well you don't exactly sound like a native with your phony stage accent."

"Stage accent!" My mouth formed a big gaping oh. I thought I mimicked a pretty convincing Irish accent. "Well you don't exactly fit in here either with your bright red lipstick and your big gold hoop earrings." I chided. To anyone else this might have sounded like an argument but this was our way of dealing with a stressful situation. We rebuked each other with no bite or venom but treated the tête-à-tête as a chess game with skillful attack and counter-attack.

Now it was Nora's turn to stand with her mouth agape. She was just about to come back with a retort when I looked up at the store in front of which we'd parked and said, "Hey, is this the place we read about in the travel guide? It is. Isn't it?"

"Hold on." Nora reached back into the car to grab the guidebook, listing sacred places, both pre-Christian and Christian sites to visit in Ireland. Ever the tour guide she flipped through the book, and found the page we'd been looking at last night back at the cottage. Though I'd been doing the driving, Nora was the navigator and map-reader. In the same vein, she had a knack for getting us right where we wanted to be by her use of books, guides and on-line help. She was like the encyclopedia for topographical guidance. Her pupils contracted as she scanned the pages and then, "Yeah. The Sacred Traveler, this is it. Let's go in and check out what they have."

I eyed the café up the block a bit and speculated as to whether I might get a decent cup of coffee there first. I could almost smell the caffeine. It had been three days since we left home and I had not gotten any solid research under way. Time was slipping by here in a most surreptitious way, and us without any rational accounting for what we'd accomplished as time played the sneak. So I heaved a sigh and figured I'd try the café once we finished in the Sacred Traveler. Armed with notepad, pen and MasterCard, I surrendered. "Let's go."

And so finally, our adventures in history began.

———

We walked through the door to the Sacred Traveler and were met with the fungal smell of old books mingled with the dry smell of old people. The place was dark and hushed, conjuring up childhood memories of Saturday afternoon confession at church when Nora and I would each, in turn, go into the claustrophobic box to confess whatever sins an eight and ten-year old may have had. This place had the same feeling, but then again not.

There was almost a lingering smokiness to the air but no scent of a fire. *Good thing too,* I thought *'cause this place'd go up in a gigantic poof with the slightest spark, there's so much stuff piled around.* Perhaps the dim light lent itself to the impression of smoke or it could have been dust from all the old looking items around the shop. There were no visible sales people manning the ornate, cash register that had giant hand push, round keys and brass on black paisley patterns on the side. Maybe it wasn't a church but this place sure did command some form of reverence. I shook with a bit of a shiver. Maybe the store was chilly.

After my first impressions settled, I looked around and found that aside from a few book titles that spoke along the lines of Pagan Europe, Ancient Ireland, and

Celtic Oracles there was little else that couldn't be found in regular tourist shops and probably in better condition at that. We poked around the shop for a few minutes looking at Celtic crosses, reproduction St. Patrick statues, rosary beads and other religious paraphernalia. Feeling somewhat deflated after the excitement of not only finding the shop, but almost having it find us with the whole car mirror incident. I thought a place like this would have plenty to offer on early lore and mythology for dissertation material. I looked at Nora and we silently gave each other the eye. We were done here.

Disappointed, I breathed a heavy sigh and choked indelicately on a huge piece of floating dust! I hacked, a sort of gag/choke, as the dust attached itself to the back of my throat and as I began to make unfeminine noises coughing with unattractive red-face, a strange little man snorted to life right next to me in a decrepit wicker chair that only seconds before I would have sworn was simply not there. The little figure had pure white hair and his face was as red as mine probably was at the moment. He was momentarily a bit confused at the commotion and his face betrayed his annoyance at being awoken so abruptly. He quickly sized us up behind his little round spectacles and decided that maybe Nora's big, gold hoop earring held promise that we might be paying customers. His face adjusted to the concerned grandfatherly type and helpfully thumped me on the back with arthritic fingers.

"There now. A sip of water perhaps would help ye, dear."

As it was with my own grandfather, I wasn't sure, because of the accent, if he was saying "dear" or "there." In that moment, this little stranger, who had crossed the American cardinal "Two Foot Personal Space" rule and actually touched me, had oddly made me feel right at home. I nodded my head in agreement that water would probably help, expecting that our newfound host would provide some for me. He remained at my side resting an ancient hand on my back and I realized the water might not be forthcoming. This miniscule man peered up at me with somewhat filmy, watery brown eyes. He inspected my face as though he were waiting for me to speak to him. I hacked again and he snapped to attention with his mouth in a neat little pucker, he poked one gnarly finger into the air as he almost did an exit stage left move toward a wrinkled, well used brown bag tucked beside his chair. The word spry popped into my head as I watched him with my fist corked in front of my mouth trying to quell the blasts from spewing all over his merchandise. Out of the brown bag he pulled a thermos and carefully filled a paper cup with about three gulps of water. This done with the same caution had he been pouring nitro glycerin. The cup was presented to me as though he were offering ambrosia.

I gratefully took the cup and sipped not only because I didn't want to choke again and give my newfound knight a view of his water spewing from my nose, but also, I did not think this odd little man would offer me another drop. I believed he was unaccustomed to offering kindnesses to people much less American strangers, but all in the spirit of a sale I supposed.

"Thank you" I croaked, trying to clear the grit from my throat. My would-be savior, in a maneuver that could only be described as a prance, moved toward my sister now that presumably I wasn't going to die in his shop. With a *how do you do* look on his face and his hands practically wringing with the prospect of a sale asked, "What can I be helpin' ye gorls with?"

As we had already made up our minds to leave, Nora made obligatory polite conversation while composed myself. "We thought you might have some books or material on Astrology."

Ireland is filled with both the ancient and Christian archaeology and history. But regardless of what Ireland once was, it now appears to be a predominantly Catholic place. Our upbringing had taught us that Catholicism and Old Ways don't mix; at least not on the surface. We'd been wise to keep our beliefs underground in that environment. My education in the Catholic schools and church had given me another label for what I'd been taught as the Old Ways, a maligned word for what was the supposed antithesis of everything good. The word cast about as the evil, dishonorable, uncivilized, un-Godly people was Pagans. We wondered at the reception we'd receive when we each attempted to research our decidedly Pagan subjects here in Ireland and despite the few books I'd spotted in the shop on Pagan Europe, I really thought his answer would be a snappish, 'No!' just prior to hustling us out the door.

His response was one of surprised amusement. He pulled his mouth into a smile that looked foreign on his face but pleasant to see all the same, in spite of the gaps that could be seen between his remaining bottom teeth. "Astrology is it? Well ye could look through the books ye find here to see if any suit. Are ye lookin' for a horoscope lass, to find love maybe?"

"Well, no um, actually," Nora said, "I'm an astrologer and I'm doing research on a particular aspect of astrology." He waited. Nora forged on. "I'm looking for material on this one facet of Astrology to support a book I'm writing." Nora had been bombarded with erroneous concepts about astrology for all of the 20 years she'd been professionally calculating and reading mathematical charts. She was accustomed to misconceptions, snippy condescension, religious doggedness, narrow-mindedness and giving long explanations as to what astrology is not. Her face and tone of voice told me that she hadn't the patience for suffering fools just now.

I knew though, that if we were going to make any progress here in our endeavors, we may have to do a considerable amount of fool suffering before we found the underground network of people that might actually be able to help a couple of heathens. I cleared my throat for insurance that my fit was over.

"Excuse me sir" I interrupted, I notice you have a few books here on Pagan Europe. Do you have any more books or information along that line? We've both come in search of genuine information that we likely won't be able to find in the states."

His head swiveled back toward me and once again I was scrutinized over his spectacles. He seemed to be deciding whether or not we were genuine ourselves. "What's your name then?"

"Ah, I'm Lee, and this is my sister Nora...um O'Leary.

Our host was growing agitated. "Um O'Leary is it? What kind of a name is Um O'Leary? Is it O'Leary or not?"

I figured ten seconds, and he'll have us out the door. "Yes." I said defensively, pulling myself up to full height. "Our maiden name is O'Leary." And I don't know why, but I added, "We're sisters." As if that lent substance to my words.

"That's better. It's proud of your name ye should be. No ums. And are ye as sure of your...Christian names as well?"

Stubborn I could be. My husband has often called me 'rock headed Irish'. I'd be damned if I was going to let this little man berate me for being, American, Pagan, or any other thing.

"I'm sure of what I'm looking for." I said. "Is it something you can help us with or should we look for another shop whose best feature isn't the aggrandizing advertisement in the travel guide?"

The little troll, as I was now beginning to think of him, raised both his twisted, knotty hands in front of his chest and to our surprise, clapped them together as he actually cackled. I wasn't sure, watching him wheeze and hoot, if he was having some kind of fit of his own. Then to our absolute amazement, he smacked Nora a glancing blow with the back of his hand across her upper arm as if they enjoyed some kind of private joke. If we weren't so shocked at this point we'd have stormed out the door but as it was, all we could do for the moment was watch with wide eyes.

"Hee hee, he heee!" Now it was his turn to choke and cough. "Call me Cath." He quacked as he wiped his streaming eyes with an ancient handkerchief trying to get himself under control. Still hiccupping giggles, he turned and cavorted almost sideways, toward a curtained doorway at the rear of the store beyond his antiquated wicker chair. He beckoned us both to follow still attempting to get his chortling under control muttering under his breath. "Aggrandizing! Oh yes, a spark te that one."

We looked at each other with speculative raised eyebrows. I gave a shoulder shrug that said, 'What could it hurt?' We followed Cath toward the back of the store where he stopped by a doorway and ceremoniously waved a hand toward it gesturing with a slight bow that this is where we should go. I pulled back the velvety drape of thick blue material that served as a door-block and came to an abrupt stop. I goggled at the sight of what the back room held and Nora walked right into the back of me and emitted a breathy "Oof."

At precisely the same time I let go an amazed, "Awe," of my own.

A quote from a television documentary I once saw came immediately to my mind when Howard Carter, the discoverer of Tutenkamen's Tomb in Egypt was asked by his partner, "Can you see anything?" Upon peering by candlelight into the newly excavated opening of a treasure filled room, he uttered an awestruck whisper. "Yes. Wonderful things."

7

Blood Will Out

Lon Dubh, Faidhe's youngest daughter was sitting cross-legged, in front of her modest hut skinning a rabbit for the pot and deciding what she'd do with the fur. She'd been pre-occupied this morning, with hints of a vision that peeped out in her mind only to slip away like the rabbit she was skinning had done half a dozen times before she'd brought it down with her sling. And like the rabbit, she'd catch this elusive vision too. She set her jaw and redoubled her efforts to separate the rabbit's skin from its meatier counterpart. Always determined to achieve her goal, Lon Dubh worked the skin with her hands while her mind puzzled the snippets of imagery that were distracting her today. These were strange pictures that flashed for a moment and just before she could identify the images, they would disappear so that she was left with only a sense of what she saw. Usually more adept at identifying her visions, Lon Dubh was not only frustrated by this illusiveness, but she disliked that her inability to capture the visions secretly made her question her skills as a potential Seer for the clan. She was keenly affronted by her powerlessness to assume the position of the Keeper of the Circle, or as a member of Tribal Council. As a result, anything that might be recognized as a weakness in her abilities or that flamed the spark of self-doubt was most unwelcome. She'd committed her life to the goal of assuming one or both of these positions as her mother had. She thought of her future with the tribe as the Keeper or as a Seer as her rightful place within the tribe because since she was a young girl she had a recurring vision of herself as doing extraordinary work and great magic for the tribe. There was no detail to the vision, she simply saw herself as a woman in an important position that she'd taken on for the benefit of not just the clan but for the entire Tuath.

Hers was a large and powerful Tuath; comprised of the Danann Clan, the people of the Goddess, Danu, and all the extended groups who made up the tribe whether through marriage, or alliance. Lon Dubh had displayed strength in her seeing abilities and often had visions that proved to be accurate and helpful to her clan so she thought it only natural that a position as one of the six Seers of the Council or the most important position as the Keeper of The Circle, would one day be hers.

"I am of the daughters of Danu," Lon Dubh told those who would question her solitary ways. "As my mother before me, I am of the direct line of the union of Morrigan and The Dagda. My blood can be traced back near countless generations to those who brought the sacred implements and planted the Stone of Fal. I have seen the visions of my future and will keep my own Council as to what they may or may not mean but know this: As a daughter of the line of Danu I have already taken an oath in my heart to keep the Circle and protect the sacred artifacts brought from the north countries."

The Stone Circle is the central focus of the magic of the Tuatha De Danann. It is the sacred Ring of Stones that serves as a portal to the other world, the place of the Universal Power. There are hundreds, perhaps thousands of sacred circles erected all over the world each with its own purpose. This particular Circle of the Tuatha De Danann was erected using the power of the Stone of Fal; a great stone brought from Falias a magical land to the north, one of four such lands of knowledge, magic and learning. The Stone was integral in the Danann conquering and taking of this green land, and so this Stone is forever linked with the royalty of the land of the Danann. It is said to have a voice and will scream the truth about the rulers and destiny of the lands. It is placed at the head of the Circle so it meets the rising sun in the east each day and stands witness as it parts each night. The placement is such that the magic of the Stone cannot flee back to the north where it originated. The other stones in the Circle join the keystone to create the portal between the worlds and to contain the magic of other sacred implements utilized within. The Circle's function is tri-fold; it serves as a shrine to the strength of magic of the Tuatha De Danann, it is a portal between this world and the other, and is also used for the purpose of harnessing the power of the magic that was brought there many generations hence.

Stories of that time hold talk of much magic and strange, other-beings walking the earth. But now, even though there is talk of a giant here, sightings of merfolk, or tales of some dragons in the land to the east, such extraordinary magic and beings seem but distant and fantastic tales to Lon Dubh.

The Circle though, she knows, is where the sacred implements of the Gods of her clan are kept, and is also where communion with the Gods is most probable. Through the portal she'd seen many spirits of ancestors return upon being summoned during a festival or during a clan ritual prior to a battle. She'd also glimpsed occasional visions of her mother in the Circle performing *real magic* although she had never been able to determine in her visions exactly what that real magic might be. *When I take over the duties of the Circle*, she thought, *all the magical secrets will be revealed to me. I know this must be my destiny. I've given up so much; it has to be.*

Her mother, Faidhe, had been on Lon Dubh's mind today and thoughts of her mother always brought unbidden, raw disappointment to the surface.

"Dual frustration." she snorted, as she concentrated with her head lowered over the rabbit. With a final slice from her sharpened tool, Lon Dubh separated the rabbit from its fur. She tried to concentrate on what she had to add to the pot with the rabbit meat; some root bulbs saved from last year's harvest and some new green shoots popping up in the weak spring sunlight, perhaps some greens from the yellow wildflower. They were always plentiful and added a mouthwatering sharpness for which Lon Dubh had acquired a taste. Her hands worked the meat, separating it now from the bones, but her mind was distracted.

Why does the Keeper come into my head today? Even though she could not determine, specifically, what these new visions were about, she knew this energy she was picking up, somehow involved her mother. Lon Dubh knew change was coming in some fashion and her frustration began to ease as it was replaced with speculation that perhaps Faidhe had finally come to recognize, due to her advanced years, she should come down from the hill and allow someone younger and stronger to take her place. Lon Dubh felt confident that she would be the logical choice as her mother's replacement. As she had told all those who would listen these ten years since she'd reached womanhood, her blood was of strong lineage, she had borne no children as her sister had, and many other potential Keepers had as well; a sacrifice she'd made in planning for the day when she'd walk up the Hill and take what she thought of as her rightful place as the Keeper of the Circle. She'd conceive her children as gifts of the union during one of the festivals, just as the other Keepers had done, as her mother had done. She was older than most who'd ascended to the Circle but was still plenty young enough to bear children and so not past the point of being considered for the service of the Circle. She reckoned on her fingers...

"Twenty four, no twenty five festivals of the final harvest have passed since my birth. A perfect balance I think." she calculated to herself. *No children yet but still at least ten seasons left before my moon blood ceases to flow.*

The maternal relationship is considered to be the most sacred of all to Lon Dubh's Tuath. It is so because it is through motherhood that life, on all levels of existence, springs. The Earth mother creates all life on earth from the lowliest insect to the mightiest tree. The human mother brings forth new life in continuation of the bloodlines of the clans, and the Mother Goddess reigns supreme in nurturance and creation of all life on earth, in water and sky.

The female, always seen in one of the three roles of life encompassed within the span of one human woman's lifecycle, is the personification of all that is. As a maiden, she is the potential of the clan's future and very survival. As the mother, she is the giver of life, the nurturer, who succors the tender spark of life so it grows strong and stronger still until such time that life takes its useful and productive place within the clan. As the wise woman, she is the keeper of history and knowledge. She is the teacher of the young so that the essence of the spirit of the clan is renewed in the maid. The wise woman is the renewal of the knowledge and is closest to the rebirth into the spirit world. So every woman is revered as sacred, a vessel capable of bringing forth a life from the spirit world, instilling the life-spark in human form and enveloping it within the flesh. This awesome and sacred responsibility is the most important role in the life of the tribe. The giving of life in continuation of clan, continuance of crop and perseverance of cattle or livestock is encapsulated in the power of the She, and her role is never taken as less than the most sacrosanct.

The woman chosen as the Keeper of the Circle must have no young children prior to going up the Hill or any children she may already have must at least be matured to the time of preparation for their first sexual rites. It is considered to be a gross offense and an act against the sacred, once the bond of nurturance had been formed in the sacred relationship of mother and child, that it should be severed too early or abandoned, unfair to both the mother and the child. The only exception to this principle is when the Goddess calls a maiden of the tribe through omen or vision to serve the Circle, as was the case with Faidhe. Only then she may leave her mother to learn from and serve the Mother Goddess.

If a woman is to take on the mantle of the Keeper of the Circle, she must be unencumbered by any commitments to a man or a child in order that her focus and ability to tend to the rituals, rites and duties of the Circle is pure and unfractured. For this reason, the Keeper of the Circle is usually very young and often times, still a maiden when she takes on the responsibilities of the Stone Ring. The ritual of the Keeper's first right as a woman, when she would first lay with a man at one of the festivals, became a great and important celebration for the tribe. And if there should be a child of that union, then the entire tribe took on the fosterage of the babe upon the day of its birth so the Keeper remained pure and undistracted as an implement of the Circle.

Because Faidhe had occupied the position as the Keeper for so long, Lon Dubh and her sister were the only two Children of the Circle alive within their clan at this time save for one that neither of the girls knew personally. That she was born under such conditions, it was another reason Lon Dubh felt her place as the Keeper was more justified than any other potential initiates. She rationalized that she was of the Circle and so had an intimate link with the magic of the realm within it. She was conceived there on a magical festival night, and was born there through the very portal between the worlds.

Despite her magical conception and claims to the Circle, in not taking a husband or to lay with a man on the sun or moon festivals, Lon Dubh had risked being ostracized by her clan. Motherhood was not only a sacred relationship but also a woman's commitment to produce new life to ensure the propagation and survival of the clan. Lon Dubh had refused to take a husband or to lay with a man in order that she would not risk bearing a child in waiting for the day when she would serve as the Keeper of the Circle.

Once she had reached maturity at the age of fifteen and came into her moon blood, Lon Dubh was expected to join the fertility festivals in celebration of her new phase of womanhood. When she refused, the clan considered the unusual behavior an abomination against the sacred. But paradoxically, it had always been the woman's prerogative to select the man with whom she would lay and as such, she made it her choice, not to choose, it required consideration that the woman's ultimate selection is the right one. The Council discussed this new wrinkle in the spiritual path of a woman. Was it ambition that kept Lon Dubh from the sacred path of motherhood, a thirst for power? The latter, of course, would be profane. However if it was a decision made of purely spiritual intent, then her actions would surely be approved by the Goddess, and Lon Dubh's fruitless womb would be tolerated.

———

As it was, Faidhe was asked by the Council to seek communion with the Gods on this matter of Lon Dubh's refusal to take a man. She had worried over her estranged daughter's decision to refrain from the fertility rights and wanted to speak with the girl to get a sense of what her motives were. In a private meeting Faidhe asked this young woman her purpose in refusing the accustomed and sacred ways of the clan. Lon Dubh's cheeks reddened as she recalled her audience with her mother that day.

"Child, where lays the sacred purpose for your refusal to take part in the festivals? Has the Goddess instructed you so?"

At that time, Lon Dubh had never in her 15 seasons been this close to the woman who was her mother; much less spoken to her although she had seen Faidhe perform the awesome rituals upon the Hill at the altar stone. She had witnessed Faidhe transform right before her eyes and take on the appearance of the Gods and Goddesses she petitioned. Faidhe held great respect in the clan and the larger tribe. Lon Dubh wanted to hold the position her mother held, to be like her and to wield the Power as she did. She was overwhelmed with the responsibility that Faidhe had impeccably carried out for so long, yet wanted to prove that she was able to do as well in service to the Goddess, if not better, given the opportunity. She was drawn to the duty of the Keeper and was frightened of it at the same time. She was so sure that she was destined to take her mother's place yet, she had never been touched with a vision or voice from the Goddess or lesser God or Goddess to confirm this path for her.

The pubescent girl twiddled a piece of straw between her fingers and silently chastised herself for not meeting the Keeper's gaze. She dropped the straw and breathed deeply. Looking up at Faidhe, Lon Dubh rose from her seated position on the floor of Faidhe's hut and knelt so that she would be eye to eye with the other woman who sat on a low stool made of sturdy branches and woven straw.

"I have not been instructed by any other than myself." Lon Dubh challenged.

"Is it fear you harbor? Or have you no desire for a man?"

"I have no fear of the act of laying with a man, nor do I lack the desire. What I do have is a keener desire to serve the Goddess on the Hill and take your place as the Keeper of the Circle."

There, she'd said it out loud and would not have her knowledge that she would be the rightful replacement for Faidhe as Tribal Seer and the Keeper of the Circle diminished by harboring it as a secret. The silence in the hut was plain. The girl rushed on speaking to fill the awful void.

"You have kept the seat of Keeper for almost twice my lifetime and in that time I have known many who would have made adequate Keepers yet you remain on the Hill long past your youth. How is it that you do not descend to your appropriate place among the Wise Women and allow such as myself to keep the Circle?"

Faidhe did not allow her shock at the girl's boldness to show on her face but she let the girl know she had spoken carelessly in the sight of the Goddess.

"It is not for you to assume what is adequate or appropriate regarding the responsibilities of the Keeper. That is the right of the Goddess alone and when I am called by Her to the honorable task of Wise Woman, I will gladly descend the Hill and not before. As for your idea that it is your place to take the seat as Keeper, it is my fervent hope that if it will be so, you will have learned much patience before that time, for the position requires much of the will of a woman. Strength in temperance, quelling of the self and personal desire is required as is a standard of craft that reaches far beyond mere adequacy."

Lon Dubh's face burned with shame for she knew in her attempt to appear stoic, brave and worthy, she had come across as brash, childish and selfish. She was mortified that her first and only meeting with her mother should take this course.

"Forgive me Mother." She lowered her eyes once again. "I will strive to practice the restraint required of the Keeper and learn all measure of the required crafts to the best of my ability so that if the Goddess has use for me as Keeper or a Tribal Seer, I will be prepared beyond what is adequate. I will take heed of your words as one who knows and consider this my first lesson in the ways of the Circle."

Faidhe was not sure if the '*Mother*' identified her in a position as one representing the Goddess or if Lon Dubh referred to their connection by blood. She felt a pull at her heart for the relationship that might have been but for the very temperance she had just now identified as so necessary to her position. She warmed to her daughter and wondered if she had any right to try to dissuade her from the path of the Keeper. She felt the maternal impulse to protect her daughter from this hard and solitary existence. Had her children felt the loss of a normal maternal relationship as much as she had? She wondered.

Faidhe studied this girl whom she brought forth into the world. She was named well for she had the night black hair of the black bird and her eyes so dark as not to see the black openings to the spirit held within the head. Faidhe could see strength within this one but with a wild streak as with a horse that can never truly be brought to hand. Lon Dubh was a gift of the final harvest festival at the end of the warm days. Conceived at the fires, she came to birth at the first wheat harvest at festival of Lugh the following year. A child of the Circle was an honorable standing. To be conceived on a sun or moon festival is desirable because the child is said to be a favored one to be given the life-spark by the fires of the festival. Lon Dubh was not only conceived during a festival, but was a child conceived as her mother and father took on the spirit of the Goddess and the God within the sacred Circle. Even this type of conception is not unheard of, but Lon Dubh, created of the Circle, was also born within the Circle on the High Festival Day of Lugh, the resplendent God of the sun. This had never happened in any times remembered. She was special, no doubt, she had the gift of communion with the spirit world, that was plain, and her birth a harbinger of some connection and service to the Goddess or more likely the God as her birth was during a sun festival, which is decidedly masculine.

But Faidhe did not see her in the service of the Circle and considered why she did not suppose Lon Dubh would ascend the Hill to the task as Keeper. She had the power of communion. She seemed committed in her abstinence in order to avoid profaning the most sacred relationship of mother and child. Perhaps it was just her own will that her daughter not serve to live such a lonely way of life.

Faidhe opened herself to the Power seeking answers as to this situation. She lowered her head almost imperceptibly to shift her state of consciousness and let her eyes slip into a half focus as she studied Lon Dubh.

The sounds around Faidhe took on an echo-like quality. The chirping birds outside were distant and fuzzy. She recognized the thrum in her head that was the precursor to communication from the place of the 'other.' Faidhe watched her daughter take on the appearance of the spirit for which she was named as they sat in the Keeper's cozy hut. She saw the girl transform, in a vision right before her, into a bird with great black flapping wings rustling restlessly behind her. An enormous squawk emitted a warning call from her razor-like beak, three sharp caws and so quickly as to be a blur, the great razor beak jutted forward and ripped into Faidhe's middle. She felt her innards being pulled and the great bird tugged at a long thin vine as if it were a worm being wrenched from Faidhe's insides. The vine hung from the bird's mouth and Faidhe recognized it as a local wood vine used for weaving nest-like baskets, sitting mats, and other useful items. The vine was a soft tendril that lent itself well to the weaving process because it could easily be molded and adapted to many shapes and purposes, but once set and dried, became a strong, almost indestructible material.

All at once, the bird was gone and the girl was just a girl sitting before her looking very young and a bit nonplussed. Faidhe opened her mouth to speak and to her own surprise, words came echoing up through her as from the depths of a well rather than words of her own. Her voice sounded eerily of grinding stones and gurgling water.

The ancient sounds of the earth belching forth out of a human mouth gave Lon Dubh a hint of the humbling Power that lay beneath the Circle with which her mother had been intimate for so long. Her skin grew moist and she went white and cold while adrenaline pumped into her system and her heart quickened. She forgot to breath.

As Faidhe forced this foreign sound past her own vocal chords the wind itself could be heard in her breath.

"Child, you are one of the Cumhacht de Cruinne, a daughter of the Universe. Your path is long and your journey extends beyond that which can be encompassed in the four directions. If you choose to forego motherhood, you will not be admonished for when it is time, you will participate in the Great Union and be among those who will propagate the life of the Triad. You will preserve the Circle. From your mouth will fall the earth, water and air and only from the mouth shall it be fertile, germinate and breed new life. You will follow the Keeper and her path shall be your path, her journey will be your own."

Lon Dubh gasped as she was shaken out of her reverie by the shock of slicing a deep gash on her thumb made by the cutting tool she used on the rabbit meat. Shaking her head to clear the memory of her only audience all those seasons passed with her mother she thought, I know that voice meant for me to take my place as the Keeper. She corked her thumb into her mouth to quell the bleeding. How else could the message be interpreted? Over and over again through the years since the voice had spoken to her in Faidhe's hut, Lon Dubh had pulled apart the message, word by word, trying to divine exactly what her future would hold. But if I am to take my rightful place on the Hill, then why has it taken so long since it was foretold to me? Best be careful, she chided herself, all things in the Goddess' time, not my own.

The intimidation she'd always felt when confronted with the Power behind that voice returned to her as if it had just happened. A healthy respect for the Universal Power, the Cumhacht de Cruinne the voice called it, is a good thing, she told herself. One would be foolish to approach the service of the Circle without respect and reverence. This too was a message she'd repeated to herself many times when she'd felt the fear she experienced on the day she'd been singled out by that voice and the Power behind it, welling up to fill her heart with trepidation. "All in the Goddess' time." she repeated aloud. Lon Dubh was now doubly shaken by the sight of the blood she'd just drawn during the memory of such a powerful event. She knew blood of the maidenhead, blood of birth, blood of fertility and blood of death held the Power of the sacred cycle of the Goddess, blood drawn intended the keeping of a promise. Did this play a part with the visions she'd been trying to recollect? Was it some kind of harbinger of the coming events she had been intuiting today?

8

The Forest Comes Alive

Faidhe descended the Hill feeling at once apprehension and elation, enthusiasm and remorse for what lay ahead of her. The crisp clear way she now saw all things remained with her and did not seem that it was only a temporary effect left after her visions of the night before. As she walked by trees, now just in bud, she saw as well as felt the new energy rising in the sap within each tree. The wind itself brushed past her with the faintest hue of blue that was reminiscent of the blue light revealed to her within the Circle. Each step she took connected her, through her feet, with the energy of the Earth Mother. It renewed her and she drew strength from it. Despite her hesitance at what the tribe's response might be to her message, now that she understood its necessity, Faidhe was more alive and invigorated by her mission than she'd been through all the time she'd spent on the Hill for the past 35 years. As she walked the path toward the village, a trip that would take but a few finger measures at arm's length of the moving sun, she found herself aware of everything that occurred around her with all her physical senses and now with her heightened vision sense as well. The volume of her existence had expanded so that she was a part of all that was around her and it was a part of her. The result of this interchange was that she found herself aware of the unguarded thoughts, senses and feelings of all the creatures near her without being burdened or overwhelmed by it all: The hunger of the bird that flew overhead, the resignation of a wood mouse caught by a small falcon as its life was absorbed by the larger creature, the pleasure of the wild lilies as they first poked their relentless green heads through the forest's soil on their journey toward the light. Faidhe was surprised at the idea that flowers could feel pleasure but then thought why should they not? She felt a thrill at her part in the pulse of life quickening all around her and keeping rhythm with her own breath as the forest awakened with the implication of spring.

As if in a dream, Faidhe quizzically turned to see whether she was truly stepping on the earth since she felt almost as if she was floating rather than walking.

To her surprise, she observed her own footprints marked not by a depression in the forest carpet, but by a faint luminescent blue almost as if she left small pools of water where she'd stepped. She knew, it was not water but her energetic essence, just as she knew if there were others present, that they likely would not see the telltale color in her wake.

The smile faded from her features as she turned her attention back to the path toward the village. There was a deep shift in the forest's energy and she was startled by the knowledge that she was being watched. Her awareness was not of the fleeting presence of an animal or ethereal spark of new plant growth. *Yes, it is both*, she thought, *but then again, this venerable energy is ancient with depth of strength that perhaps could defeat time itself*. Faidhe was so caught off balance by this primal power, which was at once benevolent, terrible, and familiar that she instinctually spoke by reaching out with her mind. *"Who are you that I am so frightened as to set my bones to quake, yet I feel as if I am being welcomed into the arms of one so intimate that you are me, myself?"* Faidhe looked around to detect from where this power emanated. All her senses bristled to attention; she caught the dark, rich, scent of moist soil with an unidentifiable hint of some type of musky tree bark. It was a smell that held all the promise of a fecund harvest after a lush season of growth. Faidhe felt her body answer to the verdant aroma as her nipples rose to points as though chilled, and her aged womb responded to the instinctual harkening of the primal need to breed.

After so many planting and harvesting seasons in petition of just this type of drive to fertility, the scent that called her urge to couple and multiply was that of the earth. It was the scent of the earth, upon which she had taken the role of the Goddess many times, and yet this aroma carried the assurance of something more. She had petitioned the God and Goddess to grant fertility to the clan, crops and cattle as she had participated in the Sacred Union by the festival flames right on the earth and intimately knew the scent of the earth as she opened to accept the seed. This familiar earthy smell mingled with its musky scent of growing things, spoke of the mingling union of the earth as the womb itself and the seed of the green and growing things. For Faidhe, this scent manifested the beginning of the great cycle of life.

She reached out with her spirit to divine the location of this robust spark and was inundated with images and secret knowledge of the forest around her. She recognized the stoic strength of the evergreen pines, and the aromatic beginnings of the lily shells, ferns and fiddleheads that grew in the shade. She inherently knew the locations of hundreds of acorns, long buried as insurance against the winter's cold, now beginning to crack, sprouting the future of towering oaks. She knew by the hidden remains of a vole that it had spent its last moments merrily invading an abandoned squirrel's hoard just before it came under the silent wing of the winter owl. All this knowledge and more flooded at her with the simple reaching out of her spirit and then as the moth is drawn to the heat of the flame, she centered on the location of this profoundly fertile energy and spied a being standing so stock-still that she might have mistaken him for one of the grand and ancient trees of the wood through which she traveled.

He peered at her out of eyes, deep and brown that shone with humor and sorrow. These eyes that seemed to hold secret knowledge of the ages, were deeply set in a face that was both ageless and ancient. His skin bore the look of tree bark where she noticed furrows on the brow that marked the wearing of care and creases radiating from around the eyes and mouth that revealed deep and genuine laughter but with all the supple texture of summer leaves. A shadow of living moss spread across the strong jaw, down his chest and swathed his genitals. He exuded masculinity. This magnificent creature was a sight from which she could not drag her eyes, and found that she did not wish to.

Faidhe felt herself drawn to the being in remission of everything else. Her recent awareness of new abilities, her mission, her daughters, the Circle, everything dissolved from her mind as she surrendered to the opportunity just to be lost in those eyes. She felt herself being absorbed to know this spirit, this man, in every way she could. She drank him in with her own eyes and began to feel as if she'd had strong drink indeed. Her head began to buzz and she felt quite light in her body.

Though Faidhe stood the length of 5 men away from the woodland man, she felt herself reach out and touch the veins that stood out on his arms, legs, torso and manhood. A familiar gesture of a lover as she traced the ridges that twined over his body like great vines. His phallus responded and although she had not moved, she found herself directly in front of the man, looking up into his eyes and laying her palms flat on either side of his face noticing only then that his brown eyes were flecked with green and the black centers were open wide as if to absorb her every thought. She felt the texture of his skin and was intoxicated by his musk. This close, Faidhe was entranced as she observed that about his face were leaves in many stages of growth some in bud, some in bloom, others in tender shoots, some full, lush and green, then still, others gloriously aflame, blazing with color just before browning and dropping to return to the leafy blanket of the forest floor. While she studied this spirit, she observed the constancy of the leaves advancing through all the seasons and stages of growth right before her.

He moved for the first time during this introduction to put his arms out to her. As solid as tree branches yet flesh as with any man, he wrapped them, browned and weathered, around her, and belying great strength, they lifted her effortlessly. With no conscious thought, she wrapped her legs around the man and Faidhe felt herself open up to him as he let her know all of him. The air eddied around them in great swirls of green and blue and Faidhe lost herself as the physical and the spirit of the two combined.

Flashes of scenes rushed through her head as they mingled both mind and body in an unspoken union. She saw thousands of growing seasons elapse in an instant. Rainstorms that brought great change over the land. She watched in her mind as they shared together the smell, texture and taste of strange bounty of forests unknown from exotic and far away places. She shared the sight of hidden trysts and timeless couplings that the life force of the forest often compels in its bountiful spirit and smiles upon as honor and respect for the proliferation of life. She became him and he knew her. She could no more have met this energy and resisted than the buck could resist the passing of his seed while catching the scent of a healthy doe that is in her season.

She, having a foot in the spirit world but still most definitely human, and He, being of the spirit world, yet having a profound existence in the physical world, the two shared thoughts and visions of this act as it had been performed through ages in furtherance of life. Flickers of familiar Circle ceremonies over thousands of years and in lands far beyond her realm of familiarity had sparked in her mind and she saw that He was present at every coupling, His spark evident within each man playing the part for the God. She observed that the Goddess was ever there within the woman who took on Her mantle, and Faidhe observed without surprise but with interest that she, herself was present at every ceremony, every union, every act of propagation and love as well. She was aware of these visions in her mind even as her body responded to this coupling as a desert responds to a saturating rain. She began to flower. The appearance of ivy-like vines showed on her arms and legs as she gripped around his neck and body. Her long-idle breasts became full and yielding as she watched his lips coax them each to quenching him. They joined for what felt like eternity, yet Faidhe felt no fatigue even after so many waves of release and acquiescence to the long neglected need of her woman's body.

When he was sure she had been sated after tears, laughter, abandon, visions and a sharing like none she'd ever experienced, he consummated the act and poured himself into her. She cried out again and again, her voice raw to non-existence as it echoed against the sky. She felt the hot rush of everything of the forest within her. She felt communion with all the spirits, trees, plants and beasts in the forests as one with herself. For a moment she had a glimpse of the knowing of all things flood into her, and then her spirit expanded to infuse itself into every bit of the entire forest from the greatest tree to the smallest speck of dust. She had intimate consciousness of her partner's existence. She was the forest, the leaves, the trees, beasts, wilderness itself and it was within her.

All at once, with the echoes of her final throat-rending scream still in her ears, Faidhe found herself standing just where she'd been when she became aware of a presence in the wood. The forest twittered with the usual sounds around her. She looked around and there was nothing amiss with her clothing and no evidence of the all-consuming deed that she had just shared except for the sense of a profound shift of the energy within herself. The sun, by her account, should have been low in the sky and the air with a chill for it must be late in the day. But the sun still hung high overhead. Faidhe looked to the man with a questioning face and communicated wordlessly. *What has just come to pass? Is this a new way of 'Seeing' or does my mind fail me?*

She wondered at this creature and studied his familiar face, yet she was sure she'd never seen the likes of him before this shared experience. Still carrying the flush of what had just taken place, Faidhe struggled to make sense of her experience and deluge of feelings.

He waited, knowing that she would come to recognition. He seemed to be all together comfortable with waiting as he stood stoic, and still as she was again fascinated with his wild beauty.

"Ah, your eyes," she spoke, testing her tender vocal chords and found them without damage as if she'd not just used them until they gave out in fatigue. A hand flew to her throat as if to verify this was so. "These eyes have watched over and protected me for all of my days. I know you for I have basked in the wealth of your toil and served my people with the gifts of your forest. I know the flood of warmth and safety I feel. You are the God of the Wood, are you not? You are the custodian of the forest...Are you not the Greenman?"

"I am." He spoke aloud for the first time. His voice carried a deep and quiet surety in resounding force.

Faidhe felt a flood of emotions as if seeing an old friend after long separation. "I am not equipped to thank you for the gift you have bestowed."

"Thanks? None are necessary for you gave as much of yourself as you received. It is the heart of the sharing, as it should be. This was an act integral to your journey."

A kernel of discomfort made itself known in Faidhe's chest. She felt remiss that her mind had so completely abandoned her task. "Are you then a part of the quest I now embark upon?"

"Come woman, set down your charge and sit by the rivulet here so that we may speak plain."

Faidhe had forgotten all until this moment, being reminded of what she still carried on her shoulder and was surprised at this for it was the responsibility of this very item that necessitated her journey. How could it so easily have been put from her mind?

He responded to her astonishment and knowingly spoke to her in his quiet baritone. "It is the beginning of what is to come Faidhe." He reflected with a tinge of sadness. "You have seen in the visions this night past in the Circle, the images of what will be. If not for this knowledge, you would not have left the Ring on the Hill and embarked upon this path. You, who have spent most of your days in service of the Circle and in Keeping of the sacred implements now serve as a living, breathing symbol of what will take place between the *Cumhacht de Cruinne* and the human world for it has been decreed that it will be through you that the balance between the Goddess and the God, shall be made right and then maintained. But before that comes to pass, there will be much that will change, indeed, must change. As your charge just slipped from your mind so the Goddess will long be forgotten.

"So it is true?" Faidhe blurted, panicked at the verification of what she'd seen in the Circle. "The visions I have endured will come to pass." She pleaded. "But, there can be no life without the Goddess! Reverence and worship are her due. Yet she will be forgotten? This is folly!"

"So it would seem to us now Faidhe, but the quest you embark upon is to bring balance between the Goddess and the God among the humans. For without one, the other cannot be sustained. The arc of energy has begun its great swipe in effort to counter balance the reign of the Goddess o'er these many ages. In the building of the earth's variety and population, this great energy She bestows has been in demand, nay, necessary to come through so many stages of life to arrive at humans; spirit beings of the flesh. And the energy of the God has been in recession due to the need of the life energy of succor and feminine nurturance. Humans though, seem to have mistaken this recession for a secondary position to the Goddess. Therein lies their error. The Goddess has brought great abundance to the world and now, with her feminine-ness and moon-cycle, has reached the time when humans must begin to progress using their own means of creativity and fertility. This means the subsidence of magic and travel between spirit and physical realms. What man has already begun to do in this withdrawal is take from the Mother Earth, not what is needed for survival, or worship, but raping her of her precious metals in order to create weapons for furtherance of the glut for power and reasons of war. What has been prophesied is evidence that as the Goddess recedes and withdraws, the void that will be created by removal can only be filled with the masculine of equal measure to the absent Goddess energy together with the masculine energy already in play. It seems human masculinity will lose its way from the spirit and the path to the spirit, for most, will be usurped by this all too human lust for power. This, as you have seen, causes the pendulum of balance, once swung this time, to move so far out of balance that my energy, the masculine energy will, but for what you will bring to pass over these next turns of the seasons, take over the world like an all-consuming fire. You, in this infinitesimal moment we have spent together are living proof of how even the most devout follower may be lost from the way of the spirit. Keep your awareness about you Faidhe, lest *you* forget the Goddess and the cauldron."

Faidhe flushed. "I would deny it possible but for what has just been proven to me. How is it that I have allowed myself to fall unmindful of the responsibility bestowed upon me? Is it the shock of all that has taken place in this last day that makes me forget my primary charge? Or is it some potent magic that misplaces my thoughts?"

"You are an adept student Faidhe. It is what you say and more. It is magic of this pendulum unchecked. You must shape the magic Faidhe to do the bidding not of the Goddess or of the God but of the balance needed for humans to continue to exist. For without the balance, 'man' as they will then call themselves will surely begin to kill all life in its consuming greed and arrogance and all will be lost. For it is so that *nature* out of balance will right itself by flood, quake, storm, fire or whatever else may be necessary to ensure its continuance and proliferation. The ill you are given to put right is a much weightier task. *Spirit* out of balance creates dis-ease and unrest on all levels of existence. There will be occurrences of the spiritual masculine energy manifesting on earth in effort to lead humans back to the spirit, however the aggressive taint of humankind or I should say mankind will turn it from how it is intended. The coming of the weapons being made with this new iron combined with the dawning of this new and masculine energy taking over the spiritual reverence will rage out of control and create much warring and even those few who are sent to plant seeds of spirituality among the humans will have a following that will lead to naught but warring over spiritual belief, and squabbling in want of power. And that will last far longer than We care to endure but for the knowledge that what you set in motion will reveal itself through time that the Goddess lives and wants to be the Mother to humankind and at the right moment in time, We may come together in balance only if humans will allow. And when or if the spirit comes to balance, it will begin to manifest on earth that humankind will begin to come into balance as well."

Faidhe was overwhelmed. She sat in reflective silence mulling over thousands of questions, sensing her time with the Greenman was coming to a close, tried to choose the most important ones to ask. "Are you the God then?"

"Yes, but I am but one facet. As we came together, I gave you a vision. You saw me in countless Circle ceremonies participating in the Great Union and you also saw yourself?"

"Yes." She blushed having been so engrossed in his explanation of what she'd seen in the prophetic vision of the Circle the night before, she'd forgotten the magical coupling they'd shared only moments ago and what she'd seen then. She wondered if she truly was addled in her mind.

In his trick of knowing her thoughts he answered, "No Faidhe, your mind is unhindered. You're adjusting to a greater perspective, not a simple task even for one who has opened to the spiritual Seeing as you have. You saw yourself in the vision through countless seasons and harvests, many lifetimes over because, as I am of the God, you are of the Goddess. You too are a facet of who She is. She is the Danu and She is a great many other Goddesses to a great many others. I am the God and I am the Greenman and I am the Dagda just as I am the man who gives seed to his wife in their marriage bed and the woman, old or young, is the Goddess. We are one, and We are many."

"Ah!" She was jubilant in her understanding and rushed to learn more. "What of the crow as was seen in my vision of the Circle? 'Seek always the black bird,' it said. 'The raven.' My instincts lead me to Lon Dubh who is named for the Black Bird. Is this quest her path as well?"

"You must trust the information that comes to you. You are of the Goddess and have been chosen to create the channel through which she will travel forward in time. Symbols are as important as the word for interpreting vision Faidhe. Hearken to whence this vision first visited upon you. And then you will know."

Faidhe studied her feet for a moment, wrapped in tough buckskin leather, lined with softened straw. Formulating her next question she looked to her teacher and found herself sitting next to an enormous oak tree standing where he had been sitting only moments ago. She was sure the tree had not been there before but then she recognized this oak served as a marker that had stood for centuries beside the path and next to the little offshoot from the river where a traveler could stop for clean water and to rest under the shade of the tree. How was it that she did not recognize where she had been before this? She briefly thought again about the state of her mind and dismissed it accepting that things were just as he'd told her; she was adjusting to a new way of being.

Helping herself to a mouthful of clear, clean water that tasted faintly of something woodsy, she smiled to herself and her body thrilled at the memory the taste brought to her mind. Then Faidhe gathered her cauldron onto the staff and was grateful that she still bore the company of all the sprites, fairies and woodland spirits. They still seemed content to help her bear the load she carried. More accepting of stepping in and out of the spirit world, Faidhe took notice that although her mind told her it had been at least a half a day since she first sensed the Greenman, the sun still hung overhead in the sky as if no time had passed at all.

When she turned back to the trail that led to the closest clan village, she could still feel his presence but much reserved. The path she traveled down the hillside was dense with spring bracken and overgrowth due to little use to and from the Circle. Travel was slow and Faidhe took that time to learn things gone unnoticed before and add them to the many new things she now had in her cache of

knowledge. She allowed herself to revel in her fledgling understanding of the forest, touching with her mind, fingers and spiritual sight all she could to learn of the
creatures and growth there. The green moss keeping company with the oaks on the
north facing tree bases would aid in healing wounds. Poisonous mushrooms long
thought to be well avoided, Faidhe learned, were strong medicine if but made to a
tincture just as the leaves from the lily shells would hold medicine to strengthen
the heart if harvested at the correct time.

The little used path widened some way past the rivulet where she'd taken her
drink and just then she sensed a new energy in the forest. This had a more complicated feel than the simplicity of the forest. The further along the village path she
traveled, the more prominent the energy until, as a flint being struck in the dark,
recognition peeled in her mind. She felt the presence and innocence of a child!
Faidhe was pleased she was quickly honing her knew skills.

Looking further down the trail, she spotted the child searching for ground
nests to collect the first eggs of the season. Egg hunting is a much-anticipated ritual
after a long cold season without fresh grown foods and little fresh meat. The villagers fashioned nest-like collection baskets and went in search of fresh bird eggs.
This child looked in Faidhe's direction as if she too felt the presence of the other.

Expecting that all the clan's folk knew her, she was a bit uncertain as to why
the child greeted her formally as a stranger traveling the road instead of a warm
greeting of familiarity.

"Good day, kind mother. Are you come for the festival of the Goddess of the
spring planting? Know you the village here or is it instruction you seek to find your
way?" The girl of about eight sun seasons suddenly grew stiff and her eyes grew
wide. Faidhe traced her gaze to the cauldron and staff she carried. The child fell to
her knees and asked, "Mother, are you the Goddess herself then, come to celebrate
with our people on the day of your feast?" With a furrowed brow, Faidhe recognized the energy around the girl had gone from a golden hue of pleasant introspection to swirling pools of excitement.

"No little one. I am Faidhe, Keeper of the Circle. I am of your clan and likely
some kin to you. Have you no knowledge of me?"

"You are not the Spring Goddess, come to quicken the lands?" Asked the girl
with not a little wonderment. "If not, then how is it that you carry her basket of
seeds for fertility and you are surrounded by the rabbits that foretell of her coming?"

As she looked around, Faidhe did see streaks of light that held an active, pulsating energy. She recognized the energy was the highly charged life force of the
prolific spring rabbit. Her way of seeing the world certainly had changed but now
that she'd encountered a member of her clan and not been recognized she'd begun
to suspect that the way the world would see her is different as well. "What is your
name little one?"

"I am Emer. If you are Faidhe the Keeper, then we *are* kin." How is it that you are grown so young as to be mistaken for the Goddess of spring and fertility? Is it magic then?"

"I am not so young as that." Faidhe chuckled. As the laughter rolled up from her chest, the sound breathed from Faidhe's mouth in a bouquet of color that extended toward the child and tickled a smile onto her lips. Faidhe saw in that moment that her laughter was communicable and tucked that bit of knowledge away with the rest. "You flatter me Emer. Have you found many eggs for the celebration?" Faidhe thought of the great spring planting at the celebration of the coming of the warm days with some regret and sense of loss, she knew that this festival would greatly differ from those of the last millennium.

"Oh I have a great many in my basket and have gathered a variety of others before this basket was filled." Chirped Emer. A shadow then crossed her face and she nervously added, still not sure if this was the Goddess of spring or not, "I have never taken more than one from any nest. I know not to hunt with greed but with gratitude and thanks for the sacrifice of the mother birds and the life within the egg so that we may eat."

"That is our way Emer. You have learned well to respect all life and take only what is in balance for your need. Would that all people could learn the lesson of balance so well. Will you accompany me on the path to the village?" Faidhe thought that when she descended to the village, it would be best that as many villagers as possible should be present to hear her news firsthand when she arrives rather than trust to the rumors that will undoubtedly spread afterward. With her new friend, she traveled toward the village. Along the way, the two gathered several more children who were a-hunt in the forest and others out for the forage of new green. By the time they reached the outer boundaries of the village, Faidhe walked with a band of children and villagers about twenty strong.

The sweat poured down his face and naked upper torso as Iarann, the blacksmith stoked his fires and worked the precious metals into useful implements to further the clan's survival. This craft considered to be an important and magical one due to the nature of the extraction of the metal under the earth itself and the artful shaping of the hard elements into bronze implements, gold adornments, iron tools and weapons. For the sake of safety, the outer reaches of the village are where the tanning huts, the smoke houses and smithing fires are situated. Most days Iarann took pleasure in working his tools at the flames built in the fire pit outside his work hut to enjoy the open air and sky as he worked the metals of his trade. On those days Iarann worked with a boy from the village clan who stoked the fires for him to shape the metal. Today though, he was alone and inside his hut because this was a day when he would complete his work on several pieces and the private, sacred words would be issued over the metal. To complete this magical work, Iarann stayed within his smithing hut walls and sent the boy who worked the bellows away to observe tradition so that the craftsman was alone to conduct this final phase of creation.

The other working villagers paused in their labor to see what brought the children out of the wood in such a large group. Engrossed so in his labor almost to the point of trance, he was the last to recognize the foreign sound of many voices so near but then Iarann reached for the nearest weapon to hand, the great hammer he'd completed just a short time before and followed the sound of the voices, both children and now more villagers, as they gathered by the wood's edge. He knew it was not unusual to suspend the egg hunt or other foraging quests due to a bear, wolf or boar sighting. Iarann prepared himself to protect the group from harm.

Upon emerging from the smithing hut, his skin tightened around his muscles as the cooler spring air touched his heated body and bare upper torso. Iarann was large even for the Danann clan and his arms, chest and abdomen showed the evidence of years of lifting, hammering and working the great weights of metal work and the wielding of tools, and implements of that craft. He was streaked with soot from his work fire and bore the wild look of a warrior wary of danger on his bearded face. Unaccustomed to speaking a great deal, as he worked in solitude most days, his voice was guttural as he called to the group and brandished the great hammer.

"Is it danger? What brings you?" He relaxed, as the first thing he notice was the elated look on the faces of the children in the group. Although he noticed there were some confused looks about the faces of some other adults who came to meet the group exiting the forest. The focus of attention in the cluster of people seemed to be a maiden carrying an impossibly heavy load of stones obviously rich with thick veins of silver and gold. He drew toward the crowd and called a hush to the cacophony of noise and voices simply by his presence. "Lady, allow me to unburden you of such a heavy load. Is it enchantment that affords you the strength to bear what many men could not?" He stopped then, his hand out to relieve the maiden of the weight, and felt his throat tighten, constricted with momentary grief at the resemblance he saw between this woman and his young wife, lost to him these past ten sun seasons.

Faidhe was struck at once with the unruly beauty of this man. She saw not only his physicality, but his energy as well. This is a man who works long in the service of his craft, tempered by the solitude of his days on the outskirts of the village. She saw in him the same fortitude it took for her to live in solitude these many long years and instantly felt a connection to him. A man of strength and equal gentility as his genuine concern for the safety of the children and other clan members showed in the energy all about him.

"I thank you for your kind offer sir but the burden I bear is my own in service of the Goddess," After only a brief pause, she quickly added, "and the God. And you are correct in recognizing that there is magic involved in how I keep the encumbrance aloft and the gifts contained within."

"How do you come by such fine ore then? And have you brought it to me to craft for you?" Iarann asked trying to recover from his momentary shock. Upon closer study, he realized now that this woman, though beautiful, really did not resemble his Ethlinn. Perhaps it was her lovely long black hair that called his wife to mind.

Slightly bewildered, it was beginning to dawn to Faidhe by the statements made to her along the way by the children and others, that people saw her and the cauldron she carried in various ways. The young girl Emer had seen her as a Goddess bearing seeds for the spring planting as did many of the children who were egg hunting, perhaps because this task made them mindful of the coming of the Fertility Goddess of the spring. Another woman in the wood bearing the sorrow of a lost child saw Faidhe as a young mother and her freight as a lovely babe at the breast. Now this metal worker recognized her cargo as what is most precious to a smithy, a shipment of fine ore.

"I am Faidhe, Keeper of the Circle and Second member of the Council of Tribal Seers. I come to the village with news and would be heard by all. Will you offer your assistance then, in summoning the clan-folk to the place of gathering where there is ample room so that I may tell my news and be heard?"

Iarann was astounded that this woman was claiming to be Faidhe for he had known of the Keeper and been in attendance to her in the Great Marriage during the spring festival some seasons before his marriage to Ethlinn. He knew that Faidhe was at least as old as he if not some small measure older. This woman was no more than a maid.

"What enchantment is this?" He commanded. Feeling cheated at the fleeting hope that his beloved had returned from the spirits. "How is it that you claim to be the revered Keeper when you have not her look or season's age about you?"

Faidhe knew her news would cause controversy and dissention but she had not expected that her very identity would come into question. She was pleased with her newfound way of seeing but if she was going to be heard and her message taken seriously, she must overcome the bedazzlement of the people.

"Question not my authority, Smithy. You who have whispered the sacred words over the gifts of the Earth Mother should recognize the magical act of separating sand and rock from ore and extracting precious metal. The Goddess has separated me from my humanness that I may come closer to the form She wishes me to take.

You see not the rock and sand of Faidhe's humanness but the more pure bronze or gold of the spirit."

She hoped the analogy to something familiar to him would suffice in explanation as to why she did not appear to him as herself.

"Have the villagers assembled at the place of gathering before the sun reaches half-sky while I convene with the other members of the Council. Enlist these others and the children to help you."

She saw in her mind's eye just how she appeared to this ironworker now: formidable and forbidding. *That will suffice*, she thought. A bit regretful that this gentle and kind soul should be abused so in his moment of confusion but also that he should look on her with fear. It had been long since she'd enjoyed an appreciative look from a man without awestruck reverence as she performed the rituals of the Circle.

She was immediately put in mind of her lament at the Circle just that morning that she would not relish having to approach her task without benefit of her feminine youth. She recognized in this moment that she must be cautious in the words she utters in petition, for the Power may grant it in ways that carry out results not in the least helpful. *Words spoken carry great power. Do not speak them foolishly or without thought.* As she heard these words in her head, they took on a quality of strength beyond a passing thought. They had a hint of command about them and she knew she would do well to remember them. Mentally, she made note, careful to commit to memory. *Words spoken carry great power, do not speak them foolishly or without thought for the Cumhacht de Cruinne, the Universal Power, may set into motion petitions in ways not in the least expected or helpful.* Only then did she turn her attention back to the ironsmith.

I am in service of the Mother in any form. I'll tend my fires first lady," he said revealing a look of awe as he lowered his head, "so as not to burn the entire village with my carelessness. Then I will do as you bid me."

Faidhe saw the look and sighed inwardly. Not wanting to alienate him and wanting to appear more human to this man without knowing why, she said "Thank you for your help Smithy. What is your name?"

"I am Iarann, son of Goibhniu."

This caught Faidhe's attention. "Son of Goibhniu? Came you to the Circle in the role of the God these many harvest seasons past?" She recollected a night by the sacred fire of the End of the Warm Days within the Circle. A gentle man selected by the Council to serve as the God to Faidhe in the Sacred Marriage, had come to her and they had joined by the fire in a sweet and memorable union. So little human contact she'd had her entire adult life that despite the fact she was assuming the role of the Goddess, she could not help but allow a bond to form with the few who touched her in such an intimate and sacred way.

"Yes, Lady. I have had the honor of taking on the mantle of the God." In that moment, he saw Faidhe just as she was on the night of their union. He remembered her tears and her tenderness. A fragile creature crafted of the hardest material to withstand the lonely existence in service of the Goddess. In frequent reflection on that one night he found he could not forget this woman who sacrificed so much for the Goddess and the tribe.

He did not remember Faidhe in the same way he remembered his Ethlinn. He'd had a brief life with his wife; one that carried moments and memories of silent looks, familiar touches, and laughter at simple things. His love for Ethlinn was rich with heat and passion. But for all the passion, she was but young girl and he came to marriage late in his life. There are times when a man pines for more than the heat of passion. He looks to be comforted in his vulnerability and longs for companionship as something deeper than mere company.

Since Ethlinn's death it was likely his own loneliness that ignited what he felt was a kinship with Faidhe in that he knew she must feel the sting of loneliness as deeply as did he. He had, not often, but on occasion since their union, speculated had Faidhe not been chosen for the Circle, what kind of a partner would she have made. And in his years since the death of Ethlinn as a lonely man's mind is wont to do, he wondered about the woman on the Hill just a half day's walk from his smithing hut and whether she were looking at the same stars as he, or smelled the same rain, or if she ever recalled the one night in the Circle when they had joined. He supposed not. She was, after all, The Keeper and he was just a faceless man to fulfill the sacred role of the God. It had not been him she bedded; it was the God with whom she coupled.

Iarann was mildly abashed that these thoughts were surfacing, unbidden in the very presence of the Keeper. Not wanting to show disrespect by speculating any further as to what it might be like to come to the bed of Faidhe and partner with her, Iarann tried to call himself back to the business at hand. *It is for naught,* he told himself, *for the Keeper is bound to the Gods and no other*. But his mind persisted and he allowed himself a final consideration: *perhaps then I could serve again for the festival marriage*...And with an inward chastisement at the self-serving thought, Iarann spoke with uncharacteristic shyness as though the Keeper could read his thoughts.

"Lady I am in your service and that of the Goddess." Forgetting himself in a wave of familiarity after being so recently put in mind of the memory of their union, Iarann impulsively took Faidhe's hand as he said this.

The shock of his unexpected and unbidden touch, thrilled through Faidhe and the blue energy that surrounded her shot forward from her body toward the ironworker whose own energy answered the call and joined hers in a clash of vibrancy, igniting a blaze that flared and crackled where their energies explored one another other.

Faidhe drew back her hand as though burned. "The place of gathering, half-sky." She said curtly. Then as if her hand had its own ideas and will, she reached out and squeezed his forearm reassuringly. She turned to her task of calling the Council, somewhat shaken and puzzled as to what had just taken place.

9

What's in a Name?

The silence in the parched room was constant but for the in and out of my breath and the occasional noisy creak as the old building settled. The steady rhythmic ticking of the mantle clock was buried somewhere in the room that had no apparent mantle, and the flipping of pages also became part of the scenery of quiet. The hush drew around us in the close back room of the old man's shop except when a mechanical voice would chime every hour to speak of the end of our stay in Ireland drawing closer, sixty minutes at a time.

The building was solid enough but I wondered at the old floor's ability to hold the weight of the thousands of books stored here. There were parts of the papered walls in the room that could not be seen from floor to ceiling having been obstructed by books upon books. There was one slim collapsible door that lent privacy to a very small half bathroom that looked as though it was installed in what used to be a closet. There was no window that could be seen, but that didn't mean there was no window, it just couldn't be seen behind the stacks, if it were in fact there. One could maneuver through the room only by means of a path formed between piles of books, desks, and bookcases. Ironically, the bookcases held not books, but boxes of what I assumed to be back-stock of store merchandise. There was some semblance of arrangement of the books although I could not make it out beyond generalities because Nora ended up on one side of the stacks where the astrological stuff was located while I settled to peruse another section offering titles closer to what I was investigating.

We had each retreated to our own worlds pawing through the books that Cath had stored in his back room. Though stored was not exactly the right word for it. Stacked, stuffed, shoved all would be a more accurate description of the namby pamby way the books and thousands of other items, objects, mementos, photos, bits and scraps had been kept in this claustrophobic 400 square foot room.

Jackpot, repeated over and again in my mind. With each new book I picked up and thumbed through, I found a new tidbit of information that would validate or at least support a line of previous research or as I discovered an entirely new concept or theory to consider regarding origins of myth, lore or customs. Like an axiomatic kid in the candy store, before long I had a stack of books in my 'to buy' pile that held information too vast for me to scribble some notes and citations. I had to follow the thread of information, once discovered, and pull on my end of the facts until I unearthed and evaluated all the history I could find on any given grain of information. I knew I would have to pare the pile down before we left the shop but I didn't know quite how I would do that. It'd be like having to choose between best friends, each having something of value to offer and both difficult to leave behind due to the emotional connection.

These were academic publications I would not find readily available in the states, written with benefit of scholarly research or archaeological evidence. Some seemed ancient, hand written in Gaelic, with yellowed, flaking pages and dissolving spines while others were more recent publications, but with no less validity to the material within. Familiar with the language of my grandparents since childhood and having studied Gaelic on my own, I could eke out a superficial conversation, however these books seemed to have been written in a form of the language I could not quite grasp. Cath had instructed me not to touch the older books, as they were fragile and very valuable. I could refer to the synopsis versions he offered that had been translated into English, German, Italian, Swedish and presumably some other languages that I could not see in the piles at the moment. These shorter versions of the older materials looked suspiciously like cliff notes and when I questioned the quality of the translation, I was surprised to learn that Cath had labored over the translations and produced the abbreviated text himself. I cast a suspicious eye toward the incongruously modern computer in the corner of the room, half hidden under papers, sticky notes, magazines and other artifacts that I could not identify. This looked very much like my own workspace at home. I began to realize there was likely much more to the meat of Cath than the shopkeeper that meets the eye.

"A linguist?" I quipped under my breath as he left us to our research, "Can't judge a book by its cover." But more soberly as his wizened form showed me its back, "There's definitely more to that old man." I made a mental note to approach him about possibly doing an interview with him on his knowledge of the ancient folklore.

We had gone down the rabbit hole and our entire existence lived in that room, unconscious of the world around us just as we'd done many times before when engrossed in a project. We had been given the gift of laser-like focus inherited from our father who, when we were young, sometimes disappeared for hours or days into his workroom and later emerged with a painting, sculpture, poem or some other impossible work of art. My eyes were tired and as the day wore on I felt a stealthy chill seep into my body. Coming back to the surface of awareness I called across the piles to Nora.

"Are you finding anything?"

We had both been sitting cross-legged on the floor because there were no chairs in the back room among the vast piles. I assumed that when Cath, or whomever, sat at the computer they dragged the wicker chair in from the display room in the front of the shop. She didn't have to answer. I craned to the left and peeked around a pile of books I'd discounted as of no use to me. I eyed a pile of books Nora had set aside that reached about the same height as the one I had chosen for myself as 'take homes,' which was piled up in front of me.

Breathing deep, I dropped my pad of notepaper on the floor with the pen I'd been using. I clawed my fingers open and closed a few times to loosen up the stiff joints. Moving to flex my back, it sang in protest. Slowly I unfolded my legs to stretch them out straight in front of me and the entire muscle department went on strike. My rear end felt flattened as though it had taken on the shape of the wooden planks beneath. The blood had drained from my legs and they let me know, with a vicious attack of pins and needles, that they were asleep with no intention of returning to work anytime soon. Despite our late breakfast, my stomach howled at the same time reminding me that it was likely well passed lunchtime. As if to confirm, the clock chimed once again and Nora and I looked at each other in disbelief as the clock continued to bong on and on announcing the hour as; what was that...7:00?

Astonished we looked at each other, passing the same thought between us. For the second time that day I found myself asking the rhetorical question: *How can it be so late?*

That's really not the right time is it Nora?" I must have looked owlishly foolish hitching up onto my knees, arms flapping for balance, as I looked around the room for the clock we had obviously ignored for the last six hours. Nora bubbled up with laughter at the sight.

"No, it shouldn't be." She answered. "At least I don't think so." Then, with a dawning of the possible situation we might be facing, her expression changed. "Would he have let us stay so late? What time do the shops close around here?" She seemed to be toying with mild panic. Now it was my turn to laugh.

"What if he forgot us and locked us in?" I was poking fun at Nora's rapid-fire questions but was really in no position to make fun of anyone as I looked like a fallen hippo trying to right herself. Or I felt as though I looked that way and I finally coaxed my legs into holding me upright on my feet and gave myself a proper stretch. I tested out my walking legs heading toward the blue curtained doorway that lead to the front of the shop and my knees gave off a series of pops and cracks in celebration of movement again. I poked my head out the door and for a moment of my own panic, I thought we actually had been locked in the shop. I looked to Cath's wicker seat and it was vacant. Then I spotted him standing at the front of the shop peering out the front window with his hands clasped behind his back.

"Um, excuse me, Mr. er Cath? What time do you close?" He turned to me with a pleasant look.

"Are you finished your reading then?" He asked.

"Well, sort of. Is it ah...what time is it please?"

"Did ye not hear the clock sound just a minute ago?"

"Yes but we didn't think it could be that late. Is it? I mean it's still pretty light out. Is it really 7:00?

"No lass ye hord wrong." My relief was only short lived when Cath announced "It'll be 8:00 o'clock now."

My face must have revealed my confusion because I felt it screw up into a wince as I tried to figure out what was going on. *Oh, summertime in Ireland, the sun is out pretty late by comparison to the U.S. so it would still be light outside.*

"I have a bunch of books I'm interested in, but I still need to make a decision on some of them. Are you closing soon?"

"You girls," he pronounced it 'gorls' "take the time ye need, I've nowhere in particular to go."

"Okay, great. Thanks." I withdrew my head from the doorway then popped it back through when my stomach reminded me to ask "Hey Cath, is there anyplace good around here to eat?"

"There's the local down the alley or if ye're for a bit more fancy, ye might try Kenny's across the way. It's a bit touristy but the welcome is fine and the stew is hot." He eyed me appraisingly for a moment and suggested, "Kenny's might be yer best choice."

I wasn't sure if this was a fair appraisal or if I should be mildly insulted at being summed up by a local as "touristy." But I was too hungry to give it more than a moment's thought. A warm welcome and hot stew sounded perfect just about now.

"Good. Thanks again."

I made an attempt to choose the most pertinent books for my research but my stomach called and I really couldn't decide which would suit my studies. I wanted all of them. Something pulled at me to pay the price and ship them home but I wanted to have the books with me for reference, in case I find some similar information at the Trinity Library or during interviews I'd hoped to conduct. *Well, I'll buy them and have them for now. Then I'll ship 'em home before we leave. Best of all worlds,* I told myself.

I got "the look" from Nora as she saw me make several trips with arms full of my selection to the front desk.

"Will you have any money left for dinner?" She chided.

We had always been a little competitive and joked with each other about who would be the first to publish and as with many parallels that happened between us, we set to writing the exact same day without knowing what the other was up to.

"I'm charging them." I said. "Better proof for a write off when I publish. "And who's talking, anyway? What do you have, about one less book than I do?" Nora pulled one side of her mouth into a smirk as I turned to make my purchase.

"Cath," I said, "as part of my research I plan to conduct interviews with natives who may have stories not easily found in books regarding sacred sites, traditions, folklore, rituals, stuff like that. Would you be interested in taking some time to sit with me so that I might ask you some questions?"

His face looked doubtful and his head was already unconsciously shaking back and forth. I imagined he'd had enough of waiting around for his payoff today.

"I don't mean now, not tonight." I added quickly. "But maybe another day, before we leave?"

He didn't look as though he relished having to talk at length with anyone. He appeared to like his quiet shop and his solitude by the way he'd let us spend so much time without trying to usher us into any kind of sale or talk to us at all during our time there.

"It's O.K." I said to fill the void, as I held out my credit card to him. I didn't want to make the moment any more uncomfortable for either of us. "I understand that you're busy with your shop and probably with your translation work. I just thought with your line of work, you might have a few stories to tell."

Cath wasn't listening to me. He was inspecting my credit card as if to burn a hole in it. He looked at me sharply over his little glasses and spoke even more so.

"I thought you said your name is Lee?"

"It is." I answered. Beginning to understand I explained to him, "My nickname is Lee. Everyone calls me Lee but my real name is Lenore like it says on the card. It's just a bit too formal for everyday use I think. But here..." I fished for my passport with photo to prove I was not some American fraud out to use a stolen credit card or whatever he might have thought. As I looked up from my purse, he was staring at me with an intensity to make me shiver. "Really," I said, shoving my passport at him. "Here see for yourself."

He took my passport without ever taking his eyes from mine. "So this is your *real* name then?"

"Yes. Lenore, like in Edgar Allan Poe's, *The Raven*." It was such an unusual name, I often found myself spelling or repeating it two or three times to people who just couldn't get that my name is not Ellen, Eleanor, Lenora, or even Nora. Sometimes the frame of reference to Poe would either bring them to enlightenment or they would back off not knowing the classic poem but not wanting to admit it, they'd let it drop. A bit too much trouble just to say my name. Hence the nick name, Lee.

"What kind of a name do ye carry now? What's this, how d' ye say yer marriage name?" I told him how to say my last name and he asked growing agitated, "What kind of name is that then?"

"It's a German name. And growing a bit agitated myself, "Listen, I have plenty of identification, and you can call the credit card company to verify that the card is good. Do you want to sell the books or not?"

"And your maiden name is O'Leary." It was a statement more to himself than a question for me as he drifted into introspection for a moment. I followed his eyes to where he now looked. Cath was inspecting the books I'd chosen for myself. Nora had come to join me at the sales counter to see what all the fuss was about. Just then, as if something flipped a switch in him, he came back to life so abruptly that it startled us. We jumped as he snatched up the old-fashioned credit card slip and slid it across the counter at me. "I'll be needin' the phone number of yer hotel if you please."

"We're not staying at a hotel and we don't have a phone where we're staying." I knew I could have given him Bridey's number but she wasn't the type to take too well to strange men calling her home in search of the American girls staying at her cottage, at least someone who is not married to either of us.

"I can give you my home phone but really, there won't be a problem with the card. I promise."

"Fine, fine." He said in a dismissive tone. Then he surprised me by saying, "If ye'll be after an interview, I'll have a story for you then if ye'll tell me one of yer own."

My surprise was quickly taken over by my enthusiasm.

"Really? Will you come to dinner with us?"

Immediately I felt Nora shooting darts into my back as I signed the credit card slip. I glanced at the total and gulped looking back up at Cath who had a triumphant look of someone who'd waited all day to spring a trap and had just pulled off the job of the century. He was literally vibrating with excitement. I turned to answer Nora's silent protest at my invitation to Cath trying to smooth things over.

"Are you too tired Nora? Would you just rather go back to the cottage instead?" I subversively showed her the credit card bill. Her eyebrows flew up and she stepped up to the counter for her purchase taking about half of her book selection aside.

"No I'm not that tired," she answered. "I just think you should make an appointment and to have all your interview questions prepared to come back and speak with Cath." Then to Cath, "I'm going to have to think about these." as she set aside 8 or 10 books from the pile. "Will it be O.K. to hold them aside for a day or so?"

"Oh te be sure." Looking only a bit disappointed. He rang up her books and put everything in a box for us.

I got the impression that he wanted to be done with the book sale and with us so I hurried to secure a general time that I could come back and learn more about this strange man and what he knows.

"Will you be available tomorrow to speak with me for a while?"

"I will. And if you have a thought to, you can bring lunch in case you find yourself hungry."

Expecting that he may have felt cheated out of a dinner invitation, I promised to bring lunch for the both of us on the following day along with my questions. I left the shop a bit shell shocked, not knowing exactly why. I mentioned how I felt to Nora and she bit at me with exaggeration. "Do you think it had anything to do with paying about $7 million for a heap of old books?"

It wasn't what I meant but I rose to the bait all in fun.

"Listen, those books are going to be worth it for my paper when it's all written and besides, it wasn't 7 million dollars it was 7 million *pounds*."

"That's even more!"

"Don't remind me. Let's go to Kenny's and be touristy. You buy."

"And how did I get that honor?"

"Because I just saved you about $3.5 million.

"Pounds." She cracked.

"Whatever." I said. Just to get the last word.

We put the box of books into our car and found our way up to Kenny's Pub. Despite it being during the summer months, it was becoming quite raw outside and we'd dressed for warmer mid-afternoon weather. It was now nearing 8:30 p.m. and the mist started to blow in with the clouds.

Kenny's was every bit as warm and inviting as promised. We found a seat right near a crackling fireplace and decided on what to eat. We both thought about getting a pint of Guinness Stout but thought better of it considering the ride home. We ordered up a couple of bowls of the most delicious lamb stew I have ever tasted with big chunks of lamb, potatoes, onions, turnips and a thick savory broth. I don't know if it was just because we were so hungry that it was so good but there was not much conversation between us at the table until the meal, complete with warm bread and soft salty butter was polished off with no remains.

I sat back feeling my stomach push at the button of my jeans, and felt like taking a nap in front of the cozy fire but knew if we didn't get going now, we'd be in trouble with the unfamiliar roads and full dark coming on. So Nora paid the check and we braved the chill on the way to the car and headed home.

"Not a bad day's work. You think?"

Nora looked as though she felt like a nap too. "Mmm," was her only answer.

"Hey, try to stay awake so we can get home in one piece. I don't really know my way around here yet. 'Specially at night. Okay?"

"Okay. It's a good thing we didn't order the Guinness."

"I know. You'd have to drive home!" I teased.

"We'd be safer sleeping here in the car!"

"Probably."

On the way home, Nora fell asleep anyway and I found myself going over in my mind what I wanted to ask Cath about during our interview tomorrow; things about his background, how he came by all the books on ancient myth and lore, if he might be able to direct us to any sacred sites with mythological connections, and then it struck me: It had been illusively gnawing at the back of my mind all evening that during our arrangements for the interview, I never asked Cath what he meant when he said he wanted me to tell him a story of my own.

I pulled up the long drive to the cottage practically driving with one eye open talking to myself to stay awake.

"It's not even 11:00 yet and I can't keep my eyes open. Tomorrow, I get a cup of coffee if it kills me."

"What?" Nora asked. Sensing we were home when I turned off the engine.

"Nothing. Help me with these?"

We'd have left the box of books from the Sacred Traveler in the back seat if not for the seeping cold and damp mist that clung to everything. Not wanting to take a chance with some of the older books, we made the effort to carry the heavy box inside and unceremoniously dumped it on the couch. We had wordlessly agreed it was time for bed. Once securely inside, we said hasty goodnights and after hastier teeth brushing, I burrowed under the heavy woolen blankets on my bed to slip easily into blissful somnolence.

———

I woke to someone shaking me. When I opened my eyes, there was an old woman standing at the end of my bed staring at me. She said nothing. She just stood at the corner of the bed between the door and me looking severe. It seemed when she was sure I'd seen her and could not pass her off as a dream, she turned and walked out the door and down the hall toward the kitchen. I was spooked and tried to make sense of why this woman was trying to get my attention. And who was she? I'd seen apparitions before. I knew this woman was not a physical being. She was unknown to me but definitely meant to get my attention. My imagination began to take the terror ball and run with it because I was suddenly inundated with images of wild beasts coming for me, calculating, prowling outside the cottage. Pacing, sneaking, sniffing to get in. Every now and then I would catch wafting smells of some kind of animal that smelled like wet fur and rotten meat. I was all at once, so hyper alert with adrenaline that sleep was out of the question but I felt paralyzed to get up and look out to see if there really was anything out there. In fact, the last thing I wanted to do was leave the childishly imagined safety of my bed to investigate whether the boogieman or boogybeast was outside my window devising ways to get in at me. So I lay in bed awake and scared until the first rays of sun snuck their way under the drawn blinds in the cottage and only then, comforted by the light I began to think how silly I was. What kinds of wild beasts could there be roaming the Irish countryside? Finally I drifted to sleep.

———

The clock stood silent on the night table. The red numbers stared at me soundlessly announcing that I had once again slept the morning away. The clock gave me a wink as the last digit changed from a two to a three. *Time marches on*, it said. *Time waits for no one*. I closed my eyes again and drifted. Then peeked at the clock again. *Catch me if you can*. I stared at the numbers for a full quarter minute before comprehension took hold, 11:11!

"Oh shit!" I spat as I flung aside my blankets and jounced out of bed. My feet hit the floor only seconds before something hard and heavy landed on my left foot. A frustrated, lip-biting "Mmmhh!" emitted from me in an effort not to start the day with even more explicit profanity. I satisfied myself with a "Shit, shit, shit, SHIT." The angry bruise could already be seen flowering, small, round and purple/black on the top of my foot.

Looking around I spotted a large book on the floor, half hidden under the bed. I picked it up and recognized one of the books I'd bought yesterday. It was a weighty, hard covered book entitled in Uncial gold leaf, *The Power of the Word*. Its jacket, if it ever had one, was missing and the binding was some kind of canvas or linen in a soft blue. Under the book title was a stylized Celtic cross. The cross itself was done in gold and was pointed at the bottom as though it were a blade. The circle around the intersection of the cross was an unbroken pattern of a vine, sprouting three-pointed leaves all around the circle. This part of the Celtic cross was done in silver.

"Hey Nora! Where are you?" I listened for the shower or kitchen noises. Nothing. "Hey Nora. You up?"

A rustling from the other bedroom and a quick intake of breath was an indication that I had just woken her. I mentally saw her reach for her glasses to check her clock and snickered in spite of my throbbing foot when I heard her spit out a *Shit*, of her own.

It was then it occurred to me that if Nora was still sleeping, then how did this book get into my room? All the nocturnal events of the past night came flooding back to me and I felt a frosty sensation raise the hair on my arms. As I headed away from the bed toward the door with the book in my hand, I looked around the room to see if there was anything else out of place. I felt foolish as I was reminded of a childhood habit I'd had of jumping out of bed as far away from the bed as I could so *the hand* wouldn't snatch out from under and grab my ankle.

I took the four steps down the hall to the left and stood at the frame of Nora's bedroom door.

"You're late." She said. Sidetracked as I was with all the nonsense of being freaked out and injured, I was totally put out of mind that I had my first interview appointment today and hadn't prepared anything. I'd planned on getting up to do some morning prepping and now the morning was almost over.

"What do you mean *I'm* late? Aren't you coming?" Nora stretched as luxuriously as a cat and rolled over on her stomach. Returning to her back, she held out her hands, palms up.

"Let's see." She said, lifting one hand, palm up. "Rush around, no shower, no food, sit with old man all afternoon." Then lifting the other hand in a weighing motion, "Leisurely breakfast, hot shower, and sunny day in the yard reading my new books." She looked at me without a trace of sympathy or regret. "I'd love to help you but ...have a nice time."

"Oh Nora, c'mon, you don't want to be stuck here all day. Come to town."

"I'll manage with a nice brunch and maybe a walk around the farm. Thanks, but...no."

"Oh food!" I said with redoubled exasperation. "I'm supposed to bring him lunch too!" I tossed the book on her bed and ran toward my bedroom. Snatching hands from the under-bed netherworld forgotten, I tore through my clothes in the closet to find something comfortable and clean then decided: *Cath can wait a bit while I take a quick shower. I won't be packing any picnic lunches today either, he'll just have to be happy with takeout or subs or something.*

While in the shower, I impatiently waited while the comparative dribble from the showerhead seeped onto my hair. It seems that Ireland is necessarily cautious with its water usage and the water-conserving showerheads in the bathrooms of the cottage are a little overzealous in the conservation department. The water tends to mist from the spigot rather than spray. A quick shower is more like a bird-bath, washing only the essentials as not to offend, but my hair is long and thick and without water pressure, the hair wash was slow going so I multitasked the shower time. I do some of my best thinking in the shower and I brainstormed about my upcoming interview while I brushed my teeth and the steam rose. Finally my hair was wet enough to wash.

Feeling less hurried now that I had a reasonable plan to buy lunch and ad-lib the interview, I stepped out of the shower and was taken up short by an unbidden recollection of the woman I'd seen during the night. Then as if conjured, in the steamed mirror I thought I saw her serious face looking back at me through the mist. Outside some farm birds started to raise quite a noisy ruckus as they flew by my window, casting black shadows on the closed blind. My attention was distracted to the cawing sound of the birds and when I looked back to the mirror, it was only my own outline in the foggy glass. *I think I need more sleep,* I thought and wiped the mirror of moisture with the side of my hand in order to throw on concealer to cover my sleepless night and lipstick.

I dried quickly and threw on my jeans and a white cotton sweater with white canvas Ked's slip-ons. I grabbed my jacket, remembering the cold of last night. Then out the door in a flurry of contractual permission forms, notebooks and standard pre-written interview sheets, I hopped into the car with wet hair, an empty stomach and a sense of guilt at leaving Nora at the cottage without a car. An entire day in the country with no means of transportation seemed limiting but as I hollered my goodbyes, she was content enough to sit in the sun that had finally come out, and do some reading. In fact I was sort of jealous. It would have been a nice day to do just that but the interviews were important and one of my primary reasons for the trip. And if I'm any judge, Cath will have a few local tales to tell. I looked at the clock, calculating how long it would take me to get to town. It was 12:40 now. About 20 minutes to get there and find a parking spot.

"Don't break anyone's mirror," I reminded myself. "Find a sub shop or something." (*Do they have sub shops here?*) "And get to Cath's store." I could be there by 1:20, maybe 1:30. That's still a respectable lunch hour. I was mentally grateful that I'd only offered to bring lunch without saying what time. If Cath was hungry before then, well he'd just have to wait or eat whatever cheese sandwich on brown bread kind of fare he was used to packing for himself. My mind continued its monologue by again going over the questions I planned to ask Cath and I soon found myself in town without any mishaps but it was already 1:10.

Today, I found a parking spot right in front of my café with the promise of coffee. A stroke of luck, I thought. I can go in to get sandwiches and a big, tall, extra-large, mondo, huge cup of coffee! Eyeing the sign on the door I dismissed it as an oversight of a forgetful clerk. I reached the handle for the café door to discover that the sign told the truth; they were CLOSED. Looking at the hours of operation, I discovered that the shop closed at noon on Saturday and did not open at all on Sunday. Today being Saturday, the café had closed a little over an hour ago. I received some strange looks from some passersby as I stood at the door expressing my disbelief.

"You have got to be kidding me! How can they be closed? Do they know how to run business over here? It's mid-day for Chri..." I caught myself and pulled out of the rant when two little, round, hat-wearing ladies, walking arm in arm stopped to have a look at the raving American. "Ahhm, good morning... afternoon, I mean"

I said trying not to appear crazy. "Can you tell me where I might find a sub shop?" Blank stares. "Um a restaurant?" Still nothing. Then hopefully I rephrased in a louder than necessary voice, "Is there anyplace in town that I can buy lunch and take it with me?"

The women began to nod their heads at the same time and speak to me in what I knew was English but I could not understand most of it. Partially because they were speaking at the same time, but mostly because their accents were so thick I made out maybe one word in five. I was able to look where they were pointing and tried to hide my embarrassment that they probably not only thought I was crazy, but stupid too. Directly across the street was an eatery with a sign clearly posted, "Food to go." I sheepishly thanked the women and tried to look casual as I strolled across the street to order lunch...late lunch.

10

A Date with the Past

Feeling harried, tired and slightly guilty, I finally made it back to the Sacred Traveler with armloads of sandwiches, juice, milk and sodas. Not knowing what type of food Cath might like, I bought a variety of sandwiches along with several plastic containers of various side dishes. In a way that someone who is late for work brings donuts in order to soften any hard feelings when they finally arrive, I thought, the more food I brought, the more forgiving Cath might be. Not much of a justification, but the only one I had, and it would have to do. Just as I reached the front door to the store, I realized that I had neglected to get myself any coffee. The idea that the café was closed and coffee wasn't available from there, somehow translated in my mind that I wouldn't have coffee today at all so it never occurred to me to order coffee with the sandwiches for lunch. Regretfully, I sighed, pushed open the door and stepped into the Sacred Traveler.

The little bell over the door gave a jingle and I winced slightly. Until that moment, I hadn't realized that I was hoping Cath would be asleep as he was yesterday and I could just look around the store until he awoke and smile indulgently when he did as though I'd been patiently waiting for him. I didn't remember a bell ringing when we came into the store yesterday, but I wasn't trying to sneak into the store then either. None of that mattered now because Cath was not in his chair sleeping, he was standing at a portable folding table that had been set up in one corner of the store by the front window.

Eyeing the setup I began to feel a bit uneasy about coming to interview Cath alone. The table was complete with Irish linen tablecloth and napkins that had obviously been stored with care for a very long time as the creases in the slightly yellowed linen were evidence of folds in the material that had been there for so long that they were razor-like in their crispness. There were places set for two with a decidedly feminine fine china, presenting a white background that shone brightly on the yellowed linen, embellished with a flourish of delicate, hand painted pink flowers that might have been violets dancing around the scalloped edges of the china pieces. There was silverware that was actually silver in several mismatched patterns but that had recently been polished. In the center of the table was an incongruously colorful bouquet of fresh flowers poked into a glass vase without benefit of arrangement but with a lovely wildflower effect. On one side of the table was Cath's wicker chair and on the other side was a metal folding chair apparently brought in for the occasion. The early afternoon sun was pouring through the front window onto the scene and made it look almost inviting if I didn't have a growing sensation that although he was so much older, Cath might have the wrong idea about this American woman who'd asked him to spend lunch with her. *I forget that we're not in Kansas anymore Toto.* My offer to spend time with this man may have been totally misinterpreted. My feelings of foreboding grew as I looked more closely at Cath to discover that he was wearing a tie under his gray woolen V-neck cardigan and his pristine white hair was obviously combed to one side with water or some type of hair product. His shirt and pants were the same nondescript type he wore yesterday but Cath had definitely put some extra work into his daily ablutions today.

Well, I'm in it now, I thought, *better make it clear right now that this is business, first, last and only.*

"Hi Cath, I'm sorry to be later than I expected, I was held up on the phone to America with my husband and son. I sure do miss them. It was hard to focus on what I had to do today after talking to them. Should we get right to it?" I asked.

Putting the bags of food down on the counter where I'd purchased my books the night before. Tugging at the papers I'd brought with me I pulled out a form that would give me permission from Cath, once he signed it, to use his stories and to quote him in my dissertation. I was a bit red in the face and flustered now due to the idea that Cath may have romantic ideas. In my nervousness, my hands just wouldn't cooperate and I dropped my folder, spilling permission forms and standard interview questions out onto the floor. As I knelt to pick them up, I found myself staring at the oldest pair of wingtips I'd ever seen, polished to the best shine the aged leather had left in it. Not wanting to look up at Cath as he stood over me, I could only continue fussing with the papers, trying to stuff them back into the folder.

A gentle hand came down on my shoulder; about to jump out of my skin at this point and ready to fend off the inevitable, I blazed a look up at him only to see pure amusement in his eyes. I felt as transparent as glass.

"Is it romance ye think I'm after? Well put your mind to ease then. I've taken pains to set out the good plates because that's how Evelyn would have done it and how she'd have me do it for a guest such as yerself. Evelyn is my wife, dead these twenty years. It's only the proper way to treat a guest here and to break bread and speak of the old tales, so then, it's only due respect to her, to the old tales and to you."

My scarlet face deepened but I was grateful for the rescue from my own imagination that had obviously gone rogue over the last few days. I was reminded of my thoughts only yesterday regarding Cath and I was right. There certainly is more to him than my first impressions of a cranky shop owner. The tension drained from me as easily as if he had pulled the stopper in a basin full of water.

"Thank you Cath. I'm honored. It's lovely. And I'm sorry about your wife, Evelyn. These must have been hers?" I asked about the dishes.

"Aye. They were a wedding gift from me. She loved them when she saw them in a shop one day but they were much too dear and we moved on, but I went back to the shop after, and bought the whole set with some money I'd put by towards our honeymoon. 'It was a good choice' she always said, 'to spend the money on something that brought joy for so many years.' She used them for all occasions throughout our marriage: family, company, holiday feasts, but I enjoyed most when she pulled them out on no occasion at all and set us a lunch. She'd say, 'Who's better than us?' And we'd eat ham and cheese sandwiches in just as fine fashion as the French Riviera Cafés on our Irish linen and Limoges China." His eyes were looking at something long ago and a smile played on his lips.

I felt myself staring and drew my eyes away from him feeling as though I were peeking in the window at his private luncheon with Evelyn. I searched the room for something to speak about and I was reminded when I spotted the lunch bags.

"Oh, ham and cheese. Do you like that? I bought a couple of ham and cheese sandwiches. I got all the condiments on the side 'cause I didn't really know what you might like." I went over to the bags and began to set things out on the counter. I knew I was babbling a bit but it gave me the moment to regroup and for Cath to come out of his reverie.

The folding table set for lunch was too small for much more than the dishes and flowers so we used the glass display-case as a sideboard to serve the food. We sat to a selection of ham and cheese, roast beef, and egg salad sandwiches on various types of bread, mashed potato, coleslaw, and potato crisp sides. I had cold milk and Cath had puckered and smacked with tart lemonade. When it was time for desert, Cath had made and served real tea from a china tea set that matched the dishes, and we enjoyed round little cream filled puff pastries named profiteroles. Although I'd never heard of them before, the girl in the lunch shop had assured me I would enjoy them.

"Oh they're gorgeous," she told me practically salivating as she convinced me I should try some for dessert. I was glad to have brought them because apparently they are one of Cath's favorite sweets. Swirled over with chocolate sauce, he enjoyed them immensely.

We spoke through lunch of my knowledge of Celtic Mythology and the stories I'd learned as a girl. I informed him in more detail about the research I was doing and about what types of sacred sites I'd hoped to find while here in Ireland. He questioned me about what brought me to this line of study and I answered him as best I could trying not to reveal too much of my family history.

"What exactly are ye lookin' for in the way of stories?"

"Well," I collected my thoughts. "We have customs, rituals and traditions in our American society today, and in Christian society all over the world that have been brought forward on the wave of Christianity. They're believed to have originated as Christian ideas and have stories behind the Christian origin of the tradition, whatever it might be." I knew now that I'd find out which way the wind blew with Cath and how far I may be able to expose my beliefs, abilities and family history. But considering the work he'd put into translating some of the books chronicling Pagan history, and all the books Nora had found on astrology in his shop, I felt I was on fairly firm ground that Cath would have an open mind. Or at least that I was speaking with someone who was knowledgeable enough not to be a participant in religious dogma and prejudice that maligned the Old Ways of religion that existed in Western Europe prior to Christianity. I took a deep breath and a leap of faith.

"I've done research on these stories and traditions and found solid scholarly evidence that these traditions, holidays, symbols, customs and even some saints are based, not in the stories taught in the Christian faith, but hearken back to much older, Pagan traditions, symbols, festivals and Gods..."

Silence, as he penetrated me with those watery brown eyes over his spectacles. I hurried on. "What I'd like to do, Cath, is find actual proof beyond recent speculation, whether it is archaeological or in any ancient texts, that these traditions and stories, widely accepted to be Christian, actually originated in a much older religion now thought to be only myth." Gaining boldness now, and warming to the rhythm of my diatribe. "One that is in fact a religion, not a cult of crazy barbarians as they are often perceived. My main problem though, is that there is very little written documentation of what happened during the Celtic pinnacle in Europe's history and before, and what is written had been done by sources outside the Celts themselves which means much of what is available is tainted by supposition or worse, outright loathing of the people, like with the writings of Caesar, so I think I'll have to rely on archaeological sites and local lore hoping for a more authentic perspective on what may have been, in order to present an alternative theory that is closer to valid historical events surrounding sacred worship, rituals stories and traditions. And I know there have been plenty of artifacts found in Czechoslovakia, Hungary, Germany, Switzerland, England and plenty of other places but I feel this sense of urgency to look at my own history and heritage to get at the truth."

"Ye sound as if this is a personal mission more than an academic subject." It was given as a statement but he was asking the question. He wanted to know what my personal stake was in this subject matter.

So much for being careful about personal information. I was so passionate about this subject due to my personal knowledge and participation in the Old Ways that it was obvious to anyone listening, this was more than an academic foray into European, pre-Christian anthropology for me. Cath had raised an eyebrow and was waiting for me to make some kind of response.

"You're right." I resigned. "It is more than academic conjecture. I have lived a life split between two religions. On one hand, a public face of Catholicism, a religion whose representatives I found, both historically and in my own experience, to be intolerant and really very unforgiving toward others outside the religion. People who hid behind their position within the church, claiming to know what's best for everyone in order to maintain some kind of power over people whether it was power over the community like the Monsignor had over the parish fold when I was a kid or the power the Nuns had over the children in school...or the power the entire organization had to usurp sacred traditions and customs of others to meet its own ends in the quest for absolute power as in the early days of the established church that held control over the masses and dictated much of its doctrine through monarchies and other political structures. It's always seemed to me that organized religion is more about power than it is about God or what's sacred, or at the very least, being right while vilifying and making everyone else wrong or diminished or second best or downright evil. Kind of, 'If you ain't with us you're against us' mentality."

I stopped, took a breath and measured Cath's response. There didn't seem to be any, other than a non-committal nod of his head urging me to continue. So I did. "On the other hand, I have practiced what my grandparents, parents and family members taught me about the Old Ways and that seemed to me to be a much more welcoming, reverent and respectful way to live a life: in honor of ancestors, nature, and any Gods or spirits that seem always ready to help. I have an inside perspective of both religions and through the years have found one in such high protestation of the other, one that I've found to be nurturing of every human and spiritual need or inclination, that I knew there had to be more to the story than the one the Christians were selling."

I stopped took another breath and was amazed at my own heat on the subject. I nervously tapped the table with my fingertips. "Well." I said. "No question about which side *I* agree with, huh?" I let out a nervous laugh.

I knew what my beliefs were but I had never really articulated them because this was a subject I had been trained to keep to myself. And through all the months I had conducted active research on the subject, I had never really focused on why

I felt so compelled to uncover the truth about much of the Christian ideology being built on the foundation of the old Pagan ways and having absorbed so much of the old practices, claiming them as their own, while at the same time, maligned those Old Ways and anyone who practiced them as being evil.

"Vindication, I guess, is what I'm looking for. And if I come to answers and knowledge in the accepted ways, through the halls of academia, and find proof that I'm not wrong or evil for believing what I do and for having this ability, then maybe I would finally feel validated after years of hiding my faith and my abilities."

I was suddenly saddened that my purpose seemed so small, almost petty, once I had arranged it and put it into words so succinctly. Was I really so compelled in my work only because I needed those who had mistreated me so in Catholic school and those like them to approve of me in some way? Did I expect letters of apology to pour in once my work was published? Were the headlines going to read, *'Two Thousand Years, All a Mistake! Vatican Apologizes.'* What was I thinking? Why did I burn so with gathering the information, knowledge and proof? I felt deflated all at once and looked over at Cath feeling foolish that I had no better explanation for why this work was so powerfully important to me.

"Cath's attention was palpable now. His eyes were penetrating in their focus on me. After what seemed like an eternity of his scrutiny, distilling all that I'd said, he asked a fundamental question.

"What's all this about ability?

Only then, I realized I'd let myself slip. So many years of not talking about my family and our *special gifts* and in one afternoon I'd spilt the beans to this unassuming old man. I took measure of the man across from me, speculating how he might receive my story and decided to give it a try. I sighed in resignation and began to tell him about my family and some of the things we'd experienced and what we could do.

"Do you believe in magic Cath?"

"I don't think there's any self respectin' Irish person, (he pronounced it por-son) who doesn't know there's more than just the earthly (orthly) things about us. If yer callin' that magic, well then I'd have to be sayin' yes."

I liked him more by the minute. *Okay.* I thought, and I took the plunge.

"My sister and I, no my sisters and I seem to be able to do and see things that other people can't.

"What can ye give for examples?"

"Well," lowering my eyes, I thought briefly and decided to risk showing him. I focused my concentration, looked back up.

"Do you go to church Cath?"

Briefly, he seemed mildly confused by the question but in a moment's time, his eyes grew wide as he looked around the small shop. I noticed his hands grow white with tension on the arm of his chair and stopped my concentration. He looked back at me, slightly bewildered. "What did you see?" I asked.

"I saw...well I'm not just sure what it was. I saw everything you see now but I... definitely *felt* as though I were in a chorch. There were flashes of the colored glass in the windows and well, I don't know exactly. What did you do?" He finished.

"I wanted you to experience a little of what I can tell you about our abilities because once I told you about what I might be able to do, then you might be expecting it and I may or may not be able to make it work. Although I have to admit, things along the magic lines work way better for me over here in Ireland. In fact I've seen all kinds of odd things since I've been here, some small but others not so small. And other things are just plain unexplainable."

Still a bit shaken, Cath seemed to be preoccupied with trying to figure out what had just happened. He came slowly back to attention and wanted to know more.

"Such as...what is it ye can't explain?"

"Well, I dream here. And I know I'm dreaming these long, epic, prolific dreams that ordinarily would stick with me throughout the day until the truth about what I dreamed was revealed, but here it's as if there is a cloud around my head or something because when I wake up, I can't remember anything about what my dreams are. Not even right after I wake up when they're usually fresh in my mind."

"Why a chorch?"

I felt as though I was in a mental Ping-Pong game the way Cath was lobbing the questions at me in a way that bounced between subjects. I considered this.

"I thought about it, and when I came into this store yesterday, my first impression reminded me of the hushed sacredness of a church so it would be easier for me to give the impression of a church because that 'feel' is already here. And that may be why you got the feel of a church, because it was my experience. Get it?"

He seemed to have really warmed to the subject now.

"Is this something ye do often? What do ye use this ability for? Does it work with everyone? You feel there is sacredness in Chorch?"

"Oh man, Cath. Slow down. No, I don't use it for anything other than circumstances that would make people comfortable like a social engagement. For example, I could give a party a little nudge toward being a success by making people feel comfortable or right at home. They would not see something as you just did but I have a greater ability to affect my surroundings than say create an image for people to see *me* differently. That's a talent that Nora outstrips my ability tenfold. It's not that I can't. It's possible, but not quite as easy for me to do with people. Animals now, that's a different story. Animals tend to take to me 'cause I can make them see me or feel me; I guess, in a kind of telepathy. They know my intentions and I can sort of catch images from them. Kind of a rudimentary communication."

Cath considered this for a long moment as he watched a couple of teenage girls, complete with the teenaged, disaffected youth package: cell phones, low-rise jeans, pierced faces and navels, cigarettes wafting, walk passed the window of his store. The novelty of the moment seemed to have dissipated. He leveled me with a look and repeated his question in a more serious tone.

"So ye believe then, that there is the sacred within the Chorch?"

"Of course. I *know* there is. It's not the spirit of the church or the religion that I have difficulty with. The foundation of the tenets of what Jesus was trying to do and teach is sound and just. It's the people since that time that have interpreted his words and established organized religion that have gotten things all messed up. A church is a holy place for sure. There is spirit there. The basic code of belief has just been so twisted through the centuries to suit who ever might come to power and keep the masses under control I feel that there is little left of what Christ originally tried to set forth. The rituals and symbolism are there but I really don't think the people who attend church, for the most part, even understand what they are all about."

"It's good ye see the forest through the trees then. Now, ye spoke of seeing things?"

"Seeing things?" Still playing Ping-Pong, I figured out what he was asking. "Oh. Well yeah, that's more often what happens with my abilities. I see stuff like people or things that may have happened in a place before I get there. These things sometimes sort of replay for me, especially if it was some kind of emotional circumstance. That makes it more ah, charged, I guess. I see gray balls that float around me all the time but sort of with a purpose like they know where they're going...and sometimes little sparkly things that wiz around. I know these are some kind of conscious energy 'cause they respond to me when I acknowledge them; and besides, I'm not the only one who sees them. Sometimes Nora will see them when she's with me and other times, my son sees them too. I've seen people who have died when I'm both awake and in my dreams. A lot of times they come to me in my dreams and we can talk there. They tell me things that turn out to be helpful to other people or warn me sometimes about things that will happen. There's more but you get the idea. Right?"

"I do. So there are a great many people making claims to these abilities these days. Why is it ye feel that ye can't speak about what ye can do?"

"I don't want to be a side show; be looked at like something from a Stephen King novel or to have to prove myself to people Cath. I know I'm different in a way that makes me different even from those who are different. I just want...I think...I know that..." The dam of years of holding back broke and the words just rushed in a flood of release. "I think there's more to me that is connected with all this stuff; the visions and things. I think it's wrapped up in my past somehow. Not *my* past but my family's past, our history. 'Cause we all have some kind of weird connection with magic, occult, psychic ability, whatever you call it but it comes through my family. And whatever you call it, it's misunderstood. The abilities we have are not parlor tricks or something to be fooled around with. Now I don't know why my cousins don't have these abilities to the same degree as we do but they do have it and my sisters do but what we have, I think, no, I know is connected to these traditions, the Old Ways and sacred places and customs and rituals. I don't know how I know that but at the bottom of all of it, what I want to find out is what I think I was born for. So my work, my writing, my education, all of it is in search of that end. Not so much to prove the Catholics wrong, or even to use the abilities for what might be perceived as constructive, but to find something concrete that will remove the stigma from the Pagan ways and the doubt surrounding anything magical because there is so much beneficial material there that could help people in a big way but not if it is still looked down upon as evil, doubted as charlatanism or chuckled about as so much woo woo."

I pointed my finger to my temple and swirled it around in the universal symbol for crazy. My confusion as to what true benefit this work would have for myself or the world at large frustrated me. I felt I was not expressing what I was feeling. In truth, I was not sure in which direction my feelings traveled. I felt muddled, and tried to focus on my goal.

"The Christians and Jews have their Bibles," I started again, "with all the stories of Christ and what came before him. There are thousands of scholars if not more who have made their life's work attempting to find the sites of the biblical stories to provide evidence that these things actually took place. Christ used a form of this magic and they called it miracles. I think it's the same thing. The Pagans have their magical stories too, kept alive in folktales. And I want proof. I'd like to find actual archaeological sites that correspond with mythological stories in order to construct and support a theory that stories of myth have come through the ages based on some actual historical events. I don't know why, but this, along with the Christian religion being somehow mixed up with the older, Pagan religion is important to me. I know I've had a foot in each camp my whole life and it's been a juggling act trying to figure out which is right or which is right for me. And it's about magic and history and family and...all that but it's about something ...more than all of that. In fact, I think it's important to more than just me. It's bigger than me." I said, trying on the words as I spoke them. "Yeah, bigger than me, important. I don't know how, but it just is."

The room echoed with silence. I looked at Cath to see his response. My eyes tried to meet his but after several attempts, gave up and settled on some grains of salt on the table picking at them with my fingernail.

"Whew" I uttered weakly feeling as if I'd just confessed delusions of grandeur. "That's the first time I ever really thought consciously along those lines... I think. And it's definitely the first time I ever spoke out loud about any of that."

Cath sat across remnants of profiteroles and cold tea, looking at me apparently having no idea of how to respond to my monologue. He carried an unidentifiable emotion on the lines of his face and appeared to be thinking of what he should say. He drew in a breath and what he said was not what I'd expected. I don't know what I expected but this was not it.

He said, "Do ye know what yer name means?"

"Huh?"

"Your name, lass, its meaning. Do you know what it means, this Lenore?"

More Ping-Pong, I thought. I bumbled around mentally as I tried to make sense of why he might be asking me this now and I said with a furrowed brow.

"Uh, yeah, it means...ah white, I think."

I recalled a time I had found myself at a website that offered meaning of names during research one day as one link lead to another through a maze of sites for coat of arms and history of heritage, heraldry and so on. Among those sites was one that gave meanings for first names rather than family names. I remembered finding my name and being surprised that it was among those listed because as a girl, when all the fashion rage was to have your name on stationary, barrettes, buttons, and license plates for stingray bicycles, my name, being so unusual, was never found written on any of the novelty items. So I remembered being surprised when I found my name on that website and the meaning of my name stuck with me.

"Not exactly white." he said, "It means, light. Not the kind that doesn't weigh much, like light as a feather, but the kind that illuminates, is a beacon. Do ye know anything about how ye came to be named?"

"Well, yeah, it's kind of funny, I've told this story before. If you ask one of my parents how I was named, you'd get one story and then ask the other, you'd get another story, but they both tell it as the honest truth, so I don't know exactly."

"Well then, why don't you just tell me both the stories?"

"Okay." I knew this was the kind of conversation that had someplace to go but I wasn't sure yet where that might be. "My father is an artistic man who loves painting, sculpting, books, word play, poetry, that type of thing. He says he had always loved the poem *The Raven* by Edgar Allan Poe. I think I mentioned that to you last night. Are you familiar with the piece?" Cath nodded. "My dad claims that he named me after the one who was long lost in that poem, *Sweet Lenore.* But my mom says that she went to high school with a girl who was named Lenore and when I was born, I had a full head of hair that was so blond it was almost white, 'A halo of ringlets' she called it. She said my eyes were so big and blue and my hair was so light I reminded her of this high school friend that she hadn't thought of for years and it just popped into her head that she'd name me Lenore. So it's kind of funny that I was named for a black bird from a very dark poem and after a towheaded girl for an angelic look about me but no matter how I look at it, I figure the name was meant for me 'cause both my parents claim the name just came to each of them the day I was born."

Cath regarded me for a moment and said, "I think ye're right about that. The name was yours even *before* ye were born, I think. But I believe ye're wrong about the 'Sweet Lenore' part.

"What do you mean? I asked.

"The Lenore of *The Raven* was 'named by the angels.' Lenore of another of Poe's pieces was the 'Sweet Lenore.'" He corrected. "Are ye familiar with the other works of Poe?"

"Uh, yeah, I guess because of the *Raven* thing, I've read his stuff since I was a kid. And, now that I think about it, you're right, I misquoted. That's from the poem entitled *Lenore* isn't it? So in a way, you could say there were angels on both sides of the naming!"

Cath nodded. "But ye can't forget the significance of the raven in the process now, can ye? Nor the reference to light? Have ye noticed a pattern of this type of, let's say, duality in yer life? What I mean to say is yer name, yer religion or religions, is this something ye find occurring often?" I had to think about it and I could think of a few occasions where it was glaring but in a more subtle way I supposed balance and symmetry had always been important to me.

"Yeah, now that you mention it, things just seem to balance out for me that way. I do tend to see things in terms of black and white, right and wrong, like that?

"What was the sign ye were born under?"

"What?" I was surprised. "You Cath? Now you sound like Nora. I'm a Libra. The scales of justice." I said with mock importance. "Why?"

He seemed to consider that and appeared to come to some kind of internal approval.

"It appears as though you have the duality or shall I say balance, there too is all. But now let me ask you a bit more about your parents. Your father, you say has the poet in him?"

By the way Cath was asking me questions, I knew he had a purpose but I still had no idea what that might be. I felt as though I were being tested or somehow having to pass muster for something. I considered this and decided to answer the questions. I'd find out where all this was leading eventually so I decided to go with the flow.

"Yeah. He has a wonderful way of expressing things in poetry. As far back as I can remember he had a way of using rhythm, wit, emotion, satire and irony to create a lyrical tale about even the most mundane subjects. He also believes that the true cadence of poetry is carried in the effort to deliver its message with rhyme. He was never one for gushing emotions but Dad can relate in his works, what his feeling are. Like the poem he wrote when my grandfather died was very telling. I never saw him shed a tear, but the poem, full of admiration for my grandfather's connection with nature and how he'd taken so fully to the Old Ways. Want to hear it?"

"I'd be honored. There are not many youngsters these days, who take to the art of poetry or storytelling."

In my forties, I was pleased to be referred to as a youngster. I smiled inwardly and supposed that, to Cath, I am a youngster. I collected my thoughts to remember the poem and do justice to my dad's work and to my grandpa's memory. I found myself a bit nervous with the recitation as if this, too, was some kind of test, but dismissed the thought. After all, I'd volunteered the telling. I settled myself down and thought of my father and grandfather as I'd remembered them talking together at the burning barrel so many years ago and the rhythm of the words flowed through me with ease. I spoke:

Dada
By: Patrick O'Leary
He knew the earth, was one with its soil
And called the birds by name
The sunny, open sky with toil
Were his, in joy to claim.
The fullest cup of nature's wine
He drank the vintage straight
The good, rich life was his, in fine
He gave and took from fate.
The fruitful earth, its treasure
Life's wisdom he did know
And from it drew his pleasure
He enjoyed, then did bestow.
Old Mother Earth takes Chosen Ones
Reveals to these, her lore
She's searching now for other ones
To wear the gift he bore.

The room was quiet and Cath seemed genuinely touched as though he were one artist appreciating the work of another, knowing how few others could understand the amount of self, one pours into a work of art.

"I thank ye for that. Yer right, he reveals himself in his words. And ye show him great respect in your rendition of the work."

"I cherish the stuff he's done." I said. "In fact, I've begun to collect his works and create a compilation ranging from the early 1950's to now."

He seemed to be contemplating something then asked, "He's from County Cork, is he?"

"Yeah, how did you know?"

"The O'Leary name. Cork is the general location where the name settled...after a while. And what of your mother?"

"My mother? Oh no, she's not from Ireland. I mean, yeah she's Irish, well at least half Irish. Her maiden name is Scully and her father's side comes from Ireland but her mother's family, my grandmother is from Sweden, Höök was her name."

A tremor went through Cath as if his entire body was charged with some energy foreign to a man of his obvious years. It seemed as if he forced himself to remain seated. Then without missing a beat in the conversation, "Is she artistic as well?"

"Who, my grandmother?"

"No your mother. Tell me about your mother."

"I don't think she's a big one for poetry."

"What is she a big one for then? What is she like?"

I thought for a minute about my mother and cast about a little to find a foothold in this conversation.

"Well, she's always been a strong role model for me as a professional woman. She knows a hard day's work. I learned from her in a different way than I learned from my dad. She went off to work and showed me that a woman is capable in more ways than just domestically. You know that old commercial on T.V. for a perfume, I think it was," I began to sing "I can bring home the bacon and fry it up in a pan, and never, never, never let you forget you're a man... You remember that?"

"I'm afraid not, but I get the idea."

"Well that was my image of my mother when I was a kid. We learned how to cook, bake and be a hostess with linens and fine dishes from my mother. Not that she really taught us how or anything like that, we just learned from her example that this is the way things should be done. She liked things that were of quality and went out to earn what she had to in order to have those things. Which was great for those big holiday family gatherings we always had, but she wasn't around all that much while we, Nora and I, were young. My memories of my mom are mostly connected with the big excitement of cleaning and decorating for Easter or Christmas and waiting for all of the family to show up for the party but the everyday stuff of school work or practicing piano lessons, we were pretty much left to our own devices."

"So ye celebrated in the Catholic fashion as a rule?"

"Well, publicly you could say that. We called them Christmas and Easter but there was always awareness within the household that there would be the additional celebrations that we didn't discuss outside our home. It seemed that's what my mother really wanted was for us to fit in with the community around us but she never objected overtly to the way we kept the old traditions with my father's family or in the home. She was present for a lot of it but kind of on the periphery, she was more involved with the appearance of being Catholic now that you mention it."

"Now have ye a sister other than Nora here?"

"Oh no, not here. I have two more sisters both older than Nora and me. I'm the youngest of four girls. Our sister Patrice was supposed to come with us on this trip but no matter how much I wish it had worked out, it just wasn't meant to be this time. The three of us, Nora, Patrice and I have grown close in our adulthood. We've shared apartments in our single days and learned how to travel as a companionable group for years. We enjoy each other's company. For the three of us, it's easy. We just sort of get along.

"And ye say all of ye have this magic as ye call it?"

"Yeah to some degree or another. We all see things, and now that I think of it, my mother does too. She told us once of a story when she was a little girl, and I remember it clearly 'cause she never really spoke about things like that. It was after her grandmother's funeral, she said, when her family had come home and my mother saw her grandmother, whose funeral they'd just attended, sitting, plain as day, at the dining room table. She turned and looked directly at my mother and then was gone. That's all she ever told us about her seeing stuff. But my sisters and I always saw things, and just took it in stride that that's the way it was. I know my sister Mary had certain uh, talents."

"And what were those?"

I didn't know why I was telling Cath all about my family, but after years of hiding, it was like a confession of sorts, a purging of all that was kept in the dark. It felt good to talk about it...to shed light on it.

"My two older sisters, Mary and Patrice, have this gift of vision, sight or psychic ability and have used it or not in their own way. Like I said, we all have this ability to some degree, and that's what leads me to believe that the gift we have is somehow hereditary and this magical energy is not random, but has come to us with a purpose. We inherited more than just our family traditions that have their roots in our Celtic heritage." Having said that, I began.

"The oldest of our sisters, Mary," I thought for a moment, "Yeah she has a fair dosage of the ability but during our childhood, she scared me. She kept books on black magic and the occult hidden under her bed. And rather than observe the Old Ways with the family, it seemed to me that she felt this other path was the fastest route to meeting her ends, which was to get people to do what she wanted them to do. She was good at that; getting people to do what she wanted, whether through cajoling, threats or bribery it didn't matter to her so long as she got what she wanted."

My mind took inventory for a moment as I recalled what life with Mary was like as the youngest sister in the family.

"Lee," she would say to me in the voice of a woman selling snake oil, "if you go up to my room and get my nail polish for me, I'll give you a lollipop." Ten years my senior, of course I did what she asked and upon returning with her nail polish, there would be no lollipop, only a reproaching tone for having fallen for the ruse. I shook myself back to the conversation.

"Her beauty was the first thing anyone would notice about her. Even now she is well into her 50's and looks much younger. But when we were kids, she was something. She had intense blue eyes and dark olive skin. Her rich and thick black hair hung down to the tops of her legs. Methodically, she grew and painted her nails, curled her hair, and painted her face. When she got ready to go out she prepared with razor-like focus as if she were casting a spell on her appearance so it would pull just the right people into her web. I didn't realize until much later that, that was just exactly what she was doing. She'd slip into seductive clothes and set out to attract those who would do her bidding. She knew she could bewitch men with her beauty and she did. There was always a parade of men of all ages sniffing around despite the fact that she treated them no better than she did me or any other member of our family. She wasn't very nice back then. She thought we wasted our power by being involved with the Catholic ways and should use the gifts we had for our own advancement. She had contempt for the men she dated for being weak enough to fall under her charm. But they kept coming. She found the centerpiece of *her* magic in her sexuality by appealing to people's base needs, wants and desires."

"Sounds as though she might have been a popular gorl." Cath commented.

"Oh no." I answered. "To the best of my recollection, Mary had almost no friends to speak of. There would be an occasional person who would serve a purpose and this would be an intense *friendship* for a brief time. Then one day, that person would no longer be at our house, or calls would no longer be accepted from them. Somehow or other, they had served their purpose or fallen out of favor. They would no longer exist. I couldn't understand how Mary could be blessed with so much beauty on the outside and be just plain mean on the inside. She worked at harnessing the magic she had but did so outside of the family traditions and rituals; without reverence. To me, this was very scary."

"And did ye get along after a fashion?" Cath prodded.

"I guess there were times when things were okay. Mary could be very charming and personable and even funny. But her scope of vision never strayed far from what was best for Mary, so if I could, I kept my distance."

And now?

"Well, I guess you could say we've gone in different directions. She's a softer soul now, but still hasn't grasped the concept of a world beyond what is best for Mary or what she wants. Justification serving as her best logic for the things she does. I hold out hope though, that someday she'll see beyond her own version of the truth."

"And the other?"

"Patrice, I felt bad for her when we were kids. She's the second oldest in our family, I guess you could say she was cursed to be close in age with Mary because she was stuck sharing a bedroom on the top floor of our house with Mary and came directly under her eye on a daily basis. This was too bad for Patrice because she had her own kind of pure beauty. No makeup needed, natural curves, long flowing chestnut hair with auburn streaks that shimmered in the sun. She emanated friendliness with an open face and beautiful smile with the most beautiful black lashes around perfect, lively brown eyes."

I thought to myself that even though they were supposed to have shared the bedroom, the space up there on the top floor was Mary's and Patrice was subject to the chaotic living style that was Mary's. Patrice was a guest in her own bedroom and not a welcome one either.

"The resulting effect for, Patrice, I think, was that she withdrew. She tried to make herself as invisible as possible in order to avoid the wrath of Mary. Having her own tendency for magic, enough energy devoted in one direction will get results I guess because Patrice folded in on herself and did, in a way, disappear within our family. I still wonder to myself how much of this enchanted disappearance was Patrice not wanting to be seen and picked on by Mary, and how much of it was Mary not wanting to compete with Patrice's natural beauty and lovely personality. But however it came about, whether her own doing, or Mary's, Patrice avoided contact with the family and constructed a web of friendships outside the family in order to not have to deal with anything abnormal. Our family was the poster picture for abnormal so she joined the Catholic family so to speak. And that was good for her. She flourished there in a rich social life with teenaged boys and girls her own age. There were parties and dances, camping excursions and all kinds of activities that reeked of normalcy. I always admired her when I was little. She struck me as so glamorous and cosmopolitan, there was always some social thing she was off to. She went to church and went to St. Gregory's High School and fit right in. Come to think of it, this was just what my mother had hoped for all of us. Patrice breezed through school and out of our lives for a long time, without so much as a whisper. She dealt with family functions by falling asleep. She was there, but not there. I think I understand now that what Patrice was trying to do was quietly stay connected to her magic while at the same time staying under the radar, Mary's, the family's, and the Churches."

"And now?"

"Now, Patrice is, well I guess she's living a quiet, normal life. I don't think she keeps the traditions of either of the religions in her life but is searching for the best way to just live a good and spiritual life. If she has the magic, still, I don't know much about it other than she has true dreams sometimes. She's still beautiful and still has lots of friends. She and Nora got that social gene that I just never had the knack for."

The sun was getting low and while I had enjoyed our discussion and the revelations and relief that came with letting myself talk about all of this, I still had no interview to show for the time. I had shared quite a lot of personal information with Cath and was curious about him as well. I felt a bit more comfortable now that I was fairly sure he was not going to try to ravish me or throw me out the door for my religious beliefs so I felt comfortable enough to ask him the question.

"Cath, what is your stance on some of the things we've talked about today? Are you religious? Are you Catholic? What is your interest in the books you have collected in the back room? Does it go beyond a business interest? Is it academic? Personal? I mean, after all, I'm supposed to be the one interviewing here and I seem to be doing most of the talking."

"Right." He said. "Ye've shared quite a bit. Well let me share my story with you by startin' with another story. Ye know ye've a kind of name that I've heard of before in a story. One such as ye mentioned just before to me. A story that has the sound of myth about it, but that has its feet planted in the ground of history. And if ye'll allow, I'd like to take some time to start our real interview with the telling of that one if ye'll let me."

Totally shifting gears now I felt as though I'd been booted out of a cozy cubbyhole of lethargy after lunch and conversation and must now be at attention and go to work.

"Oh, Okay. Just let me grab my stuff, and a pen. Wait! Can I record this? Hold on."

I hurried to the counter where, hours ago, I'd dropped my bag. I felt as though I were doing a bad Annie Hall impression as I rummaged to liberate the right tools from the leather satchel that carried my equipment. Not quite the organized professional I envisioned myself to be. But I finally settled back at the table and found that Cath had cleaned away the remnants of lunch and was waiting patiently for me. It seemed in our short time as acquaintances, he'd done a considerable amount of waiting patiently for me. And from what he was about to tell me, I really had no idea just how much waiting he'd actually done.

"All right. I'm ready." I snapped on the mini recorder and had my paper and pen at the ready.

11

There's Magic in the Air

ow! It was the only word that seemed to envelope what my mind was trying to wrap itself around. "Wow!" I said out loud as if verbalizing would somehow harness my thoughts more satisfactorily into something other than electrified amazement. I had so much to think about, to write, to verify if possible.

Cath had told me a story that was very much like the mythical tales of my childhood told by my grandparents. Some of the names were even familiar to me, but his take on the tale was that this and many other stories, passed down from generation to generation, were actual spiritual lessons couched in a tale in order to avoid persecution during the rise of the Christian religion. He also told me that this one particular tale had come through countless generations all the way down to him with the responsibility of making sure that it would be passed on verbatim to the next generation in order that it would be known at the right time in history to help enlighten the world about its history, duty, and future.

"No pressure there!" I said sarcastically. It was a great story that had all the elements of what I was looking for. It was supposedly based in fact, it had magic, it had specified locations in Ireland, it had deities, and it was an active story known to the locals. Okay, the locals who know the tale are some kind of clandestine circle or something, but still, it has all the right stuff! It was exactly what I was looking for.

Driving back to the cottage seemed almost automatic for me now. As my mind operated on trying to sort out and dissect all the information Cath had given, my hands and feet drove home in partnership with the little car. It wasn't quite dark but I could see the first stars peeking out at the night and the great moon, just about full, was huge and ivory, calling my eyes to it with obsessive frequency. The moon, I thought, has been a constant in human history. And our humanness is what seems to draw us in fascination to look at that moon. *This is the moon that called my ancestors' eyes in this very country!* I had always known I had relatives in Ireland but never having contact with them, that idea was just a fact recited as if from a book.

Now that I'm actually here, my new perspective seemed to be bringing that fact to reality. *I have relatives in Ireland!* I made a mental note to see if Nora would be open to a visit to our relatives within the next couple of days, but my mind glanced over that thought and continued its internal monologue. *I want to see that other guy first. Finny, what was his name? McDonough, that's right, Finny McDonough. I'll want to go and get his take on this story and any others he may be able to tell me about. What a score in meeting Cath. Well he turned out to be the nicest little man; and interesting. I can't wait to tell Nora all about everything.*

"Oh Nora!" I had been so engrossed in the story Cath told me I'd forgotten that Nora was at the cottage with no transportation and very little to eat in the tiny fridge. I was glad to have some remnants of lunch with me that Cath had insisted I take. My mind bounced to the final minutes of my conversation with Cath.

"If ye don't mind, I'll keep a ham sandwich for myself?"

"Oh no Cath. I brought this food for you. You keep all of it."

"My appetite's not what it once was. A ham sandwich will do me. Ye'll take what's left of the sandwiches, and the other dishes, but I'm partial to those sweets..." The statement hung in the air and the expression on his face was comical, almost boyish.

"Of course Cath. You enjoy them. Are you sure about the rest?"

"Aye. It'll be wasted if ye leave all that food here and I don't see the sense in wasting."

"O.K. then." I packed my satchel with my equipment and the leftover food. "Thank you so much for such a wonderful day. I can't tell you how much I appreciate the time you took with me today. I took one of your cards from the counter. Is it O.K. to call you if I have any questions?"

"Well, it'd be a disappointment to me if you didn't. Now I expect ye'll come see me again. And ye'll go see Finny McDonough?"

Cath had given me the name of a man he thought would have a wealth of stories that would help me in my research. He promised to tell the man I would be coming to speak with him.

"You know I will Cath. I can't tell you what a help this has been, in so many ways. Thank you so much."

Feeling such a warm kinship with this lovely man I felt almost sad to be leaving him. Now that it was time to leave, I wanted to make sure that I would not lose contact with him. A fleeting afternoon, and I was as connected to him as if he were family. Without hesitation or self-consciousness, I stepped close to him and gave him a sincere hug with a peck on the cheek. Obviously flustered with the display of affection, Cath gently pushed me toward the door shooing me off before dark. The embarrassed smirk on his mouth told me he was not at all displeased.

A blaring car horn warned me that I was drifting on the road. I found I was again staring at the moon. I had to get a grip on myself. Even though it was nearing nighttime, there were plenty of people out on the road. It was Saturday night and people around these parts did have a tendency to tip a few after a long week's work. I tried to bring some focus to driving and a semblance of rational thinking back to my mind but I found it difficult.

I opened the car window hoping the wind would refresh me. The air smelt of cool fresh water as if it had rained, but it did little to clear my head, which was dancing with all the potential of the tale I was just told. I took in a large, nostril flaring breath and I became even more lightheaded with excitement. There was a sultry feel to the night that added to my excitement.

"There's magic in the air tonight." I said to the moon. And in that moment, I realized this was true. I recognized the energy I was feeling was a swirling mixture of electrical excitement and expectancy that charged the air all around. I waited for something to happen, but nothing came. Usually when I would experience this kind of energy, it would drain right after the glimpse of a spirit, vision or a clairvoyant thought. But I was beginning to recognize that things of this nature were not status quo since I arrived here in Ireland. It was familiar, yet foreign to me. It is as if the aperture opened wider on my psychic lens and allowed more visions, transmissions or whatever they were called, through to me than what I was accustomed to in America. Transmissions that were once comparatively weak and shadowy for me now happened with clarity and strength. But at this moment, there was no transmission. It seemed this enhanced energy was with me as a normal state of my existence, sometimes surging while others ebbing to a low vibration, but always there. I thought: *If I could see the energy, I bet there'd be all kinds of sparkling lights all around me like static electricity.* But for now, all I could see was the stars and that moon.

I began to recount some of the extraordinary or unusual occurrences that had happened since we arrived in Ireland. Not least of which were the strange woman in my bedroom last night and the eerie feeling of being hunted or stalked by some beast. *What was that all about? And that smell! Then I saw her again this morning in the mirror.* With the moon as my company, lighting my way, it became clear to me for the first time that someone is trying to tell me something. In retrospect, I was amazed that I had observed all of these occurrences and put them aside without examination. But as I began to assemble the circumstances in my head, they seemed far from normal now. In fact it seemed as if I should wake up and begin to pay attention. Things are happening, magic is swirling. Maybe this coffeeless, sleep induced funk I have been in has dulled my usually sharp and inquisitive need to investigate and seek answers. The cottage incident when we had first arrived was not totally out of the ordinary, knowing where things were situated was not unfamiliar to me but when the whole place seemed to zoom back in time it became clear to me that this cottage was no ordinary place.

The conversation I had with Nora after Bridey had left us to unpack on that first day should have been an indication that things were different for both of us in Ireland. And why that conversation hadn't raised some alarm bells is beyond me. It is as if all of these signs were coming my way and for some reason, though I acknowledged them, they had not left a reasonable impression.

"What was up with you?" Nora asked when Bridey had left the cottage.

"I don't know. This strange déjà vu came over me and I just couldn't shake it. Why? Was I being weird?"

"Weird! That's not the word for it. Were you trying to scare Bridey?"

"What are you talking about? I was doing all I could do to keep from fainting. The whole cottage morphed to a different era on me. I felt like I was in two different times at the same time."

"You were projecting an image of yourself as an old lady. I didn't even think you could do that very well and now here you are putting our landlady on guard or freaking her out on our first day!"

"Nora, I swear I wasn't doing anything. You know I'm no good at changing my image with people. And why would I? I was in this freakish state of having been here in this cottage before but I could see the cottage at the same time from what seemed like centuries ago. It came on all of a sudden and I couldn't do anything to shake myself out of it. It was too weird. And, I know, without even going down that hallway" I said waving an arm toward the hall, "that your room is at the end of the hall and it's painted yellow and orange just like our room when we were kids. And the room that's mine is on the left with a double bed, a big wardrobe and a bathroom off the bedroom. Am I right?"

Nora stared at me and nodded her head. We both stood for a minute trying to figure out what was going on.

"There's something else." I added. "There is this room here off the main room that some voice came to me loud and clear telling me that this is 'the mother's room.' I get the feeling that we're supposed to steer clear. Didn't you pick up or feel anything?"

"The only thing I can tell you is when I looked at you, I saw what I thought was you trying to project yourself as an old woman. Didn't you get me asking you what the hell you were doing?"

"I got the look you gave me but I had no idea it was because you were seeing what you were seeing. I had no idea that's what I was projecting. All I know is, I felt like I was struggling to keep from falling into another time. That's how powerful the feeling was. As soon as I walked into this place, things started happening. I knew the layout of the house for no reason and then I was in some kind of time-vortex."

"What do you suppose this is all about?"

"Nora, I have no idea. But it's kind of scary that you saw something I had no knowledge of and I was experiencing something that you didn't. That's not like us to be so out of sync with each other."

My mind busied itself with these memories and other occurrences and all that had happened with Cath today as I drove the car up the long driveway road that lead to our cottage. Feeling as though I had been in the dark and someone turned on a light, I was determined to talk with Nora about all these circumstances to try to puzzle out what might be going on and why, until now, I had allowed them to be dismissed.

"Good." I said to myself as I observed that the cottage lights were still on and a wisp of smoke twisted out of the chimney. Nora was still up and I wanted to discuss all of this with her and compare notes about if anything was going on with her that I didn't yet know about. If someone or something were trying to tell us something, we'd have a better chance of figuring it out together. And if it all came to nothing, then at the very least I had to tell her about Cath's story. I was surprisingly alert now and pumping with energy.

Part II; The Village

12

The Telling

Word that there was an important stranger within their midst, one who had
convened the Tribal Council had traveled quickly through the village. There
were conflicting stories regarding whether Faidhe had descended from the Hill or
not. Some said that Faidhe had died and this new woman was here to take her place
while others spoke of the Spring Goddess honoring them with her presence at the
coming festival. There were these and countless other half-truths and outright fabrications. Many villagers told stories regarding the return of many ancestral spirits,
stemming from an experience similar to the one had by Iarann. In truth clans folk
had thought they saw their loved ones and those who'd passed to the spirit world
but these stories were those that grew each time with the telling as though the
tale had a spirit of its own and became more intriguing with each repetition of the
account. The village grew more excited in its anticipation upon being summoned
to the meeting-ground on the far west side of the village, where the tribe often
came to be entertained by actors, gamers, songsmiths, and many other types of performers. The place of gathering had an air of a festival about it as the murmuring of
the crowd heightened to a roar and the village people awaited some news, action
or entertainment.

Seated stoically at the front of the crowd, was Iarann, silently wringing his callused hands. He seemed to be the only one present with the understanding that
this was not a festival and the news that was inevitable was not likely to be light
in nature for the clans. Once he had gathered the crowd by lighting the communal
fires to draw attention and spread word for a gathering, he had taken a seat to mentally recount all that had happened in the last hours since this woman had appeared
at the edge of the forest, particularly his powerful, undisciplined response to her.
When he looked about the chirping crowd, he realized that he was not the only
one who awaited the coming news with some foreboding. Iarann looked into the
black eyes of the Keeper's strange daughter. What he saw there was the burning

recognition that this gathering would have great effect on the tribe but in those eyes, he also discovered fear.

Away from the site of the gathering clan, the hut where the Council convened was located at the center of the village. Typically where the great feasts were held, the round hut spanned about 54 tri-paces across the center that mimicked the great Circle, and boasted an enormous raised cooking pit lined with great stones in the center. To the east of the great hearth, were two large, beautifully carved oak chairs, embellished with sections of gold, reserved always for the Dagda and Danu. In front of the large thrones were six smaller, less ornately decorated chairs arranged at a table reserved for the Tribal Council each of whom had, to some degree, the ability of vision. Great wooden feasting tables were arranged in accordance to rank and honor from the highest, closest to the thrones, to the rear of the hall for lesser queens, kings and warriors during high gatherings of the entire Tuath and for common village folk during local feasts. The timber of hundreds of trees held the thatch aloft the great pointed roof, absent thatching only above where the ceremonial cooking fire would be lit and the smoke would need to escape. The walls of the feasting hut were created of thicket, which was bound tightly with sturdy rope made from the stem of the stinging nettle plant.

The hall seemed unusually empty with only the six members of the Tribal Council seated at the large feasting table. Faidhe, the Second member of the Council, sat in the seat at the head of the table and therefore commanded due attention and respect that came with the placement of the seat. For urgent occasions such as this, one who takes this seat need not adhere to the general rule of equal standing within the Council during meetings. She did not come to seek counsel with the others, as was their custom. She had come to tell them what had transpired at the great Circle on the previous night and to tell them of the fast coming changes. She would brook no opposition as could be expected from Briciu, one of the two men on the Council, nor would she even tolerate pleasantries or polite banter as was customary.

Faidhe left no time for courtesies. She stood and gave a brusque speech.

"It comes to this: I have been given prophesy in a great vision that reveals doom for our ways. Now comes the time for swift action to plant the seeds of change in order that our ways are preserved. And as the seed is unseen and underground, so too, must our ways be nurtured in secret until such time when they can come to light once again and thrive in a more harsh and hostile environment. It is left to us... to me to create a path from now into the future, casting magic and using the Power of the Word to bring our strength of faith and ritual ways forward on the breath of the religion that is to come. For this I must journey and give Council with wise ones of other tribes and peoples. So say the Gods.

She observed the amazed faces on the members of the Council and could not imagine how it was they saw her. She gauged how the first wave of her news was accepted by the expression in the eyes of her co-members and detected that as she predicted, Briciu, despite being the Sixth and least powerful member of the Council, thought somehow, by virtue of the size that came with his gender he was more powerful than his station and was brewing up a blustering response.

She ignored his reddening face and gestured Briciu to quiet himself.

"Know this now. We have no choice in this. Either we contrive to protect our ways and the Goddess along with all the lesser Gods by voluntarily aiding them under to the Sidhe, or they will be lost to all and forever. I have been given sight of the world to come and it is a woeful vision to have the land stripped of its beauty, the air and water fouled by insolence and the spirit of her people bereft of the sacred. We must forego the preservation of our current ways and shift with the changing tide. Great changes will be made beginning now and with our clans. The future of our blood, our seed, our ways, our Gods, our lands and that of humankind depends on our response to the call of the Gods on this very day." She saw in her periphery, Briciu standing up now demanding to be paid attention.

"Wise woman, you are Seer and Keeper and Councilmember. Yet, you show us not the respect due at Council? Do I not recognize your standing as I address you? This is outrage. You take high seat with no explanation. Are you to come to us then to petition changes such as you speak without honoring us with full revelation as to what has transpired that we may speak on it and come to decisions as to what best may be done?"

Faidhe's appearance grew terrible and largely magnificent, surrounded by light and fearsome as a warrior. She did not raise her voice, but the underlying growl in her tone commanded full adherence to her warning.

"Sit down Briciu! I do not come in petition or to seek counsel. I come with the word of prophecy and duty to the God and Goddess. Keep your self-honor in check, Councilmember. This is not a matter for the Council's discussion behind walls. I show the Council courtesy by addressing it first on the matter, however all will be revealed to the Tuatha De Danann in a formal telling so that the word may be passed from clan to clan and there will be many to effect the changes needed, nay *required*, by the Gods."

Faidhe returned to her task with no other thought to how affronted Briciu may be feeling at this moment.

"The signs have been coming on for many years and yet we have not recognized them. How often, of late, have we seen The Dagda or The Danu?" She gestured to the empty seats of honor at the head of the great hall as though their emptiness was evidence of the truth she was revealing. "There are those within the Tuatha De Danann who speak of the Dagda and Mother Danu as if they are characters of myth. It has been this long. The other tribes have waned over the past centuries as though they already had knowing of the coming of the end. Even we, as Seers, actually see so few of the magical creatures, fairy folk and the like, the merfolk *are* all but a myth; the remaining dragons have gone feral for lack of a tribe's keeping. Is it so long ago that the Firbolg and the Fomorii were banished to the nethers that we forget how it may just as easily happen to us? I tell you now we must make great effort over the coming years to exact changes necessary to send the spirits underground to the Sidhe voluntarily. But the most important task is to pass the mantle of Power from the She to the He within the tribe and to cast the proper magic so that the She will be protected until such time when the world is ready for Her return to take her rightful place beside the He."

Most of the Councilmembers sat in the echo of her speech with mouths agape and astonished expressions on their faces.

"The He?" Briciu repeated falling into his habit of argumentativeness. "What are you saying? That we should abandon the Mother and give her honor to the lesser Gods as does a lowly ruler or chieftain give over fealty to only those who are likely to win a battle? If it is so, that our way of life is waning, then we must do what we must to reinforce the customs, not abandon them."

Briciu, accustomed to playing the advocate of the opposition on many Council matters so that he could hear his own voice spoken in authority, spoke now of shoring up the current spiritual ways but it could be seen in his eyes that another thought ignited behind the words. It had been only a short while since Briciu was brought onto the Council and with some trepidation of most members. He was a young man with much to offer in the way of magical skill and seeing, however the Councilmembers hesitated long before giving in to the reassurances of Briciu's mother, Gara, the Third member of the Council, that he was the best choice due to his skills.

Lon Dubh, Faidhe's daughter was also in serious consideration for the position but in the end, Gara's incessant claims that the Council would be wise to choose someone "involved in tribal matters" and that Briciu would be a better choice than one who remained "a recluse and kept peculiar ways".

Since his acceptance as the Sixth member of the Council, Briciu fell away from the assumed humility he kept during the trial process and of late had displayed an attitude of enjoying overmuch his new position within the Tuatha De Danann Council. It was rumored that he accepted favors in exchange for speaking on behalf of clan folk with the Council. In fact, Faidhe had noticed he wore a fine woolen cloak fastened at the shoulder with a bronze brooch bearing the Circle, the symbol of a Councilmember. This cloak could have come to him from any number of sources but Faidhe needed only look at him to divine that this was a gift from someone who had made gains through Briciu's position as a Councilmember. Briciu was using his position to create self-comfort and to build a base of power for his family within the clan rather than to serve the clan.

Faidhe eyed Briciu and could see his energy boiling around him despite his struggles to maintain a congenial exterior. It became clear to her that Briciu would have some part to play in the task at hand but knew not what that would be. She put her thoughts on that matter aside and ignored his statements, knowing they were not in the least sincere.

She announced, "I have had the villagers assembled at the place of gathering to announce what has come to pass and to make known what will take place in my absence."

"Absence?" Gara spoke for the first time. "You intend then, to come down from the Circle Hill? Then we must accomplish our duty of deciding who will replace you. Well then, Faidhe," she said in an almost dismissive tone, "since you have important news to deliver, go then and prepare while we Councilmembers complete the more mundane work of day to day tribal business."

Faidhe was uncomfortable to notice that Gara and her son had created a pocket of power on the Council that was not at all wholesome and that she, herself had been on the Hill overlong for these members of the Council showed her not the respect due the Keeper but appeared bothered at her presence rather than cognizant of her message. This was not something she'd acknowledged before her shift in vision but may have been due only to the reality that while she was Keeper of the Circle, she was not present for many of the lower Council meetings held to determine how the day to day running of clan affairs would be handled. She did not miss the note of sarcasm in Gara's comment but Faidhe understood that the way to get things done now would not be made easier by making enemies on the Council. But she could also see clearly that, enemies she already had.

"I do not relinquish my position as Keeper of the Circle to simply return to the clan as a Wise Woman. As the Keeper, I am implementing the necessary changes within the clan in order to carry out what has been prophesied through the Circle as necessary for the survival of our ways. And as the Keeper, I will name who is to continue my duties in my absence as was shown me in my vision between the very Stones."

Faidhe made a move toward the door of the feasting hut and to leave the Council to make her presence known to the rest of the clan. Now both Gara and Briciu stood, seeing the opportunity for a great shift in power within the clan, they did not know quite how to seize the moment but it was obvious to both of them that this was a moment they did not want to pass without having some say in how the power would be distributed. In that same moment, Craiche, the oldest member of the Council stood, resting heavily on the table in front of her.

"Have you an eye toward the position yourself then Gara, or is it your daughter you think of now?" Gara and Briciu spun toward the old woman's voice, surprised to remember that someone, anyone else was in the hut with them.

Quickly regaining her composure silkily Gara responded, "I had not thought of anyone particularly for the position of Keeper, however now as you suggest my daughter, speaking only as Third member of the Council, not as her mother of course, yet having some personal knowledge of her abilities, I think it an excellent choice."

Craiche let out a wheezing chuckle at this. "I do not suggest anything of the sort. You have so long been angling to position yourself and family in places of status or power within the village that you cannot recognize the critical moment we have before us. In your grab for power, you would trample over anyone in your path. I, Craiche, *as First member* of the Council, and having *great* knowledge of a *great many* things, think you should put aside your quest for personal power and gain. Now is the time to listen to Faidhe and adhere to what instruction she brings us from the Gods. Are you blind to your own vision? Have you had no inkling of the great changes that are at our feet? Have you seen nothing of these changes your-selves? Even if your Seeing abilities have failed you in this, can you not see what is at stake here by way of common sense?"

Being baldly called out so, to have the very ability of a Councilmember's vision publicly brought into question, Gara put a squeezing hand on Briciu's arm to stay any response and softened her voice to reply.

"Of course I recognize what is at stake and only speak to preserve appearances that the Council remains intact and has a ready plan to stay any alarm over such drastic changes within the Tuath. We must think of the clans and maintain stability and be able to announce to all that the Council has voted and is in full support of what changes Faidhe is suggesting."

"Gara, my dear, Faidhe is not 'suggesting' anything. She has brought decree from the Circle and we must obey. However if it's a vote you must have, then all those in favor of affording Faidhe our full support?" Craiche looked to the group of Councilmembers and the others held raised hands. She looked to Gara and Briciu who recognized their defeat for the moment and both slowly raised their hands, each bearing a look on their faces as though they'd just swallowed a good dose of bitterroot. "Good then, shall we attend the gathering?"

Faidhe collected her strength and bent to pick up the great bowl with the fine staff. She became most uneasy as she observed both Briciu and Gara eyeing her cauldron lustily. One could only imagine what they might see within the magical concavance. She thrust the bowl over her shoulder and noted with some satisfac-tion that her strength in carrying such a weight was recognized by those who may have corrupt ideas about the Power it holds. They stood back and watched Faidhe pass through the doors of the great feasting hall.

The crowd, having been assembled at the place of gathering, began to cluster in groups of clans and families over the vast stretch of smooth grass conveniently kept short by the clans' flocks of grazing sheep. People could be seen playing the game of sticks, blowing tunes on wooden whistles, and singing songs. Indeed some new songs were already being spun about these recent happenings and versions of the stories of the *Woman from the Wood* and the *Ghosts from the Hill* were already being sung. The village had a general air of festival about it. But the tone changed as soon as the woman carrying the great bowl was seen walking toward the west end of the showground where a platform was constructed of stone and wood to elevate performers so they could be seen by all. The villagers began murmuring speculations and observations about the woman and what she carried. Those who met Faidhe in the forest enjoyed their moment of importance at having actually spoken with the stranger and related their stories over and again as to how she appeared and what she carried and who she claimed to be.

As Faidhe climbed the stones arranged in front of the platform in graduated height, the crowd quieted but still hummed. She made some exaggerated movements to place the cauldron down in plain sight, and then just stood facing the crowd, knowing that in just a moment she would have the full attention of the people. As she waited Faidhe noticed Briciu working the crowd, making his way toward the platform. He clapped backs and squeezed hands, claiming insight to those along the way.

"We have important news. Yes, very important announcement. Patience now and listen. We'll reveal things as necessary."

Less obvious on the other side of the platform was Gara, standing on the higher stones that served as stairs to the stage. When he'd finished glory mongering, Briciu had arranged himself on the stairs in an elevated position of importance as Gara had done.

Faidhe's annoyance was momentary. If the Councilmembers would serve as insurance that what needed to be done was accepted by the Tuath on the whole, then Briciu and his mother could stand where they will but she would not have them standing in the light of her announcement for their own self-importance. Faidhe raised her arms and the crowd was silenced.

"I am Faidhe, of the Tuatha De Danann, Keeper of the Circle, second member of the Council and Seer for the clans of the Tuath." She announced.

At this, Faidhe heard a great undercurrent of mumbling and saw much shaking of heads. She detected that many people of the village did not recognize her as herself. She pushed on. "I have news of great import. Listen, and I will share what has been revealed to me and required of me...when the rest of the Councilmembers have taken their places."

Fleeting confusion crossed over the faces of the Tribal Council who had gathered together at the base of the platform to listen with the rest of the village. Craiche was first to move by taking the arms of Faeg and Brath, the fourth and fifth Councilmembers, having them escort her over the large stone stairs up toward the platform. She did not stop on the step where Briciu and his mother had assembled in front of Faidhe. They watched as the ancient woman made a grand, if a bit theatrical, entrance up onto the stage itself, where Faidhe stood and then proceeded to stand behind her flanked by the other two Councilmembers.

Faidhe smiled inwardly at Craiche's simplicity in showing Gara and Briciu for what they were; self-important, glory thieves. By standing behind Faidhe, Craiche showed support for her without usurping the attention she required for the moment. Gara and Briciu fumed with scarlet faces as Faidhe silently waited while they took their place behind her with the rest of the Council. To the crowd, it looked as though Briciu and Gara simply did not know what was expected of them. It put them forward as not really knowing what was going on. *Just so.* Faidhe said in her head to Craiche. *Well-done old friend.* Then much to Faidhe's surprise, she heard Craiche's silent response.

It has been coming for some time and it was very much my pleasure! Faidhe's head turned with a start toward Craiche who was showing a broad, almost toothless smile as she acknowledged to Faidhe. *Old, I may be, but I have found that people tend to disregard an old woman who is quiet much of the time. In those moments, I am able to see truth and hear thoughts. I have knowledge of much that is not public. Yes Faidhe, I have been touched by what you have seen. Make yourself known now and we will speak later. Until then, know I am behind you!* Craiche's face crinkled in amusement at this last.

Faidhe quieted herself and called upon the Gods to support her in bringing their message.

"Kinfolk," She announced again. "I *am* Faidhe, Keeper of the Circle. I bring you news of our future and great changes already taking place. The Gods have spoken to me and shown me our future far and away from the times we live in now. Our way of life, nay our very existence is at risk. The truth is, our future as a people is short." The crowd offered subdued protest at this. "The coming of change and destruction is upon us. We stand at the threshold of the end of our days." She raised her arms at the protest "Hear me!" She claimed their attention. "Hear me now. The times of which I speak will not happen within our lifetime nor even that of our children's children, but it will happen. And if we are to preserve our lineage, if we are to offer a future to our descendants, then we must act now. I have been told that for some generations to come, the Goddess will be retreating from our awareness and practice of worship. She is not abandoning us, it is with the cycle of all things, Her time to be in acquiescence to the God." At this there was much grumbling and louder protestations. "Just as the God had been in acquiescence to the Goddess while she created abundance over these many generations past. I have been shown that though it will happen slowly, it will happen. And the world without the Goddess will lack respect and reverence for the She. The quest for power will hold sway. Bloodlust and ownership of the lands will become the new religion in the name of the He. The new God that comes will be revered as the one God but men will use the new religions of the He to suit their own needs and claim for themselves power in His name. The need to be all-powerful will make no room for difference in manner of worship. All other forms of the spirit will be cast aside as false or evil. In the consuming quest to be 'the one, the true, the powerful' men of the He will squelch the spirit of reverence and crush all existing forms of worship in these lands. This will be done in the name of the God, but it will not be the work of the God. The God, as we know him will be lost by the use of warfare, pomp and ritual, guilt, shame and derision to maintain deference from the followers. In this world, the earth Mother will not be respected but sectioned off as parcels, to be owned and destroyed, robbed and raped, as if there is no spirit of the land. Indeed, there will be poor opinion of any who believe there are spirits of the land. Those who will come after us to this land will mark the beginning of the changes. What we must do now to prepare for that day is begin to shift purposefully to a more balanced reverence of both the She and the He. Because as She retreats, we must have in place a more nourishing and active participation in the new spirit that comes: The He. As anyone knows, a masculine is very different when joined with equal or greater feminine, but a masculine alone, unchecked, can be a dangerous thing. For this reason, I must leave the Circle and take counsel with others in far away lands who have been revealed to me as other participants in what must be done in the name of balance between the Goddess and the God. I have been shown that I must take some of the clan members with me to expedite the Powerful magic that must be cast in order to preserve the ways of our people throughout many future generations. As I journey, I have no guarantee of a safe return to this land, I will name a custodian of the Circle to remain in my stead."

The news brought renewed conversation within the crowd. Faidhe held up a hand to stay the noise and pushed on.

"This new Keeper will mark the beginning of great changes within the human tribe. This person will begin the rituals necessary to help the spirits through the portals all over this land into the great underground Sidhes. Communion with the Gods and spirits and our ancestors that we have enjoyed for so long has already begun to dissipate, but the new Keeper's task will not only be one who communes with the Goddess or God and spirits, this Keeper will maintain the Circle as a portal through which the spirits will go under to the world below the earth where they stay in waiting for the time when balanced energy is possible. The result of this process will be that we will honor the Goddess no less, but that we must give the God equal reverence."

Faidhe hesitated now and drew a breath. She plunged on. "As a gesture of our willingness, nay eagerness, to begin these changes toward balance of the spirit, the new Keeper I name to follow me in service of the Circle will be Laoghaire, come to us from the calf herding clan south of the Great Hills by the eastern shore. He has not only brought wealth of cattle to our midst and has proven himself a devoutly spiritual man, he is of royal blood and given up aspirations to a throne in order that he could marry and join our Tuath. This proves he will ascend the Hill humbly in service, not hungry for the Power."

At this, the crowd broke loose offering shouts of disapproval at the idea of a man Keeping the Circle. Men had only come to the Circle in service of the Goddess during the Great Marriage. Many voices rose in discussion. The chattering continued until Laoghaire himself ascended the stairs and mounted the platform. The crowd hushed and Laoghaire, a solidly built man the age of 35 seasons, drew appreciative looks from many of the women in the crowd. His pleasant face, framed by dark rich curls that hung to his shoulders was not the least of his attractive features, but the eyes that adorned the face drew one in to want to know him. They were deep and soulful and put one in mind of the quiet and watchful eyes of the many pointed stag of the wood. One came to like and trust Laoghaire upon first meeting. Men and women alike were pleased to hold his attention or friendship. Because Laoghaire was clearly well liked within the village was therefore, in addition to reasons she had just stated, well chosen by Faidhe to be Guardian of the Circle.

Faidhe greeted Laoghaire by taking both his hands into hers. She recognized the look of awe mingled with shock in his eyes as she looked up at him.

"Be trustful." She told him. "It has been prophesied. You will be Keeper."

As Faidhe conveyed these words to him, she saw the transfer of blue energy rush down her arms and begin to infuse his body where they clasped hands. In a moment, his energy was completely calm, serene and blue. This man was truly the right choice for the position of Keeper. She thought. He is receptive and faithful. He will remain true to the Circle, the Power, the Goddess, and now the God. Just before she released his hands, Faidhe saw him in a vision across a great valley, standing atop a hill, himself aglow with the blue light of the Goddess. There he stood, a king, facing her as he did now, only it was not her he faced in this vision, in her place, stood a man swathed in green of the God, yet he was carrying her Staff, or a staff much like the one she carried. This man with the Staff and her chosen man Laoghaire stood on opposite sides of the valley, each atop his own mount and rising up between them was a great flame that grew so high that Laoghaire could no longer be seen.

As she blinked to clear the vision, she returned her attention to the increasingly noisy villagers; she saw that the direction of their gazes was the cauldron for it was illuminated with the same blue energy, to which she had recently become so accustomed, emanating from within. Faidhe drew closer to the bowl to inspect what was causing the energy to rise. Looking into the depths of the great pot, and as Faidhe reached toward the blue light, Laoghaire himself stayed her hand.

"Touch it not Lady, the flame will consume you. This flame will not burn me. I can see that what lies beneath is my claim to what you have prophesied. I know not how I see this but it is your time to trust."

Laoghaire reached into the pot and the crowd lost sight of the entire upper half of his body as he bent over the side to lay hand to his claim. When he retreated from the Cauldron he had retrieved by its handle, the Sword of Nuada and with his other hand he pulled out the great battle Shield of Lugh.

"These are the implements of magic that remain at the base of the Power of the Tuatha De Danann." As he held them up and spoke the words, Faidhe recognized the words she'd heard in prophesy only the night before. "The three implements brought to the Circle and laid before the Stone: the Cup, the Sword, and the Shield representing the Triad, the sacred three shall be ever forth altered and joined by the fourth, the Staff."

At that, Faidhe stepped forward and displayed the magical Staff that she had used in aiding her to carry the cauldron.

"This shift in energy," she said, seamlessly picking up the thread of what Laoghaire was saying, "by adding the staff to the magical implements, will accompany the shift in the care of the Circle, the Earth, the Mother. The implements will be split and the Staff with the Cauldron will be placed on the road in service of the future of the She, while the other implements, the Sword and the Shield will return to the Stone in service of the preservation of our magical ways, the She and the initiation of the He. As all who can see here today, this sacred Sword and Shield given us by the Gods will remain in the hands of Laoghaire as a symbol of his rightful claim, through prophesy, as the Keeper and as a symbol of his duty to defend and protect the Circle and the spirits, rites and rituals of the Circle now and ever forth."

The crowd was awestruck at the magic they had just witnessed. Again, Faidhe suspected that each in their own sight, had vision of something different for when the Cauldron began to glow blue to her, Laoghaire claimed to have seen flames. She knew not what they saw but the crowd was duly hushed by the Power.

Briciu stepped forward in the breach of sound and broached the question, "Tell us Lady, did the fact that Laoghaire is husband to your daughter, Colm, and father to your grandchildren have any bearing on your decision?"

Faidhe should have expected this but in truth had not thought of her familial connection to Laoghaire in any meaningful way. She had been instructed and carried out what was decreed. The idea that she would make a decision based on personal gain or gain for her family was utterly foreign to her, but apparently not to Briciu or his mother. Faidhe spun around on him.

"Should it occur to me that there is personal power to be had in the position of Keeper, and were I of the ilk to pursue position for my own gain, would I not keep secret the prophesy and continue to maintain my position on the Hill? Or perhaps you think that I must follow what has been set forth in the prophecy by vacating the Circle but deem to further my familial hold on the status of the position. Surely if that were my goal I would not go about it by proclaiming one who hails from outside the Danann clan and is a man. Would I not claim one of my daughters as Keeper? Or perhaps you think it would be more fruitful in my quest for power within the clan, to try to convince the Council that one of my daughters would better suit in my position as a member of the Council when I leave on my journey or one as Keeper and the other on the Council. But then, you are schooled in the ways of family involvement in procuring a position on the Council, are you not? Think man, were I to be of the breed that seeks power and position, would I be vacating my positions as Keeper and Tribal Council?"

Gara's face flushed, as she knew the rashness of her son's comment would further damage their already compromised position in this business.

"What Councilmember Briciu means to say, I think, is that you choose wisely in those you know already to be of good stock and faithful service to the clan. As you may have found it more difficult to decide should there have been more than one, ah, candidate for the position and among those, ones you did not know." Gara, once again, laid a hand on Briciu's arm to stay his tongue.

"As I informed Council earlier, there is no decision to be made. The prophecy has shown Laoghaire to be Keeper on the Hill. And in furtherance of the changes taking place, his family will, should they choose to, be able to ascend the Hill and live there with him in the Keeper's hut."

More murmurs emitted from the crowd at this. Gara stepped forward another few paces and said, "In light of all that has taken place, and seeing that the village is already assembled, we have much to celebrate. Shall we not make a festival of these events? I will slaughter two of my cattle in honor of Faidhe's announcement and upcoming journey and Laoghaire's ascension to the Circle."

A cheer flew up from the people and the moment was lost for Faidhe to complete her work in sharing the prophesy in its entirety. Gara had effectively ended the announcement calling attention to herself rather than the important work at hand. Faidhe would have to speak individually with Craiche and her other daughter Lon Dubh. It may be just as well that her part in all this was kept silent until such time as they were ready to leave. Faidhe would not deny the clans folk their feast and it would give her the opportunity to set in motion the undertaking of passing the right story to the rest of the Tuath beyond this village so her journey and mission would be common knowledge and could be passed on in story and song throughout the countryside.

"Well then, feasting it shall be. As the sun now sets, we shall each say praise in passing of the sun and for the coming of the sliver moon and then go prepare for three days of feasting. And thanks to Gara for the two cattle she has offered for each event; tonight we celebrate the prophesy and the changes it portends, tomorrow, my journey and all it entails and the third, Gara offers her generosity in endorsement of Laoghaire's rightful position as the new Keeper of the Circle."

When it looked as though Gara was about to say something in protest, Faidhe turned and spoke close to her ear and made it appear to the crowd that an embrace was taking place.

"Take care Gara. To offer cattle for one event and disallow another would be imprudent. I would not want your status in the eyes of the clan to falter after so generous a gesture by seeing you choose which events you will support and those you would not. And you certainly would neither want to offer offense to the new Keeper of the Circle nor the old one." Faidhe leveled a look at Gara so there was no misunderstanding between them. "You grandly suggested at a moment important to the clan that we retreat from the news to instead feast, so again, I thank you for your offer of no less than six cattle to support your suggestion." Gara was angered but knew she had been trumped. Smiling her brightest smile, she took Briciu's hand and raised it over their heads and the crowd cheered for their part in the feasting event.

"My son and I share our wealth and good fortune with our clan-folk and kin offering equal shares in our livestock in celebration of these events." It was obvious by this announcement Gara had decided that should she have to compensate for her son's impulsive brashness, he would pay his freight as well. "To the feasting hall!" She proclaimed.

As soon as she turned around to speak with her son, the smile fell off her face and the words that passed between them were not of celebration. To anyone who was looking on what took place then between Gara and Briciu could see plainly that Briciu was as displeased by what he was hearing as Gara had just been, by being cornered into offering some of her own beasts to help feed the many mouths of the Tuatha De Danann for the next three days.

13
Family Reunion

The villagers scurried about in excitement to prepare for the impromptu cel-ebration and to recount all that had taken place that day with the coming of Faidhe from the Hill and her announcement of prophecy to the magical appearance of the sacred Sword and Shield upon the platform. Some expressed concern over the drastic change in the traditional responsibilities of the Keeper. And despite Gara's apprehension that Briciu had been foolish in not holding his tongue in his opinions regarding Faidhe's choice for a replacement on the Hill, the seeds of sus-picion had been strewn and there are some who provide just the right soil for a healthy crop of dissension. Tongues were wagging about all that had come to pass but in particular about how the new, male Keeper will affect the sacred traditions, festivals and rituals of the Tuath.

Faidhe took the opportunity to approach those with whom she needed to speak under cover of the bustling crowds as they left the gathering place to prepare for feasting. She did not want to come under the eye of those who need not know what she is about, for she could feel the energy of opposition at work.

First, as Faidhe stepped from the stage, she set down the Cauldron and took the hand of Craiche in proper courtesy. In unspoken communication, she told Craiche the plan to meet as quickly as possible in a place very few would think to search even if they were over curious as to what might be taking place. Still holding Craiche's hand she turned and spoke formally to Laoghaire asking him to escort Craiche through the crowds. When he had agreed, Faidhe placed Craiche's hand into Laoghaire's and left it to the old woman to instruct Laoghaire as to what was now needed of him and what must be done with those magical implements now in his possession. And finally, as if the magic had already found them and drawn them to each other, she saw her daughter Lon Dubh and Iarann, the ironsmith standing only a few paces from each other. Faidhe drew near her daughter, expecting to feel the wrath of her disappointment at not being chosen as the next Keeper and was pleased to find otherwise. Their eyes met and Faidhe signaled to Lon Dubh to wait a moment while she thanked the smithy for his help earlier that day. To anyone's eye, she was cordial and distant as would be proper of a woman of her station addressing a villager. And Iarann, of course bore a serious and respectful expression befitting a man of his standing being addressed by a higher up in the tribe. But an astute observer would have noticed the smithy leave the Keeper's presence with nod of acquiescence and a dutiful air of purpose. Any observer would not speculate that any more had passed between the two than the simple thanks that had been feigned, it was not obvious the smithy had taken instruction and set out to do as she bid him.

At last she turned to her daughter who spoke with anticipation. "Is it now, Mother, that I am called to do the work of the Goddess?"

"Yes...Daughter." Faidhe felt the old familiar longing in her heart together with a surge of excitement at being called "Mother" when she'd rather expected a hostile confrontation. She tentatively tried on the role of her motherhood after so many years of being bereft of the attachment. "It has been long since we spoke. And I am sorrowful for what must be your disappointment in not being called as Keeper after so long preparing for the task. But I have recently been put in mind of our last meeting. Remember you, the visitation of that day?"

"I do, Lady. For it was just this morning that I too have been contemplating the very day of which you speak. I recall the voice of the Power, come to initiate me as one who will serve the Goddess. It is for this you come to me now, is it not?

"Yes, my Black Bird. Although you will not be an initiate of the Hill, you will be an integral tool in the epic changes now taking place. This is the start of the message delivered these ten sun seasons past and again but one night past in the prophesy. Will you come willingly to journey with me for the sake of what must be done?"

Both surprised and pleased at the more intimate use of her name, Lon Dubh too felt a rush of exhilaration at finally having her part in the way of the Goddess revealed to her and to feel the validation of her many visions coming to fruition. But something she hadn't anticipated was the flush of joy she felt at a moment, even if fleeting, when she took pleasure in a simple dialog with her mother. Not a foster mother, or tribal Wise Woman, not the mother of a childhood friend, or all the mothers of the village who had conspired to raise her and care for her as a child of the Circle, but a moment she shared as a daughter with her own true mother. She was overwhelmed to be spoken to so. Then Faidhe's words penetrated her delight and she realized what was being said to her.

"With you? Journey *with* you? Of course I will. Yes. In the name of the Goddess, yes!"

Faidhe recognized Lon Dubh's joy and knew precisely what she was feeling. She too was eager to come to know her daughter and salvage what there might be of their relationship. But she also knew the responsibilities that lay ahead may damper hope of what they both wanted. What will be required of Lon Dubh will tax their relationship but Faidhe could not allow her heart to stand in the way of her duty.

"Know that this will be a journey that will have need of much from you. And there will be times when you will not recognize the wisdom of what is required of you. But it is for that which you have reserved yourself these many years. You must hold fast to your faith that what lies ahead must be carried out unquestioningly. Are you willing to so completely give over of your comfort, your independence, your very free will and walk in the path even into danger for the sake of the Goddess and the God?"

"Oh, of all the people in the Tuath, you who have given service on the Hill overlong as to give up all living other than for the Gods, can take measure of my devotion to this cause. It is, as you have said, that which I have prepared myself since I was called to the Goddess in vision even as a child. So most fervently, I understand there will be sacrifice and danger and will count it an honor to serve in any way shown to me."

Satisfied that she had been right in her interpretation of this piece of the prophecy that Lon Dubh would be one of those who will make the journey with her, Faidhe instructed her.

"Come then, to the hut of the ironsmith and I will give counsel on how to best approach preparations for what must take place. Speak of this to no one and come to the hut so that you are not seen. Know you where the smithing hut stands?"

"I do, but why in such secre..." Lon Dubh saw a look of impatience cross Faidhe's face and checked herself. "As you instruct, I will carry out. Need I bring anything? Will we journey tonight?"

Faidhe softened, reminding herself of what all the change and news brought with her from the Hill must be stirring for her daughter. In that moment, she realized that due to her years of isolation on the Hill she had little skill in the way of personal interaction. To walk amongst people in the world, she would have to widen her skills in diplomacy and develop patience for the curiosity and emotions of others.

"No Black Bird, just do as I bid you now. We will come to what must be our preparations within three days' time. Now go. And be cautious."

When Lon Dubh left her, Faidhe stood for a moment, eyeing the great Cauldron resting at her feet. She contemplated just how she was going to cross back through the village with this giant consignment and avoid being seen. The sprites within the bowl peered up at her with anticipation. She contemplated and rhetorically asked them under her breath, "How then, am I to carry this great tub unseen to the smithing hut to the far eastward end of the village?" The sprites gathered at attention and for the first time, actually spoke to Faidhe.

"Lady, we will take it there for you, as you wish." They said in unison.

Faidhe startled to attention. "You speak? Why have you not done so before this?"

Again in unison, "You have not addressed us before this."

Faidhe's cheeks reddened to recognize that these sprites, sent by the *Power* to assist her had helped her immeasurably and she had not yet acknowledged them personally. She would not make that same mistake again. Faidhe guiltily looked around her, knowing that she must appear unstable, speaking to sprites that no one else can see.

"I am most grateful for your willingness to assist me. But the bowl must be safe from the eyes of others. Will it be so?"

"Oh yes, Lady. It will not be visible until you request that it be present."

"Then I humbly and gratefully accept your help, Little Ones."

Faidhe was pleased at this new knowledge. Why had she not thought to ask the *Power* for help prior to this? Why had she assumed she must work on behalf of the Gods without their help? She supposed that over the coming months, there would be much to learn about that which is new and strange.

Without warning she had been called to attention. Faidhe caught the feeling of surreptitious energy around her and knew she was being watched.

"Do it then, quickly." She pleaded to the sprites. "I will call for it when needed, take the Staff as well." What Faidhe saw as they went to work was hundreds of tiny sprites swirling sun-wise around the implements and within the bowl so quickly as to create a cloud of spinning blue light, until the pieces vanished. Faidhe heard a sharp intake of breath some distance away and wondered what her unwelcome witness had observed. Taking her opportunity in the momentary shock experienced by whomever it was that followed her movements, she pulled the dark hood of her cloak over her head and walked toward the obscurity of the woods bordering the edge of the place of gathering. Just inside the edge of the tree line, she knew it would be more difficult to trace her steps in the shadows and she depended on her mystical reputation and the awe of all that had happened this day to deter anyone from attempting to follow the Powerful Keeper into dark places.

From under the backside of the platform from which Faidhe had earlier descended with her Cauldron, a pair of eyes peered out from the stanchions keeping a close watch on the movements of the Keeper and the implements she carried.

"You would be playing a game of stealth," was how it was put to him earlier that evening. Briciu told his son of 11 seasons, "to see how we might best serve her. We must know what the Keeper is about in order to anticipate her needs. Do not let her see you, but stay close that you can return to me with all the news about who she speaks to and whose ear she has. Watch carefully for anything of magic that comes from the pot and for anything out of the ordinary for we must serve the Gods by judging also, whether the Keeper is still sound in her mind. Do this well, my son, and you will be rewarded. Do it not or be found out, and bear the punishment that will pale only under the shadow of the shame you will bear and cast on our family. Quickly now, yonder she leaves the platform. Go and achieve this for our family's pride...in service of the Gods."

Triag was not close to his father, who did not exhibit any involvement in his family beyond what would show to be outwardly proper to the clan. Triag, a clever but lazy boy, was not particularly interested in pleasing his father, but understood missions such as this served to keep his family in comfort. He had done this type of thing many times before knowing that information could be as precious as gold or a healthy cattle count in the right hands; his father's hands. A doughy, round shaped youth, obviously partial to honey cakes and sow-meat, Triag was more interested in attending the feast. He sullenly inquired, "Why is it that you are not available to gather your own facts?

Quick to anger, Briciu stayed his hand and assessed that he'd need his son's devotion to the task and, eyeing Faidhe who had left the stage and was already involved in conversation with the old witch, Craiche, decided that bribery was the most expedient tactic here.

"My son, you have seen what has taken place at the gathering. There is much to be done in preparation of the feast and in the politics of the changes happening now. This is the fabric of great stories we are making this very night. I must tend to the ears of the clan and Council to see that we are allotted our proper share of recognition. And with that, as you know, comes position and power. Hurry, and do this for us now, and you may choose your reward if it is within my power to grant it." Briciu knew that this could be a promise he might regret but he knew also that he was not above reneging if it proved too costly.

Triag now stood quivering under the platform watching after Faidhe. He knew his father would be greatly angered if he could not say where the Keeper had gone. But he was not a brave boy and the threat of a beating did not outstrip his fear of one who wields such magic as he'd seen today. So he did not delay in going about finding his father to share what he would tell him. And when Triag found him, Briciu was in foul disposition for having been assigned by Gara, the lowly task to oversee the slaughter of the two cattle that would be offered for the feast this day.

"What nonsense is this?" Briciu bellowed at the news his son related. "There is no such power to humans as this. Only the Gods may come and go in this manner. You have failed boy, and you lie to cover your uselessness."

To cover for the fact fear had kept him from following Faidhe into the wood and that he'd lost his charge, Triag had told his father the half-truth that Faidhe had made the Cauldron disappear in a blaze and that she had the ability to disappear herself. He had concocted this story in order that he could avoid a beating and might still receive his reward.

"Believe what you will, father, but I tell you what I saw. The Keeper and the Cauldron could not be tracked for they disappeared before my eyes. You saw the ability she displayed upon the show platform only today. Why then, would you doubt my telling that she has other powers unknown to us? Ask you among the clan and you will not hear tell of any person who witnessed the Keeper walk among them after the gathering in the village with her great pot. You will see I speak the truth for she could not be seen or followed because she *disappeared*!

Briciu concentrated on this last statement. "Ask, I will." He said to Triag. But there was no salt to his threat. His eyes formed slits as his mind worked on what was taking place and how it might best serve him. He spoke in breathy undertones, his calculating monologue. "The pot itself dispensed the other implements this day. The pot, come down from the Hill, exhibits the fantastic powers of which we speak. Not the hag. It is not she who holds the Power to perform this magic. It is the pot itself. One who holds the pot, holds the Power and it serves the request of the one who claims it."

"Then this information is valuable to you, Father?" Briciu had all but forgotten that his son was still with him. Realizing that he was waiting to claim a reward for this report Briciu said,

"It may be of some value, but the information I needed was where the Keeper went and with whom she spoke. But because I may have use for what you have told me, you have earned your way out of the consequences promised for your failure. Go now to the feast if you wish, and speak of what you have seen to no one!"

Triag counted himself lucky to have come away unscathed but harbored resentment at having not been granted his promised reward. For this, he was pleased that he had kept a tidbit of information to himself about the Keeper speaking at length with her daughter about her attendance on a journey. He thought to seek reward elsewhere in that it may have usefulness to some other of the clan.

———

Faidhe came to the hut of the ironsmith to join those she had called to the assembly. As she approached the structure from the edge of the forest, she made note that they were wise in keeping low the lighting from within. She made her way to the entrance and quietly let herself inside. There, Faidhe was met by First Councilmember, Craiche, who sat rather uncomfortably on the workbench Iarann used for hammering. Iarann and Lon Dubh sat together on the dirt floor by the small fire that was concealed within the smelting oven. And as Faidhe had requested, Laoghaire's family had joined him for the meeting. Faidhe was most pleased to set eyes on Colm, Laoghaire's wife who was her oldest daughter. Their twin children of about seven season cycles were a most welcome sight to Faidhe as well, for she had never before seen her grandchildren.

Morgan a diminutive beautiful girl-child bearing all the best features of her parents, thick ringlets of hair like her father cascading to her shoulders in the golden honey-wheat color of her mother's hair. Smooth and flawless skin stretched over feminine cheekbones that seemed to contrast the roundness of her large blue eyes with their high angular shape, and gave her face the appearance of an enduring, gentle smile.

Macha, a fine boy with intelligent and watchful eyes was as dark in skin and hair as his sister was light. His black eyes gave the impression of pensive thought and he was indeed a quiet and thoughtful child. The lashes, full and thick, that surrounded his eyes, Faidhe thought, would give more than one clan maiden's heart a flutter in his time. Good stock, she mused to herself; then shook off her reverie.

Faidhe began, "I bid thanks to you all for coming while having no foreknowledge of our purpose here. There is much that must be planned and we have but three days in which to untangle all that is necessary so I fear I must forego the pleasures of meeting with my daughters and grandchildren in any customary fashion until this business is settled. For that, I have great sorrow." Faidhe cast an eye toward Colm and caught a smoldering gaze in return. "Know, daughter that you are not a victim in these changes. It is not unknown to me that you carried not the desire to serve on the Hill, yet serve you will, at your husband's side. This is most important in the process of creating the magical balance necessary to cast the energy on the wave of the future. Your knowledge of herb-lore and your femininity are much needed ingredients for what is taking place. I am not unmindful of the upset this causes for you and your family but it must be so. Come now, hate me not or hate me if you will, but let it not stand in the way of what must be done."

Faidhe should have known that the years of emotions held at bay would not be quelled but for a few words. She saw Colm's face working and felt the physical pain in an empathetic swell in her heart. Faidhe knew she would have to allow Colm her rage at the circumstances and at Faidhe herself and give her time to embrace all that lay ahead, but they had little time for either her rage or adjustment to the situation in order that they might get to the business at hand. Faidhe sent out a tendril of her own energy to her daughter in a silent pleading for understanding that all that had been and all that is taking place truly is in service of the Gods and that Faidhe was just as much a servant in how things unfolded as were they all. Faidhe knew that Colm's task must be taken on with a fullness of heart unburdened by resentment and without the festering poison of anger. Faidhe watched the hopping blue blaze of her energy snap and pop as it reached in a long finger, from her own heart, out to her daughters. She willed Colm to see the purity and necessity of her faithfulness to her position as Keeper. Faidhe communicated her genuine love for her daughter while revealing the painful choices she'd made to remain faithful to her clan and the Gods as well. Then Faidhe was surprised to witness a shock of energy, slightly less vibrant in its blue hue, reach out from Colm's heart to meet her own.

In that moment Colm felt a softening in her resolve to resent her mother for years of what she felt was abandonment. For much of her life, Colm was told fantastic stories of her mother's abilities as a Seer and the Keeper of the Circle, performing rituals and achieving results never before heard of in the history of the Tuath. 'If it were I who was chosen for the Keeper,' Colm told herself often throughout her lifetime, 'I would have relinquished the position for the sake of my children when they came.' There were others who could assume the role of Keeper but none other who could be her true mother. She silently resented that she was not considered important enough to her mother to have warranted putting aside duties on the Hill to raise and nurture her.

Colm eyed her own children and speculated how much bearing this new position on the Hill would affect them, and then thought about how their lives would be influenced if she did not answer the call to the service of the Goddess now. She returned her attention to Faidhe and wondered if, or how often she had thought of her own daughters and whether she felt compelled to serve on the Hill out of love for her own? Until being called to service herself, Colm had never given thought to her mother's reasoning for such a stalwart commitment to her position as the Keeper. Colm began to understand, through what lay ahead of her, that it is possible to serve in a position and not truly want to, but do so for the benefit of others. She became aware that Faidhe was looking at her and all other eyes in the hut were focused on her as well. Colm spoke as she answered her mother's gaze.

"Until this moment, I have never been truthful with myself about my emotions toward your commitment to the Gods and the clan. I have been a jealous daughter but not for the reasons I have told myself. I have held resentment in my heart that I was not important enough to you to have beckoned you to motherhood over your position on the Hill. But my true resentment lies in my own deficiency. In my early maidenhood, I spoke long and loud and often of your great abilities on the Hill. There were many who thought I spoke out of pride at being close kin to such a one. But I did so because, inwardly, I feared the day when you descended the Hill, that I might be called. And I knew I could only pale in the inevitable comparisons.

I foolishly thought my praise might serve to keep you long on the Hill so I might never risk being called. It was with great relief that I found such a true and strong, unwavering love for my Laoghaire for it was then I knew I would not be called to the Hill, being so completely bound in heart, mind and spirit to another. I was released of my own self-doubt and fears, but even then, what remained was still a sense of failure that the Gods had seen fit to pass me by. Such confusion of the heart, while I wanted you, I prayed you'd stay away. I feared being called to the Hill, and was disappointed when I was not called. And the Gods knew my heart better than I, for they sent to me my loves, Macha and Morgan to sooth my bruised heart that I might know the love between mother and child and that I taste the sweetness of giving over wholly to that which I am committed. For these children," Colm confessed as she drew her twins to her, "I would bear much suffering, sacrifice; face any challenge. And now I see that it is my time to do just that, for you would not come to us from your place on yon Hill if it were not for the direst of need. So it is for this I know, I must put away my fears and my childhood imaginings of being cheated. My service on the Hill, the very thing I have feared, is needed to insure my children's future and their children and on. Do I understand the circumstances true?"

"You begin to understand Colm." Faidhe responded, pleased that her communication had reached her daughter's heart and alleviated her fears so the situation could be seen with clarity. "And I am pleased you have your children to comfort you as I never did. There is much we could say in this moment to make up for lost love through the many years, but we must harden our resolve now. We must plan in haste and be satisfied that our pain and loneliness was not borne individually. Understand daughter?"

"I do. But in truth, my heart is heavy again, for having come so close to you and still yet being kept to a distance."

"It may comfort you to know my own heart burdens me thus. But let us speak on this no more now for it makes our task no easier. The time is urgent, and I find that though we have not yet a plan for how we will go about all at our feet, we have but three days. So we must discipline ourselves to keep to the task at hand, and later, perhaps at the feasting, for decorum requires that we take part, then look to a time when we might speak our hearts. But for now, we must work quickly to make arrangements, and we must keep our own Council as to what these plans may be. I sense we already have need of secrecy, as there are those whose close interest in what we discuss here tonight is only to grasp at potential power and position. This I have seen, but just who will make this grab for the sacred implements and higher position in the clan or how they will go about it has not been shown to me. I have my suspicion, as do we all, but they will be revealed in the God's time for they too have their role to play in what will take place. But for now, we must speak of the magic we, in this group, possess as Seers, descendants of the Old Ones...and of royal blood." she added as she gave a nod to Iarann and Laoghaire. We must share those visions and abilities that have come to each of us so that we may puzzle out the picture of the best-chosen path we are to take. I have seen each of you in the prophesy and have been informed by two of you, Craiche and Lon Dubh, that you have had prior visions bound to this great change so let us now speak of what we have seen." Craiche, you told me that you have been touched by what I have seen. Will you reveal to us in what way has the prophecy reached you?"

At this, Craiche sat for a moment and thought how to begin. Her voice was that of an old woman as she started to speak, feeble from many years of quiet observation and reflection. But now she knew it was time to speak so she cleared her throat and pushed it passed the years of neglect to speak with authority. And as she spoke, her voice took on a rhythmic cadence of trance.

"I am Craiche, known to you all as the First member of the Council and Seer for the village. I have reached this position not only due to my age, but also for my ability to see and to divine. We, here in our village, for many years have lived in relative peace with the outsiders, due to our strength in numbers of the Tuath. We have long enjoyed a comfortable, if not plentiful harvest of both meat and crops. The Gods have been generous. The cycle of the seasons has spun through many generations. I myself have seen 63 sun seasons. Though not the oldest of our Tuath, I am near that distinction and still have my wits and a fair portion of my magic remains. I tell you, in my time I have seen much, but in my visions of late, what I have seen is the end of our time enjoyed as a village here at the foot of the sacred Circle Hill in communion with the very Gods that grant us fortune. Both here and beyond, as our people branch out from here into the other villages of our clan, I see an arm of change wrapped around all our villages to embrace this clan, as well as all those under protection of the Tuatha De Danann. I have had visions seep into my waking time as well as my dreams over some ten sun cycles and it has reached a point now that the time is upon us to act. My vision has shown to me, Faidhe coming down from the Hill just as she did this day. This vision first came to me on the day when her daughter, Lon Dubh took counsel with Faidhe that same ten sun cycles past. I have known changes were brewing since that time and have seen pieces over the years of what has taken place thus far today.

I have seen of this group, some will take action, while others see not completely, the gravity to the cause at hand. I know not who, but there are those among our clan who will undermine what will be set forth. But the effect of this alternate path is unknown to me.

I have seen a fertile sprouting from the result of a Great Marriage. And from the seed of that marriage will be one who rules the Staff. One who will honor the

God and bring about the final phase of change in our land, the change already taking root.

With the one who bears the Staff will come a time of respite for the Goddess. As She retreats underground, the clans too will find their ways of worship for her all but forgotten and so too buried under centuries of dust of forgetfulness. There will come a time of great darkness for many lands beyond that of the Danu, and the energy of the He will burn with fever. The stuff of the knowing will burn in the flame of that fever and be all but destroyed save for what will be secreted and kept in this place, the land of the Goddess. But for the gathering in this hut, our part of the world will move on from all that is redeeming in the spirit that connects our kind with the earth and its creatures in respect. I see the sacred implements as tools to be used against the consuming surge of the He yet used in unison with it. I have seen much that confounds me, as it makes not sense, for I see many of the symbols typifying the Goddess in use and in service of the God. I see much of our sacred items rejected and then come to the service of the He. I know not what the conflict is that I see in my visions only that the inconsistency is consistent. I see the worship for the He snatched from the faithful and twisted by men to create a platform for their own power and in maintenance of that power, there will be extreme suffering in many forms all over the world. There will be much torture and death waged over the detailed stories of a great man recorded in strange marks, come in the name of the He. I have done much meditating over these visions. Perhaps there is one among you who might cast a light on the message they carry?"

Faidhe contemplated for a moment and spoke. "Thank you, Craiche, for you have validated some of what I have seen. Our purpose here, in part, is to set forth what must be done to see to it that the respect for the Goddess is attached to the wave of this masculine God as reverence for him takes sway. We must insure that as the Goddess rests under the Sidhe, that the spirit of the feminine remains subversively active within this new religion. Her story must be preserved and told in ways that keep the heartbeat of the feminine steady and strong as the world burns with this new fever of the He."

It seems that we three," she continued, raising a sweeping arm toward Craiche and Lon Dubh, "have been put in mind of the very day when Lon Dubh came to my hut on the Hill for counsel on her decision to refrain from taking part in the Festival Rights. It was on this day that a powerful message came through me from the Gods. This message, I believe was the beginning of the changes prophesied. But as with communications such as this, I recall much detail in the images I saw, and naught but a shadow of what was said through me. Let us examine what can be remembered and..."

"I remember all that was said through you on that day Lady." Lon Dubh broke in. "Since that conference, there has not been the passing of a day that I have not examined those words in effort to divine what lay ahead in my future. Let us recite together what befell each of us that day. I must admit, I am curious. I have long wondered what it meant for my role in the service of the Goddess. What did you see as you looked at me with eyes so distant and a voice so ominous? It did appear as you were in pain."

Unaccustomed to sharing conversation, much less to being interrupted, Faidhe realized that she'd convened a group to puzzle things with her, she'd have to make adjustments in how she communicated because for whatever reasons the Gods have, she must be bound by what each member of the group had to add. And until all could be sorted, every bit of information contributed would be treated as equally important to their calling. Warming now to the idea that she had the opportunity to interact with others she answered her daughter.

"I recall seeing you take on the look of your name. In the vision, it was you, daughter, who in the personage of a great black bird, a crow or raven sounded warning by thrice cawing, but I knew not, until now, of what you warned. Quick and sharp then, from my very middle, was pulled with your beak a strand of the figh vine. After that, all with you was as before and the vision was gone but the pain of the extraction remained. I did not know at the time, of what the vision spoke, but I must reveal that this image of a black bird and the figh vine was made known to me once again during storm of the prophesy this night past. But before I reveal more of the meaning of the prophecy and its connection to this vision, tell us now, Lon Dubh, of the words spoken to you following this vision, those many years ago."

Lon Dubh was mildly embarrassed at speaking publicly after so long living in relative solitude. She was most conscious of all the eyes on her. It would not be easy for her to speak of such things when all of her life she had been an outcast, albeit voluntarily, from the villagers, hunting and providing for herself. She knew that many pitied her as one ailing in her mind. So she had kept her distance and silence in the years of late. She had become all but a ghost in the village. The change in her presently was visible as she made the decision to take on the mantle of responsibility. She was no longer waiting for her moment in history; it had arrived. She met the eyes of each member of the group and her very physical posture took on a commanding stance. She looked to Faidhe and spoke.

"I came late to my moon cycle but when the Goddess blood came on me, I was struck with strong visions about assuming a role of importance in service of the Goddess, but none so telling as the words spoken through you that day. You recall our meeting was to speak of my refusal to take a man in my commitment to these visions?"

Faidhe nodded.

Lon Dubh continued. "If there was any doubt that the Goddess would call me before that day, none remained after audience with you." Lon Dubh turned to face the rest of the gathering. "The words spoken came through the Keeper as the very voice of the Earth Mother for in her breath was the Power of the wind and water and stone, so great as to make me tremble. This voice called me as a daughter, one of its own that initiated me into Her service as no physical Festival Rights could have. I was told of a journey that would go beyond the four directions and it spoke of my part in a Great Marriage to 'propagate the life of the Triad.' My assumption was that I would do this and conceive a daughter at one of the Festival Rituals when I had taken the position as Keeper of the Circle. But I now know this not to be so. The voice went on to speak of strangeness I have not fully understood. It said, 'From your mouth will fall the earth, water and air and only from the mouth shall it be fertile, germinate and breed new life.' The message was finished when I was informed that I would 'follow the Keeper' and so I assumed again this meant I would be Keeper after my mother for it said 'her path shall be my path and her journey will be my own.' I know now that the mention of a journey foretold of what is taking place as we speak. I will follow my mother now and journey with her in service of the Goddess and these changes taking place, for it is as much my path as hers. In years past, these words had a different meaning for me than I know them to have now. But there is still much about the message I do not understand."

There was a long moment of silence as the group took in all that had been shared. Faidhe was speaking aloud under her breath in a habit she'd developed over many years of seclusion. "Figh vine, great black bird, two mentions of a Great Marriage. We know what the journey is for we two venture out in three days' time to foreign lands great distances from here, but earth, water and air falling from her mouth to germinate and breed new life! What can it mean? What?"

Faidhe was distracted by the whisperings between her grandchildren, Morgan and Macha. Slightly annoyed at the interruption in her thinking, she saw excitement in their energy as it swirled about them as they spoke to each other in a symbiotic cocoon of communication. They looked up at Faidhe as they felt her concentration bearing down on them. They stiffened at being the focal point of her gaze as a rodent freezes beneath the shadow of a predator.

"What is it then?" Faidhe demanded. Then caught herself and softened. "Speak children, if you can help us in what we seek, fear not, for you have been called here as the rest of us have been. So what you have to contribute is equally important. You will be Keeper Children of the Circle Hill...the first to bear the name. You will participate in all that takes place for you are the embodiment of the She and the He, born of one womb, equal parts of the whole. There will be no need of whispering for as Children of the Circle Hill, words you speak will be of consequence."

The twins stood transfixed. Not sure how to respond, they looked to their parents who gave them gentle encouragement to reveal what they know, if anything.

Unconsciously, they grasped each other's hand and spoke, not in unison but in turn. Macha began.

"Well, is it not true that when the words came through you...Grandmother," Morgan broke in to finish the thought.

"...That you had the very earth, water and air fall from *your* mouth?"

Macha spoke again. "When you told the tale, Aunt" he said, directly to Lon Dubh, you were the only one who knew the story.

Then Morgan finished, "But now, like the game of Truth or Tale, the story has been told to seven others and in so telling, has grown. And if we seven..."

"...Go and tell seven more in turn, then many will know the tale, and it will 'breed new life' as said in the prophecy of that day. But, as with our game, the story which begins as 'truth,' often ends as 'tale.'"

Morgan stepped in, "After many tellings, the story that began is much changed and takes on a path of its own."

It was a dizzying prospect for the adults other than Colm and Laoghaire who were accustomed to this form of back and forth conversation between their children, to follow the twins' direction of thought. After a moment of silence Colm tried to explain the game of Truth or Tale to the others.

"It's a game the children play by telling a story or making a statement in the morning to a friend and that friend passes the tale on and so on. By the evening, when the group of children convenes for late meal, the last to hear the tale shares what they have heard. The fun is in seeing just how much the tale has changed from morning 'til night; from Truth to Tale."

Lon Dubh almost shouted as the thoughts of a much mused over puzzle fell into place for her after these ten long seasons of contemplation.

"So the tale becomes fertile, germinates and breeds new life! Oh nephew...and niece, would that we were closer these long seasons past, you could have saved me much frustration!"

The statement was said lightly in relief and joy, but it cast a light on the fact that despite family connection, her own sister, Colm and her children were strangers to her. The silence in the room bore out the unspoken thought. As children will do, Macha answered in an honest fashion.

"We were afraid, Aunt, for you are known to be weak in the mind. But I don't see that is so, now that we've met you."

Lon Dubh was struck by the words and looked at Colm. The pain of many lonely nights reflected in her eyes. Colm's face showed shame and she cast her eyes downward to avoid seeing Lon Dubh's pain.

In a very small voice, Colm confessed to her sister, "It is true, Lon Dubh, that I feared association with you. I warned my children of drawing near. As a child of the Circle myself I missed having a normal family and being taught by my mother all that a girl child comes to expect. I tried very hard to be a part of my foster family and the village community so the stain on my heart left by being motherless did not show. You, Lon Dubh, were a constant reminder of all that could have been for me, for us, as a family, but never would be. Then as villagers began to speak of you for being weak-headed, sick-minded, I denied connection or likeness with you in any way. I distanced myself from you and did not offer a space at our hearth for fear of being touched by your sickness, if only by repute. My husband," she said, tipping her head toward Laoghaire, "prior to our marriage, made it clear that should I want that you come into our household, he would have no objections. I took this as an oath of his love for me, but I never gave a thought to what it might mean to you, to finally live with blood family after fosterage for so many years. I would not share my family or my hearth with you. I had a choice and I chose to abandon you. I know you had a good family to live with and care for you, as did I but I know the void in a person that stems from having a mother and not being able to be loved by her. For all this, sister, I have regret and now on the dawn of your leaving, my heart laments for all I foolishly threw away when it was there for the asking."

"Lon Dubh had to dig deep to identify what she felt in hearing her sister speak so openly. She had never considered that there might have been a place for her in her sister's life. And perhaps that was for the best for if she had wanted it to be so, she very well could have nurtured resentments through the years. But as it was, Lon Dubh responded with honesty as she considered these thoughts.

"Carry no guilt sister, for who could blame you for building a life for your children that was not your own joy in childhood? We each had our own path that brought us to this moment. I can only believe that the choices we have each made are our own to live with and bear the consequences of those choices. Fret not that you did not reach out to me for neither did you ever find me at your door. Perhaps I could have offered *you* solace and neglected to do so by not approaching you. It is useless to regret what we have not done but it holds true that what we have done or not, up to this point has prepared us for what must come to pass now. It was necessary, I think for us to be alone in such ways, for look now at the group gathered here. Have we not all lead solitary lives? Are we not all tempered for the task that lies ahead by what we have already endured?" She considered each person in the room as she spoke. "Smithy, you had been married once, but your chance at a family was snatched from you when your wife went with the spirits. And your very craft keeps you separated from the village at the outer reaches, far from others, alone with your metal and magic. Mother, you have been on the Hill for all but the first ten seasons of your life, alone with naught but the spirits and you own magic. Craiche, you have long been at the center of the political circle for the village but have pointed out yourself that you have spent many of those years in meditation and introspection, speaking only when called to by the most important visions. Laoghaire, you are well respected within the village, but it is never far from people's minds that you are of the clan of Calf-herders and not native to the Tuatha De Danann. So, in our individual lives, we have each remained a part of, but separate from the clan. I have to believe that this has been crafted for a reason beyond my knowing at this time. So sister, we have each been lead to this moment with our history just as it should have been. Waste not one moment in regret or guilt, for all is just as it should be. We are each pieces integral to what must be done now. Look not to the past, Colm, but to what is at hand. And know that in this moment, what you have just said to me has been taken with all the pleasure of a thirsting plant when it rains. I think not of the thirst, but of how I am renewed and strengthened by the drink. I thank you for your honesty and bear you no grudge at all my sister."

In observing her daughters, Faidhe sensed the honesty in their words. She formulated a silent prayer of thanks to the families that had fostered her daughters, grateful for the women they had become resulting from that fosterage. She could not claim credit for who they are but was proud of them, nonetheless. Emerging from her personal thoughts, Faidhe brought the meeting back to the task at hand.

"Smithy, what knowledge of these circumstances have you? We each have been brought here with purpose. Have you a tale to add?"

Iarann seemed slightly perplexed at the question as if he were observing a performance but surprised to find himself one of the players. Drawn from his observer's status, his strong auburn brows knit together and his dark eyes took on a dreamy quality as he stared into the small fire and spoke.

"You all know of my heritage. I am a half-breed son of the Smith God Goibhniu and Fionna, my human mother. My father enjoys great respect in the tribe as a gifted maker of sword and spear during times of battle. His status has largely been afforded due to his ability to swiftly forge and repair weapons of great strength and quality. I have, for reasons I cannot explain, never had desire to create weaponry as my father before me, but am called to the ore all the same. I have learned the magic of removing the precious gifts of ore veins from the earth and separating that which is useful from the stone. I have been gifted the secrets of the goldsmith from my father's brother and have developed a style so that issue of my craft is recognizable as my own. My life has been unremarkable in the shadow of my heritage and I have never felt that my craft was more than a product of sheer labor rather than the magical process it is in the eyes of the Gods. Although I have been acclaimed as a master of the metals in my own right I have never directly participated in magic beyond the sacred prayers of thanks as I cast my metal, however I have on many occasions, as I bent over my smelting flame, been lost in visions, unbidden and powerful. In the flame, dances sights of strange and far away lands. I know not if these visions are portents or just musings of a mind set to trance by the rhythm of the bellows. I feel the loss of my home in these visions as I am bidden to travel to these far away lands, but I feel also the elation of great joy over, at last, finding myself with a family of my own. But far beyond images of myself I am often visited by a mighty people who blanket the land to our east and wash across the lands in a great wave until they come to our shores, and the land of the Great Mother, to protect and be protected. They are fierce warriors both men and women alike, with the look of the Gods about them. It seems this people are made of the very things of the earth. Some have fierce eyes the color of the great waters and others grow tresses the color of the sun or the red of flames in addition to the brown of the rich soil. These are people of the many Gods but most true are they to The God and Goddess. And while I describe this people in colors of the earth, a great reverence they have for the *Power of the Universe*, as do we. But most strange of these people is that no matter that they are spread out over great distances, and that they speak even in variations of their own tongue, they all take care in ritual and in battle to paint themselves in the blue that is the color of the sky."

Faidhe started at this last bit of information for this is a color with which she had very recently become most familiar. She had begun to understand that her journey would involve preparing a Great Circle for the coming of just these people, those who would carry with them the sacred traditions, long after her own Tuatha De Danann had gone over to the spirits and new peoples arose with their own commissions in preservation of the knowledge that must be protected through the ages. So these would be the people who would bear the symbol of the Goddess and join it with that of the coming God. These ones selected to preserve the tale and carry forth the magic necessary to weave the bond between the past and the future, the She and the He.

Iarann continued. "The images I see of these people are captivating. I often see those who look familiar as if these clans are distant relatives. But entrancing as the images may be, the most enchanting sight in my visions is a bowl crafted of the most pure, and finest materials. This vessel is the embodiment of a sacred story. It glows from within of a radiant light and it's very metal glows with a warmth that not even liquid gold can equal. This is a Cauldron imbued with much of the spirit, I think. Its manufacture, indeed, is crafted of the purest of magic, a labor of humanity. A selfless production of the body and the spirit, of silver and gold, of God and Goddess, and on and on I could recite the balance of this bowl. For every point, there is an equal balance. The bowl captures my eye and heart in the beatific rendering of a perfect balance. I sense from this sacred cup, a balance to which every true student of the Power aspires, an existence of flawless centeredness...or at least the possibility of such." Iarann struggled with what he was about to say.

He tore his eyes away from the flame and rose to feed the fire with scraps and twigs from the kindling bin. A large and muscular man, he bore the look of one with strength beyond the normal but he also carried himself in a manner that was graceful and uncharacteristic of one of such size. This could be accounted for only when one knew of his heritage. He was a man both of the body and the spirit. His humility was endearing for one with such strength and power. It was obvious on his face that he had come to some kind of decision as he turned to Faidhe and spoke.

"Lady, this very day, you came from the wood bearing the finest ore of silver as I have ever seen. When I saw this, I asked if you had brought this to me to be crafted and you said the load was your own to carry. I offer you neither insult nor disrespect when I tell you I think you are mistaken. This load is for me to craft, and it is the crafting of this very bowl with which I am charged. This is part of the visions I have had that I can say with doubtless surety it is my charge now to craft this very bowl for reasons I cannot fathom. But know you this, I am bound to the tale that Lon Dubh is prophesied to proliferate and must craft the bowl in keeping of this responsibility and so must bind myself to her in her task."

Lon Dubh stared at Iarann, as he spoke to her mother, with eyes wide and mouth agape, for she had seen Iarann transform in front of her to an unyielding warrior surrounded by a glowing halo of blue, wearing impenetrable armor of gold and wielding a great golden hammer that rivaled the Dagda's own. Awestruck, Lon Dubh could not release her gaze from this half God. She had felt some connection with him at the gathering place but knew not why. She had seen him many times in the village without being in mind of him any further than a polite nod in greeting. But now, it was as if blinders had been removed from her eyes and she knew in that moment that she was already bound to this man. So much, so fast, she thought to herself. She tried to stem her confusion and be exhilarated by all that was taking place. Lon Dubh found that she was not at all displeased that she would be in some way working closely with Iarann.

"Well then, Iarann," Faidhe spoke, "it seems that you will be preparing to travel with Lon Dubh and myself in three days' time. Know this Smithy, our journey will not be an easy one, and may be fraught with danger over great distances. I am comforted to have one of your breeding and strength along the road for we will be traveling to those far away lands of which you spoke. Truly what you saw were genuine visions, both of the strange lands and of the people. For I too have been given sight of these places and the people and it is for the latter, in part, that we travel. I rejoice in that I need not explain to you that the Gods require you to embark on this journey with us, but that you have already committed yourself to this cause. You bring me news of that which I did not know, regarding the ore offered from the great Cauldron to be used to create this new vessel. It seems we each have our own piece for which to be responsible on the journey. Great endurance and fortitude will be required for this trek, for it will be the passing of many moon cycles before our work is complete."

"Is there any more need be said now?" Craiche asked as she stood with effort. "For while we have spoken here, it has grown well past full dark and there are those who will begin to count heads and take notice of those who are missing."

The rest knew Craiche was right but hesitated to leave the newly formed alliance. Within the small hut, even the children knew that the coming together of these eight clan members had created something powerful. They knew that once they left the hut, all of their lives would be changed. A silent glance was exchanged, hands were clasped; embraces were tearfully given for all that would change and for all that might have been, but never came to pass. But each in their own way was honored for their part to play in the task appointed them by the *Power of the Universe*.

"Bound are we by blood and promise, as we clasp hands here in this Circle, an oath to each other and to the Gods that we will remain so bound until the story has been told," Craiche dipped her head toward Lon Dubh. "Until the bowl has been crafted. She dipped her head toward Iarann. "And the history of the prophecy is recorded and set forth into the future. So it is said, so shall it be."

The group, standing with clasped hands felt the current of magic behind the oath and as if on cue, all repeated in unison, "So it is said, so shall it be."

At that moment, a gust of air rush through the hut, so strong as to upset a forgotten goblet of water from Iarann's work table so it spilt onto the fire and then clanged with a metal gong onto the earth serving to symbolize the ending of the gathering.

Laoghaire, Colm and the children exited the hut first, and together, they headed to their own hut to begin to prepare for what they would take with them on their impending journey to the Circle Hill as they would embark on a new, unprecedented way of life but more immediately, to prepare for the evening's feast. This would afford them a reasonable excuse for any prying questions about why they were so late in coming to the feast for that evening. From inside the hut, Morgan could be heard asking questions revealing rumors of many hearth-fire children's stories.

"Mother, is it scary up on the Hill with all the spirits? Do the Gods live there? Will we learn real magic now? Will we be able to disappear and be privy to the conversation of others? Will we be able to spy on our friends from yon Hill? What of the Sacred Spring? They say it pulls children down to the depths and swallows them up! Shall we partake in the rituals? Oh what an adventure this will be!"

Macha's eyes grew wide for though he was taller and more sturdy-built than tiny Morgan, he was less adventuresome and more prone to awe of the unknown rather than an excitement to explore it.

Colm hushed her daughter for fear that in her exuberance she might be overheard. "Quiet Morgan, speak not of these things. All in time it will be revealed to us just what our role will be."

Faidhe smiled faintly at the questions and wondered about the future her grandchildren would endure. Would it be a burden or indeed an adventure for them? She sighed and then dismissed the thought.

Next to leave were Lon Dubh and Iarann for no one could see any reason for keeping secret a friendship between the two.

Once they were upon the road toward the village center, Lon Dubh queried, "Will you come with me to my hut first, before attending the gathering, Iarann? I have not much to add to the feast but have, only today, made a savory broth of rabbit meat and woodland bounty. I will be honored if you would share my table."

Lon Dubh blushed at her newness in the invitation. She had long been unaccustomed to company, let alone male company, and in fact had never shared her table with a man. Usually direct to the point of indiscretion, Lon Dubh now found it difficult even to meet Iarann's eyes.

Iarann put a protective arm around her and said without thought that he had simply picked up on Faidhe's use of the name for her, "It will be a pleasure to share your table, Black Bird." This will be the first of many a shared meal, no doubt." From under the skins he'd donned to defray the evening chill, he brought forth a small drinking bladder and said, "I had, myself, planned on bringing what little I have to the feast on such short notice. This is well-aged mead. Though I keep the tradition of making the drink, it has not touched my lips since before Ethlinn went to the spirits when you were likely a very young girl. It is my hope that the flavor of the drink, fine as it was then, will have developed sweetly as I improved the process of its making over the years. Will then, you join me in testing its juices?"

Warmed at the intimacy of her name, Lon Dubh nestled into his protective arm said, "I can think of no other way I would rather spend this night of feasting than with warm broth, sweet honeywine and the knowledge that we celebrate the first of many meals together."

With the satisfaction of having her role with the Goddess revealed, a reunion with her sister and family, and the impending journey planned with her mother and this strong gentle man, she felt finally as though she'd found a place to belong.

Inside the hut, Faidhe and Craiche banked the flickering fire and walked out into the night looking much like two crones they were with their hoods pulled up as their heads drew close together. And walking arm in arm, whispered in low tones of what is to come, what will be needed to fortify the Tuath to bear the upcoming changes.

14

The Power of the Word

The stars were in the billions in the country sky as I returned from my day with Cath and walked from the car to the front door of our cottage. Though the night was so clear as to be able to imagine everything in my sight was surreally crystalline with clarity, yet the air was sultry enough to deposit little droplets of dew on my hair and skin as though I were indistinguishable from a blade of grass, a spider's geometrical design, or the wing of a dragonfly. I could see all in the light of the moon. I felt I was a part of everything and was exhilarated.

When I stood before the open blue door of the cottage with the door handle in my hand, reluctance to have to go indoors overtook me and I opted to stay outside, alone for just another few minutes. I closed the door again and slid down the rough wall of the cottage and crouched to see the moon making its way up the sky just beyond the eves of the roof, to listen to the night sounds and to just breathe. The smell of cattle and fresh hay was on the air, simple and clean. Enjoying a feeling of wellbeing, I was satisfied to be a part of this night in the shadow of the cottage like a bird or bug without a hustle to be or go somewhere or to do something. It had been so long since I had just stopped and been alone.

A furtive movement down the long driveway caught my eye. I realized the three brothers Bridey had told us about who rented the other cottage were out behind their house. I couldn't quite make out what they were doing but it looked as though they were uncovering some piece of equipment. It was almost comical to watch as they bumbled and shoved at each other. It was really none of my business what they were doing but I silently chuckled as the Three Stooges came to my mind and continued to watch the show. Whatever they were uncovering tipped and almost fell over in the mud. This brought on shoves and slaps from Moe. Larry tried to right the item and Curly backed into it once again as Larry overcompensated by pushing it into Curly's back. I realized, once they had stopped the slapstick, that the item was a telescope. *Stargazers?* Well I had them pegged all wrong

I guess. They were really into it by the size of the telescope. It appeared to be an all-business type set up. I thought these guys, locals by Bridey's report, were workaday humps and nighttime beer drinkers. I'd seen them out working in their yard around their cottage with boxer underwear hanging below their shorts and three days beard growth at all times. I even joked to Nora that they were the Saturday night bath type, displaying plenty of butt crack and not enough teeth. I felt a little sheepish to recall my unkind remarks. Maybe they were absent minded academics, astronomers, or students of the sky. I had a hard time trying to believe it, but there they were, outside on a Saturday night, before the bath I assumed, taking advantage of such a clear night to view the stars. I let go a little giggle at the bath comment and Moe, Larry and Curly froze.

I wondered if they had heard me or if it was something else that caught their attention. How could they have heard me this far away? Although sound does travel in the country. No noises to muffle and nothing but air to carry whispers like feathers on the wind. I did not move or breathe. How would I explain spying on our neighbors in the dark of the night? Trying to rationalize that I could sit out and enjoy the evening if I wanted, I could not quite convince myself to move. For one minute, two, they remained still. Images of my fear welled up from the night before. Panic blossomed in my chest as my mind took off full bore. What if it's the beast?

Then like long probing fingers, tendrils of that stink from last night reached my nose, once again. I was not imagining things but I knew I was sensing the odor rather than smelling it. It was crazy but I knew, just knew, that smell was searching for me. Whatever was out here brought this unbidden thought of a beast pursuing me and along with it the reek that was akin to decomposing flesh of some animal. I almost gagged but worked to quell my gorge and forced myself to remain still and unseen. To not bolt for the door of the cottage as instinct told me to do.

Just then, the brothers apparently decided the danger had passed and continued to go about their work with the telescope. At the same time, the smell and my panic subsided. I relaxed a bit, took a shaky breath and decided to go inside when a flash of light caught my eye from down below. The moon had reflected in the lens of the telescope and flashed brilliantly in my direction. I waited for the adjustment of the telescope toward the stars so I could go in the doorway unnoticed but grew suddenly very cold when I realized that the focus of the telescope was not the stars but our cottage!

I pulled myself deep into the shadow of the corner between the cottage front and the little alcove that served as a windbreak and mudroom. I once again concentrated on being still and remaining unseen, quietly chanting to any powers that might be out there to help.

"Don't see me. Don't see me. Please don't let them see me." I didn't know what they'd do if they knew they were found out as peeping Moe, Larry and Curly. Suddenly not so funny anymore, I felt the vulnerability of being in a foreign country with no phone in the middle of the boondocks with three guys leering nightly from 1/8 of a mile away. I fervently hoped that Nora had not heard the car pull up and would decide, at this moment, to come outside to look for me. I was trying to decide what I should do when a ruckus from below erupted.

There was what seemed to be a whole lot of crows or some type of large bird flying and swooping around the three dark figures and their telescope. In fact, they seemed to be attacking the men. The brothers were frantically trying to cover the telescope with a tarp while being pitched and dived upon. It seemed the men were actually being pecked by these birds as though suddenly finding themselves too close to a nest containing precious fledglings, the adult birds launched a full out attack.

I took this as my cue to get into the house unseen while their attentions were occupied. I rolled to my knees and opened the cottage door from that position and scrambled while on my knees to the inside. Once in the alcove, I closed the door behind me and stood up. I felt exposed in the bright light of the little mudroom but didn't think I had been seen coming in. After locking the outer door, I let myself into the sitting room of the cottage and double locked the inner door. My eyes as big as saucers, I expected Nora to turn around and be shocked at my appearance but she remained on the couch, back to me, reading a book. I immediately went over to peak out through the shutters in the front windows into which the brothers likely had been spying.

As I did this, Nora startled and turned around. Her eyes moved past me to the window and I thought she saw something out there that frightened her so I slammed the shutters closed. She flew up out of the couch and stood staring at the window looking more frightened than me.

"Nora," I said, "did they come up here? Were they bothering you?"

It was only then that Nora focused on me and her panic subsided a little. She looked confused and shocked at the same time. "Where did you come from?" she asked.

"I'm a little freaked right now," I answered. "I just caught the guys down the hill in the other cottage spying up here at us with a telescope! Did you have any problem with them today while you were alone?"

Nora looked from me to the window and back again. My anxiety grew at the prospect that I'd left Nora alone and something might have happened. "NORA! Did they bother you at all?"

Tentatively she began. "No... they...ah...no...I...I didn't see you there, I guess I didn't hear you come in. The window...it scared me. They what? They're peeping?"

The automatic recount of all that was done in the cottage that might have been observed crossed Nora's face. She was doing the same mental inventory of how many times she'd walked by the windows in a towel after a shower or how often she'd walked down the hall to the kitchen in less than public attire or just how many days or nights had they watched us regardless of what we were doing. She went through all five fazes of a victim of this type of thing right before my eyes. I knew what they were because I'd just experienced them myself: icy fear, embarrassment, revulsion, anger, and red-hot outrage.

"What do you mean you caught them? Did you say anything to them? What happened?"

"Wait a minute." I said, as I went to all the rest of the windows in the cottage to check the locks and secure the shutters. After that I checked the locks on the doors one more time. Once I was satisfied that the cottage was fortified as best as possible I dimmed the lights and I gave her the short version of what I'd just witnessed outside, from the telescope to the crows, and how I'd snuck into the house unseen.

Nora appeared pensive for a moment as though she were trying to solve a riddle and what she said then was not even close to what I'd expected.

"I think you were invisible." The look of fear had returned to her face, or maybe it was fascination.

"What?" Exasperated and confused that Nora was consistent in not staying focused on the problem at hand, I was sure that I'd heard her incorrectly.

"I think you were invisible," she repeated. "I was reading..." Then she stopped and looked at the book that had toppled to the floor for the second time in the same day. I recognized it as the book I'd found on my bedroom floor only this morning. She let go of whatever thought she'd had and continued. "When I heard the door, then I heard the shutters move behind me, I thought it was you but when I turned around, I didn't see anything or anyone, then right before my eyes, the shutters slammed shut like a poltergeist was in the room playing tricks. I swear I was alone in the room until you started talking and then," she blurted, "there you were!"

"That's crazy Nora. You said yourself you just didn't see me there."

"Yeah, I didn't see you because you weren't there, or you *were* there and I didn't see you 'cause you *weren't visible!*"

"This is crazy talk." I started to say as I peeked out a crack I'd slivered open in the shutter. Scanning the pastures between our cottage and the one down the hill. I satisfied myself that the brothers were at least no longer peeping with the telescope. Nor were there any birds that I could see, so presumably, the men were no longer outdoors. Preoccupied with the situation at hand, I mentally recounted what I knew to be the norm regarding peeping Toms: If they peep, they don't pursue. Don't approach and they'll stay distant. Well I had no intention of approaching anyone of the brothers but Bridey was going to get an earful in the morning.

This caution being satisfied for the moment, I turned and began to hear what Nora was telling me.

I couldn't understand why she was not more shaken by the idea that we were being watched but she obviously held the same frustration in why I could not fathom how disturbing it was for her to discover that I'd developed the skill of vanishing. What really vexed her was that I'd developed the skill, so she thought, and had no knowledge of it. I disregarded the idea because I thought she'd imagined what she saw or perhaps picked up on my panic as I willed myself not to be seen and told her just that.

"Exactly!" she erupted. "Don't you get it? You were trying not to be seen and *that's what happened!*"

I stood immobilized for the moment with my hand still on the shutter. Feeling exposed by the window, I let the louvers snap shut again and gave my full attention to what she was trying to make me understand. Nora seized the moment to further rationalize the irrational by attempting to remind me of when we were kids and I tried to make myself appear various ways without much success, but there were times when she'd told me during those efforts that I was less noticeable. As a kid, I had grumbled that it wouldn't work the way I wanted it to in making myself appear different to people so it wasn't useful to me as far as I was concerned. I couldn't disappear from class or fade into some ghostly looking thing; I needed people to see me as cool or smart. What good was having a cool power if it didn't work the way I wanted it to when I wanted it to?

"Maybe you can completely make that happen now. Lee, I'm just telling you what I saw. Things are different here. You said so yourself. Tell me again what, *exactly* happened when you were outside?"

I recounted just sitting outside, smelling the night air and being drawn to the moon.

"Oh and wait until I tell you about what Cath told me today." Sidetracked by all that had happened, I forgot completely about all that had taken place at The Sacred Traveler during lunch.

"Lee" Nora quipped, "One amazing thing at a time. You were outside, where?"

"Okay." I took a breath and focused. "I was outside leaning against the wall by the front door just enjoying the night for a minute. I noticed the brothers down the hill setting up what looked like a telescope. As they tried to set it up, they fought with each other and I started to laugh at them. You should have seen them; they were just like a scene out of The Three Stooges! But they seemed to notice the sound because they stopped and listened. As they listened, and I don't know how they heard me all the way up here at the top of the hill, but as soon as I laughed it was as if they knew I was here. And then there was this smell, kind of sneaking around the area right at that moment. But here's the strange thing though, last night during the night, I was really scared about something and I know it sounds silly now, but I smelled it again.

"Something rotten." Nora flatly stated.

"Yeah. You too?"

"Did you see the old lady?" Nora asked.

"Yes!" I gasped, nodding my head, excited now that I knew I wasn't alone in my strange experiences of last night. Some little comfort that I wasn't a paranoid lunatic or maybe I was, but at least I wasn't alone in my lunacy. "What happened to you?" I asked.

"No wait." She held up a hand. "Finish what you were telling me. There's some other stuff that I saw and learned today you should probably know."

I tried to compose myself and reflect on exactly what took place outside and picked up the thread of the account.

"I was about to go inside when I noticed that the telescope was pointed up here at our cottage. I almost dismissed it and came inside when I got that prickly skin feeling. I was crouched down and stayed there for a minute to see what they were doing. Then I saw that they were watching our cottage, not the sky then it dawned on me why they were so alert when they heard me laugh, 'cause they were being sneaky. Then I got scared because if they saw me see them...well that's when I pulled back into the shadow of the cottage because I really didn't know what would happen if I let them see me. I was so scared, I kept saying that under my breath, *'don't see me. Don't see me.'*"

Nora had a look of triumph on her face that said: *See, I told you so.* As if just my recounting was proof that she was right and I had been, for lack of a less ridiculous term, invisible.

"Alright, even if that part of all of this is true, it still doesn't change the fact that we're in the middle of nowhere with peeping Tom neighbors and little chance of anyone doing much about it. We're only here until the end of the month. Those guys *live* here. They raise pigs for crying out loud. They're not going anywhere. They probably have friends here and I don't think I'd like to tangle with anyone those guys would have for friends. They make the local pub set look like aristocracy. And Bridey? Bridey is a nice woman but she's not going to trade steady rent for temporary tourists.

"We're not tourists." Nora sniffed reflexively.

"I know that Nora, but that's how *they* see us. And besides, do you think it'll make much difference to them that we're here on an academic pursuit instead of to kiss the Blarney Stone? We're not from here, those guys are...and they're guys. You know how they feel about women here, never mind American women. I think we're on our own with this. We have to deal with this because in truth, I think that all the odd stuff we've been experiencing is somehow tied together."

"Well I'm with you on that count. Let me tell you what I found out today in that book you left for me."

"See that's what I'm talking about Nora. *I* didn't leave that for you. The apparition of the old woman woke me up last night. Woke us both up last night. And that book was in my room when I woke up this morning."

"So?"

"So, I never brought the book into my room. You were there when we left the box of books in the living room. So either the old woman had reason to bring it to my attention or you put it there."

I looked at Nora brows raised inquiringly, already knowing the answer. She shook her head to confirm that neither she nor I had brought the book to my room during the night. That left three remaining possibilities: the ghost of an unknown old woman for some reason disturbed us to call attention to a book only recently purchased, our landlady, who presumably has the only other key to the cottage, sneaked in during the night as a practical joke. *Not likely.* Or, the three men who live down the hill were stalking us much more closely and have a literary side to their nature. *Very doubtful.*

"So," Nora said, obviously reaching the same conclusion regarding nocturnal luminary possibilities, "Who's the old woman?"

"I have no clue. Let's have a look at the book." I tipped my chin in the direction of the book in question that had been flung to the floor by Nora during her rude introduction to the world of disappearing sisters...well, sister.

At this, Nora sprung to life however, clearly without the ability to finish a sentence.

"Oh, I have to tell you. This book... I started reading. Today. And the birds. I have to tell you." I waited as she struggled to catch her mouth up with her thoughts. She was only slightly annoyed at my amusement as she obviously had some news to tell.

———

"Jesus." I sighed when she finished her tale.

To which she responded, "Exactly."

"Okay," I said, now huddled on the couch with Nora fingering the book in question between us on the cushions, "Tell me again but give me all the details...everything that happened, even the stuff that you might think is insignificant. You were reading in the courtyard behind the cottage..."

"Yeah, the sun was nice and for some reason I just couldn't bring myself to get started on my books that I bought yesterday. I started to thumb through this book," she said, bouncing the heft of the hardback in her open hand as she took it from me, "after you got into the shower this morning and I got interested in the tale it supports that the ancients here in Ireland believed that once a story is told, it takes on a life of its own. It underscores the reasoning behind why the Celts or the Gaels had no cohesive written language for so very long in that they believed a story would not die if it could be retold person to person. And with each subsequent telling of the tale or whatever, the story grew in strength. No one could steal the information, nor could they destroy it as long as there was a person to tell the tale and a person to hear it. As the story, song, lesson, instruction or whatever was passed from person to person, generation to generation, it grew in its power and, they believed, became an entity in itself with power to regenerate and find a likely avenue to continue through host after host. It seems all this began with a spell or something cast," She hooked the first two fingers of each hand into mock quotations and wiggled them up and down twice while saying, "long, long ago and far, far away. And I thought to myself," Nora continued, "how strange that the story about the Power of the Word," again hooking her fingers, "should be passed along in written fashion when the whole idea in the book is that speaking the words is the way in which they hold power."

"Yeah, I got that part, tell me about the birds." I said.

"Nora mentally switched gears and recounted, "I took the book outside for a bit of breakfast reading at the patio table in the courtyard. As I was reading about the book's idea on rhythm and how words spoken with rhythm or rhyme hold additional power, a rhythm of my own kept running through my head. You know the old Boston Celtics basketball player from the 80's, Larry Byrd?"

When I nodded that I did Nora continued. Remember the commercial hype for the games used to chant, 'Byrd, Byrd, Byrd,'" she said, her head bobbing up and down with the rhythm of the chant. "'Byrd is the word.' And as that kept getting louder in my head I started to say it out loud. And like I told you, when I did, all these birds came flocking to the tree that hangs over the stone wall just beyond the courtyard at the end of the property. There had to have been hundreds of them! Crows, I think but big ones. Maybe ravens, but they don't travel in big packs like that. Do they?"

"Murders." I corrected. Contemplating the added details Nora had just told me about the birds.

"What?" Her brows knitted together.

"A murder of crows is what it's called. You know, like a flock of sheep, a gaggle of geese, a pack of wolves? Well, it's a murder of crows."

"Yeah but what's it called when it's a bunch of ravens? Anyway," she pushed on, "those birds stayed there as quiet as a tomb, all morning, just watching me. Lee I swear they were *watching* me as I read the book. That was all they did; just sit there perched as if they were waiting for something. I kind of got used to their quiet company there, until I got up to get something to eat 'cause I guess I was reading for hours when I realized that it was way past lunchtime. I decided I'd read enough and got up from the table when all of a sudden they all just started squawking and flying around over my head. It scared the hell out of me! I didn't feel like I was in danger. They just put up a ruckus. And then the strangest thing happened. I looked up at all of them and told them to settle down, that I was just going to get some food and I'd come right back. You know how you talk to a dog without really expecting a response?" I nodded again. Nora continued, "Well as soon as I said this, they all flew back to the tree and were quiet again. Not a peep. I got up from the table again and headed for the back door. That's when the biggest, blackest of them all flew down to the table and eyed me from there. I was about halfway between the table and the door when the bird pecked its big black beak at the book I left on the table. This bird was huge." She demonstrated with her hands spreading them about 18 inches apart in front of her face as she continued.

"It pecked and looked at me, peck...look. I know it sounds foolish but I got the distinct impression that the bird was actually trying to communicate with me. I felt foolish but I asked it what it wanted and it pecked at the book again. I walked back expecting the bird to fly away but it didn't. It stayed there on the table just watching me while all the other birds watched from the big tree. Lee it was so weird, but I just *knew* these birds were talking to me in their own way. I got the distinct feeling that I wasn't supposed to leave the book outside. The big bird wanted me to take it with me. So I asked aloud if that was what I was supposed to do and the bird let out a squawk that I'd swear actually sounded like the word, book. I swear I wasn't hearing things. I felt like I fell down the rabbit hole, but when I reached out and picked up the book, the bird literally nodded its head. It looked me in that sideways way that birds have and stayed there until I went inside. I looked out the window as I scraped together some lunch; thanks by the way, I'm still starving."

"Oh." I startled with the reminder of food. "I brought back a bunch of sandwiches. They're still in the car. Come with me to get them?"

I wanted to hear the more detailed recounting of what happened to Nora while I was at lunch but after the evening's happenings, I'd completely forgotten about the food I'd left in the car along with all my notes and information from my day with Cath. I felt suddenly anxious and wanted to have the information I'd gained from Cath with me and not sitting, exposed, in the car. 'Exposed' occurred to me as a peculiar way to think of it but I was learning quickly that peculiar was the norm for us here in our ancestral homeland. Besides, the food wouldn't keep in the car overnight and we were both hungry. So after a careful look around, we braved the eight or so feet of exposure from the front door to the car to retrieve my day's work and our fortifications for the telling of the remaining stories of the evening. On the way back to the front door, with my materials and promised dinner in tow, Nora clutched my arm in a desperate grip as she squealed in whispered excitement.

"There it is, Lee! Look! LOOK! There it is!

After the evening's panic of being watched from below, my eyes immediately scanned the brothers' cottage. Finding nothing there, I looked to where Nora's attention was directed and found her looking up toward the moon that had moved to a higher position now over the roof of our cottage. I found the moon, now considerably smaller than it was a few hours ago, was not the focus of her gaze but, to the left of it, upon the chimney leading down to the woodstove in our sitting room, was the biggest raven I'd ever seen. Just as Nora had described it to me, big, black and for now, silent. It sat alone like a sentinel, eyeing us. I urged Nora toward the cottage by giving her a shove. Not wanting to be outside any longer than necessary, still cautious of our inquisitive neighbors.

Nora stopped abruptly once again to say, "Hey, look at that." Our position shifted as we drew closer to the door, the silhouette of the raven came in line with the perfectly round, pearl-white moon. It created a striking picture of contrast, black and white and all at once, reminded me of childhood Halloween decorations depicting the witch flying across the moon. In that moment, I understood, without knowing how, that this big, black raven was the matriarch of the birds I'd seen in the earlier frenzy. I also understood that the magic I'd felt in the air earlier this evening still emitted ample energy. For lack of a less cliché term, I definitely felt that there was something brewing around here.

Once back inside with the remaining sandwiches and remnants of lunch preserved by the cool night air, we settled back on the couch happily munching and recounting. Nora finished her tale a second time. But this time, with more confidence now that I'd actually seen the spectral figure myself as if the bird's very presence lent validation to her unlikely experience.

"Okay," she said, re-warming the story she had been telling. "I got some brown bread and butter that Bridey left in the fridge for us and made some tea for my lunch. I was taken by surprise as I sat at the table to eat, when the bird flew up to the back window," Nora tipped her chin toward the window over the kitchen sink that overlooked the courtyard in back, "and tapped at the glass looking in at me."

In that moment, I'd been reminded of what Cath had enlightened me to earlier that very day but I kept my silence so that Nora could finish her story. For what I had considered to be an interesting story of lore to analyze for my dissertation was now becoming a living mystery in which we were active, if unwitting, participants.

Nora continued, "The bird was insistent at the window tapping so fiercely that I was afraid it would break so I tried to shoo the bird away but it wouldn't go away. I tried to get rid of it by opening the window with a broomstick in my hand, ready to swat it if I had to. But when I opened the window, the bird flew into the kitchen and landed on the counter where I'd put the book. It just stood there staring at me and then pecked at the book, stare, peck, stare, peck. Then it scared me again when it cawed at me as if it had reached the end of its patience. I was stunned into action then and asked it what it wanted. Then the bird said, 'Book.' I swear to God, Lee, this time I had no doubts, it *said* book!"

Despite the fact that Nora had already brought me through this story one time, I had raised flesh on my arms, imagining what it must have been like for her to have this experience.

"Talk about "Tap, tap, tapping at my chamber door." I said and nodded reassurance that I didn't think she was crazy so she'd continue.

"Well," Nora said, "I told the bird I'd read the book and that's what I've been doing since then. There're all kinds of fascinating things in there about the telling of a tale and how it was kept secret. Then there's some contrasting points about having to actually write some things down to keep from saying them because the power of actually saying the words would unleash the power prematurely so the people of this land, Ireland, and... it's the Celts, I think the book speaks of, devised a way to pass on the secret words without saying them, until it came to be the right time to 'unleash' the energy of the words."

"And when was that?" I asked.

"Well, it's a huge book. I'm not sure when, or even if it says when it is, but I do know that there are things that are like poems or songs in the book that are strange additions to the text and I think they're meant as clues or something but I couldn't quite figure it out. And something else. Even though the book is old, it's written in English, so it's not really old from Ireland or it would be in Gaelic wouldn't it? There are some parts that are in Gaelic but it seems that it's more of the song type of writing because all of that is in handwriting, not the print that the rest of the book is done in and those pages seem to be older paper than the rest of the book. I looked up some of the words in your Irish-English dictionary and most of the words aren't in it so I don't know what they say. There are eight of them. Can you figure out what they say?

Nora handed the book back to me with a hopeful look on her face. I looked at one of the poems or whatever it was and saw that she was right. The page and writing appeared to be very old. Thick, yellowed and fragile around the edges. I remembered buying this book for reference and authenticating the point in my dissertation that folklore, has its roots in the spiritual past and came forward in folktales, then to fairytales gleaned from folks and rewritten, Christianized, politicized and patriarchalized by entrepreneurs like Hans Christian Anderson and The Brothers Grimm. I wanted to support the theory that fairytales, as we know them, have symbolic meaning rooted in Pagan ways. I could make out a few words with my basic knowledge of Gaelic, but not so I could make sense of what the text was saying.

"No, nothing useful anyway" I said. "Maybe I'll have to ask Cath. He translated a lot of those books so he'd probably know."

"Yeah," Nora answered. "It's all pretty confusing and I doubt we'll have any idea of what the actual message of the book is until we have someone who can translate those passages for us."

"Us?" I questioned. "What about all the work you have to do?"

"Are you kidding? Talking birds, strange ghost woman, magic book, spying neighbors; something's going on here and it involves us. Do you think I can just go about my merry way writing about trines, oppositions and sesquares?"

I was relieved that Nora was with me in all of this now. Because I didn't know if she'd have believed the story I'd heard from Cath. I knew that it was more than just a folktale he was telling me but he never came right out and said that. He was telling me the tale in that form to test the waters I think. After what I'd shown him a bit of what abilities I have, I got the impression that he'd been testing to see if I was worthy of learning what he shared with me this afternoon. I'd hoped I wouldn't have to investigate alone. Now that Nora had provided what I thought to be a piece of the same puzzle I'd been working on, I felt better about what I was about to tell her and that she was more likely to believe me now too.

"So, you feel like taking a ride with me tomorrow?" I asked Nora.

"What'd you have in mind?"

"There's a man down in Midleton, County Cork that Cath told me I should talk to. His name is Finny McDonough and apparently, he's the guy in the know about some of the things Cath told me about today. I was excited about talking to him when Cath told me Finny would be a wealth of information for my research so he might be able to shed some light on what's going on because the story Cath told me today, I think, is somehow tied in with all of this. I think so 'cause it seemed that Cath wanted me to go see this guy, like it was important to him that I do. So I promised Cath I'd go see him even before I knew what your plans would be for tomorrow. Are you up for it?"

"Sure. I'm all in. What was the story about?"

"Nora, I'm so keyed up I'm halfway between dead on my feet and wondering if I'll ever get to sleep. Do you mind if we turn in now? It's already almost 2:00. And if my track record on getting out of bed doesn't improve, we might not get on the road before noon tomorrow."

"No, that's fine. Where's the map? I'll just check on a route to Midleton to see how long it might take us to get there."

"Good. Thanks. It's in the pocket of my note bag." I checked the locks on the doors and windows again and reflexively tightened the already closed window blinds before I walked down the hall to my bedroom where I surprisingly fell quickly to sleep.

———

I was pleasantly surprised to find myself roaming through a forest. This was a place of ancient beauty. I found the sensual feel of the mossy soft green under my feet a welcome contrast to always wearing shoes. This felt somehow, natural for me to actually feel what the forest was saying to me through my feet. I looked down and saw my feet covered in some soft tannish colored animal hide. "Ah." I thought out loud, "That's why I can still hear the forest: natural material on my feet from an animal of the forest." That made perfect sense to me as things often do in dreams.

All the sounds around me seemed amplified due to the otherwise uncommon quiet in the forest. A bird lightly rustled a leaf and it seemed to shake and crackle. The trees themselves were unmistakably old. Huge too. I felt if I listened hard enough, I would hear what they were thinking. And again, in that dream sort of way, the idea that trees could think was perfectly natural. I'd always thought of natural things with a sense of universal sort of kinship but this was different. These were conscious beings. In fact, all around me I could sense a palpable consciousness in the forest. Little skittering things, large and powerful beings. The openness between myself, and those all around me was as natural as coming home. In fact, I thought in my dream awareness, this is exactly that: I'm home. And just as I was overcome with a consuming joy at finding my way back, a great black shadow flew across the sun. A great, piercing caw called out in warning. I was chilled as the shadow blocked the sun. Suddenly the feeling of the forest altered to something malevolent. The homecoming was foiled. Another urgent caw. The voice, the voice is a familiar one.

"Caw. Caw. Wake up, child. CAW!

"But wait, I have questions!"

My body jerked awake to the sound of a bird cawing outside my bedroom window. *Oh,* I thought to myself, *it wasn't part of my dream.*

15

The Feast

The crowds gathered in the great hall for the first night's feasting. Word about the plans for three days of celebrating and key changes in the power structure of the Tuath was sent to neighboring settlements along with news of the amazing circumstances of the gathering place earlier in the day. It would take some time before word reached all the clan's folk to achieve a gathering of full strength but all within three-day's travel would arrive at the main settlement at the base of the Hill to hear the tale and participate in the festivities. Those further than a three-day walk from the Circle Hill would eventually hear the news as it traveled back on the tongues of those who attended the feasting. Others still would make the journey despite the fact that they would be approaching the main houses of the Tuatha De Danann well after the feasting and events had taken place. They would come, stay with relatives, and capture the essence of the all that had happened, while sitting by the evening light of the hearth-fire, hearing the tales from those who witnessed the events or by listening to songs already being created about the happenings of the day and no doubt more to come; for this was news that some would not trust accuracy of such extraordinary phenomena to a road-stranger or passer-by. And it was just too salacious a tale to miss seeing how much of the rumor was gossip, and how much could be proved as fact. Lips would flutter for many years to come.

As with all-important occasions, the celebration and feasting commenced at dusk, a time between light and dark. This was done in reverence to the Sun God and Moon Goddess. No dishonor or disrespect was given to either if the feast days and celebrations were initiated at a time between times. Cloaks were wrapped against the cold spring air as plumes of breath could be seen rising from mouths with excitement, imitating the smoke billowing out of the smoke hole in the roof of the great feasting hall. Clan folk bustled about to stake a claim on tables in the hall with a satisfactory vantage of the Council table. Musicians brought their strings, skins, pipes and whistles with the hope of gaining entrance to the great hall by offering benefit of their music and song. Early travelers from nearby villages would, by evening time tomorrow, be vying for seats at clan-members' tables hoping to be among those feasting inside the great hall and not among those seated around the many small fires that burned, dotting the field grass in the village outside the great feasting place.

Due to great care taken for feeding royalty and other guests of distinction, the meat that roasted on the great spit inside the feasting hall was typically smoked, sweet, and desirable. However, the outdoor fires at many other feasting times were most often favored due to the ease with which one could slip away to celebrate fertility couplings. This feast, however, held particular fascination within the hall walls due to the esteemed guest in Faidhe, the nature of the news she brought with her from the Hill, as well as the brewing changes in the power structure of the clan. Most hoped to catch a glimpse of the Keeper and her great pot or to see if Laoghaire would carry the Sword and Shield magically gifted to him as evidence of his rightful, if not unusual, positioning as the new Keeper of the Circle. There would be ample jockeying by many, seeking favors to be recalled, and promises of favors owed in an effort to procure a seat within the walls of the feasting hall this night.

Laoghaire, Colm and the twins stirred up a renewed frenzy of stretched necks and gawking as they arrived at the great hall dressed in their finest linens and woolen cloaks. Colm bore baskets of early season, garden-grown hardy greens and eggcakes made from the early spring nest hunt. Laoghaire openly carried the sacred Shield; and the Sword could be seen tucked into a handmade leather sheath bound to his midstrap. Again, Laoghaire drew looks from many a maiden and married woman alike as he threw off his cloak in the heat of the warming hall. They drank in his toned muscles that moved serpentine-like under the weight of the Shield. Having had no prior experience being charged with items of such sacred importance, Laoghaire did not want to risk improper reverence to his new responsibility by leaving the items unattended in his family hut, so he opted to bring them with him. This felt, to him, to be the right decision and so he agonized about putting the sacred Sword into an un-anointed scabbard however, after consideration he knew it would be a great offense to enter the feasting hall with an unsheathed Sword; particularly as he had so recently been reminded, he was not of the Tuatha de Danann but of the Clan of the Calf-herders. It would be considered not only a great dishonor to the Tuath but a challenge as well, to enter the feasting hall in a posture that could be considered to be brandishing a weapon, no matter how innocent.

As each event of note occurred, the old woman stood, unseen among the people, with open ears while she kept a silent watch, observing everything as the night began to unfold. Craiche noticed the manner in which Laoghaire brought the sacred instruments into the hall and inwardly agreed with her old friend Faidhe that Laoghaire would take to heart his position of succeeding Keeper. He had intuitively known not only to bring the implements on this occasion, but he'd been cautious enough not to offer any reason to doubt his respect and reverence for the task that lay ahead of him by the manner in which he carried the Sword. *A most astute judgment*, she thought.

A new wave of chatter broke out as Lon Dubh and Iarann entered the hall together. There was a brief question at the door as to whether they would be admitted to the hall at all for Lon Dubh had never before entered the hall to partake in any prior feast and Iarann, despite the fact that he was half-God born, had not attended his table in the feasting hall since his Ethlinn had died. Consequently, the door watchers were unaccustomed to seeing either face at the hall and hesitated as to where they expected to be seated.

More than a few were surprised to see Lon Dubh and Iarann together, however only mildly so in comparison to seeing Lon Dubh approached by her sister and publicly embraced for it was widely known that despite their blood kinship, they had never hearth-bonded. Colm also offered Iarann a properly demure hug showing due respect befitting a family member. This was to be a night with much gossip to savor and so, because Iarann was not a member of either Keeper's family gossipmongers tucked away this bit of newsy prattle to be inspected later.

"My sister and the Smithy will have no need of their rightful place at their own tables this night." Colm announced to the doormen, reminding them and all who were within earshot that although it had been generally accepted up until now to subtly ostracize Lon Dubh, she still held a place of esteem within the tribe and could take a place at the Keeper's family table, whether the old Keeper or the new, anytime she opted to do so. But even more surprising to all was Colm's announcement made in the form of a request.

"It will be our great honor if my sister and Smithy Iarann will join my husband Laoghaire, the new Keeper, and our family at the Keeper's table. Will you share in our feast, sister and honor us by taking bread and drink with us?"

Her invitation to her sister and public affection for Iarann together with an invitation to the high table closed the gaping mouths and silenced the hall considerably for a moment, only to another moment later cause a new eruption of widened eyes and elevated chattering as all within the hall speculated about the rapid changes taking place within the Tuath.

Once again, Craiche scrutinized the vignette before her and was satisfied to understand that although she had never wanted anything to do with ascending to a position on the Hill, Colm was born to it nonetheless. Regal, strong, subtle, diplomatic, Craiche mused silently. *She'll make a strong partner to the Keeper...and perhaps an excellent Councilmember.*

Lon Dubh flushed with the invitation. "The honor will be mine if my companion will accompany me so, for I have promised to dine with the Smithy and would not vacate a promise even for such an esteemed invitation as you have offered, sister."

Turning to look up into Iarann's eyes, Lon Dubh wordlessly questioned whether he would accept the unprecedented invitation. She also wanted him to know that despite her newfound family ties, her loyalty to him and their quest as travelers would be her primary commitment, superseded only by her commitment to the Goddess herself. Iarann understood and smiled indulgently down at Lon Dubh, feeling pride in his association with one who held to her commitments and promises with such integrity despite the sacrifice it may exact from her.

A bit disconcerted by the watching eyes, Iarann bent low and quietly responded with his breath in Lon Dubh's ear.

"I am grateful and much honored to be included in these momentous events. I accept your invitation once again, to join you to feast Lon Dubh, and am humbled at the privilege to be made a part of the events unfolding here this evening and in our future." Then, disregarding his innate shyness he raised himself up to his full and considerable height, and with all the resonance his large chest offered, Iarann spoke to the crowd. "Come what may, I offer Laoghaire and his new Keeper-family my thanks and support in these changing times. For, as one with an educated eye in the magic of ore, the Sword offered to him from the Gods is one that will tolerate being borne only by a rightful and true leader. That this Sword was given to his hand and his alone, together with the protection of the Shield, it cannot be disputed that the Power to protect the clan and the Circle during these changing times will be carried out as prophesied by none other than the Calf-herder, Laoghaire, royal of blood and true of heart."

Not one to speak much at all and almost never one to speak publicly, Iarann was amazed at himself for he did not know what he was going to say until the words came through him almost as if from a burning flame rising from under his heart. He thought inwardly: *How appropriate it is that the Power of the Universe should come through me as if on the fire of my craft. But now, creations will come through me and I will be used as the tool.* Iarann's brow furrowed momentarily at that puzzling thought and put it to the back of his mind. His attentions turned back to his companion as he smiled down at Lon Dubh to find her looking at him with something akin to awe. He put his arm around her protectively once again to escort her toward the Keeper's table.

Craiche, at last, took her place at the head of the long Council table and leaned in to speak with Faeg and Brath, who occupied the seats for the fourth and fifth Councilmembers. As she wished, she'd gone unnoticed in the great hall while observing the events of the evening but even now as she turned her attention to her conversation with Faeg and Brath, her intuitive awareness was still keenly tuned to her surroundings. She sensed the unmistakable feeling of being scrutinized. Undeterred, she continued her exchange with the Councilmembers and sent out a filament of energy to search for whomever it was that attempted to pry upon her discussion. Amazed at her finding, as she covertly looked around, that the intruder was in extremely close proximity, Craiche mentally shouted with all the intention she could muster.

"Reveal yourself. These are not times to engage in furtive snooping. Your clumsy attempt at intrusion is unseemly and will not be tolerated!"

At that moment, screaming from beneath the Council's table attracted the attention of those seated and milling nearby. Struggling to free his bulk from under the table was Triag, son of Briciu, grandson of Gara, scrambling on his hands and knees. His progress was hindered by the fact that he had to stop every few inches to hold a stubby hand to his head and ears. Craiche took satisfaction that her spy had been outed and that he was most uncomfortable with her thoughts buzzing in his head. Triag looked as though the spirits tormented him as he waved his hands about his head. To the crowd he appeared as though he was under attack by swarming bees.

The disturbance at the Council table, while not unnoticed, was only one in a rapidly unfolding chain of events in the moment. The atmosphere carried the boisterous electric feeling of a festival with an added undercurrent of expectation. The noise of raised voices carried with them anticipation. Heads swiveled and necks craned with each event or new group that entered the building hoping to catch a glimpse of the Councilmembers or the enigmatic Keeper. Therefore, little note was taken of the pudgy boy's behavior.

At about the same time Craiche revealed Triag for a spy, or at the very least a snoop, Gara and Briciu calculated a well-timed entrance into the hall as the height of the crowd's anticipation reached a frenzied crescendo. Each was dressed in high feast finery and both Gara and Briciu bore the brooch of the High Council. Behind them were several family servants hoisting the first of the slaughtered steers prepared for the cooking spit on a great oaken roasting branch. Briciu made much of giving instructions on how to place the beast on the largest of three roasting spits at the center of the great hall despite the fact that the largest spit was not required for the rather small offering, which was not substantial at all. Then in an overly loud voice: "Take caution now, this is fine meat." Briciu announced. "Not to be cooked in haste. This fine young steer must be turned slowly and watched through the night to be washed in its own juices to preserve the flavor of the succulent meat. This is fine stock. Take care to turn the spit slowly."

He chastised the servants only to draw attention to his own self-importance for it would not be the servants who transported the carcass to the hall that would be doing the cooking of the beast, the Tuath had several cooks whose livelihood it was to tend the meat. In fact, they'd already been roasting two hogs and some mutton sheep on smaller spits since first news of a feast had been announced. Briciu's blustering was only to call attention to his arrival and of his family's offering for the feast; grudging as it was.

Amidst all the squawking and gawking at Briciu's dramatic call for attention and at Gara's outrageous display of wealth in her manner of jeweled decoration, barely noticed was Gara's daughter Nemain, who trailed the extravagant pair into the hall. A plain young woman with pasty skin and lackluster hair, she resembled her brother only in that she had the same darting, close set black eyes that seemed to miss nothing. Other than that, Nemain was skinny and easy to overlook for her withdrawn personality and quiet ways. Dressed even in her finest robes, Nemain cast an unremarkable presence. Her one claim to talent however, was that she enjoyed a reputation as one of the few who could make contact with tribal ancestors who had passed to the spirits.

Before recent events, it was this ability, Gara had often told Nemain, which might set her own daughter upon the Hill as Keeper. Inwardly though, Gara still harbored a notion that one day, if all could be arranged with proper bribes and a bit of magic, it would be she, herself, that might yet ascend Hill to be Keeper. She had the remarkable audacity to overlook the fact that she was well past the age of an initiate to the Hill but she schemed that if the Councilmembers outranking her were to accommodate her by going to the spirit side, there may still be a chance. And with these changes of late, Gara began to think the time was likely for her to move toward that end. *Now that Faidhe planned to relinquish her seat, only the old woman Craiche remained in the way. If she would not accommodate me by going to the spirits soon, well perhaps there might be something done to help the spirits call her home. That would leave me as First Council and with few to oppose me. I would fill the remaining seats with those I could easily purchase and the other two members are weaklings that could be outvoted if necessary.* However, if this could not be contrived, and she failed in assuming the position, then when the time came she would use her daughter as the likely initiate to the Keeper's position on the Hill for the sake of comportment. Either way, Gara had always felt that the power wielded from yon Hill would eventually be hers. Nemain would do as she was told.

Now, that witch upon the Hill and her brood had attempted to spoil her plans. But Gara could rise to the challenge. If she could discredit Laoghaire or perhaps more subtly, his wife, she thought she might even be able to use these recent circumstances to suit her own purpose.

Triag, still captive to Craiche as she occupied his mind, hoped to use the distraction of his father's and grandmother's grand entrance in order to escape the grasp of the old woman at the Council table however he was imprisoned by her warning voice inside his head.

"Hold boy!" She commanded.

He found himself helpless to move. Whether it was his own fear of the stories he'd heard of the old woman's magical capabilities or if she was actually commanding his body to be paralyzed into immobility, he knew only that he was helpless to move from the spot where he stood.

"What brings you to the Council table to have ears for that which does not concern you?" The voice resonated in his head.

Triag knew better than to reveal who had sent him or for what purpose, for the consequences from that faction would be something experience told him he should not risk. He shook his head wildly in an attempt to clear the voice from within. Strong in the practice of self-preservation, Triag instinctively closed his mind to the sensation that he was being mentally inspected by the power behind that voice in his head, which did not relent.

"Boy," it directed, *"reveal your purpose and I will deal with your sponsor directly rather than exact a penalty of you."* Triag recognized a bargain in the voice's tone and knew well the language of negotiation. He tentatively tried answering the voice in his head by responding voicelessly in the same way.

"Can you hear me?" He said, furtively flicking his eyes in the old woman's direction.

"I can."

"It cannot be known that my purpose was discovered."

"Speak boy. I've only to count on my fingers, those among your kin to see whose purpose you serve. State your intent before I am forced to call you out for all to consider. Is it not better for these matters to be handled with discretion? No one need know that I have come by this information and you will be free to fulfill your task by reporting exactly what I tell you to say you heard here. I'd wager you'll not find such an amicable arrangement offered if you're found to have not only failed in your pursuit but revealed who sent you as well."

Triag willed himself to look at the old woman to see if her promise could be trusted but he knew there was no choice. His father's threat of a beating was one thing, but when he went to his grandmother to see what value she might place on the tidbit of information he'd withheld from his father, he knew the risk of involving himself in affairs she considered important. A beating could and had been withstood many times but the price of displeasing his grandmother, or worse, failing her could be steep indeed. She held the purse strings in the family; she held the position on the Council that was the key to other positions of rank within the Tuath, she doled out reward with her favor and could wreak devastation when crossed. Fresh in recent memory her response galled him when, rather than reward him for revealing what he'd heard of the Keeper-woman's conversation about a journey with the strange one, Lon Dubh, she clutched his arm tightly and interrogated him to gather every fragment of information, word for word. She repaid him by requiring that he gather more information for her by finding out what is discussed at the Council's table in her and Briciu's absence. Triag was beginning to understand that this business of spying was not paying him the dividends he expected or felt he deserved. He resigned himself that he was quit of this business and allowed Craiche to gather the scene from his thoughts as he recalled for her what had taken place in his grandmother's hut a short while ago. Craiche knew Gara was ever eager to place her family members in advantageous positions but did not suspect that she'd resort means such as this at such a serious juncture for the Tuath to further her goals.

Craiche now understood that Gara saw these changes within the Tuath, not as events from which to draw upon to prepare for the spiritual future of the clans and the Gods to whom she has sworn her oath of loyalty, but rather as an opportunity to take advantage of the events to further her selfish causes of advancing family members, lining her purse and accumulation of power. Worse, Craiche also recognized that Gara could possibly do the unthinkable and begin to use magic for her own purposes. That would be a dark choice indeed, for the Universe does not take well to diminishing the gift by serving one's self through its use.

"Go you now boy. Report to your grandmother that Faidhe, the Keeper, travels east at the third great moon, just after the midsummer festival. The journey will follow a period of transition between Keepers, old and new, for the passing of knowledge to the new Keeper. Say she takes her daughter in consolation to save her embarrassment that she'll not be left on the Hill in service of the Goddess as Lon Dubh had hoped. Report you know not why the Keeper takes the journey but only that it is to spread the word of the changes in our spiritual future. Understand you this task?"

The boy under the best of circumstances resembled a swine, but his experience this evening of being preyed upon by so many with very little reward caused him to be red in the face and sweat through his linen garb so that he looked even more swinish than usual. He snuck another glance at Craiche and slid his eyes toward his grandmother. He knew he'd been defeated and to betray this dialogue with Craiche to his grandmother would only bring wrath from both sides for his efforts. He acquiesced with a nod of his head and before he slunk away, looked again to the old woman to see her gaze settle upon his grandmother.

Gara, a woman in her maturity had taken good advantage of her family wealth and her position on the Council to avoid even light labor over her lifetime. Consequently, she enjoyed being recognized as an attractive woman who looked younger than her years. The fact that she had fine clothes and adorned her fingers, toes, and sand colored hair with gem stones and seashells added to the fantasy of her reputation as a beauty. She kept several secrets of her attraction to herself such as, rubbing beet-root juice on her cheeks to add a youthful blush or marking her eyes with a subtle line of hard coal from the fire to give the appearance of dark and lush lashes. This and a bit of spell work to keep those with simple minds enthralled and captivated helped her maintain the air of mystery about her for many knew her approximate age but thought her truly blessed by the Gods with eternal youth. And there are those men who will know better, but will often let themselves fall prey to wiles of the likes of Gara. It was these on whom she depended most for support within the Tuath; those led astray without difficulty or put in compromising positions all too easily. Gara was cautious to keep these type dealings very discreet and well hidden from Councilmembers and clanswomen. She was shrewd in her dealings but knew when prudence was needed. Those who had a bit more mental acuity were able to see her as a well-preserved, yet middle-aged woman of 42 seasons but still knew little if anything about her secret dealings within the clan.

This night, though, Gara shamelessly worked the crowd in her own way. She stood close to men of wealth and consequently of some importance, she gave an intimate touch here, a knowing coquettish glance there. Gara was not above feigning to lean in to make a comment and unabashedly brush a promising breast against a recipient's hand or shoulder.

Once Craiche finished dealing with Triag and settled her attention on Gara, she'd quickly recognized that Gara felt there was much at stake now, to have been so publicly overt in her interaction with powerful and affluent members of the Tuath. Craiche considered all that had taken place this day and inwardly hoped that the next three days were enough for the eight clan members who gathered in the Smithy's hut to set into motion all that must take place and to do it without calling any attention from those who would seek to usurp the powerful positions upon the Hill and within the Council. A chilling thought then struck Craiche. *What if one or more of these few chosen to do this work, were to go with the spirits before the work is complete? Would the Gods allow it? Will they be protected? Are there those in the clan who would blaspheme this sacred task for personal gain?* Never having to think in such a fashion, Craiche recognized with stark reality that what she was contemplating was the possibility that members of the clan might commit murder in order to seize power. This type of thing was not unheard of, but looking around the hall at faces of the Tuatha De Danann, Children of the Goddess Danu, she knew in her heart that their time of peace and prosperity would soon come to a close. Their task was not only to help the Gods and Goddesses seek comfort and shelter underground, beneath the Sidhe, but to make preparations for all or most of the Tuath to live with the spirits as well. Craiche knew there would be deadly opposition to this advent, particularly from those who honored the Goddess only by rote and not with reverence. She would have to be stoic in her faith that the glimpses of the prophecy she'd seen was received with timeliness so that the work to be done might be completed. For if there is no hope, why then was the prophecy so sent?

———

After Briciu had enjoyed his moment, having all eyes on him as he clucked over the arrangement of the beef steer on the spit, he was anxious to move away from the heat of the fire. Anything beyond giving instruction and soaking up some recognition would be too akin to work and his linens were beginning to rumple with the film of sweat that was collecting on his skin. As he turned to slip away from the fire and get to his work to undermine the new changes in the power structure, he was already deep in thought. The way Briciu was calculating events in his mind, if a male could be accepted on the Hill as Keeper, then why not himself? He could certainly count on support from his mother and her nest of allies. Briciu knew that she had long begrudged the Keeper Faidhe her Power on the Hill and felt if Faidhe had stepped down sooner, Gara was the likely prospect for the spot but at her age now, she was past hoping to take the Hill herself. Briciu felt confident that his mother would see him as the most likely to rise to the task rather than his mouse of a sister now that the obstacle of gender had been overcome. That's one thing, he thought, that the old crone Keeper had done for him as if he'd planned it himself. She supported the logic that a man should now be on the Hill, indeed must be. He'd already proven himself as a member of the Council and had, in a very short time, built his own alliances with those who enjoyed the benefit of his association. He may yet attain his goal if he could discredit the Calf-herder severely enough to unseat him and take over the Power of the Sword and the Hill for himself.

His mind whirring, and his beady eyes aglow with the fever of his inner thoughts, Briciu was abruptly jostled when he turned to leave the hot fire and walked squarely into someone with enough force to have knocked them over and soundly startle himself. His jowls fluttered and his face displayed a comical look of fear resembling that of guilt, almost as if being startled revealed his inner thoughts to those around him. When Briciu heard a few snickers he grew instantly furious at being the focus of any joke. His temper ignited as he lashed at the young man sprawled on the banqueting hall floor.

"You there, boy." He said to the figure on the ground struggling to right himself. "Has your father taught you not, how to comport yourself around important people such as you find here this night? Get up now. I'll have your name and see you whipped; or better, I'll have your family of dullards levied for their remission in teaching a boy proper respect."

Fully expecting the boy to be duly fearful Briciu stood erect with hands resting upon his ample stomach awaiting a groveling apology to assuage his publicly bruised image. The fat on his neck hung like a ball of dough as he peered down his nose at the whelp. Rage caused the Councilmember to clench his teeth as the boy stood and his gaze met Briciu's with no evidence of fear or a forthcoming apology. What Briciu saw disturbed him. A quiet pair of eyes surveyed him. Those eyes were familiar to Briciu but he could not immediately place how he knew this boy however, he was mildly alarmed that he may have offended a child of an important family within the clan but dismissed the thought for he knew if this was a boy of one of his or even his mother's many cronies, it would matter not. He calculated, there are not many others who would matter and as for those who do, the matter would easily be smoothed over. *Power is a wonderful thing* Briciu thought to himself. Yet, he wondered: *Who is this boy who looks upon me so boldly?*

"Have you nothing to say boy? From what hearth do you hail? Who is your family?" After a pause with still no response, more impatiently, "Come, come boy. Know you who I am? Let's have this business done with. Who is your family?"

Feeling publicly affronted now that the boy did not satisfactorily grovel, Briciu began to feel uneasiness tickle under his breastbone. He peered more closely at the boy to determine his connections. Had he been one of the early families that traveled from a nearby camp? *Those eyes. I know those eyes. Who is this child and how does he dare meet me with such brazen silence?*

"Ah so you must be simple then. You cannot speak. Truly evidence of your poor breeding then? You must then be a servant boy come in mock finery to serve the betters of the Tuath." Briciu goaded.

About to approach the boy, Briciu hastily checked himself when he felt a gentle hand on his shoulder and a soft voice speak into his ear. Though the voice was spoken in a low, intimate manner, it could be heard clearly for very suddenly, all in the dining hall near the cooking spits went silent as if on cue.

"The boy does come from a humble family. I, as his father will take punishment for any disrespect he has shown to you this night. Surely, it *must* be my remission in teaching Macha the proper way to address those of rank in the Tuath that has caused your displeasure. He certainly has led a simple life when compared with someone of *your* import. Pray, what is it he has done to offend you so?"

Briciu spun around so swiftly as to almost upend himself; ready to direct his wrath at the owner of this voice who had the nerve to put a hand on him. What he was met with was those same thoughtful brown eyes but flashing in these, was a twinkling of glee that exuded a humor in which Briciu did not at all feel inclined to participate.

"Laoghaire." Briciu said flatly. In a quandary how best to approach this situation without looking the fool or relinquishing his position as the one offended in the circumstance at hand. Briciu saw the situation as an opportunity to come away with the new Keeper indebted to him or better yet, to publicly place Laoghaire in a subordinate position in what was now a battle of wit and words for spectators. "Your boy, indeed has but to apologize to me to put this matter to rest but he seems not inclined to do so. Perhaps you can speak sense to the child."

"I certainly plan to, Councilmember Briciu. What is the crime he has committed that would warrant a levy on his mother, Colm and myself? Surely it is a despicable act to so deserve to be whipped at a time of celebration? I did hear you correctly, Councilmember, did I not? Whipped? I confess, I do not know my son at all for I would not have though him capable, at the age of only seven summers, to commit something worthy of such a punishment. I ask you again Councilmember, what is my son's crime so we might have his punishment meted out swiftly.

Briciu winced at the third use of his proper title offered by Laoghaire realizing that this man, although not officially, holds the highest station in the hierarchy of the clan, the very position to which he, himself, aspired. Briciu now understood his predicament. How could he justify punishing the boy for lacking to show due respect to a clan leader when he was so deftly ushered into committing the very same offense? Trying to look, at the same time, good natured and magnanimous, Briciu offered response.

"You are, of course, correct and ...ah... as you are a new servant of the Hill," avoiding acquiescing any valid title to Laoghaire but showing no disrespect, "I am inclined to overlook the whole incident in light of the celebratory occasion."

"You are a kind and generous man, Councilmember Briciu. I would be in your debt for such a favor."

At this public statement, Briciu felt a flutter of excitement, for debts and promises are taken very seriously by the Tuath. If one gave their word on a promise, it was a contract. If one was indebted by a kindness, a price could be exacted of the debtor's choosing. Of course the debtor would have to balance the degree of indebtedness with the favor owed. It was a careful balance but considered as the very best kind of debt for a man like Briciu.

Laoghaire continued, "But alas, I would *again* be remiss in my parental duty, should I let my son walk away from such a generous man as yourself without paying full penalty for his crime. Let us settle this now and decide how many lashes will be given and what type of levy will be paid for the crime." Laoghaire turned to Macha and asked firmly so all could hear.

"Macha, what is it you have done that has upset the Councilmember so? Have you insulted his family name?"

The Boy's brown eyes widened with the question posed that he had done something so unthinkable. He answered, abashed.

"No father!"

"Have you disrespected the Councilmember's ancestors?"

"By the Goddess, no Father." Macha was now warming to his father's game-like questions.

"Cursed his family?"

"Again I say, not, Father."

"Ah, then you must have taken something of his that does not belong to you."

"No, once more, Father." Macha smiled as he began to understand what his father meant by asking such outrageous questions of him.

"Well then surely it must be horrible for these are the worst things I can think of that would call for such a punishment. Son, you truly must have betrayed all that I, and your mother have taught you, to have done something that would call the wrath of so great and fair a man as the Councilmember Briciu. Confess it now and we'll get on with your punishment. What is it you have done?" He solemnly knelt down in front of Macha and took on a mock-serious tone for a moment. "A ferocious attack on the Councilmember?" Laoghaire said smiling at his son while wiggling his eyebrows up and down.

The boy giggled out loud as he realized they *were* playing a game of sorts. He took his father's face in both his hands and said imitating the tone his father used in his questioning.

"Father, I confess it. I tell you my crime: I was found to be in the place where the Councilmember chose to walk. I was in the place that was so rightfully his that he deemed to knock me out of it. Right to the ground!"

"Well, what was so important that it brought you to be in the Councilmembers place?"

"It was himself, the Councilmember, Father."

Again, Laoghaire raised his eyebrows but this time in surprise. "The Councilmember Briciu?"

"Yes Father, he was so proud of the beef steer that he'd brought for the feast, I wanted to see what was so much better about his steer than ours. He was telling everyone how fine the meat is, and us being cattlemen as well, I wanted to see what wisdom the Councilmember had to have such special stock...especially because the animal on the spit seems to be so small for such a great number of people to feed."

At this, Briciu reddened.

Macha explain further. "Indeed, Father, I would not have been in the Councilmember's space if it were not for my desire to improve the meat we produce for the clan so ours is worthy of the boasting that the Councilmember Briciu does about his stock." Then leaning closer to his father's ear, "But Father, then I realized that you already know about the animal that is on the spit so I thought you must have had something to do with why the meat is worth so much pride."

Now truly puzzled at what his son was saying, Laoghaire asked, "What mean you Macha? I know of no secret to create a better tasting meat other than constant care over the stock."

"Yes Father," Macha said, growing weary of the audience, "you must, for this beast on the spit is the very one you tended for the Councilmember just this moon past. You can see for yourself that on its haunch can be seen the mark of the very same wound you cared for with my help."

When it was clear to Laoghaire what his son was telling him, he was deeply disturbed but outwardly smiled at Macha. He stood to face Briciu and spoke for benefit of the crowd that was still intent upon the drama.

"So, the mystery is solved Briciu. My son meant no disrespect and found himself an affront to your importance only to do you honor by wanting to learn from you of your renowned herdsmanship. You would not punish the boy for doing our craft the honor of seeking to raise better cattle for the sake of the clan. Would you?"

Although Laoghaire still bore the stamp of congeniality on his face, Briciu sensed a shift in his stance and demeanor that made him wary. Eyeing the Sword at Laoghaire's halfstrap, Briciu thought better of his pride and made a dismissive gesture as though he'd truly decided to forget the entire incident wanting only now to be shut of the whole thing. As he made a bow toward the pair in mock generosity, Briciu spoke to the boy.

"So you've come to learn from the best, eh? Well even I won't fault you for that. No harm done at all. But stay not so close the flame next time, one might be knocked into the fire and we wouldn't have that now, would we?"

Making to leave the spit area, Briciu could hear the crowd examining all that had just taken place and he was relieved to have the spectacle over with. Scowling to himself, he feared that he might not have come out as the victor in the war of wits with the Calf-herder after all. Nor did he like how smoothly Laoghaire slipped out of a debt that would have been a tidy gem to have tucked away for the right time. Eager to get to the real work of the night, Briciu was unpleasantly called from his inner grumbling when he heard Laoghaire call to him once again in a tone that was low, clipped and certainly would not be ignored.

"Briciu, a word in private." Laoghaire walked past the portly official and out the door of the dining hall without a look back making it clear that the Calf-herder fully expected Briciu to follow. It was also clear that during this exchange, there was no formal title of respect attached to the address.

The outrage! Briciu was affronted but knew until he could unseat this outlander from the Hill, he would have to play along.

"Certainly, I'll be there momentarily." Briciu said. Hesitating a full count of fingers, before he followed Laoghaire out into the night not only to assuage his pride but to collect himself as well. Until now, he had not much dealing with the Calf-herder beyond cattling. Although Laoghaire was quite comfortable by cattle count, and was supposed to be of some sort of royal blood, he was of little consequence within the Tuatha De Danann...until now. He was not involved in Council matters, nor was his wife of any consequence aside from her relation to the hag on the Hill. Briciu had never regarded Laoghaire as having any value to him other than the occasions when one of Briciu's livestock needed good medicinal care beyond his own staff's abilities. Briciu always regarded Laoghaire to be a pleasant man who knew his place, was appropriately humble and who healed Briciu's cattle when asked. In fact, Briciu thought, it was a privilege for Laoghaire to be favored by such an important family as his own to call him for duty. Briciu thought it was understood, that Laoghaire could capitalize on using his dealings with Briciu's cattle to earn a name as a healer of cattle and charge whatever price he desired of others. Working for Briciu and being in his favor, in his own eyes, was reward enough for anyone smart enough to reap the benefits. And since, after his first time tending a sick calf for Briciu, Laoghaire had refused payment, Briciu thought they understood each other and considered their relationship a mutually beneficial arrangement. *Now,* thought Briciu, *this recent (and temporary) development in the clan's power structure has made this outlander think overmuch of himself to speak to me so.*

Briciu adjusted his face to his best neutral pleasant, straightened his back, a trick he used to accent his more than average height to better look down his nose, and fortified himself to speak as he must with this troublesome cattleman from some back-corner kingdom.

The Councilmember's first impression after stepping out into the cool night air was that he did not recall the Calf-herder being quite as substantial as what he saw before him. It would be difficult for Briciu to look down his nose in a lordly manor at a man who stood fully two inches taller than he. Slightly disconcerted that his usual bluster and trickery had not shaken this man into recognizing his inferiority within the Tuath, despite his recent claim to power, he was after all, only an outlander. Perhaps, if the Tuath had had some noteworthy battles of late, he might have made some distinction as a warrior. Briciu reassessed the man before him standing in the chill without a cloak and bare arms; he did not appear to feel the cold. Bearing the Sword and with the Shield slung over his back, Briciu thought with some fascination, that Laoghaire indeed, looked quite warrior-like. But as it was, Briciu's comforted himself with his opinion that Laoghaire is just a lucky minion, fallen into an undeserved position of power and affluence that he could neither live up to nor possibly know how to cultivate. Briciu decided this conversation would be endured so it would provide him with an appraisal of his adversary to see how he might best oust him from his claim to the Hill and was not prepared for the conversation that ensued.

In his usual punctilious manner, Briciu began, "Fear not Laoghaire, all is forgotten and there will be no grudge against you or yours. In fact, I see how much pride you take in your son. He seems a fine boy, if a bit enthusiastic."

Laoghaire was usually inclined to let Briciu bluster during their past interchanges. He understood that one with no real substance depended greatly on title and inflated reputation to ease inner knowledge of his own deficiencies. Those rich in cattle or in position often thought that what they had to say was important simply because they thought they were important. And quite often they took for granted that others thought what they said was important as well. He did not mind suffering Briciu's nonsense, as usually, it did not involve anyone enduring injury however this time Laoghaire was outraged.

"I am not come to beg apology for an offense that was not given Briciu. You seek to blame another, a boy, for your own clumsiness but even that affront is not why I called you out.

Unaccustomed to anyone speaking so plainly, Briciu sputtered an automatic denial. "Certainly you can see that I was generous in letting your whel...

Laoghaire flared. "I come not to trifle with the means you use, pathetic as they are, to save your over-bloated sense of dignity from embarrassment. I come to you out of courtesy for the occasion and to keep peace within the Council and between your family and the Hill. I come to offer you an opportunity to save your precious reputation and that of your mother's for as my 'whelp' has pointed out, you show disrespect, nay contempt for these events taking place by fulfilling your mother's offering of two steer with a single, diseased adolescent farrow and attempt to pass it off as quality veal meat!"

"You dare say slander and in such an insolent tone!" Briciu spat in disbelief. "Heed well to not let this travesty of new power make you drunk and commit grave error Calf-herder." Pointing to the Sword he said, "You bluster about with your new toy as a young boy with his first bow. Take care not to think over-highly of your position for it may be that you will not sit a-seat on the Hill overlong."

Laoghaire stepped menacingly close to Briciu so that his breath could be felt upon the Councilman's skin as the Keeper spoke.

"You cast threats upon the Hill then?"

Briciu immediately recognized his mistake and set about retracting his statement but he knew that to repair the damage would be difficult at best.

"Certainly not. I am not accustomed to being spoken to in such a fashion. I retort to defend my honor and family's honor." Then quick to change the subject, "Now what say you about this tender calf I offer in the highest regard for the occasion? As a cattleman yourself, you know there is no more tasty or tender meat than that of a calf. Less to offer, yes but better to savor."

"The animal on the cook-spit is no calf. It is an adolescent heifer. And as my boy pointed out, it has the unmistakable mark of my own surgery where I cut away blackness of dead muscle this moon past. This heifer did not foal this season for being so sick in her blood. You dare feed this meat to clan and kin? Give you no thought to safety in foodstuff? Know you not better than to save from eating a diseased animal before a full season has passed? We speak not only of honor here Briciu we speak of betrayal to offer tainted meat to the unwitting. Tell me this was error cattleman, or is it you are so penurious that you offer not the full weight of commitment to your promise of two beef steer for each night of feasting? As it is, there is only one beast to see to your offer and *it* must be removed from the spit."

Briciu calculated quickly what story might skulk his way out of this situation.

"Laoghaire. Keeper." He simpered. "You know I am overburdened with business of the Council. I admit I did not oversee the slaughter of the animal as such a duty warranted." He lied. "Instructions were given and I trusted that my staff carried out this task as I'd ordered. In my haste to bring a splendid offering, I did not inspect the meat closely. Your boy himself recognized it as a small beast did he not? Surely you see an easy mistake for a calf of good veal meat?"

Laoghaire was struck by the tale with incredulity so as almost to humor. "Is it your truth that you know not the difference between a calf and a heifer, cattleman? How is it you have operated animal husbandry thus far? Know you the difference between a heifer and a bull or which has teats and which hang ballocks? Perhaps we should be thankful that it is the bull's task to decide which end of the heifer to mount?"

Briciu contained his impulse to respond with threats to the jibes and tempered his response to ease out of the difficulty.

"Of course, you joke. But the truth is I was saving the real prize offering to be used as a grand gesture. Truly, I will look into the mistake and if it is so that the meat is as you say from a sickly cow, well then, I'll rectify the situation immediately and make the announcement about the offering of such value that even a herdsman such as yourself cannot deny its worthiness. I...ah...well, one such as yourself, em, born with a look that draws the eyes of the women cannot know how those of us with a plain countenance must use what we have to partner at the festivals. You must admit," Briciu leaned in to share a moment of solidarity, "maidens are much more pliant to the coupling if there is promise of money or reward in the offing so you can see how a show of a fine animal from my stock would loosen up a leg or two."

Laoghaire was amazed and horrified when Briciu gave him a conspiratorial elbow in the ribs. *Just us boys duping some maiden out of her most precious gift from the Gods.* The new Keeper quelled his repulsion and wondered how he'd never seen the gaping hole in this clansman's honor before this.

"See to it that no one is fed of that meat Briciu. Make of your excuses and presentation of proper meat what you must but see that it is done."

Briciu swallowed his gall and responded. "You take on your leadership role quite adeptly. I wonder is this charge you take on a force from your God-gifted Sword? I wager you'll have no need of large offerings, now you have this rapier, to find the maidens sinking down to comfort you by the feasting fires."

What Briciu thought was a bond that all men shared with a wink and a nudge, that all girls, save his mother of course, when they came of age, were taught that it was their gift to be fertile and to play the role of the Goddess of fertility as often as possible so that the men could bed with them more easily. Sometimes the ruse that sex was a sacred act would get in the way of him reaching his goal when he was just in the mood to rut, but he considered what a difficult task it might be for him if there was not occasion at every feast and ritual to enjoy the rut as part of the celebration.

Laoghaire worked to contain his anger but retorted.

"I have but one woman to share my fire and have no need of offering my marriage gift to any but her. Unless I am called to do so in ritual on the Hill, I would die before dishonoring my word and my oath to keep to my marriage bed. It is sore business that I find your honor so diminished that you use show and bribes to cheat a maiden out of what she'd proudly give in honor of the Goddess. You make sport of the sacred for little more than fleeting pleasure and that is insult to all we hold sacred. A change in your ways would be beneficial for you and apparently those around you. I find this attitude and the heifer business disturbing indeed Briciu. I offer this, not in judgment but rather as advice. The Goddess will not favor those who behave so."

Laoghaire offered this last and turned to reenter the hall leaving Briciu looking after him with a sour look of hatred eating at his back.

"Give me advice will you Keeper?" Briciu hissed through clenched teeth. Muttering to himself as one whose spirit was afflicted, Briciu stomped away toward his cluster of huts to locate some servants to set his budding plan in motion...and to beat in order to relieve his mounting frustration. Someone would pay dearly for the way he was feeling.

16

A Gift

Faidhe knew little of the goings on in the feasting hall as yet. She'd found the need to rest for a few moments after she'd left Craiche by her hut with an embrace and a promise to meet with her and the others of the Council at the feast. Feeling taxed after such a day of journey, magic, emotional reunion, and intrigue she required some much-needed solitude. Faidhe followed where her feet led her and breathed an indulgent sigh of relief at finding a quiet spot next to a small spring fed pond in the wood to reflect in seclusion before attending the feast. She knew it was important that she attend all gatherings over the next three days and nights to help solidify all that must take place before her journey but with still so much to be done Faidhe knew that a vessel must be replenished or it would eventually offer naught but emptiness. So Faidhe hiked up her linens and removed her doe-skin slippers to sink her feet into the cool water to replenish her energy. Though she could hear the distant sounds of the feast getting under way, she noticed that, with her attention turning inward, her ability to see the spirit of the living things around her had returned. She reflected that it never actually left however, as she tended to the task of being with other people, her observation of the spirit world remained more on the periphery of her consciousness. Now that she had a moment to quiet her thoughts, she glimpsed all manner of colors, lights and darting energies around her. Surrounding her own person she saw the lovely vibrant cobalt blue that she had come to think of as a decidedly feminine energy, yet more; perhaps a pure energy of munificent and altruistic origin. Faidhe had begun to see this color in particular among all the other colors around her and recognized it as a visual adaptation of the very life-spirit itself. The spark of life that emanates from within.

Faidhe lay back, knotting her hair at the nape of her neck to use as a cushion against the ground and to keep the specks of woodland stuff from catching in her tresses. She let the cool waters slip between her toes as she looked up to the constellations above. The night was crisp and clear. Faidhe enjoyed the far off sound of pipe and string music as it drifted on the air together with the faint homey scent of wood smoke. She found it increasingly difficult to think clearly on what must be done in preparation for what the next few days might hold. The tinkling music of the water swirling around her feet kept rhythm with the teasing notes of the bard-song just out of hearing. Flashes of the prophecy and the happenings of this day played across her mind's eye. Her beloved Circle home of 35-sun seasons until just this day seemed nothing more than a memory now.

Has it only been one day? Faidhe's mind whirred with a collage of thoughts and mixed emotions. Daughters that were always at a painful distance, suddenly and joyfully at her side. The curious vision of Lon Dubh that had been given to her these ten harvests past. The new way of seeing things she had to adjust to. The sacred Sword and Shield having come out of the very Cauldron she carried, given to the new Keeper. *How poignant*, she thought, *that the time of the Goddess's period of influence was symbolized by a great bowl, the very womb of humankind. Now, as the time of transition occurs, the symbols have transitioned to those which offer symbolic balance between the masculine Sword, and the feminine Shield, a circle typifying protection and proliferation of life. How fitting now that both the masculine and feminine will serve atop the Hill! Ah, but what of the Cauldron itself that will travel with me? It too is seemingly balanced with the masculine for as I now journey, I must have the support of the Staff to heft the great bowl even with help from the sprites. Masculine Staff supports the feminine Cauldron as carried by me a woman, and the masculine Sword wielded by Laoghaire, a man who is protected by the Shield...the feminine.*

Faidhe mused the dizzying synchronicity in the pattern of how events had so rapidly developed this day past and allowed her mind to drift and her feet to sway in the waters. She gently rocked with the waters as she listened to the night sounds and smelled the fresh water while watching all manner of life around her. She watched in a jubilant fascination as she witnessed her own blue life spark dance and swirl above her torso and was not at all surprised to see very small wisps of the same deep, earthy green she'd seen surrounding Laoghaire earlier this day beginning to intertwine with the blue. *The very balance that is taking place around me is also manifesting within me. Of course it should. I strive to bring balance to the spirits and humans alike. Naturally my own spirit will bear evidence of that mission.*

The sound of the woods around her became more prominent with the music of toads and tree frogs joining that of the cricket. The leaves of the trees shushed along being played by the breeze. The rhythm of the distant drum skins increased in volume until Faidhe became aware of the volume of the banging growing closer to where she lay. Soon, she realized that what she heard were not drums, but peals of thunder perhaps. Faidhe turned her eyes to the sky once again and saw no sign that a storm approached. Growing alarmed at the impending rumbles, Faidhe sat up quickly to devote all her attention to the thumps to determine from which direction they came. Thumps became crashes as something large lumbered through the wood from the east. The sound of saplings being splintered and snapping like so much kindling seemed to be rapidly nearing the spot where the woman was resting.

Faidhe reassured herself. *Get hold woman. Are you not chosen to walk the land to carry the hope of the future? All manner of strangeness must be endured for you are one who walks in two worlds now. Greet not your confrontations with wide eyes and a-quiver. Bear up!*

With that, Faidhe rose up to face whatever it was that came her way. Standing upright, her hair unwound in a spinning ball until it was again unbound and stretching toward the earth. She sent out a tendril of her energy to seek out and identify the source of the sound and was perplexed for what she felt through yon trees was both there and not there. It was substantial in size and Power and somehow diminished, ailing. As Faidhe strove to identify who or what came in her direction she felt both the familiarity of kin and the newness of a stranger met. She decided that whatever approached, it would be an encounter that is yet another facet of all else happening this day. She waited.

Trees split and cracked over as twigs. The fresh perfume of pine escaped into the air. Faidhe watched as the energetic stuff of life oozed as so much mist from the rented trees and noticed on the periphery of her thoughts that the dying trees let off a much lighter green than the deep green she'd just been contemplating. Bushes separated as if a huge beast trampled through on the hunt. The noise grew to deafening heights and stopped mere steps from where the wise woman stood.

"Make yourself known." She commanded. "You've created such display of your advance it would decrease the dramatic introduction were you not to show yourself now." Determined not to be fearful, Faidhe chided the phantom. "What business have you here? Have you come to hear news of the great changes ahead for us beings or have you come to gawk at the old woman down from the Hill? Make no mistake, if those who engender to foil what has been prophesied have sent you to do me harm for their own gain, I carry great weight of Power from the Gods as this is a righteous cause I am charged with. Be warned!"

Without a conscious thought Faidhe flicked her wrist and in her hand appeared the great Staff that typically bore the weight of the Cauldron. Vibrant blue emanated from her and illuminated her piece of the woods all around as she crooked the hooked end of the Staff under her left arm and pointed the blunt end in the direction of the disturbance. Poised to do battle, to any observer, she was a beautiful and terrible warrior.

A great laughter resounded in the wood. Its very echo rang in Faidhe's head and ears deep and strong.

"Daughter, you are well chosen to the task of protecting the clan and serving the Gods. Your willingness to battle does you credit but know you not the difference between the time to wield and the time to listen?"

Faidhe cocked her head to one side as if she *was* listening but she was cautiously working out in her mind who or what this entity might be. Again she sent out a tentative feeler to see if she could recognize this strange energy. The familiarity with which she was struck caused an overwhelming feeling of nostalgia to well up under her breast. But still, in her state of uncertainty, she could not identify her visitor.

Faidhe became impatient with her inability to be precise about who this energy is and her irritation could be detected in her response.

"I've not occasion to linger here about. If you have matter with me, state it. And show yourself! If you have no reasonable business with me, be gone."

Another great reverberating laughter boomed at that and Faidhe was amazed to see the figure appear faintly at first then with some vacillation, become a solid and ample being in front of her.

"You are right little Faidhe. We come with drama and showiness in our return to this lovely isle. And that is much of what it is, as you say, just a spectacle of bluster. Truly, it is evidence of the unbalance that is taking place in the world at present."

Faidhe stood astonished at what she saw before her. She felt emotions of great joy and confusion for the being she now could see was Dagda, father of the Gods and the Danu, great mother of the Tuatha De Danann; embodiment of the feminine triad, The Triple Goddess. Faidhe was struck silent at the sight, for both the God and the Goddess were joined together in a churning, swirling, ever changing being. The body smoothly transformed from that of a young woman to the great hulking mass of the giant Dagda and then to the seemingly fragile frame of a crone and again to that of a woman obviously great with child. Bewildered, Faidhe was fascinated with the being she beheld but the faces of her beloved God and Goddess constantly changing from one to the other, from youth to maturity was what held her eyes wide and affixed.

"Check your countenance Little One, for your mouth is agape." Said the Goddess being. "We have long been accustomed to fear, awe and reverence upon our appearance but not often do we encounter such an unconcealed gaze!"

This last was said with good humor but unaware that it had been hanging open, Faidhe snapped her mouth shut.

"Danu...Mother." She started, and faltered. Then, "Dagda? I...I am at a loss. Forgive me." She restarted, trying to collect herself. "Forgive me Great Ones. I am overwhelmed at being in your presence. It has been a great many years since I have had such an honor."

"And I'm guessing we appear more than peculiar to you at present." The Danu mother creature said with a smile. "Let us make you more at ease with our appearance for the duration of our visit with you now."

Faidhe witnessed the two beings within the same body turn and face each other as though one was superimposed upon the other and at the same time, both took one great step backward. The sound Faidhe heard as they did this was that of a loud sigh and tearing linen in unison almost as though the beings had to tear a place in space for it to accommodate both of them where only one had been just moments before. Upon their separation, Faidhe fell to her knees to bid them welcome and to offer respect.

"Mother and Father, giver of life and bringer of the seed, I am here to serve you. Please honor me with your indulgence and forgive my harsh words for I knew not who you were and the need now for protection of myself and ways that honor you, I fear, has grown."

Danu continued to display the triple aspects of her feminine expression. First, she appeared as a maid in her youth. Her face young, her body nubile with but a hint of budding breasts, a face pretty but not yet fully formed with character, crowned with longish unbound chestnut colored hair. Just as quickly as the eye could recognize the appearance of the maiden, Danu's shape changed once again to a woman in her full blossom of beauty. The hair, full and lustrous cascading over well rounded breasts as they spilled out, bare, over the top of a leather binding about the middle. Her face displayed knowledge and wisdom. That of which she had knowing was revealed in one continuous, smooth motion as the leather binding unraveled from about her waist and the loose white material beneath began to swell and separate revealing the belly, swollen with the growing child within the womb. Her engorged breasts gleamed with sweet milk at the ripened nipples, identifying the nurturing mother, ready to suckle. Then just as swiftly, the breasts grew thinner and slightly pendulous. The Danu's shoulders and hips thinned while her hair, at first streaked with gray, became slightly brittle, then straw-like and finally white. Her face, while still holding the remnants of beauty in her eyes was now stamped with lines beside those eyes and yet they held within them such promise, Power, and knowledge of many things. Suddenly and only momentarily shrouded in black woven wool, the old woman seamlessly transformed once again and held the juice of youth within her skin and was for a second time the pubescent girl waiting for her womb to ripen.

When she spoke, Danu's voice bore the echo of three voices at once offering the listener the realization that whichever aspect of the Goddess spoke, the information or comments came with the full Power of the knowledge of all that is born, all that creates, all that is learned, all that has died.

"Faidhe, Daughter of the Hill, child of my heart, you have been faithful and ever strong. Indeed, we have chosen rightly to offer you the task of keeping safe the knowledge of the spirit."

After a few more moments, the triple manifestations slowed and the voices of Danu collected to one voice. When she spoke next, her voice was singularly strong and she bore the outward appearance of a radiant woman fully seasoned to childbearing age but not yet bearing fruit. Faidhe could smell the scent of both the Goddess and the God in such rich and earthy splendor that she immediately thought of her encounter with the Greenman that took place an eternity ago during this very day. Faidhe instinctually looked to the Dagda, as if for confirmation that she had indeed spent time with the great masculine energy and that it was not just part of an elaborate dream. He acknowledged her unspoken question.

"Yes. You have been visited with a great many lessons, one of which was given in the wood today in the aspect of the Green, and you will be in company of a great many more before your work is complete. These visitations come to you now but as our strength grows dim on the earth-side, you will find it necessary to seek out audience with others of our kind to draw knowledge from them but to also inform them of what is to come."

"Inform them?" Faidhe was alarmed. "How can I inform them of that which has come from them?"

Dagda's face took on an expression of great sorrow. His massive shoulders slumped with a weariness Faidhe would not have thought could touch the Gods. The eyes that looked at her somehow seemed silvery in color that diminished the deep brown she had known them to be. With compassion laced sadness he enlightened her.

"It is not a plain task you have taken on Little One. But for your strength, will and commitment to us, and your faith in us, I fear we would be lost to humans at this juncture in the earthly happenings as respect for us diminishes and is usurped by avarice, lust for power and personal gain. And so our Power and influence in this world falters. Our strength to manifest here grows weak. Already the rot of greed has taken hold of many to varying levels across the lands. Even those who would still hold us in esteem for what we can bestow have faded in their quality of prayer and offering. Time spent in pursuit of other endeavors has increased while attention to matters of the *Universal Spirit* has become rote and secondary. Your task has facets great in number Faidhe. You must not only impress upon peoples of this land and those beyond, the need for balance in the veneration of both the masculine and feminine, but you must take the word and spread the cause throughout the worlds of both humankind and the spiritual to enlist those who have it, to focus their Power upon this task in order that it create the changes necessary to carry forward the cause, deep into the future. So you must arrange things in the present in order to preserve the future. This must be done physically, spiritually, and energetically, binding the old to the coming of the new so that all the Old Ways will be brought forward on a great wave of change in order to reemerge at a time in the future when it is most needed. For this, we must prepare. The gifts of the *Universe* must be carried forward in magic and in blood, Faidhe. Your blood. You will plant these seeds. Blood of your blood will play the roles needed and carry forward the words until such time when blood reunites and creates the portal necessary to birth a new era and to rebirth that which has been ushered forth."

Faidhe paled to a ghostly gray, stuck by the awesome task for which she'd been chosen and lamented what this would mean for her daughters and grandchildren... blood of her blood. She shared her self-doubt.

"I am but one woman. I have enlisted the help of few and there are many who would undermine my success for personal gain. How is it that I am expected to change the face of ritual and how people have perceived spiritual hierarchy since time out of memory? Will my family be forfeit to this cause?"

"You have more ability than you know Faidhe. Since you were a small child and saw we two dancing under the sacred spring as Sun and Water, you have had extraordinary magical ability. You have spent many a harvest season developing your skill and keeping to your duty. But in that duration, you have lost much of the natural craft to recipe and intention. You always have unfathomable skill at your behest but over the years you have unwittingly resigned your skill. Now is the time to reclaim your gifts and use them in the name of this cause. And you must remember that you have but to ask for help and it will be given. We were most pleased to see that you've begun to reclaim your gifts so instinctively."

Dagda said as he tipped his head in the direction of the Staff upon which Faidhe was now leaning. Faidhe was almost surprised to see what she held in her hands. She recalled the moment it came to her hand but was only now amazed at its presence.

"The sprites?" She asked.

"For now. As our chosen vassals, yes." Danu answered. "These sprites, faeries, brownies and Elven folk give of themselves to offer help in our service. You have but to think of what is your need and it will be instantly arranged. As you become more confident and practiced in your ability to draw upon the *Universal Power*, you will no longer require the help of the sprites, although, they will ever be available to serve you. Have a care not to call upon them for that which you can do on your own. They will not serve the lazy, but they will serve the needy. Your need to call upon them will grow less with time. You may eventually draw upon the *Universal Power* completely on your own as it serves the benefit of humankind and thus serves us."

"Who is 'us'?" Faidhe asked.

"All who live, Child. Us is the earth, the suns, stars and planets, greenlife, the trees, crawling things, the animal stock, humankind, those in between the two, centaurs, merfolk, waterlife, as well as those in the spirit, God and Goddess in all our forms, masculine and feminine alike from the smallest sprite to the greatest energies and all other forms of the living: ancient giants, the Firbolg, Fomorii and many more you have yet to come to know."

"Ah" Faidhe began to understand. "We should each serve to the benefit of all, so the subject sprites who aid in carrying and keeping safe the great Cauldron do so, not only for me, but for you and the cause before us and for the future of human-kind and spiritkind alike. Do I speak true?"

Dagda explained. "For the greater part you understand correctly Faidhe but the sprites are not subject to us just as you are not subject to us. They have free will, as do you. But they are ever at the ready to assist you in your time of need for they understand that all living energy is interwoven and if the physical plain is overwhelmingly corrupt with self-indulgence and disregard for the whole, then so too will the spirit grow weak. Then no one of us will be able to sustain our strength and the Power; and in turn will not be able to serve or nourish those who seek our help. Everything serves the other. The sprites serve you, as you serve us, yet we serve you, humankind, and the sprite as well."

"How then," Faidhe continued, "will I hone the skills of which you speak? Will the sprites teach me or will I come to the knowledge by simply acting on intuition as I did this night summoning the Staff to me in my time of need?"

This time Danu answered. "You will develop abilities you never imagined were possible Faidhe. What you are able to do is all of your own ingenuity. Often times there are those who are able to achieve or create great things to suit a particular pur-pose and will never again be able to repeat the skill. Perhaps the ability is designed by the need for the moment. What we can tell you is that you must *believe* the skill you desire is there for your use. For if you question whether the Power to create or to manifest your need will be there for you, the very act of questioning will diminish your success. You must *know* your need will be fulfilled upon petition and so it will be. Until then, the sprites and spirits are here to protect and support you."

"Why then, do I need the Cauldron or the Staff if I have but to call upon the *Universal Power* and my need will be satisfied?" Faidhe probed earnestly trying to grasp all the knowledge she was able.

"There are certain places on the earth," Dagda told her, such as the Hill Circle that bring forth or emanate a stronger measure of the *Universal Power* than others. Do you agree?"

Faidhe nodded and agreed, "It is true."

"The implements of which you speak, the Cauldron and Staff, and others still, the Sword and Shield, are but implements made with great care by drawing on the

Universal Power at a time out of memory when the Power was much greater than what we utilize now. Because these items were created of the Power using magic that had been directed and distilled a great many times over, they are not only symbolic of the Power, they are imbued with the Power to serve a specific purpose and an actual manifestation of the Power. To that end, these are conduits for the Power and greatly compound the energy when called upon to perform the task for which they were created."

"What then is the task for which this Staff was created? For it came to me so readily when I called for it when I thought I was in danger. Is it a war club?" Faidhe inquired. "Am I to carry an instrument of death?"

"An easy assumption Faidhe." Danu broke in. "But think on what it was you were protecting at the moment you called for the Staff."

Faidhe looked at Danu then at Dagda and tried to calm her raging thoughts so that she might concentrate on exactly what she had been thinking and saying when she'd called, quite instinctively, for the Staff. She focused on the moon's light, a tiny sliver reflecting on the pond water and watched the listless waves halfheartedly reach for the verdant beach. The night sounds increased as she turned her attention inward to recapture the moment when she'd flicked her wrist and knew, she *knew* that the Staff would come to her. Then she was certain that it was not her own safety she feared for in that moment, but the work she had ahead of her. She understood that there were people in this very Tuath, people of the Danu and the Dagda, who would strive to foil her plans and her journey and she called for the Staff, knowing that it is a tool that imbues one who wields it with the mark of leadership and righteousness in his or her cause. Faidhe's eyes brightened as she returned from her almost trance-like state and brought into focus the Goddess and God once again.

"It is a Staff for one who journeys with great news to be told." She now smiled. "I have been perplexed as to where I will travel and what my purpose will be in the excursion but now I feel a great release from my burden of the unknown for though I know not to whence I travel, it will be knowledge that will be clear to me when I ask for it or when I need to know. Am I correct in this notion?" she asked.

The Dagda and The Danu both seemed to breathe a sigh of relief and showed pleasure on their faces at this last. Danu took Faidhe's hand into both of hers and kissed it. Dagda stepped up behind Danu and enveloped her in his arms. Danu stepped backward toward Dagda and they once again became a creature of one, in union speaking in a voice full of echoes.

"Yours is a path never before taken Faidhe, and we understand that carving a new trail is often challenging, for vision is limited and difficulties lay hidden but know that we are with you in all our forms, great and small, to see that you have every opportunity to succeed in that which has been assigned to you in prophesy."

The God-dess placed their hand on Faidhe's breast over her heart and at the same time took up Faidhe's hand and laid it on their own breast. Faidhe could see the face of Danu before her and just before she softly pressed her lips to Faidhe's mouth, she informed her.

"A gift for you Little One, my daughter." Danu parted her lips and Faidhe's open mouth was awash with sweet breath and the fresh taste of clover blossom causing her own mouth to water with the clean, sweet flavor of Danu's kiss.

Faidhe's body flooded with sensations from time out of memory. She experienced the familiar sensation of youth surge through the muscles in her legs buttocks and torso. Her arms felt at the same time weak and vibrant. The woman's skin tingled under her hair and from her scalp to her feet, she felt invigorated as if she'd just come out of the cold pond water. From under Danu's hand, Faidhe felt her heart pumping with the strength she'd not felt for a great length of time. And if not for her encounter with the Greenman earlier this very day, she would have found other sensations in her body quite a distant memory as well. For now her body was called to full attention of her womanhood as if she'd been infused with all the stages of the Danu's femininity: twinges of her eggs ripening, nipples being brought to tender pink, breasts engorged and trickling, silky warmth between her legs. When Faidhe opened her eyes, she was met with the gentle smiling brown eyes of Dagda and felt the fullness of the promise of his seed between them against her abdomen. Faidhe felt as if she would wholly surrender once again to the call of the union but just then, with a faint popping in Faidhe's ears, the figure in front of her was gone.

Faidhe looked around her and saw no evidence that what she's just experienced had taken place at all. The trampled bushes were as before the visitation. The trees that had been snapped were upright and undamaged. There was but a dim scent of the previous overpowering odor of pine. Faidhe felt confusion at her body's reaction to the closeness of the Goddess and God but at the same time, enjoyed the moist warmth she felt below and the sensation of her sensitive nipples being teased by the slight roughness of her linens. She puzzled as to the meaning of the gift that was mentioned and wondered as to what that might be. She took a moment to organize her mind around what had just occurred and then put it away for later contemplation. For now, she had work to do. Faidhe put on her slippers and stood erect for a moment in the wood facing the moon and raised her arms above her head and called out.

"Mother and Father of the spirit, I thank you for your visit and wisdom. I feel the vital force within me that will help me to forge the path ahead of me. This new liveliness and strength is treasured as I feel renewed to my task now that all the physical pain and fatigue has been drawn away." *Ah, so there is the gift!* She thought as it dawned to her how wonderful she felt. *I have been gifted increased strength and fortitude. Or perhaps that comes coupled with the knowledge that the Universal Power is there for the asking if only I believe it will be.* And with this thought, Faidhe was put in mind of another thought she'd had in the past and was chilled with the reminder: *Be careful for what you petition the Gods may grant it in ways that are not at all convenient.*

With this she turned, using her hooked Staff as a walking stick, toward the great feasting hall, steeling herself for what lay ahead.

17

The Traveler

We were in our usual positions to navigate the road, Nora with her face buried in a crinkled map of Ireland and me exercising the right side of my brain driving on the left side of the road. Heading south for the small town of Midleton in County Cork we were both a bit dazed due to the meager five hours sleep we managed the night before. I thought briefly about stopping for coffee but I wasn't quite as crotchety today even without getting my morning dose. Maybe I was finally adjusting to the time changes here or it could have been my new crow cawing alarm clock, but for the first time since landing in Ireland, I found myself awake, showered, dressed, fed and on the road by 8:00 a.m. A respectable time to justify my feeling as though I'd actually accomplished something despite the fact that we really didn't know exactly where we were going to look for a man who, by Cath's description we would find if we would, "Just ask about town for his lately address."...Lee O'Leary, super sleuth.

The day was brilliant with open blue skies and great volumes of the kind of clouds that, when I was a kid, urged me to lie down in the grass and release my mind to find what shapes that would be revealed in the billowy folds. I resisted the urge as I maneuvered the car over the inadequate country roads. We drove by pastures that ambled up and down the hillsides sliced into square portions by stone fences that fed into one another with a small opening from one to the next. They reminded me of stone mazes for the cows to puzzle out. The weather smiled on us with 75 degrees and a fresh scent in the air that said, *"Breathe deep this is what air is supposed to taste like."*

So I took in a great lungful of sweet air. With the windows half down and almost no traffic we were able to actually mosey along and take in the countryside scenery as it scrolled across our windshield. The lushness of the fields was breathtaking and an impossible green that would not exist, were it not for all the rain this side of the island drinks in. As we traveled southward, the green pastures dotted with cattle gave way to a more yellowish green that reminded me of new shoots on a spring tree. The herds of beef and dairy cattle thinned out to make room for the sheep that became a more frequent feature of the changing landscape the further south we journeyed.

"Okay." Nora said in a no nonsense tone. "We're going to see this guy to find out more about what Cath told you yesterday, so what did Cath tell you that makes this trip worth taking? Does it have anything to do with what happened last night? Those guys?"

I thought for a minute about whether there was any connection that I could determine between the spying brothers down the hill and what Cath had told me yesterday.

"If there is, I don't see it. The story Cath told me was a folktale about the mythological roots of Ireland and how, historically, Ireland has been able to preserve its early beliefs and cultural traditions through this, ah...I don't know, kind of a secret, I guess, kept over time, a long, long time until the right time in history to let the secret out."

I was a bit hesitant to actually share the entire story with Nora, fearing that even after all that has happened she'd give me her *you're crazy* look and tell me to turn the car around. I took in a deep breath and I thought: *In for a penny, blah, blah.* I resigned myself that Nora would have to know just what I was chasing here and she'd also have to know what I'd shared with Cath about our family and ultimately what he'd shared with me.

"The truth is, Nora, I...came to really like Cath yesterday. And I know it sounds a little crazy but I trust that what he's telling me is the truth."

"And?" She waited.

"And - well, the thing is, the story he told me, I think, actually has more to it than just a tale of lore. I think what he told me is actually what's going on here with us and all this paranormal activity." I hedged.

"You mean the old lady and the smell around the cottage?" She asked.

"Well, yeah but not just that. I mean the way the cottage sort of drifted between times and the way my abilities seem to have, um, improved since we've been here. And the crow with you yesterday. The book. Everything. Me being invisible to you. Or maybe just you not being able to see me, however you want to look at it. I don't think we can ignore that something is going on with us since we've been here. And it's not the ordinary experience everyone has when they come here to visit. You have to admit that things have been pretty strange around us since we've been here."

"Lee, I don't deny any of that. I see what's been going on and there've been some little things that have happened to me that I just took in stride but haven't mentioned. So, really, you don't have to convince me. What do you know that you're holding back?"

I took the plunge. "Well, Cath told me a story yesterday that had to do with a family in ancient Ireland, before it was Ireland, before it was Hibernia, before the Christians, and even before the Celts. He told me a story for, what I thought was going to be included in my research. But as he was telling me, it sounded really like one of Grandma's tales. You know how she used to tell us and we thought she was talking about people she knew from the ol' country?"

Nora nodded and I knew she wouldn't comment because she wanted the full story now with no interruptions. I obliged.

"The way he told it, I was totally sucked into it just like I was when Grandma started to tell her stories. He said somewhere between 3000 and 4000 years ago when people were more like we are with the abilities to see and create things with, ah, magic, I guess. He called it 'the Power'. He said, like you hear in the myths, that this was a time when the Gods walked among the people and could intermingle with them. But it was the beginning of the end of that time. There was a family who was charged with a task of preserving their magic and somehow spun it together and, well I don't know, kind of cast it forward in time to hook it together with the Christian religion as it occurred a couple thousand years later. The magic of those old traditions sort of attached itself to the new religion as Christianity blossomed and actually changed the face of how it developed throughout history. The magic served as a kind of secret ingredient that enabled Christianity to take hold, particularly here in Ireland in such a way that paved the way for the Old Ways to re-emerge in society when the time was either just right, or most needed. I'm not exactly sure about that."

I stole my eyes away from the road to have a look at her to see how she was taking all of this in. There was no expression that I could read. At least she wasn't giving me the *skeptical look*. I pulled the car over to a small shoulder in the road.

"C'mon, let's get out for a few minutes." I said.

We hopped out of the car and over a split rail fence with a bit of rusted wire fencing between the rails. About 20 yards into the field there was an old dolmen stone which is two larger stones planted upright in the earth with another stone laid across the top. Aside from the fence itself, and one tree off in the distance, it seemed the only place around for miles to be a logical choice to sit. Ireland was dotted with countless numbers of these structures as a reminder of the ancient civilizations that were here for many thousands of years. I thought this would be an appropriate place to sketch out the tale for Nora.

"Let's sit here while I tell you the rest."

We climbed up on the capstone that was angled so one end of the stone was lower and close to the ground and the other end angled toward the sky. Once on the top, we both sat sort of hugging our knees into ourselves for a moment as though we were steeling for the rest of the tale; her hearing and me telling. When I became aware of what I was doing, I released my legs, stretched them out straight and lay down on the stone to look up at the sky, and then Nora did the same. I began again.

"The story goes: that from the time when all this started with some kind of prophecy, each generation from several chosen families across western Europe selected two members of the next generation to pass on the history of what happened when the Gods went away. Those two people from each generation of each family were sworn, by some kind of oath of honor, to pass on the story exactly as it was told to them, word for word, to two people of the following generation so that the story lived without deviation and would survive even if one of those chosen people died before they got to pass it on. The people who assumed this responsibility were selected very carefully for their integrity and faithfulness to be able to carry out the task. Once they had securely passed on the story to the next generation and were sure it was committed to memory, then the older storytellers were charged with spreading the story to all who would listen in a somewhat altered fashion using symbolism and metaphor so the secrets involved weren't revealed but that the story lived in the wider population. Whether in song or poem, or whatever, it was spread so that it would survive time itself, maybe in fractured form or in a mythological tale, but in plain sight so to speak, so it would reach a time when it should be told in its entirety and the power it carries is released upon the earth to bring back the Power and knowledge of the Gods before the earth is destroyed." I finished this last in a rush, hoping Nora would accept what I was telling her.

Nora interrupted. "Destroyed? Destroyed how?"

"Well, I don't really know. I just know what Cath told me about the story itself. He didn't give me all the minute details. But the thing I found out that is really the exciting part is this guy we're seeing today, Finny McDonough, is supposed to be one of those people after hundreds of generations that's supposed to know the story! He's known by locals here as a tinker or a traveler but according to Cath, he's supposed to be one of those chosen people that has learned the entire history of the story!"

I could feel my excitement rise at the prospect of documenting such a phenomenal tale. Nora became quiet. I waited.

Finally she inquired, "Why haven't we heard about this through Grandma or someone if it's such a widely known story?"

"That's just it. The way Cath tells it, we've probably heard parts of the story our whole lives from Grandma and in other ways. He said there are even common fairytales that have fragments of the story but that when the story is revealed in its entirety for the world to hear, that's when the time will be right for the power to be released. Nora, remember the book you read yesterday, The Power of the Word? Well, I think that's involved somehow. It may be that the time for release is drawing near and we're somehow wrapped up in it."

"Lee," she said. "I admit there's something going on here that I can't explain but I think you're being a bit dramatic. I know how your work consumes you and this is like the Holy Grail to someone who has the academic agenda that you do. You came here to find a link between ancient pagan religions and current day fairytales and such, and someone just hands a whopper to you on a silver platter. Doesn't that seem just a bit convenient? Don't you think maybe you should slow down and just hear what this guy has to say before you decide to buy it all? I mean after all, selling stuff here is the stock and trade of these people and Cath made a pretty penny from us. Maybe he's trying to send us to a friend to see if lightning can strike twice."

I did tend to dive, head first, into a project and think about the depth of the water later, but I was loath to admit it. I had such high hopes for what a story like this would unveil or prove, particularly if it could be somehow documented so far back in history. I was a bit disappointed that she was being so logical but Nora was making sense. I was hoping that with what I hadn't yet told her, she would at least be open to some possibilities.

"What else?" She said finally.

I knew better than to try to keep something from Nora. We were just too close in the mind for me to conceal something from her. Particularly something I was so excited about.

"Well, remember when Cath got all funny about my name the other day?"

Nora nodded.

I pushed on. "He said that there was some part of the story that had connections similar to what my name is. Or, well not exactly. Parts of the story say something about people in Europe who are waiting, even now, for someone to come along with a certain name to indicate that the time has come to begin the process of releasing the Power. And Cath said that over his lifetime, there have been only two people that had possibilities as being that sign or signal, but I guess they didn't pan out. But he said to me yesterday that my name is one that he wants to investigate." I raised my eyebrows and looked at Nora expectantly.

"What name?' She asked. "Lee or Lenore? And aren't there lots of people who've walked around with both of those names through the centuries? Why does he think you're so special?"

"Both my first name, Lenore and our last name, O'Leary together sparked his interest not because they are the secret code or whatever, but he said because of how I was named, what they actually mean, and the significance they carry together." I was hopeful she'd understand my excitement. She was blunt.

"Did it occur to you that maybe Cath is a con man?" It hadn't. And hearing her say it was like throwing cold water on me all at once. "Think about it. You went to him looking for a story and he wasn't interested in talking to you until you spent a lot of money, then he gave you a whale of a story. But not the entire story, just a teaser. To get the whole thing, you have to go to someone else and probably have to pay him for something too. Just to keep you on the hook, though, you just happen to have a role in the story. It sounds like those fortune-tellers that Nana used to take us to see when they told us we were 'connected to royalty in another life' or 'going to change the world' and we both know how that turned out.

Nana, our mother's mother was an unusual woman. She didn't cotton to the church ways and she chided our mother for trying so hard to fit in to the church mold. But despite their similar views on the church, she wasn't too fond of our father, thinking that somehow, he was the reason that we were being raised with knowledge of the Catholic religion. It was odd how Nana saw things that way because she'd married a Catholic man and had her own children raised with that same knowledge. I always felt as though she'd married our grandfather for deep love but regretted that the church was a part of the bargain. Maybe she chose to blame our father for the Catholic influence so she didn't have to recognize that it was really our mother who insisted on our involvement with the church. Denial is a great illusionist.

Our Nana kept some strange traditions in her home that mimicked those we'd seen in our Grandma and Grandpa's home but hers were traditions with a decided edge to them. Sometimes almost even scary. She's recite things in the clipped Swedish tongue while hovering over a boiling pot or while dropping some smelly additive into a home brew of skin remedy or poultice she'd make for people who came to her for such things. She was one of those in the exciting, secret circles of people who make poultices, told fortunes and spoke in harsh tongues. We were intrigued and it was novel and interesting when she'd take us to see the fortune-tellers. She would, at the same time, make fun of their accents and colorful clothes but underneath the superior attitude, we could tell that she took very seriously the news they gave her. She had particular interest in taking Nora and me to see Gardenia, a dark and beautiful woman who had been fond of big jewelry and the color purple. We were privy to many trips to see Gardenia for tealeaf readings and palm inspection. It was as if our Nana was searching for something about us. I never knew what that was or if she found it. We just enjoyed the cookies Gardenia gave us along with the tea and felt the whole thing mysterious and entertaining. But believed none of it.

"It all smacks of a con, Lee." Nora brought me back to the present. "Do you really want to waste your valuable research time on something like this?"

I was so hoping that Nora was going to be as thrilled at this idea as I was but now with a good dose of the cold water cure thrown on me, I saw the truth in what she was saying. I heaved an exasperated sigh.

"I guess I see your logic. An attitude of cynicism is a good idea until we get the truth about what's going on here."

"You're still planning on going to see this guy?" She asked.

"Nora, look. Let's not forget about what's happened to us since we've been in Ireland. *Something's* going on. Especially with the book you were reading yesterday and its potential connection to the story Cath was talking about."

"Yeah, but it was Cath you bought the book from. Maybe that's where he got the idea to tell you the story he did, because he knew you'd eventually read the book and his story would be corroborated."

"I don't know, Nora. He seemed so sincere to me."

"Well, on that score." She surmised. "Maybe he isn't a con man and actually believes the story. That doesn't mean it's authentic."

"I guess that's why they call it research." I said. "I've got a lead, let's just follow it and see where it goes. Besides, I don't think Cath could plan what happened with you and the giant raven yesterday." Nora nodded at being reminded of her run in with the corvine clan.

"Okay," she said. "I get your point. But please, let's just be cautious about this McDonough guy. Alright?"

"No argument from me."

We left the dolmen stone to return to the car. I felt somewhat relieved at having told Nora about what Cath said to me about this living story but I was deflated too at the prospect of being duped by such a sweet old man. Actually, I was a bit sad. I liked Cath and I didn't want that possibility to be true and I felt a bit traitorous to think of him that way. I decided to hold onto the truth that I'd shared much of our family history and abilities with Cath. Nora had enough doubts about everything without adding a new worry to her list about being exposed or having actually given someone a small demonstration of what our magic could do.

Back in the car we were silent with our own thoughts for a while. Nora paid attention to the map for something to do and I was glad I was driving to occupy my mind. I tried to piece together all that had happened since we'd arrived only a few days ago and I kept drifting away from the task of arranging those circumstances into some kind of logical meaning and found my mind sneaking back to the story and my possible connection with it. My mind finally surrendered after chasing around in circles for some miles and decided to let things drop until we met Finny McDonough to hear what he had to say. I suddenly felt last night's lack of sleep catching up with me.

"Nora?"

"Hmm?" She answered, still looking at her map.

"You think we could get a cup of coffee when we get to Midleton?" I was glad for something neutral to say to her that was not just inane conversation. It occurred to me that a cup of coffee was just the thing for me to focus on and then to actually partake in. It would get my brain firing so I could think about all this without being muddled. I pushed the sniggling word *addiction* to the back of my mind when I thought of how relieved I'd be when I could have a cup of coffee and finally think like my old self.

"Sure. "We should be there soon and we can ask at the store or coffee shop about where to find Finny McDonough. This should be interesting." She said with a twinge of sarcasm but then let it go.

"Good." I said. "I really have to use a bathroom too."

We pulled into the gas station parking lot at 11:30. I wasn't sure if they had a convenience store too but I just couldn't wait. I needed to go, now. It looked old, but clean enough. I just hoped there was a restroom. I pulled in fast enough that people stared. There was a slower pace around the countryside and I attracted attention when I'd zipped into the filling station too quickly to suit the locals.

"You coming?" I said to Nora.

"Yeah. It doesn't look like they have food or anything. Just looks like a regular gas station. I'll come in to see if anyone knows anything about the mysterious Finny."

I didn't like her tone of voice. I'd felt like after last night we'd be working as a team to figure things out but now after telling Nora about what Cath had said and that his story might involve me somehow, I'd felt doubt coming from her in waves, about Cath and worse, about me. I was glad she'd agreed to come with me to see Finny in spite of her doubts. It would be good to have another set of discriminating ears to listen when Finny told his tale. The worst part about everything at this point was that after hearing what Nora said, in the light of day, I'd begun to doubt what Cath told me. What made perfect sense to me yesterday in the warmth of his store, with a full belly, kind of rang a bit foolish now that Nora had pointed out some obviously fantastic coincidences to me. But I kept on because, con men or not, I was on the trail of what might be an authentic folktale anyway, if slightly modified.

I whipped into the vacant parking spot just beyond the two ancient gas pumps and jerked the car to a stop just a little too fast so the wheels gave a little chirp. Heads turned again and people stared as we headed into the gas station to inquire about a restroom. I was the first through the door and was amazed that the gas station probably looked as it had 60 years ago. The two men with unmistakably Irish faces were both in green uniforms with yellow piping and over the left breast on each uniform was a yellow patch with embroidered nametags. The older, red-faced gentleman was 50ish, with a bulging belly and brownish curly hair. His tag displayed the name Thomas, not Tom but full-out Thomas in script. The younger, kind of pie-faced one, labeled Angus, was about 20, had perfect teeth, not a common sight around these parts that I could tell, and was thin, white skinned, with a raging head of red hair. The older man, Thomas, asked if he could help us. I looked around doubtfully.

"Do you have a public restroom?"

The smile seemed to have faltered on Thomas's face just slightly and he surreptitiously looked behind us to see if we were at least going to have them pump a little gas for their trouble.

Angus reached automatically for a key that was attached to a giant brass ring hanging from a nail on the wall behind the counter and began to hand it to me. Thomas had looked as if he was going to tell me there were no public facilities until he saw Angus holding the key, looking indecisive as to whether to give it to me. After another moment's hesitation, Thomas mumbled that the bathroom could be found around back. And just for good measure to exact some price for the usage of his restroom, Thomas snapped.

"You'll be returning the key directly after ye've done yer business and securing the lock against the travelers."

Angus looked chastened when he heard that, but smiled at me as he handed me the key. I accepted it gratefully, mildly embarrassed at being spoken to in such a way. *Done my business?* I wondered if I was considered a traveler to them because we were, for all observations, to the locals, just tourists. I turned and rolled my eyes at Nora as I headed out the front door. Nora apparently decided not to ask the grouchy Thomas about Finny and followed behind me. We found our way around the building as I was thinking how odd that everything seemed to be in such a time warp here. I hadn't actually used an "out back" restroom since I was a little kid back in the '60's. And my memory of those childhood emergencies were vivid with warnings from my mom:

"Don't touch anything! Don't sit down! Flush with your shoe. Make sure you wash your hands. Use a piece of tissue to open the door when you're finished. And *always* lock the door when you're in a public bathroom." The litany came flowing back like a wave of paranoia but they were lessons well learned and I'd steeled myself for the conditions I might find back there behind the lonely door in the backside of the station but was pleasantly surprised to find the restroom although just as old as the rest of the gas station, was also just as neat and fully equipped with soap, paper towels and toilet paper. The bonus was that it actually smelled clean. But Mom's words ran deep so I followed strict public restroom protocol and came out with the giant brass ring feeling both relieved and germ-free. I was met with an expectant look from Nora who was waiting her turn with the question on her face asking *how bad is it.* My mother's words obviously echoed in her mind as they had in mine.

"It's not bad." I said in answer to the expression on her face. I handed her the big key ring and sternly warned her in mock tones to, "Return the key directly! Don't touch anything! Don't sit down! Keep out the travelers! Wash your hands."

Nora couldn't help but giggle and it broke the temporary silence that loomed large in the small car for the past few miles.

"Meet you out front,"

Then she jammed the key into the lock as the ring clanged against the door.

I walked around to the front and was obviously being eyed by Thomas who was keeping a sharp watch out for the return of the bathroom key. I entered the service area of the filling station once again to put Thomas at ease in case he thought I was planning to jump into the car and make a fast getaway.

"Do you know how far it is to Midleton?" I asked the men.

It looked as though Thomas had reached his limits in patience with me but just at that moment the service bell chimed to call one of the men to pump gas. I think Angus understood that Thomas was percolating to a lather and ignored the bell to answer my question so Thomas was forced to go help the paying customer.

"You're just outside of the Midleton line. If you follow Rte. 25 another few miles south, you'll come to the center of town."

I did a double take at Angus and he smiled at the shock on my face that he'd spoken to me with a clearly American accent. Not only American, but also obviously a Bostonian. He said you're as "yoah" another as "anuthah" and center as "centah" in the typical Bostonian way of dropping the "r" from the end of a word.

"Where are you from?" I demanded in a friendly tone.

"Southie." He smirked.

I laughed out loud at the irony that Angus lived just a few miles from where I'd grown up and I came all the way to Ireland to meet him.

"Oh not Southie; that's just too cliché!" Southie is a part of Boston that is widely known for its Irish population.

"Yeah I know. I get that a lot when Americans come through. You know Southie?"

I cocked a thumb over my shoulder to indicate toward the rear of the station where Nora was *doing her business* in the restroom.

"My sister and I, have an aunt who still lives in Southie. And we grew up in Dorchester." Although both areas bordered each other and were both predominantly Irish when I was a kid, there was always a bit of rivalry in Irish pride between South Boston and Dorchester. I guess that rivalry held fast to Angus's generation because he didn't seem to be all that impressed with my Dorchester background but asked after our aunt.

"An aunt huh? Where's she live?"

"South Broadway," I flipped back in an off-handed way that said, *I know Southie, and I know the neighborhood.* In other words, *I'm cool.*

He nodded as if to say I was okay by relation. If I had a living relative in Southie, then, it was as if I could be kin. I was amazed that the old, hard lines still existed in Boston and even more so that it had reached all the way across the ocean.

"How did you come to work here?"

"Family. I come over every summer. Have since I was little. It was my folk's 'keep 'im busy and off the streets program'. Now I'm older, I work steady each year for my uncle." Poking his chin in Thomas's direction.

"Ah. A cuddly man." I said trying to keep a straight face.

"Ah he's alright." Angus defended.

"Listen," I recalled my original question, "Midleton?"

"Oh yeah, just keep on 25 and you'll see where it comes out to town."

I spied Thomas finishing up with his customer and hurried to ask further."

Angus do you know of a man named Finny McDonough who lives in Midleton?" He seemed to ponder that for a moment and said,

"Should I?"

"Well, no I, ah, I know this sounds weird but someone sent us to speak with him but they didn't have an address for him. They just said when we get to town to ask around. That people would know where he is. So I thought I'd ask."

I reached up impulsively to spin the wire rack holding a variety of maps. They were of local towns with local attractions. I didn't think I'd find the directions mapped out, *(Finny McDonough's house, E-4)* but I didn't think it would hurt to have local maps with a bit more detail than the AAA map we'd been using. I selected a few maps and asked the price just as Thomas re-entered the station with Nora right behind him holding the key and ring. He saw me purchasing the maps and Nora return the key. Thomas seemed to be assuaged a bit at these events but just to make sure he gruffed at Nora.

"Are you after lockin' the door then?"

Her eyebrows shot up and her pride reared at being spoken to like she was a child. She leveled a 'Nora' look at Thomas as only she can do and with an overly sweet response dripping with condescension she replied.

"All safe and sound." Giving him a placating pat on the forearm.

He seemed to deflate at that, and appeared a bit embarrassed that he'd made such a grouch of himself over the use of the restroom.

"It's just that the travelers are always comin' in more and more and usin' up the facilities and such. It seems lately every Tom, Dick and Tinker is about the countryside sniffin' round fer news of the road and they all come te freshen like it's a boardin' house I'm runnin'." He looked forlorn.

I was glad to have purchased the maps at least, now realizing that it could be infuriating if everyone came in to impose for directions and bathrooms but didn't buy anything. They would end up costing the poor station owner money. I guess he was just trying to run a business. With this more empathetic attitude I tried to save the moment.

"Nora, Angus is from South Boston."

The dry moment between my sister and the station owner had passed as her attention settled on the younger man.

"Really? Did you tell him where we're from?"

"Yeah. But he seems more interested with where Aunty Helen lives." I chided in fun that it hadn't escaped me he'd disregarded our Dorchester roots. "But he was just about to help us find Finny McDonough to redeem himself by helping two hometown women abroad."

Angus responded amiably to the ribbing. "I'm sorry, I don't know if I can help you with that. How about you Uncle? Do you know a Finny McDonough from Midleton?"

"Most folks do. Ye have learnin' to do? Thomas replied looking inquiringly.

"We have an appointment with him today but need directions." I said, wanting the instructions to Finny's house but not wanting to reveal my business.

At that, Thomas almost guffawed. "An appointment is it?" But immediately caught himself for being rude and suppressed his mirth though his eyes continued to twinkle. "I can give ye instructions to where yer likely to find him."

I opened my newly purchased map of Midleton and located Route 25 with an index finger. Can you show us from where we'll pick up 25 on the map?"

Thomas seemed to grunt approval not only that I'd bought a map, but also that at least I knew something about where I was going...for a tourist. I silently thanked Angus for telling me the correct road earlier because normally Nora does the navigating and I'd have no other idea of where I am or where I'm going if not for Nora's instruction. He began reciting the instructions and pointing to the map with his big sausage fingers. Nora and I listened and watched his finger etch along roads on the map until his final instruction. "...and as ye go around the church into the back, ye'll see the graveyard. Ask after him there. If he's not there, you'll find someone there who'll give you further instruction."

I looked at him to see if he was pulling my leg and decided that Thomas was not the leg-pulling type.

"Is he a grounds-keeper at the cemetery or something?"

"Well he might make a penny or two doin' the odd job there but that's not somethin' I'd be keepin' track of."

I didn't quite understand what it meant that we'd find Finny in a graveyard that he may or may not work in but I nodded my head as though it made perfect sense.

"We really appreciate you taking the time to help us... and Angus, it was really nice meeting you." I said.

"You know, this is the cleanest gas station I think I've ever seen." Nora added sensing something more was needed. "The restroom was a pleasure." I thought she was laying it on a bit thick but Thomas's chest swelled with pride of ownership.

"Well, it's Agnes, insists on the extras in the toilet. Agnes is the wife. And it's herself says those things make the difference."

I wondered if he considered paper towels or soap as extras in a restroom but somehow, I liked Thomas better for having a thoughtful wife. It meant that she loves him and maybe sees the redeeming things about a man that only the intimate can. I especially like that he gave her credit where it was due. My opinion of Thomas had warmed. I offered genuine smile to the gentlemen, took my new maps thanked them once more. Then Nora and I headed back to the car and today's adventure.

We were stopped by Thomas calling after us saying from the filling station door. "Ye'll give Finny McDonough my regards if ye've a mind to do it? And tell 'im how ye came by instructions?"

I hesitated for a moment, trying to comprehend what Thomas was saying through his accent. When I understood that he's wanted me to say hello and tell Finny who sent us, I smiled.

"Okay, we will." Then we were in the car and off down route 25 toward Midleton and the Holy Rosary Cemetery. "Well that was easy." I said referring to finding directions to Finny on the first try.

Part III; The Beast

18

A Challenge

Gara watched Laoghaire with the intensity of a cat watching its prey as she searched for any weak spot: in his family, commitment to his new position, or anything she might turn to her own purpose. He was wealthy in cattle; there was little possibility of a bribe there. He had relinquished his claim to a royal position in his own clan to marry Colm so an offer of title would not sway him and he'd already been given the most respected position and title within the clan. His commitment to his woman is evident. She had not even heard of him taking part in the fertility festivals with any other than Colm even though it would be perfectly acceptable for either of them to take another for the rites. So there is little room to persuade him with promise of the delights of her own womanly experience beyond perhaps a simple dalliance; nothing that Gara could see blossoming into an alliance between the two.

What a pity. She thought as she contemplated what such a liaison might involve should she be able to coax Laoghaire to her bed. Gara allowed her eyes to drink in Laoghaire's bare upper torso as he playfully hoisted each of his children onto his shoulders. She noted how his muscles moved with apparent ease to sustain his twins aloft. She meditated momentarily on the strong legs she viewed underneath his tunic-like linens until her thoughts turned to what other gifts those linens might conceal and how she'd take slow pleasure in revealing them. In that moment, Gara sensed attention directed at her in a focused manner. She became immediately aware that this attention was not just a passing curiosity she'd often felt due to her being a powerful woman of the clan, but rather a concentrated energy meant to seek out her attention in a most direct fashion. Gara scanned the faces of those around her to determine the source of the bold attention when she glanced across a face with a gaze that was most candid and not at all friendly. She steeled herself for the approach of one whom, prior to this very day, had never amounted to having any value or consequence to Gara. But she knew not what to expect from such a one as would confront her now. Perhaps this was the opportunity for which Gara searched. While a dalliance with Laoghaire might be an enjoyable distraction, the path to Gara ingratiating herself to the Hill may be through this one who approaches. Gara pulled herself up to her full height and pasted a smile on her face while extending her hands to the advancing woman.

"Colm." Gara soothed but there was salt in her words in order to establish the order of command. "I bid you good fortune in your unexpected rise to notoriety and offer my assistance to you in taking on the hearth duties of the Hill. Worry not over the simplicity of your wifely position. There is no shame in your lack of experience or in needing help in tasks for which you have had no preparation. I am at your service in helping you in the proper ways to direct the clan in rituals and protocol. As I hear it told, the retiring Keeper will have not time for such training. Once again, I fear, you are to be left on your own to learn and fend, as she takes on important duties."

Colm approached Gara and did not stop until she was standing within an intimate distance from her. To the general crowd it appeared as if Colm had taken on her new role as the Keeper's wife quite adeptly and was sharing pleasantries as well as any other involved in the politics of the Tuath. Inside the cocoon of their moment together, Colm was pleased that she could feel Gara's impulse to step back but was not surprised when she did not. Though the smile did fade from Gara's face when she saw the hot frosted glare in Colm's blue eyes. To her own credit, Colm stood eye to eye with the formidable Councilwoman and did not blink.

"Perhaps you view the position I come to as one of notoriety, Councilwoman, but for me, it is an honor by which I am humbled. I care not for claims to prominence but only that I perform the tasks of the Hill to *which I was born* with the utmost reverence for the responsibility."

Gara's mouth fell open at being addressed so by one, whom she'd never considered of any more consequence than a sparrow, either easily crushed or chased away. Not one to take such starch lightly, Gara retorted.

"Forgive me child if I miss my mark. I only offer my assistance to you as you have ever been in fosterage and in need of the support of the clan. It was merely sense to assume that without the consistent training of your birthmother, you would still be in need of aid to properly conduct the required tasks of the Hill."

Gara's words set Colm's cheeks aflame. For she had been a child of fosterage and despite the reason for her mother's absence, she was never able to let go of the feeling that she was perceived with pity and ever in need of charity from the clan in spite of the fact that she's created her own family and her own hearth prospered. At this point Colm did take Gara's proffered hands in an unyielding grasp and smiled a steely smile.

"It is easy to understand how a woman of your history and age would see me as a child Gara, as you are of an age that could *be* my mother and I am of seven and twenty seasons! But do not mistake my relative youth for lack of knowledge. I thank you for your offer of help Councilwoman, but I'm sure it is not unknown to you that I have earned respect and acclaim as well as good barter in the Tuath as a healer and one who has much knowledge in the way of herb lore and application of alchemical magic. And fear not for my performance of duties on the Hill for who better now to instruct me in those tasks than my birthmother and honored Keeper for many a season past. As for her absence due to 'important duties' I will learn well from those she deems suitable to teach if the need arises. I think though, that perhaps it was not in quite such a laudable capacity for which you offer your assistance. I see by the plainness of the expression on your face as you calculate what value your wares may be to my husband as well as the area in which you would like to offer help, and be assured I need no help in this or any other area from you. While there are some gifts of skill the Goddess bestows to women of your advanced age, the experience you hold pales in consideration of honor, love and commitment I bear my husband. So lust you may for the power the Keeper maintains or perhaps only you crave now for the appeal of a powerful man's bed, but keep you your unwholesome thoughts at bay for a man such as Laoghaire will not be tempted even were your wares not quite so well used."

Gara was so completely unprepared for such an affront that she was left standing with her hands still outstretched in the position they had held when Colm released them leaving the memory of the strength of her words in red imprints upon the older woman's flesh. Gara had to ask herself had she actually been called out by a relative underling in the clan. Colm had left Gara as quickly as she'd approached her but she'd let on with such a fury that Gara stood in utter surprise and the expression on her face was one of unreserved shock. She collected herself quickly when she pulled her hands to her chest and closed her gaping jaw. Her expression then took on a fleeting look of deadly wrath before she composed herself.

So long had Gara been accustomed to wielding power and having her way through bribery, manipulation or sheer force of will, she was appalled to have been accosted by such a one as this scrap of a girl particularly with such unguarded honesty. What she did not calculate was the depths to which Colm's love and dedication reached and any threat to her family would be dealt with in a ferocity no one would have expected possible from one who is so typically compliant and quiet. But Gara had no regard for Colm's love for her family, she knew now that battle lines for authority in the clan had been drawn. Diplomacy may still be useful but any hope Gara had of manipulating or wheedling her way into a position on the Hill had been dashed with the surprising turn of events that Colm might actually be a formidable adversary and that Laoghaire may not be as easily manipulated as most men she'd thus far encountered. Gara would now have to depend more than she cared to on her spies as well as the support of her family and fellow clan folk to find a means to bring down this power usurping family entity.

———

It took her some time to walk through the deserted village to arrive at the feasting hall. As she drew near, Faidhe could see many orange fires glowing with the promise of a night of festivities. People were still trailing into the village and would be, no doubt, for the next three days. Music could be heard from within the hall as well as many whistlers and skinners keeping time from their places around the outdoor fires. Dancing could be seen in silhouette here and there but to Faidhe's senses, the images were all now in streaks of energetic colors rather than dark shadows of the night. Already, Faidhe could sense the coupling of some of the revelers even at this early hour of the feast. She passed the outdoor hearth fires by which clan folk warmed themselves and cooked what meals they had until the offered meat from the indoor spits could begin to be carved and distributed much later. Slipping silently through the crowds watching from under her cloak's hood, she went unnoticed.

Faidhe walked into the feasting hall door and stood to be recognized by the door- keepers. She was at first assaulted by the noise and smells in the hall and so turned inward to quiet herself and prepare for participation in such gathering. Her attention was called when the doorkeeper barked.

"What family girl?"

Faidhe waited for someone of the others around her to respond to the man's question when she grasped that he was speaking to her. Faidhe reached up and removed her hood to reveal her face and the doorkeeper's own expression went stiff with embarrassment apparently over his abrupt tone as he assessed Faidhe's fine clothes.

"Pardon, if you please. How may I help you fair one?"

Now it was Faidhe's turn to be taken aback at being called by such an endearment by a stranger, even if he is a clansman.

"Doorkeep," she replied, "I come to give counsel and to hold seat with my family at yon table."

Faidhe indicated toward where she could see Lon Dubh sitting with Iarann, quietly conversing with Laoghaire and the twins seated under the table having a game of sticks. In that moment, Laoghaire looked toward the entrance and hesitated for a moment before recognition crossed his face. He then immediately came toward Faidhe and the doorkeeper. The others at the table stopped their conversation and looked to see where Laoghaire headed.

He greeted her formally. "Councilwoman, Keeper and Seer for the Tuath. We are humbly honored and welcome you to share in our meal at our hearth table. Will you take food with us now or will you take your seat at the Council's table?"

At this, the doorkeeper renewed his attention toward Faidhe and his expression could only be described as puzzled.

Faidhe noted that from his expression and Laoghaire's that there was something in her countenance now that had changed since her meeting with the Goddess and God. She felt different but she must somehow appear different as well. Deciding to think about that later, she answered Laoghaire with equal formality.

"It is I who am honored to be welcomed at your hearth table, Keeper. It will please me to take food with you and all those at your side. I bid you though, I have responsibility with respect to the Council and ask to impose whether we may join your hearth table with that of the Council so that we may publicly unify your relationship with the Council openly to all eyes showing that you are direct in taking on your responsibilities as Keeper swiftly and with authority with your wife at your side."

"It will be as you say, Keeper." Laoghaire dutifully replied.

"No." Faidhe answered. "It must be as you say, Keeper. Understand you from this point forward, you are the Keeper and must make it known that you wield that Power with purpose much as you would wield the very Sword you carry as a symbol of your rightful place as a tribal leader and protector." She warned, pulling him close as they slowly strolled arm in arm toward the Council's table, "Remember, we have but little time to place you firmly on the Hill. You must keep your guidance from me to hidden sessions and make all decisions public with surety so few will harbor doubt regarding your new position."

"There is wisdom in your perceptions, Lady. Please excuse me while I make arrangements for the changes required."

Laoghaire strode back to the doorkeeper to formally request that arrangements be made for the two great tables and bench seats made of heavy oak be placed together in front of the great chairs reserved for the Danu and the Dagda so that the two groups may be joined for the feast. Laoghaire chose the spot in front of the great thrones as a symbolic gesture that these changes are made with the blessing of the Goddess and the God. Having taken care of this change, Laoghaire recognized that the evening should be called to order with some kind of a blessing or announcement to formalize the occasion. This, he knew would be his responsibility as the celebrations over the next few days were in large part due to his taking a position of great authority in the Tuath. He would have to begin making meaningful decisions in this time of transition that will lay the foundation for him to not only perform his scared duties for the Tuath but also pave the way for the Goddess and God in all their forms to come under protection as the great spiritual energies shift the weight of Power.

At the moment Laoghaire came to his decision to formalize the feast, and stepped toward the raised platform upon which the great chairs stood, Briciu could be seen just ahead of him in stepping up onto the platform. The portly man raised his arms to gain the attention of the feasters.

"Clan folk, hear me! Hear me!" He said louder and the clatter and voices of the indoor feasters slowed to a murmur. "Clan folk, I have news. In honor of these most favorable circumstances, I have opted to offer not only such fine meat as you have seen on the spit this night in recognition of the auspicious changes taking place within the clan, but in honor of our changing ways and out of respect for the coming of a man to the revered position of Keeper, I am here to celebrate, give respect and support for these new ways. To give honor to the God by having a man ascend to the Hill is new, yes, but also a necessary step in securing the future of our deities."

All those seated at the combined Council and Keeper's family tables looked at each other to determine if anyone there knew what Briciu was up to. It did not seem that any seated had knowledge of his plans. Gara, may have known what Briciu intended but she was not present at the table just now. Laoghaire, who had been just about to step up to make an announcement himself was standing just in front of Briciu at the foot of the platform. He felt a sense of foreboding at the seeming support for the changes in the hierarchy of the clan Briciu was announcing.

"Look you," Briciu said, pointing toward Laoghaire, "upon the new Keeper of the Stones. He has taken leave of his holdings in cattle and his home to serve our people and the Gods. In honor of this new, masculine role of Keeper, I offer my prize bull to the slaughter for the feast with a challenge, in respect for all these changes." This was met with a round of exclamations from the crowd. Briciu basked in the recognition of his costly gift and the attention he was claiming.

"Further," he continued, raising his hands once again to regain attention from the crowd, "to provide Laoghaire an opportunity to prove himself in his new position as the leader and protector of our Tuath, and to allay any who may doubt his abilities or think him ill placed due to his lack of clan heritage, I offer Keeper Laoghaire this challenge to present his skills to claim this prize I have presented. So my gift is two-fold: I offer my prize bull to the spitfires with a challenge and I provide Laoghaire an opportunity to dispel any fears or doubts in his abilities as a clan leader or claims that a male should not ascend the Hill for what he lacks in magical skill, we shall see if he makes up for it in other skills."

More murmurs among the people while Briciu beckoned Laoghaire up to the platform to join him. Laoghaire cursed his positioning at the time of Briciu's announcement. It appeared as though this challenge was approved by him and that he was awaiting Briciu's address to all those in the hall. Seeing no hope to diffuse the challenge, Laoghaire stepped up onto the platform with Briciu to speak.

Laoghaire shrugged off the insult against his heritage as unimportant but refused to allow his family's livelihood and home to be taken as easily as Briciu suggested. Laoghaire had no doubt but that Briciu was angling somehow to take possession of his livestock and have it look as though he was doing a favor to relieve Laoghaire's family of all their holdings. Having already taken precautions to avert such claims, the Calf-herder answered.

"Though it is not customary or practical to bring livestock up to the Hill, I realize that the cattle of my family is counted among the Tuatha De Danann as part of its collective wealth and I would be loath to see all that I and Colm have worked for be lost to you, the clan that I now call my own family. For this reason, I have sent word to the kingdom of my mother and father asking that an honored member of my birth clan be sent to tend the cattle here so it will not be lost to all of you who I count as my own kin and clan. For as was decreed in the marriage promise when I came to live among you: If for any reason the marriage dissolved and I was no longer considered to be of the Tuatha De Danann, or if I die before my children have reached first rights, the cattle I brought to this clan would revert back to my birth clan in the same number of cattle heads until such time my children come of age. Although these new circumstances are unlike those that are predetermined within the contract, I did not want any question as to who would take possession of Colm's and my cattle in our absence so I have opted to have a worthy member of the Calf-herder Clan come and live in our home and keep the stock in our stead until such time one, or all of my family have fulfilled our obligation to the Gods and we descend the Hill to return to our humble place among the Tuath. So worry not with thoughts of what wealth might be lost to the clan, for I have provided for the clan in our absence."

This received sounds of approval from the crowd and having said his piece about his family business, Laoghaire captured the allegiance of many who had not even given a thought to the loss of wealth the clan would sustain should something happen to him. They seemed to view him now as a thoughtful leader and provider in the way he averted any claims on his cattle that his birth clan may have in his absence.

Briciu was inwardly chagrined at this new admiration for Laoghaire and his missed opportunity to graciously offer to take Laoghaire's herd from him but thought his more important plan; his primary goal had not been foiled. The Calf-herder brought Briciu out of his inward thoughts when he took control of the very challenge.

"What say you Briciu? Name your challenge and be it within my power to claim the bull for the pleasure of the clan, I will do my best to meet the challenge with the blessed Sword and Shield given me as symbols of that leadership and protection for which I must display proficiency. How must I win the bull for the clan? A challenge of strength? Bravery? Endurance? Speed? Wisdom?"

Laoghaire knew that he could not refuse a challenge given in circumstances such as these. To back away would plant doubt in the minds of the clan folk regardless of how many cattle head he brought to the Tuath, and rightfully so. Despite the support given him by Faidhe or the gift of the implements, should he back away from a challenge it would show him for a coward and weak, he would be finished before he started as the new Keeper.

"You rightly guess, Laoghaire, that the challenge will give you ample opportunity to display your abilities in all the areas you mention. I'm sure the clan will enjoy the entertainment you will provide them as well." Briciu beamed the smile of one who had won a most satisfactory amount in a wager. "I have taken the liberty of having my prize bull brought up from his stable hut so he might be viewed as a specimen in his prime with enough meat for all here to have their fill. And you Laoghaire, will have time to prepare yourself before the challenge commences."

"I bid you give me notice of the challenge Councilmember so that I may know how best to prepare. What feat must be performed to win such a prize from your herd?" Laoghaire was familiar with Briciu's prize bull. It was truly in its prime and had sired many a healthy head in the herd; it had plenty of rut left in him. Laoghaire knew that the challenge must be difficult indeed for Briciu would no more give up his prize bull to the slaughter than he would offer all his worldly possessions to a stranger. He must be secure in that no matter what the challenge, Laoghaire would likely not be able to fulfill the obligation. The new Keeper arrived at the inspiration for Briciu's challenge: *So this challenge will discredit me as worthy to assume the position of Keeper whether I accept it or not and whether I've been chosen to carry the implements or not.* He knew he'd been foxed by Briciu's experience in political showmanship. He had no choice but to follow through.

"Well Briciu, what lies ahead for me in your challenge?"

"Your task is quite simple, to win the bull for the clan, you must show your prowess in speed, strength, bravery, endurance and wisdom as it seems those are the things you claim are what suits you to be our leader and protector. You should prepare to meet the challenge with these skills alone for you'll need them all when you step into yon enclosure with the prize and fell the bull for the clan."

With that, the crowd was in an uproar. The challenge, they knew, would be impossible for one man to fell a bull of such a size and temperament. The people seemed up for a game of challenge but did not want to see Laoghaire killed. Sensing this response, Briciu again raised his arms to quiet the crowd.

"Clan folk," he shouted, "we are coming to new territory in these times with a man of strength taking the position as Keeper. I doubt not that it is time for a man to ascend the Hill but should we not relieve ourselves of the concern as to whether he is fit for the service using what he, himself claims are his abilities that suit him to the job? Were I a one to rise to the position, would I not be expected to be tested in areas of diplomacy, trade and strength of magical ability?"

It became apparent to Laoghaire, and a few others that Briciu had hopes of positioning himself to move into the Keeper's hut by highlighting his own strengths as being more valuable to the position should the current Keeper fail to meet the challenge while at the same time insuring that, should he be considered for the position, he would be challenged on the skill areas in which he excelled. Briciu was not a foolish man. He was formidable in his cunning ways. He had also very craftily brought to the fore that Laoghaire had not been known publicly for having any magical skills. It was not difficult to see how Briciu, with so few likeable attributes, came to a position of power within the clan. Laoghaire raised the arm not bearing the great Shield to quiet the clan and when he was sure he had the attention of all, he looked to Faidhe as she sat at the head of the newly combined tables in front of him. She nodded her head at him and Laoghaire didn't know whether it meant for him to go ahead with the challenge or that she was assuring him that things would come out with him as the winner of the challenge. He looked to her for guidance and knew all he could expect was her support at this moment. He then looked to Colm who returned his gaze with a face stricken with grief over the mere prospect of her husband accepting such a challenge. His heart felt for her anguish.

Laoghaire asked the Gods for strength and he was awash in calm as he came to a decision. He addressed the crowd in a normal speaking voice and all those in the hall strained to listen.

"I accept this challenge as an initiation to my position as leader and protector of the Tuath. For it is as it should be that I prove myself to be the one true to the position for was I not called to it by the Gods? I will meet the challenge using all that has been gifted to me in the way of agility and strength, as well as the magic bequeathed to me directly from the Gods in the way of these implements. For whatever they saw in me that was lacking, they had the wisdom to give me the tools to compensate for that lack. I will not set aside the implements and disregard the gift from the Gods. I will use all of my skills and all other means available to me for as a leader and the Keeper, you as a clan should expect nothing less from me when I rise to meet any challenge. So," he ended with a flourish, "eat, drink, see the spectacle of the bull for by this time tomorrow, should the Gods will it, he will pass on his fertile strength to us as we taste his meat and juices!"

With this last, the crowd cheered and most stood. The festival like atmosphere of the moment took the clan with promise of entertainment, a challenge with a steep price, good meat and long nights of reveling ahead. Many began to make their way to the door in order to have a look at the great bull that the new Keeper would meet in battle. The confidence he exuded in his speech infected all who listened so no one truly believed that Laoghaire would meet the challenge with the likelihood of meeting his death. The Tuath seemed to look upon this challenge as an exhibition of strength or demonstration for entertainment purposes. There was one man who understood exactly what this challenge meant. Laoghaire turned to face Briciu and away from the crowd to instruct him.

"Have not a thought Briciu for driving a thorn into the bull's sensitive areas or to blow flint dust up his nose to increase his ill temper. For as part of my preparation my men will check the bull for any such practices. I will meet this challenge honestly and earnestly but doubt not that if you use deceit or trickery in any way, I will expose you for it and call upon the Council to remove you from your seat on the basis of lack of honor."

Lack of honor was a most serious accusation and would not be ignored. Briciu did not seem disturbed by the warning so Laoghaire felt that, at least, he would be meeting the bull without the added concern for it being in a rage due to pain or discomfort. That being settled, Laoghaire then took care for the clan and caution for his family.

"And should I fall to the bull I am leaving instruction that you be held to your debt of two steers for each night of feasting none of which has been paid as of yet. And be assured also that should I die this night, my clansman from the Calf-herder Tribe will arrive to keep my house and stock in order for my family. If you had an eye toward *helping* my family out of their livelihood."

Briciu attempted to sputter denials but was so obviously gleeful at his apparent success in takeover maneuvers that he could sparse keep from gloating at Laoghaire's anger.

"Perhaps all these preparations for your loss of the challenge would not be necessary if you had the power of judgment to expect a challenge and be prepared for it. Your lack of experience as a leader is painfully obvious Laoghaire." He turned to waddle down from the platform. "Make what preparations you must." He exited with a smug wave of a pudgy hand as he was met by his mother who grasped his arm and appeared to usher him toward the door with the flow of the crowd already heading that way.

Laoghaire returned to the great table to find that those who met his eyes there were those who attended the meeting at the Smithy's hut only a few hours before with the addition of the fourth and fifth Councilmembers Faeg and Brath.

"So much is happening so quickly." He voiced to no one in particular.

"Father," Morgan looked at her father with beseeching eyes, "how will you kill the bull? He's very large. Have you some herdsman's knowledge that allows you to overtake the animal? Is this why you bear the name of the Calf-herder Clan as your own?"

Laoghaire knew his daughter was right and was grateful to have this reminder. His very name carried with it the meaning for his family's trade. He had come from the clan of the Calf-herders and his parents the king and queen of the clan. Theirs is a wealthy clan and their cattle, a much sought after currency for with care and know how, the number of the herd would only grow and the fur, skins, horns and hoofs were useful to the clan or for trade. Useful too are most of the animal's innards and bones. This hardy stock required little supplemental feeding beyond the grass feed. Trade and barter were a constant with the tribe known for excellent stock and healthy cattle was insurance against a hard winter or starvation. Laoghaire, his name meaning simply *Calf-herder*, was born to the cattle clan and raised with much knowhow breeding and handling of the stock. He'd been a herdsman all his life and found himself now smiling at his daughter who had very plainly put him in mind of that fact. Laoghaire lifted his daughter with one swooping movement up over his head and brought her down quickly to plant a kiss on her forehead.

"Yes daughter, I have much knowledge in the ways of cattle and how to bring the bull to hand. I will be swift and merciful in his slaughter so he suffers not." Morgan smiled for her father at the news, feeling comforted as he put her back on the earth to return to her game. "Councilmembers," Laoghaire addressed those at the great table, "a herdsman I may be but I sense there may be more to this challenge than the task of felling the bull. Am I amiss in questioning whether there might be advent of magic cast around or over the bull to secure that I will not meet the challenge?"

Brath, the Fifth member of the Council was shocked. "What you suggest is irreverence in a most wicked way. Surely you do not suspect that there is a one among us who would see you fail?"

Laoghaire realized he had spoken in haste without a caution to who else was at the table. "You are such a good and trusting man Brath. That you would not think it possible only speaks to your own character in that it would not occur to you to pilfer the Power to suit your own purpose. But in these changing times, it is always prudent to understand that not everyone has only the clan's best interest in his or her thoughts. There are those who may be tempted to abuse the Power for more than simple needs, wants or desires. We must be cautious in that we do not allow ourselves into a position where we are taken by surprise for lack of forethought to what might occur."

Faidhe agreed.

"Well said, Laoghaire. We must ever be prepared for the unexpected. There are some things that can be done to assist you in your preparation for this challenge. Have you any natural magic Laoghaire, upon which you can draw?"

"Nay, Lady. None. I fear it is a dearth in my competence as Keeper, just as Briciu claims."

Laoghaire looked at Faidhe and noticed for the first time with his full attention that she appeared different to him somehow than she had earlier this day. Still powerful, still lovely, but something…his mind toyed with what it might be, waiting for the thought to rise to the surface but he was drawn back into the conversation about the situation at hand and let it go for the moment with one last glance toward Faidhe.

Craiche stood to speak for the first time.

"There is much to be done and we should keep to our business lest we allow ourselves to be caught up in the merriment of feasting and challenges." Turning to Brath she voiced her request. "Councilman, while we none of us find it appealing to imagine anyone abusing the Power for selfish gain, Laoghaire is wise in taking measures to avert such mishaps as could manifest from such misuse. Since the challenge comes from Councilman Briciu, it should be given to him in courtesy in the way of a witness to his action that it might be said he was not engaged in any magical discourse just prior to the challenge. Will you go then Brath and stay with the Councilman Briciu to assure any who may accuse him of such, will have no basis for the accusation?"

"You suspect the Councilman of such?" Brath said.

"I have seen nothing to make me suspect him so, but I repeat, at these changing times we must have the Council showing solid support for one another and the changes as they occur. We cannot be bogged down with deterrents to our work as would occur if the clan were to be plagued with problems arising from any such accusations. The Council must be free to conduct business arising from the changes."

"I see your method Lady. But did not Briciu leave with Gara? Can they not vouch for each other's whereabouts?"

"It is true, they were seen just now leaving the hall together but think man," Craiche urged, "would not a mother's first instinct be to fend for her own son? In fact, if one were to accuse Briciu of such a corruption would we not be remiss in our support of our fellow Councilmembers should we neglect to provide Gara with a witness to support her innocence of any wrong doing as well?"

Faidhe agreed, "You are quite right Craiche. I believe that as Brath goes to support Briciu, Faeg should also seek out the third Councilmember and provide Gara with the benefit of her company as well." Faidhe turned to Faeg and instructed her so that there would be no further discussion. "Go now with Brath and offer your company to Gara as Brath seeks out Briciu. Keep your eyes astute for anything that may be construed as a possible affront to the new Keeper and the Gods' changes taking place this very night. And support your charge by advising them against doing anything that might be perceived as dishonorable behavior should you see it about to take place."

The two were given their instructions and would not question or disobey the orders they had been charged with but both Councilmembers recognized that they were, in actuality, being asked to spy on the others of the Council and neither were pleased with the task. Nor were they comfortable with the prospect of telling either Gara or Briciu what to do or what not to do. As they left the feasting hall together, they spoke of their reservations to each other.

"Brath," Faeg queried, "I know that Gara is rumored to be unkind to those who cross her but know you of any of her deeds that would bring upon her such scrutiny? After all, she is the third Councilmember, soon to take her place as the Second Councilmember. And she has worked long for the Clan on the Council. Should we not tell her of the true nature of our venture?"

"Gara has long worked for those Council issues that benefit Gara. You know this but your heart is tepid to our commission at the thought of reprisals from her. I too dislike this task as it feels we betray our own but as these changes take place we must take stock of not who wields power, but who is likely dedicated to the Gods. Faidhe has long been in service there on the Hill and has not lived a soft life. Craiche, you know has truly worked on behalf of the Clan taking not much in the way of comfort or payment for the task. Gara has used her position on the Council to direct decisions that will make her standing stronger or that will benefit her trade in cattle or barter. Yes the clan will often benefit as well but do not be fooled; Gara has made herself quite comfortable in her position. And need I point out to you the driving force behind Briciu's reason for doing anything will always be for what benefits Briciu."

"This is true, but..." She trailed off. Faeg knew that Gara and Briciu could be more than unkind to any whom they thought were in opposition to them. What struck Faeg most troubling was that she had, on more than one occasion supported Gara in voting on minor Council issues in return for personal favors. She fell sway to Gara's assurances that this was how things worked and that all those on the Council conducted business in such ways. But Faeg knew that all Councilmembers did not operate this way nor would it be well accepted should these dealings be brought up publicly. Faeg struggled with her conscience and offered a half-hearted response.

"Of course you are right and the changes taking place following the prophecy are most important. I suppose it is my own reservation at the possibility of seeing the Council afflicted with dissension that weighs dark on my mind. I suppose we should be honored at having a task that will help to bind the Council together. Ah, there is Gara by yon corral. Surely, Briciu cannot be far from her. Let us go and tend to our task."

Craiche had been aware of the relationship between Gara and Faeg and was certain that although they were small issues which did not affect the Clan adversely, the favors that Gara had granted Faeg cost the fourth Councilmember much in the way of sleep and wear on her conscience. Craiche also knew that Faeg was at heart a good person with the Clan's best interest in mind, but that she had compromised her integrity with Gara and so Craiche hesitated to enlist her to keep watch on Gara due to the fact that she was not entirely sure that she would be absolutely devoted to the task. But in these times, one must allow for the hope that a fundamentally good soul will come to tell the truth to redeem him or herself despite the personal cost. *Faith. Faith in the Gods is one thing; faith in another human is a more difficult risk,* she mused as she watched Brath and Faeg melt into the crowd. Then she renewed her attention to the task at hand.

"Laoghaire!" she snapped. "Say not you have no magic for it is within us all. Doubt not that you have some form of the Power available to you. It has simply not yet been determined how it may be of use to you. Iarann," she called to the ironworker, "bring forward yon skin of honey wine."

Craiche took a furtive glance around them to see what audience they might have and was relieved that many of the clan had ventured outside for the moment to view the bull. Then looking to Faidhe, the Keeper understood her message that they must go unnoticed for the business at hand by those who remained inside the feasting hall.

Faidhe closed her eyes and imagined a veil draped around those at the Council's table. This done, she called to the Power to keep their activities unseen and unheard to all those outside the magical veil. She extended her hands above her head and claimed the Power to do as she bid so that no clan member would wonder where these eight were or to what business they tended. As she finished her petition she opened her eyes to stares of awe from everyone with the exception of Craiche who was pouring some of Iarann's mead into a drinking bowl on the table.

"Lon Dubh" Faidhe summoned. "The lamp."

Realizing that she was being called upon to participate in the proceedings, she jumped to action to bring one of oil lamps that lit the hall around the giant table to where Faidhe and Craiche were beginning to formulate the basic structures to cast energy for a particular purpose.

"What shall I do with it?"

"Wait until she is finished pouring, then give it to Craiche." Faidhe gestured toward the old woman as she dug into her own sealskin pouch. She brought out a large green leaf; folded to envelop some dried vegetation. "We haven't much time." She said holding the leaf packet out to Lon Dubh. "For your part, take this and stand by Iarann just now.

She shifted her attention. "Laoghaire, place your Shield on the earth to your left some five paces away from where you stand and your Sword five paces to your right." Faidhe instructed as she placed her Staff on the earth about five paces in front of Laoghaire. "Now stand you in the center of the implements." She coached Laoghaire. With a point of her finger, Faidhe shot a blue spark to the earth behind him and as the spark ignited into an immense ball of blue light, the great Cauldron appeared.

Impulsively, Colm and Lon Dubh looked around at the others in the dining hall and wondered that such doings had not been seen. All had taken place within the veil but Laoghaire, Iarann and even Craiche hadn't noticed whether they'd been seen or not, for they each watched Faidhe with amazement at the Power she so obviously could call with ease.

Faidhe dismissed their expressions of astonishment. "No time for explanations. Colm, come with your children and stand around Laoghaire in a circle. Just you three, and hold each other's hands and close your eyes. Think you now on watching your father, your husband as you see him fleet of foot and smooth with strength, stout of heart, and confident with expertise, see him dispatch the great bull with ease. See him do it over and again until it is assured. Begin to circle Laoghaire in a sunwise direction and speak low of how you see him conquer the beast."

As they began the process, the children looked at their mother for direction and copied her movements to gradually pick up the rhythm of the moment.

"Now," Faidhe continued, "we four will stand just inside the perimeter created by the implements on the earth in the spaces created between where they are positioned. Lon Dubh, you with the figh leaf and aromatic herb, there betwixt the pot and the Shield, I, here 'tween the Shield and Staff, Iarann, stand you with yon vessel of mead midst the Staff and the Sword. Craiche, get you with the lamp betwixt the Sword and the pot.

Now, we each are a living representation of the sacred three, earth, air, water, and now the fourth, fire. Iarann, take a draught of your honey wine made of water and gifts of the earth and travel sunwise to Craiche so that she may taste of these elementals, then move on to Lon Dubh and myself that we each draw from the vessel of water and earth to stir their energies to answer our call."

Iarann stepped to Craiche and held the pottery vessel to her lips until she'd taken her fill and repeated this duty with Lon Dubh and Faidhe as he journeyed around the outer circle of participants until he took his place once again between the Sword and the Staff. Faidhe noted that above the heads of Laoghaire and his family was beginning to form a cone shape of green energy or light seemingly spinning in the same sunwise direction as the small circle of people. Faidhe was pleased at the rising energy.

"Lon Dubh, open the figh leaf and crush the herbs, grown of the earth in your palms until you can smell their fragrance. Craiche, come you to where Long Dubh stands and hold your lamp so the herbs can be burned over your fire to release their aromatics. Fire meets earth, releases the scent to the air. Good, now let all the herbs meet the fire and as that is accomplished, Craiche walk all the way around the circle until you regain your place".

"Lon Dubh next, walk you through the smoke made from the burning and bring its waft toward me as you now complete your circle. Once I'm imbued with the scent of the herbs from the earth burned in the fire to create a scent in the air, I stir the air around the circle and bond it with the water so all four of the elements are beckoned and at work."

At this, Faidhe began to move around the circle toward Iarann and took a final draft to finish the mead in the ewer and handed it back to him. Having done that, she walked in the same direction around the circle and then regained her place between the Shield and the Staff. Once in her place, Faidhe again lifted her arms and called in a firm and commanding voice to be heard over the chanting-like voices of Colm, Macha and Morgan.

"I humbly summon the Power of the water, earth, air and fire to carry our petition to the Goddess and God...the God and Goddess. The She and the He...the He and the She so that we witness the elements take on the spark of the *Universal Power*. Mother we call upon you to use your triple aspects, maid, mother and wise woman, earth, air and water, Cup, Shield and Sword, to hear and carry out our petition" In that moment, all the implements took on the faint blue glow of the same light with which Faidhe made the Cauldron appear.

"Father we call upon you in your time of emergence and recognize the rise to your time of influence and call upon you to use your strength of fire and the Staff to grant victory for your servant Laoghaire. We ask that you instill him with your strength that he might own success in conquering the beast."

At this, the green cone above the heads of Laoghaire and his family burned brightly as it spun furiously in the same direction Colm and the twins traveled.

Faidhe carried on. "We petition these energies, for protection of this servant of the Hill in honor of all that is revered and sacred."

With this Faidhe began to make three revolutions around Laoghaire and his family as they continued to fervently work to create his success through vision magic. The faint blue grew from the implements stronger and more vibrant as she did this. The light created a dome over all the participants from the earth just behind the implements to an apex at a height of about two men high at the very top.

Faidhe threw off her cloak as the heat within the dome became quite perceptible.

"We ask," she proceeded, "that in his time of confrontation, Laoghaire is as fleet and agile as a cat to avoid the horn and hoof of the beast. We ask that, in his time of aggression, he carries the cunning and strength of tenacity of the lone wolf on the hunt to fell the beast. We petition that, he wear your protection as a garment, cast about him so that should the beast be anointed with the magic of another, Laoghaire will be impervious to injury and unmarked as he must be to rightfully claim seat as leader of the children of the Danu, The children of the Dagda, The Tuatha De Danann."

Faidhe walked the circle three times again and repeated each petition and finally repeated the revolutions a third time so the petitions were thrice extended and each sent to draw upon the *Power of the Universe* utilizing the energy of the elements, the implements and the Gods.

"With power and energy granted, we ask that your child Laoghaire, son of the Calf-herder Clan be granted protection, prowess and practical use of all his knowledge in the time of his challenge and need to be successful in conquering the bull."

Just as Faidhe returned to her place in the circle the point on the green cone above Laoghaire and his family had elongated to touch the ceiling of the blue dome that encompassed them all. As the two met, giant veins of white lightning like energy ignited and coursed through the shell of the dome and the cone alike. Loud crackling sounds traveled through the very bones of all in the circle.

Faidhe looked at her cohorts and saw the unbound hair of the participants standing on end, charged with the magic within the circle. She turned her attention to Iarann and focused upon him so intently that stamped upon his face was the fright he felt at seeing her countenance charged with the spirit of the Gods. She directed her energy at him so that he might understand that because he began the circle of the ritual he must initiate the close of the ceremony by releasing the energy of the water. Whether Iarann understood or if he was merely startled at her appearance, she did not know but in that moment, Iarann dropped the pottery goblet to the ground where it shattered into many pieces.

Faidhe then nodded to Craiche who knew that to end her part in the ritual, she must douse the element for which she'd petitioned and wetted her thumb and long finger with her tongue to pinch the flame out.

Faidhe and Craiche looked then to Lon Dubh who held nothing in her hands but instinctively bent to scoop up a handful of dusty earth from the dining hall floor. As she stood, Lon Dubh let the sand drain from her loosely closed hand back onto the ground releasing the power of the earth.

To close the circle of magic, and release the Power to work however it may, Faidhe let out a long exhale of breath to release the power of the air and the vibrant blue and green lights subsided, as did the crackling sounds within the dome.

Sensing the shift in energy Colm, Morgan and Macha slowed their circling and chanting to a stop and dazed, they opened their eyes. They looked around in wonderment as though they had no recollection of what had just happened or what they had just done. Colm stepped toward Laoghaire who remained still and appeared to be sleeping or would, had he not been standing.

Gently, Colm rested a hand upon Laoghaire's shoulder, and called to him.

"Husband? I sense that you still hover beyond this world. Bask for the moment in the pleasantness of the glow of magic to regain yourself but do not linger there in the Otherworld. Do not fall to the allure of the peace that side offers for you have much to do here." Then more urgently she shook his shoulder. "Fall not to the draw of the magic of the initiate's first circle."

Colm knew well the seductiveness of the magical energy. Should one be not disciplined to release the Power after having petitioned for a cause, it can be as the drink for some who linger over long in the glow, or who partake in the rituals for petty reasons if only to experience the euphoria that often accompanies the magic. Some inexperienced or untrained unfortunates have even been found to vacate their human form to wholly cross to the Otherworld leaving behind only a dead husk of flesh within a magical circle.

"Come now Keeper, you must answer my call to ground yourself and return to the task for which you were just now initiated for we are not yet ready to release you to the Gods."

Colm tried to sound lighthearted but began to show the mark of concern on her face but her worry soon diminished as she saw Laoghaire's eyes begin to flutter open and his nostrils flared with a great intake of breath.

"Worry not, Wife." he answered Colm as he beamed a most magnetic smile. "Think you I can be gotten rid of so easily? I have much to do in this world." He slipped his arm around her waist and drew her close. "Beginning with seeing to my duties as your husband as soon as I have felled yon beast."

Colm was not at all displeased at the evidence Laoghaire's body showed of the magical energy as he pressed against her but was also quite aware of the eyes upon them.

"Doubt not, Husband, that I am eager to see to it you do not renege on your duties but I'm certain that, for now, you must reserve all of your strength for the effort you must put forth for this challenge." She drew closer to his ear and lowered her voice. "But trust you this, after you have felled the bull, know that I will claim title as the one who felled the man who felled the bull!"

The others in the veiled circle busied themselves with the task of returning the lamp and pieces of the broken pottery to the great table. Faidhe removed the Cauldron from sight in a blaze of blue and picked up the Staff. Laoghaire had taken a moment to get composed as he picked up his Sword and Shield. He then took a seat at the great table until all evidence of his connubial promise subsided. Colm tended the children with an admonition to speak not of what had taken place.

"This is part of being children of the Hill and you must keep the need for silence upon these matters outside of those you see here. Understand you this import?"

"Yes Mother." The twins claimed in unison. "We understand."

"Good then, my little nymphs." She gathered them to her as she, too sat at the table. "We must keep to the visions we conjured and repeat them in our minds and hearts when your father takes to the paddock to kill the beast but speak not aloud. Keep the images to your minds."

"Yes again, Mother." This time with a bright smile at the prospect of experiencing more magic this evening.

Faidhe called the group to order. "Take your places at the table. Lon Dubh, mete out some of that stew to those seated if you please and Iarann, tear off some of the bread supplied to the Council's table to share amongst us. A bit of food will serve to ground us from the magic and will also appear quite natural to those around us that we share our meal at these tables. For there will be some who will sense a difference in the energy around them once I remove the veil around us so we, once again, join the feast."

Many people had come back inside the great dining hall and more were streaming in through the door opposite where the group sat. Faidhe looked around at the clan and willed them to see nothing amiss. She raised her arms still standing at the head of the table and released the energy that was holding the veil of secrecy around the group. This done, she sat down and spoke to Craiche who was seated to her right in a quite casual tone as if they'd been idling the feasting hours with conversation, food and drink.

"I think you might find willow bark more suitable to that tincture Craiche. You must try it the next time someone comes to you ailing of a griping stomach." Then turning to Iarann, who still looked a bit stunned, she said, "Smithy, have you a bit more of that honey wine to share? I tell you it has been overlong since I have enjoyed such sweet flavors."

Taking his prompt, Iarann poured some of the remaining mead from the skin into Faidhe's waiting tankard.

"Yes Lady. It gives me much joy that such esteemed clan members as those who dine at this table enjoy my draft. You flatter me with your kind words."

"Nonsense." Craiche spoke up; holding out her cup as well as she gustily processed a piece of bread with her remaining teeth. "Faidhe speaks naught but the truth. This is fine mead indeed Smithy. You have a second vocation should you engage in production of this craft beyond just a leisure pursuit." Craiche's cheeks were aglow with the flush of magic as were many at the table, but to any onlookers, as they suddenly found that they noticed the group at the table, those seated looked flushed from warm stew, conversation and good mead. The group drew a few odd looks from the passersby but beyond that, there was not a glitch in the rhythm of the evening so far as any outsiders were concerned.

Just then, Faeg and Brath could be seen walking across the great hall together trailed by Nemain, Gara, and Briciu who still seemed to be working the crowd as they made their way toward the Council table. Laoghaire, upon seeing them approach, stood to excuse himself.

"Clan and Councilmembers, please forgive me but I must bid your favor in releasing me from your company. I must tend my preparations and inspect the bull but first I must seek out some of my herdsmen to assist me. I give you my thanks for what we have shared at this table this evening."

All seated knew he meant not for the breaking of bread that was shared but the outpouring of support and the gift of magical protection. Taking up his Shield and with his Sword once again hanging from his halfstrap, he turned to Colm and his children to plant a gentle kiss on Colm's lips. He breathed his words into her ear.

"A good man must always tend his duties. Do you not agree, Wife?" Colm's answer was equally playful as she responded.

"No Husband, it is a good man who tends to his duties well and until said duties are complete to the satisfaction of such a one who rightly issued the task. So go you and prepare for your little challenge so you may rise to the more important one later this night."

Laoghaire raised an eyebrow at his wife's randy words and planted a kiss on the crown of his children's heads just as the Councilmembers and Nemain reached the table. Laoghaire stood erect to meet eyes with Briciu.

"Councilmembers, I make my excuses for not joining you to feast and conduct business as I should on this night for I have pressing work to do to prepare for this unexpected challenge; but please do sit with my family at the Keeper's table. If you have not yet eaten, I suggest the boar. Its meat is sweet and wholesome."

The jibes about the challenge or the meat were not lost on Briciu as he headed for the Council side of the table to take a seat, as did Gara, for neither one was eager to resume conversation with the family members of the new Keeper. To their surprise, they watched as Nemain walked toward the Keeper's end of the table and took a seat alongside Colm and across from where Lon Dubh sat with Iarann.

"Good feasting to all at this table." She announced. "I thank you for the invitation to feast and drink with you. Are you not excited at the news?"

All members of the Council and the Keeper's table stared at Nemain. Not only because she was rarely occasioned to have much to say, particularly when her mother and brother were in proximity, but the oddity of how she presented her question was apparent.

Colm responded first. "Of what news you speak Nemain? That of the new Keeper?"

"Can it be that you do not know?" Nemain looked around at those seated to read their faces. "Ah so it is unshared news I bring you from those who speak to me from the Otherworld." She eyed her mother and brother for a moment, as it was a rare pleasure she had when she could have attention focused on her rather than them. "I have been in communion with my ancestors earlier this night and they have given me news of the Keeper." Colm then became deeply interested in what Nemain had to say.

"What news of my husband then? Know you the outcome of this challenge?" She sliced a look toward Briciu, but was intent upon Nemain. "Is it such news that can be shared?"

Craiche gave Colm a warning look to remind her from whence this news came is to be taken with caution as Nemain, although not known for any involvement in politics, is Gara's daughter and may have her own agenda where messaging news is concerned. But Colm did not notice for she was entirely focused on Nemain.

After Nemain had enjoyed her moment of suspense and that even her mother and brother had no idea of what she was about to say she answered Colm.

"I did say my news is given about the Keeper but I was not speaking of your husband, Colm. I bring news of the Keeper Faidhe from the side of the spirits. They are quite excited at the news themselves you see." Lighting her eyes upon Faidhe to speculate as to whether she had shared this news or not Nemain asked, "Have you not shared your news Lady?"

Faidhe cursed that her early departure from the clan would be released to those who would benefit from the news and disrupt her cause. She wondered if Nemain knew that she meant to take Iarann and Lon Dubh with her. She decided not to let on anything to see just how much the girl knows.

"I'm sure I know not of what you speak, child. Can you be sure this news is come true from the spirit? Not to asperse your abilities of course, but could you not be sharing news of a dream thought to be news, perhaps?"

"I take no offense at your query, Lady. Could it be that you have no knowledge of this news yourself? By the look on your face, I see you do not but it is plain to see that the news is true. I bring you joyful news and you will now know why the spirits rejoice and share with me that one from the Otherworld will come soon to the flesh."

"You speak true child, I know not of what you speak. So if you will, be plain and share your meaning."

"Yes Lady, of course. With respect, you are breeding. You will bear a child of your union with the God from this very day!"

Faidhe was stricken. She felt exposed to have her moment with the Greenman so openly discussed but even further, how could this be so? She had union in spiritual nature only. Her mind whirred with the memory and recalled the Greenman's mention of giving her a gift. Then her mind sped to her encounter with the God and Goddess only a brief while ago. Had she not seen the green tendrils of energy herself growing outward from her body? Of course, the energy she carries is masculine.

She was shocked as she acclimated within seconds to the news. *Oh Gods, I'm with child!*

"What news is this?' Gara flared. "This cannot be so. She spoke to Nemain in a factual if not dismissive tone. "Faidhe is five and forty seasons, at least. Surly you're mistaken girl. Or, for if you are not, she will certainly not carry to birth at her age."

"I'm not mistaken." Nemain stubbornly replied. Turning to Faidhe she said, "Have you no notice of her youthful appearance? She is but a few counts on one's fingers older than you Mother, and though you too are beyond forty seasons, you still avail yourself of the clothing and pleasures of a younger woman. But notice you not that since she has come down from the Hill, the Keeper does not merely dress or act as a younger woman, she has taken on a more youthful vigor?"

Those at the table were stricken speechless. All eyes were on Faidhe and she was compelled to speak in the silence.

"Though it had not yet been shown to me, I cannot say that it is not possible. Just this day I was given a great gift of union by the aspect of the God as the Greenman. And later this very night, I was visited by none other than the Dagda and the Danu both of whom breathed their blessing of what I can only perceive now as the gift of youthfulness to bear this child as only a much younger woman could. So I thank you Nemain, for bringing this news for if the spirits are excited with the prospect of bringing a child of the Gods to the flesh, I am honored to be the vessel to bring that child forth."

In that moment, Faidhe was put in mind of the vision she'd experienced earlier when she clasped Laoghaire's arms upon the speaking platform. She saw herself as a man, standing with a Staff facing Laoghaire across a great mountain divide until the flame of the masculine energy flared so until there was no longer a view of Laoghaire upon the opposing summit. Then the phrase, *blood of my blood* echoed in her mind as well.

"I had not been privy to this information in the prophecy but this can be none other than part of laying plans for the future coming of great changes."

The silence at the table was loud in the midst of all the music and merriment of the feast as each member of the table tried to calculate what this might mean for the Tuath while others, still calculated what a child of the spirit might mean to benefit them.

19

The Traveler Met

We followed Thomas's directions and found our way to Midleton without any trouble at all. As we drove in to town we noticed the immediate change in atmosphere. The countryside was open and freeing with a fresh scent to the air but the closer we got to Midleton, the grayer the scenery became. There were small homes and shabby storefronts seemingly a manifestation of the meager livelihoods people eked out in this town; just enough to stave off the cold, nothing fancy, utilitarian at best. I felt almost claustrophobic as we came to the end of the access road into Midleton and entered the town, proper. The feeling of sadness of years of poverty and day after day of unanswered prayers weighed on me here. I was overwhelmed with mental images and audible snippets of years of sorrow, broken hearts and broken dreams. Frustration and resignation. Desires, futile desires, want for a drink with despair flooded my emotions. I fought being a sponge absorbing all this toxic melancholy as I was bombarded by the tsunami of emotions of the lives that desperately carried on behind the doors and windows of these meager houses. I became aware that my fingers held the steering wheel in a white knuckled grip as I wrestled with this fiendish depression.

Glancing at Nora, her expression told me she was having a similar experience. I could also feel her impatience at having to endure this unpleasantness. I started to talk to her in a falsely cheerful tone as a distraction to the oppressive waves of sadness.

"Let's stop at the first decent looking restaurant or coffee shop. A larger town like this will definitely have coffee somewhere. I'm about as ready as I could be for a pick-me-up. Maybe we'll get some pastry or lunch or something for Finny McDonough too. It's almost lunchtime. You think that'll be something he'd like? You hungry yet?"

I knew I was chattering but it seemed to be working.

"There! Pull over. There's a bakery." Nora pointed.

"Oh good."

I swerved to the right side of the street temporarily forgetting the rules of the road and pulled into a parking spot in front of the bakery conspicuously backwards. Nora's eyes goggled at me and I had to laugh. It was a nervous laugh that seemed to relieve a bit of the pressure in the car.

Now that I'd parked and we were just a few steps away from the bakery, I began to think of going in to the store as a major task. An overwhelming feeling of anxiety started to blossom in my chest. Thoughts scurried across my mind like rats in the night. *Is it safe to go out there? This place looks dangerous. We're so far from home. What if something happens to us?* My mind raced with fears, doubt and insecurities and showed me pictures of all kinds of threatening events that made me just want to turn the car around and head for the safety of our cottage. Or better yet, catch an early flight home. Then it hit me all at once, that smell! Ugh! The rotten meat and wet fur smell. It was all throughout the car surrounding us, permeating our clothes, oozing into our skin, eating away at our will...*Get out of here! Get Out of Here! GET OUT OF HERE!* **GET OUT!**

"Listen!" I said. "We have to do something to start to protect ourselves from all this..." I waved a hand around in the air searching for the right word to describe what I was feeling. "Stuff." I blurted, settling for a word though not eloquent, related my message well enough. "You smell that?"

"Oocck." Nora agreed with a disgusted sound expressing her opinion of how she felt about the odor. But in her eyes I could also detect the same fear that was sickening my heart. She looked around the car as though searching for an escape route while rolling up her window. I didn't know if she was trying to block out the smell or protecting herself from some unspecified danger. Although I didn't know exactly what Nora was experiencing, I did know it was probably panic similar to my own. I felt the urgency to leave now so intently that my stomach was threatening to heave.

"Let's do something here. Is this what people who live here feel like all the time? Are we picking up on their pain? Can't we protect ourselves? We can recognize the sensations without being overwhelmed, can't we? Let's do something." I repeated. I didn't like the whine I heard in my own voice.

"Like what?" Nora's answer smacked of resignation. I liked even less the tone in her voice or the implication that we'd be so easily sucked in empathically to the feelings of the town around us without a fight. I clawed at her hands impulsively to grasp them in solidarity.

"Take my hands. Close your eyes and think of good things. Think of Grandma and her stories. Think of Mom's cooking. Think hard, concentrate on people you love. Think of your proudest moment or your greatest achievement, your best orgasm, anything good in your life. Block out this feeling of hurt and pain. Don't let it in. Don't feed into it. Block it." She looked at me a bit bewildered and I shook her hands violently.

"Ow!"

"Do it! Close your eyes and concentrate!"

As we squeezed each other's hands, I gave her a nod of reassurance that I didn't feel at all. Once she'd closed her eyes, I took a deep cleansing breath ignoring the smell and closed my own. In my mind, much more quickly than I have expected, a scene popped into my head:

Christmas lights and a table laden with so many treats it might have moaned. When we were kids, our family celebrated Yule/Christmas with mixed traditions. Our mother was half Swedish and she followed the Scandinavian tradition of having our house open to family, fully decorated, and a smorgasbord table covered with myriad traditional treats: cardamom wreath bread, real fruitcake, whitefish casserole, and real nog from an old family grog recipe. In part, we did the smorgasbord thing because it was my Nana's (Mom's mother's) birthday too.

For a moment, I was actually there in our beautiful Victorian house in Dorchester. I smelled the smells of steam heat radiators and Swedish meatballs mixed with the fresh scent of pine boughs and a fir tree. A calm washed over me and lent me the feeling of being cleansed, as the earth is fresh after a hard and fast rain. I heard the echoes of aunts, uncles and cousins from both sides of my family talking and laughing.

Then, the scene changed and I found myself in my childhood bedroom where I felt warm and safe listening to family noises one floor below while I enjoyed the rare treat of having my childhood pet, Baron, a handsome German shepherd, in my bedroom with me. It was one of those special moments in my childhood that all was right in my world and I had a sense of having found a perfect place to fit into time and the universe with my family. The winter solstice, when time hung between two worlds. Perfection. Magic.

From that feeling of safety and comfort, a new scene took shape for me and formed into a kind of a song or a chant, but not quite, almost told as a story. That's it, a story in my head. It was so dreamlike and so real at the same time. I actually saw the words spontaneously form from the Yule scene of family in my mind's eye. The words rose and they were recited and arranged themselves visually, almost dancing as they repeated in my head. The voice that told the story was familiar to me but I couldn't make out who owned it because the lines were recited in repetition so that before the line ended, it began again so the recitation sounded as though it was performed by many, though I knew it was one voice that told the tale but try as I did, I couldn't recall whose voice it was. I only know that it told the tale with the sweet and lilting accent of Ireland:

There is a sheen on contented faces, kindled by dance and food
*And the smell of **laughter** is on our breath*

The warmth of the fire that burns with tales of centuries past,
Pales in the glow of friends and family
The log crackles with history's tales and pops with holly berries
All wrapped with garland of the Ivy Queen
The spirits and memories of those gone over, come to dance with us and join
Frey
*Our passion, the essence of our **laughter**, love, sto-*
ries and song, collects on the panes –
And as the cold taps at the window, white ferns paint the glass
The gathering is sheathed from the night so...
The inevitable darkness must wait
We notice not, the moment the old year departs and the new one is birthed
Still we eat and drink and sing and laugh
The night has no choice but to settle
To wait
To watch for the Light to return
As do we, to greet the year anew

I abruptly opened my eyes to find an expression of utter joy on Nora's face. As if she felt a shift in my body or my energy she began to stir. Reluctantly, she opened her eyes and as she looked at me her nostrils flared.

"Evergreen?" She said.

"Yeah." I answered. The scent of salty air and seawater filled my nose. An image of blue waters licking at a sandy shore flashed across my mind.

"Beach?" I inquired.

"Mmm huh." Nora nodded her head.

We'd mentally shared a glimpse of aspects of each other's strident visions, different but with unified purpose. We looked around the car as though testing the air. We assessed our emotional frame of mind to discover the feeling of despair and foreboding replaced with kind of a sense of well-being and contentedness.

"Did you get the song type thing?" I asked her.

"No, I didn't hear any music. Just waves and lots of distant laughter, people and us kids having fun and being together just enjoying the ocean and sand and warm sun on a long lazy day." She looked wistful.

"Yeah me too; but mine was different. It was a strange thing to watch." I said, energized by the experience. "I was thinking about our family Yule celebrations when we were kids and all of a sudden, right from the scene in my head there were these words dancing above everything but a part of everything at the same time. It was almost as though they were created from or a part of the *feeling* of the family and the special time but a combination of all the scents and sounds of the day too.

Like the words could be heard, but were visible and emotional at the same time. A visceral manifestation of everything that those celebrations were for us, but not just us, for every generation for centuries before us. Kind of a manifestation of the family when it was all together."

I stopped, realizing that any description of the words would not relate the feeling behind them or the creation of them. I tried again.

"It was so powerful! And the word 'laughter' was different from the others. It was beautiful in script and colors as though that were a most important aspect of all those people and gatherings through the years, beyond all the food and trappings. Laughter! There was one other word that had some kind of significance too. The word 'Frey' stood out in fanciful lettering that sort of moved and flowered in bright colors of yellow and blue. It was almost a living word with personality...Ahh, I know I'm not saying it right." I stopped again, in reflection. "Kind of weird to go buy pastry now isn't it? It seems so mundane. Let's not forget this okay Nora? Something just happened here. We did something, ahh..."

"Important?" Nora put in. "Big? Meaningful?"

"Yeah, I think. This means something. If we stick together and harness whatever power we have, we might, ahh...Shit! I don't know. It feels like whatever is going on here is happening...It's like trying to assemble something without knowing what it is and without any instructions but we have to trust our intuition and each other to build whatever the thing is. Because I think the thing, is important. Make sense?"

"Sort of. Like trust the internal compass, not the map." She took a stab at her own analogy. "You feel any better?"

I looked up toward the ceiling of the car as I took my emotional temperature.

"Lots. Let's get going though. But wait!" I hesitated. "I want to write this down first, before it goes right out of my mind. I don't know if it'll be word for word, but I want to get the basics of what I saw down on paper."

I rummaged through my satchel for a piece of paper and pen to record the prose I'd just heard and seen. It seemed necessary that I begin recording in earnest what was happening to us here in Ireland. Until now, I'd just been scribbling a travel journal but it seemed more urgent to me that I document what was going on now and what we were doing or rather, what was happening to us. For now though I had to get the vision-prose recorded before it was lost. I could concentrate on the detailed daily journal later.

Feeling energized, we entered the small bakery through the old wooden and beveled glass door to be met with the cheery tinkling bell over the door, a round faced counter girl and scents very similar to those I'd just experienced in the car. The bakery had a yeasty, sweet smell holding promise of decadence and chocolate topped with something gooey. And the distinctly enticing scent of real brewed coffee. I felt infinitely better!

Armed with three large Styrofoam cups filled with the magic elixir, a bag of a half a dozen scones, a few brownies and some bready kind of pastry frosted with a sugary drizzle and covered with slivered almonds, we piled back into the car. Just the smell of the coffee made my mouth water for a crumbly pastry dunked in the hot juice. But even the foam cups were too hot to hold and I had to scramble to put them into the cup rack, the only obvious luxury feature in the car. Two cups there and one on the dash, I blew on my fingers resenting the fact that I'd obviously have to wait to sip my coffee or else burn the skin off my tongue. Nora grabbed the dashboard cup and stuck it between her feet on the floor to secure it while we drove. Inhaling the coffee scent as deeply as I could without hyperventilating, I shoved the car into drive and pulled back over to the left side of the road to find the Holy Rosary Cemetery and Finny McDonough.

———

The church and cemetery were a brief four minutes beyond the bakery. The church, a huge overblown ordeal of construction was, I suppose, meant to be imposing and it was. Covering about three or four acres in stained glass and stone, the church would inflict the fear of God into anyone within a country mile. Following Thomas, the gas station owner's instructions, we found the road leading around to the back of the church to find the cemetery entrance. The steep road twined up and up until finally we came upon the hidden entrance behind the church. I pulled as far off the road as I could to park because there was no parking lot on this side of the burial ground and someone had abandoned an old jalopy truck on the other side of the entrance to the cemetery that took up what little space there was outside the gate.

My little Pagan heart beat quickly in the shadow of the looming church. I stood beside the car to scan the cemetery for an office to inquire about Finny McDonough. Trees and shrubbery grew thick in back of the church and in the shadow of the great stone structure and together with the darkening sky, conditions made visibility poor. I stretched hopefully peering over countless Celtic crosses and headstones in the graveyard deciding that I really didn't want to go into the church or rectory on my business here. Knowing it could not possibly have cooled enough to drink yet, I reluctantly eyed my coffee and closed the car door to scout out the mysterious McDonough.

Just as I ventured toward the cemetery, almost on cue, the town's gray attitude opened up a dismal patch of sky over Midleton to baptize us with a raw and relentless mist as though the town itself didn't want us to get away with deflecting the natural state of loneliness and despair.

"It figures." I mumbled. And feeling responsible for the rain, I said, "Sorry Nora. Whyn't you wait in the car. I'll see what I can find out."

"Yeah, okay. I came all this way to sit in the car beside a cemetery and let you go crashing around Ireland by yourself to find a guy who's likely going to try to pick your pocket for a story that you're likely to let him. Right."

Grammar aside, I got her point and was grateful that she was with me whether she agreed with my quest or not.

"'Kay. Thanks. Let's go see what's in there. Wait a sec." I turned back to the car and grabbed my camera out of the back seat. Then we started back toward the entrance to the graveyard. Once we passed through the gates, the blanket of quiet was almost corporeal. The inevitable crows one finds in a graveyard covered a distant tree but were eerily silent as they hopped from limb to limb and twitched their feathers and wings. There were no other apparent visitors brushing away leaves from the stones of loved ones, no one busily digging to nestle some budding flower. No sniffling family dressed in black hovering over their dazed goodbyes. Nothing. The only sound we heard was that of the hissing mist that collected on our hair, dampened our clothes and pricked cold needles at our skin.

Nora wondered out loud just what I'd been thinking.

"Wonder why the guy'd hang out here. He *must* work here or something so let's look for a maintenance shed or equipment barn."

We walked through the entire landscape, stopping on occasion to read an interesting epitaph or focus on a likely picture. After about a half an hour, we'd determined that there was no such maintenance staff or at least, no one on duty at the moment. Nora punctuated the fact.

"No sign of life."

I looked at her to see if she was trying to be funny but saw by her expression that she wasn't even aware of her pun. I gave a little giggle and she looked to see what I was laughing at. It took her a second but she caught on to her unwitting humor.

"Oh!" She said. "Ha." Then, "Time to go back?"

Unenthusiastically I agreed as my attention was drawn to the tree full of crows as they set up a ruckus about something.

"Maybe it just wasn't meant to be. Maybe just as well. Yeah, let's go. Thanks for coming, though."

I felt deflated having been deprived of my answers and adventurous tale because I knew there was no way Nora would go on this goose-chase a second time. I was hesitant to give up on finding Finny McDonough but was also eager to get back to the car and flip on the heat for a few minutes before we decided where we'd go next. And I was hopeful that the coffee would still be at least warm and the pastries still sweet.

Nora knew I was disappointed but didn't really hide her relief that the mysterious Finny was nowhere in sight.

"Where to?" She asked as we headed toward the car.

"Dunno yet. Let's just grab our coffee and warm up for a few minutes."

Seeming to have enough of a plan for the moment, we walked back to the car in silence. I thought we might look at the maps to see what else there may be to investigate in this area. As I opened the driver's side door to the car I saw Nora walk toward the ramshackle abandoned truck that was parked across the way. Focused for the first time on the thing, I noticed that the door on the back was open and inside of the wooden house-door that served as an entrance to the trailer like box on the rear of the truck's bed, cooking utensils and pans hanging from hooks on a peg board could be seen. Then I noticed that there was actually a screen door obviously belonging on a farmhouse somewhere was also attached to the rear of the vehicle. The wood door was open to the air and I could see shelves of canned food and a hot plate on a larger shelf that may have also served as a table. Images of the traveling professor, the Wizard's counterpart in The Wizard of Oz popped into my head. The construction of the truck boggled my mind; it was an amalgam of several different parts cobbled together to create a mobile home of sorts on the back of the old vehicle. The roof was a fiberglass cap to a pickup truck that sat atop sheets of scrap aluminum welded together. This raised cap sat on what looked to be pickup truck with a bed that had been extended in length by using more pieces of scrap aluminum or metal taken from other vehicles and patched together. *Frankenstein meets Wizard of Oz.* To my absolute amazement, there seemed to be some kind of smokestack on the opposite side of the truck belching out plumes of peat smoke I hadn't noticed before. Then it occurred to me. *Oh my God, someone lives in that thing!*

I wanted my coffee and food but kept an eye on Nora feeling all at once, the isolation of our location. *What the hell was she doing over there?* As she turned the expression on her face was an odd mixture of exasperation and resignation. There was a moment of hesitation when she seemed to make up her mind about something and then she slowly waved me over to the truck/house.

"Bring the coffee." She shouted over between her cupped hands.

A stab of excitement and adrenaline bolted through my solar plexus.

"Is it him?" I knew the answer already. The expressions on Nora's face betrayed what she'd just been thinking even if I hadn't felt her mixed emotions at the reality of finding the illusive Finny. She nodded and waited for me to collect our offerings and join her outside Finny's front or was it back door.

"Hello?" I called into the door. Not knowing the protocol for entering a truck/trailer we waited to be invited in or to see if its owner would come out to speak with us. I had mixed feelings about what I was most hoping for.

From inside the truck I heard the same lilting accent I'd long associated with home, safety and being protected. This was a County Cork accent for sure. This man sounded very much like Grampa, our paternal grandfather.

"Are ye the gorls I'm expectin' then?"

I looked to Nora and in a whisper, asked her just to be sure.

"Is he Finny?"

"Yeah. I think so." She whispered back.

I gave an impatient facial expression to ask, *Well what the hell does that mean?*

I called into the back to ask if anyone there might know a Finny McDonough and a guy's voice, she nodded toward the truck, said,

"'Ye might be findin' him here.'"

Rolling my eyes at the uncertainty I asked in the direction of the open door.

"Are you Finny McDonough or do you know where we might find him?"

"That depends on whether you'd be the gorls I'm expectin'." Then a snicker.

"Mr. McDonough," I said with little patience, "it's cold and wet out here and we're here to speak with you on the recommendation of Cath...ah." For the first time I realized that I didn't know Cath's last name, nor could I remember if it were on his business card. "...Cath. If you are Mr. McDonough, you will be expecting us."

I didn't know if this was a man pulling my leg or if it was actually the man we'd been looking for but I was just about finished with the game.

"Then I guess you'd be the gorls I'm expectin. Yer wastin' time out dere. Are ye comin' in or not?"

We took that for about as much of an invitation as we were going to get and, coffee and pastry in hand, we walked toward the humble entrance to Finny McDonough's home. I peeked in beyond the open door into the truck bed to see a surprisingly cozy space within. Stepping up onto a wooden box that served as a step and onto the rear bumper of the truck, I was the first through the door, which up close I could clearly see had been cut down to accommodate the tiny entrance to the trailer because I had to stoop down to a crouch to squeeze into the living space. It reminded me of the little doors depicted at the base of oak trees in my childhood stories. Nora followed right behind me and I understood her raised eyebrows because like me, she was not expecting the pleasant interior to such an outwardly derelict construction.

Once inside, there was just enough room to stand comfortably and there seemed to be much more room than what I thought was reasonably possible. The space was utilized to the nth degree but each area of living could be easily determined. The kitchen was obviously just inside the door with all the cooking accoutrements hanging on the back of the door and on the peg-board. Shelves of food were neatly organized over the hotplate and tiny sink area. So obviously, Finny had rigged up some method for having water in the trailer. A shelf served as an eating space with a stool tucked under one side of the space beneath it while not in use and on the other side under the shelf was a small, dorm room type refrigerator. The living room held an oversized leather chair and matching ottoman fit for a king that was strategically placed next to a wall of pine-board shelves that groaned with books, papers, and most surprisingly, on a fold-out shelf for use in the easy chair, a laptop computer! All the shelves were constructed with an apron across the front to prevent any books or goods from falling off when the truck was in motion so presumably the truck was mobile! There were several floor-to-ceiling box-type shelves that held neatly folded clothing, linens and personal items. Built in to the shelves was a partition that jogged out about 18 inches behind the great leather chair that, I assumed, must have hidden, the toilet area. The interior walls to the soldered scraps on the exterior had been insulated and neatly covered with sheet rock, which very much made the truck feel warm and inviting but the real homelike warmth came from the tiniest potbellied stove I'd ever seen that stood about 18 inches high in its own spot in between the kitchen space and the living room space sitting atop an elevated slab of slate and attached to it was the pipe vent that could be seen as the smokestack from the outside of the abode. On the slab next to the stove was a rectangular copper box holding several blocks of peat and some pre-rolled logs of newspaper with a cardboard box of kitchen matches. There were a few pictures on the walls, actual pictures with frames, not just pin ups. This was truly someone's home. And that someone was nestled in the leather easy chair with a smirk upon his lips and a glint of mischief in his eyes. It appeared that he was thoroughly enjoying our expression of amazement at the unexpected and snug interior of what I'd dismissed as an old abandoned jalopy. Trying not to appear so dumbfounded as to be rude, I closed my mouth and tried to remember that I was a guest and that this man was gracious to have invited us here to do some research.

"Mr. McDonough? My name is Lee O'Leary and this is my sister, Nora. We're very pleased to meet you." I realized that I couldn't shake his hand due to the fact that I was still holding two coffees and a bag of pastries. "Oh, these are for you." I said. "I hope you like scones. There're some other things in there too. We brought you a coffee too but it's probably cold by now." I didn't really know what else to say as the man in the chair hadn't said anything since we entered his home. "Uh sorry, but it took some time to find you. This is an unusual location for a home. We almost left, not knowing that someone lives here." Losing my arsenal of small talk, I sort of petered out of conversation. I turned to Nora for inspiration and she looked at me as if to say: *This is your show; don't look at me.* So I looked expectantly back to Finny... Still nothing. I stepped forward and handed the bag to Finny who opened it and peered deeply into the top, taking his time inspecting the goods within. Once he appeared satisfied, he rolled the bag closed again and got up from his chair with some considerable effort as it squeaked in its leathery voice.

Finny stood about 5'2" and if Cath was an older gentleman, Finny seemed ancient, road worn. But to his credit, he stood with a straight back and I noticed he had an incongruously thick head of downy, white hair. Still silent, he slid effortlessly past us to the kitchen area placing the bag on one of the shelves. That done, he reached out and took the coffees from my hands and placed them on the table/shelf and removed the covers. He then turned to Nora and took the one she was holding and repeated the action. As we watched this ritual I wondered if he planned to reheat the coffee. Cold or reheated, I didn't care, I'd enjoy it either way. Taking a cup in each hand, Finny extended the cups out the open door and poured them on the ground. Turning, and carefully putting the empty cups in the little sink, he dumped the last coffee onto the existing brown puddle outside his door and placed the third cup, stacked inside the other two, in the sink.

"Poison it is. And ye'll lorn that though ye think it wakes ye, it'll sure close yer eyes te yer seein'. I've been sent word of yer comin' by me brother Cath who tells me as ye've got the seein'. So ye'll not be poisonin' yer gifts with that stuff of the racin' mind and heart."

I caught myself just before wailing but I wanted to wail at the little man and the *nerve* of him to dump out my coffee! And then his words sunk in.

"Wait. What? Cath is your brother? He never said anything about that."

I did the automatic mental calculations when informed of a relation between two people. Was there any physical resemblance; do they sound alike and so on. I thought Finny had a much heavier accent than Cath and his eyes; unlike Cath's warm brown, were an incredibly pale shade of blue. Cath was small but substantive, while Finny was tiny, bordering skinny. Finny's fingers were extraordinarily long for one so small but they appeared to be painfully gnarled with arthritis. This feature made his hands appear grasping, almost scary. But beyond these differences, there was definitely something familiar in Finny's mannerisms and facial expressions that spoke of his kinship to Cath. And if it can be said, he *felt* to me of the same comfortable presence as Cath did, once I got past his gruff and crusty exterior. I hoped that Nora would be able to pick up on this sense of sincerity that seemed to emit from this soul despite the wizened exterior, much like the interior of the trailer felt like a home despite what it appeared to be from the outside. I felt the same sense of comfort coming over me here as I had during lunch with Cath and I hoped that Nora would feel it too. I wasn't sure if she'd picked up on his comment about "the seein'" but I had to assume that was their word for our magic. Now that Finny had let the cat out of the bag that I'd told Cath about our abilities I knew I'd have to share with her that I'd given Cath intimate knowledge of our family and demonstrated a bit of our magic. If she could feel the sense of comfort I did, then it would soften the blow when I finally explain everything to her.

"It'll be tea we'll have. Ye've done me a fine torn bringin' those treats. From Cassey's Bakery was it? Sure, she's got the touch fer the scones she does. Not a bit dry, and a pinch more sugar than most. I'm partial te sweets."

We stood gaping at Finny as he set about filling a kettle with spring water, I assumed, from a glass jug and setting it on the flat top of the potbellied stove.

"Go on now and sit dere." He demanded pointing at the ottoman.

I guess he wanted to insure that neither of us would presume to sit in his chair. Dutifully, we squashed our rear ends onto the footrest and tried to make ourselves as small as possible in the confined space. Finny unhooked three well-used tea mugs from the underside of one of the shelves and pinched samples of tea from a few different canisters then from another. I noticed that he'd pinched different amounts of various leaves in each of the cups. A scurrying thought of possible danger crossed my mind. At that very moment, his blue eyes lighted on me as if he'd heard my mind.

"Tea is more than fer the flavor in the drinkin'. Ye drink the mixture of the leaves, as'll do ye the most good. There'll be no harm come te ye from tinctures such as these. Ye, Miss O'Leary, blond one, have the need of clear sleep and this'll ease its comin'. And the other Miss, corly brown," I realized that he was referring to our hair as identifying features, "will benefit from lettin' the truth passed yer guarded heart."

Always very proud, I could feel Nora stiffen next to me and responded quickly before her indignation could get loose after such a personal observation from a stranger.

"Well Mr. McDonough, snowy white," I said following suit with what I hoped was humor, "please call me Lee. And regarding my sleeping patterns, it seems you're a bit off track in your assessment. I have such trouble waking up since we've been here that if you give me something to aid me in sleeping, first, I won't be able to drive home and second, I'm afraid I'll miss the rest of my trip by sleeping through it! So if you don't mind, I'll say no thanks."

"I didn't say as ye couldn't sleep. I said ye have the need of clear sleep. Are ye dreamin' since ye've been here?"

I thought for a moment of the fractured and confusing dreams I'd experienced lately and a flash of my dream from last night popped in my head for a millisecond and then was gone.

"Well, I *do* dream but I can't seem to remember them very well when I wake up. Sometimes I feel like I want to grab at the thoughts and that just makes them slip away from me."

"Ha!" He said triumphantly as if I'd just made his point for him. "Yer workin' too hard when yer sleepin'. Ye need te be able te sleep and rest while yer *other* gathers what comes yer way. Then ye'll rest easy and wake fresh with all the lornin' is sent ye. That coffee takes a time te leave off and let ye get back te the livin'. Have ye been long on the evil tit?"

I was having difficulty trying to keep up with what Finny was saying and to decipher his accent at the same time. To buy a little time I tried to repeat what he said translated into Americaneeze.

"Are you saying that I'm not really getting sleep, ah, deep enough because I drink coffee so the dreams I have can't be remembered and on some level, I know this and I try harder to stay asleep to catch whatever message is in my dream? Are you saying that my dreams are important; that they're trying to tell me something?" I could feel my face screwed up with concentration and consciously released the expression. I decided to ignore the 'evil tit' remark all together.

"Ye've got the idea in general, as they say. And are ye tellin' me that ye're a woman of yer age and in yer entire life, with the seein' ye have, ye've not yet discovered that yer dreams are the ticket te great lornin' from other times and other places? Is this why I've waited me entire life fer ye? Te have te teach ye all as though ye were naught but a slip of a gorl with not a stitch of sense?"

I was nonplussed and Nora, who was about to boil over, began to stand up when Finny caught himself.

"Ah now, I'm runnin' off at me own excitement. Cath has said as ye've got a talent and it's been a great while since there's been such a one as yerself te hang me hope on. I'm sorry, lass. Believe this from an old man who's waited a long lifetime and has grown crotchety with the wait. Let's have our tea now and begin again, shall we?"

During the discussion, Finny had prepared the tray with milk and honey, napkins and three spoons and poured the hot water over the loose tealeaves then handed Nora and me our respective mugs. I noticed the plate of Keebler cookies on the tray and wondered about the scones and pastries.

Nora decline the spoon Finny offered. "No thank you I take my tea black."

"Nonsense! Finny responded. "That's a terrible cup of tea! Ye've got te honor all gifts in the taking of the sacred."

He poured a bit of milk into her mug before she could protest and then squeezed in a gold stream of honey leaving the spoon in the liquid for her to stir.

"The water's one, heated by the fire, that's two, to make the steam, poured over the leaves, that's three, conjures the aromatics, that's four. All yer elements dere but ye've te add the others as does honor te yer ancestors. Ye call yerself an O'Leary! Ye must have a nod te the dairy and a bit of the sweet gold te bind whatever's yer desire or te keep pure and sweet yer intentions in the cup."

Nora and I looked at each other. I wondered if she'd drink the tea or set it down in indignation. I shrugged my shoulders, picked up the milk and poured with a mock flair then ritually poured a column of golden honey into my cup as well. I offered Nora one of her own well-used expressions. "When in Rome..."

I raised my mug slightly in his direction as he settled now into his chair with his own cup."

Thanks for your hospitality, Mr. McDonough."

In my first sip of the tea, I tasted something almost familiar, but couldn't quite place it. I sipped again as deeply as the hot liquid would allow. The rich aroma rose to my nostrils and I couldn't take in enough of it. First, I felt my hunger dissipate and my muscles began to unclench systematically beginning with the skin on my forehead and the muscles in my neck. I was unaware these muscles were holding tension at all then I felt the release all the way down my shoulders and back. I felt my lungs expand easily with a breath that uncoiled a knot in my chest I hadn't even known was there until it was absent. My legs and feet enjoyed the sensation as relaxation poured down them as if gravity turned them to warm liquid. Another deep breath and I felt just fine. A profound sense of well-being and relaxation allowed me to enjoy the best cup of anything I'd ever had in my life. *Before we leave I have to find out what this tea is and where I can get some.*

The stove let off the homey scent of peat and wrapped me in soothing warmth while the contrasting cool draft from the open door rippled in lifting my hair slightly and giving the air a clean flavor. I felt completely at ease for the first time since...well, since I don't know when. I could feel my face take on the expression of a dreamy smile as I looked over at Nora. I observed without alarm that she was crying silent tears. I continued to watch as the droplets progressed down her cheeks. *"You okay?"* I asked, only marginally aware that I hadn't spoken aloud. Nora wouldn't look at me but answered me in the same fashion.

"Yeah. I'm okay but I can't tell you how out of control I feel. I'm like an open wound here. I feel so exposed but...okay. I reached in slow motion across what felt like miles, even though she was crammed onto the same seat with me and took her hand in mine. I felt as though I were in a dream due to the surreal way I experienced my senses. When my hand touched Nora's two things happened: she began to cry in earnest sobs and I entered into a realm that I can only describe as: I was visiting the house of her mind. I felt what she was feeling and I knew that her description of being exposed didn't begin to relate the experience she was having.

I found myself inside the metaphoric house of Nora's world. Her mind, heart, her very existence. I observed that she'd kept the doors carefully closed and locked with the window shutters slats closed tight. Nora had only allowed cautious moments of exposure to keep tight-fisted control over everything that happened in her house. Shades of some windows in the attic are open to light of learning. Knowledge is carefully let in and collected. A first floor window is open a crack to get to know a friend. I see a figure, her husband, with a foot in the door but the door had been chained from the inside. Windows at the front of the house could be opened briefly to perfect the window boxes so all will look right to the outside world, then would surely be secured again when all appears to be well and blossoming. Furniture arranged for interior comfort. Multiple storage boxes neatly stacked, labeled and arranged in all the storage spaces for easy access for whenever a tidbit of knowledge is needed.

Nora seems frantic. The house is groaning as the windows begin to creep up on their own. The doors rattle slightly as if they're going to fly open any moment. She looks around and realizes that someone, me, is in her house. She heads toward the back of the house away from me.

At the back of the house, well hidden from the windows is a mantle. The mantle is decorated with well-worn pictures of loved ones above a tepid fire in the hearth that illuminates the pictures. I look for my face among those on the mantle and don't find it. The house is neat as a pin, no clutter. Nora stands beside the hearth wringing her hands at the prospect that someone is in her house. Even me. I look above the pictures to a small, round window over the mantle. Odd, I think, because the window is cut into where the chimney would be right above the heart...no hearth. It's out of place. It's different than the other windows, having no shutter. It seems that there have been several attempts to put up elaborate window coverings to close it off but they've all been knocked down to the floor. Amidst the rubble of the failed covers I can see a curtain that has fine calico print but on closer scrutiny, within the print, I recognize written in the tiny pattern are harsh words Nora had said to me over the years. Another pile of refuse appears to be bricks with a depiction of the time Nora told me that I was an accident of birth never really wanted by my parents. Piled still higher are wooden slats from a broken shutter that have upon them remnants of a childhood taunt that cut me deep, "No wonder you have no friends." I see these and more failed attempts at barring the window from eyes and access into the room where Nora's heart...no hearth burns. Something appears to be posted above the window and I draw closer to see what it is. A small piece of manila construction paper torn from the corner of a larger piece is nailed above the window with a poorly drawn picture of a skeleton key in crayon and beneath the key are the words scrawled in childish letters: "Lee's window." I turn to Nora, who is standing fretfully, still wringing her hands with tears profusely flowing from her eyes.

"I didn't mean to hurt you." She said.

"I know that." I comforted.

"I was scared."

"Of what?"

She hucked in a shivering, heaving breath. "Of being different. That your loneliness would rub off on me. That people would reject me the way they do you. That I wouldn't be in control of how I'm perceived. That people would find out who I really am. You just kept coming. No matter what I did or said, you just kept loving me. It was almost embarrassing because I didn't deserve it especially in the way I pushed you away in front of other people. And because you found me loveable, you always had a secret entrance into me and you made a space for yourself right over my heart. I had no control. You just kept coming in. You were so vulnerable. So trusting. So wounded. I saw how you hurt and never wanted to feel like that so I made sure I didn't. I used the mask and made sure people respected me. I made sure I had all the childhood friends in the neighborhood even if it meant that you didn't have any. I separated from you publicly, in school and in the neighborhood but secretly admired how you lived so wildly and free on your own terms. I worried for you though. I thought you were brave."

"Nora, I wasn't brave. I just did what I had to do to survive. Just like you. And as kids and then as adults, you were always the place I knew I could call home. I kept coming, because you kept letting me in."

"No. I was mean. Look. Look at the mean things I said to you." She nudged the refuse on the floor with her toe. I blocked your entrance with cruel things and you kept coming in and loving me."

"Nora, you always let me in. Don't you remember?"

"No," she blubbered. "I didn't."

"Yeah, look." I pointed to the key above the window. "Don't you remember when you made this for me? We were little, still living in Jamaica Plain after Grandma died, before we moved and the family split up. We were on the top floor in our bedroom and you made this key for me. You told me it was the magic key to our secret world on the other side of the mirror in our room. Anytime I was in trouble, you said, the magic key would help me to escape into any mirror nearby and from there I could find my way back home to the mirror in our room. You gave it to me and even though I knew there was no real way to go into the mirror, the magic was in your love and protection, having that strength to draw upon helped me so many times. In that simple gift, that you gave to me freely, I had the key that connected me to you always. Maybe not into a secret mirror world, but your words were always there that I'd be able to come home to where it's safe, home away from trouble, home to you...always. Maybe you didn't know it at the time or maybe you didn't remember it, but you made a promise to me that day. There it is." I said pointing to the key. "And you put the window there. Not me. You gave me the key and an invitation to come home...whenever."

Startled, Nora looks at the window, and remembers her discomfort at truly letting anyone in. She gasps.

I look to where she's looking and am surprised too, to see the little round mirror from our early childhood bedroom hanging over the mantle where the window had just been, the magic paper key right above it.

"But I was so mean." She protests. "Why didn't you see that?"

"No. Enough! I did see it but I knew something else too." I point to the mirror and in it is our reflection as the children we were at the moment the key was given as a gift of magic and of the heart. Cocooned around us is a beautiful, soothing bright blue light. We watch together as our images in the mirror transform within the light to reveal a great dark bird where I stand and a hawk in the place where Nora is. The birds flutter their wings and the raven blasts a caw before it takes flight into the forest background in the reflection. After a moment, the hawk follows upward into the mirror-forest.

I turn away from the mirror toward a sound behind me and in the opposite corner in the room from the hearth is a great leather chair with Finny nestled in it, sitting quietly, apparently sleeping.

I opened my eyes with the echo of a voice ringing in my ears. *Birds of a feather, Lee. Birds of a feather.*

I checked to see where Finny was and felt a bit confused that he was right there in his chair with his eyes closed, just as I'd seen him in my vision. Was I aware of him here so he appeared in the vision? Was he actually there in the vision? Did Nora and I have some kind of parallel experience? Nora will have to tell me what she experienced, if anything, so we can compare notes. Looking at Nora sitting next to me with her eyes closed, I saw the tears still streaming down her face. Something in her countenance shifted and she appeared to be paying attention to something, but did not open her eyes. I was fairly certain that we'd experienced this vision together but I wanted her to open her eyes so I could confirm that what I'd just seen was something we'd actually shared.

Nora fiddled her fingers together in her lap and her head was bowed as if she were in prayer. Finally, as her eyes opened she continued to bow her head and look at her hands in her lap.

"I forgot about the key." She whispered through tears.

My heart leapt at the knowledge that we had the same vision.

"You saw it?" I asked.

"Yeah. I saw it. I mean, I didn't forget about it, I just didn't know that it held such significance. I thought it was a kid's game."

Nora seemed shaken and inhaled a trembling breath. She watched her hands as she fiddled at nothing in her fingers. Then she looked at me with red eyes and pointed intent.

"Lee, I'm so sorry. I remember saying those things but I didn't realize the impact of what my words may have had on you. I was trying to protect myself and wasn't consciously trying to hurt you. It's no excuse but it's all I have to justify how I could have hurt you like that, especially knowing how lonely you must have been."

"Nora, stop, please. If you have to say you're sorry to help heal yourself then I'll sit still and listen until you feel you're done but please, if you're saying you're sorry because you think I hold a grudge, or don't understand how you feel, please stop. I know you love me and no matter what you say, it's what you do that I see and have always seen. And you've always been my support, my partner in magic, my friend, my sounding board and beyond. If you weren't, there'd be no window, I'm sure."

This was all such an odd turn of events. We'd gone in search of Finny who was supposed to give me a story and we ended up rummaging around in each other's heads. I suddenly realized that Finny's eyes were open and we had an audience to this very personal exchange. I searched for something to say sufficient to the moment to bring us to some semblance of normalcy and to give Nora a chance to collect herself.

"Uh, good tea. What's in it?"

"Ye don't have te be doin' that Miss O'Leary. Yer sister's capable of dealin' with situations without ye runnin' interference fer her."

"What? I'm not running..."

I looked at Nora and was a bit shocked at the truth of Finny's statement. I was running interference for her. In fact, we had been complicit in our respective roles; Nora would take little or no crap from anyone as a way to protect herself and I would assume the role of smoothing things over to avoid an eruption in any situation.

"Well, she's upset and vulnerable right now." I said instead of denying the truth. "I just think she should have a minute to compose herself."

"And what makes ye think she's not able te fend for herself if that's what she's needin'?"

"I don't think that. It's just that I...we stick up for each other."

"Is there someone takin' advantage of her now that she needs ye stickin' up for her?"

He wasn't attacking me, it seemed as though he genuinely wanted to know about this dynamic Nora and I had unknowingly developed between us.

"No, but..." I looked at Nora and wondered why, for the first time, was I so protective of her feelings and why had I assumed the role of the protector between Nora and the world when she was obviously the one who had the experience with people and friends.

"And why is it that ye don't feel yerself worthy of an apology that ye've long desorved? Is it ye don't see yerself as valuable?"

"No!" I was becoming defensive. "She doesn't have to apologize to me because I know she didn't intend to hurt me."

"Then what was the truth of why she did it?" He pushed. "Of course it was her intention to hort ye. Otherwise, she'd not have said such things te ye. Apologize she should and ye should let her. From what I've seen, ye've got a true bond but ye've te work out the problems with naught else but the truth. Ye've got work te do now and this is no time fer savin' feelins in place of plain truth and honesty."

I was becoming overwhelmed and threw up a hand.

"Wait. Stop. Can we stop for a second? I need to know, Nora, you saw the mirror from our old bedroom and the attempts at blocking me out of the window?"

"Yes. And all the ways I've kept my life organized by keeping up appearances and making sure that I have very tight control over who gets in and how far."

"Okay, so we saw the same vision or whatever it was then. Right?"

"I think so. I saw you there and we saw the same things."

"Did you see anyone else there with us?"

Nora's eyes flashed toward Finny and we both looked at him.

"You were there too?"

"I was."

"How? How could you have been? We've been able to communicate like this to some degree because we're sisters. Although never like this before. How could you be there with us? How is that possible?"

Then it dawned on me that my childhood theory of the Irish being able to do magic was not entirely false. My enthusiasm began to perk.

"There are others? Like us, I mean? You can do magic? What do you know? Is this part of the story?"

"I believe me brother is right in his ideas about ye bein' one we've been waitin' for. But from what I've just now seen in the little round reflection of yer mirror, I've gotten some questions of me own. But as ye've come te get a story, I'll give ye what knowledge I have, as the bloodline here in Ireland has come to an end for the tellin' of the tale with me and Cath bein' old as we are and without any young folk for us te pass it on. And I'm hopin' yer ready for the hearin' of it. For as soon as the tale is told ye, ye'll be takin' on a responsibility of honor with it. Are ye ready then?"

Nora and I looked at each other and exchanged a look that said we hadn't a clue if we were ready for any of what he was talking about but by the same token, we both knew we weren't leaving Finny's little home without getting some clue as to what the hell was going on.

"I guess. Nora, you ready?" I asked.

She answered in a tone that was soft and inquisitive and noncommittal.

"Okay Finny, let's hear what you have to say."

"That ye're both here is an unexpected part of the way of things but now as I see ye both, and find yer foreign born from America, things may make a bit of sense I'd not seen but for yer visit. But now what's required is that the two of ye must swear that ye'll take yer part in the tale with reverence and gravity."

"Our part in the tale? What do you mean?"

"As I see it, and as has been told by many upon many a generation, yours are the ears for which the tale was told and the tale is not only fer yer ears, but it was told about ye as well. And so ye'll have a stake in how things play out. Will ye take the tellin' of the word and give me yer word that ye'll shed yer modern logic and doubts until ye've hord all?"

"I can't speak for Nora, but I've been open to hearing this tale from the minute I heard there was one...probably before that. In fact, Cath told me some of it and that's what brought us to you." Then like light dawning, a thought occurred to me. "Hey, since Cath told me some of the tale and sent me to you to hear the whole thing, does that mean the two of you are the ones from your generation that have been keeping the story?"

"That'd be right after a fashion. We're brothers of the McDonough clan, long known as the tinkers and travelers of the Isle. We've kept a humble existence te keep watch as time unraveled. Forst, we kept watch in all the parent countries waiting for some tidbit of news that could be the start of what was prophesied. There was much excitement at the discovery of the Great Pot in '91. We thought forst, it'd be England that'd give us The Named One for 'twas a great long time in fairly recent history that England held Power and rule over much of this part of the world but then the advent of America shifted our attentions, but after the discovery in Denmark, we thought to look to the Scandinavian countries for the Named One and wait we did. But then, we watched across the ocean, in the teens and orly 1920's as the battles of suffrage brought change about in America that we thought might be a sign. The Suffrage brought the vote to women and as such gave them a voice but no evidence of The Named One. Then, for a while there seemed to be somethin' brewin' in Germany that seemed a promise of the Power comin', though that was a devistatin' thing as it torned out. And then again in the 60's as we witnessed the women's movement rage across America we had hope that we'd see the release of the Power as women developed a voice in how things were to be run. As it was though, borning braziers became more the issue than did the idea of resorgience of strength for the feminine. But the freedom of expression in sexuality at that time held hope for us too, but still it came to naught. Then, in the '70's, we thought we'd real hope when a woman named Shirley Chisolm ran for President of the United States. And she had the countenance we though was a sure clue as te the coming of The Named One but as the story has it, she was not unassuming and did neither come to the Isle as to confirm her connection te the tale we hold, nor did she bear a name that could be reconciled with the tale so that was that, as they say."

Nora and I sat on the giant leather footrest and both had the expression of total confusion on our faces.

"Mr. McDonough...Finny," Nora asked. "What do you mean? I'm sorry, but Great Pot...Denmark...Germany...suffrage...Shirley Chisolm...the women's movement? I'm lost. Lee, do you know about any of this?"

I tried to mentally piece together what he might be getting at but really had no clue. Shaking my head. "No. I think Cath told me something about The Named One though. Remember I told you that the people who knew the story were waiting for someone to come along with the right name?"

"Yeah."

"Well, Cath said my names both first and last were a combination that he was interested in investigating and even more than that, he said that because our family has...ah, abilities, that makes us even more of interest to him."

Nora's head spun a sharp turn toward me. "Abilities? What might Cath know about that?" She said with widening eyes.

Having come through all that passed over the last 24 hours, I was fresh out of feeling regret or remorse for sharing something I'd kept secret for so long and after what we'd just been through with Finny, the cat was really already out of the bag.

"Nora, the time was right for me to share with Cath some information about our family and some of what we can do. He seemed to know about us in a way anyhow, so I shared and it felt right and he listened and seemed to be familiar with what I showed him to a degree. Besides, Cath knew about magic just like Finny was part of what just happened between us here. That's why he sent us to see Finny...I think. Because of the magic?" I directed this last in a question toward Finny.

"Yer right about that and we'll see what else ye might have in the way of knowin' tucked away for just this day but for now, let me shed some light on that which ye don't have of the story. Will ye have more tea before I start? For once I begin, ye'll be bound te stay 'til the end of the tale."

"Nora? You in or not?' I asked, trying not to sound as though I had any attachment to her answer. I knew I would stay no matter what, but I fervently hoped she'd stay too.

She seemed to be deciding something internally and after what seemed like a very long minute, she leveled her eyes at me. Nora was crying again.

"You have supported me in everything I've ever done. You've been there for me even at times when I didn't deserve it. After being reminded of just what we've meant to each other for a very long time, I'm in - for you. I'm in for the adventure. I'm in to learn about all the things out of the ordinary that I've chosen just to take in stride or use to my advantage without questioning any of it. I know that on some level, you're probably right and that Grandma and Grandpa knew something of all of this and that's why they kept us involved with the Old Ways and the old stories. All our lives, you've worn your connection to your magic on your sleeve and people shunned you for it without ever really knowing why they did it. Me, I hid it away and buried it to the public so they wouldn't reject me. Lee, you've been *my* home. You're the place I can be myself without ever fearing that I won't be accepted."

She took my hands in hers, and quite clearly I saw in my mind's eye, the small mirror above her hearth with the view of a forest in its reflection. She gently pulled me toward the mirror and we both stepped up onto the mantle base. Before I knew just what was about to happen, she took a willful step toward the mirror and all at once, I could see her standing in the forest on the other side of the reflection. But at the same time, I was still holding her hands. Nora gently pulled on my hands and in that moment, I too was on the other side of the mirror, standing in the forest.

"Now, I'm in, Lee. Really in."

I giggled at the pun and at the same time, marveled at all that had taken place. I knew that the strength of her promise was not belayed in the simplicity of her words. This was a promise sealed with magic. I knew that the element added gravity so as to make the promise more than just that, but rather a vow. And although I wasn't clear yet as to the significance of us crossing over into our magical world of childhood imagination, I knew we were in a place where I was the raven and she was the hawk. And I felt sure that held meaning as well. We were taking baby steps with this newfound freedom to utilize our magic like a fledgling bird tries its wings.

Slightly surprised to find that we were still sitting on the footrest, I turned to Finny, then looked out the little trailer door to the cold and gray afternoon.

"Okay Finny. We'll hear the tale and share with you what you need to know, if there's anything to share. We'll fill in the gaps for each other but you have much more to tell than we do and I think that'll probably take a while so if you'll excuse my rudeness either you break out the pastries we brought to have with that cup of tea or we have to go and get something to eat. What do you say?"

"Och!" He spat with clear disgust. "'Tis me's been rude gorls. I know the rules of hospitality and have all but ignored them. Let me put another brick into the belly."

Finny piled some peat into the potbellied stove and refilled the teapot to heat.

"I'll be takin' a few minutes to collect the tale and put meself in the right frame of mind like. That'll give me time to put on a lunch and we'll break some bread together proper. Will that do ye?"

"Yes thanks. Can we help?"

"Not that I don't appreciate the offer gorls, but yer me guests and I'll have none of it. Besides, I've naught but a bit of space and we'd more likely be fallin' over each other than getting anything done. Sit ye now and let me prepare."

20

The First Telling

It was a bit awkward trying to balance our plates on our knees but the cold beef and horseradish sandwiches Finny had prepared for us were just delicious. The beef had been cooked to perfection and lightly seasoned to taste just right.

"Finny, this is good!" I marveled at the quality of food he offered in this tiny little broken-down makeshift trailer.

"That'll be fresh farm beef yer enjoyin'. Ye'll not have had the likes of it from yer market shops. Tender and flavorful it is. And this cattle isn't after any of the injections and such. Just pure, fresh meat." Finny practically smacked his lips.

"You have a farm?"

Nora asked around a mouthful of sandwich while delicately trying to catch a drop of juice from the edge of her bread with her lips.

I was pleased to see that Nora seemed to be relaxed and enjoying Finny's company as well as her food.

"Better." He twinkled. "I've a woman friend who keeps a small farming concorn who's taken it as her own chore te see me fed. And in retorn, I tell me tales at her groups and clubs and such as like. She thinks me a gas man."

"A gas man?" I queried.

"Sure, a gas man. Ye know, she finds me funny with me stories."

Lamenting that I'd come to my last bit of beef and horseradish sandwich, I asked, "You tell stories to everyone? You mean you don't just have this one big story that you've been keeping?"

"Now how would I fill me belly that way, havin' a tale with naught but an audience of one in a lifetime te tell? There'll be plenty of stories that'll bring a hot meal or a sip of whiskey...or company of the right sort."

He twinkled again and I felt a little flushed at the insinuation that, although Finny was so advanced in his age, he still kept time with the ladies. Not like his brother in that respect, I supposed.

"Uh, Finny, can I ask you something?"

"Yer wonderin' how many years I've a right te claim?"

"Well, I'm a bit curious. You mentioned before, that you kept a watch on suffrage in the U.S. and I know that was in the 1920's. You must have only been a very young boy then. How could you have taken on your responsibility at such a young age? And you also said something about America coming into power. I can't figure what you meant by that either.

"Well, I suppose there's no harm in tellin' ye that I'm a wee bit older than I look." I thought he looked pretty old but didn't think it was proper to say so.

"Well, then" I sputtered, "you must be in remarkable health to have seen and remembered all that went on then as...um, a teenager?" I was still fishing.

"Aye. Good health." He repeated and slipped the question like an oiled fish. "Tell me about yer journey here te find me. Was it a pleasant drive? Exceptin' the weather of course."

It was not a very stealthy change of subject but I let myself be led away from my curiosity.

"The weather was actually pretty nice until we came to Midleton. Then it changed to dark and raw. But other than that, the ride was kind of pleasant. We even stopped to sit outside, for a while, on one of those dolmen stones you have all over the countryside."

"And what brought ye te the great stone?"

Nora and I looked at each other and she spoke first.

"Lee felt that the story Cath told her had some substance to it and I thought she should be more cautious about trusting...strangers. We stopped there so she could try to explain to me how important she thought it might be to come and listen to what you have to say."

She was matter of fact in the truth of it and didn't seem to feel any compunction about admitting that she'd mistrusted Finny or his brother. Their blue eyes met and Finny nodded. I don't know if it was just in his understanding her caution or that he approved of her wanting to shield me too, but he seemed to take no offense.

"And then?" He prodded.

"And then we came to town to find the bakery and you." She finished.

"That's not exactly right." I interrupted. "We stopped at a gas station to ask for directions first. Oh, and Thomas from the gas station said to say 'Hello' to you."

"Said te say hello, did he? Ha. Doubting Thomas? Coverin' his bases more like."

"No really" I protested. "He made it a point to send his regards."

"Well I'll not be so harsh as all that with the lad. He means well but tries te keep a distance from the traveler's reputation."

"Yeah, he mentioned something about the traveler's. What's that all about?"

"Thomas is me grandnephew and his skin's grown thin with the lifelong association of bein' kin te the family renown for bein' of the lowly station. Humble we are, and he took some ribbing as a boy for havin' a connection. He has a good woman in his wife Agnes though. She keeps him level and grounded."

"You're related? He didn't mention that. In fact, his nephew, Angus, said he didn't know you at all. You'd be related to him too wouldn't you?"

"Angus'd be blood te Agnes, not Thomas. Though he loves the lad, I'm sure. Now!" Finny said, with an air of leading away from any more small talk. "When ye left Thomas at the station te come here, did ye encounter anything that was out of the norm for ye? Did ye see, or hear anything...unusual?"

Nora answered by describing what she felt as we came to Midleton. I knew what she was describing because it was exactly what I'd felt too. Her lips peeled back in disgust.

"Loneliness, despair," She said. "Dejection, poverty, fear, doubt, anxiety, utter hopelessness. Absolute craving for a drink, horrible stinginess of heart, a complete lack of sympathy...Oh, it was awful. All these feelings just gnawing away at anything light-hearted or hopeful. It was...it was just awful...awful."

She looked as though the feelings threatened to come back and haunt her even now. I touched her hand and she came back to herself looking mildly disturbed.

"We both felt it." I said. "It was like an attack on us as we drove into town. I guess we were feeling the sadness of the town itself."

"No ye were not!" He snapped.

Nora and I startled at the vehemence in his tone.

"If anything'd tell me sure that yer te take the hearin' of the tale and play a role in the coming of the Named One, then that'd be it. There're places across this great land that have sacred spirits kept alive always with purity of reverence but those who'd have the Power for themselves in all this, have curdled their lust into something malevolent. It taints the very spirit of all it touches te keep it from naturally comin' together with its destiny te release the Power for the porpose for which it was cast. Understand, this part of the land, this town is one of those sacred places and so there's opposition at work here. Now did ye see or experience anything when this happened?"

"The smell?' Nora looked at me to confirm that part of our experience.

"Yeah," I agreed. "There was a nauseating smell that overtook us that was like decomposing flesh together with a feral smell like some dirty wild animal. In fact, that happened twice, no three times since we've been here: once on the ride here and once during the night when an apparition came to us and the next night when I caught our neighbors spying on us."

This caught Finny's attention. His head swung around and he leveled a look at me that scared me. A tickling sensation began to release adrenaline into my midsection just as it had on each of the occasions I'd experienced that smell.

"Finny, what? What is it? Do you know anything about what that smell is?"

He ignored my questions and answered with, "What's this about yer neighbors...spying? How? How de ye know? Have they knowledge that ye caught them? Where is it, exactly that yer stayin'?"

"Finny," Nora interjected "why are you so concerned? What should we know about that smell or the brothers? Are we...is this part of the story that you're going to tell us?"

Finny's shoulders slumped and he looked defeated for a moment. *"Brothers."* He mumbled to himself. Then, just as quickly, he straightened his back and took our plates over to the sink.

"Some years back," he started, "there seemed to be one who came to us with great possibilities in the way of the Power and some of the pieces of her name fit as well. Chiaro Vorace was her name, from Italy. Although some of the pieces didn't quite fit, we thought it was just us that we didn't see the symbolism in the way it was meant to be read. We met with Chiaro many times and she had a history that could be interpreted in such a way that we truly thought we'd found the one we'd been waiting for. You see, we're not only waiting to tell the tale but we're to tell the tale to the one about whom the tale is told...to a cortain degree. The catcher of the tale if you will. And this Chiaro was a dark beauty from Italy, with potential in her name and from one of the parent countries."

Nora broke in, "Finny, you said that once before. What do you mean by the parent countries?"

"These are the countries enlisted by the one who cast the story. The great mother, Faidhe journeyed through lands, directed by her intuition, if ye will, te lay the groundwork for the great casting of the Power and the tale te be told. These parent countries are those we've kept a watch on for a great many years, generation after generation with the hopes of meeting the Named One in a timely fashion. Among them are, Ireland, Italy, England..."

"Sweden and Germany!" I shouted with excitement. Finny and Nora looked at me in surprise.

"Right." Finny said.

"How did you know?" Nora questioned.

"The books I studied at Cath's store. All of the really old ones that had been translated were done in those languages: Gaelic, Italian, English, Swedish and German. You guys have been ready for someone to just come along and walk into your lives all this time but you never knew where they'd come from?"

"We didn't know from which country they'd travel but there were cortain aspects to their history and personality we'd keep a watch for so we'd have some indication when the right one would come. Forst, we knew the Named One would be female; 'A daughter of the future' as it was told. Then, we also knew to watch for one who carried the mark of the Power in her name and so when Chiaro came te be at one of me story tellins and expressed great interest in the mythic tales and in particular of how people in some ancient stories still were able to speak and communicate long after they'd died, we were interested in her, ye see because the one who the auld tale is meant for, will come asking for the very knowledge of the occult. Occult meaning things hidden – the Mysteries, not that Hollywood rubbish and nonsense ye'll find in the picture movies. Then, knowing the meaning of her name added to our excitement."

"What does her name mean?" Nora asked.

"Well, the forst, Chiaro, is literally translated: white or bright so we saw possibility there. And then her other name, Vorace carries the meanin' voracious or greedy, but could also mean ravenous, and that we thought could be interpreted as one who is raven-like. So she held the possibility of bein' the Named One as she had a bit of the Power in that there was some ability she had te communicate with the departed. In fact, that's what she said she did for work since she'd lost her position as a secretarial worker at the Vatican for participatin' in this very craft. The fact that she'd worked for the very *establishment* and had a gift of the Power as well, gave us the extra proof we needed that she came to us with porpose beyond lornin' of mediumship. Chiaro found ample material in Cath's library te keep her occupied and we met with her often but we still weren't sure as to what te think.

"Finny, Cath told me that there was something in my name that caught his attention but I'm not entirely clear on why it's of interest. And I really haven't explained what I know to Nora yet either. So can you tell us exactly what the meanings of light and ravens or ravenous have to do with the tale?"

"Yeah." Nora chirped in. "Can we start at the beginning of the tale so I can understand just what all of this is about and how we play into it, if at all?"

"Aye, yer right gorls. I'll begin with the explanation of why yer name called our attention. Then I'll move te the meat of the tale. As part of the tale, there is a section when great and powerful magic is cast forward in time, to the right time, when the recipient would come te the flesh and be named as an indicator te those who carried the tale through a great many generations, that the receiver of the magic had been born and would eventually be drawn te the place where the tale began. The seat of the knowledge, so te speak. There were te be specific attributes the name would be imbued with and the porson herself would be the personification of those attributes."

Finny sat back in his chair and folded his hands in his lap. His eyes slid from looking at anything in the trailer and took on an inward gaze as he began to rhythmically recite:

'At her borth she will don her name as the mark te be borne, a gift of balance from the heavens above and those below the Sidhe. In her name, she'll carry the Sword of light and knowledge te pierce through ignorance. In her name, she will keep commune with the secret wisdom of dark bird of the Heavens as a Staff to carry and spread a message of balance. Her name will sing of evidence of the strength for the one who would be king and the king of the mount. She will serve as the cup to catch and hold the blood of the four corners. In her heart she'll stoke the fire, in her belly she'll carry the blood. From her chest she'll breathe life back into the forgotten and all who meet her will hear the voice of the earthen meadow. She will be the embodiment of all the elements. And with her, will be honor in the flesh and feather, offered as a Shield, ever at the ready to spy out, hunt down, and tear the flesh from the Beast.'

"The Beast?" I crowed. "That's what came to my mind the first night I smelled the animal smell. I thought or imagined there was some kind of skulking, hunched over Beast-thing stalking around outside our cottage. I could smell it, so awful, and the fear I felt was almost paralyzing. But that's what my head and scared little heart called it. The Beast."

My hand rapidly patted my chest to demonstrate the memory of my fear. I could see Nora nodding out of the corner of my eye.

Finny looked deeply pensive. Then he leveled his gaze on me.

"Chiaro Vorace is dead."

I didn't know how to respond to the statement. It was a bit shocking but I wasn't sure how she fit into the conversation at this moment. I was at a loss to even find the right question.

"Dead? How? What does it have to do with...?"

"After we'd spent some time with her, she told Cath and me that she felt as if someone were following her. She told us that whatever it was that we thought she might be connected to, she'd rather just continue her search across Europe for the metaphysical. Since she was looking for stories of hauntings in Ireland te be in the places where the veil between the worlds are thinnest, she said her goodbyes te us and continued on her way through Waterford, Carlow and Wexford and Wicklow counties on her way te Dublin. She kept in touch with us for a bit and we thought, though nothing out of the ordinary happened when we'd taken her to Lough Corrib, home of the Tuatha De Danann, that once she came near Dublin if she found herself drawn te New Grange, Knowth or Tara that we'd hear from her again and be more secure in the idea that she was the Named One. We were willing to speculate that despite the fact that we could find no connection in her name te that particular passage in the prophecy, which indicated her name would *'be that of the one who is king of the mount,'* it was our own failing in understanding the connection. But then she was killed in Wicklow County. Mordered."

"That's terrible!" Nora was aghast. "How did you find out? What happened to her?"

"Well, we're not sure if it happened with porpose or if she was a victim of some terrible killings that were going on in the county at the time. But the way she was killed was done with the intent to defile any respect or reverence for a woman. If ye know what I mean. She was treated in a most vile way and killed in a very bizarre fashion for anyone who may not have knowledge of such things. Her killing was ritualistic and with torture ye see, and it had the authorities baffled. We saw it, me brother and I, as a possibility that the *Beast* as it were, is an actual force set out to intercept the Power as it comes to the Named One. A force of opposition perhaps. I'm not exactly sure; in fact I'm not sure at all. It could be that her death was just one of the many that took place in Wicklow County during that time period. But the ritualistic nature of her killing with the added irreverence for her female anatomy and the fact that after Chiaro's death the killings stopped, gave us reason to think that there was a connection between her magical abilities, her potential as the Named One and her brutal morder. So ye' see, I must let ye know that there may be some very real danger in yer takin' on this tale. But the other side of it is that ye're so very likely the recipient for the story, that to not take on the responsibility will have disastrous ends for humanity."

The atmosphere in the tiny room was close and heavy with the last four words hanging in the air. Nora and I sat leaning our weight into each other for support as if such news required us to lend and receive such buttressing.

Just then we were both startled out of our reverie when we realized someone was clunking up the makeshift stairway and into Finny's home. My first thought was that whoever it was would easily block us from the only exit. Immediately followed by a lightening like thought communicated between Nora and myself that we might have to draw battle lines right here and now. My third thought was how unlike Nora it was to be so quick to the ready in a circumstance that we might actually have to fight for our lives. We are, after all, middle-aged women. In my younger day I'd held jobs and done things that walked the edge of the razor when it came to danger and excitement but that was then, this is now. Granted, we'd both been blessed with genes that gave us youthful appearance but to actually engage in a physical altercation was a different thing all together. My mind then quickly started to calculate where we were in terms of isolation and how near was help? Then I recognized the white-topped head as it worked its way into the field of vision just outside the door.

"Cath!" I hollered, probably a bit too loud, in my relief that we'd live to see another day and in my excitement to see his friendly face again so soon. Although at this point, it seemed like eons had passed since our cozy luncheon.

The electricity in the tiny room had begun to dissipate and I was surprised to find myself on my feet holding the knife Finny had used to cut the meat for lunch. I didn't remember picking it up, but there it was in my hand and at the ready. Nora was also on her feet facing the doorway standing between Cath and me. She seemed just as shocked to find herself holding a large cast iron pot cover she'd grabbed by the handle from the pegboard wall just within her reach. I relaxed and felt foolish for having been so easily carried away by my fears. Nora stood at attention holding the heavy cover in front of her against any potential attack until I broke the moment and tried to minimize my embarrassment with a little nervous laugh. The nervous tension in the room broke when I heard the crows cawing outside as if they laughed with us at our embarrassment.

"Look at us!" I said. "All jumpy from a little story."

Nora turned to me and noticed, for the first time, that she had the large pan cover in her hands and I with the knife in mine. She looked a bit bewildered but there was also an expression in her eyes that I'd never seen there before. Her appearance and energy emitted a surging fierceness difficult to describe, almost like a soldier denied the opportunity to strike down an enemy. And for the second time during this trip, she reminded me of our maternal grandmother. As she took a moment to breathe I noticed something else. Cath and Finny were looking at each other with expressions of their own. Cath gave a single nod to Finny before he spoke. He turned and closed the little door behind him to shut out the squawking crows.

"I've been working since we saw each other last. Ms. O'Leary. Based on information ye told me of your family and yourself, I took some time and resorched your name both in ancestry as well as you personally. I've some interesting things to reveal so if ye'll relax your guard," he said indicating our impromptu weapons, "and have a seat, we'll get down to it."

"Finny, did you know Cath would be here today? I didn't know you'd be here today Cath." And I was not at all displeased that he was but he seemed much more serious today and I felt some apprehension but we did as he requested.

Finny responded. "It wasn't the original plan, lass but when I caught drift of the strength of yer energy, I called for him te be here for the tellin'. As this is the forst time all the pieces fit and someone with any potential has made it through the dark magic cast about Midleton te detor them. The idea that ye felt the desperation and were able te find yer way through was a big hordle indeed. Tell me now, ye felt the panic and caught this scent of the Beast, as it's the Beast's energy has set out the detorrent in the forst place, but how is it ye made it through te me without bein' paralyzed by the fear?"

"We did it together." Nora explained. "It was almost instinctual, when we were at a point that we wanted to just keep driving through Midleton and do anything but come here, at least I did." Nora looked to me to see if our urges were synonymous. I agreed with a nod and she continued. "Lee and I took hands and meditated on good things in our lives. We sort of, I don't know, pushed the panic back and created what I saw in my mind as a cocoon wrapped around us."

"Bubble." I broke in. "Like a force field of family love with us inside of it. But not just our immediate family, it seemed as though all the families from all the ages in our lineage were there in spirit to help insulate us against, well, against everything. That's what I saw. But we both had different experiences while we were doing that meditation as Nora called it. Funny thing was, we both could smell aspects of the other's vision. And that was a relief. No more rotten meat!"

"Good then. Ye're connected, as ye should be. And ye've identified the presence of the Beast through the sense of smell. Even better." Cath answered as he pulled the stool out from under the little table shelf to sit down.

"Finny," Nora inquired. "You said you'd called for Cath when you met us but you haven't called anyone since we've been here. In fact, I don't even see a phone. Are you sure you guys didn't have this all planned?" I thought Nora was being a bit over cautious and still hadn't come to trust that we were part of what was happening here but after the news of our predecessor meeting such a violent end, I realized that I wanted to know the answer to that question too.

"I didn't say as I called him when I met ye, it was when I felt the strength of yer energy out in the graveyard. Ye had enough of it te find yer way here te me home past the opposition and ye called the bords te ye as well."

"How did you know about the birds? We didn't say anything about that?"

"Ye didn't have te say anything, I watched them gather on the oak tree as ye arrived and strolled through the graveyard. Have ye met the dark ones another time?"

"I have, uh well we both have at different times yesterday and last night." Nora explained. "I had a bunch of crows, I think they were crows, land on a tree yesterday while I was reading one of the books we got from your store, Cath. And then one big one in particular was brazen for a bird, and vocal!"

I continued the explanation. "And I saw a whole bunch of crows or black birds, whatever, attacking or diving at the three brothers, I told Finny about before, that I caught spying on us. I thought they'd found out that I saw what they were up to and all of a sudden, all these birds just started diving at them making all kinds of noise. That's when I slipped into the cottage and I don't think they knew I was there but that was one of the other times when that smell was obvious. Then later that night, the big one, a female raven, I think, was just perched on our chimney. It was kind of strange to see 'cause our crows in America don't really come out at night the way they do here."

"Alright then," Finny said, "Cath, come sit here in me chair with me."

He scooted a little forward and to the side to make room for his brother. Cath didn't protest and abandoned his stool. The chair was large enough to accommodate both of them comfortably, if a bit comically, to see two men of such an age sharing a chair. Then I thought about Nora and I doing exactly the same thing on the footrest and wondered if we too, looked funny. We were practically knees to knees with the old men and face to face in the tiny space. The air in the little trailer seemed to have shifted and the little room had a feeling about it that we were finally getting down to business. Something felt complete in the four of us being together: these two old men and us two women.

Cath pulled a paper out of his breast pocket along with his little round specs.

"We'll start with yer names gorls. As it torns out, our confusion on yer bein' here together has been settled and the answer is in yer names, just as it'd been told it would be. But as we were lookin' for one porson all this time, it took a bit te figure out how two pieces solved the puzzle rather than the one we were expectin'."

Cath looked at his paper again and said to Finny, "Ye'll be pleased te know that the name Nora means honor, and the name Lee carries the meaning, meadow!"

At this, Finny startled so obviously that I was concerned for his health. I watched as his face paled and he stared off into space for a full half minute. He turned to Cath as if for assurance that he'd heard correctly then looked to us and spoke.

"After a very long lifetime of waitin' and figurin' and maybes and disappointments and doubts, I see now that it's all been true and it's all comin' together as we speak. 'Tis a joyful and fearful thing te know. Now," he composed himself, "the Name O'Leary, have ye knowledge of its meanin'?"

Yeah, I think." I recollected what I'd learned. "The O means son of or grandson of, so somewhere along our line, our name was just Leary. Right?"

"Aye, but it's just *of*; the O means of. The gender connection not withstandin'." Finny shared, "But it's not the answer in entirety. Yer name, from orly times is directly translated te mean 'keeper of the calves' or 'of the Calf-herder clan'. 'Tis a name that settled here in Midleton for a great many generations but did not originate here. Have ye hord of the King Laoghaire?"

"I think anyone who has studied anything about Ireland knows who King Laoghaire was." I said. "He was the king who opposed St. Patrick on the Hill of Tara but finally allowed him to preach Christianity in Ireland. As I recall though, the king remained true to Paganism himself. Right?"

Cath responded. "Yer right lass. And 'tis his line that ye come from."

"Yeah, right." I scoffed. "The royal O'Leary girls!" Cath's expression didn't change. He seemed to be waiting for me to accept the news so he could continue. "You're not serious." I said. Still, he said nothing.

"Ye'll have te take what yer bein' told as plain truth lass or we'll not get through all, this day. Will ye allow me te get through this segment of the tellin' so we can get on te the next?"

This was the no nonsense Cath from the bookstore I remembered meeting, business-like and focused on closing the deal.

"Sorry." I said, chastened. "Go ahead."

"Well, as history has it, the motto often found on the coat of arms fer yer family name goes: *Laidir ise ber righ.* Translated, it means: Strong fer yer king. Now there may be many ways te interpret the portion of the tale that says '*Her name will sing of evidence of the strength for the one who would be king and the king of the mount,*' but it has always been speculated that it'd be likely that the *daughter of the future* would come te us bearin' the name of Laoghaire or more lately: Leary. Yer name is but a slight variation and would carry the same motto which was often sung and heralded by the clans at gatherins or before a battle ye see. And now fer yer Christian name, Lenore. Ye know we've touched on a conversation regardin' its origin in yer line and te yer knowledge, yer the first te bear that name. The very way ye were given the name is in keepin' with the foretellin' of yer comin': *At her birth she will don her name as the mark to be borne, a gift of balance from the heavens above and those below the Sidhe.'* Now ye told me yerself the story of bein' named fer yer likeness te an angel by yer mother and for the very raven herself in the poem by the same name, by yer father, a blood Leary 'of Laoghaire. As fer the meanin of the name, Lenore, itself means light or enlightenment. I forther quote the tale, '*In her name, she will carry the Sword of light and knowledge to pierce through ignorance.'* And moreover, '*In her name she will keep commune with the secret wisdom of the dark bird of the Heavens to carry as a Staff in spreading a message of balance.'* This balance is what we spoke of at length durin' our meal. Do ye remember what was said?"

I nodded as I answered, trying to take in all the information being given.

"You said that it was notable that so much of my life was a balance between two opposite ideas, philosophies or whatever. Light-dark, Pagan-Christian, all coming into play as a battle between good and bad, right and wrong, all based on perception. You said that being born a Libra was another facet to that balance being the sign of the scales." I looked to Cath for some endorsement that this was the information he meant to call to mind.

"Aye, it's all these and more for without balance between forces, one will eventually overwhelm the other or at the very least, create a discord in the spirit of things as to cause dysfunction or disease in the great way of things. Tis yer innate need for balance that has caused ye such conflict throughout yer life. Ye've a sense of fairness that many discard te make gains or get ahead. Much of the segment of the tale quoted te identify the *'daughter of the future'* is evident in you. Now as for yer adopted name, Lee, 'tis one ye use for all ye meet, yer public name so te speak; am I right?"

Another nod.

"And this next part speaks of the meanin' that ties in te the less formal name, Lee. *'And all who meet her will hear the voice of the earthen meadow.'* And as I just now told ye, the name Lee, in some parts, means meadow! So every part of the telling ties te yer names just exactly as it was told."

"I see how you'd find all of that in either my names or what I told you about my life but what about the rest of what Finny told us about that quote? There was a whole bunch of other material there that doesn't seem to fit."

"Such as?" Finny replied.

"Well, I don't remember exactly, but wasn't there something about a cup of blood and what about all that about hunting down and tearing apart the Beast? That all sounds pretty dark to me. How does that play into it? 'Cause that doesn't sound like anything I'm about to do."

Nora interjected just then.

"I heard some familiar items mentioned in what you recited, Finny. I made out a Sword, a Cup or Cauldron, a Staff, and a Shield, right?" She didn't stop to see if they agreed. "Those are the four suits of the Tarot deck. I'm familiar with the deck because it directly relates to the astrological signs and planets. Two symbols are masculine and two are feminine. They're synonymous with the elements, air, fire, water and earth and I heard those all somewhere in that quote too. These elements are also connected to the four quadrants of the Zodiac, three signs to a season, spring, summer, fall, and winter...Libra is an air sign." She added, not really explaining what she was getting at.

"And so what does that mean?" I asked.

"I'm not quite sure with regard to all this." She waved a hand toward the men. "But I do know that of the four quadrants of the Zodiac, Libra is a cardinal sign which is a sign of action and it falls under the suit of Swords in the Tarot deck. So the idea that, whoever this prophesy is about, will wield a Sword, sort of makes sense. And to have them wield a Sword to create balance has even more clarity if that person is a Libra. But to create balance between what? She asked looking expectantly at the brothers.

"Between the Old Ways and the Christian, between the masculine and the feminine, between the Heaven and the Orth, between the spirit and the mind, between above and below." Finny stated, as a matter of fact. "And I think what me brother was getting at when he announced that the name Nora means honor, is that we've been mistaken these years in misinterpretin' the meanin' of this last phrase to be about Lee. *'And with her, will be honor in flesh and feather offered as a Shield, ever at the ready to spy out, hunt down, and tear the flesh from the Beast.'* When in fact it's been about Nora, and that's why ye've come to us as a pair when we were expectin' only one."

Nora's eyes grew huge. "So, what, I'm supposed to run around with a Shield tearing flesh from some Beast?"

Cath replied in a calm voice that helped to sooth the moment.

"Ye have te understand, these words aren't true or literal as they say, and yet they are. Ye'll not be expected te carry a Shield, but ye'll be a Shield...her Shield." He dipped his head toward me. "And I've no doubt that, with the name ye bear as honor itself, ye'll have pledged yerself te yer sister in that capacity sometime in the lives of yer souls so that ye two are bound together in the task at hand. She is the Sword and yer the Shield. One masculine, one feminine. And judgin' by the stance ye both took when I came to ye this day, I'd say that was just so. Ms. Lenore with the nearest Sword te hand. And standin' in front of her was Ms. Nora with her cast iron Shield!"

Now I understood the knowing glance between the brothers at our reflex to protect ourselves. They'd begun to see us take on characteristics of our preordained roles in all of this. I marveled as I began to see it myself.

"What sign were ye born to then Nora?" Cath asked.

"Me? I'm May First, a Taurus. It's an earth sign." Then after a moment, her eyes widened and she said, "Oh. Oh, I see. It *is* kind of like a puzzle isn't it?"

"What?" I said. Not liking being in the dark. Nora and the men nodded as if in agreement to each other. "What?" I demanded more insistently.

"Like the sign of Libra is of the suit of swords in the Tarot, the sign of Taurus is of the suit of pentacles in the Tarot." She looked at me for recognition of her point but it evaded me for the moment. She prodded, "The pentacle...The pentacle is the Shield, Lee."

"Oh." I was amazed as the connection dawned on me. "I get it. I was trying to make some connection to the fact that you were born on Beltane, the old religion's cross-quarter day."

The men nodded to each other.

Then Cath said, "If I'd more time I'd have found out more about ye but as it was, I'd all I could do te get some of yer lineage from my resorch since yesterday."

I was trying not to feel as though my privacy had been invaded to know that someone was prying into my family history but my curiosity was piqued and I was more interested now in anything that would shed light onto this deepening mystery. It seemed the more we found out, the more confused I became.

"What did you find out?" I asked.

"Ye've an interesting lineage." Cath mused.

"Well," Nora said, "It's not every day that someone finds out that they're descended from royalty!"

It's not yer paternal side I'm speakin' of." He looked at me. "On yer mother's side, ye told me yesterday that she was half Swedish. Through the years I've purchased every bit of software available te help with me sorch for the Named One and before that, it was a much more tedious process. This new technology is wonderful thing and I've quite a few paths at me disposal te find out about lineage and bloodlines, records, birth, death, marriage, employment and...well ye see the idea. What I've found is that yer mother, who had a bit of the seer in her, as ye tell it, was born of Martin and Sigrid Scully, whose maiden name was Höök. Ye told me as much. Have ye knowledge of the meanin' of the Swedish name Höök?"

"Yeah," I said. "It means Hawk, right? It's actually spelled with the dots over the letters. What's that called?"

It took a moment but the shocked look on Nora's face impressed upon me the weight of the vision she and I had just shared as its significance came rushing at me like a tidal wave. We looked at each other and for the first time began to recognize the spiritual identification of her as the hawk and me as the raven. The thin space between slim and none was uncomfortably squeezing out any room for doubt that we were connected to this tale.

Cath continued as our minds tried to organize and assimilate this new paradigm into our perception of who we are.

"It seems yer bloodline comes te ye from two of the parent countries. On the paternal side, yer blood can be traced by records te a point and then orlier, by vorbal accounts carefully memorized by each generation and handed down as part of the tale te be recalled. This line identifies ye as relations of the Laoghaire of the Mount. This is no small task as the Learys of the world have been prolific progenitors indeed! And despite the magnitude of that undertaking, at least I had the records te go by.

Each of the parent countries keeps their own recollection of their portion of the tale and we keep the total account of all the portions that create the one tale in total. Ye gorls have blood of a distinctive line of the Irish as ye know. And the Swedish as well. 'Twas a bit trickier te mark the Swedish line on yer maternal side te say the least, as the records of lineage are less easily acquired than those here in our home-country, but the mark left by the Swedes and their story of how te identify the descendants of the tale would come with an unmistakable name heralding the beginning of the shifting energetic tide of the power of the feminine with the name of a great warrior. That name, ye see, is Sigrdrifa, known as the Shieldmaiden of the Valkyrie."

Nora asked the very question that was formulating in my head.

"Are you saying that our grandmother is that marker in time?"

"She bore the name, Sigrid, a variation of the older Sigrdifa, and yer sister told me not two minutes ago that she was of the Höök clan in Sweden, did she not?" He continued to drive his point. "The reason, I've surmised that the two of ye are te rise te yer task is due te the fact that yer the forst that we know of te carry *two* of the lines in yer veins harkening te the time that the tale was cast. When ye told me, Lee, that ye never knew why yer cousins didn't carry the strength of yer, ah, magic as ye call it, yet they did have a trace of it, I thought te look te yer lineage on yer mother's side as ye told me she had a bit of the seein' as well. And it's no coincidence that the Swedish blood from yer maternal grandmother's veins, carries the tradition of bein' the Shieldmaiden. As it seems, Nora, that'll be yer task in all of this. Now mind ye, it's not the nonsense ye hear in the myths about the Valkyries bein' reduced te the waitresses te the Gods an' such blather. In the beginning they were seekers and carriers of knowledge and as the world changed they adapted and developed other strengths as was needed in the new aggressive times. And fierce warriors they were, who held the power over life and death with their gifts of magic and battle know-how. But as I say, times moved on and the great wave of masculinity took sway and the great she-warriors' place in history was relegated te only a fraction of its truth. But, to their credit, I suppose, the Swedes held the old traditions with reverence to both God and Goddess right up until the 11th century. A stubborn lot!"

"Cath," I asked, "Nora and I have had a shared vision, I guess you could call it; that revealed Nora as a hawk and me as a raven. That sort of makes sense to us that the name Höök would have relevance, but what does the name, or a hawk have to do with all of this? How does that fit in? I don't recall anything mentioned so far about a hawk."

Now it was the old brothers' turn to look at each other for support. Finny forged ahead by explaining.

"There're several forms of this tale. One is the living telling for which Cath and I hold responsibility in this country. Then there is the written version that only speaks *about* the tale in verse and explains the Power of the magic that can be released in cortain words in a sort of a cryptic fashion, ye see."

"The Power of the Word?" Nora asked, relating what Finny said to her new understanding of the material she'd read in the book so far.

"Right, lass. The secret tale was enveloped in the written word, but not spelled out, so te speak. Just as parts of the tale have been told fer centuries in myth, lore and fairytales, which regenerates the energy behind the tales, keepin' it alive and fresh. But the actual meaning of the release of Power with the tellin' speaks of us tellin' ye the tale and the Power within ye will be released. But there's a third way the tale is told and it's usin' neither words, song or writin' but a precious depiction of all that happened and all that will come te happen and it's there in that particular tellin' of the tale that at the time of the comin' of the raven and the hawk together along with one other, that will bring forth the full Power of the originator of the tale."

"So we're here with you to hear the tale." I mused, "But you sold the book to me without really knowing if I was the one you were looking for. Wouldn't that have been a waste if we were the wrong people?"

"Not so, lass." Cath responded. "I'd many copies of the book made through the years and when the book is read by any interested party, it'd sorve te keep the tale energized. As it was, yer interest has already storred things up what with the bords and the increased resistance around Midleton. See the unleashed energy not only strengthens yer abilities but the opposing energy as well. So ye must be careful and stay together, as it seems so long as ye have each other yer strength is potent."

"So where is this depiction of the story?" Nora asked. "Am I right in assuming that if we have the benefit of all three ways to learn the story that we'll be in a better position to do whatever it is that needs doing?"

"Right ye are, Nora. Ye'll need all three perspectives te fully release yer Power and te guide ye through what lies ahead."

"Is it something you keep at your store, Cath?" I asked.

"The artifact is an old one. It is great and beautiful bowl fashioned of pure silver and due te its age, takes on a gold hue, which was part of its design, te, represent the female and the male. Silver, the feminine bein' the color of the moon and gold, obviously masculine, bein' the color of the sun, symbolically representing that, although it's the gold color that ye see, the foundation of the tale is primarily feminine as is the Cauldron."

"Cath," Finny broke in to remind his brother of Nora's original curiosity, "The question was of the hawk."

"True and right ye are." He said to Finny with a tap on the knee. "The hawk and the raven are depicted on one of the many panels of the artifact together with the great woman of Power, Faidhe and her two daughters. The woman carries one of her daughters at her right side upon her shoulder and the other tends to her head on her left, signifying that though they are separated, they keep te each other in their thoughts. Upon Faidhe's left breast, over her heart, she holds a man's life in her hand but as ye'll see there is also the depiction of a dead dog representing that this one, though held by Faidhe, was lost te the temptation of taking Power from the Otherworld without care or reverence. Faidhe is destined to depend on her daughters te have a care for the future as it is depicted in the bords who must fly te the future. Upon her right hand is the living thing she will use most to deliver through time and space, her message until 'feather comes to flesh' and the Named

One is initiated. The bord ye see, is a harbinger throughout all history and the reason is that they are able te travorse all the elements, earth, air and water so they're chosen by her as carriers of messages between past, present and future; between spirit, dreams and flesh. Ye'll begin te see the pattern of the three as the story develops for ye. This bord, she holds in her hand is the dove, the very symbol of the Holy Spirit of the Christian faith. These three bords represent yet another trinity, a concept sacred te the old ones with the Old Ways, in the Maid, the Mother and the Wise One, as well as te the new religion with the Father the Son and the Holy Spirit and humanity, the mind, the spirit and the flesh, the hawk, the dove and the raven. So the birds ye'll see on this one particular relief represent the raven of the old religion, the dove of the new religion and the hawk that will come te defend the unity between the two. This panel though, was not the forst made, it was created as one of many in the process of making substance of the magic that was cast in the tale."

Nora and I sat mesmerized by what Finny was telling us. Not because of what he said but in how he said it, I think. He had a way of telling a story that captivated his audience. Well, at least I was captivated. Not only was the rhythm of his voice inviting, but I thought he must also have a type magic about him that created a mental image of what he was saying for those who listened. He could lull one into the rhythm and then create the opulent and detailed images directly into his or her mind almost like downloading material into a hard drive. I did not wonder that he'd come to be successful as a storyteller. I had to ask him if what I saw were my own thoughts or if my suspicion about him being able to reach into the minds of his listeners was a talent he had. After all, he had actually experienced Nora and me in our meditation as if he were a mental witness. If he could observe, then why not transmit, so to speak?

"Finny, as you were describing what was on this picture or relief as you called it, I saw a large, shiny bowl and I was reminded of the Gundestrup Cauldron. Is that the type of artifact you're talking about or is my imagination just being creative?"

"No lass, it's yer mind beginning te open up te its own potential. And ye've begun te recognize things by peelin' away the logic and goin' with yer natural ability and instinct te see things as they are rather than what ye think should be. The Gundestrup Cauldron is the artifact te tell the tale as ye thought."

"Really? The actual Cauldron? I've read about the Cauldron! It was found in ah, Denmark. Right? In a bog?" I was growing excited to find that I actually had some knowledge of part of the tale. "But it was broken or in pieces. Wasn't it? Until someone put it back together?"

"Aye, the separate parts were pieced together but what they found was not the complete arrangement. The bowl is made up of five large rectangular pieces and seven smaller rectangular pieces or panels te create the cylinder or sides and the base of the bowl is a round panel depicting the forst magic cast in the tale te be told.

But there's one panel missing te complete the tale as that part hasn't been written, told, created or...eh, lived as yet."

Nora jumped in after taking in everything in relative silence up to now. "Are you guys saying that we have to make the final panel to complete this artifact?"

Cath answered, "Well, yes and no. In the literal sense, we don't think so but in the figurative sense, we believe the story has yet to be complete depending on this, ah chapter, so to speak. So the space had been left empty for two reasons: one, so that no one could put the entire Cauldron together te usurp its magical purpose for his or her own and two, so that ye'd not be bound by or to any means by which ye might take on yer task in all this."

"So you're saying the rest is unwritten?" Nora asked.

"Exactly." Cath agreed

And we don't know what's to come? I added, hoping that the men had some indication of what was to happen next.

"Not in the scheme of things," Finny responded. "But we're hopin' ye'll be open te takin' some time te work with us on developin' yer abilities. Both of ye. As ye'll both have cortain skills te work on and likely others te be discovered."

All at once I realized the magnitude of what these men were asking us to do. If all of this was based in reality, we were expected to battle an unknown adversary that had probably killed before. If I understood correctly, I'd be playing a key role in some magical movement to bring about unity or balance or else. Religious movements never proved to be sedate, historically speaking. I began to feel overwhelmed with questions about just how much I didn't know. I contemplated our time here in Ireland and my family back home. I reviewed my reasons for coming to Ireland and my lifelong angst in always knowing there was more to who I am and why I have these abilities. I weighed whether I could surrender to one path completely and give up the other. Finish the quest, so to speak and put my academic goals on a back burner, or maybe completely off the stove. How much time and money I'd already devoted to my Ph.D. would I lose if I took the path Cath was suggesting? Could I do both? Knowing myself, I'd have to devote all of my attention to one project or goal. It would have to be one or the other. My grandparents and parents crossed my mind. The poem or song that came to me in a vision earlier today ran through my head as well and made me think of all those ancestors that came before me with such a singular purpose in time for it all to come together right now in me. Something was definitely happening and Nora and I are a part of it. I considered Chiaro and her horrible end and she hadn't even wanted to participate in this venture. Rushing into anything was not part of my plan now that I knew this adventure could carry such a steep price. I didn't know what to say or do and I didn't feel that all the facts were in for me to make such a weighty decision.

"What would I have to do?" I said. "How long will it all take? What about my son? My family? I don't want...I can't. I don't think I can do this. What if I don't do anything? What if we just go about our lives and forget all about this tale and everything? What would happen then?"

Both Cath and Finny contemplated their hands on their knees but I knew it was my question that captured their attention. Cath pursed his lips and raised his eyebrows before he spoke in a subdued voice.

"Ye can do that. And this is the part of this business that we've no tellin' as te what's the next step or what's the right thing. We've only known that in all our long lives, we've been waitin' fer ye and as ye came te us, we understand that the time fer creatin' the balance is upon us and it's critical that somethin' be done now or we'd be sure te see the destruction of life as we now enjoy it. Fer the Power is there and is askin' te be called. 'Tis me fervent prayer that it'll not be the Beast that claims the callin' of it."

My back was growing stiff from sitting on the footrest and the cold seemed to have, once again, crept into the little trailer. It had grown late into the afternoon and even the meager light that had peeked through the little makeshift windows earlier, was no longer evident. I forced my bones to stand up so I could stretch. My knees each let off a cracking protest to having been seated so long and my back sang out as well. I'd have paced but there was no room. Growing agitated and feeling trapped, I said, "I can't. We can't. I have a life, a family, what am I supposed to do, just forget all that? Besides, you don't even know if this is real. Do you? Do you have any proof that what you say and what this story is all about is anything more than a fairytale?" I could feel the heat in my face and a sense that I was close to panic.

"Come now gorl, and I'll fix ye some tea. It'll heal yer conflicted mind." Finny suggested.

"I don't want your tea!" I snapped. "I want to know my own thoughts without your tricks in a cup to make me feel what you want me to feel." I was close to tears when Nora's voice broke in.

"Oh my God, Lee." She said and waited for me to look at her. "Gardenia! Remember? I was talking about it just today on the ride here." Then more insistently, "Remember? She told us all kinds of things but the things she told us *every time* are the same things that we're hearing now! 'You come from a royal line in another life.' And 'You will grow into yourself and come to change the world.' Sound familiar?"

"Oh come on Nora. You told me today that you thought it was all a con."

"Lee," she tried to pacify me and took my hand to pull me back down into the seat, "you know this is all coming together and won't be denied."

My misery was slightly appeased at Nora's touch. I knew she was right and I was hoping that this was all something I could just write about and get a degree for my efforts. But the deep down truth was I just didn't want to have to deal with anything that could make me feel this scared and small. My mind kept returning to the childhood hand reaching out from under the bed to grab me and suck me into the underworld of the unknown.

"Stop that!" Nora warned as she grabbed both my hands into hers. "Remember what you need to do. Think about your strength, our family; think about a better world for your son and generations to come. Whatever you have to do, but fight it! Can you smell it? It's working on you right now."

She was right. I was feeling the panic but didn't recognize that the smell had returned. What I was feeling was a force trying to get me to turn my back on what my blood said I was born for. I squeezed my eyes shut and the threatening tears rolled down my cheeks as I did.

"Okay," I said. With an exhale I purposely expelled anything toxic, unwanted or negative from my mind and heart. Feeling a little lighter I took a second deep breath and as I prepared to let it go, I felt a dry, warm hand slip over Nora's and my hands and a moment later another joined the knot of hands. I opened my eyes and I saw that it was Cath's hands that I felt; then Finny's did the same.

Calm washed over me in a soothing wave and with it, several vivid images invaded my mind so rapidly that I was barely able to identify them. I saw a great black bird flying, as a lone silhouette against a crystal blue sky. I saw myself in my bed at the cottage with a woman standing at the foot of the bed, praying over me, willing for me to hear her. There was a flash of a man, glowing with green light standing atop a hill and as his ash-wood Staff penetrated the fertile earth, it immediately sprouted roots that created a vast, formidable network under the entire country of Ireland.

Then, a gathering of people, dressed in strange clothes. Some are small and average, unnoticeable while others caught my attention because they bear lights of green and blue and maroon around them that seems to emanate from them. Some are seemingly familiar but just out of reach of recognition. Nora is here. *Nora, can you see all of this?* But wait; then again, that's not Nora. And the woman from the bedroom visitation is here. I feel a deep love for her. She glows the most vibrant and beautiful blues and greens. She is young and lovely. And, oh look! She carries the same Staff as the man on the hill! I see a large stone with a cleft standing at the top of a hill by the ocean. I hear it singing through the opening. On one side of the fissure is perched a raven and on the other I see a dove. Between the two sides the sun can be seen as if the sun is being held up between the stones. A woman and a baby. The woman dressed in blue robes. I see many births, I get the sense that what I see is men and women all over the world as they welcome thousands of children, generation after generation into the world. Great light, then darkness, deep darkness. Then, rapid flashes from hundreds of wars raging through centuries scroll past my awareness. Men covered in blue dye or paint charging to battle. A great army of men clad in breastplates and helmets, carrying long semi-cylindrical Shields, javelins and daggers march across many lands and consume them like a plague of locusts. Giant men with blonde and fiery hair, streak to the shores of foreign lands behind the silent prow of long boats. Armored men bearing heraldry, stampede to war on horseback. Clear visions of knights in white robes bearing a long red cross teem throughout western and eastern Europe. I see intellectual struggles ignite into war. Then, the more familiar scenes of World War I cross my consciousness and then more precisely familiar depictions of World War II come to life in great detail. I begin to recognize an increasing sense of familiarity in all of what I see. Bits and fragments of information and history coalesce and understanding creeps into my psyche. I begin to see a movie-like timeline throughout the ages, like an enormous string of beads surrounding me in a simultaneous historical movie showing me all of history at once; but still too many pieces are missing. Or maybe it's my understanding of the scenes before me that is faulty. I feel myself struggle to create a full picture in my mind that will tell me all. I hear my ears ringing and my eyes feel hot and bulging. I reach and strain to make sense of what I see, mentally searching for a connection or a clue. My muscles ache as I strain to reach understanding. I hear the scratchy chalkboard sound of my teeth grinding and fatigue defeats me. Overwhelmed, I have to pull back, first mentally, then with my hands.

As I did, I felt the loss of that connection with the others and also the relief.

My body shook with exhaustion and I was filmy with a coating of fevered sweat despite the dark and chilled trailer. As I shivered, all four of us sat in the echo of silence as I slowed my panting and sought to bring my heart rate down to something near normal. Beyond my physical discomfort, the first thing I noticed was that it was full dark outside. I struggled to make sense of how that could be by calculating just what time it must be. Even with the gloomy weather, during the summer season in July, the sky should still, at least, be a late afternoon gray but looking out the little truck window, I could see only black.

I opened my mouth wide to unhinge the tension in my jaw and peeled my pasty tongue from the roof of my mouth and asked through a blazing headache, "What time is it?"

21

Initiation by Blood

The bull stood at about eight heads and was an excellent contributor in creating strong, healthy stock among the clan herds and consequently, lining Briciu's purse with ample wealth in breeding fees. Proud horns were used for more than display, as this bull kept his cows heavy and milking each season by battling off any prospective competitors. Used to having the best of the grazing fields, cows and watering spots, this beast grew large, confident and extremely jealous of his territory. He had not enjoyed being aggressively herded down from the hillside fields and confined in a paddock with noisy, gawking humans so near. Twisting and bucking to keep those so near from approaching, he let them know that he was in ill temper.

Briciu stood slightly away from the log rails of the paddock contemplating all that had taken place this evening and puzzled the meaning of this news that the hag would bear a child of the Gods. Could his sister have been mistaken? Not likely considering that the woman had indeed grown to appear as a younger maid so even his mother had sparked envy in her eyes. Briciu felt a momentary rush of satisfaction at his mother's notice that Faidhe had a genuine flush of youth. He thought, *She must have been gifted this child from the Gods, so it's best to wait and observe the progress of how the child might be of use. One does not want to anger the Gods after all. But this usurper, Laoghaire,* Briciu smiled to himself, *he is a different thing. I will enjoy seeing you gored and bloodied and if it's possible, before you die, I will make sure you know that I will have your wife just for the pleasure of it before she joins you in her own death. Poor thing, I think I'll make it appear as though she takes her own life in her grief. How sad. Then your stock will be my next order of business. No relation from some back corner kingdom will stop me from my due.*

Briciu's smile widened to a grotesque deformity as his eyes revealed the diseased thoughts that roiled behind them. Standing in the shadows, no one witnessed the evidence of the putrescence that infected Briciu's mind like a fever since his mother had laughed at the foolishness of his plan to take position on the Hill and ridiculed him as nothing more than her pawn. Until now, Briciu had been content to wait for the right moment to make his move toward power and continue to reap the benefits of being a Councilmember to add to his wealth and comfort. He'd done his mother's bidding, and kept still at her behest even at times when he wanted to wield his power. He'd restrained himself through the years from lashing out at Gara when she'd been overbearing because she served a purpose. She had power and wealth and was useful in bringing him to power of his own but he'd waited overlong to be rewarded for his duty to her dealings. And now, all this change upon the Hill proved to bring all those years of scraping, restraint and obedience to his mother and her wealth to naught for she still intended to maintain the Power for *herself*! At her age! This was all too much. His pride had kept count of all injuries and insults she'd thrown at him through the years and he outwardly remained her puppet so long as it benefited his advancement but his patience had grown tender as he nurtured the memory of these offenses. His desire for revenge and to lash out had reached a point that he could no longer tolerate doing nothing but he knew better than to overtly strike out at his mother. Spurred by a festering hatred of always being thwarted and dominated by Gara, Briciu plotted revenge against at least one member of the clan that could be acted out publicly, legally and immediately to assuage his mounting feeling of loss of control. It was a plan of which he was proud. He would see his enemy bloody and have it done publicly without need for covering up his handiwork. It would bring him one step closer to taking the Hill and having ultimate Power to cast his mother to her knees. He fantasized about her public humiliation one day. *Yes, this plan is a good one. Killing Laoghaire will satisfy my pride for now and ultimately bring me closer to my rightful position.*

Although he was sure that his bull carried enough strength to crush Laoghaire, he felt smug reassurance at Laoghaire's inevitable demise when he recalled the tidbit of insurance he'd afforded the situation just to tip the scale in favor of the bull in the event that Laoghaire actually had any ability as a warrior.

"Test the bull all you care to Keeper." Briciu spat under his breath. "For it's nothing you'll find amiss there. The beast has been gifted the drive to kill you with all the cunning and rage he can muster but not by means that you can detect. How childlike you are to come to battle with naught but your human strength. You bring no magical skills to cast or protect. You show how unworthy you are to claim Keeper of the Hill."

Briciu recalled the servant man that he'd beaten this very night after his last encounter with Laoghaire. His rage had flared so, at his perception of the insolence of this latecomer who dared speak to him with authority, that the beating was overdone. It was not important to Briciu. It was not the first time his rage had been unleashed and someone had died as a result, but this time Briciu had used the servant's blood, so fresh from the kill, as an offering of sacrifice to bring success in his plan. He would not murder Laoghaire, but he would take pleasure in his death all the same. A ripple skittered through his body as he recalled the relentless erection he exhibited as he beat the servant and then utilized his blood. The bloodlust together with the Power of magic in the sacrificial spell created a consuming physical need in Briciu. He'd decided not to relieve the need but rather savor the force of his surging desire as he disciplined himself to direct that energy into the magic as well. It was his promise to himself that he would make sure once the magic had done its work and the bull rid him of the impudent Laoghaire, Briciu would, at the first possible moment; slowly and meticulously avail himself of Laoghaire's prized wife. The anticipation of the subtle ways that he would inflict pain on her excited him more than the thought of relieving his sexual tension. But to be sure, that was his final intension and he'd breech her in ways that Laoghaire had certainly never done. Perhaps he'd keep her living long enough to use her for some of the ideas he'd kept in his head while he drove into the women who would lay down for a price. Never daring to test their willingness to engage in such reviled acts, he acted out the scenes only in his head. Briciu would not risk his reputation or position to quench his desire for his aberrant cravings but now at the thought of conquering his adversary after spilling blood in magic, the physical drive was all but overwhelming. Even now, as he stood in the shadows watching Laoghaire's men inspect his prize bull, his erection could be seen pushing against his fresh tunic as it had done against the other that was so recently covered in blood and torn away in primal triumph. He felt himself quiver as the evidence of his murderous act writhed against taut skin in search of a dark place to bury its fury and release its poison. But Briciu knew from experience that one release would not satisfy the surge that pumped in his loins. His eyes surveyed the crowds in search of the fair-haired Colm to give his weapon a direction in which to point.

If one were to observe him in this moment, he or she would know that something had broken behind those eyes but no one was looking at Briciu. No one suspected that his mind had been eroding over the past years or that as a result of all the recent change combined with several affronts to his authority and pride by his mother and now Laoghaire, his ability for normal thought had slipped away from him but his skills for planning and calculation had not abandoned him.

Those that had come to watch the proceedings were inspecting the bull in all its glorious fury. Though they had difficulty in drawing near to the beast, the men could see that there was no inflammation in the nostrils so that they were assured no irritant had been used. By the way the bull reared and twisted at their approach, they observed him landing heavily on his hoofs so they were satisfied also that the bull had no sliver of wood or other material pushed into the tender underside. They could not be assured but were reasonably certain that the bull had not been overfed apples to drunken him as he had clear eyes and no sign of an unbalanced stride.

Laoghaire's men reported to him that they were satisfied there were no measures taken to inflame the bull. He would face the bull's strength and speed but would not have to contend with pain or fear and rage that had been inflicted by false means. Upon hearing the news, Laoghaire thanked the men and asked that they stay with the bull until he joined them for the challenge to insure that the bull remained unaffected. He then withdrew to return to his hut, away from the crowd of clan folk who were eager for the entertainment of the challenge, to open his heart and mind in prayer as he elevated his arms wide over his head.

"Goddess and God, I come to you humble in my service. You have offered me your protection through my family and other of your worthy servants in the Circle of Power this night. The privilege of being witness to your Power gives me the strength and assurance that I will take on this challenge and be successful. I utilize the gifts you have given into my charge as you see fit. I accept the challenge in your names as a fitting passage to prove my worthiness to further serve you as a leader and protector of the people and as Keeper of the Hill." As Laoghaire lowered his arms he noticed a faint blue glow of light around the Sword at his waste and had it not been at his back behind him, he'd have seen the Shield aglow as well. He was clear on his plan as he returned to the crowd to begin the event of his challenge.

The smell of cooking meat permeated the area around the feasting hall as smoke poured out of the hole at the top of the structure. It appeared that all three cooking spits were in use and the prevailing scent was that of cooking boar. Laoghaire observed as he walked past the hall toward the paddock that two oversized impromptu spits were being erected over the main outdoor fire pit. He took this as a good sign that the clan had faith in his ability to fell the beast for the spit and overcome the challenge to his position as the Keeper. Faith in his ability meant faith in his leadership. Laoghaire could almost thank Briciu for presenting him with a situation that would so readily afford him acceptance in his new position. Almost.

As he walked toward the paddock, Laoghaire saw a great many people gathered on and around the tree logs that made up the paddock fence. More with his instincts than with his eyes he scanned the crowd for his family and smiled the thought that he looked not only for Colm and the twins but to all those who had participated in the magical casting of Power with him such a short time ago. For the first time since he'd come to the Tuath, Laoghaire truly felt the bonds of family in his heart for clan members beyond his own hearth. That Circle magic had seasoned him somehow. Perhaps opened his eyes to the Power that lived around him daily, for he saw the glow about his Sword and he knew exactly where the members of his family were to be found without even seeing them. He felt a pulse of surety and quiet knowledge, without doubt that he would be protected and given the strength to complete this task. For reasons beyond his understanding, Laoghaire also knew that this task was a most important one in all this. The thought nibbled at his mind and he tried to make it come clear but another more insistent thought pushed it out of his mind. *Colm.* He thought. *I must see to Colm; she is in danger.* As he sought out her energy, Laoghaire could actually smell her scent and vaguely acknowledged that this animal craft of scent had shown itself along with his other developing strengths. Spotting her unusual light hair among the many dark heads, he started toward his wife with a rising panic but realized when he reached her that she was in no apparent need or danger, but stood stoic in anticipation of what lay ahead for her husband. *Perhaps,* he thought, *I sense her unease and concern for me in this challenge.*

"Husband, I hold you to keep to your promise in paying your duty to my satisfaction." She teased. But her gentle smiling face took on a serious expression and in a low voice she beseeched him. "Go you then and see to this trifle in order to come to me so we may tend tribute to the God and Goddess and consummate our place anew as we pay reverence to their very presence in both of us. I long for the purity of our coupling now more than on our first moment in union for there is energy on the rise between us. I feel it all about me and it mounts in strength. We are bound by this Power husband, you and I. Know that I and the children are here casting our magic for your protection so no harm shall befal you. I refuse to think anything other than your utter victory will be the outcome. And should it seem that evil will prevail, I would cast my very self between you and harm and absorb it as your Shield, my love. Know this as my vow."

"Colm, grateful, I am for the protection of your magic." He whispered back in a lover's tone. "See here in my eyes the truth that I will come to you this very night and we will grant each other all desire, taking on the very spirit of the God and Goddess to pay them tribute in thanks for our success in this challenge. Take this Shield in representation of your vow as you cast your protection upon me."

Knowing the Shield would be of no use for this challenge upon his own arm, Laoghaire placed the Shield upon his wife's hand and felt certain that it completed the connection between them. Two halves of the whole.

"For I trust the strength of your words as you say them to be none other than the absolute truth. I pray the Gods that I'll have no need of your protection but I take you at the strength of your vow. As the Sword is wielded against yon beast, I will emerge from the paddock cloaked in your magical protection, for you ever have been and would that you will evermore be the living Shield for this family."

As those words left Laoghaire's lips, a great and gusty wind rose up and swept the words away.

Laoghaire felt a presence at his back and turned to meet Briciu's fuzzy gaze. His first thought was that Briciu had overmuch to drink this night for his eyes did not focus but floated just below his own as if there was something interesting about his cheeks Briciu attended to. Briciu also had a scent about him that was disturbing; it was...something familiar yet indefinable, something fetid and wrong.

"Laoghaire. You do us honor by taking the challenge in such a heroic fashion. Give not a care for your woman for this task will be done quickly, I'm sure. So then we may all return to the pleasures of this night."

At that, Briciu's eyes did focus directly upon Colm. Laoghaire felt an immediate resurgence of his earlier protectiveness toward Colm and stepped decisively toward Briciu. As he did, the smell of death came off the man in waves so overpowering that Laoghaire felt his gorge threaten to rise. Laoghaire stood his ground between Briciu and Colm. He needed time to puzzle out this new scenting ability and what meaning it carried for him but was distracted at Briciu's seeming fixation on Colm. Laoghaire stalled in his position.

"You seem to have a blithe outlook on the impending slaughter of your prized animal Briciu. Did you not tell me you had no involvement in the slaughter of the animal earlier this night?"

"I did say that." Briciu forced himself to focus on the usurper. "I had no idea of the nature of the beast that came to the spit. Do you still accuse?"

Inwardly, he knew he must be careful for the final blow had not been struck; it was not the time to gloat, not yet. *Laoghaire must step into the paddock with the bull and absorb all the rage, wrath, strength and power from the beast that will relentlessly seek him out until his blood is spilled and his gore is flayed. No one can or will stifle the bull's bloodlust until it has been sated. The magic itself will not be satisfied until the deed is done. Then...then it will be released so that I will be even more closely positioned to take over the Power. I will have patience until the magic has claimed its mark and then it will award me my just reward.*

"I assure you Laoghaire, Keeper," Briciu coaxed, using all his discipline to keep his eyes from slipping back toward Colm, "this bull will more than appease your suspicions that I held back on my family's oath to provide ample meat for the feasting. Should it not? You have but to claim it."

Laoghaire wanted to ask the man why he wreaked of death if he hadn't shared in the slaughter but then had a thought that maybe he was not catching scent of Briciu's physical odor, but perhaps in this newfound magic come to him since he pulled the magical implements forth from the Cauldron, he had gained the ability to smell the very rancor of the man's spirit. At that, Briciu showed Laoghaire his back as he waddled away adjusting something under his tunic. Laoghaire was unsettled by Briciu's behavior; he seemed too pleased with himself and had bordered on disrespectful in his overt assessment of Colm. The Keeper feared there was more to the challenge than he could see but he had to trust that the magic of the older Councilmembers and his family would hold strong and see him the victor. Laoghaire turned to Colm.

"Take this Shield, wife and hold it as a symbol of strength against all evil and ill wind that would befall us and our family. The Shield is a symbol of the Gods' strength as you are the strength of our family. Hold this for me wife, in your role as my Goddess and I will return to you in victory to take my place with you as the God. So long as you are here, I will return to you. So maintain strength, my Shield, for I have a promise to keep."

Laoghaire pulled her toward him using an arm around her waist and kissed Colm deeply while the crowds whooped in encouragement. Upon his releasing her, he turned without further connection and stepped up and over the paddock gate. He strode, not toward the bull that had calmed only slightly in his tossing about, but to the middle of the paddock and withdrew his Sword from its sheath as he walked. Internally he prayed for strength to overcome his challenge, agility to strike when the opportunity is right, and wit enough to recognize when the opportunity presents itself. As he prayed, Laoghaire could see the blue glow around the Sword and he recognized that his vision had taken on a strange manner of viewing his surroundings. In his periphery, he saw the light of Faidhe, blue and green glowing brightly. He could also see a similar light around Colm, Macha and Morgan, yet it was streaked with specs of gold as well. Iarann and Lon Dubh had a cocoon of light envelop them in deep hues of blue and Craiche could be recognized by her energy that was an incongruous, lavender and white dancing about her in youthful swirls. *My family*, Laoghaire thought. *My heart.* But then a menacing disturbance shook his calm. The odor he had endured earlier emanating from Briciu had increased tenfold within the paddock ring. Laoghaire's eyes searched the crowd for Briciu's location and he was disturbed to find the man only four or five paces behind Colm. Worse, his countenance was swathed in a murky, mud like energy, sluggishly oozing around him and shooting tentacles out toward the bull in the ring to shroud it as well. Then all at once, Laoghaire recognized the fetid smell as one of decay such as that indelible stench that sticks to clothing and skin after being mired in the bog to loose an animal that has been caught in the sucking mud. He saw now, and knew that although no evidence of foul play had been found about the animal, a truly profane act had taken place. But there was no time for contemplation. The hues he saw surrounding these people had to be evidence of magic at play. Briciu had cast magic, not for protection or in petition, but a much darker energy was at work here. Something foul and for personal gain.

Initially, the beast had not recognized his territory had been invaded but let wrench a bawling mewl of outrage when he fixed his eyes on Laoghaire within the paddock circle. The bull had taken two short jolts forward on all four hoofs as if dancing in celebration at having, at last, a target to unleash upon. The massive head plunged up and down to display the magnificent horns as the fore hooves scratched the dry earth raising a small cloud of dust. Most unexpectedly, the bull then unveiled its genitals as if making ready to mount a cow.

This brought a great deal of surprised chatter from the spectators and Laoghaire was distracted at the gayety of the mood. Looking toward Colm for reassurance, he noted that both the bull and Briciu now had murky red bolts of ooze roiling through the energy around them. Enraged, as the clarity of truth came to him that this sexual energy binding the beast and Briciu was somehow attempting to penetrate the blue hue that surrounded his unwitting family. Laoghaire stepped steadily forward toward the beast now with its head raised, sniffing the air for some whiff of estrus. Firmly, he stayed the bull using an old herdsman's trick of inserting the fingers and thumb of his left hand into the nostrils and brutally clasping the delicate, soft tissue in between. Shocked, and momentarily rendered immovable by the grasp, the bull was absolutely still.

Laoghaire raised his Sword in his right hand and keeping his solid grasp on the bull with the other, in a single movement stepped to the side of the standing bull to pierce it in one savage thrust to the heart. The stench lifted and the bull took a few moments to understand that it was dying. As the legs folded under him, the animal's eyes met Laoghaire's and the Keeper saw no trace there of the wild beast that had residence only moments before. Laoghaire released his hold on the bull and his Sword and placed his bloodied hand on the bull's head to say a humbled prayer of thanks to the Gods for his victory and to the animal for its sacrifice in battle.

A violent wind screeched through the area and as it subsided, calls for help could be heard nearby where Colm and the twins stood. Quickly retrieving his Sword, Laoghaire leapt the fence and when he reached his family he saw the calls for help were to healers in the crowd for aid to the sixth Councilmember Briciu who had apparently fainted at the loss of his prize bull...and let loose his water.

22

Mother's Love

"What is the meaning of what I saw Faidhe? What was this evil that assaulted my nose around the bull and the Councilman Briciu? What was this foulness that encroached upon my family? How was it that I saw these things that were not obvious to others? Please, if I am to protect my family and the Danu's people from spells and casting as well as fight the source of such things, I must know fully of the nature of my enemy. For truly, I understand now that as Keeper, not only will I be required to my duties of the Hill but that I must also utilize the magic in the Sword and the Shield against these forces. I see now that I am to be a warrior in every sense. It is urgent that I understand in a fashion that is expedient for you take to the road all too soon to teach me at leisure."

After the challenge, Laoghaire had bid Colm take the twins and be in the company of Craiche, Lon Dubh and Iarann until such time he could council with Faidhe about what he'd seen and smelled about Briciu. He'd known the man was troublesome and perhaps underhanded in his quest for power and position within the tribe but had no idea until the challenge the extent the man would go to achieve his purpose. Laoghaire wanted to understand fully what had taken place between him and Briciu this night not only for the sake of the Tuath, but in particular regarding the safety of his family.

Faidhe contemplated what she, herself had seen. She bid him give her a moment with a raised hand. Laoghaire was anxious as he waited for her to speak. In the dim light of a hillside fire, the two met in private counsel so that all that had happened this night between Laoghaire and Briciu could be shared and examined. Laoghaire had beseeched Faidhe to take counsel with him immediately after he was sure his family would be safe. It was no easy task to slip away through the cheering throngs that sought to slap Laoghaire on the back or clap a hand to his shoulder in support and congratulations over his swift and agile work of taking down the fierce and potent bull. Laoghaire had instructed his men to bleed the bull in preparation for the spit and directed the crowds to help in the task. Although many men had been persuaded and eagerly helped with the dressing of the bull, many still clung to the new Keeper's person as if they thought some hero's musk would rub to them should they associate with greatness. Faidhe made short work of the swarm with a wave of her hand and they fell away as sheep move from a nipping hound. Laoghaire wondered if it were magic she cast upon them or was it simply their awe of Faidhe that sent them scurrying at her simple gesture. Perhaps both.

Now, in the relative darkness just outside the rim of light given off by the meager fire, the two sat in silence, each trying to work through what meaning the sights and circumstance of this night might hold.

"I too witnessed evidence of magic being cast this night." Faidhe began. "But it is not the magic of protection that we cast about you that I speak of. Our magic cast with good intention was a light and airy sight swirling about you with a fresh tint of the love felt for you as the magic was consummated in the Circle for you. It is not this magic I speak of but of the other that you saw as well. This was of other stuff. Not cast in love, light or for the best of the Tuath, rather it was a large and looming energy that held a thick and congealed binding power of blood magic. This energy was cast upon the bull you slew in the challenge. I saw the need in that energy to not only take your life but to rent you wide for the pleasure of it. This magic was cast from a perverted greed and the vengeful sickness of hatred. It came to you with an oath not only to tear you asunder but also to defile all that you love. I think this is the reason you saw what you did in that 'muddy energy' as you called it, surrounding not only the bull and the originator of the magic, but trying to grasp at your family as well."

"So this energy has been thwarted and my family safe, but what can be done about the hatred and betrayal that Briciu has brought not only to the Tuath but to the Council? And what of his mother? Does this profaning of sacred magic dwell in her heart too? Speak to me Faidhe, for my oath to the Hill will be held on my honor but should the price for that honor be the lives of my family, I will be damned to protect..."

"Say you not these words, Keeper!" Faidhe interrupted this oath curtly. "For to be so quick to damn yourself so soon upon taking an oath to the Gods and the Hill will not be taken as valor or with favor! An oath to the Gods is given and taken in the face of all situations, not just the ones that suit. You must think as a diplomat, a spiritual leader and more like a king now, Laoghaire. Your duty is to your personal comfort not at all. To abandon your oath to the Hill will be seen perhaps not equally as profane as the dark magic cast this night for personal gain but profane, nonetheless. And know you this, the dark magic cast with blood and obvious lust as well, may not have been vanquished."

Laoghaire lowered his eyes then Looked directly into Faidhe's eyes with conviction.

"From each situation I learn that the duties of a Keeper now have been redefined to include skills of a diplomat, a scholar, a magician, and warrior, all. The task at present will require me to double my awareness and efforts to keep safe my family and expand my fealty to the Tuath without compromising my oath to the Hill. I do not foreswear my oath but spoke from frustration at my lack of knowledge in these matters of the Power. I feel small in the shadow of all I must learn and much diligence is now required of me to keep safe from failure for the sake of the Gods and my family." Laoghaire then asked the question to which he did not want the answer. "Tell me what mean you that the dark magic has not been vanquished?"

"An energy raised and cast with the stain of blood is not easily put aside. As blood, once spilt, is not easily removed from a weave or a hide-skin, neither is a magic cast with blood easily dissuaded as the blood carries in it the spark of life and infuses the magic with a life of its own. The goal of the Power cast with such fierceness of hatred against you was not achieved and so it will seek out means as an arrow unstoppable until it meets its mark, to complete the task. As you took the life of the bull, you shed its blood and so altered some of the energy of the ill Power away from its original intent. A counterattack if you will, and it was done in self-preservation with the aid of our Power of protection. Our magic has achieved its goal and kept you from harm during the challenge so that energy has likely been disbursed. The other, the shadowed Power will continue to manifest in any way it can until it is satisfied; the bull has been killed but it was an unwitting vehicle for the magic, the force behind dark magic has not been sated and will strive to meet its mark. But magic gone awry like this will find its mark in the most unlikely ways. Often it is unknown where it will strike, or how."

Laoghaire sat silent for a moment contemplating what he had just been told. When he spoke, his words were careful and specific.

"What then, must be done to extinguish the evil Power? Is it I need give of some offering to quench the consuming need to kill me that has been loosed? Must I die to protect those others it seeks? My family?"

"First, my son, the Power is never the source of evil. It is the hand that wields the Power that determines whether it is for good or evil. You will do no benefit by dying in hopes to quell the fury of this spell for it not only sought you but your family as well and it will not rest. Your death will only insure one less warrior in the battle against the tide. Your offering will not alter the force that has been cast, for it is only the one who summons the energy who may set about the work of diminishing its strength and even then, it is not often that any work of this nature can be recalled without consequence for if a Power is cast lightly or without commitment entire, the Universe will not take lightly that such Power was summoned and used for frivolity or for a purpose only faint in the heart of the one who casts it. If one opts to withdraw energy from Power cast with intent, then there will most certainly be a price to pay. This is folly to discuss for when we consider the ruthless force with which this Power was directed, and the baseness of its intent to defile all that is dear to you, then we must acknowledge that the initiator of this murky casting will not easily be persuaded to remove the spell, for even if he spoke the words and displayed the actions to remove the energy from the spell, it would be but a hollow display when sized to the sheer force of his hatred for you."

"What then? What must I do to counterbalance this dark magic and make safe my family?"

"I fear, Laoghaire, that there may be naught you can do." Faidhe's words came to Laoghaire's ears but her face told him she was not entirely faithful to the truth.

"Come Faidhe, we have but little time to waste in this dance about the truth. Know you a way that can bring this thing to rest? For if one exists, reveal it to me so I may put an end to this evil and make right the situation for my family...your family, our heart. And you know truly, they are my heart, for without them, I am but a husk of a man and would be of no use on the Hill or to the Gods. Speak Mother and tell me what must be done."

Laoghaire could see that sorrow overtook Faidhe's features and she quarreled in her own heart. Her face betrayed that there was much she knew but she only vaguely answered his uncertainty.

"There is nothing you will be able to do, Keeper, save to keep sacred your oath to the Hill, evermore. In this only, will you reserve favor and perchance avoid the landing of this blight upon your family."

———

Faidhe wept. Alone now by the dying fire on the outskirts of the village where she had met with Laoghaire, she contemplated her fate and how things had come to this without her knowing. So much had taken place in the past turn of a day that even with her glimpse of the prophecy and her insight into the world of the Gods and spirits, she was overwhelmed. She thought of the new babe to be taken to breast at this stage of her life when she should be preparing for a life with the women of wisdom. Her heart responded with logic that reminded her how all things done in the service of the Gods have symmetry to them. *But with this new spark of life, comes a renewed youth for you to bear the burden. But then, I am to be ripped from my home and newly found family to travel a harsh road. And with that travel comes a life with your daughter as an initiate of the Hill. Yes, she will serve well and be joyful in her role but for the sorrow it will bring her, she will likely hate me in the end. What you will have brought her is a life within a family she has, thus far, never known.*

Faidhe allowed her heart only a moment of self-pity and then turned her mind to contemplate this new task that had been cast at her feet. *And what of this dark magic? I know the way to battle blood magic can only be truly altered or diminished if the initiator of the foulness is ritually sacrificed. But the one who draws the blade across the profaner's throat is forever stained with the tainted blood. The paths of the two souls lay connected from lifetime to lifetime. This I cannot allow Laoghaire to do for it will render him unfit for the Hill. As his body must be unblemished by spilt blood, his heart and soul must also remain untethered from any debt of service to such a person as Briciu. Laoghaire must be pure to the service of the Hill. No, this, is my burden to bear and when I am successful in the duties of my journey and the veil grows thin enough for the Gods to go beneath to the Sidhe, perhaps my years of service will be penance enough to be equal to the price I must pay for the taking of a life outside of battle and they will mercifully take me with them when my task here is done so that I may be shut of the debt owed to the soul of the one whose life I must take.* A whisper of a cold breeze toyed with her hair at this last statement as if to acknowledge the possibility of what she thought.

With a shuddering intake of breath, Faidhe steeled herself for what lay ahead. As silently as a ghost, she stood from the embers left from the dying fire and went about arranging for what must take place.

———

Gara stood in her son's hut as he lay in his swoon and fretted over what would come of her reputation now that it was suspected that Briciu had never actually committed the beef steers to the celebrations as promised. The men at the spit had come to her with the news that Laoghaire and Briciu had words over the small animal on the spit and when Briciu ordered that meat rescinded, it had not been replaced. Briciu ordered the men to wait until after the challenge for the slaughter of the promised beef. *Well that might be rectified easily enough now that the bull had been felled and would come to the spit. But what of this other chaos, how had things come to this?* Gara reflected on the evening.

Briciu had just left the platform in the feasting hall after presenting the challenge to Laoghaire when Gara had accosted him, taken him by the arm and led him outside with the masses as they scrambled to inspect the great bull. When she had questioned him in harsh whispers on his foolhardy public challenge of the new Keeper, he had truly concerned her with his absurd idea that he would win the challenge and be in line to take the Hill himself. At this she laughed outright.

"You?"

She scoffed and brought her voice down immediately as she saw she drew some attention. Gara pulled Briciu behind a large tree and continued with venom in her tone.

"How do you dare think yourself prepared in craft, knowledge or even good sense to seat yourself upon the Hill? You tantrum about in times that don't suit, you flap your tongue only for the sake of attention and must be directed as a beast on a lead to come to anything resembling sound judgment. Proof of this is in your ridiculous challenge that brings unwanted attention to you at a time when you should be working surreptitiously so that no fault, blame or suspicion can be cast upon our family when the new Keeper fails in his position. He will fail at a time when *I* deem appropriate and not before. Remember you this, boy, you are a product of *my* making and *my* power. I put you upon your seat in the Council to work what might be convenient for *me*. If you have made yourself comfortable in that position, all is well, but forget you not, you will do as you are told Briciu. And to do more than this or other than this, you will meet with not only the loss of my support to keep you within the Council, but you will feel my wrath should you get in the way of my plans to come to the Hill myself."

"You?" Briciu spat. "You? But you are near as old as the woman come down from the Hill! And it has been said that now it is time for a man to come to the Hill. Who better than me, in my youth and as your ally? You have long considered my sister Nemain as a possible initiate to the Hill so you might work from behind her, as she has no more brains than a camp kitten. Do you not see the sense in my plan? My placement on the Council, the connections I have forged with others of the Tuath, and my experience in diplomacy makes me the likely choice. Given a few bribes in the right hands and with the strategic passing of the crone, Craiche from the First seat of the Council, I would have the position on the Hill and you will fill the slot of First Councilmember. Then together, we could hand pick the ones that will fill the remaining two seats on the Council. Perhaps even Nemain would be suited to one of those positions. Surely you must see the benefit of this plan?"

"I see a spoiled, ambitious boy who has overgrown dreams of running matters that he has not the wisdom or knowledge to carry out. You think overmuch of your own importance Briciu. Tell me, what of your challenge and plans should Laoghaire take down your bull? Have you put in place a plan to recompense that loss? Or to form alliance with the new Keeper to make amends for your challenge should that happen? How will you continue your animal husbandry without a mature breeding bull? You will be beholden to the very man you challenge to provide you with good stock seed from his herd should your bull be felled. I'm sure Laoghaire will not readily come to the aid of a man who so obviously contrived to see him dead or maimed or at the very least, one who publicly opposes his position as the new Keeper. And when he takes the Hill, the kinsman he sent for will have even less concern over the well-being of our Tuath. He will see no favor in keeping your herd robust. You have done yourself an ill turn in this Briciu. All due to your foolish ideas of grandeur to play at being important."

Briciu raised his voice. "He cannot be the victor of the challenge! I have seen to it that my plan will play out in my favor."

"Lower your voice!" Gara chastened and was pleased to see him flinch at her hissing tone. She did not like this evidence that Briciu had grown strength in his backbone. She pressed her point. "And what of the meat we've pledged for these proceedings? This was a pledge we made together in front of all eyes of the clan. I gave you no leave to postpone the slaughter of the pledged meat rather I gave you direct order to see to the slaughter of the meat with your own eye. You cannot make up for your stupidity in losing the meat in the first place by reneging on our promise. What you do or say publicly casts an echo on me so you will see to it that from now and forward the only words you speak from your mouth are the ones put there by me." Gara's cheeks were aflame with her surging anger. "What of our reputation should we be put about as oath breakers? You are a fool, boy! On so many levels you fail to think ahead and cover yourself with a reasonable story or a plan to follow should you fail. Worse, I am now bound to you in your folly. And this, *this* is the kind of work you think will bring you to the Hill? Nemain has the sense of a camp kitten to be sure, but she would at least have the good judgment to consult with me prior to taking on anything of such import on her own. Come now and think no more on your own else I shall see you stripped of your title and have your herd brought under my protection and have it put about that it is for good of the clan since you show such a reckless disregard for the good of all. Take my arm boy. For now we shall go about the people by the paddock to hear what winds blow."

Gara now stood in Briciu's hut searching her memory for any indication during their conversation by the tree that Briciu had taken matters upon himself to draw upon the Power to defeat Laoghaire in this foolish challenge. She knew that if this magic she'd sensed was indeed initiated by her son that she would have to work quickly to put distance between herself and him. For if she sensed the magic at work, then certainly, others had as well. To be so associated with such blasphemy would undo all her work that had gained appropriate seats on the Council and developed relationships with powerful members of the clan. No matter what information she held over wealthy or useful clan folk, she knew that no one would stay at her side should she be put about as having anything to do with casting ill magic over the new Keeper. *Even this night just after our conversation behind the tree, Faeg and Brath approached us, sent to keep watch as eyes for the Keeper. Despite my previous dealing with Faeg the mouse of a woman came to me in earnest to the task of spying, all the while making small conversation as though I would not know her traitorous heart!*

She cursed her son for a fool but was equally disturbed that she had not any foreknowledge of what he had been about. She did not know that he'd step so far out of line as to commit magic of this nature and to so publicly make himself an adversary to the new Keeper. But the issue that frightened her most was that he had willfully challenged her own plan to come to Power. He had spoken against her in favor of his plan for his own gains. He was as dangerous as the magic he'd made over the bull: a wild and unpredictable thing. Gara fretted over what she must do to rectify this disaster and how she might bring things about so that she was quite distanced from any blame.

The mother looked upon her son resting on his sleeping pallet. *You have been marginally useful to me through the years but I think you have outstripped your usefulness.* She looked at his stained tunic and her lips pulled back in revulsion. *How would you expect me to think otherwise? You are a burden as a son and no longer serve any purpose as an ally. You bring shame and embarrassment upon my name. That I will not tolerate. You have cost me dearly in all this and have fast become a liability but perhaps,* she calculated, *before I cast you out, you may yet offer one last service to me as I ingratiate myself with the new Keeper and turn you in as the deviant offender you are.*

23

Mirror, Mirror

After leaving the place where she'd met with Laoghaire on the hillside, Faidhe found her way to the tribe's main outdoor boiling pit; a place where water is heated for washing, stretching hides, cleaning bones, the making of broth and various other purposes. By the pit, many tools and implements could be found and Faidhe had selected the carven bowl for its shiny, dark wood. Its base was smooth and black when filled with water so it made a fine reflecting surface into which Faidhe could look. The simple bowl would suit her purpose for she hesitated to call upon the sprites to bring the Cauldron for a task that she could otherwise conduct. Faidhe instinctively understood that the Cauldron should be reserved for only the most sacred and important of tasks. Faidhe took the bowl and stole away to the spot at the lake where she had just this evening at the rise of the moon, seen and spoken with the Dagda and Danu. Here, she filled the bowl with water from the lake and waited for the surface of the water in the bowl to become smooth. She sought to conjure the images of what must take place in order for her to contain this dark magic before she must take to the road in two days' time. This Faidhe could perform with a few simple aromatic herbs and a drop of salt marsh rose oil from her satchel of necessities taken from the Hill.

Faidhe peered at the surface of the water, now fully smooth and spoke the words that would bring the images she sought as she pinched the herbs between her fingers to release their bouquet into the air. Then a single drop of oil punctured the smoothness of the watery mirror to create small colorful rainbows in the ripples of water. As the water settled back to its calm, Faidhe observed ghost-like impressions dance across the surface. As she was drawn into what the mirror revealed, her eyes were as dark as the reflective pool itself and her trance state was evident.

The woman felt a ripple of frustration, as the information she sought would not easily be revealed. She knew not how to render the dark magic impotent without damning herself to an eternity bound to the one she aimed to dispatch. What was revealed to her were images of Laoghaire, once again, atop a mount peering across a great divide toward one who stood atop the neighboring mount. Laoghaire stood with his great Sword, and Shield and twining about his legs, arms, and body were great twists of the fighe vine. The one who stood across from him carried Faidhe's great Staff appearing so large, that it could be recognized even across this sprawling distance. Faidhe could see her own likeness in the person across the divide, and yet, not so, as with some trick of the eye, it was she, and then it was a man, she, and then the man. And when the image settled, clearly, it was a man that wielded her Staff, one of conviction and who emanated crackling green energy. He had his own message to be delivered and heard by many and so with the Staff, he demanded to be paid attention. In a swift and sure motion, with the ash wood Staff, he rented the lush grass with a great stab into the very Lady of the earth. From this consummation, vast and enormous roots traveled rapidly under the earth to spread all throughout the land. This new root could be seen sprouting at Laoghaire's feet then twining up his legs to combine with the weave of the fighe vine. This marriage of the Staff with the land propagated a seedling of something not yet known before this time, a highbred of the two: the Mother earth, herself and the message behind the man with the Staff.

Just then, the water rippled with the kiss of a breeze and the image fell away. Faidhe was intent upon the reflection and was not ready to give up on coming by the answers she sought. Instinctively, picked up a shard of jagged rock and dragged it across the fleshy tip of her finger. Squeezing tight the wound, she allowed one drop of blood to fall into the water. As she looked into the beyond of the mirror, she saw a raging snowstorm, the like of which she'd never seen. Commanding all of her attention to focus on what must be done to protect Laoghaire and her daughter from the wickedness of the evil that had been loosed, she saw an image from the blinding snow begin to take shape. At first Faidhe thought that she'd once again lost the spiritual connection and was beginning to see her own reflection but then from what seemed like the other side of the water's surface came into focus the face of a woman. Gara appeared to be looking right into Faidhe's eyes and it startled her. In that moment of surprise, Faidhe lost her concentration and the mirror, once again simply reflected the moon.

Startled as Faidhe was, she saw something in the eyes of Gara before the image was lost. She was quite sure that when Faidhe recognized Gara in the reflection pool, that Gara had seen and recognized her as well. *What could this mean*, she calculated. *What had Gara to do with all of this?* She was reluctant to do what she must but to do nothing was even less appealing to Faidhe especially now as time grew short. She asked the Gods for guidance and poured the basin out onto the ground with a prayer of thanks and release for the energies used to help her visions with the mirror.

Faidhe stood and put a protective hand over her abdomen and was pleased to feel the little spark of life that was harbored there. For the sake of this child and those she had already borne, she knew now what she must do to bring clarity to her plans. Faidhe trusted her intuition to guide her through the village to find Gara and swore to herself that she would not come away without the answers she sought.

———

Gara was on her knees, listlessly poking a stick at the cold and barren hearth in Briciu's hut wallowing in what she perceived as recent occurrences both unjust and unfair. *What plan had the Keeper, come down from the Hill? And to appoint such an unexpected replacement! Imagine, the news of a woman her age, practically in her dotage, to be breeding!* The unkind thought was not at all sincere. Gara had no desire to carry or raise a child but she felt a constant nagging jealousy at the gift of youth Faidhe had been given. Although, she thought herself to be beautiful in her maturity, Gara's good looks gave one a sense of coolness and distance, an unapproachable hardness whereas Faidhe appeared as a woman in her youth with look of good humor, warm and approachable but with all the wisdom of her years. The kind of beauty to draw the eyes of men of all ages. Gara spiked a hungry pang of envy to know that no amount of her own magic could equal the gift Faidhe had received from the Gods.

Gara liked it not that she held envy for anyone, much less another woman over beauty. She devoutly turned her mind to the more pressing matter in trying to plot a plan that would get rid of Briciu for her but one that would preserve the façade of honor for her family and maintain her position of power without loss of her regard in the Tuath. She'd been deep in calculations when she quite unexpectedly found herself in the midst of visions unbidden. She saw her son in the servant's hut and witnessed him beckoning a man hither to aid him in gathering some items. Gara recognized these items as those used to summon, and cast a spell of strength and aggression. She watched as she discovered in horror, what her son had done to the servant and how the blood had been used.

The Councilwoman had known of her son's temper and she'd helped him hide his mistake when, as a boy of only 12 or 13 seasons, he'd killed his friend in a rage over the loss of a game. Briciu had sworn to her that he won the game and his friend had cheated him. He implored her to understand that it was a point of honor and that the boy had died in the argument was a tragic mistake. Gara was quick to believe her son because the alternative would be to face a Council tribunal and have her family honor brought into question. *Better to cover the accident over than to answer prying questions,* she decided. For she did not want it known that her son was over-fond of the pain and discomfort of others. She knew to keep Briciu well under her control and also to keep him ever away from being alone with his sister. He was dark, yes but it was a power that she thought could be harnessed as useful. Through the years, Gara had hoped that her son's inability to maintain his rage had been tempered with position and family. When he reached 16 seasons, he began to raise and trade cattle, and brought a fine profit. He'd taken a wife to his hearth and soon after announced the coming of his child. Gara thought to breathe relief that he'd outgrown his childhood temper. But soon after his son was weaned, Briciu's wife met her own untimely death. While the rest of the Tuath offered heavy hearts for the young man, Gara knew in her own heart that the poor waif of a girl had not really gotten in the way of an errant stud bull to be trampled; just as surely as she knew on that day that 15 seasons ago, the young boy found at the base of the overhang by the ocean had not found his way there by any hand of the Gods. Now that Gara had glimpsed the recent doings of her son, she realized that any usefulness he may have offered was outstripped by the danger he posed to her now.

As she shifted the dead coals with a stick to see if there was a vision offering an idea how to best distance herself from Briciu, Gara leaped back from the cold, ash filled hearth and had fallen hard on her backbone as her buttocks hit the ground; her legs sprawled out in front of her. With the jolt, her teeth came together with a loud clack and she cried out as she had sharply bitten her tongue. She drew her knees up to her chest and huddled by the cold hearth, she contemplated why and how had she'd been visited by a vision of the Keeper Faidhe, so soon upon learning of her son's unpardonable deeds. *This was more than a vision. She saw me, looked into my eyes! What means this Keeper woman coming to me unbidden? Does she know what I have seen in the darkest depths of my son's heart? Does she think me in collusion in this foulness he has wrought? Is she the way out of this for us to preserve our name and position? What must I do now? What can I do? I know not but that I have to be shut of this oppressive weight that is my son. If only I could heave him off yon cliff and be shut of this business and return my thoughts to the Council affairs at hand.*

Gara grew cold at the thought of murdering her own son. She knew it was not something she could bring herself to do for she knew the price for such an action would be steep indeed. Her skin gathered into puckered points and she felt the hairs on her neck crawl to attention. There was the faintest scuff of a heel step behind her and alarm warnings of self-preservation came to jangling attention. Picking up the nearest hearthstone to hand, Gara rolled to her knees and in one movement, turned to face the imposing figure standing just behind her.

"You wake, my son. How is it with you? Are you more well now for having your rest?"

Briciu offered in a singsong voice that echoed of something off key.

"Mother, what brings you here? Come to look after your ailing boy? How kind that you tend my hearth so lovingly. It shows the warmth of your motherly love." He waved a theatrical hand at the cold and dark hearth.

On her knees and at a disadvantage, Gara hid the stone in the folds of her linens. She made to stand up and ready herself for whatever battle was coming but Briciu bade her stay where she was in mock formality. He stepped closer.

"Please, don't exert yourself. It is a fine sight indeed to see you over a hearth. It has been overlong since you've cooked a meal for me or done me a kindness in a motherly fashion. But then who could expect the great and powerful, lovely enchantress, Gara to stoop to anything as mundane as to warm a hearth fire with loving words of support for her only son?"

Briciu placed a rough hand atop Gara's head and shoved back her efforts to get to her feet.

Gara looked up at her son and realized that what she was looking at was thinly veiled consuming hatred that smoldered from his eyes...and something else. There was a hint of something gleefully savage in the pulse of his energy. And the smell coming from him made her wonder why she hadn't noticed before that he must have loosed his waste as well as his water. She lowered her eyes to the drying stain on his tunic and made the discovery that what she mistook for loss of his bladder was in fact more likely evidence that he'd lost control of his ability to comport himself in normal society. Then cold dread captured her ability to move when she observed that her son had grown aroused while standing in such close proximity to her kneeling position. Gara turned her head away in revulsion and was put in mind of the harsh words she'd spoken to Briciu when he was but a boy. She grew impatient with the child as she observed him too many times with his hands beneath his tunic rubbing to work up his seed.

"Where is your honor boy? You carry on this way and spill your gifts onto the ground and the Goddess will not see fit for you to couple with any woman. Spill not the juice without purpose. It is not what the Gods intended for if you are over fond of pleasuring yourself, you will be cursed with being less of a man when it comes time to lie with a woman. Is this what you will? Would you deny me my reputation by having a son who is put about as a one who has not the will to honor the Gods with a strong spear at the festival fires?"

As those words came back to her, Gara realized that her son was hovering over her with his manhood showing no signs of the malady foretold. She knew she had to think quickly for even now, her eyes were drawn back to the hulking man as he began to hike up his tunic where he stood only mere inches from where she knelt.

"Briciu, stay your hands and mind your place in this Tuath. You must not be taking actions beneath your station. Know you the laws of this land? Defile an unwilling woman and disgrace your honor. It is known that any man who forces the rites is an abomination. And though the Gods may choose to mingle with their own, it is not seemly that a man should lie with his mother but for the very act of survival or in sacred ritual for propagation of crop, cattle and kin. And even then, it is only rare. Know you now, I forbid you to take the role of the God with me."

He taunted in mock formality.

"You think over much of yourself, Councilwoman, I have no desire to play the God with you. For anything that would fall from your womb is doomed to a life of degradation and would be better a carcass put to field for the carrion birds than to take such pecking as a child of yours." Briciu, by now had entirely hiked up his linens and fully exposed his manhood taught with intent. I would sooner become a eunuch than plunge into the blackness of your womanhood. But to stopper the screeching sound that has cascaded from your mouth these long years will be more the pleasure just to enjoy the muffling of the badgering I've endured all too long."

Gara understood what Briciu meant to do and realized too late that her son had gone bad in the mind. She made to scramble away from him to get to her feet and he held her firm with his hand fast in her hair. Gara clutched the rock but it would do her no good for he was towering over her. She thought to scream but knew that her son's servants would not dare enter without his permission. She was one for absolute privacy in her own hut and she knew that Briciu would not be disturbed in his and even if someone were to come to investigate the screams, his servants would bide his word for now she saw how they would be in great fear of him. Too, her pride could not allow for the shame that she should be seen so vulnerable by a lowly servant or slave.

Briciu paused a moment to revel in his victory just before he allowed himself to take the final plunge into the abyss of the perverse darkness he'd held at bay his entire life. In a rasp of wild vehemence, he bent close to his mother and warned Gara.

"Woman, you do harm to me and I will take slow pleasure in beating you bloody. I have naught to lose now and I will have my way to regain my opinion of myself as a man."

Regaining her wits now, Gara realized that the spell Briciu cast this night must now be clinging to him for her son was mindless himself with power and aggression that was all entwined with the sexual rites. He must have somehow tangled himself in the spell and rather than wield the magic, it now gripped him in some fashion. Gara also knew that the blood spilt for this spell would mean no release from it until its purpose was satisfied. She would be his captive until rescue was made and during the coming days of festivities, there would be less than few who would search for either of them soon. Gara's reaction to this thought took even her by surprise. She gagged at the stench of his closeness as he leaned over her but it offered her an opportunity to bring the rock she still held tight hard and swift across Briciu's temple.

The shocked look of disbelief took over his face and Briciu understood as he crumpled to the floor that, once again, his better had trumped him. The disappointment of failure crossed his face and was replaced with a chilling expression of hatred, just as the light left his eyes.

Gara felt her gorge convulse but she managed to stay her control and spit several times on the floor instead. As she tried to compose herself, she looked to the figure in the doorway.

"Ah," said Faidhe. "I am come too late."

"My son is ill." Gara started, stating the only obvious thing that came to her mind after such a shock of violence had been inflicted upon her and still not quite comprehending what had just taken place. So many years of covering the truth and manipulating circumstances came as habit to Gara and she stood to right herself and to make an attempt to diminish the appearance of anything untoward. This was no small task as Briciu lay openly exposed on the floor with a sizable gash on his temple and the rock that had likely opened the wound was still in her hand. Gara's hair, usually impeccably quaffed was a tangled mess. Her eye was already puffing with the impact of the blow Briciu had given her and her lips were bruised and swollen with minor cuts from her own teeth due to the rough treatment they'd endured during his attempts to dominate her.

Faidhe took in the situation.

"You will survive your injuries Gara, though I doubt it not that your pride has suffered much. But your son is likely dead, if not, he will be soon enough. One does not sustain this type of wound and live long with his wits about him. How came you to this moment? For surly his is a battle wound, is it not?"

Seeing a way to excuse her from penalty for bringing physical harm to a clan member, Gara thought to confide in Faidhe and lay bare the story of what had just taken place but then was conflicted over whether she might be accused of being somehow in collusion with her son to bring about the death of the new Keeper, or worse, to have misused the gift of magic to bring that death about. She stumbled over what to say.

"No. I, ah, came to see to Briciu's health after his swoon to losing his prize bull. A shock to him, I'm sure."

"Come Gara, play me not the fool for it is beneath even you to try to dissuade one from what is obvious in this situation. Know you now; the eyes with which I see are privy to much beyond what is seen by all others. I tell you in honesty that though I may not know all, I can attest to the darkness in the spell Briciu has cast this night, for I saw its caul upon the bull and Laoghaire as well as Colm and her children. And too, I saw from whence this abomination of dark spell was cast."

Gara watched, as Faidhe took on the look of the Goddess Morrigan, dark in expression, beautiful and grand. This aspect of the Goddess, Gara knew, was one who reveled in battle and often chose who would die at her whim. So long had Gara been removed from consort with the Gods beyond rote, that she'd come to think on reverence given them as something feigned and habitual rather than with genuine thanks and veneration for the good fortune they bestow and the Power they possess. But now, Gara witnessed Faidhe's countenance, large and terrible, swirling with crackling energy and her dark hair a-slither and afloat with a hint of mysterious things hidden beneath her robes and understood what true Power of the Hill must be if this was but a sample.

Gara hoped to turn this recent event to her advantage. "Lady, Keeper, please, old friend. If you know what misery my son has wrought on my good name and honor with his treachery, then you must know too, how he has woven this curse so that it has taken hold of his very self and turned him to things unnatural. I cannot be held for his doings for he has turned his darkness upon even me. I too am a victim of his plan, gone afoul. You must understand, he has ruined himself in the eyes of the Gods and his place in the Tuath must be rescinded."

"Silence! Even now you think on only that which concerns you. Whatever ill has come to you is only a fragment of that which you cast upon those around you for your own gain. Woman, see you not what times of import come flying fast at us now? Your son has created a monster of a tide that will stop at naught until it reaches the shore and likely wipes out everything in its path. Blood has been spilt! And ill magic has been cast for the sake of personal gain! There could be no more a foul combination of circumstance and it was at your knee this one learned to be a man." Faidhe, dark with wrath pointed at the lifeless body on the floor.

"So you too must pay the price for your part in this. The most sacred of laws is to keep the maternal relationship above all else. You have put aside that honor in furtherance of your own agenda and it has come back upon you with vengeance. Weep not for yourself and harm done you, weep rather for this wreck of a man who has so offended the Gods that his life is forfeit in attempt to right the ill magic he has cast. For if he lives even now, to turn him out is not a solution open to us. You know what must be done to reverse the effects of the ill-cast spell."

Gara seemed an empty husk and appeared every one of her years at this moment. "You are right. It must be done. Take him." She uttered in a small voice, yet not so small that relief could not be detected.

"Take him? You misunderstand Gara. If you have any hope at all that your son's spirit will not wander, Godless, forever lost, then you must partake in the ritual to reverse what he's done, to retrieve the evil that lurks even now, to destroy the new Keeper and his family and to desecrate all that we hold sacred."

Gara's facial expression alone told Faidhe that she had no desire to partake in any ritual involving her son. She could not comprehend that this would compromise her own spirit in life here and after this world.

"See if his heart still beats." Faidhe ordered. "For it is all for naught if he has no breath in him."

Gara made no move to go nearer her son and with a sigh of impatience, Faidhe nudged her aside to see for herself if Briciu lived. With a silent prayer to the Gods, Faidhe bent low to listen for his breathing and to see if his heart still kept the rhythm of the living. It was slight, but it could be heard.

"He lives." Faidhe announced. "For now. I have business to attend in preparation for all that must take place. You must acknowledge now your task, in order to reclaim your son's spirit from eternal displacement and your own from the price the Gods will exact for your part in this, you must do naught else but to prepare yourself and Briciu for the ritual that we must now hold. This must take place now before the moon sets and before this man breathes his last breath for then we know not what will come of the energy cast in this malicious madness. Understand you your task?"

Gara stood unsteadily on her feet and weaved back and forth as a marsh reed in the wind. A drawn look was stamped on her face and a distant stare in her eyes impelled Faidhe to grasp Gara by her forearm and shake her to attention.

"Gara! Councilwoman, heed me! You will not relinquish your responsibility in this. It is your task and can be delegated to no other. None other than you and myself must act to dispel the foul fury Briciu has roused. Wake, woman. This is the stuff of the duties of the Hill. Want you the title of Keeper so much now? Understand you the real sacrifice of a servant of the Hill beyond playing at Priestess of the Circle? Move now! Put yourself right! And prepare your son for his death."

24

The Story Continues

Despite the fact that it was well past 2:00 a.m. when we finally returned to our cottage, I seriously doubted that I'd be able to sleep when we got home from our trip to Midleton. Once inside, we continued to be silent and absorbed in our own thoughts as we double locked the doors, checked all the windows and drew closed, all the shutters and blinds. That done, after a bump of a hug to each other, we retired to our own rooms. I flopped on my bed and fell blissfully into a deep slumber. If I had any dreams that night, I have no recollection at all of what they were.

But early in the morning, I found myself back in the familiar woods I'd been to in some recent dream. I had peripheral awareness that I was dreaming and I was curious to look around and see what I could see. I felt elation and a strong sense of coming home as I walked a path toward a gnarled and moss-covered tree that grew next to a cheery little brook. I went to sit on the tree's roots and thought to put my feet in the water when I realized that the shoes I wore were not any I recognized but some kind of suede leather booty. As I pulled them off my feet, some flattened straw fell from inside them to the earth. I was amazed at the detail I experienced for what was a dream. My feet toyed with the water so they could adjust to how cold it was. Joy was the pervasive feeling of this dream. Joy and comfort. I mused at how wonderful I felt as if nothing in the world mattered and nothing could sully the mood. I was home. Just as I leaned back on the great tree for support, from the path behind me I heard a low familiar voice.

"Hello Black Bird."

I turned. And though I thought it was not possible to feel any happier, I was over-joyed as I jumped up.

"Mother. We've missed you so much!"

I was on my feet and dashing toward the old woman standing just there on the path. As I drew closer, she signaled me to stay my enthusiasm, her hand extended, with palm facing flat toward me.

"I am pleased, Little One, for when we last parted, you all but cursed me for your part in the prophecy."

Then, in the way that things are understood in dreams without logical reasoning, I knew that somehow, this woman was my mother but then again not. I took in her appearance as she held me at bay. She looked like someone who carried many burdens with strength and dignity. Her eyes were stamped with deep lines at the corners that crept all the way down her cheeks as she offered a melancholy smile but the expression in those eyes told a tale of great sorrow. In my struggle to take in her appearance and to make sense of her words, I realized that I was angry with her. I had the urge to turn away and leave her out of righteousness but internally I was not an accomplished 40 something year old woman traveling to pursue and earn a degree; I was a girl of 15, awed at her mother's presence. I enjoyed that she called me 'Black Bird' and 'Little One' and I didn't want to be angry with her because I missed her and loved her and I knew that I'd left her, when maybe I should not have, and I felt the shame of that decision. I also knew that she could help me understand all that was going on.

"Prophecy?" I asked.

"Yes, Lon Dubh. You still must play a role in this as you have sworn. You gave of yourself to the Goddess and the God to be an instrument of their will. You swore an oath of service and though you have lived many lives in training since that oath, now is the time you must hold true your oath and be wielded as the living Sword. For it was yours to wield then but for circumstance you should have followed me to the Hill had not the prophecy dictated otherwise. So it is yours/you now. This task involves those you love and have loved through many lifetimes but this time you bear the responsibility of deciding whether this will be the last of lifetimes for any and all."

"That's what the old men told me too but I just don't know how." I felt panic begin to rise.

The woman touched me but she never moved. I felt her hand on my shoulder as she said, "Hold now child. Stay your fears for there is help for you and your sisters: my little Colm Dove...and the others. But you and Colm together - you must remember and relearn all you can, using all your wits and sources. Remember what you will for there is much training you have had already, during many lifetimes over in preparation for this day. But you must finish what you started as blood of my blood. Give not over to sorrow or fear or pain; give not over to what trickery the Beast lays out for you. Trust that what poison it has woven, in the end will unravel so long as you remain, this time, steadfast in your oath. Go now child. Remember your oath."

I heard a muffled sound in the background; a snuffling like a pig digging for truffles. I ignored it.

"But I don't want to go. I want to stay here. I want to come home."

The woman appeared distracted by the sound and turned back to me to speak with urgency.

"Wake now Black Bird, for you do not dwell in this time that is not a time, in this place that is not a place." (Snuffle) *"You have not yet the preparation and we draw unwanted attention. Go now. And learn."* (Snort) *"It is for this message I come to you at great risk to you both. Know this. Learn to draw upon the Power to fulfill your needs for it is ever available to you. Trust your intuition."*

"No! Wait! I have questions. Please, let me stay and learn from you for a little while." Then a loud but distant squealing echoed just before I shouted and woke myself up feeling cheated and at a loss I looked up to see a concerned Nora standing at my door with an unasked question all over her face.

"I'm okay." I said with a sigh. "I guess we have some things to talk about don't we?" And then not waiting for an answer I heaved myself out of bed, defiantly putting my bare feet down right next to the dust ruffle hanging from the bed, symbolically throwing down the gauntlet. The decision was made. I'd stay. I'd learn. I'd fight. I had to know if Nora had come to the same decision.

"Let's get some breakfast and talk about last night."

———

We were rested and fed but were mutually quiet during breakfast. The one thing we'd discussed and decided was to take some time away from the brothers to travel around a bit but really to sort things out between us before we worked our way back around to Cath's store back in Lahinch. We started in Ennis to do a little shopping and ambled toward Bunratty but skipped the tour of the castle to go to the Hunt Museum in Limerick. Neither of us could seem to get into the mood for idle touring but neither could find an appropriate opening to speak about what lay ahead of us. Perhaps in my desire to experience that sense of family and coming home, once again we eventually set out, to find our relative, Margaret's house in Killarney, County Kerry.

We had written directions to Margaret's house but found the roads a bit confusing so after a few phone calls to Margaret and a sinking realization that we might have some difficulty in communicating with our cousin, due to the heavy Irish accent, we managed to find the modest group-type home where she lived with eight other women.

I found myself searching Margaret's face for some glimmer of familiarity, some hint of blood relation but was disappointed to find that, although she was my Dad's cousin, my second cousin, I saw no reflection of my family's features in hers, no sense of home. This spec of a woman about 70 years old barely reached 5'2" and had lackluster mousy brown hair that was likely a rinse. She dressed in inexpensive but current clothing and was neat and crisp in her dark green slacks and light green sweater with flat black slip-on shoes. I guessed that she was far enough removed from us that some spark of familial connection wasn't going to leap out at my heart. Pleasant though, she was polite and gracious but devilish difficult to understand. We ate a light lunch of scones, jam, and tea with Margaret and her good friend Sheila, a smallish, plumpish, mannish looking woman, with thick glasses and a deep scar on her right cheek, who also lived in the house. I almost lost my composure when at one point, as Nora began to cut into her scone, Margaret reached over to Nora's hand, took the scone from her and tore it in half with her fingers. Nora's eyes bulged so wide that I wondered if, after such a molestation, she would actually eat the pawed over scone.

"Dere's da wey ye braik da sco-in." She said in directing Nora that the scone was not to be cut from top to bottom, but rather from one side across to the other. "As aboove, so den below." Margaret said, almost as a prayer. To my surprise, Nora took the scone with a nod and slathered it with jam before eating it. Not only that, but I noticed she added some milk and honey to her tea. I speculated, because we were assimilating to these small ways, that somehow or other, they mean something if only symbolically.

Margaret carried the conversation almost non-stop while Nora and I desperately tried to decipher what she was saying. We knew it was our turn to respond when Margaret would finish with, "In't dat right, Sheila?"

To which Sheila would respond. "Ooh, 'tis. 'Tis."

Then they'd look to us expectantly, waiting for some kind of answer or comment. Nora was much more successful than I was during this volley due to the fact that she could turn the conversation neatly to photos and knick-knacks around the sitting room so that Margaret would pick up the conversation to tell about the trinket or person in the photo. We both tried valiantly to be polite and conversational but we could have laughed right out loud when Sheila flatly stated, "We're havin' trooble oonderstandin ye."

Having chatted for a while and been schooled in the proper way to cut a scone, if not proper table boundaries, we began to make moves to be off again and had just about made it to the front door, at which point, Margaret shocked us both by grasping at my arms and bursting to tears pleading at me, "Are ye da ledie frim da rohid?"

I looked at Nora hoping she'd give some hope in the translation department. Her eyebrows were so far up her forehead; I knew there was no help for me there.

I took my cousin's hand.

"What is it Margaret? What are you asking?"

Giving me a frustrated look, she tried again through her tears.

"Are ye - da ledie - frim - da - ro - id?"

I looked to Sheila for some help.

"I'm sorry, we're having some trouble understanding you too. Can you tell us what she's asking?"

Sheila, in her sensible shoes and stretchy polyester slacks, walked with purpose over to the ancient telephone table and pulled a piece of paper from the notepad there. After scratching some quick words onto it then handing it to Nora who was closest to her, nodded her head with a no nonsense finality that clearly meant she'd put an end to the problem.

I looked to Nora for an answer to the mystery and she looked a bit bewildered as she read the words on the paper.

"Are you the lady from the road?"

Now it was my turn to be bewildered. But I turned to Margaret shaking my head and assured her.

"I'm sorry, Margaret, I don't know what that means but whatever it or she is, I don't think it's me."

Margaret was still looking at me with furrowed brow and teary eyes. She didn't understand me either. I shook my head again.

"No."

I was sure she understood the universal symbol for no. At that she looked downright miserable and I couldn't help but hug her in comfort for whatever I lacked in not being 'the lady from the road.' I felt sorry that she was hopeful about me being someone or something that meant something to her and that I'd disappointed her. We said our goodbyes and promised to write as we walked out the front door of the little group home in which Margaret would likely spend her last days, because when I hugged her, I knew she was very sick with something wrong in her midsection and would likely not live much longer: a year, maybe two. I sighed as we parted and I don't know what prompted me to do it but at the last moment, I turned back through the door and reached over to her forehead and with my thumb, I planted the graphic that I'd seen on the cover of the book, *The Power of the Word*. In three quick motions I etched the design and kissed her goodbye on the same spot. Margaret gripped the tissue in her arthritic hand to her heart and began to cry again. Through her tears, she waved enthusiastically at us as we drove away.

We took the long ride throughout the day to recount and take inventory of our Ireland experiences. Between stops to take listless strolls through one store or another, we ambled along the roads we talked about Margaret's odd "lady from the road" question and both agreed that we felt drained after our visit with her as though our energy had been tapped. The conversation led us to discuss much of what we'd seen and experienced the night before and worked our way through some difficult patches when it came to the emotionally charged memories of the mental tour through Nora's house and hearth. Most of what might have been said about that experience was alleviated when Nora struggled with a verbal apology over old hurts and I waved them away.

"Nora, you know I love you and throughout our lives, you've been my really only, someone...always. I know you love me too. I mean I *know* you love me. So don't think about 'sorry' 'cause it's nice to know but not necessary no matter what Finny says. So let's not dwell on that stuff, let's take the messages we get and use them for the information they offer. Okay?"

There was no answer from Nora and I knew she was struggling with the emotion of regret or forgiveness but I knew that to create the bond between us I figured we'd need, all that relationship crap would have to be behind us. Thinking of that vision, I wondered aloud at the significance of the hawk and the raven.

Relieved at the change of subject Nora mused, "Well, Cath said the bird has been used as a spiritual symbol in many different faiths. And the idea that it can travel through three of the elements is significant too. Let's see, what do we know about birds?"

I answered, "Both the raven and the dove are in a biblical story of Noah's Ark, in the Old Testament. And the pre-Christian Scandinavian, Teutonic and Celtic pantheons are full of the ravens in connection with various Gods and Goddesses. And they are often depicted as a medium to witches and wizards because they are supposedly able to travel and communicate between the spirit world and the earthly world."

"Native Americans believe in the power of totem." Nora continued. "A person is imbued with the power of an animal when that particular animal has marked them in some way or has come to them in a vision or the animal is drawn to a person so a continuous appearance is noticed against likelihood...Like seeing crows and ravens all the time, sometimes at night." She said in her sardonic fashion.

"I guess that could be right in this circumstance. You know, once, while I was doing research, according to one book I came across written on Native American totems, my totem is the crow based on my birth date."

"You surprised?"

"Not anymore; not after all of this. Anyway, what about the crow or raven and the hawk? I guess the dove, now too. Let's start with the basic Celtic or Irish symbolism and see what there is there. And, we'll have to look to the Nordic history and myths to check out the hawk now. I don't know so much about the hawk. Also, it seems that you've taken from the Swedish side of the family for your position or title as the 'Shieldmaiden' so we have to investigate that some too I guess. Then, let's examine the Catholic religion and the earlier stories of the Old Testament. That's what we're supposed to be doing isn't it? Create balance between the old and new? Let's look at symbolism through history on those three birds and the

Sword and Shield implements see if anything develops to help us recognize what we're supposed to be doing."

"Okay. Let's make a plan for when and where we can do that kind of research but let's just ask Cath and Finny first to see what they can tell us." Nora said.

It felt good to have made a decision, at least, about making a plan. Without coming right out and saying so, it seemed that we had begun to accept the fact that we were in for some kind of battle and we'd do well to arm ourselves with knowledge if we planned to see it through.

As we drove we speculated further on what the visions regarding the man who carried the Staff might mean and what the roots and vine could be as well. We both carefully avoided talking about the Beast as though its mention might bring back that sense of desperation. I knew that hesitation to take on this subject was being fearful and that was not good but for now, I was comfortable to leave that subject alone.

I eventually attempted to bring the conversation around to the dream I'd had that morning to put out a feeler as to whether Nora had any inkling or indication of the idea that we have a relationship to the old woman we'd both seen in our cottage some nights ago; or that the woman is somehow connected to this magical struggle throughout centuries.

"So how'd you sleep last night?"

"Okay. Why?"

"Just asking."

"Liar."

I smirked. "Okay," I said, knowing it would be foolish to think I could slip passed Nora's antennae. "Did you have any dreams? Not mundane dreams but loud dreams or telling dreams, you know, in connection with all this..." I waved my hand around in a few circles as if from searching in the air, I'd pull out the right word, "this mystery?"

"Ah, not that I recall. Why? What happened?"

"You know the old woman that came to us that first night when the Beas... ah, smell came?"

"Yeah."

"Well, I had a dream this morning and she came to me...no that's not right. I found myself in a place that I know I've been to before. Either in dreams or I don't know - whatever, but I recognized the woods where I was. It felt like I was home. You know, like I belonged there and I haven't felt like that since we all lived in the triple-deckers in Jamaica Plain with Grandma and Grandpa and everyone. I was so happy to be there in the woods. And that woman was there. It was weird because I knew I was dreaming but in that same way, I also knew that it wasn't a dream. This place and the woman, they were real. Or they felt real." I hovered in thought for a second and shook off the struggle to try to explain the feeling with a small shake of my head. "The woman was my mother. I know it sounds strange but I just know it was a connection I'd had to her at some time. She called me 'Black Bird' and she came to tell me that I've been through other lives to train for what we're going to be facing. She said to trust to draw on the Power and it'll be there when we need it."

"We?" Nora asked for clarification with the one word.

"Uh, yeah, because apparently, she's your mother too. She actually called us by different names but they were as natural to me as hearing us called Lee and Nora... she seemed to know about Patrice and Mary too, I think."

"So she called you Black Bird and did she call me Hawk Bird?" Nora quipped. I had felt such joy and happiness at coming home to this place and seeing this woman for whom I obviously felt a deep love, I wanted Nora to understand the awe I felt for having had such a visitation. I chose to ignore the note of sarcasm in her voice.

"No, she called you 'Dove, Colm Dove.' And she called me something like, Lawn Doove and Black Bird too. The dialect was a funny sounding language that was something like Irish, but I don't know, it was different too and the weird thing is I knew she was speaking in a different language, but I understood her anyway and I think when I spoke, I answered her in her own language. What I think is important though, is that she told me we were sisters when she was our mother. And that we gave some kind of oath at the time, to fight this battle whatever it is, and we've been here many times over, training, so to speak to learn to use our magic. And it all has to do with 'the prophecy'."

"Lee, I know I have to get my mind around thinking in a different way now. Things like this aren't impossible and I guess I have to learn to trust things as they come to us. I know this *mentally* but it still has to pass through my analytical process for now, so bear with me while I play devil's advocate. "What makes you think it wasn't just a dream?"

I considered the question and genuinely searched for the answer but I found that there was no one thing to point out.

"I can't say why Nora. I just know. It was almost like all of the questions about our magic and all that's happened here in Ireland, and our relationship since childhood all came to light and made perfect sense. It was like all the tumblers fell into place and a big locked door swung open so I understood why we're different from other people and why you and I know each other's minds and why we have magic. I mean really understood, not just know about because of what Cath or Finny told us but it made sense and felt natural to me that she was our mother and knew about our magic and encouraged it. It was like ..." I gave up trying to explain. I just didn't have the words to relate the overwhelming *rightness* of the dream.

Nora recognized my mounting frustration and impulsively patted my hand apparently to alleviate my struggle with trying to explain. I briefly but distinctly felt the union of our minds when Nora unknowingly or perhaps intuitively cut out the need for words and took from me, what I struggled to say.

"Oh," she said, somewhat unsettled, then let go of my hand as if it were hot. "Okay, I get it."

It was kind of unnerving to me that, lately, people had been able to reach into my mind and see or feel my thoughts so easily, but it felt so natural with Nora that I almost didn't take notice at the rate at which the ability had grown between us.

We drove in silence for a while and then Nora said, "Okay."

"Okay what?" I asked.

"Okay we can skip the rest of the tourist stuff and head to Cath's. Didn't you just ask if we could do that?"

I smirked, as I understood what had just happened.

"Not out loud." I answered, and pulled over so we could check the map to find the quickest way to Cath's store from where we were.

———

Over the next few days, Nora and I devoured book after book in Cath's little back room library searching for any and all information to be had on the symbolism of the raven, crow, hawk and dove. Much was revealed to us regarding the crow and raven, which symbolically were synonymous. Another facet to the duality of my existence, I supposed. I was fascinated to have found the raven connected to aspects of prophecy, solitude, messengers of the Gods and a solar symbol. All these in some way tied into what my role is in all of this newfound knowledge. Perhaps the most telling bit of information was the use of the phrase "Raven's knowledge," which was commonly used in earlier times to mean the human gift of second sight. I found peace and comfort in the familiar act of research and each time I was called away from the books I felt annoyed at the break in continuity. The steady stream of information made me feel better protected and more armed to do what needed to be done and I hoped that Nora was finding equally telling information about the hawk. At the same time though, I realized that all facets of this new training were important. We brought The Power of the Word with us from the cottage in order to read, study and discuss its contents while using the McDonough brothers as a sounding board for our interpretations. We toggled between reading and research and telling Cath and Finny, all we could remember about our family and abilities as well as everything unusual that had happened to us or around us since we'd arrived in Ireland.

Finny left his ramshackle truck/home in the back of the church for the duration of our training and returned with Cath to stay in his little apartment above the store. He worked with each of us both separately and together to help strengthen our abilities so that we had some modicum of control over calling the Power as I'd come to think of it now since my dream with the woman. I struggled with doubts I'd had since childhood and felt like a fledgling bird about to be cast from the nest without knowing whether my feathers would support me in flight. I felt awkward and self-conscious at each turn when Finny introduced me to words that were intended to result in a specific action. The logical part of my brain protested that I was a grown woman, taking lessons in magic. *Where's Hagrid, Harry and Hogwarts!* I scolded myself. Despite doubts, we worked to discover what we could do with this Power and how it might be used, not only to protect us from what might lie ahead, but also how it could be wielded to help us achieve our goal. It was difficult to clearly define this last, due to the fact that we weren't certain as to what our goal was but we were hopeful that our path would be revealed to us soon.

Cath, on the other hand, took time each day to school us on the story and fill in as many details as he could. What we discovered was that even though these brothers knew the tale and could tell the story, we were still left with many questions because, as with the first part of the tale regarding how the Named One could be identified, the tale was handed down in language that was ambivalent and needed to be interpreted with much speculation. I was fascinated as we read through The Power of the Word with Cath as though it were a textbook as he guided us through the language and helped us to extrapolate from it how and when details from the spoken tale of the prophecy took place in history and within our own lives.

"As ye know," Cath explained, "the Prophecy as it came te Faidhe was the foretellin' of many changes in the shift of balance but the primary event it spoke of was the coming of the Christian philosophy and religion. Now in her plan te keep the two forms of worship, the Old Ways and the Christian ways from driftin' apart Faidhe knew she had te cast powerful energy te bind them tegether. It seems though, that there was a barrage of hurdles directed in te her path that continuously tried her ability te keep te her given task."

"Like what? Nora asked.

Cath appeared to sit in contemplation. We waited almost a full minute and I began to doubt whether he'd heard Nora's question. I was just about to prod him again when Finny entered the living room where we were seated. In that moment, Cath raised his head and Finny answered.

"Like havin' te exact the price of the one who cast the magic that unleashed the Beast upon humanity for that deed. And like havin' te enlist that very one's mother te the task of killing her own...te start."

"Will you tell us that part of the story?" Nora asked the brothers.

"I will." Finny replied. "Sit ye back now and I'll share the unfortunate nature of Faidhe's forst night down from the Hill where the Corcle of Stones and the sacred implements were kept. The implements are those that we've spoken about orlier in conversation, the Cauldron and the Staff. They were kept under the safety and protection of the great Stone of Fal. The keystone of the very Corcle itself. The Sword and Shield came te active use in the Stone Corcle only after the Cauldron and Staff took te the road with the Lady horself."

Nora and I started at the phrase Finny used. What he said was so like the strange expression used recently by our cousin Margaret that I had to ask.

"Finny, someone asked me recently if I was the lady from the road. Is that some Irish expression or term that we Americans don't know about?"

"There are so many stories that contain snippets and fragments of the actual tale that there are many references te the Lady from the road. This item along with many others ye'll find in portions of the children's tales such as Snow White and Sleeping Beauty; both are essentially the same tale ye know. They've just been spread by mouth from one region te another changing from story teller te story teller until they'd branched off te two varied stories but they kept the tale alive throughout Europe through the centuries. Porhaps the largest change that has been inflicted upon the fairytales is that they have been patriarchalized te the degree that the Lady from the road is the evil witch or the wicked stepmother travelin' te wreak havoc and poison the princess or ruin her chances te marry out of jealousy rather than keepin' true the character of the one who cast magic in the beginnin' for entirely different reasons. But as with the masculine energy takin' sway, it was no surprise that the Lady Faidhe and her magic in these stories were demonized as the personification of evil. And as such pervasive tales, there are a great many folks; particularly here in Europe who feel there is more te the tales than just fantasy. And right they are. Some have actually developed societies te interpret the old tales and legends along with the ancient myths te cobble together some sense of it, ye see. But it's only as Cath and meself are the final two of our generation te know the real tale entire, any stories of the Lady from the road are just smoke and mirrors for people who're holdin' on hoping fer somethin' grand te happen. There're tales of the Lady, Faidhe, though they don't know her name, retorning with wrath te settle injustices against women; there're others that speak of her retorn as some kind of time of the world's end. And that may not be so far off the mark but for that, Faidhe will not be retorning. She's gone under te the Sidhe at the time of the great transition. But let me get te the tellin' of the forst night when Faidhe came down from the stone Corcle and about Briciu, the caster of the ill magic that spawned the Beast. For ye must know all ye can about the origin of this force that'll sure work against ye in all that ye do. Knowledge is Power in this case gorls. So settle back and take yer lornin' from this part of the tale."

"So what happened to this Briciu? He was obviously found out. Why didn't someone put a stop to him right then?" I asked what I thought was a sensible question.

"Ah, the logical question." Said Finny. "But not so easily dispatched. Let's examine the part of the tale that involved Briciu and the Beast. Then we'll see about the rest of the tale as it's depicted on the Cauldron."

Finally. I thought. We'd been working and meditating and studying to make sense of what portions of information we had learned from the men but I sensed Cath and Finny were withholding telling us more of the tale until they were comfortable not only that we were invested in the whole commitment but I think there was some concern over the energy behind the Beast. I got the feeling that the more we knew and the more Nora's and my ability grew, that the energy from the other side would be growing in strength too. For these reasons I had, up to now, let the men lead the way with the course of training despite my eagerness to know more about the tale. Not wanting to sound too impatient, I casually answered, "Okay, shoot."

Nora snorted as if to tell me I was transparent as glass in feigning a relaxed air about learning the more juicy parts of the tale. I knew she was right. All four of us had become somewhat open books to each other in a very short time. I shrugged in resignation to being very keen on hearing more and settled in to the couch in a more comfortable position in preparation for what was to come.

...Faidhe returned to the hut from the cattle house at the back of Briciu's paddock where she'd retrieved some tools to use in what lay ahead. She'd left Gara with the unconscious Briciu in his hut where she was placing the last touches on cleaning her son's wound as he lay now back on his sleeping pallet. Faidhe observed that Briciu's fresh linens were somewhat threadbare, but clean. Gara looked unsettled and uncharacteristically unsure. Faidhe instructed her to place the tools, a gelding knife, an ax, a length of rawhide leather and a nettle weed rope on Briciu's chest. While Gara tended mechanically to her task, Faidhe stood on the opposite side of the sleeping pallet from where Gara nervously fiddled with the instruments on Briciu's chest. Lunging across the stricken man, Faidhe reached quickly to clasp onto Gara's arms and called a loud and strong plea so that Gara was startled and instinctively tried to pull away.

When Gara fell backward and landed for the second time this night on her backside, she heard the dull thud of Briciu's body as it whumped onto the soggy earth in front of her. She realized that she, Faidhe and her son were no longer in Briciu's hut, but outside in an area so thick with vegetation that she could scarce see the sky. Faidhe proceeded to take up the rope and heave Briciu over in order to bind the man's arms with it. She instructed Gara to assist in preparing the man for the ritual they were about to perform.

"You need not have redressed your son for he will go through the ritual without being clothed. Though I do understand that your last act as his mother might be to revert to the things you remember doing for him in a better time. To dress him, to bathe his wounds, to feel as though you are taking care for him. Understand you this, Gara, what we are about to do is the soundest way you will convey any love you have left for your son. Work with haste now, for we have not much time left to the moon. Remove his clothing." Faidhe instructed.

Gara stood staring at Faidhe, her mouth slack with the shock of all that transpired and was taken completely by surprise when Briciu turned swiftly and tried to get himself to his feet. Enraged that this was not easily accomplished with rope binding his arms and his many years of soft living, Briciu began snarling and snorting throwing his head this way and that actually attempting to push the women over using his head. Wild and insane, the madman finally got to his feet and presented a volatile problem for the women. Gara, recognizing that her son, once again was aroused with his fury, backed away and attempted to find an escape.

As she turned to run, from behind her the panicked Gara heard Faidhe's commanding voice uttering some foreign sounding words and after a moment of a sickening mushy sound, all became quiet. Gara stopped and turned to see what had taken place, hoping with her whole being that she would not be found here in this dense grove of vegetation alone with her son. What she observed was Faidhe standing over Briciu, who was on his knees. In her hand was one end of the rope that bound Briciu's arms. Gara followed the rope with her eyes down to the prostrate man where she was shocked to find the rope not bound around the man's arms but traveling right through wounds opened through the tissue and muscles on the upper part of his limbs. Gara watched as Faidhe secured the rope tightly and walked around the man three times. She pointed a single finger that shot a bolt of blue toward his forehead while she chanted.

"Be still the man, be still the Beast,
Take heed the spell that has been released.
Bound in blood to feed desire,
I bind the misguided to submerge in the mire."

Briciu knelt still then and as the blue spark drew back from where Faidhe pointed at his forehead, what remained was a vacant and distant stare.

"Remove his clothes now." Faidhe called again to Gara who was frozen in her place slack jawed and wide-eyed. "Make haste!" Faidhe commanded and Gara jumped to life.

⸺

"The ritual was performed so that the mother of the man drew the gelding knife across his throat and took his head te remove consciousness from the magic. Cut off the head, and the rest will fall away so te speak. Then the ax was used to separate the heart from the loins by severin' the lower extremities te remove the abominable and aggressive drive from the spell. There was a binding of braided leather wrapped about his left hand te symbolically stay the hand from ever again being lifted in the castin' of magic. Finally, the man was cut through each nipple te leave off the poison from one side of his heart while allowing purification in te the other." Finny finished.

Cath interjected. "Ye'll have te understand, this was all symbolic and the women worked te release the man and the energy from the bindings of blood magic however, what they couldn't bring themselves te do was what we suspect was needed. The letting of the evil and the cutting from the loins, should have been done prior te the beheading. But they couldn't bring themselves to do torture and apparently it made a difference, for the energy was loosed on that night te the world; diminished for the ritual and not able te take hold in any living thing but loosed energy all the same. And from the very beginning when the transition of the human world from the feminine te the masculine started te take place, it's been bound with the taint of this magic as well. But now, we fear the wrath and rage of this Beast energy has come te some kind of process toward manifestation or awakening of some such."

"What makes you think that?" I said, asking but not really wanting to know the answer.

"Well, in some recent years, the very body of the man, Briciu, a Councilman from the Tuatha de Danann who was the caster of the ill magic that spawned the Beast and who died from this ritual that we've known about for most of our long lives, has surfaced at Croghan Hill in County Offaly and been removed from its place of burial in the bog where the women submerged the heart of the cursed one who cast the magic."

We were silent as we absorbed the idea that what was up until now just a story with some intriguing magical side effects, was now tangible. Yes there was the Gundestrup Cauldron but that was an artifact, not an actual person. Despite the fact that it depicted actual people and circumstances, it was tantamount, in my mind anyway, to reading a history book. But the discovery of this body and the realization that it had been an actual person whom we'd heard about as an integral part of the tale was not only fascinating but hit home that we were dealing with something very real.

"Where's the rest of it...him?" I asked.

Cath said in an uncharacteristically soft voice. "Now that's somethin' ye'll be hopin' never te find out, lass. For never do we want te witness the reunion of the loins, heart and head of this magic come te grow and feed on mankind's malfeasance over these past thousands of years with every act of aggression, every act of oppression, every time a man raised a hand in violence te a woman, or worse. The energy has grown ever stronger but not come te a central source. Should the parts of the magic come together in a revorsal of the separation of the body, we fear the worst in that it may unleash the coming of the blackest kind of evil without any foreseeable recourse.

Silence echoed in the room as these last words hung on the air. An attempt at lightening the mood was useless so I suggested that we pause or have a bite to eat and got up out of my seat on the couch to head toward Cath's kitchen.

"Mind if I fix a snack?" I said without waiting for an answer.

The four of us took a break as we sat around Cath's modest dining room table munching on a snack of oatmeal cookies and milk. The little second floor apartment was surprisingly neat and tidy in contrast to the jumble that was the store downstairs. As a change of subject to allow the section of the tale we'd just been told to sink in, Cath spoke of other aspects of the tale that he felt were evident in history.

"Working from the present and goin' backwards, ye'll take note of how women in the west have come to recognition in their own right for rights and equality. As we watched the success of the suffrage movement in America, we saw the glimmer of the start of things te come. We'd no idea that it'd be so long before things heated up te the point of action. There'd been so many times throughout history that the Goddess's energy'd poke through all the masculine dominance only te be squelched by the overpowering strength of the opposing energy. So we waited te see if there'd be more te come and it took another forty years before the women's movement got up a head of steam in America. I see now, lookin' back that we should have guessed that the Named One'd come out of the foreign born as opposed to one of the parent countries. As America would be a melting pot, so te speak, fer all the blood of the parent countries te have the opportunity te mingle and have the added energy te come forward with the strength of power needed. But we didn't know about how that would work." He stopped and seemed to contemplate that thought for a moment. "Hind sight is 20 – 20, as they say, eh?"

The unspoken words hung over the four of us at the table but no one needed to say them but we all wondered, how much else is there that we don't know about?

Shaking off what we could do nothing about I asked through a bite of the chewy cookie.

"So when else in history has the Goddess's energy 'poked through' as you say?"

"Look te yer world history, particularly in the European theater." Cath replied. "Take any occurrence as will put a woman in power from politics te the least little thing. All throughout history, especially after the advent of Christianity, ye'll see moments that will earmark the struggle for the feminine te take hold for example, as the Christian movement began, women were the forst priests, so te speak. They re-enacted the ritual of bread and wine as it was considered a domestic undertakin'. In their homes, women preached the gospels and spread the words of the stories about Jesus. Then, after a while, some men saw that the movement was catchin' on and they thought te organize the movement and call themselves bishops. They quickly relieved the women of their duties te take over the esteemed position in the newly forming chorch themselves. Not only had they taken the responsibility from those who'd done the work of bringing people te the faith, but they then made it a crime for the women te participate in any meaningful role in the chorch.

"Why am I not surprised?" I answered.

"Take too, in te consideration, all that has been said over Mary Magdalene's controversial role in the chorch. It makes sense that the Christ would have an equal in coming te the flesh as a facet of God why then, would he not have a feminine partner if he were te be bringin' news and concepts of the spirit te human kind. At the very least, he'd have a view of women as equal in standing te honor all that God had created. But once more what should have been revered was sullied with the reputation assigned, not orned, mind ye, but assigned as a whore."

Just then Finny broke in. "And when the mother of Jesus came te some kind of recognition, it wasn't' until the early twElfth century when we hord word that she was someone te be honored and respected. A time just after the last of the convorsion of the Pagan Swedes fell te the new God. As one door closes, another opens, as they say. But even as the Catholics came to revere the Madonna, factions of the chorch split off denying Mary any deification or reverence."

So you're telling us that if we examine history, we'll see all kinds of evidence that there has been an ongoing struggle for the balance to right itself?"

"Boggles the mind, doesn't it now?" Cath said with a knowing smile.

My thoughts turned to what else might be right under my nose in my research and in history books. I thought about European leaders that have been women and great women of history and wondered about all the parts of the world that still accept women as deities and the underlying energy that denoted the ongoing struggle for balance; then I was struck with epiphany of sorts.

"Hey, Hilary running for President!" I blurted. "And Sarah Palin! Aside from Shirley Chisolm and Geraldine Ferraro, they've been in the running for high office in our country. But it seems that no matter which ticket they've run on, they're never really taken seriously or at the very least, they had to work twice as hard as their male counterparts. Is that one of the things you're talking about? You know, women struggling but coming to some kind of power or recognition?"

"It's the idea, but the type of woman that will come te that position, will necessarily need te be a woman of integrity. Hilary has been too long in the man's type of game and too willin' te compromise te come te that position and make a change for the better. She's too close te the masculine way of doin' things te be a true representative of the feminine, I think. But that's just my opinion. It's more than gender te be considered te rightfully define the feminine. And the others, the Palin woman, well, it seems she's te play a pawn's role in the man's political game. Attention is called to hair and clothes, te diminish takin' her seriously. But the idea that a woman is comin' that close te a position of authority in a most powerful country is evidence of great changes in the cosmos; ye may soon yet have a woman in the high position. The fact that you've come here, now and the storrin' of the Beast along with the many things that are happening over the globe show us that energy is accumulatin' for something te happen on a large scale. So gorls, let's get te work and prepare te be as ready as time will permit, for whatever is coming our way. Back te work.

———

Cath began. "As ye might know by now there are three parts te the tale woven within the one. Just as it is so in much of the Old Ways, the three parts, and the three ways of telling the tale will repeat in its pattern and is significant. The forst part is the tale of the Prophecy and what changes were te come as a result of that warnin'. That's the most important part te work through due te it's complicated method of deliverin' the message hidden in poem, riddle or what all else. That'll be found in part in The Power of the Word. The second, the tale of Faidhe and her travels te make the arrangements te cast the magic so that all that was sacred in the balance of the masculine and feminine would not be lost, but rather be bound te the wave of the new teachin's of the masculine religion for which the seeds had been germinated at the time of the Prophecy. And the thord is the tellin' of how one would come at a time when the world was in need of the balance of both the God and the Goddess. A time when the world is perched upon a precipice between salvation and ultimate destruction due te the overwhelming spirit of the He run amok so te speak, with the quest for power that has somehow fermented te consuming lust, greed and avarice without compassion. The need for the Power of the feminine would be great, but when the evidence of the retorn of the Goddess started to become apparent, the opposing forces in the nature of masculine human kind would surge with the effort to deter the reemergence of the Goddess. What is happening in parts of the Middle East is an example of how the masculine is fanatically surgin' te overpower the feminine in its dominance of the women where accepted custom in dress and behavior is warped out of logical measures and human rights are obliterated. The fever of this sickness is bornin' so brightly that the surge has traveled from interior boundaries te attempt te rule over all who would oppose their dominance. So the scourge has reached beyond borders and infected other countries. But that's just one example of what's goin' on all over the globe. Look at Russia, China, Africa, Cuba, Eastern Europe; it's as though we've lorned nothin' in all our years of civilization and near as much as the whole world's gone mad with greed and dominance and power."

Cath stood up from his place at the table and began to pace into the living room space adjacent to the dining room.

"And if that weren't bad enough, the thread throughout all the tales, the wild-card, was the unexpected casting of magic by one who embodied all the poison of the negative aspects of the masculine. An infection, if you will, of a quest for power gone putrid that hums just beneath the surface of every institution on this planet that serves man and strives to keep oppressed the women."

At this point, the subject seemed to so upset Cath that he was gesticulating wildly with his hands.

"This is in evidence all over the globe. At its worst, it is bound up in the desecration of all that is sacred in the feminine. It is insidious as it hides in politics, religious organizations, family institutions and so many other places fertile for this type of domination. This cancerous seed has cast a bated hook to many a man and woman through the ages and from it was birthed all that is skittering, sneaking and underhanded with regard to the sanctity of a union between a man and woman. This energy is the gleeful tittering at shame and perversity and feeds the need for men to overpower and overwhelm women and children and each other. It has diseased whole communities and is the fruit of this poison seed planted with ill cast magic. This is the stuff of the Beast, gorls." He said with a finger poked straight at us as if to emphasize that we need to pay attention. "This has permeated society on every possible level and is so ubiquitous that it has been accepted as the natural way of life. From the simple attitude that men are physically stronger, therefore better than women to the reeking and festering cesspool of pornography, slavery of prostitution, rape, reduction of sexual intimacy te no more than a physical act of release, mere physical gratification devoid of any mingling of the spirit, no sacred act te the union. This energy has taken over the world from the most open societies in the form of objectification of the feminine to the opposite end of the spectrum where ye'll find woman covered from head te toe in saris and robes yet they're no more than chattel and are no more respected by their men than the pervasive sellers of flesh looking te sell the bitch fer a good priced fuck."

I noticed as Cath was speaking this last, his lips were spewing spittle and peeled back in disgust while his nose wrinkled as if he smelled something unpleasant. With that thought, I realized that in fact, I detected the signature stench of the Beast. There was a flurry of activity and I saw Finny move toward Cath faster than I ever dreamed possible for the little man. Nora and I were alarmed as we witnessed Finny grab Cath's hand and shake his arm only to be thrown off like a rag doll with a shrug of Cath's shoulder. Finny lunged again and gave Cath's cheek a pinch so hard that the skin around his eye became pulled and distorted but with his other eye, Cath seemed to be looking directly at Nora and me and I'd swear the man looking at us was not Cath at all. My skin puckered in chilled gooseflesh while my body felt as if my bones had jellied. The delicate skin on Cath's cheek began to flush a deep red, then purple. I grew alarmed by this rough treatment but the pinch seemed to do the trick. Cath's eyes cleared and he seemed himself again. Finny took the brunt of Cath's weight as he leaned into his brother in a semi-swoon.

I was not only amazed at Finny's apparent strength as he carried his brother but alarmed as well at the unexpected turn of events. Released from the sudden shock of the moment, Nora and I ran to the men to help bring Cath to the couch.

"Such a force. I felt it sorchin' and as I told ye of what energy lurks, it was seekin' me out. I felt it strugglin' te take me thoughts, take in where we are and whom ye are. I had te fight te keep te me own head."

Cath was gasping and copious beads of sweat made a popping appearance on Cath's forehead while a massive purple bruise threatened to close his eye.

I sat on the couch and held Cath's hand attempting to calm him while Nora prepared an icepack for his cheek.

I asked Finny, "What did you see that made you jump at Cath the way you did?" He looked at me as if I were an idiot.

"Ah then, I suppose ye don't know Cath as well as I, but if ye did, ye'd know that this is a man who's never in his life spoke a curse word, much less call a woman, any woman, such a vile name, even in quoting a lesson. I caught the scent, but wasn't sure if it was just as a part of talkin' about the Beast, but when I hord the corsin' comin' from the mouth that'd never uttered a bad word about anything, much less corse in front of ye gorls, I knew."

Nora gently put the icepack made up of ice cubes in a plastic bag, wrapped in a damp dishtowel onto Cath's cheek. He appeared to be refreshed by the coldness of the pack. Cath sat up and taking the icepack from Nora to hold it himself.

"I've somethin' te tell ye gorls. I fought the force that wanted te take me and with the help of Finny, I was able te fend it off but in that moment that I felt a bit overwhelmed by the force of this thing, I saw the way it sees ye gorls and it's not good. Ye're right te think that something is stalking ye. It is. It senses ye but hasn't yet been able to determine who or what ye are yet but it suspects and it's sorchin'. And when it's sure of ye, its plan is te do te ye what it did te Chiaro. I'm thinking that due te what I saw, we were right in our suspicions about her death."

Cath looked as if he were convulsing with tears but then he heaved himself up from the couch and ran more nimbly than even Finny just had only moments before, to the bathroom. And we all lost our appetites for oatmeal cookies or any-thing else for a while.

———

When Cath had returned from the bathroom we expected him to call it a day for today but instead, he came with piles of papers obviously printed from the Internet together with several books offering information and interpretations on the mean-ing of the Gundestrup Cauldron. He invited us into the living room where we sat and read much about the piece of art.

"Ye must lorn all ye can as soon as ye can gorls, but I think the less we actually say in a vorbal fashion, the better it'll be te keep that energy at bay. Ye know now that the Power of the Word, especially the spoken word carries great weight."

A few hours later, Nora and I sat on the floor of Cath's living room with papers strewn all around us. Pictures could be seen giving several angles of the panels on the enigmatic vessel.

I stood to the concert of my popping bones and joints as I stretched and pre-pared my questions.

"Okay, you guys, enough with the delays. You said the Cauldron is the picto-rial of the tale and you brought this stuff out for us to read on the heels of a pretty upsetting experience Cath. I want to know what the connection is and which panel reveals the role of the Beast in all of this."

Nora nodded her head and stood beside me.

"I'm with Lee on this one. It's time we had some clear idea of what happened then so we can know what's happening now. All the practice of magic in the world isn't going to give us the education we need to defend ourselves or to know what we need to do if we don't know the whole story. Truth time."

The men looked at each other and nodded. Finny agreed.

"They're right Cath. Let's begin with the forst panel te explain about the Beast."

Cath moved to the pile of papers on the floor and shuffled until he came up with one bearing the picture of a round panel from the Gundestrup Cauldron.

"This, gorls, is the base panel te the bowl. It bears the picture, not only of the forst magic cast in the aftermath of the Prophecy, but it holds the part of the tale when the actual Beast was released te the winds te blow free and germinate." Cath poked a finger at the picture and explained the graphic. "Ye'll see a bull with a man and a Sword tegether with two dogs. There is some vegetation depicted as well. This is a parallel scene te one other of the panels in which ye'll see..." Cath paused and rummaged to find the page he was looking for. "The depiction of three bulls tegether with three men appearing te attack the bulls with a Sword. Each man is flanked by a wolf and a cat and ye'll see a bit of vegetation here as well."

He passed the pictures to Nora and signaled us both to sit down once again. Nora inspected the pictures and handed them to me.

The pictures were a bit fuzzy but I could plainly make out the items Cath had described.

"Okay." I remarked as a cue for him to continue.

"Each of these panels is a combination of symbolism and realism. We'll explain now as te how these two panels came about and how the symbolism is te be interpreted." Cath flicked his head toward the kitchen door while looking at his brother and Finny disappeared through it. "Get yer comfort now gorls and be aware as I'm tellin' ye this part of the tale for any signs that I...ah," He looked around for Finny. "That I may need another pinch."

A chill rippled up my arms as I recalled the thing that looked out at me through Cath's eye and understood the hazard of speaking this part of the tale out loud. Though we hadn't been directly warned, we saw first-hand how speaking about the Beast could raise energy for it, and we'd read plenty by now in The Power of the Word book about how speaking words and prayers will energize thoughts to action. Understandably, that was the reason for the pictorial to tell the tale in the first place.

Nora interrupted. "Wait! Isn't there some way to prepare for that possibility? Can't we, I don't know, join together to keep that from happening?"

"Ye read me mind." Finny said as he reentered the room holding some items in his arms. He sat on the couch with Nora and me, arranging the items on the coffee table in front of us: a bowl of water, a shaker of salt, a bundle of dried sticks and a candle with a box of wood kitchen matches. Finny looked expectantly at us as we waited for him to do something. "Well?" He said. "Get ye te work."

"Oh." Nora said. She grasped at the same time as I did that if we were to protect ourselves as well as those around us, we'd have to know how. We looked to Finny for instruction.

He breathed an impatient sigh. "Follow yer instincts gorls. Soon enough, that'll be all ye have te know what's te be done."

I exhaled to center myself and reduce the chatter in my head about what was the right thing to do and in that moment my hand reached for the matches at the exact same time that Nora's reached for the bowl. With the scraping and slow motion igniting of one match, I lit the candle as Nora added salt to the water in the bowl. After shaking out the match, I picked up the bundle of sticks and jabbed the leafy end into the candle's flame while Nora took the salt and walked around the room sprinkling a steady flurry around the edges of the living room. I realized by the sweet, fresh odor of the sticks and leaves that I was burning sage. A familiar scent from my maternal grandmother's house. I got up from the couch and followed in Nora's footstep carrying the smoldering sage sticks around the edges of the room allowing the smoke to permeate all corners of the space. Nora picked up the bowl of salted water and we circled the room together sprinkling the water around its circumference. This ritualistic procedure served to calm and clear my mind and put me at ease. I felt safer within the circle we'd created. Nora and I returned to the couch where Finny sat and Cath pulled up an ancient Queen Ann chair to sit across from us and begin his interpretation of the Cauldron panels that would occupy our complete attention for the next few hours.

"Here, on the base panel," Cath began, "is the history of the magic cast that brought about the scourge of the Beast. Ye'll see here a man atop the bull in the posture of attacking the bull with a Sword. This is the depiction of yer very ancestor, the forst and last, I'm afraid, male Keeper, Laoghaire. As ye'll find in Celtic mythology, a known troublemaker named Briciu challenged Laoghaire to a contest of strength. Now ye might find several different accounts of this myth but the challenge was designed by underhanded means, morder and some very dark magic te kill Laoghaire, usurp his cattle, take his position and te violate his wife in a most vile manner. The initiator of this magic was himself a troubled soul and he committed morder te use the blood of sacrifice te add strength te his magic and bind the magic te its task until its completion. Here ye see the bull that Laoghaire was challenged te kill with only his Sword as a weapon. The bull, powerful in its own right, was tainted with this Powerful magic. Fortunately though, the man, Laoghaire is depicted above the bull meaning that he was above the dark magic and was not killed. Due te the magic cast by others who represented the Goddess and the God symbolized in this vegetation here by the trilobate leaves. The three leaves representing the cover of the triple protection this man has cast about him. The dogs ye see here, are most often representative of connection with the Otherworld in Celtic mythology and are often companions of the Mother Goddess. To find them here in such a way, one dog living and one dead, is an indication that the energy of this panel discards the connection with the Mother Goddess yet still opts te draw energy from the place of Power, from the Otherworld. A gravely disrespectful and dangerous way in which te draw."

"This other panel," Finny continued, "one of the five inner panels, depicts three bulls attacked by three men with Swords. It is the same scene as the other panel however the difference is ye'll see the scene in triplicate te represent the magic of sacred design. Look closely and ye'll see this one man in the center, who represents the actual figure of the Laoghaire, is clothed and the other two are not. This clothing is the depiction of the protective magic cast around Laoghaire so no vital parts would be injured. The animals here," He said, pointing to the three cats and three wolves, "represent the skills given him in the protective magic: agility of a cat and strength and hunting abilities of the lone wolf. And here, ye'll see vegetation between the figures representing the sacred fighe vine, the symbol of the coming together between the flesh and the spirit which is just so, during any ritual, magic, or petition of the spirit. A prayer, a mass, a blessing: all the same energy mingled between the human and the spirit. So here, it represents the magic cast in the name of the God and Goddess to assure Laoghaire's victory over not only the bull in the challenge, but more importantly, over the ill magic cast using the bull as its agent."

After a moment's pause, Nora asked, "So why is the panel depicting the evil magic or the bad spell or whatever, why is that the base of all of this story? Why is it not just another panel in the sides like the rest of them?"

"Can ye puzzle for yerself why that might be?" Cath questioned us both.

"Well," Nora reasoned, "it sounds like the basis for lots of good stories with the archetypical, good versus evil. But this was recorded for more than the purpose of a good story. Right?"

"Wait!" I shouted. "Excited at putting together some feasible logic. "It's part of the symbolism. Right? The whole thing is put together using symbols and at the *base* of all this is the good triumphing over evil. Right? Is that it? Is it to inspire hope that good will triumph?"

"Well," Cath speculated, "Laoghaire did not die that day but neither did the malevolence of the ill cast energy. Perhaps it's a reminder te keep us ever vigilant."

"Laoghaire came out victorious in this challenge even though this Briciu guy obviously cheated and used murder in his magic." I surmised. "You say the malevolence of the magic didn't go away, and that's what the Beast is now?"

"Simply put, yes." Finny answered.

Over the waning hours of this day, we delved into the symbolism on the panels and the possible meanings hidden within the flora, fauna and characters depicted. We asked questions regarding the characters in the tale only now becoming familiar to us. It was like a patchwork quilt that held secret the final pattern until all the pieces were sewn together. I had questions that I could forecast would last far into the night for each question brought about a new part of the tale. I inquired as to the several panels in which a wheel was depicted when Cath interrupted.

"It's getting well on past dinnertime. Let's send down te Kenny's Restaurant for a bite and Finny can again take the role of the storyteller fer ye gorls as we eat, te fill in the tale as we interpret the panels."

My stomach growled in agreement as if to remind me that it had been several hours since my last oatmeal cookie.

"Sounds good to me." Nora agreed.

25

Happy Birthday

It was about noontime in Ireland on August 1st and after breakfast, we called home from Bridey's phone to our respective husbands. Nora was disappointed once again to find no one at her house to answer the phone. It was my turn next and my heart was gripped in a tight fist of homesickness when I heard the voice of my husband, Walter and our son Lucas in the background. Haltingly, I tried to sketch out for my husband the possibility that I may travel to Denmark to follow the fantastic story I'd caught hold of. Using the excuse that I couldn't run up Bridey's phone bill so I didn't go into any detail about going there to find the Gundestrup Cauldron but I promised to buy a disposable cell phone so I could call and speak with him at length and in privacy. I glanced over my shoulder at Bridey, where she was pretending to busily dust some infinitesimal piece of dirt off the ancient hall chest behind me. I knew she was listening so I only spoke about some of the more typical research-based things we'd done, and said my love yous then asked to speak with our son.

In a rush, all at once, I was overwhelmed by how much I missed my family. The gravity of what lay ahead hit me hard, that I was indisputably responsible for the future of these two whom I love more deeply than I ever thought was possible. It was one thing to abstractly think about 'saving the world' it was entirely another to bring that scope down to one's own family. My chest tightened again at the far away sound of his little voice.

"Mom, when are you coming home? I want you to come home."

In my mind, I could see him standing by the phone in our bright and cheery kitchen, such a contrast to Bridey's dark foyer filled with somber and solid antiques. He was dressed in his blue striped shirt with the signature stains down the front, over mismatched green shorts and his left sneaker was untied. I imagined his thick blond hair, corked in places; so long, it was threatening to cover his enormous blue eyes in the front. Although he was still a baby to me, he was eight years old and in his estimation that was too old to be crying to his mom and I could tell he held on to his emotions.

"I've got some work to do, Baby. But I'm coming home to you and Dad as soon as I'm finished." I felt pain run down the bridge of my nose as tear ducts filled and my throat tightened. "You be good for Daddy and help him do things only you and I know how to do around the house; you keep him straight on the routine, okay? And I'm going to buy a phone today so you can call me anytime if you want to talk. I'll call later tonight to give you the number and to say good night."

"Promise?"

"Promise."

Silence. Then, "Mom?"

"Yeah, Honey?"

"I dreamed something was chasing us."

Fear blazed across my solar plexus and I steeled myself to speak evenly.

"Did you? Who was chasing us?"

Silence. Breathing. "It was a b...It was a big monster." I breathed a sigh of relief. For a moment, I thought he was going to say 'a Beast' but was reassured to find that it had only been a run of the mill bad dream.

"Lucas, I'm sorry I'm not there to give you a hug after your bad dream. You tell Daddy that he needs to give you extra hugs and kisses to send you off to good dreams tonight. Okay?" I knew he was a bit old for this particular kind of reassurance but he didn't protest and he seemed comforted for having heard my voice coming with a promise to call again soon. Walter was good for the typical maintenance stuff of parenthood but he adhered to the *tough it out* school of thought when it came to eradication of monsters, kissing of wounds or soothing fears. I could almost feel Lucas's need for me over the phone, or maybe I was just projecting how much I missed him.

"I'm giving you a hug right now. Ready? Here it comes."

I balled up all of my energy and pictured my beautiful son in our kitchen at home and sent out a blast of energy, imagining it shooting west across the land, over the ocean and finding its way to the east coast in Massachusetts right to Lucas's heart. For a moment, as I envisioned all of this, I found myself hurtling into my kitchen flying at Lucas like a fastball. He looked right at me for a moment and his big blue eyes grew even wider with surprise. I barreled up to him and was able to stop just before I plowed right into him. Momentarily shocked from the experience, we looked right into each other's eyes and I wrapped my arms around my son. It felt somewhat like what I thought static would feel like if the fuzzy perpetual energy of static could actually be felt. I realized that my husband did not see me and quickly made the mental adjustment to understand that I was not physically in my kitchen back home but through the effort of trying to comfort my boy by sending him a hug; somehow, I had been able to be there in some weird kind of energetic form.

The instant I began to think logically about how this was impossible, I found myself shot right back into Bridey's hallway, standing next to Nora with the phone still in my hand.

"Lucas?" I said. "Did you get my hug?"

I didn't want to reveal anything unusual to Bridey but I wanted to see if Lucas had experienced what I thought just happened. Hoping against hope that he wouldn't be even more frightened.

Lucas's voice gushed through the phone so loud I had to pull it away from my ear. "That was cool! Do it again!"

"Ah, not right now Luke, maybe we'll try again when I call you tonight before bedtime. I knew explanations were impossible at the moment so I tried to shift his attention hoping if he had seen me, he'd let it go for now.

What time is it there now?" After a few seconds he answered.

"It's 7:14." He answered. "In the morning." He added. "But Mom, can't you just do that one more time? This time I'll be ready?"

"Ah, I can't right now Luke, I'm using someone else's phone and we can't stay on too long. Okay? I will call later, though. I'm not sure what time I'll get back to you tonight but I'll try to call you as close to your bed time as I can so we can say goodnight and I'll give you another hug then. What time is Dad breaking all the rules to let you stay up until anyway?"

He giggled at this and told me in a conspiratorial whisper.

"I stayed up until 11:00 with Dad last night. He fell asleep watching T.V. with me so we both slept all night on the floor! Dad said it was okay 'cause it was like we were camping out."

"Traitor!" I heard Walter mumble in the background, but I could hear the smile in his voice. Then more giggles from Lucas.

"I love you, Baby." I told him. "Can you put Dad back on the phone?"

"Okay Mom. Love you too." Then with a return of caution to his voice he asked, "Mom, you dreaming over there?"

"Yeah Baby, but just good stuff. Promise."

"Okay. Here's Dad."

We made plans to talk later with a tentative time for me to call and said our love yous again and then our goodbyes. After I hung up I felt a sense of vacancy and longed to be with my family as I stood there in Bridey's foyer. Behind me, I heard Nora talking to Bridey about settling with her to pay for the phone calls.

"Nonsense." I heard Bridey say and my attention was drawn to the conversation. "Ye'll not be givin' me any money per call. I'll just get the bill and settle up with the credit card information for the price of the calls. Done all at once, no fuss."

I was glad to hear it because there was one more call we needed to make today before we went about our plans.

"You dial." I said to Nora. "My ear is hot from holding the phone so tight."

I made the excuse because in truth, I felt a little shaky. I didn't know if it was melancholy for missing my family or if I was shocked over the realization that I'd just impossibly traveled home and back within a few seconds. I had to check myself to question whether I imagined the whole thing. As Nora dialed the phone, I dug my fingernails into my palms to keep from growing dizzy. I knew my fingers would be visibly shaking if I tried to dial the phone right now.

In thinking about the experience, I remembered that Lucas was wearing exactly what I'd envisioned he had on, the blue striped shirt and green shorts. So that wasn't much help for validation; it could just be an over active imagination. What else? I thought. *Walter was at the sink or washing the dishes when I was talking to Lucas. What did he have on? Think...No, I didn't notice. What else? Play dough! There was a blob of homemade play dough on the table next to the phone. They were playing at the breakfast table when I called. I'll have to call back tonight and check if I actually saw them there or if I just imagined the whole thing.* This was all such a shock to me and it all happened so quickly but despite wanting to double check with my family when I speak with them later, the idea that it might be real was settling in. *'Many lives in training...must remember what you've learned.'* The voice of the woman in my dream came back to me. Then I was reminded of possibilities I'd so recently protested: *'I couldn't' see you Lee, because you weren't there!'* Nora had insisted. *'Energy enough te call the bords to ye.'* Finny had said. Could it be possible that I had just traveled in spirit, conscious spirit back to my home in Plymouth to be two places at one time? Holy crap! *Beam me up Scotty.*

"Lee. It's ringing."

Pulled from my thoughts, I went to the phone with Nora and we both listened into the receiver between our ears as we held our heads close together. The phone rang with a tinny sound that often happens in overseas calls.

"Hello?" Came from miles away.

We both sang Happy Birthday into the phone to our sister Mary and laughed a bit at the silliness, but we didn't want her to think we forgot her birthday because we were already on sketchy territory with her due to the fact that we had not invited her to come along on this trip to Ireland. She knew that we'd tried to move the earth to arrange things so Patrice, our other sister, could make the trip, as it had been routine for the three of us to travel on weekends and vacations together many times and Mary was a little sore that she'd been excluded, even though Patrice ultimately didn't come this time. Although there had never been much interest prior to this trip on Mary's part to travel with us, she'd been particularly keen to find out more about our itinerary in Ireland. Usually, when Mary expressed an interest in someone else's plans, it meant she was looking for a 'what's in it for me' angle. It just wasn't that kind of trip and I found it a strain to spend more than a few hours at a time with her. I had hard research to do and although she would not see it as truth, Mary could sometimes suck the air out of a room with a consuming need to have things arranged as she would like them despite anyone else's needs.

We got past the initial awkwardness then there was a bit of chitchat about being here and there and I could see that Bridey was caught up in the gayety of the moment because she forgot to pretend she was dusting and was looking right at us with a twinkling smile.

When we hung up Bridey commented, "It's an auspicious day your sister has been born on: August 1st. It's the day of the first harvest, Lughnasadh." Bridey surprised us with her mention of the cross-quarter day, an important day of note in the old Celtic calendar. Back in America, probably due to the emerging feminine energy, there has been a resurgence of Neo-Pagan and Wiccan type religions for some years now so knowledge of these old religions are making a come-back with the advent of all the New Age information available. We just hadn't expected to find obvious evidence of these ideas here in Irish Catholic Ireland. Maybe the Old Ways were more prevalent than we had expected.

"Yeah, we knew about that. We always thought it was kind of funny that so many members of our family are born on those kinds of holidays. My birthday's May First." Nora said. "May Day."

Bridey seemed to think about that for a moment, and then turned to me. "And yours?' she inquired.

"Nope, not me. Just a plain old birthday in October."

"October the 31st?" She quizzed.

"No." I answered and began to feel a bit protective. Maybe it was from a lifetime of keeping family information close to the vest but more likely since the situation at Cath's home the other day, I didn't want to talk about our family and Bridey suddenly seemed a bit too interested. I moved to take our leave, but Nora chirped her reply.

"No, not Lee; that'd be our sister Patrice. She's the one born on that day, well actually, November First but only just after midnight. It's a weird, pattern in our family that so many of us have been born on one of those kind of holidays."

Bridey's smile faltered and her eyes momentarily slit.

"Is that the truth? Right on the day? How many of ye have been born te those days?" She insisted.

Then suddenly aware that I no longer wanted to be here in the woman's home and having this conversation. As I grabbed Nora by the arm I said, "Jeeze Nora, we've already let half the day get away from us. Let's get going and let Bridey finish her cleaning." I gave her a yank and we headed for the door.

Bridey looked like she wanted to find a reason to call us back and ask us more questions but I waved her off.

"We'll see you later Bridey. Thanks for the use of the phone."

———

"What are you doing?" I asked Nora as we hopped into the car.

"What do you mean?"

I couldn't believe that she'd just blurted out information about our family birthdays so soon after finding out some possible significance for those very days just last night during our meal with Cath and Finny.

"Why are you so quick to be open with people about all of that when you don't really know who they are?"

"Are you serious?" Nora asked defensively.

"Yeah. I'm serious. How do we know who anyone is now? How do we know who is innocuous and who is one of those kooks Cath told us about? The ones waiting for the return of Faidhe, or the ones who've turned the whole story into something about witches and devil worship and who knows what other crap. I, for one thing, don't want to try to convince a bunch of zealots that, not only are we not the second coming of Faidhe, but that we are not interested in any of their weirdo cult nonsense. Remember what Cath said. These people are subversive and carry on a normal appearance while doing cryptic and arcane stuff in old stone circles. They might be harmless but they might have some traces of magical abilities in their bloodline somewhere in our family tree. I think it's just best to keep things quiet like we've always done. In fact, I think the need for secrecy is more important now that we know we'll be dealing with more than just being outcasts. It's just as possible that we could be in danger from these cult type people as well as the whole Beast thing."

"But it was just Bridey, Lee. You think she's one of those crazies?"

"Nora, I don't know what to think. I'd just feel better if we kept all of that stuff to ourselves especially since we still don't know everything that we'll need to. And don't forget, we still have family back home that doesn't know anything about all of this. What if that energy sniffs out people in our family because we're raising its awareness over here?"

"I never thought of that." She said in a small voice. "I haven't been able to get in touch at home. You think everything's okay there?"

"We'll go get that phone right now so we can call at our convenience and you can touch base. I know Lucas will feel better if he can have direct contact with us. You know how he's always so connected to us? He seems to sense that something's up. I don't know why we didn't think to get a phone before this. Just because there's no phone at the cottage and our cell phones wouldn't work here doesn't mean we can't have our own connection to home."

I thought about how to approach Nora about my little excursion across the ocean but decided to wait until I had some kind of confirmation from Lucas and Walter before I started ringing any bells about it.

"You notice how Bridey's always hanging around when we're on the phone?"

"Yeah, but I don't think it's anything. I think she's kind of lonely and likes to hear about all that goes on in other people's lives."

"I guess." I said. But I wasn't convinced. I'd begun to build a protective crust around my way of thinking and I hadn't liked how Bridey was so interested to learn more about our family. *Better safe than sorry,* I thought.

I put the car into gear and drove down the long bucolic driveway past some lazy cows to head for town and arrange for a phone and phone card that would provide service for us while we're here in Ireland. As we pulled toward the end of the drive, we didn't see the curtain slightly pulled aside in Bridey's front window, but we did see the three brothers in their front yard stop to watch us as we drove by.

They were shirtless, blubbery, white skinned men who, to accommodate their bulbous bellies worked only in sweatpants cut-offs with boxer shorts hanging below the bottoms and work boots to finish off the ensemble. This made me shiver as I was reminded that these repulsive men were peeking into our privacy. I wished I hadn't looked their way when my eyes locked with one of the brother's beady, black little marble eyes and I felt, even now, as we were a safe distance away, that I was being violated somehow. I steeled myself not to drag my eyes away. I felt some kind of challenge in my mind that I must not relinquish my stare. I would not demure to this withering leer as he ran his tongue over the smirk that played on his livery lips. The gesture called to mind unnatural ideas. I kept my eyes on the largest man Moe, as I had come to think of him, as we drove by so that my head turned almost all the way toward the back seat as we passed, so the man was sure to know that I had not given any ground. Maybe he'd get the hint that we weren't anyone to be messed with but it didn't seem that way. He seemed to be almost entertained at the challenge when he jutted his stomach in our direction. I wasn't sure if he was straightening his posture to stand tall or if the motion held more lewd undertones. *Gross!* I thought and stepped on the gas.

Part IV: The Exodus

26

Wayfarers, All

The days of feasting had drawn to a raucous close. The great hall was littered with the refuse of reveling, and song. Up and down the hillside that bordered the village was evidence of sleeping camps alongside visitor's fires of those who could not find room at the hearths of kin. The number of visitors would likely dwindle over the next days as travelers took to the road to return to their own huts and villages carrying news of all that had taken place.

Faidhe had arisen before dawn from the palette laid for her by her daughter in Lon Dubh's hut. She had few things to pack but was intent upon insuring that everything needed would be taken, for what could not be carried must be acquired during their travels and she was not familiar with the territory of the road. Despite her strong capacity as a Seer, she had no experience with travel or protocol with strangers. Faidhe felt the pinch of anxiety gnaw at her but pushed it back by keeping her quiet focus on checking and rechecking that her party of three would have all they would need as they traveled the road on their sacred journey. This steady focus helped Faidhe to avoid thoughts dwelling on what had taken place with Briciu, Gara and the servant's body. She pushed back thoughts of seeing Briciu's torso sink into the boggy mire. She suppressed the memory of gleaning from Briciu's mind where the body of the sacrificed servant could be found, for even a brief moment in Briciu's mind caused Faidhe great disturbance. But the servant's body would raise questions should it be found and it was necessary for Faidhe to dispose of it. She and Gara did dirty work two fold that night not only did they dispatch Briciu in the killing ritual, but also took the murdered servant to a neighboring bog and ritually released the man's spirit by thrice cleaving his head with the same ax used to detach Briciu's head and his lower extremities from his body. In truth, Faidhe knew not the location of the bogs where the bodies were disposed of and did not question the wisdom of the Power for the places it had chosen. She and Gara performed their tasks and with the help of the Universal Power, had returned to the village in short time. As far as Faidhe was concerned, the matter had passed. The less she thought on the entire situation, the better. *No sense devoting energy to a situation for which there is no help.* Faidhe was resolute that no other of her family or friends would bear the burden for her actions of that night. She would tell no one so if or when the time came when answers about Briciu's disappearance would be called for, all those in the alliance would be truthful in their ignorance of the Councilman's whereabouts. And Gara, a most unwilling participant in these doings would say nothing of her own role in her son's actions or disappearance.

Faidhe's concentration was disturbed when Lon Dubh entered the hut dressed in hunting attire. Having spent much of her adult life independent of the clan, Lon Dubh had spent many days and nights in solitary hunting in the wood and upon the road. She was well prepared to pass some months on the road wearing leg skins for mobility and a woven woolen smock to eliminate the need for a cumbersome cloak while traveling. She wore a sheathed knife at her leather halfstrap and across her chest was strung her favorite leather sling for hunting small game. Upon her back was a sheepskin pack containing practical items for survival on the road: flint rock for fire and spider weed for kindling, a sharpening stone to renew her knife for skinning hides and whittling arrow shafts, mending bones for skin craft and clothing repair, spool sticks of spun wool and linen, strong sinew enough for three bows, a fishing net loosely woven of figh vine, linen tunics for warmer weather, a woolen cloak, extra skins for shoes, and her wind whistle for music and song. The rest of the pack was filled with foodstuff of which there was plenty to be collected from the serving bowls and hearth spits following the feasting. She also carried salt to dry and preserve some of the meat in caution against spoilage.

Surveying her daughter, Faidhe approved of her sensible planning for the journey and for Lon Dubh's lack of vanity in having chosen practical clothing over what would be considered fashionable. Their journey could be made more comfortable should they travel from village to village as a Seer and Councilmember of the Tuatha de Danann with her daughter but there was need for discretion so they must avoid unwanted questions and keep to the wood and road. They would likely leave the village with many others who were preparing to leave this day. There would be eyes on the road that would not otherwise be there if not for the feasting. It would be difficult to go unseen or unrecognized, particularly if her lovely daughter had chosen to dress in finery of her station rather than with prudent attire for the road. It pleased Faidhe to recognize that Lon Dubh was aware of their task and had taken to it with commitment.

After checking her own pack roll one last time Faidhe wound the straps onto her shoulders. Covering it with her cloak, she pulled on her hood and knew that in the dark of the dawn, there would be few who would take notice of her. Lon Dubh took the cue and pulled a hood and neckpiece of tanned deerskin over her head, so to any onlooker she would appear just another kinsman hooded against the morning chill and packed to take to the road.

As they set out for the edge of the village, Faidhe was aware of one who watched them take their leave. She did not turn to acknowledge the woman standing in the doorway of her son's hut. She knew Gara watched but also she knew that there was no longer need of secrecy with the woman. Gara would change little in her underhanded ways on the Council, but Faidhe left for her journey comfortable in the knowledge that Gara was now as a snake without venom. She could not undermine the pact vowed to by the alliance of eight that was united in a sworn bond these three short nights ago for she was inextricably tied to their future. She was now bound by the magic that was unleashed and still working. Gara now understood that Power and magic are not a game to be toyed with or brokered, she knew that for her own spirit to be loosed from its bondage in the act of taking her own child's life, she would have to see success come to the eight of the alliance and so, was obliged to support their every need.

Gara liked it not that she was in the service of the others, now and the thought was bitter to her but she knew she would acquiesce. A tremor of a chill shook her when she recalled the idiot look on her son's face and the thread of drool that seeped from the corner of his slack mouth just before she stepped behind him and firmly grasped his hair to carve the knife deep into his neck. It repulsed her to be reminded of that very action he had subjected her to only a brief time before she took back the life she gave him 27 seasons past but part of her took satisfaction in her revenge.

———

A hulking outline of a man could be seen lurking in the tree line just ahead in the shadowy dawn light. He stayed his horse when it whickered at the approaching women. The man obviously desired to remain unseen and would have frightened an unknowing traveler with his size alone, but the women approached him and his heavily laden horse and Lon Dubh boldly embraced Iarann in greeting.

"May good and safe travel be granted us all this fine day and ever as we travel, kinsman."

Faidhe witnessed this and was pleased to see the bond developing between Lon Dubh and Iarann. She felt blessed to be making up for lost family time and felt a tug at her heart that she could not stay longer to get to know and instruct Colm and Laoghaire further on the tasks to be undertaken upon their rise to the Hill. As it was, they had to snatch moments so she could share with Laoghaire what she had foreseen regarding him in the prophesy and instruct him as best she could on what is required of him. She could only hope that Laoghaire would trust his intuition to lead him in how and when those things must take place. She was not shown these details and so she considered that the timing and process would be revealed to Laoghaire alone. Colm was versed in alchemy and spell work and Faidhe was confident once she made adjustments to life on the Hill, she'd do well in her role, but Laoghaire did not know the wealth of Power available to him and he would struggle on his own to develop his skills. She shook off the regret with a sigh and formally greeted Iarann as was proper in blessing their journey.

"I too greet you with blessing and goodwill kinsman, for as the sun rises we embark on our journey in his direction. May He shine upon us with warmth and may the Mother's pale face keep us by night. Gods and spirits be with us so that we may carry out what they require of us."

"I thank you Lady. Gods grant it be so." He replied. "I have with me many tools but they are necessary to my task of crafting." He gestured toward the animal. "The horse will bear the burden of the weight until such time the bowl is complete and we have no further use for the tools. And at that time Lady, perhaps you will be grateful to sit a-horse when you are great with the weight of the child you carry."

"You speak with optimism, Iarann, that we will have need of your crafting for only the time it takes to breed a babe. Think you, we will have completed our journey in such short duration? For if you spoke true and you will craft this pot to tell of our journey, we will travel to the birth of this babe and beyond."

Iarann's surprise was evident in his response. "Surely you will not travel with the babe once it is born. Even with the mildest of winter season, a newborn will not thrive at his mother's breast when she is weakened from hardship of the road."

Though Faidhe had taken on a youthful countenance of late, her expression at this last comment revealed a haggard face. Faidhe shot back in a voice that was tight with gall.

"This child has a destiny, as do we all. The Gods see fit to bring this child forth through me and we each do what is necessary. As for our journey, it ends when we are finished and not before."

Iarann and Lon Dubh stared at Faidhe for a moment and saw her quickly turn away. They briefly eyed each other as if to ask the meaning behind her harshness. They shrugged but Lon Dubh's eyebrows knitted with concern as the three travelers turned toward the road heading southeast out of the village.

———

Colm rolled across the sleeping pallet reaching a lazy arm across to her husband. Still half asleep, she let memories of the last three nights and days play across her mind: the warm strength of her husband as they slipped down by the hearth fire in the afterglow of his victory over the bull was a memory she particularly luxuriated in contemplating. Whether it was the magic in which they had participated, the excitement of such momentous changes, or the stewardship of the sacred Sword and Shield that imbued them with some exotic energy, she did not know but the vigor and enthusiasm they brought to their marriage bed on the night of the challenge brought Colm to fully understand for the first time, the power a woman possesses in her sexuality. She had devoured Laoghaire in every way possible and still had not felt completely sated. She roused him again and again until he good-naturedly begged her rest for his manhood lest she wear his staff down to kindling. For the next two nights after that first, they had found new vitality and passion for each other in a most voracious way.

This morning, Colm savored her recounting in her torpor planning to coax Laoghaire to pleasure once more before they arose. Checking quickly with one eye to insure that the children were still asleep on their sleeping skins, she rolled to further stretch an arm and bare leg to his side of the pallet, thinking she'd just climb atop him to see what would be done. Both eyes opened with a start when she discovered that Laoghaire was not there. Momentarily feeling cheated of a last intimate moment in her own hut before they made their journey up to their new quarters on the Hill, she attempted to quell her desire and focus on the remaining tasks needing attention before she woke the children. Standing for a moment in the hut that had been the only one she had ever called her own, she allowed the damp morning air to wake her as it nibbled at her bare skin. Colm filled a bowl with water to wash her face and rinse her mouth. She added a bit of fresh tasting liomoid root to her mouthful of water to refresh her mouth. Her hand lingered while she washed Laoghaire's seed from their frolic of last night from her folds below and momentarily closed her eyes at the sheer pleasure of her touch and the sensation of cool water. *What is it that calls my body and thoughts like a wanton?* She contemplated, and gave herself a final rinse before she forced her thoughts to the business that needed tending this day.

Removing her linen tunic from a branch stub jutting from one of the hut's supporting tree columns, Colm stretched her arms high over-head to allow the garment to slip down onto her body. She felt the course linen material graze her nipples and although she'd already prepared most of what they would take with them this day, chastened herself not to be distracted from the remaining work.

Her shift fell into place on her body; she resigned herself and began to roll up the skins on the bed in a great mass in order to remove, burn and replace the straw beneath them for Laoghaire's kinsman who would come to live in the hut and tend their cattle in their stead. Colm smiled and closed her eyes in gratification as a pair of arms wrapped around her from behind and she took the hands in her own guiding them to stroke her breasts. Behind her, she felt the promise of her man in quest of coupling nuzzle up against the indentation between her legs just below her buttocks. Colm nestled her backside closer into the solid urging behind her. She thrilled with pleasure as the hands left her breasts and one tended to lifting her linens to expose her from behind while the other impelled her to lean forward and rest over the great roll of skins just in front of her. When she did, two arms firmly wrapped around her hips and Colm felt herself being lifted as her feet came off the floor far enough to accommodate Laoghaire's height. She inhaled deeply as she felt herself being entered. She allowed herself to give over completely to the desire and need that had nagged her since she awoke, nay, since the first night of feasting. Having never experienced sexual rites in just this way, she felt a sensation of strong pleasure every time she returned his thrust and felt her loins tightening each time he reached deep in her, just so, in one particular spot. There was a moment of unreality when she saw morning vapor actually rising from her heated skin then heard a guttural animal sound and was vaguely aware that it was coming from herself. She moaned louder at the frustration of both wanting to open more completely to the coupling and needing to use her strength to keep a purchase on the skins to meet every thrust. Then in surrender, allowed deep release to the abandon of the moment. Seemingly, her frenzy had a mutual effect on her partner as he quickened his rhythm and Colm felt his heated release spasm as he frantically plunged into her some last few times.

"Laoghaire!" she breathed. "You take me as a deer in the rut. I'm conflicted at my physical delight and yet the loss of gentle reverence and ritual, which I have grown to love and crave. How is it we are infected with such raw desire for each other? She asked of her husband as she turned to face him. Jolted with a fear and revulsion Colm screamed, as she looked, not into the face of her loving husband but into the beady eyes and leering, piggish face of Briciu.

The scream pierced her own consciousness when she awoke on her sleeping pallet to find that Laoghaire was indeed not beside her. Colm felt panic rise in her chest, thrust back the skins and bound to the floor. Hands shaking, she fought with her tunic and revolted at the slickness she felt between her legs that only moments ago had been so pleasurable. Her traitor hands would not put the garment right and Colm was reduced to whimpering while trying to clothe herself. She was barely aware that her children were not in the hut either but was momentarily relieved that they were not awakened by her scream. Colm willed herself to gain control. *It was but a dream.* She reasoned with herself. *Briciu has not troubled us since the night of the challenge. A challenge he lost. Only a dream.* She repeated over and again until she gained control of her hands. Once clothed, Colm looked to the bowl for her morning washing ritual and was saddened to think such a routine pleasure was now tainted. *I cannot wash as I had just done in my dream. It is too close, too close to...*

Colm took a soft chamois skin and headed for the lake to be cleansed of the feeling of being sullied and violated. There was work to be done but this cleansing had to take place if she was to concentrate at all on what was necessary to move her family up to the Hill quarters today. Colm fought back tears and knew not why a dream could abuse her mind so, but she could not shut away the thought that she must be cleansed before her husband set eyes on her this day. She would not bring the stain of such a foul dream with her on the very day she is to take her place as the Keeper's wife and partner on the Hill. She told herself that the dream was unbidden and harmless but inside, she would not allow herself to recognize her true shame in that she wholly enjoyed the act of rutting in her dream. *When I thought it had been Laoghaire who took me in such a way...* shame set flames in her cheeks that she surrendered entirely to being flayed open and skewered like a sow in heat to the rut. What she had given over to was not a ritual of procreation with reverence of any kind. Colm lamented that in their newfound relationship, neither her sister nor her mother were here to help her puzzle through the overpowering sensation that the dream had a more consuming feeling to it than something merely ordinary.

Colm was resolute; she would cleanse at the lake and then she would seek out Craiche for some understanding of her dream and she would ask her how to set about a tincture to keep her from dreaming until she could think on it no more.

———

"Come boy!" Gara snapped. "Get you some movement behind gathering your things. Your father has taken to the road as a coward in the loss of his challenge. And rightly so, that he should so dishonor his family. You will come to my hearth and be raised proper. For who knows what damage your father has done you. Hope well that he has not filled your head with nonsense. I will have no more self-gaining ideas from a boy of mine. Come with me and I'll preserve what honor you may have in our name. Do it not and you'll likely find yourself on the road in search of your father, for there is no other to whom you may turn."

Triag jumped at his grandmother's command. He loved his father little, if at all and would not miss the routine beatings but still, he wondered at the truth of what had happened for he knew his father would not take to the road with only one servant at his call and surrender his hard won position, hearth and cattle. It did not surprise Triag that his father had abandoned him but property and title were not something Briciu would surrender voluntarily; not for shame, honor, or reputation.

Triag picked up his pace in packing his belongings. He cared not whether it was his father's house or his grandmother's house in which he lived but he decided he would be silent with his questions about his father for Gara was in foul disposition this day. There was one to whom he could turn for answers but he would let things settle a bit before he approached his aunt to see what light could be shed. It was a dangerous balance, but if he could uncover a bit of information that might be held over his grandmother's head, life would be easier while living under her rule. Push too far, and she might be good to her word and he would find himself upon the road as a beggar. That did not suit him at all.

"Yes Grandmother. It has been too long since we have spent time together. I have missed your wise words. Thank you for showering your Goddess-like kindness on me while my father takes to his diplomatic journey."

Gara recognized the unabashed sycophant that was her grandson and graced him with a generous smile. She liked a boy who knew his place. His praise and adoration would be as a balm to the festering sore that was the memory of her son.

"Come my little suckling, we shall gorge on honey cake and sweet fruits from my stores. Then we can discuss how you will make new friends with Laoghaire's children."

So that had been it. Triag thought. *Grandmother has seen fit to bind allegiance to the new Keeper and has allowed him to cast my father to the road. Let us see where this will lead.* Triag decided to test the waters with Gara to see if they maintained family fealty or whether they had broken all ties from his father.

"Yes Grandmother. I was thinking to extend a hand to Macha for the ill treatment he received upon the first night of feasting."

Gara thought for a brief moment and leveled a look at Triag.

"It is a good thing to make associations where they are needed, Grandson, but give a care not to give over too much. Extend a hand, yes, but offer apologies or admit wrongdoing is to place you at a disadvantage. Understand you, my meaning?"

"Yes Grandmother." He answered as he pushed his tunics and game sticks into the packing skin with some other of his belongings. He would have one of the servants retrieve the rest before his aunt, Nemain moved into the hut that was his home for all his life.

Gara was wise in moving Nemain to Briciu's quarters. In case there was any suspicion as to where Briciu had gone, she did not want to be one who gained from his disappearance. Nemain would take over the properties and cattle and Gara would maintain control over Nemain. Now she could direct her thoughts to the vacancies on the Council and how she might salvage a place for herself in all the change that has taken place. She knew that Faidhe had not told anyone what had happened with Briciu for she had not wanted anyone to bear the burden of association with murder whether it be ritual or necessary did not matter to Faidhe. She was determined that none other of the Council or her family should know. Gara would keep it as such for now, but she would share Faidhe's part in ritually slaying her son if necessary, strategically leaving out her own role of course. It would serve as a piece of information with which she could seek advice from the First Councilwoman, Craiche. It would perhaps help to forge a more intimate trust between the two if the old woman knew that Gara could have pointed an accusing finger at Faidhe but refrained from doing so for the greater good of the Tuath.

"Come boy." She spoke to him in colluding tones. "We have things to do."

———

Nemain brought her belongings from her mother's hut to the main hut in the cluster of structures that were her brother's. She wondered at how she'd come into such fortune as to be given her brother's property by her mother when Gara herself could have absorbed everything as her own since her brother had abandoned his station in the Tuath. As it was, Nemain would steward the cattle until her nephew was of age, but he would receive only the headcount as it presently stood. Nemain would be entitled to anything over that count to take as her own and the huts, paddock and out huts and servants would remain as her own as well. She gleefully stepped into the structure to celebrate her first day of freedom from her mother's critical eye and sharp tongue. Her celebration was cut short by images of one of her brother's servants, the short one with peculiar hair, beaten and cleaved in the chest, dead on the floor. Nemain, always sensitive to the voices of those gone over, searched the hut with her mind to call the murdered slave's voice to her. Nemain opened her mind and beseeched the slave, to communicate with her. *Brintu; that was his name.* She caught snippets in her mind of a gruesome scene here in this room, and indeed found her feet standing on the very place he had died, but try as she might, she could not raise his voice in her head. Nor did she receive any answers about her brother's disappearance from other spirit contacts she was accustomed to calling upon. There was an unusual silence from the Otherworld. One with which Nemain had no experience. *Briciu has gotten up to something foul.*

"Haven't you brother?" Nemain inquired aloud. To her surprise, her mind was at once flooded with some kind of communication at last. But straining to listen, hear and understand, Nemain was not able to decipher the garbled message she heard. It sounded to her as skittering gibberish one hears from a madman, fractured words that made no sense. She liked not the overwhelming intrusive feeling she experienced as this voice greedily pushed into her thoughts. Nemain closed her mind to the racket and tried to shake off this unsettled feeling.

Looking down at her feet, she inspected the ground there more closely and could see that new flooring sand had been swept over the spot. As she moved the sand with her toe, a dark brown stain remained and Nemain had discovered a mystery to work out. After a moment's thought, she replaced the sand, covering over the stain and set out to find her new servant staff and to at last establish herself as the new head of her own hearth and hut.

She was confidant of her skills and would return and improve her understanding of what had taken place here in her brother's hut. But for now, Nemain's thoughts were full of building her fortune and making a home for herself. She would settle into her new position and first, replace the ostentatious weaves and pottery Briciu surrounded himself with in order to reaffirm his self-importance. She would choose new pieces to her own liking.

———

Laoghaire had struck out early to meet his kinsman. Word had come to him on the last night of feasting he could expect the arrival of his cousin and childhood friend, Cuan, by sunrise today. Laoghaire wondered at the speed at which his cousin would be arriving, for the message Laoghaire sent to his home in the east should have taken six days' time, at least, just to reach his kin even had the messenger been a-seat a fleet horse. He was curious as to how his cousin would arrive only three days after his message had been sent.

Seated at the outer reaches of the village, pondering the implements given to his charge he fingered the smooth surface of the shining Shield and gripped the jeweled handle of the Sword that fitted his hand as if it were forged for him alone. Laoghaire was in great need of taking some time to contemplate in solitude all that had taken place. He wondered at the where-abouts of Briciu who had been noticeably missing since he'd lost his bull and the challenge. Laoghaire thought to prepare himself for some type of retaliation from the Councilman for he did not seem the type to so easily give up, but then, Briciu had always been over much concerned about his pride and that had been sorely wounded. Perhaps he *had* taken to the road with his servant. That seemed to be the general opinion around the village, and too, it was what the man's own mother had put about as well. But...Laoghaire felt uncertain.

Faidhe would not give her opinion as to what she thought Briciu had gotten up to. She spoke only of this dark magic he had cast and that she was grateful there had been protective magic around me for the challenge. He thought there might still be dealings with the likes of Briciu. *Cast not a net over waters not worth fishing,* he thought and was taken aback at the recollection of the expression that had been his mother's meaning; don't dwell on things that you can do nothing about. Sighing, he resigned himself that no good would come of worrying over Briciu for the moment.

Travelers could be spotted here and there leaving the village after the feasting had done. Laoghaire heard the low hum of voices and distant morning sounds of early risers packing up to take to the road. He had enjoyed the feasting and communing with visitors for the last few days but was relieved that the burden of being somewhat of a celebrity was drawing to a close. He would not miss the noise, rowdiness, odor and waste made by the crowds either. But, he supposed, he'd miss them soon enough when he takes to the Hill with his family and is secluded without his daily routine of tending his cattle and the pleasantries of passing time in idle conversation with other villagers following evening meal.

As if beckoned to rescue him from his thoughts of solitude, Morgan and Macha could be heard giggling and planning to sneak up behind their father to surprise him with their presence. Laoghaire sat completely still feigning deep concentration until, when the twins were only a short distance behind him, he turned quickly roaring at them and they took off in the opposite direction, shrieking with delight. Morgan brandished her stick recklessly in the air as Macha turned holding a rounded mat made for sifting grains as if it were a Shield to face the mock challenge.

"Stay there, you beast." Cried Morgan poking her stick at her father. "We are children of the Hill and we have the Power to bind you to our will."

Laoghaire played to his children's game and stopped in his place to fall down to the ground.

"Nay, you are too powerful, I cannot fight you. I am defeated." He cried as the children pounced on his back. Quickly reaching around, Laoghaire grabbed the twins and began to tickle them unmercifully until they squealed for relief from the assault.

Through sighs of contentedness after such laughter as all three lay on their backs watching the clouds, Morgan said, "It is our fortune that the real beast could not turn on you through our magic as you have done with us this day."

"Truly it is a good thing." Laoghaire answered. "For you may have had to eat only of sow liver for the feast!"

With wrinkled nose, and sounds of disgust Morgan protested, "Then truly, we are fortunate. Not only did we save you from the beast, we saved ourselves from that which is worse than all else: Sow liver!"

In a more solemn voice, Macha put in, "Yes it was our magic that saved you from the bull but it was Mother's who saved us from its master."

"Macha!" Morgan hissed. "You promised never to speak of that. It frightens me."

"What's this about a rescue?" Laoghaire was fully attentive now. "Did the Councilman Briciu or someone of his staff attempt to harm you in some way I do not know of? Have you seen him these last few days?"

The children tensed at Laoghaire's change in tone.

"Councilman Briciu?" Morgan asked looking to Macha for confirmation. "No. Why do you ask about him? He is gone, is he not?"

Laoghaire clarified his question. "Did you not just say your mother saved you from the bull's master?"

Morgan was reluctant. "Yes...No. Well, not the Councilman Briciu, Father, the creature that controlled the bull until you killed it. Remember you, the large and looming beast that sought us out as you battled the bull?"

"I saw no such creature. You say it was your mother who saved you from its approach? Why did she not tell me of this? Do you jest with me? Is this part of your game of imagination?"

The children grew worried at their father's agitation.

"Father, please," Morgan pleaded. "I do not think Mother knew it was there. We saw it come toward us but we said nothing because we would not break our concentration in the magic we used to keep you safe. Mother did not see it, I'm sure, but she held the great Shield you charged her to hold and it seemed that while she held it, we, all of us, were protected from the force that held the bull and tried to overtake us as well. The force came at us but was repelled just as the Councilman himself fell down as if struck as he approached us from behind."

Laoghaire listened earnestly to his children explain what they had seen and experienced. Knowing they must have seen some aspect of the dark energy Faidhe spoke of, he was sorry to have frightened them.

"You have both acted with such bravery and honor my children. I have not properly thanked you for the magic you cast to protect me. For truly, were it not for your strength and attention at this critical time, I may not have met my challenge with the bull. And all while you were facing peril and great fear. For this, I am mightily grateful." His words were outwardly gentle but Laoghaire had concern that this energy had sought his family in the challenge as well as himself.

The children joined hands with each other and bore the pleasure of his words on their faces. Each taking a hand of their father, they looked into his eyes and said in surprising unison and with a maturity far beyond the reach of small children, "Know you not, that we are of your blood; and you of ours? We will bring you through time itself and ever be where you are, to protect you so long as the Power is within us."

Laoghaire's skin chilled to puckers at the echoed quality to the dual voices. For he knew, not only had his children meant what they'd said, but also that there was the Power of an oath behind their words.

"Hail! Kinsman." Came a shout from behind him. Laoghaire lost the thread of his thought as he collected his Sword and Shield from the ground to stand and greet his cousin as he walked up the incline from the wood line below.

"Macha, Morgan, this is your kinsman and cousin, Cuan." Laoghaire introduced. "He is great and large, is he not?" Indeed the children were awed to see a man who so resembled their father but was a half a head taller and some stones heavier. He wore great fury skins that might have been from a bear and strange deerskin boots that strapped up the lower leg. On his face was the start of what would be a full and bushy beard but in his eyes could be seen the unmistakable twinkle as in their own father's eyes and that which could be seen in Macha's eyes as well.

"Come now little ones," Cuan's voice boomed. "I am not so ugly as that, am I? Surly your father resembles a toad more closely than I." He teased as he scooped the children up with a thundering laugh and kissed them wetly on their faces until they squirmed to be released.

Putting the children down, Cuan raised himself to greet his cousin in an affectionate embrace.

"What's this? Cuan asked. "You come to greet me as if we are at war?"

Laoghaire housed the Sword and shifted the Shield to return his cousin's encirclement. By the expression in Cuan's eyes, Laoghaire now knew why his cousin came so soon to the Tuatha de Danann. It was not the message sent from Laoghaire that brought him here, his cousin brought news from home and it did not look to be happy.

"Stay your tongue, Cousin." Laoghaire stated quietly. "We'll have time enough for news from home. Come you first to receive a proper welcome such as can be given, as this is short time I have within the village. Perhaps it is fortuitous that you come now."

———

Craiche left the Tuath under a slowly waxing moon on the third night of feasting leaving Faidhe to her final night with Laoghaire and Colm before their party of three took to the road. Walking slowly, stooped with age and the burden of knowledge that her old friend had yet to bear great heartache, she offered prayers of blessing for Faidhe with each painful step. Craiche prayed that Faidhe would at last come to know the love of a family unit as she traveled the road. For once again, her babe would be snatched from her arms at birth so that she may continue to do the bidding of the Gods. May her daughter's company sooth her and perhaps, she may find warmth by the fire with the son of Goibhniu.

Leaning heavily on her walking stick, Craiche found her way to the foot of the Hill and began the uphill trek to ready the Circle and hut for the new Keeper. The magic needed for Laoghaire's task in preparing the implements and utilizing the great Stone of Fal, might be beyond his fledgling skills so Craiche took it upon herself to be sure that when his time came to protect the Sword and to raise the Stone, that he would succeed with confidence. Then, in all that is to follow, Laoghaire will achieve without self-doubt to weaken his success.

It had been perhaps hundreds of times over many years Craiche had taken the walk up the Hill for ritual gatherings and festival ceremonies. Her feet knew every step of the path but this time her steps were leaden for she also knew that this would be her last time to make this uphill journey. She set about preparing her mind for the magic that would be required of her when she reaches the Circle atop the Hill. She set one foot in front of the other and settled into the halting rhythm of her gait.

27

The Journey Begins

The threesome traveled east away from the village until mid-day when they came to the innermost edge of the bay and were able to turn south toward their first destination. Faidhe was relieved to be heading south now instead of east for she knew intuitively that the bodies of the two men she'd sunk in the bogs lay somewhere to the east of the village. Though both spots were far beyond many days walking distance, the Seer was troubled by simply drawing nearer them in an eastward direction. Whether just the idea of having gotten rid of the bodies or something more vexing, she did not allow her mind to ponder. Faidhe kept her own counsel as to where the troupe would travel. In truth, she was bound to follow her intuition rather than any formal plan on the road and had to trust that where they traveled would be where they would best suit the divine purpose.

Their first stop, Faidhe had known was necessary to initiate Lon Dubh in her task of proliferating her story. There was a clan of some repute who held the honorable distinction of bardship that could bring a story to the very mind and heart of a person as they listened to either word or song. It was to this old family, Faidhe knew she would entrust the telling of the tale. They would exact a heavy price, she was sure, for to tell this tale, they must endure erudition and continued spell-work to insure not only that the tale is told, but so that those who tell it will pass its meaning and magic, undiluted for however many generations would be necessary until the magic bound within the story is to be unleashed. Not many, even from the middle village south of the Mounts, who are as renowned for their love of the gems and gold as they are for their bardic genius, would agree to be bound by blood, oath and magic to a tale such as this. The price will be steep, but stones and gold were of no consequence to Faidhe. She had the sense, now that they were on the road, things would fall where they may. There would be many prices to exact and pay before her task is done. But the risks of striking a covenant with the Duibhe, the clan of blackness could be steep beyond the price they exact for the tale. These people, driven by their lust for gold and gems had long before now, for the most part, taken to live under the Seven Mounts of the south where they mine for precious gifts offered by the earth. Though some folk, a few women, the aged and some storytellers still keep to the middle village above ground, it is argued that the bulk of the ancient clan had been in the dark beneath the hills so long, they had, whether by magical design or by nature, shrunken to a people of smallish stature to more conveniently work in the mines.

Despite the story-telling abilities, industrious nature and shrewd business sense, the ambition for the treasures has driven many of the womenfolk away from the underground life in search of other endeavors which has left the clan aging and dwindling without new blood to replace the elders. Though they are said to live extraordinarily long lives, the clan has taken to promises of flesh from other clans and peoples as a more precious payment than gold and gems as payment for services. Their tribe needed new blood to work the mines.

Faidhe could not risk the life of the babe inside her to be hidden away under the hills nor would she chance to anger the Duibhe by refusing their request should they come to hear of her breeding condition. It was not yet time to have the babe's purpose revealed, for Faidhe did not know what lay ahead in the future for him. She did know without question she would not promise him to the Duibhe. Faidhe would keep the babe she carried private until negotiations for the spinning, keeping and telling of the tale had been completed.

Lon Dubh would be the one to set these terms, for it was her task to weave the tale to tell of the Goddess's reign and plight. She must forge a spiritual connection with the ones chosen to spin the tale so that they may commune no matter where Lon Dubh may be, until the tale has come to completion. There will be much for her to learn in a relatively short time before they reach the seven mountain ranges of the Duibhe to the south. Faidhe contemplated her daughter's path in this journey and inwardly resigned herself to the idea that they each would do what they must. Faidhe's heart was heavy as she turned to observe.

Lon Dubh could be heard behind Faidhe, prattling on about village happenings and much of the doings of the feast nights. To have willing company and finally have knowledge of how she would serve the Goddess's purpose, Lon Dubh seemed to have dropped the stoic silence in which she'd kept herself over the years and her voice and laughter came in a deluge.

Iarann, though a solitary man, seemed not to mind at all. It had been many years since he'd enjoyed idle chat and laughter with anyone, much less a dark and mysterious beauty. He was pleased to breathe the air and take notice of blue sky and birdsong. Faidhe's silence prompted Iarann and Lon Dubh to make fast friends; they found they genuinely enjoyed each other's company.

"Jest not Smithy," Lon Dubh warned with a glint of mischief in her eye. "I know words of flattery will turn the ear of other maidens but I am not so easily swayed by pretty words and trinkets."

"Surely," Iarann retorted a bit flummoxed. "I do not jest. I have made a clasp for your cloak by winding some fine polished bronze shavings and have strung it with small pearl-like seashells. I was put in mind of the task on the first night we supped together as you oft held your cloak around you tight. I though you could find use of a clasp and had some bits to work with. Will you not make use of the piece?"

Lon Dubh took in her breath as she spied the clasp. It was of delicate beauty but the strength of the piece could be seen as the back of it and the crosspiece were of sturdy material. The tiny seashells were indeed shiny pearl-essence to catch the sun between the gold tones of the bronze. She would not have thought that such strong hands could conceive of such fine and delicate work.

"Oh Iarann! It's lovely." Her gaze went from the jewelry to his eyes looking to see what she would find there and knew her own filled with tears. "It...it would not suit to have such finery while we are on the road." She said blinking furiously as she turned her head away.

"There will be a time for it, if only to remind you of the shores of our bay and the calm of our village lake for I have selected shells from both places." He said as he turned her to him and secured the clasp to her hunting skins. "We need not be practical each passing moment."

Lon Dubh smiled up at Iarann's kind face and saw him smile through his red beard. This bred a smile on her own lips and she touched the clasp as he leaned down to kiss her on the forehead. Now she cried in earnest.

"Thank you. I have no words for how grateful I am...for everything."

Faidhe observed the scene and was warmed by it. She knew that Lon Dubh was grateful for the companionship and attention and for at last, having family close at hand and all of those emotions were tied up in her thanks for the trinket; for Faidhe too, understood all of those feelings of late. It pleased her that there was warmth and love growing between her daughter and Iarann. She watched as the colors around them glowed and swirled with a warming golden hue. She sighed in relief that at the least, this company of companions would not be a hardship.

"Come now, long enough we have lingered over kind gifts. Let us speak as we travel the day's next half before we settle to camp for the night. Iarann, you have spoken of a bowl of fine crafting and have been given the purest of silver from the great Cauldron to begin this task. Know you a plan to begin the design? Has it been revealed to you, how this bowl will be of use to us?"

Iarann hesitated before answering Faidhe.

"Lady, I...as I have admitted, I thought I had not any special Power other than my smith craft, but I have found, since I began to forge the fine silver, I am creating panels in a manner that is unfamiliar to me entire. My hands craft when my mind is absent any thought as though I work in a dream only to wake and find magnificent work before me. It may be of my father's blood I hold these talents but more like, I think I am but a tool to manifest this bowl. I have worked these two nights past upon the bowl and have, each morn, woken by my bellows with a completed plate depicting events which have taken place since your arrival to the village."

"This troubles you?" Faidhe asked. "You seem uncertain about the work."

"Nay, Lady. It does not trouble me. I am humbled by my role in forging the plates, and I know the meaning for each depiction in detail. I find myself happier than I have been in a great many years in creating things of beauty and to have purpose beyond making tools or weapons. It is strange to me though that my trance in the creation renders me without recollection of ever doing the work and that the plates, which should take many passing days to complete, are fashioned in the fleeting of only one night."

"It seems Smithy," Lon Dubh commented "you have the honor of being touched by the Goddess in your craft."

"Just so." Faidhe agreed. "You must show us the panels at evening-hearth and explain to us the details you have wrought so that Lon Dubh may include all that is put down into her tale."

The men sat on mats next to the darkened hearth. They both bore faces of sorrow but Laoghaire's eyes were rimmed with red and he fought the rage that welled inside him.

"How did this come to be? Bonds have been forged and alliances between clans have afforded peace for the Tuatha Laoghaire for many generations. My mother and father were loved and respected as fair and generous leaders with a great many trades from their shores. Who would benefit from such butchery?"

Cuan's chest tightened for his cousin's anguish. He loved his mother's sister and her husband the king. He was angered at the news of their murders and his first thought was for revenge but Cuan knew his duty was to retrieve his cousin to take seat of the throne in order to insure protection from fighting factions of the clan who thought to have a chance at a Chieftain position. Laoghaire is king proper now that both his parents are dead.

"My heart calls for the blood of the ones who did these murders so foul, but my first duty is to see you take your place at The Hill T'airg of your own clan before it is lost to lesser savages scrabbling to gain only power for its own sake. The likes of cattle thieves and such without care to the propagation of clan, cattle and crops so long as they can take what they want at sword-point and call it legal because they have usurped the throne in your absence."

"I cannot! You know I have left the Tuatha Laoghaire to take up life and hearth here as a humble herdsman. It seems that I am plagued by power that will not allow me a simple life. And now, I have been called to honor a place here with the Tuatha de Danann as I have given my word I will do. It is my time to take the Hill here and carry out my duties as the Keeper of the Circle until such time it is my duty no more."

"You cannot? You abandon your kith and kin at their time of need? You do not avenge your parents such an indecent and degrading death at the hand of a stealthy coward who took them in their sleeping chambers?" Cuan grew red in his face with disbelief that Laoghaire had not taken up his new Sword and set off to wage war this very day on those he merely suspected of doing this deed. "Laoghaire," He tried to speak reason. "Your father was castrated! Your mother violated and defiled in most degrading ways and left to be displayed for all to witness her dishonor! Is it so important to you to be cast among the great and famed Tuatha de Danann that this matters not to you?" Cuan stood and began to pace, dwarfing the hut with his bulk.

"Cousin." Laoghaire spoke with a calm that belied his tortured feelings. "My parents were not dishonored in their deaths. The one who committed such filth owns the disgrace. But I will dishonor them if I break my word to my wife, my adopted clan and myself. I must take the Hill here and perform my duties. My heart cries out for the clan of my birth and my parents but I am bound by my word and honor to keep to my oath." Laoghaire stood and took his cousins hands in his own. "Cousin. Cuan, you are my blood. And I cannot tell you what duties lay ahead of me but I can tell you I am in need of your help so that I might complete these tasks rightfully. Will you stand by me?"

Tears now streamed down the hulking man's face. "How can you ask this of me Croi? I am charged with bringing you home. What of *my* honor? What of *our* clan?"

Laoghaire was tortured by the pleading in his cousin's voice and was particularly touched by the use of his childhood name. It was an intimate path to his heart that called home to him all that was lost in the murder of his parents.

"I can never truly give of my all to do what you ask until I have completed what is necessary here. I must do this for this clan, for our clan for the very future of all of us. Then, I swear to you, with the same strength of oath with which I carry my obligations here, that I and my family will come back to Baile Laoghaire and to the Hill there and put things to right."

"You swear it, cousin?"

"You have my word."

"Laoghaire. No!" Came the protest from the door to the hut. Colm, looking tired and worn, had retrieved fresh straw for the sleeping pallet, which now fell from her hands to the floor. "Have you gone mad? What of your oath to the Hill and the Circle? Is this betrayal? How can you swear this without having spoken to me? You have sworn, and we are bound to take the Hill this very day. How can you even think of doing other than what we have avowed?"

Laoghaire recognized the uncharacteristic panic in Colm's voice. He knew there were unsettled feelings of resentment between Colm and his cousin, who had tried to talk him out of leaving Clan Laoghaire to marry. Colm had been insulted when Cuan had suggested that she, a girl with no cattle, would aspire to marry one with many riches and claim to the throne for the chance to elevate her station in life. Cuan knew this not to be true but he was wounded that someone could take the heart of his closest friend and family member.

"Colm, there is news." Laoghaire began, but Cuan interrupted,

Stepping between Laoghaire and his wife, momentarily forgetting that Laoghaire was now rightfully his king, Cuan said,

"No cousin. Let me. Colm," He started in a habitual harsh tone. "Kinswoman," He softened, and started again. "Cousin, I have wronged you in our past dealings and for this, I beg your forgiveness."

Colm was wholly taken aback for she was prepared, once again to stand and fight an old battle to win the right to be recognized as one who loves her man for himself and not for the dishonorable reasons cast at her by Cuan. She was speechless yet still did not trust the words she heard from her husband's cousin. She turned her face away from him.

"The news I bear is wretched and I come with a man's heart seeking justice and vengeance for the slaying of a much loved king and queen, not the jealous heart that foolishly drove my own kin to a foreign clan so that he could live life with his love in peace."

At the news that Laoghaire's parents were dead, Colm looked to Laoghaire whose face worked to control tears.

Cuan pushed ahead. "True, I once hated you for the fact that Laoghaire picked your love over our bond of friendship, but I was a foolish boy who thought to bind my pain with blame and hatred to avoid bearing the grief of losing my kinsman."

Cuan knelt in front of Colm and gently took her hands. "Cousin, I should have come many seasons ago to beg yours and Laoghaire's forgiveness. I do this now, not to suit my purpose in bringing Laoghaire back to the Dun, but whether he does or no, I hope you will forgive the boy his wounded heart and embrace the man as kin."

Colm was awash with emotions. Still confused from her morning dream, she knew not which emotion to trust.

"Your parents are...dead?" She asked of Laoghaire, remembering the gentle-woman and the kindhearted man. "What happened?"

"Tend to the request that is at your feet Colm." Laoghaire retorted, all at once weary of the old battle and under the new pressures of being pulled by so many important responsibilities. Colm was forced to focus on the man on his knees in front of her. She looked into his eyes, so like her husband's yet she felt the habitual steeling against his jibes and insults as a hard defense set across her chest in the form of her folded arms. She remembered hating him for foiling her opportunity to be a part of a family, to have Laoghaire's parents as her own. He had sullied her reputation throughout the Tuatha Laoghaire as one in search of status and title. She recalled the biting words of the boy she remembered. But now in front of her she saw an open heart full of regret and pain. She began to remember what her heart would not let her see all those years ago, that the boy who hated her was, himself, without parents and counted Laoghaire's own mother and father as his foster parents and Croi Laoghaire, his cousin, his friend was as his brother. Colm allowed herself to see for the first time what her presence might have meant to the boy, for she threatened all he had cherished. In this moment, she had not thought about what she was about to do or say. As she saw the man for the first time as anything other than an enemy, she felt shame at how she ignored the young boy's feelings and thought only of her own. Colm could have put a hand on Cuan's head and feigned a wounded woman who'd suffered greatly but who would bestow forgiveness, but she did not. She fell to her own knees and looked up into Cuan's eyes, feeling all the weight of the impending move, the loss of her newly reconciled family, the confusion over her accosting dream, she burst to tears.

"It is I who beg your forgiveness, Cuan. I was young and alone, yes, but I was a woman who should have recognized your need to keep your family as equal to my quest to build a family of my own. I should have taken you to my heart and soothed away your fears that I was the enemy. Instead, I made your fears real and took Laoghaire from you. But at the time, my love for him outstripped everything, for his love was as the air, earth and water to me; I did not think it possible for me to live without it. But in my own need, I had no care for yours. I am truly sorry for this and for all the years we have lost since, that you have not known the warmth of our hearth or the laughter of our children."

The two embraced in sobs and Laoghaire placed a hand on the head of each to share in the moment.

"Come." Laoghaire said, "We have little time to lay plans and prepare for our trek up the Hill. Although it is still early morn, time is growing short for we have much to do before the spring festival and all the ritual we must enact at that time. Each night we draw closer to the time when the sun takes over the moon and the day grows long. For it is upon this particular night, I am told, when the full face of the Mother, Moon shows herself that we must draw from both the feminine and the masculine energy at the moment they are at the pinnacle of equality to set into motion the rituals and magic to protect the sacred implements, and this land from the wave that will soon come and leave her peoples awash in the mire of change and confusion."

———

Craiche entered the hut that had, only three days prior, been the home to Faidhe for 35 long seasons. She took no time to reminisce or lament for all that had come to pass. She devoutly averted her eyes from being drawn to the sleeping palette, bursting with fresh, sweet straw to avoid the temptation to succumb to her fatigue. She took from her materials, a pouch-skin of special salt rendered from both the earth and the sea mixed with sweet-herb known for cleansing things of the spirit. Spreading the mixture around the circumference of the hut, she cast strong magic of protection utilizing the spirits of the earth, air and ocean that imbued the blend to hold fast the energy of shelter from all corrupt and devious energies. Craiche was well aware of the evil that had been loosed on the Tuath. She'd seen its malevolent force and knew that the foolish heart that unleashed this beast would not have the strength or the know-how to retrieve it even had he still lived. This spell-work was most vile, for it contained all that lurked in the heart of the one who cast it. A spell cast in greed will only grow in strength as its consumptive nature absorbs all it can and affects all it touches to the same end, for its own sake creating additional greedy hearts and inflicting its desirous nature upon the weak. This lust for all things: power, money, possession is trouble enough as it infects the heart and minds of humans, but a spell cast in perversion of the gift of sexual rights will seek to employ the physical aggression of those it touches in order to maintain dominance and oppression. This magic cast with the taint of both greed and perversion portents grave results especially at the time of the masculine sway that is now beginning to take place.

Craiche had to protect those who will come to the Hill to perform the rituals that will serve to bring the Old Ways and old knowledge with some small knowledge of magic to the future. These rituals must take place and a balance of honor must be in place to counter act this mistake of a curse that has been unleashed on humankind. So much, so much is dependent on Laoghaire and his task in maintaining the implements so that no magic or deceiving hands may use them for ill. Yet he must maintain position as leader of the people even far beyond the Hill. He must preserve the Power of the Hill and make certain that it never falls to the hands of those who would use the Power of this other magic, the dark magic.

She finished her salting of the inside of the hut and went outside to rim the perimeter as well. The sun rose as she chanted and mumbled the words that would enforce the protection of all who slept in this hut while they are in the hut and as they travel beyond its walls. Having cast the circle of salt two times, Craiche went back and created a third rim of protection, pacing slowly, sunwise around the hut. Having completed her plea for protection, she proceeded to the great Circle and was shaken to actually see the Keystone split asunder. She had seen it rent in her vision but it was something overwhelming to see this Stone upon which her tribe had based its spiritual foundation and that had been brought here from the north lands to settle a village at the Lake of the Ivory Heron many, many generations ago. The great Stone held within it the magic to help both the spirits and Gods travel to and from the Otherworld. It made the Circle, a sacred space in which to commune and petition the energy of the elementals. It held within it the Power to identify true leaders and rightful sons and daughters to wield the power of leadership. What, now that it is so altered, does this mean for the future of the Tuath and its people of the Danu, and even yet, all people?

At the altar stone situated in front of the Keystone she laid out tools and implements in a ritual fashion. Slowly and methodically Craiche cleansed herself with water from the sacred spring and enjoyed the refreshed feeling she experienced as she drank the water; it infused her with renewed strength to complete her tasks. After eating of some bitter ground herbs, she waited patiently at the latrine pit, dug into a rise on the backside of the Hill until she was satisfied that her body was completely purged of earthly sustenance. Once again, cleansing and drinking of the spring water, she returned to the alter and removed her linens to stand naked and begin the necessary ritual to give surety that Laoghaire would have the crucial knowledge, magic and Power to perform all that was required of him.

It was mid-morning by the time Craiche had finished her intricate weaving and casting of spells; the final act to secure the magic would take place and then Craiche would be finished. She would pass her skills, knowledge and Power onto Laoghaire to mingle with his own untapped energies. The essence of the newly made energy must then be used in whatever way Laoghaire creates to see all duties to the Hill completed. The old woman was lighthearted and felt a sense of satisfaction and completion of her work here and lay herself down upon the altar stone amidst implements, bowls, aromatic plants and tinctures. Placing on her chest, the large shallow bowl carved of stone, filled with clear water from the spring, Craiche could see the reflection of the sun in the spring water.

"As above, so below." She uttered.

Then she allowed herself to enjoy the sensations of the cool rock beneath her white skin and the cool breeze as its movement teased the tiny hairs on her body into a dance. The old woman watched the frothy clouds parade across the blue sky and settled her mind to trance. She listened and paced her breathing until she felt the pulse of her heart slow in its rhythm. Keeping ever Laoghaire in her mind and heart, she chanted the words necessary to bequeath to him her Power and knowledge. Feeling the vibration of her voice set tremors of motion into the water bowl, she allowed her life force to resonate into the bowl itself. As the very last pulse of life left her body, she released her breath and it sent ripples across the water in the bowl itself that continued to pulse a slow and rhythmic beat on the surface of the water.

Craiche had known she conjured the ultimate magic, for to give of one's life to seal a spell is a wholesome act of love. Unlike magic cast in blood, this type of sacrifice is selfless and though blood is dense and binding, love is pure and so the magic will be as well. She gave of herself without regard for reward or penalty. She gave freely and the only regret she felt in the end was the sorrow she felt in her heart for Faidhe, whom she knew to have sacrificed her own promise of a peaceful passing at the time she would leave this world. She would not pass to the Otherworld with her ancestors, for in an effort to diminish the evil casting wrought by Briciu, Craiche knew that Faidhe must serve the Power until such balance as can be had is achieved. Faidhe will not go to a restful death but rather walk in a netherworld being neither alive nor dead but her spirit would live in between.

She will ever be aware. She will witness the pain and suffering of all her descendants she will witness their joy and not be able to share it with them. She will ever be near, without hope of being born to the flesh again, for she will not ever truly die, but live in the Otherworld, ever tending this world, never being allowed to wholly pass over. Craiche selflessly gave of herself to death but it paled, in her judgment, to the sacrifice Faidhe had given in her attempt to harness the dark magic and render it ineffectual.

The real grief, despite her sacrifice, is that Faidhe had not succeeded in banishing or even harnessing the foul force but only in weakening it so it may not spill any more blood than it had already on the very night it had been loosed…weakened for now. But it will feed on weaknesses of people and find its way into their hearts and minds as insects and worms to rotten wood. It will settle there and grow so that its minions will wreak its evil upon the world. It will grow in strength with the suffering of the oppressed and the contamination of the sacred. It will take glee in usurping a good heart and turning one against another. It will seek power in any fashion. It will grow in strength in particular when it can corrupt that which is created to do acts of purity and selflessness. All are its victims but none quite so boldly will it target as those in positions to do the most good for human kind. For this reason, Craiche felt sorrow in her heart for Faidhe, Laoghaire and their family members whose task it would be now to keep balance in the spiritual and fight this seemingly unconquerable ever growing force that is now, true wickedness.

28

Reading the Cauldron

I felt safer after getting our phone with a renewable card that would allow for 500 minutes of conversation. We could call home in privacy; we could call Cath or Finny if we needed to and we were not cut off from everything at our cottage on Bridey's property. It probably wouldn't help us in a battle with the supernatural, but still it was a measure we hadn't had before.

Reaching into the back seat to my ever-increasingly full satchel, I struggled to drive with one hand and with the other, pull out a fistful of printouts Cath had given us about the Gundestrup Cauldron.

"Let's go over some things, okay?" I handed the papers to Nora who took the wad and righted the papers into a neat pile.

"Okay." She agreed. "I'll organize them into exterior panels and interior panels. The outer ones all have one main figure or more and the inner ones that tell certain aspects of the family's respective journeys. Here's the base panel with the bull and Laoghaire. Here's the internal one showing the same scene but with the triplicate image. Here's the one with Faidhe and her daughters and the symbol of the birds."

There was a moment of silence when we formulated in our minds that these depictions, if my visitation dream was true, were of both of us in a lifetime passed. We looked at each other and realized with a chill that the birds, the raven and the hawk were also somehow relevant in all that was currently happening to us.

"Weird." I said.

"Umm." Nora answered.

"Anything there that'll help us know how to fight the, ah, negative forces?" I said, not wanting to tempt fate or poke the proverbial sleeping dog.

"Dunno yet" Nora said. "We still need plenty of time with Cath and Finny. We only have thumbnail sketches as to what each panel means."

"Any thoughts? Intuitions?" I asked.

Rummaging through the papers she answered. "Not really. Let's just see what else we've learned. Okay, we know of the origin of only three of the plates so far, so there's way more to the story. I think we have to get serious about a learning schedule. We've done research about birds and bowls and started to develop our abilities but I think it's time we went to the brothers and set down a pace to get through the tale so we can figure out what to do next."

———

Bridey kept watch on the cottage up the driveway being rented by the two girls from America. She carefully stayed behind the curtain as she watched the three brothers mosey from the work in their front yard, one by one, around to the back cow path that lead toward the back acreage behind the upper cottage. She knew they had no other business on the top land up the path where the cows grazed. She knew where they were going. Bridey just kept a watch as the men slid out of sight behind the cottage. She glanced down the driveway hoping that the American girls would not return just now. She wasn't ready to expose her purpose just yet so it would be quite inconvenient if the girls should show up while the men were in the cottage. She had to be sure...to be sure. The brothers would help her make up her mind if these girls were connected with the Old Ones. *The buffoons are sloppy though. I'll just let them do their work and then I'll slip into the cottage to tidy up so the girls wouldn't know anyone had been in their place.* She breathed a humph in exasperation at the clumsiness of the men. *They'd almost given themselves away the other night with their damn spyglass. What would I do if the girls'd gotten scared and moved to a hotel somewhere? As it is now, I can go through their things, see where they've been, and keep watch on how they come and go.* She didn't dare go into the cottage while the girls were sleeping to see everything they carry with them during their trips. That would be too dangerous but, *that satchel the blond one carries is mighty curious. They hadn't bought the regular trinkets and tourist things. They had some curious old books though...That blond one, she was a queer type on the first day they came. I swear I saw that one shape shift or some such. She has the gift for sure and with the name too. That, with the books and the phone calls this morning...*Up until now, she'd been able to hear their conversations to relatives back home. *I know she was up to something on the phone today as well, that one.* And when the phone bill comes in, she'd be able to get addresses if she needed them. But Bridey lamented that she may have pushed too far with her curiosity this morning.

"Damn." She cursed softly chastising herself on that account because now the girls have mentioned getting their own phone. *And they hightailed it right out of here when I caught wind of the telltale birth dates. Did she lie about her own birthday? Well that's easy enough to check with the credit card information. We'll see Miss O'Leary when your birthday may fall.*

Another peek out the window. Still no brothers coming down from the cottage.

"Get done your work and come down from there." Bridey hissed under her breath as if someone might hear her if she spoke too loudly. Something had to be done when she'd decided that the men were taking too long. Bridey knew the brothers would take it as a signal to leave the cottage if they thought she was coming up herself so she made an elaborate showing of coming out of her own little house and turning to lock her door. Tucking the key into her apron pocket along with the key to the cottage, she went to the fence out in back of her house where a bucket hung on a hook and she filled the bucket with seven blocks of peat from her own peat stacks. Bridey then began to walk up the long driveway hill past the brothers' house toward the guest cottage with her store of peat. She had guessed that someone would be keeping watch so she walked slowly to give the men plenty of time to be alerted to her coming and vacate the cottage.

She began to think the men were completely foolish when she was more than halfway to the cottage and there was no sign of them but then she saw movement on the cow path and ignored the sight of them as they nonchalantly strolled down the hill.

Once inside the cottage, Bridey tisked to herself all the while, at the sloppy job the men had done by going through the girls' personal items and not taking care to put things back to right. There were books and papers strewn about and the dressers had been ransacked.

"Those idjits!" She cursed aloud when she saw that the lingerie for both girls had been closely inspected. In fact, they'd need to be laundered. "Ugh."

Bridey thought there was no help for it now but that she would have to clean up the mess and leave the girls a note that she's just tidied up a bit and restocked their peat as part of the service. She knew the girls, would likely not want this type of service as many who rent the self-catering cottage prefer their privacy and for things to remain undisturbed. Particularly the academic types, they're a bit fussy about their papers and books and such. *Well, they'd been here near two weeks now,* she reasoned to herself as she pulled the caddy from under the kitchen sink holding dust cloths and cleaning solvents. *I'll just give all a proper cleaning and have a look for meself at what to be seen.*

⸺

When I told Cath and Finny about my dream of the woman who called herself our mother and that I'd also seen her in some of the visions I'd experienced, I was incredulous that the old brothers had known something of our past, so to speak, and did not share with us the part of the tale that illustrated a reincarnation or a return of the principal people in the original story.

"What do you mean? You knew? How could you know and not tell us? Don't you think that's kind of an important tidbit to overlook? Oh, by the way, you're really not you. You're someone else on a 4000-year old mission and the life you have now is really just incidental! Are you kidding me?"

Finny retorted with sarcasm even Nora would be proud of.

"Well now. Ye seem te be takin' the news much better than we'd imagined. Given all the work we've still te do, and how calm ye are at the moment, I see now, the error of our ways in not sharin' the news with ye so ye could blow yer fuse right from the git go and be totally useless te the lornin' ye still have te do."

I was struck silly with the wry sarcasm sweet old Finny had thrown at me. I had to take a moment to work out in my mind if he was actually ribbing me or if I just heard him wrong. Nora's snort behind me told me that I hadn't heard wrong. This was Finny's way of telling me to settle down and trust them; the brothers know what they're doing. My face flushed and I was kind of embarrassed at my outburst. A contrite smirk convulsed on my lips and my indignation melted away. I was left with the task of trying to get my mind around the idea that I was myself and I was someone else...lots of someone else's, in fact. That much I could fathom; I'd always believed in multiple lives but I'd never expected to actually be informed of my own, much less be given an assignment to carry out from the days of yore...or pre days of yore.

The only solace I had was the idea that if I was on a mission across time, I guess I'd expect to be traveling with Nora. It made sense, and was a comfort to know that we were in this together. I looked at her and she locked eyes with me knowing what I was thinking, we easily joined our thoughts without effort and all at once, I saw lifetime after lifetime of the two of us together in every combination of relationship: mother and daughter, brothers, teacher and student, husband and wife, father and son, son and mother and on and on so that we knew one another mind, heart and soul. Through these times over and again, we had developed a bond that had been forged like tempered steel, stronger with each relationship over perhaps hundreds of lifetimes. For a moment, my heart cried for all that I had known of those others and missed. But then, I saw Nora in a different way so that in her, I saw all of those whom I had known and loved.

Then, like a bolt of lightning, I was struck with the simplicity of the knowledge that the spirit transcends the flesh. Who we are, who we truly are, has nothing to do with gender, age, religion, status, class, money, or race. Who we are, has only to do with how we conduct ourselves with the spirit of others. Spirit has nothing to do with religion, masculine and feminine have nothing to do with gender, wealth has nothing to do with money, quality of character has nothing to do with any type of cast system, and the value of a person has nothing to do with class, status or education. These are things that I knew cerebrally, but I did not go beyond the acknowledgement of the thought. I never truly let the thought effect the way in which I saw the world. To me, people were who they were and what they did; they were one-dimensional. But now, it was as if a veil was lifted from my mundane way of seeing; like all the lock tumblers falling into place on a safe, my eyes swung open wide and I had the ability to see people for who they are, really are, not who their skin and everyday life dictates they are. I looked from Nora to Finny and saw a stoic being with will and tenacity. I saw an advanced spirit that sought to serve and had little use for monetary riches. I looked to Cath and saw a wealth of knowledge swirling about him. This is one who had come through century after century learning wisdom of the human spirit and its history. I recognized how each man's spirit had manifested in how they chose to surround themselves: Cath in the Sacred Traveler and Finny in his humble digs behind the church. The infinitesimal spirit, hidden behind the grandeur and trappings of the church. Then I recognized the energy of both men as familiar to me.

"I know you." I whispered. Trying to place who they are...or were.

"She's come to the knowing." I heard Finny say to Cath in a muffled far away voice.

I woke up on Cath's couch feeling the scratchy material under me right through my clothes. I felt as if my skin was being scraped with sandpaper and I wanted nothing more than to rip off my clothes and dive into a cold pool of water somewhere. I started to sit up and was gently held down by Finny's one hand placing pressure on my chest and the other placing a cold compress on my head.

"Stay firm now. Ye'll have a banger of a headache if ye get up too quickly. The spirit can sustain quite a bit more than these frail vehicles we have te get us through life. Give yer body a bit te adjust te the shock."

"What's...What happened?" I was unclear about how I got onto the couch, the pain in my skin distracted me and then my memory began to reintroduce me to what I'd seen."

From the other end of the couch, sitting at my feet, Nora answered.

"You fainted. You okay now? How do you feel?" There was an anxious look on her face but when I instinctively reached out to her to see what she was feeling and knew that she was not worried about my fainting but was nervous about something Cath and Finny had explained to her.

"What did they tell you?" I asked.

Nora looked to Finny and then behind me to where I knew Cath was standing. "Never mind them!" I grew irritated trying to sit up in spite of Finny's warning. "God, my skin hurts." Then feeling on the verge of anger I demanded, "What? What's going on?"

Nora looked from Cath to me and began.

"They say that you made a leap in your learning, Lee. It wasn't expected at this point but you've sort of transitioned to having your eyes opened or your awareness sort of jump-started so you recognize things differently now. They say you'll begin to remember things now and the learning of your skills and the tale will come much faster. In a way, it's what they've been waiting for."

My head was banging but I forced myself to sit up all the way. Each time I moved, my skin hurt as if I'd been badly sunburned all over. I rubbed my eyes in an attempt to clear the blur from my head and wished I hadn't touched my face.

"Jesus, my skin is killing me. What's going on? I have to do something. I need some...Cath, I have to get... I..."

Springing up from the couch, I ran to the bathroom and turned the water on cold and fast. Trying to take off my clothes without touching my skin, I gave up and just stepped into the tub and sat down splashing the water on myself as the tub filled. I contemplated turning on the shower to let the water flow over me but I thought even the force of the slow, Ireland shower would feel like needles on my skin and hurt too much so I satisfied myself by sitting and softly splashing while the tub filled up.

"Lee?" Nora knocked on the door "Can I come in?"

"Yeah. It's open." Nora came in the bathroom looking at me as if I had gone crazy but with concern in her heart.

"I'm okay." I said as she took a seat on the closed toilet. "I just needed to cool off. My skin is on fire. So, I fainted?"

"What do you remember?" She asked. Another knock on the door interrupted us. Cath called in for permission to enter the tiny room.

"Come in." I said feeling a little ridiculous sitting fully clothed in the tub of water. Cath entered with a glass jug of clear liquid in his hands and said nothing. He walked over to the tub and gently added it to the water already in there. Immediately I felt a tingling all over me as the burning began to subside. I dunked my head under and enjoyed the relief from the pain. Wiping my eyes and nose as I came up sputtering.

"What is that? It's working. God, thank you!" I sighed, and luxuriated with relief.

Finny came in without knocking carrying a cup of something and handed it to me with instruction.

"Drink!"

I did and felt infinitely better but began to feel silly sitting in the tub with an audience all staring at me waiting for me to say something. I looked at them and contemplated that I still saw them as the same people they were yesterday, but I had, if I wanted to, an option to see them in a different way as well. It was almost like putting on 3-D glasses and having the ability to see them more clearly and real-istically. I began to remember the shock of understanding and gaining memories from lifetimes past and felt gnawing fear, as my mind was flooded with history of other lifetimes.

A bit on overload, I avoided the inevitable.

"So what was in the jug, Cath, eye of newt?"

"No lass, just some water from the sacred spring of yer people. The spring upon the Hill by Lough Corrib still offers a drink and is said te have the healing qualities. It's the same water I offered ye on the forst day ye came te the shop."

"And the same as what I use for makin' tea and tinctures as well." Finny put in.

"What happened? Why was I burning?" I asked of Cath.

"People have different physical reactions when they've been opened te a new awareness. It seems that ye've had a wakenin' of yer understanding of the way things are. It's one thing te believe a particular thing, it's quite another te bear wit-ness te what ye believe. I've seen degrees of the wakenin' take place before and recognized yer energy spiral outward as yer awareness grew. What did it for ye? What was the point of yer new understandin'?"

I looked to Nora and told them what I'd seen.

"I saw you Nora, but I saw beyond you, to many others that have been you in past lifetimes. But in each of the lifetimes, you and I had been related or connected in so many different ways, but almost always together. Remember one time you had a dream that you told me we were on a Polynesian island and you were my mother there?"

She nodded.

"Well we were there. We learned worship and alchemy and respect for the Huna spirits and the land. We were there. Your name was 'Lo lani and mine was A'ia'i. Your dream was a memory. I know because I remember! And Cath's right; when you told me about the dream, I figured it was possible that it could have been something like another lifetime, but it's a whole different thing to actually have memories in my own head of so many different lifetimes. It's overwhelming. It's amazing. I feel like I've expanded somehow, grown, that I'm...I don't know...more."

I was silent then, and allowed my thoughts to percolate. Then, an intake of breath with an epiphany.

"I remember! Oh my God. I remember the Cauldron now. I remember! Oh, I know what they mean. The panels. I remember." Shooting up to get out of the tub, I sent volumes of water sloshing over the edge. "I can tell you Nora. I can show you. Oh. I know who you are!"

Cath grabbed my arm to support my wobbly stance."

Slow now. Slow and steady. Let's get ye some dry clothes and see te getting ye something te eat. It'll ground ye a bit te have something in yer belly. Finny?"

Cath directed the suggestion to Finny who agreed and headed for the kitchen to scare up some food. Nora had grabbed my other arm to steady me and I realized I was dripping water all over the floor.

"I'm okay. I'm okay." I reassured them. "Cath do you have a bathrobe or something I can wear until my clothes dry? Uh, you do have a dryer don't you?"

"Right." He said and left the bathroom with a glance to Nora that said, 'Stay with her.'

I didn't know if that meant he had a drier or not.

"Really Nora, I'm okay. Just let me get out of these clothes. I took a towel hanging on the rack and started to dry my hair. Cath returned with a decidedly feminine bathrobe and I assumed it was a preserved piece from the closet of his late wife, Evelyn. He hesitated and then handed the robe to me and with his other hand, shoved a mop at Nora and left abruptly. I took a tissue to blow my nose and then proceeded to peel off the wet clothes and wring them our over the tub as Nora mopped the puddles on the floor.

"You know," I said, pulling on the robe. "I have snippets of memories of the panels on the Cauldron. I have kind of a recollection of what they mean. But I also have a vague idea of what our job is in all of this. It's not all clear but we're supposed to somehow bring balance back to the world before it goes crazy with war and religion and pollution and raping of the earth. I know this but have no clue how we're supposed to do it. I just know that we're somehow supposed to use the Cauldron or keep the Cauldron to bring into the world what's needed to do the job." I untied the towel I had wrapped around my head and scrubbed my hair dry.

"You finished?" I asked Nora.

"Just about."

"Let's go get that food and take another look at the pictures of the Cauldron."

"You sure you're okay?"

"I think so." Slowly, I took inventory of how I felt. My skin no longer hurt. I saw my sister as I always had but upon concentrating on her, I could slip on those 3-D glasses and see beyond her physicality to her real self to who she is on the inside. I checked for any remnants of my headache and that seemed to have been replaced with a sense of well-being. "Actually, I feel pretty good. Let's go eat."

———

Listening to the mundane sounds of normal life as the drier tossed my clothes somewhere off the kitchen, I collected my thoughts. Sitting in Cath's dining room in a crispy cotton robe with delicate little wildflowers sprouting up from the waist.

"So," I started, "the Cauldron is a combination of symbolic iconography and a pictorial of actual events that had taken place; often both combined in one panel. But the entire Cauldron as a whole is also symbolic of the human condition as we know it in a way."

"Explain." Nora said around a bit of Irish bread with butter.

"Okay. Look at the photo. See these outside panels? They consist of three females and four males. Think. What do the numbers represent?"

Nora thought for only a moment until her face bore dawning realization.

"Oh, I see. The number three is typically identified with the feminine. Like in the tarot, the Higher Arcana card for the number III is the Empress. It's a wonderful depiction of female energy and speaks of matters of the spiritual. There is water in abundance in the card, which is decidedly female if you think, amniotic fluid. There's the symbol of Venus, also indicative of strong female energy, fertility, the life cycle is such that everything has a beginning, middle and end and the very existence of women is broken into three cycles: the maid or maiden, the time prior to her menstrual cycle, the mother, when she becomes fertile and able to reproduce, then finally, the wise woman or crone, after she no longer can bear children but is filled with the knowledge of her experience and learning. She's no longer physically fertile, but she's once again productive and fertile with an evolved spiritual awareness. A woman's ability to produce children empowers her because it's through her that the spirit enters the flesh and only through her that man is born. You can't have one without the other."

"And what about the number four? What does the Tarot say about number four?" I continued to prod her not only so she would understand what I was thinking but also so that I could deepen my awareness with Nora's know how of the symbols that just now started coming clear to me.

Nora took her cue. "Then the number IV card is the Emperor; he represents dominion over earth, manifestation, and the earth plane. As with the many things connected with the earthly plain, we tend to view them as coming in fours: the four seasons, the four directions, the four winds, the four elements, even the books that tell the story of the man proclaimed to be the Spirit come to the flesh, has been whittled to four, Matthew, Mark, Luke and John. Four men, I might add. In this card, the Emperor is vigilant to keep the balance of earthly things and things of the spirit. All too often, man can be lured to the delights of earthly pleasures and neglect things of the spirit. Man must rely on his intellect to remind him not only to abide by the laws of the earthly plain, but to keep divine law as well. The thing is, though, man often finds it difficult, if not impossible in his pursuits of earthly things, to maintain some modicum of spiritual balance. And so, comes the expression, 'It takes a woman to bring a man to God.' The human experience is only complete when the energy of both male and female come together; the flesh and the spirit, so to speak."

When it appeared that Nora had finished, I urged her to continue. With my new understanding of the message the Cauldron delivered, the analogy was not quite complete. "And?"

"And what?" she said.

"What is it that happens when the two numbers or energies come together?"

She hesitated with an expression of concentration on her face.

"The Chariot!" she blurted. "The number VII in the tarot deck. Three combined with four. The journey. The human struggle for balance. The coming together of the spiritual and the earthly. It is representative of the seven levels of the spirit as described in the seven chakras, the seventh, being the crown chakra. It is a card of action in making a decision as to which path to take. But despite the drive to do something, it also represents a time for reflection, rest and solitude to gain inspiration for which way to take action, which path to take, or whether to take action at all. In the card itself, the Chariot represents the human body being driven by the will of the spirit. At its best, it represents the aspiration to connect with something higher than the self, at its worst, it represents a wrong use of Power."

"Good." I responded. "This is the symbolism behind the seven panels on the outside of the Cauldron, the coming together of the male and the female, the body and spirit in balance and with purpose... a higher purpose. Of course, they each represent something more concrete as well, like the panel depicting Faidhe and her daughters in both their human and bird forms making the statement that the women would be connected to her in particular ways and would be representative of these particular animal energies for a purpose."

Cath agreed. "Right ye are lass. Have ye any indication as te the meanin' behind some of the other panels in the pot?

I thought for a bit trying to collect fragmented thoughts and snippets of cognition in connection with the other panels. My eyes slipped from focus on anything in the room and my thoughts turned inward to the images in my mind.

"Ah, yeah. There's the one with a woman with her arms folded. Her arms are folded because she'll do no more. She's gone over to the Otherworld. She, she surrendered herself for the greater good. She gave herself over for the sake of this guy."

I rustled the papers and pulled out the sheet with the panel to which I referred and another with the circular base plate, pointing.

"See this guy here, over her left shoulder? Well, he's the same as this guy here on the base plate; so he must be Laoghaire. She gave up her life, I think, for him. And this man over her right shoulder struggling with a lion that represents, Power or maybe the responsibility of Power...I think. Something like that. She passed on the Power or responsibility to him even though she knew he'd have to reconcile his instincts to use the Power to force things to his will with his innate qualities to assess and conquer through inspiration and innovation. She took it on faith that he'd overcome the urge to use this Power to seek revenge or to ease his personal situation."

I felt information flowing through me now and was soothed by the rhythm of talking. I felt myself shift into gear in what I came to think of, in my years of teaching classes, as academic speak. Picking up another picture and pointing to it.

"This panel is a depiction of Laoghaire's struggle with that very thing. See here, he has hold of two sides of himself. The figure over his right shoulder is shown with the dog of the Underworld at his feet. It represents, as you know, abuse of the Power by using it for personal gain or without due respect for all use of magic to be used with reverence for the sacred. That figure is touching a boar on the top of the panel. The figure over Laoghaire's left shoulder has a horse with wings under his feet. The horse is representative of freedom and one with wings, particularly so. The Pegasus, if you will, is offering Laoghaire freedom from the despair and misery of magic misused should he only choose to take the path of elevation or the high road so to speak. Obviously, this figure is touching a boar as well. The boar is representative of the problem Laoghaire must deal with, but it's not the task dealt him by the Powers that be. Laoghaire must choose how he'll deal with this boar: the Underworld or the high road. The boar comes to represent, in other areas on the Cauldron, a dark and malevolent force of energy. Without evil, we couldn't know good. Without free will, we could never rise to make the right choice, to right a wrong or to make mistakes. So the boar has its place in all of this."

Choosing another panel, I said, "This one is the third depiction of a woman. It is a woman in love and willing now to open herself up, as depicted here by her open arms, to the knowledge of a man. She wears a torque around her neck signifying that she is a woman of distinction. She will finally give of herself to the sexual rights and yet she is conflicted somehow between these two men."

As I was speaking, I was flooded with images in my mind and emotions that came as a torrent with the images. The story came to me on a river of feelings. Tears flowed freely down my cheeks and I felt the emotions of this woman being torn apart by her love for the men and a sense of deep disappointment and betrayal. I knew who this woman was on some level but I kept myself from fully acknowledging at the time the full truth behind this particular panel.

"So each of the people on the outer panels, the three women and the four men are a reference to an actual circumstance but they're also symbolic?" Nora reiterated for clarification.

"Seems so." I said.

"Did you guys know all of this?" She asked of the men.

"Aye, we did. We do." Replied Finny. "It'll make for much easier going now that ye've an understandin' of the depictions. And for the most part, there's little we can add that'll be of great importance."

"So how did you come to be the guys to carry all of this forward?" Nora blurted the question I'd been trying to figure the answer to myself.

"Yeah you guys, when I had my 'wakening' as you call it, I had a momentary glimpse of recognition but as my attention was drawn to other things, it's sort of faded from my mind. How did you become the ones to hold the story? Can you tell us?"

The brothers looked at each other and agreed with a nod.

Finny answered. "We'll tell ye as it's part of the tale anyway. But understand, we're not the focal point of the tale, we're just the tellers so if ye don't mind, ye'll not question us overmuch about our porsonal lives and such. Only as it pertains te the tale. We'll not have ye gawkin' and gapin' at us, if ye please. Just listen and lorn what ye may."

Duly warned, Nora and I flashed an amused look at each other and agreed. "We promise not to gawk and gape, so shoot." I said.

And they did.

29

The Brothers
Tell Their Story

*I*t had been a long trek indeed for the moon would be pregnant in three night's time and when Faidhe and her party set to the road, the moon had been hardly more than a sliver in the sky. They would enter the Middle Village by daybreak where Faidhe would, with discretion, ask favor of a few nights lodging in exchange for whatever services she and her party might offer. This would be careful business, for the Duibhe were not known for their hospitality. However, for their interest in coming out on the better side of a bargain, they were renowned. Despite the Duibhe's quality gemstones, silver and gold, their most viable means in trade for survival, barter had fallen off over the years due to the insular practices, the clan seemed to have become overly abrupt and abrasive, lacking decorum and social skills. Many simply feared going into the thicket and wood to come to Middle Village now for the reputation of strange goings on had grown like a legend around the Duibhe. In spite of all the rumors, once settled, Faidhe would put about her inquiries of her want of a storyteller but would keep her lips tight about her condition, the Cauldron and much else until an oath was taken by the weaver and teller of the tale so that there could be no trickery in the binding of the agreement.

It had been long since the east and west villages had been abandoned, a time out of memory in fact. For the convenience of travel from all the mountain ranges, Middle Village was the only remaining evidence seen above ground that the Duibhe had ever been a thriving community with myriad occupations. Now, but for a few, too old for the mines, left to plant and hunt food and even fewer storytellers, all the Duibhe clan depended on the mining and the trade of their wares for their livelihood. Though they were known to have exceedingly long life, the clan was slowly dying out for there were no longer any women of childbearing age to replenish the bloodlines.

As Faidhe, Lon Dubh and Iarann entered the outer limits of the village, they saw much in disrepair and many abandoned huts with sagging roofs and clumps of the dried out thatch missing. Many a smoke hole that back at home, would be writhing with smoke at this hour of the day, were cold with only a rain-washed memory of cooking char from the hearth. The place had a lonely feel to it and tempted one to pull his or her cloak about them as they entered. Upon the ground sat what appeared to be an idiot boy that had obviously been the product of a mating between the full blooded Duibhe and some other clan for he was not stocky with the gnarled and twisted musculature of the Duibhe, distorted and developed through centuries of heavy mining. Nor did the boy have the telltale low brow and bulbous nose of the Duibhe for his face was delicate and although small in stature, his body seemed to be of normal proportions. Lon Dubh looked at the boy who seemed to gaze right through her with his eyes but lent her a toothy grin just the same. She shivered and looked anxiously around for any signs of industry or hearth craft and found none. There were no typical sounds of village life to be traced only the sound of the clopping hooves of Iarann's road-worn packhorse.

As she drew her eyes away from the boy, Lon Dubh shuddered.

"Where is everyone? Do we enter the wrong village? I sense a feeling of despair here...mixed with, a desperate, grasping feeling. Do you sense it as well Iarann? Or am I just chilled and hungry and my spirit is disappointed at finding naught but a few straggling souls here to see to our task?" She instinctively reached out and took the blacksmith's giant hand.

"Nay Black Bird, you sense true." He said as he gave her hand a reassuring squeeze. "For I feel my heart drawn down with a heaviness that pulls me near to despair. Look at this boy here in rags, likely mindless for lack of teaching and care. Where are the elders? Where are those who would greet visitors? Where are the womenfolk at morning hearth-time? I see naught but one or two straggling curls of smoke above these hearth holes. This town is all but empty. Pardon my question Lady," he said to Faidhe. "But are you certain we have come to the village of which you spoke? For you did say it is a village of strength and riches. Did you not?"

Faidhe knew the seven clans of the Tuatha Duibhe would be coming from their respective mountain ranges to the Middle Village for the rights of the fully lighted night. The old rites were not abandoned even for the mining, which had become all-consuming to these clans; for the Tuatha Duibhe held fast to the wax and wane of the moon, sun and seasons for two reasons: to keep the blessing of a steady flow of jewels and gold from under the hills and to petition for new flesh to come to the clans so their blood would not die out.

"In three days' time," Faidhe answered, "you will see all there is of the Clans Duibhe. We will strike our bargain here and Lon Dubh will take one to her head and heart in order that the tale of our journey and our task will take on life. The bargain will be struck and sealed on the rising of the round moon. Lon Dubh, you must be on the watch during this and the next days for those who you find suitable as recipient of the tale."

"What will I look for?" The daughter replied. "How will I know from these strangers who is suited? Have you seen in the prophecy anything of a sign to guide me?"

Faidhe drew in a breath and sighed for patience.

"Question not, daughter. Just do. You must learn to trust that if it is yours to perform you will be given the knowledge when needed. Trust."

"Yes of course." Lon Dubh said certainly, feeling nothing of the kind. She startled as her eyes met with those of the boy they had seen seated on the earth by a dilapidated hut. He had silently followed them to beg as they walked through the village, Lon Dubh thought. But he asked for nothing; he seemed content just to follow along as though they were some kind of entertainment. For a town such as this, she reflected, that's probably what they are to him. Lon Dubh was taken aback when suddenly she felt a touch slip into her free hand and when she looked down; she saw the boy's grimy little hand in her own. Looking into his eyes again, Lon Dubh was surprised to see along with marked intelligence, pure contentedness and a simple expression of jubilation. The boy smiled his toothy grin and leaned his head onto Lon Dubh's arm in an obvious sign of affection.

"Get ye gone!" Iarann started.

But Lon Dubh, after a lifetime of loneliness and still basking in any kind of human interaction bid him, "Leave the boy alone. He means no harm. And besides, I think he is not accustomed to the face of a woman. He finds me comforting... I think."

"What of the face of yon Lady? She is for certain, a beauty. Why does he not trouble her so?"

Lon Dubh took Iarann's question to be evidence of his mild jealousy and was not displeased that he might feel as such. But she held her thoughts at bay.

"A beauty she is, for certain, but even you, close as we have been for the passing of almost a full moon cycle, have kept a respectful distance. It is that she emanates the Power and people sense that she is not one lightly approached. You have seen her project the face of the Goddess and it is most beautiful but awe inspiring and forbidding as well, is it not?"

"Aye, it is true." He admitted. "But beware that waif, or you will find yourself a-swarm with scalp bugs and naught but an itchy head for your kindness. It would be a sorry thing to see your raven hair shaved for the likes of yon imp."

Lon Dubh didn't want to reject the boy's friendliness and didn't see the telltale signs of the scalp bugs on the boy but released Iarann's hand and pulled her long black braid over her left shoulder, far away from the boy who, though he showed no evidence of any ability to speak, seemed to understand what Iarann had said and repaid him with a sulky expression that would have been right at home accompanied by a growl.

"Hey, ho!" Came a greeting in a gruff baritone voice. "Be ye friend? Or be ye foe?" An ancient Duibhe hailed the group as he rested against an oak tree under which one of the few obviously maintained huts was nestled.

Faidhe held up her open hand in greeting and returned the salutation.

"May the Gods bless your kith and kin, heart and hearth, crop and cattle." The eyes bore good humor but caution lurked there too and his hand could be seen to hover near an aged wood-ax that also leaned against the tree. The old man's eyes shifted from Faidhe to Iarann appraisingly scanned the horse and more intently, Lon Dubh before they slid back to Iarann whom he addressed.

"Ye are of strong stock. No mistake, sure yer almost double an outland man in size but have ye such a high opinion of yerself that ye'd need such fine horseflesh and two women all to yerself?"

Iarann was appalled at the reference to the women as if they were some kind of property and moved to have words with the Duibhe but Faidhe raised her hand to stay his response.

"We seek shelter and trade. Kindly man, know you of a hearth open to trade meat and drink for a song or story perhaps?"

The little man wheezed through his long, white beard that had yellowed from the intricately carved pipe clamped between his teeth.

"Do ye know where ye be woman? We've plenty enough stories that ye'll find naught to waste a trade of good meat and drink on another!"

His eyes twinkled now at the prospect of a trade that might prove to be good sport and he made the mistake of dismissing Faidhe as foolish to tip her bargain by letting it be known that she had little knowledge of the trading prowess of the Duibhe.

"But have ye any other skills we might be in need of, I'm sure a deal can be struck. What say you man? Have ye any special skills? Or better still, have ye anything worth a trade we may have interest in?" The squat man let his eyes take a lingering walk over Faidhe and Lon Dubh while he slowly grunted to his feet. "Mayhaps we have yet a bargain to be made. Mayhaps we do." The man stepped closer to Lon Dubh.

Iarann was insulted at the inference and grew agitated.

"See and hear me now!" He thundered. "We are not beggars and these are women of the Tuatha..."

"Thank you Iarann." Faidhe broke in and gave Iarann a look that said, 'Be still.' Turning to the Duibhe, decidedly shifting the attention to her and her daughter as those with the trade in mind.

"My man offered you no insult. We are women in search of a trade for lodging, meat and drink, sir. If you be not the one we should strike with, then please, if you will, direct us to one who is and we will trouble you no more."

Iarann, feeling slightly bruised at being cut off, understood that Faidhe did not want to reveal their position or their purpose until she was sure it was the proper time and with a well-chosen recipient. He stepped back and was silent as he observed the scene before him.

Faidhe inspected the small man's threadbare clothing and was inspired.

"I think there is much we have to offer for spinning of wool and skin-crafting are only a portion of skills we can trade. So if a story does not suit, perhaps some clothing or healing simples will protect against the cold and ailments of all kinds. Will you direct us to who might be pleased of these services? Or shall we send the boy to find those who will be grateful for a trade of these goods and assistance?"

The old Duibhe scowled at the prospect of losing first bid at a trading opportunity and gave the boy a threatening look. Shrewdly, the old man pasted a congenial look on his face and offered to bring the party where they might find a meal and some ale.

"Are ye passin' travelers with the risin' of the sun or will ye be takin' our hospitality at least until the moon rites."

The innocent enough question could not hide his lascivious appraisal of Lon Dubh once again. Iarann understood that the moon rites would also involve sexual rites and stepped between Lon Dubh, who still held the boy's hand, and the Duibhe. Bending down close to the small man's face, Iarann asked in a low rumbling tone,

"Is it your own meat and drink you offer us?" Unaffected, the squat man returned the glare and stated, "Either way, be it mine or be it not, ye've need of me te lead ye te where it may lie. So if ye've a mind te do me harm, sir, 'tis a far stretch te the end of Tuatha de Duibhe territory. I think ye'll not find it a pleasant trek wi' the likes of the clan at yer heals."

Iarann's countenance grew looming and terrible at the threat and now the Duibhe did take an uncertain step backwards shifting his attention to Faidhe who was watching Iarann's energy take on an uncharacteristic maroon color with kinetic sparks running through it.

"Woman!" The Duibhe said, "I am Diog, of the Tuatha Duibhe. Clan Do-pib, I offer no insult, only to lead you whence you may find the trade you seek. But surely you must know that a woman such as yourself or that of your companion here will be worth a mighty price indeed to our clan. We seek not to trade in servitude, only in service. Should you find it convenient to idle here but for a short while, only long enough to bear and wean fresh stock for our clan, you will be treated as royalty and after only a short interruption, sent about your journey, laden with such riches as you've likely never seen."

Satisfied now that she had been recognized as the leader of the group and that Faidhe was the one with whom negotiation would be made; she finally directed her attention to the newly introduced Diog. "Have a care not to assume that the life of royalty is a temptation and neither should you assume that we seek riches beyond that which we request. You tip your trade too soon friend. For it seems you are in need of what we may offer a great deal more than the reverse. I'm sorry we are not able to accommodate your needs for I am priestess to the Goddess's Circle and may not lay with a man for reasons other than for her purpose and would that I could, no man's seed planted in my womb at this juncture will make a babe, for the Goddess has given me other direction. And my companion is sworn virgin to the Goddess as well. She will not relinquish that which she has not been bidden by the Goddess to do. While I feel sorrow for your plight, we cannot strike this trade. I offer your clans comfort of spun wool and healing remedies; and perhaps some hearth craft as well to breathe life back into your village so that it might attract to it the type of population you seek. Do I miss my mark, sir, in presuming that it is childbearing women you require?"

His face reddened for having been so smoothly duped out of his bargaining upper hand, Diog grudgingly admitted that the primary goal of his clan, beyond mining for riches is to find suitable women with whom to mate and carry on the bloodstock of the Duibhe.

"Aye." He admitted. "Tis our purpose as even our young ones are well past their middle life and the new ones we've bred," he said with a wave toward the boy, "are of Elf mixture and have neither the strength for the mines nor the will required to dwell overlong in the darkness. We thought the mixture a wise one, as they have longer life than the other outland clans as do we, longer even than us, but they care not for industry, only for frivolous endeavors such as music, green things or watchin' the skies. All but useless to the Duibhe." He said this last with a click of his tongue.

Lon Dubh looked at the boy and was surprised to see Diog's exact expression on the young boy's face. She laughed outright when he imitated the tongue click to perfection. In a flash the boy was away flipping back on his hands to feet over and over, light and fast as a buck to get away from the old Duibhe who sought to rescue his dignity by clouting the boy for his insolence. The boy stopped flipping, whooped and hooted with a gleeful hop at the old man's anger adding a few extra tongue clicks for good measure before disappearing into the underbrush at the edge of the woods.

"Damn Elven blood. Those whelps are good for nothin' but hidin' amongst the trees and stealin' food. Be watchful of those ones, sure. They'll steal what ye have even if they've naught use for it themselves."

"My sling!" Lon Dubh gasped; checking herself with her hands to discover what else might be missing. "My knife!" She looked toward where the boy had disappeared into the forest line and saw nothing but heard a whoop of laughter echoing through the trees.

———

Diog led the party to a vacant hut and instructed them to remain there while he announced their arrival and made arrangements for food and fortifications.

"I trust him not." Fumed Iarann as he tied the horse to a low branch of a tree nearby the hut.

"He will do as he said he would." Faidhe comforted. "I have seen it in his energy. Though he liked not negotiating with a woman after many seasons of only men making decisions and structuring their laws. I see it has become a point of pride for these lonely souls, for it is better to reject that which you cannot attract to soothe the pain of being rejected. What better way to dismiss a hurt than to render the inflictor insignificant? We will meet challenges here abouts but I think the choice to plant seeds for the tale here first will prove wise."

Lon Dubh looked around the interior of the abandoned hut and marveled at the haste with which someone left the encampment. There were flint stones waiting to spark a fire, and there were several carved bowls bearing evidence of dried oat-mush. She lifted an old drinking bladder and convulsed with retching almost to vomiting when she'd sniffed the spoiled goat milk it contained.

"Oh! Sickening! What manner of place is this? Is there no order or sense of purity? It is no mystery, if this is how these people live, that they attract no women, for one must be pure of heart and mind and body to pay honor to the Gods. These wretches have been consumed by greed for gems and gold and have all but forgotten the spirit and basic cleanliness. I wonder at the illness we might suffer from putrid food and drink. If this is what the future of masculine dominance holds in store, perhaps it is best they do not continue their line! Perhaps the Goddess has seen fit that these Duibhe should not continue in light of what is decent!"

"Careful daughter. These are dangerous words you utter. For if you do not agree with how others live, it does not give you leave to decide they are not worthy to live. As a servant of the Goddess, it is our lot to help all others learn how they may improve and how else they may choose to do things, for it may only be due to lack of understanding or options that these men have taken to the hills for their survival. Perhaps what they need is not condemnation but information. Can you teach by example, daughter?"

"I can. But will they learn? If this Diog is an example of the people here, I do not think they will be over eager to take instruction from a woman."

"Then you shall learn as well daughter for you must find a way to encourage these people to live and breed for it will be their charge, 'one of their blood' to carry the tale. This I have seen in the prophecy. My mind and heart tell me that the life of the story that must carry forward must be planted here first. Only then shall we quest in earnest for the other chosen places to plant the seeds of the story you must proliferate. Feel you the need for the first casting to be here?"

"I know not what my feelings be, Mother. I must search for my place in all this. Though we have traveled this whole moon cycle, and I have devoted much contemplation on my task, I have not yet been granted clear vision on my duty in this. I have *need to quiet my mind to listen to my heart. But I do not think I can conduct clear thought in environs such as these." She looked around with a sneer of distaste.*

"Ye must come wi' me now." A gruff voice came from the crooked doorway to the hovel. Ye must be seen by the chieftains in three days' time for any bargains te be struck. It seems yer te be honored guests until the High Seven reach Middle Village from the mines so as a decision can be made as te what we're te do wi' ye. Come ye this way." He looked at Lon Dubh with a cool expression of one who's been insulted and she wondered how much of her comments he had heard.

He turned abruptly and walked with purpose without looking back to see if they followed. His strong gate looked somehow comical on one so squat. Lon Dubh couldn't help but smile at the dignified waddle and immediately regretted her comments.

Diog led the party a short distance down a once well-traveled path, now beginning to be lost under wood growth. They came to a large hut that appeared to be four rounded huts combined into one large hut so that the structure resembled a clover plant with four sides. The assembly was in fairly good condition so that Lon Dubh held out hope that they would not be housed in the squalor they had just witnessed. Her hopes were dashed upon entering the first section of the quartered hut that was in much worse disarray than the last. Encountering an overwhelming odor of rotted food or decay of some sort she covered her nose and moaned. "Oh!"

With a swipe of his arm, Diog cleared a corner of the table situated in the center of the hut by knocking drinking vessels which held half evaporated and molded liquid and wood bowls caked with grime onto the floor. He then placed a woven basket on the table and bowed mockingly at Lon Dubh waving his hand toward the basket.

"Yer food. As for the drink, I've farther to travel for that. Ye'll wait here in the hut of the High Seven until their return in three days. I trust ye'll be comfortable." He waited expectantly for a response, almost daring them to complain.

"This will be, uh, we uh, thank you for your hospitality, Diog. We appreciate your kindness." Lon Dubh said in absence of her mother saying anything, and in light of the fact that Diog was obviously addressing her.

"Oh, and one more thing." Diog said removing a folded swath of material from under his arm. "Let's see if yer mending skills are worth a trade." He whipped the cloak at Lon Dubh, which she caught in one hand without flinching. "Enjoy yer meal for it's not likely ye'll see another from us until we can judge yer skills." Then he was gone.

Lon Dubh said as she inspected the contents of the food basket, "It seems I've insulted our host. I must resolve to keep my comments at my own counsel for one can never know when such words will fall to into ears where they can cause insult or pain."

"Then, Black Bird, it was worth the trouble if it is a lesson learned." Faidhe told her.

Iarann came nearer Lon Dubh to inventory the content of the basket. Reaching in, he pulled up two small, stale loaves of bread, and a strip of salted, dried salmon. His face showed indiscrete outrage that these women should be treated so.

"It is but a small thing Iarann." Faidhe said, reading his expression. "Lon Dubh must have time to contemplate and discern her direction in all of this. We shall give her leave to do so by gathering the gifts of the forest for our own sustenance as we have done since we left our home by the lough. Goddess and the wood have ample gifts to offer. Let us collect them. Lon Dubh you remain here and open your mind and heart to search for the one who will bear our story. Use your intuition daughter and find the one for whom you seek. And kindle your mending skills." Faidhe added as she gestured to the rag of a cloak in her daughter's hands. Lon Dubh's eyes grew wide but she said nothing and nodded.

"We've need of your fishing basket, Black Bird. Perhaps we can bring up some fresh salmon to aid you in your thinking task." Iarann tried to sound encouraging as he rummaged through her sheepskin pack to pull out the pliant net-like basket woven of sturdy but supple fighe vine. "We shall feast soon enough." He promised and kissed her on the forehead.

"Do not be over long." She pleaded, not liking the sound of the whine in her own voice. For, though she had spent much of her life in solitude, she had never been far from another member of her Tuath and had never been within the bounds of a foreign clan, much less alone. She found the taste of fear strange and unpleasant.

"We will be as long as we will be daughter." Faidhe answered. Lon Dubh did not feel encouraged. "Iarann and I shall leave you to find your way then." The older woman called back as Iarann untied the packhorse to once more take to the woods.

After the two travelers left her, Lon Dubh tried to calm her fears by organizing what must be done. First, she thought, if we are to be quartered here in this oversized hovel I have need to cleanse my surroundings so my mind may be at peace to search for my direction. She set to work cleaning the table, which was made of a rough-hewn oak trunk, split in half and rested upon a grouping of stones. It is most unusual for a hearth-hut to have a table such as this, she mused. This structure, set off in the woods, is large and would accommodate many. I wonder what purpose it served back when there was life in the village.

It took the better part of the morning and early midday, but Lon Dubh had organized what appeared to be an eating hall under all the rubble and refuse. Certainly miniscule compared to the great dining hall of Lon Dubh's own Tuath, but an efficient one, nonetheless. She followed her nose and the scent of water to a nearby spring and made several trips hauling water back to the hut to soak the bowls and drinking vessels in a large pot she'd found in another quarter of the hut. When she realized that soaking would not cleanse the caked on muck that covered the bowls, she kindled a fire under the pot and easily scraped the viscous grime away after being boiled a while.

She was intrigued to find this separate room for cooking with a double hearth: one with an arm for boiling and over the other, a large spit for meat. Between large round stacked portions of tree trunks cut for the purpose, were hewn planks that created shelving for storage of food stores, bowls, stirring sticks, salt and other cooking materials. Some herbs and foreign smelling substances were carelessly forgotten on the shelving, thick with dust and pollen and would have, no doubt, been rancid or ransacked by woodland animals and rats, had they not been kept in pottery bowls, covered and sealed with beeswax. Someone, at one time had taken great care in this kitchen.

Lon Dubh stacked the newly cleaned bowls and vessels on the shelving after she'd scrubbed clean the pantry, and organized the herbs and spices near to the boiling hearth for easy access. Taking a newly cleansed wooden bucket that had obviously, at one time held some kind of ale by the yeasty smell to it, she went back to the spring several times to refill the large hearth pot with clean water for drinking and cooking. They would have to use the pot for all she had was one bladder to contain water and she dared not open, much less use any bladders she found in the hut after her last experience. Opting to load all the items she thought could not be used onto the old cloak Diog had given her to mend, she dragged them to where, once again, her nose led her to what appeared to be a latrine at one time, but had more recently been used as a waste dump. One by one she offloaded trash, broken potteries, unidentifiable food refuse, and bladders, both full and empty and buried them using the shovel left there for that purpose but judging from the dumping area, no one seemed overly concerned about burying the refuse. After leaving the waste dump, she began to fill the cloak with small firewood and kindling. Once she'd loaded on all she thought the cloak would bear, Lon Dubh dragged the wood back to the hut and stacked it under the end of the shelving nearest the hearths.

She then set to work constructing a sturdy broom of fallen birch branches for they are close and supple and suited to the task. Using a bowstring from her pack, she bound the branches to a solid stick handle, and let her mind wander while sweeping and scrubbing filth she did not care to speculate as to what it was. As she swept, Lon Dubh could feel the pleasure of accomplishment rise within her. She allowed her sense of joy to spiral up from the earth as she whirled round and round to clean the floors.

Remembering that she had a task to perform beyond the rhythm of cleaning, she set her mind to concentrate on who her recipient would be to begin her tale. She swirled and tried to envision the face of the one with whom she'd connect, 'heart and mind' as her mother had put it. Blank...nothing, she swirled and swept, swept and swirled, trying to conjure an image, a hint, a clue as to what she must do. (Swirl.) Nothing still. Round again. The broom swished and touched down, as she twirled again. Faster and around again. She pushed all her energy into her thought. Trying to bring up an image as if from the earth itself. (Swirl, swirl, swish.) She felt herself rise from the earth as she turned and thought rationally that she had worked too hard and had not eaten, now the spinning that she could not seem to stop, nor did she want to, had made her light as a feather not only in her head but her body as well. She felt a swelling of energy within her and as it reached a climax, the vision of a face shown behind her closed eyes. Then, nothing.

———

Lon Dubh woke to the face she'd envisioned however it bore an expression of panic and concern. The face was shaking in and out her field of vision and then came the realization that it was she who was being violently shaken back and forth. Hearing strained whoops and hoots that sufficed for language; she recognized the face of the boy who'd stolen her sling and knife.

With surprising strength, he pulled her upright to a sitting position and pointed furiously to the front of the hut through the dining hall. In perfect imitation, he put on the expression he'd used earlier to mock Diog and clicked his tongue.

"Diog is coming?" She asked?

A whoop, jump and a nod answered her question.

"Do you know why?"

Nod.

"Am I in danger?" She asked with growing panic of her own.

Shrug. Then he gave her a chill when he mimed with his hands a great pregnant belly and pointed to Lon Dubh's own midsection.

That was all she needed to spur her to her feet. Dizzy, hungry and a bit shocked, she was unsteady and the boy took her arm around his shoulder to shore her up. Again, she was surprised at his strength but reminded herself that this boy is half Duibhe, and they are very strong indeed. That got her moving at the thought that Diog might mean her harm but the boy gave a few muted hoots and urged her into one of the two rooms she had not yet explored. It was filled with several sleeping biers as if for a war encampment or a large family. The stale smell of the room hit her in the face and she turned to the boy.

"There is no way out here. We cannot hide, he will find us." The boy pulled her to the very far wall and knelt down pushing a panel of woven saplings aside to create a small door of sorts. He gave her one last look and was gone through the space. The sound of the door to the hut being pushed back abruptly, got Lon Dubh moving right behind the boy who waited only for a moment until he saw her and gestured that she follow him into the woods, which she did.

Once behind a thicket of brush, the boy nimbly scrabbled high up a giant oak tree that was only 20 paces behind the hut. He turned to urge her to follow but Lon Dubh had not climbed trees since she was a girl and it was a foreign concept to her but this boy lived and survived with the Duibhe. He obviously knew this territory better than she. Not to be outdone, she picked her way up the knots on the trunk and up the branches to join the boy. She concentrated on climbing up behind him, careful not to misstep, and moments later found herself sitting in a platform built in the crook of two giant branches. Her view was of the backsides of two boys who were peering out through a lookout cleverly designed of leafy branches and virtually invisible to anyone on the ground. Lon Dubh was immediately reminded of Diog's words 'Elf blood' he said. No wonder their nature was to take to the trees, she thought.

Reaching out, she gently tugged on the rags that served as a tunic to get her rescuer's attention. He turned to her and pointed to the lookout. She came forward to have a look and as the boy moved aside for her and she was impressed by the construction of the lookout as its placement was strategically designed so that the angle gave her a perfect view through the hearth-hole right into the hut's kitchen.

Lon Dubh wondered at how long these boys had lived life like this, on the periphery of this dead town, keeping hidden and yet surviving without being forced to the mines. Just then she stopped breathing as she saw Diog enter the kitchen with a look on his face that was half annoyance, half wonder as he inspected the work she'd completed on the hut. Just then, he saw the cloak he'd thrown at her not repaired and some worse for wear. His face gathered gloomily into a frown as he tossed the cloak aside and stormed out of the kitchen. Moments later, he could be seen exiting the hut through the dining hall, obviously angered that either she was not there or that she had not yet taken to mending his cloak. Either way, she was glad she was not there when he'd come.

"Why did he come?" She asked of either boy, not expecting an answer. "Surely he did not mean to harm me. How could he have known I'd be without protection?"

For the first time, Lon Dubh acknowledged that there were two boys: her rescuer, whom she met before and another who bore almost an identical face to the first. The second boy turned and spoke in a voice so sweet it almost sounded like music or singing to her.

"He's kept watch all day. He watched you, we watched him. He saw your family leave and followed them for two fingers of the sun, then, when he was sure they were far enough gone, he came back."

"Do you suppose he wanted to do me harm?"

"Suppose? No. Know? Yes. He is crafty and cannot be trusted. Even the others no longer allow him to the mines. He is shamed for bringing the mark of a hoarder onto the clan Do-pib and he works to repair his name with the Chieftain Do-pib. Perhaps to bring new blood to the clan, an offering of flesh. He is lustful, that one. He is not above trickery to bring a woman to do his bidding. Our mother fell to his bargaining and gave birth to us but he would not release her because he said we are no good to him if we cannot mine for the Tuath."

"Release her? She is captive?

365

"No. She is dead. She gave up her immortality to be released from her promise rather than to break her vow. She promised to give Diog either a daughter for breeding or a son to the mines and he would not release her for we are obviously not female and are no good to the task of mining. Being underground away from the sun and the air brings us near to death and useless with a pick or a shovel. He said we did not fulfill her promise and she must bear him children until one is good for breeding or to the mine. After two children, our mother realized that Diog only meant to keep her here, captive to his wants and needs, a slave to his lust."

Lon Dubh's heart wrenched for the boys. *"I'm sorry for you. You are brothers then. What are your names?"*

"I am Fion and this is Cathbad." He pronounced this last name, 'Cat-baud.' *"My brother does not speak with his mouth much but he studies everything, understands much and knows plenty."*

"Thank you for helping me." Lon Dubh said sincerely and with a slight chill looked back over her shoulder toward the path she'd seen Diog take.

———

"So wait a minute." Nora interrupted. "You're saying that these elves are your ancestors? You're saying that there really are elves? Or were...you have actual Elf blood in you?" She was trying to get a handle on the reality that this great underworld of fantasy that had occupied our childhood had been confirmed. Trying to reel herself in, she tried not to gawk and stare as they had warned us not to do. "I mean" this is incredible. Isn't it Lee?" She said just now remembering that I was in the room. "These guys are descendants of actual Elves!"

"And dwarves." I said, still entranced in the mood of the story.

"Huh?" Nora questioned.

"The Clan, Duibhe, is the tale of what has been told and retold over the years about the Dwarves. Right?" I said allowing my eyes to focus on the people in the room, as I found my way back from the tale. "Mining and gems and living underground. The Duibhe are what we know as Dwarves, right? You have Elf blood and Dwarf blood; am I right?" I was more insistent this time. I could feel tears streaming down my face and my heart was twisting in my chest as understanding dawned on me. "Only you're not *descendants* of Fion and Cathbad, are you?" I was sobbing now and Nora left her chair to sit with me on the couch where I'd settled in for the telling of this part of the tale. "You aren't souls that I recognized like Nora and I who've passed through life after life with a beginning, middle and end. You've been waiting and living all of these years for us, for *me* to come along. You've been waiting with this message for thousands of years. You *are* Fion and Cathbad, aren't you?" I was filled with wrenching sorrow for what these men must have experienced. "Oh my God, what has your life been like, never living with your own kind, never fitting in, seeing whole generations come and go. Evelyn. Oh Cath, your Evelyn. She was just mortal like us and you had to watch her grow old and die. How many lifetimes have you watched everyone you care about go away? I can't bear the thought that you have suffered so much for so long and had to watch the world move on to a time when all is lost to the sacred world you tried for so long to save." Outright blubbering now I was inconsolable that these dear men should have suffered so long.

Cath said, "Not lost; only forgotten for a while." He laid a gentle hand on my arm. Instantly my sorrow was quieted but not broken.

"You were there to help me then and you were the ones I was so connected to when I felt so lost and alone. How could I have forgotten about you?"

Finny explained. "It was best. Such emotional baggage, so te speak would have been overmuch te bear, comin' in te each life knowin' about the last. Ye lorned what ye did and kept it te yer soul. That way, ye'd only have te remember, when the time came. Ye both know the secrets of a magical existence; it's time fer ye now te remember all. We've been over cautious about the Beast and that's a force ye'll have te deal with, sure, but what yer role is in all this is te bring light te the world; light of knowledge in preparation for balance. So feel for us what ye may for it hasn't been easy, but know that we've spent this time in waiting and preparation for a porpose and we'll not see it defeated now. So now," he said with an air of finality, "get yer mind back te the tale so ye have an understandin' te be movin' te the meat of yer task."

"Wait!" Nora interrupted with the exuberance of one who is experiencing a light bulb moment. "The Duibhe, you said means darkness. Right? And there were seven chieftains, one for each mountain in the area that's now, what, Cork? County Cork?" The men nodded. "Are you saying what I think you're saying?"

The brothers nodded in silence. Cath added, "We told ye that the story had been perpetuated in many different ways through the centuries. Every time the tale is told, any version or any portion, it charges the energy behind the magic cast te bring us te this moment. So as many a story ye can think of that may fit within this tale, or any details ye recognize, as incredible as it seems, has added and is adding te the energy ye'll be needin' te apply te yer task; whenever and however that may come about. There's the Arthurian legend come te light in the 12th century just at the same time the Christian Mary, was recognized and bolstered as important in the written version of the Christ story."

"The Christ story! You mean the Bible?" I inquired. Part of this story is in the Bible?"

Finny nodded in ascent. "Aye, there's quite a tale te be sure. There're many things less well known about the beginning of Christianity that held the Goddess's truth but were either changed or removed so that women held a secondary role of servitude or appeared to, as the decisions were made about what stayed in the Bible and how it might be interpreted. So, through the centuries, residual energy from the Old Ways ebbed and flowed and women and the Goddess alternately were Powerful and deeply involved in the manifestation of Christianity and then they were deemed unimportant, unfit or in the most flagrant case of Mary Magdalene, dismissed from being the equal partner in the new teaching as a prostitute. Yet with all that's come te light with that particular part of the tale recently in publications such as The DaVinci Code, The Laughing Jesus, Jesus and the Lost Goddess and so many more, ye can practically feel the energy swirlin' about ye as these old fabrications designed solely te protect the masculine dominance and power over the mass of Christians begins te erode. People are beginnin' te seek the truth. An example is the little known that women were the first te celebrate the communion with bread and wine as we mentioned before. So in effect, they were the first priests as kitchen duties fell te the women in the communities so bread and wine were blessed and sorved by the women until men came along and appointed themselves as bishops te take over the duties and decided that it was no longer a ritual te be held in the domestic setting as Christ had forst intended. This knowledge is just now comin' te light as people begin te resorch for themselves. Even the much hidden knowledge that all the Christian holidays and rituals are based on orlier, so called Pagan rituals, is beginning te be common knowledge. But we knew some time back that energy was on the rise and would be more than a surge in the wakening of peoples' understandin; it would be a wakenin' passionate, wholehearted wakenin' te the truth of things so that we knew the time for the tellin' of the tale had come. We knew te keep our eyes open for ye and have been waitin' since the 19th century."

"Aye," Cath added. "Look at the timin' in all this even without considerin' the Bible itself. When the very fairytales came once again te the public beyond folklore and folktales, was in the 19th century. Right about the time we started te see a permanent change in women's rights and politics in yer country. The Brothers Grimm, and Hans Christian Anderson, were offerin' more than the entrepreneurial spirit when they wrote down and published their collections of stories; patriarchalized, sanitized and Christianized as they were, they did the trick of resurging energy te the tale. Then, later on, ye'll find that Edgar Allan Poe was useful in this respect but in a varied way. And later still, yer beloved Walt Disney helped in these past five or six decades tremendously with the making of several films for people, especially children, te see over and over sparking imaginations: the birthing place of magic. These pioneer storytellers are receptive to the energy of the story and find their own way of spinning the tale without even knowing that they were part of the process."

The mention of Poe caught my attention. "What else besides my name did Poe have to do with this?" I asked. "I thought it was just a poetic reference that created the circumstances for my name."

Cath fielded this one. "If ye've ever read his works, ye may have noticed that in addition te his dark flair for the dramatic, he's definitely got a grasp on the mystical and makes reference te mythology as well as the mysterious and fantastic. If ye'll take a book of his works and thumb through some of his titles, ye'll mark that this was a receptive soul, a misfit in his own life, as ye'll recall ye've been through many of yer own lives. We've no way of knowin' for sure but we'd suspected that he was one of the chosen ones te live many lives throughout the centuries. For he hits upon too many of the ideas and truths of the tale in his works te be a coincidence."

Nora and I responded in unison to Cath's statement. "The chosen ones?"

"Aye lassies. Look te his works. Among the titles ye'll find the likes of *The Island of the Fay, Mystification, The Angel of the Odd, The Power of Words, A Tale of Ragged Mountains, The Raven, Lenore, The Sleeper* and more te ignite the idea that there's a recognizable connection to anyone with but an inkling of the knowledge. And beyond the titles, there're several works that give forther indication: *A paean, Evening Star, The Lake To-* and several others. If one looks, a knowing, whether he was aware of it or not, a knowing was there. And he fits the pattern of folks who have lived life apart from the whole in general. So we speculate, but who knows which member of yer family he may have been."

"What?" My head swiveled so fast it literally made a snapping sound. "What do you mean? Our family? Are you saying we're related to Edgar Allan Poe too? That can't be." I argued.

Finny broke in. "What Cath means te say, is not that yer blood related to the writer, but that along the line of history, it's likely that this man, with this knowin' is one of the original eight souls, chosen te come through time and be a part of the mosaic of this tale. As ye've come through time together, so have members of yer family, chosen in the beginning te make the trip back several times until such time as it is right for all eight te come together as a blood family once again. So it's more than possible but likely, that Poe was one of the original eight and that would mean that he'd be one of yer current family members now. Is there any who might have the gift of words?"

I looked at Nora and then to Cath. We all knew who would fit the criteria but once again, Nora and I said in unison, "Dad."

I explained to Finny, "Our dad has always had a gift with words. Poetry, specifically, is how our father has always expressed himself, his emotions and his musings on the world. He loves language and has an appreciation for anyone who can create, using wordplay as the medium. He's always admired Poe's work. He's the one who chose one of Poe's poems to give me my name." Warming to the idea now I said, "In fact, he knew lots of Poe's works by heart."

"Maybe he was just remembering." Nora said in a soft voice.

A creeping dawning was hammering at the back of my mind. Logic was not allowing me to gloss over what Cath and Finny were finally telling us about our past and our family. I was afraid to ask the question but powerless to keep it to myself. Against my better judgment, my mouth asked the question that I wasn't sure my heart was ready to have answered.

"So if Nora is Colm, and I'm Lon Dubh, does that mean our mother is Faidhe? And if our father was Poe, then who was he in the original tale? And who are our other sisters? Our family only makes six people; who are the seventh and eighth?" Now that I allowed my mind to go there, it flooded with what seemed like hundreds of questions but before I could continue, Cath cut me off.

"Well now. Ye've come right te the point. Haven't ye." He nodded with approval. Don't forget yer grandmother, come through with her name te be the harbinger of things te come. But beyond that one, there's a cortain other marker that was indicated in the prophecy that Faidhe cast as part of the final magic te set all in te motion. The passage goes like this:

At the time in space when the wheel is turned,
Sigrdifa comes through when darkness is spurned

At the forst harvest, when the summer wanes
The pair comes te the flesh te spark borthing pangs

Of the Laoghaire still so named, at the spoke of the milking lamb
Who takes union with the elder coming at the spring tide - fish and ram

They borth the forst who comes with a debt
On the day of the Lugh, this one is met

The next is come through, the worker of ore
On the eve when between worlds, opens the door

Then comes one marked by the Beast
Borne to this time on the bulls own feast

Lastly the one holds the light and the knowledge together within
She will complete the corcle, to set it te spin

As the hub that unites and brings the wheel complete
And precise is the time when the task is replete

Open is the balance when the light's strength takes sway
To complete the wheel and birth the sun's long ray.

The child brings vast change as the great wheel spins.
And the Fifth Civilization is ushered, as maturity begins."

I recognized some of the characters through the story Cath and Finny had been telling us and some from the memories that were coming back to me in snippets from that other lifetime. Still finding this long distance memory a bit disconcerting, I struggled to fathom that these people from the tale were actual members of my family. Somewhere, someone started a boulder rolling down hill and I was helpless to stop or control it in any way. It seems, now that we've opened this door, there is no closing it. *Can't un-ring the bell.* I thought.

I rubbed my face hard with my hands and reached for a pen and paper from my satchel.

"Can you say that again Cath slowly so I can write it down and we can try to decipher it?" When he repeated the poem, Nora and I sat together on the couch staring at the words; both of us hesitating to say anything aloud for fear that saying something, anything would make that boulder tumble down the hill even faster. Then a thought occurred to me. "Hey, if this is part of what you said was a spell, cast by Faidhe to bring these people back into this time all together, why does it rhyme in English?"

"Very astute of you." Cath responded. "Ye've seen the orlier vorsion of this work in The Power of the Word only it's written in an archaic form of the Irish. It's one of the quirky magical knots tied into all that's taken place. These words, spoken by Faidhe all these years ago did not have the rhythm as ye've hord here but in translation, almost as if she'd spoken the words directly to the future language, as might have been a clue te us as te where yer family'd come through in time. For the words don't rhyme in the other parent countries either, only in English. But being that England actually had a role te play in all of this as sort of a receptacle for the keepin of all the information, if ye will, we couldn't have known it'd be America where ye'd hail from. Now, te work so we can get back te the tale. Let's have a look at the piece so ye can figure who's who in yer family."

"Okay." I said, sharing the poem with Nora. This one's obviously Nana, Sigrid/ Sigrdifa but what does it mean she comes through when darkness is spurned?"

Nora mused, "Well, she was born in 1899 at the turn of the century. What was going on in history when she was born? Wait! That's it. When she was born!" She shouted. "Nana was born on the winter solstice! The longest night of the year but then the days start to get longer from there, so 'darkness is spurned!' Maybe this is where our birthdays come into play."

I sat dumbfounded for a moment and came to life when I recognized the significance of my family's unusual birthday patterns.

"You're right! The birthdays! Let's see." I said grabbing at the written poem, reading the next lines to put the newfound information to the test. "Okay, here it is. 'At the first harvest, when summer wanes.' First harvest, that's the fall equinox. Both Grandma and Grandpa were born on the fall equinox; same day, same year, different counties in Ireland." I shared with Cath and Finny. "We always thought it was just meant to be that they would be together that they'd made the journey to earth on the same day together and found each other in their teens to spend the rest of their lives together. Born on the same day, do you suppose they were the twins?" I asked rhetorically, having already made up my mind that I was correct in my assuming. "Who's next?" I asked Nora, who had recaptured the paper from me and was studying the poem.

"Wait," she said, poking a single finger into the air directing me to let her read. "The second line to Grandma and Grandpa is part of the clue. It says, 'At the first harvest when the summer wanes, the pair comes to the flesh to spark birthing pains...Of the Laoghaire.' So it must mean they gave birth to whomever Laoghaire came in as. ...At the spoke of the milking lamb. The spoke refers to the wheel they talk about in the poem that must be the wheel of the year?"

"That's what I thought." I said. "The Celtic wheel of the year." Consisting of four fire or sun festivals and four moon festivals, eight markers creating balance between seasons and masculine and feminine throughout the year as seasons pass. "So Dad must be Laoghaire because he was born on February 1, on the eve of Imbolc; the time when the milking ewes is celebrated. What's it say after that?"

Warming to the solving of the puzzle, we read each clue with excitement as if we were on a game show hoping to earn big winnings. Nora revealed the next part. "'who takes union with the elder coming at the spring tide – fish and ram'. Fish and ram is the time between Pisces and Aries."

"Oh!" I shouted. "Spring Equinox!" Barely containing myself enough to stay seated. I excitedly continued. "Mom's birthday, Mom's birthday. So who is she?" Hot on the clues, we tried to decipher "'takes union with the elder. The elder must mean Faidhe. Right?" I asked. "But wait, wasn't Craiche older than Faidhe? If it were Faidhe, then it would say *an* elder not *the* elder. It must be Craiche. Right?" I looked to Nora to see she had the same opinion. "You think?"

"Could be. Let's see about the rest to see if that makes sense. 'They birth the first, who comes with a debt.' So this one must be Mary; she's the first and the rest makes sense 'cause, 'On the day of the Lugh, this one is met.' Lughnasadh is August First, Mary's birthday. Today, in fact. We just spoke with her. Oh hey, before I forget, there's an eclipse of the sun here today. I wanted to see if we could detect it as it occurs." We all looked at Nora with bemusement. "What?" She asked defensively. "As an astrologer, I live for these things. And it passes over the British Isles today. I'm not sure it'll happen at the right time of day, but do you think we could take a break and have a look?"

"Well, yeah, but we're sort of doing something here. Let's finish this, okay?

"Okay. Sorry. Where were we? Comes in with a debt?"

"Yeah, but what does it mean that she comes in with a debt? How does that tell us who Mary is in all this?" I asked.

"Let's just keep going, we might find out more." Nora said. And she continued to read. "The next is come through, the worker of ore.' That must be Iarann! 'On the eve when between worlds, opens the door.'"

"That one's easy." I said. 'The eve when between worlds, opens the door' is Samhian, Halloween, Patrice's birthday. Patrice is Iarann!" I blurted with excitement at solving a part of the puzzle but then it struck me that what I had said was more than a game. "Iarann is Patrice." I startled at the surprise that genders had been crossed and my expectation that people would remain within gender boundaries was dashed. In fact, I recalled several lifetimes I'd lived as a boy or a man so after a moment of adjusting to the idea, I could truly see how some of the attributes of the gentle soul of Iarann had found their way into the person who is now my sister, Patrice.

Living on Cape Cod, Patrice had made quite a successful business of designing jewelry and working with silver and gold to create intricately woven, handmade pieces of art, interspersed with fine and unusual gems. The most revealing connection is that some years ago, Patrice dated a man who had made his own mead as a hobby. She long since abandoned the relationship, but pleased herself with a lifelong hobby of mead-making and had come to perfect the process so that she had her own cottage industry bottling the golden drink. I thought of how many other little things like this would be revealed as I discover my family all over again. I, once again, felt a pang of regret and I wished Patrice were here with us.

Nora broke my reverie. "'Then comes one marked by the Beast, born to this time on the bull's own feast.' Marked by the Beast? Bull's own feast? Well the bulls own feast makes sense to me if it's my birthday. May First is May Day on the wheel of the year and it falls, into the sign of Taurus the Bull. But marked by the Beast?"

Finny interrupted our process for the first time. "Ye'll remember the part of the tale when the Beast had marked Laoghaire's wife Colm as one who'd bear the brunt of his revenge after Laoghaire was killed?" We nodded and then understanding dawned.

"Laoghaire gave Colm the Shield and that's what protected her so that she and the twins were safe from the Beast. Is that what you mean?' Nora asked.

"It is. But there was more. If ye'll recall, Laoghaire, fresh from the Corcle of magic and having the Shield of Nuada gifted te him as a tool te protect his clan, issued the words te Colm, whether he knew what he wrought by intent or cast by accident, he assigned her te ever be the Shield for the family. And she assumed the task, sealed with an oath and a kiss. Neither te be taken lightly. So Nora, yer responsibility te be the Shield is due te a very old oath. Ye've come te be the Shieldmaiden from both sides of yer bloodline. And it's no coincidence, I think, that yer born te the sign of the bull. In fact, I think ye'll find few coincidences where yer birthrights and life tasks are concorned."

The playful mood of the game was subdued. We were both beginning to understand the depth and gravity of the task we'd taken on and the strength of ancient oaths given along with the value of an oath kept.

"What's next?" I said quietly.

Nora returned to the poem and found her place. "'Lastly the one holds the light and the knowledge together within. She will complete the circle and set it to spin.' I guess that's you Lee; you're the last one in the family."

"Yeah but the last verse doesn't say anything about *my* birthday. I wasn't born on a special day. So how can I be part of the wheel? How do I complete the circle?"

"Ye'll know that a wheel can't spin without the hub?" Finny interjected. "But in order te be useful, the hub must connect with all the spokes for they don't connect te each other without the hub, and therefore the hub cannot be a spoke as well, lass. You were the hub in spinnin' the tale in the beginning as Lon Dubh, and in fact, in yer forst life, ye were born te the center of the sacred Corcle as a child conceived in the Corcle and born in it as well. It makes sense that ye're the hub now in the center of the wheel so te speak. So it's only logic that ye have not the special borthdate as ye say."

"So then," I said, "if we are all accounted for, except for who Mary might be, so is she Faidhe? And then who is the final spoke? There are eight spokes in the wheel of the year. The cross quarter days and the equinoxes and solstices" I seized upon the thought that Mary's identity might help us to determine something other than where my mind was leading me. Counting on my fingers I ticked off the names from the original tale: There's Nana, who was Sigradifa. We don't know much about her yet but she had some pretty strong magic. Then there's Grandma and Grandpa who were born together on the same date and here in Ireland; they must have been the twins, Morgan and Macha. There are two of them, they might make up the other spoke, but they were born on the fall equinox so that doesn't balance out. They gave birth to Laoghaire who was Dad, so that makes three spokes. Then Dad married Mom who was Craiche, probably, who was not a blood tie to the family but was one of the original eight. They gave birth to Mary, Patrice, Nora and me who are all identified except for Mary. So who is Mary in all this? And what is the debt that she has? Does it have anything to do with the other spoke?" Then I had an epiphany. "Oh wait. The Cauldron had seven panels and one was missing. Maybe this a reflection of the multi-tiered way things work in Celtic magic that you were talking about? Is this empty spoke, sort of the same as the missing panel on the Cauldron?"

My uncertainty began to gnaw at me and create an irritating panic just below my breastbone. I tried over and again to make logic of the construction of the wheel filled in by my family members but I wasn't ready to face what I knew that meant.

"Read the rest." I snapped hoping for an alternative outcome to the one I was trying not to contemplate.

"'As the hub that unites and brings the wheel complete, and precise is the time when the task is replete.'" Nora looked at me expectantly and I was snappish with growing agitation.

"Keep going!"

"'Open is the balance when the light's strength takes sway, to complete the wheel and birth the sun's long ray.'

Cath broke the silence that hung in the air after the last words echoed.

"If yer comparin' the Cauldron te the wheel then ye could see it that the rest is te be played out te finish the story of the final panel. And so, too, has the blank spoke been filled, and filled by you as the prophecy states, 'te complete the corcle and set the wheel te spin. Put things in motion, if ye will."

The dawning of what was being said drained the blood from my face. My mind did the trick of trying to justify an alternative to what I knew was being said in this part of the prophecy. I looked to Nora for reassurance and I saw only worry and concern where I sought comfort. She knew what I knew and there was no denying the inevitable.

"No." I said in a firm and decisive voice as if my word and will could hold back the floodtide of realization. "NO!"

"Lee," Nora soothed, "If it's his destiny, you can't change it."

"It's a mistake!" I said panicked.

"His name, Lee. You named him yourself. You knew exactly what his name meant and that's why you chose it." Nora reminded me.

"It's coincidence."

"And his birth date. You can't deny that. You know that he's the final spoke."

"No," was all I could find to say but the word had lost its starch and was more of a plea.

Nora repeated the last lines in an effort to convince me what I already knew in my heart. "'Lastly the one holds the light and the knowledge together within.' "You know you did, Lee." 'She will complete the circle and set it to spin.' Without you, the final spoke would not have been born. 'The child brings vast change as the great wheel spins. The Fifth Civilization is ushered by this spirit child, as maturity begins.' Lee, you know what this means."

I crumpled on the couch and buried my face in my hands. "No. I want him to live a happy, normal life. I want him to be the sweet boy he is, untouched by any of this. The responsibility, the Beast, the theological confusion, the stigma of the magical world. All of it. He's too innocent. NO!"

"Maybe it's the only way he'll actually have a future Lee." Nora offered the voice of reason. You can't deny that all the clues point to him. Astrologically speaking, his birthday is the summer solstice; the final spoke in the wheel. And the part of the prophecy that speaks of you says that you 'hold the light and knowledge within.' You gave birth to him. And what does his name mean? Say it Lee, what does Lucas mean?"

I sobbed a lifeless almost inaudible answer. "Bringer of light and knowledge. But..."

She kept pushing. "And what did you give him for a middle name?"

Pleading now. "But it was supposed to be me who fights this battle."

"Lee." She persisted. "His middle name?"

"Ray." I reflected on the day I gave birth to my son. He was so blond his hair was almost white. His whole body was covered with golden hair and he just looked up at me with perfectly clear blue, intelligent eyes and cherry red lips, the picture of perfection in my biased eyes. His name just popped into my head. Lucas Ray. 'My Ray of sunshine,' were the first words I said to my son. I still struggled to convince everyone – anyone that "I am the light to lead. I am the Sword. This doesn't have to fall on him. He's just a baby!"

"You can't will someone not to fulfill their destiny." Nora persisted. "Do you remember when he was born and I did his astrological chart for you, how I remarked on how unusual it was that he was not only born on the solstice but that he was born at exactly 9:25 pm?"

"Sort of."

"That precise minute on June 20, 2000 meant that he was born on the exact moment that the night and day were at equal strength and the beginning of the year and the end of the year were also at equal length, two seasons behind, two seasons ahead. It also meant that he was born into the sign of Gemini, the twins: male and female together. It seems he's a living pinnacle of balance.

"I would think though that to mark the resurgence of the balance between the God and the Goddess, the herald would be a female." I said, grasping at straws. "It makes more sense to me that way. Doesn't it?" I implored the brothers.

"In part lass, yer right." Cath explained. "Yer sisters and you have come through in a poetic balance so te speak. Havin' been born te the balance of the wheel, ye've each been born te a particular astrological sign, so that, although yer all female physically, ye each represent a balance in yer borth. One born te water, in Scorpio, one born te air in Libra, one born te fire in Leo and one born te orth in Taurus; two masculine, two feminine. But even more important is the relation each of those signs and elements has with the sacred implements." He stood quiet for a moment while that information sunk in for us.

Nora spoke. "Water-Cup, Air-Sword, Fire-Staff and Earth-Shield. We each represent one of the implements." She seemed to marvel at the paradoxical simplicity and complexity of the web of connections and how the magic was spun to bring it all about.

"Why me?" I demanded. "Why is it Lucas who was created to do this task whatever it is? Why not one of the other kids born to our family? It could have just as easily been one of Patrice's kids. Why Lucas? Was it just because I conceived him at a time when he'd be born on the right spoke?" I grew increasingly agitated.

"There's more lass." Cath said with the taint of pity in his voice. "And it's a great lot fer ye te take in but the time is now and ye must hear it all."

"No, there is no more. I'm not listening to anymore." I was practically shrieking now. The others waited and I knew my denials weren't going to change a thing.

I smoldered, "What else?" Not really wanting to hear what else, at all.

"Yer family represents the wheel, to be sure. And you and yer sisters represent the elements and implements. Ye've the blood of two of the lines from parent countries so yer family is blessed with the knowledge of the auld ways and the gift of magic runs through yer veins with that blood. You yerself and yer sister as well as yer son have been marked with names that when called, cast a meanin' about who ye are and what is yer task here in this life. None are coincidence. All carry meanin' and import."

"And." I said rudely.

"And," he began, "Do ye know the meanin' of yer husband's sir name?"

Exasperated, "What, this again?"

"Aye lass. This again."

I heaved a sighed. Not at the brothers but at the situation. Tired of the whole thing, I struggled to concentrate.

"It's German. I said. Feeling uncomfortable at the recognition that this was one of the parent countries and immediately identifying that my husband was also half Italian, another parent country. Cath and Finny watched in silence as they waited for the dawning recognition on my face. "My husband?" I asked.

"Aye. Yes. Finny answered. "Yer marriage name, Kieseling, means stone. And the story, as ye may have hord from myths and tales, tells of a time when the Sword and Stone come together in magic. This is another facet te the tale and the magic that was cast by Faidhe. She took from her knowledge of the prophecy and the advice of Sigrdifa, yer ancestor from Sweden, the country of origin of the Stone of Fal and took the heart of the magic from the sacred Corcle te recreate the Power and force of the implements in human form. The Stone, as ye may know was the keystone of the Corcle; the Stone of Fal brought te Ireland from the North Country was split asunder during the prophecy. One half was used te support the final magic cast by Faidhe and the other half was utilized elsewhere. But the identification of the rightful king is indisputably tied te the Stone in both myth and in legend and now in flesh."

I watched in my mind's eye as Finny's story-telling abilities painted pictures in my head of all that had taken place with the Stone's halves incongruously inter-mingled with my childhood memories of the animated film of the Sword and the Stone, another version of the Arthurian tale.

"So what does this have to do with my husband?' I asked. My voice was flat.

Cath touched my shoulder in genuine concern. Maybe to steel me for what he was about to tell me.

"Yer husband carries the blood of the other two parent countries, Germany and Italy. Although he may not have shown any signs of magical ability." Cath arched his eyebrows at me as if to inquire whether his comment was correct. I shook my head in the negative.

"Not that I know of." I answered.

"Well we'll see about that eventually I suppose. We're making a leap of our assumption here without tracing his heritage, but what we believe is that your hus-band, the Stone, carrying two of the bloodlines and you, the Sword, carrying two of the bloodlines have borthed the child of the prophecy. The one who will be king. He will be quite powerful indeed. He has the Power in his ancestral blood dis-tilled through the centuries but strengthened fourfold as a descendant of Faidhe, Laoghaire, Colm, Lon Dubh, Iarann, and Macha come tegether in the veins of one being. Ye've seen how yer cousins have but a fraction of yer magical ability with only one of the lines. Yer son's Power will have increased exponentially having the union of all four lines running through one heart."

I was quiet. I felt broken. I recalled the knowledge of what my son's middle name actually means when I looked it up after I'd gotten home from the hospital. I could see the print on the page as if it were in front of me now: The meaning for Lucas, his first name, means 'bringer of light and knowledge' and the meaning for his middle name, Ray, means, 'the one who will be king'. The satisfaction as a new parent I'd felt in the moment I found the meaning of his names was complete hav-ing felt I'd chosen good strong names for my son; but now, my desolation at the prospect of giving my son over to a battle for the survival of the human race was overwhelming. I wanted to know how this was possible. Had I ever truly fallen in love with my husband? Or was I just a victim of destiny? Why did he not know magic? What will happen when these great changes take place? What is the Fifth Civilization? What is expected of me now? What did it all mean? All I could muster was, "Tell me."

30

The Inheritance

It was only mid-morning and yet it had already been such a long day. When he thought his heart could bear no more burdens he'd found himself atop the Hill, alone in the great Circle standing over the lifeless body of the oldest member of the Council. Only lately having formed an intimate bond of magic with this woman, Laoghaire felt the crushing reality that the relationship with Craiche would grow no more and her mentoring too was no longer available. He had depended on her guidance to establish himself upon the Hill. The fresh wound of grief over having lost his true parents may have been soothed, if only slightly, by the presence of this woman but now, all the weight of the changes over the past three days came crashing down on Laoghaire. Falling to his knees, his hands fell, open palmed to the earth as the Sword and Shield clanged and echoed to the ground. Laoghaire turned his head skyward and let forth such a keening wail as to set the leaves on the trees a shiver. This lament was full of rage and sorrow, the depth of which he had never felt or understood before.

In that moment, he realized the solitary life Faidhe had led and the countless sacrifices she'd made for her people and the Gods. He was utterly bereft for her, for Craiche, for himself, his people, the loss of his parents, and his family for the arduous task that he knew lay ahead of them.

Laoghaire wailed for what he now could see clearly as he stood at the altar in the Circle. He wept for the passing of his life, as he'd known it. He had not only lost the comfort of his parents' love, but now, he bore the burden and responsibility of being Keeper to the Circle for the Tuatha de Danann and a king by birthright to his own people of the clan Laoghaire. He felt as a ship without moorings, adrift on uncertain seas. He prayed bitterly for the first time in his life that he may be exempt from the choices he must make for himself and his family. He was disturbed by the nagging voice in his heart that urged him to abandon all of the responsibility and simply live well with the benefits of his newly appointed titles.

Unaccustomed to self-pity and even more a stranger to this new insistence that he should shirk his duty for a life of comfort, Laoghaire shook off the weight of sorrow.

Looking at the sun, he was shocked to see that he'd spent overlong at the altar with the lifeless body of Craiche. He was empty. An emotional husk. As he stood up by the altar to collect himself, he observed the woman lying there. He tried to divine what the purpose in her dying just now could have been. *For she obviously died a peaceful death here in full ritual,* he thought as he inventoried the various items she'd used for the ceremony. Then he spied the pulsing bowl of water upon her breast.

Wait! Her heart beats. There is life in her still for the bowl pulses with the rhythm of her heart. Laoghaire bent to listen for Craiche's breath and found none. He returned his gaze to the stone bowl of water to puzzle the heart pulse he saw there. Upon impulse, before he had a moment to think about what he was doing, Laoghaire picked up the bowl cupped between his two hands and drank the palpitating water within, to the very last drop.

As he drank, Laoghaire could hear whispers surrounding him; echoes of Craiche's voice, as she'd cast the magic to pass on her knowledge and Power to him. Snippets of conversations she'd had both mentally and verbally with many clan-folk during the last three days and nights, things she knew regarding members of the Council, the whereabouts of Briciu and what Faidhe's task was in her journey. Laoghaire, only moments ago, was an empty man broken by sorrow, was now infused with Craiche's Powerful abilities and knowledge of many years of experience and practice. He felt passing discomfort at the possibility that he might unknowingly abuse that Power and was immediately given an answer that shed illumination on the fact that those thoughts of personal gain he'd experienced moments ago were remnants of the dark magic Briciu had cast. His relief was only momentary until he saw the larger picture of what that evil magic will do to humanity as Briciu's attributes creep into and eat away at the fearful hearts of millions who would be fertile grounds for such disease: lust, greed, laziness, anger, gluttony, envy, pride and much more. For a fearful heart will seek to be relieved of its fear and these infections in the heart will flourish as they feed on the fear and ultimately sicken the mind.

Knowledge he never imagined flooded his existence as he absorbed all that Craiche had left for him to gather. Along with her forceful energy, he absorbed instruction and understanding as to what he must now do with newfound authority and responsibility and what he must do with the Sword, Shield and the Stone of Fal. Preparations must be made, for in twelve days' time, he will hold his first celebration of the Circle at the rising of the full moon. There is much to be done in preparation.

"Thank you, Old One, for it was a sacrifice in love to give over of yourself in such a way." Laoghaire said to the departed Craiche as he gently patted her hair. He knew he should move to make preparations for all that was to take place but he stayed a few moments longer at the old woman's side. "Take heart, Mother," he whispered to her ear, "I will use well the gift you have bestowed."

"I know well that you will Calf-herder but know that you will use it but briefly in the role of Keeper." Came a response. Laoghaire looked quickly to find the owner of the voice and saw by the rented opening in the Stone of Fal, an image of a woman he recognized as Craiche but she had obviously been relieved of the binds of the human body for she had not the stooped posture of the old Craiche but was erect and her face was clear of the years of careworn crevices. She did not appear to be younger, but rather more invigorated and fresh. About and through her was a faint glow of light energy as she spoke to Laoghaire.

"You know now, that our time here is all but finished and it is your duty and responsibility to move past the celebration of your first rite here at the full moon and assume your rightful place, not as liaison to the Gods as we thought, but to take our magic and assume your place as king on the mount as is your birthright. There was no coincidence in the timing here. As these changes take place and the time of the Tuatha De Danann moves on, you must bring the Power to the throne to see that all that is prophesied comes to pass. Faidhe will do her part in seeing that the honor of the God and Goddess is protected until such time the world is ready to truly give respect to them once again in a way of reverence, rather than fear or contempt and scorn."

"How is this my path when I have just come to the Circle as Keeper? Was I not chosen to wield the Sword and the Shield for the purpose of protecting the Circle and all that is sacred to the Gods? Is this not my task?"

"It is. And you will, but not in the way you assume, King. For your primary task is to bring your family's blood to your place of birth. For they too are important spokes in the wheel as time turns. You must insure them a future line in blood to come to the Mount when the circle symbol of the Shield is joined with the symbol of the hilt of the Sword and the symbols together will represent the union of the Old Ways and the new, the feminine and the masculine. But when the symbols are bound, as the Circle and the Cross and the Goddess laments her banishment, the blood of your progeny will serve on the Mount and will represent the Goddess at a time when one will come from the east and will be known by the Staff he carries, for it will be that he carries a message of the new God, the masculine God and your blood and namesake will acquiesce to the one who carries the Staff of Lugh, his birthright as descendant of Faidhe. But, still, your blood will carry on until such time that it stirs again in the heart and veins of your descendants and the living balance shines the light of knowledge upon the world."

"I surge with the Power you have bequeathed, Craiche, and from what you tell me, the Staff of Lugh, which Faidhe carries is to continue to serve the Gods and from what I have seen, the great Cauldron of Dagda will serve the purpose of the Gods but what use these implements if I am to relinquish them as I have seen?"

"You will understand your purpose, Laoghaire. The Sword was not given for you to use in leadership, nor the Shield for you to keep the Circle. You are charged with the sacred placement of these implements so that they may be of use when the Goddess has need of them. The time has come when the God and Goddess have need of human intervention to preserve the sacred implements in the living blood for if there is no longer reverence or respect for the Power of the Universe, the time for these deities is passed. Faidhe has been the Keeper and her blood, mingled with your blood will be the future that will create these implements in the flesh. You have need of creating and partaking in the rituals that will insure this. Beware, though, you have an unexpected battle with the essence of evil that now takes seed in the hearts of some. With this, you must find your way on your own." With that, Craiche reached a hand to touch Laoghaire's face and she bore a look of something Laoghaire thought was akin to sorrow or perhaps pity.

"Craiche!" He shouted. "I bid you wait!" And through the air, rippling as wave on the lake, she was gone. Laoghaire turned to where her body lay on the altar stone only to see the final shimmering of the air as her body seemed to be taken by the air and rushed under the altar stone to the ground beneath.

With a heavy heart, Laoghaire retrieved the Sword and Shield from the ground in front of the altar stone. He first held up the Shield and then placed the Sword in front of it. What he saw would, many centuries later, be known as the Celtic cross; the very symbol Craiche spoke of that would be the world-wide symbol created by the descendent of the human Faidhe and her union with the Greenman aspect of the God. It made sense to Laoghaire now that this man, who would be known as Padraig, would carry Faidhe's Staff to deliver his message of the new Masculine deity, and forever be identified by the symbol synonymous with the union of the masculine and feminine Gods. Laoghaire also knew that this man, known as a holy man, would forever be linked with the masculine color of the Greenman for it was his spiritual ancestry. This comer to the land of the Danu will endeavor to conquer the Old Ways, but unwittingly will fulfill his destiny by binding the old to the new so both shall be brought forward until such a time when the Old Ways will once again surface. Sadly, though, Laoghaire knew that time would be long in the future and many would suffer, labeled as evil should they deviate from the all-consuming masculine fire in the name of religion that will burn with fever for many centuries after this new masculine religion is established.

Wrapping his fist around the grip on the Sword, he tightened the muscles in his arm as if gaining strength from the implement. Hefting the great Shield with his forearm through the three bands on the backside of the armor, he postured a stance of preparedness for battle and he felt the Power course through him. Maintaining his position at the altar stone, Laoghaire knelt as he had before only this time he was not driven to his knees in despair; he voiced a prayer of petition that he be given the wisdom and strength to carry his family and his people through the times to come. When he felt the throbbing surge of the answer to his prayer pulsing through him, he stood and reverently laid the implements upon the altar. Laoghaire gave no thought to his actions, he only followed instinct as he carried out a ritual completely foreign to him but entirely familiar, nonetheless.

As Laoghaire removed his tunic and skins, placing them at the foot of the altar, his skin strained against the cool spring air and tightened over his muscles. Evidence of the Power vibrating through his heart and veins was almost palpable as he took strong, long strides across the Circle toward the sacred spring. Invigorated by the wave of energy flowing through him, the weight of his substantial manhood did not deter it from standing proudly in an impressive show of masculinity as Laoghaire brought this male essence in physical form to the sacred spring for the first time in legend or memory. Without hesitation, he dove into the spring, and was barely aware of the frigid water sinking sharp needle teeth into his skin. Laoghaire was invigorated, strengthened and refreshed by his initiation into the sacred world of the Power and the spirit. He spoke not with his lips but his heart in commune with the sprites, spirits and Gods. He took Council from the disembodied voices while he floated in the sacred waters for what may have been only moments or possibly centuries. Laoghaire raised himself out of the waters knowing he had been initiated and accepted into the ranks of those who serve the Gods. All of his hesitation and feelings of self-doubt had been washed away. He was certain of his direction now, and was equally confident that he had the knowledge and Power to succeed in his task.

After having been cleansed and initiated in the water, Laoghaire strode to the great Stone of Fal where it stood in two halves beyond the altar stone and stepped into the divided center. He climbed up into the split between the Stone and stretched his legs to place a foot on each side of the split in the Stone. As he reached up with his hands to touch each half of the Stone with his outstretched fingertips, he struck a pose that would be exactly the rendition that, many centuries later, one of his future incarnations would create, known as the Vitruvian Man. As he took this stance, the great Stone began to hum, then vibrate, and finally give forth of a screeching wail that would forever more, identify the true, rightful and righteous king of the land. And with the shift in leadership from the Spirit-Goddess to the human king, the energy of the isle had now decidedly taken the pendulum full swing and was now careening back toward all things masculine.

King Laoghaire jumped down from the Stone, retrieved the mighty Sword from the altar and with one powerful swing, struck the bottom of the Stone to sever the two halves completely. Magically forged, not from the ore of the earth but of a great meteor star that plunged into the earth from above in a fiery blast when the earth was still being born, the Sword flew and great sparks ignited as the metal cut through the Stone as a blade through butter. Laoghaire stood and moved not at all, as the two halves of the enormous stone fell in opposite directions and shook the ground as they landed.

31

Long Distance

"Hey Baby. It's Mom. How're you doin?" I asked, knowing that my antennae were on full inquisitive mode listening for any word, phrase, voice inflection or clue that something might be wrong.

"Oh, I'm okay." Lucas answered. "Is this your new phone?"

"Yup. Want to take down the number so you can call me?"

"Kay. Let me get a pencil. Mom?"

My stomach tightened. "Yeah, Hon?"

"When are you coming home?"

"Well, I'm not exactly sure, Luke. I have to finish up my business here first."

My throat tightened. I missed my family furiously and wanted so much to be home to be with them and to protect them, especially now. I wanted to talk to Walter about everything that had been happening and all that we'd learned. I wanted him to tell me it was all hogwash even though I knew it wasn't. I also knew that he'd probably think I'm crazy. My husband knew about my ability to communicate with my sisters and that I'd occasionally see unusual or ghostly things around the house only because I'd told him so. He never saw anything himself but he was accustomed to my family's peculiarities and also to Lucas talking about such things. But this, I had no idea how he'd take the news about any of this.

"Lucas, you know I came here to do some important work. I've found a really big story that was just made for me. *What an understatement!* I think it's exactly what I came here to find out. So now I have to do all the research and stuff before I can come back."

Silence...

"I may even have to be here a bit longer than I planned at first, but I'll be back before school starts. How's Dad?" I said changing the subject.

He's good. He's been snoring really loud though. I hear him at night sometimes."

"Does he wake you up? Is it that loud?" I said, relieved that we were onto innocuous territory.

"No. I'm awake and I hear him...Sometimes I sneak into your side of the bed next to him."

"Well if he's so loud, why do you get so close?" I asked with good humor.

"I feel safer in there with him." And there it was. The first quiver in his voice that told me all was not well.

"What do you mean, 'safer,' Baby? Are you having more dreams or are you just missing old Mom?"

"Mom, can you come home just for a little bit like you did before? I know you have to do your work, but...I keep dreaming bad things and sometimes I'm not sure if I'm dreaming or if it's real."

Like you did before. I felt my face drain of blood and my hands and feet went cold.

"Tell me what you mean Luke. What're you dreaming that's so bad?"

It never occurred to me to dismiss my boy's dreams as nothing more than missing me, or a child's method of manipulation to get me to come home. I had always taken for granted that the communication between us could be nothing less than open and honest because, if I'd had a link to Nora and what she was thinking and feeling, the link I have with Lucas is ten-fold. He was telling me the truth and as I tuned into what was going on with him, I found myself, with less dash this time, once again back home in Plymouth, simply sitting next to my son on the old *This End's Up* couch we have in our family room.

I surveyed the room and saw Lego's strewn on the table that matched the couch with remnant dishes, from a cheeseburger and homemade fries, dinner that had obviously been eaten in front of the television. Seated right next to my son in his tee-shirt and pajama bottoms on the sturdy couch with yellow flowers, still talking into my phone.

"What are your dreams about, Baby?"

Lucas lit up with joy and surprise as he looked at me. He answered me still talking into his phone as if it were the most natural thing to talk to each other through our phones while sitting next to each other.

In a hushed voice, "The monster keeps sniffing around for me. I keep running from it to hide. I find a hiding spot and make myself really small but then there's another monster or more monsters and they look for me too. I can hear them sniffing and squealing trying to find me so I pull out blanky and cover myself up with it 'cause they can't see me under blanky. But they keep coming. They come almost every night now."

Blanky is Lucas's name for his baby blanket. It was my baby blanket and all of my sisters before me. Since I am the youngest in my family, it was mine last and so it was mine to pass on. Since infancy, his blue blanky was never more than a few feet from where Lucas was. Still now, he keeps it with him, like Charles Schulz's, cartoon character, Linus Van Pelt, it's his constant companion. He'd always loved the comfort of the blanket but it never became an issue when we left the house or when he started school so we let him keep it around. He slept with it and cuddled with it and sometimes he unconsciously rubbed it with his thumb or ran it back and forth under his nose while he was reading or playing with his toys. I could see how it would represent security for him in his dreams at a time he felt threatened.

"Where do you hide Luke?" I asked. Looking for more details about the dream without trying to focus on the monsters.

"Oh, I hide in the woods on the ground behind a great big tree." He said in a tone that sparked of amusement in getting the upper hand on someone. "Or some-times I hide in the lake under the water. Sometimes I even fly! I like that 'cause the monsters can't get me in the air if I can get high enough. But if I don't think I can get high enough to get away from them, like if they might grab my legs, I just go to the big old tree or hold my breath and go under the water but flying is good 'cause even if they see me, they can't get me when I'm up in the air. But I don't like to get too high 'cause I start to get scared and fall. Hiding works but mostly, I know as long as I have blanky, I'll be okay."

"That's good. You keep blanky with you then." I watched as my son rubbed the backs of his feet together as he perched them cross-legged on the table in front of the couch. I noted to myself that his legs are getting long and how much this foot-rubbing motion reminded me of his father.

"Can you see me Luke?" I had to be sure.

His blue eyes inspected me with an expression that said 'Of course I can see you.' Then he nodded his head.

"I can see you...but you're not really here. Are you? I mean this is real, but you're not *all* home; are you?"

I thought how aptly he understood this situation. Kids are so open to things adults would dismiss as impossible.

"I'm here Luke. But you're right; I'm not all here. This is better than just talking on the phone though. Huh?"

He leaned into me on the couch and I felt that static sensation I had expe-rienced earlier when I'd touched Luke in this state. I felt no weight as his light blond head leaned on my shoulder but there was an electrical type sensation of him touching me nonetheless.

"Sometimes I think I'm in bed with Dad, but I wake up in the morning and I'm in my own bed again. So I don't know if it was real that I was in your room or only wishing I was there. Dad doesn't remember me coming into bed so I guess I just dream that too."

"That can happen sometimes." I said trying to sound reassuring.

"I know, but Mom, sometimes I wake up in the morning and I find leaves and stuff in my bed. That's kinda weird and it scares me like maybe I'm really in the woods when I think I'm dreaming? And if the woods are real..."

I understood where he was going. If the woods are real, then the monsters are too. I remembered aspects of my own dreams of being in the woods and I felt like I'd come home to a wonderful place. I remembered meeting Faidhe there as well and not wanting to leave. But there was a kind of squealing in the background while I spoke with her and she said something to me. What was it? That I don't live there or I don't belong there where she is. Something like that.

"Lucas, I think your dreams might be a little like what we're doing now. They're real, maybe, but you're not *all* there. And maybe that's why you don't wake up with Dad in the morning, 'cause you stay in your own bed but part of you goes to be safe with him. I don't know, but maybe that's it. You just keep blanky with you both here and when you sleep. That way you have it always, if you need it. Okay?"

"I do, Mom." He said and pulled a corner of the cobalt blue satin edging out from behind him on the couch and flicked his thumbnail back and forth over the soft, satin material edging on the blanket that was now threadbare from generations of washing but mostly from the constant use over the last eight years. "What do I do about the leaves and stuff?"

"Well, what kind of leaves? Do you think you're picking leaves up on your feet in the woods?"

"No, it's not like that. I don't get all wet when I hide under the water and I don't get scratches when I fall into the trees or anything like that."

I marveled at his logic and reasoning for one so young. Obviously he'd already puzzled this out on his own to have discerned that if he were physically tied to what happened in his dream state, that he'd necessarily come back with other evidence of his being there.

"It's like, sometimes I wake up and someone leaves a branch or twig of something inside my blanky with me. That's something else; when I wrap myself up in blanky in my dream, I wake up with it wrapped around me too. One time, I found a funny looking round, gold thing with an eyeball on it. You know, like on the dollar bill?"

I remembered seeing that type of symbol from the ancient book; *The Power of the Word* so I knew what was happening with my son was undoubtedly connected to all that I was experiencing here.

"Luke, listen to me now." I said, trying to sound calm and ignore the knot in my stomach. "Have you ever seen anyone else while you're dreaming about being in the woods?"

"Sometimes I think I see someone moving there, like in the corner of my eye but when I look, I never really see them. It's not the monsters though. I know 'cause whoever it is, I'm not scared of them. They're just kind of there. Watching me, or something."

I recognized that he already trusted his instincts and depended on his feelings and intuition to determine what was happening around him. Maybe much of this will just come to him naturally. I knew that the fact he chose to seek safety and hide in one of three places: in earth, air or water in his dream was an instinctual choice, even if he didn't know it. He was relying on ancient knowledge, part of his heritage. Perhaps he'll just know about these things like some genetic memory that will come to him as easily as learning to speak or walk or eat. I passionately hoped this was the case.

"Okay, here's what I want you to do. Save all the leaves and anything that you come back from your dreams with. Find a box or something and collect all the leaves and sticks, everything you find like that and put it all into the box. You may need to use this stuff one day but I'm not sure how. You may know how though. Sometimes it'll just come to you how things work out. Right? Like using blanky to protect you? You listen to your instincts about those things Luke. It could be important."

Not wanting to scare him but wanting to leave enough of an impression so that my words would stick with him, I took his little face in my hand. Again I felt the electric buzz in my palm. I looked right into his blue eyes. What I saw there was an expression too old to belong to my eight-year old son. I noticed the dark circles under his eyes and knew he wasn't sleeping well.

"I love you, Baby. Now that I have the phone, you call me if you need to or just want to. And don't forget, we can visit like this too, I think. I'm not sure how this works and I know other people can't do this, but we must be able to for a reason, so if you need to, call me on the phone and let me know what happens with your dreams. Like I said, I don't really know what it's all about, but I believe you and maybe it has something to do with what I'm doing over here. I guess there's something I need to do to make sure that the monsters don't bother you, so hold on and be brave for me? I'll be home, *all of me* just as soon as I can. Okay?"

"Okay Mom. Will you tell Dad it's all right for me to sleep in your room with him? I don't want to ask 'cause I don't want him to think I'm a baby."

I could read between the lines in what he was saying. I knew because he wouldn't tell his father anything about the magical things that were happening. At least not while I was away. Lucas knew that I was the one who paid attention to all the unusual stuff that happened and we had a link that his dad just wasn't privy to. If he were to say anything at all to his dad, it would be that he had a bad dream and leave all the rest out of it.

"You got it, Buddy." I said. "Now take down this number and then you can put him on." On the table, in front of us was the pen and paper Lucas had gotten earlier. He reached for the small spiral notebook pad of paper with his left hand and without being consciously aware, he held out his right hand for the pen that was about five inches out of his reach and the pen was drawn to his hand. He nestled back to the couch with the phone cradled into his shoulder.

"Okay, what's the number?"

As I observed this action I knew that he wasn't even aware that anything was out of the ordinary. I wondered if this was a recent occurrence or if he's always had this ability and I just hadn't noticed. *No. I'd have noticed something like that.* I had been aware through the years that he answered questions I hadn't asked out loud or he asked me things without verbalizing but I just chalked it up to a very strong connection between a mother and her son. But then, there were times when perhaps I'd convinced Lucas, or more likely myself that incidents similar to what I'd just seen were somehow explainable, ordinary circumstances. In this moment, I couldn't avoid recalling one such occasion that had nagged at my sense of normalcy more than the rest.

When Lucas was about five years old he was at summer day camp and I was at home, painting our family room. I had a bolt of panic and understanding that he was scared and needed me. I got into my car, shoeless and covered with forest green paint to drive the half-mile from home to the camp. When I parked at the 86-acre site, I walked straight to where I would find my son. There were two boys on the ground in front of a giant swing set with the camp nurse squatting over them. One of the boys was my Lucas. I was calling ahead to him with my mind, trying to determine if he was all right. In that moment, he looked directly at me and started to cry. As I drew closer, I saw that the boy next to Lucas had a severely broken arm. Apparently, the other boy had jumped from the swing when it was at its summit and landed on top of Lucas who was walking in front of the swing set toward the lunch tables. The boy, some 20-pounds heavier and a few years older had, 'bounced off' Lucas, as the other children told it, and fell hard on his arm and shoulder. The appearance of that boy's arm was sickening to see, broken in several places. I squatted to my son and put my hand on his back.

"Hey Spooky" I called softly to him using our pet name for him. "You okay?"

Without taking her eyes off her watch as she took the other boy's pulse the camp nurse answered my question.

"He seems to be fine; more shaken up than anything. Although I don't know how."

I picked Lucas up off the ground and he wrapped his arms and legs around me in the 'koala bear' as we called it. Uninjured but upset at the circumstance, he cried into my neck telling me he didn't mean to do it but the boy hurt him.

"I can fix it Mom. I can fix it." He repeated. "Let me get blanky and put blanky on him and I can fix it with the light."

I felt badly for the other boy but my heart broke for my own son. He'd had the wind knocked out of him and taken a pretty hard hit but he felt guilty that the other boy was badly hurt and he wanted to lend comfort in the way he knew comfort: blanky.

"Lucas, just because the boy fell on you doesn't make it your fault he's hurt. I know it sounds harsh, but he should not have been jumping off the swing. We all know that's against the playground rules. Right?"

"I guess."

"No guessing about it. What if you weren't so lucky and were really hurt? That's why the camp has those rules, so no one gets hurt. But it's not your fault that boy is hurt just because he fell onto you."

"He didn't really fall onto me, Mom. I felt him coming toward me and I knocked him away."

I considered what my son was telling me at the time and looked at the respective weight and age of the boys and concluded that I was lucky to be carrying my son away from the swing set instead of following an ambulance to the hospital like that other mother probably would be doing.

We stopped at the camp office to sign Lucas out for the day. I received strange looks from the attendants there who apparently were just in the process of calling my home to inform me that Lucas had been involved in an accident at the camp. They couldn't figure out how I'd arrived before they had a chance to call me. I lied smoothly that I'd intended to pick him up early anyway to attend a family party in the afternoon and I just happened to be there at the right time. The two staff members eyed my bare feet and green spotted outfit but easily accepted the story and Lucas and I went home together to spend an afternoon blowing bubbles, drawing with sidewalk chalk, and trying to put the emotional business of near misses behind us.

In retrospect, I speculated that I'd known Lucas needed me and we had that link between us. It wasn't unusual for regular people to have experiences like this and we were a family with additional abilities in the psychic area so, no big deal. But until now, I'd managed to ignore what Lucas had said about pushing the boy away and what the other children had said about the boy 'bouncing off' Lucas. Then, all the peculiar talk afterward that Lucas wanted to 'fix it with blanky and the light.' Just the term 'light' started clanging in my mind now with my new understanding of what his name means and what his role in this life is.

Until this trip to Ireland, had I seen my son use telekinesis to move an object I'd have just thought that he had inherited his abilities from our side of the family or more likely, ignored it as I had the incident at day camp. But now, I know that the manifestation of his abilities, especially at this point in time, is evidence that what Cath and Finny have told us about the Power surging now is true.

After telling Luke the phone number I asked him to put his dad on the phone. I felt the faint electrical feeling run through my lips as I kissed him on the forehead and gave him another snug before watching him run out of the family room waving the phone in front of him.

"Dad, Mom's on the phone."

In that moment when Lucas had left the room, I found myself mildly disoriented and lying on my bed in our cozy little cottage in County Clare. I was quite exhausted from all I'd endured today and even more exhausted at the emotional toll that being away from my family exacted on me.

"Hello." Came my husband's voice.

"Hi, Handsome. How's your life of despair without me there?" My husband is a handsome man but not in the overt way some men are or that women are likely to notice before a second look. Not tall, but well-muscled, he has an easy smile and an open face with lovely brown eyes that are framed with a network of laugh lines reaching down his cheeks when he smiles. For all the years I'd known him, he covered his face with a burly man's beard but one day he shaved it off without a word of warning and the face that was underneath was like tearing up carpet from a floor to find beautifully aged hard wood underneath. A very pleasant surprise. Thick lips and high cheekbones, the smile I was accustomed to seeing only in his eyes all those years could now be fully appreciated under an impressive, full mustache. A full 13 years my senior, his salt and pepper beard, I thought was distinguished looking, he'd shaved off because he thought it made him look older. Either way, I was still in love with my husband after 12 years of marriage and was relieved to know, prophecy or not, fate, destiny, whatever, I truly love this man.

"Miserable but we'll muddle through." He played along. It was good to hear his voice. I wondered if I tried to project myself back to my home, would he see me in the same way as Lucas." I decided it was probably not the time for that with him. *Not yet.*

"How're you guys doing together? I hope you're not just working around the house all day. Are you taking any daytrips or anything? It is your vacation after all."

"Yeah we get out every other day or so. Today, we went down to the Plymouth Plantation and explored the Mayflower II at the bay."

"Oh good. Lucas loves it at the Plantation." I said.

"I know. He told me all about how 'Mom does this' and 'Mom shows him that.' This is where Mom takes me for lunch after we go on the boat.'"

"You sound a little jealous!" I teased.

"Well you're a tough act to follow."

"Don't try to follow. Just build your own traditions and memories with him. Don't forget, it's been Lucas and me for eight years, 24-7 while you're away all day every day or away on business. It's going to take you two more than a week or two to develop your own relationship. So he's probably just going to his comfort zone in things he's familiar with that we've done together. I do think though, that you won't make any progress with him if you make him dinner and plunk him in front of the T.V. to entertain himself." I bit my tongue as soon as the words flew out of my mouth.

There was a bit of silence after I said that. I knew Walter was wondering if Lucas had told me that he ate dinner alone in the family room or if I was checking up on him as though I'd had no faith in his parenting abilities. Of course there was no way he could know that I'd been there and had seen for myself.

We'd had words in the past over the fact that I thought Walter could devote more time to our son. He resented what he thought was me telling him how to be a father. It was only an issue because his own parents had divorced when he was very young and he never really had a role model for how to be a dad. So he was sensitive at anything that could be perceived as criticism. I could feel the old argument brewing so I continued before we had an issue.

"He loves your cheeseburger and homemade fry special. I hear that you're quite the chef at breakfast too. And what was it that you guys did with play dough today?" I took a chance mentioning something I wasn't completely sure they'd done, I could feel him let it go and the momentary tension shifted.

"We used your recipe to make play dough. I made a few different colors and we made all kinds of things with the cookie cutters and Lucas made some really good dinosaurs or maybe they were dragons. I didn't know he could do stuff like that. I made a few things myself. It's been so long since I just sat down to make something creative. I forgot how much I enjoy it."

"Excellent." I said. "Did you squash them back into the dough or will I be able to see them when I get home?"

"No. We cooked 'em. Luke showed me how you can cook the dough to make it hard. He's a smart kid!" Walter said, almost in surprise, like he was getting to know his son for the first time.

"I know. Did you think I was making it up all those times I told you he had talent? He takes after his mother!" I chided in good nature. "Sometimes I forget that he's only 8-years old. How does he seem to be doing without me there? I mean, I know he's having fun with you, but this is the first time we've been separated for so long and he seems to be trying to be brave about it. Have you noticed anything about him having trouble with the separation?"

"He's fine." Walter said with a little exasperation.

"I know he's fine, but I also know that he wouldn't tell you if something was wrong because he wants you to know that he's not a baby. But really, Walter, is he, ah, sleeping okay and everything?" My husband started to dismiss me as overly protective but then he remembered something.

"No, he's fine...Well, he does have some kind of ah, dreams or something that I never remember him having before."

"What do think that's all about?" I prodded.

"I don't know but he seems to be kicking and mumbling a lot. You think he's having nightmares or something?"

"I don't know. Do you wake him up and ask him what's going on?"

"Well, no. I just hear him and go back to sleep when he calms down." I kept silent for a moment and hoped it would dawn on Walter that if I'm not there to comfort Lucas that it's his job to make sure everything is okay; tired or middle of the night or not.

"You think he's having nightmares because you're away?"

"Could be." I fought the urge to lead Walter with questions that could be misunderstood by him as blame rather than helpful like, 'Is there something you can do about that?'

"Then, maybe he can sleep in with me if he wants to."

"Oh, that's a good idea. You could ask him if he'd like it for you guys to hang out together." I said, relieved that it was Walter's idea so he wouldn't give me all the macho crap about not babying Lucas. Walter had had a lonely childhood of independence, much the way mine was but for different reasons. I vowed to be there to love and nurture my children so they'd know that whoever they are, they are loved and accepted. Walter, on the other hand, was of the mind that he was tough and independent when he was a kid and to expect anything less from his own kids was coddling. But I knew, underneath the tough exterior, he'd had a soft spot for a lonely, scared little boy. And he admired that Lucas hadn't asked him to snuggle with him when he was scared. It was an ass-backward feature of the paradoxical male as far as I was concerned; (As long as you don't ask for it, you can have it) but in the end it didn't matter as long as he'd be sleeping next to his snoring father, Luke would be comforted.

"So how's the research"? He asked.

"Oh, I can't tell you all that I've uncovered here." I said, trying to sound enthusiastic. "You know the two old men I told you about?" I didn't stop for his answer. "They have been a wealth of information on mythology, historical lore, archaeological sites and so much else. I think we're going to finish out the week here and then do a bit of traveling to follow the vein of this story. Nora's getting a bunch of info too. This was the best idea for fact finding. I think when I get back, I'll complete my dissertation and then use what I've gathered to write a book about all of this myself. There's so much history!"

"That's great! You said you'd be a bit longer than you thought the last time we spoke, though. I only have so much time off you know. How're we going to manage your tuition, me taking time off, and the trip if you don't come home soon?"

I winced. I knew that our finances were on a shoestring as it is and to stay extra time, even a little might put us from a little behind to seriously in debt.

"I know, Walter. And I want to be home like you wouldn't believe. I really miss you guys but I don't want to pass up this opportunity, 'cause I know I won't be fly-ing back here anytime soon so I want to make the best of the time I have here, while I'm here. You have a couple of personal days you can tack on to the backside of your vacation time. They'll give you that. I mean, after all, you've worked non-stop for them all these years and you've never taken so much as a sick day. But if that won't work, can you call my mother to ask if she might be able to take care of Luke if I'm not back by the time you absolutely have to go back to work? You know she'd jump at the chance to take him for a few days."

"Okay, okay. It'll work out. You just do what you need to and get that degree you've worked for all this time. Then you can be Dr. Kies-e-ling." He said in a mock German accent. "Zen Heir Dock-tor, I shall retire und you shall be ze bread winner."

I giggled a bit and was grateful at his understanding. "Thank you Walter." I said sincerely. I started to choke up again at having this wonderful man as my partner, flaws and all. He is a good man and I know it. I told him so just then too. "I love you, you know. And thanks for understanding how important this is to me. And all my boyfriends over here can just save all their offers of an exotic life of luxury and their broken hearts for someone who isn't as lucky as me to have you and that other little guy.

"Does this mean I have to send away the harem when you come home?" He joked back.

I pretended to consider.

"Well, let them stay until the day before I come home so you'll have help clean-ing up the bachelor pad disaster I know the house must be by now." I spied the time and realized that I'd been on the phone for almost an hour. "Oh, Walter, Nora is waiting to call home too. I didn't realize I was on with you guys so long. I gave Luke the number if you guys need or want to call me but I guess I have to go. Okay?"

"Alright, I love you."

"I love you too. Give Luke a snug for me tonight too. Bye."

The room felt vacant now that I no longer had the telephone connection to home. I rolled up to sit on the edge of the bed for a minute and reflect on the con-versation. How was I going to explain all of this to Walter? I knew that eventually, it would all break loose if my son was going to be instrumental in whatever is going to happen to change the world. I would have to find a way to inform Walter without him thinking I'd gone completely crazy. I had a feeling when all of this, whatever, happens, we'll need to be a unified partnership to support Lucas in whatever way he'll need. I sighed and pushed myself off the edge of the bed to bring the phone to Nora. She'd want to check in with her husband too. Especially since the last few times she tried, she wasn't able to reach him. Now, at least if he isn't there, we have a number she can leave so he can call back when he gets the message.

———

While Nora was on the phone in her room, my mind wandered from my husband and son back home to the rest of my family as I busied myself in the living room. I inventoried my childhood and found so many things that made sense to me now as a result of the discovery that my life has a purpose. How many people stumble through life trying to figure out their purpose and never come to the knowledge? In the wake of all that I'd discovered about my heritage, my past lives, and my reason for living in this life, my mind swirled with memories of my childhood and dreams I'd had that shook me to the core but I'd had no idea why. Things were taking on a clarity I'd never experienced before. I had answers to questions that very few other people had the privilege of knowing.

Looking back down the long corridor of time, I reached to the part of my memory that held snippets of that first lifetime. My life as Lon Dubh, a.k.a Black Bird. Even my name made more sense to me now. I wondered at those blurry memories of the original eight people that were members of my current family. I tried to make connections of characteristics between the old personalities and the people I knew and loved as my family now.

I easily connected Colm with Nora. After all, we'd been through many lifetimes together and we were inside each other's lives and minds for so long it came naturally to me that I'd always known her. My other sisters though, Patrice being Iarann was a shocker at first, but the more I thought about what I could remember about the giant man, the more my heart warmed. I began to see that Patrice was strong and stoic in her ability to listen and nurture. She was immovable in her ideas of propriety but always let you understand that her decisions for herself were not a reflection of anyone else. She did not judge. She was caring, and kept a special eye out for me when we were small because I was a magnet for the school bully types, but she always maintained some reserve when it came to fully participating in family affairs and functions. I came to see how the center of her sprouted from the gentle man I so loved in another time.

Mary, on the other hand, I could not reconcile her to any of the family I could remember. She was eccentric to say the least and she could be very charming. One could have a fun time with Mary as long as they understood that the fun and the time were about Mary. How could this personality possibly be a product of my family of long ago? I counted on my fingers and reached for my satchel to go over my notes. Drawing out the spiral notebook, and flipping to the page with the wheel I'd scratched out, I observed the names and dates of the people who'd come in on the spokes of the wheel.

I studied the wheel and cursed my memory for having such spotty recollection. Realizing that my frustration was getting in the way of doing anything productive, I set about lighting a fire as I mused about this last spoke in the wheel. I thought it might be important. *Of course it was important!* We're all here with a purpose. Faidhe would have made sense as the eighth spoke in the wheel, but Cath and Finny made it clear that Faidhe was not, could not be reborn because she was paying a debt for her part in the death of Briciu. So if she had originally planned to be here at this point in human history, someone would have to take her place. Craiche is the obvious replacement for her but of course, she had already been identified as Mom. Which made a kind of sense that she'd come in and spend a life with Dad, who is Laoghaire. They had created such a bond in her sacrifice for him to be able to carry out what he needed to in a time of crisis.

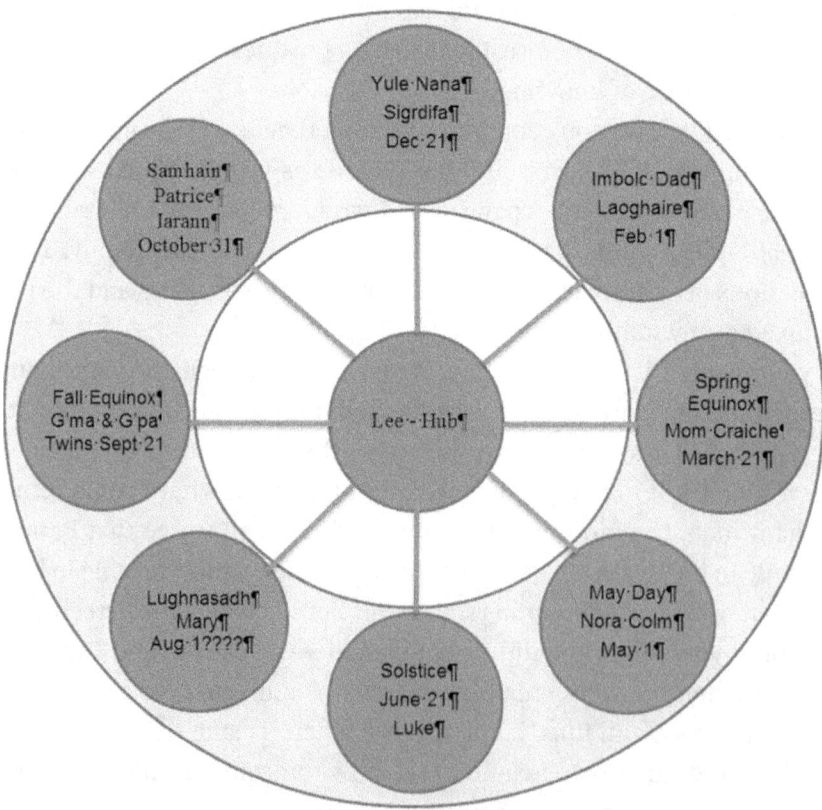

I repeated the line in the prophecy that spoke of the one who came into this world on Mary's birth date, August first. "August first, Leo. Larger than life, flamboyant, sucks the air out of a room, kinda self-centered. Hmm. Comes in with a debt."

I remembered the words as they were spoken in Cath's Irish accent that so endeared me to him and that had become such a comfort to me. 'They borth the forst who comes with a debt, on the day of the Lugh, this one is met.'

*Comes in with a debt. Comes in with a debt. If a debt kept Faidhe out of the wheel then a debt must've put Mary's counterpart into the wheel. Faidhe incurred her debt at the killing of Briciu so...*My mind toyed with me and the likely answer slipped passed my consciousness like mercury slithers between the fingers. Debt out, debt in. Suddenly, I drew a huge shocked breath.

"Oh." I shouted as the obvious dawned and I realized that Mary, my sister, is Gara! "Gara! I spat. Are you kidding me?"

Eerily, the pigs in the pen down the hill that the three brothers kept started to squeal up a ruckus. *How appropriate,* I thought. My skin puckered all up and down my arms and I felt my nipples gather together in stiff points of their own at the sound of the squealing.

Even through a millennia I remembered the caution and mistrust I'd carried for Gara. Some tumblers fell into place in my brain and it all made sense to me now that my sister Mary had been so flagrantly different from the rest of our family. I wondered at the purpose all this would serve.

———

The phone was ringing. A dark hulk of a shadow lay slumped on the couch in the darkened living room. Behind drawn shades, the 1950's music pumped at full volume through the house so the walls all but shook and the sound of the phone was almost drowned out. The coffee table and room were littered with beer cans, empty bottles of Grey Goose vodka, half empty Chinese food cartons and pizza boxes. The room was rank and smelled of something unclean.

A guttural squeal erupted from the hulk on the couch and ended in the feral bellow of a wounded animal as if it were in pain. In the background, the answering machine picked up the call. *Hello you've reached... Please leave a message and we'll...Have a great day.* The same voice as the outgoing message could be heard after the beep.

"Hi Will? It's Nora. Are you there? I know we haven't called much since we've gotten here but now we have a cell phone so we can make calls when we want to. When you get in, here's the number so you can call me when it's convenient." After giving the number she said, "I miss you...Hope everything's okay...Call me... Bye."

———

I knew from the look on her face and the short amount of time she'd been in her room, that she wasn't able to reach Will. Her face bore the stamp of worry and hurt, but at the same time she was a little miffed that every time she did call he was not at home. I knew she worried what he'd been doing.

Will was not all that pleased with Nora coming to Ireland with me. Never a very confident man, he found reasons to think Nora would be searching for someone to "hook up" with while we were here. Irrational of course but insecurity made for some strange suspicions and could lead to some unpleasant arguments as well.

Nora had her own successful business and was fairly independent. Will was the type of man to be attracted to her success and independence but resent it at the same time. He complained that she spent too much time at work and with clients one day and then he berated her for not making more money with her talents the next. He knew that she had special abilities and accepted that we were different, but he'd resent that she would help people with their lives through her astrological consulting, but she wouldn't give him winning numbers to win the lottery. He knew it didn't work that way but it didn't stop him from hammering her with the lament that she helped everyone but him.

Nora maintained a reserve with her husband and he knew we two had a special bond. Will was jealous of the close relationship Nora and I had but when it was convenient for him, if Nora objected when he went away on gambling junkets with his friends, he was always happy to tell her to spend some time with me.

I felt her pain when Nora came into the living room where I'd just lit the woodstove with newspaper and a few chunks of peat. She knew that an insecure man with a chip on his shoulder made room in his heart for things that didn't belong in a marriage. They'd had their problems but never had Nora been guilty of the horrible things Will would accuse her of when he wanted to lash out and hurt her. I knew Nora was looking forward to this trip for several reasons beyond gathering information for her book, one of them being to create space between her and her husband so that the absence might jumpstart things between them.

Careful what you wish for. I thought. *Sometimes the Gods grant it in ways that are not convenient at all.* I wondered just what might have been jumpstarted as a result of the deadly combination of her absence and his fearful heart.

"Come on. Let's have some wine. It's been a really long day and I think we deserve it. You check the doors and windows, I'll pour. I have something to run by you."

I pulled on the cork from a cabernet that had been waiting for us in the cottage with a flower basket sent by Walter and Lucas to greet us on the day we arrived. The cork gave with a pop as I tugged the old hand driven corkscrew.

32

She Spins Her Tale

The smaller pot cheerfully bubbled over the crackling hearth-fire and the dried and salted salmon wiggled back to plumpness in the writhing water with some of the preserved herbs found on the pantry shelves. The concoction danced with some roots, bulbs and greens Lon Dubh had foraged while she loitered in the forest with her new companions waiting until she felt it safe to return to the hut. Steam rose from the pot tantalizing the noses and stomachs of the two boys. Lon Dubh prepared the meal for the emaciated looking boys and enlisted them to set about gathering fresh grass and straw for the sleeping palettes she'd discovered in the back room during her escape from Diog only hours ago.

A second, larger pot heated more water for washing the linens of the seven small palettes. Lon Dubh was careful to use not hot but warm water as not to shrink the woven linens down to nothing. As it was, the sleeping palettes were smallish platforms and she did not intend to cause further discomfort for her party by creating even smaller beds than necessary. She thought that Iarann would have to use three or four beds across to accommodate him. She intended to take her mattress to the floor once it had been swept clean but she could not fathom even resting her head on the ancient linens caked with unspeakable filth. They would be laundered clean then stretched and air-dried over the branches of the bushes in a sunny clearing just beyond the dooryard of the hut. She would fill them with fresh picked sweet grass over straw with the help of the boys so they would smell fresh and crisp with the scent of clean air and green grass. Lon Dubh opened the thatched shutter in the sleeping room to air out the stale muskiness from it as well. Once she finished putting right the sleeping room she returned to her cooking pot and found two heads above it with nostrils fluttering wide to take in the savory aroma rising in vaporous tendrils.

"Take some water from yon pot and make ready yourselves to give thanks and break your fast." The two boys looked at Lon Dubh with suspicion at her suggestion that they near the wash pot themselves. "Know you this." She said with an inflexible tone. "It is grateful I am for your help in avoiding unpleasantness this day and also for your toil to help fill the cook pot and the mattresses but I will not have spent this day making this space worthy for the Goddess's blessing and allow you to dishonor yourselves by partaking of her gifts without first making ready with proper cleansing and thanks.

The two scruffy boys looked at each other with an expression of guilt and then both looked longingly to the roiling pot of delightful scents and resigned themselves to washing for what appeared to be the first time in a very long while. At first, they attempted to splash an obligatory drop or two of water in the general direction of their faces and looked expectantly toward Lon Dubh. She returned their looks with a withering glare that told them they'd better properly clean up or prepare to go hungry. The Elven boys sulked over to the pot of warmed water and each filled a bowl and took it outside with them to do right by the Goddess.

Some while later, the two boys returned looking no happier than when they'd left however they were pink in the cheeks and the only dirt that stood out on their hands was that which could not be scraped away from under their fingernails. They'd even washed knees, elbows and feet.

Lon Dubh graced them with a smile that spoke volumes of her pleasure with them. She set aside their washing bowls and doled out two large and steaming bowls of fish stew. She added a generous helping of quick bread she'd made with the remnants of ground wheat stores that was not so infested with bugs that it was beyond use. This, sweetened with honey she'd also found in the pantry shelves, was baked right in the fire in a pottery bowl with a cover. The steaming bread set the boys stomachs to growling just at the sweet scent of it. Lon Dubh ladled out a third bowl of stew and added a torn crust of the hot bread to it for herself. The three sat at the freshly cleaned table in the dining hall to enjoy a meal together and talk of their plans. Lon Dubh stayed the boys from eating by taking each of their hands and said:

Mother, we thank you and your cohort for the woodland bounty
We thank the great salmon for her sacrifice to our table
We offer appreciation for the sprites who gift us the pleasure of their herbs
We thank the bees for sharing their harvest of sweet honey and the Greenman for
His gift of wheat bounty God and Goddess in all forms, we thank you.

At this last, Lon Dubh spilled a bit of her stew on the hardened earthen floor of the hut, tore a corner of bread and cast it there as well. That said and done, she smiled sweetly at the boys and they waited for some sign that the ritual was over and that it would be time to eat. As she raised her bowl to her lips, the boys tore into their meal and did not stop until every bite was finished. They were invited to take as much as they liked and so they did. It gave Lon Dubh great pleasure to see the boys take their fill with such gusto. She wondered at the feeling of satisfaction a mother must have in seeing her brood eat with enjoyment of the meals she creates in union with the bounty from the earth. She breathed a contented sigh and then they spoke of the prophecy, her tale, and struck a bargain for the keeping and telling of this tale as it unfolds throughout her journey with Faidhe and Iarann and how the earth's spirit will change, is changing, and what must be done to prepare for the impending shift from communing with the Goddess and reverence for the fruitful gift of the feminine to a time when all talk of the Goddess would be considered wickedness and all things feminine would be reviled as weakness. Indeed, revered women would be reduced to the value of an animal or mere property of a man.

"But it seems that this attitude has already begun to take hold. For even in this place, we see the absence of the female essence has created a culture of men that has all but been besotted with greed, avarice and a view of women that resembles that of a brood mare more than a venerated bringer of life to be held in the highest regard."

Lon Dubh sighed as she rose from the table. The boys followed her with the bowls into the hearth room and began to clean them in the remaining warm water from the large pot. Cathbad replaced the bowls on the shelves in the dining hall and Fion banked the fire under the stew so it remained lit and low. Neither boy wanted his time with Lon Dubh to be finished but she seemed to lose heart for her tale for the moment or perhaps she lost heart for all that was to change and take place. They said nothing but their eyes communicated some message between them as Cathbad returned to the kitchen. The boys came up behind Lon Dubh each taking a hand in theirs. They led her to the entrance of the fourth room in the hut that she had not yet explored.

"I cannot bear another room in disarray my little friends. I am done with cleaning and cooking and fetching firewood and water this day. Whatever lies beyond will have to wait for I have not the strength to dive into further chaos."

The elves were insistent that she should enter the last room of the hut and practically pulled her with them through the doorway. It took a moment for her eyes to adjust to the dim light slipping under the thatched shutter of the room and between the weave of the saplings and vines in the walls. The room seemed larger than the others but Lon Dubh knew it was only an illusion for the room was vacant but for a few large items, each fitted with a stool. The first item she identified as a wheel threaded with recently peeled and washed flax that would spin a thick and supple linen thread. The next was a crude spinning system for wool designed of a weight stone which was suspended by a piece of cleaned and combed wool as it threaded through a large stone set upon a wooden stand made of tree stumps. The large stone had a natural hole in the center obviously worn smooth by centuries of water perhaps at the base of a waterfall somewhere, and offered a smooth surface through which the wool could be twisted round and round without catching. Someone had been spinning both flax linen and washed wool in here very recently. There were several skeins of wool and even more of the flax all ready for the loom, which was the third apparatus set up in the room. It seemed that someone had worked skillfully on the spinning of the threads but there was no evidence that the work would benefit them for the loom sat unthreaded and empty.

Lon Dubh clearly understood that someone had worked long and hard to spin all of this material and whoever had done this was skilled at the work. The threads were neat and even, spun without sparse spots that were likely to fray. The wool was strong without lumps but thin enough to weave tightly and offer a lighter more efficient garment.

"You?" she asked.

"We harvest the flax and we shear the sheep ourselves." Fion answered. "We can sell the yarn and thread to some who can make use of it or sometimes we trade our work for food. We can't let Diog know that we shear his sheep or he'll charge us. As it is, he has us herd his sheep to the high country and keep them grazed and watered. He pays no attention and no harm done to use the wool he does not. We are clever with the spinning but we have no knowledge of how to weave our craft on the loom to make real clothing for us or to sell. Traditionally, the weaving was a craft that women excelled at due to the fine work. Our mother taught us how to gather and clean the flax and to wash and comb, even dye the wool. Eventually we learned to spin the fine flax or the wool and when it was spun well, she made our clothes with her loom. We have the fine bones and small fingers for delicate work but no one to show us how to weave so we never learned. We are stymied and so we spend most days harvesting, peeling and cleaning the flax and wool and come here to spin. It's dry and safe from Diog for he'd never find himself in a place of work. Can you weave?"

Lon Dubh fingered the fine yarn and admired the labor it took to create such delicate threads. "You are part Elven." She murmured to no one in particular. "Of course you can spin. Elven weaves are renowned for creating exceptional concealment in the wood, part craft, part magic." She had a spark of inspiration. "Know you any magic? Any kind at all?"

The brothers looked to each other and their faces belied the truth. Lon Dubh knew what it meant for the boys if the greedy Diog knew of their skills and value should he find out how to bend them to bring him profit. "For no other reason than that we might work this craft together in order that we may follow through with our plans. You will be repaid a plenty for the keeping and telling of the tale, but more than our promises to each other must bind us, for the fabric of this tale must be made of strong stuffs. Let us mingle our minds and hearts in the creation of our bonds and of the tale. Make haste little ones. Shadows grow long and I would not have Diog come back whilst our work is not yet finished. Fion, take up yon wool and drop-stone. Spin for me your yarn, straight and strong. Cathbad, my quiet friend, take up your silken flax and spin your wheel until you have no harvest left to spin. I shall take up the loom and together we will create. I will teach and you will learn."

The group took seats at the three stations facing toward each other and began the work of spinning and weaving. Until the sun hung low and shadows spread toward night, Lon Dubh spoke as in a haze to the boys of much she knew from Faidhe and more she'd learned only as she spoke the words. The tale spilled from her lips and the three communed at times with words and other times through silent communion all the while the clack of the loom and the whoosh of the wheel synchronized with nimble fingers. Over their heads formed a cone of bluish light that emanated from the crown of each participant's head and all three columns of light converged at a point above them. Lon Dubh watched with amusement as the story she told formed visions between the three of them and they watched silently as events could be seen as though they were just now taking place. Hands were busy in an automatic fashion as the bond formed between these three and brought forth events and details of the story that even Lon Dubh had not known. They observed together glimpses of the bowl that Iarann was crafting and saw the people and events that are and would be depicted as the Cauldron is created. There was a growing tendril of fighe vine interwoven throughout the scenes as they appeared and developed before their eyes. The vine sprouted new leaves and grew ever longer as each new vision appeared. The vine looked as though it snaked through the fabric of each scene and gave the appearance that it was weaving a connection between the translucent images. The vine could be seen weaving itself into the shape of a great bowl and as the bowl hardened and strengthened, it took on the form of a shining silver Cauldron that would be the finished product when Iarann completed his work. Depicted on some panels of the Cauldron could be seen the fighe vine in pure silver. And Lon Dubh knew that the vine was a symbol for the Goddess's energy. Its roots, an unseen network that flourished beneath the earth until such time it is touched by the sun and then proliferates in fertile beauty. Earth Mother and Sun Father together creating life that is most difficult to stamp out.

The concept of the vine brought her to the memory of her mother's vision of Lon Dubh on the day of their first meeting. She took on the countenance of her namesake and the fighe vine was pulled from the womb of her mother in the grasp of her own mouth. How prophetic that she would nurture the roots of this living vine for this mingling of energy to take root. 'The journey extends beyond the four directions.' She knew now that this journey she was on would plant the roots and would venture not in any one direction but in all directions and into where time and the future would take it. Her task now was clear that she would tend the growth of this vine until its tendrils are interwoven within the fabric of time that the mesh of the feminine and the Goddess will be inextricably bound with the masculine. Symbiotic. One will not survive without the other. And one day, when they are near to equal in strength, they must join to battle the energy that threatens all.

Lon Dubh's attention was drawn back to visions in front of her. Above the shining Cauldron could be seen much of what the future held for the Goddess, the new God, the Tuatha de Danann and the raging fever over the new masculine God as it would sweep all the land and far beyond and into time reaching further than Lon Dubh's ability to fathom.

The three watched enthralled as the added ingredient of evil magic was infused into the fabric of time and history. They saw and understood that at the time the story of the new God came to light, there was also a competing energy for Power in the God of the bull. They saw the symbol of this evil magic manifest into the symbol of the bull and for a brief time, at the time of the new religion's birth, the sickness of the other infected the hearts of those who would hold power over others and there would be much senseless killing over the belief of the One God or many and that argument would rage on and burn out of control. Man would fight for the right to lay claim to the true God and all the while murdering, stealing, raping and conniving in the name of their God. The dark magic would take up residence in the hearts of men who would betray a brother, sell flesh, kill babies, and commit even more outrageous acts, having the audacity to claim it all justified in the name of their God. But in truth, it could be seen in visions as the three looked on, that the murky, brownish-maroon, mud-like color of the evil magic had eaten its way into the hearts of many. The hope they saw for the future was that the pulsing green and blue hews of the divine aspects of men and women were also present in the hearts of many. It was understood that they would and must keep the breath of life in the story for if it died, this dark red infection might take sway and then the best of humanity would be doomed. They saw that every time the feminine energy surged to be recognized and valued, there was also a surge of the evil to squelch it for it feared the time when men and women would be equally revered. It understood that that would result in diminished power for itself. And each time the evil energy held sway, there was a subtle showing of the feminine emergence when and where it was most needed to shore up the masculine and bring reason and logic to the warring hearts.

The three sat long into the night spinning and weaving while they learned of what was held in the hearts of each. A bond was intricately woven so the three could see and speak each other's minds. The tale as it happened thus far had been released to the brothers and part of possible futures had been revealed to them.

They understood the magnitude of their oath to each other and the burden they would bear for the sake of the Goddess and humankind. In that small room that had been where these young boys helped their mother, another relationship was birthed. A bond was set, an oath taken and a love fledged that would bear lifetimes of tests in sorrow and in joy.

As the sun lit the dawn, the three observed their night's work. They had spun enough material for Lon Dubh to weave tunics and cloaks for the boys. She had also created a masterful and showy cloak to replace the one she'd used for collecting firewood, intertwining various shades of the wool to create a design in the center of the garment and had edged the wrap with the blond linen so that it displayed rich handcraft indeed. The final piece of clothing was woven using the linen and finest wool yarn to create a sturdy square of fabric that would lend warmth for winter nights and comfort for having the soft linen fibers enmeshed with the wool. This blanket, she knew, would be a gift for one most important. She knew of the one, but did not yet know him or her. She could not recall the facts she garnered about this one in the previous night's meditations but she knew that this was a one she would watch and care for. She thought perhaps he or she, she wasn't sure of that either, would be a child she would birth through the great union that was spoken of in the prophecy. Perhaps she would, after all, give of her virginity to the Goddess to produce the child for whom the fabric was created. She thought of Iarann as this last thought crossed her mind and took comfort in the possibility.

After such a long and arduous night of crafting and magic, Lon Dubh was drunk with fatigue. She looked around for the boys who had left her but she had no idea for how long. Dazed now, she observed the boys who looked drawn and exhausted as well but she followed as they led her to the sleeping-room where they had filled the laundered linens with the grass they'd harvested yesterday. The room smelt fresh and inviting.

"Oh, you boys are so dear. Thank you. We have truly earned our rest."

Fion replied. "You sleep here Raven. This is a sacred space now and you should be safe. We will keep watch from above in our perch. We have learned much and will be true to our promise. There are things for which we must prepare. One of us will journey with you and the other will remain here. You rest now. Sleep well and take comfort that we will be as roots of the vine."

"Thank you my loves." She kissed them both on their heads and truly felt blessed to have a bond with two such creatures as to truly know and love them both so completely as only the depth of the communion they'd shared could make possible. Trust and faith were not in question and intimacy of the heart had allowed them to fully know who they all were in their hearts.

"I have never known such contentment even at this precipice in our lives as we take the fool's leap headlong into the future. Let us rest now little ones."

She stopped at this and excused her rudeness. "Forgive me, my friends, you are both near or equal to my own age, yet you maintain the appearance of childlike youth. It will require some concentration on my part to adjust my thoughts of you as children."

"It will be of use as it has been so many times in our lives that adults ignore our presence and dismiss us as unimportant." Cathbad said. "We are able to gather much that is of use in the way of information as well as goods. We will age and grow old for we have the blood of the Duibhe in us, but it will be a slow process for we are of the elves and immortality is their gift and curse. So do not feel remorse for seeing us as youthful, for we are that in the scheme of things."

Lon Dubh goggled at Cathbad for these were the first words she'd heard him speak. "I thought you were dumb, ah, I mean..." She turned to Fion, "You said he does not speak."

"I said he doesn't talk much." He replied with a grin. "You'd be surprised at how much people will say in front of one they think not only cannot repeat it but one they think has no mental capacity. We gather much knowledge in the wake of my brother's silence."

Her day of toil and the night of magic had completely sapped Lon Dubh of all her energy. She felt deep fatigue and could push her body no further. "I must rest, my friends. I must rest now." She turned and fell across three of the palettes and was in a deep sleep before her head touched the mattress.

———

It had been three days since the party of three had arrived in Middle Village of Clan Duibhe. Amazingly, Lon Dubh still slept in the stupor of travel, work, fatigue and magic. She was absolutely unaware, as the clan leaders of the Tuatha Duibhe had returned to their place of residence when not working at their respective mountains. The men returned to the Middle Village expecting to find all as it had been left, but when they entered the great hut in the dining hall, they were both surprised and suspicious to find the evidence of Lon Dubh's cleaning spree.

Fion and Cathbad had kept a fire burning for when Lon Dubh eventually woke up so that porridge could be made and there would be warm water for her to wash. So, although there was no evidence of anyone inhabiting the hut, there was a fire in each hearth and the smell of cooking bread met the broad and ample noses of the Duibhe clan leaders.

The Duibhe had returned to the village for the monthly moon rights as they had every full moon throughout history. They understood that something was very different this time and set about finding the intruder who invaded their quarters. Lon Dubh, still asleep, was found lying across the sleeping palettes much as she had been three days past. She was startled awake by the gruff sounding voices edged with outrage at her invasion of their gathering hut.

Lon Dubh felt a tug at her arm and it took her quite some time to surface from her deep sleep. She wasn't quite sure she'd been dreaming but she could swear that someone had kissed her so gently and sweetly on her lips that she woke to the sweet thought that Iarann had returned to her. Slowly she breathed deeply and luxuriated in the feeling of being well rested. She had the sense that she was not alone and opened her eyes expecting to see the face of the man she'd been dreaming of or the friendly faces of her new companions, Cathbad and Fion.

"Oh!" She awoke with a start and her eyes flew wide. "Forgive me. I am caught unaware!" Lon Dubh was understandably confused at her awakening after such a long sleep. It took her a moment to remember why she was in these surroundings and who these odd, sturdy little men were and did they mean her harm?

"I have been ah...your companion, Diog has offered me this house as a temporary living...ah, I am Lon Dubh." She tried again as she stood up to make her situation right with these men whom she knew were the tribal leaders. "I must take my leave for now but I shall return and explain."

She nervously bound out of the sleeping quarters and through the dining hall past all seven men leaving them to puzzle for themselves with jaws agape just what had happened.

Lon Dubh ran for the latrine area and relieved herself. She took moment to compose herself and walked to the pond to wash and rinse her hands, face and mouth with cool water. She knew of these men but not enough about them to understand whether she would be in danger. She knew that they had a reputation for being superb traders and they toiled long and hard. They had spurned the likes of Diog for hoarding so honor must be a part of what they value. She would return and speak with these elders and seek their protection should it be necessary if Diog tried to lay any claim on her as he had the Elven mother of Fion and Cathbad. She wondered at the whereabouts of her new companions and then about her mother and Iarann. She thought, surely, they should have returned by now, it is mid-day and they should have scouted and foraged enough to fill two cooking pots over. She had no idea that it had been three days' time since she fell into a deep rest and more since her companions left to forage. Had she known this, her concern would have been unmistakable and suspicion may have crept into her dealings with these men. As it was though, the three days on her own and with the vestiges of the Power of her own spun magic had left its stamp of change upon Lon Dubh. She had had an awakening of self-recognition and after a lifetime of wanting to serve the Goddess and fill the shoes of her mother, she had begun now to recognize herself as having value in her own service to the Goddess and not just due to her familial connection to her mother. Still, her mother and Iarann had been gone over-long and if they did not return soon, she would have to calculate how she must carry forward the work of their journey. Lon Dubh tried not to show her concern as she returned to the hut to face the men who were no doubt waiting for some kind of explanation.

As Lon Dubh entered the doorway, she saw the seven men seated at the dining table; facing them with a look of a bitter storm brewing on his face was Diog. She observed that the clan leaders were none too happy with Diog but they turned their attention to her as she stood in the doorway. All 16 beady, black eyes were on her and she thought to excuse herself and quietly back away but she was the daughter of the exalted Keeper and chosen servant of the Goddess. She must teach herself to stand her ground while out in the world. She is of the Tuatha de Danann and would not be cowed by these men. She would own herself and her birthright as a woman of the Goddess, a child of the Circle. She would be paid attention. In that moment, Lon Dubh composed herself and donned an imaginary robe of all that came with her heritage as if it were so much finery.

"Gentlemen." She stood with her hands gently clasped together as she spoke in a voice low and sure. She saw the look of awe and terror on some of the faces before her and understood that she now wore the face of the Goddess as she had lately seen her own mother do so many times over. Inwardly she reminded herself to be strong and then she spoke.

"I am Lon Dubh. I come to be here in your home at the invitation of your man Diog. I and my party have come to strike a trade and have made a bond with those who have met our terms. For this, we are pleased. Diog has offered us hospitality and in return, he has been promised payment with the gift of fine weaving."

Lon Dubh walked boldly to the room where the spinning had been done. She was amazed that the room was empty but for the cloak made for Diog and the finely woven blanket she had completed both folded neatly and positioned in the middle of the floor where all the magic spinning had taken place. During the time she had slept, someone, presumably the brothers had not only cleared the room, but also taken the blanket and dyed it the richest hue of blue she had ever seen. *It must be of woad, she thought. Or perhaps indigo from the east. The boys have been busy while I slept!* When she returned to the dining hall, her surprise did not show on her face. Diog accepted the fine cloak woven for him with the look of shock and surprise on his own face for he thought Lon Dubh had left to find her fellow travelers and had not expected to be paid what was promised.

"Your village has been a haven for me while I conducted my business, and for this, I have repaid you with what I hope will be pleasing for you. As you can see, your stores are in order, your hearth is kindled and as you have seen, your sleeping linens are fresh as is the stuffing inside. There is fresh bread; clean water and I will be pleased to fill your bellies with rich and thick mutton stew should there be an offering of such meat to the pot. I have hearth skills but no meat, I fear, for I have traveled far and have yet still farther to go. So should you know of whence such meat can be found, I will avail you of my hearth-skills in a fashion such as you've likely not had in some time in the name of the Goddess and in her honor on the night of her bountiful moon."

Then she fell silent to allow her words and offer to sink in. She would see now how her dealings with these men would be received.

It was Diog who spoke. Ever willing to ingratiate himself to the clan leaders, especially his own leader of the Do-pib clan so he was quick to offer a shank to the hearth for the promised stew.

"I have recently taken a he-sheep to the slaughter. It will be my honor to offer tender leg of mutton but barely two seasons of age."

At this, Lon Dubh gave Diog a withering look and he knew it was well deserved for the spare, all but inedible food he had offered her party and all the while having good and fresh meat.

"Is it well then, gentlemen?" She inquired of the seven. "Will you accept my offer of a hardy meal in payment for your hospitality? For a deal has been struck with two of your kin and I would have the bargain sealed by sharing a meal with you. For though we are so close to the gathering of the Goddess moon, my good fortune will be doubled should my work for the Goddess be brought under the protection of your worthy clans. Surely the Goddess will smile upon those who help her cause."

Lon Dubh knew she struck a nerve with this last statement. The little men still honored the Goddess moon every month. They prayed for continued wealth and especially that women-folk would return. If they so honored the Goddess, then she could see no reason they would not take the opportunity to please her by offering their protection and support and by filling well their bellies. The first of the Duibhe stood and spoke.

"I am Do Pib, chieftain of the Clan of the burning pipes. Diog, I give you leave to bring your meat to this hearth and offer this woman what assistance she may need."

Diog liked it not that he was commanded to assist this woman whom he had only a short time ago assessed as a possible concubine to serve purposes of his own.

"Certainly. Right away." He groveled as he left the hut shame-faced and red.

Do Pib mumbled something disparaging under his breath and the others chuckled. He turned his attention back to Lon Dubh.

"Allow me to introduce the chieftains of the clans of Tuatha Duibhe. Here, my ugly friend is Grauma. His name carries with it the meaning most appropriate, for it speaks of his black humor and his dismal outlook."

"I need no introduction from the likes of you!" The little man groused and shoved Do Pib aside. "How long do yer think we'll be cursed with yer company, woman? We'll not be coming back to flowers and frills here abouts. But if ye'll be a decent cooker, then well get to it and let's have it."

Her eyebrows arched in surprise near to her hairline, Lon Dubh responded without batting an eye.

"Well it's very nice to meet you too, Grauma. And you are very welcome!" The rest of the men muffled chuckles and covered grins with hands as many feigned a cough or two to cover their amusement at Grauma being so easily read. His gruff voice and exterior was all bluster and Lon Dubh knew it.

"I am Bas Fill of the clan Bas Fill. We are known for our luck at cheating death. If we get sick, we recover. If we are injured, we heal quickly. If we are poisoned, we often appear as dead, but then wake again to live another day. And the liveliness is instilled in every bit of us Bas Fill men, if you know what I'm about." Bas Fill said with a bawdy wink.

"How fortunate for you." Lon Dubh responded. "You must be blessed."

"And allow me to introduce the others." He said boldly, as he cast a broad arm toward the others, likely fancying himself a desirable catch for having shared this last tid-bit about his manhood.

"Sli Bain heads the clan Sli Bain. They are known for seeing the way and where to cut the earth to find her gifts and harvest what she offers. A good talent, that." He clucked with approval.

"Here be Snatsta, leader of clan Snatsta. They've a particular talent for cutting the stones as they come from the earth and bringing the true gloss so they're pleasing to the eye. Another valuable skill I'd say." Lon Dubh nodded to the men and Bas Fill continued the introductions.

"Diol Pa is our resident deal maker. Head of the Diol Pa clan, their skill is in the making of a bargain on both sides of the bench. They can sell and they do right by what they pay for wares as well."

"And last, we have Daigh of the clan Daigh. He has knowledge and wisdom about him. He knows about things but he can be stubborn to the core. Once he makes up his mind, there's no convincing him otherways. Sometimes it helps in the bargaining process if we send Daigh to do our negotiating, anyone knows there's no negotiating to be done and either the deal goes our way or it does no going at all. I tell you, we are pleased to merry meet, merry make and as we near our Goddess moon we're more than pleased to take a meal with you. And your name my beauty?"

"I am known as Lon Dubh. I was named for the Black Bird." At this, many of the men drew back for they knew the tales of the Goddess Mabh who selects those who would die before a battle and feeds on the eyes of the dead in the form of the crow or raven.

"Fear not my new friends, no one is being chosen for the feast today for it is my promise to fill your appetites, not the other way around."

Lon Dubh did not dissuade the men from their ideas about a mysterious woman come so close to the eve of the Goddess's full moon. She thought it was not unhealthy that these men should respect and revere her womanhood rather than plot to use it instead.

"If we are to sup in the name of the bounty the Goddess has bestowed, then I will tell you as I have told the others; you must come to this house properly cleansed in reverence for her for this house has been made of a sacred space to do her work and her bidding. You will be well protected and blessed herein but only come to her house with the proper respect."

Lon Dubh stood her ground and looked down at the men daring them to speak against such formalities.

Bas Fill broke the silence. "Well I'll clean up for the likes of the Goddess and yerself little lady. I'll warsh all of me in case the Goddess or anyone else might like to get a glimpse at what gifts I might give back." He said with another wink. "It is, after all, a night for the festival rights. Is it not?"

The other men were awakened to the idea that there was a woman in their midst and it was indeed a night that sexual rights might be practiced. The thought seemed to hit them all at the same time and they each hurried for the door toward the shore of the pond to cleanse the month's worth of grime from their bodies.

Lon Dubh smirked at her ability to bring these men so easily to her bidding. She was aware that she was already growing fond of them but that she needed to have caution until her mother and Iarann returned. She was here alone after all. Except, she thought, for her new friends. She walked to the hearth room and looked out through the smoke hole up toward where she knew the boys could see her if they were in the great tree. She could see nothing but she heard a sound behind her and turned quickly to see Diog behind her holding a bloody club in his hand. Stepping toward her, he raised the club and Lon Dubh realized that it was not a club but the promised leg of mutton.

"Come my worthy partner. In short time we will produce a stew such as you've never enjoyed and we'll see what can be done about mending your relationship with your clan."

It was Diog's turn to raise his brows in surprise. He momentarily saw the wisdom in cooperation and heaved the weighty shank on the substantial table.

33

Lady's Day, King's Night

Laoghaire sat in the center of the great stone Circle using colored pastes and dyes to create the images he'd seen emblazoned on the Shield as he'd seen when he received his gift from Craiche. He was not skilled in this craft but he took great care in his efforts to create the images as close to those he remembered. Symbolically, he knew the images held meaning and would carry with them certain energies to help along the cause in total but he did not entirely understand what he was doing. He followed his intuitive inner voice to create the new ritual. Laoghaire knew it was important that his task be complete before the rise of the next full moon, for the magic that grew and collected as he set the figures upon the Shield would be released to the Power at the gathering of the clan at his first ritual as Keeper.

He was mostly silent for the last three days since he and his family had come to the Hill. Adjusting to this new world of magical energy and all that had taken place over the last week was overwhelming for him. He contemplated the travel he would embark upon and how it would affect his family so soon after the first upheaval of being snatched from their home in the village. He felt a deep sorrow in his heart for what had taken place with his parents and now harbored a deep foreboding at the knowledge that not only had Briciu set forth such a treacherous curse upon the world by his act of dark magic but also in the attempt to quell its havoc, the balance had been upset and changed the possibilities of what was to be cast forth in the future. Though she tried to keep others from knowing what had happened with Briciu, Craiche knew, nonetheless and consequently, now Laoghaire knew as well. Faidhe would not be reborn to the future as she had planned, but the likes of Gara, he would now have to contend with and be responsible for until such time Faidhe completes her own journey and can arrange energies in the cosmos to insure the proper outcome at the proper time in the far distant future. Laoghaire felt a profound regret at what he knew must take place now and that all the Tuatha de Danann will be displaced and the Gods and Goddesses they had so loved and revered would retreat to the Sidhe.

A civilization lost. He thought.

Redirecting his thoughts back to the task at hand, Laoghaire painted a water vessel onto the Shield. He thought as he drew the figure that he would harness the Power of the seas to his task. His mind took on the rhythm of trance as he set to his drawing. His thoughts wandered with the sentiment behind what he drew and phrases came to him but made little sense. Laoghaire made himself content with allowing the thoughts to come. *One who can harness the strength of the ocean can maintain rule. A king over land and sea. The sea can rise up in ill temper and swallow the land. And the land can boil forth rising far above the reach of the ocean. Balance between the two. Land and sea. Strength in balance. Strength in the land. Strength in the sea. Unpredictable is the sea. Strong is one who can conquer the sea. Strong is the king of the sea.*

In that moment he caught a mental image of a descendant of his hearth in uncounted generations to the future. Despite the passing of such length in time, this man bore the look of Laoghaire himself or perhaps what his son Macha grown to manhood might resemble. The man bore marks of the twining fighe vine from wrists to shoulders, from ankle to thigh in the color of woad as a symbol of his worship of the Goddess and adherence to the Old Ways. This man also bore the brooch of the Hill T'airgh that was his father's own in signifying the keeper of the calves and king of the eastern shores. *Land and sea.* But Laoghaire understood that the one who bore the brooch in the future ruled not only the eastern shore but was the High King to all the Isle of the Danu. Not a lesser king as was his father. Laoghaire understood this to be a pinnacle moment in the future that very much depended on how he conducted himself at present. He saw some logic now in why he must leave his current post as Keeper of the Stones and take to the road with his family to bring his bloodline to the mounts of his father's people, his own people. The time of the Tuatha De Danann is coming to an abrupt end. It must. In order for the magic Faidhe casts to prosper and for the seeds of the feminine to take hold in the religion to come, his blood of the Sword and Colm's Shield must meet the blood of the one with the Staff once again and mingle with the blood of, not the Cauldron at that time, but a new vessel, called the Chalice, made of not the silver of the Cauldron he'd seen being cast by the smithy as Craiche's knowledge flooded into him, but of the gold of the sun which will carry the blood of the new masculine God to mix with the blood of the old Gods so they may create a new religion that will carry forth the Old Ways into the new future.

Laoghaire understood on a fundamental level that the visions he saw would take place but he found it difficult to fathom a time he knew to be so distant in the future. And he had the sense that the juncture he foresaw would be still many hundreds of sun seasons yet before the time when the culmination of this magic he conjured would come to full fruition. He was humbled to think of time in such vast increments that he would affect the distant future with what he cast now in this sacred Circle.

Laoghaire came back to himself and he observed that the watercraft he'd begun to paint on the Shield was now complete. He had no recollection of finishing the work but he witnessed the evidence as he inspected the work. Amazed he was, at the detail in the craft and as he looked closely, he could see the ship rise and fall as though aloft the ocean. Closer still he drew his attention to the figure, squinting his eyes to be sure they did not betray him. Upon the boat he observed casting about in the waters, he saw a party of familiar faces in Faidhe, Lon Dubh, Iarann the smithy and with them a young boy, small in stature looking pale and sickly. The party, he knew would be making a voyage and he knew he must time his departure from the Tuatha De Danann to ready a ship for Faidhe to have at her disposal upon the eastern shore of the island. He knew also, that the cargo they would carry on the ship must be readied as well. Laoghaire looked from the vision of Faidhe and her party to the Keystone of Fal split asunder not 20 paces from where he sat and pondered how he would go about moving the great pieces to where they would be needed. This he must have solved by the spring moon festival for it will be upon that night, after he performs his first Circle ritual for the Tuath that he and his family must depart from the place that has been home to the Tuatha De Danann for generations out of memory. He was chagrined at the prospect of uprooting his family yet again and leaving the clans but even more so at the knowledge that he would have to have such a one as Gara and her corpulent grandson with his family as they travel. He felt compassion for the boy. Laoghaire now knew what had come of his father but the boy put him in mind too readily of the one who spawned him and the evil he wrought on human kind and on those Laoghaire loved.

———

"Nephew, how good it is for you to come and see your aunt. Or is it that you miss these rooms already in the absence of your father? Could it be other than a friendly visit? Grow you weary of belching forth compliments for your lady patron? Believe you, I had come near to insanity for having to walk lightly around whatever word or sound that might set a flame to the kindling of her temper. I envy you not, to be under her eye but if I am given a choice, that you bear the burden or I, nephew, I hope it does not disappoint you that I would subject you to the lady before myself."

Triag stood at the doorway of his former home looking around with amazement at the speed with which Nemain had transformed his father's rooms into a feast for the eyes in richly dyed wools, skin and sheep pelts. He was almost aghast to see his father's favored tapestry on the floor to be trod upon. Then, Triag took a tentative step forward and nudged the rug with his toe. He looked at Nemain with the question on his face.

"Yes nephew, it is there with a purpose. You will do no more harm to the tapestry than the sins it covers beneath its weave."

Triag wasn't quite sure what his aunt meant by this last comment but he understood that he was being invited to step upon his father's tapestry. He momentarily recalled a particularly unfair beating he took when someone had gotten soot ash on the wall hanging and his father had blamed him. First, Triag stepped onto the rug and waited almost expecting his father to come into the room and catch him. Then a smile spread across his pudgy face so his eye all but disappeared into slits. The boy broke into a comical dance, shuffling his feet across the tapestry, then escalated to a full out celebration of being released, for the moment, from tyranny and ended with three or four jumping stomps on the piece for good measure.

"Triag, how is it at Gara's hut for you?"

"Oh!" He replied automatically, "I am bestowed with everything a boy could dream to have."

"Come now, boy, no need to offer Gara's words by rote. We are family, you and I, and it can be not much different for you moving from my brother's house to live in my mother's. Believe you, I know what it is like to hold my tongue from the truth and the frustration that Gara can inflict. One moment giving favor, the next a sharp tongue cutting at the thing she knows will sting the most. Am I not on my mark, nephew?"

The boy looked at his feet on his father's rug and subconsciously stepped off the rug, realizing that he had little reason to celebrate.

"My grandmother is a kind and generous woman," was all he could say.

"Spare me your lessons in public decorum, Triag. Have you no more backbone than this? I had always taken you for a boy with drive and a measure of more cunning than my brother." Nemain flared then composed herself. "We two are what's left of this family. Gara speaks now of supporting the new Keeper and it seems that things will settle down here soon enough. We have work to be done, you and I, for you will come of age in three short calving seasons and we must count cattle to determine what your inheritance from your father will be. Then, we must take careful steps to see that Gara does not abandon her senses entirely and allow Laoghaire to fully inhabit the Hill and the Council to the exclusion of our claiming our rightful places among the hierarchy here."

Triag's face betrayed his shock at Nemain's boldness. She laughed at the expression."

Did you not think the mousy Nemain capable of independent thought beyond Gara's words put in her mouth? Naïve boy; I am not such a sheep. There is wisdom in keeping silent and allowing others to think what they may. Then no one looks in my direction to intrude with questions I prefer not to answer. Know you my meaning? Think you that Gara would have given over of your father's holdings to me if she had a thought that I would deem to keep my earnings at the end of the three season's stewardship when you come to full manhood? Think you that she will allow you to keep your inheritance? You know she already has some kind of plan that will give her leave to absorb part or all of what we both will have worked to build. It is who she is. Now, with Briciu out of the way, we too stand to come to wealth and perhaps title. We are smart, why should we not have what is ours without the unpleasantness of answering to Gara?"

Triag's mouth was agape at this newfound knowledge that his half-wit aunt had outfoxed both his father and his grandmother in such simplicity.

"All this time?" he asked the simple question that covered so much.

Nemain nodded and flounced down right in front of Triag on a mountain of lounging cushions covered with costly furs.

"I have magic far beyond what I have revealed. I have developed my skills when no one thought to see what I was doing. You see, when one is considered unimportant, that is when the most harm can be inflicted upon an enemy, with the element of surprise. Has anyone taken a care to see what magic you have, Nephew?"

"No, I...my father always said I was useless to him for I could not have ears in places I was not present."

"Ha! The imposter. Had you ever wondered boy, why he'd need your ears should he have the talent himself? Or if he expected you to provide this service in his stead, why then did he not teach you how? I'll tell you why. Your father never could listen or speak in his head to others, but I have the ability to speak with those on the other side and sometimes to extend ears where they may not be welcome should my intended target have the ability. The trick is to listen to what people are saying in their minds without them knowing it. I can glean from your simple mind that you spoke internally with the old woman of the Council." Nemain watched for the boy's reaction and again laughed out loud at the expression on his face.

"I know another secret too." She said conspiratorially. "Gara, the great temptress and Councilwoman has not this ability either."

With this, Nemain made a feigned look of shock on her own face.

"So boy, here's what I propose: I will help you to hone the skills that you have, so that we two may communicate while Gara is unaware. She may expect us to work together to some degree, but she is not a stupid woman. Should she see us together overmuch, she will grow suspicious or jealous; it is her nature. For she is looking to you to be groomed as her new puppet for she thinks she already has one in me. She will be penurious with time you do not spend in her bidding. Are you open to making your own fortune, boy? Will you not benefit from the skills

I can teach you? Will it not be in your interest to know what is in Gara's plans as you ingratiate yourself into her confidence? You and I will be in communication. We will know each other's minds. For this reason alone, you will know you can trust my plans for us. Together, we will build our own empire. What say you, nephew...Triag?"

A lifetime of scraping and scrabbling to please Gara and his father to keep from enduring their wrath kept him frozen in indecision. The idea of learning magic and developing his own wealth appealed to him but the penalty should he be caught or even suspected would be steep. Nemain may have a plan that could work in time but what if they were to be found out before they could gain a foothold in their lessons? They would surely both be in such disfavor as to be put on the road themselves.

"Ah, Sweeting," Nemain crooned. "We will not be caught because we will not be foolish. See? I can already read your thoughts. You will be adept at your learning and let me tell you how we will do this. You will appeal to Gara's sense of superiority and greed. I know she did not give these huts and cattle to me in earnest. In truth, she has her own reasons for wanting to distance herself from your father's possessions at this time, but we have no need to examine that for the moment. You will go to her and ask permission to watch over my doings here to insure that your inheritance will be well preserved. Tell her that you worry over my lack of thinking ability and that I should be supervised. Surely, she has expressed this concern on her own by now." Nemain raised an eyebrow to her nephew to verify her suspicion and the look on Triag's face revealed that it was so. "See nephew? I understand the woman. She had much power at one time, but the winds are changing here and we must make a place for ourselves while we can. You must make her think you come to me of her accord. Then we will be free to practice your magic. Make no mistake, we will work at building the herd and keeping the stock healthy but we will also keep in communication as to how we might, one day, relieve Gara of her burden of livestock, just as she would have done us. You will be strong, and possess magic. This I will do for you. I will not keep you weak and bribe you with sweets so that you grow fat, lazy and weaker still, ever like your father." She said with disgust. "I will show you what it is to be a man, to earn, to cast. Come here Triag, my love, be not afraid. Come to me and I will show you how to be a partner, not a slave."

Nemain's crooning words wrapped around the boy and anesthetized him to any reservations he might have had in participating in a plan to usurp his grandmother. He was seduced in ways that appealed to him for what he'd always wanted was to be loved and respected and powerful. He'd felt a mischievous thrill as earlier he stepped on his father's tapestry but that was a mild delight in comparison to the ecstasy he felt now at the prospect of learning magic, and coming to his manhood wealthy in cattle all the while outsmarting his grandmother, right under her nose.

He would be receiving benefits from Nemain while at the same time earning praise and rewards from Gara. A sly smile spread across Triag's mouth and he greatly resembled his father. He nodded his allegiance to Nemain and she held out her arms for him and he joined her on the cushions in an embrace that was not at all wholesome, for Nemain's intent was to so completely have this boy's allegiance that he would not ever occur to him to betray her. She calculated that she was only half-blood to her brother for they were both born of different fathers from various festival rites. So, she justified that any real relation to this boy was but a trifling thing and he wouldn't come to full manhood for some three years yet. Anything she showed him could be deemed part of his education for any man to be of worth to a woman, he must know how to please. She would give to him the intoxicating blend of power, pleasure and wealth with the added ingredient that Gara had kept ever distant from her minions: good self-opinion.

———

Colm had done her best to create a new home for her family on the Hill. At first, the children were curious about the Circle and the sacred spring and all that could be explored. She was left to make ready the hearth and sleeping pallets. She and Laoghaire would have to share the smaller pallet that was Faidhe's until such time she could weave larger linens for a new bed. The children had brought their own linens from below, as Laoghaire's cousin Cuan would have no use for the children's pallets. Faidhe had kept a meticulous kitchen and had taken very little to the road so Colm had many herbs, early greens as well as simples, tinctures and unguents at her disposal left by Faidhe. It took short work to put things in order to her liking on the first day they arrived up the Hill.

On their third eve on the Hill as they prepared to sup, Colm inquired as to whether Laoghaire might need her on the next day for she wanted to keep busy with the gathering of flax and spinning of linen to create a new marriage bed for the two of them. She knew it was silly, but she felt unsettled in sleeping with Laoghaire in the pallet that was her mother's and did not want to spend any more time in that bed than she had to. It was as if she sensed that the energy between the two of them had shifted and chastised herself for thinking that somehow Laoghaire knew of her dream of Briciu and was distant for his disappointment in her. Although Colm knew this was not the case, she was eager to bring up from their former home, her loom to set to spinning a fresh bed for her and Laoghaire to symbolize a fresh start.

"Husband, are you well? You have been tending yon Circle all this day until far past dark and now upon your return, you are still yet far away."

After a few moments, Laoghaire was pulled from his thoughts and attempted to smile at his wife.

"I am well, my heart. I have seen and done much this day. On the morrow, there is much to do still. And many morrows after that I fear. There is so much that I must learn and arrange before the festival rites. This will be a Powerful ceremony for as you know, it is not only a full moon sky, but also the day when the days begin to be longer than the nights. It is a telling ceremony for these times, is it not? The full moon of the Goddess on the very day that the sun of the God begins to take sway?" He did not wait for her answer but continued. "Colm, I know you work early and late to make right this place for our family but I think there is not much for you to do here until I have learned the necessaries of the Circle and the children have explored as far as I think is safe for them to venture alone. I will better turn to my work if I know you are not alone and waiting for me to finish what I must. Should you decide to venture down the Hill to inventory anything you may not have taken in our haste to leave the village, I will welcome being relieved of the guilt of leaving my beauty alone overlong. And should you tarry to visit, all the better that you should have words and company to bring back news to me of village doings."

It was as though Laoghaire knew what she intended even before she had fully understood it herself. Brightened, she replied, "I would so like to bring my loom from below, for we are not sleeping well in our small pallet and neither are we making full use of our marriage bed." Colm's eyes dropped to the ground at this last for it had been three nights since they came to the Hill and they had not yet consummated their new home. She was concerned.

"Fear not, my dove, I am overcome with my new responsibilities. We will come to our marriage bed with renewed zest; be sure of it. But be patient with me for we have much to do before the Circle Ceremony. And much to plan for after."

Colm was troubled at the mention of what comes after the ceremony for she understood that Laoghaire meant to journey to his own village on the eastern shore and was not sure what he intended after that. No one would fault him for going to his village upon hearing what had happened to his family, indeed he'd been praised for staying to the Hill to engage in his new duties until after the first ceremony, but Colm had not the courage to ask him as yet what would follow.

"Yes Laoghaire, I will take the children down the Hill on the morrow and I will seek counsel with Craiche for I am plagued with dreams and I would know what tincture will cure me of these parasites."

Laoghaire stirred at the mention of Craiche for he had not shared of her passing or what she'd bequeathed him. He knew not why he had yet to tell Colm, he just kept silent about all that took place in the Circle.

"You take your visit Colm. And bring your loom along with fresh washed wool for I feel that it is much cooler upon the Hill than below. It may be that we'll have need of more woven woolens."

Colm smiled as she observed the children run to join herself and Laoghaire at the outside hearth with red faces and woodland scratches of adventure.

Colm called to the twins, "Get you to the cleaning bowl you imps. You'll have none of this quick bread or tender sow loin until I can see your hands and beautiful faces 'neath all the sweat and dirt!".

Laoghaire was relieved that the conversation had turned from Craiche for now, but he knew he'd have to share with Colm all of what he knew upon her return.

———

Faidhe felt some urgency around how long they'd been gone from Lon Dubh but was soothed as her consort, the Greenman, came once again to her side as she foraged in the wood for food.

"Worry not, woman for your daughter is cared for and in the hands of friends of the green. These Elven folk are necessary to her journey and she will be in need of communion with them. Trust that what you have wrought will be so. You bade her follow her intuitions to find a worthy partner in the telling of this tale, and so she has. Come and sit with me a while and I will tell you of a future for our son."

Faidhe carefully shook the handful of early green berries she'd picked into the small pouch at her halfstrap and sat down next to the Greenman eager for news of the babe that quickened in her womb. She had concern for she'd seen that this child was not destined to take the long journey with her but would be fostered in a strange land with which she had no familiarity. This news both relieved and terrified her. Faidhe struggled to ignore the strong scent emitting from this man that called her to lay with him even now with a babe in the womb. Drawn as she was to his scent, she noticed the great horns he displayed atop his head. "What manner of husbandry is this? For when last we met you bore no antlers as a buck."

"I am the proliferator of all life in the wood and green, Faidhe. I take on the likeness of the great stag as well as the great trees. For this is the time of the spring fertility in the wood; is it not?"

"It is. I understand, without your call to propagate, there would be no new seedlings, no flowers, no new foals or fawns. Faidhe felt herself being drawn ever closer to the man. She steeled herself to the subject at hand and shook off the call to couple for she was most eager to hear what lay ahead for her child. "My attention is yours but would that I were not distracted so by the urge to be in union with you." And as soon as she uttered the words aloud, the urge had greatly diminished.

"As you wish, Seer. Let us tend to the information you seek. The babe you carry will be a guest as he is fostered in the lower reaches of the great land to the east, beyond the large island and due south on a peninsula. There he will be fostered and eventually father a great many children as will be his nature considering his heritage. This babe must be in fosterage and thrive until manhood for it will be of his blood, when this place where he is fostered becomes a great empire of the region and far beyond, a descendant of our child will be a warrior of conquering for the peoples of that empire. This child you carry will be blood ancestor to this leader and to others who establish a stronghold for the new religion on the western shore of the peninsula. This warrior's role on the peninsula is vital to our cause but more so in his conquests up the western coast of the great island to the east of here for he will find himself in the land of the Picts and in the way of his ancestor, will father children there as well. Some few hundred seasons after this, the great one you have seen in our visions and in the vision of prophecy will be born of that blood. This is the one for whom the Staff will be preserved. He will find himself drawn, as the land of the De Danann calls him like a moth to the flame. He will have our blood in him and will have the gift of seeing and vision as you do yourself. This heir to the Staff will be named Padraig and will mark in time the union of the Old Ways of the Gods and Goddesses and the new religion of the one God. This one alone will establish the union and will plant the Staff in the soil of the isle of the Danann and the two religions together will take root and proliferate the old religion with the new as the symbols of the hilt of the sacred Sword and the circle of the Shield come to be known as the symbol for the new religion in this land."

"I am to cross water then?" Faidhe asked clarifying information she'd intuited but had no idea how she'd be able to arrange the voyage.

"You will gestate this babe, conceived of the green land, on the ocean as you voyage south. This balance will offer him and his descendants dominion over land and sea."

"Ah." Faidhe commented. I have seen in the prophecy this combination of elements, earth and water used often in both vision and symbol. It is a mighty combination then, is it not?"

It is and will be in the new religion as well. It is only for us to understand the need to maintain balance between the two within our creation of all things. For to lean too heavily on one element or to harness the Power of one over the other, will work against our cause in keeping balance in all things for as you know, these are the foundation of the existence of the human kind. One being feminine and the other masculine so this child must be imbued with all the energy and Power from both these elements."

"Why then, teacher, will we not use the other two elements as well for a complete balance in the forming of this one?"

"This will be the child of the earth, and will spawn those of his blood who will tend the masculine aspects of the human condition: warring, conquests, and so on. The other two elements will come in to play when the descendants of our child come to the spiritual on their own, as will be their destiny. For one of the descendants of this child will bring the new religion to the isle of the Danu where the union of old and new will be created and another descendent of this child will found the stronghold for this new religion in the very region our child will be fostered. The flesh must come to the spirit. That is our quest in all of this. Which is why, once you have completed your work in the large island to our east, you will journey by water and follow the trade routes to the south until you reach the inlet between the two vast lands. Once through the inlet, you will eventually come to the shore of the peninsula where you will leave our son to set things in motion."

Iarann had taken to building a large fire. The strong pull for him to make use of his tools to create a panel for the Cauldron would not be delayed. It had been this way for him since he had taken on the task of creating the Cauldron he'd seen in his visions. Only when the overpowering call to create a panel came on him, was it revealed to him what images would be depicted on each. As had happened each time he set to his tools to complete a panel, he had no recollection of creating the images; he was left only with a knowing of the meaning behind images and symbols. Only after the panel was complete would he be released from the grip of the trance and he was free to inspect the plates and admire the craft that had been so adeptly constructed in an extraordinarily short amount of time. Iarann was always amazed at the finished product for it was fine work he did not recognize as his own. Iarann often found himself wondering if this was how it had been for his father, the God Goibhniu, who was renowned for the speed at which he'd constructed magnificent Swords and instruments of battle.

Iarann enjoyed hours instructing Lon Dubh on the symbolism and meanings for each panel, which depicted the events that had taken place since the first day they had come to be friends. In fact, as his hands did the work of crafting this most recent panel, his mind kept busy thinking of Lon Dubh and how she fared in his and Faidhe's absence. He was aware they'd been gone overlong but he also understood that Faidhe had her reasons for keeping to the wood. Now that he was set upon with the all-consuming need to create this panel, he resigned himself to the idea that all was as it should be, for the construction of the bowl is key to all they do now. At least, he thought, it is my key role in this story. And with that thought, he was besieged by visions of a woman of great and terrible beauty. She beckoned to him and he could not resist. All about her were bodies of the slain and she paid them no heed. This woman wore the color of the sun in her hair and bore eyes the color of ice, vibrant and forbidding. Upon her head she wore a hat of armor adorned with great red wings. As she reached for Iarann's hand, he could not resist and he held out his hand for her after only once looking back toward Faidhe and

Lon Dubh. All at once, many wheels that were set about her took to spinning at the moment that Iarann's hand touched the strength of this woman's hand.

When Iarann awoke, it was full dark and his fire had gone cold. His head lay upon a silver panel that, to his astonishment was complete with several animal figures and a key human figure bearing great antlers upon his head. As Iarann sat up to inspect the piece, he was aware of a second panel beneath his hip for it pained him as he made to move. The smithy tried to fathom what time in the night it might be and how long he'd been lying on the earth. He wondered then with mild panic, *where is Faidhe?*

"I am here, Iarann." Came her voice from behind him. "I see you have knowledge of my quest here in the wood. And, it seems, you have had visitation of your own." Faidhe added as she nodded to the panels in his hands.

Iarann tried to focus his sleepy eyes to see of what Faidhe spoke. There on the second panel, he saw himself and the woman of whom he dreamed with the wheel held between them and several strange animals around them.

"What means this visitation Faidhe? I fear this woman for she holds great and fearsome power as well as bewitching beauty yet I felt myself sparked with the need to touch her, to lay with her, to be consumed by her. This kindles fear in my heart."

"You have your path in our journey as do we all, Iarann. It seems, at the endmost part of our journey you will serve the Goddess through such a one as this as I have served with the Greenman himself. It makes sense that she will have chosen you for you are of her ilk through your father's lineage. We travel to the land of the origin of the Stone of Fal in the North Country after much travel to foreign places abroad. She has claimed you for her own to suit her role in all that must be done."

"Who...why...?" Iarann, still groggy, could not even formulate the questions he wanted to ask.

"As the Keystone to our Circle comes from the cold country to the north and it is the Power of the feminine we seek to preserve, we travel not only to plant seeds for the future but to initiate and activate Powerful feminine magic which is strongest for our peoples in the Goddesses of the northlands, the Valkyries. It is from these northlands that our Tuath hailed so many generations ago. These Valkyries are our kin and I know this one who has claimed you, for she is one of many whom I have contacted through magic to warn them of the prophecy and prepare them for what must take place upon our arrival to the gateway for their territory. Her visitation with you can mean only one thing. The prophecy I have foretold has come to them as well, in some form, for the panel you create expresses the Valkyries will participate in casting the magic needed to preserve the Goddess. This is pleasing to me to know for certain our journey will not be for naught in that region for it is a cold and harsh place. And there will be a price for their magic I'm sure. Would that we'll be able to pay it; for their magic is great and will be needed."

Closing the subject Faidhe stated, "Come Smithy, we shall travel by the moon for it is time we return to our Black Bird. She will have had three days' time to have made the transition from a novice to one who has come to her own in her role as a servant of the Goddess. Let us visit with the men of the Seven Mounts for they will be returned to Middle Village for the rites."

———

Gara spied Colm walking toward her former hut as she returned to the village with her children. It took a moment for realization to dawn, how unusual a sight this is for Colm should be tending her highly important duties with her husband upon the Hill, she thought bitterly.

"Triag!" She called into her hut behind her. "Where are you boy?" She was slightly annoyed to remember that she'd sent him to Nemain's hut to keep count on the cows that were already bred to the prize bull for spring calving prior to it being felled to the spitfires. It would be prudent to choose bulls of his stock and take care to raise them with good feed and close attention so that the prize bull should not be missed overmuch.

Gara hastened to the huts belonging to Nemain to retrieve Triag for it was part of her plan to take opportune moments such as these to forge friendship between the Keeper's family and her own. She was shrewd enough to understand that due to Briciu's blunders and some minor missteps of her own, it would not be an easy task but there was hope for her grandson, who was but a few seasons older than the Keeper's children, to ingratiate her family to the other.

As Gara approached Nemain's huts, she could see no sign of the cattle being brought from the fields for the calving cows to be accounted for. Without announcing her arrival, Gara burst into the hut for she felt she owned the premises and was taken aback to see her daughter and grandson using sticks for some strange game between them.

"What nonsense this?" She demanded. "I give you leave to learn business practices of the family and I find you both gaming? Perhaps I made an error in judgment to have confidence in your abilities to take over your family duty to cattling, daughter. And you," she smoldered. Are you not here to see that this kind of laziness does not take place?"

Gara immediately recognized her mistake in revealing that she'd sent Triag to keep watch on Nemain's actions.

Ignoring the obvious Nemain stood from the cushion furs and approached her mother feigning excitement. "Mother, come see what Triag has taught me!

It is a counting system for the herd to keep track of every head! Look here; these sticks in this pile are the heifers coming to spring calving. Each of which will be a product of the prize bull. We have counted nine that are obvious and there may be more but nine that we know of. These sticks here are young bulls that will be rotated from the outer green fields to allow the heifers prime rye and wheat grass to calve with proper nutrients." Nemain pointed to another pile of sticks. "Here, these sticks are bulls ready for spring mating for these mature cows, to gestate and be ready for the fall calving. We propose to have these cows mate early to come to calving early and give the young ones time to grow strong before the end of the warm days."

Gara was taken by surprise that Nemain not only grasped these concepts but also seemed well versed in the process. She looked to Triag and he answered all her unasked questions.

"My father is a herdsman." He said with a shrug. "I learned things as I watched."

Gara was pleased to see that things would run smoothly here and she would no longer have to keep more than a cursory watch over this stock.

"Have you a total count?" She inquired of Triag ignoring Nemain.

"We have, Grandmother, and we may expect that number will have grown by 20 come the end of summer even considering those gone to the slaughter."

Gara seemed satisfied for the moment and spoke again, only to Triag as if Nemain was of no consequence.

"Come boy, I have a task for you. Do it as well as you have taught your aunt this day and there will be extra sweets for you tonight. I wish for you to visit with the Keeper's children for they are down from the Hill this day. Inquire of them if they have any need of our help in provisions or any other such."

Nemain perked up and spoke in her dimwitted fashion.

"Oh Mother, mean you that the Keeper is in the village? I do so hope that Colm is with him. I find I have need of one of her unguents for I am helpless with a rash of the womanly kind."

Gara winced in disgust at the thought of her daughter's hygienic address but thought again that a union of friendship between her daughter and Colm might be the connection she desired.

"Go you both, then and speak of what you might but have a care not to be overbearing in your inquiries. Remember you these are people newly raised to title within our Tuath. Keep ever mindful of respect."

"Of course, Mother." Nemain gushed in the way of a simpleton about to go on an adventure.

Gara looked to Triag who had been well versed in his duty as Gara saw it, for him to ingratiate himself to the Keeper's children at every opportunity. A friendship between the families would eventually be beneficial.

"Yes, Grandmother." He answered her dutifully, playing just enough of being exasperated that he would have to further endure Nemain's company for Gara to believe he was still doing her bidding.

You played that well nephew. Triag heard Nemain say directly into his thoughts.

Well played yourself, Nemain, for Gara would not seek to ask of your affliction and whether Colm succeeds in healing your womanly difficulty. Shall we tell her how you came by your soreness?

Nemain struggled to stifle the giggle that threatened to escape her lips but after years of practice she maintained her discipline and remained in her character as a simple girl.

Triag maintained his discipline too.

"Come, Aunt, we shall approach our new alliances together. I will help you explain to the Keeper's wife what needs you have but I tell you I'd prefer to spend my time with my new friends closer to my own age." He lied as he took her hand pretending to be over solicitous of his dimwitted aunt.

Gara was pleased at how things were going. Good stock on the way, eyes on her dull daughter, a possible connection to the Keeper's family, perhaps two. She felt secure enough in how her plans were taking shape to possibly visit the Keeper's kin who is staying in Laoghaire and Colm's hut. *Perhaps I will have dire need of his herding advice in light of being abandoned by my son who used to tend to these things.* She thought, already putting Triag and Nemain out of her thoughts. *Yes, I think I might take time to fix my hair, wash with salts and have the servants prepare a meal of special quality this night for this man is a guest of the Tuath and it is my duty as the only member of the Council who seems to be available to the task to tend to his needs.* At this she smiled to herself and wondered at what needs a man of such size may have. She felt justified in that it had been overlong that she had use of a diversion to erase the foul memory of her failure of a son and having missed out on the festivities of the feasting due to his rude interruption and having forced her to contend with cleaning up after he'd made such a mess of everything. Glad to put it all behind her, she allowed her mind to wander to possibilities of creating her own connection with the Keeper's kin and felt a cunning satisfaction that the connection she had planned would be much more enjoyable than that which she envisioned between Nemain and Colm or that of the children.

34

Spring Equinox

The return trip to Middle Village was comparatively brief for Faidhe and Iarann in that they stopped for nothing and carried a brisk pace. They found their way back before the moon had set high in the sky and prior to the start of the evening rituals. The rhythm of the beating drum skins could be heard in the distance first as Faidhe and Iarann drew closer to Middle Village. The closer they came to the hut where they'd left Faidhe's daughter, more instruments could be recognized and beneath the mournful whining music of the skin-pipes, the additional lighthearted sound of Lon Dubh's whistle became obvious. A hardy smoke could be seen rising from the smoke hole in the thatch above the hut and the rich aroma of savory lamb was easily identified in the homey scents wafting from the hut that appeared to be well lit from within.

"It seems I worried overmuch for the welfare of our Black Bird." Iarann uttered with a suspicious expression. Without comprehension, he felt a spark of protectiveness bolt through his midsection as he recalled that he and Faidhe had returned to participate in the rites of the full moon upon this quarter day. An event that called for one to take the role of the Goddess and another to assume the role of the God in a marriage of union following the celebration of this particular spoke in the wheel of the year. That thought put him in mind of his vision earlier this day of the woman beckoning him to her, for they too had some communion pertaining to the wheel of the year he thought. But the longer he walked in the plain of the wakeful, the less clear his vision became. The music had stopped for a moment and at once, Iarann was at attention again listening intently for signs that Lon Dubh may have need of his assistance but his thought was dashed as he recognized his Black Bird's sweet lilting laughter tinkling as bells from within the hut as she called another reel to be played. Unexpectedly, Iarann felt an uncharacteristic jab of jealousy at that.

"She is learning quickly as is necessary, Smithy. And it seems she has had more success with finding food than ever we have. Have you any salmon left in your catch basket?"

"Nay Lady, for it was a small catch and we had need of our own appetites to sustain three day's travel. Early spring offers meagre foraging. I have eggs and some nuts forgotten by those who buried them. I will be glad to taste of the meat that calls to me even at this distance." He said as he began to head in the direction of the cheery hut.

"Stay firm Iarann." Faidhe called. "We must allow Lon Dubh to find her way to her rightful place in assuming the role of the Goddess for these celebrations. Though she has not taken any man thus far, if it is to be so, then we cannot sway the energies with our presence. I can see by her energy moving about the hut that she has indeed grown strong in her magic and in womanhood. If she is ripe to offer the Goddess her maidenhead and a child of the moon celebrations, then we must not interfere. This night may be her rite of passage into full womanhood. And though it would not have been my choice for her to couple with those in this clan, it may be a facet to her negotiations in the keeping of the tale. I would not presume to know the Goddess's plan."

Iarann looked forlorn at the prospect of Lon Dubh going through such an important passage without benefit of a family member or friend to share the moment and guide her.

"As you say, Faidhe. But I hesitate to leave her at the will of these untamed little men. Know you they will respect her in the ways of reverence?" He had not even noticed that he had called her by her familiar name without the more proper title of Lady or Keeper but Faidhe noticed and had mixed feelings on the endearment. She would dearly love to share a tender moment with Iarann during the moon festival this night but was conflicted that such a union would somehow interfere with the energies building to create the child growing within her.

"For some time they have not had the benefit of feminine company," she answered pushing past her personal thoughts, "but these men keep the ways of the Goddess and understand that naught but reverence will bring them more of the feminine blessings they so need and desire. She will be safe...or learn how to make herself so."

Faidhe could sense the tension in Iarann's energy cooking off him in waves of swirling emotions as they both tarried in the woods with growling stomachs waiting to observe Lon Dubh take upon her the function as priestess for the Goddess in celebration of the full moon sky. They would not wait long. The music stopped completely as the moon neared its zenith in the sky casting pale shadows from the trees all about the watching pair. They spied as Lon Dubh exited the hut first, wearing about her shoulders her woolen cloak fastened at the neck with the clasp Iarann had fashioned for her. The priestess's hair was unbound and cascaded long past her shoulders down her back. Faidhe gasped as she observed that Lon Dubh had woven a crown of fighe vine and it adorned her head catching glimmers of light from the moon as it reflected off the shiny leaves like precious gems.

Behind Lon Dubh came two small figures from the hut, one Faidhe observed was the boy Lon Dubh befriended as they came to the village and the other was obviously of the same line if they were not, in fact, brothers. Both boys were wearing fresh and richly woven linens bearing between them a woven piece of woolen material beautifully dyed to the most vibrant color of blue that Faidhe immediately recognized as the Goddess's blue. The smallish pair were followed by seven mature Duibhe, not dressed in any finery but obviously spruced for the ritual.

The gathering of ten assembled in a circle around an ancient altar of Stone slabs in a grove of trees some 50 paces beyond the hut. The grove was not regularly tended and it was so overrun with forest growth, vines and brush that it would surely be missed if one did not know where the altar was placed.

Lon Dubh took high position behind the altar while the two smaller figures flanked the front of the altar. The rest of those gathered at the foot of the Stone slabs completing the circle that included the altar, elves and Lon Dubh. The circle they formed symbolized a living, breathing rendition of the Lady Moon on this special night.

In a dramatic moment Lon Dubh reached to her clasp and released her cloak to allow it to tumble upon the forest floor. There she stood in the night, an imposing figure emanating the Power of the Goddess and all but glowing as the bright moon reflected off her alabaster skin as she stood for a moment clothed only in the sky to draw in the moon's light and energy.

The two Elven boys stared openly as if mesmerized. Lon Dubh looked to her new friends and instructed them mentally to spread the blue woven wool on the altar. When she was satisfied the task was complete, she flicked her hand toward each boy and at their feet, small flames sprang to life in oil pots that had long been placed there for ceremonies such as this. The boys drew from their sleeves pellets of hardened herbs and oils mixed and pressed to burn long and fragrant and placed them into the flame of each fire. Eventually, the sweet aroma would drift and enchant all in the circle as it set forth from the flames. Next, from beneath the altar stones Fion and Cathbad withdrew a dark stone with a natural basin worn into it. Though it was large and heavy, the boys struggled little to place it upon the blue altar covering where they gently filled it with water from skins. The sound of the water tinkled so that one could imagine a continuously singing brook nourishing a lush and green forest giving of great bounty for all living creatures.

There was a collective intake of breath as the grove around them took on the appearance of just such a forest in full, fruitful summer bounty and all watching imagined they felt the warm sun on their skin and tasted of the fresh water from the brook and all were revived with a sense of youthfulness not experienced in centuries for some.

Faidhe was intent upon her daughter's countenance and actions. She had not herself witnessed one of these celebrations for 35 seasons for she had only performed as a priestess and had never been able to see the work of the Goddess through one of her initiates. She had tears of joy silently streaming down her face and was renewed to the awe and beauty of that to which she'd dedicated her life. As Faidhe watched, she became aware that many others had joined in the wood to participate in the ritual. About a hundred or so squat, dark folk of the Duibhe clans were scattered around the circumference of the grove. Not far from where she and Iarann stood, there was a toothless Duibhe who turned to them.

"I thought I'd miss takin' to the part of the Goddess in all this as 'as been me role for se long, but what an honor te watch; this 'un's got the Power about her. No mistake."

It took Faidhe a moment to realize that this ancient Duibhe with nary a tooth left was actually one of the scarce womenfolk left to the tribe.

She responded, "Then sister, we have both come to the time when we have been duly replaced in our roles in the Circle and come to an honorable vantage where we can look upon the Goddess's greatness and bounty."

"Well said. Well said." Came the old Duibhe's response as she gave Faidhe and Iarann an unabashed up and down. Before returning her attention to the ritual she spoke again. "I'll wager ye'll have a time fer yerself this night even i' yer not takin' te yer back in the great bonds of ceremony. He's a big 'un, that." The Duibhe woman eyed Iarann appreciatively if a bit lasciviously and twinkled her eyes at Faidhe.

The old woman turned back as not to miss the proceedings for at that moment the crowd once again drew in a sharp breath at the priestess's beauty and vibrating Power. She stood at the altar with hands outstretched high over her raised head as if to drink in the light of the moon. As she lowered her hands, Lon Dubh removed the crown of woven vine from her head and held it up to the moon so the bright orb was centered to her view within the circle of the crown. As she lowered the circlet to place it upon the altar around the stone bowl, there were further gasps as a perfectly round luminescence was encompassed within the crown and appeared to sit above the small pool of water contained within the bowl. The water in the bowl reflected the small moon replica and illuminated the human circle gathered in the grove far more efficiently than the fire in the oil pots.

Lon Dubh spoke words of praise and thanks to the Goddess and the God in a voice that echoed with deep, resonating strength. Then came a moment when Lon Dubh's eyes, half closed in trance opened and shone only with white, as the moon. Her voice, still deep, took on a quality that inspired awe and fear in the onlookers. In an arcane language, unknown to even Faidhe, the priestess spoke blessings to the worshippers and from the palms of her hands, sent out blue rays of light touching some members of the crowd with the beams. She then concentrated the beams from her right hand onto the blue woven altar covering and with her left hand, drew white light from the orb above the bowl of water. She alternately moved her left hand to draw light from the flames at the boy's feet in front of the altar and then back to the moon-like orb above the bowl. Continuing to say prayers and petitions of protection the priestess imbued the weave with a glow of warmth from both the firelight, symbolic of the sun and the white light of the moon. It could be witnessed that the magical light wove its way in and out of each and every crossing of thread until the piece appeared to glow with a warm radiance from within.

After withdrawing her hands, she folded her arms at her sides, hands by her shoulders, and for the second time in her daughter's presence, Faidhe watched as Lon Dubh took on the countenance of the great mother Raven, the Morrigan. Still appearing human at the core, all around her could be seen the impressive out-stretched wings of the Raven as Lon Dubh deliberately and slowly raised her arms. A shrill and frightening caw blasted from the impressive beak and the Raven was gone.

A mature stag, just then, entered the grove at what might have otherwise been a silent moment of shocked reverence. As he walked directly to Lon Dubh in greet-ing, it was known that this was a stag of the spirit, for his antlers were fully devel-oped which is not possible for a buck to have his antlers so fully formed this early in the spring. And all about him was a nimbus of green as around Lon Dubh was a radiance of blue. The stag came to Lon Dubh and she allowed him to nuzzle her affectionately. She scratched him under the chin and about the ears and smiled in understanding as she touched her forehead to the stag's own head.

Both Faidhe and Iarann recognized the antlered beast for they each knew this was the creature with which they were familiar. She, knowing him as the Greenman and he, knowing the stag depicted in the very plate for the Cauldron he had fashioned this day. They both forgot to breathe while they waited to see what would take place and then sighed relief without even realizing it, when the stag left the Circle and Lon Dubh once again appeared to be fully herself. The light emitting from the fighe vine crown upon the altar began to diminish and as Lon Dubh spoke words of release to the Power and to the congregation the appearance of a verdant summer forest, once again returned to the overgrown grove. Only the blue altar covering seemed to main-tain a faint impression of the glow it gave off during the ritual. The Circle ceremony had ended. There would be no sexual rites in the form of a great marriage to serve the Goddess this night, at least not in the ceremonial manner.

———

The people of the Tuatha De Danann began to make the trek up the Hill on the night of the full moon for the spring festival celebration. As was tradition, the gathering would begin at sundown at a time between two times and the ritual would begin at the setting of the moon at a balance point between day and night. The ceremonies would take place and there would be revelry and celebration for the three days to follow. This was a much-anticipated ceremony as the entire clan was eager to see what skills the new Keeper might display and how he might fare in his task following the former Keeper of much experience and renown for her magic.

Typically a time for high energy, this particular festival sparked much talk and speculation. Although it had been only a short time since the excitement when the Keeper came to his position and took the Hill, the forthcoming celebration garnered excited preparation for feasting, merry meading and eagerness for the fires that follow the rituals.

Gara gave particular attention to her preparations for this festival for she'd planned to arrange things so that she would finally bring Cuan to slip down with her by the fires and she would be more secure of their friendship once she'd given him a sense of the pleasures that lie ahead for him. She tried often without being overt to make contact with Cuan since her first visit to his hut when the moon was just before its half. Gara had envisioned an evening of flirtation and conversation that would endear her to the younger man. She had ordered her servants to put a simple chicken to the spit for an intimate dinner they two could share. She'd even sprinkled the bird with a savory powder oft used to bring its recipient more readily to enjoy coupling but when she'd arrived at his hut, on that first night, Cuan already had company in Colm who was preparing a meal at the hearth. Gara was surprised to find Colm still in the village for when she saw her earlier it was Gara's assumption that Colm would have taken her children back up the Hill before dark.

"A welcome to you, good lady." He said. His broad and friendly smile spread from his mouth to his eyes. "I am Cuan, cousin to Laoghaire and am here in his stead. What be your purpose here?" Came Cuan's polite welcome to the stranger outside his hut. Colm looked up from the hearth and became very curious indeed to find Gara at the door bearing a pottery bowl as if she were a homey matron. Colm resisted her urge to come closer to listen but remembered decorum forbade her interference for this was no longer her hearth. But she was not pleased to see that Cuan looked past Gara's age and unscrupulous character and like many men, saw only a woman of a sensual nature.

The woman at the door straightened her back and did not falter at the change in arrangements for the visit she'd planned.

"I am Gara, a member of the Council of the Tuath. I come to offer thanks and gratitude at your generosity in helping our Laoghaire to rise to his place on the Hill without cause to worry overmuch that his cattle will not be well cared for. I doubt if you have received a proper welcome from the Council other than myself, for we are in disarray over these recent changes. I am offering you my services to assist you in guidance to where such as you might find goods, barter and services while you stay here in our village."

Cuan heard Colm muffle a cough behind him before he answered.

"It is a generous offer indeed, Gara. Though I have been visited by many a friendly maid these last nights, I can say I have never been so flattered as to have a woman of the Council honor me so, unless I include the honor of my esteemed cousin come to warm my hearth with my good king's hospitality. Will you take bread with us?" He gestured to the interior of the hut where Colm could clearly be seen.

"No, I thank you sir, I have only time for these words and I must be tending other matters. Just know that I am here to guide you should you need one of my experience and know-how for the best trades and dealers within our village and beyond...or whatever else your needs be." Gara gave him a smoldering look filled with promise at this last comment.

"Lady, is this dish something you have brought to relieve me of the task of mundane cookery?" He flirted. Colm rolled her eyes while she tended the hanging stewpot.

Gara intended to leave with her chicken for it was obvious that the evening she'd planned would not take place and then it occurred to her to think better of it. Who knew what might happen if Colm and Cuan find themselves inexplicably drawn to the straw for having shared the enchanted dish. The possibility of stirring up trouble for Laoghaire and wife stimulated her and she turned back purring,

"Why yes, I all but forgot to leave my offering of welcome." She replied as she handed him the dish. "It is a goodly sized bird and will bring your mouth to water no doubt. How fortunate that you have some family with which to share yon foul. I do hope you both enjoy the bird." With that, she gave Cuan a silky smile and bowed a head in Colm's direction. "Lady Colm, it is my hope that our meeting last can be something put by as a poor start to what was and is a sincere offer of help to you as well, if only in the way of support and friendship should you need it."

"I thank you for your offer, Gara," was all Colm said. Remaining neutral as to her feelings toward the other woman and continued to work at testing the bread in the pottery dish atop the fire's hot embers.

Now in her hut, preparing for the festival, Gara came back to herself as she remembered that first night at Cuan's door. She regretted that she was not privy as to what had taken place between Cuan and Colm that evening. *It would truly have been a nugget of information I could have used. And wouldn't it be sweeter should there have been a child of an unsanctioned union come to the new Keeper couple. Ah, there may still be something to come of that yet. We have but to wait and see what winds blow.*

Gara prepared her finery and packed it away for her servants to carry up the Hill along with a tent to be assembled for her in some private location upon her arrival as they neared the top for she did not want to appear road worn after the half day's travel. She would rinse and prepare in her tent and be radiant. For after making excuses to run into Cuan and to catch his eye since that first night, she was determined that she would have him this night by the festival fires. For even though Colm had visited his hut some few times between that time and this, Gara could be reasonably sure that had there been a spark kindled whilst Laoghaire tended his new duties, Colm would spend this night with Laoghaire and no one else so that Cuan would be free to attend to other things. This was one alliance she was looking forward to forging. She had the servants pack some cured meats, strong mead, some fruits and cheese, along with the tent so all would be ready when she brought Cuan back to her impromptu quarters after the evening ritual.

———

The Circle was domed with the light hue of blue as Laoghaire sat on the ground in front of the altar Stone, as was his habit since he'd taken to working his tasks in the Circle. He could feel Craiche's presence but had not seen or heard even a whisper of her since the day she last spoke with him from between the rent in the Keystone. Laoghaire looked to the space that had housed the Stone for as long as the Tuatha De Danann had inhabited these lands. What he saw there was an empty space next to the remaining single half of the Keystone lying askew on the ground.

Laoghaire contemplated how the sight of what had taken place at the Circle and what he'd planned for tonight's ritual would affect the Tuath. In truth, he had been awed when the one whom he'd summoned came to do the work of transporting the great Stone halves to locations foretold.

At first, as he conducted tests for summoning just the proper process to move the Stones to their new locations, respectively, Laoghaire had little success. Limiting his thoughts to only methods of human ingenuity, he imagined brute strength of many men, rolling contraptions, and all other manner of moving the great Stones. In his frustration, he tried to summon images of how the Stone was brought from the north all those generations ago with the hopes that he could spy out the spell or magic used to lift and transport the megalith.

Stymied by his unsuccessful attempts to reproduce the magic needed, he blurted, "Would that I could know of what giants carried this Stone. I'd summon the strength of thrice 60 men upon whose backs these Stones could be heft! For I would say, 'I beseech you stand up and take these Stones upon your back as light as goose down they are to one so strong. It could be done with a snap of your finger as you dance a jig. For to complete this task for God and Goddess I will give you my thanks.'"

With that, Laoghaire's heart leapt as all around him, the Stones of the Circle began to shake and tremble. A great and terrible sound came rumbling and screeching as the Stones of the Circle tumbled and rolled toward each other, crashing and smashing into one another and each rolling up atop the next scrambling into a semblance of a human form in its bulk, towering over Laoghaire who was struck with fear until he spoke of logic to himself to take charge of that which he had wrought.

"You there!" Laoghaire hollered up at the being. "Are you the strength for which I summoned?"

The being seemed not to hear or notice Laoghaire but was rather engrossed in the discovery of its new form. It inspected arms and wiggled the smaller finger stones that formed of the rubble that had broken in dust and splinters as the great Stones violently smashed one another. Its head moved from side to side and peered down at the newly shaped body below. One leg lifted, then the other just prior to a testing of the hips as the whole body swayed to one side, then the opposite. As the being experimented with this new shape it moved in all directions testing walking ability, jumping, arm movements so that it resembled a great dance of the rock giant.

Laoghaire stood at a distance, careful not to find himself underfoot of this creature. Realizing his purpose once again, Laoghaire stood atop the altar stone left standing alone on the eastern most side of where the great Stone Circle had been.

"You there, Great Giant of the Stones!" Laoghaire called with authority. "I have summoned you to the work of the Gods. I celebrate in your presence and ask that you hearken to me."

The giant seemed to have heard something and suspended its dance, standing still for a moment. Quickly, it turned to find the origin of the voice with a great and thundering sound that could only be imagined emitting from such a creature.

"Who summons us?"

Laoghaire swallowed hard and answered, "I do. Laoghaire, Keeper of the Stones."

The monster began to laugh in an ear-splitting sound that echoed to the very sky and back but Laoghaire stood his ground.

"I have need of your strength, friend and the Gods have granted my request to offer you form to help in this endeavor."

"You have deemed to up end us who have been in our place for generations beyond time where we have stood so proudly to greet each day and night?"

"I have." The Keeper answered firmly, almost defiantly.

"And it is you who has given us the gift of movement?"

"I have, with the blessing of the Gods."

"Then, we are in your debt. We have long been stoic and are grateful to be at your service. What task can be done for you and your Gods?"

"I have - we have need of your strength, to transport your brother and sister here to places where they will be needed and places out of reach of those who would misuse their Power and Knowledge." Laoghaire hoped he had chosen his words wisely for he did not wish to anger this creature but he wanted to implore the creature with some sense of kinship to his task so that it would take care in its execution. Then it occurred to Laoghaire that it was not known, though this creature appeared to have human qualities, if it could, in fact, feel or understand kinship. But it knew and expressed gratitude so it did have something akin to human emotion. "Have you a name, friend?"

The giant stood with its arms hanging at its sides and appeared as though it contemplated the long forgotten answer to this question. One great arm consisting of two longish Stones lifted to the head and appeared to scratch in thought; then it answered, "My name...my name is...Dam...Damhsaigh...Damhsaigh Cloch!"

At that, the giant broke into a jubilant dance once again as though it had enjoyed a goodly bit of humor.

"Damhsaigh Cloch, know you of these Stones?" Laoghaire interrupted. "Know you of the great changes happening in the earth, sky and underworld?" The giant was recalled to the conversation at hand and stopped to ponder the words once again with arms hanging and questioning appearance to the face.

"Changes? Yes." The answer came in a slow and profoundly deep voice yet almost in a whisper. "Changes. I have a task to do."

"Yes Damhsaigh Cloch. You have a task to do. And once you've finished your task, you may return here to settle or choose a place more to your liking to watch as the changes take place. But know you this; the spirit of your shape for this place and time cannot be permanent. You must agree to your task and enjoy the gift of freedom for a time, but you must return to your original state when you have served the Gods."

The stony face took on a furrowed brow at this. "Who are you to command us so?"

"I am he who summoned you to your task. I am Laoghaire, Keeper of the Stones and king to my clan, Tuatha Laoghaire. I am charged with the placing of the Stones of Fal as well as the placement of the sacred implements, the Sword, Shield and Staff in preparation of these changes."

With brow still furrowed, "We know our Stones, human. The Stone of Fal speaks of true kings and harbors much Power. You have magic, for otherwise we would not be here but we would not bring about such changes in the placement of the Great Stone for one we do not know. A sorcerer you may be, here to make tricks. Show us the implements we have kept o'er these recent times as proof of your rightful place here among us."

Laoghaire was following his instincts during this discourse but hesitated to expose the sacred implements to a force so strong and unpredictable.

"I have not the Staff for it travels with the Cauldron in service to the Lady, Faidhe until we are reunited. The Shield has been worked and is being prepared in the care of my wife who has been chosen as its steward. I have only the Sword of Nuada in my charge."

Laoghaire stepped down from the altar Stone and pulled the Sword from the alcove beneath. He held the Sword, not as a weapon but flat across the palms of his hands as he held it out to be inspected by the creature as it drew close.

"Lady Faidhe? You said Lady Faidhe. We remember Faidhe who kept us well for a moment in time. She had the Sword and now it is you?" Laoghaire nodded while the creature seemed deep in thought scrutinizing the Sword and the Stone of Fal in two halves. Then faster than Laoghaire's eyes could track, the Sword was adeptly snatched from his palms and plunged into the half of the keystone laying closest to where he stood.

"You say you are a king and so you may be, but only one pure of heart, unblemished in battle and destined for high kingship may wield the Sword; so says the Stone. Proof of your purity must be given despite our joy at being freed from the earthly site. Proof we must have of your authority to call us and use the Power of the Sword and the Stone. Draw forth the Sword from yon Stone and your task shall be completed. Do it not and there it will stay until such a one may release it from its stony scabbard and bring his line to high kingship of the isle."

Laoghaire found himself wholly frightened at the speed with which the enormous rocks came bolting toward him and relieved him of that which he was charged to defend with his life. A momentary blast of fright consumed him as he felt doubt creep into his belief as to whether he would be able to pull the Sword from the Stone that would be known as the means to identify kings of this land. He recalled the screech it had issued forth on the day of his baptism to the Circle. He brought to mind images of the wise and respected Faidhe and Craiche. He fortified his confidence with the memory that the Sword and Shield came to his hand from the great Cauldron of the Circle and breathed in a preparatory breath, walked toward the Stone and climbed atop the behemoth. As he did this, the Stone began to vibrate and hum, the sound growing louder until his ears heard only discomfort.

Without hesitation, Laoghaire reached for the hilt of the Sword, which was the only remaining part visible above the Stone and effortlessly pulled the blade from the Stone with only a minor hiss of the sound of metal singing as he did so. Slightly amazed, and not a little relieved, Laoghaire looked to the Stone giant again.

"Is this proof enough that the Power emitted from the Sword, the Stone and myself are all issued forth of the same origin and are harmonious in this cause for which I summoned you?" Laoghaire jumped down from his perch to put a halt to the din raised by his position on the Stone.

"It is, human. We will carry out our task as you require, for it has been long that the Stones of ourselves have kept company with the Stone of Fal and have been a place of protection for the implements and their Keepers. We will bid goodbye to the end of this time and make placement of the Stone's halves as you desire to make way for this new arrangement."

"I thank you for your help Damhsaigh Cloch. Need I instruct you as to how to come by the places of which I have been foretold?"

"It is of this Power and of this earth from which we have come. We will speak to the earth and Stones along our way to choose the path that will bring us to the presaged destinations. Then, we will find our way back to our home on the large island for it is whence that we came before being honored by the Danu to be useful as a portal gate here."

With that, Damhsaigh Cloch bent and picked up one half of the great Stone and heaved it on one large shoulder as if it had no weight at all. He bade Laoghaire goodbye.

"We will enjoy our travel as we move about the land. You have proven to be a man of honor and we are pleased to take on this task. We will take great strides and tarry not for it is your intent that we are returned here before the ceremony of the sky?"

"It is. You have much knowledge Damhsaigh Cloch. It is my privilege to count you among those who serve the Goddess and God with me. I am fortunate to have met you and look to our meeting next."

With no further comment, Damhsaigh Cloch took a great step toward the east and set about the journey creating thunderous, earth shaking, concussions as lumbering strides moved the giant out of sight and earshot.

Now, on the very night of the spring festival, Laoghaire wondered at the response the village folk of the Tuatha De Danann would have, to the knowledge that the very Circle of Stones no longer stood on the Hill. He wondered at their response to the news that the Stone of Fal would be made of use in lands away from here. He wondered at the welfare of these people with whom he'd lived and cared about when he and his family take to the road and the hierarchy of the Danann all but falls apart. He made mighty efforts to push this thought from his mind as he made final adjustments to the materials he brought from below the altar Stone to arrange for the evening's ritual.

35

On the Road Again

As we rustled about the kitchen to scare up a couple of wine glasses I noticed Bridey's note stuck between some canisters on the counter, almost as though it was placed there with the hopes that we wouldn't come by it for a while. The instant I read the note, I was angry and outraged at the presumptuous gall of the old woman.

"Hey Nora, come look at this. It's from Bridey." I showed the note to Nora and we both knew intuitively that someone had not only been in our rooms but through our things as well.

"You feel that?" Nora asked.

"Uh huh. Creepy." I responded. "Why didn't we feel this before?"

"Probably too wrapped up in our phone calls."

We went to our respective rooms to take inventory. I first noticed that my suitcase, which I had tucked neatly under the bed, was now placed on the chair by the foot of the bed.

"You see anything missing?" I called out to Nora as I opened the wardrobe door and made note that the strappy shoes that I'd left in my suitcase were lined neatly on the floor with the rest of my footwear.

"No. Nothing seems to be missing but some stuff has definitely been moved." Why do you think Bridey went through our stuff?"

Try as we might, we could not find any valid excuse for Bridey to have gone through our drawers and personal materials as part of her cleaning routine she'd informed us of in her note:

Dear Girls,
I've been to your cottage to give a thorough cleaning, as I will once
every week to keep things tiptop. You have replenished peat and your

linens have been changed. I took the liberty of putting a few of your personal items to the wash and placing them away for you. Enjoy!
Yours,
Bridey

Had we just received a note from Bridey about the cottage having been cleaned, we would have been polite and asked her to refrain from cleaning until the end of our stay but she'd trespassed in touching our personal things. Even if she'd provided laundry as a service, which she did not, it would still not be acceptable for her to enter the rooms and rummage through our belongings to accomplish that task. And we definitely got the sense that our belongings had been disturbed to say the least; all of our belongings, not just items found where she'd likely look for soiled laundry. And besides, the things that were moved in my drawers were definitely not dirty, so why would Bridey be pawing through our drawers for dirty clothes?

We were outraged at the constant sense of violation we'd felt since arriving to stay in the cottage. First with the three stooges spying on us, then Bridey hanging around to listen to our phone calls. Now this. I felt conflicting messages in what I was sensing in our temporary home. As I looked around at what I had once seen as a cozy, cheery little haven, I now eyed pictures and heat vents with suspicion, wondering if my showers or dressing routines would show up on the Internet or something. *Okay,* I thought to myself. *Don't get paranoid. Use your head. What happened here?*

I'd closed my eyes and I caught snippets of images as I concentrated on finding out just what had taken place here. I saw our papers and books strewn about the sitting room and our clothing thrown about the floor and beds of both our rooms. I couldn't see who was doing these things but I saw the frightening aftermath of our undergarments and pants having been turned inside out and stained with stuff that I preferred not to speculate about but I had my suspicions about who had left their marks on our things.

Bridey had left the note, which would support the idea that whatever went on here, whether she was involved or not, she knew about it and covered it up; a scenario that did not make me feel warm and fuzzy toward her. By covering up the fact that someone had ransacked our place, she put us in potential danger and there was no excuse for that even if she was trying to save her little home business.

"What do you want to do about this, Nora?" My back was up but I also knew that we'd have to tread lightly if we wanted to retrieve any part of our deposit.

"Fuck the deposit!" Nora said with an uncharacteristic vehemence in response to my thought.

"You go girl." I said lightly. Usually I was the one to slap a hand on a service counter or to demand a refund for something but I understood that in this circumstance, Nora was right. We may be better off just eating the expense and moving on.

"But where to?" I inquired, following the train of thought.

"Well we have traveling to do." Nora thought out loud. "We could go up to Galway to Lough Corrib where the original Circle was. We could head over to Sweden or Denmark to see what moves us there."

"I guess..." I was searching for the right idea or a plan that clicked for me to give me that 'AHA! That's what we need to do!' feeling. But nothing really jumped out at me as the right move.

"We really haven't finished up with Cath and Finny yet. There's still stuff to learn." Feeling apprehensive about making any kind of move at all but knew we couldn't stay here even one more day.

We both stood for a moment with thoughts racing as to where to go and what to do when we heard a thump outside the cottage that made us both jump. We instinctively clasped hands and walked toward the front of the cottage to see what made the noise out by our car.

"Wait." Nora whispered and shut off the lights in the kitchen and sitting rooms so we could be less conspicuous as we peeked out the window. The noise was not repeated and we saw nothing untoward out front but in sending forth a tendril of thought to seek whatever might be out there, I recognized that one of our piggy neighbors down below the pastures had escaped its confines and was snuffling at our car in search of food.

In that instant, I knew the pig had not escaped but had been let loose to find its way up to our cottage. I had a quick vision of hands unlocking the gate and slapping the pig on its way. Apparently, this has been a ruse used by those men down in the other cottage in the past to have an excuse to come up and have a look around and size up the guests in the cottage. Unbelievably, this gave me a moment of hope that maybe we're not the sole focus of these men and their unwanted attention. I thought that maybe, this is something they do with all the guests of this cottage.

Knowing we'd have company all too soon, I pulled back from the window and moved to shut off the rest of the lights in the cottage.

"Help me Nora. If there are no lights on and they think we're asleep, they won't bother trying to knock on the door. If they're using the pig as an excuse to come up and get closer while we're here, we can watch them to see what they do."

"Pig?" was all she said as she followed my instructions to shut the lights in her room.

I sent a mental picture of what I'd seen to Nora, hoping she'd understand and not have to ask any further questions. The quieter we could be, the better. As Nora returned from her bedroom, she met me at the hallway window between our two rooms. This window was set higher in the wall than the ones in the bedrooms so without having to crouch we peeked out the bottom of the window through the space under the closed blind. For a while we saw nothing and eventually we saw a fat little pig walk around our car and over to the pot of flowers by the door to snuffle around for some hidden treat.

"He's kind of cute." I said.

"It's a pig!" Nora answered appalled that I could consider such a piggy creature cute.

"No, really, look at hi..."

"Shh!" She hissed. "Look over there!"

I followed Nora's finger pointing down the hill toward the path that lead up behind our cottage. There was one of the brothers, I thought, quietly working his way up the path.

"There!" I said. Closer to our home was another silhouette of a man that had started up the hill likely before we'd even heard the noise outside. "You think it's all three?"

"Probably. What do you want to do?" Nora asked. Her voice had a quality to it that sounded foreign on her tongue. It caused me to look at her and I saw that same far away expression on her face I'd noticed the first time we felt threatened here in Ireland at Finny's little trailer. It sent a chill through me to see a side to Nora that no one would ever suspect was there. Her eyes never moved other than to watch her prey. Around me I could feel her energy gathering heat as if someone had just opened an oven door and the blast came rushing out, drying my eyes and blowing my hair up in drafts of rising air. Then, I began to smell something most unpleasant.

"Nora? Do you know what you're doing?" I felt jittering nerves dance in my stomach and reached out with my mind to see what she was thinking and all I saw was her view of the two visible men in the dark. There was an awareness there too of me being in close proximity. It was as if Nora had identified me as non-prey and kindred, not as quarry and her entire body was wound like a spring ready to loose on the kill. The heat energy intensified. I didn't know what she intended but something was going to happen and it felt big. My eyebrows, lashes and the hairs inside my nose started to curl with the heat.

Just then, lights flashed across the window and a car pulled up to the front of our cottage. The driver side door flew open and out popped Bridey. The lights broke my connection with Nora but I felt the discomfort she had experienced when the lights shone in her eyes and broke her concentration.

"Nora." I shook her arm. "Nora. Bridey is here. Don't do anything. Nora, listen to me." I shook harder and Nora reached up with an iron grip and peeled my hand from her arm. She literally vibrated with the unleashed energy. I was unsettled by what I felt coming from my sister in waves. We both looked back toward the vignette in the front yard. Bridey was shooing the pig down the hill with her apron and storming a stride toward the men. There were three of them in fact. One had already been behind our cottage before we even were aware of anything going on.

"Get ye goin' now ye amadans!" As Bridey shouted, it seemed her accent grew thick with her excitement. "Ye'll not be about yer skullduggery here. Now go on with ye and get that animal in order as well. Ye'll be scarin' me guests here half to their maker skulkin' around these parts after dark. Ye'll ruin me business and then ye'll be out on yer ears for all me trouble!"

Bridey stood her ground with arms folded across the ample shelf that was her chest. Although we couldn't see her face, she held a stoic stance that brought to mind an expression of set determination.

The men seemed to loom in response to her challenge and move to cluster together in a group of three neither advancing toward her nor did they retreat down the hill toward their cottage.

I was so engrossed in the scene, I wasn't aware that Nora was no longer next to me until I saw her walk into my field of vision and take her place next to Bridey.

"Nora! What are you doing?"

I ran down the hallway to the front door. I had to stop running to reverse my direction through the breezeway to get out the front door so it appeared to the men that I'd walked out the door in as calm a fashion as Nora had.

Perhaps this lack of panic or fear is what made them question their upper hand in brute strength because none of we three women gave any appearance of being intimidated or fearful. We simply stood awash in the light of Bridey's headlights to face them without words as they stood just outside the field of the light. Kinetic energy could be felt enveloping us and pushing outward and an opposing energy could be felt pushing back at us. I have never felt anything with such a force in my life. This was real magic. Someone else in the world had abilities equal to, or even greater than our own. Practiced energy.

Suddenly, I recognized what was happening and realized that we'd been duped into revealing ourselves as having some kind of uncommon Power. Nora's and my hairs were standing on end with the electric current snapping through the air. Bridey's hair had been snatched into a bun and remained in place but there was no doubting that magical energy was at work here and whether Bridey, sandwiched between Nora and I, was contributing to the magical energy, I couldn't tell. I reached behind Bridey and grabbed Nora's hand to communicate to her that we were being tested right now. Not only did they know for sure that we had magic, but they wanted to push us to find out just what our strength was. *Don't' do it Nora.* I pleaded. *Whatever it is you want to do, don't. Please. They're ready for it. They want to know how strong we are. If they're stronger than us right now, before we're ready for this kind of thing, they will kill us right here tonight. Can't you feel that? It's coming off them in waves that they want to savage us. Fight it Nora. Fight your urge to unleash your energy. Nora. NORA!* With that I squeezed her hand and let go to give her a hard pinch on the back of her upper arm. When we were kids, this maneuver never failed to get her attention.

Nora looked at me with undiluted fury in her eyes at being called away from her focus. For a moment I thought she might unleash that fury at me so she could fully devote her attention to focus her energy on the enemy. I could see something register in her eyes as soon as she'd taken her gaze off the largest of the men who had obviously focused his attention on her. She understood what I was telling her but it seemed her eyes were being dragged back to focus once again on the leader of the brothers.

"Nora!" I called aloud and her eyes snapped back to me. Quickly I moved to stand in front of Bridey, facing her and Nora with my back to the men.

"What the hell is going on here?" I demanded. "It's practically midnight and we have pigs and people traipsing through our yard. What kind of a place are you running here Bridey? And you! I spun around on the men. If you think we're going to put up with this kind of nonsense, think again. We called down to the local police when you scared us half to death out here. What will you tell them when they arrive? We were out walking our pig? I don't know what you guys are up to but whatever it is, we want nothing to do with you. So go home to your own property down there and stay away from ours. While we're here, this is to be considered our home and if we find you trespassing around here or near here, first, Bridey, we will demand our money back and give you a brutal negative rating online and second, you three, after we report this incident tonight, we won't hesitate to inform the police every time you so much as *look* in our direction. You get my meaning, Tubby?"

I hoped he caught the meaning in my last statement and understood that we were on to their peeping habits as well. I knew I was rambling and probably looked like a madwoman but I couldn't risk a showdown here at night, unprepared and outnumbered. I didn't know where Bridey fit into all of this, but I wasn't sure she could be counted as an ally.

"So, unless you want to answer to the police when they arrive, any minute now, I suggest you get your sorry, fat asses down the hill and away from us. How's that for ugly American, you rubes?"

The looks on their faces were mixed wonder, sly consideration over the police threat, and unabashed hatred. My comments did their work though and that seemed to break the standoff for the moment but it didn't have the immediate affect I was hoping for. Moe stepped toward me with a smirk on his livery lips. He was a large man, and tall. He bent toward me in mock formality.

"G' night, Miss."

It took all my discipline not to turn away gagging at the stench that emitted from his mouth. It was the Beast's own brand of stink. Now I knew for sure what we were up against in these neighbors. In an insane moment, my mind conjured up the words to the old Mr. Roger's television show. *"Please say you'll be my, say you'll be my, won't you be my neighbor."* I shook of the urge to laugh, annoyed that such an emotion should come now at a most inconvenient moment especially since, unfortunately, they likely knew or had an idea who we are as well. I swallowed my gorge and faced up to him with all the strength and dignity I could muster. I threw all my energy into creating a stance and appearance that spoke of fearlessness and there actually was a momentary lapse in the smarmy expression on his face. I got the sense that he didn't like what he saw in me so he shifted his gaze back to Nora.

"G' night to you too, Miss. And I'll especially look forward to meetin' wi' you again to tend our unfinished business." At this, all three turned to go back down the hill.

I waited a few moments to make sure the men were headed away in earnest. Nora never took her eyes from the men.

"Bridey, we'll have a word with you please." After making the statement, I walked toward the door of the cottage indicating that I expected her to follow. "Nora," I called to my sister. "We have work to do. Come on." I didn't want to be outside just now, feeling exposed and open to scrutiny.

Once inside, I retrieved the cell phone from where Nora had left it on the table in the sitting room and called information for the number of the local police. I didn't want to offer empty threats as a line of defense. Maybe if these men knew that some authority was aware of them, they might not be so bold. When I hung up the phone, I observed Nora and Bridey sitting in the living room not speaking but apparently waiting for me.

"Are you alright, Nora?"

"Yeah, a little drained, and a bit ah, frustrated, I guess you could call it. But aside from the bruise on my arm, I'm okay."

I ignored the jab and gave a perfunctory "Sorry." Then got right to business.

"Bridey, you cleaned up after those animals here in our cottage today but you stood against them tonight. What is really going on here? And we want the truth before the police get here. If I think you're smoking us, I'll report that you and your boys broke in here today and then returned for something underhanded tonight. Cause basically, that's the truth. Right?"

Bridey contemplated her answer for a moment and seemed resigned as her shoulders sagged.

"It is girls, but hear me out as to the reasons. Will you?"

We waited in silence for her explanation. Bridey took a deep breath and steeled herself to tell us her story but held the expression that she didn't really think we'd buy it.

"I'm an orphan." She stated. "I've lived here for a very long time and I depended on the kindness of foster families throughout my childhood. I've been brought up with countryside knowledge of a family of special people who were and are thought to bring special gifts to the country at a time when they'll be needed. I had suspicion that you girls might be members of that family so I kept a close eye out for your comings and goings. The thing is, though, I'm not the only one that's been keeping watch." She indicated the men down the hill with a toss of her head in the general direction of their cottage.

Nora and I understood now that Bridey was likely one of those people following the tale of the Lady from the Road.

"What makes you think in all of Ireland, all of the world, Bridey, that this family would just happen to be one of your tenants?" I ignored the fact that, in a way, this is exactly what happened.

"Well, I suppose that you'll either think me completely mad or you'll understand what I'm about to tell you. Based on what I've seen and heard and gathered about you girls, I'm inclined to suspect the latter, so in for a penny, in for a pound... There is a woman, named Faidhe who is a respected and revered holy woman on this isle. She had been the very heart and spirit of Erie since the time when the island was full of magical happenings. There are many who have heard tell of a legend that this woman will return at a time when she's needed and do all sorts of miraculous things. It was thought that during the troubles, she'd come and settle the differences in the North. It was thought prior to that she'd come and stamp her foot to send the English ascendancy packing, and when the famine cursed us, it was thought that she'd come with her Cauldron to feed the children, or her wrath was awaited when the devil Queen of England killed so many for honoring the Old Ways but of course, none of that happened. This was not her mission. This land and farm I own has been in my ownership for a great while. I chose this land due to the fact that it's midway between where Faidhe originally lived to the north and where she and her daughter traveled to begin their work in telling the tale, marking this land with the essence of great magic that would change the history of this country, and those lands beyond it. I created a space on this land, beneath this very cottage when it was first built, so the Lady Faidhe would be able to more easily pass from the world of the Sidhe and do her work on this level of existence."

"Bridey," Nora said, "we've heard of Faidhe and the Lady from the Road." She was careful not to betray the real tale or anything beyond what might be common knowledge. "But this cottage is over 200 years old. You mean when it was renovated you dedicated it to Faidhe. Right?"

Bridey sighed a weary breath. "No. As I said, I am an orphan. My first foster mother was a woman of a dying tribe of people long ago. I was born to a time, as I said, that magic still blessed the earth and this woman Faidhe and her daughter took to the road."

Nora and I looked at each other trying to decide whether this was the fantasy of an old woman who fervently wanted to believe in her tale or if it might have some truth to it.

"I have lived on or worked this property for over three hundred years and much longer in the country as the world changed, waiting and watching for a sign that what my brother had foretold had come into its time. It is my belief now girls, that you are involved in this circumstance due to signs and clues I've recognized. And I believe that those amadans down the hill also play their part in the story which is why I've kept them close by charging them no rent as they work the pigs for me."

She looked at us with a resigned look that she knew we'd think she was crazy but there was a spark of hope in her eye as well.

"What about your brother? Who was he and what happened to him?" I asked.

Bridey inspected our expressions to see if we were just humoring an old woman until the police came, but she must have seen that we were not mocking her and she decided to continue her story.

"I had a brother who was directly involved in the doings of the great mother Faidhe and the tale her daughter had spun. I had another brother that would come visit when he could and tell me the latest news he received. But eventually, I got word that my brother abroad had been killed and my other brother wouldn't believe it so he set off to find him in strange places far away. I lost contact with him when he left and as the world moved on; I assumed the worst about him as well. So I set about my brother's work in keeping alive what I know of the story and the hopes that one day, the Lady herself would return. I put about sending out what little magic I have to call any players involved in the tale to come to these quarters here and so those men, the three brothers down the hill came to me eight years ago now and have been here since. I've kept watch for signs of other likely persons and aside from a scattered few possibilities, you girls are the most likely that I've seen to fit the bill. And given your display out front this evening, I'm not off the mark. Am I?"

I made to deny anything out of the ordinary but Bridey would have none of it with a hand in the air as if to ward off my denial.

"Be still now and don't deny that you both made a powerful display out there this night. Your hair a flying and the air cracklin' fit to burst to flames. That, you can be sure was not my doin.'"

I noticed her accent creep back into Bridey's speech, as she grew excited.

"Ye've got the books with the old learnin' and the family birthdays markin' the old calendar that has te mean somthin' especially with ye bearin' the name of the much loved King Laoghaire of the very time I spoke and again centuries later during the travels of St. Patrick. And you, Miss O'Leary, can you tell me with an honest heart that there was nothing magical happenin' while ye were on the phone with yer boy this last time? I can smell magic when it's about and you were up te somethin'; of that, I'm sure!"

I was about to answer when a set of car lights slowly moved up the very long drive painting the wall in our cottage with long shadows from the blinds. As I looked out the window, I identified the car as the local police shining a spotlight across the pastures and up toward our house. I turned to Bridey.

"Is there anything about any of this that you feel the police should know at this point in time? Will filing a report about the brothers help us in any way or will we be better off just leaving this alone and fighting our own battles?"

Bridey looked like a deer in the headlights. Undecided as to what to do about the police she didn't say anything.

"Bridey" I pushed, taking a risk, "I believe you...about everything. And you're right about us. Now tell me, do we want the police involved for protection here or not?"

"Well," she sputtered to action, "I've always kept a low profile, not knowing who might be on the side of right and who may not be. Uniforms don't always tell the truth about who wears them if you understand my meaning."

I said, quickly reciting our story, "Okay, Nora, we were scared at the racket outside and it turned out to be the strange men lurking were our neighbors. We called Bridey, our land lady who came up to vouch for the men when they explained to us that they'd come up to find their escaped pig. We feel very silly about the whole thing and apologize for calling them. Get it?"

"Right." Nora said.

"Bridey?"

"Yes." She agreed just as a hard knock came on the outer front door.

I made a show of bending the blind in the window next to the front door to peek out and see who was knocking at such a late hour.

"Yes?" I said through the window.

"Did someone at this address call for help, Miss?"

"Yes, that was me." I said, still speaking through the window.

"Is everything fine with you, Miss?"

"Yes officer. I, we made a mistake. I thought there was a prowler but it turned out to be our neighbors down the way."

"Will you open the door to speak with me please?"

"Okay. Just a sec'." I answered. I walked to the front entrance and unlocked the inner door. I left that door open and unlocked the door in the breezeway leading to the front yard where the young police officer stood.

"I'm sorry officer, I was a bit nervous at the noises I heard outside and I called you guys before I thought to call down to Bridey, our landlady, to see if she knew what the noises might be. As it turns out, one of her pigs got loose and some of the men from the cottage below came up here to get it back."

At that moment, Bridey poked her head around the corner of the door jam.

"Well hello to you, Seamus." She greeted. "How's your mother feelin' these days?"

"Oh hullo Missus. She's much better thank you. And how's yourself?"

"Very well. Very well. I'm afraid I'll be paying for a new latch to the pen down below though. I've nearly scared my guests to the horrible fate of hotel living with a suckling on the loose! But we're all over it now, Seamus. Thanks for coming."

Officer Seamus's baby face seemed to hesitate looking down the hill at the men's cottage. "You sure there's nothing…You're sure," he started again, "that it was a pig they were after?"

"Oh yeah, we saw him up here sniffing around our car and our plant pot over there. We're city girls though," I exaggerated, "and we didn't think of farm animals when we heard noise out here and then we were startled to see strange men out here. We'd never met our neighbors and didn't know who they were. Again, officer, I'm sorry to have jumped to conclusions but better safe than sorry. Right?"

"Right, Miss. No trouble then." He tipped a nod to Bridey. "Missus."

"Good night, Seamus. Give my best to your mother, will you?"

"Will do. Good night to you then."

I closed and locked both doors and turned to Nora. I pulled her aside by the arm and whispered, "Should we pursue this story here or should we all take a drive?"

"Let's call first and see what they think." She answered and continued. "There are some discrepancies and a big pitfall is that we never heard of a sister. It could all be a wishful fabrication of someone who wants badly to be a part of the story."

"Okay," I said. "You want to call?"

"Alright. Where's the phone?"

I pointed to where I left it after I called the police and Nora swiped it off the end table while heading down the hall for privacy. I remained in the living room with Bridey.

"Bridey, we know a bit about the story you're telling us but we've heard it told in a slightly different way. We'd like to take a drive tonight to settle these differences. Are you willing to come with us? I know it's late, but after being revealed as having a little magical energy, I don't think it's safe for us to stay here now. I think you know those men mean us harm and if you know the story, you probably have an idea what kind of malice they hold in their hearts. So, we have some friends we'd like you to speak with so we can compare stories and figure out what's going on here. Will you come with us?"

Before she could answer, Nora returned to the living room and announced, "They're not too happy about the late hour and less happy about being revealed to one of those 'crazy Lady from the Road' people but I insisted and we're to meet them at Kenny's Pub."

"What's this now?" Bridey squawked. "I'll not be traipsin' around the countryside at this hour. And who are these men you're about with while you have husbands you should be sure not to forget? No, I'll stay put, thank you very much." Bridey headed for the door as quickly as her sensible shoes could take her.

Nora called to her. "Bridey, after what you've just witnessed, and waiting what you've described as a great many years for just this kind of visitation, aren't you even curious, why we believe your crazy story and what we might have to show you?" She didn't turn but that stopped Bridey from her speedy exit.

Nora continued, "You remember the day we moved in here and we picked rooms? Remember when Lee knew just where everything was situated in the cottage? Didn't that make you a bit curious about how she knew things like that? Or later when you were telling us a little history about the place and she appeared to look like an old woman? I know you saw it and what's more, I thought you might have recognized that old woman. Am I mistaken Bridey? Did the face Lee bore that day look familiar to you? Could it have been the face of Faidhe?"

Bridey turned now to face us as Nora continued. "What if I asked you about that purple room over there, the 'mother's room'? Would you tell me that room is where you created that sanctified space in the cottage to call likely people from the prophecy to this property so you could keep watch?"

Bridey walked unsteadily back to the couch and sat heavily at the mention of the prophecy.

"Blue," she said.

"What?" Nora responded.

"Blue, blue, the room was blue when I did it over but it's faded now to this purple." Nora and I looked at each other wondering if Bridey was slipping a little in the mental department. "It's true then," the tiny woman wondered aloud. "It's not just the fantastic musings of an old widow. You've come to answer the call. Are you the embodiment of Faidhe then?" She said to me.

"Come on Bridey." I persuaded. "We'll take a ride and I promise, you'll know more about all this when we're done than maybe even you want to, but for now, I don't want to stick around with the three stooges down there and wait for them to come up with some bright idea about coming back for another visit. For that matter, Nora, let's grab anything we don't want to leave here to be rummaged through if they decide to come back when we're not here." I went to my room to check for items I wanted to take with me.

"Nora picked up where I left off by taking Bridey's arm as she seemed a little unsteady now at the realization that what she'd heard her entire life as a tale actually had truth to it.

"Let's lock up and we'll leave your car here. We'll meet our friends and you can decide for yourself what fits your story and what doesn't, but mostly, I think, we'll want to hear about the brothers down the hill and how they came to live here eight years ago."

Returning from my bedroom, I had an expression of resignation on my face when I dropped my fully packed suitcase on the floor by the door.

"I guess I'm not willing to leave anything behind to those, what did you call them Bridey: amadans?" She smiled faintly at that.

Then I said, "Well Nora, if this is the beginning of our adventure in Europe, you better go pack too."

She took off down the hallway to collect her things while I packed up all our new books back into the box we'd gotten from Cath's store. I closed the peat stove to subdue the fire that had been lighting the room with its orange glow and turned on the overhead light in the kitchen for safety. I grabbed the cottage and car keys from the kitchen counter and as an afterthought, grabbed the bottle of wine that had by now had ample time to breath, corked it and shoved it into my satchel to bring with us.

I didn't feel entirely comfortable bringing Bridey with us to meet Cath and Finny and I'm sure she wasn't thrilled at the idea of traveling to town this late at night with two American women but we both had our reasons to rely more on trusting the other than not. And like it or not, this woman knew bits of the story that we didn't figure anyone to know. She seemed to know about the dying tribe of Duibhe and something about two brothers traveling with or associated with Faidhe and her daughter. Somehow, she'd come close to facts about the real story and insinuated herself into the mix but the fact that she'd created magic through which Faidhe could communicate and possibly had drawn us and these men that are some minions of the Beast, judging by the smell of them, we thought we'd better run all of this by Cath and Finny.

We were an odd group looking to be seated at this late hour. Two middle aged women and a decidedly older woman, looking to meet up with two old men.

"We've done with serving meals some time ago," the woman who greeted us the door of Kenny's restaurant told us. We looked beyond her to see if our friends had arrived and in fact, they had taken a table at the far end of the dining room, away from the crowds in the pub, by the cheery fireplace where Nora and I had sat the first time we ate at Kenny's.

"That's okay," Nora told the pleasant looking waitress. "Our party is waiting for us there. We'll seat ourselves." She stepped around the woman, whose nametag identified her as Sinead, and made it clear there would be no protest at us sitting in the empty dining room. "Bridey," she said, and put out a hand to let Bridey go first into the dining room.

As Nora and Bridey slid past Sinead, I said, "Thank you. We'll start with three pints of Guinness please." Slipping a bill into her hand that would cover all the drinks including the ones in front of Cath and Finny. I said, "Keep the change." Sinead seemed to mind less that there would be an extra table to clean up tonight.

"Right," she said. "I'll take care of that for you." And off she went to the bar to fill our order. I felt a bit out of place as curious people from the considerably younger pub crowd gawked over to see the older folks who commanded a special table in the closed dining room. I turned my attention to the men we'd come to meet.

Nora was already taking care of the introductions. "Cath, Finny, this is Bridey Flynn our landlady at the cottage where we're staying for a while. Bridey, these are our friends, Cath and Finny McDonough."

"McDonough? You're goin' about as Tinkers then?" Bridey asked in a tone that sounded like an accusation.

I was somewhat familiar with the term and I didn't think it was a complimentary one connected with people who lived a life on the road offering to fix household items and things made of steel or tin for a meal or cash. I was a little disturbed that Bridey was being so rude to these dear men. My friends.

"Can ye think of a better way?" Finny replied. "We've kept humble and away from the eye of any who'd think te look in high places. Well that's been my way of it, anyhow. As for him," he tipped his head toward Cath; he's done some time as a Druid when his magic suited, and his gift for words came in handy right enough as a monk transcribin' the old works. Had a hand in the book of Kells he did. He kept fed in the chorch. Hidin' 'neath the holy robes and scripture but always keepin' safe the words. Then later he elevated te teachin' theology at the Trinity for some time. It's been a lifetime of written words for Cath and a lifetime of the spoken word by the road and travel for me. I've been a bard for much of this life one way or another; keepin' te the road and remainin' anonymous but all the while listenin' for goin's on that'd be of interest to us."

Bridey retorted, her voice taking on the accent she'd obviously devoted effort to diminish, "And ye never gave a thought to comin' fer me?"

"What are ye sayin' gorl." Finny denied. "We've been centuries over tryin' te find any clue as te whether that goat Diog was tellin' us true or no. In the end, we gave ye up for lost as he'd told us ye were dead in the aftermath of the push te the Sidhe. We believed him due te the fact that he was just as keen te see if we knew of yer whereabouts as we were to find out news from him. We figured ye'd be better off gone te the Sidhe than te spend se much as a day wi' the likes of him. Insane, he was, when he found that there'd been a girl born te the clans and he'd been told as ye were stillborn. Concorned he was that we was denied claimin' credit for ye. Despite that so few of us can actually breed, it would na' have stopped him from exactin' a price for ye and sellin' ye off te the same type of slavery as our mother endured. Not a moment's concorn he had for our dear mother whether she'd taken her own life in misery and neither did it matter te him that ye'd be in the same misery. Gettin' his due was all too dear te the likes of him."

"De ye mean te say that ye've been livin' right here under our noses all along?" Cath's voice practically squeaked with the stress of many years lost.

"Not precisely. Tell me all." Bridey said as she took her seat at the table with the men leaving Nora and I standing somewhat befuddled and in disbelief at the meeting of these three.

"Ah, excuse us." I said with a little indignation. "Are you forgetting something?" Just then, Sinead came with the pints of Guinness and placed them on cardboard coasters on the table with a bowl of snack mix. She looked to Cath and Finny to ask if they needed anything else.

Finny replied, "Aye lass, I think we'll be needin a dram of Jameson's for me and me brother here, in fact best bring us all a taste. It seems we've a bit of a reunion te celebrate. And I know it's beyond the kitchen's time but d'ye think ye could scare up a bit of bread and beef for us too?"

I saw in Finny's face how he'd gotten over for so many years with his farm women and others seeking stories. Although Sinead was a girl no older than 22, she blushed at Finny's attention and direct gaze that was filled with mischief and promise.

"Yes sir." She said. "Right away."

I goggled at Nora with amazement that he'd all but massaged her rump but never raised a hand or said anything reprochable. It was all in the way his eyes danced to make the young woman practically squirm at his attention. We both looked at him with our mouths open in wonder and he seemed quite pleased with himself.

"What? An old man can't be friendly?" was all he said as we plunked ourselves down at the table.

"Okay, spill." I ordered. "What's going on here? Are you guys related? Is Bridey's story true that she's been keeping what she knew of the story going? C'mon, give it up."

Cath put a hand on my arm. "Let's us wait until we've all our order, then we can speak plain. That is," he said out of the side of his mouth toward Finny, "if me brother can keep his ears from jutting out for all te see!"

At that comment, Finny put on a feigned look of innocence and winked at us trying, not too hard, to conceal his smile. When Sinead returned with silverware, a loaf of bread, some slabs of cold rare roast beef and five shots of Jameson's whiskey, I noticed that she'd applied a bright red color to her lips and combed her hair. I peered a bit closer at Finny and noticed that as he looked at Sinead, his ears actually did appear to poke out of his white hair in small points.

"Holy smokes!" Nora said and distracted me from examining Finny's ears more closely. "We'll all be loaded." She looked at Cath, Finny and Bridey who were holding up their shots of whiskey in a toast and raised her glass too. She looked at me with a shrug and said, "When in Rome."

I shrugged too and lifted my glass. The five of us wished each other health. "Slainte," and bottomed our glasses. The heat from the whiskey immediately blossomed into my chest and then took its place in my cheeks as I felt the flame ignite in high red color I always experience when I drink anything other than beer or wine.

"Woo!" I exclaimed after the liquor went down. My eyes watered and I reached for the Guinness to help cool my palate.

I noticed now that tentative and surreptitious hands began to reach across the table between Bridey and the men. There were reassuring pinches of fingers, fogged glasses and subdued sniffing as they all took a moment to realize that this reunion was miraculous. Cath reached his handkerchief under his glasses to swipe at the wetness there and Finny gave a rousing honk into his own handkerchief. Bridey let the silent tears flow and brushed at her nose with a cloth napkin from the table. I noticed then, as she pulled the wooden pin from her hair to release the bun that her hair fell over her ears to cover slightly angled points I was sure had not been there before. Cath too showed evidence of extra size to the tips of his ears. Perhaps I'd never noticed before but I would have sworn that the points concealed under his fluffy white hair, were not there before tonight.

Feeling inept and out of the loop, Nora and I just waited. They'd get around to us eventually. For the moment, we quietly gathered our patience while the others gained control of their emotions. Without thinking about what I was doing, I picked up the salt from the table and walked clockwise three times around the table spilling the salt on the floor. With the complimentary book of matches, in the ashtray I lit the table candle that had been doused after the dinner hour. No one seemed to take notice, but I felt better for having created a ritual space for this reunion. It struck me that these three people, coming together created a shift in the cosmos somehow that coupled with Nora and I might send up some powerful energetic flairs and the last thing we wanted now was to be noticed by the energy behind the Beast. We had no way of knowing who or where other agents of the Beast might pop up and one night with the three stooges was enough drama for me.

"What about a bit of ceol?" Finny said as he pulled out what looked like a small flute. "The boys here have a concertina and there's a lass that plays a handy fiddle. I sore miss me harp but it's been a great long time since I've born the weight of the strings. If ye've ever gone te the Trinity, ye'll see evidence in the Book of Kells of Cath's devotion, and a harp of me own design there as well. This is more compact and convenient to carry he said gesturing to his tiny wind instrument. It's been all together too long since we've pushed the chairs back. Wouldn't ye say?"

"Now?" I squawked. "Don't we have work to do?" I looked to Cath for some semblance of reason. "We came up against something very powerful and downright evil tonight...In the flesh, not in a dream or energetically. Those guys that she's been harboring for eight years came on us with bad intent and some pretty forceful magic without so much as breaking a sweat. And that's not all; they went through our stuff in the cottage. Who knows what they found out about us? They probably know who we are now, and they know we have some kind of magic. And the big one, I think he's the leader, he seemed to have a particular interest in Nora. I don't like it and I don't think we should be sitting around, getting drunk or playing music!"

"Drunk? Who said anything about getting drunk? There's a time, lass, for rejoicin' in the family ye've been given and we're goin' te mark this occasion in thanks of that joy." Cath tried to calm me.

"But shouldn't we *do* something?" I protested.

"Aye lass," Finny put in. "We're doin' it. Remember when ye got the whiff of the foulness as it tried te ward ye off comin' te Midleton with fear and terror, and ye two gorls held tight yer hands and thought of sweetness te weaken the hold yer fears had on ye?"

"Yes." I answered. Nora was fully attentive now too.

"Well, that's one of our most powerful weapons against the Beast. Love, family, pleasant memories, laughter, music, poetry, sweet smells, all of that type thing will help charge yer batteries so te speak. It makes perfect sense when ye reflect on it. When is it that people make the most fervent...ah, love? Is it not in the face of death after a wake or funeral, as an affirmation of life?"

"Well, yeah."

"So then," Cath broke in, "at the advent of a great competition for the success in the task that lies ahead for ye, will it not make sense for us te drink of the whiskey made successfully in the town of Midleton in spite of the fearful hold the foul energy has placed on the sacred place? And then come tegether with family te revel in each other's company with drink, food, music and dance and, if Finny has his way, a bit of earnest flirtation as well?"

I was reminded of something I'd heard or seen sometime recently but couldn't quite put my finger on it. I mentally withdrew from the conversation for a moment until I could place it.

"Hey this sounds like the scene I saw in my meditation when we were in the car fighting off those terrors. Remember, Nora? The poem that I wrote down? You guys remember, don't you?"

I rummaged through my satchel to pull out the pad of paper where I'd recorded the verses and shuffled back through scads of notes I'd taken since I recorded the words from my meditation. "Here, wait. Here it is! And there were those words that sort of came alive and sort of lived or had personality or, oh I don't know, I'm not saying it right but I think, that was a clue that came to me when I needed help fighting off the Beast and the fear and the smell. It was telling me what you're saying, I think. Listen:"

> There is a sheen on contented faces, kindled by dance and food
> And the smell of Laughter is on our breath
> The warmth of the fire that burns with tales of centuries past,
> Pales in the glow of friends and family
> The log crackles with history's tales and pops with holly berries
> All wrapped with garland of the Ivy Queen
> The spirits and memories of those gone over come to dance with us and join the Frey
> Our passion, the essence of our laughter, love, stories and song, collects on the panes
> And as the cold taps at the window, white ferns paint the glass
> The gathering is sheathed from the night so...
> The inevitable darkness must wait
> We notice not, the moment the old year departs and the new one is birthed
> Still we eat and drink and sing and laugh
> The night has no choice but to settle
> To wait
> To watch for the Light to return
> As do we, to greet the year anew

"The word laughter was alive, I guess it could be called, but the word Frey was beautiful and rhythmic. It moved with different designs and colors in the lettering. It was almost, I don't know, proud or showy. But that's not right either. Am I making any sense?"

Finny answered first. "I believe when ye told me about this piece, I thought its meaning would be revealed te ye in time. Perhaps now ye'll understand how being here and takin' time te celebrate as was done in the times long past, is a way te keep darkness from the door."

"Do you know the meaning of that living word, Frey?" Cath asked.

"It means a conflict or commotion. So in the case of the verse here, I took it to mean to join in the activity of the gathering."

"It would if it had been spelled, f-r-a-y but the word ye have here is F-r-e-y. And it's written with a capital letter. Was this intentional? What I mean te say is, ye've copied it just as ye saw it?"

"Yeah. Does it make that much of a difference? I mean I wouldn't have noticed the spelling; it's never been a sticking point with me so I really hadn't noticed if it was misspelled. I just copied it as I saw it."

"Frey, I think may have been a riddle of sorts within the work. Spelled as it is, with a capital letter, it is the name of a Norse God of crops, fruitfulness, love, peace and prosperity. So the piece is tellin' ye that as ye prepare for a battle, a fray, 'join the Frey,' and all that he stands for and put that on as yer armor. And it seems, yer heritage from the Swedes is callin' ye for your attention prior te this battle for it's a Norse God ye've mentioned. Is there anything else in the piece or the meditation that would support the callin' te the north?"

"Well if by north you mean our Swedish heritage, then yeah. The whole meditation was about our Yule celebration as kids: smorgasbord, grog, Swedish meatballs, candle wind chimes, and our Nana would always bring her little Yule Tomtien, or the Swedish Santa Clause as she called him. It was a handmade ornament of a Santa looking character that was as old as old could be, holding a pine bough in one hand and a sprig of holly in the other. So I guess it would make sense that the poem or the verses would have meaning connected with the Yule time. Plus, it was always kind of a double celebration at that time of year because Yule was Nana's birthday too. Oh yeah, birthdays," I was reminded. Switching gears I said, "Nora, I didn't get to tell you, I figured out who Mary is! I think."

"Who?" She said shaking her head at the dizzy speed things seemed to be happening.

"Let's finish this first and then remind me. Don't let me forget."

"Don't worry, I won't."

"So," I continued, trying to sort out Cath's train of thought. "The vision that came to me was speaking of fighting off the darkness and joining Frey. You feel the darkness is a metaphor for the evil and joining in laughter and song and dance with family is a strong tool to be used against the evil. But you feel that the scene, which is also very much a part of my heritage was a calling, of sorts, for me to look to my Swedish traditions and history to figure out how to fight the Beast?"

"In a way," Cath answered. "But don't be sidetracked. The Beast is evil, no doubt, and ye'll spend a fair amount of energy trying te get around that detour but think te what your primary goal is in yer task here? Remember?"

"I, um...we're supposed to, ah, save the world?" Came my pathetic answer.

Cath didn't lose patience. "Think, lass. You're developin' yer Power for a battle sure, but what is it ye'll be fightin' for?"

"I don't know! We never really identified how we're going to save the world or what we'll be fighting." I began to grow agitated. "I just know that this evil thing is out there and it hates me. Hates us. Hates anything that can't be manipulated or turned to its own purpose. The thing that I hate is that my son is involved in all of this. He's so sweet and so innocent. He shouldn't be involved in any of this. So, if I'm honest, the real reason I'm in this now is to fight for him. To protect him. To keep him safe. And if the rest of the world benefits, well fine, but he's my priority here."

At this Cath seemed satisfied. "Well then, there you have it."

"Have what?" I snapped.

"There's your purpose in all this. Remember the verses in the prophecy regardin' yerself?"

"Which verses?"

"'*She will sorve as the cup to catch and hold the blood of the four corners.*' This ye've done. Ye carried the child who is made of all four bloodlines of the original families involved: Yer son Lucas is Irish, as the direct descendant of the forst High King of Ireland and the last. He is Swedish, of the blood of Sigrdifa the Valkyrie from the land of the origin of the Stone of Fal, the Keystone of the Circle. And her consort, Iarann. Both these bloodlines he got from yerself. And then from yer husband, Lucas is Italian of his father's line, descendant of the very child of Faidhe and her consort, the Greenman. And he is German through his father as well. This being as a descendant of Lon Dubh as she crossed the European continent te find her own way in all of her troubles after she felt betrayed by the Gods. So ye've fulfilled that part of the prophecy in bearin' yer son te the world." He continued. "'*Then 'she'll breathe life back into the forgotten.*' Whether ye knew it or not, yer life has been about resorchin' and writin' about the Old Ways. Bringin' te light what has been forgotten as well as bringin' life te the boy whose very name means te bring the light. And later, it's repeated in the prophecy of your rebirth inte this life and the task it was said, '*Lastly the one holds the light and the knowledge together within. We know that te be yer son whose very name means light and knowledge.* And the rest: '*She will complete the corcle, to set it te spin. As the hub unites and brings the wheel complete, and precise is the time when the task is replete.*' Again, referring te the borth of Lucas. '*Open is the balance when the light's strength takes sway, To complete the wheel and birth the sun's long ray.*' The last part is about passing on the responsibility to yer son rather than assuming it yerself. But as the balance, in the scales and in much of the dual gifts ye've been given, ye must be fully open te giving yer son what he needs te take on his task in all this. He can't be protected from his destiny, but you can give him all that he needs te assume his responsibility in the last two lines of the birthing prophecy, by doin' yer own task with an open heart and full heat of passion."

"And what is that?" I inquired, fighting the hot stone that was sinking in my gut.

"Ye must go te the Cauldron located in Copenhagen, Denmark, the old gateway te the land of the Valkyrie and unite the tale of the prophecy and the tale of Faidhe tegether with the depiction of it all with the Power of the Word te release the Cruinne Cumhacht, the Power of the Universe and direct it te your son as the recipient. Ye were the Cauldron that borthed the light of yer boy inte this world, now te complete the duality, ye've got te borth the Power of the Universe through the sacred Cauldron and direct it te yer boy. It will ultimately be his role te create the balance needed for the world te survive and move on to the Fifth Civilization."

"I asked you about that before. What is the Fifth Civilization?"

"The lines in the prophecy regardin' this statement, *'The child brings vast change as the great wheel spins. And the Fifth Civilization is ushered, as maturity begins.'* It is believed that ours, Finny's, Bridey's and mine, was the third civilization lasting 3000 years, with two eras prior to it, the second Civilization lasted 4000 years and the First Civilization, which lasted 5000 years. During our time, the Third Civilization, is when magical creatures roamed the earth and certain animals bore spirits similar to ours in that they were able te communicate in various ways with us. Every aspect of the orth was recognized in a great tapestry of life as havin' a porpose and equal in its importance te the fabric of the tapestry. There were Centaurs and Mer-people of the sea, along with giants and dragons who were mighty and regal creatures so long as they had human interaction. There was great diversity in the mingling of the human and spirit worlds and the coexistence of human and flora and fauna. But as humans began te change, and the time for the Power was over, most of these creatures and magical peoples went under te the Sidhe and much of the old knowledge was lost but for what lived on in the women folk, old stories and some remnants in the books of religion written long after. But as ye know, even these women were destroyed as witches, and the stories varied, so not much of the original stories or spirit behind them remained. The world was left te struggle under the yolk of masculine lust for orthly power, dominance, control and riches. This period was the Fourth Civilization come te full fledgin' during the age of Pisces, the fish, or more widely known as the time of the Christ, whose symbol was the fish. This time lasted only 2000 years. As ye know, at the torn of the century, that time began te come te a close as we come now te the dawning of the Age of Aquarius."

Nora piped in now that the conversation had turned to her familiar territory. "The Age of Aquarius is being ushered in now and will be recognized as the age of technology and science. There will be a period of transition as the age of religion begins to fade out. You know how they say the fire burns brightest before it burns out? Well, it seems the fight against religion, all religion, being superseded by the advancement of technology and science will rage the hardest in these transitional years. Aquarius is about universal knowledge so the time for male dominance will begin to diminish as well but not before it, too burns hard and hot in protest of being viewed as archaic and ineffectual as we reset our ideas about religion and masculinity. This combination of religious dogma, masculine dominance coupled with huge gains in technological knowledge creates a very precarious time for humanity as we adjust to the change from one civilization to another. Imagine what could happen when even just one religious zealot uses modern technology to assert dominance for his point of view throughout the world!"

"We don't have te imagine. Bridey said quietly. "Look at what's happened in your own country with the twin towers. And throughout Eastern Europe and other places as zealots try to destroy all that is not under the yolk of their beliefs. Imagine nuclear technology in the hands of those people? Is this what the Lady Faidhe will come back to correct?"

"Bridey," Finny answered. "Cath brought ye what news he had of the story as I traveled with Faidhe during our time and ye had some of the tale right but he could not tell ye all that happened due te the promise we'd made with Lon Dubh." At this statement, Finny tipped his head in my direction before he continued. "And te keep all between us three and only release te others, facts about what was happening on one level but nothing of the inner workings of the prophecy."

At this I was surprised to recall that the person he spoke of was me. I had not begun to think of myself in terms of Lon Dubh reborn. I still thought of her as a person other than myself whose faded memories were stored in my head. I tried not to dwell on this issue and redoubled my efforts to focus on the conversation at hand.

"The truth is, Bridey, Faidhe will not be coming back as ye've expected all these long centuries. It's come te this." He said, spreading his hands toward Nora and me indicating that we were the women of the prophecy. "And what ye may have hord about the Lady from the Road could be applied te what these gorls are about te take on."

"But Magda, my foster mother, she told me she'd met the Mother, Faidhe. Magda told me of her graciousness as she passed her role as priestess to the Circle to someone other than herself. I was weaned on the stories at Magda's knee. And yourselves kept me informed of when she'd taken you on the road with her, Finny. Cath told me of your travels to the Mounts of T'airg and on the ocean to far away lands until we'd lost hearing of you and then heard tell you were dead. You confirmed Magda's tellin' of Faidhe's adventures on the road. How can it not be true?"

Cath responded, "Bridey, ye've been true te what ye knew of the tale even when ye thought we were lost to ye and the cause, and ye're a stout soul for keepin' life in somethin' that was not your keepin' but there's much ye don't know or don't have the truth of what little ye do know. But ye were right in knowin' that there's something about these gorls that bore attention. And we'll have time a plenty, I hope, te go over it all with ye, but that'll be for later and we've details te iron as these girls take te the road, but for now, we've voices te raise and music te play and it's been centuries since me feet have trod their way through a jig. I can't tell ye what joy I have in me heart te see ye Bridey. Let's see how many other hearts we can fill this night. Finny?"

In the single name, Cath made the request that we forego any serious conversation and give over to the abandon of joy.

Finny raised his whistle to his lips and let out one long, slow, mournful sound that immediately struck a resounding recognition in my heart. I felt, as I had in my dream of the forest, that I'd come home. With the one note, all notice in the pub was drawn to our little group as if we appeared to their view for the first time. People stared in quiet anticipation as they answered Finny's call to attention. When the one note came to its subtle finish, not a sound could be heard in the pub and all eyes were on us. After a dramatic moment of silence, Finny laid lips to his pipe and broke into a rousing song that spontaneously brought the crowd's hands to clapping. A young man wearing a black leather jacket, jeans that fit just right and engineer's boots approached the table. He had a massive head of curly black hair and walked with a swagger that dared anyone to make comment that he carried his concertina under his left arm. Pulling up a chair next to Finny, the man sat down and adjusted a few buttons and widgets on his instrument and tapped his foot three times to catch hold of the tune before he jumped in. As though the crowd was released from restraints, people had begun to push back the tables and chairs in the dining room. A girl who looked no older than 15 years old joined the two men. Cath offered her his seat and she sat straight backed while she fitted her fiddle under her chin. Smiling a broad grin, she plunged into the music with skill of someone who played, not with the precision of years of lessons, but with the casual ease of music in her fingers from birth.

The floor resounded with tapping feet and Cath put his hand out to me to join him in a dance. I was shy and tried to refuse but he'd have none of my protests that I couldn't dance.

"It's only a memory lass, for you and I have spun this way before. Come now and remember who ye are."

With that he firmly placed his arm about my waist and guided me into the circle created by the pub patrons. Starting slowly with a few bouncing steps to the right then two stepping back we began to bounce and step in a circular motion until we completed one revolution around the circle.

Cath had been right. It was as though my feet knew what to do and the strange steps were so familiar to me that I felt almost free as I bounded around the floor with him. There were snippets of comments I heard as we rounded the center of the circle.

"Oh they look like they're flying. Look at their feet!" I heard Sinead comment, "She's American!" As though that meant I shouldn't be able to dance. Her fellow employee of Kenny's Pub responded that, "It must be from all the barn dancin' they do there in America."

I laughed right out loud and enjoyed every step of the dance. Cath then spun me into the arms of a man in his 30's wearing work pants and a shirt with the name Liam over the pocket. Liam seamlessly continued the dance but with much less finesse. It was as though without Cath's grace on the floor, I had somehow lost a bit of my own, but we muddled through. I noticed that Cath and Nora were now tripping the lights and many in the crowd joined in. There were moments when someone or other would take center circle and put on a display of fancy footwork to the varying types of music being played. It felt like hours that the raucous celebration played on. Bridey and Cath danced, Nora and I danced with each other, several from the crowd switched places dancing with us all. At one point, Finny took a break as the others played and he came to me holding out an old cloth with something in it for me to see. I looked into what he had wrapped there and recognized what he showed me.

"My whistle!" I exclaimed.

"Aye. He responded. It's time ye came back te yerself."

After the initial excitement of recognition, I felt momentarily confused. "Wait. That's not mine. I made a mistake. I...I think must have seen it..."

"Don't over-think it lass. Just allow yerself te relax inte the moment. Here." He said as he handed me the whistle.

"But I don't know how to play." I felt mild panic that I'd be expected to play here in front of the crowd.

"I know, I know. How could ye? Yer just like everyone else. Right? Ye couldn't possibly have any hidden talents." His eyebrows rose high on his forehead as he waited for me to see how ridiculous it is to place restrictions on what I might be able to do before even trying, considering all I'd learned about myself over the last weeks.

I snatched the whistle from him resigned to his common sense and felt the familiar piece in my hands. The wood had been well oiled and preserved and the whalebone mouthpiece shone white as if it had been carved in recent years. Testing its tone, I raised the flute to my lips and breathed a tentative note through its ribs. I recalled the sweet sound as someone might hear a familiar voice. I blew another note and allowed my fingers to rest comfortably in their places. I felt my mind turn inward as the crowd, music and noise faded to the faraway of my consciousness. I let my mind show me pictures of memories when I'd held this instrument in my hands as it comforted me in my loneliness and chirped of every joyous moment I'd ever had. It was the voice of my heart. My fingers skipped over the notes like water tumbles over river stones, each proclaiming its own distinctive sound in the song of the forest. As I stood alone in the woods with my music singing the songs of my heart, I could smell the river water and the moss. I felt the dew settle on my skin in the early morning mist as the sun toyed with the vapors and made millions of tiny rainbows. With each breath I pulled into my lungs I could taste the unspoiled air filled with sounds of birds talking, leaves rustling and growing things. When I recognized that all had hushed, I let out a final note to my heart and opened my eyes surprised to see that every person in Kenny's Pub had stopped dancing, laughing, drinking and playing music. They were all staring at me. I had thought I'd go unnoticed in a corner, hidden by all the activity and noise, but now, obviously, I had disturbed the party to the point that I'd embarrassed myself.

"Oh." I said. "I'm so sorry. I was just trying to see if I could still play this. I'm sorry. I'll stop. Please keep playing. Keep dancing."

Unexpectedly, many in the crowd began to applaud and then everyone joined in. The man I'd danced with, Liam, pulled me over to where there were several people playing instruments now, and sat me down with the group. My eyes grew large and I was purple from embarrassment.

"No I couldn't. Please. No."

To which Liam said, "Don't be modest now. Yer as good, at least, as any here. And with the different sound of it, it's really quite lovely. It's as if the music speaks." He paused thinking that what he said didn't make sense but it was almost accurate. "Ah, no matter." He accepted his inability to express exactly what he meant. "We'll have none of that modesty now. We've all enjoyed what you've played and we'll be lookin' for more. Now play; won't you?"

I put the flute to my lips if only to keep people's eyes off me. I searched for the knowledge of some songs in my head but found that I only had to follow my fingers where they lead me. The music began again and the Guinness flowed. We all danced and took turns with each other. The entire crowd seemed not to notice at all that Nora and I were comparatively older and that the other three siblings were ancient.

Nora had met one person who seemed to mind not at all that we were a bit older. In fact, after a while, I noticed that Nora was dancing quite a few wheels and reels, always returning to this man as her partner. He was tall and on the thin side sporting a beard and an amiable smile. After I'd taken a break from playing, Nora introduced this mystery man as Eric. I was surprised to discover that he was not a native, but traveling from the states like us.

"Lee, this is Eric. He's an American from South Carolina." She said. Announcing it as though she'd just discovered something unusual. Cath grabbed Nora and hauled her back out to the dance floor leaving Eric with me.

"Hi. Nice to meet you, Eric. What brings you to Ireland?"

"I'm traveling to a few places in Europe and then to Norway to check out the country of my ancestry."

He didn't sound like what I expected from a southern man. I didn't really detect the deep southern drawl.

"Have you been here before? You seem to know a lot about the dances here."

"No never. I've lived all over when I was young. My father was in the military and we traveled a whole lot but I've never been here before." *That explains the lack of accent*, I thought.

He continued, "I came here with my friend, John who's Irish...well, Irish descent. He wanted to come to Ireland. But I find the dances are basically the same as shag dancing back home. If you know how to shag, it's pretty easy to pick up the variations of these steps."

Eric was talking to me but he could not take his eyes off Nora. He watched as she danced with Cath and smiled as he saw her misstep and easily laugh at the fun she was having. Careful not to be rude, he looked me in the eye and shook my hand.

"It's been very nice meeting you." He said. "Please excuse me?"

"Sure." I said, and he walked over to Cath and Nora, politely taking her off Cath's hands to sweep her around the floor once again where the dancing crowd swallowed them from view. I watched Nora and Eric dance and laugh together and felt that the only thing that would make this night complete was if Patrice were here too. She could use a laugh with family and a bit of romance. I felt a momentary stab of loneliness for her and felt myself wishing that my sister Patrice had come on this trip with us if only to engage in some fun with us on this night. It was like a tongue worrying over the space where a tooth used to be. Patrice's absence felt like a gaping hole. I sighed as I waited for Cath to make his way back to me.

"This has been so much fun, Cath. You were right. I feel memories and strength coming back to me. It's almost like how sap runs in a tree during the spring. I'm not thinking about making it happen while I'm having fun. It's as if the music and dancing and people are the seasonal trigger to spark the sap that causes the blossoming that will eventually become fruit. Does that sound silly? It just seems like a perfect metaphor for what I feel like right now. It's like genetic memory is at work and I just instinctively know what to do. It feels so strange but perfectly normal at the same time. Make sense?"

"Perfectly." Cath said with a contented look on his face.

"So what's with your ears?"

A smile touched Cath's eyes before it reached his lips.

"Ye'll know our heritage on our mother's side will bear this trait. We've been able te keep those who don't expect te see this or those who don't know of us, from recognizin' the features that would give ourselves away much the same way ye perform what you call the mask. But there are those from yer own bloodline, distant relatives perhaps, who may have a bit of the Seer in them, will on occasion give a second look as though they weren't sure they saw what they think they saw. But for the most part, people don't see what we don't want them te see. As ye've done yerself throughout yer lifetime. But on occasions such as this, when we're free te pick up the Old Ways and music and especially when we find ourselves tegether with our own kind in addition te bein' this close in proximity te genuine Power and old souls, well it's all we can do te keep from takin' te the hillside te slip down by the fires in keepin' with the old traditions of festival."

"Cath!" I was a bit taken aback to think of Cath participating in those old taboos. But I rechecked myself as I remembered that feeling of genetic memory as I ran through the woods as a girl, sweaty in the face and covered with dirt and grass stains, chanting things I didn't understand in languages that were not my own. And again as I had experienced only minutes ago. How right it felt when I allowed myself to just let go of all the rules, fears, insecurities and doubts. When I let myself just be myself without all the expectations of society and the shoulds and shouldn'ts of the religious framework, I was able to see clearly and just be who I am. I nodded my head and shrugged in Cath's direction to indicate to him that I understood. "You're letting go, just being who you are."

He nodded back. I looked to the crowd and wondered about Nora. It had been so long since I'd seen her laugh and having fun. So long she'd kept herself tied down under the heavy bonds of appearances, propriety, duty and pride. Now, her hair flew free and her face was in high color. She'd worked up a dewy glow from dancing and looked genuinely happy for the first time since we were ...well kids. She was radiant and beautiful.

"I guess that's the true her without all the crap." I wondered out loud. This made me reflect on the condition of her marriage of a quarter century or more. What does that say about her life at home if she can be so happy here and I haven't seen *this* Nora since our childhood? Then I cast a wary eye on this guy Eric, feeling a bit protective of Nora, wondering if he expected to 'slip down by the hillside fires' tonight as well. Well, I thought: *She's a grown woman and she'd do what's right for her*.

"Right ye are lass." Cath spoke. I wasn't sure if he was responding to my statement or my thoughts. In that moment, Nora looked directly at me as though I'd caught her doing something. I smiled at her and nodded my head to let her know that I have no judgments and whatever she needed to do to make herself whole and happy would suit me just fine. This guy Eric, on the other hand, if things go down that road tonight and he's not the gentleman he appears to be, I'll be hard put to keep from roasting his Norwegian ass over one of those hillside fires.

"Is that the sun?"

I couldn't believe what I was seeing. Through the windows of the pub, the sky appeared to be turning from inky black to bluish gray. The features of the buildings across the way were discernable now and there were stirrings of an occasional car driving down the street.

"Cath, how can that be? We've been here all night?"

"Aye lass. Even though it was a late hour when we arrived, it seems we've been quite caught up. Watch ye now what happens as ye've broken the reverie. Watch as people come te themselves once again."

He was right, people seemed to have somewhat confused expressions cross their faces and a few at a time, they slipped out the front door of the pub. "They'll have little or no real memory, only a feelin' of what took place, a sense of happiness, contentedness and well bein', but they'll remember very little and like yerself, they feel as only an hour or two went by when it's been the night entire."

"Like Brigadoon?" I inquired. Referring to the old tale of people who got caught in the enchanted village in Scotland that only came into existence once every hundred years, but what seemed like a night spent in Brigadoon, passed one hundred years in the outer world.

"Perhaps on a very small scale this night might've carried some enchantment, sure. Don't forget, though, Brigadoon was fantasy story built on the tales of the memories about the enchanted wood of the full-blood fairies in their own element. Te be caught up in the place where the fairies dwell is te be lost te your own time and the rhythms of this world. Fairies are kin te the Elf but we're only half-blood Elf. So this adventure was not quite the same as Brigadoon, but near enough for academics I suppose." At this he wiggled his eyebrows and ran up the points on his ears for me to see. "We've created this place and time between places and times only with the help of yer Power and ability Black Bird. It was yer need te create this space that made it so."

I jumped a bit at the casual usage of the name from the tale and it brought me back to the situation we had come to discover and I was put in mind of more serious things.

"Cath," I said. "I know who Mary is. I don't know what it means or whether she'll play a part in this that will work for or against us but the way I figure it, Mary is Gara. Now I think we're all here for a reason or purpose, and Nora and I obviously are at the center of the action, but if there is any need of real support, I'm not sure Mary can be counted on for anything that won't benefit Mary."

He seemed to contemplate how this news could affect our task and dismissed it as unimportant for the moment. "Ye'll have other things te tend before ye come te face what roles the rest of yer family play in all this. Some have fulfilled their role in just bringin' all the souls together in this life. Yer grandparents have passed after bringin' Laoghaire through te this time; and yer grandmother, Sigrid has played her role and gone as well. Perhaps too, yer parents in Laoghaire and Craiche have served their purpose in borthin' ye four girls, each representin' one of the elements. And yerself borthin' the bringer of light and knowledge. Yer sisters may have sorved their porpose by simply bein' here te open up the energy that formed the wheel and te just be a part of the wheel so it could be set te spin. I think it's fair te say that ye two gorls still have a role te play in all what's te happen, just as yer son will take the lead soon, but as for the others, perhaps it's best te proceed assuming that their role is accomplished, and if not, then it will be revealed in time."

"Cath." I was struck with a profound concern and sadness at his mention of Lucas taking the lead in all this. "Lucas is only eight years old. How can he possibly take the lead in all this?"

"Ye've both come here without any knowledge of all that's taken place but ye've lorned in a short time about new capabilities and a porpose that is yer own."

"Yeah," I answered, unsure as to what his point might be.

Yer boy is eight years old at this time, and once ye've accomplished what's necessary in Denmark te release all the Power te him te be at his disposal, he'll have resources available te him that are beyond our reasonin' te even imagine."

"Well he may have that Power, but he's just a boy. How will he know how to engage the Power? How will he be able to battle things like the Beast? Inside, he has the heart of innocence. How can he stand up to people and forces that are so ugly and foul that even just knowing that they exist would bend the mind of even the most brave?"

"True, things are beginning te happen at present in the world that prove the stirrin' of the evil energy but the prophecy states in the last line regardin' Lucas that *'The child brings vast changes as the great wheel spins'* so ye know that it is expected that he is still in his youth when these changes begin te take place. It's the final line in the prophecy that might lend ye some solace: *'And the Fifth Civilization is ushered, as maturity begins.'* Now ye have a bit of knowledge on the Fifth Civilization and we'll go into it in more detail before ye leave for the north, but the last of this line states it all takes place 'as maturity begins.' This would indicate, if it allows that these words are taken from the orly traditions here on the island and carried through the centuries in the Celtic ways, that the boy has until he's halfway through his twelfth year, when he comes te the beginning of manhood te lorn how te use and hone his skills and the Power. In the Old Ways, that would be at a point in his life, when the rights of passage would have been performed for him and by him.

"So we have until," I thought for a moment, "2012 to help him learn and practice what he needs to know. But that doesn't mean the other forces will leave us alone until then. They're already trying to stop us here and now. What if they've already found him over there? He said he was dreaming about monsters. What if that's them trying to get at him?" I felt panic beginning to rise. "What if they get to him before we can even get to Denmark? Who's going to protect him? My husband doesn't even know there's any danger!"

Cath put his hand on my shoulder to calm me slightly.

"It may be that the Beast is hunting as an agent of opposition te the energy that yer boy brings te the world, but remember that the true force he fights against is imbalance, an inequality in all phases of life on this world: in the spiritual and religious, masculine and feminine, and in all other manner of life. The Beast is real, and then that would mean that there is an equal force around, te protect him as well. Yer son has many things around him te care for his well-being; not the least of which is Faidhe herself. So tend ye te yer task and things will take place in their time, as has been prophesized. The end of this Fourth Civilization will take place on December 21, 2012, the very day yer boy comes te the halfway mark between his 12th and 13th borthday."

"Hey, that's the date that the world is supposed to..." I stopped, realizing what I was about to say and understood the significance of the date. "That's the last day of the Mayan calendar, right? That's the day when it's all supposed to come to an end?" My face went cold and I had to sit down.

Preparations for this battle came to motion again in this time when yer grandmother, Sigrid, was born on the Solstice of 1899 and yer boy was born te complete the wheel exactly 100 and one half years later. That's when things started happening in the world that set us on a course with having te pay attention te the way we've been living, particularly during the Fourth Civilization. Not only with religious zealots and women's rights, human rights, but the very orth we live on stands on the brink of destruction. Everything will have come full corcle on the Solstice in December 21, 2012, the dawning of the Fifth Civilization but also with the dawning of the Age of Aquarius or the age of technology, we must be mindful. This is where we think it will be imperative te create balance and harmony in this world. Can ye imagine just what horrors humanity will create with leaping advances in technology? There must be an additional balance added now which promotes reason into the goals for any new advancement. So ye must finish yer task in gettin' the necessary Power te your boy and then train him with yer knowledge so when the time comes, he'll have all at his disposal te create the equilibrium in humanity necessary te keep it from destroyin' everythin'."

While I chewed on Cath's words, Nora could be seen across the room talking quietly with Eric by the window as Eric's friend John slept nearby with his head on a table. She seemed to literally glow, but was speaking in tones that betrayed her sadness and shook her head refusing to take a paper he was handing her, presumably with his phone number on it. Their energies could be detected as almost smoke-like vapors of color extending and stretching toward one another and entwining in colorful swirls as the energies embraced but physically, the two people stood apart, not touching. *That must be what they mean when it's said that people have chemistry.* I thought. It seems Nora would be true to her commitment to her marriage and lamented what might have been with the tall Norwegian. I contemplated that there was so much good in this world that's revealed in these minute moments so easily forgotten. From where I sat I could see love budding, and integrity of a promise kept despite the fact that the promise had outlived the energy of the love behind her marriage. What was truly the right decision: deny an honest love that might grant happiness for two people or hold to an old promise that was given by a young woman who no longer existed to a young man who, over time has grown bitter, cold and unbending? I looked to Finny where he sat canoodling with Sinead and could see there, two souls engaged in a union of mutual discovery, not a dirty old man letching after a much younger woman. And there was Bridey whom I once perceived as a devout Catholic with strict moral judgment who actually strove for an unfathomable time with heroic resolve to keep a story alive that is based in early Pagan traditions.

Perspective. It's all in how one sees things and what one knows I thought as I consciously acknowledged for the first time that I had a new way of seeing colors, auras and truth about people's inner selves, not just what is displayed in the physical world. It's as simple as changing perspective, I thought. I wasn't sure if I was just bone tired or if the answer to all of humanity's problems could be as simple as merely changing perspective.

"So, Cath, I think we'll spend a few days more with you and your family at your home, if you don't mind, to finish up those loose ends to the tale and the prophecy, maybe to test our skills a bit; then we'll set off to Denmark. We'll just have to take things as they come but I guess what I'm feeling is beyond resignation to what I have to do but I know now that for all our sakes, but mostly for Lucas, I just have to accept that this is a commitment I have to make." Then with poignancy only I recognized, "I've had a change in my perspective. I'm ready to do whatever it takes."

I watched as Nora gave in to be polite and slipped the paper Eric had given her into the back pocket of her pants. He bent to kiss her and hesitated only a breath away from her lips. She took his hands while she turned her head slightly to kiss him slowly and gently on his bearded cheek. He understood and accepted her faithfulness signaled by the chaste kiss by returning one on Nora's cheek. He walked away from her looking utterly bereft, to wake his friend John so they'd be on their way.

In a moment, our party was the only group left in the pub aside from the owner of the establishment and Sinead. After being assured that they would have the place cleaned in no time and would need no help from us, we paid our tab with a generous tip and allowed ourselves to be shepherded out the front door into the morning sunlight.

We had stayed the darkness with laughter and music and song. Now that the light had returned, it was a brand new day and the world appeared very different to me.

Part V: The Beginning of the End

36

The Road Less Traveled

Finally, after some weeks on the road, Laoghaire began to recognize landmarks indicating they drew close to the place that would be his kingdom. It had been slower going than he'd expected for they drove Laoghaire's cattle as well as traveled with the children. The cattle required grazing and water and the children required regular rest and food. Laoghaire reflected that much had taken place and he hoped during the long trek, Colm would come to understand that he'd had no choice in leaving the land of the Tuatha de Danann. As it was, she had withdrawn from him to do little other than tend to the children. They had not reconciled their marriage bed and she wept often. She would, on occasion, speak with Cuan, but the conversation would wither as Laoghaire approached at which time Colm made excuses about some task or other that must be done.

"I'm sorry cousin, your wife is heartsick for her homeland but more, I think she pines to know that the village and clan of her birth will not think themselves abandoned by you. She worries much of your legacy and how your time as the Keeper will be remembered."

"She is deaf to my words that had I any other choice, I would have done all in my power to save the Tuath from such upheaval. She thinks I have betrayed my oath as Keeper and will not give me regard that this is my primary task as Keeper. Would that I could do other, I would have stayed with the Tuath and lived out my term as Keeper to return to my happy home in the village to love my family and tend our cattle until my dotage. Can you not speak with her for me Cuan? Bring her to reason that all of what I do is in keeping with my oath to the Hill. Implore her to see that I took not the Stone from its place on the Hill lightly or without purpose of the Gods. My wife has ears for your words, cousin. Will you speak on my behalf? For I am but half a man without her counsel and warmth and I am afraid that her sadness fools her to see me other than I am. I cannot bear for her to think me less than honorable. The rule of my kingdom and my attention to the business of all that changes in these times will suffer, for I am distracted so by this distance between Colm and myself.

Cuan's heart felt his cousin's pain.

"Patience." He advised. "There has been much for her to bear. A woman's reign is over her hearth and home, friends and relationships. Her security and sense of self often stems from her family and her bond with the Gods. Colm had barely met her family of blood and lost them in three days' time. After that, she moved and settled to a new home, distant from all her friends and support and during that time, she felt lost to you. You took your responsibility to the Hill seriously and Colm was thrown into a life of isolation and loneliness. She felt you no longer needed her or desired to speak with her for you showed no evidence or interest in either while you tended your new duties. She did what she could to bring you back to her and her bed but your concerns and energies were elsewhere. And now this separation of her from her clan and Tuath and ruination of her chances of ever returning to her Tuath or home by initiating what can only be recognized as annihilation to the Hill, Stones and Tuatha de Danann. This last, she feels is the worst, for she counts this not as service to the Gods but turning your back against them and in her following you, she feels she too has turned her back."

"But things are not as they seem!" Laoghaire retorted.

"Cousin, I do not question your choices. I see that this business rents your very heart. I know not what takes place in the high world of the De Danann or in the mind of the High King Laoghaire but I see how it has brought all on your family that if not for your oath to the Hill, you would have fought to your death before subjecting them to such hardship. Give her time and she will come to her own peace with what was necessary. It may be a while until she trusts that the new home you offer her will be hers for the rest of her life. It will take time as well for her to realize that what you have done was not for your own benefit but that truly your honor and oath bade you to render things so."

Laoghaire's shoulders sagged with surrender to his cousin's words. "I will try to allow her time to heal, but I long for her words, her touch, to be with her, to be whole again, for I am adrift without her. She draws her strength as you say from her place in the Tuath; I draw my strength from the knowledge that each day I wake to this earth and the sun, my Colm will greet me. All I do and all I am, functions only because I know she is beside me."

"You must trust me in this cousin. All your wife needs is time to sort her feelings and return to you. For now, she has thrown herself into the care and future of your children. This is the best way she could expend her energies now. You keep to the order of things as we draw to Hill T'airg and Baile Laoghaire. You will find your family more amenable once they have found themselves at home and acquainted with new family."

"Thank you Cuan. I will take your counsel. It is true, I feel happier for drawing closer to where I will call home at last, so I must believe it will be the same for my wife. I only regret that I had not come sooner so that I might have spoken with my mother and my father once again. But that is a sorrow I must bear. Thank you again cousin for your help with Colm and for driving the cattle as we travel to our home." As he strode away, his mind was already turning to much he had yet to attend.

As Laoghaire retreated, Cuan allowed the smile to fall from his face and his troubled expression was revealed. Soon after Laoghaire had moved to the Hill and taken on his new responsibilities there, Colm began making frequent visits to the village with the children. It seemed at first as though she'd missed her home and conversation with other people. Visiting often to where Cuan occupied her former hearth and many times, she cleaned and kept a cook fire at work. Cuan enjoyed their newfound friendship for they had missed many years communicating as kin. They talked about much that had taken place since Laoghaire and she left Baile Laoghaire. He knew she was grateful for his taking this place among her clan to help with the livestock so she and Laoghaire might maintain their livelihood. Before long, it became regular occurrence she cooked at his hearth and made talk over meals. More frequently Colm came to the village without the children or at times allowed them to visit and play with other village children while she visited with Cuan. When Cuan began to look forward to her visits and felt disappointment on those days when she did not brighten him with her presence, he understood that nothing good could come of the feelings he knew were growing. Worse, he believed that, in her turmoil over her husband taking on so much new responsibility, she had become all too familiar with his own presence as a companion. Cuan had known plenty enough women to know when an attraction has been established. What was truly dangerous about his situation is that this woman is surely at home and comfortable with him and at her own hearth. All the awkward discomfort of new beginnings of a courtship had been circumvented. Time and again they found themselves quite comfortable in a homey setting, talking about clan doings as though it were a normal arrangement.

Cuan knew Colm could easily be persuaded in her loneliness to come to him so he battled his growing feelings for her and fought the urge to take her in his arms. She did not love him; he knew it was merely that he had stepped into a position in this home and with the cattle that had been his cousin's place. It was all too easy for Colm to mistake the comfort of familiarity for love and desire. He hoped she would come to that realization before one of them made a move for he knew if things advanced in that direction he would be in a hard way to evade showing her his true feelings and worse still to keep from giving in to his consuming urge to bring her to his bed.

Many women he had pleasured and been pleased to keep time with but this was different. Perhaps it was that which he could not have was the only thing he wanted, but he loved his cousin and his king. He would not betray Laoghaire and bring his life to ruin.

It would have been so much easier for him had he been able to stay at the village of the Tuatha De Danann while Laoghaire made his way back to the east coast of the island to claim his throne but it was not to be so. Cuan's mind returned to the night of the amazing spring festival. *What magic! What chaos.*

Gara had come early to his hut as she had made it habit to do of late. Cuan understood that she was giving him permission to pursue her. She was an intriguing woman of means and power who let it be known that she had more than a passing interest in sharing her bed with him. At another time in his life Cuan would not have thought over-long before accepting her offer. She was the kind of woman who enjoyed a man as a short-term distraction but made it clear that it would be well worth the time spent with her. Cuan found older women to be both knowledgeable and enthusiastic for their part in honoring the fertility Gods. But he was vexed by his consuming attraction to his cousin's wife so he had not returned Gara's overtures. This seemed to increase his appeal to her for she had redoubled her enticements of food, gifts and attention. Women of her stature and beauty did not often endure a hesitation at their offer to share a bed.

"I will have my servants bring a tent and other items on a litter to insure my comfort following the festival ritual this evening, Cuan. If you are not otherwise engaged, I will be honored if you will share in the springtide rites with me."

Cuan thought with some amusement that she must have grown weary of playing a game of chase with him. Some aloofness is desirable to women but this woman made her wishes known in such certainty to bring the truth forward as to what his feelings and intentions are. Cuan decide that he could use a distraction of his own from his nagging want for Colm's touch.

"It will be my pleasure to attend you in the rights this night Gara. I sincerely hope I can assure you that it will be your pleasure as well."

"Very well. I am pleased and will take my leave of you to make preparations for the festival. Until the fires then." She said as she turned to go.

Cuan walked along the field, using his walking stick to keep the herd together and in motion. He reflected on his memory of Gara's offer and then his mind was drawn to the Circle ritual and all that broke loose when the clans of the Tuath arrived atop the Hill to not only discover that the ring stones were no longer in place but that the Stone of Fal had been split in two and all that remained was but half of the Stone. Were that this was all that had taken place in the way of change, things may have been contained but as it was, the announcement that the Keeper and his family would leave the Hill to return to his clan, taking the remaining half of the Keystone with him, chaos ensued. But not before the ritual itself which was really quite something to witness.

As Cuan had arrived to the place where this Tuath had gathered for many a generation, it was just before sunset. Voices were raised in accusation and anger. Clan members were running to and fro frantically shouting.

"The Circle is gone, the Stone has fallen." Cuan did not know the depth of severity of this announcement for he had not been a part of this Tuath and had not worshiped on the Hill, but he did know about great stones of Power and understood the panic that hid just beneath the surface of this gathering.

Cuan's first instinct was to seek out Colm and the children to lead them from the gathering lest they take some injury from an alarmed clan member who sought to lay blame for the dread they were feeling. He knew that it was not his place to fend for his cousin's family for it was his cousin's doing that all this had taken place. Just when the massive group came to sides, arguing both for and against waiting for the ritual to take place to seek answers, appearing calm, Laoghaire stepped into public view from the path leading from the Keeper's hut. His gait was slow and paced. He spoke to no one and made eye contact not at all but his presence brought all who laid eyes on him to a curious silence. Despite their despair over this latest change in the very foundation of the Tuath, they were eager to see how this new man would conduct the ritual. Many stopped abruptly in fascination as Laoghaire walked tall, holding the Sword in his right hand, clad in only linen cuffs he wore to cover him tied at his arms and legs. The energy of the Power that near pulsated as it emanated all around him. As the Power surged through him, Laoghaire's manhood stood as an impressive demonstration of the striving force that drove him in his task to welcome the spring and celebrate the rites as if to mark that changes will take place but life will continue.

Laoghaire reached the altar stone and stood until the crowd quieted. He lit a blaze, in the readied wood under a black pot filled with water and aromatics. With the Sword pointed skyward in his right hand, a smooth gesture of his left hand sent a blue spark toward the wood and it was set ablaze.

"I have news for you." Came his voice in a booming resonance that made known the Power he represented. "The gift of the Stones that was given into our charge, born of the quarries on the great island, has completed its time in our service. Long have the Stones of the great Circle served as a portal in this land to offer commerce and communion between the Tuatha De Danann and the Gods and spirits. But the very presence of a man to keep the Hill marks the point at which time itself is moving on. These great changes portend even more transformation for the people and animals of the earth. Our way of life here will not remain as we have known it for generations out of time; untouched by hardship. The time of the Mother among us is passing and as she goes to her rest, the active spirits and Gods go with her. We will no longer have the portal through which to commune with our beloved Gods and ancestors. We must still honor and worship our deities but no longer will we be blessed with casting eyes upon those who are of the nature of the Gods." Laoghaire headed off the idea that the changes brought on reprisals from the Gods. "Fear not that we are punished, for in keeping faith in out ritual and honor for our Gods, we will be rewarded. We will have their faith in us that we will honor the Earth as she provides for us. Each day we will give her thanks; for even in the Goddess's absence, she cares for us. We must honor the sun festivals and be grateful for each season the sun marries the earth and we have the blessing of bounty from this great marriage. We will see the face of Bel when the Sun kisses a child's cheek. The voice of the Morrigan will sing to us as the raven's song is sung. The great hand of Lugh will come over the horizon everyday as the Sun lights the Earth. We will not lose hope or faith in our Gods simply because we can no longer see them. For if we but open our eyes and hearts, we will see them in the bounteous beauty around us. We will hear their voices in our hearts if we but silence ourselves to take their counsel. We will continue to see their gifts in all that is around us and should we take heart in these gifts, we will see the wisdom in what the Mother and Father offer to us for food, medicines, tools and many wondrous uses of nature. We are like children, fledged to the world to forge our own way now. We will keep to our hearts the lessons and love of our God-parents, so as we strike out on our own, they are with us always and ever there in spirit as we beckon for them."

The crowd began to fill in the space around the altar and without being aware of it, they formed the Circle where the great stones had formerly stood. The living, breathing Circle of flesh created a new energy where the villagers were not merely observers of the ritual, but they created the sacred space in which the ritual would be conducted. Many strained to see and as those in the rear pushed forward, the old limits of where the megaliths stood were breached and the crowd drew near to Laoghaire in an intimate gathering for the worship.

"As we gather here for the spring festival, we are doubly blessed, as on this night, we also have the presence of the Lady moon in her most pregnant and fertile state." Laoghaire lifted his hands and cuffed arms toward the full moon in the night sky. "I look upon her face and she graces me with her silvery light. Illuminating that which is dark in the night, giving me guidance and lighting my way. As I walk my road in this life, it is oft dark and I know not which path to take, this Lady offers counsel and direction as she lights the way for me, and though I may not see her at times, I know she is there and will return for me to once again offer her illumination that I may drink her wisdom and be satisfied. But she will return to me in her time and in her own cycle. Not to answer my own will or purpose. And so, clansmen and women, if only we can keep mindful that though we may not see our Gods, we must take heart that they are there and will reveal themselves to us in their own time."

The glowing and pulsating Keeper had captured the attention of all the Tuath now and commanded their silence by his voice and actions. Standing alongside the remaining half of the Stone of Fal.

"The sister Stone to this one here has been delivered to its new place of standing. There it will await its purpose in the highlands of the large island to our east." At this, there was some grumbling and murmuring from the crowd. Laoghaire raised his hands to quiet the crowds. "Hear this now!" He commanded. "I tell you what has taken place, not for your approval. I tell you to instruct you as to how you may continue to live and prosper under the blessing of our Gods. Understand the opportunity of growth offered us in learning a new path and survive. Understand it not, and resign you to your fate." He began again. "As instructed, I have sent the other half of the Stone to be useful in later seasons. This half will come to the seat of the land and serve its purpose now in speaking announcement of the one High King of this land. One who will be pure of heart and carry communion with the Gods in the manner of our ways until such time it is his duty to pass the flame of knowledge to another who will come to receive it. So it has been told to me, so it will happen."

A low murmur pulsated through the crowd and gained momentum until some shouts could be heard. Some ugly accusations were flung from distorted and angry faces.

"You spirit away our Circle and you take the sacred Stone for your own purpose." One frightened voice called.

"Where is Faidhe? She would not allow this!" Demanded another.

Then, as prejudice will subtly pulsate beneath the surface when times are quiet, it will strike to sting at times when people are threatened. Laoghaire heard the venom.

"Your kind of magic is not needed here outlander! Who will be this new High King? We see what you attempt here."

Laoghaire had known this would happen. It was all as he had seen in his visions but it saddened him nonetheless to actually hear the people he had counted as his family, turn on him so. He watched as several of the men moved to place themselves between himself and the half-Stone.

"Stay your place men!" He lowered his voice but the steel for the command was enough to stop the men mid-step. "I bring you news of what has been commanded of me and of us and you can think no further than a dullard, laying ownership to that which was never yours. The Stones of the Circle are gone at the behest of the Gods who command them. The Stone of Fal will be placed where it will serve the purpose of those Gods as well. And if they see fit to make changes in how this sacred isle is ruled, then it is not up to me as the Keeper to question and it is not up to you to question out of some mistaken sense of entitlement. We have been blessed with the care and keeping of this Circle and now we are once again blessed with the charge of bringing our love and faith for our Gods to the generations of the future. It is not for our convenience these Stones are in our charge, it is so that we may serve those Gods who imbue us with life and bestow us with blessings. Step not between me and the duties I have sworn to carry out. I do not wish to shed blood of kin, but I am sworn, and I will do what I must."

Laoghaire was met with mixed expressions of surprise, disgust and undisguised hatred but mostly, he recognized the look of fear stamped upon the faces of people he has long counted as friends and kin. With a sigh he continued.

"I tell you these things to lend you understanding. So you will take comfort in knowing that these changes are to preserve our future and that of our Gods. Faidhe now travels to lands afar to make way for our Gods to take to the Sidhe. Anyone wanting to travel under with the Gods has only to choose to do so when that time comes. Anyone wishing to remain will be free to continue a life but with a lesser active measure of support from the Gods. And know this now, as I have been informed, it will be my blood that creates the high throne." The grumbling returned. "I am not pleased at this duty, for it will further change the lives of my wife and children as we must travel once again to the land of my birth."

More grumbling and shouts erupted from the swollen crowd as people pushed to gain a place closer to the action. Laoghaire address the accusations of abandonment of his promise to keep the Circle.

"I do not abandon you or the Circle! I take my direction from the Gods and follow my path! I go to arrange the future so at a time when the seeds I plant come to fruit, all is as it has been prophesied. I do not choose this path, but I will follow it as I have sworn."

Laoghaire removed the linen cuffs from his forearms and untied the laces holding the linen around his legs to uncover what he had hidden beneath. In the color blue of the Goddess, Laoghaire revealed twining fighe vines writhing up his arms and legs, tattooed from his wrists to his shoulders, hips to ankles.

"I mark my body for the Goddess for all to see that as I raise my arms, I will be reminded for whom I speak and to whom I vow my service. These are vines that will grow and blossom so long as I live as a tribute to the Gods under whose rule I serve. The tri-leaf, symbolic of the three faces of the Goddess will be the mark of my blood and so will be the mark of my name as my sons and daughters and their sons and daughters take the seat of high throne in this land. As I take my family to the seat of the high throne, I bring with me the marks of my service, the marks of the Goddess, the marks of great change in this land, now and in the future so there is no mistaking to whom the High King offers reverence and fealty."

A hush fell over the crowd as the kinetic energy around Laoghaire shone bright blue and small flashes spit and glimmered within the glowing aura. People watched in fascination but were soon distracted by a far-away beat hammering in the distance. Some strained to listen and the steady rhythm grew louder. Then attention of all had been drawn away from Laoghaire and was commanded to attention of the approaching noise. The sound grew louder and more menacing; with each percussion, the ground vibrated. Some of the children covered their ears and loved ones reached for each other's support as the very earth shook beneath their feet. The sound approached from the east and many were perplexed for there was no path leading from the east side of the hill. There was naught on the east face of the Hill but thick and dense wood and growth that would not allow for any travel. Yet the ominous thunder grew closer still until through a small clearing in the dense trees Damhsaigh Cloch appeared and stood for a moment observing the crowd as the people appeared shocked and then exploded in shouts of panic and began to scramble and run.

"Laoghaire raised his arms and his voice. "Stay firm!" He boomed in a voice so magnified that it caused the awe-struck masses to freeze momentarily and look to him. In that moment, the blue light around Laoghaire extended out and around the crowd and enveloped the Tuath.

They instantly responded to the soothing light and serenity took sway. "Stay firm, I say." As he held his arms outstretched to the crowd in a calming motion, the fighe vine markings on his forearms writhed and shimmered with a blue luminosity on his skin as if a growing living thing.

"We are kin and no harm will come to you, for this is the living Circle you have revered and served all your years. The Circle too is servant to the Gods and the Goddess. Recognize now the great honor you have witnessed to see this living Circle, Damhsaigh Cloch."

With the sound of the name, the giant's attention was brought to Laoghaire and in the magnificent and grand timber, the stony voice responded.

"Ah, Laoghaire, our young Keeper. We have delivered of the half-stone and positioned it to be at the ready in waiting for the Lady to enact the purpose of the Gods. We come now to you, on the celebration of the spring festival to complete our duties before we return to the place of our birth and rest on the large island."

The Tuath went completely silent. Damhsaigh Cloch bent to pick up the remaining half of the great Stone and hesitated as the Stone was lifted presenting the top most part of the monolith to Laoghaire.

"Understand you that one last time you must trust this sacred implement into our care?"

Laoghaire thought only for a moment at this and plunged his Sword, up to the hilt into the great Stone as though it were merely driven into sand. Before Laoghaire released the hilt from his hand, the Stone began to sing its shrill song. Holding his hand there to ensure all had heard the song of the true High King of the land, he released the jeweled hilt and as the din receded.

"Go you now friend." Laoghaire said to the stone being. "With our blessing and gratitude for all the generations you have kept us and the implements well, even as we have kept you. My heart weeps for the passing of this time and rejoices that our work here has made preparation for the return of our ways in the future. Do this for us and go to your rest with your stony kin to serve as a great reminder to future generations uncounted, that there will come a time when the Goddess, God and their lesser Gods will be thought of with reverence and come to balance, for all else is unthinkable. I eagerly look to the time when I am reunited with the sacred Sword and Stone as they two together will demonstrate my position as the first High King to the isle and my distant seed will produce the last High King as well, marking the time of great change in this world."

A booming yet thoughtful voice returned. "You have honored us well with this task and we rejoice in the gift of motion Keeper. We will remain true to our promise to relinquish the gift as you have been true to your words of oath. We will deliver the Sword and the Stone to its new standing and rightful place in the land of the Calf-herders by the sea, then we will travel to the causeway in the north once again to cross to the great island and take our rest with our brothers and sisters in the monument Circle of the Winter Solstice where we will await the time when we will be called to service once again."

Damhsaigh Cloch hefted the Stone with the Sword hilt over the grand shoulder. The sound of grinding rock could be heard and then the giant was gone, leaving only an empty impressions in the earth where the Stone of Fal had fallen and the diminishing thumping of the great pounding steps as they moved to the distance.

Laoghaire did not wait until the crowd recovered; he continued his duties at the altar of the spring festival.

"More changes are to come but these will be as introduction of new traditions. There is no Circle in which to conduct the fertility rites. I have seen new rituals born in my visions. Times may become lean and the earth, not so fruitful. In order to insure a bountiful growing season, we will return to the village where I will take my queen to the threshing house and we will consummate the growing season by planting the seed of the king in the fertile ground of the Queen over the stores of wheat and grains. We will do this in the expectation that the Gods will continue to grant fertile growth of our crops, kin and cattle. And for those who choose to stay here and live out life in the village, once each year you will choose your king and queen to insure a healthy season. No longer will there be one Keeper to serve as the proxy in the great marriage, for all over this land, for each clan, for each Tuath, there will be a chosen couple, likely to be fertile to serve as the Goddess and the God in the great marriage."

"When you abandon us, who will be our spring king and queen?" A nervous voice rose from the crowd. At this, Laoghaire caught motion of a person snaking through the crowds and recognized the woman coming to the fore and answered swiftly.

"I do not abandon you. The right to serve the Gods has been taken out of the hands of the one and been given into the hands of all. You will hold ritual at your own hearths. You will conduct fertility rites and honor the passing seasons by the wheel of the year within the village. Each year at the ritual times the village entire will choose the queen and king for their youth and vigor and likelihood to bring a child to the clan as a gift of the coupling."

With the mention of youth and vigor and likely child, Gara stopped her advancement toward a place of public observation. In one sweep, Laoghaire had dashed her fleeting hopes of assuming the position as Queen of the Tuath. She thought herself the likely person especially since the Keeper was conveniently vacating the Tuath. She thought things could not be more advantageous had she calculated the situation all on her own.

Laoghaire continued, "My family and I will take to the road, this very night after I take my bride Queen to the threshing house and bless the wheat stores with fertility. We will travel with a small party taking my good cousin and clansman Cuan, and the cattle he has watched over for the days since I took to the Hill." Calming the grumbling that threatened to turn hostile, Laoghaire continued. "We will take only those heads that I came with to your clan. All other stock that has grown in numbers through these years will remain with you. Also, Councilwoman Gara will accompany us on our trek to the Calf-herder kingdom to the east for she will have important business there. The wealth of her cattle will remain with the Tuath as well to benefit the De Danann kin. Of course, her grandson Triag will accompany her since his father no longer resides with the Tuath for we would not separate one not yet come to manhood from foster mother and kin." He said directly to the Councilwoman, "Gara, you may pick people of your choosing to safeguard your cattle in your stead for it is not known how long you will be needed to attend these high affairs in the east. You may choose, also, a servant to bring with you on the road."

A look of confusion stamped Gara's face. She had no prior knowledge of such a journey and was not prepared to travel nor did she have any desire to leave her home and place in the Tuath where she worked long to establish her comfort. She understood there would be no argument with the Keeper during the festival ritual and bowed her head to him in public acquiescence but her mind was already working to see how this might be undone.

Elsewhere in the crowd a note of panic flew from where Triag stood across the Circle to Nemain but she communicated to him, *Fear not my dearest nephew for this will work to our favor. You will travel with Gara and keep me apprised of what takes place. We will not lose our ability to know each other's minds even over distance.*

We will ever be available to each other. I will assume responsibility for her cattle and make a place for us here. You will tell all that you see and find your way into the Keeper's trust and family so that you might communicate back to me of any magic you learn at his side. Can you not see how great strength of Power emanates from him? Also, we desire to know of the Sword and how best we might calculate to draw it forth from the Stone. It will be but a short time you will travel, I promise. Then you may return to me and we will assure that we are of the chosen ones to come to the positions of queen and king here. All will be well. Her words reassured him and he let his mind move to what lay ahead and what he would bring with him that would be useful.

Laoghaire continued to address the Tuath as this communication between Triag and Nemain took place.

"Now you have seen the Circle is gone and the Stone is no longer here with all of your own eyes and sensibilities, you must know that things will change and take place as has been foretold. Make haste then, to the village 'fore the moon sets in the sky so that we may invoke the magic here that will sustain the Tuath in good bounty. For then we must ready the cattle and ourselves to take to the road this night."

Laoghaire searched the crowd for Colm and found her with their children dressed in her ritual garb, holding the Shield in front of her.

"Come my Colm. We must make for the threshing house and to-it. The trek to the village is necessary to bless the Tuath with bounty and abundance before we take our leave."

Colm smiled dutifully and turned to the children to usher them toward the path leading to the village. Her face displayed calm, but inside she had been infected with dread of the task that lay ahead of her.

Colm so loved her husband, but she'd been tainted with the constant troubling memory of her dream of Briciu that it had robbed her of her sleep and consumed her with both desire for her husband and shame for the way in which she desired him. She turned her heart from him so her shame would not touch his position of the Keeper who must be unblemished and pure of heart. She had convinced herself to turn her attention elsewhere, anywhere so as not to bring shame to Laoghaire's legacy on the Hill. She had taken solace in her new friendship with Cuan and felt it a safe relationship for he was kin and clan and there would be no thought to an unseemly relationship there. That had been well for a while for Laoghaire had been so busy with his duties but now she was called to duty in the Great Marriage to represent the Goddess! She was sure that she was so unworthy that the Goddess would reveal her for the fraud she is by not entering her so Colm could not take the role of the Goddess for the ceremony. One thing she could be grateful for was the new concept that she would not have to call the Goddess's energy publicly under the eyes of all the Tuath as the ritual had always been conducted in the past. All would witness the coupling of the Great Marriage in the Circle before going to indulge in the rites by their own fires. At least his new way, she would be saved from publicly bringing shame to her beloved and have him called about as a fraud. But still, the act was ahead of her and she knew not how she would lay with her husband and not be exposed in her dishonor.

Now as Cuan reflected on all that had taken place the night of the spring festival, he herded the Laoghaire's cattle closer to his home near the shore. He recalled the look on Colm's face as she led the procession down the Hill to partake of the springtide ritual. If he read her face correctly, she feared the coupling as much as he was loath to think of her with another, even if the other man was his most beloved cousin and friend. He remembered that she looked at him almost pleading for some intervention as she walked past him heading to her village from the Hill for the last time.

———

"There are few who have uttered the word no to you Gara, and I understand that you are unaccustomed to hearing the word, but be assured, you may count me among those few who have no trouble at all telling you that you will not have your way."

Colm was matter of fact in her impervious nature to the approach of the older woman. Colm liked her not, owed her no fealty and would not be a tool for her wheedling and manipulative ways. While they traveled on the road, Colm felt out of sorts and displaced from her home but could muster no sympathy for Gara who was no doubt feeling some of the same discomfit and misgivings. The former Councilwoman had changed her tack from trying to reason with Laoghaire that her wisdom and experience would better serve those left behind than on the journey east, to asking Colm to speak on her behalf to Laoghaire.

"My answer is the same as it was yesterday and all the days before, Gara. Why do you not take on whatever is your responsibility in this journey with grace and dignity? Can you not offer your services as a woman of the Tuath without complaint? You have worked long and made your own comfort of your position for many years. Now you are called to a task of duty and you show not your honor by your constant pressure to be shut of your responsibility. How did you keep your place on the Council for so long and no one noticed how little interest you have in doing right by the Tuath if it comes not with payment or reward for yourself?"

Gara's weeks on the road had taken a toll. Her fine linen cloak proved too fragile and quickly became somewhat frayed. As well, her delicate slippers were no match for the walking she had done for she had imagined a woman of her stature would travel in a litter and so had not packed wisely for the road. Her hair showed proof that the adept hands of her handmaid did not travel with her for Laoghaire was adamant that she was able only to bring one servant and she chose for one who could carry much because Gara had no intention of carrying a pack for herself. She was no longer able to luxuriate for hours in a bath and at the mirror bowl, or eating fine foods and applying concealing tricks to her face to conjure a youthful appearance. She was required on the road, as all were, to walk the paths and cook over open fires, to forage for food along the way and when necessary, to keep watch on the animals. Theirs was a small group and all were required to do their fair share. Gara had been mistaken in thinking that she could send her servant or Triag in her stead to work, for they too had responsibilities in their trek.

Gara's beseeching expression toward Colm turned to restrained rage and her mouth clacked shut in shock that anyone would speak to her so. She turned briskly from Colm and walked off without another word. Although Colm would be pleased to be shut of the woman accosting her daily with requests as though they were friends or kin, she would neither be a pawn in Gara's balking at whatever she'd been called to do for the Tuath, nor would she bring herself to question Laoghaire's reasons or authority in all of this by agreeing to speak with him on Gara's behalf. Though her heart cried out for their old life together, she would not disrespect his new standing and the importance of that role to the future of the Tuath. To speak with him or even agree to do so against what he had decreed would allow one to think that his own wife may question his reasons for making the choices he had done since his rise to the Hill. In addition, Colm was in ill temper when it came to Gara, for she often consumed Cuan's time when Colm herself looked to him as a sympathetic ear to sooth her nerves and nagging doubt about herself. Just being in his presence calmed her for he so resembled Laoghaire yet she could be with him and allay the constant guilt she felt when in Laoghaire's presence. It seemed lately she was sure of nothing. She agonized over so much and was insecure in all of it: How to bring herself back to her husband? How would her children take to another such change? What would be her role in this new life? How would her husband's people accept her after she'd taken him from them those years ago? Would Laoghaire forgive her for all but demanding of him to take on the role of Keeper in her Tuath while his parents were being slaughtered? So very much more nagged at her mind. She felt, she must look as haggard as Gara for all her worrying and lack of sleep. But as she looked to her children now, she saw how they still ran and laughed and played as though they were on a great adventure. She was proud too, at the way they took on their responsibilities without complaint. Colm sighed in resignation and subconsciously pulled her fingers through the tangles in her hair and thought that she probably worried overmuch about her children at least, and continued on her march toward her destiny. She felt better for the moment of relief from her constant fears and worry.

Only now, as she drew near the place that would be her new home, did she allow herself to reflect on her time on the spring festival with Laoghaire. He had been so gentle, so loving with her despite all the Power that he obviously possessed. She looked to his face and saw the God in her husband. Expecting to be exposed as a harlot and a fraud to assume the role of the Goddess, she was taken entirely by surprise when Laoghaire laid her atop the grains in the threshing house and looked on her with such love that she near came to tears.

"I cannot." She uttered. And the look of pain that passed over Laoghaire's face felt to her as though she had run the blade of his Sword through her own heart with her words.

"Wife." He responded. "I have been a lesser man to you in these times, I know. I have been consumed by my duties and I feel the distance between us as though our whole world has changed since we took to the Hill. I will mend that rift between us for I know it is at my feet that the blame shall fall. But this, this is our duty to the clan. Let not the shadow of my neglect cast darkness on the future of the Tuath. Hold not your bitter feelings toward me against the kin you hold dear. Open your heart wife, to the Goddess and let us be as one in the God and Goddess to ensure the futures of clan, cattle and crops. Know me now as your God and I will know you as my Goddess and later we will couple as king and queen, husband and wife when you allow your heart to forgive me and once again, invite me to your bed. Cast off your wounded pain and allow the Goddess her due, my love. And know that God, king or man, my life is yours, and I hold true my vow for the sake of the Tuath, but in truth, it is for my honor and you, my love and for my children, my family that I give all."

In that moment, Colm allowed a moment of forgiveness for herself, she reasoned that what had taken place was but a dream and she had not the control to suppress her dream. She knew that her love for her husband was not shaken and she thought that this moment might cleanse her of the terrifying and sullying moment she had shared of herself with one such as Briciu. She saw the face of the God in her husband and felt as the Goddess assumed her place within herself. She saw the blue energy that surrounded Laoghaire then, emanate from her own form. She reached her arms out to Laoghaire who mounted her and let out a whimpering breath of relief that, again at last he had bonded with his wife, his queen, his Goddess. They came together in love and abandon amidst the shushing of the grain seeds as their movements made a nestling indentation in the grains that formed to their bodies as they consecrated the planting season for the Tuath and found each other again, for the moment.

As she remembered her joy at their reunion, Colm pined to confess her wicked moment to her husband and trust that he would understand and love her still. But it was the fear she harbored that he would look on her with disgust that kept her to herself and suffering the distance between them. Even as he spoke to her she fought to keep her tongue still for she knew if she looked to his eyes, she would tell all and then what would she do if he spurned her?

For now she had no family at hand, no Tuath to return to, for most of the Tuath was not at all pleased at the turn of events when she left with her family. All she had was her children and her love for her husband. It was that love that kept her from telling him anything for she would not have his reputation and legacy damaged through her own shame.

This war waged in Colm and she could not see that her own thoughts of logic tried to persuade her to go to her husband and trust him to love her. It was the infection she'd taken on in the curse of Briciu that kept her fear living and growing. The danger in what had taken place was that he had not taken her physically before his death as he'd wanted because she and her children were so well protected, but his remaining essence held enough strength, after sating its vengeance on Laoghaire's parents, to come to her dreams and plant the seeds of fear, doubt and insecurity within her. On this, the infection could incubate, feed and grow. Much like a beautifully ripened piece of fruit will quickly grow putrid from one small point of bruising. Briciu's infection grew in Colm as she began to see herself as he had seen her, an unworthy whore, a wanton, rather than seeing the natural innocence and rightness in her sense of self and her own healthy sexuality and desire for her beloved husband. This fear and self-image would have grown rampant if not checked by her own rational intellect and her occasional conversations with Cuan who always reassured her of Laoghaire's love for her and gave even higher praise to her abilities as a woman, a hearth-keep and an alchemist. Cuan's words acted as a soothing security for her. The night of the spring festival had almost burned the infection from her completely in her joy, but those small nagging doubts nibbled at her in the following days of isolation on the road, until they grew strong and now, as they drew ever closer to the land of her husband's people, she began to believe the doubts and fears as utter truths once again.

"My aunt has taught me much in the way of magic." Triag boasted. "I can light the fires, even as your father did on the night of the festival. It is but a lowly form of magic that any who have the Power can do. It is one of the first things one learns. Can you not do it? Have your parents taught you nothing of the magic? I would think that if I were a child of the Circle, I should have great magic by now. And you have not the Power to make fire?"

"Show it."

Morgan stepped between Triag and her brother whose stance had taken on one ready to do battle with shoulders back and clenched fist by his sides. Always the one to spot adventure and trouble, Morgan did not like it when her gentle brother was being goaded into doing what she thought was beneath him. Although much smaller than her twin, Morgan proved to be much more outspoken and daring. She also knew how to turn around a challenge and smoothly put the challenger on the defensive.

"Prove your words. You say you can make fire as done on the Hill, show it. Else we'll know you as a braggart and a mis-teller. I'm sure the people in our new home will be well warned of your stories, should you not be able to show proof you have the abilities you say you can do."

Triag was older than Morgan and Macha, but they were the only children on the drive east, so they found each other and did children's things. Triag was enamored and entertained by Morgan. She was energetic and fun with a daring streak that he found most attractive but mostly he liked that she was openly honest and wholesome. This was not anything he'd been exposed to in his own family. It was refreshing to speak with one who asked nothing of him in the way of contrivance as every member of his own family had, since he was old enough to listen and speak.

Her brother was another story. He was as tall as Triag, and lighter, but he was finely built with a solid, trim frame and unusually developed muscle tone for one so young. Although Triag was the older boy, Macha could outrun, jump and throw Triag. The only way the older boy could win at wrestling was to throw all his weight into it and even then, if he didn't win quickly, he'd become winded and tired and begin to flag. So Triag resorted to the intellect to goad Macha in areas he felt he could win such as this test of magical abilities. He knew it was not something he should reveal, but he wanted to prove himself in front of Morgan. He wanted to impress her of his worth for he knew he could not compete with her brother physically, and he so wanted to insinuate himself between them. He never thought of befriending Macha and having a relationship with both of the twins. That had never occurred to him for it was never his family's way to consider genuinely befriending a rival instead of trying to best him or her with trickery or deceit if necessary. But now, Morgan had sided with her brother and called Triag on his word.

Triag turned to face her and he had gone scarlet in the face. It annoyed him that he wanted to impress her so but he would enjoy showing her something that he was sure Macha could not do. Triag never took his eyes from Morgan's and his face took on a strange look as though he was straining. There was a momentary odor of boiled eggs, and a small cluster of dried weeds beside where the three children stood ignited into a crackling flame. Morgan jumped a bit as a breeze blew the flame toward her tunic skins. Macha stepped toward the burning weeds and stomped them out. Never taking his eyes off Triag, Macha stepped in front of his sister and faced his adversary eye to eye. In that moment, Triag resorted to his father's tactics and raised his head slightly as if to gain advantage in height.

"Come Morgan, we have chores to tend. Should you want to practice your magic later, we will do it with reverence, as we've been taught."

This statement deflated Triag once again, letting him know that they did have magic and that he had allowed himself to use the Power for a petty display such as this would not be looked upon with admiration. This young boy, this child that could so easily outdo him in so many areas and he was the brother to Morgan, more even than just her brother, her twin. How would Triag compete with this boy? What could he offer Morgan that her brother could not? Triag watched the twins walk away from him and he began to grumble.

"Am I not a man? Have I not learned the secrets of the pleasures from my aunt? Can I not peer into the minds of others? I will not be bested by this boy."

In that moment, his honest feelings of affection and friendship for Morgan turned from something natural to a tainted competition that rendered the girl a prized piece of chattel to be won by the victor of two warriors. His jealous heart would no longer tolerate being bested by this boy when he himself was almost to the rights of his manhood. He knew of and had done things that other boys his age had not even thought of. He would have his prize and he would take her from the one who would feel her loss the most. At this thought, all hope for any salvation of this boy was lost and it showed in the expression on his face.

37
Welcome Home

"Bless this house and all who enter." Bridey said as she passed the threshold of the front door to Cath's humble home above his store. "It'll be a time before I'll likely settle with the idea that you've both been this close to me for so long and I had not a clue as to whether you were even living. You went off to find what had happened to Fion, er, Finny and left me without so much as a whiff of when you'd give a thought to come back." Bridey walked into the house as if she'd lived there all of her life. First removing her shoes by the front door and reaching behind the kitchen door without looking to find the apron that hung on a hook there. She pulled the cotton covering over her head and tied it behind her back. "Cathbad, help the girls with their suitcases into a room where they can stay as decent women under a man's roof. Then come and sit yourselves down here in the kitchen so we can talk plain. I'll fix us some food before we take our rest. It seems there's still work to be done?" She said with a lifted eyebrow as she pulled the ancient cast iron pan down from its peg on the wall.

"Aye, there's work te be done." Cath answered and showed us to a small room off the dining room furnished with two twin beds and a small dresser. When we returned to the kitchen, Bridey murmured and mumbled as she inspected the contents of Cath's old refrigerator and backed out of it with her arms loaded, holding brown bread, butter, eggs, bacon and a pitcher of orange juice. She gave Cath an exasperated look marked with pain and he understood.

I wanted nothing more than to know ye were safe, Bridey, but when we returned from the mainland, it was long after the world had moved on and all but a few scattered folks of the Tuatha de Danann had gone under te the Sidhe and the Duibhe had long since scattered from the hills or gone under themselves. It was as though any magical creatures or people of the auld blood but for the most stubborn were compelled to go under when Faidhe cast the magic that called for the change. We had come te full grown manhood and all trace of you and Magda's family were gone. We'd gone lookin' fer ye and found that the obstinate mule Diog still had breath in him stayin' te the hills as if he were the laird himself. Old and filthy he was, livin' in the old caves of the very hills. We inquired after ye and he was near te a fit knowin' that he'd been duped out of his rightful claim on ye. As if it mattered at that point. But stubborn and proud he was. There was no love lost between us and the likes of that one. The coot! But he did tell us true that Magda and her lot were long gone or died out. Where did ye get to Bridey?"

"Cath, would you be a love and get me something of sheepskins for my feet?" She said as she lit the top burners on the stove. "It may be August, but your floor is as chilled as if it were the slate of the old cottage floor." She commenced arranging the food and pans to begin cooking. Bridey reached above the stove to a shelf that held among other things, a small box of wooden matches. We watched as she lit the old cast-iron oven and arranged thick slices of brown bread of the interior racks to make toast. Once that was done, she placed several slices of bacon onto the heated pan on top of one of the stove burners. The sizzle rose with the scent of fresh bacon and made my stomach take notice.

"It wasn't as if ye never heard of my whereabouts." She answered as she slipped her feet into the slippers Cath had given her. "Have ye not taken the tale of the daughter of the Druid, Bridget? I was not blood kin to the old Druid as you know, but he took me to house and taught me well the ways of the Druid long after the Tuatha de Danann went under and the land was populated with the influx of the coming of the Celts. Of course, the old man'd have no way of knowing the blood that ran in my veins, he just knew that I'd a natural aptitude for the magic and such so he helped me learn the skills and indulged me in my desire to keep the old knowledge within the population of womenfolk who wanted to learn in the face of the wave of masculine ascendancy. Mostly, I was hopin' that those with the magic still in them would come and I'd learn of the Lady and her whereabouts if she still lived for it was centuries, by then after time moved on. So if she were no longer livin' I'd keep watch for signs of her return. Well, I was doin' my best to gather the women folk and educate them and earned a bit of name for myself as the daughter of the Druid, and as a Goddess to some with the old thinking, for the magic was, for the most part, a thing of the past out of the memory of the mortals but for a few who knew the ways, but then as times moved on and it seemed prudent to go with the flow of things, I went from being known as a Druid priestess or Goddess of the hearth and home and animal husbandry, to being known as a Christian nun who established a convent for young girls to teach them the ways of the new God. I did much the same as it seems you did yerself, Cath, in movin' with the times and tides as things changed. So," she feigned a sniff, "from Pagan priestess to sainted convert, I did what I needed to keep alive the tales of the Lady from the Road as time moved on from the Old Ways. There were times in the very early days, I actually took bread at the first Dun Laoghaire to see if I could hear news of either of you and the Lady Faidhe, but it was as though any word of the Lady or anyone who traveled with her was kept tight as I went about living my life to carry on, as best I could, what I thought was needed in keeping the tale alive with the hopes that I'd be enough to stir the energy when it would be needed."

Bridey turned and put a platter of buttered toast on the kitchen table, followed by a jar of marmalade from the fridge and a plate with a mound of bacon came next. She put a pile of forks and knives in the middle of the table with a stack of plates and instructed Finny, "Make yourself useful and spread these plates so I can get these eggs on the table while they're still hot." She began to mumble again. "Lord knows there's not a single fresh egg to be had here in these cartons you buy down to the superette. Nor a decent slab of bacon in these little strips they offer as breakfast ham! I'll bet neither of you has had a good home-cooked meal in some time. Look at you!" She said giving Finny a poke in the ribs. "Ye'll spend some time on my farm now, I expect. Now that we know that my call put out some time ago brought the three brothers to my door. I don't suppose you have a plan as to what we're sup-posed to do with them now, as we know maybe not who they are but what they're likely about? And no good is what they're about in all this, I'm sure."

There was a look of astonishment on both Cath and Finny's faces. They looked at each other and Finny took on a sly smile.

"She was always bossy. Now I remember how we did Diog the favor in not tellin' 'im about her. She'd have cleaned and pecked 'im te death in no time!"

Cath's lips began to quiver as he tried to subdue a snicker. "We appreciate all ye thought ye were takin' on in our stead, Bridey, but do ye not think that we've lorned a thing or two on our way through these last civilizations? Can we not eat a bit and take our rest before we set out on our trail te glory?"

Bridey stood for a moment, pan in one hand, and the other on her hip, looking down at the men menacingly.

"Oh, go on with yerself." She answered with a playful pinch to Cath's shoulder as her cheeks turned crimson. "So long I've felt as this was my own burden to bear, and not knowin' in the least, what to do with it, I'm just runnin' off at the mouth. Eat now. Eat." She waved her free hand at us while she returned the empty egg pan to the stove. When she sat down at the table, and we were all together, it felt as if we should say something.

"Uh," Nora said. "Should we say grace or something?"

"Right lass," Cath answered. "It seems a right time te give formal thanks."

We held hands and a palpable current ran through the connection. A faint blue aura created a dome over us as Cath spoke.

"Thanks we give for the sacrifice the animal gave for us te eat of this bacon, and thanks we give to the wheat grains of the harvest for the bread. Thanks we give for the potential in the life in these eggs, and thanks we give in the gift of the butter and the sweet juice of the oranges. Thanks we give for the company and connection at this table. And humble thanks we give for old family and new. Let's us break bread." He ended with a squeeze of hands and we each briefly reveled in the simplicity of the moment before we began to eat.

"And thanks to Bridey for cooking." I said.

"Amen." Nora agreed.

It felt meaningful. Not only the prayer but the connection as we were bound together in ritual. Then the moment folded into subsequent sounds of toast crunching and forks scraping. The meal was one that I'd eaten hundreds of time before in my life, eggs, bacon, toast and juice, but none had ever tasted so fulfilling as this meal, taken with friends so fast made, and so long known that I couldn't tell if it was the drama of the moment or the unknown quest we had ahead of us, but the sense that we were all in this, against something, together, about to make changes in the fabric of the world, I wondered at how Christ felt at the last supper. I pondered the odd thought for a moment and then lost myself in the joy of the meal. We all ate in silence and when I'd finished my bacon, saved for last, I looked up and asked what I thought was an innocent enough question.

"So what happened? Back then I mean. There are some things I remember, but mostly, not so much."

Cath began by putting down his fork and wiping his mouth with a napkin. He took a swallow of juice.

"I hated that Finny was going to leave with Faidhe and her party and I had to stay behind. We were both pledged te Lon Dubh and the story but one of us had te stay on sacred soil, while the other traveled and took on the tale. We two were porfect for the task, for we had the means of communication between us no matter what the distance. So what happened to one, the other would know about and after so long in not hearin' from Finny, and thinkin' that he was either dead or gone under te the Sidhe as time began te move on...I could still *feel* he was alive, but had hord nothing from him for far too long. This is when I left ye Bridey, to search for Fion for I knew he was not dead. And then after findin' him finally, ye were lost te us then as confusion and chaos took over for a time during the transition."

Finny leaned forward putting his weight on his elbows on the table.

"Aye, it was all so fast. One day, the most important thing we did was te keep Diog from knowin' that he had a gorl child and te scrape up enough food te keep livin'. Then we were castin' magic and takin' oaths and separated in three days' time, leavin' family te fend on their own and lettin' go of the only home I'd ever known te be on the road te places far and foreign. I was in the mix of great things and great people; excitin' it was but so scary and the ocean! Oh how sick I was.

But my misery is not important te the story so much. Let me tell ye as te how things happened for my part.

———

Faidhe and her party left the Clan Duibhe on the morning following the springtide festival and had traveled in relative peace as the days grew longer and the moon drew toward the night of the dark sky once again. The party had grown in ranks by one for Fion had joined them to learn of the tale as it unfolded. They traveled east toward the shore of the isle to find passage on a ship to sail to foreign lands as described by the Greenman himself to make ready the paths for future generations.

Iarann and Lon Dubh brought Fion into the unit as if they'd gained a child to watch over and protect. Despite the truth that he was about the same age as Lon Dubh, his appearance as a boy suited the group well for they would avoid prying eyes that would be curious about who this odd collection of travelers might be. If they appeared as a traveling family taken to the road with but one horse and no servants, they stood a better chance of being left to their own plans without fear of robbery or slave raids that had taken place with more frequency of late like a dark shadow cast over the land. Once they left the territory of the Duibhe, the party was no longer under their protection and would have to resort to their own resources should they be accosted on the road.

Of course, they were not in fear for their lives, Faidhe thought as she contemplated their plan; it would simply cause complications if it were necessary to use magic and Power for protection. There was need for discretion now. Anyone or thing looking to thwart the changes Faidhe was introducing would have but only to take her life or that of the child she carried to defeat her mission. Use magic she would, if necessary, but better to move surreptitiously and without drawing undue attention. She drew her cloak protectively around her middle as if it would shield her babe from harm. With that thought, Faidhe's heart grew heavy once again for she knew that this child, as with her others, would not be hers to hold and suckle.

Pushing the thought from her mind, she planned for their approach to the territory of the Calf-herder Clan. The rest of her journey would depend on procurement of a ship and keeping safe her babe and fellow travelers. She would have to somehow come to the clan-folk of Calf-herders and convince them that she is kin to their king apparent and will arrange for accommodations there until Laoghaire and the rest of his party arrive. This was a double-edged sword for if people know who she is, those who plan to stop her from making such vast changes in the hierarchy of her own Tuath or others who might now be tainted as agents of this new dark magic will know where to find her. But then again, she needed the ship and must be recognized as important enough kin to Laoghaire to gain access to him to make ready the plans for her departure. Faidhe knew that the people at Dun Laoghaire would be suspicious of any newcomers to the territory after the brutal murder of their leaders. She must be able to assure these folk that her arrival heralds the impending appearance of King Laoghaire, himself. She must be taken in as kin for if she is not established as such before the arrival of Laoghaire; it is not likely she would gain anyone's ear to tell of their relation. For the people of this clan will likely be thrice protective of the new king in light of what happened to his parents. And too, there may be those who mean Laoghaire harm by aiming to usurp the throne to whom her presence might be seen as a threat.

Fear and suspicion seemed to be pervasive as this evil storm grew in strength. Faidhe had failed in neutralizing the evil Briciu had unleashed. She now had this opposing energy in addition to all else to contend with. This blood spell seems to collect power as it plants seeds of fear, suspicion and doubt in the hearts and minds of people, then it feeds off that fear to gain potency. Even as their little group traveled, she got the sense that the world was pulling into itself in fear as if to ward off an evil chill. Faidhe speculated her welcome at Hill T'airg and Dun Laoghaire would not be a warm one.

Faidhe made her decision.

"It is not quite nightfall, but let us camp here for the night. We draw close to the territory of our kinsman, Laoghaire but I sense that we will need to approach with confidence of our rightful connections. Let us spend this night under the quiet waning moon before we take the leap of the fool into our life's journey."

"Yes Lady." Iarann answered. I am pleased to have one more night with our little group before we plunge into the throng of strangers. I have completed much work on the panels but have been distracted and have not had the opportunity to meditate on them for over long. It seems it is when I am able to be alone and at peace in my heart and mind that I fall to the trance that enables me to do this work. I am pleased when my work takes my mind off other matters."

Lon Dubh agreed. "It is a good choice to rest here this night, I think. Fion and I will take the opportunity to go over all that has happened thus far in our family up until we took to the road. We must all sit and add our individual experiences to the tale for it is not a one-dimensional piece of work. The tale is a living, growing, changing entity in itself and must be created in the mind of the teller as such. Should it not?"

Faidhe cast a wary eye on Fion and wondered that he might be entrusted to keep and tell the truth of the tale. Even her part for what she had attempted to do to release the blood spell was her burden, but now, as a disease in their midst, the burden would spread to another. She tried to protect the others from what had taken place, but she saw how things so easily slipped from her control. Through a dream visit, she knew of Craiche's sacrifice to Laoghaire, and that they both knew of her attempt to quell the dark magic had cost a man his life. Now, she recognized that it was her own shame that made her hesitate to share this piece of the tale with the Elf-boy, and not for his protection as she'd tried to convince herself. She breathed a deep sigh.

"Yes daughter, it is time we shared of all facets to the tale."

With this, she felt a bloom of dread blossom in her chest for regardless of her intentions, not only had she taken a man's life, but had bound him in sacred ritual to bring him to the slaughter. Faidhe had intended to bind the blood spell he had cast with his death, but she had obviously failed in her efforts so that would mean what kind of recompense in the debt she owed for the life of a man such as Briciu? Though it was not her hand that spilled his blood, it was by her direction and order that he was slain. In truth, Gara had killed him, but it was she who had been attacked by him. Her price for his death might not be so heavy, but for her own part, Faidhe knew that she would not leave this life or spend another unscathed for these actions. Unconsciously, she rubbed her abdomen as if to protect her child from the world he would be born in to. Faidhe was abruptly brought out of her inner turmoil when her daughter picked up the conversation and made to prepare for their camp.

"Excellent, we shall make a celebration!" Lon Dubh crowed. "We shall eat of our stores and build a fire to warm us and illuminate the tale. Fion, you shall play your tunes and I will blow life into songs with my whistle. We will dance and share what little of mead we carry. Let us join together as family around a meal-fire and prepare for the future winds."

She seemed truly happy having come to her calling in service of the Goddess, and as they traveled with their growing party. She sees all as an adventure, Faidhe mused, and Iarann basked in Lon Dubh's glow of excitement. How blindly they trust in giving over their lives for this journey. How blindly they trust in me!

Fion was swept up in the impending festivities and went about collecting dry wood for the fire. Faidhe watched as they, all three, went about preparing to make camp and break bread over the tale before they would bed down for the night. Let them enjoy what camaraderie they can for the moment. Faidhe allowed. For they deserve what happiness can be taken now before we set course for our destinies.

———

The party drew near the gates of the ring fort built atop a hill to house the Calf- herder clans. Dressed in their finest linens and woolens, the party of four approached appearing as regal emissaries. Faidhe road horseback, bearing her brooch as Keeper, Seer and High Council as would someone of stature. She didn't expect any outside the Tuatha de Danann would recognize the significance of the Power behind the brooch but a piece of such quality and of gold would identify her as someone of stature. Lon Dubh too wore her fine woven woolen cloak bound at the neck with the clasp fashioned for her by Iarann of bronze and seashells. Iarann wore his physique as the mettle of his worth adorned with the golden torque of his family about his neck identifying him as one of high breeding and regard. Fion, who lead Faidhe's horse, wore the fine linens woven by Lon Dubh on his mother's loom and could have been a well-dressed servant or a child of one of these women.

The sentry at the gate called to the party to stop and call clan. A safety measure that was typically a formality but in recent times it was once again a precaution to know all who enter the gates and what family connection or business any traveler had with the Calf-herder clans. Faidhe responded from horseback. I am Faidhe, First Councilwoman for the Tuatha de Danann. I have news for you. Bring me the ears of those who would hear of Croi of the Clan Laoghaire, heir to the throne and rightful new leader for these territories."

The sentry seemed confused with the statement and was torn as to what to do. He took in the incongruence of the small number of the party and the meager way in which they traveled, and the obvious finery in their manner of dress.

"Wait," was all he said and he turned from the gate and disappeared from their view.

After some lengthy time waiting at the great gates of the ring fort of Dun Laoghaire, a commotion could be heard from the interior and at last the sturdy double gates were opened. A tall, well-built man with an easy smile and pleasing good looks came to greet the party with several men in a well-armed party of his own.

"My name is Dha' Teanga. I welcome you as kin, but in these times, I must keep you in careful regard. You understand, we have suffered greatly of late and our clans are in some disarray. Before you enter, we must know your business and what news you bring." He said while eying their clothing. He seemed particularly interested in the golden torque resting heavily on Iarann's neck and the gold brooch displayed on Faidhe's cloak.

"I am Faidhe, kin-mother to Croi Laoghaire through his marriage to my daughter." She thought it best to reveal her connections to the Calf-herder clan as her primary claim for admittance. "We travel with news of the return of the Croi Laoghaire, come to light the pyres to send his mother and father to the underworld." But she also wanted to be recognized as an important figure in her own right without revealing any information that was not necessary. "I am First Councilwoman for the Tuatha de Danann, and would see to it that all is arranged for the heir to the Calf-herder throne when he arrives."

"Forgive me." Dha' Teanga smirked. "But you have the look of a girl I would gladly bed at the night fires, and have not the look of a matron of the First Council seat of any tribe. Much less be of age to be kin-mother to Croi Laoghaire. For I have seen his wife some eight or ten seasons past, and she is no girl by this time, surely she herself is twenty and five season at least."

"You dare!" Iarann roared, stepping toward the insolent man and in one movement, lifted him off the ground by his throat. All six of Dha' Teanga's guards drew their swords in a singing blaze as they made to lunge for Iarann.

"Hold!" Came Faidhe's voice in such silken calm and so even a tone that it commanded the attention of all but Iarann who was intent on snapping the other man's neck. "You meant to test our strength Dha' Teanga. Well here you have a sampling of

what hides 'neath these gold pieces and fine robes. We are a small grouping of great force of strength, come to herald the coming of your king. Will you risk treating us afoul? Know that I grasp your need to test our truth in these times and forgive your insult but now that you see we are not your average road worn troupe, and carry finery of Council with strength of the Tuatha de Danann, and are assuredly kin to your kin, call down your guard. We have shown you no insult or disrespect, only stood to protect our own from such. Laws of hospitality rule that you must not lend further insult but must allow us to enter, and shall afford us rooms, food and drink until our kinsman arrives. So if you value your neck, give signal for your men to stand down and we shall proceed."

Fion, unfamiliar with the mask of magic that could be donned so easily, blinked up at Faidhe and though he was under her protection, stepped back all the same with his mouth agape at the Power that emanated from the woman. It was not unnoticed that several of the guards had done the same.

An unlikely smile spread across Dha' Teanga's red face. He managed a slight nod and the men sheathed their swords. Only then did Iarann allow Lon Dubh to coax him to put the other man down by urging his massive bicep toward the earth in her delicate hands and then by taking his giant hand in hers to convince him to release the grip on Dha' Teanga's neck.

"Well played, Lady." He croaked. "Though I meant only to see what weapons you may conceal." His eyes took an appraising stroll over Faidhe's womanly figure as he said, "I stand by my observation that you are one quite flush with youth to be kin-mother to Laoghaire."

Faidhe ignored the words for she knew that though they were couched in a polite compliment, she understood that this man still held doubt as to her claim and all but revisited the comment pertaining to the night fires. She gazed at the man and held his eyes in her own unwavering appraisal. This was a man who received much in the way of what he wanted due to his pleasant looks and obvious intelligence. He had ambition, this one. And Faidhe could probe further into the motivations of this man but now was not the time. For the moment, he held power over their entrance and she would not reveal her magic before or unless it was absolutely necessary. Holding his gaze she waited for the other to speak.

Dha' Teanga knew this was a test of wills but had to calculate the possibilities that these were people of importance and whether Laoghaire might, in fact, return to try to regain the throne. In that case, things would be a bit complicated within the clans for he had already laid much preparation to assume the role as chief attendant to the affairs of the throne while things were yet undecided and in flux after the murder of the royals. In truth, Dha' Teanga disagreed with the open-handed way the old king dealt with the Tuath but he loved the old man and respected him. He had lent the king good counsel through the years as his own father had before him but now that the old king was gone, and his only son saw fit to abandon his place some years ago, Dha' Teanga felt he had every right and duty to assume some role of leadership for the sake of the clan. At least this is what he told himself. He assumed power easily in the absence of any other willing or able to take it since Cuan had run off after his cousin more than a whole moon ago instead of taking the lead and sending other emissaries to deliver the news of the demise of the royal couple. Just as well, he thought, Cuan has strength but he is no leader. He is infected with fealty to his cousin. Dha' Teanga had been close to the affairs of the throne for so long, he thought it was his right by this time to assume responsibility for was it not he who was best and closest confidant to the royals?

"Let them enter." He said to his men without taking his own eyes from the woman Faidhe's. "Give them suitable rooms in the small stone house." Then to the party, "Refresh yourselves there and wait until I send word for you. When I call for you we will discuss how you came to be on this path ahead of Croi Laoghaire."

Faidhe liked it not that they were all but prisoners rather than guests and she did not miss the lack of title with which this man addressed Laoghaire. She smiled sweetly at the man and responded.

"With thanks." And with a bow of her head, still not taking her eyes from his, she signaled for her party to proceed with a hand gesture. Iarann brushed by Dha' Teanga and took Lon Dubh's arm leading her through the gates, behind some of the swordsmen and dwarfing all of them. Another of the swordsmen reached to take the reins of Faidhe's horse and snatched his hand back quickly as Fion growled as fiercely as a wolf and held fast the reins to lead the horse himself. As she passed through the fort gates, leaving Dha' Teanga behind her, Faidhe graced Fion with such a radiant smile that he blushed furiously.

———

The stone house was in fact an elaborate cluster of beehive type structures within the fort. The interior of each of the hive domes made comfortable rooms in which they were to be quartered. There was a much larger structure within the fort that appeared to be an improvement on these quarters that might have been accommodations for the royal couple themselves. Faidhe understood that their lodgings were not chosen for their comfort, but for the fact that stone rooms would not allow for them to easily escape, should they be of the mindset to leave the compound to cause disturbances within the fort. She also knew that they would not be leaving through the one main doorway for there were two armed sentries posted there.

Iarann took the packs from his horse and allowed a servant to take it to be fed and watered. Turning to one of the guards he inquired. "Will we be attended or are we prisoners, outright? My Ladies will be in need of water and washing bowls, mead and bread."

Though the guard stood his ground, he gripped his sword hilt all the tighter. Iarann's large countenance and looming presence gave those who did not know his gentle nature cause to inventory their own lack in size or skill, for unarmed as he was, Iarann gave even a brave man pause before answering him. The guard hesitated, observed the women and boy through the stone house door and came to a decision.

"I shall inquire as to what other accommodations will be brought. But for now, I will order water, washing bowls and see that your hearth is lit."

Iarann nodded approval and thanks and bent low to enter the main doorway to the stone structure carrying the packs over his broad shoulder.

There were a few mats and cushions in the main room and sleeping palettes in the other rooms in the rear of the formation. Each room had a rounded doorway that led to the next area so one could walk a complete circle through all the rooms and return to the main room with the only doorway leading to the outside. Every chamber in the stone house had but a sliver of a window space worked into the design of the building's structure. It allowed for movement of air and a very small view but obviously would not allow for egress. Of the three rooms in the rear, each contained two sleeping pallets but they did not choose rooms for they did not know if they were to be housed here or if it should be where they waited for further instructions or an audience with higher-ups in the tuath who would hear their news.

They all waited in silence as servants brought in several bowls of water, wood and kindling for the gigantic and unusual stone hearth that was built into the space between all of the rooms in the structure so that one great fire would warm each of the separate quarters and therefore, each could privately maintain simple cooking tasks. There was no smoke hole in any room for the stone walls of each room's exterior constructed a natural path for the smoke to travel skyward. The girls left the bowls of water by the hearth and a boy servant brought spider weed with an ember from an existing fire in a bronze pot to set the hearth ablaze. Once this was completed and the fire was burning with strength, the group was once again left alone.

Lon Dubh pulled the heavy skins down to cover the doorway that would afford them some privacy.

"I like it not that we are kept to these rooms that have the look of a prison about them in spite of the embroidered cushions and warm hearth." She complained. "How are we to know truly that Laoghaire comes this way? Is he not charged with Keeping of the Hill? In all your years as Keeper, it was not often you left the summit and even then it was to travel for much heralded great gatherings. For what reason should we expect Laoghaire to come at the news of his family's misfortune? Does he care not for the gravity of the duties of the Hill? How came you by this information Mother? Mother?"

Faidhe had found her way in to the northern most room and was peering out the slender window space. There, she observed several new timbers and tree trunks had replaced an older section of the fort fence that had been splintered and tossed aside like a child's game of sticks. Not far to the right of that scene, in the centermost area of the town could be seen a great monolith that had been plunged so violently into the earth that great clumps of sod and dirt were crumpled up the sides of the Stone higher than even the tallest of men. Atop the boulder Faidhe caught a glimpse of the sun reflecting brightly off a shiny object. She breathed an inward sigh of relief at the sight of the great Stone and its contents. She observed as the men working there used the remnants of the splintered fence to create a step-like structure to allow a person to climb to the top of the Stone to examine the sparkling object on its top.

"Know you the prime purpose of the Stone of Fal daughter?" Faidhe spoke while continuing to peer out the window slot.

Lon Dubh shifted mental gears to give her answer. This was how she learned much in her travels with her mother. The questions would come and she would answer to her best ability and logic. Then a discussion would follow. She searched her memory for points of study.

"It is said to hold the great Power of the clans and to be brought from the north by the Tuatha de Danann, granted as a gift of the Valkyrie and Norse Gods as a tool in aiding the Danann in running off the Firbolg and assuming stewardship of the sacred isle."

"And?" Faidhe inquired.

"And in that respect, the Stone will seek the purity of heart for those who may lay rightful claim to rule these lands. It is said that the Stone gives to the hand of one so pure, the power to rule and protect by indicating the chosen one with the call of the Stone. It will trumpet for all to hear, and none to doubt, the heralding of the one true leader. But thus far, there has been no one person to rule the lands; we have lived in relative peace since the Danann came to the great Lake of the Ivory Heron. There has been no great need, for all tribes, tuaths and clans have ruled within their own hierarchy. We trade and barter and keep to our own lands but have lived with the Gods and the knowledge that we held the Power of propagation and protection."

"Have you not noticed the fearful caul that is cast upon these lands daughter? Have you not felt the pull of doubt in your own heart in spite of your newfound role as a Priestess of the Goddess?"

"I admit, I have had frequent doubts in many things of late."

"You do not endure this affliction alone, Black Bird. But trust not that you have cause to doubt your abilities. For you would not have been chosen so if it was not your destiny to come to this task. It is the doubt itself that infects your abilities. It is a part of the new foul wind that blows across this land. Bringing with it seeds of putrescence that will take hold in any heart that offers a warm place for the unwholesome weeds to grow and choke all that is redeeming in the heart and mind of a person. We have our task in this battle but this new filth has been enlisted to hinder our task and soon, will take over to make what we must do ever the more difficult. So it is time for the one who is pure of heart and so offended by the tainted energy as to never be turned to greed or lust any other of myriad tools used by the darkness to call one's heart to sickness. This one will take the lead and fill the throne for us. This one will Keep all the tribes and tend the garden plucking out these weeds so it will bear fruit at the time of greatest need.

This one will join us in our duty to sow the seeds for our future and through the gift of this great Stone, that will one day birth the coming of the one who, through innocence and true purity of heart, will wield the Power of all four of the implements and be supported by all the force of energy behind the Stone." Faidhe's eyes came back into focus as she turned from the window slot and looked right at Lon Dubh. "The Stone is here, now. And it has been brought here to herald that this king, this one man will be the High King of the entire sacred isle. That High King will be Laoghaire."

As if magically conjured by the words spoken by Faidhe, a holler from a young voice, still cracking with adolescence came from the front gate.

"A cattle party approaches! Kinsman Cuan is among them."

"Come," Faidhe said. "We must prepare and make ourselves ready, for this night we reunite with our family and I'm loathe to announce that we are already one short of the eight pledged to this cause." Faidhe responded to the shocked and pained expression on the faces of her daughter and Iarann. "I did not wish to dampen your spirits with the news, but you must know now that Craiche has given herself over to this cause. She has gone to the Otherworld but we may yet draw strength from her, as she's come to me in dream visits. But we have not the time to mourn proper for our friend this day for we are to support Laoghaire in mourning his parents and assuming his kingship before we take to the ocean. And for this we must be sure that Laoghaire comes to his reign with dominion over both land and sea to insure the future of our plans. For strong is the king who holds reign not only over his lands but over the sea as well. It will be some time before they come for us. Make haste, we have much to do in preparation. Iarann, bring us yon packs. Lon Dubh, bring out your herbs and salts for these bowls. You there, boy, Fion." With this, the Elf jumped to attention at being more than a spectator. "Build the blaze and count your magic in with ours, now. You have participated as an aid to the altar of the Goddess in the spring festival rites. Commit you now to this cause as a warrior of its ranks?"

Fion looked at Lon Dubh and felt his heart squeeze a bit. The memory of what they shared in the spinning room had bound them as though they were blood. He could no more remain on the sidelines and be merely a witness to her tale than he could watch as someone took to beating his own brother. He looked back to Faidhe and with steel in his eyes, voiced his oath.

"My own mother gave her life so that a girl child could be born to the Goddess. She made my brother and I take oath that we would never lose our hearts to the slovenly ways of the Duibhe. She held my hand and made me swear with her last breath that I would keep to the sacred ways and never forsake the Lady Goddess or as we had known her, the Queen of the Wood. We kept our sister safe at a hearth of a Duibhe woman who kept to the Old Ways in reverence of the Goddess although it was not the Elven way, but near enough: not in petition for wants and needs as did the men. I waited and wasted away in the lands of the Duibhe knowing all the while, our life's

destiny in service of the Goddess would be revealed so that our sworn oath by my mother's deathbed would be kept. Then, my brother and I found your daughter with the raven black hair and eyes so deep. We protected Lon Dubh from Diog, as we were not able to do for our mother and came to know our destiny through her. My life is hers for the Goddess and I hold true to my oath to take this tale to its rightful placement. What meager magic I possess will be used for the safe passage of my Lady Raven and her tale until its rightful end."

Lady Raven, she gave pause to his choice of words. How appropriate, she thought. Lady Raven. She returned her cool observation toward the Elf and Faidhe observed the pulsating aura that emanated from the boy in swirls of gold and white. She saw in him a true and strong heart and in his words he was honest and resolute. Having seen weaker resolve in many a grown man, she was satisfied that this boy would be true to his word and oath. She needed to trust him with her parts of the tale and this would have to do for they were in short time and had much to do before the coronation of the first High King Laoghaire.

"Come then." She said. "Let us work."

———

Fleet of foot and quiet as a breeze, Fion squeezed his slight frame through a window slot in the rear of the building to seek out information regarding who they were dealing with in Dha' Teanga. Keeping to the knee-high, planted stalks of grain in the village garden to remain unseen, Fion found his way to the front fence and had a look through a knothole to observe the cattle party as they drew near. With his keen eyes he observed a woman with wheat-yellow hair carrying a round shield strapped across her back and there was something familiar about her face. But she bore a haunted look in her deep blue eyes that would otherwise be so lovely. There was a large man, with curly black hair and a great beard, though not as commanding as Iarann, but formidable and who took absolute control of the animals as they were herded. Fion saw two children; a boy and a girl ride the shoulders of yet another man who might be kin to the other. This one bore the look of kindness and wisdom and though he laughed with the boy and girl, his face too was stamped with lines of care-weary thoughts. A peculiar leafy design painted his arms and legs. Then Fion thought he saw the design move and dance about the muscled man's extremities as though the vines grew with life. An old woman walked alone, scowling at her feet, swatting uselessly at the flies that traveled with the herd. There was another who was dressed in rough woolen cloth garb who had the look of a servant as he trudged behind the older woman carrying several packs. The one of all who caught Fion's attention was the last person in the troupe. This was a small man or large boy who brought up the rear of the cattle heads and was partly obscured by the moving animals. Fion squinted and concentrated wholeheartedly on this figure for there was something about this one that did not sing a true note. As he forced all his attention toward this figure, Fion momentarily caught a glimpse of this one's thoughts and found a mishmash of adolescent thoughts about the young girl in the group all askew with images of a woman with whom this boy had practiced unwholesome acts of sexual gratification. There were also sickening thoughts of revenge and torture all mixed up with the pleasure of the gratification together with a festering resentment for so many. Fion pulled back his thoughts with such intensity that his head pulled violently back from the knothole in the fence. His face contorted with disgust and he spat on the ground as if to clear his mind of what he'd witnessed.

"Bah!" He spat again. "Worms!"

Fion looked back out through the fence to find the pudgy boy standing stock still at the end of the herd, looking around with suspicion and a sly look of guilt stamped on his face for he suspected something of his thoughts had been breached.

Fion noted that this one would bear watching but care would be needed for he has the knowing of such tricks as mind-watching. The Elf could do this with his own brother with ease but not at all with his sister. Both he and his brother were greatly surprised at how adeptly they could both communicate this way with Lon Dubh but had no knowledge that this could be done with others. Perhaps they couldn't do this with the members of the Clan Duibhe because the clan did not have the ability but Fion was learning that these Tuatha de Danann from the north part of the isle carried Power as did the Elven folk but in much greater measure than his own.

The gates opened and again, Dha' Teanga met the cattle party this time with a larger company of armed guards. He greeted the large man by clasping his arms and then embracing him as kin.

"Cuan," He said, "we are pleased at your safe return. Have you delivered our tragic news to the son of my beloved king? How come you by this cattle?"

Fion caught the ring of insincerity in the man's voice. It was obvious as he cut his eyes to the tattooed man who was putting the children down from his shoulders, that he knew him but failed to greet him. As the second man approached, Cuan wasted no time in heralding the arrival of his cousin and son to the dead king, Laoghaire.

"My cousin and my king's son has returned to mourn for his parents, and to assume his responsibility to his people."

Some of the younger warriors looked interested in seeing the one they'd only heard about since they were children and inspected Laoghaire by taking measure of his size and how he carried himself. Laoghaire greeted Dha' Teanga in a reserved fashion and did not clasp his arms or lend embrace to the greeting.

"Dha' Teanga, my father's aid and assistant, I greet you at the gate of my father's lands with a wounded heart that I may not be hailed by my father and mother. But I thank you for carrying your duties long past that which would be required, now that you are aid only to a dead man. You will be rewarded for your loyalty."

There was no mistaking Laoghaire's meaning that Dha' Teanga's show in meeting the party at the gate and assuming authority with the guards reached well beyond what was acceptable for a man of his station within the Tuath. And the unpolished manner in which Laoghaire spoke of Dha' Teanga's position in the Tuath gave a clear indication that the man was all but dismissed by Laoghaire. Additionally, there were no formal introductions or presentations of the party with whom Laoghaire traveled. There was no question as to whether the party would enter the gates as Laoghaire took Colm's arm and led the party through the front gates of his home. Almost as an afterthought Laoghaire turned to Dha' Teanga.

"The cattle are in need of watering and should be put to field. Once we have been refreshed, I will send for you so I may hear from the one who was closest advisor to my father what thoughts you have on how my parents were so carelessly guarded that they were so easily taken by surprise and so violently slain."

Laoghaire knew that the other man had no part in the murder of his parents but he was in foul disposition for now that Laoghaire drew close to his childhood home, the reality that his parents were dead and how they died, tormented him. The fact that Dha' Teanga was no friend to Laoghaire nor had he ever been, was much magnified in this moment. He never liked how the man insinuated his way into affairs of his father's house and more than slightly disapproved when his father had appointed Dha' Teanga to the position that was held previously by Dha Teanga's father before him. Laoghaire remembered harsh words he spoke to his father on that occasion.

"Intelligent he may be Father and as you say, practiced in diplomacy to be sure. I grant you all of this, Father, but this man cares overmuch for his own position and will compromise what's best for all, if he sees an opportunity to fatten his own purse. I know that he is not above using your name to benefit himself. This I have seen for myself. Please Father, consider another as your aid; perhaps one who displays loyalty as a primary trait. I know you loved Dha' Teanga's father and will miss him much, but this is no reason to choose his son to high position."

"It is his skill in diplomacy that I need in these times, my son." Laoghaire's father answered. "You take to the land of your new bride, and I grudge you not in that choice, but I must have such a one as Dha' Teanga who has built many relationships already with neighboring clans and has much knowledge of trading goods he has learned by keeping vigilant to his father's teachings. I know you like him not but in your absence, I need one who is ready to take on the position his father had done without flaw for so many years. Just know, Croi, I see the man for who he is. I understand that he puffs of pride in position and status, but confidence can be a benefit when dealing with outlanders. He is well liked for his easy smile and respected for a strong hand. He will suit my needs in your absence as an aid and advisor...until such time as you return, then I will be most pleased to take you into my confidence on all affairs of these lands and the plans I have for the trades open to us from the large island and the mainland beyond. I will keep strong your place as heir to the throne and disregard your choice to surrender your birthright in the hopes that one day you will return with your wife to take your rightful seat upon the throne here. And should you decide never to return, at the time of my death, I will pray to the Gods that your cousin, Cuan is ready to ascend to the position. I will keep him apprised of all that happens here and you may rest easy that he is involved with all affairs, though he is some measure more tolerant of him than you, he is none too fond of Dha' Teanga and will keep him trustworthy."

Laoghaire knew he had no solid reason to dislike Dha' Teanga and did not like to think on himself as being envious that this man spent years with his father that he, himself had not. As he reflected on this conversation he had with his father just prior to taking to the road to go with Colm to the Tuatha de Danann, he recognized that it was not jealousy that made him dislike his father's aid, but that he had never wholly trusted him and it was this that caused him to offer terse words upon his return to his home. Though he realized this, he did not offer words of apology as he ushered his family to their rest.

As the party headed for the front gate, Gara stumbled over her deteriorating slippers and Dha' Teanga impulsively caught her with a strong arm. Her hand went reflexively to fix her hair as she fluttered her lashes at the handsome man.

"Well, finally someone who offers a lady a hand and some kindness. For all this travel in the wilderness, I am so fatigued as to barely be able to take steps to find comfort within these gates."

Dha' Teanga tucked this tidbit of discontent away for possible use later and lent a firm arm to the woman who, at first glance appeared old and haggard, but upon closer scrutiny could be seen as one with age upon her but who had pleasant looks and was seemingly a woman of means for she traveled with a servant and much in the way of material goods.

"Allow me to assist you Lady in any way I might as you find your way to rooms your kinsman Croi Laoghaire deems suitable for you."

The look she afforded him at this comment told him what he desired to know; that Laoghaire was not friend to this woman, perhaps kin somehow, but Dha' Teanga could read people and this woman was not here of her own accord or desire. Perhaps this would be useful information if Laoghaire indeed had returned to take the throne and strip Dha' Teanga of the duties of his position he'd so impeccably carried out during all the years of Laoghaire's absence. If only for the blood of my birth, he thought, I should be rightful heir to the throne. A better son to the king was I. Here at his side I could be found day and night, working long and hard to build relationships for the clan and assisting in the acquiring of lands for my people and my king. Accustomed to being an important person within the tuath with access to the king's ear, Dha' Teanga was not about to let his rank and position slip away without working at some plan to assure that things turned to his favor. He put on his most congenial face as he turned to the woman and spoke gentle words to her.

Fion had seen enough and slipped back into the grain on his knees to carefully head back toward the stone cluster of buildings where his party had been quartered. He rushed from the edge of the grains to the small window opening, where he began to climb but froze when he heard Dha Teanga bark in a whisper to the guards at the door to make sure that no one came out of the rooms.

"Keep silent the news of another party's arrival here prior to that of the king's son. In light of all that has happened, I must make safe the clans and these people within are still strangers to us. Keep your guard and say nothing."

"Sir," the guard inquired, "If these folks are to be kept here, should we not allow for food and drink and perhaps pots for their chamber comfort?"

Dha' Teanga thought for a moment. He doubted that these people were who they claimed, at least the one that rode a-horse, but nor could he find reason they might be otherwise and he did not want to lend anything that could be seen as insult. They were obviously people of stature and so agreed to have them treated as such as long as they stayed within the walls of the rooms they had been given and until he could determine whether they were truly kin to the king's son. And in case they are, then he would have to decide how to deal with that detail if it should stand in his way of maintaining his position of influence in the clans. As Dha' Teanga moved away from the door of the structure, Fion scrambled to squeeze his body through the window before the guard could enter the building and notice that he had been missing.

———

"You are sure?" Faidhe inquired of Fion as he related his story of the cattle party that had just arrived.

"I am, Lady. One man great as a bear and another with twining tattoos on his arms and legs that hold some magic, I think, for to my eyes, they move as if they grow from the very earth."

Faidhe remembered her vision of Laoghaire with those very tattoos and uttered without being conscious she'd said it out loud.

"Mayhaps they do grow from the very earth. Mayhaps they do."

"Lady?" Fion called her back to attention.

"Yes. Please go on. The women. There are two women, you say?"

"Aye, one with the look of sadness about her but very fair and with hair the color of golden wheat and eyes the color of the sky. She has a familiar appearance I cannot place. And the other is older, a wise woman perhaps or kin mother to the other travelers. She looks none too happy about the toll the road has taken. She has not the look of one who fares well on the path or in the wood. And she is not protected with practical sense of what may be necessary as one travels, for her slippers appear as they were once fine embroidered silk. And there are children as well, three of them. Two are

friendly with each other and might be kin to one another but the other..." He hesitated as he thought of Triag.

"Speak plain Fion. Who is the other?" Faidhe pushed.

"The other is an older boy who has much flesh on him for one so young and he has, well I think he has ability to the mind-watching.

"Mind watching?"

"Aye. As my brother and I do. The ability to communicate without speaking. In our heads, like, to know what the other is thinking."

"Ah." Faidhe said, as she understood Fion's meaning. "And what makes you think this?"

"I was peering at him through the gate-hole and caught a glimpse of what was in his mind. This one has the muck of the bog in his head. It near made me sick to be touched by his thoughts. He has not the reverence for the Gods but this one has been touched by the magic in some way. I saw him in ritual practice with another and not one with wholesome intent."

Once again, Fion's face took on a contorted expression of disgust as he described the boy.

The reminder of mind watching, as Fion had called it, gave Faidhe an idea. She understood that Dha' Teanga intended to keep their presence unknown and they were but well-kept prisoners. Having fought the urge all through the years to attempt to communicate with either of her daughters this way, it hadn't occurred to Faidhe until now to reach out. She called to her daughter Colm in her mind as she tested what she'd already known was Colm's ability. She spoke to Colm by extending a tendril of thought to reach out and find the other wherever she might be within the compound.

"Daughter. My Colm Dove, hearken to me. Hear me now."

As Colm arranged the rooms in the large stone structure that had been Laoghaire's parent's home, she stood up from the sleeping palette she was plumping and was still. Cocking her head as though listening she looked about the room to see if she had company.

"Is someone there?" She called. Again, came the voice.

"Colm, my daughter, hear my voice in the name of the Goddess."

"Mother? Is that you?" Colm answered aloud.

"It is, daughter. But speak to me in your thoughts so that we are not discovered by those who might be curious about their new queen."

"Queen?" Colm inquired. Grasping at trying to understand this new experience.

"Pay no heed to that now Colm. Know you this: We are held without choice to leave in the small stone structure not far from where you are quartered. You must send word that you are expecting kin here and that you should be notified immediately upon our arrival. This should reveal our presence to you so that we may join you and take care of our business at hand."

"Mother!" Colm shouted in her mind so that Faidhe winced at the pressure in her own head. "Mother I have so needed your counsel. My unworthy heart plagues me and now

you tell me I must be queen? I am fearful of the very health of my mind. For I know not if you speak to me now or if it is only my mind plying me with tricks to do me comfort."

"Take ease child. The fear and doubt that eats at your heart makes you question your path. This is easily remedied. Send for your husband's cousin and have him inquire as to the kin you await. He will carry the voice of authority with these clans and he will arrive at the truth of our presence here. Wait not daughter; time allows for opposition to our cause. Make haste now."

Colm dropped the linen pillow from her hands to the palette and made for the doorway.

"Willa." She called to the servant that had been assigned to her comfort. A roundish, young girl of about 15 seasons could be seen coming toward the sleeping chamber in which Colm and Laoghaire would be housed with a large urn of water and a bowl for washing.

"Yes Lady?"

"Willa, know you my husband's cousin, Cuan?"

"Of course, Lady."

"I have need of his attendance. Will you have him summoned and brought to me here?" Willa looked around the chambers and inquired as to the propriety of such a meeting with her response.

"Here, Lady? In these chambers?"

Seeing the error in her request Colm corrected herself and tried to cover her mistake.

"Of course here. I have need of conference with my cousin and it is not so formal as to be taken in a receiving room, this is a place of comfort where I may speak plain with my kinsman." She highlighted that he was her kin and no impropriety was intended with her request.

"He is just now tending to the cattle head brought in with your party. Shall I send for him in the fields or will you wait until the herd is counted?" It was obvious by Willa's face that in the clans of the Calf-herders there is not much to warrant being disturbed in the fields.

"I hesitate to disturb him in his duty. However, this is a matter that will not wait. I will thank you to send a fleet serving boy with my summons now."

Willa dipped a curtsy at the tone of Colm's voice and left all personal doubt she had to be dealt with as an issue to be handled by the royals and not a servant girl such as her.

"Yes, Lady." She acceded and left the water urn and bowl to tend to her task.

It took all of Colm's reserve to resist marching out of her chambers and over to the smaller stone structure to demand the release of her family but she knew if her mother was indeed there and her call was not just a trick of a wanting mind, that they would be released shortly without raising questions or creating a diplomatic upheaval. The wait for Cuan's arrival was over long for Colm's liking but in truth only a short while before Cuan appeared at her chamber door.

"Colm?" He spoke her name softly and the one word seemed to be full of hope and pain. "You have need of me?"

Colm, too distracted with her own hopes, did not notice that in that moment had she called him to her, Cuan would have lost his resolve and betrayed his beloved cousin to have this woman as his own love.

"Oh Cuan!" She ran toward him and he flung the skins down over the doorway. "Yes, let us not be heard." She mistook his action for his understanding of her need for privacy. "It has come to me that my family, taken to the road the very morning you came to the village of the Danann, is here within the gates of this clan."

Cuan stood dumbfounded at his own foolishness that he'd expected, after several private dinners followed by many nights of sleeping in close proximity on the road, that she would choose now to call for him under the watchful eyes of all the clan. His face turned red with the flames of his own shame at what he would have done in this very room had she but given him a sign that she felt the same.

"Be not angry, cousin, to be called from your duty for I have reason to believe that my mother and sister are here and are not free to come to me of their own will. Their party is in a chamber house much like this one but with many less rooms and more modest accommodations. They must be allowed to come to us here as kin but knowledge of their presence must not be revealed for it seems it is important that it is not known that my family has knowledge of magic of the Danann. Will you herald the expectation of my family and put about a request for any news of my family's arrival here so that we may see to their release?"

"I will Colm, but why is it you do not ask yourself or have Laoghaire inquire after your family? You are the Queen here now."

"I fear that though you may think so, cousin, there will come the truth shortly that many do not feel Laoghaire is rightful king as he left so long ago to be my husband. And I know there are many who feel ill will toward me for it was not a kindly reputation I had all those years ago when I first came to the Clan Laoghaire."

Cuan's eye dropped to the floor in shame once again for he knew it was his own doing that many in the clans thought on Colm as a wealth hungry, title stealing, blood chaser that would go after any and all to further her own position in life.

"I will do as you bid, Lady, my Queen, for I know and you are kind not to accuse, that it was at my word that you suffer such an ungracious reputation. I will do anything you request of me of course it is my duty, but I am eager to undo what wickedness I have attached to your name. Allow me to see to this myself and have your family brought to these chambers so that you might be comforted by their company." Cuan turned to leave and from behind he heard Colm call to him.

"Cousin, Cuan, I bear you no ill will for we both made mistakes all those years ago. Carry not shame or guilt in your heart. We will begin anew here as we must."

Cuan's heart was lighter for the kind words but still tormented by his love and desire for her all the more for her forgiving heart. He pulled back the skins on the door to leave and caused the girl Willa, who was listening by the doorway, to jump back in surprise.

"Have a care there, girl. You'll not want to lose your position as house servant and be put a-field for your lack of discretion!" He growled. "Listen not at chamber doors for false or misinterpreted words may not kill, but they are known well for causing great harm." He said protectively, still punishing himself for the trouble he'd loosed on Colm and Laoghaire with his own words all those years ago. "Heed this, if nothing else girl, you'll not want to be prying at the door of your queen to make yourself comfortable in the Dha' Teanga's favor. Appear not so shocked, you think you are the first to be taken to his bed for news of what is said in these chambers?"

For the first time, Colm looked around her and realized these were the rooms of the murdered royal couple, her husband's parents. While at the same time, Willa looked on Colm with new eyes in speculating how this might change things within the Tuath and what it might mean to her survival, particularly now that she'd been caught listening at the chamber door. Upon Cuan's departure, the servant girl spoke.

"Please forgive me, Lady, I had not the knowledge that you and Prince Laoghaire had come to claim the throne. I have been told most of my life and the whole of what is in my memory that the Prince had left his throne under spell of the wicked... ah pardon, Lady, to marry in a place far, far away. Since you're arrival, all have speculated that you have come to pay respects and light the pyres. In truth, it was only at Cuan's insistence that the pyres were not lit some time past. For it has been well past a whole moon cycle since the king and queen were...ah since they died. In fact, we had given up all hope even of Cuan's return as it had been told us that he had decided to stay and live with your clans and the lighting of the pyres was to take place on this very night. It is a wondrous thing that you should arrive on this day. There has been much in the way of mysterious doings since our king and queen have left us."

Willa chattered nervously as she made up the sleeping palettes and poured the water adding scented oils to the bowl. Prattling on in the hopes that she would make an alliance with the new royals and possibly save her position in spite of being caught brazenly listening at the door.

"Once Cuan had left in search of your husband, the only real authority we had that was knowledgeable and organized was Dha' Teanga. The rest of the clans were not versed in higher things for we mostly just serve and keep the cattle. We have been so well taken care of for so long. Matters of diplomacy and trade continued to be taken as Dha' Teanga's responsibilities so most are his allies and many just deferred to him as the one to take these matters on. In fact, he put himself about as taking on stewardship of such things until such time as one of the royal line should come to claim their right."

Colm had been doubtful of herself of late, and had questioned her place in the tuath as well as her abilities as a Keeper's wife, a woman, and a worthy partner but she felt emboldened by her natural protective nature when it came to any who meant harm to her Laoghaire. She saw an opportunity in keeping this girl close.

"Is it true you have a relationship of the fires or rites with this steward to the throne? Dha' Teanga?"

Willa couldn't help but betray her pleasure at sharing the rites with the man and probably more than just the rites so Colm would have to be careful if there might be genuine affection between the two or at least on the girl's behalf. But in situations such as these, it is often a matter of comfort of station or status to bed with a higher up in the clan beyond the festival rites, so Colm thought Willa's arrangement with Dha' Teanga was likely more of a mutual understanding than anything akin to love. Colm speculated that if there were news to be had, this girl would know much of the man and his ambitions.

"So the pyres will be lighted this night?" She kept the girl engaged.

"Yes, Lady."

"If that suits my husband, we will be in need of proper preparations. I await the arrival of some of my kin from my village. I expect they will stay with us here in these rooms when they arrive for the lighting of the pyres. Please arrange for four more, I think."

The girl hesitated and Colm asked, "Is there issue with arrangements for my family?"

"No my Lady, it's just that with the other two guests in these rooms and the personal servant, there is not the room for so many."

"What other two guests?"

"One I assume is your mother, an older woman and her boy and manservant."

Colm knew quickly who might fit that description.

"Gara? Within these walls? Who ordered this so?"

"I know this not Lady. Not for certain. She just seemed to find placement here and began to make order and arrangement so she has privacy for herself and her boy. She has been brought food, mead, and water and has made demands for some very particular sweets as well. The servant has been quartered with the rest of us in the kitchen house. We thought because she spoke with authority that she must be a revered wise woman and made no question of her requests. It was out of reverence for her age and stature that we served her so, before even yourself, Lady. But now that I understand that you are to be Queen and our Laoghaire will take his father's throne, I can only apologize and beg understanding for the error."

Willa stumbled to alleviate any blame that might be cast her way by paying so little head to the status of one potentially so important. Especially in light of the fact that she'd heard all the old rumors of the mean spirit and ill temper of the woman who stood to be her queen. The girl saw her sought after position as a house servant dwindling with each passing insult to the new queen's station. She tried to rally and shed light on who may properly be blamed for the blunder. Willa brightened with the thought of what might be her saving grace.

"In fact," she said, "this woman, Gara, did mention that Dha' Teanga has extended every courtesy to her needs."

Colm flared momentarily and looked frightening to the girl. Willa reminded herself to remember this moment, should she ever have a thought to undermine or betray this woman. She is formidable and Powerful. The girl almost felt pity for the woman Gara who had obviously overstepped her welcome and authority but then took a bit of comfort that this Lady Colm's wrath might not be directed at herself. She felt emboldened.

"Shall I make other arrangements for these members of your party then...Highness?"

Just then a disturbance could be heard in the outer chamber foyer. Both women looked up to see the beautiful and familiar face of Lon Dubh at the door.

"My sister!" Colm squealed with joy. "Come you to me that I might look on you and bask in your company. It has been but a moon since we last embraced but also a lifetime of care has rested on my brow; I pined so for news of you and my mother." Lon Dubh entered the room and the two embraced in a sincere reunion. With moist eyes they greeted each other and spoke news of the road. Colm asked how long ago Lon Dubh had arrived and the darker woman shared her story of where and how they had been quartered. Colm asked if all were well in the party, Lon Dubh began to speak but her eyes sliced toward the servant girl and when they realized they could not speak freely, Colm turned to Willa.

"Go now and make arrangements for the elder woman and her boy to be housed where my family has until now been kept and then arrange to have all comforts for my family to be brought here so they may wash, eat and rest to be refreshed for the services this night."

"As you wish." The girl chirped, happy to still offer any service to this would-be queen if it meant she was still positioned within the royal house.

———

"We must make haste in our journey, Laoghaire." Faidhe spoke plainly. "You had the Stone sent here and have done a wise thing in planting the Sword of Nuada for the Keeping of the magic and to claim the kingdom. My heart is leaden with sorrow for you in the loss of your mother and father in such a ruthless manner. But this loss can only highlight for us the nature of our path and the decisiveness needed for us to take to our destinies. Mourn for your clan but do not let your grief cloud your vision as to what must be done here. Light the pyres and claim the throne this night for you must not leave room in the minds and hearts of your clans for doubt and fear or mistrust for these are the new tools of evil. As you know, the one who took the lives of the king and queen has sown those seeds well and deep. Give those seeds no chance to sprout."

Faidhe sought out Laoghaire even before she gave a thought to seeing her other daughter. She found him alone in the receiving room of his parents' home. He was *sullen and in a dark mood but she could not waste time to tread lightly on his wounded heart. She knew of an opposition that worked within this tuath against the possibility of the rightful heir taking the throne and ultimately garnering fealty of lesser kings to create the first position of the High King in the land. What takes place in the next moon here could possibly mean success or failure of the entire plan she had arranged for many future generations.*

Laoghaire had focused on her one comment on 'the one who took the lives of the king and queen.'

"What knowledge have you on who did this to my mother and father?" Laoghaire roared to life. "Who has done this thing? Tell me so that I can cut them down!" He demanded reaching to his halfstrap for the Sword that was no longer there.

Faidhe remembered that she saw in a vision what had happened to Laoghaire's parents but had left the lands of the Tuatha de Danann for the road by that time. She had not the time then to explain to Laoghaire what had come about.

"I am sorry kinsman. I am still finding my way in communicating with others. Often, I assume that if I have knowledge of something that others do as well. Let me tell you how your parents met their end and how they played a role in all of this. But you will not take comfort nor will you be able to exact revenge."

"I must know and then I will decide what action might be taken." Laoghaire announced.

"On the night you fought Briciu's challenge, you fought more than a raging bull."

"This I know. I was given this information in the gift of love and magic Craiche passed to me upon her death. I also know, Lady, of your attempt to quell the dark magic and what price you have paid for the trying."

"As you say, this is my debt to pay. The magic cast against you that night was a blood spell. One intended to take your life and allow Briciu to ravage your family. My daughter in particular was to suffer profane acts of the rites and yours and Colm's children to suffer and die as well, to stamp out any possibility for the future of your seed and blood to continue. Briciu was diseased in his mind but that did not make the magic less potent. The spell was binding and would not stop; but it was thwarted through our protective magic. You killed the bull, which released the magic and Colm held the shield of protection so Briciu was not able to follow through in hurting and killing your family...your family with the Tuatha de Danann, that is. If you count back, it was the very night of the challenge that your parents were killed as the spell attempted to find its mark. It was this dark magic cast that loosed this evil on your family. Despite my attempt to quell the darkness by taking the life of the one who cast it, this malevolence has been loosed on the world, for the spell will never bear the fruit that had been intended. At first, your duties were to be in Keeping of the Stones and continue to hold balance between masculine and feminine so that a stronghold for the Old Ways could be initiated as the new masculine God comes to Power, but with the addition of this evil energy, we now have the additional task of binding our faith and

sacred practices with that of the new God so that when the world will need it most, the Power will be available to our kinfolk, generations from now, to rise and fight the evil as the energy behind the blood magic comes to enough strength to manifest once again either in this powerful spirit, or in the flesh. Either way, history will play out the challenge in some way once again."

Laoghaire was completely silent and stared out the window at visions unseen. He appeared to carry fatigue that delved much deeper than road weariness. Tears threatened to overwhelm him as his face worked to maintain impassivity.

"Claim your birthright this night and get on with the business of taking rule of this island." Faidhe urged him. "For all arrangements must be made and secured for our passage so that this babe within me gestates over water and comes to swaddling as we come ashore in the land where the news of the masculine God's birth will be launched in these lands and far beyond. I have been so instructed to take this voyage and for your part, you have the authority and must make it so by making arrangements for our passage on some vessel. Even the Tuatha de Danann did not have need of dominion over the sea, for we had commune with Mananan, Mac Lir who rules our sea but as the Gods withdraw, we have need of other means to rule the waters and your father has developed a network of trade that will afford us the access, over water to these far lands."

"And what now of my family? Are they to be forever plagued by this dark energy? My wife seems to be repulsed by me and keep kind words only for my cousin and our children. We have, of late, known each other only in the sacred rites, as was our duty. How am I to hold the fellowship of a kingdom and strength of a king when I cannot even raise the love of my own wife?"

"Laoghaire, the doubt you experience in your heart and mind now is what I suspect your wife feels also. Your thoughts keep you from going to her and being honest with her and so you both continue to live in fear of loss or fear of doubts you carry. Like a festering wound, you will both let your love die of infection when all that is needed is for you to open the wound and clean it out. Go to her and speak with her the truth of what you question about her in your heart. Debride the wound. Tell her the truth and accept nothing less from her. Painful it may be but it will be the only way to find one another and continue with your lives together. Do not allow this infection to kill a good and wholesome love for the lack of talking to each other! For then the magic will have met its mark and killed all that you love anyway. Waste not any more time in this my son. Go now and speak the truth to your wife so that you may heal your hearts and gain strength in living out your destiny."

Laoghaire felt the first stirring of hope in his sluggish heart and his confused mind. The idea that his marriage was dead and his wife had no love for him had created a covering of sadness around him that had begun to harden into a shell of bitterness and disappointment. Without realizing it, he allowed himself to surrender to defeat without a fight.

"You are right Lady! I have, without even being aware, let this heaviness live in my heart uninvited. What stealth it has to steal into the foundation of my being without question. I thank you Lady Faidhe for your keen perception and honest words to wake me from this poisonous slumber! I must go." Laoghaire abruptly turned to leave the receiving room.

Faidhe watched him go and was satisfied as she saw the aura vigorously pulsating around him, once again and the figh vines tattooed upon him all but came to life as they twisted and twined about his well-structured limbs. She was, for the moment, content and followed Laoghaire in search of her daughters and grandchildren.

———

"So Laoghaire took the throne and you went with Lon Dubh, Iarann and Faidhe on the boat? Where did they go to?" Nora pressed as we cleaned the dishes from breakfast. "Did Laoghaire and Colm settle their differences? What happened with Gara and Triag? Did they cause any more trouble?"

Finny threw up his hands as if to protect him from the barrage of questions. "Now, ye've told me that I've a way fer tellin' me stories and I'll thank ye te let me get around te things in me own order. Let's us finish wiping off here and get te the sittin' room te continue." He said as he dried the cast iron pan Cath had just washed and handed it to Bridey to return to the hook on the wall. I washed and wiped the kitchen table and replaced the salt and pepper to the small shelf over the stove. Bridey surveyed the kitchen one last time before she took off her apron and returned it to the hook on the back of the kitchen door.

"It'll be short time again, and we'll be making ready for lunch! Are ye ever planning te sleep this day?" Bridey asked.

I looked at the ancient plastic clock whirring on the wall in Cath's kitchen, aged yellow by years of kitchen cooking and it told me that once again, we'd been caught in that weird time misstep that allowed hours to fly by like only minutes.

"Oh. She's right! I said, amazed that it was almost noon. We've been up all night and all morning. Why am I not falling down, or asleep on my feet?"

"Yeah." Nora added. "I'm not ready to sleep yet either. Are you guys up for more of the story; or do you want to sleep and come back to it later?"

"I've been overdue te open the store." Cath announced. "I think I'll go down for a while and see if there's need te open the doors. Likely, I'll be back shortly, for if I have other pressing business, it's typical that I'd have a slow day at the cash register. I create me own reality, ye know!" He said with a wink and headed for the front door leading down the stairs to his shop as the rest of us settled in his living room to continue the story.

38

Unions, Olds and New

Triag had slipped away from the rooms he and his grandmother were assigned within the strange stone house. He went to have a look around to see what he could divine and report back to his aunt. And ever he kept an eye for an opportunity to catch Morgan alone without the troublesome company of her brother. There was no sign of Morgan but he thought it a stroke of luck when he found himself in the receiving room, secretly privy to the conversation Faidhe and Laoghaire were having regarding the man's fearful heart, but even better, he found knowledge of the Power behind that fear and it came from his father!

Triag was careful this time not to be caught in his spying. He had learned well at his aunt's instruction how to veil his mind from being noticed as he listened. Information he divined as he hid behind a stand of large urns was that the witch, Faidhe had killed his father for his part in trying to best Laoghaire in the challenge with the bull. It was not an affront to Triag to learn that his father was dead; rather, it was a wound to him, he told himself, that such a personal attack on his family had gone unavenged. This exchange between the old and the new Keepers allowed Triag to justify the growing adolescent plan in his mind to kill Macha in some foul way that would shame him prior to allowing him to die and then taking Morgan as some kind of a wedded slave to his whims.

The boy did not realize that the plans he plotted grew in him like an infection. He did not recognize that these ideas and change in his recent behavior were not his own thoughts but echoes of his father's plans of assault on Laoghaire's family. He did not understand that the corrosive nature of the magic unleashed by his father had begun to utilize the blood bond between his father and himself, and would direct his own actions until it had been sated and satisfied. He was not the only puppet over which this evil and twisted magic held sway.

Triag waited until the two elders left the hall and near vibrated with glee at the news he brought to his aunt. *"Hear me aunt. Can you speak plain?"*

When she caught the loud communication, Nemain was toying with one of the young serving boys in her mother's huts where she resided once again. She abruptly ordered the boy out. "Leave me." The bewildered boy began to dress, relieved that he'd escape her clutches at least for now, when Nemain spat at him, "Go I say! Take leave and tend to your robes elsewhere and await my summons. Out!"

"*I am here nephew.*" Nemain called back in her mind as she settled back on the plush furs she had tossed about her sleeping palette. Idly playing with her nipples as she lounged. "*How goes the travel? Have you news?*"

Nemain's eyes grew wide as she received the information Triag sent to her. Reflecting on the news, she had suspected that Briciu was dead and had, in fact, received garbled transmissions from him that were similar in some ways to those she received from others who had passed to the Underworld but they were different as well. These communications came in a confused fashion along with sounds similar to animals in a frenzy of sorts, sounding much like a sheep or a pig being lead to slaughtering. She was not able to ask questions of Briciu or rather, there were no answers to her questions. But when she lived in her brother's huts she had grown accustomed to his confusing messages and assumed he was dead, but the news that Faidhe had killed him was shocking and could be quite useful indeed.

"What else?"

"The old woman of the Council, Craiche is dead as well."

"*Who Killed her?*" Nemain asked, never considering old age as a factor in the woman's death. She formulated suspicions of a takeover, wondering what role her mother played in all this and speculated as to how it might benefit and further her own plans.

"*I know not, but it was said that she died in 'giving a gift of love and magic.'*"

Nemain sat up at hearing this. *A gift of magic? If that is possible, then it may be possible to forcibly transfer magical abilities as well.* She put that thought aside to think about later. "*Nephew, what comes of this trip Laoghaire makes to the eastern shore? Know you yet if this is truly a permanent move? Know you yet, his plans for you and my mother? Will she be allowed to return home?*"

"*I know that Laoghaire plans not to return to our lands. He is to take claim of the throne here, but his plan is to rule all the land, including ours once he has taken seat of power here. Something Faidhe said about claiming kingship through the Stone of Fal and the Sword of Nuada shall give him right to make such claims without challenge. I have seen the Stone here as we entered Dun Laoghaire this very day.*"

"*Ah, so it is true. We have seen that the Stone does have a voice as the legend says. And you say it will speak again. So Faidhe shows herself as enacting a plan that will give to her hand power over all the lands through this one who might have lineage to claim it?*"

"*Not so, aunt. She has plans of taking to the sea to birth her child on shores elsewhere. She plans, as far as has been spoken, to leave these shores in short time and to take those she traveled with across this land over the sea as well.*"

"Then she is to leave the reign and rule of this land to Laoghaire? Is my mother an honored guest in all this or is she traveling in protest?"

I know she has not been treated with any high regard. As for myself, I am left to my own idles. I am allowed to wander and keep conversation with the Calf-herder's children. A momentary spark flared in Triag's loins at the thought of Morgan and Nemain caught the reaction.

"Ah nephew, have you interest in making yourself a royal connection?"

"In much the same way you connect with your servant boys, aunt." He blazed at her with a flame of childish jealousy.

"Oh nephew...Triag, these boys are but distractions until you come back to me. They are but tools to keep me able while I await your return. Until then, keep you close to the Keeper Faidhe and watch for any sign of magic she performs. For we need to know what she plans and how she goes about achieving it. You must go unnoticed and keep me informed. Perhaps, we can find out how to make use of the possibility of a gift of magic to our benefit." By this time, the two were calculating how they might usurp magic and Power to be had in these changing times. Each shared what they chose with the other, if it would serve them to do so and both kept valuable nuggets of information for themselves. They both fiddled with their growing excitement over possibilities and shared a moment of mutual physical gratification as they contributed images of their fantasies of dominance with one another. *"You know nephew, Gara may still prove useful to us, but I can't help but think on how many benefits may befall us if some unfortunate accident should occur and she were not able to return here to reclaim her position and titles..."*

Now that his excitement had been sated, he had no further desire to be in contact with Nemain. *"I must go now. I will reach you with news."* He told his aunt and closed his mind to her as he went about rearranging his clothes. Triag was unsure as to the sincerity of Nemain's suggestions but they had both enjoyed the images of a fallen Gara during their mental tryst and experienced intensified excitement at the end of the communication. What he did know was the objectionable relationship he had with his aunt gave him arousal and shame at the same time. He mused that there seemed to be something at work when the two combined their energies to bring about such behavior, as he had never even considered such activities with anyone before. He knew he enjoyed the sensations and the physical pleasure but he wasn't at all certain that he liked what was happening to him. His mind turned once again to Morgan.

———

Because Fion was half Elf, he was fleet of foot and could travel through crowds all but unseen. He had abandoned the rooms within the stone walls for inspection of the village and was able to travel among the crowds as an unnoticed child for the most part. He took in the great Stone with the jeweled Sword hilt atop it that had been placed in the village center. By the repairs in the fencing, he surmised that someone or something had recently crashed the great fence to splinters to allow the Stone to be placed there, for the earth and grass around the monolith had been greatly disturbed.

Fion liked not the smell of crowds and people. He felt trapped within the fences for there was little moving air and few trees within the village. He longed for the woods but made sure he learned all he could about this way of living. Never in all his life had he imagined so many people and so few trees in one place. He walked idly along, telling his brother Cath about all he had seen and learned. Fion told him about the other party from the northwest and the mighty King Laoghaire and his murdered parents. He gave his brother images of Lon Dubh's sister who, too, is beautiful but has long, golden hair and eyes as blue as the ocean! *So much to see brother! Share what you will when you see our sister.*

In that moment, Fion caught a glimpse of that familiar mind filled with what felt like to him, worms: slimy and writhing. Immediately, he closed his mind as not to be discovered by the other but as he felt his way around the village for the source of the flow of thoughts he detected, he was lead back to the stone walls in which his new family was housed. Fion crept up to the window space and peered into a great room. The room appeared empty, but when he carefully let his mind feel around he traced the energy to the boy hiding behind an array of large empty urns used for water or possibly wine for ceremonies or festivals judging by the large size. Fion dared not seek out the boy's thought for fear he'd be detected but as he watched, the Elf saw the boy engaged in upending his clothing to reveal his manhood. Fion turned to leave and spare embarrassment for them both when he once again caught a wave of what the boy was thinking. Fion stopped to listen with his mind and realized that the boy, so engaged in his excitement had lowered his defenses against someone like himself being able to listen. Fion caught sight and sound of the images and conversation the boy was having and was repulsed but forced himself to stay until the end for he felt the danger in this one and the other with whom he communicated and knew the information might be important.

When the boy had reached the end of his communication and made to rearrange his tunic, Fion slipped away unnoticed but feeling soiled by what he'd seen and heard He sought out the rooms within the walls to wash and seek counsel.

———

Dha' Teanga paid a visit to Gara after she had been settled in the smaller stone house. He gave the woman ample time to wash and dress and stew in her discontentment at the treatment she had received in being tossed out of the main house and being severed from wealth of foodstuffs and servants she had come so close to commanding in her brief stay at the royal's quarters.

"I may be able to help you to sow the seeds of dissension among your people regarding Laoghaire's fitness to take the throne here." Gara speculated as she furiously tried to calculate what this man really wanted, what use he might be to her, and whether she would be better off not crossing the Power of Faidhe, Craiche and Laoghaire, not to mention that rabid wife of Laoghaire's but always the businesswoman she explored any opportunity that might pay her dividends.

"But tell me Dha' Teanga, why would I want to put about such rumors of the rightful heir to the throne here? It seems the people here have seen enough pain and turmoil since the slaying of their leaders. What benefit or purpose would it serve to prolong their confusion? Would it not be best to mend the suspicion and chaos with the naming of a new king who is the claimed successor to the throne?"

"You have been insulted and mistreated. Have you not? I saw to your comfort in the house of honor and you were disgraced by being shuffled here as an unwanted guest. I see that these people seek only their own gain and comfort and cast you out with jealous fear. You obviously hold power. And unless I miss my mark, you are a woman who keeps valuable information for times such as these." Dha' Teanga raised his eyebrow as he handed Gara a goblet of fine wine imported from the lands to the south. "I believe you would want what is best for all, including yourself, dear lady. Often, people need stability in established leaders." He continued warming to his own voice now. "Having mastered trade through the ocean here, I have negotiated fineries that even the old King himself never dreamed of. I have spent years growing our trades and bringing riches through many other avenues beyond the trade of cattle." He said this last with a sneer as if the idea of cattle herding was distasteful to him. "Croi Laoghaire is but a boy when it comes to the knowing of such things. True, he was like a younger brother to me as we were raised in the same manner and often, the old King Laoghaire would reveal his wish to me that he would have liked his son to be more like me. What better endorsement for me to maintain the position of steward to the throne? I ask you, these many seasons past, where was Croi Laoghaire in these important affairs?" Dha' Teanga began to shake his head. "No. No. It cannot be arranged. He has not the experience or knowledge for such things. I know and love my people. They trust me. It will be better for all here if Laoghaire should light the pyres this night." He poked an emphatic finger toward Gara to make his point. "A task I should tend myself, for the old King Laoghaire was a father to me but for the blood of my birth. He should light the pyres and take his family back to those he gave his loyalty to long ago. Tell me, lovely woman." He devoted full attention to her now. "You have much in the ways of his history, and knowledge of what I might use to lay my claim this night." Now Dha' Teanga took the goblet from Gara's hand to place it away and stepped closer to her so that he could caress her cheek and shoulder with the back of his hand. "We are people of business and intrigue, you and I. We make the best type of partnerships, those without entanglements that do not suit us." His hand moved from Gara's shoulder to her neck and deftly untied the lacing there, to slide his fingers inside her tunic to her breast. Reaching his mouth closer to her ear, he whispered, "Help rid me of this familial inconvenience and you will be well rewarded with wealth and status. For it seems you have been brought here in disgrace and will not be able to return to your former station."

Gara stiffened at this for that very thought had plagued her for much of the journey here. She did not know if she would be permitted to return to her home particularly now that she was aware of Faidhe's presence here in these territories. She then reassured herself that an alternative plan never hurt in situations such as these but she would wait to see which way the winds blow before making any solid commitment in any direction.

Gara smiled and allowed Dha' Teanga's arms to engulf her and his hands to probe where they may. It had been a great long trip, and she thought she well deserved what pleasure she could procure for herself especially after being so rudely rejected by that great oaf Cuan. It seemed, once they set upon the road, he had lost all interest in the possibility of lying with her. Her pride had been wounded and her body was hungry. She could scarce control the greed in her fingers as she relieved Dha' Teanga of his skins and linens.

"Greetings, Lon Dubh. I am pleased you have arrived in these parts safe and unharmed. I have been told that you came through the lands of the Duibhe unscathed and have chosen one among them to travel with you on your journey." Laoghaire anxiously looked about the room in which he and his wife would be housed. "Forgive my intrusion, sister, but I have need of my wife. I respect that you have not long to visit and linger here with Colm, but I have much to attend this day and must consult with her now. I will not take long, but for this now, will you allow us a moment of privacy?"

"Of course, Laoghaire, I will take my leave. It is truly a pleasure to see you here safe as well, brother." As Lon Dubh embraced her sister, Laoghaire noticed the desperate way in which Colm clung to the other woman and he noticed for the first time that Colm's face was red from crying. A bolt of fear shot through his solar plexus once again, immediately followed by guilt that he was somehow to blame for his love's unhappiness.

As soon as Lon Dubh exited the room, Laoghaire pulled the heavy skins down over the entrance. Colm was put in mind of how his cousin had done the same thing a short time ago and how alike the two men are. She knew her attraction to Cuan was only a pale imitation of her love for her husband, but still, the attraction brought with it guilt and shame. In her mind, by her dreams and in her heart, she knew she was untrue to her marriage. How could it be seen as anything else to have sullied the rites with such dreams of one so foul as Briciu, the very man who would have seen her husband defeated and dead! Colm cast her eyes downward and heavily took a seat on a wooden bench across the room by the window.

Laoghaire shored himself up by repeating in his mind Faidhe's explanation of his feelings of fear. He steeled himself from the overwhelming sadness he felt upon seeing his wife so repulsed by him now. Clearing his throat Laoghaire began.

"Colm, my wife, my love." The expression on her face was pain and his heart clenched, knowing with certainty that she no longer loved him and bore him much resentment at taking her from her home and seemingly being an oath breaker. Laoghaire thought: *She could not love a man like that. Colm is too pure. Worse, she had lost respect for me as a man and as a husband because she thinks me to be such a man.*

Laoghaire shook off the thoughts that had plagued him all the while they traveled and renewed his effort to fight his way out of this ooze of doubt and fear.

"Colm!" He spoke more sternly than he intended with the struggle to be loosed from his insecurities. She looked at him with such fear and dread in her own eyes that Laoghaire couldn't bear the thought that she should fear him. *It must be worse than I'd thought. Not only has she lost her love and respect for me, she is fearful of the man I've become.*

"Colm." He began again, softening his tone. "I come to you an empty man with only sorrow in my heart. For all these days past, over the last moon and longer, we have been strangers but for our duty to the Circle upon the night we took leave of our home. In truth, that was the last moment of joy I have felt in all this while. It is irreverent, I know, to have taken my own pleasure in the moment we assumed the roles of the Goddess and the God, and I fear I add to the things you may collect to use as evidence that I am one unworthy to be entrusted with your heart but there is naught I can offer you now but the truth.

Colm was silent so Laoghaire pressed on. "When we lay as God and Goddess and the threshing house of our home, I renewed my love and commitment to you. I saw that moment of sharing and proliferation of life for our clans as a renewal of life in our hearts for each other. But since that time, you have grown more distant from me than ever. I understand that in the moment the spirits came into us, you saw me as the God, but I held hope that you saw me and knew me as your husband as well as the God. Speak to me Colm of our future and whether you will remain here to be my queen. Or have I come to you too late and another resides in your heart? I made an oath to be the Keeper and to protect the Circle at all costs, but I am burdened with the greatest sorrow I have had to bear to understand that in keeping my oath, I have neglected you so that you might love another. But know you this, my love; I am not an oath breaker. I come to my homelands at the behest of my oath to the Goddess and the God. It is in the keeping of the Stone and my charge of the Sword that we have been brought here. But what is the Sword without the Shield? Bearing only the Sword, I am but a battle slash away from death without you at my side. Colm, you are my Shield, my other half. You are the very breath in my chest. Without you, I am but half a man. And for this I bear the shame of offering you myself as only a portion of what you deserve, but it is all I have; that and my hope that it will be enough. If it is not, I will release you from your vows and you are free to return to the breast of your family. But with all my heart, my desire is that you will stay with me and rebuild our love. Wife, will you come willingly to these lands and be my queen? Will you help me to know how we may erase the divide between us so we may once again come together as we once were? Please tell me it is still possible to make this so."

By this time, Laoghaire had slipped down on his knees in front of where Colm sat. He longed for her touch and her forgiveness. He took her hands in his and looked up into her eyes searching through his tears for any hint that she would see him as her husband again.

Colm removed her hands from Laoghaire's and his heart shriveled.

"Laoghaire, do not look at me so, for I cannot bear the pain in your eyes, and the sorrow that lives there before even I have told you of my betrayals." At this, Laoghaire seemed no longer able to sustain his weight on his knees. He turned and sat on the floor, facing away from Colm while his heart broke. "No, do not ignore me. You think you love me but you cannot. When I tell you of what part I have played in harlotries, you will no longer want me here among your clans."

"How have I hurt you so that you tear my heart from me with your words?"

"It is not my desire to hurt you Laoghaire. Would that I could die this day and spare you the insult of duty to one who so clearly does not deserve your heart. But my children keep me from alleviating your pain in such a way."

"I speak to you of love and you speak of duty. Is there truly nothing left of us? Tell me all so that I might find solace in understanding, at least."

There was a lengthy silence from Colm and Laoghaire understood this to mean she felt no compassion for him to grant him this request that she reveal to him how she lost her love and respect for him.

"Please Colm, I must know."

"It is cruelty to have to reveal myself to you so. But I will if it will make my leaving the easier for you." Laoghaire's head bowed in defeat. "I have been most unworthy of your love. Upon taking oath to the Circle, I should have been understanding of your absence and your strength of oath to your duty but instead, I whined like a babe at my loneliness and took to the village at every opportunity. I abandoned you to take on your duties alone and in that time, found friendship with your cousin Cuan. I returned often to our huts to take counsel with him and speak with him. I found myself longing for our old life, selfishly making my own comfort at the hearth there in the village and leaving you to the Hill on your own."

All the color had drained from Laoghaire's face and although she could not see it, she could tell by his shoulders and posture he was sunken and defeated at this last news.

"So you have found love with Cuan, then? Are there any who know you have shared the fires with him?"

"What? No! Not like that. No Laoghaire. He spoke comfort to me that you would return to me. I longed to hear him speak of your commitment to your duty and that your honor held you to your oath but that you would come to me when all had been settled. I needed reassurance and could not come to you for such. It was my own selfishness that brought me there to Cuan. Why did I not stand with you through your duties on the Hill? Why did I not see the import of what was taking place rather than feel only misery that you had abandoned me. I felt unworthy of your love right from the beginning for it was on the morning we were to take to the Hill that I betrayed you and so never feeling worthy from the beginning, I sought out other places to mend my wounded heart and shame. I could not speak to you of my disloyalty when you had so many other burdens of the Hill to attend."

"So there is another? Not Cuan?"

She was silent again.

"Who is this one with whom you left our bed to engage? It is hard for me to fathom that you would have been abed with me so completely just the night before we took to the Hill and that very morning you lay with another?"

"No my love! Never...never willingly." At this, Laoghaire rose to his knees once again and turned to face Colm.

"You were ravaged? Who in the tuath would even think such a thing? Why would you not tell me of such an abomination? For the first time, Colm reached out to touch her husband's face. She longed so to take away his pain and hesitated to say more but she honored his plea to tell all.

"No, I was not ravaged. At least not in the way you speak of. In truth, at first, what I thought was a dream has been so repeated in my head, I know not whether I have convinced myself that it was a dream only to alleviate my guilt. I have neither reason nor excuse for what I did, other than I must be the most unworthy woman in the tribe to have taken duties on the Hill. Remember you the lust we took to our bed for the time after the challenge? Laoghaire nodded. "It was this hunger I awoke with on that morning we were to move to the Hill. For what I remember is that I awoke in our hut and wanting for more and allowed myself to be taken as an animal to the rut without reverence to the Gods but for the pure fever of the fire. It must have been the fever for otherwise I have no understanding of why I would find myself in such exposure and in such a beastly way with one so foul and repugnant as..." She swallowed and lowered her eyes once again. Then barely audible she uttered the name "Briciu."

"What's this?" Laoghaire roared. Colm shrunk from his wrath and he saw it. "Colm." He got his voice under control. "My wife. Dreams sometimes come unbidden and make no sense when they do."

"But I don't even know anymore if it is a dream of what I speak or my mind tricks me to thinking so only to ease my guilt. But whether in thought or in deed, the affront has been committed. I am not worthy of your love or to be your queen and I am much less worthy to take reign of the Shield."

"Hear me now." Laoghaire took Colm by the shoulders and shook her gently to snap her attention to him. "Briciu is dead." She looked at her husband uncomprehending. He was dead on the very night of the challenge. Ask me not how he died but know that you could not have done what you say, for the man was not living at that time."

"But I felt him. I smelled him. I had need to wash him from me so foul. I could scarce look at you from that day on for my repulsion at what I had done sickened me."

"Wife, if you had been touched by this man on the day you say, it was a part of his ill magic that tainted you. Faidhe says it had tainted all of us in some way. As our faith in our ways begins to take on doubt or confidence in our love begins to crumble, doubt creeps into our hearts and causes sickness there. For my part, I know I have been sick in my heart with grief, sure that you held no love for me and that you were justified for my neglect drove you away. Is this true or not?"

"Oh my husband, my love, my heart has been drowned in my guilt over such unfaithfulness that I was convinced you knew of my betrayal and would release me at the earliest moment you could be shut of me. In fact, it has been so long since we took to the flames, I thought it likely that you'd take others to compensate for my neglect. Forgive me, but I could not bear to come to our marriage bed knowing I had soiled the purity of our vows. My one moment of joy was in the celebration of the rites with you for I too was soothed in the moment we came together as God and Goddess. That moment was more pleasurable, powerful and potent than any feeling of lust or desire. The union with you has been the only real thing to give my mind hope and clarity from the cloud of the torture of the other moment."

"This is not unfaithfulness. The man is dead. I believe you have had magic visited upon you to plant seeds of doubt." Colm winced at the analogy. "This menacing magic works on us to magnify our greatest fears. It sneaks into our hearts and minds as a poisonous vapor to break down with fear all that is good. And that is the hideous strength of this thing; whether what we fear is true or no, just the thought that it might be, grows until in our minds, it is so. We will consult Faidhe for guidance."

He saw the look of fear return to Colm's face and responded. "You have no shame to bear for having this visited on you. Your mother will know better of such things and what might be done to relieve your discomfort so you can be shut of the foul memory. We will arrange for such a meeting this very night after the ceremony for my parents. But there is one more thing you must know so we will have no hindrances between us. I have told no one, though there are those who know of it. I have kept it to my heart for there is guilt I carry over the gift I have been given and what it has cost another."

"What is it, husband. Let us speak all now so that we leave no shadows behind which further doubts can lurk. My heart could sing with the joy I feel in the knowledge that you can love me still."

"Remember you the time upon arriving at the Hill you had desire to speak to Craiche?"

"I do! It was to take her counsel over this very matter we have discussed."

"She could not be found, not because she was tending Council affairs over the great changes as many speculated, it was because she gave of her life and magic on the day I took the Hill." Colm appeared uncomprehending. "She died that morning in a great ritual of love so that I could take the Hill with all her knowledge and skills for magic. Her abilities are my abilities now. Her knowledge is my knowledge. It was such a gift of love and so intimate in the knowing of another so completely, I owe Craiche a great debt. I must follow through with my duties and oath with full devotion so her sacrifice is not wasted."

"I have been so foolish." Colm said as she brushed away the single tear that fell for the old woman. I thought you left the Hill for selfish reasons but now, as I begin to see clearly again, I know this is not so. You have never been anything but honorable and I have done you damage in doubting you so. Let us plan for this night, husband and rejoice in that we have found our way back to each other. Swear to me we will never let this fear grow between us again."

"On my oath." He said, and planted a sweet, lasting kiss on her mouth that stirred her, body and soul, and made her believe.

———

"Mother?" Lon Dubh tentatively approached her mother. "I have been thinking. Now that we are on this road in service of the Goddess, you must bring your babe to swaddling in lands afar, and Iarann has the task of recording these times in the great Cauldron's panels, and Fion is to take the tale to assure its future for generations to come, but I am wondering what my task is in all this. I know I am here for a purpose, but I have no clarity in that purpose. Am I to give of my virginity to the Goddess? Will I claim position as Priestess at the next festival and give to the rites of myself or have the rites been under revision since these great changes so that there are no more fertility rites celebrated by the priestesses as you had served? Will I bring a child to the Circle?"

Faidhe knew the time would come when Lon Dubh would begin to wonder at the whole truth of her task. She vowed her life to service of the Goddess but now was not the time to reveal the path her life of service would lead down. Faidhe thought it best that her daughter be well on their journey before her future should be revealed. "Remember you the first meeting we had daughter?"

"Of course."

"Remember you the first lesson in the ways of service to the Goddess?"

Lon Dubh knew where this was going and was chastened. "Yes Mother." She said with an exaggerated sigh. "Patience, patience, patience." She smiled a sheepish grin at the older woman and Faidhe knew that Lon Dubh would let it go for now but there would come a time when she must know what will be her destiny. Faidhe did not look forward to those times. She briskly changed the subject.

"Let us arrange our possessions in the rooms provided. You and I will share this room and give Fion and Iarann the quarters with the great hearth. Fion can stay here with us should Iarann need to work in privacy, but it may be that the boy will prefer to sleep under the stars. Although he is half Duibhe, I believe he takes mostly from the Elf in him and does not enjoy being within walls."

Again, Lon Dubh seemed a bit perturbed at this but saw the wisdom in that the man would make better use of a large hot fire to tend his task in working the Cauldron. But she was finding it harder to ignore the fact that such close proximity to the man for such a prolonged time had awakened in her the desire to take to the fires. She wasn't sure if it was the man or the proximity that has awakened her, or if it was her part in the fertility festival of late that brought her to this state but no matter, for now, she would just do her duty and let things unfold as they may.

"Yes. That will do." She answered and swiftly changed the topic. "Have you ever seen such walls as these Mother? Built of stone with great square rooms? I marveled at the first rooms we were housed in, large and rounded with the space for the hearth in the middle, but these rooms are so elaborate with stone floors, window space and multiple hearths, so many rooms, as well!"

"Yes, daughter, I have seen stone structures such as the first place we were housed in my meager travels but as you say, a fine stone building such as this, I have never seen. I know that Laoghaire's father had a reputation for great trade. Perhaps the idea for these structures came from lands afar. If it is one thing that is fruitful here on our isle, it is the multitude of stones She bears. It is wisdom to use that which is plentiful, is it not?"

I feel protected within these walls through which no sword or arrow could pierce. How then, could two such well-loved and protected people as the leaders of these lands be taken so completely and unawares?"

"Neither stone walls, death, nor time itself can offer protection from the unrelenting energy that has been set upon this clan. You will do well to remember this.

And though we deterred it from its initial goal, it sought its mark in this house and as it regains strength, it will continue to seek out and destroy for that is the consuming evil that had been created. I can all but smell the stench of its residue here."

"Mother, I think we must make of our herbs what we can to cleanse this place of this and make light the air again. It feels to me that there is a weightiness to the people here that goes beyond the sorrow over their loss of leadership. I begin to catch the scent of which you speak."

"You are right Lon Dubh, and perceptive to recognize the menacing signature. Let us now make use of our herbs to cleanse these chambers and to make packets for burning at the ceremony this night to alleviate these folk of their discomforted hearts and anxious minds for it sits upon them like the scent of smoke long after the fire had done its damage but makes the fear of another flame live in the heart so that normalcy of everyday life is not possible."

As the road-weary troupes settled into the village, all in the clans prepared for the lighting of the pyres and looked to what might be the future of their Tuath with the unexpected return of their king's son and the appearance of the mysterious Stone that had so violently breached their sanctuary so soon after the murder of their royals. All within such a short span, these were forceful and frightening times for the Tuatha Laoghaire.

39

From the Ashes Arises a King

It seemed all about the stone house, there was renewed energy for the making of cakes and loaves, lighting the hearths and general excitement at having new clan members about whom to gossip and speculate. Willa took to her good fortune at being kept on to serve Colm as a personal chambermaid with a sense of fierce protection of her charge and sought to please Colm by anticipating her every need. Water boys were sent to the river to fill many a great urn to have fresh water at the ready. A fresh drum of wine was ordered brought from the cool underground stores to pour for the royal family. Traditional drink made of apples was brought out for the funeral ceremonies in preparation for the pouring of drink to the ground for those lost to the living and in petition for regeneration of the life-fire within them. By this time the apple drink had fermented nicely and would loosen tongues to provide even more spirited song and storytelling of the fallen King and Queen Laoghaire after the burning.

The sadness over the death of the beloved couple and the fear that gripped the clans following that bloody night had spread throughout the village so that people walked silently with downcast eyes and children kept close to hearth. Men and women found less joy in their day-to-day living and even the elders of the clan were less inclined to stop and speak with a clan member or to idle away a work task with pleasant conversation. It was as if the village had witnessed the horrible display of their leaders and had turned inward with fear. Yet, since the arrival of the new parties, the clans looked with eagerness to witness the rise of the new king and whether Dha' Teanga would stand by this one who hadn't lived in these lands for ten seasons or more. The clan began to feel hopeful again. This new blood infused into the clans came with a breath of air and tongues were wagging again as people prepared for the lighting of the funeral pyres, at last putting this awful thing behind them and looking with renewed anticipation toward the future.

Faidhe and Lon Dubh had sent for Colm and had been duly chastened by the unwitting Willa.

"One does not send for the queen." One withering look from Faidhe and Willa amended her announcement. "But I will tell her of your request and she will come if she so desires."

Working to define the line between protecting her charge and knowing her place, Willa's reddened face was obvious as she left the room trying without much success to keep her chin up under Faidhe's steady glare.

When Colm came to Faidhe and Lon Dubh's room, she ran to her mother with tears of joy. Burying her face in the other woman's shoulder.

"I have so missed you and strange it has been for I had only those three nights to know you as my mother but I have felt a great loss at not having the benefit of your wisdom during these upsetting times. And to have just now found that I could have spoken with you all along, I lament the time I have wasted in not taking your counsel sooner so that I might have avoided wallowing in my own self-pity instead of taking on my responsibilities as a woman of the Stones should have done."

"We have all been keeping step to the rhythm of one who takes pleasure in confusion and mayhem, daughter. You are not the only one to have been caught in the snare of this damnable spell. We have all been slowed in our desire to make haste as though our feet are in the confines and thickness of a bog." At the mention of the bog, Faidhe shuddered a bit and realized the relevance of her words and pushed on.

"Come, it is for this reason we call you Colm. Lon Dubh and I have prepared leaflet packets full of cleansing herbs to rid these walls of the unseen mark of this evil that lurks. We three will take part in releasing the purifying qualities of these herbs throughout these walls so that we may rest easy here. This night at the funeral services, we will add to the ceremony by burning more than the flesh of Laoghaire's mother and father. We will put to rest the underlying dread that has so completely captured this village. Take you these packets to cleanse your own rooms by burning the herbs there. Make sure the scent and smoke finds its way into all the corners. Have your girl bring these to the kitchen and servants quarters and do the same there." Faidhe handed Colm several packets of dried leaves filled with the cleansing herbs.

"Have a care to give excuse only that the scent is pleasurable to you and not betray the true purpose of the sachet. We'd not have any fear of magic hinder us in these parts for the knowledge and use of magic is not as prevalent here as in our home. There are some who have great mistrust for knowledge of the magic and herbs."

Colm took the herbs and tucked the packets into her tunic.

"Shall we take a moment of thanks at our reunion and offer our thanks to Craiche for her sacrifice?"

"Sacrifice?" A deep voice from the doorway startled the women. Iarann stood in the opening, dwarfing the entrance to the room. His presence outdoors was something to behold but the enormity of his size was greatly magnified when he was observed indoors. The smithy bent to avoid hitting his head on the rounded door opening as he entered the room. He carried his saddlebags of heavy tools and equipment over his shoulder as if they weighed nothing at all. The only sign that could be marked of the great weight he carried was the display of the large man's muscles as he moved with the surprising fluidity and grace of one half his size.

"What of Craiche? What sacrifice has she made in all this? Is she not here with your party?"

He flung the bags to the floor with a clang of metal and stood bare-chested looking both savage and handsome; his gentle eyes and concerned expression were an attractive contrast to the brute strength his physique revealed.

Lon Dubh dragged her eyes away from the spectacle of his attraction and looked to Colm with an expectant expression on her face, as did Iarann. It was obvious now to Colm that Lon Dubh and Iarann did not know of Craiche's death but it was equally obvious by her mother's expression that the news was not a shock to Faidhe.

Colm haltingly started, not knowing how much she could say without revealing so much that Laoghaire would lose comfort for people knowing what had passed between him and Craiche.

"The old one has gone under and will no longer travel with us in this world. She gave of her life willingly to this cause and crossed over neither by violence nor her own hand. It was her aim to give of her life so that her wisdom could remain and be of use through one with youth and position. Before she left this world, Craiche made certain that Laoghaire would have benefit of her vast knowledge."

Faidhe added, "Our sister was honored in a ceremony of the great Circle after offering her lessons of magic and history to the new Keeper and king. The out-pouring of love and giving of her knowledge drained the old one so that she had completed her time here. We love her and honor her contribution and sacrifice. It will not detract from the services this night if we are to remember our sister and her strength of character on this night of remembering those we have sent to the Otherworld in the shadow of these changes."

They all stood for a moment reflecting how quickly and drastically all of their lives had changed in a very short time. It was not unrecognized how much they had all come to love one another despite being relative strangers until just lately. They felt honest sadness at the passing of their friend.

Lon Dubh snapped out of the reverie first and slipped her hand into Iarann's much larger mitt, callused with years of heat and hammering.

"We have prepared your room and have insured that you have a great hearth and plenty of fuel in case you are called to work your craft. Come, let me show you." Iarann hoisted his bags and allowed himself to be led to his chambers as Lon Dubh chattered about the stone walls and the grand structure. Faidhe called after her.

"Daughter. Do not spend overlong with Iarann. We still have cleansing and to preparations to attend."

———

Morgan stepped from stone to stone planting her able feet so she'd not slip and fall into the stream as it danced happily by the children where they played. Outgoing and friendly, she chattered on about the long trek from the northern part of the isle with the cattle as she pushed back the hair from her face and concentrated on her feet. She and her brother had gone exploring as soon as they were able after helping Cuan see to the grazing of the animals.

"So that's how we came here and we're to live here now in our father's lands." She said with finality as though the statement said all to her listener. The older boy watched her intently and scanned the horizon for a sign that anyone else might be about keeping watch on this girl, daughter of Laoghaire. For the moment, it was just she, her brother and himself. After the images he'd seen of this sweet girl being violated so, he could not fathom the disease that must live in the mind of one who could conceive of such things. And her brother, so stoic and silent; his strength could be recognized as could his father's. Fion had appointed himself protector of these two for the time he would spend here in these parts. And he would be sure to arrange for their safety when it came time for him to leave. He smelled the scent of magic about them and knew there must be some protection in place already, but after what he saw and felt from that other boy, he knew caution would not be wasted.

"Come Fion, are you afraid of the water?" Morgan taunted. "Will you not step these stones with me?"

Due to his Elven blood, Fion appeared to be a boy despite his years, but he was part Duibhe as well and it is common knowledge that the Duibhe are none too fond of the water for washing or otherwise. But for Morgan he braved the water and deftly skipped over the stones so quick as to appear to stand in the middle of the stream atop the waters to engage in the girl's game and to get to know these children better.

"Oh Macha did you see? Fion you look as if to fly you are so fast! You must know these parts well; your feet find the stones so easily. You do not have the look of my father's clan. Are you from here? Are we kin to you? Know you our father, Laoghaire?"

Macha broke in. "Morgan so many questions! My ears ring from the sound of your voice. Can you not just listen to the river talking and let our new friend speak of his business when he may?" He chastised his sister but there was no salt in his words. In fact, he envied her ability to be social and make friends for this was not a skill he possessed as his own.

Fion took no offense to the questions. "I have come here from the west with friends. We journey through here and will be on our way soon enough."

"Oh it is all so exciting! So many people to meet. We have ever only been in our village with our own clans." Morgan gushed. "I suppose these are our clans as well but none that we've ever known. I'm sad you will be leaving soon. But this is a port city. My father says people come here from all over to trade and rest as their great boats pass through. Where will you go?"

"Your brother is right, Morgan. You have many questions and that is good for learning about your new home but for now, let us play." He avoided answering questions for Fion didn't know who was listening or who needed to know of his journey or not. For now, he simply wanted to stay close to the children to ensure that they remained safe. He would deliver news of what he saw in the mind of the other boy when the time was he was sure the children were safe. He dazzled Morgan and made her forget any more questions when he showed her back-flips, hands over feet so fleet and sure of foot that she stood with her brother stunned and open-mouthed as they watched. Fion then ran up the side of a tree and flipped into the air to land lightly again on his feet. The three grew to like each other very quickly in an easy friendship.

The remains of Laoghaire's parents were brought up from the cool of the storage cavern dug into the earth where they were held in waiting for the burning ceremony. Their remains had been cleaned, treated with herbs and wrapped in oiled funeral linens in preparation for the fires. The coolness of the underground helped to slow the deterioration of the two and the herbs and scented oils in the linen wraps kept the insects at bay. They had been placed high above the village on pyres built atop the great Hill T'airg. Wood fuel, peat and oil had been placed under the pyres to guarantee a great flame that would be hot enough to consume the two quickly.

There would be celebration this night for the passing of two much loved leaders. Laoghaire had trouble sorting through his emotions for he had the sorrow of missing his parents, the pride of helping them pass to the Otherworld and the joy of knowing his wife loves him still. This coupled with the looming responsibilities he would take on this very evening on the heels of all that has already happened, caused his head to spin. But overall, Laoghaire had joy in his heart for having returned home with his family. He came to his rooms after seeing to the proper displaying of his mother and father and was greeted with the fresh scent of burning herbs. His heart grew light at the sight of Colm tending to their children as she helped them dress in their good linens for the funeral and feasting this night.

Macha was teasing. "Morgan doesn't need washing Mother, she was quite cleaned up after she tried to keep up with our new friend on the stepping stones and fell into the stream!"

"Oh yes! You should have seen him!" Morgan exclaimed! "He had feet like the wind and oh, he is nimble! I did get wet but it was worth it to learn how to fly over the water as he does."

"It seems as you've had a better lesson in swimming!" Macha teased.

"What's this?" Laoghaire involved himself in the conversation. "My little wood nymph is learning to fly?" Both the children ran to Laoghaire, sensing the change in him, they were glad to see an easy smile on his face. He greeted them and asked if they had seen their grandmother and aunt as yet.

"Well, we've time before the ceremonies and I still have to wash and dress. They will be so pleased to see both of you. Find your way to their quarters down the corridor there and have a visit. I must dress and tend to some business with your mother."

It had not gone unnoticed by the children that their parents' relationship had changed and been somewhat cool of late. Now they eyed each other with a gleam at the return of the phrase their father had used when he cared not to reveal to the children that he wished to lay with their mother but wanted them to understand that he desired privacy with her. The children smiled at each other and their eyes grew large as they skipped toward the door to leave Laoghaire and Colm alone. As they stepped through the door, Macha turned and unhooked the skins and allowed them to fall over the opening there.

For the third time that day, the skins had covered the door and Colm came to Laoghaire. Without words they found each other and took a long sweet time in remembering all they had missed of one another. This was not the fury of hot passion but a sensual exploration with all the tenderness that one who sought to please could muster. There were tears and depth of passion known only to those with love in their hearts. There were unspoken sorrows and words of promise and commitment. They shared the union of the Sword and Shield and around them swirled the energies of love, joy and excitement at their reunion all the sweeter for the waiting they had endured. And the magic of the moment solidified their pledge to one another and to their commitment to keep and proliferate the magic of the Stone and the Circle as had been prophesied.

———

At full dark, all the clans gathered and the flames roared. The children and Fion had been given packets of the herbs to distribute throughout the clans with instructions that, in respect and memory of the greatness of the king and queen, all should go and burn these at their own hearths and cook-fires. None had questioned this for in general, the mood of the clan became jubilant and they were inclined to continue the feeling with any excuse for a celebration. Many packets were added to the pyre flames and indeed made all among the ceremony feel hopeful and happy; emotions they had not felt for some time, but until this moment, had not recognized the lack of them.

Lon Dubh brought her whistle to her lips and played a lamentation low, loud and clear. Fion looked up at her and reached into his tunic to bring out his own whistle to join the song and his own lyrical sound. A beautiful girl from the village of about age 17 seasons, stepped up so the light from the fires let shadows dance across her face as she opened her mouth and in an ancient tongue, sang the words of passing in a most clear and sweet voice that carried and drifted over the masses and stirred hearts to attention. At the final low note, the song ended and there was silence but for the crackling of the fire as it worked to consume all there was for it. Off in the distance, not near where any living soul stood, there was a great howl that could be heard as a shrill, inhuman voice keened to inform all the clans of the passing of the royal couple to the Otherworld.

At this the crowd broke into a raucous jabbering for all had heard tell of the keening of the Bain Sidhe but few had heard the actual call until this night. And despite the gooseflesh raised on many arms, there was great relief and joy at the knowledge that the passing of the royals had surely taken place. Those who had brought strings and drum skins began to play while bards of the villages told stories and the songs they'd written of the adventures of the late king and queen. Many onlookers clapped the rhythm and others took to the dance in circle groups. This was not a festival but there was feasting and carrying on by the fires in an affirmation that the living would not waste the joys of life. Out of respect for the dead, they would pour drink on the ground and consume greatly, they would eat with gusto for the dead who could not and they would heatedly couple with the hope that should a life spark in a womb this night, it could be the rebirth of one of those passed so that they never truly are beyond our reaches, but born to enjoy life's treasures once again.

Laoghaire had much to be thankful for this night. He engaged in many a sincere embrace with his clan members, danced and ate mightily and joined in the chorus of many songs. After the passing of half the night, the pyres had burned completely and the ashes from the fire pit along with the remaining bit of bones were taken and cooled in an iron pot. The next day they were to be placed in a specially made box for ritual burial at the great mound site but a short distance from the Hill T'airg. Before the burial, his parents would spend their last night above ground in the comfort of their old sleeping room with their son the King and his wife, the new Queen.

As the villagers returned to the confines of the village hill fort, spirits were high and there were songs circulating about the new King Laoghaire, come now to take the throne. All in the immediate village walked in procession around and behind the two men carrying the iron pot containing the royal remains as they marched back to the gates of the village from the hill. Laoghaire had been so approachable on the funeral hill there were those in the crowd who felt comfortable enough to begin to ask him about a crowning ceremony.

As the procession entered the gates of the hill fort, Dha' Teanga could be seen standing wide legged and arms crossed, next to a large fire lit in the center of the village near to the great Stone that had been planted there some, half-moon past. The spectacle caught Laoghaire's attention and called to mind that Dha' Teanga had not been seen at the funeral ritual. Laoghaire gravitated toward the firelight. As the villagers attempted now to engage him in conversation, Laoghaire looked past them to puzzle out what had caught his attention. All went quiet when Laoghaire walked toward the other man and the crowd followed. As he did, he noticed that there had been guards, armed with bows and spears posted high along the fence. This may have been expected, as the villagers left the encampment for the funeral ritual on the hill, there would be those who stayed behind to protect the village especially in light of the recent death of the long standing ruler in this land, but Laoghaire had an idea that a less traditional reason for these men to be posted. He approached Dha' Teanga, waiting to see what might be said but wanting also to know why the man had committed such an effrontery as to deliberately miss the burning portion of the funeral ritual. As he approached, the other man could be seen giving a nod to the men posted above along the gate walk. This confirmed that Laoghaire was correct in assuming there was more to the armed men than the formality of protecting the empty village. He inwardly chastised himself for not having taken care of the posting of sentry men himself.

"Dha' Teanga." Laoghaire called to the other man. "You have posted armed men. Have you heard word that we are soon to be under attack? Is it your loyalty to the memory of my father and keeping safe his lands that kept you from attending his funeral ceremony? If this is so, I commend you on your diligence for I know you loved him well and would not have missed seeing him to the passing for any reason other than loyalty." Laoghaire said loud enough for most to hear. Keeping diplomacy but letting the other man know that any other reason for posting guards and missing his King's funeral would not be acceptable. At Laoghaire's tone, Cuan and Iarann came to his side, followed by Faidhe, Colm, and Lon Dubh.

Fion stood with the twins but kept them to the side of the group out of harm's way. There he felt the concentrated attention coming from someone and both he and Morgan turned to see the face of Triag, cast with shadows from the fire, where he was standing with his grandmother. It occurred to Fion that the boy and his annoying attention had not been at the funeral rites and from that it could be deduced, that neither had his grandmother been there. He made mental note of the boy's whereabouts and returned his attention to the drama unfolding by the great Stone in the village center.

Croi Laoghaire, son of Ri Laoghaire of the Calf-herder clan, I am Dha' Teanga, son of Crionna of the Calf-herder clan. As steward of these lands and families, I exercise my right as advisor to the late King Ri Laoghaire, to inquire as to your intentions in participation in the affairs of these good people and operations of these lands and ports." The man stood his ground, looking majestic in his stance and was obviously pleased with the sound of his own voice. He awaited an answer to that which was not quite a challenge but called the attention of the clan folk to the pressing situation of who would take the duties of the throne in hand.

"What right is it that you speak of Dha' Teanga? You claim rights of me as an advisor to a dead king? I do not recall hearing tell of a blood connection so close in our clans that you rise to a station that would call the only son and heir to the throne to answer to you."

Laoghaire stood close enough to remind Dha' Teanga that he was not a villager who cowed to Dha' Teanga's position in the clans, nor was he the young man the advisor remembered as a fool for abandoning the affairs of his kin for the love of a woman.

Slightly taken aback that his adversary did not writhe in discomfort at being called to answer publicly about his intentions, Dha' Teanga inwardly scrambled a bit to define just what right he had to extract any information from Laoghaire, much less demand it of him. After a momentary pause.

"The right I earned when I assumed responsibility for these ports, land and people at the death of my king and queen. While you idled in your fanciful lands of the Tuatha De Danann almost a full moon-cycle after being sent word of the tragedy here, business continued, port fees collected, shipments arrived smoothly, cattle husbandry continued, gates were protected and life was kept from panic.

These lands have been exposed to any with a fighting force and a thought to take seat of power here while both you and your cousin, the two most likely to fill the seat, were doing naught for these people. All was kept in hand by my rule." He righteously thumped his chest. "Should you have never returned and turned your back on your people, it would have been my hand that lit the fires for my beloved leaders as it was I who remained ever at his side and I would have continued to keep these lands prosperous as I have always done."

Laoghaire let the insult pass for it wounded him that he was not at his father's side but particularly, he bore the guilt that this foulness visited upon his parents was due, in part, to him.

"But I *have* returned. And you did no more than was your duty to your people, Dha' Teanga. Of course you have accomplished all that you said, for that was your task assigned to you by my father and mother because they so loved your father who did the job before you. Are you saying that because there was confusion for a time after the death of my parents over who would be paying you to do your duty, that you should be commended for not abandoning the task that was your sworn responsibility? And think you that because I did not come to these lands straight away with the news of my parent's passing that I did not grieve for them or care for my people? Or perhaps you would have thought it more prudent to do what my grieving heart cried out to do rather than be true to my duty and make certain before I came to these lands that their murder was not a grab for power. Perhaps you did not recognize the need to take care that my cousin and I were not the next targets of foul play for you were too eager to see yourself in position of rulership. You took residence in my parent's home, made comfortable yourself with their servants, helped yourself of their wines and continued to draw payment for your services despite the fact that you had no *right* to do so. You see Dha' Teanga, I have had eyes and ears about these lands since early in these times and when I determined it safe for my family to travel here, is when we came, not before. I ask you Dha' Teanga, were you as concerned for the welfare and safety of the heir to the throne as you were for the commerce of the ports? Have you grown so accustomed to the kindnesses my family has afforded you that you took them as your right? You speak to me of your right to ask my intentions toward the throne when there should not be any question in anyone's mind as to whom the throne belongs. Even now, you dare to order the King's Guard to stand against his only son and heir to the throne."

At this some of the men lining the fence shuffled uncomfortably when they recognized that what they were doing might be seen as treason rather than protecting their lands.

"I'd say Dha' Teanga, if I were not availed of the intelligence I have regarding the death of my parents, I would be looking more closely in your direction for you behave more as one drunk with the illusion of his own importance rather than a well-meaning official, loyal to the memory of his rulers."

"Pretty words from the pretty prince." Dha Teanga responded. "You have abandoned your position here as you abandoned your sovereigns. You have not remained to keep safe your family nor have you learned the trade that keeps these clans well fed and comfortable. Through many years of hard work and diplomacy we have trade, which brings us goods from land afar and we are able to bring our crafts to markets which increase our stores through barter and payment. I have remained loyal to my royals all the while you were absent. I have kept these peoples safe within these gates and their individual wealth has not suffered for the King Laoghaire's rule on shares has not changed since his death. So I have proved myself as a worthy leader to these people."

Your words betray your notion that you were in a position to change the laws that were my father and mother's; for how else would the rules on shares of crop and cattle be changed since the event of their death, unless you thought yourself in the position to change them. And this must be so, for you claim to be a righteous and "worthy leader" for having allowed the rules to remain intact. So I ask you Dha' Teanga, on what do you base your claim to have the right to demand anything from the heir to this throne and these lands?

"I stand firm. You have abandoned your family and people while others have seen to the operation of these lands and ports. You are not worthy to claim title here for you have been a deceiver of other clans for whom you swore your oath and then have abandoned them for more fertile pastures here now that it suits you." This was the first accusation thrown down to back up what was forming as a challenge for the throne by Dha' Teanga and at this, there was grumbling and murmuring from the crowd.

Laoghaire cast a glance in Gara's direction knowing it was she, from whom this last bit of information had come, and he stepped closer to the other man.

"I have had enough of this disregard for respect due my mother and father on the night of their passing to the Otherworld. Their bones are not even cooled and you challenge me for the throne. Let us see this for what it is. You are challenging me for the throne are you not?"

"I do so for the sake of my people, Laoghaire."

"Well then, you must do so for the sake of all the peoples in the land for I come to the Stone of Fal, brought here to make voice that a High King will be chosen in this village to rule all of these lands until such time as such a rule is no longer significant."

At this, Laoghaire gestured to the great Stone standing in the village and all the people broke into explosive conversation over the mention of a High King of all the land.

He continued, "What do you know of this Stone that breeched the very village you claim to have kept safe Dha' Teanga? Is it a common occurrence for you to awake and find your countryside rearranged? Had you not thought to find out more of what comes to your village in the night on the heels of the murder of your leaders? Or had you thought that to patch the hole in the fence was enough?" Laoghaire looked atop the Stone and asked. "Tell me Dha' Teanga what is it that I see perched atop the Stone? Have you knowledge of this?"

The usurper straightened to defend his appraisal of the Stone. "I have had it investigated. Yes. The Stone seems to have no other special qualities as to be identified as the very Stone of Fal as you say. There has been no singing or noise as I, or my men approached the Stone. I am convinced that it is merely a Stone but for the oddity atop. It appears to be the hilt of a Sword but there by some hand of magic for it cannot be removed. Even the strongest man we can find in the village has not been able to remove it." He said with authority.

"Perhaps one from outside our village may be able to draw the Sword for he is known to have great strength as you have witnessed." Laoghaire said with a knowing smile as he gestured to Iarann.

"Let him try." Dha' Teanga announced. "It is quite secure." He said with confidence for he had ordered pulling, prying, hammering and many other methods to remove the well-jeweled hilt from the Stone. He was convinced no one would remove the Sword.

With a nod from Laoghaire, Iarann approached the staging made of wood that led to the top of the great Stone. Many watched with amazement at the great man's agility as he climbed to the top. Iarann reached for the Sword and the handle was lost in the grasp of his great hand. As he pulled, people watched expectantly for the giant man of great strength to pull the piece from the Stone. Iarann placed his foot atop the Stone to get a better purchase on the hilt and pulled now with both hands. The Sword did not move, not even slightly. Iarann gave a final try as he fully stepped up onto the Stone with both feet and pulled with all his strength. He stood with beads of sweat on his brow from the effort and gave a shrug as if to resign that the effort was useless.

Laoghaire turned to Dha' Teanga who responded, "And this proves what? That the blade is entombed within the Stone? What has this to do with the matters at hand?"

"Did you not hear me state that this is the Stone of Fal? The very heart of these lands and one of the gifts from the Gods of the countries to the north? From the lands of Odin and the Valkyries, this Stone and its magical qualities gifted to the peoples of the Danann. It granted them rule over this island and success in banishing the Firbolg and is said to have the special Power to sing when stepped upon by the one who will be king of these lands. The Sword you see planted within the

Stone is the Sword of Nuada, yet another gift of those lands from the north which is also said to be given to the hand that will rule until such time as those who rule are too foolish and at that time the Sword will no longer reside with men but will find its home in the hands of the Goddess once again."

"You quote me myths and children's tales?"

"Are you saying that you deny the truth in the tales of how the Tuaths came to these lands and you deny the Goddess in the sacred stories?"

"Of course not. We keep the reverence of the Goddess here in these lands." Dha' Teanga looked around a bit nervously. In truth, he had been a man of business for so long, he thought of those who were devout in their worship to be childish in their beliefs. It had been many generations in any lands beyond the Danann territories since anyone had seen the Gods and even longer since real magic beyond herb lore had been habitually practiced. It seemed these cosmopolitan, populated places with worldly traffic and commerce had grown too hectic for the worship beyond rote and token magic.

"Then you won't mind trying your hand at the Sword to see if you might be the one the Gods have called to the Stone to claim High King over this island."

Dha' Teanga's mind sparked possibilities. He thought that the arrival of this Stone here in his village might have been some kind of a sign that he was to take possession of the throne. At least that was how he was going to twist the tale. After all, he convinced himself, he had run the village and stood to open the ports all over the island for trade with many lands should he become High King. He thought with a leaping heart that the timing was such that the Stone arrived after the death of the royals but *before* the return of Laoghaire and his cousin. Would that he'd have climbed the scaffolding himself, he may have drawn the Sword easily from the Stone. But this, now, he could draw the Sword in the eyes of all and legally lay claim to the throne in the eyes of the village and the Gods. Yes, he thought, this was his calling.

"I will inspect the Stone to determine whether there is any trickery about. We will see if the Sword can be drawn forth by my hand." Dha' Teanga walked to the base of the wood platform past Iarann, who had climbed down and was once again on the ground, and began to climb as all watched. He thought in eagerness as he climbed: *If I am to be king, I will do right by these peoples and bring much trade and wealth to this land. I will keep well the lessons I have been taught by Ri Laoghaire and be known throughout the world as a great king. With the backing of these legendary stories, I will have my place in history as the one who came to the throne, not of a royal line but through the choice of the Gods!*

These visions of grandeur danced in Dha' Teanga's head as he climbed and reached the top. He stepped upon the Stone, fully expecting to hear beautiful voices sing as he did so and hesitated only briefly when they did not. The would-be king reached for the hilt of the Sword and it felt so right in his palm that he was sure it would slide easily out of the Stone and be his right to a king making. Dha' Teanga pulled gently and the piece did not move. He tugged again to no avail. He grasped with two hands as Iarann had done and pulled until his face was red. He stood.

"It is a trick. The Sword is a part of the Stone and made to look as a separate piece. The myth is but a child's tale, told for generations out of memory. It proves nothing of who is worthy to lead these people."

"How then, came the Stone to this village? Know you of any army strong enough to raise a Stone such as this in one night with naught a witness?" Laoghaire asked shouting up to the other man.

"Come you here then, and see for yourself it cannot be done." Dha' Teanga immediately regretted the invitation for what if the other man could best him and pull the Sword? He would be made a fool. But even at the dawning of this realization, Laoghaire was halfway up the platform.

Colm held her breath as she watched her husband adroitly scale the wood steps to reach the top of the Stone. Laoghaire waited for Dha' Teanga to step off the Stone so that he could gain a purchase on the Sword handle but the other man did not move. When it was clear to Laoghaire that his adversary wanted to remain to insure there was not trickery involved, he simply reached over to the hilt and smoothly removed it from the Stone with one hand. The ringing of the metal could be heard only by the two men atop the Stone for the rest of the crowd let out a collective gasp so the Sword's voice could not be heard.

The two men could be seen conferring but their words could not be heard. Laoghaire held up the Sword for inspection while the other man appeared to examine the piece. Laoghaire then replaced the Sword into the small hole left in the Stone and allowed the other to try again to remove it with no success. Upon this second try, Dha' Teanga stepped down from the Stone onto the platform with Laoghaire and announced, "There is some trick here which I do not see."

For the last time, Laoghaire reached over and without aplomb, removed the Sword and held it up for all to see. The gemstones in the hilt sparkled in the firelight and the intricate knot work designs in the blade caught the light as well. It appeared as the knots and jewels came alive and the figh vine tattoos twined up the man's arm so it appeared the Sword gave life to the leaves and the leaves on Laoghaire's arm made the man and the Sword appear as they were of one piece of beautiful art. Without a word, Laoghaire stepped up onto the top of the Stone with the Sword raised toward the skies and the Stone let out a sound so loud that the vibration shook the very earth beneath the feet of the clan folk. Some fell to the ground and covered their ears while others could not tear their eyes away. Others still fell to their knees in praise of the Gods for their new king.

Dha' Teanga lost his balance with the shock of the noise and began to fall backward off the platform, a fall that would surely mean his death. Laoghaire, who by now was completely surrounded by a radiant blue hue, reached his free hand to stay the other from falling. In that moment, Dha' Teanga was touched by the Power emanating from Laoghaire and his eyes widened as he snatched his hand away in fright. Once sure he was in no danger of falling, Dha' Teanga bent to his knees and Laoghaire stepped off the Stone to face him.

"My King." The shaken man trembled and kept his eyes lowered as he uttered the words. "King Laoghaire, you must know that I only confronted you for the sake of these peoples. But now I have seen a glimpse of what is truly in your heart and have faith that you are the one chosen by the Gods to rule this land and lead us to our destinies. I offer you my humble service in whatever station you deem suitable. I will show you the same loyalty I offered your father for I loved the old man and your mother. Please pardon the liberties I have taken in my position in his absence. I had mistaken you for something you are not. At this, the kneeling man looked up at Laoghaire with tears flooding his eyes. Can you forgive me my insolence?"

"Get up Dha' Teanga. Get up. I have been faulty too, in my assessment of you. I needed someone to blame for the death of my parents and admit I was jealous in my heart for the time you spent with them that I did not. I know my father loved you and would not have done so if you were other than a trustworthy man. I see you had intentions to save these people from the selfish man you thought me to be and for this, I could either call you treasonous or a loyal king's man. I choose the latter. Let us go and be enemies no more. We will drink a cup of wine and pour some on the ground for the pleasure of my parents. I hear you have some high quality wine at your disposal." Dha' Teanga reddened at this last jest and started down the scaffolding.

Gara stood with her hands on her grandson's shoulders while he squirmed to be loosed from the fingers that dug into his skin. The woman's face was pinched into a mask of anger and hatred. She watched as her chance to develop an alliance of power within this village had just melted before her eyes as even this man of ambition publicly knelt to Croi Laoghaire. And if Laoghaire is now to be king of these lands, she saw her opportunities slipping away from her in any arena on this island. She would have to strike out on her own and go where she might, to be shut of this family that was altogether too far reaching for her liking. She began to formulate a plan.

40

Tapestry

I yawned a jaw-cracking signal that my fortitude to stay awake was coming to an end. Eyes watering, I realized that Nora and I were leaning into each other on Cath's couch while Bridey softly snored in the old Queen Anne style chair.

"The Sword and the Stone." I murmured. "Seems like another tale was usurped by England."

"Well that might be somewhat true." Finny agreed. "But not so much usurped as spread."

"What do you mean?" Nora asked as she shifted her weight to a more comfortable position.

"It was not but three days after the Sword was drawn from the great Stone that our party was offered passage and took te the sea in a sturdy trade ship of Laoghaire's inherited acquisitions. We did much travelin' over the ocean as the ship we called home for many months forst went north up the eastern coast of Ireland te parts of the large island you know as England and Scotland. We then traveled south, past the tip of the mainland that is now France and came te port several times in what is Spain te drop fine hammered gold and pick up rich red wines and silver and who knows what all else was te be the trade. Much of this trip was a sickened blur for me, as we with Duibhe blood in us don't fair too well on the waters. I was sure to plant feet every time we came to port though, and when we did, Lon Dubh and I told tale for all it was worth but we spent little time in any Spanish or Italian ports enough te make the tale stick, but we salted the European countries with seeds of the tale and some took hold. Though we landed in Italy with purpose, we spent very little time there and we quickly traveled north from Italy on foot. We had more time te tell our tale on the road and in what you know as Germany and into the Norse country for that is the path we traveled. Ye can see that many a fairytale has come from these areas, England, Germany, the Norse countries, for the story was readily accepted as we traveled and told tale in those parts. But right from the start, it was more easily and widely accepted in the large island or England at forst, for it seemed as we dotted the shores along there, the people were most receptive te our bardship and as many of the crew of the boat were there to confirm our story, so far as they witnessed the part about Laoghaire, his Sword and the great Stone, people took te the tellin' and thorsted for more. The folk there had been hearin' tell of unusual stories of their own so they were eager te hear of the tales we brought with us and they readily believed us and exchanged stories of their own similar experiences. In the south of England, we heard tell of a dancing giant that came te rest at the Great Stone Corcle there. We calculate this was Damhsaigh Cloch of the very Sacred Circle of the De Danann gone home with all the secrets and history of the magic taken place there at the Lake of the Ivory Heron. This Corcle is why we figure England is a great wellspring of all the old tales brought to it by the dancing giant and then reinforced as Lon Dubh planted her seeds of the tale along her way. We were told too of a giant, great of size and made of stone, takin' te the countryside from the causeway te the north in Scotland. The people there told also a tale of a Great Stone bein' planted by night near what would eventually be known as Birdoswald, much the way the Stone was planted in Laoghaire's village. This was the very half of the Stone sent by Laoghaire te the northern parts of the main island te be utilized for a porpose many, many generations later."

"What was that?" I asked.

"It was planted there in preparation and waiting for the borth of one te come te these lands te spread news of the new and masculine God. This one would be born of the blood of the ancient Gods and a very descendent of Faidhe and the Greenman. He would bear the Staff of Lugh and bring the message to the sacred isle. His color would ever be the green of the masculine God and his name would be synonymous with both Ireland and the Christian Chorch."

"You mean Saint Patrick?" I asked.

"I do."

At this, Bridey opened one eye and gave the first indication that she hadn't been fully sleeping but was listening all along.

"A good man Patrick, if a bit grouchy. But he had much responsibility and that could draw the humor from anyone's heart."

"You knew Saint Patrick?" Nora goggled.

"You can't expect that we'd have been designed to live so long and to have taken on the mantle of the care of the changing spiritual landscape and not have a hand in the shaping of such things? Granted, I was one working with half knowledge of the story but despite that shortcoming, I came to a position that afforded me to be aware of the inner workings of how this new patriarchal society would develop in these parts and so was granted a hand in how these things came about. The man himself baptized me when he came to my part of this land. He argued new religion against old with the man I called my father during that time, the Druid Dubhthach, a Chieftain of Leinster. We spoke of the Christ, Patrick and I. He respected me as an Abbess as I did the labor of bringing women into the fold for as they say, it takes a woman to bring a man to God, so as long as my girls accepted the new God, we went about our lives keeping the Old Ways and weaving them into the new and brought into hearth and home to continue under the banner of the new God. Patrick was ever so pleased at the converts I'd brought to the Church. How could I not know him? He kept distant from the women though as if they'd scald him if he drew too near. He was only slightly more comfortable with the women of the Abby for they'd not be so overtly drawn to his eh, magnetism. But that didn't stop them from flittin' after him like a bee to the honey."

"But I tell you now Finny," Bridey said shifting her attention to her brother, "Now as you're telling me that he was a descendent of Faidhe and the Greenman, it makes more sense to me, for the man had the gifts of a Seer and the magic was about him but it must have been most difficult for him to resist his more natural urges. In truth, I think it all scared him. Once, as he visited with my father I served them cheese and ale and he spoke of haunting dreams and visitations that brought him back to the isle and of being aware of happenings prior to the event. It was a calling he spoke of to return to this land. It was a sickness in his heart he'd felt all his life until he came home to Ireland and her people even as a slave. But in his heart, he knew he had these special abilities for a purpose but he was greatly troubled with his gifts for he was not at all sure he was not of the 'devil' for he never thought himself worthy of the miraculous Powers he'd been gifted with, so he always questioned the meaning of the Power he wielded as to why it had been granted him. Was it of the devil to tempt him or was it a gift from God, he wondered always."

"He told me once in a moment of confidence that when he'd first come to Ireland as a slave many years before, he'd committed what he called 'a great sin' and was so overwhelmed with the power and strength of the call of the flesh when he stepped foot here, that it frightened him. He landed in the area of Laoghaire's lands as a slave and lay with a woman in the countryside there by the fires. He had no control over the draw to the coupling as was in his blood of auld. The Power overwhelmed and frightened him so that he thought it could not be wholesome. For such Power in the hands of a human could prove to be destructive. He saw it as his own failing to be so consumed of the flesh and so convinced himself that it was the devil's doing to tempt him. And that's why he so devoutly went about his duty to bring those of his beloved Erie to the Lord to make his Power count among the good rather than the other."

"Man," I said, "who would ever believe that old Saint Patrick and I had such a problem in common! Not the sex part but the conflict. But I get what you say about being called home to Ireland. Even though I am not a native to Ireland, at least not in this lifetime." I corrected myself. "It's as if everything I am has come alive and been woken up since I got here. My memories, abilities even my mission in life at this point has been revealed and defined for me."

"So it was the same for Patrick. He was of the same blood as you and sorved the same Gods as you will in yer respective missions." Finny reminded us.

Then it struck me. "Hey! It was Saint Patrick I saw in the meditation I had in your trailer! He carried the Staff and planted it into the ground here in Ireland. I remember thinking that it was a union or binding between the message he carried and the earth here, because as soon as I saw the Staff enter the Earth, a huge network of vines sprouted and took root. It was mostly underground though, the vine I mean. It was the symbol for the proliferation of the old religion and reverence for the feminine. I think I know what it means now. It *was* a union...The Great Marriage!" I shouted as the symbolism of the vision became clear to me. "It was a combining of the old religion and the new. The Staff he carried as a symbol for his message of the masculine God plants the seed within the fertile ground of Mother Earth, the symbol for the old religion and from that union, life of the old religion was propagated as the new religion took hold in these lands, largely due to Saint Patrick. But it was no coincidence that the vine's roots grew deep and silently underground. So it worked! Faidhe's magic to keep the old religion alive within the new one worked! I'll bet Patrick had no idea, did he?"

"I rather think not." Finny answered. "Despite the fact that he carried Faidhe's ash-wood Staff, left for him in the Stone of Fal in his homeland, the upland of Scotland, all those years before. He'd not have been honored te know he was not only propegatin' the marriage between the Goddess and the God but ordaining the symbol of the Sword and Shield as the new way of recognizin' the religion he was ministerin'. He did know that it was the symbol of the Corcle though combined with the sign of the cross. Either way, he was strivin' te combine the two but the effect was not what he'd planned. He thought te usurp one, the other would hold sway but what he really did was to marry the two so the other wouldn't completely be lost."

There was an echoed moment of silence as we all sat in the room contemplating under physical and mental exhaustion, how someone in the room had actually known Saint Patrick and that same someone had been recognized as a saint herself. We mulled the unlikely truth of how others of us here were in some very distant way, related by blood to Saint Patrick. Further, we sat silently knowing that the role he'd played in the mission he lead here in Ireland had served to keep the Old Ways alive just as if it had been a graceful dance choreographed by Faidhe herself. I couldn't help but wonder then, how much of what is happening is making us dance to Faidhe's design right now? I mentally giggled as an image of myself as a living character in the fairytale Sleeping Beauty and how it had, in certain versions, the heroine and sometimes the witch putting on shoes that made her dance until she died. The irony touched me as I realized that in one life, as the tale I told proliferated, the story branched into many tales of lore and as it survived, I actually was a character in an original fairytale!

The same fatigue that made it difficult for me to wrap a cognizant thought around all of this also made it much easier to accept everything as fact. Although, I'd had a lot of practice lately in accepting the impossible as fact and these things were growing easier to believe and understand by the minute.

I felt my eyelids involuntarily slip closed over rough and scratchy eyes. At last, the night of dancing and morning of fantastic stories had begun to catch up with me. I looked at Nora and she had the O'Leary raccoon eyes, deep set with dark circles that was as typical of our family as was the big round shape we all had to our eyes. I knew I must have the same tired look about me too.

"Time for sleep, I think." She said as if she'd read my thoughts.

"Yeah. Let's take a nap and start again when we wake up." I said, intending to retire to the guest room we'd been given. That was the last thing I remember before being awoken by a steady thumping noise that translated in my dream as *the rhythm of Iarann pounding his hammer to bring the softened silver into shape for the final panel he was constructing for the Cauldron. I saw the familiar panel displaying a depiction of a Cauldron and many people lined up for what seemed to be a ceremony of sorts. I understood as he tapped and pounded his fine hot chisel to create the images, that this was the most important panel of all. "This is the pinnacle piece." I said to him in my dream quality voice. The blacksmith didn't answer me he just kept at his work.*

"I have been pleased to keep you to your work until now, Iarann, but this piece, I fear. For when you finish this one, I know our time is at an end. I feel great sorrow for the love we should have between us. Things are different now, I know, but still, we have love for one another that is pure, for there is no true love that is tainted. We came together as family and that is what we are. Not as we had expected, but now I have forgiven my mother for her part in this, if there was ever anything to forgive. It is we who vowed to walk the path of the Goddess. It is we who pledged our lives to do her bidding. You will do your part, like it or not, as I will do mine until we share in the Otherworld, Heaven, or Valhalla or where ever two such as we will find rest. Will you not break from your task of metals and wake to your task of flesh? We are two of the three on the road, and we have come through this journey that has extended far beyond that which can be encompassed in the four directions, beyond time, two of those needed to spin the wheel and now two of the three needed to release the Power of the Cauldron of your design. You have had your slumber. You can evade your destiny no more. Wake now Iarann, wake to your Power, your birthright. Wake, for you are reborn to your sworn duty to the Goddess and you are needed to finish your work of the Cauldron. Wake, Iarann, WAKE!

My eyes flew open with the echo of my own voice in my head. There was the steady breathing of someone sleeping next to me. *I am on the road.* Came my first thought as I tried to adjust my eyes and realized that it was dark out. I heard the rustling of someone stirring near to me.

"Patrice?" I called and thought, *No that's not right.*

"Mph." Came a muffled reply.

"What time is it?" I said to mask my confusion. *On the road? Patrice? Wrong sister.* I struggled to capture the essence of my dream but already it was disappearing from my mind like soap bubbles popping. *The Cauldron and Iarann. The final panel.* I committed these phrases to memory for later examination.

A bolt of intrusive bright light poured in from the front stairs as the front door flew open. I realized that the rhythm of the hammer in my dream must have been Cath's steps trudging up the stairs.

"Whoa!" I shielded my eyes. "Shut the door please!" I snorted and saw that all four of us must have fallen asleep where we sat some eight or ten hours ago. We obviously slept through the day because it was full dark now. "Cath? Where've you been?"

The old man closed the door behind him and turned on a small lamp that sat on a round table next to the chair in which his brother was seated. We all made stirrings to stretch, and the room filled with creaking and popping bones and groans as we stretched and waited for a turn in the bathroom.

"We must've fallen asleep!" Nora said, stating the obvious.

After turning on a second lamp in the room, Cath announced, "I've news for you. I've made travel arrangements and ye've work te do."

"Arrangements?" I fought to bring my mind to the present conversation and a strange tinkling alarm disturbed my efforts. I looked around the room to see who would respond to the sound. "Oh," I said, as I realized it was our new cell phone ringing in my satchel "That's my phone, hold on." I rushed to answer. "Hello?"

A feminine voice surprised me.

"Lee?" I tried to shake off the cobwebs and my brain searched its files for identification of the unexpected voice drifting over miles of ocean to reach me.

"Patrice? I was just dreaming about you." I said without being immediately aware that the statement was not entirely true. But then it occurred to me that in a way, once upon a time, Patrice was Iarann, so maybe it was Patrice I was dreaming about.

"Oh, I'm sorry. Did I wake you? I'm not exactly sure what time it is over there but I didn't think it'd be too late. I got the number from Walter as soon as I got your message."

"Message?"

"Yeah, I got your message from the airline about the ticket you guys got for me but what's all this about Denmark? I thought you were strictly keeping to Ireland?"

"Uh, can you hold on one second?" I didn't wait for her to respond and stuck my hand over the phone. "Cath, did you contact my sister Patrice about traveling to Denmark?" He nodded that he had. Then, light dawned and I understood the meaning of my dream and what was said in it. Iarann made the Cauldron. He'd traveled with Lon Dubh in partnership in their quest. In my dream I was Lon Dubh speaking to Iarann, but it was really a request that Patrice wake up to her role in all this and my own realization that her help would be needed. I knew there was a reason I'd felt that Patrice should have been on this trip all along. Maybe Nora and I had to be firmly established as Sword and Shield first. But now the longing to have Patrice here grew to a more urgent strength. I asked Cath, "How did you know?"

"Keep te yer conversation, lass. Ye know what's necessary. Make it happen."

I returned my attention to speaking with my sister. "Pat? Ah yeah, in a nutshell, we met some...family members over here in Ireland and we've become really good friends with them. They've been helping both Nora and I in our research and given us some very interesting and solid background to our own family's involvement in some of what I'm researching. It's been so exciting and fascinating to say the least. Our research, well, my research, has raised the need to travel to Denmark. These people here are so interested in following the thread of my research, 'cause, well it involved their branch of the family, they made arrangements for us to travel north to Denmark and they also had the connections to arrange for you to meet us there too."

I was tap dancing as fast as I could to make (*as soon as the shoes were fast on her feet, she began to dance*) the story sound credible. I shook off the thought and looked at Nora who was now listening to the conversation without any knowledge of what I had dreamed so I shot her a quick mental vision of what I thought was happening and what I was trying to do and her face looked confused. I shrugged at her indicating that it was the best I could do.

"Listen," I continued, "I know it's short notice, but when we told our, ah, cousins how we really planned this trip for the three of us and you weren't able to come, and we've mentioned you about a million times how we wished you were here to see this or that, they insisted they use their airline and travel connections to bring you here. They've kind of been in the travel business here in Europe. Consider it a free vacation. All you have to do is clear your schedule even just for a few days if that's all you can spare. You can stay longer, but don't pass this up, Pat, please. All expenses paid." I inwardly winced because I didn't know where the money would come from but I had to convince her to come and trust that it would just work out.

"Who are these people?" She speculated this was some kind of joke or she smelled that something just wasn't right about what I was saying.

"They are our family who live here. Remember we were going to visit our cousin Margaret when we got here? Well, we've met a whole lot more than just her since we got here. Nora and I have been living at a cottage belonging to one of them and we've spent a great deal of time learning and researching with the other two. Funny thing is, they have been doing similar research over here and have really put us on the right path to discovering so much. But they have given us this opportunity to follow leads to Denmark and we want to share it with you while it's possible. Can you get away?" She didn't say no right away so I pressed her. "You have to admit, Pat, you really wanted to come with us in the first place and we want you here. The only thing holding you back was the money, right? Well, it's not exactly the same, but I'll be doing research and we'll be checking out our heritage and history in Denmark instead of Ireland. What? No, I know we're not Danish, but it seems we have our Swedish heritage due to a connection through Denmark. And Copenhagen is just a skip away from Sweden. By the time you meet us, we'll have an itinerary planned and a place to stay. We'll meet you at the airport. What do you think?"

I signaled to Nora for reinforcement. She complied by taking the phone from me.

"Listen, Patrice?" She spoke with the no-nonsense tone that allowed her to come out on the winning side of any exchange for most of her life. "It's Nora. Yeah. No really it's good. It's all been good here. I know it sounds almost too good to be true but really, don't pass this up. You can get away for a few days. Consider it an early birthday present. Just throw a few things, comfortable things, in a suitcase and meet us..." She looked to Cath for information and he handed her a computer printout of the travel itinerary. Then, after a moment to figure out dates and times, "Meet us at the Copenhagen Airport in three days. That's plenty of time to arrange things at home and to get on your flight at Logan and meet us." She listened into the phone for a moment and rolled her eyes a bit. "No, no, that's the face price of the ticket. These people do a lot of traveling and they have all kinds of connections with discounts and fare breaks. All we had to pay was the tax. Yeah! I know." She began to sound enthusiastic over the supposed good fortune. I knew that Patrice was sold. She'd gotten past the, too good to be true, aspect of the invitation and said she'd be here.

Remembering my dream, I put my hand out to Nora and she gave the phone back to me. "Patrice, one last thing. I was just wondering; are you working on anything special right now?" Patrice fashioned handmade jewelry in her own designs. I wondered if my dream of Iarann had any actual connection to anything Patrice might be making.

"Why do you ask?" She sounded curious.

"I, ah, well. Are you?"

"Yeah. I started working on something different a few weeks ago. It's not jewelry but it's something I'm trying out to see if I can craft it and then to see if there is a market for it. It's a small relief I started right after you guys left for Ireland. 'Cause, well you know I was disappointed at not being able to go with you so I tried to satisfy myself by reading up on Celtic history and art and I found some pretty interesting artifacts I started to think about replicating. You know, torques and brooches, jewelry type stuff but then I kept being drawn to this one artifact made of silver so I decided to try my hand at a wall relief that can be framed or not. I have the style down pretty close I think, but I plan to overlay it with gold when I finish. Actually, you'll be surprised when you see it; you're kind of featured in the work, well both you and Nora with me, over there the way it should have been. So, why are you asking?"

I just had a dream about a new piece of work you were doing and wondered if it was so."

"Oh you're doing it again!" Patrice would comment on the abilities Nora and I had to know each other's thoughts in this way. She referred to our ability as "it."

"Yeah, I guess I am but the thing is, Pat, I think you should bring your work on this relief with you when you come. I think we might find it very useful here."

"Really? You think there's a market for the reproductions? "Well it's a reproduction of style, not an actual copy of the other pieces I used as a model. I only have the one piece so far and they won't be cheap considering the materials. Do you have someone in mind?" Patrice thought my suggestion meant there was a commercial market for her work and I didn't stop her from thinking that was the idea.

"Yeah." I said. "Definitely bring it with you."

She began to grow excited at the prospect of coming to Europe and potentially growing her business; it was evident in her voice.

"I'm so glad you decided to come. You have our number; call if you need to, otherwise, we'll just see you in three days. 'Kay? Take down these confirmation numbers and information so you can download your tickets. See how these things work out? You're going to get your passport stamped after all."

We said our goodbyes and I hit the end button on the phone.

"God that was brutal. I hate lying but it's *really* hard to lie to one of my sisters. They almost always know something's up. Nora thanks. She wouldn't have trusted the 'free trip' story if you hadn't convinced her." At the thought of the money to pay for Patrice's ticket and the additional tickets Cath had purchased for us to fly to Copenhagen from Dublin, I turned to him and opened my mouth to speak.

"We'll have none of that now. It's only a small price after all has been done, te get ye te where ye're needed."

"But how..." He cut me off again.

"Wait now, I've been up the better part of two days. Let's clean up a bit and sit for a meal." Cath was right. I'd delayed a much-needed trip to the bathroom being captured by all this activity.

"Okay." I said, heading for the bedroom to retrieve my toothbrush and hairbrush. "But we have to figure out how to pay for all this on our own. You guys can't afford to be paying for all this."

Bridey, Finny and Nora having already visited the bathroom headed for the kitchen where they began the process of putting foodstuffs out onto the dining room table for us to munch. I thought to myself: *All we seem to do here is eat and sleep.* I knew it wasn't true, but it really seemed like we were constantly hindered by the frailty of the body's need for sustenance and rest. *It gets in the way.*

At the thought, Finny called out to me, "Perhaps it's why they're made te be so enjoyable. Otherwise we'd forget te take care of ourselves."

"Hey. Get out of my head. I'm in the bathroom!" I said. I flushed, washed and brushed quickly, eager to return to my conversation with Cath. I started right in when I returned to the group. "So why is it you feel the need to pay for our passage to Denmark? Or why is it that you think we can't do it for ourselves?" I guess I prided myself on being independent and didn't want anyone paying my way.

"Forst, I know that ye'd have taken a great deal more books on the forst day we met but ye both were very selective in even those you did take. The very reason you came te Ireland, as ye told me, and while ye found a treasure trove of what ye came for, ye still only took a handful of what ye actually wanted. That was the forst sign. Ye're stayin at a self-caterin' cottage instead of a hotel with the room sorvice is the second clue. Ye're keepin' te the pub fare or yer makin' all yer own meals for food. I've been judgin' the likes of tourists and how they spend or don't spend for longer than ye've both been livin'. I can tell frugality when I see it."

"But our financial situation isn't a reason for you guys to pick up the tab. You don't appear to be so well off yourself."

"Ye'll have te consider that we' three have been around a great deal longer than the average porson. In our time, at least this is true of Finny and meself; we've accumulated more of money and property than we know what te do with. And it seems as though our sister has done none too poorly with a goodly chunk of land she's parleyed inte a self-supportin' farm and business so much so that she can afford te keep a second home for the likes of the ones stayin' on her farm. So don't worry about where the money is comin' from, just know that ye've a need and it's been filled. Come te think, much of our financial good fortune was as a result of the forst trip ye took te the Norse region."

"What do you...Oh, you mean Lon Dubh? How?"

"Well, once ye'd arrived there and the purpose in casting magic for the future was accomplished by Faidhe, things in our part of the world began te change.

Moved on so te speak. It took some time, but gradually, clans fell apart, the Tuatha de Danann scattered te the winds for the most part. It seemed the regular order te things was pulled apart. Many of the established tribes became nomadic and disbursed. Magical creatures and Gods were seen almost never. Diog, the old coot, was the last of the Duibhe clans te stay in the hill territories and when he died, the remains of the old mines were ours. We didn't dig but the stones and metals he'd stored were ours fer the takin' after his passin'. Industrious the Duibhe were and Diog was a right pernicious hoarder. We knew, of course, where he'd kept his treasure hoarded. We'd seen him admire it many a times from our perches in the trees. So many years after I left Ireland te find Finny in the Norse lands, we retorned home te ownership of gold and gems enough te support a small country."

"So, excuse me for saying so but why haven't you lived a life of more, ah, comfort?" I tried not to insult the men but the truth was, Finny lived in a ramshackle trailer and Cath lived in an apartment above his store that had 60 or 70-year old décor and not the kind that could be described as antique design.

"Well, we're livin the way we choose. And that's comfort enough." Finny answered. "And we've lived many an orlier year on the road as tinkers so the true treasures we've found are a good story, a melodic song that evokes a stirrin' in yer heart, and love of another. Although the love, most valued of the treasures, carries a steep tax, it does. For those who live a lengthy life as we do, it's bittersweet to find love and be helpless te stop the inevitable thief as time steals the youth from the one who is so loved. After the grief of losses te me heart in that way, I keep a distance. But a heart seeks te be of kin and every few centuries, there are those who adopt us so te speak such as ye met the day of our forst meetin'."

"You mean Thomas at the gas station?" Nora asked.

"Aye. But it was Agnes, his wife's grandfather and grandmother who took us in as family. We met James and Katherine McDonough at a McDonough family gathering. It was the name of McDonough as ye may know that were known as the tinkers and travelers and there it was easier te travel with me stories and have a nomadic life. No need for family counting or borth connections. With the tinkers, ye come inte a camp and state yer clan and yer welcomed as family. So it was with James; Cath and me made friends as close as brothers and so it was that we became uncles to their children and grandchildren, one of whom was Thomas's wife Agnes."

Finny's eyes shifted a bit uncomfortably toward Cath. Cath cleared his throat and finished the thought. "It was Katherine McDonough's sister Evelyn as did me in. It was love struck I was, as I'd never been, what with my monk's past and scholarly endeavors. I'd kept the ritual of the festival rites on occasion but never had I felt a love such as with my Evelyn. It would not be ignored as caution would have warned and although I appeared much older than she, she loved and cared for me so. And I could give her no children, as it's rare that we hybrids can reproduce but she didn't care. She loved and took care of me as I did her. But she aged and grew old and sick."

Bridey made a tisking noise that called our attention. We looked at her expectantly and she enlightened us.

"It's as though we've spent centuries crossing near each other's paths but never coming together." She looked flustered. "It's, well, I have a friend in the organization, ye know, the Ladies from the Road? And her name is Agnes. Her husband's name is Thomas and he owns the gas station just outside of Midleton. I'm thinking, as we've been this close, as te live within miles of one another and te know the same people. How is it we've never...well, it makes no sense to cry over it now."

We contemplated what Bridey had said for a moment and then it dawned on me, "Hey" I piped up, "Midleton in County Cork. That's where you guys lived back then? Middle Village?"

"Aye lass. And it's where we forst met ye." Finny said. "It's where ye cast yer forst real magic with us te create the bonds that've lasted through thousands of years. It's where ye created a sacred space that would always be a haven fer us. And it's upon the very spot where that magic was cast that the chorch where ye found me was built."

Nora added, "That's where our grandfather was born. How is it that if the Laoghaire clan was established and settled in or near Dublin, that the Leary and O'Leary clan ended up predominantly in County Cork and in Midleton?"

"Well now, here is where we have te add a bit of imagination te the mix of the tale, as we weren't there but have found facts along the way te cobble tegether what might be the truth of it" Finny continued. "And our lovely sister's given us the information needed te fill in the blanks a bit more respectably and in truth, it makes more sense te understand the symmetry of what may have been. Bridey, it seems, tells her tale from the perspective of her knowledge of Saint Patrick but we know of a tale as has been told from the perspective of another that goes something like this: The final changes from the real magical ways came with the wave of Celts that moved across the mainland and wound up in our part of the world here in Ireland. We were fixed right with a great deal of wealth. But it was not so for others of our time. As foretold, the clan of Laoghaire remained intact and assimilated well with the influx of new folk whether the Celts or invaders from the Norse countries or later, the folk from the main island, the clan Laoghaire survived".

"The last King Laoghaire had many children and one of his daughters was said to have taken the fires with one of the herdsmen, which was beneath her station. In fact, it was rumored that the one with whom she coupled bore a glow of green light all about him as they took to the fires on the hillside. The king was distraught, not that his daughter had lain at the fires, as was still custom for these Pagan lands, but that it was known that she had lain with a slave boy. As she told it, she could have no more resisted the lure of this boy if her Da was standing over them. She knew it was magic had brought her to the boy and caused her to lay with him. But her father could not bear the sight of his daughter, big in her belly, birthing a slave's child and sent her west with two of her brothers to none other than the area of Middle Village for her to give birth and also to establish stronghold for his name where he'd heard tell of riches te be found in the hills there. A great pot of gold and silver, he'd heard, in the tales of the myth. And so the child, we suspect may have been born te Patrick and Laoghaire's bloodline, rejuvenated the energy of balance and magic once again for that time. The Laoghaire name that was found mostly in Dublin area propagated quite well in Midleton and County Cork for many centuries te come. And rule ebbed and flowed from high kingship te chieftains and lesser kings but as history has it, Croi Laoghaire was the forst High King in these lands although ye'll not find that in any history book, and his descendant, Laoghaire of the time of Saint Patrick was the last of High Kings in Ireland te wear the twining blue tattoos of the figh vine before Christianity took sway. All just as Faidhe had planned right up until her very descendant, Patrick came and stood on the mount opposite Laoghaire and challenged him by lighting a fire of the Christ at a time when according te the Old Ways, all was to be ritually dark in the land. And by doing so, began the reign of the new religion on this sacred isle."

There was silence in the room as the last words of Finny's story hung on the air and we absorbed all that the story meant.

Nora spoke. "So that's how our bloodline came to be. And how we are of the Laoghaire's from Midleton in County Cork. It's amazing! There's such an intricate web of how all of these times and tales come together. I'll bet there's so much we don't know or never will know. All of these connections and coincidences that aren't really coincidences at all but part of the fabric of this tapestry Faidhe began on her Hilltop Circle."

"Well said, lass." Cath commented. "Whether he knew it or no, the branch of the family that was sent te Middle Village came under the protection that ye blessed it with yerself so long before. It truly has been a tale that is woven throughout time with many colorful threads te highlight history's secrets. But as for this old historian, I've need of rest now and will bid my brother te tell ye of another thread that may run through yer tale that comes with a less pretty hue as te bring darkness and shadow as much as the other brings light. The history of the beast runs parallel te yer own in all this and so ye must be made aware. Finny?" Cath said, as if giving his brother his signal to tell the other side of history. The old man walked away from the dining room table toward his private thoughts and sleep.

41

Passages

At the sight of Dha' Teanga on his knees to Laoghaire and the sacred Sword, once again, in her perceived enemy's possession, something in Gara's mind shifted. In this moment, she could have given over and surrendered to her fate here in this new situation and played her part, whatever that would be, but as was her habit, her mind shifted to survival mode and in this moment, she was desperate. Because these were not her people and this place was such that no one knew of her powerful position in the Tuatha De Danann she had neither wealth, position nor power here. This clan knew not of the cattle she owned, nor of her family situation or her position on the clan Council that had given her ample opportunity to be involved and maneuver most circumstances to her benefit within her own wealthy clan. Here, she was an outlander, without even a marriage connection, dependent on the goodwill of those such as Laoghaire, who had shown no interest in her at all. Or Colm, who flatly refused to help her in anyway. There was Cuan. He had shown promise at one time but it seems his loyalty to his cousin had proven even more powerful than her magic. For she had at one time cast a spell to bring the big man closer in physical union to herself but recognized that blackmail might be of more use to her, should she leave the spell to work on Cuan and Colm. But that seed never bore fruit beyond the lovesick looks of longing she would see on the big man's face as he looked toward Colm. The plan had ruined him for her own purposes, for he now had no interest in her as a sexual partner and so she had no one to speak for her to Laoghaire or to defend her against him.

I am a prisoner here. She thought, and her mind began to panic at her inexperience with utter lack of resources here. *I must return to my home.* With that thought she began to hatch a plan.

Gara gave no thought to the truth that she had not been imprisoned and had been given ample private quarters in which to reside. She and her grandson had been given food aplenty and she had enjoyed good drink and fresh water. They had been treated with due respect as any guest of the new King Laoghaire. But Gara had focused on that she had not felt she was treated as an *honored* guest. And although she was free to come and go at her pleasure, she envisioned her stay here as being held against her will rather than doing her promised duty to the Gods and her clan. It was a prison to her in that she held no position. She had not been able to get a grasp on anyone of import and had no experience in simply being a part of the whole.

Gara decided in that moment to leave. She must arrange for her own travel and it must be soon for if she is to regain any position in the Tuatha De Danann, she must make haste to return there and take the reins of what must now be chaos. The Council was ravaged, the Hill defunct, the Circle gone. Any semblance of leadership for the old clans is gone. She must return with a dramatic claim if she is to take hold of any new form of rule that will inevitably have happened to reassemble the sense of normalcy within the clans. She had the cattle of her son and her own to return to. She was the wealthiest woman now and most powerful in status but for the old one Craiche and she had suspected that Craiche would not be any problem. It occurred to her now that the only reason she had been required to make this inane trek to the eastern seacoast was so that she could not establish herself in just such a position within the Tuath. *Of course* she speculated. *This had not to do with Faidhe and her business with Briciu nor was I needed in any way by Laoghaire or his family in order to be ripped from my home so. This was because they were in fear of my ability to gain power in their absence and they are afraid perhaps, as ruler of a more powerful clan that I would stand against them as they try to establish a stronghold on the entire land from this port. It is my rightful place in this land that I should lead. It is to this calling I should hearken not to be dragged about the countryside for the sake of oaths made by others.*

The thought that they were situated in a port city gave Gara an idea.

"Come Triag." She barked. "We must return to our quarters and see to making our future." When the boy squirmed under her grasp upon his shoulders, she dug her fingers deep into his flesh to make him obey. "Listen you to me, boy. If you have any desire to return to your life of comfort within the bosom of our own people, you will do as I say."

At the thought of returning home, Triag paid attention. He looked toward Macha and Morgan where they stood near their family with another child, perhaps of the village. The two children seemed happy as clan folk offered condolences and congratulations alike to Laoghaire. Triag thought a speedy retreat toward home might be just the plan he'd hoped for. He was disturbed by the images that plagued his mind and worried that if he was made to stay in this place, he would not be able to quell the thoughts or the physical drive that urged him to do what he knew would be an abomination and sure to get him killed if found out. Triag dragged his eyes away from the twins and in a monotone voice obliged.

"Yes, Grandmother."

———

A couple of days after the spectacle of Laoghaire pulling the Sword from the Stone in the village center, the town was abuzz with talk of the coronation celebration that would take place this night. When she felt she would not be missed, Gara tucked what gold and jewels she had taken from home into the sleeve of her linens and covered up with her most elaborately woven cloak. She had insisted that Triag dress in his finery as well. Feigning a desire to explore the market at the shore where ships docked and unloaded their treasures from afar, Gara took the opportunity to inquire about ships at port that were scheduled to leave within a short time. After some research, the woman found the captain of one boat that would head north along the coast before setting about the large island and then touring and trading along the mainland.

"This is to insure passage for my boy and myself." She said as she slipped a sizable yellow stone into the man's hand. "This is so no one is privy to news of the passage." She slipped a larger stone into the man's calloused hand. He looked questioningly into her eyes as if to assess whether this woman's passage would be more trouble than the price she offered.

"I've booked for six others already and it's not a fare I can turn down. I haven't the room." He said and pushed the stones back into Gara's hand.

"I have not yet given you a docking fee for when we come ashore." Gara pressed yet another stone into the sea captain's hand. "I am a quiet woman and have but one boy to travel with me. I have no great demands other than our privacy and I wish only to travel to the port nearest the Lake of the Ivory Heron, Lough Corrib as you sail north. So you see, we will not burden your stores or your crew for much more than water and a little food for we need travel only a short while with you. With such a long voyage planned, it will be a great while before you return to these waters, and any who may ask about my name will be long moved on and you will bear no inconvenience for the passage of one woman and her boy other than the weight of these stones here."

Gara took the man's hand and placed a fourth, very impressive stone of a deep red tone into his palm. She gave a little shove of encouragement with her mind, willing the man to agree to take her and Triag to home waters. Still, the man hesitated. Growing impatient, not wanting anyone to see or recognize her talking with a ship's captain so that her steps home might be traced, she barked. "Well what'll it be, man? This is likely more wealth than you'll see in a year's voyage." Completely tipping her desperation, she gave up the pretense of being a shrewd bargainer and said, "Very well then, upon setting sail, you will receive my final payment of a matching firestone to that last one there. It is all I have and all I can do. Either agree or give me back all my stones so that I may take my business elsewhere."

At this, the captain looked up a Gara with bloodshot eyes and studied her well. He looked again at the stones in his hand.

"Agreed." He said. "But we'll take port in the north most shore in the north channel. It's as far as I'll go and it's a stop I hadn't planned to make." He said gruffly to let her know this deal was take-it-or-leave-it. "Ye'll be on foot from there te get to where ye will. We set sail at first light. Come before sun up on the morrow next if ye want to be gainin' the ship without witness. Mind ye, we leave at first light whether ye be here or no. And, woman, have a care how ye be showin' such wares around. Ye may not be se fortunate as te come across such as meself and be takin' a thump on the head for your troubles. It may be that this port is known for its welcome and the good nature of the old king, but things has changed since his death and there's been a darkness te the night beyond the passin' of the sun, if ye take me meanin'."

Gara looked surreptitiously around her. "I do take your meaning and thank you for the advice, Captain." She took his hand now in both of hers. "Perhaps one who is wise in the ways of these ports and waters might take an interest in the safety of a lady in her travels?" She shined a bright and meaningful smile at the man who knew her meaning and for the first time smiled back at her. His teeth were bright in his sun reddened, leathery face. His eyes took an appraising walk over the woman's figure and clothing. His face betrayed his thoughts that this might prove to be a beneficial fare for him in more ways than one.

"Seein' as the other areas of below decks will be occupied, it's likely ye'll have te stay in me own quarters for yer part of the voyage...As me guest like.

"Captain," Gara answered and took the man by his arm and confidentially leaned in to his ear as though they shared a secret. "It will be an honor to be your guest." She graced the captain with another smile she hoped was full of decadence and promise as she felt his muscular arm beneath his linens and gave it a conspiratorial squeeze.

"If ye'll come te the hut by the stone jetty at gray sky, just before sunup, I'll have two of me men there waitin' te carry yer things and te make sure yer safe aboard. Be there not and yer on yer own, fer as I said, I've other passengers te attend." The Captain added in a softer voice, "Although I doubt if I'll enjoy their company as much as I will yours, Lady."

"And the boy." Gara added just to make it plain that there would be two on the voyage although she hadn't cared much if he stayed below decks or with the crew.

The captain landed his watery eyes on the boy and assured Gara. "The boy too."

Gara left the area with Triag satisfied that she'd found her way out of these parts and back home to where the world was right and sane. Back to her land and cattle and comfort. It was a risk, she knew, giving the Captain the gems but she felt confident in the magic she'd cast the night before that would ensure she'd find the correct captain of the correct ship to take her to her intended destination. Gara felt assured of passage on his ship but was pleased that he took her offer to have her company on the journey as an added guarantee. She only hoped now, that her idiot daughter hadn't completely lost all control of her holdings in the short time she'd been away. *Short time. Ha!* She thought. *It's been an eternity.* Gara felt content at the prospect of leaving the backwards world of the clan Laoghaire where he would now be king and she held no power at all but was practically a prisoner. In fact, she may even enjoy the laughable king-making festivities this night knowing it will be her last one here.

Deep in her thoughts and plans now, Gara made no note of a figure standing at a nearby table making a trade for some exotic spices. The figure appeared to be a small man interested in making a bargain with some furs but as Gara and Triag passed the table, Lon Dubh, dressed in her traveling leggings and leathers, turned her face away as not to be recognized. She made note of the conversation she just heard and resumed her business with the trader.

———

The three women worked together to cast long and deep magic of protection around Laoghaire's kingship and family. For the first time in a great many days, Faidhe called to her the Cauldron and the Staff to infuse the artifacts of royal lineage for the Clan Laoghaire, the golden torque, brooch and circlet that would be Laoghaire's crown with strong blessings of health, harmony, protection, strength, influence, wisdom and justice. The women spoke the blessing over the great Cauldron which they had filled with spring water and set to bubble over a wood fire infused with herbs and some very potent herbs and spices acquired by Lon Dubh at the port market earlier this day.

All three took a purchase on the Staff as they stirred the concoction so the aromatics would rise and each of the elements would add its Power to the spell cast with a long arm to bring the magic well into the future of kingship for the isle. The women took on the triple aspects of the Goddess herself, one still a maiden, the next a mother and the older one, though still bearing fruit, of age to be the wise woman. They chanted the words and stirred the pot. One by one, they dropped the artifacts to be blessed into the pot for purification and infusion of the characteristics to be displayed by the king who would wear them.

Colm dropped the brooch of the Hill T'airg into the Cauldron with her petition.

"Grant that the heart which beats under this brooch will beat strong and true, ever offering harmony and protection, meting out wisdom and justice. Grant the heart that beats under this brooch will rule true and generous to its people, battle fierce with the fury of the legendary lion when words of wisdom fail, and grant that its wisdom may never fail. Grant that the heart will be the heart of a High King, filled with confidence and bravery, kindness and understanding. Grant that the heart of this one High King will share stewardship of its kingship with the equalizing and rational fire of thought that burns in the head." All three continued to stir and Lon Dubh tossed the golden torque into the pot and offered her portion of the entreaty.

"Grant that the voice that emanates from the throat upon which this torque rests will carry the resonance of Power of the word of one king throughout this land. Grant that the voice of this king will be heard throughout time as in legend and tale to carry from this first High King to the last. Grant that the one who will bear this torque about his neck will have his words heard as king's words by all in this land from the first High King to the last. Grant that his voice will carry authority enough to hold the people of this land together as one people, one clan from the first High King to the last. Grant that the voice of this king will utter the wisdom of both the heart and the head. The women stirred the Ash wood Staff around in the Cauldron and could hear the artifacts being swept along the metal Cauldron with the sunwise current they created. Faidhe spoke as she dropped the gold circlet that would be Laoghaire's crown into the mixture.

"Grant that the one upon whose head this crown sits will have care and caution of thought to rule his words. Grant that the one upon whose head this crown sits will remember his oath to the Goddess and the God to strive for balance in his rule and to forget not the Old Ways. Grant that the fire in the head of this High King will be cooled by compassion and will be stoked by injustice. Grant that this High King has a thirst for knowledge to feed his words. Grant that High King from first to last will have ears for the voice of his heart and know when to listen and when to speak and when to act so he is blessed with the love and loyalty of his people from the first High King until the last so his task as High King may be completed. Bless his head and thoughts."

Lon Dubh added, "Bless his throat and words."

And Colm said, "Bless his heart and passion."

After a moment's hesitation all three women said in unison, "Blessed be."

For the clan folk, the donning of the artifacts will signify the passing of kingship from Ri Laoghaire to Croi Laoghaire. But Faidhe did not want to leave the importance of this task up to trust that the artifacts alone would insure his success in taking over kingship of the entire island. The casting of magic will make certain, expedience in the acquiring of fealty from neighboring kings, queens and chieftains to come under the protection and rule of Laoghaire so that there would be a gathering of power under his name rather than a challenge. Circumstance would provide Laoghaire with opportunities to display to his would-be rivals, the benefits of coming to the side of his Sword in battle and to stand protected behind his Shield. Now, Laoghaire will be ready for all that his kingship will involve when he takes the artifacts and the mantle of rule at his king-making ceremony.

"I am blessed to have been with you both to see my husband come to the throne." Colm broke the silence as the women fished the artifacts out of the Cauldron, dried and wrapped them with linen. "I had lost my way in despair for a time but now, as I stand with you both, I feel centered and right again. I can only attribute my honest love for you both in such a short time to the knowledge that we are not only kin, but also kindred. If you take my meaning; it is within the realm of magic that I find myself secure and sure of my path.

She said directly to Lon Dubh, "I find that when I cast with you my sister, I am most suited to the task and feel a bond such as could be no stronger had we been birthed as twins from the same womb and seed." Unused to being so honest and intimate with any other than her Laoghaire, Colm flushed.

"I take your meaning and feel as you do Colm. I know not if it is the joy of knowing my sister that strengthens our bond in magic or simply that we share the bond of being children of the Circle, that we were conceived in magic and born as children of the Goddess and God as well as of our earthly parents, but our bond goes beyond being sisters or the earthly aspects. I feel we share one heart and one mind as we open to the magic of the casting. Though I have known no other as closely, it frightens me not. It is a comfort to me. It will be especially so, as I journey now to places afar, now that I know you are here in the world and only but a moment's thought away. And know you this: Should you feel the cold fingers of doubt creep to your heart and mind again, you have only to reach out for me and I will lend you my strength to force back whatever troubles you. Think of it not, just do it and our bond will comfort each of us."

Both women took a moment to swallow the lump welling in their throats and to blink away tears. It was in the aftermath of the Powerful magic they had just cast with the Staff and Cauldron that the residual energy still swirled about the women. As the words were spoken they were sealed as oath as Lon Dubh and Colm took each other's hands and joined hearts. Neither felt awkward, they bonded as a lifetime of each woman's memories flooded the other's mind and heart and they knew each other in that moment.

"Would that we had more than three days' time each visit we are granted with one another. Would that we be granted lifetimes together to make up for the one we forfeit in our commitments in this one." Colm uttered.

"If it were mine to say, I would make it so." Lon Dubh answered. In that moment, Faidhe spilled the waters of the magical ceremony out onto the earth and the steam rose throughout the small hut they had procured for the ceremony, filling it with the scent of the herbs and spices and sending the flames sputtering as the water bubbled furiously around the edges of the fire. The sisters looked at one another; their eyes locked as they continued to clasp hands. Their hair rose with the steam of the pot and they knew from that moment, they were connected by a bond of the heart, of magic and now by oath. And for the second time in a short while, the two women uttered the words in unison: "Blessed be."

Faidhe looked up from her work just in time to see what had been cast and thought: So they will have with each other what I have had with neither. Am I forever cursed to be on the outside, never partaking in the lives of my children? Then she shook off the thought, chastising herself that she should be honored to have been the vehicle through which these stalwart souls would be born to the Earth.

———

Nemain sat with tight and puckered lips at the news Triag was sending to her. She took a moment to figure as to how the return of her mother would affect what she had set in motion and liked it not that she would lose her eyes and ears for the news of what takes place as Faidhe works to set her puppet, Laoghaire, upon the High Throne. Nor did she cherish the idea that she would have to contend with her mother earlier than it would take for her plan to be in full vigor. She sent the question to her nephew: *How long will it be until you are returned to us?*

I know this not. He answered. I do know we are to set sail at first light on the morrow and we will sail up the coast to be set a-port at the northern most port in the North Channel. From there, Gara will have to arrange for a guide or a litter to bring us home. Likely it will be a guide, for I think she has not the means for a litter.

It will be inconvenient and more of a fight than I will have wanted so soon. I still search for proof of what I know is a deed at her hand. But what I have will be enough to damage her standing, if it must. Keep me apprised nephew. I have easily taken over the remaining sheep left here to Council. Some of the Tuath have left these parts in search of kin in other lands but fear not, I think your grandmother's times of blackmailing and manipulation is over. Much has changed here with the exit of the Keepers and their family. The void has been nicely filled with a few well-placed bribes and promises. You would be surprised at how many of Gara's associations were only too happy to see her thrown to the wolves. She has done harsh business for over long and many are glad to see her in turmoil now. I must go now nephew. Keep me apprised.

Nemain closed her mind to her nephew and turned to the spot where she found blood on the floor of her brother's house.

"Brother." She called. "Brother, come to me now. There is much I need to know now so we must perfect our means and method of communicating. You must harness your energy and focus if you still desire to have value in this world. I will need your full help if I am to work the magic of bringing your spirit back and you must give to me what I need to have full control of all that takes place here, for our sakes and the sake of your only seed if we do not succeed in bringing you to the flesh."

A milky, filmy substance began to form over the bloodspot and appeared as though it was trying to take some form or shape. A jabbering whisper of garbled and disconnected words could be heard. At this, Nemain smiled a wicked grin.

"Brother, let us work together. I have known you to make an appearance simply to see someone mocked or embarrassed. For this, ultimate power in position, and magic with a hint of revenge, I would think you would try harder!"

The taunt did its work. The appearance of Briciu came into full form within the misty film but as it did, Nemain drew back a step as she noted the look of malice and contempt stamped upon its features. It seemed that the thing was both her brother and not her brother. It was unlike any other spirit or entity she had communicated with during times past. This being was completely devoid of humanity or conscience but oh, she could feel the wave of Powerful energy emanating from it wash over her like an intoxicating bath.

"I will figure how to tap into but a portion of this Power brother, we will see you make your passage back to this world, and then together, we three will rise to rule and then you may see to your revenge. Nemain had never cared overmuch for her brother but the Power she felt from his communications was seducing her to do what she otherwise would never have thought to do. She was dabbling now in magic beyond her abilities and comprehension without benefit of tutelage from a wise woman or any attempt at protection magic. She was toying with uncontrollable energy, foolishly grasping only at what might be gained without thought to the consequences.

———

At the sacred time of in-between, when the daylight wanes and the night takes hold, the flames of celebration were lighted near the great Stone in the village of Clan Laoghaire. Croi Laoghaire stood naked for his king-making so all could observe the unscarred body of one who would be king, indicating the protection of the Gods throughout his lifetime and so a sign that he is worthy to take High Throne.

As part of the king-making, Laoghaire must make a union with the earth to swear his allegiance to the Gods so that all under his protection will prosper. He will need their blessing also if he is to stand through inevitable battles that will occur until all have come under his Shield. *But better for them under my Shield than under my Sword*, he thought, for he knew he would be the victor of all his battles so long as he carried the sacred Sword. He had no desire to slay fellow countrymen in such a way, that their battle was lost even before it had begun.

It was Laoghaire's hope that word of the fair and balanced rule he intended for his people would travel quickly so there would be few challenges from those who quested after power for personal gain or repute and admiration.

In times past, king-making was done with some kind of union with a symbol of the earth and an oath taking. Laoghaire had heard stories as a child, of king-making ceremonies where the intended ruler copulated with a horse to display his strength of dominance over the earth. This was not to be so for him, for his rule would be to promote balance and reverence, not dominance between forces: male and female, earth and spirit, king and queen, God and Goddess. He would take his queen to lay with him on the night of his ceremony. As he passed from prince to king, to High King, Laoghaire would do as he could from the start to make changes for his clan folk and this sacred isle.

For this reason, Laoghaire had consulted his wife and queen for it would be a display for witness at the close of the ceremonies. A consummation of kingship and a symbolic union between humankind and the earth. When he had shared with her his sentiment behind the ritual, she had agreed that she would once again play the role of Goddess to his God, queen to his king. He explained to her as he would to the clan folk when he took his oath this night.

"As the world passes from the supremacy of the feminine to the dominance of the masculine, we must take great care in maintaining respect and reverence for the feminine. The She must not be dominated but protected and revered without condescension. Her wisdom must be respected and preserved. We must make changes as the masculine ways take sway, but we must take caution that the changes are made in such a way that all is not destroyed. Changes to preserve the Old Ways!"

So they stood publicly at the ceremonial fire as Laoghaire was ritually washed and his body was marked with ancient symbols in blue stain made from woad. The magical symbols were painted with meaningful intent to bring strength and virility to crop, cattle and kin during his reign.

Colm was wrapped in pristine linens of the finest weave so that it was as sheer as dragonfly wings and soft as the spider's web. One stretch of linen was draped as a veil over her head and crowned with a wreath of woven vines and springtime wildflowers. Several other stretches of linen were knotted about her body in a form-fitting manner as to trace and expose all the curves of her womanhood. The two stood for all to see and they were magnificent in bare simplicity. Laoghaire drew attention as every muscular curve was accented by the flickering firelight as it cast deep shadows into the crevices of his form. When the painted symbols were completed, he raised his arms holding the sacred Sword in his right hand above his head and the crowd silenced. With one swift slash of the great Sword through the base of the fire, all flames were snuffed out from the ritual fire as if the Sword stole the very breath from the flame so it could not kindle. Raising the Sword once again to the sky Laoghaire called to the people.

"The flame of the past has been doused and we stand in darkness. Take this time to lay aside fears, quarrels and hardships that weigh heavy on your hearts. Put to the past old wounds and infractions. Now is a time of passing away from stale sorrows and passing into a new time for our people. We keep honor for our ancestors and revere their memory but we mourn not the dead for they are with us and in time, may return to us as life anew sparks from our seed and wombs. One night past, we said goodbye to my mother and father our King and Queen Ri Laoghaire with full hearts and blessings as they passed to the Otherworld. This night we bless their son as he passes to his destiny as King Croi Laoghaire to his people. I serve the Gods who have granted this stewardship of the people of this island to me when they issued to my hand this Sword." At the mention of the Sword, the blade began to glow an aura of energetic blue. "My father's flame of life has been doused, and here in this hearth tonight a flame is kindled anew."

Laoghaire lowered his Sword once again and from its point issued a blue spark that set the glowing hearth aflame once more, bright and hot.

Over the gasping of the crowds, Laoghaire spoke boldly. "I am sent here to you, my clans' people to insure the flame here is kindled anew each cycle of the sun as the seasons pass so we do not forget, in the changes that will come, to keep reverence in our hearts for the Gods and each other. I have seen our days in the long future and our beloved sacred isle will change greatly but neath her blanket of long times past, buried under generation upon generation of dust, she will lay sleeping until it is her time to wake. She will spark once again just as this flame has been rekindled here this night.

My kingship for which I take oath this night is to ensure that our isle and our people reach beyond time and are not erased against many forces that will try to place her under a yolk for their own bidding. We will not be broken. It is our task and duty as Clan Laoghaire to keep the ember of the sacred aglow 'neath the ash until such a one will come and douse the fire of the past as I have done here this night and usher in a spark and flame anew in these lands to bring forth our pride and spirit to be once again born under his own banner, that of the Circle and the Sword together."

With this, he took up the Shield from Colm and lay his Sword atop the other so the symbol of the Cross and Circle could be seen by all. He made note of the new figures that had been etched on the Shield and looked to Colm in question. She nodded in reassurance and he accepted that he would understand the images when she explained them to him. He had after all, entrusted the Keeping of the Shield to her as the feminine half of their union. He continued to address the people.

"It will be long after our bones have slept in the ground but what takes place here in our clan and how we keep reverence and faith for the Gods and the land, will be our legacy for this one who will come in the name of his God and keep flourished the spirit in this land. For it is this spirit of clan, and unity and reverence for the sacred in all that is the He and the She."

As Laoghaire finished speaking, Colm had been aided in her climb to the top of the Stone of Fal where she awaited the next part of the ritual. From below she heard Laoghaire's words: I consummate this bond between myself and the earth, air and sky. Atop the very Stone of Destiny I will lay with the Earth Goddess and She with me, witnessed here by you, my clan and illuminated by the fires. So in the eyes of the Gods and the elements we play the role of the spirit as we join flesh and consummate our bonds to this land, her people and her Gods. This is my oath to you, my clan, as we build our triumphs of the future on earth and sea."

With his final word echoing, the crowd watched as his agile body scaled the wooden scaffolding to the top of the great Stone. The view from below provided the crowds with only a glimpse of Colm's gauzy linens, unknotted, as they cascaded over the edge of the Stone. For just a moment, Laoghaire could be seen standing in all his masculine readiness over the woman, his wife, who represented the Earth Goddess and a subdued hum arose from the Stone. He kneeled to take partnership with Colm as the King God and his back could be seen gently lowering toward her. As he did so, the Stone vibrated a deep and consistent hum that shook the earth under the feet of the clan folk.

Although Laoghaire could not be heard, it was seen that his expression was one of complete bliss and reverence as he uttered quiet words to Colm during their union. It seemed as if none in the crowd moved to make their own way to the private fires, but all stood practically breathless awaiting consummation of the kingship that brought newness, excitement and changes to the people. All perceived this change as a positive thing in the shadow of the recent deaths and feelings of foreboding in the village.

In the final thrusts, Laoghaire's back arched and he threw his head straining toward the sky. The Stone's vibrations grew in intensity in this moment. The blue symbols writhed on the king's back as his muscles contorted. Evidence of contentment covered his body in a dewy sheen of exertion that reflected the flickering flames further giving the impression that the symbols moved as the sweat blurred the edges of the woad and the symbols ran together. High on the Stone he disappeared from view as he leaned over his queen for a long moment and the vibrations from the Stone ebbed once again to a low hum.

Atop the Stone, Laoghaire took oath and vow quietly with Colm.

"My wife and queen, Earth Goddess, I am on this day as breathless in your presence as I was on the first day you cast your spell on my heart. When I thought I had lost you, I wandered in darkness, and misery, fearful and weakened at the thought of living a hollow and meaningless life without the warmth of your love and touch. I understand now the error I made in thinking that in order to be true to my commitment to the Gods that I had to be separate from you. I should have seen that I was wrong when I took to the Circle alone rather than to share and partner with you all aspects of my journey for what use is the journey to me if you and our family are not only its end but by my side throughout? I was distracted by my call to responsibilities but I see now with open eyes that you and our children are my first responsibility and so with any new endeavor as ruler of these lands, no matter how crucial or important, you shall be at my side and rule as my partner, my queen, my wife, my love."

"And I was lost in a childish need for your attention, never giving thought to the magnitude of your calling to the Hill. I should have been with you offering my knowledge rather than pining for you in your absence. Never again my love will I be blind to the presence of such evil as to cause me to doubt myself or you."

At this, Colm took the linen she had worn draped over her head and wrapped Laoghaire's loins to cover his spent manhood and threw the end of the material over his shoulders to bind it with the gold brooch she had taken from one of the knots in her linens. As she fastened the brooch she gave explanation.

"These pieces are symbols of your kingship but have also been blessed with attributes you will be known for and this one especially, worn over your heart, will be a symbol of your strength of character, the lion's heart, true, brave and pure in purpose. It is for this symbol I have added the picture of the lion to the Shield so the blessing is cast in triplicate: in your heart of flesh, on the brooch in gold and depicted for all to see and recognize as the symbol of your strength and protection on the Shield. These too, have been so blessed by my mother and my sister for you so you have triple blessing on all three symbols of your kingship."

Colm placed the heavy gold torque on Laoghaire's neck and stood to wrap the remaining linens, now slightly smeared with blue, about her while Laoghaire remained on his knees. Offering the last artifact to him, she raised her voice so all could hear. "On this night, you, Croi Laoghaire, take your place in story and song as the true and rightful heir to the throne here on the coastal shore of this island. As I place the crown upon your head, you meet your destiny as it has been given you by the Gods."

She placed the circlet on his head and the Stone once again let off a shrill and loud screeching vibration in celebration of the rightful king taking his place in history.

Laoghaire stood next to Colm now and took the crown of flowers from where she had laid it on the Stone.

"On this night, I accept my duties and crown as King Croi Laoghaire of this land." He signaled for Colm to kneel. As she did, Laoghaire held out her crown of flowers over her head.

"In acceptance of this kingship, I crown you Queen Colm of the Clan Laoghaire, Earth Goddess, and of the royal line of the Tuatha de Danann. You will rule with me as my partner, advisor and confidant. Shield to my Sword. Laoghaire bent to pick up his Sword from the top of the Stone and gently touched her head once with tip of the blade. A shivering blue spark danced from the tip to Colm's head and shone brightly at the spot between her eyes and disappeared. Let all who witness this celebration hear me now for the news I bring you is that of your queen. She is Goddess to my God, queen to my king, feminine to my masculine, spirit to my flesh and will be revered as such. And from this day forth, we will hold a celebration of the coming of the Goddess Queen, Mother of the Earth at the time of the second planting.

There was a moment of silence before the crowd cheered a great roar. There was much revelry and celebration of the new royal couple and the sense that those in the village had been released from the fearful clutches of something unclean and evil. The new king brought decisiveness and strength as well as youth and new blood to the clan. The clan's folk were hopeful for a positive and prosperous future. And they were relieved to be out from under the dark caul of death and uncertainty that had touched them of late.

During the celebration, small boys went about brandishing wood swords and twig crowns and the girls carried straw shields wearing linens draped over their heads or flowers in their hair, each emulating the new leaders. There were many who energetically took to the fires as they would during a quarter celebration. Villagers shared what food was to be had and there were more than a few seeds planted to further the Clan Laoghaire that night as people took to the fires with whomever attracted them for the time.

But for Laoghaire and Colm it would be for them as it had always been. Each to each other and on this night, the words they spoke were as their vows to keep only to each other until separated by death. The memory of the last feast they had attended was distant and all but forgotten as they danced and laughed together with their children and clan.

—

The boy watched his mark as he danced through the winding group of people, placing himself so he'd be sure to pair up with his prey. When finally he came to his chosen partner, he smiled what he hoped was a winning smile and danced her out of the grouping, spinning her and laughing all the while he ushered her to the edge of the crowds.

Morgan wore a white veil of linen as her mother had earlier, with a crown of ivy around her head. Dizzy with the spinning of the dance, she pulled to a stop and tried to understand what Triag was doing.

"Stop Triag. I want to dance with the others."

"But what I am going to show you, the others do not know. Come with me and I will show you a secret." He cajoled.

Morgan looked to where everyone was dancing and then toward where Triag was leading her. One area had light and laughter, people, music and dancing. The other way was dark but for a few small fires outside homes beyond the village center.

"What is it?" She asked.

"If I tell you, it won't be a secret, now will it?"

"If you show me it won't be a secret either. I don't think I want to." She said and turned back toward the music. Triag grabbed her arm and held on securely.

He assessed how many people might hear her if she yelled or screamed. *Too close,* he thought and released his pressure on her arm.

"No! Please, don't go. I really want to show you. Just you. This is special Morgan. And I want to share it with you. Won't you let me? Please?"

Again Morgan looked to the crowd and felt her intuition warn her, but she'd always felt badly for this boy. He was so odd and awkward.

"How far is it?" She asked.

"Just over here." He said. Feeling encouraged, he took her arm and began to lead her past the trading huts where there were no other people, then between two of the huts and behind them to where there was a courtyard of sorts where someone had begun an early garden. Amidst the plantings, Morgan saw a small fire and a mat laid out nearby.

"Triag, what is this?" She inquired, truly befuddled as to what he was showing her.

"This is our coupling fire." He said and began to urge her toward the arrangement.

"What? No! I am not of age and neither are you. It would be wrong and I don't want to. You know what is said: If a woman refuses the rites, as is her duty to bear children, she must answer to the Council. But I am not yet a woman and may refuse without question." Morgan turned to go but a moment too slowly.

"Those were the rules of the Tuatha de Danann." Triag grabbed her and spun her easily. "This is not the Tuatha de Danann and there is no Council here."

With unexpected strength, Morgan shoved the boy so he stepped back pin wheeling his arms to maintain his balance.

"No, there is no Council here but my parents rule here and no matter who you were back with the Danann, forget not who I am now. I am a maiden of the Goddess of the Earth and daughter of the king of these lands." She grew fierce and stepped toward the boy. "You will not harm me."

Triag watched as the little sprite of a girl seemed to grow in size and took on the appearance of one much older and wiser than the girl he knew her to be. She was formidable. Any thought he had to take this girl, by force if necessary, shriveled at the sight of her countenance.

"I...I would not harm you." His petulant voice denied. "I...I wanted to love you." He said and now sounded as bewildered with the situation as if he'd just awoken to his own actions. "Morgan, I..."

The girl turned away from him and with straight back marched back down the alley way between the huts toward the rest of the clan. After she had gone, Triag stood staring at the fire scene he'd set up, wondering just what he thought would take place. He whimpered a bit and in a fit of rage, furiously kicked dirt over the flames and put out the fire. "FATHER!" He shouted in ball-fisted frustration before he left the courtyard.

In the silence that followed, a small figure emerged from the shadow of the buildings and Fion could be seen watching the last of the boy lumber away.

"Good girl." He uttered with admiration. "You have the strength of your heritage. You will not easily be maneuvered."

———

Lon Dubh came to the rooms where she knew she would find Iarann.

"Why is it that you do not celebrate at the fires?" she asked. "Do you carry still, pain in your heart for the loss of Ethlinn?" Lon Dubh was curious to puzzle out the big man's motivations. She knew he had love in his heart for her and although she had not overtly offered her maidenhead to him, she was sure that should she lie by the fires at any one of the rituals, that he would be her partner of choice. She wanted to know if he would accept the honor should she offer it.

"Always will I feel the sting of the loss of her company but I will not dwell on the loss for look at all I have gained in these times of travel with you and Faidhe. I come to see your hearth as my own and feel blessed that we travel as a family. Faidhe is an admirable woman and carries her duties to the Gods as a mantle of honor. She carries the burden of this quest and a babe in her womb with dignity and single-mindedness. I know not where she gathers the strength to do what she must. And I accept that she is so occupied with all that her task entails that she has little or no time for the likes of you and me. It is your company on this journey that I cherish, Lon Dubh. If it had not been for the privilege of learning who you are and making a family with you and your mother, I do not know if I could bear the burden of making this trip, knowing what is ahead for me."

"What's this? Are you a Seer now so you can see your own future in this journey? What can it be that keeps grim those eyes that I have come to love as I feel their warmth when you gaze in my direction?"

Lon Dubh felt a thrill at uttering the word love aloud to Iarann for it had been long in her mind that she would take to the fires and make a life with this man. And it was true; she was warmed by his glance and embrace. She had come to be comforted in his company and protection for all this long trek.

"No. Not a Seer, but in my task of fashioning the silver plates for the Cauldron, it has been made known to me that I must reserve myself as a key player in the great ritual that will take place when we reach our final destination. Would that I could be free of this commitment, I would proclaim my love right now to my fellow traveler and hope that she would have me as my heart longs to share itself with her. But I fear duty stands in the way and it will not be so."

Lon Dubh's own heart leapt, finally hearing the words for which she'd long awaited.

"I am sure that whatever your duty is, you will find your travel companion willing to wait a while longer to have finally come together with the love she has anticipated and been so patient in her wanting. And should the ritual of which you speak be a Great Marriage, then it will be so and perhaps there will be another babe in this family to sooth for the time that has been lost."

Iarann's eyes turned to Lon Dubh and the pain could be seen in them. "Do you know this in your heart or do you just sooth a man so that he will not be broken by the loss of his own hope?"

"I know well the heart of your travel companion and although she longs for your touch and to have her duties to the Gods done well and finished, she is quite willing to wait until all is ready for the exact moment when you will be free of your commitments to stand as God to her Goddess. For one thing in all this is certain, when that union takes place, it will be a Sacred Marriage."

"You have discussed this with your mother?" He asked eagerly.

"Not to detail but you can be sure that she and I are of equal opinion that your position in this family should be solidified by such a marriage that reaches beyond a union of the Circle."

"My heart sings at this news. I can scarce contain my joy at hearing you say so. I will keep to my task of smelting the silver Cauldron to bring all to fruition and bring closer the time when this marriage will take place. I mind that all must be done and finished as the Goddess has proclaimed and only then will I come to my bride for only then will she be ready. Until then, all will be as it has been and we will travel as a family until we make it so for in my heart we are already as a family."

Lon Dubh could not resist embracing Iarann in her absolute joy at hearing him profess his love for her. She buried her head in his chest and told him of how pleased she was at his integrity in honoring his commitment no matter how difficult it might be for all those involved.

"Leave me now Black Bird. Let me begin work on this final panel for this one vexes me in all its complexity. I must concentrate deeply to forge the details of this one for I sense this panel carries more strength of meaning than the rest."

"As you wish Iarann. I will grant you all the time you need to complete your task and to come to the end of this journey with the knowledge that you accomplished all that was yours to do with the highest degree of care and attention." She pulled him down toward her and planted a gentle kiss on his cheek before leaving his work chamber.

42

Bon Voyage

The sea captain had been true to his word and two men had been sent to meet Gara and take her safely aboard his ship. Unseen, she and Triag slipped from Baile Laoghaire in the early morning, taking with them all they possessed that could be carried. The two men were strong and made light work of carrying Gara's goods to the captain's quarters. The knowing smirk on the dark one's face irked Gara for it seemed that the men thought her some kind of chattel there to warm the bed of their captain rather than an honored guest of the most powerful man on the boat. Gara's pride decided to let these men know right from the start who she is and that she'd not stand for any disrespect.

"Thank you for your service." She said. "After you've brought fresh water, that will be all."

The men glanced at each other with mirth in their expressions. It was the taller one who spoke in a gruff, thickly accented intonation. "Water is it? Me Lady." He said with a low and mocking bow. "Y'er a right high one wi' yer airs and fine speech. Are ye not?"

Gara collected herself and gathered her strength, quelling the anger that rose within.

"I am of the Tuatha de Danann, a Councilwoman and set to take the place of the former Keeper in affairs of all that is sacred in the Tuath. Cross me not, seaman, for not only am I an honored guest who has paid smartly for passage on this vessel, and I am of kinship to the woman who is now called your queen." She stretched the truth here, and although it was not likely, it was possible that there was some familial relationship between Colm and herself if lines were traced back generations, even if only by marriage. Gara had no compunctions in dropping a name if it would advance her own cause. "Further, my good friend and your Captain will not take kindly to any mishandling of his guest."

The smaller of the men saw a shift in Gara as Triag had; he stepped back at a glimpse of what he thought was something dangerous. He did not wish to tangle with this one even if all she claimed was not true. But the taller of the men was either arrogant or too stupid to recognize the venom in this one that could be lethal, and so he continued to taunt Gara.

"I know what ye are woman. I've been the world over and y'er a one with high opinion of hersel' but yer really no more than an elder, probably put aside by yer mate, disgraced for not having any use as a wise woman and come to slip awa' beggin' a space of the kindly captain, hopin' yer wares be not too spoilt so as not te find y'ersel' cast o'reboard when he's had done wi' ye. Or mayhap ye'll spread y'ersel' te the mates then if he's ha' done wi' ye? Lets us see, mayhap I'll be givin' ye a try now and see?" He was taunting Gara as he made a move toward her.

Gara had her hand on the dagger she had tucked under her cloak and was contemplating whether she would cut his throat now or acquiesce in order to get through the journey back to her home and comfort and power, taking consolation in the knowing that she would kill him at some point during the voyage. Gara's mind flashed to Briciu and how she'd dispatched her own son after a similar skirmish. She thought that would be just the right kind of demise for this offal and relished the thought of watching his lifeblood pulse from his neck. She looked at the man and was taken aback herself when she thought she saw the very eyes of her son looking back at her. What's more, she imagined she saw a glimmer of conscious enjoyment in those eyes at the recognition. A chill ran up Gara's spine and the flesh on her arms raised into bumpy points even under her heavy traveling cloak. Just then a voice came from the entry to the captain's quarters.

"Here now. You should be long on your way mates. Off with ye now and prepare to heave away. We'll be castin' off at first light."

Heads down, both men gave a perfunctory, "Aye Cap'n." and left.

"Well it seems as though my men have not the manners to treat ye with the respect a lady such as yourself deserves. My apologies. Perhaps it will be best if you and your boy stay protected in these quarters until we're well under way. I'll be wantin' no harm te come te ye."

"Captain, that man was about to do me harm."

"No missus, he was just havin' a bit of sport with ye, I'm sure. I see ye've not a spec of color left in yer face over it. Worry not though; he'd not take liberties in captain's quarters. He'd sure enough lose his situation as a mate on my vessel if he did. No. I'm sure yer quite safe here abouts. Although, I do think as we're about te be very good friends, I should know yer name proper?"

Gara had not missed the inference that it was the captain's quarters that held the man from doing her harm and was not comforted by the fact that she'd be protected only if she remained cooped up within the stark wooden walls of the small room.

She lied. Not wanting to have her own name overheard anywhere that would prove inconvenient to her but choosing to maintain a name that might carry some weight of power, particularly when she'd landed and was in need of help to make the trek back to her home.

"Oh, of course, I am, ah, Craiche. The boy is Bannoch. And you good Captain?" She started to warm up to her benefactor in an effort to deflect attention away from Triag and herself or any story he might be looking to divine from her. "If we are to be good friends, as you say, what will I call you?"

"For now and for propriety, you may call me Captain Long but we'll see if there's a name more fittin' you'll choose te brand me with at a later, more leisurely time when we've cast off and are on our way up the coast."

He said as he stepped closer to Gara and snaked his arm around her to fill his ample hand with a goodly portion of her buttocks and squeezed with a good-natured assessment of what he might find there later.

"For now, though, I've things te tend and ye'll have te find entertainment here within this chamber. I'll send a bit of water and food, but mind, if ye've never been on the waters, ye'll not want te be takin' in too much of the water until ye know how yer innards will take te the sea. Meantime, there's a pot and make sure of it, fer I don't want any dealin's with a green-gilled seafarer makin' a mess of me cabin." That bit of business out of the way, the captain left Gara and Triag for the time being, cloistered in the small room.

Gara looked about and was unimpressed with the quarters kept by the captain of the ship. The opulence that she thought would have come with the title was absent. There was a small bunk and some interesting gadgets for navigation, no doubt. Now that she'd made her escape from the village, Gara looked to the travel time ahead of her with some grim reality. She was locked in this room at the behest of the Captain for whatever he desired and totally dependent on him for food and drink. She would have to prepare to keep him content and hope that not only will he be an honorable man but also that the trip would mercifully brief.

———

Gara and Triag occupied the captain's quarters as best they could without getting in each other's way. They stayed out of sight and were not disturbed beyond when the smaller of the two men who met them earlier, brought them an urn of water and some small loaves of hard bread made especially for long treks and sea voyages for the dryness of the loaves that would deter mold.

Had either of the two looked out of the door at any time before cast off, they might have caught a glimpse of the other travelers of which the captain spoke as they boarded the ship. To any who were not familiar with recent happenings in the land, the travelers appeared well connected for they came with important people to see them off. There could be seen a couple and their child, and another woman whose appearance was close enough to the first for one to assume they were sisters. But to any who had witnessed the king-making and the festivities but one night ago, these folk would be recognized as the Queen Colm's family being seen off by none other than King Laoghaire and Queen Colm.

Prior to boarding the ship, Faidhe spoke in serious tones to Laoghaire who stood with a stern expression as he listened. Colm embraced her sister and cried openly for it was the second time in less than a planting season that they had fast bonded and been torn apart.

"This time I take solace, sister in that we may speak and communicate as our mother has taught us. It is a skill we must hone as we use it for we shall use it often. Promise me?"

"I promise," Lon Dubh answered. "Never again will we be separated by a little thing such as time or distance. And you! Little ones, come to me here and let us touch hearts for I'm sure you'll be quite grown the next time we meet." She bent low and hugged her niece and nephew tightly; helpless now to even attempt holding back tears as she embraced Morgan and Macha. Lon Dubh stood, trying to compose herself.

"Brother," she whispered to Laoghaire in a tear soaked rasp, "I had no cause for concern over my sister's welfare in the past and admit, there is no cause for concern now other than I have come to know and cherish her and all her family. You have a good and faithful heart Laoghaire; have a care not to give it all away in service of your position. Keep a slip of it reserved for the most important task, that which is your most precious charge. Know you my meaning?"

"I do, Lon Dubh. I have taken my oath that my duties as a leader will never stand in the way of my heart: my family. I have learned well from the scalding pain of the loss, if only briefly, of my family and the grasp that they are as necessary to me as the very air I breathe. It is for this reminder that my wife has added the hearty lion pictorial to the Shield so that it shall not easily be forgotten that my family is my home, life and kingdom first. Now embrace me woman, and I'll see you off to your journey with a full heart knowing that my wife is happy and that you travel with all the knowledge you will need to navigate the waters and traverse the road ahead of you. Always the independent one, I trust you to find your way."

As Faidhe gave Colm last minute words and advice, and tearfully embraced her grandchildren, Laoghaire clasped arms with Iarann.

"These waters are blessed by the Sea God, Mananan Mac Lir for passage of my father's trade as was done with his father before him. I hold that the agreement between Mananan Mac Lir and myself will continue in good faith as it had for my father, but the sea is fickle and we know there is always a possibility that the ship and its precious cargo may be lost to us. But the ship's course is set and will not often be in open, ocean far from land. Iarann, you are half-God and an able man.

I see how love grows in your heart for the companions you keep. Use what you can of your strength and heritage when necessary to bring your charges through to the finish of their oath. Protect them in my stead so that this upheaval, pain and separation will not have been for naught."

Laoghaire's eyes pleaded with the big man and Iarann understood the king's sentiment. He had these same thoughts himself prior to embarking on this leg of the journey.

"I will have a care for all in my charge but knowing these women as I do, they will need little protecting for they are both able and strong and offer strength of will and determination as fierce as any warrior. But worry not; I will foreswear my pledge to them only if my oath in the keeping of the prophecy should demand that I do so."

"I will have to take contentment from that." Laoghaire replied, and the men released the hold on each other.

Faidhe felt content that all had been set in place here on land and now she could look to what lay ahead of her. With a saddened heart, she left part of her family behind as she and her party gained entry to the ship.

The rooms below deck that the four had been provided were small but comfortable. As important guests they had been afforded every comfort. There were fine blankets of wool and silk upon the sleeping bunks that had been aired to a fresh scent. The quarters had been scrubbed clean and they were supplied with fresh water, dried fruit and honey cakes enough for all the guests. Covered waste pots had been discretely placed behind a curtained area for privacy in such close quarters. Captain Long introduced his passengers to Searbhonta, a boy of about eleven years of age, who would be their personal helper and take care of their needs while on the voyage.

The captain had been paid handsomely to fulfill his primary charge, to bring these passengers safely to harbor in the lower basin on the south side of the mainland. He would follow his regular trade routes with the exception of one stop for which he must head due north. Other than that, he expected calm seas as customary for the spring season and the winds promised to be with them as Mananan Mac Lir continued to smile on them. Payment from King Laoghaire for the passage of these important people when he could have simply ordered it so was the first benefit, but then the added payment in jewels from the woman for her passage was an additional bonus but to have the trip be unhindered in its original trading schedule would prove to be the most lucrative passage to the mainland that the Captain had ever made. He would drop his goods of linens and hammered gold and take on oils, wine and spices in trade. Surely the Gods were smiling on him. He took this all as good omen that the trip would be successful in its completion. And although it would be the end of the warm days here at home by the time they reach their destination, it will be still mild in the warm seas to the south of the mainland. Good fortune all around he thought, as he bid his guest to excuse him to ready for cast off.

———

Triag found himself both in the way of and repulsed by Gara and Captain Long getting to know one another so had ventured out of the Captain's quarters once they were underway. A jolt of excitement burst in his mid-section when he spied another passenger whom he recognized as the boy from the village who had befriended Morgan. He briefly wondered whether it could be possible that the girl was on the ship and dismissed the thought as unlikely and foolish. When he also spied the big man from his Tuath, Iarann and Lon Dubh together on the deck, he wondered with curiosity at where they might be headed and whether their presence had anything to do with himself and his grandmother. After a moment of calculating, he supposed that they were headed back home to the Lake of the Ivory Heron as he and his grandmother were doing. Triag knew Gara would like it not that one of the family members of the Keeper was returning but it was not his problem to consider what his grandmother may or may not like. As long as she got him home, he would leave it to Nemain to dispatch his grandmother and keep her from power. If she could not, well, he would strive to remain neutral and appear innocent so he could land on the side of whomever was the victor in the grab for power and affluence in the Tuath. Either way, he would have his cattle and home so he decided to keep the information of the other travelers to himself for now and to avoid unnecessary questions by keeping out of sight of the other travelers.

———

After the passing of half a moon cycle, the ship finally came to anchor just offshore from a beach where land appeared close enough to swim ashore. When Gara felt the rhythm of the ship beneath her feet change, she ventured a look out the door of the cabin and was overjoyed to see land. She hurried to pack the few items she'd left around the cabin and readied to disembark. Gara pushed back her momentary agitation that Captain Long had not told her, despite her constant questions about when they would come to port, that it would be on this day. Just as she was about to bring her things to the deck and send hasty word to find Triag, the captain entered the cabin door.

"Where're you going pet?" He asked Gara.

"I see we've made anchor. I make ready to leave and arrange for a guide to lead me home. I thank you Captain Long for your help in my journey. You have been true to your word."

"Not se fast, Lady. This be not your port. I told ye as I'd be makin' port along the way, going about me business." At this, Gara was deflated. "Bear up now, bear up." The Captain tried to bolster her morale. "We'll not be over-long in port here, a day at the most, and we'll be on our way again soon as a wink."

"I'll go ashore then to breathe the air and walk on land." Gara snapped in exasperation.

"I'd surely take ye there meself but as ye remember how sick ye were on the first days of the journey? If ye'll not be wantin' te return te that state, Lady, I'd stay aboard. For now as ye have yer innards all set te the rhythm of the sea, te go ashore and back, ye'll risk bringin' on the sickness over again and sometimes it comes worse than the first bout." The captain was lying quickly with the hope that Gara would stay on board. He knew it would be tricky business to keep her unaware of what was actually going on, that in booking passage on his boat, Gara had actually done precisely what Faidhe had needed of her. Rather than be afflicted with Gara's complaining at being told she must travel with them on their path, when Lon Dubh had told Faidhe the news that she'd overheard Gara booking passage on the very boat they had intended themselves to board, they decided to let her travel as far and long as was possible without the knowledge that she was not going home but would embark on the journey they had intended for her. The captain was given strict orders to keep her aboard the boat until they were well away from the shores of the small island and there was no hope of her getting off the boat to find other means home.

"I'll tell ye though," the captain cajoled, "as many of the crew will be goin' ashore te trade, I'll have ye come out and walk the deck with me and te breathe the air when they've gone. I know it's a hardship te be locked away all this time. But it is for yer own safety. A beautiful woman such as yerself among all these men deprived of a woman's touch, even if ye are their Captain's guest, ye might drive these men mad."

Gara thought of the gut-wrenching nausea that kept her bent over the pot in the tiny room. Even the small amounts of water she took in to keep from withering would not stay long in her. But just as she swore she could not bear another hour of the sickness, the contractions in her stomach began to subside and she gradually began to feel well enough to take light food and drink. She had no desire to return to that state and decided that she could take a bit more of the cloistering to get her way home.

"How long until we come to my port Captain?"

He dodged the straight question with and evasive answer.

"I know we've taken longer than ye expected te come te the proper port te get ye te yer home, but patience, Lady. It's the lifeblood of me business te stop and trade. Remember now, as I told ye strait and true 'fore I took yer bargain, that I'd make no special allowances. Ye'll disembark no sooner than yer destined to fer I have me trade stops and I'll not waver. Now let's look forward to a pleasant stroll above decks when the men have gone ashore. Shall we?" He wrapped his arms around Gara's waist and pulled her close. "And after we've had a time fer ourselves this day, I've arranged fer a surprise te be brought aboard fer ye te enjoy this night. Let's be pleasant now and make the best of things."

Gara was not appeased but allowed herself to be convinced. The Captain had treated her well and had some knowledge in pleasuring a woman so that Gara was quite pleased. He had offered her some extraordinary gifts in the way of scented oils and exotic spices and so she comforted herself with looking forward to a walk on the deck, a gift or bobble of some kind, and some pleasures behind closed doors later in the evening. Gara softened and for the moment, melted into the man's arms.

———

Faidhe and her party of four made their way ashore from the anchored ship in the tiny craft as the seamen rowed into a cavern between craggy cliffs that opened to a sandy beach. As they disembarked Faidhe stepped upon the beach and immediately felt the Power in the Earth. She had not realized she'd missed the connection with the Earth's energy until now when she was able to reconnect with it. And at some great distance, she was aware of the Circle Stones that had been her home for so long, for she felt their energy now, somewhere in this land. She recognized the faint tremor of their presence and bent to remove her buckskin shoes to better feel the Earth's energy. The seamen and guides that had been assigned to go ashore with her stopped and watched the haunting woman perform this ritual with interest but kept their distance.

A strange tree nearby to the shore called Lon Dubh's attention in that it appeared to have sprouted black, fluttery leaves. Upon closer scrutiny the seamen recognized that the tree was completely covered and inhabited by crows, ravens and black birds. Lon Dubh smiled and raised both her arms toward the tree.

"Greetings my friends and protectors. Your welcome warms me."

In that moment, thousands of the birds swarmed from the tree and flew about cawing and squawking their welcome to the party and flew off in the distance to perch on yet another tree.

"We travel this way." Faidhe said, and began to walk in the direction that the birds had flown. A few of the men were glad to depart company with the strange party and headed to the coastal village to do trade. The other of the seamen followed Faidhe and her party further inland. Some of the more observant men noticed that the older of the women, the one who had taken off her slippers, was carrying an elaborate Staff that they had most certainly not seen before this moment. Some thought nothing of the oddity while others displayed expressions of curiosity.

None mentioned it. They all followed the woman and her party, as the entire group followed the flight of the birds.

At mid-morning, the company arrived in the area where they found many willing to gossip about a great Stone having been planted deep into the earth by night and stories swirled about a stone giant that did the planting, which then set off to the south with great booming strides. Faidhe spoke with tribal leaders to gain information regarding the giant and to request permission to view the Stone. Since just prior to the planting of the Stone, there had been Seers in the tribe here who had caught glimpses of the coming of just this woman and her party, there was no question in allowing her to continue on to see the Stone. The name of Faidhe had been familiar to those in this village through glimpses of the prophecy seen here and there was much buzz of excitement upon the arrival of such a woman bearing the name. The rest of the party remained in the village to trade, collect necessaries and to exchange stories while Faidhe was permitted to view the Stone.

Alone, Faidhe was seen leaning on her Staff and mounting the higher stony territory where she had been told the Stone would be found. About mid-day, still in her bare feet, Faidhe arrived at the site where the Stone had been erected. She immediately recognized the monolith as half of the Keystone of the Circle: the Sacred Stone of Falias. Faidhe understood that the part of her journey that involved her spreading words of what must be done was finished. The Staff, which indicated a cause to be talked about, must now be held for the one who will come telling of new changes, not of the Goddess, but the God. She knew she must relinquish the Staff in waiting for the one who will come. Subconsciously Faidhe's hand touched her stomach as she thought of the descendant of the child inside her who would come to carry the Staff. A fierce wave of love for her children pierced her stoic countenance and she cried bitterly for the children she left, lost or would leave all for the sake of this cause. Exhausted, she broke down.

"Danu! Dagda! I have given my oath to do what is required. And I will sacrifice my comfort of home and family and love for the sake of the many. I have seen the prophecy and know what must be done but if there is a way that my blood in generations to come may be spared the suffering of loneliness that is the price of service to you, I bid you tell me now how it may be done."

Her voice echoed in the trees and off the Stone that stood so tall in the clearing. She waited for a response but only sighed when she was answered with silence but for the quiet cawing and preening of the thousands of perched corvine birds that had led her to this location of the Stone. She collected her emotions and with tired bones and cheerless heart Faidhe approached the Stone with Staff in hand to fulfill her task here.

"Old friend I return to you now in my last intercourse with you to do the bidding of the Gods. I retain the Cauldron and have assigned the Sword and Shield to other worthies to suit their purpose where they be. But you and I, old friend, we have this last bit of business before I move over the waters. As a seed, I plant this Staff of Lugh for future usage in the hand of one who will be named as noble priest to bring word of the coming of the time of the God to these lands. We transit away from the time of magical awareness and the reign of the Goddess and use what Powers that be now to temper the fury of the masculine energy with a living reminder of the spirit so that the Power of the masculine is not unleashed on the world in full strength. When this man comes, blood of my blood and blood of the spirit, he will hear the voice of the spirit as I do and will be drawn to and understand his journey. He will serve the God as I have served the Goddess, unselfishly and unfailing in his efforts. He will find his way back to the land of the Mother and he will plant his seed with the Staff of Lugh in the fertile ground of the land of Danu so that the message he carries will take hold and grow firm and strong. For despite the one-sided teachings of the God in that time, there is no He without the She and the She will be succored and nurtured, unrecognized throughout the Fourth Civilization's time of the God until such time at the dawning of the Fifth Civilization when She wakes and takes her place in the world when it will most need her. Keep safe the Word, keep safe the message, keep safe the Staff until such a one as my grandson of many grandsons in the future will come to claim it."

As Faidhe finished her spell, she raised her arms holding up the Staff as if to raise the Power to bring all she'd cast to fruition and in that moment, a strong gust of wind stirred the air and dust and the great Stone appeared to waver as if under water. Faidhe placed the Staff against the Stone and it was absorbed into the Stone in ripples of green glowing light. The Staff was gone; the Stone stood still and all was quiet.

After a moment, Faidhe turned to make the trek back down to the village and had anyone been witness to what had just taken place, they would have been shocked to see how fatigued she appeared and that the woman's hair once again began to be streaked with strands of gray.

Lon Dubh, Fion and Iarann stayed with the village folk and told stories of their journey. Music was enjoyed and before they would leave the village this day, there would be two or three new songs to tell of the prophecy, their travels, the Duibhe, King Laoghaire's Sword in the Stone and Queen Colm's marking the Shield to herald Laoghaire's lion-heart, the sacred implements, the great Stone giant and the preservation of the Circle of Stones, Goddess's triad and the sacred feminine. Here marked the first of many stops throughout this land and others to tell the story. Where there was a barrier in language, Fion proved to be useful in creating an understanding in visual context for the tale to be understood in the mind of each recipient as Lon Dubh spoke the words. This proved the Elf to be a perfect selection to both keep and tell the tale as the years slipped by. For as they traveled from this day forward, the details of the story grew as well for as was prophesied many years ago: It was a living story that would grow and proliferate from the mouth of Lon Dubh. She would spread the tale of the earth, air and water. So with her new family, she took to her task with a natural ease. She played her whistle and at times sang songs she'd learned from village to village. The songs and stories took shape and then took on life of their own each time, having added details of the last village to the tale. Lon Dubh looked to the time when she might tell the tale of the ceremony when she would give up her maidenhead in the Great Marriage. She longed for the time when she would take Iarann as her man and he would give her children. She looked to a time when their oaths were kept and their tasks were finished and they would return home to once again live on the small island together with her family. She'd waited all her life; she could wait a few moons more.

——————

There was a great rush of wings that attracted the attention of the village folk as Faidhe returned from the site of the half-Stone. Iarann was first to jump to his feet and to her aid.

"Lady, are you well? You look spent. Fion, water. Hurry!"

There was so much commotion with the birds flying overhead and the booming command of the large man, no one took notice of the impossible speed at which the Elf could travel. He was back in moments with a water urn and drinking bowl he'd commandeered from the front of one of the huts. He found Faidhe perched on a log, resting in Iarann's huge arm. Gratefully, she took the water and sipped gradually until some color returned to her face.

"It is done here." She said. "We must move on as the waters take us, seeding the rest of the lands we encounter as we go. The next and greatest task, I must face alone, once again, but that will not be for some moons."

"Rest, Mother, do not speak." Lon Dubh interjected. "We have but a short time before we will need to return to the shore to be taken back to the ship. You will need your strength to travel."

"It is not so far now." Faidhe answered. "And you are right Black Bird. We have much time on the waters to discuss what has taken place and what must be done next. I will rest a moment and then we can be on our way."

Iarann put in, "I will carry you to the shore. You are weakened and have taken on frailness since we took to the water. Preserve your strength and let me walk for you."

"Thank you Iarann. You are generous but on this path, we must each walk in our own shoes." She smiled at the joke as she fingered her own shoes tied to her waist strap. "You must preserve your strength for the time when you keep to your oath and there can be no other to stand in your stead. We must each bear our own. But I say again, thank you for all you have given me." Faidhe took her daughter's hand and looked to her face. "Let me rest here for a moment. Then we'll move on." Faidhe closed her eyes and succumbed to her exhaustion of travel, fasting and relinquishing of one of the implements to the future. It seemed that with the loss of one of the implements, she lost a measure of her youth and strength also.

———

After some lengthy moons on the ship, much of Fion's color had fled his cheeks for he was plagued with his Duibhe half needing to have the land under his feet. He was not grateful for Diog's Duibhe blood that ran in his veins for it caused him to battle the uproar in his stomach that threatened to shrink his skin to his bones. Sick or no, the Elf knew his responsibility and made quiet his insides to make contact with his brother to share with him all that was news as he had done many times since he had left the shore of Baile Laoghaire.

Hail brother. I veil my mind and must speak quick and plain. I feel your openness to me. Allow me to deliver my news without question for now. She has completed her task in the passing of the Staff to the one who will bring the word of the He to our land. The babe grows in her belly and thrives but it seems as a drain on her vitality that we saw so energized only a few moons or so ago. It seems as though a distance grows between Faidhe and this world as if she is a boat that has slipped its knot and drifts distant with the tide. I see her peering into the great Cauldron, which she calls to her often now since the Staff was relinquished. She searches with far away eyes as if looking to find our next venture within the depths of the pot. Faidhe and I wither in the flesh: I for lack of keeping food in me, and she as the hungry babe takes all goodness of the food from her.

Our lovely Black Bird is taking to her mission and spreading the tale about the countryside as we travel down the coast of the large island and now down the main-land coast. I assist her with every telling so there is an understanding, deep within the mind of the village folk despite a difference in our tongues. Some differences in language are more notable than others but the tale is being absorbed and adapted to the beliefs and understanding of each of the tribes as we meet them. The tale will multiply and regenerate in song and many versions as will be necessary. As you are aware, I open my mind to you at each telling so we have equal share in knowledge of the tale as it unfolds so you may keep the knowledge alive in our own land for the future's sake. I admit though, every time I take this union in the tale with Lon Dubh, I feel myself draw closer to her as though we have a contract of spirit. I feel as close to her as I do you my brother. There is a bond of the heart that has grown right from the first day we sat to spin our tale together. We spun a tale as we spun wool and flax all with the binding stuff of magic sealed with an oath. I love her well and must take caution that it does not interfere with our task.

I have won the heart of the Smithy, so gruff and stern to the exterior. He protects us all and teaches me some of his craft when he is able. He is gentle in his way and brings a smile to Lon Dubh's eyes, but below decks often is he now. I sense that this last panel he toils upon so long, troubles him somehow for he goes about with a crease in his brow and hears not when he is addressed. Concern is written on his face.

The woman, Gara, took not well the news that she was destined to travel with us on this journey. She grew weary of waiting and suspected the ship's Captain held her prisoner for his own entertainment. When we were well away from the port of her choosing, it was revealed that we traveled south along the coast of the large island rather than north to a port close to her home on the small island. She had plans of her own and though she felt sorely betrayed by the Captain and his part in keeping her aboard, she chooses to stay with him still in his quarters rather than to retire to the room that is hers below with us. She knows not yet that the boy knew of our presence on the ship and said nothing to the woman to warn her. I wonder myself why he said nothing. I feel a conflict within the boy, Triag. He has disease in his heart and he struggles as a dry leaf on the wind to be shut of the tormented thoughts he finds in his head. It is not often that I venture into his thoughts for it leaves me feeling sickened in my own head with his putrid thoughts and then again, I am useless to take food; even more so than the wretched waters make me. I keep my caution with that one for I fear there is a malevolent force dictating his moves. I would not wish for him or whatever evil is about him to know my mind as I open up to you brother. The boy communicates with someone as we do but has taken precautions to guard his mind. I catch occasional glimpses but his skills grow and it becomes difficult for me to hear his thoughts.

The Captain was true to his promise to Laoghaire to keep safe our secret voyage from the woman and now it is too late for her to disembark and find a way home. He balances his business and the woman, who is quite a handful of ill temperament, all the while keeping to our bargain and supplying us with ample food and comfort in our travels.

I miss greatly you and our sister, Cathbad. Would that I were with you through these times but we have taken oath and must see to the end, this venture. Share with our sister what you might but take caution not to reveal her existence to anyone for you know what fate she'll suffer should news reach Diog that a girl child is within his grasp. Keep well yourself and safe our sister, Brigit for I understand as we mark our journey with happenings to create change that will be felt far and wide, but will bring about vast and speedy change especially within our own land first. What effects initiated by the Power in splitting the Stone of Falias and removal of the Circle from our land, had set forth changing events and will continue until such upheaval will cause *great upset in our land that will over time send out ripples of energy and continue to cause changes in the world for time long into the future.*

Cathbad responded in kind. I miss you also brother. I will be brief. Changes already do take place here. As word of Laoghaire taking seat of High King spread through the land, there were some who banded together with an eye toward unseating him and usurping the place for themselves. Laoghaire has made short work of those tribes and clans who never truly banded together in strength of numbers enough to rally a true effort. He wields his Sword and the crows amass on the battlefield to pick the bones of his enemies. Colm, the queen is ever at his side, even on the battlefield, with her Shield. More travelers take to the roads these days and even in the land of the Duibhe, the stories come to Middle Village of the great and good magic that King Laoghaire and Queen Colm possess for the land prospers and but for the few skirmishes I mentioned, there is quiet in the land. Raids are few, cattle are fat and the first harvest will prove to be plentiful.

I visit Brigit as often as I can and share with her our news. Fear not, ever am I careful not to reveal her to Diog. Gods keep you safe and bring you home to us, my brother.

———

Some half-moon ago the ship had passed through the inlet between two vast lands just as had been foretold to Faidhe by the Greenman. The voyage across the waters was drawing near to its end. Faidhe was large with the child and grew near her time. The ship had come to port once again and she fought the urge to go ashore just for the sake of feeling the earth beneath her feet. Her mood was foul and she would not be good company to the others who would go to trade, tell tale and see what there was to be seen in this strange and exotic land. Standing on the deck, she smiled and waved to Iarann, Fion and Lon Dubh as they set off in the boat that would take them ashore. Faidhe watched the boat grow smaller to her sight as the crewmen rowed in unison.

Triag too was in the boat with the others as he had taken to going ashore when possible. He had always found his way back to the boat and made no attempt to leave them. Likely because Gara had remained ever on the boat and kept her arrangement with the captain. Now that she knew danger from the crew had been the Captain's ruse to keep her aboard, she had come out of his quarters to take air on the deck and at times would join the rest for a meal, but for the most part, kept to herself within the confines of the Captain's room. As the small boat pulled further away from the ship, Faidhe cast eyes upon the boy and felt unsettled that she'd not been able to identify just what bothered her about him. Had she been at her full strength, both physically and Powerfully, she might have recognized a familiar odor of something putrid about the boy.

Faidhe waved again to her family with one hand and massaged her complaining back with the other. Deep set circles weighed down her eyes and her stomach looked deformed, bulging out so far from her wasted and thin body. Faidhe relished the air as the breeze rippled across her loose linens but she felt faint and longed to sit down. She thought to go below deck to her quarters but would not leave the sight of her family until they made shore. Her back pained her but she remained disciplined to see her family ashore.

Both hands now massaging the overworked muscles that carried such a heavy weight, Faidhe turned unexpectedly toward the deck rail and emptied the contents of her stomach over the side.

"Ah, I thought to be done with that moons ago. I hope I've not taken some spoiled food," she said to no one in particular.

A voice came from behind Faidhe to chastise her.

"It has been long since you've been in the throws. Remember you not what harshness a woman's labor can be? I have but to look at you and know it is time for careful doses of mistletoe to sooth your pain and slow your blood."

Faidhe turned to the voice and saw Gara looking well and refreshed.

"The ocean air has done you good Gara. What brings you to the decks?" Faidhe said flatly, annoyed at the other woman's observations. "I remember well the pains of labor and the untidiness of birth. I judge you are right in your assessment. My babe pulls tight at my innards just now," she said and stopped speaking with pursed lips to endure the contraction. Just then, a gush of water could be seen to spread at Faidhe's feet.

Gara drew back as not to cause a stain to her soft kid hide slippers. When her eyes returned to Faidhe's face, she saw not the woman she had long perceived as her enemy but that the woman was a skeleton covered with a thin layer of sallow flesh. A coating of sweat covered her face and scalp that caused her hair to cling to her face that was drawn while she stood in the throes of pain. Gara stepped forward to support Faidhe but knew not to touch a woman in the peak of a labor pain.

"Be not so stoic, Faidhe. Your babe is upon you. Come to my room and take your rest."

Faidhe wanted to say no and return to her room but the pains were hard on her now. As soon as the first ended, the second commenced. She threw her arm over Gara's shoulder and allowed herself to be led to the captain's room.

Gara stripped Faidhe of her soiled linen and made her comfortable on the bunk that was now covered with luxurious silks from trade along the coast. She poured water from an urn into a bowl and added a good pinch of valerian root to sooth the spasms and battle the fatigue of childbirth.

"I have no mistletoe to help with the bleeding but hopefully it won't be necessary." She dipped a soft linen cloth into the water mixture and held it to Faidhe's mouth for her to suck. "Here, this will refresh you. Worry not that it will make you sick. It must be taken for it to do you good."

Faidhe took the saturated cloth and allowed it to dampen her lips. She tasted the familiar root and took it in slowly. While the Seer endured the next wrenching pain, Gara wet another cloth and dampened her face with cool water. Her expression was one of disgust. Faidhe saw this and responded.

"I have birthed children before. You are kind to help but need not stay through the mess of the delivery." Go about what you had planned for your day. Leave me, I will tolerate my path."

"You mistake my thoughts." Gara answered. "I see all you have lost, sacrificed and endured in the name of the Goddess. Now as I see the wreck of your body for the sake of bringing this child forth, I see that your position is not one of glory but one of duty. I am not of the stuff for this kind of work. I think you bring me along on your quest because you see some role in all of this for me but I tell you Faidhe, I am not made of that weave. I have not that kind of strength."

Faidhe let forth a heaving bellow and gritted her teeth to force her words through her pain.

"Speak not woman. This is not a time for thoughts of you! Can you not see any part of the world through a view that is not your own?"

"Be still now. Be still" Gara soothed, ignoring the outburst. Oddly matched we are but we have a history in common and I would no sooner leave you to bear this birth alone than you would have left me to battle my son. Try to relax and breathe deep as the ewe dropping her lamb. Let us see when this child plans on arriving."

Gara placed her hands between Faidhe's knees and pressured them apart. "Raise your backside and slip this under you now." As Faidhe did this, Gara treated her hands with some oil made from olives to easily examine the other woman. "I have not experience in this other than birthing my own children and watching my men bring cattle to calving but together, I think we can manage." Gara looked and probed with a touch so soft as one would not think her capable to use. "This one wants to come fast. I see already his head. You must have been in labor before you were aware."

A primal groan issued from the depths of Faidhe's chest and Gara thought she sounded like a calving cow indeed.

"This is a sound that is familiar to me. You are dropping this babe now. Get up now. Get up. It's time for you to squat and let the earth pull down your babe; here Faidhe lean on me. You must bear down and help him."

Faidhe focused all her attention to the life she would bring forth. Grabbing Gara's shoulders she pushed down hard with her muscles at the ebbing of the contraction, showing all of her teeth with the effort.

"I see the head, Faidhe. Good now wait and rest." Gara instructed and soaked the cloth in the treated water for Faidhe to wet her lips and sip. Monitoring the next contraction, at the optimum time, Gara felt Faidhe lean heavy on her shoulders once again and spoke in excited tones.

"Push now. I see the face. This is a determined one. Yes. Just a little longer, and good."

Faidhe screamed as she bore the tearing flesh down below. Gara spoke rapidly to distract the mother's attention from the pain.

"Here is the shoulder; the worst of it is done now. Just a bit more." And in a bloody gush, Gara caught the child in the bedding silks as he slid out of Faidhe. "You have a son Faidhe; a fine, fat son! And I don't wonder at that; he's been so greedy with your food. Wait now and lean back. Wait for the last of it." Faidhe rested waiting for the final contraction as it ejected the placenta and Gara tied off the umbilical cord to deftly sever it with a small curved dagger.

Briskly wiping and cleaning the babe caused him to open his eyes and mouth and let forth a squall that forced Faidhe to collapse in tears while at the same time, Gara let out a laugh of jubilation at the new life she'd just helped bring into the world. With genuine joy in her eyes, Gara placed the boy on his mother's chest and gently covered Faidhe with fresh blankets after cleaning away the soiled ones.

"Rest you now and suckle if he will. I doubt it not that this one will continue to drink you dry. I will bring you broth and see if there is milk that has not yet turned." Gara turned to go with her day's work all over the dirty coverlet and blankets she carried.

"Gara? Thank you for your kindness. I would not have enjoyed going through this alone."

"These moons on this boat away from the politics of the Tuath have helped me to enjoy simpler things of life. I feel as if this, today, meant something more than mere decision making over grazing rights and such." Gara stopped and contemplated what she wanted to say next. "I know we have not been friends but you have helped me in the past. Thank you for letting me help you and return the favor. This was a ritual as we both once again stood in the passageway between the Otherworld and life. We ushered my son out of this world for the good of all and I presume we two ushered your son in for likely the same goal. I'm pleased that the latter task was with the bringing of life rather than the other."

When Gara left the quarters, Faidhe was silent as she inspected her son's nose, sex, fingers and toes. He peered at her expectantly with wide blue eyes. After a bit of contemplation on what Gara had just revealed to her, Faidhe raised her eyebrows and said, to her son. "Hmm, so many surprises today!"

43

Trail of Sorrow

Lon Dubh and Iarann devoted a great deal of time trying to nurse Faidhe to health but they knew the sickness was in her heart and there was little they could do for her beyond keep to their tasks on the road.

They had come ashore to their destination over two moons ago when Faidhe was all but dried up with no milk for her babe. In the last days of the voyage, the crew had taken to bringing aboard fresh milk of goats and cows to supplement the decreasing supply of nutrition provided by Faidhe for her son. Not a moment too soon did the ship come to the port where the party would disembark and more likely regular milk could be found for the child.

The unlikely party of six and the babe, bid farewell and thanks to Captain Long and the crew before heading inland, led by the crows to find the place the babe would call home. Gara gave the Captain a particularly warm goodbye and slipped the promised firestone into his hand.

"I will take it not, lady for we had a bargain and it is I who came out the better for it. You may need the price of a guide here abouts." With that, he pressed the firestone he'd taken from her almost ten moons ago into Gara's hand together with the one she now held out to him and closed her fingers over the stones.

"You have offered me more in the way of warmth and knowledge of humanity far beyond what my position of power ever had in my own land." Gara confessed. "When I had the choice to slip away and leave upon many an occasion during the voyage, I opted to stay warm with you on your ship. You paid me attention and kindness though in your position you could have just as easily abused me. I have learned that power can be most powerful when it might be wielded but is not. I hope to retain the warmth of your kindness in my memory for I now have the understanding of the meaning of a vow and debt owed, and I must count on my memories of you to sustain me on the journey ahead." Gara planted a warm kiss on the seaman's lips and headed for the waiting group. All were warmed by the transformation in the woman but for Triag who inwardly considered her now to be weak and unworthy of any position of regard back home. He had been greatly angered at the discovery that he would not be seeing his home any time soon but after conferring with Nemain, he understood that this would be a convenient way to learn of Faidhe's business in these lands and to divine any magic used here abouts. He would stay quiet and observe while traveling for no one noticed him much these days.

Gara paid little mind to Triag for she was visited often by the memories of her time with the captain as they continued north from the peninsula where they had landed and were heading for a hard trek through the mountainous land to the north. The woman tried to hold onto her memories of warm days and nights of pampering and attention but the farther north they traveled, the more difficult things became, the more distant the memory and the woman fell on her old habits of harsh words and self-preservation. This would be an even more treacherous journey now that the cold months were hard upon them. And the further north they traveled, the colder it would become.

Faidhe's own mind was plagued by the memory of where she'd left the babe with a young woman and her husband who already had two children of their own and had recently lost their third born. Once they had left the ship, within two days' time the crows had led the party to the humble home of the couple that took them all in for a period of time. The crows and ravens had lingered in the trees surrounding the couple's home and as friendships grew in a short time, the decision was made that the child would stay with the couple as the traveling party took to their duty upon the road. The infant had sniffed the young mother's milk, still full and leaking from her sore breasts so soon after the death of her own child, and had taken to her to suckle. He seemed an insatiable being, questing always for the pleasure of food and to be held. This both pleased and pained Faidhe at the same time. She knew this moment was inevitable but was helpless in her sorrow as the moment arrived. Not a word was told to the couple of the boy's heritage or destiny for his future would be for the fates to carry out now.

Faidhe remembered as she walked north, the smell of the babe's hair and the expressions he made with his intelligent eyes as they changed color from blue to deep green, his satisfied cooing he made while he ate and the soft skin she soothed while she held him. Pulling her warm fur hood over her face to hide her tears, she never once looked back to the farm where the crows had led her to abandon her son and she walked heavily toward the challenge of the mountains ahead leading one of the mules they procured to carry their newly acquired supplies.

After more than two moons on the trek over and through the great mountains, the group came to a village nestled at the base of the last range of smaller hills. The clothing they had acquired for the trip was warm and sturdy but after several days of rain, the party was not only grateful to see a village but cheery smoke puffing from several hearth fires as well. They approached the village cautiously for they were strangers in a strange land and now could not depend on clan calling to be welcomed. These folk were inland and unaccustomed to the varied population of the seaports. Occasionally a trader might pass through to sell wares, but this village was well protected against travelers, wayfarers or raids and such by its very place-ment with the harsh mountains at its back and it was placed far above any raiders coming across the open land in front so any visitor would be announced well in advance and any attack would be well prepared for. But the party came unexpect-edly from the mountain range above the village at the close of the ruthless winter months so the villagers were taken unawares as the party descended the foothill into the village. It was the flurry of crows and blackbirds that alerted the villag-ers of the strangers amongst them with the raucous cawing and daring dives they made, calling attention for all to see the newcomers to the village.

Iarann took the lead as he pulled Faidhe's mule along behind him. It had been some time since all the packs had been removed from one mule to the other to accommodate Faidhe, rather than supplies. She'd given up her stoic trek and had ridden in quiet solitude for at least a moon now. Her spirit waning, she left the hunting and gathering to the others and called the great Cauldron to her less in these later days but for the most scarce times in the mountains when food stores were gone and none could be found in the raging snows. Only then did Faidhe call the Cauldron to bring food, wood and drink for survival. A party traveling over the mountains in winter without benefit of magical intervention would surely have perished. Still, Faidhe took little food or water for herself. She meditated often and kept herself isolated from the others. It appeared as if she grew physically smaller and perhaps weaker, though it was difficult to determine under all the fur and clothing worn to keep out the cold. Anyone with magical knowledge might under-stand her isolation and fasting as signs of a woman purifying her heart and mind while gathering strength to perform Powerful magic.

Lon Dubh recognized her mother's practices as being in preparation for expending vast magical energy so went about her daily chores for travel and sur-vival without being overly concerned for Faidhe's well-being. The young woman had been preoccupied with meditating on thoughts of her own. *It has been moons uncounted it seems since we left the harbor town and my mother's son. She readies herself but does not reveal my task in all this if it is to be more than to tell the tale as I have witnessed it. I communicate with my sister and she tells me of all good hap-penings for her family and the new clans. She grows in her magical abilities and has received instruction from the Gods as to what must be done with her magical charge, the Shield. We each play our role in all of this and I wait in vain for the voice of the Gods to speak to me. Iarann and I grow close but there has not yet been any talk of giving of ourselves to each other or of a marriage. I feel the ever-increasing pull to couple and bear a child to the Circle but I have not been so instructed. How am I to separate the will of the Gods from my own? I am a woman of the Goddess and have been telling tale faithfully as is my oath. I have been Priestess to the Circle at every festival without the customary ritual coupling of the fire rites. I will no longer wait for a voice to speak and tell me what will be so. Duty is first, and I have performed my duty. I will wait no longer for it is a woman's choice and I so choose now to give of my oath and promise to the Goddess, to participate of the Great Marriage of the Circle at the next ritual. I will inform Iarann that we will, at last, lay together, and may be wed if he wishes, for he too has promised himself to the Gods and to participate in a great union and I choose to believe that this is what was prophesied and we shall both be participants in the Great Marriage. Let it be so then that we fulfill our destinies together and perhaps replacing the babe that was given away in all this will bring a healing balm, once more to my mother's heart.*

So deep was Lon Dubh in her thoughts as they approached the village, she was visibly startled when two large men bearing long, pointed spears confronted her party.

"Halt!" came the call when the party was practically upon the guardsmen who were themselves surprised at the arrival of the relatively large party of six and two mules. No one was expected on the path leading from the hills, as it was too early in the season for herd folk to bring flocks to the hills. In fact, lambing wouldn't take place for another half-moon, yet.

The larger of the men began to hurl orders at the group barraging them with guttural words in short clipped bursts. Now pointing his spear at the travelers, the guard who looked initially surprised now took on a fierce and menacing stance.

Iarann could be seen to swell to his full height and loomed a full foot over the guardsmen who appeared intimidated but stood their ground. From behind Iarann, Faidhe slipped down from her mule and quietly walked toward the men. With a wave of her hand she caused the men to see that, despite an impressive show from Iarann, they were merely harmless and tired travelers in need of lodging and supplies. The men easily accepted the slight magical push that Faidhe had used on them and stood down their defensive stance.

Lon Dubh inwardly chastised herself for not having the presence of mind to have done something similar. If she is to call herself a Priestess to the Goddess, she must step out from her mother's shadow and begin to think and take action for herself rather than waiting always to see what her mother will do. Iarann stepped up willingly to the lead to protect them and even Fion had moved to his side at the guardsmen's approach. Not much if anything was to be expected from the other two, Gara and the boy who are here for no other reason, it seems, than Faidhe's insistence. *If I am to take on a role of leadership in some way, I must begin to think independently and as a leader. Especially if the unthinkable should happen and my mother is no longer able to conduct whatever magic is necessary in this journey. I must speak with her this day about what must be done should she fall to the sickness that wastes her.* It was the first time she allowed herself to consciously recognize the signs that all was not well with her mother. Looking upon her now, Lon Dubh saw that once again, her mother's hair was more gray than the lustrous black as it was only this time in the past sun cycle a few moons after they'd boarded the ship. Looking with closer scrutiny now, the Seer looked not only her age, but rather past it as opposed to the fleeting youth and beauty she'd displayed not so long ago. Lon Dubh shuddered at the thought that the responsibility for all that must take place should fall to her if her mother's health should fail. *But was that not what you waited for back in your own village? Did you not desire for your mother to come down from the Hill so you could take her place as Seer and Keeper?* Then immediately another thought came to her, this time in her mother's voice. A lesson Lon Dubh learned from her mother and oft repeated. *Be careful what you ask for. You can be sure the Gods will grant it in ways that suit their own purpose, not at all convenient to you.*

While lost in her own thoughts regarding her mother, one other of the group watched Faidhe keenly as she presented the Power to subdue the guards with a wave of her hand. Triag kept a close eye on all magical occurrences in order to report back to Nemain what he was privy to. Some minor things he'd told her of and others, like the type of manipulation Faidhe had just used, he'd keep to himself. Triag knew knowledge was a powerful tool. He did not intend to share all with Nemain, just the things he knew he would need her to perform if he could not do it himself. He'd seen the Cauldron of plenty provide for the group as they traveled but for the moment, dismissed that as unattainable. He'd seen minor magic such as fire making many times. The small magic, he'd practiced and managed to ignite fire on his own after observing how to conduct the gathering of energy and to focus his thoughts on generating the heat. He managed to spark lighter things at first such as spider weed and then with practice, small kindling and eventually, he could create small plumes of fire out of pure thought. Now he had a new trick to practice. If it were possible for the woman to do it, then he would attempt it too. Feeling satisfied as he tucked away this piece of information for later practice, Triag was unaware that someone else had witnessed his thoughts as they occurred to him and this one was Fion, the only one of the group who had not dismissed the boy as inconsequential.

It was dangerous to dismiss the presence of this boy and Fion knew it for he'd witnessed the evil that writhed in the boy's mind beneath his bland exterior.

He knew also that the putrescence grew in its sway over the boy as they traveled. Fion shuddered. As they approached the village, he vowed to speak to Lon Dubh about the growing problem that would surely lead to trouble for the group. Just as soon as they were settled in this town, he would speak with his friend and tell her what he knows.

The group passed the guards and headed into the town following the swarms of cawing birds that preceded them. The taller of the guards looked at the birds and Lon Dubh felt a thrill as his icy blue eyes then settled on her. His stare was unabashed in its probing nature.

The guard, Sonne, was curious about the group but found his interest keenly piqued in this young woman with the raven black hair. Not many strangers made their way to this village so well protected by the mountains and rarely were women outside the clan ever seen. Never had he seen a woman wearing traveling breeches that so snugly fitted to the female shape as this. Never either had he been so completely captured by the open way this woman met his eyes and wordlessly challenged him. She carried a bow and sling of her own as well. *This woman must be some type of warrior.* He thought. All this may have just been that he was bewitched by the beauty of a woman not of his village, all of whom he knew and found to be dull and lacking strength of personality. Sonne found himself immediately smitten with this dark eyed beauty whose energy positively vibrated with strength and Power. He did not take his eyes from the woman and much to his titillation and amusement, her own eyes did not waver from his as she passed him by.

———

After taking a few days to settle in to the village, the mother and daughter sat at the hearth fire within the small quarters they had been given and the older woman listened.

"Mother, I have done all that was required of me as a child of the Circle beginning with living a motherless childhood and estrangement from my only sister. And since being called to the service of the Goddess, I have selected an appropriate partner to tell the tale and take it into the future generations. I have left my home as you have and traveled to far lands to spread the tale in support of the Goddess and her return to reign at a time when the world will have need of her balance and wisdom. I have relinquished my duty and privilege to honor the fertility Gods and lay with a man. I have watched you give up your own son and witnessed the very blush of life drain from your veins and I find myself asking whether it is fair for so much to be expected of one family. Now that I come to feel the warmth and love of Iarann, I begin to sour to the idea that we are each of us destined to live a separate, lonely and unfulfilled life. I ask, Mother, when will this journey be finished? When can the tale be told in its entirety? When do we return home and live happily from that point, together? Why must we travel so far north through this frozen land before we may head toward our home? I can keep my silence no longer."

"It is good that you are warmed by the love of Iarann. Goddess knows, I have not been the friend to him I might have been. I am pleased you have found with him, the family you lacked in childhood. It is good you have each other and your friendship with the Elf. These types of family connections and friendships, I never had during my service. Take caution though daughter that you tire of your duty to your oath before it is satisfied. We travel north now to return that which belongs there to those of the Norse world, those from whom our Power and abilities originated when we brought the implements from their lands so many generations ago. The very Stone of Fal so long generated Power for our clans to do magic and offered special energies to the Circles of our lands so we could enjoy commune with the Gods and spirits of Otherworld. Those implements were given into our charge with the knowledge that one day, we would be anointed with the responsibility to disburse them throughout our region to lay the foundation for the future of humankind. That time has come as we are drawn nearer to the threat, which unchecked masculine reign poses to our survival. In this, we have sworn and we will carry out our tasks. You my child, have not been charged with the care and preparation of an implement, but are charged with an equally important task. The tale you tell and the rituals you perform will live long after there is no longer flesh on your bones."

"Do you know when my task will be over, Mother? Is this something you've seen in the Cauldron?"

"I fear child, that the visions granted me in the Bowl are no more a telling to me of your destiny in this life than I would see looking at the sky. This I can tell you though, we turn to the lands to the north to pay them their due."

Having had enough of cryptic messages and unanswered question as added burden to her growing frustrations Lon Dubh blurted, "Who? Who is this we owe such a price as to give of our lives? Why are we not offering these sacrifices to our own Gods in our own lands?"

"Child, we may call different names of our Gods and we may attribute favor coming from this one or that, but all the Gods, be they of Goddess or God, be they Gods of plant, stone, air, water or sky, they are all the same. Just as you are aunt to Morgan and Macha and sister to Colm, daughter to me, yet you are all the same in one, no matter how many titles you are given. See you not, that in making this pilgrimage, we honor our Gods and all Gods?"

"Then why must we travel so far to fulfill our oath to the Goddess? Why was it not possible for us to do this service in our own lands?" Lon Dubh did not like the whine she heard creeping into her voice.

Faidhe softened to her daughter's frustrations and answered the questions rather than chastising her for losing resolve after such a short time in service.

"We have a strong kinship and connection with the people from the northlands. They have given us the implements and charged us with mingling the blood in our veins with the blood of pure humans and so we were sent forth many generations past, to the sacred isle to that end. We defeated and banished the Firbolg from the island with the aid and use of this Power granted us through the implements. The isle is a place of wealth and beauty, but chosen mostly for the energy that emanates from the land itself, conducive to the raising of the magic. We are a people who have magical nature and who have mingled with both the Gods and humans. We have coexisted with other magical creatures while the humankind is all but unaware, for the most part, of the spiritual presence of such creatures: sprites, spirits, fairies and such.

Many generations back, to time out of memory, our people were of the northlands that came to the island with the sacred mission to mix our blood with the humans of the land and so we have. But even still, we maintain our connections to the Old Ones of the north so our blood thins not too quickly. On the festival days, Great Marriages are still celebrated in the Circle to create children with renewed blood of the Old Ones. But now, as the times change, it is important to maintain and mix the blood of the Old Ones with the newer blood of humans for the time has come that the magical spirits, the manifestation of the Gods on this earth to end. We prepare for the implements to be stored until another time of their need, but more importantly, it is time for the Gods to go under to the Sidhe while all that takes place on the earth will be conducted by the humans alone."

Faidhe continued to explain and Lon Dubh was fully attentive to learn.

"Your sister, Colm, with her yellow hair and light eyes is the product of one such a union between the God folk of the north and myself when a chosen representative of the North folk traveled to our village to take the role of the God with me in the Circle. She is of the North blood and it is fitting that she be a Shieldmaiden for Laoghaire and her people for that union has mixed the blood of the North folk with the blood of the natives of the island in a royal line. She is of the Valkyrie, a magical warrior clan of the north ruled for the most part by Goddess women, as is our clan. We have learned and retained many of our ways brought from the North Country to the island."

"You too, child, are of a special mixed breed, born to the Circle, for you hold ties to the Gods of the sacred island to serve your own purpose in all of this. One can say that you and your sister have each been born of the spirit and of the human to follow your destinies to lay the foundation for the future of human kind."

Lon Dubh seized the opportunity to discuss her own purpose and destiny and to reveal to her mother the recent sense of urgency she felt to couple and procreate.

"It comes to this now. You speak of my lineage and my destiny. I know not whether there is a child foretold in my destiny but I feel the strength of the call for me to take to the fires in our ritual next. I have been true to the Goddess in my calling but I am ready now to lay down my maidenhead to the ritual fires and partake in what I see as the enactment of the Great Marriage. I know there will be strong magic released at the time I give of my virginity but I know not yet to what end. I only know that I must partner in a half-moon's time at the festival of the lambing and the milking of the ewes."

Faidhe's face darkened and she looked older still. "I have not foreseen these tidings Black Bird. Know you the burden of travel while carrying a babe? We do not stay long in this village. And what of the sacrifice should you be called to give over of the child? This is a pain I have endured three times in the name of the Goddess and I would not will it on any other for it is a desolate path to receive the gift of life and then to pass it to another with only an empty womb and an aching heart for comfort."

Faidhe felt a foreboding at this turning point in their journey. She had foreseen that she and her daughter at some point would be in disagreement so fierce that there was a risk of enduring her daughter's hatred equal to that of her love. She did not want to lose her daughter so soon after reuniting with her. She tread cautiously choosing her words so that Lon Dubh would receive advice but ultimately make up her own mind about her decision.

"Understand you daughter that if this is what you see as your future, then I will be your advisor and happily take the role of your Mother to initiate you into the rites if you so wish. I will be pleased to help you enter the world of fertility. I do hesitate to see you take the path I have in risking breeding at a time when we still have much harsh travel over land ahead of us."

"It may be so that I will not breed. Often the girls who come to the rites do not catch with a babe on the first time."

"Daughter! Speak not in this way. For you know that to lay with a man who represents the God as you play the role of the Goddess, the purpose is the mingling of two to make another! Have a care not to enter into this rite lightly for your own purposes. Think more on this Black Bird, please. And after your earnest meditation on the possible outcome of this action if you still wish to proceed, we may approach the elders here in the village to see what traditions they follow that might coincide with our lambing festival. We might merge our customs and celebrate with the peoples here your coming to full womanhood."

Lon Dubh promised her mother to think seriously about her decision and then asked one last thing of Faidhe before she left her to prepare for her storytelling session.

"I wish to approach Iarann about these events. We have spoken briefly on this matter before, but it has been some time since we did and I'd like to take his counsel into consideration before I make my decision. Please say nothing to him, Mother. It is a special relationship between us and I wish to discuss this with him now."

Faidhe was a bit surprised that Lon Dubh had discussed this with Iarann before she had come to her own mother but agreed to the unusual request.

"As you wish, daughter. You have waited long for a family and you should be able to conduct yourself within that unit as you see need. I will not speak with him until you have come to some decision about all of this and returned to me with whatever you have decided."

"Thank you Mother. I know you have your doubts but I feel this is right. Now I must go and find Fion to prepare for our storytelling. Already there is a large number of villagers gathering to hear our tell. Such a strange tongue they have in these parts. I can understand almost none of it and without Fion, they would understand little or none of the tale. He is a special creature in how he makes known a story right in the mind of people as if they were witness to the tale themselves!"

With that, Lon Dubh left the small room where the women had taken counsel with a light heart. Faidhe noted that despite her daughter's promise to meditate on the subject, her decision had already been made. There would be a fertility ceremony. She was only grateful in that she would be available to counsel her daughter through the occasion. An honor she would not have been available for if she were still Keeper of the Circle tending to other things back in that other life. Faidhe sighed deeply with the weight of this new wrinkle in her journey bearing down on her heart. She picked up a twig and idly poked the fire.

Lon Dubh stepped out of the hut and in her preoccupied state, bumped into someone who was hovering there. When she'd composed herself from the stumble, Lon Dubh stood and looked directly into a pair of blue eyes that peered back at her with a mixture of surprise and unconcealed admiration. After a moment, Lon Dubh recognized the man as the guard she had seen at the village entrance the day before and flushed at the brazen way he looked at her now. Embarrassed by her own reaction, Lon Dubh broke the gaze and tried to step around the man to find Fion and get to the storytelling.

The man understood her intent and stepped again in front of her to prevent Lon Dubh from leaving. At this, the woman grew reflexively angry and the guard held up his hands in an opened-palm fashion to show her that he meant her no harm but wished to communicate. Lon Dubh hesitated not wishing to insult a member of their host village and watched as the man reached beneath his garment and pulled forth his closed hand. With his other hand he took Lon Dubh's by the wrist and placed into her palm, a small black object that felt cool to the touch despite the fact that it had been stored close to the man's heart. As Lon Dubh turned the object in her fingers she felt the rich and smooth quality of stone and her sharp intake of breath let the man know that she'd recognized the quality in his carving and was pleased. Lon Dubh looked once again into the man's eyes and her own held a question. The man pointed to something above Lon Dubh's head and behind her. She followed the direction with her eyes and recognized that the trees around the village were full now of silent crows, ravens and blackbirds. She looked back to the piece in her hand and inspected the beautifully carved raven in some kind of polished black stone and smiled at the man who nodded his satisfaction that she'd accepted the gift as he pointed to the stone raven and then to Lon Dubh.

"Svort Fagel." He said. Then pointing a finger to his own chest, he said, "Sonne."

Lon Dubh knew she was blushing furiously. She stammered. "It's lovely." but did not want to assume it was a gift and thought the polite thing to do would be to compliment the man's work and return it to him. When she attempted to hand it back the man appeared agitated and took a step toward her to wrap her hand in both of his much larger calloused ones to close her palm around the piece.

The language barrier was difficult without Fion's help and Lon Dubh was confused about what he was saying but there was no mistake at this moment that her body responded to his closeness and touch. She resisted the fearful urge to try to pull loose and run away and found herself immobilized even had she truly wanted to break away. In that moment, she feared if she looked into his eyes, he would see just how frightened she was and so kept her eyes on his hands and did not move. She tried to repeat the man's name to acknowledge that she'd understood him but all that came out was a barely audible whisper.

"Sonne." She cleared her voice and repeated his name with strength. "Sonne."

At the sound of his name, the man leaned in so that Lon Dubh could feel the man's breath on her cheek and smell the wood fire smoke in his reddish beard and fur-skins. Though the air was quite cold outside, Lon Dubh was a furnace, burning up with the furious beating of her heart and an uncomfortable awareness of her womanhood below. She thought the man must be able to hear her pulse for she could hear little else inside her own skin as her blood roared through her ears. Sonne let go of her hands and with the back of one strong finger, stroked her cheek and swiftly walked away.

Lon Dubh was found standing, struck, in the very spot he'd left her minutes later when Fion appeared to go with her to attend the storytelling. Unaware of how long she stood there, trying to gain control of her senses, Lon Dubh could feel the spot, still scalding, where he had touched her skin and she found the scent of wood smoke intoxicating as it lingered in her nostrils. She had to open her hands to determine if what had just happened was real or imagination or even magical. In such a moment she was assaulted by a cacophony of emotions she'd never before experienced but there it was, an ebony stone carved with precise detail to a perfect replica of a raven even with visible delicate tail-feathers etched in the stone, beautiful and polished to an almost gem-like gleam. Lon Dubh breathed a heaving sigh and tucked the bird into her own skins right next to her own heart and tried to focus on the task of storytelling at the gathering that Fion had arranged. Feeling suddenly jubilant, she threw an amiable arm around the young man's shoulder as they walked together toward their evening's work.

Fion asked to speak with Lon Dubh about a pressing issue as the pair entered the large hall where she was to tell her tale. Lon Dubh spied Iarann already there and felt a sudden wave of guilt. Only a day or so after she'd made up her mind to lay with Iarann for her first rites and at the next festival, she had completely forgotten about him the moment someone paid her a little attention and offered her a gift. She felt the smooth stone next to her skin and her body responded with a jolt of electrical thrill that buzzed from her loins to her solar plexus. She tried to ignore the feeling and her thoughts but found that she could not look Iarann straight in the eye. *I have done nothing wrong.* Lon Dubh distracted herself by looking to Fion.

"After the tale, we will share bread and you will tell me what troubles you so for I can see on your face it is ill news you bring to me."

Inwardly pushing away her guilt, she chastised herself. *I have approached no one. I have not promised myself to anyone. It is my choice to offer myself at the fires to a man of my choosing.* Her inner struggle continued as Lon Dubh prepared a vessel of water to calm herself. *But you have not even known this man for a day. You do not know him at all. If you are conflicted now and cannot even hold the gaze of the man you've chosen to lay with at the fires, perhaps you are not ready to surrender yourself at this time.*

"Forgive me for now though Fion. I am not myself and must keep my mind to my duty of the tale."

She did look at Iarann then and after traveling so long together, he knew something troubled her. He communicated with a look of concern to ask if she needed anything. Lon Dubh smiled at him and shook her head no. She comforted herself that this man was one she loved. Of this she was absolutely certain. Anything she might have felt in that moment with Sonne was fleeting and nothing in comparison to the love, trust and true connection between herself and Iarann. Her smile broadened as she beamed at the large man across the hall. She felt the warmth of the love in his eyes as they smiled back at her. Then, in that very moment, her insecurities, self-consciousness and doubt returned as she saw Sonne the guard enter the hall. *Of course he'd be here. All the town folk have been offered the gift of her story. Why would he not come?* Lon Dubh returned to paying great and focused attention on pouring water into a tankard and taking exaggerated caution in not spilling any as she gulped.

The hall quieted and Lon Dubh felt the pressure of hundreds of eyes on her but she was most painfully aware of only four of them: Iarann's and Sonne's. Thankfully, just then, two women stepped toward her bearing a large, two-handled vessel as an offering to the storyteller. In small ritual-like movements the women uncapped the vessel and poured out a large bowl of the foamy golden liquid. The urn-like container was placed on an ornate stand obviously carved for holding the ceremonial urn. The two sturdy looking women then offered Lon Dubh the bowl and she graciously accepted, thankful that she could focus her attention on something other than the eyes upon her. The taste of the drink was yeasty and effervescent, almost bread like. The storyteller almost immediately felt lightheaded from the drink. Although it did not taste the same, it had the same quality as mead to sooth the nerves and calm the mind. Lon Dubh settled into a sitting position, took another sip of the golden drink and began her tale.

This time, there was an added facet to the tale that Lon Dubh was unaware she would tell. As in the past, when the tale has been told, the teller is enveloped in a semi-state of trance and much of the tale, rather than being told by her, more accurately comes through her; so often times she is all but spent and remembers little at the close of her tale. She relies on Fion to remind her of questions that had been asked and exchanges of information that took place during the telling. Now, at the end of the tale the audience more clearly understood who their guests were and that it is a magical purpose for which they traveled. They felt sorrow for the mother who gave up her babe and the Keeper/king who lost his parents. They imagined the love of the king and queen of the faraway island. There was wonderment at the Elf-being and his ability to tell a story with pictures in the mind and much speculation at the riches of the Duibhe. They were awed at the young Priestess of the Goddess, as her growing magical abilities had been revealed in the story. But the latest twist to the tale gave Fion pause and he blankly stared at Lon Dubh as she announced that she awaited the festival of the lambing when her own clans celebrated the birth of the spring lambs in celebration of the retreat of harsh winter and the coming of the spring. The announcement was made as part of her tale that she would stand as virgin Priestess for the Goddess at the sundown ritual and take to the fires with a first coupling to bring her to full womanhood.

The room was hushed and waiting as Fion stared at Lon Dubh in disbelief not only that she had boldly breached protocol and assumed to publicly conduct celebrations as they had at home in these new lands without some kind of prior permission, but also the announcement of her plan to partake in the fire rites was a complete shock. He unabashedly stared so that all in the room waited in silence for him to conduct the meaning of the storyteller's words to them in his pictures. The only movement or sound that could be detected was when Iarann instinctively stood to his feet at the announcement looking at Lon Dubh and then to the man who had taken his seat close to her to look upon her with obvious admiration.

Lon Dubh emphatically nodded to Fion and he commenced to translate to the crowd what had been announced. As understanding of Lon Dubh's intentions became apparent to the crowd, some of the women folk seemed unnerved and obviously displeased. With Lon Dubh's dawning understanding that the matriarchal ways of the Tuatha de Danann are strange and somewhat frightening to the peoples of other places, she asked Fion to explain.

"Tell them I will not overstep protocol of the village to usurp claimed or married men. Tell them the phrase, 'man of my choosing' is only significant to highlight the respect due the Goddess that she does as she chooses. Tell them I seek to do them honor by sharing our customs and blessing their herds. I wish only to celebrate our customs with them and honor their customs at the same time. It is a union of friendship between our tribes that we seek, in thanks for hospitality offered to us in our travels."

As Fion assembled his thoughts and conveyed the message, the women calmed and the men seemed less anxious about a woman that seemed a bit too free and powerful. For in their own tribes, men were dominant in choosing with whom they lay and were discomforted by a woman who thought to step above her station. But the reminder of her Priestess status and the promise of blessing the herds helped the men to stand down their misgivings.

Lon Dubh asked, "Have you an early spring celebration here? Something at which we might mingle our customs?" A flood of images came back to her through Fion of feasting on mutton, the making of a solid milky substance in vats and drinking of the brew she had just now enjoyed. Smiling, Lon Dubh was pleased that she would be able to celebrate in a communal festival much the way she would have at home for her rites of womanhood. She scanned the crowd and her eyes lighted on the one person who offered her the most comfort with her presence for these times yet she lamented that her sister would not be here to attend her in preparation for the ritual. Faidhe stood with Iarann now and could be seen whispering something to him. Iarann's face looked mildly concerned, but he smiled reassuringly at Lon Dubh as their eyes met. Not that she doubted he would be happy, but now that she knew he would accept her offer, Lon Dubh tried to reassure herself that this is the right decision and the proper way to go about her initiation. She wished she had spoken with him privately first, but she had already known that he had love for her. What could stand in their way? She smiled back at Iarann and sighed a breath of relief while trying to keep her eyes on her friend and tribesman; but all the while she could feel the persistent pull of Sonne's energy urging her to look his way. Though it took much discipline, Lon Dubh managed to keep from giving way to the urge. She kept her eyes on her mother and Iarann and watched as they left the hall together, Iarann with his strong arm wrapped around Faidhe as if to protect her from the pressing crowd. Lon Dubh extended an elbow to Fion and he escorted her out of the hall and toward the hut they had been given to lodge when a group of women gathered around the pair and clucked over them in clipped tones of their language. Lon Dubh was separated from Fion as the women ushered her away to a hut unfamiliar to either of them. In her last glimpse of Fion, he conveyed to her that the women intended to keep her in their tradition of preparation for the rites. It seems that she is to be kept in a house separate from all the others while she engages in various rituals leading up to the ceremony of initiation. Lon Dubh called out to Fion with a broad smile as they led her away.

"Tell my mother to come to me, Fion. I'll need my pack and her counsel."

Fion raised a hand in acknowledgement and turned to find Faidhe and deliver the message.

———

The boy had witnessed the storytelling, not because he was at all interested in hearing the overblown tale of the self-important Tuath and these women, one more time, but because it was easier for him to insinuate himself into the thoughts of others while they were open to the Elf directing images into their minds. He entertained himself while he enjoyed skulking in the thoughts of others to divine private things about them while they were unaware of his snooping but he especially liked that he could catch glimpses of what was in the Elf's mind while he was working to tell the tale with the woman. While the young woman, her mother and the Smithy were impossible to read, this one held information about the inner workings of the group that could be accessed. He knew things about the others and sometimes, Triag could catch snippets of information while the Elf was unaware.

After the entertainment, another thought occurred to Triag. He was coming of age now and he too should be able to come to his manhood at the rites. He had grown in height and had trimmed down considerably in their travels for their was much walking and food was scarce unless good luck prevailed and the old woman called to her Cauldron to feed them rather than making them work by hunting, fishing and foraging for food during their trek. *I am grown to manhood.* He thought. *If Lon Dubh could arm twist this village into preparing a festival for her passage, then I too will insist that I be given my due. Why should I not?* Forgotten for the moment were the bits of information he'd gathered at the storytelling. Triag set off to find his grandmother to tell her of his plans so that she could advocate for him with the others. She was not of much use to him these days. She seemed to hold none of her earlier strength or motivation. He was sickened at her wizened appearance as though the road had taken much from her, he thought she could at the very least, attempt to wash and weave her hair, or to mingle in society and make the both of them comfortable during their stay. She seemed interested only in procuring her own necessaries and had not attempted to refine her appearance for over long. *If she could find someone of stature for our stay here, to join with...Ah but she appears old and defeated. Who would want her now?* Triag fiddled with the hair showing on his upper lip and square jaw that was now visible without the extra layers of flesh. *I will approach my grandmother and appeal to her familial pride.* He decided and set off to tend this business right away.

"I am of age, Grandmother." He told Gara when he found her huddled in their hut next to the fire. "And just because you insist on dragging me across the world for whatever your reasons does not mean that I am not a man and that I do not deserve the rites due me in my passage. I have supported you on this trek without questioning you when all others of our clan showed you naught but disrespect. If you doubt that I will continue to do so as I come to full manhood, know you this, that I will not abandon you. As long as you find it necessary to travel with the Seer and her family, I will be with you."

Of course he kept close and hidden, his plan that he would stay with the group until he had gotten the information he came for: Why they traveled and what magical purpose did the woman Faidhe have in keeping them close. As soon as he knew the secret of the journey, learned as much of magic he could, and spied out a possible way to procure the Cauldron for himself, he would return home in high means to deal with Nemain and claim his cattle, title and land.

"You need not block my passage into manhood for fear that in my independence I will abandon you in this journey. I will not. But deny me this and I swear, I will leave at my earliest possible chance and return to my home."

Gara did not think that Triag had the means nor the determination to find his own way home but she did have to admit, as she inspected the boy as if truly looking at him for the first time in a long while, he had grown to a young man and lost all the doughy flesh he had at the start of the journey. She could see no reason to deny the passage. It may in fact, afford her a bit more status to be traveling with a viable man. He might be seen as good stock for mingling new blood with tribes along the way. And of course, she could not have him abandoning her on the road. He was one of the few things she could count among her assets at the moment.

"Of course you will join in the rites my boy. In fact, I was thinking of your passage not over long ago. The moment presents itself and so I shall speak with the others on your behalf."

Triag knew that Gara had seen his view so easily because it somehow suited her own purpose but he felt a moment of pleasure at her recognition of his approach to manhood and was pleased that she would speak of it to the others to arrange for him a place at the first fires. It was not so much that he'd take a girl or woman that excited his eagerness to come to the fires, although he would richly enjoy the moment of taking a girl for his pleasure, but as a man and a clan member, he would have a voice in how things are planned and carried out. And as a member of the traveling group, he would no longer be the lowest in status, for the Elf is not a member of the clan and so he would necessarily fall beneath Triag in the order of things. This, at least, was how Triag saw how it would take place. He was drawn back from his reverie and had to focus his attention once again on Gara as he heard her say, "...suitable girl for marriage?"

"Marriage! No! Certainly not. I am but 12 seasons and half. I look to the rites and to my passage but wish not to burden myself as we travel with a bride to feed or worse a squalling babe. Don't presume to think for me Grandmother. As a man, you'll find me quite capable to think for myself."

Gara agreed with Triag that it would be a burden to travel with extra people but if we were to be well connected through a marriage here, then we might find a way to remain here and end the trek that has taken so much from me. But Gara knew that if Faidhe had plans for her, that she would not likely slip her responsibilities. She sighed at the loss of the possibilities of a wealthy young girl owing fealty to the grandmother of her husband.

"Very well, Triag. As you wish. I will see what might be done to make arrangements for you." Gara then wondered to herself if there might still be a way to a prosperous connection. Perhaps a tie between Lon Dubh and her grandson might be arranged. The timing offers a unique possibility. Perhaps that is the way to insure for my future. She began to hatch her reasoning to be presented. Perhaps Faidhe could be convinced. After all, they did have a dark bond in the spilled blood of her own son. And Gara felt she had begun to balance the scale when she mingled her hands in the blood of the birth of Faidhe's child. She might be able to coerce Faidhe into understanding the potential benefit of continuing to pay off that blood debt with the blood of her daughter's maidenhead. The more she thought about it, the more sense it made to her. Certainly, Faidhe must see the symmetry in such a union. Gara felt life creep back into her heart as she reached with one hand for her bag to find some decorative pins for her hair and with the other, filled a bowl with water planning to wash and primp. Then she rummaged through her things to find her collection of small throwing bones to read for signs as to what might take place should such a marriage be arranged. Anyone passing by the hut would hear constant clicking as Gara shook the bag of bones and tossed them to the hard earthen floor peering intently looking for some sign of a possibility that her plan might hatch.

44

Forsaken, In Love

The seven women had taken Lon Dubh to a hut that was constructed at the edge of the village directly over the mouth of a cave. The front of the hut appeared as any other she'd seen in her short stay in the village: constructed of stone at the base, wooden tree columns and a tightly woven material that seemed to be some mix of plant growth and wool. This high up the mountain range, the people would naturally have to make use of what materials were readily available. The hut was protected from the wind for the most part due to its location in an alcove like jutting of the rocks at the base of the mountains but the interior was severely cold as it seemed the very cave to which the hut was attached breathed cold air from inside the earth that drafted through the hut.

Lon Dubh was amazed when she realized that the women expected to remove her clothing in this icehouse and even resisted their efforts but the women made it clear that her resistance would not be tolerated. When they had relieved Lon Dubh of her clothing three more women came into the hut bearing a large trough-like pot and several more paraded into the hut, dumping urns of steaming water into the tub. Shivering as she watched the parade, she noticed surreptitious glances and comments being made about her between some of the other women. The youngest, appearing about 15 seasons or so, came nearer to inspect Lon Dubh more closely. Emboldened when she drew no further resistance from the naked woman, the girl came closer and began to gently pinch at her skin commenting to the others all the while. The girl traced her finger along the defined muscles in Lon Dubh arms and legs. She rippled a single finger over the hardened double line of muscle that patterned Lon Dubh's abdomen and commented to the others while rubbing her chin perhaps alluding to the masculine appearance of the other woman's musculature. They all laughed but Lon Dubh drew back as another of the group, a large, round woman with rough hands came closer and hefted Lon Dubh's breasts, shaking her head in the negative and Lon Dubh snatched the woman's fleshy wrist in a viselike grip when she had appeared to be reaching for the sacred spot between her legs.

Lon Dubh did not mind a bit of friendly jesting at her expense and she understood that it was likely the women were commenting on her hardened body, trained by the road and hunting and its resemblance to any male counterpart whose body served the same purposes. But she would not be mocked...or violated.

"You'll find nothing there for your entertainment." Lon Dubh growled as she glared into the other woman's eyes.

Gusella, an older woman of the mountain tribe, Lon Dubh could tell, was one of status, age and of great size. She was accustomed to doing what she wanted and to whom, it seemed, at least among the women, for a flair of anger ignited in the woman's expression at being handled so, but when her eyes met Lon Dubh's, she saw something there and thought better of her instinct to strike the woman as she would have done any other underling of her own tribe. Gusella, made some kind of comment that Lon Dubh thought sounded crude judging by the woman's tone along with her wicked smile and the shock on some of the other women's faces, she was sure of it. Lon Dubh held Gusella's arm a moment or two longer before releasing it letting her know, guest or not, customs or not, she was not one to be trifled with or bullied. Lon Dubh suspected if this woman was one who helped all the girls in her tribe into womanhood, she was a poor choice. It was obvious she was the type to make sport of the young initiates and any girl just coming into her moon blood would not likely have the bravery to stand up to an elder in a position of authority and speak out against such treatment. Instead, the girl might take the abuse as part of the rite of passage.

Although Lon Dubh's height did not come close to the other woman's, it appeared to the women in the hut that they stood equal ground just as Lon Dubh had intended when she willed Gusella and the others to see her as formidable. Despite her nakedness, Lon Dubh was no longer cold in the cave hut and it may have been the hot water poured into the tub that heated the space a bit but it seemed that the energy she emitted to deliver her message to Gusella had heated the hut considerably more.

The tension in the room lessened when the young girl who had approached Lon Dubh in the first place pulled at her hands now and gestured to her that she climb into the warm tub of water. Lon Dub allowed herself to be led and it was the most luxurious sensation she could remember as she slipped her road-weary body into the hot water and felt all her muscles uncoil. All the women then gathered round the tub; all but Gusella, who at this point had decided that she was no longer interested in the newcomer's preparations. They washed Lon Dubh clean from head to foot. Her hair was unpinned and washed as well. The cleansing had been completed and the women were drying and scenting Lon Dubh with oils unfamiliar to her when Faidhe entered the hut. When the women saw her, their eyes instinctively cast downward. Gusella and Lon Dubh were the only two in the room who looked at Faidhe, one with undisguised happiness and the other with flagrant disregard that can only be displayed by the self-important or ignorant; in this case, both.

Gusella rose from her seat of disinterest with the whiff of another person to berate. In clipped and guttural tones of the language, Gusella started to talk at Faidhe making movements to rush her out the entrance again. Apparently the preparation of the initiates was tended by a finite amount of attendants. As the large woman used her size to convey Faidhe's unwelcome presence, she stopped in her tracks, which was no small trick considering her cumbersome form. In her head, Gusella heard the voice of the small woman with gray hair. It spoke not in her own language, but she understood the message, nonetheless: *You may be the largest hen among these birds, and it may grant you some status here but understand you now, we are not beggars on the road and will not be interfered with. It is a sacred path for which my daughter has been chosen and she follows not the steps of the Goddess for your sport. Remember you that these women are your sisters and when you treat them not with respect at this tender time of passage, you will surely reap the payment for your deeds when you are old and weak and you have need of the their kindness. Mayhaps they will be of better heart than you and will not mistreat you in your time of need but will you depend on their good heart when yours has been so bitter to each of them when they were frightened and looking for a kind word and guidance into womanhood? I see your future, hen and you will one day come to depend on these others for your food and health as your misdeeds take their toll on your body. Look you to these girls and count on your fingers the occasions you have ill-used each of them. Will you look forward to your dotage knowing the loneliness you will bear or the vengeance you will suffer? I think it will be well for you and all who come to you for wisdom if you contemplate how a woman should encounter her first coupling. I see your pain and how your own first coupling was closer to a fearsome rape. The vow you made never to be taken so again has been corrupted into something monstrous. You were hurt and mistreated but you have no need to inflict that pain on these others. See to it that the girls who pass through here in the future generations come to their rites understanding it is an honor and a singular ability to create new life. Go now.* Faidhe stepped up to the large woman who was wearing an expression of fear as tears streamed down her ample cheeks and fell on her even more ample breasts but was helpless to move. She placed a hand on the woman's heart and another on her head. *And let kindness grow in your heart.* Then Faidhe moved her hands to slip one between the woman's legs and lay one over her womb. *Then you will heal.*

Gusella, at this point began to sob uncontrollably and fell on Faidhe who appeared to be but a wisp of a woman next to the rotund one but Faidhe held her up regardless of size. Through her tears, Gusella appeared to be apologizing to all the women in the hut but most shrank from her almost expecting some trick for they could not fathom that Gusella would apologize for anything. It was the youngest girl, once again who held out her hand to Gusella who gratefully took it. After she settled down a bit, Gusella nodded to Faidhe and Lon Dubh, patted the young girl on the hand and left the cave hut to the other women.

"These people have strayed from the ways of the Godly already." Faidhe said in a matter of fact tone. "Are you well, daughter?" She asked as she brought forth Lon Dubh's pack to hand it to her.

"Yes. I would not allow this preparation to take on an irreverent course leading all involved to treat it not as a rite of passage but a sport for entertainment. Although I fear for many of these girls and women who are still but virgins if they have not been properly initiated into the sacred rites of coupling and birth. It's as though the process is done without their having any knowledge of why. Just now, I have had the ritual cleansing but none of the attendants seemed to know or acknowledge that the bath is also a symbolic birth into the next phase of life. There were no invocations or blessings said over me as I bathed! And the robes they give me are of the necessary red to symbolize the blood of the rupturing of the maidenhead and impending blood of birth but there was no ceremonial celebration as the robes were donned. It is strange, but I feel I must teach them why they do the rituals they carry out so that they might understand and pass it to subsequent generations." Then in a moment of inspiration, "Mother, think you this is part of my path in choosing now to come to the rites?"

Faidhe stopped cold as she handled her daughter's possessions, pulling items from the pack and looked to Lon Dubh.

"I had not thought of it in quite that way. But you may be right. There may be some purpose that I have not foreseen in your coming to your rites in such a way and in this community." It seemed that Faidhe was in a much less solemn frame of mind following that thought. "I bring you a gift, daughter. A gift procured from the Cauldron for your passing into womanhood. From mother to daughter, I give to you an apple from our beautiful orchards of home. Red as the symbol for blood, and so like the shape of a human heart. Apples contain five seed pods and as I cut this apple across its middle, you can see all the potential in the seeds waiting to blossom. I will take and eat the half of the apple containing only empty husks of the pods, for my time of bearing fruit is done. You will take and ingest your half of the apple, seeds and all to insure fertility for you during your seasons of bearing. You have begun your bearing time late, daughter, so Gods grant it that you will be fruitful in the time you have now."

Faidhe offered the apple half to Lon Dubh after cutting it with her whalebone handled knife. They ate of the apple gift in silence until it was completely gone and the ritual of fertility had passed from mother to daughter.

"You are to be housed here for the next seven days and nights preparing with many rituals to have the Goddess enter your being. Then, following the preparation time on the seventh night, you will conduct a ritual to invite the Goddess to you and your partner and the God into this space. You will then spend three more days here with your partner engaging in the coupling before you may leave the cave hut. All will be supplied for you: wood, food, drink, robes, oils and anything you may need to create your sacred space. Then, as timing wills it, you will come to the group on the third night and conduct the Blessing of the lambs for the feast of Imbolc. This will truly be a sharing of two cultures Black Bird. Will you have need of anything else I can bring to you?" As if by the very calling of her daughter's name, Faidhe noticed the small black stone carving of the raven among Lon Dubh's clothing and picked it up to inspect the fine work. "Is this your work, daughter? It is fine indeed."

"It is mine." Lon Dubh answered, not truly answering her mother's question. She did not know why but she did not tell her mother of Sonne and his gift. Rather she let her mother think that she'd carved the piece herself.

"It is truly a sign that you have come to your place and time for your fertility rites then. This is certainly the symbol that you have come fully to your Power. I bless the ritual and offer you my counsel and attendance. I am pleased for you Black Bird. You have full use of any herbs, tinctures or greenery I have to prepare for what lies ahead."

"I will have to let you know as the rituals are created and my needs are revealed to me what use I will have for various items. I have brought fighe vine for a head dressing and I hold my ritual dress for a wedding ceremony if it should come to that. I also have my fine, spun wool wrap dyed by my dearest friends in the Goddess's beautiful blue."

She pulled from her pack the blue swatch of spun wool she had created while in magical trance and much else in the way of spells as she weaved on the loom.

"I spun the wool and weaved the material back when I hardly even realized my feelings for Iarann when we were in Middle Village. I should have known as I wove the threads that the protective magic I put into it was for a purpose. Although I didn't allow myself to know it at the time, I wove this with much love for the child of Iarann."

Faidhe took this statement in stride. "I was not aware that he'd shared his commitment with you. He seemed hesitant to me but I am pleased that the two of you have grown so close and that you bear him no grudge for his commitment."

"Grudge? Why would I bear him grudge? He has told me that he has finally completed his task of constructing the panels for the Cauldron. He has worked over long on the final panel and told me with some joy that he has finished his commitment of creating the silver Cauldron, which tells the story of our family and this journey. His commitment has been fulfilled now, has it not? I have made this woolen wrapping with every intention that it will swaddle his babe. We have grown close and are a family despite the lack of marriage. What reason would I have to bear him a grudge? Really, Mother, we have had all these months together to learn of each other and for love to grow. When I accept him as the God in the fertility rites we will officially be family and I hope we shall be wed whether there is a babe or not of the couplings."

Faidhe stood stark still and said nothing. Staring only at Lon Dubh as though trying to make sense of what she'd just heard.

Lon Dubh waited for some kind of response and grew frightened when her mother did not say anything but stood only gaping at her.

"Mother, what is it? What is there about Iarann that I do not know? Why should you think I bear him a grudge? Has he changed his mind about loving me? Does he now wish to be distanced from these rites? Mother! Speak to me!"

"I will daughter. First, I must know, how came you to the decision that you must attend the fertility fires here in this village?"

"I know not exactly. As we came to the guarding gates at the edge of the village, I had communion in my mind, as thoughts tend to gather on long treks. I had come to a finite decision that I would give up the virgin's role and come full-fledged to womanhood. I admit it had not been pressing on my mind before this but only a thought here or there. But as we came to the town, my mind was made up."

"Then it is to be so. The voice within has led you to your path and you will remain here and prepare for your ritual. Goddess has spoken to you. Tend your duties here. I will return to you to advise you at the proper time." Faidhe stepped forward and gave Lon Dubh an uncharacteristic hug, then strode to the door with purpose.

"Mother wait! Lon Dubh called after her. What's wrong? I must know. Is Iarann...?" She did not even know how to formulate her question. *Is he what? Is he coming to the fires? Has he changed his mind? Does he not love me?* When Faidhe had swept out the hut's entrance, despite the presence of the other women in the hut, Lon Dubh felt truly scared and alone.

"What do you say woman?" Iarann uncharacteristically roared. "How can you think this of me? Of your daughter? We both know of the girl's bloodline. What is this foulness you accuse me of committing?" Usually quiet and mild; Faidhe was taken aback at the vehemence of his response. Her eyes became slits as she took measure of the man before her.

"No. I do not see that you have breached your trusted role in all this. You are true to your commitment to be consort to the Valkyrie, Sigrdifa."

"You know of this?" Iarann asked astonished.

"I do. But the issue for the moment is how Lon Dubh has come to understand that you have spoken of your love for her and that it will be you that she has chosen to come to her in the role of the God for her rites at the fertility fires? Have you and she spoken on such things?"

Iarann's mind was abuzz with what may have given Lon Dubh this impression. He loved her, of course, but how could she have so completely misunderstood his intentions.

"Does she not understand that this type of coupling is avoided unless so called for by the Goddess for very specific reason? And even then, marriage is never a consideration even if there is a coupling of two so close in blood. You are sure she spoke of marriage...with me? Faidhe nodded. "She does know that I have been committed to the Valkyrie. I have spoken of my commitment to her. Of this I am sure."

"Are you? Is it possible that you spoke to Lon Dubh of these things and she may have misunderstood your meaning?"

"I suppose, but how could she assume that I could be the one to take her maidenhead when she has come to mean so much to me as my daughter over these many passing moons?"

It struck Faidhe all at once like a blow to the middle. "Have you ever discussed with Lon Dubh your role as the God with me in the Circle?"

"What? No. Why would it have ever come up between us? She is your daughter and charge. Have you not schooled her in her own lineage?"

"Forget you that I did not raise her? That I only came to know her at the very same time as you? In all our travels, I have never had occasion to discuss it with her for you and she seemed to grow so close I just assumed that it was knowledge shared in the village or by the two of you who lived in the same village for so long. I thought your relationship grew out of the knowledge that you had sired her."

"I had assumed the same, that you had shared this with her. For we have had conversations regarding..." Iarann stopped, remembering the conversation he and Lon Dubh had as he toiled on the final panel so long ago, before they had even left the shores of their home island. His face turned to ashen gray as he recounted the words between them and realized that he spoke of his love for Faidhe to Lon Dubh. He told her of his wish to wed and couple with her so they could truly become a family. As it dawned on him how Lon Dubh could have misunderstood the conversation, particularly if she was not aware of his prior relationship with Faidhe.

"No!" He said. It was all he could muster to say in explanation. Not wanting to reveal his true feelings for Faidhe in this moment, he withheld telling her the whole truth.

"We spoke of my commitment to the Valkyrie. I believed that she understood I was not able to come to union with any other woman until my commitment to the Great Marriage with Sigrdifa is fulfilled. How could she think I would breach my promise?"

"As I understand it," Faidhe explained, "Lon Dubh thought your commitment was to see to the creation of the Cauldron and only that. You told her of the completion of the final panel and she assumed that freed you to come to the fires with her. She believes you and she have an agreement on this. Can you explain this?"

"I can. But will it suffice for you to know that she was mistaken in her interpretation of my words. I care not to reveal to you what was said, Lady. As it was a private sharing of feelings and love."

"Ply me not with timid hearts and embarrassment, man. This is serious. All that we have wrought may come to naught if we do not untie this knot and puzzle out who it is that will come to the fires with her as the God. Make no mistake in this; it is her time to come to full womanhood." Faidhe opened her hand and showed Iarann the carving of the raven. "This talisman was revealed to me in the prophecy. I knew when I saw this among her things, that it is truly her time to not only come to the rites, but that Lon Dubh will bear a child of the union. Of this I am sure. The Gods have chosen this time, we must now determine who they have chosen for her. We must also understand that this will likely breach our relations with our daughter to the point that we know her no longer for she will truly feel betrayed and abandoned. I have seen this also. So give a care not for your privacy, Iarann but for the future of all of this." Faidhe's voice softened and she dropped her shoulders and hands in resignation. "Now, you must tell me all."

Iarann contemplated what this meant and decided that it would be a relief to finally unburden himself and tell Faidhe of his love for her.

"Sit with me by the fire." He said as he gestured to her. "Let us share the drink of these mountain folk as I share with you what I know." The two settled together and it was easier for Iarann to speak when he did not have to look into Faidhe's eyes or try to determine what she was thinking as he confessed to her his hopes that she loved him. He poured the drinks and began.

"It was a strained conversation and now as I look back, it was crafted in such a way that two people, shy in their professions, could speak of their feelings of love without coming straight to the point. She spoke of knowing the mind of my travel companion and that I could have faith that she loves me. And I spoke of being overjoyed at looking toward the end of my commitment so that we might come together and finally be a family. I see now how we were both mistaken in the other's meaning."

Iarann's face was now flushed as he waited for Faidhe to understand the underlying meaning of his conversation with Lon Dubh. Then, deciding he'd caused enough trouble in hoping his meaning would be understood, he turned to Faidhe and took both her hands in his.

"I spoke of you Faidhe. I have long desired to come to you even as you tended the Hill. After my Ethlin died, my mind thought of you often and when you came down the Hill, I thought that the Gods wanted us to be together especially when the crafting of the Cauldron fell to me so that we were destined to journey together. And it was an added blessing that we traveled with our daughter. I took it as a reward for many years of loneliness for all of us that we would finally be able to be together as a family. And it has been so. I kept my distance when I learned of your union with the Greenman, knowing that your duty to the Gods came first, I waited until you no longer carried the child to tell you of my feelings. But then, you tended the child and so I waited. And as your heart ached for the loss of the child, I did what I could to sooth you and let you heal. All the while understanding through my conversation with Lon Dubh, that you loved me and wished to be together as I do. So then I thought just as I waited for you, it was then you who waited for me to be free of my commitment to Sigrdifa who had chosen me as her consort when we come to the Northlands. For as a chosen consort, as you well know, I cannot lay with another until my commitment to the Great Marriage has been fulfilled."

There was a ringing silence as Iarann finished his telling in a hurried flurry of words as if to expel them quickly would somehow make them less painful to say. They both sat staring into the fire, contemplating all that had been said and what it meant. After what seemed a long while, Faidhe broke the silence.

"It changes nothing. We must still follow the path laid out for each of us. Any love we feel for each other cannot be acted upon. Sigrdifa has claimed you for she understands that in order to complete our task as the few remaining tribes with true magic, we must have the proper accounting for bloodlines to represent the clans of the island and their forbearers of the Northlands. There must be the proper mingling of blood to bear us into the future. If the proper souls are to return, they must return to vessels that will allow them to have and wield the magic as *we* know and understand it, not the wisp of a dragonfly wing it will soon be. The prophecy has told it, and now I see it, as we travel these lands, magic is diminishing rapidly and women are being fast disregarded. Gods will no longer mingle with humans and the world will fall under rule of brute force and power of dominance. We must all be true to our commitments regardless of personal desires, in the face even, of love." She looked into Iarann's eyes with deep sorrow and spoke with resignation.

"I am a marked soul dedicated to help the Gods under to the Sidhe but owing a debt so that I cannot continue on my path in returning. I will not remain of this world nor return to it if all is to be set forth as it must be." She allowed the tears to come and it seemed that they would never stop. Iarann wrapped his arm around her and pulled her close to him. He was not sure what she meant but understood that she was telling him they would never come together as he had hoped. He wept with Faidhe.

"It may change nothing in the way of our duties to the journey but we will still travel together as we have. If it must be, then that will be enough. I will comfort myself in believing that if it were not for our duties, then we would come together and love one another as a man and woman do. Knowing that this is your wish too will comfort me and that will have to be enough. I do love you Faidhe. And I love our daughter. Let us now bury our grief in finding how we might best bring her to her rites so that she may be happy and come to her full Power. Let us find the right man to be the God for her and hope that her time at the fires will be for her as it was for me: a wonderful moment of passage into which a beautiful child is born."

Faidhe tried to dry her eyes with his comforting words. "But who will be that one for her?" Just then, Fion entered the hut. He appeared to be a bit shaken.

"Lady, Gara and her grandson, Triag are here requesting to speak with you." Fion could not help the involuntary way his lip peeled back in disgust when he said Triag's name. Faidhe was curious at the contempt one such as Fion could have for a boy but dismissed it for the moment.

While on the second part of the journey, Gara had come into line regarding taking on her responsibilities without complaint and Faidhe was grateful for the woman's gentle hands during the birth of her son. But when she could, Gara had kept to herself for most of the trek and arranged for separate housing for herself and Triag. It was as though Gara accepted her role to be played but wished no further relationship with the traveling party than was necessary.

"Show them in." Faidhe said simply and was surprised to see both Gara and Triag dressed in formal robes. "What's this? Faidhe asked.

Gara appeared a bit nervous but stood erect to present herself. Triag took his cue and stood with a straight back as well. Faidhe noticed for the first time that Triag had grown considerably since they had taken to the road. Or perhaps he had thinned and only appeared to have grown but in either case, he was growing to a young man for she saw in his face a maturing of his features and the telling hair beginning to darken his upper lip.

"You have grown, boy. I think the road has been good for you." Faidhe voiced her thought. And then reflecting on Gara and her own appearance, said, "Although I fear the road has not been so kind to those of us with some years."

"Nonsense." Gara began. "We are still in fine form. A few lines and gray hairs to show as prizes for our experience." Gara came forward. "May we sit with you by the fire?"

"By all means, clanswoman. The night is unforgiving in its bitterness. Come warm yourselves. I admit it is an unexpected moment to see you by our fire. It is not your habit to gather with us when we are taken to a village."

"It is true. We have kept to our own when we might. But it is not that we do not enjoy your company. It is only that though we are of the same Tuath, we are not kin and so have never felt the familial bonds that you enjoy with these others. It is fortunate for us that perhaps that can be changed at this time. We come to hopefully strengthen the bond between our families and continue on our journey with renewed fealty for our connections."

It seemed as though Gara were trying on the words for the first time. As she spoke, she warmed to the subject.

"We have been reminded only this night that though we are far from home, we owe it to our clans and heritage to keep the rites and rituals of our lands alive. On that matter, I come to make you aware that my grandson is now of age to take to the fires with his rite of passage to manhood. I come to pledge his service to the God and Goddess so that he might come to his first rights with Lon Dubh." Gara saw the look of astonishment on Faidhe's face and rushed on to complete her say. "It will not only strengthen the bonds between our families but we will continue on our journey as a unit when we leave this village suffering no more children of our blood left behind."

Gara knew this last was manipulative and risky but she would not feel she had done her best to advocate for her grandson unless she had played all her angles.

"And each with our own interest in the welfare of a child born not only to the rites but of the Circle as well for if Lon Dubh catches with child, it may be that it takes place during her time as Priestess at the celebration of Imbolc. We may be doubly blessed if a child should come of this union and we may all rejoice in the new life come to both our families. It would not be seemly for us to offer one so highly regarded in our Tuath to the foreign blood and strange ways of these mountain folk, would it?"

There was silence in the hut while all Gara had said was absorbed. It came as an abrupt shock when it was Fion who had stood to speak with a vehemence not often seen.

"It cannot be so!" He shouted.

The Elf's face took on an expression that reminded the others that he was also of Duibhe heritage. His brow thickened as it furrowed and his nose appeared to have grown as his eyes closed to slits as he stood toe to toe with the boy, Triag who had also stood, instinctively knowing the Elf would challenge him. Without taking his eyes off the boy, Fion addressed Faidhe in a voice that was barely a human growl.

"Lon Dubh has chosen me as her partner to the tale and we have had union of our minds a great many times. We know each other's hearts and minds and her choice to take to the fires at this point in our journey beckons to me as my signal that we should finalize our union together and know each other completely. I will take to my rites of the fires, as has been done with the Elven folk since time out of memory. My right at the fires was not afforded me in the mounts of the Duibhe or Middle Village. Though I have had occasion to lie with women, I have not yet come to the ritual fires and am of the same age as Lon Dubh. It is only fitting that both of us who have come to the fires so late in life is a gift from the Goddess that we two are destined to be partners complete in mind, spirit and body. And I will seek to marry her following the rituals should she have me."

He took his eyes from the boy and turned to Faidhe looking to her eyes and speaking directly to her mind. *You must understand, mayhap not myself, mayhap not Iarann, but both of us better in any account than one such as this one. It may be that you know, but it may be not, that this boy carries putrescence in his mind and must never lie with one with Power such as Lon Dubh for it will be usurped somehow and used, twisted and turned to something unnatural. This I know for I have seen this boy's mind and heart.*

Faidhe nodded to Fion and spoke.

"Come here boy." She said to Triag. "Let us hear from you what it is you know of the rites."

Triag seemed a bit surprised that something was expected of him in these discussions for it had been long since his grandmother had taken his voice from him in matters of the family. Fion remained standing while Triag bumped him slightly as he came forward and took a seat by the fire enjoying the attention afforded him by the elders.

"I know it is customary at 12 seasons plus half that a boy comes to manhood and may come to fires to couple, often times with a maiden coming to her own rites but at times with a woman of experience so that he may learn well the ways of the fires. I know that once a man visits the fires for the first time, he is viewed with the respect due a man and is considered for more important tasks such as hunting, cattle care, and decision-making. I have taken my responsibility on the road with the elders of my Tuath without complaint or hesitation. I have taken to the care and welfare of my grandmother on this path and before we left our home, I had taken on the duties of our cattle in my father's absence."

With this he cast his eyes downward in what he hoped would be dutiful shame in the fabrication of his father's abandonment of the tribe.

"Though I was but a boy of barely 11 seasons, I took on my tasks responsibly and to the best effort I had. I complained not that I received no recognition for my part in this journey nor did I ask what my role was beyond caring for my aging grandmother and clinging to what little family I have left. Now that it comes to my time to pass to manhood, I wish to do so with honor for I feel I have taken on the role of manhood and proven myself as one worthy of the Tuatha de Danann despite the idea that it is not unknown to me that many of this group carry no respect for my father."

With this he looked pointedly at Faidhe, leaving her to wonder what the boy knew, if anything about his father's death.

"But if I am to complain at all, it is only to say that I have done all in these travels to prove that the actions of my father are not a light I choose to stand in. I am hopeful that though I have gone largely unnoticed that it will be perceived as a positive thing that I have called no additional shame to my family or our clan."

Gara goggled at her grandson stunned that he had the ability to formulate such a speech. For if she contrived to manipulate the others, she could not have devised a better combination of modesty, and humble inventory of deeds to inflict a sense of guilt at being an unnoticed, uncomplaining member of the traveling group. It was as though Gara herself had seen Triag for the first time as a potential ally rather than a tool or bargaining asset.

"Well said, Grandson." Gara gushed and threw an uncharacteristic arm around his shoulder. "Although I dare say your grandmother is not as aged as all that, but I'm inclined to forgive your choice of words in light of the fine speech and that you do our family proud with your service up to this point."

Then to Faidhe. "So you see, the timing is clear and the sense it makes to create a bond between the two families seems equally as clear. The decision to bring my grandson to the fires has been made, for I, as his family elder have approved and come to officially ask that the union between our families be formalized. Iarann, as the elder male from our Tuath I ask that you stand to advise Triag as to what he may expect at the fires and what is expected of him."

Gara was fortifying her claim on the union of the two families with this request for it is usually the boy's own father or the father of the woman with whom the boy would lie that is chosen to instruct the boy and oversee the preparations of the rituals. Choosing Iarann brought the arrangement closer to being solidified.

Iarann was reeling between the news he'd just received from Faidhe about Lon Dubh thinking he was in love with her and knowing how hurt she will be when she discovers that he is her own sire. Worse, the betrayal she would feel when she discovers that his love is for her own mother, the woman with whom she had inwardly competed her whole life. Then, to add this next layer of unexpected circumstance to the first, he was quite shaken but he managed an even tone.

"As an elder, I will be honored to instruct and help Triag prepare for his first rites." Then reiterating his reasoning for accepting the honor he added, "In absence of your father and without knowing with whom you will lay, if or until the father of your chosen partner might take on the responsibility, I will see to your instruction and preparation. It seems we are to impose upon our hosts for another place of ritual to prepare you for your rites."

Gara offered, "If it is necessary, I will give of our hut where you and the boy may stay and I will remain here with Faidhe while preparations are being made for the two initiates."

Gara would take every opportunity now to speak of her grandson and Lon Dubh as coming to the fires together. She saw the logic in her argument and did not think it would take too much convincing to insure that Faidhe saw things her way as well. If she were to stay in the same hut as Faidhe that would give her all that much more time to work things to her advantage. She was pleased to hear Faidhe answer.

"Very well then Gara, go and prepare your hut for Triag and Iarann, prepare your things and when Iarann comes to your hut you may return here where you'll stay for the term of the initiates. Until then, I will speak of your offer with Iarann, my daughter's sire, and with Fion, my daughter's dearest friend about his offer as well. We will find proper coupling partners for all who come to the fires at this most unusual time of the year for such occasions."

"Certainly Faidhe." Gara responded. "Iarann, I will await your arrival and you have my thanks for taking on the responsibilities of seeing to Triag's preparation for such an important rite. Come, boy." She said to Triag almost as an afterthought, and was surprised when Triag stood and bowed to her saying, "Grandmother, thank you for speaking on my behalf here today. I look forward to the time, and may it be soon, that you will no longer look on me as merely a boy but that you may turn to me as the man of our clan and that you may depend on my support as I have depended on yours." When Triag was satisfied at the shocked response on his grandmother's face, he turned to Faidhe.

"My thanks for your consideration, Lady. I know the significance of this passage for not only your daughter but for our clans as well. I will be thankful for your input and abide by what you decide." Of course Triag did not think any alternative decision was plausible. He knew the half-breed Elf was not a viable match for Lon Dubh for it was common knowledge that half-breeds of differing species could not likely sire children and so to come to the fertility rites with one known to be unable to breed would be considered an insult to the Gods. He felt confident that things would go his way. To Iarann he said, "And I am grateful to you, Smithy, that you will lead me in my path to manhood for it has been you, over these past seasons to whom I have turned for example of what is required and expected of a man. I will not take your lessons lightly."

It was such a shock to all those in the room to hear Triag speak, much less speak so eloquently and respectfully. Iarann answered formally.

"Go then and prepare. For when I come to teach you, it will be seven days and nights of preparedness and ritual to bring you to the gates of manhood. Until that time you have my experience, wisdom and support, and when you enter through those gates in passage, you will come to your manhood on your singular path with the maid, the mother and the wise woman. May she be merciful."

Not until that moment had Triag considered that there was an actual spiritual element to the process of becoming a man. He had never considered that with the invocation of his rites, he would actually come to see the face of the Goddess. This formality from Iarann, whom Triag knew had come to the Circle as the God at one time, gave him a moment of pause at what might actually be ahead of him in these rites, for surely what they held would be very different from his dalliances with his aunt. Both he and Gara nodded and left the hut.

Faidhe broke the brief silence by reasoning her thoughts aloud. "Well the timing certainly indicates that this is to be considered. There is also the reasoning for why it was necessary to have the boy along on this trek. It would seem plausible that the two families of the same Tuath should come together."

"Please, Lady! Fion started the instant he thought Faidhe was actually considering letting such a union take place. His face curled once more into a mask of disgust and he actually bared his teeth, which seemed to grow fierce and pointed at the mere thought.

"You cannot allow Lon Dubh to lie with such a one! I have seen this boy's thoughts and they are sickened with foulness so that it would be a breach of the sacred to allow him to take the role of the God. I have seen the way his eyes look on the sacred feminine and it will cost your family dearly to take this one into your fold and mingle blood with him. I have no valid say in these matters and I respect your foresight in prophecy but on my honor, I will do what I can, with you or not, to keep such a one from coming to the fires with Lon Dubh." In a fury at this point. "The Power your family holds is an attraction to this one for I know he wishes to usurp it for his own use. He plots and contrives to undermine you while caring not for his grandmother as he says. He speaks with pretty tones and words but those words are hollow of any honor."

Iarann put a huge hand on Fion's shoulder. "Calm yourself now boy."

Fion growled, with a ferocity that shocked both Faidhe and Iarann. "I am not a boy! Though my size is deceiving, I am a man offering to marry Lon Dubh and carry the weight of the tale until I die so she may come to her duty in her service to the Gods. Can you not see that I am the only choice for her to maintain her commitment and to fulfill her destiny? We will travel the road together and I will finish out the tale and keep to my promise that it will survive the ages." His fury broke and the tears of his emotions betrayed him.

Iarann spoke. "I am sorry, Fion. You are stoic in your word and your honor is unquestionable. You are a true friend to Lon Dubh and have become very much a part of this family. I had not seen before, the burden it must be for you not to be taken seriously as a man due to your heritage. It is abominable that you have never been properly brought to your first fire. And it is clear to me now that you not only love Lon Dubh, but that you are in love with her. Forgive my callousness." Then he looked at Faidhe and continued. "If there is reason you have seen that this one, Triag, is not fitting for the Great Marriage, then it should be taken into the decision making process." Knowing he had no say in matters of a daughter's first rites, he waited for Faidhe to say something.

"I agree, Iarann. If there is information to be revealed on the character of the one who has petitioned to attend first fire with my Black Bird, then I shall hear it. Know also, Fion, that your offer, too, will be seriously considered. It may be as you say that the best match would be one with whom we know Lon Dubh already has a bond and so obviously cares for. But it is my understanding that you cannot offer a woman children. Is this so? Or do you know different of yourself?"

Fion bowed his head and his voice softened considerably. "It is true that though I have coupled with women, there have been no children thus far but should the Goddess will it, I have every faith that there will be a child born of the coupling. It is rare but not wholly unheard of that a half-breed such as myself has sired a child. Though I have not seen it for myself, I have heard of such things. This point alone should not be the only thing considered when coming to your decision."

He quieted then as though he'd run out of the ability to convince even himself that he would be the best choice for Lon Dubh.

Faidhe responded. "You know I am not one to soften words Fion. I do not simply placate you when I say you will be considered and I hold great respect for you that you strive to protect Lon Dubh from harm even if you are not the one chosen. For it is of absolute love you feel for her that you fight so valiantly and argue so convincingly. These things will not be taken lightly and you can believe that is the truth. I know it is time for her to take to the fires for not only has she come to it herself, but the talisman I saw in the prophecy has been presented so I am sure the time is now for these happenings to take place. We shall see to it that you are prepared."

Faidhe picked up the carved stone bird and held the figure to warm it in her hand as though it would tell her something. The bird sent her no message, but it was Fion who began to speak to tell her all he knew.

45

The Fires

L on Dubh had spent much of the last seven days and nights alone in her preparations for this night. She was bitterly disappointed that her mother had not
come to see her personally but rather had sent word to her through her attendants
of what rituals were to take place and which greens, essences and oils to use. Lon
Dubh had tried to mentally contact Faidhe but found she was unable to connect
this way either. So she tried to wait patiently for the time her mother would come
with news for the last time they spoke, there was question as to Iarann's thoughts
on her initiation to womanhood but Lon Dubh had decided: *Not to hear news must
mean there is no ill news to hear.* But still, she missed her mother's presence and
battled her insecurities wondering why, as her mentor and advisor her mother had
seen fit not to come to her at this important time.

Black Bird had made friends with her attendants but had not seen the young
girl, Vannina, who was so kind on her first night in the cave hut. Though she'd
only met the girl for a brief time, Lon Dubh had liked her instantly and for all the
following days looked for her face among the women who came to attend her. The
language barrier kept her from being able to ask after the girl with any clarity so she
contented herself with the items that Faidhe sent to her and the few words labori-
ously repeated to her in the strange and guttural tongue.

As the days progressed, Lon Dubh found that longer trance states helped to
quell the chattering questions in her head. She was visited by visions of both past
and possible future occurrences. One such vision that dominated her meditations
was that of a plump and beautiful babe being handed into her arms. Lon Dubh was
not sure if the babe was hers but that she came to recognize the babe by its bright
blue eyes and full head of sun-colored hair much like her sister Colm's but the
babe's attributes seemed brighter somehow, more vibrant.

Communication with her sister helped to comfort Lon Dubh in the absence of
her mother. She learned of great preparations for the ritual that was being planned

for the Clan Laoghaire and of the ritual symbolism Colm had introduced to the Shield of protection for the clan. Pleased that her sister's family grew in popularity as leaders of the isle, and that there were no further malicious attempts on the lives of anyone within Clan Laoghaire.

Colm told her: Laoghaire is to conduct the ritual at the festival of Imbolc at the Great Stone. Our ewes have dropped many a lamb this year. It seems we are to be prosperous for many of our herd grow fat already for the spring calving. Word has traveled quickly throughout the island of the good fortune bestowed on us here and many representatives from factions and clans all across the island will come in great crowds to the rituals here likely in the hopes of taking the good blessings cast here home to their own people and herds. My role in all of this has become one that serves as the Goddess to Laoghaire's God in the fertility fires, which are celebrated during all the festivals now. Though in this transitional time much has changed, there is also much that has remained of the ways of the Tuatha De Danann in all that we do.

Lon Dubh responded: I am pleased things are well with you and Laoghaire. I have thought often these days of your seclusion of first fire rites and who might have attended you. I lament that as your sister, I was not a part of your first rites. It is strange, I am a grown woman but I feel the fluttering in my middle, as any young girl must before she becomes a woman. Sister, I have grown into my role as Priestess for the Goddess and conduct the rituals for the festivals whether we are just ourselves on the road or come to a village. I share the tale as ever and I spread the ways of reverence for the Gods at each festival, using what greens and symbols are available to me. But now at last I have been called to my first fire and I sense that great changes are about to take place. I feel a foreboding that I have petitioned the Universe for such a union and it has been granted me. But still, I know not if it is normal doubts of one who comes to this passage or if my alarm is warranted. It may be that I have expected our mother to more closely attend me and I have not seen her since the first night of my seclusion. But still, I sense something I do not see is at work here.

Colm responded: Ah, I feel the same loss that I am not there for you in your time of passage. It may be that we are all meant to be separate from one another. Does it not seem so, sister? It may be that this is why our mother has not come to you. We have been required to grow ever stronger in our self- reliance.

Perhaps you are right Colm. But my waiting is finished. I am bathed and robed and the time has come for my first rites. I have but to add the ritual oils to the wood to send the signal of smoke that the Goddess has come into me and that I am ready. It is good that we have spoken. You are a comfort to me Colm-dove. I must go now and prepare my mind.

A slight rustle caught Lon Dubh's attention and she turned to see Faidhe standing in the hut. "You are so beautiful Black Bird. Your hair gleams like the feathers of the raven!"

"Mother, I was afraid you would not come to me. I must ask, as my mentor, why have you not come to me before this?"

"You are not a young girl without knowledge. What is to take place here tonight is no great mystery to you. Your choice in keeping yourself from lying with a man has been your singular path and so too has your guidance to end that path been to your individual story. It was fitting that you created your own journey from the time of your decision to the time you come to the fires as well. Everything I might have shared with you would have been for novice initiates and not served you on your path. I am here daughter to give you news for which you will need to summon your strength. Understand you that the path of a Priestess of the Goddess is one followed faithfully and often painfully. You may not understand the purpose but you have vowed to serve and so you must."

"You are not being clear, Faidhe!" Lon Dubh's fear was revealed in her anger. She fought the cold sinking feeling in her gut that foretold of something amiss. "Speak plain, for if I am to continue this night with my initiation, I will have truth in what is to take place. Is it Iarann? Has he forsworn his love for me?"

"You will continue with these proceedings this night Lon Dubh." Faidhe pulled out the small black raven carving and placed it in her daughter's hand. "The creation of this talisman is proof that your intuition told you true. The Goddess has chosen this time and place for you to give of your maiden's blood for her."

Lon Dubh stared at the piece in her hand trying to make sense of what she was seeing and hearing. "How came you by this? Did you take it from me? For what purpose? She felt panic and some hidden guilt rising and tried to quell it with her anger. "Speak now. What is it you have concocted for me to bear?"

"You have sworn your life to the Goddess, have you not?"

"I have but..."

"Then you must listen and know that none of this was contrived. One other than the one of your choosing will come to your first rites this night. There will be no marriage for you with Iarann. It is forbidden unless it is the will of the Goddess that it must be so. The union of particular families is part of her intended web for the future. The blood of your maidenhead will bring a babe of mixed blood whose line will come to use at the time of the prophecy. Your babe, as mine, will provide the blood breed mix right for the coming of one in the future who will hold all the Power of the Universe to push back the other, the darkness of the unbridled masculine.

Lon Dubh was furious now and this volatile emotion after seven days and nights of preparation for the Goddess to enter her took on a most ominous quality. Faidhe watched as her daughter appeared to grow larger in her presence and her face took on a mask of rage. Heat in the cave hut was instantly stifling as her fear and emotions were finally unleashed. Urns of oils and libations burst and racks of dried herbs and vegetation flared into flames and were instantly reduce to ash. Lon Dubh's hair blew up with the drafts of heat produced in her frustration that there was naught that she could do to steer her own destiny.

She shouted and her voice was great and terrible as is echoed her wrath coupled with the Goddess's Power just beneath the surface.

"Iarann loves me; I know it is true. He is of magical blood, he is my chosen consort; you tell me why he is not allowed to come to my rites." She took a step closer to Faidhe, looming as she expected an answer.

"Iarann may be who you have chosen, but he is not who the Goddess has chosen for you. I regret that I did not know of your feelings for him sooner for I would have told you of your kinship to him so that the love you have for each other would have grown in its proper way."

Her frustration returned at the course of conversation but it diverted her anger as Lon Dubh strove to puzzle out what Faidhe was trying to tell her without being forthright.

"I don't understand. Just tell me plain what has happened to change Iarann's mind so I may deal with the truth. If I am to come to the fires this night, I must know the truth of my own circumstances. You say he loves me but not in the right way. He told me of his love so what is different. Explain this now!" She said finally in a flat voice and a pointed intensity that would not be ignored.

It was not a request and Faidhe knew the time for carefully cushioning her words was over.

"This is not how I wished your first rites to unfold. Iarann will not come to you this night because he loves you as your sire not as your mate. He is your father and has loved and cared for you this trip entire, grateful that he has had the opportunity to know his daughter, a child of the Circle. It was he who took the role of the God for me in the Festival of the End of the Warm Days that set you to grow in my womb."

Lon Dubh's knees went out from under her and she crumpled on the earthen floor. She swooned, trying to make sense of what she heard as though it was just too much to comprehend at once.

"Then who was it he spoke of that he loved and wanted to come to a marriage understanding? If not me, then who?"

Then it struck her another blow. All the pieces fell into place in her mind and she felt scalding embarrassment for how she felt such a fool after professing her love for this man while he told her all along of his love for her own mother and she was blind to the truth.

"All along you two? You must have had a great entertainment at my expense. Did you keep this until now because you needed me in all your plans?" Her fury began to mount again.

"Think child, on what you say. Think on our conversation of only seven days past. I knew not of your feelings for Iarann until only then. I was remiss in educating you on your heritage. I have not been attentive to you on this journey as I should have been. Had I been more of a teacher to you and less involved in my own pains, I might have spared you this, but it is done now and you must move on in keeping with your oath to the Goddess.

Lon Dubh breathed in and out several times to regain her composure.

"You needn't keep reminding me of my oath, Faidhe. I will take to the fires and do what I must for the sake of my oath, for the Goddess has been my one true mother."

Lon Dubh wanted her words to sting Faidhe and chose them to do just that.

"I am true to her but know this, I have learned well how to follow my individual path to do her bidding for my childhood entire, without you. This I will continue to do. Now who is this one who will come as my consort so I may adjust my final meditations? No! Do not tell me. I will have no more of these proceedings tainted by your input or words. You have not seen fit to come to me as mentor or advisor and I was at a loss, but now I am grateful. I have come to this moment alone and I will meet my destiny in the same way. Whoever it might be, I will be the Goddess and partake in the rite. No more. Leave me."

Faidhe searched in vain to find something to say. She felt diminished and small in her daughter's present state. She left the hut taking some small comfort in the evident Power that her Lon Dubh displayed. Despite all that had happened, Goddess was with her daughter in no small way. This would be a Powerful coupling.

Triag had finalized the steps required of a man coming to his rites. He had meticulously followed instruction given him by Iarann and absorbed all of the magical processes and symbolic rituals, Iarann noted, as if perfection were his goal. Despite their many months on the road together, Iarann knew very little of this boy but in the past seven days, he had discovered that he was driven and attentive. He was eager to learn and was polite and respectful and although Iarann could not find fault with the boy's attitude or performance, he could not ignite the slightest warmth or affection for him.

Iarann found a nagging annoyance at the boy's fussy demeanor and could not help but feel that the eagerness to learn was just a façade. He felt the boy had other motives for his interest in the proceedings and wondered at Faidhe's decision to let him couple with one who is so much older than he is at his first rites. *But then,* Iarann justified, *better that he come to the fires with a strong grown woman who has seen much of life rather than a young girl easily overpowered and manipulated.*

With that thought, it was as if a flash of light went off in Iarann's head. *There is the truth! That is what has troubled me about this one. He is so eager to come to the fires for the power it will afford him! He wishes to dominate! Ah so this is why Faidhe has chosen for him to lay with a powerful woman of the clan. She will not be dominated.* Though he understood Faidhe's reasoning, he still liked it not that this boy would assume the status of manhood. Now that he had placed his misgivings about Triag, Iarann felt something treacherous lurking just beneath the surface of the polite and respectful pretense.

Iarann helped Triag into his ceremonial robe, offered to him by the village folk. The boy had prepared flawlessly and was ready now to embark upon his final meditations before the ritual oils would be spilled on the fire to let people keeping first fire vigil outside the hut that the God has entered him and he is ready for his rites. It was time now to tend to Fion for whom he had volunteered as attendant and mentor for his rites as well. Iarann thought it only fitting that as the closest person Fion had to a male family member, if he could stand as advisor to such as Triag, he could do at least this for Fion. He gave last words of advice for Gara's boy and left the hut with a sigh of relief.

Upon Iarann's exit, Triag's face took on a sour expression and he spat, "Ugh! Another minute of his babbling on about reverence for the feminine, sacred this and honor that. I think he actually believes it all. What nonsense! But finally, now all I have to do is wait a sufficient amount of time and pour the oils. Then I'll come to my reward. Three days, I will have my "Goddess" to serve me." He gloated aloud. "Hardly payment for having to endure that great oaf for seven days. Had I been able to enter his mind, it may have been worth the boredom of pretending to listen and take his guidance. But no matter," Triag lounged now on the great many skins placed on the large pallet, throwing his hands behind his head. "Three days of uninterrupted pleasure."

He thought briefly of Morgan and shrugged. *One is as good as another.* He smiled wickedly at the thought and began to fantasize about how Lon Dubh would have to be true to her duty. She would necessarily have to stay for all three days and submit as many times as the "God" so desired.

———

Lon Dubh knew as the sun set that she would be expected to be ready for the rites but she felt as a trapped animal and paced the hut trying to tease through all that had just taken place. Alternately she was embarrassed and furious with both her mother and Iarann. Her heart ached for the loss of the unity she thought she had with her family and trying to wrap her mind around the idea that Iarann did love her but not as she had desired. But now that she knew the truth, she had to be honest with herself that a life with Iarann was truly not what she desired. Could it be that on some level she had taken comfort in her relationship with Iarann but knew that it was not a relationship of passion as she had often seen with her sister and Laoghaire? Oddly, with that thought, her mind glimpsed Sonne, the gatekeeper who came to her on the night of her tale telling. Her hand opened to reveal the stone raven still clutched there. Her mind raced with all she had to consider. After some lengthy time, Lon Dubh surrendered to her oath and commitment to the Goddess and mechanically poured the oil on the fire to signal with the smoke it would produce to those watching outside the hut that she was ready.

Perfunctorily, she walked to the chilled cave to which the hut was attached and stood behind the skins draped across the opening. She looked at the pallet piled high with soft skins and furs for her first coupling. She impulsively flung the stone raven at the skins as though the act could make her misery go away. Turning away from the bed, not wishing to think on what will take place there, she stood in the center of the cave to wait for her partner. *Whoever it is, I will meet him standing and endure the rites as the Goddess. The respect and reverence due her will be my balm for the affront to my pride. The one who comes to this cave will meet the Goddess, not the woman. If it will not be as I had planned and with whom, I will serve the Goddess and have done with all of it.* She then did her best to allow the trance state to take over her mind and exorcise her hurting heart and fuming anger toward her mother and Iarann so that she would be mentally separated from the proceedings. That way she could better endure the physical aspect of what she now perceived as no more than a necessary task.

Lon Dubh stood in the cave aware of the cold but it did not touch her for she emanated heat. As she fell deeper into her trance, she was aware of someone in the hut beyond the cave entrance. She was aware of everything physically around her, and she too was aware of being showered with blessings from her mother, Iarann, Fion, Laoghaire, Colm, Macha and Morgan. And to her surprise, there was even the energetic blessing, albeit, a tepid one from Gara. Lon Dubh was aware of these energies and scattered thoughts from others of the village folk as well. These blessings spoke to her spirit and soothed her pain. The longer she allowed the blessings and prayers to wash over her, the deeper Lon Dubh fell into the rhythms of the Earth. Through her bare feet, she connected with the Mother-Earth and felt the rising tide of the urge to couple take over her consciousness. In these moments, she allowed herself to drift away from her conscious thoughts of pain, embarrassment and betrayal. More loudly she could hear the pulse of the rhythm of the Earth until her heart pulsed in time with it and she became the very rhythm. She was overtaken by the awareness that many such rituals had been performed in this cave much the same as her own people utilized the Circle. The cave represents the womb of the Mother, Earth. These people saw the mountains here as great breasts from which they are suckled and given all the bounty of sustenance. This is a sacred space of the feminine. And so the God enters the feminine in the ritual coupling. Her understanding that these people had similar customs and sacred rituals to her own Tuath comforted her in some way. With that knowledge, the rhythm then took her mind high into the air and as if she were a bird soaring above the earth, she could see as the raven sees, her home village, the shore of the Lake of the Ivory Heron, the Circle, now devoid of its Stones atop the sacred Hill. The pulse grew ever stronger as Lon Dubh witnessed glimpses of the couplings of hundreds of girls come to their rites through generations of her family. She recognized that this was indeed a pinnacle moment between an age of the old and one of the new. A dawning of things greatly changed. This realization had come as a thought both formulated in her head and one spoken in pictures to her mind by the will of the Goddess. Deep inside, Lon Dubh was aware that the Goddess had indeed entered her and on the heels of that thought, she felt a pair of warm hands tugging at her ceremonial robe.

An awareness then that her eyes had opened occurred to her for she saw all the symbols on the red robe she had embroidered over the last seven days and nights curiously spring to animation. Each illustration representative of an aspect of fertility and birth, and phases of the feminine as the maid, mother or crone were perfectly formed in delicately spun, dyed wool; they came to life to enact some ritual or aspect of womanhood. Figures of women offering their maidenhead, next in full belly, then squatting to take on the birthing position, revealing the sacred opening through which a child's head crowned. Lon Dubh watched in wonder as the embroidered illustrations all over her ceremonial robe moved and danced to the rhythm that pulsed in her veins.

Without taking her eyes from the play that was being enacted before her, Lon Dubh understood that her God had entered the cave and removed her robe from behind her to reveal her finely muscled body. She felt warm hands lightly brush their palms just over the skin of her thighs and as the hands reached the tops of her legs, two thumbs briefly brushed over the coarse hair between them, then they skipped smoothly around to her buttocks, teasing her skin into raised points. The hands explored their way up her flat belly and cupped her breasts to thumb her ripe nipples flushed deep red with the blood that raged through her veins urging her to be entered. Her nipples, longing to be suckled, answered the call and rose to meet the hands that beckoned them to life. Lon Dubh imagined she felt her breasts engorge with milk and wondered at all these sensations.

The ceremonial robe had been tossed to the floor and Lon Dubh mused about what she saw on an illustration on her robe. She watched the embroidered figures as a male figure graze his hands over a woman in just the same fashion as she'd just experienced. The two figures were standing in a circular frame of holly sprigs with red berries to represent the sacred blood of the woman's moon cycle, the ruptured maidenhead and then the blood of birth. These holly sprigs were interwoven with sprays of the sacred mistletoe plant with white berries representing the milky white seed of the male, come to manhood. The tiny male figure stood parallel to the female and it appeared that his phallus strove toward her just as her breasts and hips appeared to be drawn toward him.

On some inner level Lon Dubh was grateful that she had the illustrations to call her attention so she did not have to look into the eyes of this other, this stranger who came as the God to claim her maidenhead. At the same time, she allowed herself to be caught in the tide of the ritual for her body was rife with sensations wholly foreign to her. Drunk with trance, she allowed her hands to do what they instinctively chose to do. She watched as the figures in the pictorial used their hands to explore one another. Her own fingers were curious as they discovered the smooth soft skin of her partner's staff and the contrasting hardness of its desire. She shivered as gentle fingers found the slickness of her life-giving cup and the shield of flesh still intact protecting the entrance to her womb. Breathless and pulsating to the rhythms between them now, Lon Dubh gasped as the inquisitive fingers grazed the swollen fold located just in front of her feminine opening. Although she was aware of the sensations that could be felt in this area, she had never experienced them so powerfully. Closing her eyes, she was in fear of passing out or falling down from the sheer force of the feeling. There was the sensation of vertigo as she fell backward. Her landing was softened by a very strong arm catching around the small of her back and laying her down on the mountain of furs provided for her palette in the cave. Lon Dubh was mildly aware that she had fallen because she was no longer able to see the depictions of fertility on her robe but now looked at the ceiling of the cave. Still without a sense of the identity of her partner, she gave over helplessly to the skilled hands that coaxed the mounting sensation of a tightening in the cup of her womb and down her legs. She was awash in the warm, soaking, wave of sensations when her partner abruptly stopped.

It was then that a figure came into Lon Dubh's view as he knelt above her. First, she thought she saw the depiction from her embroidery on the ceremonial robe and then she was sure she looked on the face of the God. An errant thought crossed her mind as to whether her partner saw her own face or that of the Goddess and with the thought, her visions cleared as the two figures came into focus and she recognized her partner.

He gave her no time for reaction for in one smooth, graceful movement, he leaned over and lay atop her supporting his weight with his forearms while positioning his legs between her own. He lowered his face to cover her mouth with his; gently, but firmly he kissed Lon Dubh and she was aware of his scent and his breath smelled of sweet herbs. She was compelled to kiss him back. Without fully understanding what was happening, she felt his sword at the mouth of her cup gently nudging as he moved with the rhythm that caught them both.

With the movement, the mounting sensation returned to her loins with greater intensity now. Her body responded and she raised her hips to its call and all at once, his sword breached her maidenhead. Lon Dubh cried out with the simultaneous pain and a masterpiece of pleasure. He did not move at all now but for the slight and gentle nudging while deep inside to bring her to experience her full pleasure and then slowly, so her newly abraded skin would not cause her pain, they both surrendered to the rhythm of the coupling while exchanging kisses.

He pressured kisses on her neck, breasts and mouth and she pushed him back and ran her hands over his chest and arms all the while staring into his eyes, and searching his face caught in a delightful swoon of the coupling that causes one to see all the beauty and perfection in their partner. Totally absorbed in his face, she called his name for the first time, acknowledging the man and abandoning her own promise to submit to the God in the act of fertility but to separate from the man.

"Sonne." She said.

He smiled down on her and it was as though the sun had come out after a dark storm. She knew not whether it was the magic of the coupling, or the smile he bestowed on her but Lon Dubh found herself completely content and wishing that this moment could be captured for eternity. She would preserve this moment of bliss if she could.

"Svort Fagel." He answered. "Min shatz." A look of intensity came over his face and he impulsively wrapped both his arms around her holding her tightly and plunged deeply several times in a short frenzied burst emitting a low and throaty moan.

"Ah, min shatz, min Black Bird." and enveloped her in his arms, covering her face and neck with gentle, earnest kisses.

Sonne brought one hand out from the tight spot between the warmth of Lon Dubh's back and the mountain of furs on which they consummated to inspect something he'd found buried there. In his hand was the raven he'd carved from a smooth, black river stone for this woman who consumed his mind since he'd first seen her. The smile touched his mouth first then his eyes smiled with creases that ran down his cheeks lighting up his face and Lon Dubh's whole world.

———

Faidhe sat by the fire in her hut and sent blessings and prayers to the initiates who were coming to the first rites this night. She did not question the ways of the Goddess but often reflected on the symmetry of things when left to the Power to sort out rather than rely on her own calculations on what must be done. The fortuitous turn of events that took place seven nights ago when Faidhe spoke with Fion in her hut only moments after Gara and Triag had left, reinforced Faidhe's faith that things would manifest to serve the Goddess's bidding and inwardly chastised herself for believing the illusion that she had to arrange everything on her own.

When Gara and Triag had left the hut after the pair petitioned for Triag to participate in Lon Dubh's first rites, Fion saw the carved stone raven that Faidhe had inadvertently taken from Lon Dubh's possessions and recognized the piece he had seen the village man give to Faidhe's daughter.

"I have seen this piece you call a talisman. Do you know from whence it came, Lady?"

Faidhe seemed preoccupied while asking Iarann to bring more fuel for the fire. She was already calculating how she could seek information on who her daughter's first partner would be but managed to answer Fion in a half attentive tone.

"It was carved by Lon Dubh."

"I mean no disrespect, Lady. But I think this is not so."

She watched Iarann leave the hut and when it struck her what Fion had said, it got Faidhe's full attention in the form of curiosity.

"What mean you, Fion? I have asked Lon Dubh only today if it was her work and..." Faidhe conjured her memory of the conversation because she had remembered something that rang odd about her daughter's answer in that conversation. *What was it? What had she said?* Looking at Fion with the evidence of a puzzle on her face Faidhe answered her own question. "I think you are right, Elf-kin; she answered not my question but only led me to believe the bird was her own work when she only told me the bird was hers. What do you know of this piece?"

"I had not intended to eavesdrop or witness what had taken place between the two but I grew weary of waiting for Lon Dubh to come to me so we could attend the hall and tell the tale on that night. I walked to find her here, just outside your hut but she was not alone. I saw a figure standing very near her and I stopped to observe if she was in trouble or if she should need privacy. In that time, I know she had been offered and accepted a gift from the man. He did her no harm so I stood in the shadows until he departed. As I approached Lon Dubh, she knew not that I was even there as she inspected the gift given her by the man. I saw then, that it was this carving that the man had given her. I did not wish to intrude and so did not ask her of the piece. I had other pressing business to discuss with her and take her counsel but she was not in a mind to pay me attention at that moment. Then that evening, after the telling, she was hurried away by the maids to her seclusion for the rites so I was never able to question her about the raven stone or take her counsel."

"Fion, who was it that gave her the stone?" Urgency crept into Faidhe's voice. "Can you remember? Would you recognize him should you see him?"

"I know not of him, Lady, but I do remember him for he was the one who challenged us as we first came to this village. He was the large guard with the yellow hair who stopped us at spear point."

Faidhe gave this a moment's thought.

"Fion, we will see to it that you are brought to your first fires with all the honor afforded by the Tuatha De Danann as one of its own. I must ask you first to retrieve Iarann and tell him to keep Gara and Triag occupied until I call for Gara. Then I request you to use your communication skills to inquire as to who this man is and see to it that he is brought to me. Will you do this?"

"Of course I will. Will you need me to assist in your conversation with the man when I have brought him to you?"

"That will depend on whether he has any level of magical ability or not. Should he have a spark, I will be able to manage. Should he not, then, I will have been mistaken and you needn't bother. Go now. Time, we have not." As an afterthought, "Fion, why was it you intended to speak with Lon Dubh? It is an issue for which I can provide counsel?"

Fion stopped in his flight toward the door. He appeared to contemplate and seemed grateful for the opportunity to share what he knew especially now that Triag had boldly come to petition for the opportunity to take his first rites with Lon Dubh.

"I know not if you can counsel me Lady, but it is likely time I shared my knowledge. Remember that it was you who asked me and not I who bring tales of another of our party. I would not have it seem I speak of such things out of a competitive heart but knowledge of what I have seen will be of use to you as you make your decision regarding who will honor Lon Dubh as she claims her womanhood."

Fion shared with Faidhe all he had encountered in observing Triag communing with some other, telling of the boy listening in on Faidhe while she discussed with Laoghaire the demise of his own father.

"There were other thoughts as well. Most disturbing thoughts of King Laoghaire's young one, Morgan." Fion described Triag's thoughts and intentions toward the little sprite of a girl and also what he'd observed when Triag had arranged for what he'd called his 'first fire' with Morgan. "But to the girl's credit, she was strong and stoic in how she dissuaded him, but there is evil in this one, I am sure of it. I also sense that any struggle for reclamation for the innocence in this one is long past. He is spoiled in mind and heart."

Appalled at what she heard, Faidhe was silent while her thoughts reeled at this news. Just as she was about to send Fion to find Iarann, she sensed a presence outside the hut. Signaling to Fion to be quiet. *Be still,* she rose swiftly and glided across the room in absolute silence.

The Elf was amazed at the agile movements of the woman who had so quickly wizened since he had met her. One might take her gate to have the look of youth, but Fion recognized the presence of magic in her actions. In fact, it just now occurred to him that he'd seen in her rapid aging, a transition of this one from things human to something more akin to ethereal, much like his tribe, the Elven folk.

Faidhe pushed open the door to find Gusella, the woman she had chastised for her the ill treatment of Lon Dubh and other initiates to the first rites of fertility. Taken by surprise, Faidhe signaled the woman to enter the hut. Gusella moved through the entrance sideways to accommodate her girth and although was much larger than even most men, she presented as contrite and respectful to Faidhe.

Fion was in the habit of translating for the villagers, the minds of his fellow travelers as with the tale-telling.

"This one comes to thank you for her healing from her anger and asks that you re-teach her the ways of preparation so that she can be a better advisor to her underlings."

"Thank you Fion. Gusella and I have means to communicate. If you will, please go and seek out Iarann and ask him to do what I have requested so that I may have some peace before I am to share this space with Gara. Then, if you will, tend to that other matter for me?"

"Certainly, Lady. As you wish." And he was gone.

Faidhe turned to Gusella. I *sense that you have reflected on the gift of healing given to you.*

Gusella was awed at Faidhe's ability not only to communicate with her this way, but by the fact that she could so easily look into her heart and mind to know only the truth of her thoughts. Faidhe knew things of her that she had not even allowed herself to consider. She nodded to indicate to Faidhe that she had reflected.

I am come to you for you saw in me de young girl I once was. You saw in me de pain in mine heart and reached to heal me. You knew of mine shame in mine first coupling and told me why I am so hard to make friends wit mine girls. I do not want being dis way. I just am safer being strong. I am strong over others and I am safe. But now mine anger is gone. I feel light and soft. As if to express her thoughts more clearly, the large woman hiked up on her toes and fluttered her arm to impress upon Faidhe her sense of freedom being released from her anger.

I understand Gusella. Your fear keeps you caught in your pain. And fear is the breath that fans the flames of anger. My own daughter has made clear for me that many of the girls in your charge over the times you have been their advisor to the rituals are still virgins though they have endured a coupling, if they have not come together with a man in respect and reverence, they have still not had their first rites.

Gusella bent her head in shame and quiet tears cascaded from her eyes.

Understand you, Gusella, I mean not to chastise at this time, but to teach. For you too are one of whom I speak. Though you are of maturity, you have had only one experience to the rites and it was one of cruelty. I know your womb was stripped barren due to the brutality you endured. But this does not mean you are not fully a woman. I believe I have a solution to the emptiness you endure. Let me tell you and then I will teach you all there is by showing you how to bring an initiate to her fires in self-love so that her first coupling is truly a communion of Goddess with God. Learn of the rituals and what they mean. Bring the sacredness back into the understanding of what the sexual rites are meant for. Then, as you teach your initiates they too will respect themselves and never a one of them will again come to the fires afraid or endure what you have. Then you will come to any coupling as a full woman, pure in the Goddess's energy.

Gusella responded. I had always suspected dat de damage done to mine body vas too much for me to have de children. But I never again gave or took from any man. I took out mine rage on all others who came to de rites. I vas bitter dat dese girls would have de beauty in deir experiences and bear fruit. I let de poison in mine heart consume me. How can I give back what I have taken from dese girls?

You cannot. But you can teach them differently by your example. I will teach you all I can and then, you will heal yourself completely. Come to me on the morrow and bring your most recent initiate who has already experienced the first rites. I will begin to instruct you in the ways of the rituals of my people. I think we will reenergize your own understanding of the rituals of your own people as we work.

Tank you, wise woman. Tank you, Faidhe. An emotionally exhausted Gusella left the hut feeling hopeful about her new outlook and role as a woman of power...and the possibility of kinship with another woman.

Now, on the night of Lon Dubh's first fires, Faidhe sat in her hut not far from where Iarann and Gara sat as they each sent blessings to their respective family members as they came to their fertility rites. She sensed that Lon Dubh had truly taken on the Goddess in her coupling and that her choice in bringing Sonne, the man who had carved the very talisman she'd seen in the prophecy was the exact soul the Goddess had intended for this ritual. She had found from Fion's investigations that this man was not of these mountain people, but from beyond the northern peninsula of the mainland. He was of the land of the Valkyrie but had come to these lands when his mother married into this clan. A man of size and strength, he was not merely a guard, but a keen strategist, who brought the peoples to move to this location so that they were insulated from attack. He had come through the ranks of the warriors in the village to be known now as the ruler of the men who protect these clans. *He will offer good blood for this union and is of the blood of the Northlands!*

Faidhe's eyes were closed now as she wondered at Triag's first rites. Three days was a long time for any woman to be expected to couple with this one. He may experience disappointment that it was not he who was chosen to come to Lon Dubh's bed but should he decline the coupling or leave the proceedings before the third sundown, he will not have come fully to his manhood. So there would be some learning for the boy to do. Faidhe was confident that the choice of initiate made for his partner was just perfect...for the both of them. A smile crossed her lips as she watched in her mind's eye, Gusella walk to the door of Triag's hut in her ceremonial robes equipped with a week's worth of training and guidance from Faidhe on how to be a strong, firm, self-reliant teacher fresh in her memory.

Faidhe sent also, blessing and prayers to her latest family member whom she had come to love well in these recent days. Fion was one with whom Lon Dubh spent much time and Faidhe had had little communication with the Elf on their long voyage but over the last seven days had come to see him as stoic, faithful, honest and true to his word. Ever eager to help no matter that his own desires often took last place in order of importance. She was pleased that Iarann had offered to mentor Fion for she knew it was a task both men enjoyed. The absence of Lon Dubh allowed for relationships between the rest of their traveling group to blossom. And now, though he could not get a woman with child, he would have the ceremonial recognition of coming to manhood. The initiate chosen, brought to her with Gusella was also a most satisfactory choice. Though she'd already been through her first rites, the sweet girl Vannina had benefited from training during the last seven days with Faidhe and Gusella to come to the fires, not for fertility, but to understand and experience all the ritual, symbolism and ceremonial aspects of allowing the Goddess to enter her and to be a partner to the God for the rite of passage of her consort just as Gusella would do for Triag.

Faidhe was quite content with the work of the last seven sunsets. She reached out to Iarann and took his hand, sharing her sense of well-being at work well done. Now she had but to wait the three days of initiation and prepare for the festival of the lambing of the ewes. This should be quite a celebration for these folk due to the fact that they had depended on the wool and of sheep and goats for much of their food and clothing. She suspected they must offer much praise, thanks and reverence for this festival as their petitions are heard. And I think after these first rites, Lon Dubh will be a forceful and able advocate for those petitions. She will come near to her full Power now. For the first time in a very long while, Faidhe felt at peace.

46

The Lambing of the Ewes

On the morning after their third night together in the cave, Sonne and Lon Dubh heard movement in the hut beyond the mouth of the cave. There were polite coughs and additional clanging of urns and bowls that allowed the couple to know that they were no longer alone. On the previous days, when they awoke, there was wood, a warm fire and fresh food, water and fur skins left for them as though they had appeared through magic and all refuse had been removed in the same way. The couple had never before been aware of those who came to replenish their food and drink for as it should be, it seemed they were the only two people in the world.

But now, they could hear the large tub pot being filled with water and the savory scent of mutton broth called to life their stomachs, which began to complain with the physical activity they had fueled over the past three nights and days. Whether they wanted to or not, they were being summoned to rejoin the clans.

Lon Dubh took a final moment to drink in the silhouette of her love as he lay, face down on the furs next to her. He buried his head in the furs trying to avoid the inevitable. She propped herself on one elbow and traced her finger over his well-muscled shoulder, then down the middle of his back and over the taught haunch of his buttocks. As a horse might twitch a fly, his muscles responded to her touch. Lon Dubh ran a light finger over the scars on Sonne's back and shoulders that she had by now memorized. Each jagged tear and healed over puncture; wounds from battles he had recounted to her in his strange tongue and a kind of pantomime. Lon Dubh enjoyed being told some stories for a change instead of being the focus of one and she found that she wanted to know everything about this man.

Sonne had come to these clans from the North as an outlander child with a handful of others. He had a natural aptitude for the sword and spear craft and quickly outshone all others in his ability to be victorious in battle not only through skills of fighting, but more so in strategies of battle. By making use of the land-scape, and seasons, Sonne had brought this clan to virtual insulation from being overpowered by warriors from surrounding villages who might wish to raid his adopted village for their herds, goods, slaves, or worse, womenfolk for breeding. His skills had earned him an esteemed place in this clan as the leader of the warriors. Much respected and loved by his men, Sonne had taken watch and walked the surrounding wood with the rest of the village protectors, never feeling his rank put him above the duties he expected of his own warriors. For this reason, he was on gate-watch the night Lon Dubh and her party came to the village.

Still persevering through the language barrier, both Sonne and Lon Dubh began to learn words and phrases of the other's language but surprised each other by finding their own way of communicating by mental images flashing to create for the other a picture of what they were thinking much like the way Fion helped people to understand the sacred tale. Lon Dubh had been amazed that this man had some magical abilities in communication as well as his extraordinary carving and fighting skills. She wondered to herself at the symmetry of all she'd endured. To find herself partnered with one who came from the Northlands, likely of the same clans as the one who'd sired her sister. But neither of these two she held so dear now had any deference to those origins yet were hearkened to its calling all the same. Lon Dubh had no doubt that her Sonne had been her destiny in all of this. That all of her experiences and travels, the prophecy together with Sonne's experiences had brought them both to this place to be right here and now in this very moment together. Though she knew this to be true, she still could not shake the sense of betrayal she felt that her mother had somehow deceived her. Lon Dubh had tried to be grateful that she'd found happiness in her first coupling with Sonne, yet the resentment she bore for Faidhe was not easily released.

The sounds outside the cave entrance had subsided and Lon Dubh knew that their time together in this warm cocoon of discovery was about to end, wishing to delay the unavoidable end of their exclusive time, she straddled Sonne's backside and bent to plant warm kisses on the back of his neck. Rising to the invitation, Sonne turned over to face her, allowing her to see his pleasure in being awoken so. Lost in his eyes, she knelt above his phallus allowing his entry one last time before they were swept back into their lives of responsibility.

Perhaps it was because they both knew they would have to return to the lives they had prior to discovering each other that made this last coupling one energized with the fever to make this final union last in their minds but the two understood wordlessly that the magic of their cave-time was nearly over. The fantasy of this place, suspended in a time that time did not pass, in a place that seemed removed from all the world, they drank in the essence of one another's souls and each found a home in the other. It was neither pre-measured nor contrived but in the moment they truly felt as one in the coupling, both Sonne and Lon Dubh uttered their vow to give of all of themselves to each other.

Sonne reached for Lon Dubh gently rolling over atop her and whispered, "Min Korp, *my Raven*, Jag finns ihalig utan min Korp. Bor mig med. *I am hollow without you my Raven. Stay with me.* Lata mig er karlek som min maka. *Let me love you as my wife.* As Sonne spoke these words, pictures flashed in Lon Dubh's mind of hands clasping bound loosely in the strong and supple fighe vine symbolic of an unbreakable union. The hands were seen clasped over a family bowl of bounty which is part of her own people's ceremony of marriage when two are wedded over a bowl filled to overflowing with a bounty of gifts given to the couple from their clan folk to start their own hearth. Before she wordlessly answered him, Lon Dubh gave a thought to her journey with her family and felt a momentary pang of regret.

Yes. Oh yes. I will stay with you and be your partner. I will love you as your wife and we will look to our future and all it may hold, for I too am but an empty shell, as all my life I have been but for the knowledge of you now as you warm the inside of me from womb to heart and to the fire in my head that craves to learn more of you. You have shown me what it is to be a woman complete; and the knowledge that I have been but half a soul in life until now is only tolerated by the thought that I have been well saved for only you could have given me this gift of entry into the knowledge of womanhood. We are a fit made as if designed by the Gods for one another and I burn with fever to know more of you... all of you and to share myself with you in the same way.

The knowledge of the pledge between them, made by each of the lovers brought them to an impassioned frenzy in the last moments of their coupling and in the moment that Sonne's back rounded in one final thrust, Lon Dubh felt the gift of life rush into her. Along with the familiar sensation of his seed flowing, her reward for loving him well, Lon Dubh knew with absolute certainty that in the moment they had committed to one another, a life giving force had rushed into her and the spark of life was ignited within her. She knew not whether Sonne was aware of this gift in the moment of complete openness but she was certain that the magic had been cast and a life would come of this union.

Lon Dubh reflected that this was her destiny all along. Despite what she thought her path was or even what Faidhe thought, once their eyes met, there was an inward attraction that called them to one another.

Upon seeing Lon Dubh for the first time, Sonne said he was immediately drawn to her. Perhaps it was a vibration of one who recognizes strength in another or it may have just been destiny he recognized but from the very first moment he saw Lon Dubh, he could think of little else.

For her part, Lon Dubh mused that she had been slowly coming to the realization that she would give of her maidenhead in service of the Goddess. The truth of her path had been revealed to her the very moment before she met Sonne's eyes, when she had solidly made up her mind that the time had come for her to come to the fires. She now felt sure that had she not been so involved in trying to orchestrate the moment herself, she'd have been shown the Goddess's path, which would have led her to Sonne without the scalding shame of trying to arrange a marriage with Iarann. Again, with the thought of Iarann, she felt the pang of regret that she had not known him as her father and now, she knew that she never would.

Not wanting to begin this day with regrets, Lon Dubh rose from the furs and followed her nose to the food with Sonne right behind her. They ate and fed each other gustily and each in turn washed the other in the tub to prepare for two events on this day: One for Lon Dubh to reenter the village as a full woman and the other to make plans for the ritual in celebration of the lambing of the ewes this evening.

Lon Dubh, as the Priestess to the Goddess will conduct the ritual for the village folk. There was work to do in preparing the right materials and finding where rituals such as this were conducted in the village. Much as she wanted to delay returning to the world and facing the issues she had with her family, she knew it must be done.

With a sigh, she dried herself and kissed Sonne and began to dress thinking that she'd seek to find Fion first. Now that she'd accepted her return to the village, she found herself eager to speak with her good friend, Fion and that she had missed him greatly.

———

Lon Dubh sought out Fion and was pleased to find him happy and to hear of his own path in coming to manhood. She spoke with him regarding the preparations for the ceremony in which they were to participate all the while battling her sadness in knowing that she must say goodbye to this one who she had come to love so well. So many emotions roiled inside her: happiness for his good fortune in having a lovely girl such as Vannina for his first rites, heartbreak at knowing they would soon part, gratitude when she heard that Fion had volunteered to be her consort in her own first rites. Lon Dubh was overwhelmed when she found out how close she'd come to having one such as Triag come to her bed. Her repulsion was only outstripped by the resentment she held for her mother, that Faidhe had actually a considered such a union. But the one emotion that eclipsed all but for her newfound love for Sonne was the heartbreak she felt at the loss of correcting the situation with Iarann and truly getting to know him as her father.

"Come Fion." She said fighting the tears welling in her eyes. "We have much to do to prepare for these folk a ceremony worthy of their expectations. We have told them much of our tale and of our magical quest so I'm sure the ceremony is something they will count as one that will insure the fertility of their sheep herds. We must not disappoint. Let us don our best-woven robes and cloaks and come to the ritual this night both as new initiates to full rites. It will be the first time we will have conducted these rituals as such. I'm sure it will be something special my good friend."

Fion was pleased to reunite with Lon Dubh, to share of their experiences and speak of all that had happened for them in the last ten sunsets, but he sensed that there was something she did not share with him. So accustomed to being in each other's minds, he recognized that there was something she did not wish him to know for she closed her mind to him and kept her thoughts reserved. This sparked a sense of foreboding in Fion for a reason that he could not quite place.

"Did all go well with your first fires Black Bird? Did he...are you well?"

"Oh Fion," She brightened. "I am very well. I am happy. I could not have designed for myself a better first rite ritual than the one I had."

"Your mother chose well then."

The smile fell from her face. "It was not my mother's choosing. It was my destiny to come to the fires with Sonne. And the Gods be praised that destiny won out over her meddling!" It seemed Lon Dubh had more to say but stayed her thoughts and changed the subject. "Come Fion, I do not wish to have these harsh words with you. We should be rejoicing in the exhilaration of our newly found maturity. Let us plan an extraordinary ritual for this night." She hugged him with love and affection and he gripped her tightly for he understood by her closed mind that they would no longer enjoy the easy relationship they had known thus far.

———

Due to the frigid weather in these elevated mountains, many of the rituals performed during the winter are done behind the protection of the woven walls of huts rather than in a protective grove of trees. For the festival of Imbolc, the large hut where Lon Dubh had told her tale would be the location where the blessings and petitions would be held. Though it was not nearly large enough to hold all the village folk, it would serve for those who came first to the ritual and the rest would have to attend from the cold outdoors and only hear of the ritual through the mouths of those who were privy from within. The hut was growing dark as the sun grew closer to the horizon.

The ritual would start at full sunset. Fion and Lon Dubh worked together to build the hearth fire so they would have sufficient light and heat. Lon Dubh had dressed for the festival in her embroidered robe. She had become full woman and would proudly display her red robes of fertility in keeping with the theme of the festival of fertility but the cold dictated that she would also wear her woolen cloak for comfort until the hut filled with people and the warmth of their bodies and breath together with the heat of magic served to keep the cold at bay.

Familiar faces could be spotted throughout the gathering people. Lon Dubh saw Gara arrive with Faidhe and her heart jumped with the shock of seeing her mother for the first time after her rites. Lon Dubh spotted the pretty face of Vannina smile sweetly at Fion and she thought, *Good! A good choice for both of them.*

Iarann arrived a short time after and joined Faidhe. Lon Dubh felt a momentary pang of loss for she truly did love Iarann but took comfort that it was not the passionate love she had not until recently truly understood. She felt rather than saw Sonne enter the crowd and smiled brightly at him as he took his place near to where she stood. Lon Dubh felt it when Fion seemed to falter in his meditations for the ritual. She looked to see what vexed him and saw his eyes concentrating on Triag who had just entered the hut virtually beaming with bravado and Lon Dubh followed Fion's thoughts that he liked it not that Triag sniffed at the girls in the crowd as if they were fruit on the vine, ripe for the picking for his own pleasure. Fion seemed to have taken comfort when he saw Iarann move to take a fatherly stance over Triag and put a large, firm hand on his shoulder. It was enough to reign in Triag's energy and quell his randy thoughts of coupling at the festival fires for the first time but anyone could tell that he liked it not that his newfound rights of manhood were held in check by a clan elder. Though guarded by Iarann, Triag's eyes sought out Vannina's face and his concentration on her took a jolt when none other than Gusella joined the young girl. Triag kept his eyes to himself after that for fear that Gusella would mistake his attentions and seek him out for the fires.

Typically, back on her island, Lon Dubh would serve this type of ceremony from a stone alter but there was not such a structure here. Instead, Lon Dubh was to stand on a mound of earth piled high near the hearth in the center of the large hut so she could be seen and heard by all in attendance. Lon Dubh had collected some tools she would use for her ritual and stored them at the base of the mound so they would be near to hand when she had need to use them. As the abundant crowds filed in, there was room only to stand. People gathered and spoke quietly as Lon Dubh stood atop the mound and meditated on bringing the Goddess into her for the ritual as she had done so often before. As the energy in the hut shifted, the crowd hushed and all attention was on Lon Dubh who threw off her woolen cloak of white sheep's wool as she raised her arms high above her head. There was a low hushed undercurrent of comments as the red robe, in all its fine and laborious stitch-work, was revealed. There were a few in the crowd, mostly descendants of those who came to this village from the North with Sonne's clan who were able to see the magical subtleties in the embroidery as the images of fertility sprang to life. The Priestess lowered her arms and held them out to the crowds in a welcoming gesture.

"I come to teach and show you the ways of the Goddess. To reinforce the ways of a people with reverence for those Gods who protect and love us. For in these times when the Gods are surely receding and the sun sets on their time to walk here on the earth, we must keep the news and the memories and the ways of their worship alive. As we have traveled across the ocean from the West to the South and have come North over land to you, we have learned that quickly the ways of the Goddess are being forgotten. It is the Seer Faidhe's path to cast the magic to preserve these ways. It is my path to continue to teach the tale so that it lives. And so it will be."

Lon Dubh let her red robe drop to the earthen floor and her bare skin near glowed in alabaster perfection. As the crowd watched, right before their eyes, Lon Dubh took on the Goddess and was transformed to the figure of a great black raven with extended wings rustling with Power and tension. The black feathers were majestic for within the black could be seen every color in nature swirling in the soft feather patina, the most prominent being the rich blue hue seen in the sky on a clear summer day. The Goddess creature moved to speak and the crowds were awe-struck when from her beak emitted only a regal cawing, yet her words were still understood through Fion's images:

"I bless these peoples and they come under my protection. Herds will multiply, foraging will be plentiful; enemies will be struck down until the progeny of the clan has multiplied and is assured a long future. Those will come to know some ways of magic for in their history and mixed with their blood is the blood of the North Tribe and the renewed blood of the Old North Tribe in those come from the island to the West. For the sake of the future, my daughter, the Raven has chosen to stay and meet her destiny here. And so the child of the old blood will be born; destiny will find its way. It shall be so."

Few understood the meaning of what was being translated. Most just stood in awe as they watched the great bird rustle her wings and grip the mound with fearsome talons. Faidhe understood that journey of the mother and daughter had come to an end and that the relationship, as she had seen in the prophecy had been severed. A dark and heavy remorse enveloped her heart as the stark realization came to her that she had let much precious time to build her relationship with Lon Dubh slip past her as she wallowed in her own pain. All too late Faidhe recognized that the time she had on the road was the time she was given as a gift to teach her daughter in her skills and magic until such time when she was fledged to the Goddess's task. She could have taught her daughter how to make use of those wings and talons but now Faidhe mourned her failure to see. The lament of losing one child had cost her the opportunity to know another. And now, she knew it was too late for her daughter was full-fledged woman and Priestess. The Power she would possess and wield as she honed her skills would surpass that which even Faidhe possessed but she would have to learn to wield the Power on her own.

Lon Dubh returned to her natural appearance and though the hut was enormous and filled with a great many people, there was not a single sound to be heard. Sonne stepped forward and was stopped by Fion.

"Sir, you cannot come to the Celebrant while the Goddess is still fast within her unless she summons you."

"Let him come."

Lon Dubh's voice called to Fion still laced with traces of the raven's caw. Sonne strode up onto the great mound and felt the strength of Power that emanated from this woman, his love. With the slight movement of one hand, a bowl that had been placed at the bottom of the mound moved smoothly on its own from its position there to the top of the mound between Lon Dubh and Sonne's feet. Her open palm reaching toward the mouth of the bowl, Lon Dubh summoned a piece of fighe vine which snaked up and around her wrist, of its own volition.

The Priestess looked into her lover's eyes as if to question whether he truly wished to go through with the union. Sonne held out his hand across the bowl between them, just as they had seen in vision that very morning and clasped Lon Dubh's left forearm with his right one. They faced each other and the vine weaved around their arms. As it did, an illumination could be seen coming from the bowl at their feet. As the two peered into the bowl they could see snippets of their future together; a future that appeared unremarkable, but happy in each other's company. Unremarkable with the exception of the child they would bring into the world. A child that would teach each of them what it meant to have a family to call their own. A child upon whom to bestow all their wisdom and learning. The child Lon Dubh had seen in her visions and dreams. The one she'd always hoped for, yet never dared to think she would truly ever have.

Sonne, who was bursting with joy at the sight of his son within the bowl, addressed the clan in their own tongue but all who were there understood even before he spoke.

"We have been given a gift from the Gods, for of our union we will have a son." He placed his hand on Lon Dubh's lower abdomen. "And so we bind ourselves to each other here with all you as our new family, we will remain. We are bound." He looked at Lon Dubh and she nodded.

"Yes. Here I will make my home and keep to this union with reverence always for the Great Marriage that has taken place. The Goddess has offered me a true family of my own with the gift of this beautiful child. I vow to honor this gift and keep true to my sacred roles as a mother and wife. We are bound."

Faidhe felt deflated and diminished as the impromptu wedding just unfolded before her eyes. She once again felt the sting of Lon Dubh's words for her vows sounded to Faidhe as accusations, reminding her of what she had not done for her daughter. She had not expected Lon Dubh to bind herself in such a way and realized the full impact of the truth that the rest of the journey would be endured without Lon Dubh. Tears filled her eyes as she pushed her way through the crowds toward the door that would release her from hearing anything more.

Colm inspected the work she'd done in preparing the Shield for the coming ritual. The lion she'd created in her spell of strength and protection was intact and located just below the ship that Laoghaire had painted. The ship was itself cast in magic, which carried the meaning of the words that had come to her husband in magical trance, *Laidir is e' lear righ.* Strong is the king of the sea. Colm understood this as an incantation to protect all the descendants of their family now and in future times as they crossed the ocean. For according to Laoghaire's visions, much of what they prepared for now would come to fruition in future generations in lands across the sea. She thought then of her mother and sister in far off, strange lands and wondered if life was to be so for her children and their children as well but took comfort in knowing the relationship of mutual regard Laoghaire had with Mananan Mac Lir, God of the sea, would stand to protect all those future descendants long after Laoghaire and Colm and even their children were dust and ash. Colm inspected the final drawing that she had added to the Shield. So that forever the magical protection of the Shield would not wane, she added the counterpart to the Shield at the top of the great plate, the Sword. A symbol that not only would the Shield protect the family and all it planned for in this magical time, but that they would all act in its defense and fight with honor to preserve what it has set forth in these times.

The moon hung high in the sky and it waxed almost to fullness. Colm thought it was fitting that the moon should light her way on the journey to the great cavernous site where Laoghaire's ancestors had been returned to the Mother-Earth after their funeral burning. The earth was not frozen in the Western passage where Laoghaire's parents were laid to earth, for the fires inside were kept burning each day to light their way to the Otherworld. Colm brought the Shield into the warm caverns to the very spot where Laoghaire's parents' ashes had been buried. She followed her intuition and thought it right that the Shield, provided to protect their descendants, should be watched over and protected by them. The fairly recent burial spot provided a soft area that could easily be unearthed by Colm as she used deer antlers to loosen the earth and a flat, bronze bowl to shove the earth aside.

By firelight, Colm toiled and spoke words of prayer and blessing as well as petition to all of Laoghaire's ancestors who had been buried in the network of cairns in this part of the island to add their strength of spirit in protection of the future of the clan. *For it has been passed to the human species, those who have been a part of this land, to take the mantle of proliferation of life. The time for the magical era is at an end and these implements are bequeathed to the spirit of the human-kind, spirit of the earth, spirit of the spirit so that the essence of the Shield, the protective magic for which it is a symbol, and with which it has been imbued, will be taken back to the bosom of the Mother never diminished in its silent potency and will be ever available to descendants of every generation henceforth. The time has now come for the implement to deliver its protection, not to the one who holds it but over the ones who keep alive the name of the Goddess and the God. Add your stout hearts and strong spirits to this protection of the clan Laoghaire. I bury this Shield here with you in the Earth so that the protection will cast a hand over all from now and long into the future so this land may once again see the rise of the She to stand with the He in love, reverence and respect, so that the one who will come at the time the prophecy has shown, will come in strength and purity under the protection of all who came before.*

Colm barely remembered the ritual magic she imparted in the family cairns as she found her way back to the village under the setting moon. She recalled something of a feeling of taking flight under the moon with great reddish brown wings that carried her home and something else she recalled of a beautiful blue light emanating from the ground where she buried the Shield. And though she knew not why or how, she simply knew that if she returned to retrieve the Shield, it would no longer be there. She had a sense of rightness and completion, now that her task was done.

Upon her return, Laoghaire was frantic that he had not been able to find her following their coupling at the fires of the festival. He was equally relieved to see her and angry with her that she had wandered off without telling him of her plans.

"I am sorry Laoghaire. I followed the intuition that came to me. I did as was necessary in all of these times just as I'm sure you would have. I know you must have been worried, but have faith that what I have set forth this night will help to insure the safety of our family and future generations. I should have spoken with you but the force of the magic that was upon me to place the Shield would not be ignored. Did you feel nothing of a need to place the Sword?"

"I felt nothing of that type of calling. But I do sense that something has shifted. Some sense of almost finality is creeping to my bones. I have not been called so as you have been to use the implement, but as I stood at the great Stone this night, I did feel a great shift in the energy. Did you feel a sense of change as we coupled at the fires?"

"What I felt was a calling to my sister and my mother. I felt both of them reaching out to me in pain and sorrow. I know I have a connection to them both and so you must too. Perhaps it is a shift in whatever is taking place with them on their journey that creates this sense that time is rushing forward now. For that is what I feel, like a stone hurdling down a hillside, and there is no stopping it save for the Gods themselves to stay the behemoth from crushing all beneath it. But it is all a part of what we set in motion I believe. I no longer have the Shield but it is properly placed. I know Faidhe no longer holds the staff for it too has been properly placed. Things are unfolding as they should. Let us be thankful in the knowledge that our children are safe and so is our future."

Iarann sat across from his daughter in the hut she would call her home in this new village and watched as she worked to say what she had called him to hear.

"Deep sorrow plagues my heart for all I did not know and all we did not share. We grew close but not as we should have for my knowledge of our kinship was incomplete and I wasted time with wrong ideas of love and marriage."

"Lon Dubh, no time spent in your company was ever wasted. We have spent near one whole sun cycle helping, supporting, and learning from each other. We have bared our innermost thoughts and shared the hunt and meals. We have been a family. Not one moment would I trade or change. My love for you has grown with each sunrise as I see the woman you have become, strong, stoic, honorable, committed. The pride in my heart that you consider me your friend and love me is immeasurable. No love is ever a mistake. And the idea that one love holds more value than another is where the fault in your logic lies. To see you with Sonne on this night assures me that the love you thought you felt for me in that way was naught but you answering to the Goddess calling you to your destiny. Your mind would not quiet itself long enough for you to listen to her call for if you had allowed it; you would have known your own heart. We both know you love me, as I do you, but you have never loved me in the way all can see you love Sonne."

Lon Dubh continued to keep her gaze on the glow of the fire.

"I am right in this, daughter. You know it is so."

"But Iarann, as far back as the village of the Duibhe I began to think of you in such a way. I spun a swatch of fine woolen threads into a swaddle for your babe. How could the Goddess have allowed the magic to be cast if the babe is never to exist?"

"Perhaps the babe you spun this wrap for will exist. Remember, if you weaved this piece for my babe, I still have a promise of my own Great Marriage to keep. Mayhap that child will have use of such a protective covering more than a babe of your own will need."

Lon Dubh reflected on this. "With every stitch, I imbued the cloth with protective magic. When I wove the cloth, I knew the babe for which it was woven would be of your blood and would be in great need of the Goddess's protection. This swaddling cloth was made for a child of your blood, I'm sure of it.

She knelt next to Iarann after retrieving the blanket and gave it to him. "Fion and Cathbad took it upon themselves to dye the piece this blue. The color indicates the presence of the Goddess for as you know, it is her energy that has blessed the blanket and been woven into every knot. It is odd though, that I was so sure that somehow, it would protect a babe of my own. It may be that it is our kinship mislead me to mistake the blood in my brother's veins for the blood of my son. It matters not now. The swaddling cloth and all the protection that is bound into it is for your child, Iarann. Take it and may it bless all in your line."

Lon Dubh kissed Iarann on his cheek and found them to be wet with tears. She wrapped her arms around his neck and he embraced her so tightly that she felt she might crack from the pressure. They both knew that this was goodbye.

—

The winter's grip had not been broken in these high mountains despite the celebration of the lambing which, at home, would be an indicator that spring was but a short time away. Faidhe wasted no time now that her daughter had been wed and promised to these clans. She summoned her party to her hut and instructed them to ready themselves for the road.

"We will wait not another sunrise. Upon this night we leave these clans and strike out for the final part of our journey. Take what you must in the way of woolens for warmth and find ample skins for your feet. We have been given sturdy cloaks and furs for as we move north from here, we travel into the mouth of winter."

Iarann and Fion intuitively had already planned for the journey, knowing that their time in this village had come to an end. But Gara's face bore the look of weariness with the knowledge that they once again traveled the road and Triag's face grew sour with anger, likely for the injustice that he would not be able to take to the fires as he had planned for his first unguided foray into adulthood. Faidhe was not alone in noticing how much Triag resembled his father when he bore this expression for she looked at Gara and saw on her face that she too noticed the look of Briciu about Triag's face.

Faidhe spoke first. "Count it not an injustice, Triag. There is much to manhood that does not involve fertility rites not the least of which is keeping duty and responsibility first. You may like it not, but here is your opportunity to show all that you have truly achieved your status. Go and pack your things and ready yourself for the road with foodstuffs and drink. For now that you are a man, you are expected to carry a man's load and earn your equal keep in what you carry and what you contribute."

For once, Gara was grateful that it was not she who had to prod Triag to do what is expected of him. She was equally grateful now that Iarann, as clan elder and mentor to Triag would have say in how Triag would conduct himself. For since even before they had come to this village, Gara found it increasingly more difficult to maintain control over the boy. Now that he had come to his manhood, she knew the task would be near impossible. Perhaps it was just her age upon her or perhaps she realized that she was simply too selfish to devote responsibility for another being, but she was weary of all of this and desired to be shut of her debt.

"Do as you are committed, Triag. Take heart in the honor you have been given in being on this journey. Understand you that manhood is not all power and glory; sometimes, nay often, it is about work and duty. Take you on those strong legs to prepare for all we will need...Please, my son."

The momentary tenderness surprised not only Triag but all who witnessed the interchange. The boy nodded in acquiescence but his displeasure could be seen in the set of his mouth as he left the group to set about his task.

When all had been prepared and the traveling party returned to Faidhe's hut, great alarm rang through the group at the appearance of Faidhe. She had appeared small and wizened, slumped by the fire. Iarann strode two lengths to where she sat and lifted her in his arms. His alarm increased at the realization that she felt almost as though there was no weight to her frame.

"Lady? Faidhe?" In a gentle voice, almost too low to belay the panic he felt that she had quietly died while preparing for the last part of the journey.

"I am here." She croaked. "Put me down!"

Fion spoke. "It is the implements. Is it not? I recall when you placed the Staff in the highlands of the main island, you returned to us weakened as you are now. Have you relinquished the Cauldron Lady?"

"You observe rightly, Fion that the implements and my life force are intertwined but the Cauldron remains with me for there is still work to be completed with the great pot. It is the Shield that has been placed, as has the Staff so that its energy and Power will be available for the recipient when the time is right. But as each implement is placed, I come that much closer to the time when I must release the greatest force of Power and magic any of this earth has seen. I become closer to the Goddess and the spirits with each passing event. Fear not, I will not see my death before it is my time."

The group was relieved at Faidhe's assurance that she would not die but they were wary of the almost transparent look she had about her with thin and pale skin and bluish glow that emanated from her. It appeared that as Faidhe's human constitution diminished she became more ethereal, wraithlike and unearthly so all in the group took on a hushed reverence for what they saw happening to their clanswoman. All, that is, but for Triag who's attentiveness to the old woman had increased when he heard of the great magic she foretold and of the Cauldron that would, no doubt, somehow be involved in the magic. Triag decided that the way to wield the Power he sought would be gained by witnessing the magic and then laying hands on this great Cauldron. He would be the picture of a dedicated clansman come to manhood, helpful in every way so he would be assured a place near to the rituals when this Power was to be released.

"Lady." Triag addressed Faidhe. "If you please, I have packed for the needs of my grandmother and myself, but will be honored to carry what things you have need of on the road as well so that you may regain your strength and preserve it for whatever hardships may lay ahead."

"Very well then." Faidhe answered. "Let us be gone."

Fion stopped her. "But Lady, do you not wish to see your daughter before we leave?"

Faidhe looked long at Fion before answering. "We have each of us said what we must to Lon Dubh. And if she finds that she did not say all that was in her heart, well then, that will be one of her lessons from which to learn."

With that, Faidhe wrapped her cloak tightly around her, pulled her fur hood over her head and left the group looking after her to the empty doorway through which she'd disappeared.

Part VI: The End of the Beginning

47

The Valkyrie and Cold Goodbyes

The trek had been long and the winter's breath had been particularly cold and its teeth, pernicious. Well into the spring season and well in to what should have been the warming days of summer, the group plodded through raging storms and deepening snow. Illness settled into Gara's lungs and she took little meat now but for the juices cooked into her broth. Faidhe tended to Gara's cough with warm, moist poultices to loosen the grip the illness had in her chest but so long traveling in the winter, there was little, if any, medicinal value to the poultices beyond the soothing heat and steam they offered.

Gara rode the pack animal while the others bore the burden of carrying what the animal would have if not for the passenger. When the group had reached the northern most point of the mainland, at the point of a peninsula, they were met by a waiting group of regal looking women dressed in great fur skins, unusual head-dresses feathered with white heron wings, some carrying battle shields and swords others with solid looking staffs or spears. When the women spoke, their voices carried authority and echoed of the hint that they were women with one foot in the world of the Goddess and one in the world of humans. Perhaps both, perhaps neither but one found that once they put eyes on these creatures, they were not easily drawn away for the Power of self-reliance, and assurance was both alluring and intimidating. Each of the women were similar in their majestic appearance but with individual garb and features that helped one to understand that though they were of the same tribe, perhaps, each of these beings was formidable on her own.

One particularly beautiful woman came from a boat that waited on the frozen shore and knelt to Faidhe in an incongruous show of respect from the being who stood as tall as Iarann. "I am Sigrun, first daughter to Sigrdifa, the Bryhildr of our kind. She awaits your audience, Lady. Come across the waters to the shores of the springtide where you and your kin will be seen to.

All who stood watching seemed to take it in stride when Sigrun held her hand out to Faidhe and as it was accepted, the two women simply faded from sight. For Faidhe's perspective, she was in one moment standing at the northern most reach of the mainland in a world of endless snow, and the next moment was in a land of green beauty with music of the birds in concert and scents of fresh blossoms enough to intoxicate her. Behind her, she could see only a great expanse of calm blue waters. Truly, her head spun as the warmth of the sun kissed her skin and she noticed for the first time that she no longer wore the warming furs but a tunic of the most delicately spun flax so that the breeze tickled her skin as it danced through the material.

"Faidhe." A voice spoke in echoed quality and Faidhe followed it to its origin. A woman of golden beauty stood from her ornately decorated chair to welcome Faidhe. "*Valkommen till min hem*, Faidhe. Welcome to my home." Fair of skin and flushed cheeks, this woman stood, tall and Powerful with flowing sun-kissed hair that was loosely bound in elaborate plaiting that reached down to the back of her knees. It must have weighed heavily yet seemed to float about with fluid movements as if under water. Upon her head was a crown of gold adorned with two small shields placed just above the ears on both sides of her head and one larger one at her brow, a perfect golden replica of the sacred Shield Faidhe had protected as Keeper of the Circle. From the sides of the crown Faidhe observed the outstretched wings of a hawk that seemed in one moment a living creature upon the Valkyrie's head and the next, a trick of the eye showed the wings to be a part of the crown, but then again, the fluttering wings seemed to spring directly from the Valkyrie's own head. The woman's clothing was of finely stitched material that could have been either skins of the softest chamois or a weave of the finest thread that ended at the bottom in a lacey fringe of softened animal hide or well loomed threads; Faidhe could not tell which. What drew Faidhe's fascinated attention was the lovely blue color of the woman's bodice, laced tightly to accent her waist and call attention to the blue of her eyes, icy in the center and deepened to a richer hue around the edges This gave the woman the appearance of exceptional vision and being able to peer directly into Faidhe's very soul.

Faidhe could not recall any time in her adult life when she had felt stricken so small and humble as a human, not even when she'd come face to face with the Dagda and the Danu. She knew she was in the presence of a great source of Power.

"I know how you've suffered, Faidhe. I know of your children and the losses you have endured. Take heart in the knowledge that we will all be better for your loss. You have been true to your vows, Faidhe and you have given much in sacrifice. It has not and will not go unnoticed. But you have also broken the laws of keeping clean the hands of the initiate of the Circle by causing the death of one who had created an opposing force to our intentions, and for this, as you know, a debt is owed. But in this debt, you were given no choice, for to fulfill your vow to the Circle you had to forsake the law to harm none outside of battle. Because you kept your vow, knowing you would pay a price, you will be given leave to nurture the souls of your daughters. This is your reward but so too, it will be your punishment. One you will endure until such time all has come to pass that you put forth in your magic. As you send us all to our rest on the other side of the gates of the Otherworld you will remain here. As you lay the foundation for the future generations for the ones who will reopen the gates, you will teach and nurture your daughters, but they will know you not, hear you not, see you not and love you not. It is for you to give all of yourself to them in preparation for the task that will fall to them. It is for them that you cast your magic. It will be they who are found at the other end of the lines of blood we bring to seed now. Take heart in knowing your son will grow, and prosper and his line will multiply just as Raven's will and Colm's as well. My own line with Iarann will complete the four needed to bring the implements' Power, energy and strength to the recipient humans in order that our son will be born of the wheel and bring light to the world. He will bring the knowledge of truth. He will reopen the gates. He will fan the ember and rekindle the flame of magic and true spirituality in the world. He too will battle the heated energy of the He that will rise up in all its opposition to these changes. You will see to his welfare, Faidhe. You will set all into motion so that when his time is come, the wheel will spin and through the stars, the boy will be twice-born. Once to the flesh and then when the stars align, again to the spirit. Through him, the world will begin to remember the Power of magic. They must, for if we fail in this, Faidhe, all the world will burn in the heat of the unbridled greed of the He, and then be cast into a frozen wasteland of the deepest harshest winter until the end of days."

Faidhe was shaken and drained, not only from all that she heard about her fate, her debt and the future of her children but the description of a world lost to a raging, never ending winter, recalled her vision of nothing in the world but wind-whipped snow and blinding white as she peered into the scrying bowl so long ago. On the night the evil was loosed by Briciu she searched in earnest for answers regarding her daughter's future and all she could see was ice and snow. She shivered despite the warm surroundings and wondered how she would find any shred of strength to finish her journey.

"Come Faidhe," Sigrdifa comforted. Take sustenance from the Mother to gain strength for the rest of your journey and task."

Somewhere in Faidhe's consciousness she knew it was strange, but it all seemed so natural at the same time as she watched Sigrdifa unlace the clothing at the top of her bodice to reveal her breasts. Without understanding how, the next thing Faidhe was aware of, was that she was suckling from the warrior Goddess and tasted of the finest mead as she felt her strength return forcefully to her body.

In the next blink of her eye, Faidhe found herself back across the waters with Iarann and the others who had obviously received food, drink, attention and care on the shores of the land of the Valkyrie. Faidhe found urgency now in giving him instruction to assemble all the panels of his silver Cauldron and to remain with the Valkyrie women. She grew a bit impatient as he stared at her seemingly not comprehending what she was saying for he stood repeating "Lady! You look well!"

"Yes, Iarann. I am well. I am pleased to have gained some strength for what is ahead. Now that we have established this, can you do as I ask?" She felt a pang of guilt at this but knew her time was short and everything must be prepared.

"As you wish, Faidhe." Iarann left to retrieve from his pack the pieces of silver he'd labored over so long. He took his small hammer to gently curl the edges of the panels so they would be permanently placed together and form the silver Cauldron that would tell the story of their journey and task. When he returned to Faidhe, the entire group had assembled and it occurred to Iarann for the first time since they'd arrived at the northern-most part of the peninsula, that this would mark the end of his journey with his family. He'd always assumed that he would participate in a ritual with this Valkyrie, Sigrdifa, and return to a life with his kin but the look on his companion's faces told him the truth, that this was his time to say good-bye.

Trying to ignore the inevitable, he laid the bowl at Faidhe's feet. "As you asked, Faidhe." But lost his reserve when Fion let out a ragged sob and buried his face below the big man's chest. The two stood in the embrace letting the tears flow and the blizzard storm raised its fury in sympathy, and began to howl for the men who wanted to but could not. When Fion composed himself enough to show his face, he stepped back.

"You have been a great friend and mentor. I have been blessed to know your wisdom and gentle soul. What the Gods did not offer me in lineage; they gave to me in the gift you have been to me. As no other can claim a better father they have had. You will be greatly missed. Gods grant that you are rewarded with happiness in your life here with those that are your kin from generations passed."

"You too have abundantly filled the space in my heart reserved for the son I have never had. I will miss you Fion."

Iarann wiped a huge hand across his face to remove the tears and turned to Faidhe. "Woman, Gods know I have loved you well from afar and kept to my work in hopes that it would be enough so that one day we would be in one another's arms. I know not if you have these feelings but it matters not for we each have our path and they lead in different directions now, but go not on your way thinking that you have not known love, for though your children are distant you have given of the highest love in sacrifice for them and they too love you well. You have been a mother to Fion and kindled a passable friendship with Gara as we traveled. For this I am grateful," he said to Gara and returned his attention to Faidhe. "You have made the best of a life of service and have created a family of strength to accomplish the task you were given. Take heart in what you have done here for our Tuath and the future of the She and humankind." Iarann stepped toward Faidhe and effortlessly lifted her into his arms. He kissed her lips lovingly as his heart ached in his chest for what she must still endure. "I can suffer this no more." He whispered to her ear and set her gently on the ground. Iarann turned swiftly and walked toward the waiting group of Valkyries to bring him to his destiny across these waters to the mystical shores and his new life of the unknown with Sigrdifa.

———

"Lament not, son of Goibhniu." Sigrun, daughter of Sigrdifa comforted the large man. "You have been given a great honor in being chosen to initiate the line that will bring the blood of the Auld Ones forward with a great purpose to the human kind. Sigrdifa has her choice in a great many warrior humans, or kings, thinkers and scholars but she has chosen you for this task for your loyalty to the Goddess and your gentility of soul but most importantly, that you have balanced well your blood of the Gods and that of your human mother. You have great strength in your size and heritage, yet temperance is used in all you do. As you temper the metals with which you work, so you temper your own desires to balance them with the needs of those around you. The human frailties of desire neither for the flesh nor for wealth or power consume you. Yet you have been offered opportunity for all of these and kept your ways of reverence despite your human half. And though you are of God-stock you sought not the honor that could have been yours. Your human blood is of good stock and so you will give Sigrdifa healthy seed to bear good human fruit. A child of your line will be taught how to survive on the earth by human method as you have learned. Your child will be strong of body and mind as well as pure of heart. This line will serve Sigrdifa for when her time comes, she will take the fool's leap to the human plane and forego all her spiritual gifts and memory to usher a life to humanity that will bring forward the four implements in the flesh to the time of need seen in the prophecy."

Iarann knew this was his fate and listened. He knew he was given great honor in being chosen for his part just as it had been for Faidhe, but he liked it not that he had been summoned away from his family in such a way. He asked, "Is there not another who can serve as well as I?"

"Have a care, human. It is this family for which you pine that you will ultimately help and serve by honoring your duty in this Great Marriage. As always, question not your role in these doings, trust that your role is to serve to lessen the pain of humankind in the future."

A melodic and echoed voice called to Iarann then, by reminding him, "Remember you well that each member of humanity is your family, not only those you have been given honor to know well. All of human kind has the Gods' spark of life, and so they are all kin to you even if you know them not or love them not. You are they and they are you, Iarann, son of Goibhniu."

Iarann found the source of the voice and was overwhelmed by the light that shone from the being.

"Sigrdifa?" He inquired. "Forgive me. I meant no disrespect. It is only that I have lived a humble life and displayed no great talent for magic. I thought there might be one better suited to this task."

She beckoned for Iarann to take the step from the outer reaches of the magical land to enter fully into her world of the spirit, for he would necessarily have to come to this duty voluntarily.

"Come, Husband. This is an honor for you to complete the blood lines that will serve as a living portal through which light of truth and wisdom of knowledge will be born. But should you wish to relinquish your part in this, there are others who will serve. You are not captive. The choice is yours. I took your reserve in laying with any on your journey as evidence that you had already accepted your place in all this."

Iarann was quiet as he reflected on the words of the Valkyrie. He remembered Faidhe and all she endured to come to her duty. He reflected on Lon Dubh keeping to her virgin vow and her surety that his own babe would be a joy to him and then he thought of Fion's open heart given selflessly to both himself and Lon Dubh. He thought of Laoghaire and Colm uprooting their family to put all into place and the sacrifice of the old woman Craiche, giving all of herself for this cause. He remembered even Gara who had made the trek for reasons unknown to him but even she had given up her comfort and home. They all had given up everything that was safe and familiar.

"For them, I come to you with purpose." He said. "For the love of my family, I give them up and keep not my own heart's desires to hold them close but keep to the purpose to which they have relinquished all they have known." With one giant stride, Iarann stepped fully over into the world between worlds where Sigrdifa resided and was lost to all human eyes.

"Thank you, Husband. Your stride into these worlds will insure my own stride back into the world of the flesh when the time is ripe. For now, though, come and know the pleasures of this place for it will be but a moment in time before you are to return to the earthly world with our child to teach all you know of love, loyalty, reverence and survival. Survive it must and multiply, in order to bring the line of the proper blood to fruition so that I may come fully to the world of the flesh when the time is needful. So you see, Husband, I too give up completely of what is mine to love and be comforted by, to meet the need of humankind."

In that moment, Iarann felt a sense of kinship with this woman and understood that in order for any of those involved to succeed in this task, they all had to put their own needs and desires last. The temptation of the individual is strong but the need to recognize that there is no individual; that all life is born of the same source must be acknowledged. But the more the individual strives to suit its own needs, and desires the further from the source it strays. And the more difficult it becomes to recognize anything of the Gods' spark or the life-giving source within the individual.

"Sigrdifa, I no longer view you as a consuming source who chose me for selfish reasons. I once thought you picked me as a dalliance or toy-thing holding my love for my family hostage and for this harsh judgment, I am sorry. I saw my purpose with you as in opposition to my own and so viewed you as something you are not. My understanding is clear now, as is my path. I say goodbye to what was my old life and come to you with a full heart. Teach me of what I need know and I will come to you as the God and your husband. I will carry out my duty in all this willingly and grateful to be of service."

"First, you must learn the language and ways of the North for it is in the Northlands you will raise your child. Once your people had hailed from here many generations ago and you are a descendant of those who went to the Southern isle with the four gifts of Power and the very Stone from the Mother-Earth that helps to conduct the Power. You are of old blood and of the spirit world. You must teach our child well of the Old Ways so that the blood line is continued in the Old Ways as long as possible in the reverence for the Goddess and the God with respect for the land and all its inhabitants. This old blood will soon enough burn with the lust for conquering and capturing of the lands and goods. If we are to succeed, the blood must be tempered by knowledge of the spirit and reverence for the Goddess so not to be consumed entire by the He fever."

———

Though it was but a brief time Iarann spent in the land of the Norns, with his Valkyrie wife, he learned the language, history and future of the Northlands. He tended Sigrdifa in the Great Marriage and rejoiced at the birth of his son, Frey. The boy was suckled and grew plump with health and his cheeks were red. He smiled easily and learned quickly. Iarann took pride in how well his son grew and when the boy was but four seasons in Norns, they said goodbye to Sigrdifa as Iarann knew would happen and they both took to the lands of humankind so that Iarann could teach the boy of humans, tribes, clans, Tuaths, cattle, farming, foraging, hunting and metalwork.

They emerged from Norns to find themselves in the wood at the base of a great tree. The air was cold and Iarann's first thought was to protect his son from the cold. Realizing he had returned to the world carrying exactly the items he'd left with, Iarann reached into his pack and withdrew the lovely blue blanket that Lon Dubh had given him woven by her for his babe. Iarann wrapped the warming weave around Frey as a cloak and they set off to rediscover the north world together keeping always to themselves the story of where they had come from until such time, Frey did not remember the land of Norns or the face of his mother. He knew only the love and care of his father.

In their travels, it was made obvious to Iarann that though only a handful of seasons had passed in Norns, it seemed many more than several hundred season had passed in the land of humankind. He heard stories of the He God they called the Christ that had come just as Faidhe had seen in her prophecy. Iarann learned that some of the Old Ways of celebration were kept within the new ways of the Christ as Faidhe had planned. He met men of the clans of Northlands and made himself useful with the smithing of new and hardened metals in much improved forges made for great heat. This large man and his fine young son were accepted into this north tribes and helped greatly to keep and rekindle the spirit of the Old Ways well into the 12th century, long after Christianity had taken sway over most of Western Europe and beyond.

As he matured, Frey was considered a man of much knowledge and many talents. He learned the ways of marking for words, drew detailed pictures with a talented hand and mastered reading and crafted metal as his father had taught him. He married well in the north tribe and sired a great many children in Sweden as was his destiny and purpose designed by his mother. Kept from any practical knowledge of magic, but he was taught by Iarann, just as he taught his own children to watch for signs that any they had birthed might possess magical abilities. This tradition was kept throughout the many generations of Frey's descendants until such time as Sigrid Höök herself watched her own children and their children for signs of magical knowledge near to eight hundred years after the time when the large man of smithing-craft and his son returned to the land of the living.

As a twist of fate or perhaps it was his heritage calling to him, Frey always had an affinity for water travel that had found him, on more than one occasion, on the shores of a large island to the Southwest and a smaller island even further to the West. In his travels, he heard stories that echoed the ones told him by his father, Iarann before he had died in the Northlands.

Frey was called to the smaller island for the stories he heard told there by country folk but his favorite version in particular was told by a smallish man he'd seen one time who told the tale with such skill that Frey swore he could see the faces of all those in the tale; one of them, he fancied belonged to his father. The story drew him but he was mostly drawn to the calling to a sense of home he felt there on that small island. He felt forever torn between his two worlds: the one that was his home in Sweden and the one where he felt at home on the shore of the lush, green Ireland. Well into his waning years, Frey traveled over the ocean many times searching for and never quite finding the place that he would feel finally at peace, only the hope and anticipation of it as he traveled between the two lands.

48

The Bog

Time moved on for Laoghaire and his family. All these long seasons Clan Laoghaire had enjoyed a bustling port business with Dha' Teanga's help and a prosperous, healthy cattle trade with the ever loyal support of Cuan. A fit and equipped fighting guard was trained and ready, though not often there was work for such a defense force. The countryside was at peace and the land as a whole, enjoyed mild winters and early springs.

Time found that just as Laoghaire and his family had moved away from Lake of the Ivory Heron, those of the Tuatha De Danann had seemingly, without planning it, found an unexplainable reason or urgent call to visit other places or to migrate to far-away lands. Quickly, the name of the Tuatha De Danann slipped into the realm of story and myth. As if they had known their time had begun to come to a close, some of the magical folk went the way of Craiche and decided to ritually pass to the Otherworld while others who were half God-creature and half human, quietly and without notice, slipped the mooring of the human familial ties to join the world of the spirit. Once the Stone of Fal, the heart of the island was removed from the magical Circle, the once great region of the Lake of the Ivory Heron had become all but abandoned. Slowly then, throughout the rest of the island, except for the most tenacious members, communities of magical creatures the likes of the Duibhe and others, grew scarce and fractured and had begun to scatter as well.

In her thriving community, where the Stone now resided, Colm heard often from her sister with news of her life and her family but it had been long since she'd heard anything from her mother and there had been no news from any region of what progress had been made in Faidhe's journey. More than ten seasons had passed; Laoghaire's hair was salted with gray, Colm had taken well to her role as queen but lines were stamped around her eyes that might have revealed an inner sorrow of the loss of her mother and sister or perhaps that she had given birth to no more children following the twins. Colm's own hair had taken on a dusty hue that dulled its sunny color and though she remained regal in her appearance, her age was coming nearer to 40 seasons more quickly than she could believe. The twins had reached maturity. Macha had married a lovely girl from the clans and started building a family of his own. Morgan was astute in her practices of magical knowledge and family history, taking lessons from both her parents in the application of all areas of the mysteries. Practical and realistic as was her grandmother and aunt, she had plans to succeed her father as Keeper of the Sword should he not hear from Faidhe or the others before his death. She refused her many offers of marriage to keep the family vows to the Circle but had taken to her first rites of womanhood with gusto indicative of the Valkyrie blood in her veins though she did not have the physical look of that side of her heritage. She would ever remain a youthful looking sprite of a woman, small in stature much like Faidhe. And like her too, Morgan would be an independent and self-reliant woman.

The family lived in comfort and the clan Laoghaire prospered; life carried on but there was always an air of expectation as they waited overlong to hear of their own fate and that of the lost party of travelers, until one day, just as Colm had known intuitively to retire the Shield, Laoghaire understood that he had a final task to perform in his role as the Keeper. He bid his family farewell and removed the Sword from the Stone where it had been housed for many seasons. It slipped from the Stone just as easily as it had done for him in many seasons past.

"We will journey with you." Colm pleaded.

"No. This is my path and mine alone. Ask me not how I know this or that it is time. I know only that I must return to the land of the Tuatha De Danann to complete this task. I must journey on foot and bring only my thoughts and wits to guide and keep me. What will follow, I know not. Only that I must go."

Colm's heart grew heavy but she understood the call of the implement in his charge.

"Will you leave in the morning?" She asked, trying to sound as though her world entire was not crushed under the deep foreboding she felt that not only was she losing her love, but that the world as she had come to know it was about to change in no small way.

"I must leave this day, my wife. I have long known that one day my duty would summon me so and have made preparations for this. Should I not return..."

"Stop! Say not these words."

"But, Colm, we both know..."

"I know what is possible and will not allow any strength to the thought by having you voice the words. For you know there is Power in the Word, Husband. Laoghaire, say them not for all of these past seasons I have been aware that this day would come. I will not give weight to any thought or plan that anything other than your return, when your task is done, will be our future. And should the Gods have planned otherwise for you, I will drink that cup when I must, but poison not this moment with speeches of anything other than when all our duty is done and you have returned to me."

The two entwined fingers in silence and went to the privacy of a small garden Colm had planted inside a small grove of trees she'd had placed between their stone housing and the great wooden fence surrounding their community. There, beneath the shelter of the walls and trees, they lay with each other smelling the sweet herbs she had planted there in rows of raised beds framed in felled trees. They basked in their own silence and the sensation of touch as the sun of the early planting season warmed their bare skin. Silent tears fell from Laoghaire's eyes onto Colm's face as he smiled on his love and drank in her face as though memorizing it, should he see it nevermore. Colm closed her own eyes allowing her hands to serve her own memory and she breathed in the scent of her man as though she could absorb him with her breath and keep safe his life. The two were suspended in time while all else in the world mattered not and they pushed back any idea or knowledge that there was anything in the world save for they two and the senses in which they basked while they gave of themselves and plundered one another for all the treasure they could keep safe in their memories.

Laoghaire said later, as Colm secured his halfstrap holding the Sword to his waste and he readied to go, "Know this: I leave on this day with your scent on my skin and your breath in my mouth. I take you with me in this heart" tapping two fingers to his chest, "as surely as I know that I live in yours. Tell my children, I will see them again and know that your eyes will cast sight on my face again. Of this I am sure."

Colm stayed her voice and said nothing so not to reveal the painful lump in her throat. For at this moment, she would be a queen and not reveal her own emotions and pain. She would have strength to send her husband on his quest remembering not the wretched face of a wailing woman but his partner, sharing of her confidence that he will return to her. She placed a kiss on his mouth that, even after the indulgence of their union in the garden, was laden with the intimacy that said all she could not. In the same moment when their lips parted, they both turned and walked away from one another, neither looking back.

———

With the silver Cauldron now assembled, Faidhe and her diminishing following, Fion, Gara and Triag set out from the place where they'd returned to the earthly plain from their brief stay in the outer reaches of realm of the Valkyrie. They made the final trek following Faidhe's intuition in search of the ancient and abandoned space within a Circle of stones arranged for rituals long past in a protected area of dry lands in a frozen bog. The time had come at last to prepare the Circle here for the ritual that would open the gates to send the Gods and all but a few magical creatures under to the Otherworld of the Sidhe. This Circle and others, the world over, will be utilized in the task leaving only the essence and memory of their existence save but a very few who would remain.

Despite her second gift of seeming youth and strength given her at the start of her trek after visiting with Sigrdifa, Faidhe was forced to stop now, and was to anyone who observed her, suddenly pale white and gave the appearance of a ghostly apparition wrapped in woolens and furs. During the length of the entire trip, Faidhe had looked alternately sickly and radiant, youthful and hag-like. She had made many physical conversions as though she were transitioning through all the phases of womanhood, as maid, young and beautiful, then full-ripe with child, as a mother and crone-like, nearing death. But in this moment, she appeared to fade in her very substance to an ethereal being a creature with naught but a tenuous hold on the earthly realm... On her knees, she gasped for air as a fish might have done, denied its breath in water. Tears flowed from her eyes as they watched something no one else in her company could see. She put up her hand to stay Fion's approach to help her as she struggled with her vision. When the moment had finally passed, Faidhe looked to her companions and they were shocked to see her almost translucent appearance. Her eyes bore the look of one deeply shocked as they flooded with tears of blue that matched the aura surrounding her countenance now.

"The third implement has returned to the Mother." Faidhe said. The additional shock of hearing her voice in a far off, gurgling echoed quality only added to the impression that she was more of a spirit than of this earth.

"What did you see, Lady?" Fion asked Faidhe as she allowed him now to help her back to her feet. He noted without comment that her arm as he grasped it, felt as if he gripped only fur and cloth, yet she seemed to be aided by his help as he lifted her to a standing position.

"As we draw near our task, the implements have been utilized and returned to the energy that created them so that their Power can be used through the one remaining implement, the Cauldron. I have seen Laoghaire tend to his responsibility in returning his Sword to the Goddess. He was alone and protected of course as long as he carried the Sword no harm would befall him. I saw him in our homeland, the territories of the Tuatha De Danann. The areas have been greatly changed. It seems we have spent much time across the waters in the land of the Valkyries. Much more than the few moments we thought to be there for the forest encroached where the Circle once stood and the village is all but abandoned and in disrepair. I saw our kinsman, Laoghaire as he returned to the village of our home and observed these things. It seems when we took the Stone of Fal and the implements from the Hill, we took the heart from the Tuath and it has disbursed as I had seen in the prophecy. The Tuatha De Danann has scattered and is no longer. Laoghaire was strong and vital, handsome still, but with age on him that speaks of many season's passing, so it seems the world has moved on as we have remained untouched by time as we lingered with the Valkyrie."

Faidhe's eyes turned inward as her mouth formed the words to share what she'd seen. "He took a currach, abandoned on the shore of our Lake of the Ivory Heron and though it was not sound and was in disrepair with years of neglect, it served to take him to the middle of the Lake where he returned the Sword to the womb of the Mother where no other hand will wield the piece until such time as the Lady herself offers it to another who might be worthy; if ever there will be such a one." Faidhe stood in silence for some time while the others waited to hear the rest if there was any to be told.

"Lady?" Fion finally prodded. "Is it so that with each implement that returns to the Mother, that you recede further to the world of the spirit? For each time one of the four has been placed out of the use for the human world, you become...less. Removed, somehow or more wraithlike. Is this not so?"

Her eyes found Gara and then landed upon Triag. She held his gaze until, though he thought himself a man, his testicles crawled deep inside him with the icy fear that exploded inside his chest. In the next moment, Faidhe turned and began the trek through the snow once again toward their destination of the Circle within the bog.

"It is so, Fion." She said to him and as she walked away, he saw the back of her furs glide over the top of the deep snow as though she no longer walked, but flowed.

———

That night when the rest had fallen to sleep in their camp, Triag took his first opportunity to call to Nemain to see what had truly taken place. He could not fathom that he had somehow missed many seasons of time while they spent but a few hours in the realm of the Valkyrie, as Faidhe had suggested.

Aunt. I have heard disturbing news. I must know if what I have heard is true. Are you there? Do I reach your thoughts? Do not ignore me Nemain. I know it has been some time since I last contacted you but I have been made a man at first rites and have been through much you would not understand. But now, as we near our goal, Aunt, do not abandon me. For we near the time when this great magic will take place. I have news of the Cauldron and it is well that the Power from all the implements is to be gotten from the Cauldron. We will reach our destination after the next sunrise and then this great event, perhaps even the transferring of Power will take place and be revealed to me. It is for this moment I have endured all this suffering while you keep comfort in our home. Do not ignore me Nemain, for if you do, I will take this magic and Power for myself. I do not need you in this. I have grown in my abilities and will do this without you. AUNT!

He had panicked at the idea that his aunt no longer lived and that he was in this situation alone but Triag's skin gathered in cold moisture when the voice he'd called for answered him in his head. It sounded not feeble but subdued, and the transmission was of a cold, slick and oily quality that reminded him of something grasping that one might step on at the bottom of a swamp...something with teeth.

So you live. What have you for me?

Triag was stricken with the familiarity of the voice in his head. It was Nemain, but it was also...he grew sickened. It was also his father. *Nemain, what have you done? Have you involved yourself in some kind of spirit conjuring? For I know my father is dead. I heard this from the lips of one involved in his death. I recognize that he is with you now in your very being somehow.*

So you are a man now. The voice was patronizing. *Bring us this magic and you will taste victory. We are weak and sick of being trapped in this filthy female. Bring us this magic and we will have glory for the ages as we come back into the flesh and revel in it. But we want to be a man again. We need to be a man. Bring us the magic, bring us the Cauldron and we will concoct a human blend that will serve us well.*

Triag knew he was being seduced by something. He knew that there was Powerful magic luring him into the seduction but he was not in the least way interested in fighting it. His skin was cold and he was frightened by this Nemain/Briciu thing that was in his head but it felt so good for him to be seduced and to sink into the fantasy of returning home, all powerful and left to a life of decadence and indulgence after so long being on the road as naught but a servant boy.

I will do as I have planned in this. And I will have the magic for I will be a witness to what Faidhe does in this great ritual for which she prepares. I will remember her incantations to bring the magic about but when I come home, these things will be of such value, that I will have my way in things now that I am a man and one that is practiced in magic. You just be ready for me when I do Nemain. Either I have the life I desire or no one gets what they want. You hear? You HEAR? You need me Nemain and so too, do you Briciu. Know you who is now in control.

Of course, Triag. Bring us the words, the Cauldron and the magic. We will unite and be all Powerful for all time.

Triag closed his mind to Nemain. He did not like what he felt but he was helpless to resist the dark and cloying seduction of the draw to Power. And it was so that since they had waited with the Valkyrie women as Faidhe took her meeting, he had greater powers of observation and was all at once drawn deeply to his darker urges as if the energy of these urges had had time to gain strength and multiply while he was out of this earth's realm. It took much discipline to stay his hand from striking her when his grandmother spoke or to keep from plunging a knife into the Elven whelp's heart. Even this day when the old Seer woman had fallen, he fought the urge to hike up her furs and plunge his manhood into her that very moment in the snow. A small voice that seemed to be who Triag used to be, spoke from deep inside him to question these thoughts but that voice was but the boy he once was, not the man he had become. The man was strong and powerful. Soon, these women and the Elf would understand who he is.

As the sky grew gray with the sun that would soon rise, the small party of four approached the bog for which they searched, found beyond a dense wood. At the center of the frozen bog could be seen remnants of an ancient circle created by small random stones placed as though a space had been created for a sacred ceremony or ritual hidden behind the thick curtain of trees. Although there were thick drifts of snow everywhere else, the center of the bog Circle remained clear of snow. Faidhe indicated that they should stop here as she glided to the center of the Circle. Seemingly listening to the voice of the Circle, she picked a spot and from beneath her cloak, she brought forth, in a nimbus of blue light, the silver Cauldron fashioned and created artfully by Iarann. Inside the pot were a few items that Faidhe had kept safe all through her journey: a small knife with a handle fashioned from a bull's horn, a black feather she'd found in her hut many seasons ago when first her daughter appeared to her as the great raven, and a white feather from the colm bird, her other daughter's namesake. The dove that she'd learned through the prophecy would serve as facet of the new, He God to come. The third feather, a red one from the tale of a hawk that she now knew was to represent the line of the Valkyrie Queen, Sigrdifa. She brought forth also, a few items belonging to her family members and fellow travelers along with some salt, a skin of water carefully preserved from the Lake of the ivory Heron, sage grown from her own circle garden and a striking stone to create spark for fire.

Faidhe ordered the Elf, taking no time now for politeness or niceties. "Fion, take the boy and find two large stones to serve as a base for our altar. Then find a larger stone, for the dolmen crown. Here we will conduct the Great Ones home and set in motion all that is to come. Then seek wood for a fire. Dry wood will be scarce under all this snow. We will not need much; do what you can."

"Yes Lady. As you wish." Fion looked to Triag and need not have called him for he was intent on what Faidhe had brought from the pot and upon what she'd requested. On his feet already, prepared to search for the stones, he turned back toward the woods through which they had just come.

"This way, Elf. I saw stones that will serve and they are nearby a felled tree that will have branches above the snowfall and so should be dead and dry." Fion was suspicious at Triag's willingness to do what was asked without a sour face or complaint but relaxed a bit when he heard Triag mimic under his breath in a disgusted, sing song tone. "Yes Lady. As you wish, Lady. Let me kiss your skirts, Lady."

Iarann was the one who usually accomplished this heavy work; he made carrying heavy items look effortless. The two smaller men sweated and grunted as they alternately tried to carry and roll the stones into place in the Circle. The larger stone to be laid across the top of the other two required that they up-end the flat stone with a joint effort of strength and let it fall to the earth with a resounding thud many times to bring it to its new home in the Circle. Neither knew how they would lift it into place atop the altar for it was much too heavy for them to lift with one man on either end of the stone but they watched in fascination as the miniscule woman who appeared to weigh no more than a lamb, bent over the stone and held her open palms over the flat surface, igniting blue sparks between Faidhe's hands and the stone. Gara, Fion and Triag watched as the stone gradually began to vibrate and hover erratically until it lifted completely off the ground and was raised evenly to waste height. Then, smoothly, Faidhe set the stone atop the other two so lightly that the only sound was a momentary grinding of rocks making contact as the flat stone settled. When the task was done, Fion walked over and tried to shake the top-stone without success. He imagined that it was more than just its weight that held the stone in place now.

Triag seemed not intrigued with what Faidhe had just done with the stone, but was more interested in the silver Cauldron that lay, still on the earth. Gara noticed the train of his sight and came to her grandson, snaking her arm into his in a gesture of affection.

"There is naught for us there now Triag. Once I would have planned differently but now as we come to the close of all this, I see that there are greater things, larger things, things of more importance than riches or power. I have taken overlong, my boy, to come to you with words of wisdom and likely you have found your way to manhood without benefit of encouragement from me but if there is one thing I might say and have it be more true than any other thing I have said to you it is this: I cannot take credit for the man you have become for I was not there to monitor who you grew to be. I served myself in survival and called it caring for you. Know this now, Grandson, we are about to become part of something that will serve the many and will count not one piece of gold or head of cattle for us but it will be the most important thing we do in this life. You have proven yourself worthy and true my son. In this moment, my heart swells for I know what it is to be selfless in my actions to truly serve and to be so proud of the man you have become. When this is done, we will be home to one another, you and me for we are all we have."

Gara noticed a strange look come over Triag's face and wondered that she'd waited so long to speak these words to her grandson. Was it so unfamiliar to him to hear words of kindness without raising suspicion? She sighed inwardly and supposed it was so. *I swear that when we have had done with all of this business here, I will do what I must to pay penance for how I have neglected those in my care. I have lived both in high riches and in absolute need and I have been most content in these times of need. Would that I can hold this lesson and keep in my heart that it is the relationship forged that has true value not power over another or riches to be ill gained or taken from another.* Gara sighed again as Triag deliberately unbound himself from her clasp and moved away from her.

"Your neglect has caused more harm than you know, Gara." Faidhe's voice took her by surprise. "He has turned. One who sees well, the minds of others has told me, that Triag has traversed far down a path that will lead to his own destruction. Our own Fion has been privy to the thoughts and communications of the boy and has shared with me that his mind is infected with greed and hunger for the most monstrous kind of power. He has ill-used the magic in his blood and communicates now with dark ones who would undermine our purpose and usurp the magic for their own gain. If you truly wish to assume responsibility for your part in this, then you must do as I instruct." Faidhe handed to the other woman, the ivory handled knife.

———

"Come Triag." Gara called to her grandson. "We must seek special growths in the wood that can be found under the snow. Faidhe requires this of us. Let us hope that the ground is not solid with cold to make our task impossible."

"Are you sure she did not instruct you so and you call upon me to do your work?" Triag probed.

Gara looked ashen and her face was drawn into a mask of despair. "I blame you not Triag for it is something I would think little over doing were it not for the changes that have taken place in my heart during our journey. I know I have given you no reason to trust me or to love me but know that all I request of you now and all I do myself is only for the good of the group and the magic that will be cast and enforced this day."

"What is the great magic your Faidhe will cast?" He said luring Gara into revealing something she might know that he does not. "What are you to gain for all your efforts? Has she promised you something for your toils and troubles? Where is my treasure for my part in these travels, Grandmother? What will I receive for playing the servant boy to your whims for these seasons? What have you brokered for my presence here that I have not been privy to?"

"You have every right to be angry and feel yourself ill-used. In truth, I deserve all you accuse me of. I have not been true kin to you or an advocate for your needs. But I plead you Triag, in this, our service is most surely required. Let us find these roots hidden underground for the casting of this magic. We will serve Faidhe her last deed, and then we may go about repairing all that has gone awry with our family. Let me prove to you that I ask you not to do my bidding but that I ask to serve in this process for it will be our last duty to Faidhe in this life. On this, I swear."

He'd never heard such words from Gara and knew not whether to trust them but there was a tone of earnest affection or was it regret in her voice that he allowed himself to be convinced to forage for underground growths of a special nature in the wood. Then he would assure himself a position to observe the Powerful magic that Faidhe would cast in order that he might repeat the ritual to gain or usurp her strength of magic for himself and perhaps even lay hands on the great Cauldron of the Dagda should it appear, for his own use; if not that one, then the silver one, at least.

"Very well, then," he acquiesced trying to sound exasperated. Then he flashed his grandmother what he hoped was an amiable smile and they headed toward the trees together.

The two spent several minutes maneuvering over the snow and searching for the right type of tree under which to look for the plant Faidhe required. It was difficult to discern one tree from another as the winter had stripped them of their leaves.

"There, Triag." Gara pointed. "That tree appears to be the type we need. At the base there, push back the snow and see if there are the telltale little green sprouts we seek."

"What sprouts are present in all this snow? This is a fool's errand. There is naught that could grow in this frozen land."

"Enough!" Gara snapped. "Argue not with me over things of which you have no knowledge. It is for the very magical strength of the roots of these sprouts that we seek the impossible winter plant. Stay your tongue and not your hand boy. Take this bowl to move the snow. Do as I say!" She poked a carved wooden bowl at him to be used as a shovel and then to hold the plants as they are uprooted.

"Ah there is the Grandmother I have come to know and despise. All this talk of love and family, I should have known was naught but a display. I will find your sprouts, then keep your distance from me and speak to me no more. I am shut of you and all of this after the ritual. I made my way here without your help, so too I'll find my way home. We are family no more. Keep you to your new loyalties. Good luck with the hag and the Elf."

Gara's expression was as if she'd been struck in the face. "Just there." She pointed to the base of the tree trying to change the subject. "Kneel then and find the sprouts and we'll be shut of each other." Triag ignored the offered bowl but noticed a catch in her throat as she last spoke. He knelt to shove the snow back from the tree with his hands to reveal the leafy earth at its roots. Gara neared him as if to peer over his shoulder and withdrew the small ivory handled knife she'd been given by Faidhe. In one swift movement, brought the knife round from behind.

"I'm sorry," she said. She meant to mend their harsh words and hand him the knife to dig up the roots for which they were sent.

Striking with lightning speed, Triag grabbed her wrist and easily snapped it. He spun around and Gara yelped with shock, not at the pain in her hand, but at the eyes that peered at her now. It was her grandson's face but through the eyes of the boy, she saw something dark and frightening looking at her in triumph.

"Not this time, Mother." Came the unmistakable voice of Briciu. "I was ready for your treachery this time and," he tisked mockingly, "the same old tired trick." Came the voice that was oiled with the sound of death from beyond the grave. "*You* will be the blood to seal the magic this time. This magic will insure my return and you will not keep me from it."

"No." Gara shrieked. "I am only to keep you from the ritual. I would not use the knife to do what you think, Triag. Triag! Hear me now. I know you are not gone over completely."

"You lie!" It spat. The thing speaking through Triag brought the knife up Gara's gut and with one savage slice, ripped her open to shed a rain of red upon the snow. In that last moment of exaltation, the Triag/Briciu thing caught a glimpse of Fion's thoughts that the ritual had begun. Gara's excuse to bring him to the deep wood was just a ruse. There were no additional items needed for the magic. The ceremony had begun!

Panicked that he might have missed some necessary element to the ritual, Triag squealed and plunged his hand under Gara's clothing and withdrew it holding a small pouch with a drawstring which contained the firestone she'd bribed the ship's captain with to book a voyage to their home. He shoved the pouch under his own garments and struggled around his obvious excitement over the spilt blood. In a halting run back toward the bog clearing, covered in steaming blood, limping, growling and snapping like a mad animal thinking that all may be lost if he is too late to the Circle.

———

The ritual had begun with a recitation of the story of the travelers brought together by the prophecy. Faidhe initially thought that this would be Lon Dubh's role in these proceedings but in this she was wrong so Faidhe recited the story as though reading from the pictorial on the silver Cauldron as Fion listened. This was part of the magic to be bound in that a story must be heard as it is told; otherwise, there is no Power in the Word if it is not heard. There is certainly energy in thought, but to make it manifest in the earthly plain, it must resonate to the senses of the earthly plain. In this case, in order to call all the Power she could to the tale, for the first part of her magical ritual, Faidhe used the salt of the Earth, Water of the lake, the striking stones to spark the Fire that would burn the sage to scent the Air and called to her all the Power and energy behind the elements. Faidhe recited the story to engage the tongue and hearing as she read the Cauldron with her sight and ran her fingers over the cold metal figures that Iarann had meticulously crafted.

With a flick of her wrist, the large black Cauldron of the Dagda appeared and in a blue show of sparks and bolts of light, a translucent blue image of the Staff appeared over the great pot and descended, disappearing into its bowl. Next, a bluish vision of the Shield appeared with barely perceptible images that were lately painted on it, then its image also lowered into the Cauldron. Finally, the Sword appeared over the mouth of the pot pointing skyward and a storm of blue sparks put on a show that lit the surrounding snow so brilliantly, it took on the color of the Goddess's lovely blue and the entire bog was illuminated to a near blinding radiance just as the sun peeked over the horizon. When the image of the Sword was returned to the Cauldron, the pot itself began to vibrate with blue energy until the resounding sound of the metal of the Cauldron began to ring as a resounding gong. As Faidhe watched and chanted the words of her spell, Fion covered his sensitive ears to keep his head from splitting from the sound of the ringing bowl.

The black Cauldron was completely illuminated with white-hot blue energy and began to rise from the floor of the Circle. In that moment, the energy from all four of the implements began to spin in a great ball of Power and shot, like a lightning bolt, into the smaller, decorative silver bowl of the ironsmith's making. The ringing stopped; there was absolute silence in the surrounding forest, and only the shadow of blue flashes of light danced in front of Faidhe and Fion's eyes while their noses took in the burning scent of great energy spent.

Faidhe raised the silver bowl, placed it on the altar stone and began to finger the final panel Iarann had created. With this panel, she chanted the words of her spell to bring the members of their union of eight back to the flesh at the time the world and the Gods would have need for the strength of magic to return. First, the red feather from the tail of the hawk, she held over the pot and it sparked in a shock of blue and fell into the silver bucket. "At the time in space when the wheel is turned, Sigrdifa comes through when darkness is spurned." Next, into the pot she dropped a couple of pieces from what appeared to be a game of sticks worn smooth from use, into the pot and they too disintegrated into a blue flash of light. "At the first harvest, when the summer wanes, the pair comes to the flesh to spark birthing pangs." Holding a frayed piece of leather taken from Laoghaire's half strap and a seal skin medicine bag given her by Craiche in friendship so many seasons ago, Faidhe announced in a strong and steady voice, "Of the Laoghaire still so named, at the spoke of the milking lamb, who takes union with the elder, coming at the spring tide – fish and lamb." Faidhe placed the leather scrap inside the seal skin bag, then tossed them into the Cauldron with a blue sizzle igniting from its depths.

It was a risk, Faidhe knew, but she also knew that due to her involvement in Briciu's death she had broken her vow to harm none and so she took the chance of utilizing Gara to take her place in the eight who would return. Although Gara too owed a debt for the life of Briciu, she had not broken a sacred vow in committing the ritual magic to slay the beast. But it would have to be so, for there was no other in all this who would play the part. Fion and his brother must stay to proliferate the story. Two is best for if one is lost...She would not allow herself to think in those terms, particularly not here in the Circle after raising such high magical energy. *It must be so.* Faidhe resigned herself that Gara need be the one and fingered the figure on the Cauldron that would represent her and dropped one of the woman's firestones into the pot, which created quite a smoky explosion of blue light as Faidhe recited, They birth the first who comes with a debt, on the day of the Lugh, this one is met."

When the cloud of smoke cleared she continued. "The next to come through, the worker of ore, on the eve when between worlds, opens the door." Into the pot clanged a small tool used by Iarann to fashion the figures on the plates and in return a strong blue flame erupted out of the Cauldron. In a quiet voice, Faidhe seemed reflective now as she held up the white, dove's feather and quietly spoke the verse. "Then comes the one marked by the beast, born to this time on the bull's own feast." After only a moment's hesitation she dropped the feather, which ignited and erupted into an explosion of blue flames and rolling smoke billowing from the silver vessel.

Though Gara would come through now in the position Faidhe had thought would be her own, the first born in the family of living implements, the situation had changed so that another would necessarily have to take the role of bringing through the Light; this responsibility could not be left to one such as Gara. Without question, Faidhe knew it would be her Lon Dubh. "She will be able in her knowledge, and will bear her name in that life as the Raven she is. One who is of the light and from the light, but knows the darkness and will not fear it. She will know herself as the one who will be the living Sword as I can no longer be."

Faidhe reflected for the moment on what this might mean for her daughter, then holding the black, raven's feather, an actual piece of her daughter's spiritual being, Faidhe fought her tears as she finished what was necessary. "Lastly the one holds the light and the knowledge together within, she will complete the Circle, to set it to spin." The black feather left Faidhe's fingers and drifted gracefully spinning on the air, down into the blue light now burning so brightly in the pot that it glowed as blue-hot coals. A rumbling could be heard reaching up from the depths of the earth and a column of light spilled upward from the mouth of the pot and raised to the skies as far as the eye could see. The column of light began to curl and slowly turn sunwise in a circular motion, creating a large blue orb of light, spinning in the atmosphere. Faidhe and Fion watched as the ball of light took on the appearance of a large blue wheel of light with seven visible spokes all joined in a deeper, more substantive blue in the middle. Faidhe took the salt and water, and put them into the pot. Then calling a ball of flame from her ritual fire, she cupped a small flaming ember in her hand, crumbled some sage over it, then added the ember and the aromatic to the pot at which point, the great blue wheel began to spin with frightening speed.

"As the hub that unites and brings the wheel complete, and precise is the time when the task is replete." Faidhe then dragged her fingernail through the burn that had been left by the ember in the palm of her hand and watched as her blood welled up into the wound. She held her wound over the pot and allowed three drops of blood to fall into the Cauldron. "Open is the balance when the light's strength takes sway, to complete the wheel and birth the sun's long ray." This time, a long ray of blue emitted from the pot with what seemed to be a core of red from Faidhe's blood. As the light shot out of the Cauldron, it took its place as the eighth spoke in the giant, living, pulsing, spinning wheel and Faidhe raised her hands up over her head in an open, V-shape toward the wheel. She raised her voice to the skies and finished casting.

"The child brings vast change as the great wheel spins, and the Fifth Civilization is ushered, as maturity begins."

The great wheel spun round and round and as it did, it appeared to grow tighter and smaller until it came down to a point and hovered for a moment at what appeared to Fion to be right between Faidhe's open arms as though she were holding the light aloft. Fion watched as Faidhe held what appeared to be a raven on her left hand and a dove on her right. Just as that thought registered to Fion, he saw a hawk fly right through the middle of Faidhe's outstretched arms and he heard the simultaneous call of all three. Not understanding his own thoughts, Fion shook his head to see the spinning wheel positioned right at the empty space under the dolmen stone of the altar between the two stones that served as its base. Faidhe, now appearing to be merely a faint outline of blue light, was almost undetectable within her clothing and furs. As the wheel spun at the mouth of the dolmen, a portal of sorts opened up under the dolmen and an entrance between this world and another could be seen. She chanted the words to keep the spirit of the Goddess alive and active while she weathered the firestorm of the masculine He.

Keep silent but alive the magical ways,
Keep the living traditions under the wing of the dove.
Keep the Goddess safe in her slumber while the He-God takes sway,
and wake the Goddess in her time when planted is the seed of the wheel
made in love.

Faidhe raised her voice and called to the Gods, the spirits and myriad magical beings. She looked at the same time, near to invisible and expanded with great Power. Her hair flowed in all directions with some hidden energy. Her very body seemed to vibrate with the same resonance that the Dagda's Cauldron had done earlier. Or, it could be myriad voices, Fion could not tell which.

"Take refuge now, under the Sidhe and be safe while the world begins its slumber under the dust of forgetfulness until such time the wheel sets to spin again with the coming of the Light, and when the time for memory and magic returns."

In a cacophony of noise, whispers, animal sounds, keening, moans, voices and whooshing motion, a great energy rushed through the portal created at the base of the dolmen and within a brief moment, all was quiet, the portal had closed and the bright spinning wheel was naught but a memory. The sound of the silence was deafening.

Fion found himself face down on the Circle floor. After a moment of gathering his bearings, he rose to his knees and searched the Circle for Faidhe. She was rumpled on the Circle floor by the silver Cauldron, now set by the dolmen opening.

"Lady!" He ran to her and fell to his knees to assist the fallen woman. "Faidhe!" He called, grabbing at her furs to help her up. "What?" Fion looked around to make sense of what he felt. The furs, naught but empty skins over linens and woolens. His eyes scanned the Circle and saw nothing to tell him of Faidhe's whereabouts. Looking even under the dolmen and foolishly into the Cauldron, Fion grasped that with the casting of her final magic, Faidhe too was gone, her purpose served. With this understanding he fell hard on the earth and allowed the full realization of what had happened and his current situation to sink in.

After a short while, Fion began to be aware that there were rustlings in the snowy brush beyond the Circle in the bog. He searched his surroundings and was frightened when he saw Triag rise from his vantage where he'd been watching, hidden in some bushes and stride toward the Circle, covered with blood and with a knife in his hand. The boy did not look himself; he was distant in his eyes, but worse, he resembled one who had gone full-bad in his thoughts. He spoke in tones Fion did not understand and made wretched sounds much like a swine bull. It took him a few moments but Fion became aware that Triag was looking at him and quickly heading directly for him. The Elf scrabbled to his feet and was instantly away to the edge of the Circle. Undeterred, Triag lumbered after him taking useless, wild swipes with the knife in the Elf's direction. After a few futile attempts to catch the fleet-footed Elf, Triag squealed again in frustration and gouged his fingers into his own face.

Apparently deciding that his revenge against the Elf for unknown crimes or insults would have to wait, Triag turned toward the Cauldron. Fion started toward Triag, knowing he would fight to the death to keep this other from taking the pot but was stopped when he saw Triag reach for the bowl and a tremendous explosion blew the boy back along with the stones that had been the altar. When the dust cleared, the altar was merely strewn cracked pieces of stone and the Cauldron had been separated by the blast into the original panels, undamaged but scattered upon the bog floor. Triag reached for the pieces of the Cauldron and was again jolted, but this time with a shock of blue light which sent pain into his body that caused him to writhe and convulse uncontrollably until he fell to the ground. Some few moments had passed and Triag woke from his stupor.

Fion watched as again from a cautious distance, as Triag tried to retrieve the pieces of the Cauldron and again was sent flailing. Determined, Triag tried to reach the pieces with the knife and it was snatched from his hand by an unseen force landing at Fion's feet. With this, Triag literally growled and bared his teeth at Fion, whose skin puckered with the sight. Fion picked up the knife.

The Elf understood whose blood was on the knife and the other man's clothing. He understood that he alone must fend for himself and for the Cauldron.

"You have no weapon Triag and no one to seek food and wood with you. The Cauldron is safe and protected." He hollered across the expanse of the Circle hoping he could talk sense into the Beast he saw before him. "Each time you try to retrieve the pieces there, you come closer to your own death." Fion didn't know if this were true but hoped that Triag would think it so. He watched the other man as the calculations of risk crossed his face.

Seemingly, Triag accepted the idea that he would not retrieve the Cauldron, but unfortunately brought him back to his original goal of killing Fion. He looked at the Elf with half focused, bloodshot eyes of rage.

"You cannot catch me Triag. I am half Elf and fleet of foot." To demonstrate, Fion moved so quickly across the Circle that it appeared to Triag that he had simply disappeared from one spot and reappeared in another.

"I am here now." He said from behind Triag who turned with a start and began to charge in a fury toward the Elf who moved in a blur at the very last moment before Triag plowed into the air where he stood but a moment ago.

"You are cumbersome and move like an oaf, Triag. Surrender. You will not get the Cauldron and you will not catch me. If you could, what would you do? I have the knife and have always bested you in any physical display." Fion knew this was risky for it had been some time since they had been involved in a challenge. Triag had grown much stronger with manhood since those days. A reminder of his losses may just spur more anger at the memory of having been bested over and again but he pushed on.

"Save your energy man; I foresee that we both have a long trek to survive. I choose not to expend my breath in fighting a useless battle and you seem to be breathing a great deal harder than I. We are done here. Go home, if you still have one. As will I."

Fion was relieved but held his breath to see Triag head back toward the Cauldron. This time, his adversary was thinking ahead of Fion and he cursed himself that he had not thought to take them for himself when he saw the other man bend to pick up Faidhe's clothing and furs but then understood that Triag was expecting to find Faidhe in the furs when he let out the ultimate howl of frustration at being daunted in all aspects of his fury and ran off as a wild beast with an uneven gate into the brush, then into the woods.

———

Fion sat by the Cauldron in the Circle, not knowing what his next move might be. Should he attempt to pick up the pieces of the pot and safeguard them? He thought not, after witnessing what had happened to Triag, he did not wish to endure such a jolt, nor did he know what might be done with the pieces if he were able to collect them.

"Lady," he called out. "I seek guidance. What am I to do now? This was not foretold to me. Now that your magic is cast and our journey is finished, what am I to do?" He listened for an answer and heard only the wind in the trees. *Is there no one there to guide me now?* Fion thought to himself, half calling and half hoping he'd be blessed with an answer.

Fion? Is that you? FION?

Cathbad? Oh I had forgotten in all these events. Cathbad, I am so pleased to hear from you. It is done brother. It is done.

Forgotten me? Hear from me? Brother, is it truly you?

Of course it is me. Why are you so distraught? Have you seen from our home, evidence of the great magic Faidhe has wrought?

I have been searching for you these great many seasons. I have heard naught from you in so long and in the changing times, I have left our island to seek you out. Now these many strange occurrences of light take place in the rocks and stones of the mountains and then for the first time in trying for so very long, I hear from you.

Many seasons? What mean you brother, for it has been but a setting of no more than five or so suns since we spoke last.

Has the fairy drink taken your mind brother? It has been the passing of more than ten full seasons since we spoke last! I knew you were alive, still, for I sensed it but I could reach you not. The world has changed much brother. I have taken to your original path of travel in seeking you out. I have been the mainland over many times in tracing your steps and the others. I have seen much of your travels in the stories folks have told. I have seen also Lon Dubh or Lady Raven as she is called now. She spoke words of great sadness at the news that your party and companions have been lost to our knowledge.

The idea of fairy drink jolted Fion with the knowledge that if as much time had passed as his brother said, it could only mean the brief time he spent with the others in the land of the Valkyrie passed differently than here on this plain. *Cathbad. Where are you now, brother?*

I am three days north of the village in which Lady Raven and her family live. I have spent time enjoying the hospitality there during my search for it is a brutal winter. We have seen none such as this since the season after you left on your journey.

Brother, listen. I have but few supplies and I know we have an enemy in Triag. He is wrong in his head now.

Ah, as is his aunt. It is said that she haunts the old De Danann village feasting on insects and vermin, talking to herself and her brother, robed in rags and filth awaiting the time when she will be the wielder of great power.

After knowing Gara and Triag, and hearing of the son of Gara who had released the ill magic of the Beast, the reflection on the thought of yet another member of that family crawling with the ill deeds of the dark power, both Cathbad and Fion shuddered simultaneously at the thought.

Let us forget that ill for now. Are you well Fion? I travel with a party from Lady Raven's village. We will find you now and thank the Gods for your safety.

Yes, I am well enough. I am on the northern most peninsula on the mainland and I am alone. Cathbad, I am the last one of our group save for Triag. All others are gone. There was a choked silence in Fion's mind as a response to this news. *I will prepare for harsh travel as best I can and begin to head South to meet you. I so yearn to see Lon D...Lady Raven again.*

Fion, we are North in the mainland and to travel that far south once again would be folly. If we are to return home, we must meet and go West to the seaports in time for spring. Our lands have changed greatly and in all this, our connection and kinship to the blood kin of Faidhe and her descendants is finished. There is work for us still in our homeland and in Middle Village. It is now our duty to let these adventures settle into the tale for which they were endured.

Fion thought of Lon Dubh and Sonne, now many seasons past hearing of him or knowing of his travels. He recognized the time of the bonds of the union of the original eight members from the tale had passed. Craiche surrendered to the cause, Iarann gone to the Valkyrie, Lon Dubh wed to a distant tribe, Faidhe gone to the Sidhe before his very eyes. *Very well brother, we will find one another and do as you say. The time of the union of the eight has passed and we must retire now to our oath and insure that the story will remain active. We will speak of Colm and Laoghaire soon enough for my heart can bear no more ill news if I am to have strength to journey once more.*

Fion prepared what little he had to take once again to the road. He came to the decision that the Cauldron was protected by Faidhe's magic and so it would remain where she left it. As he glanced at the pieces scattered on the ground, he spied a piece of a water-skin tucked under a shard of rock that had shattered with the force of blast when Triag attempted to take the Cauldron. Fion removed the rock and discovered the water-skin, fully intact, with a lump of salt, a clump of dried sage and Faidhe's striking stones. He could not fathom that these items survived the magic, much less the blast but nevertheless, there they were. He did not hesitate. Reaching for the items, he knew Faidhe had intended him to have them. Not only were they magical, they would insure his survival on the trek homeward. He put the items into his pouch tied to his halfstrap. Then he cleansed the knife of Gara's blood and put it too, at his side.

After a moment of silence and reflection in the Circle, Fion took up what supplies the group had left, bid goodbye to Faidhe, Lon Dubh, Iarann and even Gara as he took the first steps on his journey toward home. Just then, at the edge of the circle, he spied a role he recognized as Iarann's sheath for his small hand tools for working the silver that apparently, Faidhe had purposed in her magic. One tool was missing from the folds of the role, and though he had no use for them, sentiment would not allow Fion to leave all he had left of his dear friend behind. He tucked them close to his heart and started his trek once again.

49

A Little Slice of Home

We arrived in Dublin and took up residence in a hotel that appeared very impressive. It seemed that the hotel had gone through some recent renovations and had sunk all of its money into marble floors, magnificent art, and gleaming polished wood in the lobby but ran out of funding because when we checked into our three adjoining rooms, one for Bridey, another for Cath and Finny and Nora's and mine, the accommodations were little better than disappointing. We didn't complain; we weren't going to be there for long. The rooms were together and they'd suit us over the next few days until we boarded our flight to Denmark.

Mama?

I stood bolt straight in our bathroom as I was putting away my toiletries. *Lucas?* I looked foolishly out the bathroom door at my phone lying on the night table.

Mama, I think you're in trouble. The monster is mad at you and Aunt Nora. It's really, really mad. You should be careful 'cause they're after you.

I didn't dismiss his knowledge. *What happened? How do you know, Baby?*

They were sniffing around me last night but the lady was there to scare them off. But now, they're here even in the daytime when I'm not even sleeping. Dad doesn't know about them but I can feel them. Sometimes I can hear them sniffing around trying to smell around me, you know, like a dog does when you play hide and seek. I keep my blanket with me all the time now. I wear it like a cape 'cause, well you know how Dad doesn't like when I have blue blanky around that much. He thinks it's for babies. But he doesn't mind me wearing it like I'm a superhero.

I know, Baby. I know. You said 'them,' Luke. What do you mean by that?

The monster is...He hesitated searching to find what he was trying to say. The monster is just big and bad. You know, a monster. But the monster can get into people who are...well, not bad, but people who don't lock their doors to be careful about doing bad stuff. If people are kinda mean, it makes them real mean. If people are sneaky, it uses them to sneak for it. Like that.

We were speaking in a kind of shorthand now and I understood what Lucas was trying to say. The Beast was able to exploit people's character flaws and weaknesses.

Mom?

Yeah, Hon?

I think Uncle Will left his door open.

My skin went cold at the thought that someone so close to home might be used as a tool for this evil. *What do you mean, Luke?*

Dad and me drove over to Aunt Nora's house to borrow Uncle Will's ladder and he was, well, you know.

Drunk?

Yeah. But I could tell, Mom, he was way more than drunk 'cause his eyes were all floaty like when he gets like that, but his underneath eyes, the ones that grown-ups and other people don't really see...you know what I mean?

I think I do, Luke. What about his underneath eyes?

Well they kept looking at me while Uncle Will was trying to sound normal to Dad like there were two Uncle Wills there, the one who was drunk and the other one who snuck in the door. And there was something in his head. I kept seeing what he was thinking and it really scared me. Mom? Lucas started to cry and my heart was breaking.

What, Luke. What scared you?

Well, Uncle Will was all mixed up and crazy. Like red in his head. Not just from the drunk part 'cause I've seen that before, but all kinda crawly in there.

Fion's words to describe Triag's mind struck me now. *Worms.* I thought involuntarily.

Yeah, that's right, worms and stinky stuff.

I rubbed my face to try and think on what I'd do. I was a half a world away from my son and felt helpless to protect him but I knew if I was going to protect him, I had to stay here and finish this business. *Do you think you're okay with blanky to protect you, Luke? Do you feel like Uncle Will is going to come after you?*

There was a hesitation while he either thought about his response or was searching to see what things felt like around him. *I think if they really tried, they might make him do something, but Uncle Will is really drunk and he's with some lady that I don't know and he's busy with her so I don't know if the monster could use him the way they want to right now.*

'Busy' was our family phrase for when Walter and I were sharing private moments. Luke understood that when we were 'busy,' he did not come into our bedroom unless it was an emergency. My heart broke again, this time for Nora. *A lady?*

Yeah, when we went to borrow the ladder this morning, there was a lady at Aunt Nora's house. She wasn't nice or anything. She was on the drunk side too but not as bad as Uncle Will. I could hear her thoughts that she just wanted us to leave. She hated us 'cause we were related to Aunt Nora. She hated us but I could tell, she was scared of me. She knew I could tell what she was thinking and I don't know if it was her or the other thing underneath that knew I could tell her thoughts.

My stomach sank for Nora. It sounded like this woman wasn't just a one-time thing and had been around for a while if she were territorial enough to hate Nora and anyone from her family but that'd be something to think about for a later time. *Luke, you said there was another lady who helped to keep you safe last night.*

Yeah.

Do you know who she is?

Yeah, she's the old lady that you know. I see her in your mind right now. She says I'll be okay for now as long as she stays with me but she says you and Aunt Nora have to go to the place of the Shield. She says you should ask our ancestors for help. Then for sure I'll be okay.

Our ancestors?

Yeah.

The Shield?

Mm, hmm.

My mind ticked away at details from Cath and Finny's account of what happened to the Shield and I tried to make sense of what Lucas what saying. *Okay. Luke. I think I know what to do. Where are you now?*

I'm in the car with Dad. He's taking me to walk the Freedom Trail.

Okay. Does Dad seem okay to you? I was a bit concerned that if the Beast could utilize character flaws and human weaknesses, that there might be some hidden weakness in Walter that could be exploited like Will's alcoholism.

No, he's good.

Okay Lucas. I'm going to do what Faidhe wants. That's the lady's name. Aunt Nora and I will go to where we'll find help for protection. I'm going to call home later on the phone so I can touch base with Dad. I'll talk with you again then. Until then, keep your blanket and know that you have the Power to protect yourself if you need to. Do you know what I mean?

I think so, but Mom, the monster is after you and Aunt Nora now. It knows what you're going to do. It's afraid of what you're going to do when you go to call someone named Dren."

"Dren?"

Yeah. Someplace where Aunt Patrice is coming to see you to call Dren.

Oh my God. Call Dron? Cauldron, Luke? Is that what you mean?

Yeah, I guess so.

How did you know about that, Luke?

Well, when the monster is trying to sniff me out, I can hear what it's thinking sometimes. Cause it tries real hard to figure out who I am or what I am. It knows I'm yours and Aunt Nora's and Aunt Patrice's and Grandma and Grandpa's and...Oh I don't know how to explain but it knows that we love us and that we can open the door on people instead of sneak in through it like it does or something like that, so it's trying to figure out what I am. 'Cause it doesn't' know.

Do you know Lucas?

I think I'm...I'm full of...I'm full of light, I think. If we open the door, the light comes in. Right?

The lump in my throat threatened to choke me now. *That's just right Luke. You're full of light and sometimes that light scares people who are comfortable being in the dark because you'll make them see things about themselves that maybe they'd rather not. But that light is also full of everything that's good. And that will help to keep anything bad away. I love you, Baby. We're going to do everything we can to make all of this stuff go away.* I didn't want to lie to him even if I could now. He knew my thoughts so I added: *Or if we can't make it go away, we'll try to make it so we always have the Power to win the fight.*

Okay Mom. Love you too. Promise to call later?

Absolutely. But I gotta go now Luke. You stick close to Dad today; I mean like glue, you hear me? And I'll talk with you later.

"Nora!"

"Yeah?"

"Get Cath and Finny. We have to go out."

"What are you talking about? We just got he..." She took one look at my face and immediately went to the door that opened into the next room, which belonged to the men. They came into our room when Nora called to them.

"We have to go to Knowth right now." I said.

Finny looked a bit bemused but Cath understood right away. "A little help from your family is it?" He asked already knowing the answer.

"You told us that the Shield was buried at Laoghaire's parent's grave site, right?"

"I did."

"And that the Shield was planted there to protect the clan Laoghaire?"

"Also true."

"Do you know where that is?"

"I've an idea. What is it yer plannin' te do?"

"I'm not exactly sure, but we have to go there now."

I avoided looking at Nora and tried to shut my mind from communicating what Lucas just told me about her husband.

"I'll get the car. Meet me downstairs in front," I said, as I grabbed the phone and stuffed it into my satchel habitually checking for the precious book, The Power of the Word, and all my notes. This time I also checked for the envelope Cath gave me that held the airline tickets for our flight to Denmark. I mused how strange it was to whittle all ones valuables down to what could be held in one bag. I left the room both shaken and comforted by the conversation I had just had with Lucas.

While I was getting the car from the hotel garage, I felt gooseflesh crawl all over me. I was spooked to be in the garage by myself and couldn't jam my key into the car door fast enough. I looked over my shoulder constantly and although I saw nothing, I couldn't help the feeling of encroaching dread. As soon as I was in the car, I slammed the door lock to assuage my sense of being a sitting duck. I started the car and threw it in gear to back out of the parking spot and meet the others out front. I felt infinitely better when I left the gloom of the garage and entered the daylight.

"Where's Bridey?" I asked when I saw only Nora, Finny and Cath waiting for me in front of the hotel.

Finny answered, "She says she'll stay here. We'll tend our work and she'll tend hors."

"What's that supposed to mean?" I inquired.

Cath answered with a shrug of his shoulders threw his backpack onto the floor of the passenger side and climbed into the front seat of the car to give me instructions on the best way to travel to the archaeological site, leaving the back seat for Finny and Nora.

"Torn north onte Rte. 2, Lass." He directed.

"Okay," I said. "Cath, I have to ask you something. You know how you said you once thought Chiaro Vorace might be the one you were looking for?"

"Yes." He answered but it was more of a question.

"And you said she was from one of the parent countries and she had, ah, abilities?"

"I did. She was and she had."

"Well do you think it's possible she was a descendant from the line?"

"I did at the time. It is possible. I suppose she might have been."

"Well then, why didn't the Shield protect her? You said she was in County Wicklow and heading toward Knowth when she was murdered, right?"

"She was."

"So is it possible that she was of the bloodlines but somehow wasn't protected?"

"I can't answer that, Lee." He knew I was serious and he could figure why I was asking so he didn't mince words when he answered.

"Here's what I think, but it's only me own speculation. I think Chiaro had the blood in her that was of the line from Italy and was drawn here. I don't know why it'd have been stronger in some than others. Perhaps somewhere along the line, she'd have had ancestors of two lines as yerself and so had the seein'. But my feelin' is that regardless of that, she was not of the line of Laoghaire as ye are. For ye must remember that the Shield was given forst te Laoghaire along with the Sword; as the pair te fight and defend in any battle. And the original curse that was cast by Briciu that started on that one night of the challenge was intended te kill Laoghaire and te wreak havoc on his family and the magic that was cast in protective measure was done so te counter act that darkness...the protection was cast te protect clan Laoghaire. The branch of the bloodline from Italy was of Faidhe and the Greenman. Not a drop of Laoghaire's blood at all. So perhaps though Chiaro had the seein' in her and was drawn here by her studies much the same as yerself, she was open and exposed te the evils of the Beast."

"So we're protected?"

"I'd say I think ye are more so than Finny and me."

"What the hell does that mean? Are you saying you guys are in danger?"

"I told ye Lass, it's all speculation. I can repeat the tale word for word te ye but if there's nothin' said about these things, then well, that's all I've got. But I will say this: You and Nora have come through in yer line as the living Sword and Shield for a purpose. Ye've both come here at a time when the Beast's energy is rising and has, from what ye tell me, either been reborn as ye have or has the ability te take over willing hearts te do its bidding. Maybe a bit of both. And now yer te be joined by the one who is the living bowl as well as constructed the tale in bowl form at a time when the energy is te be rightfully released from the Cauldron; so it seems te me that things have been arranged so ye'll have all the protection ye need te shine the light on the dark places."

My skin puckered again at how close he'd come to using the exact phrase that Lucas had done not one hour ago. Cath sounded stern that I had some doubts but he put my heeby jeebies to rest for the moment.

"Go north here." He said.

And I did as I found my way out of the maze that is Dublin City. We traveled in relative silence and as we found ourselves surrounded by countryside, I began to breathe a little easier until I heard Nora take a quick breath and whisper, "Oh my God."

"What? I asked.

"It's one thing to know it, but it's another thing to see it." She said looking out the window at the impressive double Hill of Tara off in the distance. "I'm having wicked Déjà vu. The view of those hills is something I know I've seen before and not in a book! We lived not too far from here. That view is so familiar!"

"We?" I asked for clarification.

"Nora seemed to be searching her mind to put her finger on what she was trying to figure out. "Yeah..." All at once, she cried a ragged and sickening "Oh!" It came out of her like the wail of a keening woman.

I recognized what was happening to her. I'd experienced it not too long ago and I didn't envy her in this moment. Until now, Nora understood, cerebrally, everything that had happened to us before in the other lives, but hadn't remembered it and lived with it in her head as I did. The sight of the Hill of Tara was enough to trigger her memory and it was all flooding back to her now. I'd felt as though I was going to split out of my skin when it happened to me and wondered if it would be the same for Nora. Pulling over to the side of the road, I asked the men, "Is it always the same? I mean is it the same for everyone who remembers?"

Finny answered. "Let's us just give hor some time." He said and rolled his window down. Cath reached into his backpack and pulled out a floppy looking thing. It took me a minute to figure out that it was a skin about the size of one of those suede wine sacks we used to sneak into concerts when we were kids but it was more primitive looking.

"Is that...?"

"Aye, Lass." He said as he poured some water from the skin into a small paper cup, which he also took from his pack. "It's where I got the water that helped you in your time of remembrance. Now it'll help Nora."

"Are you saying it's the same one? How is that possible? It'd be way too old to last all these years."

"Aye, and it's not possible that it'd always have fresh water aplenty to pour either, but its gallons by the hundreds I have poured, fresh from the skin and so has Finny. It's a magical gift that offers healing waters and never dries. Here now," he said and shoved the cup at Nora. "Drink!"

I watched as Nora tried to drink from the cup but had difficulty through her sobbing. I stared at my sister because in our whole lives together before this trip, I'd seen her cry only two or three times and those were the times that our grandparents had died. Now she wailed and sobbed as her eyes overflowed with tears. My heart hurt for Nora and my own eyes welled up in sympathy for her.

Though her weeping didn't subside, she managed to take sips of the water and was intent on getting as much of it into her as she could. I guessed that it went a long way to easing her pain or sorrow as her memories came back to her. We waited, and I knew how uncomfortable she must be because Nora was not one to display any emotions publicly and now, here she was practically blubbering with an audience. She hung her head out the car window and took in huge gulps of air between sobs. I tried to detract attention from her.

"Hey Cath, is that where you got the water you gave to me in your shop when I was choking?"

The old man looked at me with his faded brown eyes and recognized my attempt to offer my sister privacy in her moment.

"Aye Lass. 'Tis. I was in a spot that day. Not really wantin' te offer ye a bit of the water fer the sake of givin' of it needlessly. As it was gifted te Finny by Faidhe for survival on his trek back home. It's been used almost exclusively by both of us now te keep our health te preserve us for the tellin' of the tale. It seems as the water works only te aid people if it doesn't interfere with fate. So ye see, I was cautious in givin' ye some water fer it shouldn't be squandered. But ye seem te have survived so it was obviously yer fate te come te me shop, rudely wake me, and then bless us all by not dyin' on the floor!"

I half smiled at his attempt at humor but tried to ask him a serious question.

"Does the water really heal? I mean, I know it helped me but..." I didn't know quite how to ask the question.

"If yer talkin' about my Evelyn, I did give it her, and often. It helped to ease her discomfort, for which I'm very grateful, but as I said, it would not interfere with her fate. Her time was her time." He said with finality. We sat in quiet reflection for a moment until Nora broke the silence.

"Let's go, I need air."

No one questioned her. I put the car in gear and followed Cath's instructions that brought us the ten or so miles northeast to Knowth. Glancing occasionally in the rearview mirror, I kept watch on Nora who looked out the window and took in deep breaths of air as she let the breeze from the car window flow over her. She edged her head out the window to increase the flow of air on her and looked at all she saw with fascination through leaking eyes.

Nora had seemingly composed herself by the time we reached the tourist site where we paid to enter the burial cairns but were disappointed to see that the main cairn we wanted to see was closed to the public presumably for some kind of maintenance. We waited for the next tour to begin with hopes that we'd be able to approach the family burial chamber somehow. None of us had any clue as to what we were going to do once we got inside but we'd deal with that when we get there, I supposed. *Faith, O'Leary. Have faith.* I told myself.

"Finny McDonough! May all the saints be praised! Is it yerself?" Came a forthright voice from a substantial woman striding toward us in a no-nonsense fashion. "Where have ye been, lad? And who might these women be?" She looked Nora and me up and down with a cool appraisal that smacked of territorial lines being drawn. "Hello, Cath." She said, but never took her eyes from Nora and me.

"Now Callie, lass," Finny clucked. "We've come for the tour, like, and we were hopin', well I was hopin te get one of yer special tours if ye get me meanin'." I watched Finny, who was a full 5 or 6 inches shorter than this woman, and likely 60 or 70 pounds lighter, calm her ruffled feathers using a few words and by taking her hand with one of his own and stroking her arm with the other. I was amazed when I saw Finny's ears poke out little points through his white hair and the ferocious woman's response was to almost melt and lay down for him right there on the spot. My mouth hung open as I witnessed this interaction and I looked to Cath who was trying to appear innocent, looking discretely toward the sky with an expression on his face that was purely smug, his mouth straining not to smirk and his eyes glinting with humor.

"You knew about this?" I asked him in a whisper.

"Hopin' was all." He answered. "Timin' and preparation is all, as they say." He continued to glint and smirk.

I returned my attention to Finny and Callie when I realized her interest was once again on us.

"Callie, darlin', I'd be pleased if ye'd greet our cousins from America, quite a few times removed, that is."

It seemed, here in Ireland, that one could avoid a multitude of prying questions and gain acceptance, simply by claiming to have blood relation of some distant and nebulous connection.

"This is Nora and Lee O'Leary. And who knows, it may well be that they're related te you as well, in some distant way." He finished with a flourish.

Callie hesitated a moment to size us up and try to determine whether she was being put on or not. Her eyes focused like lasers and her breasts pointed at us like a couple of torpedoes ready to fire if she determined we were enemy combatants in sheep's clothing. She seemed to have some kind of sixth sense about whether we were friend or enemy and all at once, Callie's expression changed to a rosy cheeked, cheery countenance as she shoved her fleshy hand toward us.

"O'Leary is it? Well then, there's a lot of us out there isn't there?"

I was thrown a bit off balance as I shook her hand, but understood what she was saying after a moment.

"You're an O'Leary too?" That sort of explained the sixth sense I recognized in her.

"I am. And you're very welcome to a special tour," she said. Then with a flirtatious glance at Finny, "But I'll not be showin' ye all the mystery that's te be seen in these great mounds!"

Now it was Nora's turn to stand with her mouth unhinged.

"You mean..." Nora started. She seemed to be ready to do battle over the thought of this woman and Finny or anyone using the cairns for such dalliances.

Finny stopped her percolating protest.

"It was only a bit of celebration of the Old Ways now wasn't it? And with a descendant of the Laoghaire himself? It's quite possible that Callie is of a distant relation te ye and she does right by hor ancestors by visiting with the tours every day and carin' enough te say a few words over the auld ones on the festival days as well."

He cut through all the bull of desecration or sacrilege or anything else that Nora's implanted mores might have used to protest. He didn't wait for any kind of response from Nora or myself, he turned to Callie and took her arm in his own while solicitously holding her hand at the same time.

"Shall we, to the east entrance then?" He said.

"Well, sure, but I have the next tour so I'll have te be back in an hour's time. This outing is leavin' now," she said with a nod toward the tourists who were leaving on the excursion for which we'd bought tickets. "They'll be going toward the west entrance as the only sights open te the public now are some satellite cairns. It'll take us sometime te get through the small entrance of the east side so it's not much time we have. I knew I put on my old climbin' clothes for a reason this day." She said. And my idea that she had a bit of ability was reaffirmed.

"By all means, lass, lead the way." Finny said. She blushed and flustered slightly at Finny's attention and his flattery in calling her lass as she was obviously at least 10 or more years older than Nora and me and though we looked much younger than our years, no one would accuse us being spring maidens, that's for sure.

"Callie," I called to the woman who'd all but forgotten about the rest of us in Finny's company.

"Yes dear?"

"Thanks for this, really. It means so much to us to come here and to be shown this site by someone who might...well that's so knowledgeable. Thanks for taking the time with us."

"Oh certainly, dear." She said sweetly.

Nora remained quiet as we were led to the cairn entrance at the far, east end of the large mound of earth. Callie asked us polite questions about where we came from in America, what parish our family attended when they lived in Ireland and when our relatives "took te the sea crossin'." She did her best to be solicitous but anyone could tell that her attentions were primarily on Finny as she metered out her information.

"Knowth Passage Cairn covers about an acre and is surrounded by about 17 smaller cairns. These are burial sites for many people of notability from long times past."

After being cautious about having no one see us, we gained access to the main cairn at the eastern side of the large mound through a very tight passage that was about 100 feet long. We were all quiet as we struggled through the last part that required we alternately stoop and crawl except for Cath and Finny who were apparently still fleet of Elven foot and small enough not to be hindered by the tight space. Nora and I managed on our hands and knees but I found myself marveling at Callie who was older, larger and less fit than all of us yet she managed to slip through the tight entrance with the ease of experience. I'd wondered how many times she and Finny visited this area but dismissed the thought as we reached the end of the entrance. At the end of the passage, the area opened up into a wider, much larger chamber with three distinct recesses that were obviously separate burial areas. In one recess, we saw a large, flat stone bowl, beautifully carved with swirls and what seemed to appear as a hand to me in the concavity of the bowl.

Callie prattled on, giving her tour guide's speech on interpretations of all that was to be seen here in the east passage cairn. She spoke of the stone bowl being a receptacle for ashes of cremated family members and how the cairn was constructed to allow light into the chambers, on or around the days of the year that are the fall and spring equinoxes. We all followed her politely and listened quietly to her explanation on the cruciform construct of the east passage and the carvings, curbstones, etc.

I asked occasional questions and Callie was happy to show off her knowledge. Time slipped by quickly and I was surprised when Callie announced that she had to leave us and prepare for her public tour.

"Oh, so soon? We have to go? I was really hoping to study some of the carvings a bit more closely." I pleaded. "Callie, we really appreciate you taking the time for this tour. Could we ask for just a few more minutes to spend in the burial area?"

Finny piped up then. "Well now I think we can do a bit better. Now Callie, seein' as these gorls are practically family and you and I are, well you know what we are, would ye trust us te stay here and not ruin the place without your supervision? I promise, not a soul will ever know we were here. There's no current work goin on here and no tours will come this way. We'll not leave a trace, nor will we break the rules and take pictures. As ye can see, not a one of us is carryin' a camera anyway."

I watched Finny's ears poke out once again and observed Callie's corresponding gush of infatuation. Realizing that Finny was not just flirting, but casting some kind of sensual charismatic spell, I was both enthralled and flabbergasted. Before I knew it, Callie was hugging Nora, Cath and me goodbye and warning Finny not to disappoint her for some upcoming tryst.

"I'll certainly not, my dear." He said with lascivious undertones and incredibly reached around to give her behind a friendly squeeze as he kissed her cheek. An impossibly large woman, she all but flittered down the tight passage carried by her giddiness at Finny's attentions.

Finny watched Callie's backside as she made her way toward the exit and turned to us with a satisfied smile on his face.

"What?" He said as he interpreted the unbelieving expressions on our faces. Cath just shook his head and smiled to himself.

"C'mon then. We've work te do."

Nora finally spoke. "It' not really cruciform."

"What?"

"The passage. Callie said it's cruciform and I guess it is, in a way, but it was constructed after Laoghaire died. This is in the form of the Sword, not a cross. And the bowl isn't a bowl so much as a Shield."

Nora appeared slightly dazed as she looked around the chamber and then it occurred to me that she'd been here before. I understood that she was fully remembering things now.

"Tell us." I said.

"I came and buried the Shield with Laoghaire's parents here in this chamber. The force of the Shield was imbued with magic to protect the bearer of the Shield in unison with the Sword. So it was placed to be utilized as protection for the clan Laoghaire, and all its descendants with the ferocity of the lion, both here and where ever they may travel...even across the sea." She was reflecting inward with a far-away look, watching the memories in her head. "Strong is the king of the sea," she mouthed to herself. "It was around ten years after I buried the Shield when Laoghaire knew it was his time to leave and relinquish the Sword so its Power could be utilized by Faidhe. It was then that I returned here to this site after he left. I don't know; it made me feel closer to him somehow, that I was here with his parents and the Shield. But when I returned here, this Shield was here in stone. I was amazed because I knew no one had brought it here. It's much too large and heavy to have been brought in through the narrow opening. I had a hard enough time bringing the actual Shield through the entrance, never mind a stone that weighs several tons. It's a manifestation of the Power that exists here."

"How do you know?" I asked.

She looked at me with those hawk's eyes. "I know." Looking around she pointed, "I had these chambers added, here to the left and right of the main one, for Laoghaire and myself and here for Morgan and Macha and Macha's family. The chambers created the shape of the Sword hilt here and the stone Shield here at the head formed the symbol for the battles we fought and would fight for generations in the future as well as the symbol for the union of the He and the She Gods."

"What battles do you mean, Nora?" I asked.

"The battle to keep the Goddess from being forgotten. The battle to help Faidhe send Gods and most of the magical creatures under the Sidhe. The struggle to do battle against the force of evil released by Briciu. And you know, maybe it wasn't Briciu that was the evil force on that account, but maybe he was the most viable tool to be used at the time by the opportunistic energy that saw its time come when the world was changing. He was the doorway for true evil to worm its way into the world. Let's face it, there've always been human frailties but this thing took over and capitalized on Briciu's self-centeredness and brought about the blood magic at the exact same time the prophecy was announced and the pendulum was about to swing away from the Goddess and the feminine. So I think the battle we have on our hands now is not only to release the magical energy in the tale and the Cauldron to be utilized in the world today, but to battle the force of evil that's taken over in these modern times."

"Good and evil, the archetypal battle." I said. "Light and dark. He and She. We're back to balance again. So this is no small battle and we're here today for a reason. I spoke with Lucas today and without going into any long explanations, Nora, he told me that the Beast, or the monster, as he calls it, is coming for us before we can get to the museum in Denmark to release the magic. He said that Faidhe told him in his dream that we had to come here for protection. I don't know if it's from the Shield or from our ancestors but that's why we're here. So what do we do?" I asked, looking at Nora.

"How am I supposed to know?" She shot back at me.

"Well, you buried the Shield here. We're here for protection under the Shield. Your immediate family is buried here. You designed the site. *You're* buried here for crying out loud!" I began to feel frantic in my imaginings that we'd never succeed and Lucas would come to some horrible end. Finny and Cath moved to calm me down.

"Stop lass." Cath said. "Stop it! Can ye not smell it?"

All at once I could smell the telltale stench and instinctively grabbed Nora's hands, but the smell didn't diminish. Nora began to pull me by my hands toward the great stone Shield. We held our hands, still clasped across the Shield, she on one side me on the other and she started to recite some kind of a chant in an uncertain voice and grew more assured as she continued:

"Blood to blood, kin to kin
We call the protective Power within
Daughters of the clan we serve and we rule
I claim this Shield now to protect the Light as Her tool"

As I looked across the stone, I observed my sister appear to me as though blinders had fallen from my eyes. There I saw Nora, Colm, a regal queen bearing the burden of the death of her beloved husband, laying him to rest in this cairn, memorializing him with the very symbol of the Sword for which he gave his life in duty. Upon her head was a headdress of hawk's wings with what appeared to be shields on either side.

I was a little awestruck, I said, "The Shield-maiden then, now, always."

Just as I thought our calling to the clan was complete here, Nora bent to the Shield and appeared to pick up, not the stone, but a blue outline of light in the shape of the Shield and absorb it into her very being. I was amazed as I watched, she still appeared to be my sister but to have grown somehow more, radiant or empowered. These were weak words to describe the subtle but infinite change I saw taking place in Nora. Then she pointed toward the stone once again and when I looked to where she pointed, I was amazed to see a blue outline of the Sword, lying over the Shield with its blade toward the exit and its hilt toward the back of the cairn. I didn't hesitate. It was as though I either instinctively knew what to do or I was being guided. Words bubbled up from my throat and I called:

"Blood to blood, kin to kin
We call the protective Power within
Daughters of the clan we serve and we rule
I claim this Sword now to protect the Light as His tool"

I wasn't sure what it would feel like to try and pick up something made of light but when I did grab the hilt of the Sword, it felt just right in my hand. I held the piece, pointed up toward the corbelled roof of the cairn and felt myself absorb the Power and energy from the piece directly into me. I felt energized and Powerful. It felt as though all the tumblers fell into place for me and I was no longer fearful, or unsure. I knew exactly what was necessary to complete our task and I was invigorated with the Power of that knowledge. In a far off, distance voice I heard Nora say, "I am partner to the Sword-wielder then, now, always.

As she and I met eyes across the Stone, we recited simultaneously, "Protectors of the Light."

The illuminated glow that had temporarily lit the chambers subsided and as my eyes adjusted I looked around for some evidence of the monumental thing that just took place or a clue as to what comes next. I took a closer look at the carvings on the stone shield in front of me.

"Hey look at that. It's different. I thought it was a hand on the stone before. Now it's like a sun and a moon." Then all at once, my interpretation of the pictures shifted so I recognized and had the knowledge of the actual meaning intended in the carvings.

"Oh." I said.

"Oh, what?" Cath inquired. "I've been studying this piece for years, listening to various academic interpretations. I'm inclined te see it as the sun and moon meself, as the balance between masculine and feminine, the Mother Moon and Father Sun."

"Well it is, Cath." I answered. "But look at it this way."

I moved so the graphic on the stone could be observed from a different angle that placed the moon above and the sun as if it had just come from or through the moon. "If this is the moon here," I pointed. "That is the Mother and she is the portal..." I waited to see if he'd put it together.

"Oh." He repeated my word at his own discovery. "Yes, I see. On the Shield is the story, really of what its protection is for. The moon is the mother, the birthing canal and she gives birth to, eh, not the sun, but the Light!"

"That's it." Nora said. "In all its simplicity, we're going to protect the Light. The return of the balance in a renewed respect for the feminine and balance in the world as a modicum of humanity returns and so on."

"But the truth of it is, you're the Shield, and I'm the Sword, Lucas is the Light. So it's him we have to protect because he'll be the one who begins to restore the balance."

I looked to Nora for her response and found her to be looking around the chambers again. Tears began to stream once more as she walked over toward the chamber where she and Laoghaire were laid to rest.

"I knew when he left that he wasn't coming back. He'd promised me that I would see his face again and I held onto that with hope, but I knew when we said goodbye that he wouldn't be back." She reflected and gave a rye snort. "I did see his face again though, didn't I? I guess it was one of the first faces I saw when I was born into this time, so he kept his promise. But I lost my Laoghaire when he returned the Sword."

Cath and Finny looked at their feet. They knew what had happened to Laoghaire but I didn't have that information in my memory anywhere. How could I? Lon Dubh had never returned to Ireland. And Colm and I communicated less and less over the years. I voiced what I was thinking.

"The last time I saw any of you was when Cathbad came to our village in the mountains searching for Fion. At that point, the news was that you, Laoghaire and the children were all doing well. I didn't know what happened." It wasn't a question, but I waited for Nora to tell me how Laoghaire had died.

"As I slept one night, some moons after, ah a couple of months after Laoghaire took to the road with his Sword, I woke with a vision of him standing at the edge of the Lake of the Ivory Heron, the Lough Corrib, in our homeland. He was road worn and thinner but still sturdy and beautiful. I didn't hear what he was saying but he spoke some words over the water where the veil between worlds is thin and then took a currach out to the middle of the lake. Once he got there, he said something else and threw the Sword into the depths and I couldn't be sure what it was, but I thought I saw a hand come up from the water and grasp the Sword before taking it down to the bottom. The boat began to take on water and it was difficult for me to watch Laoghaire struggle to bring it back to shore but he succeeded. Once he put his feet on shore again, he turned to face the water. He looked like he was in reflection on all that had come to pass when this thing, this dirty, filthy thing scrambled from the bushes and plunged a shard of stone into Laoghaire's back. He was totally defenseless and couldn't reach to stop the flow of blood. It was as if as soon as he finished his task with the Sword and had returned it to the Gods, he was at once vulnerable and the lurking evil took its opportunity."

"What was the thing Nora? What killed him?"

She turned those hawk's eyes on me once again and spoke words that made perfect sense, but made me go cold.

"It was Nemain. After the world moved on, she stayed where the Tuatha De Danann had once flourished, waiting and watching for Triag to return. She went crazy and took up residence on the Hill saying she was the new Keeper but there was nothing left to keep. She performed all kinds of dark rituals and magic. And as Finny has told us, she dabbled in bringing Briciu back from the dead but got tangled up in her own dark magic somehow as some kind of host to his spirit, so as soon as Laoghaire was no longer protected by the magic of the Sword, my protective magic with the Shield was not enough to keep him safe against the Beast's blood quest to kill him. I knew he was dead and so I sent Cuan with some others on fast horses to retrieve his body so he could have a proper burial here." She turned inward again and was quiet for a moment before she said, "I guess I should have been grateful that Nemain was insane and half dead from lack of food and neglect. Once Laoghaire was dead, she left him there without another thought when he could have been desecrated in so many ways like his own parents had been. Maybe my protection helped in some small way and I know he was watched over by the Gods because Cuan told me when they arrived at Lough Corrib, they found him just where I told them to look, but he was completely surrounded by hundreds, maybe thousands of crows and ravens, but not touched by a single one."

She looked at me with almost a grateful smile at this, as if somehow it was my doing that he'd been protected, but I hadn't even known he was killed. It wasn't my doing, but evidence of the Gods' presence at his time of death.

Nora finished her story. "Even though he was there for a long time, out in the open, *no* animal or bird feasted on his body. The men were able to wrap his remains intact and bring him home to me. It took some years but when these chambers were ready, I was able to place his ashes here with his parents and with the symbols of the Sword and Shield."

"Nora, I'm sorry." I said.

"That was then, this is now." She answered with a forlorn smile.

I thought of her husband Will and fought to keep my knowledge of what he was up to out of my mind for the moment. There was no reason for her to lose two husbands in one day.

"Are we finished here?" I asked no one in particular.

"I think so." Nora replied.

"Right." Cath said. "It feels as though all the energy here is calm and quiet. Let's be gettin' back. Bridey'll be wonderin' about us."

I opened the door to our room and stopped dead in my tracks. Nora came up short behind me and saw the room torn apart. Our clothes were shredded and thrown around the room, all our toiletries were shattered and squished with fragrant shampoos, pastes and such smeared all over the walls in vile euphemisms for women and their body parts. I was relieved that because I carried my satchel with me no matter where we were going, there was really nothing in the room I valued that couldn't be replaced. On the heels of that thought, I was panicked.

"Cath! Finny!" I yelled down the corridor as they opened the door to their own room. I saw it register on Finny's face as he opened their door that the same had happened to them. The dawning realization mobilized us all toward Bridey's room door. Cath banged on her door and called to her.

"Bridey? Bridey! Open yer door, woman. C'mon now, we've need te see yer face."

There was no answer. I ran back to Finny and Cath's room where the door still stood open. I barged through and unlocked the door that connected the rooms to get into Bridey's room, hoping it was not locked from her side. I felt the presence of the others behind me and turned for reassurance as I pushed the door open. I wanted to see Bridey but was frightened at what we all knew could be found there in her room. I took a breath and saw a shamble in her rooms just as we'd found in ours but no Bridey. I stalked across the room toward the bathroom, dreading what I'd find there and had a similar moment before I opened that door too. What a mess; but no Bridey.

The emotions I felt were a mixture of relief and fear of the unknown.

"Where is she?"

"Let's us take a minute to regroup and inspect what's been done here. She may have gone for a bite or something." Finny said with lame hope.

We all knew it wasn't likely, just as we all knew who did this. But there was nothing else to do so we stayed together and searched each room for any clue we could find.

———

I sat on Bridey's bed and sent out my mind in search of where she might be, whether she is still alive and what she might be able to tell us if she is. I couldn't find any glimmer of what I sought. There was no hint, clue or premonition. Nothing. I tried not to think of that as confirmation that she wasn't alive.

"I think we should call the front desk, Cath." I said. "But if there is some kind of upset with Bridey being missing, then we'll have to stay here and we won't be able to get to Denmark. I know it sounds awful, but if the Beast is getting stronger, then that's all the more reason why we need to get on that plane. That was probably its goal in doing all this." I opened my arms at the obvious. "This is just what Lucas said: That the Beast is really mad and scared about what we're planning to do in Copenhagen. If we're tied up here for days, maybe more with police business, we're screwed."

"Delicately put, Lee." Nora chided.

I was about to say something when I heard scratching at the door of Bridey's room. We all looked to each other and Finny signaled for us all to be quiet. As quick as one can imagine, the two old men were at the door and before I could even wonder what they were about to do, Cath pulled the door open and Finny was charging the person on the other side.

"What do ye think yer doin' ye old fools!" Bridey hollered up at the men from the floor where she lay surrounded by several bags. "What's wrong wi' ye!"

Apparently, when she was upset, her accent thickened because she was practically spitting "ye" with the best of them as Cath and Finny helped her to her feet.

"Leave me be ye amadans! Are ye daft? And why are ye after hittin' me like a couple of bulls?" She saw the condition of her room and looked to Nora and me with recognition on her face. "I've seen the likes of this mess before now haven't I? Those mucs are here now aren't they?" She asked as she collected her bags and came into the room to look around.

I didn't know what a muc was but it sounded about right and I nodded.

"They did this to our house before but they didn't tear things up then so they must be escalating or feeling more desperate. So they're here and they know where we are. We thought they took you." I said to Bridey. "Or worse."

Bridey thought about that for a moment and shivered a little revulsion of all the thought implied.

"I've known those three for eight years and the idea of being in the same room with them doesn't appeal to me at all. It's good as I've been without my own clothes since we left the farm, I took to shoppin' for some clean clothes and unmentionables to change into while I'm here." Another scan of the room and Bridey sat hard on her bed. "We'll have to stay together from now on until you get on the plane. One of us alone won't be safe now."

I remembered feeling panicked in the parking garage and just now realized that I felt their presence. You're right Bridey, I think we need to stay together. What do you mean when *we* get on the plane? You're coming too."

"I'm not. I've been pleased to find my boys again and to fill in blank spaces in history for you but I've no place over there. And you'll not be needin' to fret over my safety while you should be lookin out for your own. Now I'll be sorry to miss meetin' another of you girls but I've a farm to tend and, it seems, a house to let, so you go about what you must and promise ye'll come see me anytime you find yourself back in Erie. You know now, you always have a place to stay."

I started to protest but Bridey wouldn't allow it. "I've a farm hand and his boy tendin' te the hayin' and the milkin' and the sheep will keep a bit on their own, but I have to go home, and soon. So when you board your plane tomorrow, I'll take your car back home and see it's returned at the airport. Anything you'll need sent home again, I'll send by post for you too."

"But those men..."

With a hand up to hear no more she said, "Those men have abandoned the cottage and my neighbor tells me they set it ablaze and left, apparently in search of you girls. Now as you've come through and they know who you are, they'll be on your trail, not mine. I'll be needed back home to see to things there."

"It's decided then," Finny agreed. "Now lets us see to what can be done about these rooms."

———

After disposing of most of our clothes and salvaging what little we could, the rooms were cleaned up with a little water and elbow grease. The soap and shampoo washed right off the walls and there was little that we couldn't replace during a trip to the hotel store. Nora and I did a quick shop for a few days' worth of clothes and returned to the rooms to find little evidence that anything had been wrong.

The last thing I did before we all turned in early was to keep my promise to Lucas and call home. I spoke with him an assured him that everything was going according to plan. He filled me in on their day at the Freedom Trail. He told me in hushed tones that he knew people were staring at him and paying attention to him.

"When I listened to their thoughts, Mom, I could hear that something was trying to tell them to get at me. One guy looked nice and smiled at me, but I could tell he hurt other kids before. He took them and did things to them that hurt."

I could feel the blood rise in my face and I watched the strange phenomena as I saw my hands begin to be outlined with a bluish glow. I felt the Sword working within me, ready to strike any who would harm my son.

"Don't worry Mom." He said. "I stuck right with Dad and everything was fine. He even held my hand! It was good. You know what was funny though?"

"What Hon?"

"Everything the tour guy was saying, I already knew. It was like I already learned it in school or something. But I don't remember learning it. I just knew things. It was really cool. I was telling Dad all kinds of history stuff as we were walking the trail and he said I was really smart."

"You are smart Lucas. And we're both so proud of you. Keep doing what you're doing and keep yourself safe until we can come home and be with you. It won't be much longer now."

"Dren?" He said, knowing it wasn't the right phrase but enjoying it as if it were a private joke.

"Yep. I'm going to 'call Dren' and together we're going to kick some butt. We're leaving on a plane to get there tomorrow. And when we're done, I'll be home to you as fast as I can."

"Good. Wanna talk to Dad?" He seemed content that it was almost over and took comfort that I'd be home soon. God, he has such faith in me. I wasn't going to let him down.

"Sure, Baby. I love you. Sleep tight."

"Kay, love you too. Bye. Oh, I almost forgot, tell your friend that Faidhe says she can go home. Those guys won't be back."

I shook my head at how fast he was coming into whatever it is in his future. He could see into people's minds, shed light on their thoughts and he was developing a wealth of information from places unknown. *Bringer of light and knowledge.* My mind whispered. But none of it surprised or bothered him. He just took it all in stride.

"I'll tell her." I said. "And Luke, I really am proud of you."

"I know Mom. Here comes Dad. Bye again. Hold on."

"Hello. Is this the world traveler?" Came Walter's voice over miles of airwaves. It was like a breath of fresh air to hear him.

"Hi. You're showing him a good time aren't you? And all kinds of educational trips too. Good for you."

"Hold on one second." Walter said. "Luke, go brush and get ready for bed." He waited a few seconds for Lucas to go, then back to me he said, "Okay, what's going on?"

Trying to keep some level of normalcy, I answered with newsy stuff about our trip.

"Well, tomorrow we're going to study an ancient Celtic cauldron that's closely tied with my research and..."

"Lee." He interrupted. "Not about your trip. What's really going on?"

"What do you mean?" I asked. Feeling exposed for some reason.

"I see something happening with Luke. He dreams all the time now and talks to people who aren't there. He knows things no eight year old should know and like just now, how does he know about what's going on there with you?"

"Oh, you heard all that?"

"Mm hmm."

"What can I say that won't sound like I'm crazy?" I waited. Walter said nothing. "It'll all sound crazy so I'll just tell you." I searched my mind for how to begin. "You know how my family sees things and we know each other's thoughts sometimes?"

"Yeah."

"And you know how Luke and I can communicate sometimes without talking?" There was a hesitation and he answered,

"Not really."

"Well we do. Sometimes we dream the same dreams, sometimes he answers my questions and I don't ask them out loud. I've always known when he was sad or hurt. It's always been like that for us. But there's so much more going on now than just mother's intuition, Walter. Our whole family but especially Lucas is in danger. What we're doing over here now has to do with all of that and we're trying to make it so that we're all, all right."

I knew this wasn't going well. I knew I sounded loony and I wasn't explaining myself at all clearly. I took a deep breath and tried to start again but Walter spoke first.

"Does Will have anything to do with what you're talking about?" I was shocked and alarmed but seized the opening. I grabbed hold of his understanding like a life preserver.

"Yes! He's an example of what's out there that could hurt Luke. He's not himself is he?"

I glanced at Nora through the open door connecting our rooms, sitting with Bridey on a bed in the guy's room and felt a momentary pang of sorrow for her.

"No. He's not. But it's not just Will, is it?"

"What do you mean?"

"I'm not blind. Everyplace I've had Luke lately, people stare at him and I can feel, well, I feel that something is behind those friendly faces that's not...the friendly faces are not sincere. So I've been keeping him close."

I can't remember Walter ever talking about 'feeling' things before and again I took the opening.

"Okay, so here we go. Everything I'm about to tell you is the God's honest truth. I can't waste time trying to convince you. You just have to trust me...I've been in contact with Lucas practically since we left home in our minds and sometimes, I can kind of project myself to be with him too. All kinds of strange things have happened since we came here. Our abilities have increased...a lot. And I've discovered things about our heritage that mean Lucas is very special in his abilities. Lucas has magical abilities that outstrip my sisters' and mine in a big way and they're about to get bigger. Because of this, there are people who will want to either exploit him or hurt him or worse. Those people can even be people we know and wouldn't imagine wanting to harm him, but like Will, they won't be themselves. There's something that changes them and capitalizes on their weaknesses. Something we know as the Beast. Lucas calls it the..."

"Monster?"

"Yeah."

"He dreams about the monster. I hear him. But the scary thing is, when he dreams about it, I swear I can..."

"Smell it."

"Yeah. And sometimes I know what I'm dreaming is what he's dreaming too. If this is what it's like for you all the time, I don't know how you stand it. It's just too weird. How'd you know about the smell?"

"That's what we've been battling over here. It's part of an ancient force of evil and we're directly in its path because Luke is the opposing force of Light..."

I waited to see if he was going to get fed up and deny all of this as nonsense. When he didn't say anything, I pushed on.

"We've been here trying to learn all we can about what is going on and how best to protect Luke. The long and the short of it is, he's coming into this Power and it's unavoidable so it's up to us to help and guide him 'cause there're big things coming and we're a part of it."

There was still silence on the line. Never one to travel too far from the borders of Normal Town, Walter had always known about my family and our abilities but just accepted and ignored it. He never asked about it and never participated in any of our rituals. He never wanted to know about it. So I figured he just might roll his eyes and think this was another weirdo facet to being married to me.

"I've been having dreams too." He said.

I didn't expect that but it made sense. If Cath was right, it was his blood of the German and Italian heritage that brought all the old bloodlines together in Lucas. "What are you dreaming?"

"I, ah - there's a woman. She's a little wisp of a thing. She looks like a fairy or something. Sometimes she's young and other times she's old. She tells me some of the same things you're telling me. I've been talking with her practically since you left for Ireland. At first it bothered me, but then she started telling me about things like where to take Lucas and that I should keep him with me all the time and I should pay more attention to him. She sounds a lot like you! I say I dream about her but it's more like visits; the dreams are so real! She told me there was something I needed to know about Will so I drove over there with Luke...and...well..."

"Walter, I know about him. Luke told me and you're right. He's one to be aware of and keep distance from. I know all of this requires more explanation but I don't think I'm going to be able to fill you in now. Nora doesn't know about Will and that other woman so I can't really discuss it with you now. But please, talk to Luke and he'll let you know what's been going on. If everything goes well, we'll meet Patrice in Denmark tomorrow and hopefully put all this to rest."

"You're not so much doing research anymore are you?"

"I'm getting more than I bargained for in my research, Honey but not for school or publication. This research is for how to survive. Anything we considered normal is probably a thing of the past. We have to deal with things as they are now. I know you probably feel like you fell down the rabbit hole Walter, but you're a part of this and you have to let yourself trust that we are part of something larger than us. Our normal lives are taking a path to serve the greater good but at the center of it all is Lucas. And we can't let him down. So you stay with him and keep him safe without scaring him. Talk with him about what he knows, sees and feels. Learn from each other. You have to because I'm not there now and he'd usually come to me with all this but now it has to be you. I've found out so much about our lineage, both yours and mine, and they're tied together. But just trust me; ask Luke about what he knows and I'll try to fill you in when I can."

"I don't understand any of this."

"I know; you've always worked to avoid the un-normal and who knows, maybe on some level that was because you knew you were so close to the rabbit hole? Why else would you have married me? But you can't avoid it or deny it anymore so you have to take the plunge and allow yourself to talk with the woman, ask her questions and try to remember her answers. If she's who I think she is, her name is Faidhe. And talk to Luke too. He knows who she is and he may be able to help you understand.

If nothing else, I was relieved that Walter understood the gravity of the situation. That was obvious in his tone. He'd just have to feel his way around for the rest.

"I love you. We'll get through this together. I'll let you know what we find out and how things go."

I thought about how I'd tell this man who clung so tightly to chronological, concrete thinking, how I'd been through many lives and learned of magic and was a living Sword, just vibrating with blue light to smite the enemy with my sisters, the living Shield and Cauldron. Not to mention that my whole family was a living bloodline and portal for the spirits to utilize to fight an ancient prophesy of world destruction.

"I love you too. Be careful," was all he could muster in his state of bizarre-world overload.

"I will." I said and pushed the button on the phone to hang up. I turned my attention to the others and Nora was looking straight at me. I held the phone out to her asking wordlessly if she wanted to use it.

She declined the offer. "We both know there's no one there for me now."

I didn't bother denying it. "Let's take turns keeping watch tonight. Bridey, it seems as though you're right. My son seems to think you're in no danger if you go home. It'll be the rest of us that will need to be on guard in our travels."

50

Homeward Bound

The Beast guided him in his survival. He stole what he needed or killed for it. Food was in supply despite the cold and frozen spring. The Beast did not discriminate between the flesh of creatures and the flesh of man. If Triag happened across a person or party, he put forth his devious skills of feigning friendship, cajoling, usefulness and manipulation, learned well from his grandmother over the years, to be accepted then trusted. Once his purpose was served in gaining food or information on how to find passage back to his island, often the fate of his new companions was to be robbed, slaughtered or both.

It was a frustration for Triag to realize that without Fion to aid in translation with the people of these lands, he was at the mercy of broken phrases he'd picked up and primitive signs to gain the information he sought. There were a few occasions he came across people whose minds were available to him and he took full advantage, not only to find a seaport with ships and trade, but he would glean any bit of information that would be of use to him.

When alone, Triag would allow his true nature to run amuck and he would fly into unprovoked rages at the thought of the Elf and how he'd been thwarted from obtaining the Cauldron. The hatred grew and consumed him, in Triag's mind the Elf could be blamed for all that frustrated him. He believed it was Fion who had usurped his rightful place as Morgan's true friend. He would have taken Lon Dubh in his first rights if it weren't for the Elf's interference. He had convinced himself that if it were not for the wicked Elf, he would not have such a difficult time finding his way home. Soon, in his mind, all that was a hindrance or frustration to him bore the name of Fion. Some evenings, Triag lit fires all around him with his magical ability and danced naked in the ring of fire admiring his beastly arousal at the many mental scenarios he conjured of killing, gutting and defiling the Elf. "The cursed Elf with the mocking eyes."

The rages and rituals Triag performed over the moons that Triag traveled, were encouraged by the aunt thing that seduced him homeward. If it were not for her constant voice in his head, Triag may have been lost to their cause and have gone completely over to the call of the savage. But as it was, Nemain stoked the fire of hatred in Triag and he was able to keep up the façade of sanity for as long as it was necessary until one day, at the cost of his grandmother's remaining firestone, he stepped off a ship to once more feel the energy of his homeland meet his feet.

Now with hair on his face and not much flesh on him and tightly muscled, had there been anyone in the village of the Tuatha De Danann to greet him, his clan members would not have recognized Triag. More than 14 seasons had passed since he left these parts and all that was left of the Tuatha De Danann were the ruins of the village and the wreck of a woman he had known as his aunt.

"What's this?" He raged. "For this I have given up my youth and birthright? I come home for a victor's welcome and all that remains here for me is a wreaking, hag, black in teeth and festering of vermin? Where is my kingdom? Where are my cattle? What of all your talk of reward? I have been deceived!"

Triag's ill temper escalated at the sense of betrayal that all his hard work and sacrifice, as he perceived it, was for nothing.

"Witch, I shall snap your neck for this." He growled. And it was no empty promise. He saw nothing but his own revenge as he approached Nemain who seemed not the least menaced by his threat.

As Triag reached the spot where Nemain sat upon the altar in the former Circle on the Hill, he forcefully grabbed the woman by her upper arm and pulled her to her feet. He noticed that there was naught but a thin layer of flesh on her bones and was repulsed by her. He would exact his revenge for all the mistreatment he had endured and he would enjoy the taking of this one slowly.

"Snapping your neck will be too quick a death for you, Hag."

In a movement that was faster than Triag's eyes could register, Nemain had him so securely by his neck that she was able to raise his weight enough that he stood on his toes with the force of her strength.

"You will calm yourself, boy. I did not remain and live in solitude here for no reason. You have done no more than any of us in this. The truth is, times have moved on and much is changed here. The magic is ebbing now and we must do what is necessary to cast for our future. Now, you will tell us of the ritual Faidhe used to raise the Power of the Gods and what she did and said when she cast her magic. We must know exactly in order to duplicate what was cast and use it for our own benefit. We have waited long but it may be that the time we will have to wait is not over. We will do what it takes to obtain all the Power due us as the rightful heirs to that Power."

Triag was struck not by the strength of the woman but by the putrescence of the smell gurgling up from her innards as she spoke. There was nothing of the plain woman he had known remaining in this husk but as he looked in her eyes, he recognized a glimpse of who she used to be but more disturbingly, he knew he recognized a filmy, hazy-like existence of his own father in there as well. There was something unnatural and otherworldly about this creature, but there was a soothing attraction as he was captured in fright, by the draw of those eyes. His body relaxed and he felt a gush of release as he realized his body had let go of its waste.

"Ah now, there's the boy I remember." She crooned, as she settled his weight back on his own feet. "I have raised your father and he is a bit petulant at sharing this body with me. There has been a price but it has been served. The Laoghaire is dead and Briciu has had his revenge although not the glorious revenge he'd hoped for but the blood has been spilled at my hand to allow for Briciu's return to the flesh. It is now up to you and me to create the vessel for him to return and be whole. This is first."

"What are you saying?" Triag stepped back when he realized what Nemain meant to do.

"Are you in such short memory, Nephew?" Forget you the very act I offer you now is one that you so often begged me to allow not so long ago?"

There had been many a season passed for Nemain and they had not been kind to her. Triag had figured he spent some ten of those seasons in ageless suspension while he waited for Faidhe to take her Council with the Valkyrie woman. For Triag, only four or so seasons had passed in his age while Nemain had aged beyond 14 additional seasons and that time had stripped her of her youth. Neglect, exposure and poor food supply had taken its toll. She looked to be much older than her 32 or 33 seasons.

"I will not!" He roared in revulsion. "And likely you cannot. You are withered and probably past all bearing."

Nemain cackled at the comment. "I am not so old as that, boy. I still have the blood of the mother and I am ripe for the seed."

He was appalled and disgusted as she pulled aside the rags she wore to expose the loose skin of her belly and the matted triangle below. She looked at him with those eyes again and Triag felt the pull of a perverse draw to her eyes and her voice. What was worse, he felt his manhood grow with the very idea of such a repulsive union. A part of him shrieked inside to escape this insanity but he felt himself succumb. Triag didn't know what it was that called him to such an objectionable union but he allowed himself to give over to the perverse pleasure in the very idea that what he would do with Nemain was aberrant.

The three remained in the remnants of the village and waited until the child grew stronger. By sheer conviction and tenacity of their goal, Nemain and Triag raised the child some seven seasons until such time he was strong enough to play the role of the vessel for Briciu. They performed the dark magic necessary, using all manner of foulness to extricate the Briciu essence from Nemain and give him a human form once again. Once the deed was complete, the union of their sordid plans bound the three. They formed a repugnant triune that would serve to sustain the bloodline necessary to carry their plans to the future.

When the boy had reached the age of eight seasons, the family had conducted their magical ritual they hoped would guarantee them passage into the future life at just the right time to be ready when, as Faidhe had said, "the Fifth Civilization is ushered." They had devised a tale of their own sort in that Triag told them over and again of the magic Faidhe cast and the words used along with the implements she had conjured. They speculated on the best replacement ingredients to use in order to prepare their own dark ritual. The plan would come to fruition on the day when the sun, as Nemain informed them, would go dark and dim in the daytime sky. They would cast magic for the return of all three at a time in the future when these others, Lon Dubh, Colm, and Iarann were to come in, for it would be these three, Triag knew from the mind of Fion that would know where to seek the Cauldron and how to release its Power. This is the time they would petition to return. Precisely with these others so they might regain what they saw as rightfully theirs.

The three had prepared a charred black bowl, carved of burned and cured wood, a staff made of whalebone washed up on the shore and carved into the phallus of a man. The very stone shard Nemain used to take Laoghaire's life was utilized as the sword and a leather sheath, to cover the sharpened stone was used as a shield of protection against Faidhe's magic for to cover the knife that still bore the magical blood of Laoghaire was powerful and just the type of protection they sought: protection from being foiled by their enemies. In place of the bird's feathers, which Triag knew had significance in Faidhe's ritual, these three used hides of the only remaining animals at their disposal in the region. Those of long dead sow carcasses. Nemain contributed the withered balloch skin she'd tucked away from the bull Laoghaire had felled so long ago, saved for just such an occasion while Triag and the boy scoured the refuse of long dead cattle for a scrap of unscavenged skin to offer the fire. Finally, they came up with the snout of a bore bull and a sow's ear untouched by the elements or foraging animals.

The three stood around the fire in front of the altar in the desecrated circle of the old ones gone under to the Sidhe. Nemain lit the fire and placed upon it, the blackened bowl. Within the bowl was a crusted layer of salt from dried sweat accumulated for the ritual from all three participants. Added to the bowl were saliva and urine from all three and semen from Triag. The other two had contributed parts of themselves as well for Nemain had saved the afterbirth from the birth of the child and from his unnatural birth, Briciu used the stump from his belly Nemain had saved when it had dried and fallen off. All of these objects were the antithesis of the purity of Faidhe's ritual, which was designed in love and self-sacrifice. These pieces drew from the underside of magic but were no less Powerful.

As the sun from the daytime was eclipsed in the sky, they had not much time and worked to build a fire large enough to consume the bowl and all within it in a brief period of time before the sunlight returned to the sky. The fire torched skyward and the sun faded. Nemain spoke stolen verses that mimicked Faidhe's incantations in bringing the three participants back to reclaim the Cauldron at the right period of time.

When the fire had consumed the bowl and all its contents, Nemain raised what appeared to be a dark ball of energy from amidst the flames. It was not light, but the absence of it. The orb appeared as grayish black and murky smoke. As it came from the flames and began to spin whiddershins, counter sunwise, it lodged at the space between the stones at the base of the altar and from beyond the portal could be heard bleating and squeals of pain ridden animals.

Nemain uttered the final words of the ritual designed by all three and just as she completed her role in the ritual, Triag unceremoniously brought a blade out from under his robes that by this time were rags, and slit her throat from behind.

"I'm sorry aunt, but there was blood spilt at the last ritual and I couldn't take the chance that this magic would not be sealed without it once again. You will be our portal to the next life. We will be birthed through your magic and your sacrifice. Be proud, aunt."

He allowed her body to drop heavily, without regard, to the ground and flayed open her midsection. Savagely cutting, he ripped out her feminine organs and tossed them to the fire where they sputtered and sizzled along with the rest of the refuse from the ritual.

"It is only fitting so that we will be born to our next life, a womb is given in the offering. That done, Triag turned to his son.

"Now Briciu, we will see what kind of father you have taught me to be."

The look of fascinated interest the boy wore on his face as he watched Triag cut open Nemain and utilize her fertility organs to consecrate the magic they had wrought, suddenly went cold with fear. For though he was a strong spirit, he'd been reborn with the frailties of a human boy. And although he'd been well taken care of until the ritual had taken place. Briciu knew he was now at the mercy of Triag.

Triag mocked. "You are reborn Briciu and you will come again to this world as you have petitioned but I have heard it said, 'Be careful for what you petition, for the Gods may grant it ways that are not at all convenient for you.' Come now, we must find our way in the world and find us suitable brood-cows to carry the line of our seed.

———

On June 30, 1954, during an eclipse of the sun, on an island in the Shetlands, located halfway between Ireland and the Norse lands, a woman bore three sons into a heartless life without a mother. When they were born, she gave them life and then bled to death through the careless incision made to pull the babies from her womb. For the mother, it was a mercy to be shut of the life with the man she'd married. The boys' hard father wanted nothing to do with the whelps and sent all three to be reared in a Catholic orphanage in Ireland.

51

Birds Take Flight

Being lulled by the engines of the plane vibrating under me, watching clouds streak by the window, I mused to myself how we'd come to this all so quickly and yet it seemed like a very long time ago that I was at least close to being a normal person, living a normal life with money troubles, expanding crow's feet, and an overly stressful schedule. Now, I'm halfway around the world with two relative strangers and virtually no worldly possessions other than what I could fit into a well-worn satchel. Even more fascinating was that all of it, the magic, the Beast, the quest, that fantastic tale, all of it felt absolutely right. I marveled at how many other people in the world lived uneventful lives to the naked eye but who might also contribute to the world in ways that no one else will ever know about or appreciate. I thought of Laoghaire and Craiche, Iarann, Faidhe and even Gara. There'd be no history book passages about them. No one would name an alley in Boston after them. There would be no story on Biography or the History Channel. I guessed true altruism often leads one away from family, halfway across the world without fame or fortune or even a suitcase for that matter. But my quest in all this did have a personal payoff. In truth, I wasn't really in this to save the world at all. There was one small group of people for whom I would give my life, the people who made *my* world and one person in particular for whom I would go to the ends of the earth and beyond. In that moment, I knew Faidhe far better than I probably ever had during a time when we saw each other daily. I would give all that I am for my child and in that knowledge, I understood her choice to enter into a debt by spilling blood, her choice to walk a lonely path, give up both love and her future for the sake of her children.

I shook my head and pulled out of my thoughts. I guessed we needed a plan.

"So what did you learn about those brothers? Maybe we don't know where they are right now, and you might be confident that they won't be back to hurt Bridey, but I'd feel better knowing where they are and what they're doing."

Cath said, "Well, given what information Bridey's had, I did some diggin' te find out what I could. Historically, these are three men, brothers, born in Unst, the northern most inhabited island of the Shetlands of the British Isles. Easily traced, they were, due te the fact that they're brothers all born on the same day."

"Triplets?"

"Aye. Bridey was no fool in gettin' all the application information she could before lettin' the cottage te these three. She knew they were brought te her region as a result of her magic cast te draw key players in the retorn of those from the past so she insisted on gettin' all the background on them she could. And they, wantin' and drawn te be where they knew they'd eventually come inte contact with ye gorls, found they had to oblige and be truthful. It was easy enough te discover their origins by findin' the date of their mother's death on the island and tracin' their line through their father from there. It seems these are not random people; chosen as easy prey for the Beast te take advantage of their character flaws. It seems they are of a much-maligned bloodline here in these parts. The O'Tarbh clan, meanin' son of the bull, a rag-tag bunch, known for strange habits and such, left Ireland on their own before they were thrown out at the time yer St. Columba," Cath said this last with a nod to Nora, "came te these parts and shewd them away for their unholy behaviors."

Finny broke in, "Now given' the name, I'd say we're dealin' with direct descendants of Triag for it was he who saw all that Faidhe cast in her final magic and at that moment was so intent upon puttin' hands te the Cauldron. I did get a glimpse that he and Nemain were plannin' te take what he'd seen there and put it te use. And although I didn't see another porson there, I most definitely felt the presence of another. And that presence was one I'd not felt the likes of again until recently when I had call te pinch me brother back to his senses. So I'm of a mind te think that it's the one called Briciu that set this all te works in the forst place."

"Cath," I inquired. "What do you mean *her* Columba?"

"Apparently," Nora answered. "You and I have lived many lives together, Lee, but this was one I remember but have no real recollection of you during that time. I was Columba. Get it? Colm means dove. Saint Columba was a big deal in the Catholic Church, bringing affairs of Rome to Ireland, sometimes called Columcille, Dove of the Church. He...I had a mentor in a certain St. Finian, the mysterious man who developed the monastic life from humble beginnings." She looked at Finny with a sheepish grin as he twiddled his thumbs and a smile played around his lips.

"We've all kept our hand in through the years, I suppose. I'd no idea it was you or rather, I should say I'd no way of knowin' but as ye'd had account of comin' from the royal line of the Laoghaire at that time, as great, grandson te the last Laoghaire himself, I had some idea, due te the name, ye see."

"So Nora-St. Columba, what? Exiled these O'Tarbh people from Ireland?" I asked.

"Might as well have; they left before they were thrown out." Finny answered. "And they went, but it seems at the time when you gorls were comin' back inte the world as Faidhe had ordained, these three, amadans, as Bridey calls them, were born te this time as well and were retorned as infants te this land te be raised in the arms of a place, most devoid of anything nurtuin' or lovin'."

"Are you saying that these men, these brothers have come into this world the way we did? They have a conscious purpose? What is it; to get the Cauldron? Or is it worse, is it to get to Lucas?"

"It's likely both, Lass. I can't imagine that they don't know about the Cauldron. But it's possible they had no memory of the past until recently much the same as yerselves. Likely they've been drawn te knowledge of cortain things as ye've experienced. So we must assume they know of the same things we do. But I don't think they'll be tryin fer the boy until they capture the Power of the bowl. They'll likely understand that he's too strong for them if they approach him without the Power the Cauldron can offer te even the playin' field so te speak." Cath responded.

"Where are they now? Can you tell?"

"I can't. Or I haven't been able to up 'til now."

Nora speculated, "Well I think we can assume that they didn't come all the way through time to fail now. We'll probably be seeing them sometime soon if they know about the Cauldron...where it is, I mean."

"I've been put in mind just lately of a surge of dark energy and the most repulsive of unnatural vision of a ritual vile in its makeup that came te me some time after Cath and I retorned here to our home all those many years ago. I could see there was dark magic cast with ill intent by Triag. It was a glimpse through his mind, at least, that I saw what took place. The magic was cast during an eclipse of the sun in these parts. It makes sense te me that the magic cast by these minions of the Beast was cast during a time when the light is taken from the very orth. It seems, according te the resorch I've been conductin' these three were born te our current time during an eclipse of the sun in 1954. And just lately, on the day of August 1st, there was a solar eclipse once again, and it seems te have increased the abilities of these three te the point where they can seek with their minds and destroy with impunity. Their Powers are growing just as yours are, but this recent surge of the darkness under the same state in which they were fledged from the past and born into in these times has given them added strength and perhaps, they've come te their memory as ye gorls have done."

I got goose bumps as I thought, while we were singing happy birthday to Mary, those mucs were just down the road growing in strength. I remembered the look the fattest one gave to me, as we pulled away in our little car that day and shuddered in revulsion. Then a thought occurred to me.

"Hey, August 1st is Mary's birthday. If Mary is Gara and these things are Triag, Nemain and Briciu, and she was so involved with them as their mother and grandmother, is she a threat to us, to Lucas?"

Finny looked at Cath and they didn't say anything for a full minute until Cath's answer hit me like a slap across the face. "We don't know."

"What?" I shouted. To any observers, until now, we were just four people quietly having a pleasant conversation on the plane but now people turned and craned necks to see what was going on. I lowered my voice. "What do you mean?"

Cath educated, "Well it seems she's a wild card in all this now isn't she? She gave life te two of these and reared the other. She was involved in the shedding of the blood of one but had been chosen by Faidhe to come through in her stead. She is now the flesh of the line, not only of Laoghaire and Colm, but also of Sigrdifa and Iarann, just as you are yerselves. We see that the three of ye that will unleash the Power of the Cauldron are of the Bowl, Sword and Shield but Gara is the living Staff. She will be the one te deliver the message. What the message is, we haven't any idea. Perhaps if ye consider that now, at the time of the resurgence of the She, the Goddess, it's fittin' that there are four of ye sisters and only three of the brothers, a juxtaposition, if ye will of the make-up of the sacred number seven. But Mary carries the Staff which is an implement, masculine in nature, she could be the decidin' force in which way things will lean now as ye are called te the Cauldron."

My mouth hung open, as did Nora's. "You mean after all this, our futures and the future of the world hinges on what Mary does?"

"Cath pursed his lips and weighed his answer. "I can't know for sure, lass, but it may be that yer sister is a microcosm, so te speak, for the world. There is potential for her te side with great evil or te come down of the side of the light. Things are balanced on, ye'll pardon the expression, the edge of a sword and whichever side wins the struggle and is able to wield the Power will have the edge. The one who has had the blood of both camps in her heart may determine the outcome. She may be the living example of the struggle of humanity itself. Free will. Choice. Will she wield the Staff for good or ill? Will she be seduced by what the evil can offer her or will she be warmed by the light?"

Nora and I looked at each other. I was not at all certain as to what Mary might choose to do.

"Where is the Staff?" I asked. "The last we heard of it, Saint Patrick carried the message. Where did it go after he died? What did he do with it?"

"There're many a story as te the whereabouts of the piece, but as we've witnessed the burning of the Staff we understand that the Power of the Staff, its essence, if you will, as with, the Shield and the Sword may be found where Saint Patrick was at his most Powerful, at Tara where the other half of the Stone of Fal is located. It's all speculation of course. But the other implements have been revealed to us as we've needed te know of them. It's likely that the Staff will come te use when the time is ripe for it...or perhaps not until it's been decided which side has grasped the Power.

This last was an ominous thought.

It seemed our trip to Europe had become an endless parade of car rides, hotels and airports without any of the intermittent sightseeing to break up the whirlwind of travel. Once we'd landed in Copenhagen, we opted to rent a car for our purposes but it was a strange experience to sit in the back seat while Cath drove us to our hotel. Though we didn't have much luggage to carry between the four of us, I with my satchel, Nora with all our toiletries in a small carry on and Cath and Finny each with only a backpack, but we still figured the public train system would be a bit more exposed than we wanted to be, especially this close to our goal. We had no idea where those brothers were at this point and didn't know what they knew about the Cauldron or our travels so we didn't want to give them easier access to us than was necessary.

Cath seemed to know his way around the city very well and the hotel he chose for us was a lovely, luxury Radisson. I was a bit intimidated, looking at the opulent exterior of the grand hotel, thinking that we'd look like a group of vagabonds walking into the lobby. But, as Finny pointed out, the security in a hotel like this would be much harder to breech than the one in Dublin and it was only a stone's throw from the National Museum of Denmark for our research and from the airport to pick up Patrice.

The finely manicured woman of about 40 years or so greeted Cath at the front desk.

"Mr. McDonough, sir. It's lovely to see you again." She spoke perfect English with a hint of what I thought must be a Danish accent. Nora and I looked at each other with raised eyebrows. This didn't seem to be the type of place I'd ever envision Cath to frequent but apparently he had; and he made enough of an impression that he'd be remembered. But then I reminded myself that in a swanky hotel like this, if he'd stayed here even once before, it would be in the hotel computer and they would greet returning guest this way. Just a cordial greeting, I decided.

After looking at her monitor and punching a few buttons on her keyboard she informed us.

"Gentlemen, your suite is ready for you and your nieces. Have you any luggage?" I saw Finny begin to move toward the desk where the woman smiled pleasantly with perfectly straight teeth awaiting his response. I saw his ears poke through his hair and grabbed his arm while answering our Scandinavian hostess.

"We'll manage our own, thank you. But for now we'll just need directions to a casual clothing store and some club sandwiches sent to our room?"

"Of course." Blondie said to me and punched a few more buttons on her keyboard. "Will a variety of four do for you?"

"Yes. Thank you. And something to drink?"

"What would you prefer?" She asked, but I noticed now she was very pointedly looking at Finny and showing her dimples in all their glory.

"Surprise me." I said and jerked at Finny's arm. "Business first old man." I whispered. "Behave yourself. I won't have Patrice coming here and being put off to think you're some kind of letch."

"No such a thing!" He scowled at me and craned his neck to look over his shoulder at the desk manager who made me feel like Olive Oil in comparison.

"I'm not saying you're a letch, Finny. I'm just saying we don't want you to be perceived that way. Besides, the less attention we draw, the better."

He gave Heidi Klum a resigned shrug as we took our hotel map, which listed the stores and restaurants and stepped into the elevator.

The hotel was comparatively tall in this city and I was surprised as we went up and up in the elevator. Even the few times when I'd stayed in a hotel, I always had the parking lot view from lower floors but as we exited the elevator, I was dazzled by the sky lit view that met us from the solarium at the end of the corridor. There were only four well-spaced room doors on this floor and I was absolutely bowled over as Cath keyed open our door and we entered a suite that was more luxurious than anything I'd ever seen. We had an unparalleled view of the city. It seemed that this was one of the few, if not the only tall building in Copenhagen. There were windows on three sides of the large sitting area of the suite in which there was a nesting of chairs and couches artfully arranged to view the fireplace on one side and view of the city on the other, a bar, complete with wet sink and refrigerator, a dining room in the main area with a table large enough to comfortably seat 12 people, adorned by a real crystal chandelier. The floors were hard wood, cushioned by thick and opulent oriental rugs. The magnificent flowers in the room were fresh lilies and orchards. The lilies gave off a perfumed scent that made me think of Walter and Easter Sunday. He'd always bought me rubrim and Easter lilies because he knew I loved their scent.

"Wow," was all I could manage for the moment. I wandered into one of the bedrooms and continued to be amazed. Each bedroom had its own private bath. This one was equipped with a marble floor and open shower with a European rain showerhead and a separate Jacuzzi. I came back out into the main area of the suite and noted that the look on Nora's face was akin to what I assumed was on my own.

"Cath, what's all this?"

"Well," he answered. "It's not often, but on occasion I can justify a treat. And what better time to have a treat than when it can be shared." He seemed pleased that we were impressed and added, "Who's better than us?"

"No argument from me." Nora answered. "Where do we stay?" She said getting right down to it.

"There are four bedrooms in this suite." Cath said. "I figured we'd be better off all together after what happened in Dublin. Safety in numbers, ye know."

My response surprised me as much as it did Nora but just as if my grandma were right beside me, I said, "Ni neart go cur le cheile." I looked to Nora with tears in my eyes. I hadn't thought of my grandmother in a long time, but right now, I felt her right there with me. "You feel that?"

She nodded.

"I guess our little ceremony at the burial site was heard after all." Nora voiced my very thoughts. A knock came at the door and lunch was served. "Let's get some food and then get some clothes so we can shower and change and plan for what we're going to tell Patrice about all of this."

———

Back at the airport after the first solid night's sleep I'd had in a while, I felt a little disoriented in a jetlagged sort of way. I was showered and clean with new clothes, but somehow, I felt almost hung over. Nora looked a little dazed herself.

"What now?" I asked.

"The plane is scheduled to arrive on time so let's us find a place with our backs te the wall and wait." Cath said.

Finny had been particularly quiet this morning and had not even looked around for the attractive woman at the front desk as we left the hotel lobby. He seemed pensive and sort of humming with nervous energy. I wasn't the only one to notice.

Nora asked, "What's with you, Finny? You seem a little nervous. Do you feel something? Are the brothers near? Do you think they know where we are?"

"No, Lass." He said and resumed looking around the airport with an anticipatory expression on his face. Then it dawned on me; he was nervous about meeting Patrice. Of course, that was it. He'd known her all those years ago as Iarann and although he'd always fully expected to see us again one day, he had little time to anticipate it when we showed up at his doorstep. And even then, he wasn't sure it would be us but now, he'd had plenty of time to think on Patrice's arrival. Besides his brother Cath and Bridey, this would be the closest thing he'd experience to a family reunion. Cath had known Iarann only briefly but Finny had built a bond and paternal relationship with him. I figured it would have to be strange because

Patrice is the epitome of femininity. She'd have nothing of the physicality of Iarann except for those soulful eyes.

If I let myself be truthful about my own feelings, I was a little anxious about seeing Patrice too. Now that I knew who she was, I wondered at how it might affect how I see her or how we feel about each other. I was a bit nervous that our relationship would somehow change.

"There it is!" Nora announced and hustled me out of my thoughts. I looked to where her attention was directed and I saw the screen that displayed flight information wink from a show of "On time" to "Arrived" for Patrice's flight 8303 from De Gaul Airport in Paris where she was laid over for a while.

"Let's go to the gate and keep your eyes open for any signs of you know..." She said and we all trooped together toward the gate where we'd finally come together with the sister that should have been here with us all along. But I guess that wasn't meant to be at first. She'd gone through a prolonged breakup of a 25-year marriage and had been rocked off her feet both financially and emotionally. We thought the trip would be a perfect remedy for the emotional part, but aside from making arrangements with her X to care for her sons, Marcus, Mather, and Jonas it was mostly the financial part that had kept her from coming...until now.

I took Finny's arm in my own and pulled him close to me to shore each other up. I saw Nora do the same with Cath and I felt such a warm kinship for these men but all at once, the man next to me seemed small, old and frail.

"There. There she is!" I couldn't help myself. I was so excited to see my sister after all that had happened. I was so happy that I'd begun to see long tendrils of blue light stretch from my chest area out toward Patrice. I looked around quickly to see if anyone had noticed but it seemed that Nora was also extending light and Finny's emotions could be seen in a pulsating thrum of energy around him as well but no one seemed to notice the light show except myself and I think Cath could see it as well or at least he seemed to be aware that something was happening. Maybe it was just his connection with his brother but I knew he was aware of something by the nervous smile that was plastered on his face.

Patrice looked like a movie star with square sunglasses casually perched on her head holding back her cascading chestnut hair, revealing perfectly applied lipstick to match the color tones in the flowered print sheath dress that miraculously didn't appear to have been worn on a grueling, nine-hour trans-Atlantic flight. She looked fresh and happy as Nora met her first, doling out a hug as they greeted each other in high-pitched voices of excitement stating the obvious.

"You made it!"

"Finally. I'm here! How are you?"

I stepped up behind Nora and waited. Finally Patrice extended her arms to me and gave me the airport hug with the pat on the back. I hugged her tight and didn't let her go after the obligatory three or four seconds. I just breathed a genuine sigh of contentedness to see her again. Patrice pulled back slightly and looked into my eyes with a bit of concern. I was crying.

"No worries. I'm just so happy to see you."

Smiling with another quick hug she gave me a few pats on the back again with an, "Oh," that was meant to be comforting.

"Pat, these are our very dear friends...no family. This is Cath McDonough, owner of the Sacred Traveler. All his planning is the reason we're all able to be here together."

Cath extended his hand to Patrice and cordially said, "It's a true pleasure te meet ye, lass. As yer sisters have nothin' but the kindest words fer ye."

Patrice was immediately drawn in by the accent and took his hand in both of hers. She smiled her brilliant smile at Cath.

"It's so nice to meet you, too. Thank you for making this all possible. You'll have to tell me more about how your travel business works. All this is such an unexpected treat!" I knew she thought the name of Cath's business had more to do with world travel than a sacred journey, but for now I let her think what she liked.

"Patrice, this is Cath's brother and also our family and dear friend, Finny McDonough." I practically had to shove Finny toward Patrice and when I did he slowly raised his eyes to her.

"I can't express to ye what it means te be able te meet another member of this very special family. I feel as I already know ye." Patrice's smiling eyes faltered only for a moment. I couldn't tell if she was remembering, or recognized something about Finny or if it was just my imagination but then she did something uncharacteristic for Patrice. She reached out and wrapped Finny in a genuine embrace. I worried that his face was buried in her breasts and nervously checked his ears but there was no sign of the telltale point there. I saw he needed to gain control of his emotions and apparently so did Nora, who jumped into the moment hustling Patrice toward the baggage claim.

"Okay, you guys," she said, "Patrice, let's get your bags and get settled at the hotel."

Patrice was duly distracted. "I'm so tired. I never knew that just sitting could be so exhausting. I hope we don't have to go right out again. Do we?"

"Cath?" I questioned.

"Ah, no. Not right away. We've a late appointment at the National Museum of Denmark so ye've plenty of time te rest and refresh. We'll be able te fill ye in on a few things te catch ye up while we're waitin'."

As we all headed toward the baggage claim I observed Cath surreptitiously hand Finny a handkerchief into which Finny honked a few times to compose himself.

After Patrice got over her awe of the hotel room, she stepped right into the luxury shower and complimentary robe before sinking into the down mattress cover for a nap. We'd ordered lunch for all of us and by the time it had arrived, Patrice was awake, refreshed and dressed, if a bit groggy.

After lunch and tales of her travels, we told her the more innocuous details of our trip so far. During a lull in the light conversation, Finny offered in a sober tone, "I've somethin' for ye, Patrice." He told her.

"For me?" She inquired.

"Aye. We've been told as ye have a talent for the smithing. As luck would have it, I happen te have an antique set of tools ye might find useful."

"Smithing?" Patrice questioned.

"Aye. Ye've been workin' with the metals te make various adornments and such. Yer sisters have told us of yer most recent project of makin' plates of silver in a fashion that's reminiscent of some artifacts ye found in yer studies?"

Patrice began to understand that Finny meant her jewelry crafting and more recently, what Patrice thought of as wall relief plates.

"Oh. Yeah. I work mostly with gold and semi-precious jewels so my pieces are unique and affordable."

I recognized Patrice's typical explanation of her work. She was humble and didn't really give herself enough credit for the exquisite jewelry she designed and crafted. I knew Finny had a point to all this so I kept my opinions to myself for the moment and listened as she continued.

"But the most recent project is silverwork. It's new to me and I've been experimenting with different ways to fine-tune the detail in the relief. It's funny, I just started this project and I'm using tools I already have for jewelry but I was just thinking the other day that if I can find a market for this type of art that I'd have to buy some more appropriate tools."

Finny took from his backpack what appeared to a roll of blue felt tied at two places with a cord of twine and placed it on the table in front of Patrice who looked at him with questioning eyes.

"Open it." He said.

"Where did you get these?" Patrice said as she unrolled the felt and saw a tool stored in each individually sewn pocket but for one empty slot. Her face was serious and reflective. She reached out and picked up a small awl, feeling it and testing its heft in her hand. "These are..." She searched for something. "These are...made for...larger hands I think. These are...they feel so...Uh, I don't know. They feel so right. I think they'll...Wait."

She strode to her room. Returning with her carry-on bag, Patrice pulled out something wrapped in tissue paper and unwrapped it, revealing the plate she'd been working on. She didn't bother to show it to any of us, she just snatched up the delicate awl and applied it to the back of the plate buffered with a patch of leather and grabbed a small hammer-like tool from its pocket. She tapped a few times and turned the plate over to inspect the results.

"These are perfect! They'll be even better when I can work them with heat." She exclaimed to the room in general. Then to Finny, "Where did you get these? Are they expensive? How much do you want for them? I have to have these."

"They are yours." Finny replied.

"What?" Patrice said, shocked. "No I couldn't. You've done so much for me already."

"I insist. They are yours. Truly."

I recognized the very tools as Iarann's. Although in our travels back then, he'd had three such sets as he'd worked on the Cauldron. I had no idea what happened to the other two sets but as Finny had held onto the water skin from Faidhe and my whistle for me, I had guessed he had kept Iarann's tools through history too.

"Wow. Patrice, can we see the panel? It's so detailed." Nora said as she peered over Patrice's shoulder at the silver plate in our sister's hands.

"Yeah, sure. Just don't handle it with your bare hands. The oils in our fingers make the silver tarnish faster, I think." She said as she handed the piece to Nora with a sheet of tissue paper.

We sat on the couch together and inspected the work. It was rectangular in shape and immediately on the piece could be seen the same style of craftsmanship as on the other pieces of the Gundestrup cauldron. Patrice was still marveling over the tools she'd been given and I could see her struggle with the idea that she truly wanted to have them but couldn't find an acceptable way to take the gift without feeling obligated. She began to roll the felt jacket around the tools with a forlorn look of longing and Finny offered her a compromise before she could refuse to accept them.

"If yer not of a mind te take the set as our gift te ye, then please use them te finish yer work on this piece so it can be presented in completion. Ye'll want this sample piece te be finished and at its best will ye not?"

Good Finny! I thought. *Get them into her hands to finish off the final panel. That's all we'll need.* "Patrice," I asked before she answered Finny, "What is on the panel? It looks so much like some of the work we've been researching. Can you explain it to us?"

"Oh sure." She said. "After you guys started getting me all excited about going to Ireland, I started to look up Celtic history, places we could go and interesting things to learn about. You know, doing a little research of my own. But then when I found out that I wouldn't be able to come, I felt that I could at least make myself feel better by enjoying some of the art over here. Funny thing, though, the piece I kept being drawn to, is a piece of Celtic art, but isn't from Ireland at all. It's this big silver bowl and in the silver it has panels in raised relief, kind of, of various people, animals and symbols. I felt so disappointed at not being able to come with you guys that I copied the style of the work in the bowl on this panel of the three of us together. See? There's you Nora, in front of us with the curly hair. If you look really close at your hand, I made you holding the sun and moon as a symbol for you as an astrologer. And there's Lee with her pen, always writing about something. Look there. See? I made her wielding the pen like a sword. You know like the pen is mightier than the sword? And here's me with the bowl that I copied the artistic style from. Oh and see, way there in the back? I didn't feel right having the three of us on the piece without Mary being there too so I added her just to be fair, even though we never planned on her being here. There are some birds in the sky flying over our heads because in the original piece, there were always animals and so I chose to copy the birds in one of the other panels. See here's a dove, there's a raven and that one's a hawk. Of course I can make anything a person wants on the relief and it can be as big or small as they like as long as they're willing to pay for the silver and labor. This is just a prototype that I was fooling around with but I think it has a real likeness to the old style on the bowl I took my ideas from. I wish I brought the books I had with the pictures of the original bowl so you could see the similarity in style."

Nora and I acknowledged the symbolism in the ways Patrice chose to depict us with a nod to each other and then handed the piece off for Cath and Finny to inspect. The graphics on her panel were no surprise: Me with a pen as a symbol for the Sword and Nora with a depiction bearing exactly the symbol we saw on the stone Shield in the grave cairn at Knowth and of course Patrice with her Cauldron but we looked for what Mary's role might be on the panel and found no hint or evidence that Patrice held the secret to how our fourth sister would enter into all of this. Not wanting her to sense that something more than admiration for her work was our focus, I responded to Patrice's comment to keep the conversation flowing.

"Don't worry Pat." I said. "I think we're all familiar with the bowl you're talking about. Not as familiar as you are of course. But it's a pretty famous piece."

"It is?"

"Yeah." I answered. "It's not in Ireland and it's not a big tourist attraction, but to people who have studied Celtic culture or anthropology, this is kind of a big deal piece. There are lots of theories and speculation on where it's from, how it was crafted and what it means. It's called the Gundestrup cauldron."

"I should have figured *you'd* know about it." She said jokingly rolling eyes at the often useless or archaic knowledge I had about things. "I didn't realize it was famous but I can see why. It's just beautiful. To be honest, I didn't read much about it. I saw the pictures and just fell right into trying to replicate the style from the pictures. It was kind of weird the way I just kind of heated up with drive to start something completely new and foreign to me. It was like a...I don't know, like a..."

"Calling?" Finny suggested.

"I guess." Patrice said. Trying on the expression for what she felt. Her head bobbed up and down a little as she thought about it. "Yeah, a calling, or a passion like my hands just knew what to do and they wouldn't rest until I put them to work." An odd look came over Pat's face for a moment like she thought about saying something and then thought better of it.

"What?" I asked.

"Ah nothing. It's silly."

"No, what?" I pushed.

"Well it's just that with the idea of the 'calling' as Finny said, I have had the most bizarre..."

"Dreams?" Finny cut in again.

"Yes!" Patrice said to him with some amazement. "How did you know?"

"Like what?" Nora asked. Patrice sat recalling her dreams and appeared as though she was trying to discern what she would tell us and what she would reserve in mixed company.

"Well, there's the bowl. Always the bowl. What did you call it? The Gunnerstrup cauldron?"

"Yeah," Nora answered. "Gunde. Gundestrup."

"Okay, the Gundestrup cauldron. In my dreams, I'm always carrying it through the woods, in the hills, on the ocean. Everywhere I go it's so important to me. I see the panels on the bowl and they seem to come to life when I look closely but when I get too close, I can't really see the figures anymore. Then there's this woman. She doesn't say anything but she's always calling to me to follow her. I see her and she crooks her finger, beckoning me to follow her. And then finally, when I think I'm going to reach her, I end up coming to a place that's, well it's strange. It's all like a dream inside my dream where everything is surreal. There are people there and sometimes I think I know them but then again I don't. Sometimes you guys are there and sometimes...I'm not sure. It gets kind of fuzzy there. It's like once I cross over into that place, I can't seem to hold on to the dream or the Cauldron. I look and look for it there and I can't seem to find it but then I see Nana for just a flash and she's gone. And then when I wake up, I can't seem to think of anything else but to work on the panel. It's kind of consuming. To tell you the truth, I don't even think I'd have come here if you hadn't told me that there might be someone who is interested in my panels. It just seems to be the path I need to take with my art right now. Well, you know how it is with my dreams. I never have dreams like this for no reason."

It was true. No matter how separate Patrice tried to remain from our abilities, she could not deny that when she dreamed the loud dreams, it always meant something. Unfortunately, she had never allowed herself to follow through and develop her skill so she always ended up finding out what her dreams meant only after some major event or tragedy happened before the pieces of understanding fell into place for her.

"It's true." I said. You're not having these dreams for no reason. Tell me Patrice; are all your dreams about this woman in the woods and the silver bowl? Or do you dream about anything else? Something less pleasant."

She seemed to shift a little uncomfortably in her seat in the plush couch. Her eyes shifted slightly to the men in the room and I understood that our old family dynamic of keeping quiet in front of outsiders held her back from speaking.

"Pat. Cath and Finny know all about us and our family," I told her and watched her eyes widen a little. "In fact, they probably know more about us than we do. You see…"

"Cath shot off his chair like a catapult. "I think we might be ready for some tea after that lunch. We have some time still before our appointment. What say we go down te the luncheon lounge and have some tea with say a sweet or two?" He looked at me and for the first time ever Cath spoke into my head. *Ye've got te let her come into her own, Lee. Ye can't try and convince her of who she is or was. Not this one. She's got te come te her own memories.*

I was just getting used to the idea that Finny was Fion and could speak into my head as he had back then, but was struck silent with the unusual prospect of someone from this time period other than Nora or Lucas talking in my head. I turned to Cath and without argument. "Okay. Let's go get some tea."

Patrice looked as though she knew something was odd about the exchange but seemed content to follow along with the treat of having a fun afternoon in the lap of luxury at the hotel. She wrapped the panel again in tissue paper and carefully tucked it into her purse. It seemed she was so attached to the panel that she would not leave it in the room. Her instincts and intuition were sharpening. I only hoped she came to some kind of self-recognition quickly. I didn't know how we would release the energy from the Cauldron if she had no knowledge of what was going on.

———

We sat in the opulent lobby café enjoying piano music and watching passersby. We had tea and an assortment of pastries guaranteed to slow the blood and thicken the rear end but they were fabulously sticky and decadent. We lounged and conversed about so many things but inevitably the conversation found its way back to recent happenings in the world in connection with magic.

"I know you guys are always connected to your gifts and it makes sense that you'd be more aware of all that stuff in the world, but are you saying that there's more to your magic than just a family quirk of nature?" Pat asked.

"What I'm saying is I don't think we're a quirk of nature." I answered. "I think we have these gifts in a time when the world is ready for these things to be accepted to a certain degree. If we had been born in Puritan America, for instance, just think how we'd be received." I explained. "Since we were kids, the subject of magic has come to be perceived less as evil and more along the lines of enter-tainment in shows like Bewitched and Disney movies and more recently, movies like Practical Magic and even the movies, Chocolat or Dancing at Lughnasadh that hint at the Old Ways. Now, we've got John Edward connecting people with the departed. We've got books about kids and magic hitting an all-time record for sales. There are hit television shows about sisters that are witches and other magical shows about the archetypal good versus evil. Go online and you'll come up with thousands upon thousands of books and movies about magic and the supernatural. And these aren't just the obscure weirdo books. These are best-selling books. Look at Gabaldon, or the Rowling and Tolkien books made into wildly popular movies. The range of style goes from fiction to fantasy and others incorporating scads of research to weave a tale of speculation about the norm like the Da Vinci Code exposing the mystical goings on of the church and secret bloodlines. I think these are all clues that the world is ready or even preparing itself to accept the reality of magic as more than just a superstition or fantasy entertainment. The advent of the Celtic revival and Neo-pagans and even the Wiccan religions are a sign, I think, that people are changing and beginning to wake up to their own calling to their own abilities, if even on a much smaller scale than our own."

"I think Lee's right." Nora added. "Remember when we were kids and all the science fiction movies about space travel were the rage. Then, before we knew it, we were in space and then on the moon. Then Star Trek came along and now so many of those far-out concepts have been created in today's technology. I think when people start to think in a certain way about a subject it promotes energy in support of its manifestation or maybe the other way around. Either way, maybe this is our time to begin to use our abilities for constructive purposes."

Patrice answered slowly. "I'm sorry you guys. It's just...I don't really...It's that I've never felt comfortable with all of this. And even though I know sometimes I have a dream or two, I just never really wanted to open that door. Really, it scared me half to death on 9/11 when I'd heard about the attacks. The whole night before, I dreamed about the name Osama Bin Laden being repeated over and over. What good is something like that if I have no idea what it means and I couldn't help anyway?"

My nerves jangled at the term, *open that door,* Patrice used. It was too close to how Lucas described how the Beast gets in to a person's mind and heart to utilize any weakness it might find.

"Why does it frighten you, Pat? What is the worst you think might happen?" I asked her.

"Well, I guess it frightens me and more than a little. I mean, not with you two. I know you guys and trust you'd never to do anything underhanded or malicious. It's just...it all goes back to a time up in our room when Mary was dabbling with a séance and enlisted me to help her with it. She opened some communication or door up there one night and things started flying around the room and the radiators were banging, I was so frightened I just never wanted to open myself up to something so scary - so unknown. We were lucky 'cause everything calmed down after a while but how do we know where that spirit went or who it was? We don't. We were so completely in the dark about any of what she was doing. There was no control against what forces might have come into our lives that night. That was it for me. Never again! Why would anyone want to do something like that? If we were meant to live with dead people, the world would be set up so it was normal. And it's not."

"Jeeze." Nora mulled over what it must have been like for Patrice. "I didn't know about that. It must have been something."

"Yeah it was something." Patrice answered. I watched her give a little shiver.

"Well we learned one thing from your story." I said. "You gave Mary support in what she maybe couldn't do alone. Your added presence, the two of you together, increased what your abilities were separately. Just like Nora and me. We sort of plug into each other and are stronger together. So I'm willing to bet that if the three of us concentrated on something to work for the good of humanity or even something small but for something positive, I'll bet our abilities will increase in strength that much more."

Patrice contemplated that for about a millisecond. "Yeah well, maybe but I'm not about to try." She seemed to be trying to shake off the memory of that night with Mary. I wondered what else she might have seen in that room up there with Mary all those years ago.

"Anyway." I said to break the tension and try to turn the conversation to something more comfortable for Patrice's sake. "Isn't it near our time to head to the museum?"

———

"Dr. McDonough!" A man in his mid-forties met us at the entrance to the grand mansion that was the National Museum of Denmark. This man was the type that made young girls in his presence blush and older women unconsciously fix their hair and check for food in their teeth. He stood about 6'3" with a full head of dark and shiny hair. His eyes were an intense blue with a humor and kindness that matched the smile on his very pleasant mouth. It was too much when he showed his smile and deep dimples appeared on his cheeks.

I was reminded of romance novel covers and flowing white blouses undone at the bodice. I had to shake myself out of it when I recognized that all three of us, Nora, Patrice and I had whipped out our lipstick, a family trademark, and deftly applied it without benefit of a mirror. The smirk crawled across my face in wry humor. I think I was the only one to notice but then it occurred to me as we were being introduced, that Adonis here had addressed Cath as Dr. McDonough. I dutifully took the museum curator's hand and put the information aside until later when I could ask Cath what he was up to when Cath shocked me again by introducing my sisters and me as Doctors ourselves.

"It's nice to meet you Dr. Strykersen. Thank you for allowing us this very special honor." I shook his hand and felt my knees get a little jelly-like. I pulled my hand back as if it were on fire. I watched my sisters as they took their turns being introduced and noticed that when Dr. Strykersen shook Patrice's hand, he leaned in and was overly solicitous. I understood what was happening when I spied Dr. Strykersen's energy take on a transformation that was vaguely familiar. He must have some God blood in him somewhere up the line mixed with a healthy blend of human stock. This man was deadly with the ladies and probably had no idea that it was simply something in his heritage.

"Oh it's my pleasure entirely. We're always honored to have such an esteemed anthropologist as Dr. McDonough come to visit us. We're pleased to have his colleagues come for studies as well. He's practically a legend around here."

"Really?" I said looking at Cath and wondering just how much more there was to him.

"Well, it seems he's been a welcome guest here since he was a young man. He comes to study the artifacts and we are inclined to let him considering his generosity to the museum."

"Oh, of course." Nora piped in, warming to the role. A look told me she noticed too that there was something a little otherworldly about the museum curator.

Fortunately for us, Patrice had fallen into Dr. Adonis's dimples or was counting his perfectly white teeth, but she made no notice of the exaggerations and outright fabrications that were flying around our group.

Finally Dr. Strykersen announced, "Well your room has been prepared."

He led us to a wide staircase leading to a lower level of the museum. Once on the lower level we listened to our shoes click on the polished floor as we wound through a series of corridors and stopped at a sealed door with a security panel that required a code to open the lock. After punching in the code, Dr. Strykersen stopped and ushered us into the large room in which there was a conference table and chairs.

"We're just about to close up shop, so if there's anything else you'll need, you can contact either me or my assistant on the intercom." He pointed to a sophisticated looking wall panel that obviously was the intercom.

"Ah, yes. Thank you, my boy. Thank you. I think we'll have all we need here. You're always so thoughtful. We've some inspections and notes te be goin' over but I don't see as how we'd be keepin' ye overlong."

"No trouble, Dr. McDonough. I have plenty to do. Take your time. As you know the rest room is in the rear and you'll have to buzz to be let out. I'd offer you refreshments but...you know the rules."

"Certainly. Certainly. We'll want for nothing. Thank you again, Erland."

Patrice heard the name and seized it as an opportunity to keep the young man from exiting the room. "Erland? That's an unusual name. Does that have anything to do with Ireland? It sounds so similar...familiar almost."

Once again, Dr. Strykersen devoted his full attention to Patrice and stepped toward her.

"No. It's an old family name given me. It has something to do with an ancestor who came to these parts, Sweden actually, centuries ago with his son, so the story goes. He was a foreigner to the Norse lands but was accepted into the family for his remarkable ability to work the metals. Our name Strykersen, meaning "son of a trader or craftsman" started there, it's said, but my name, Erland has been passed through generations here and there. It means foreigner and so the story goes that the first grandchild of this big man was named for his family's foreign origins. That's the story but who knows after so many generations how much is true?"

Erland's accent was enough to melt any woman, let alone his appearance but Patrice was looking at him intently now with a look of concentration on her face. With a furrowed brow she was completely absorbed in what he'd told her but she remained silent, boldly inspecting the man's face.

I flashed a look to Cath and he took my meaning.

"Ah thank you again Erland. We'll be a while and'll give ye a shout when we're ready." That seemed to have broken the moment and Nora grabbed Patrice's arm.

"Let's sit here and get ready." Over her shoulder she called to Erland, "Nice to meet you Doctor. We'll see you on the way out." It sounded more of a hopeful question than a statement.

That was enough for Dr. Strykersen to get the hint that we preferred to get down to business and he bowed out of the room with a polite, "Pleasure," hanging in the air. The climate controlled hush of the door closing with a shush was the last sound we heard before we were locked into the museum basement.

Cath turned from the door to be confronted by our questioning faces. "What?" he inquired almost comically. "Ye know as I've been after scholarly endeavors for many a year.... many a century for that matter. Did ye think they'd find the very cauldron and I'd not come te see and inspect it? I've been comin' here for quite some time through many a curator. They know my name as a philanthropic donator and a doctor of anthropology so they afford me the privilege of visitin' the piece on occasion."

"So that's why you know your way around Denmark so well. And that's why they know you at the hotel too. Isn't it?" I accused.

Patrice looked mildly confused. "Anthropologist, centuries? I thought you were a travel agent." She looked around the room from her seat at the head of the conference table and spotted an article covered in a brushed cotton swathe surrounded by several pair of cotton gloves. Patrice got up from her seat and began to head toward the article on the table.

"Did you say cauldron?" She asked appearing almost in a trance at this point. Before anyone could stop her, she removed the covering from the article on the table and took in a breath. "Oh, it's so beautiful!" She gasped. Then her face took on the furrowed brow look again. She gave Nora and me a questioning look and after turning her eyes back to the cauldron said, "I see..."

I didn't know if that's all she meant to say or if there was more to come but I stopped trying to figure out what ever she saw when Patrice hit the floor hard with a sickening whumpish sound as flesh and bone met something much harder.

52

The Three Little Pigs

The three men drew some glancing looks from others who also boarded their flight but those who found the black, penetrating eyes staring back at them quickly found something else to absorb their attention. Oddly dressed for travel and carrying no luggage, the men boarded the flight, took their seats and waited in silence.

When passengers discovered their seating in close proximity to these men, people tended to seek out the flight attendants to check for alternative seating. Fortunately, the flight was not full and those people were accommodated. An unusual circumstance that so many people would prefer different seating but there was no way those travelers or flight attendants could know that it was actually the men who were emitting a conscious message that they wanted no one sitting near them. Their unvoiced message was obliged and once the regular pre-flight routines had been dispensed with, the plane taxied to take off to its destination across the ocean.

Incongruent to their appearance, all three of these men occupied themselves with books to pass the time. Alternately during their flight, they read, slept and eyed the flight attendants, not even bothering to conceal the overt stares that revealed the thoughts in which no woman would want to be featured. Though their father had not raised them, they had genetically inherited his attitude that women were created for one thing and that was to serve men. If women did not keep to their purpose then they were easily overpowered and were quite disposable.

Since their childhood, these three had lived a life of relative seclusion but they had always had a link between them that was strange and disconcerting to those in authority around them. The nuns at the orphanage where they were raised rarely found themselves in prayer for the sake of the boys but prayed often for their own protection, as the boys grew older and less manageable. They were always physically large for their age but it was not so much their size that the priests and sisters of the orphanage found intimidating; these boys seemed to know things there was no reasonable way for them to know or have gained the information.

On one occasion when being reprimanded for not doing their share of work, the largest boy, Simon, spoke in quiet tones smiling at the priest who stood with his switch, ready to punish, until the priest's face first took on a mask of fury, shame and finally fear as the boy recounted his own sins to him in detailed accuracy. It became obvious to the priest that this boy and his brothers could bring him and a few of the others at the orphanage to more trouble than he desired. In that moment, there was an unspoken understanding between the boys and the priest that the boys would be left alone while others picked up the slack for their shirking of duties.

Similar understandings were reached by the sister who doled out the food, another who tended the classroom and the Mother Superior who had the poor judgment in younger years as a novice to have a physical relationship with one of the boys at the orphanage. Some 30 years had passed since her indiscretion and there was no legitimate way these boys could have come to know her secret along with those of many others; these strange boys utilized their insights to full advantage. More times than not, more enjoyment was had from the discomfort of their victims rather than the price they were paid for their silence.

Alone, any one of the brothers might have been easily dealt with by a tragic accident or transfer to lonely places but as it was, the three were sizable even in childhood, and they never allowed themselves to be separated. Together, they were a fearsome force of intimidation. They reveled in their ability to know things about certain people, although dealing with open, honest and forthright people proved a much less satisfying enigma for these men. If someone is truly honest or kind, there is no hidden skeleton on which to capitalize, the brothers were at a loss to read a person if things secret and hidden or shameful were absent. Nor did they understand a person who was truly loving and honest so they tended to avoid such a person as a rat or cockroach avoids the light of day.

Lately, the brothers, Simon, George and Vincent had an awakening of sorts, to their Power. They didn't have any idea as to whether it was their proximity to the American girls in the guest cottage who drew their attention like a bull to a red flag or if they were just coming into their own strength of power, but they knew they had had some kind of surge in their abilities. They made no connection at all to the eclipse of the sun that had taken place recently, they just knew that their abilities had grown in strength and now they knew who and where their enemy was. All this time searching by intuition for a glimmer of recognition of some faceless, nameless person and now, thanks to Bridey and her customer records, they easily learned about the women in the cottage and where they lived. That, together with this new recollection of a lifetime from long history past, and they finally knew who they were and what they had to accomplish. They had to eliminate anything in their path that might be a deterrent to them to come to their rightful power. They did not cross thousands of years of history only to fail now. They would seek out their enemy and crush him and her. They now followed the scent of the one who could stand in the way of their plans. With this recent surge of memory, insight and strengthened power, the world would see an unstoppable force coming to its justified rewards just as soon as their one true adversary was out of the way. Then, they thought, with the knowledge they had of people's inner most secrets, there would be many to flock to their feet as sycophants to the power they would display. They would enjoy adoration and fear and it would grow. Soon, they would be well known. There would be little to stop them in reaching their goal for power and renown. Their egos would be fed and they would receive the adulation and prestige due them. Their time had come. They would wield their power like a club. They had just one task to perform to allow all things to flow their way.

———

Excerpt from Nora's notes: According to the information we received from Bridey, these men were born in Unst, an island in the North Sea on the northern most reach of English territory, on June 30, 1954. Through his research, Cath further discovered that these three men were born at 12:25 p.m., the exact time of the solar eclipse on that day. I don't know the circumstances of the birth but all three birth certificates for these babies show the same time. The mother's death is recorded on June 30, 1954. It leads me to think the mother died during a c-section birth for all to have the same time of birth.

Looking at the astrological chart for these people, Simon, George and Vincent O'Tarbh, I see immediately that they have a distinct imbalance in that they have five planets out of ten, clustered in the ninth and tenth houses. Mercury is retrograde so the mind doesn't work like other peoples' do, they do not think in linear terms but rather see themselves as a part of everything or perhaps everything as a part of them.

There are five out of ten planets in Cancer. This is unusual. They are more subjective than objective where they would see, think and feel everything in terms of only what is important to them and their focus would be limited to supporting that subjective perspective. *Note: This clustering is sometimes found in the chart of serial killers.

The spiritual focus of someone with this chart would be so direct and single minded that they would believe in something, whatever it is, so strongly, that they would expect everyone else should believe it also.

The sun and moon are in the ninth house which would give them tongues like razor blades with the capability of deeply hurting people with their knowledge. These men have the possibility of success in the priesthood, or perhaps as writers. At their best, they can be universally appealing to people but conversely can be controlling, bossy, surreptitious by avoiding confrontation with deceit and cunning. They also have a strong capacity for being very intuitive. (Cult leader?) Cancer at its worst rules greed.

They have Chiron in the house of the mother. They are very challenged in this area of the chart and it is no surprise that these men lost their mother at birth. This challenge is in a person's chart so they can learn about family, emotions, communication, relationships, parenting, attachments, taking care but would fail dismally if they did not choose to take the challenge and learn from it. Often, people with this type of challenge, if they learn and utilize it for positive purposes to grow as a person, become some type of healer, he or she supporting others in their journey to heal. This challenge coupled with the five planets in the ninth and tenth houses could create an ego driven strive for power and prestige. With this chart, an unevolved person would likely look for a kind of renown.

This is a challenged chart. This person or persons are at odds with himself and those around him. He will have been his own worst enemy and views the world or people as always working against him. This would be particularly difficult for someone with Saturn in Scorpio as in this chart for this person, control of others and situations would be very important.

This person or persons would be driven to learn. Make no mistake that these men, though possibly unevolved souls, are unintelligent. Quite the contrary. Sagittarius rules the ninth house. These persons, at the very least would understand maps of any kind, maps of development and personality in psychology, geographical maps of history and how the world evolved, astronomical maps of the stars, (maybe why they had a telescope) even astrological maps or charts of people's life template. The nonlinear way these guys think would suit understanding of people, history and such, very well. It would be a mistake to underestimate the knowledge base of these people. This knowledge could be very effective as a weapon or a tool to suit personal purposes. They are most comfortable alone but are learning now how to connect with others and to fit in, if only as a means to an end. They will participate in society if it suits them but they are still coming from a place of "I" in their chart and learning what is needed to go to a place of "we."

Again, some serial killers learned how to fit in and look quite normal. So much so that neighbors, family and friends are often very surprised when people like Dahmer and Bundy are caught because they were so unassuming and appeared normal. From what I've seen though, these three have not quite mastered the fitting in, just as they have not likely met the challenges of Chiron in learning about nurturing relationships. We may have that working to our advantage.

Because there are three separate subjects born to this chart, there would be three distinct personality signs or rising signs. One would be born with a Capricorn personality. This one would undoubtedly be the boss. He'd call the shots and no one would challenge him for too long. Another would be born to the sign of Cancer personality.

This one would be a surrogate parent or caretaker to the others. This would not be an enviable position. Considering the personalities of the other two, this person would go unappreciated and likely wind up as a servant, bowing to the desires of the other two and likely suffering abuse for his efforts. The third would be born to Aries. This one would be the hothead, a fighter or man of action. A fourth, but unlikely possible sign in the opposing positions created by triplets might be Libra but I consider it less likely than the others named above.

In summary, we must be very careful if one, or all of these men confront us. They are intelligent, cunning and intuitive. And from what we have recently learned, they have become stronger in their power and ability due to a recent eclipse of the sun over Ireland. Granted it was only a partial eclipse but if this is how they gain power, through darkness, we can count ourselves lucky that it wasn't a total eclipse of the sun. I think they were testing their newfound abilities when they came up to our cottage on the last night we stayed there. It may have been arrogance or they may have come to some kind of recognition of their other life and mission just as we had come to our awakening. So we expect some kind of challenge from these three but they have the element of surprise. We have to remain vigilant because the Beast can come at us in the form of overwhelming fear, three big men who can physically overpower us, or who knows what energy lies behind the smell that comes? We saw that thing take over Cath and it was scary. Does this mean that these men can harness the Beast and direct it to do their bidding through anyone who might be a weak link? And if it could get to Cath, does that mean it can get to anyone? Is everyone our potential enemy then?

I'll share the information I've divined in the charts with the others. Maybe there is something here that can be used to help protect us further.

53

Unleashed

Patrice rolled over onto her back and as Nora fanned her face, Finny tried to give her sips of water from the skin he'd kept in his backpack. "No." Patrice protested. "Just let me stay here on the cool floor for a minute. I'm fine, really. Just let me be."

We gave her some space and Nora and I sat on the floor by her side while Patrice's eyes investigated the ceiling as she tried to organize her thoughts. After some time she sat up. "Have you always known?"

We knew she addressed us both but Nora answered. "No. I think Lee and I have always had an intuition that there was some history or past lives between us but we never knew for certain or with any clarity. I found out while we were here but within the past few days I came to a full recognition as we approached the Hill of Tara."

"Your home?" Patrice said, then stopped, looking introspective and confused. Although she didn't seem to be definite about the information, this comment cleared away any doubt that she'd had her own awakening to the memory of our other life.

She looked at me with an expression of expectation on her face as if to ask when I'd learned of our past. When our eyes met, Patrice's expression changed to that of a person searching her memory. Her eyes slid to the floor and I waited until she found what she was looking for and her eyes snapped back to me. "Black Bird?"

I nodded and felt my throat tighten. I said, "It'll take some getting used to, but after a while, you'll just see us as the beings we are rather than connecting us with any physical form we may have had in the past. How do you feel?"

"I think I just want to stay here connected to the ground. I think if I get up, I'll just wind up on the floor again. It's almost like I'm getting some kind of relief from the confusion from just sitting on the floor."

Patrice let her dazed eyes travel to the two men in the room. "Do I know you?" Her brow furrowed with concentration and then brightened, as she seemed to look at the area around the men's heads. I knew that she was looking at their energy. "Are you Fion? She asked, but didn't wait for an answer. "Fion." She said. It was a statement this time. Patrice now took the small Dixie cup of water that Finny was offering to her and the color began to return to her face. "This is wild you guys. I feel like I'm drunk or... something."

"I know, Patrice. It's a lot to take in and you had no warning. At least we knew we were in search of something and we found out about things gradually. You were hit all at once without a clue."

After contemplating what I'd just said for a moment Patrice responded. "You know, I don't think that's entirely true. Since you guys left I've been obsessively creating this panel and had the constant feeling that something was brewing. Something...that would create a big change in my life. I thought it was the panel and a new business that would create the success I'd need to build an independent life for myself and now I know it was the panel, but not for the reasons I thought. Now I actually understand the symbolism in the new panel I made, just as I can tell you the story behind each of those old ones. I guess our lives are going to change. Huh?" She tried to get up but resigned herself to sit for another while and just reached out to take my hand with her left hand and Finny's with her right.

Nora advised her. "Don't try to get up Patrice. I needed the wind on my face. When my memories came back to me, I had to just sit and let the wind wash over me until my headache subsided and my thoughts reconciled. Don't fight it."

"It's a good thing you didn't experience my torment. I thought my skin was going to split open and peel off. I had to sit in a tub of freezing cold water until I sort of, ah, readjusted. Apparently, you need to draw from the earth. That kind of makes sense since all that we've experienced so far depends so much on the four elements. I needed water, Nora obviously needed air; you're gaining strength from the earth."

This realization begged the obvious question, what would it be like if Mary came to her memory? How would she withstand the only remaining element if it were necessary for her to do so? I shuddered at the thought.

Nora answered that thought. "Maybe because we were connected by blood in the past, and Mary was not, we won't have to answer that question. You were my sister then and you were also blood to Iarann. Maybe that's why we're here and she's not. Maybe she won't have to be a part of any of this."

"That's a hopeful thought," I said, "but she's a spoke in the wheel. She's born to one of the elements and even though I was born to Libra, an air sign, I needed water. You Nora, you were born to earth but needed air. Patrice is born to Scorpio, a water sign and needed earth, I guess, but Mary is the only one born to Leo, a fire sign and fire is the only thing left in this process. It must mean something."

Cath interjected, "Perhaps you three needed the support of one another or it was a symbol of your connectedness, but that the last, Mary, stands alone. It'll be her own memories and recollection and independently, she'll come te her decision which way she'll blow her flame, ah so te speak."

"Well," I said, "everything else had been revealed to us; I guess we'll just have to wait and see how that piece of the puzzle will fit. But for now, let's do what we came to do." My words were the catalyst to get Patrice up off the floor. She stood very slowly and was still shaky but we put her in a chair by the cauldron.

"The wheel." she said. "You mentioned a spoke in the wheel. I had put the wheel in the original panels quite a few times because it was significant. Often during our journey, Faidhe and I spoke of her plans to send our Old Ways to the future religion so it wouldn't die out and also of the return of the eight in the union as spokes of a wheel. See here's a wheel and there's another. This one is only half visible. See here?"

We did see. There were many renditions of the wheel in the panels on the Cauldron. Patrice began to explain the final panel as she referred to it. "Here is... here is Faidhe. She was..."

"We know who she was Patrice." Nora cut in. "We know, through our individual memories and then through Cath and Finny, pretty much the whole story as they filled in the blanks. But I think if we wait for all your memories to come back to you, we'll run out of time for what we have to do here."

"Okay. 'Course you'd know." Patrice answered as she put on a pair of the cotton gloves provided for us. This panel is Faidhe, performing the magic for all the magical creatures and Gods to go under to the Sidhe to preserve and protect them. See the line drawn with the fighe vine here? Below that is the Otherworld depicted by the dog here. Those on the bottom have gone under. These four on the top, well, that's us. We're riding horses to symbolize the freedom from being tied to the Otherworld or the Underworld. We're back here with a mission. As you can see, Faidhe has her feet planted in Otherworld, but her head is above, where we are. She is between worlds so to speak, never able to be wholly in one or the other. And see these three down here? Those are the three Faidhe knew about. She knew there was trouble with these ones and she suspected they'd find a way to return here when we did."

Finny interrupted. "Aye, she tried te keep away the one who planned te steal her magic from the ritual in order te avoid such a disaster. But as the fates had their way, the tables turned on that plan and Triag killed Gara. That left him free to observe the ritual and mimic the magic."

Patrice pointed to the three on the panel and continued. "See these instruments those three have? These instruments are topped with the head of a boar, which was somehow an animal that was utilized to help them come through again. They did find a way to mimic Faidhe's magic and use a back door so to speak to come back. They didn't come through the cauldron of magic that Faidhe used. They came in under cover of darkness. They slipped in stealthily, like the serpent here that is depicted over their heads and see? It has horns on it like a bull. While on the other hand, see we're high above on horses and in the light."

She finished pointing to the left of the snake-like creature where the four horse riders could be seen in open space in opposition to the three others who were under cover of the serpent, aspiring to come to the earthly plain by subversive means.

"But look. This is an interesting aspect that reveals the uncertainty of Mary's position in all this." Patrice pointed to a figure standing next to the three under the serpent. "See the headdress she's wearing? That's a boar. Now look here to the four horse riders. We each have a headdress: Lee, there you are with the raven on yours and Nora; there you are with the same crescent moon and sun symbol on your headdress. This one is me; with my smithing tools on mine, but this one of the four horse riders is Mary she's wearing a headdress with a boar. Though Mary is above and riding with us, she still bears a connection to those below and it's apparent in her headdress here. This figure that represent Gara or Mary, which ever you choose to call her could go either way in this, and side with us three or those other three. It's unknown what she'll do."

The room echoed for a moment with silence until Patrice began to rummage in her purse for the newly designed final panel. She brought out the tissue-covered panel and the blue felt packet holding the tools Finny had given her only today.

"It's not the best conditions but I'll add one last detail here. Patrice pulled out a tool with a small ball on its tip exactly like the tool in her headdress on the last panel in the cauldron. Placing the leather strip between the back of the silver panel and giving eight or nine solid taps with the hammer-like tool she'd used earlier, we watched as our sister added a distinctly snake-like figure placed under the feet of Nora, me and herself. "I don't know if it's just my will or wishful thinking, but it can't hurt to stamp out the snake this thing hides under. Do you know what this thing is?" She asked almost as an afterthought. When no one answered her right away, she stopped her work to look up at us.

"What? Do you know what this is? I was familiar with the whole 'Beast' concept back then. Does this have something to do with that foul energy? Nora? Lee? C'mon now. You obviously got me here for a reason; don't hold back now."

Finny stepped up to answer. "Right ye are in that the energy of the Beast is about and so much more forceful than when it was first loosed. But now as the three who ye've depicted here are in the flesh as minions of the Beast," he gestured to the picture on the Cauldron, "they've come to their own understandin' of their own history and power. Only their source of power is as ye say, from the absence of light. It's a slitherin' dark thing feedin' on the weaknesses of people. The three are the very initiators of the Beast's energy, Briciu, his sister, Nemain and his son, Triag. They have committed blood magic and morder te be here at this point in time. Now is the time of a reckoning te see what will come of the world. Will it be consumed by greed, avarice, lust, domination and so forth? Or will light take hold and usher in the Fifth Civilization, what some have come te think of as the last times granted for humanity. Some will think on this as the end of days."

"What, like the bible end of days?" Patrice asked. "I know all this is important to humankind but now that you put it in these terms, it's too hard to get my mind around. So what are we, like the four horsemen? Ushering in the end of days?"

Always better versed in the readings of the Catholic Church, it occurred to me that Patrice recognized the symbolism on the cauldron in a way I would not have thought of. That symbol, together with the date of December 21, 2012, and some of the prophecies and oracles from different times and places seemed to carry a similar vein throughout. Immediately, the pictorials in the predictions of Nostradamus came to my mind. He had several illustrations with his quatrains containing the wheel. And, I seemed to remember something about that 2012 date in Egyptian lore as the date marked for the end of time as well. If I focused on just us and our family, I could keep my thoughts under control, sort of, but as I began to think of all the rest of the world and the billions of people and that somehow, what I do now will matter a great deal to all those people, I could feel the panic begin to well up in me. Instinctively I grabbed for Nora's hand and she immediately knew that I needed her support.

"Wait!" She called out. "Do we have any salt?"

Patrice stopped her work and watched as Cath pulled a new canister of salt from his pack and Finny reached for the sage. Water was already available in the skin but we could not utilize fire here in the museum. We'd have to put in place our protection without the use of fire. Nora took the salt, I took the sage and Cath handed the water to Patrice. "Do as ye see and feel." He ordered, and stepped to the center of the room with Finny by the table.

Nora paced the circumference of the room and laid an unbroken stream of salt all around the edge. I followed her with the sage; crumbling the leaves in my hand to release the aromatic scent into the air and dropped the crushed leaves on top of the salt put down by Nora. Once we finished the circle, we stepped to the middle and looked to Patrice who looked like a deer in the headlights. I felt for her. She'd been flung into this world she always took pains to avoid and now not 30 minutes after she'd come to remember that she was someone else and a man at that, she would have to participate in a ritual that was completely foreign to her and then, to perform magic with us to release a great Power from ancient times. But I had to give her credit; she began to walk around the room in the sunwise fashion she'd seen Nora and I do. She did not sprinkle the water from the skin, rather she poured an unbroken stream right over the salt and sage until the circle was complete. "This much I do remember. This is protective magic right?"

Patrice's cheeks were highly flushed. She seemed invigorated by the magic once she'd started.

"Now this." She said, and took the panel she had just completed and made to put it into its slot on the cauldron.

Cath and Finny shouted in unison. "No! Not yet!" Patrice stopped in her tracks, her hand frozen just inches from completing the cauldron.

Then Cath asked, "Have ye a thought as te how ye'd like te arrange all this?"

After a moment, I was surprised to realize that I did have a thought, a few in fact.

"I'd pictured this moment that we'd all be around the cauldron and I'd read the words in the Power of the Word because it was really my tale to tell, then we'd read the panels, well Patrice would, so we would each see, hear and tell the story. And Nora, her job is to hear the ritual telling. I'm sorry you guys," I said to Cath and Finny "it's the way I'd envisioned it but I never really thought about either of you two being a part of the ritual. Was I wrong?" I looked to the other faces in the room and found Nora's to seek reassurance.

She shrugged and admitted, "It's how I saw it too Lee. Do you guys know if that's just egocentric thinking or is this how it's to be done?"

"I'd say the latter." Cath answered. "We're here te see as the tale is told and we've had our tellin' te you gorls as was our promise. It's yer family's task te release and wield the magic. So arrange yerselves te the work te be done and know that we're here te help, guide and support. Ladies," he said with an open palm leading us to our places at the cauldron.

The three of us went to the table and Patrice, still wearing her gloves, lifted the piece off the table. Nora and I moved the table aside to make enough space so that the Cauldron could be on the floor and the three of us could stand or sit around it while holding hands. After throwing the rest of the cotton gloves on the floor, Patrice placed the Cauldron on the cotton mat created to protect it from any damage. I retrieved the Power of the Word from my satchel. Then we all sat around the cauldron and Nora listened with me as Patrice told her tale as depicted on the cauldron and pointed to various panels to unwind the mystery of the symbols.

When she finished I opened the book and began to read from the archaic speech written there. Many of the words rolled off my tongue despite the fact that I had no idea which part of the tale I was reading. As I read on, I felt myself slip into a trance, fully aware of what was happening around me but at the same time, I began to understand the ancient words I was reading and I knew my sisters did too. I thought about how foreign it was to understand the language but also to read it for the first time because when it was my native tongue, there was no writing. As I began to understand the words, I realized that Cath had phonetically written the words of our old language. I read the words spoken by Faidhe all those years ago in the initial ritual and my mind opened to what she'd seen in the original prophecy as the ancient words revealed the mysteries.

My sisters and I learned of great changes that would take place, not only for us but that would begin to manifest in our country as soon as this magic is released. We took the warning the prophecy declared that as soon as the literal gauntlet was thrown down, there would be a great shift in the power of nations beginning with the most powerful. Then the shift would become global as the time between now and the dawn of the Fifth Civilization closes in. Upheaval in politics and those hiding behind morals and pretense of an upright lifestyle would be exposed as deceivers, cheats and thieves. Those, drunk with the power of rule will watch a nation tumble from greatness into chaos. The real challenge will come as the mighty fall, how will the masses seek to rebuild? How will the enemies of this once powerful nation respond? Much will lie in how those masses, the people, not those in power, respond to the crisis. Will the world live out the Fifth Civilization without integrity or will it choose to listen to the small voices of conscience? Will it follow common sense of what is right and wrong? Will women be released from the slavery of objectification? Will men sever the connection between power, money and sex? Will the need to dominate melt toward a desire to cooperate? Will acceptance for diversity in spirituality, faith and religion be adopted or will new age of technology and science become the new god so that the other will be ridiculed and marginalized? These shifts and changes will be fast upon us and as I read, I saw so many opportunities for those in current power, political, religious and otherwise, to make choices that would be sustained by the light yet over and again they made choices to feather their own nest, maintain personal power and flagrantly ignore the duty to their people for personal gain. They chose the dark. They chose dominance. They chose justification. They chose deceit.

I felt myself growing angry as I learned of situations where people had been killed, subverted and the masses had been deceived. My ire grew and I knew that a certain amount of indignation was warranted but I knew not to let it consume me now. I began to understand that it was not only the ill heart of the deceivers, but the resignation and acquiescence of the people made me even angrier that as a whole, the people grew complacent to drink, eat, play and watch television, ignoring their responsibility to keep those in power in check. They were bought off by video games, getting laid, addictions and sleeping in. I felt now that it had been so long since moral conscience had raised its head, real moral conscience, not judgment of others but judgment of the self and true desire to a personal best that I was afraid that people no longer even took an honest self-assessment. We all observed as we saw divergent paths ahead of us as a civilization: one led to struggle and order and the other, remained complaisant, lazy and greedy, led to oblivion.

Images began to rise from the cauldron as shadows of the past and people and history were revealed to us. As I continued to read, the book was no longer necessary. I had the information stored or more likely, the cauldron had, because as I spoke, pictures illustrated the details of the tale we had no way of knowing from our memories. We saw the death of Laoghaire, and the lives of his children. We witnessed the ceremony the dark three performed. We saw the foul way in which Nemain was dispatched and discarded as if a portent for the future of women. We saw the life of Iarann across the Kattegat Straight from Denmark into the realm of the Valkyrie in Sweden. We saw his son, Frey and Patrice wept. We saw my life with Sonne and our beautiful children and I was shocked to recognize for the first time that Sonne is my Walter. My heart soared that I was so rightfully paired with my husband to create this *bringer of light*. But then, so too, Nora was stunned to recognize her long forgotten friend, Laoghaire's cousin Cuan as her most recently introduced dance partner, Eric, the Norwegian. I would no longer be concerned over coincidences as I learned that there likely are none. People come into and leave our lives for a purpose. It's up to us not to let the opportunity pass and to strive to serve the reason. I observed, as we all absorbed this information, Nora's hand reach around to her back pocket. Of course, the number she had stowed there on that night of dance and revelry was no longer on her person but I knew in that moment, she would eventually make contact with the man. I was pleased for her.

As pictures continued to parade up and out of the cauldron, we learned all there was to know. Blanks were filled in and understanding was met. We knew there was no easy way to defeat the dark. It would be an ongoing battle with darkness because where ever there is light there will be shadow but there was hope in that even in the blackest darkness, a small pinpoint of light will draw the eye and call the human heart.

It seemed when we all accepted that we were now a part of this awakening of humanity to this great battle, the pictures subsided and my voice echoed in the room with the last of the words spoken in the archaic tongue which translated to mean: As of 2008, the Sun passes through Ophiuchus between times known as, November 30 and December 17 and during this time, the great changes will begin to manifest in preparation for the Light, coming of age and the rearing of the head of darkness in its war with the Light.

"That's this fall." I stated the obvious. "What's going on this fall that will be so huge?"

Patrice responded, "The elections, maybe?"

Nora spoke up. "Do you know what Ophiuchus is?" She didn't wait for an answer. "It's the thirteenth constellation. It's a part of the Zodiac, but it's hidden. Now the Zodiac is made up of the sun cycle, twelve months and twelve Zodiacal signs but during the ancient times, right up until the Druids were killed or absorbed by the church, there were thirteen months, thirteen signs based on a moon cycle; Ophiuchus is the thirteenth constellation. Actually, it's two constellations; one, is The Healer and the other is the Serpent. The two constellations together formed The Serpent Holder. The Healer is supposed to have had the gift of raising people from the dead and utilizing the benefits of plants and medicines to heal people. It's become particularly noticed because over the centuries, the stars that make up the healer are famous for solar flares that burn brightly and then settle back to typical light expected of these stars. But interestingly, this hidden, thirteenth constellation will be aligned just at the point where the center of our galaxy meets the celestial equator. This gap is known as the Dark Rift. Some people believe that earth being in direct alignment with this Dark Rift, the end of days will begin. But maybe judging by the two constellations, the Healer and the Serpent, it's when the hidden is revealed and light is shed on the darkness so to speak. The Healer and the Serpent will both have influence on humanity here on Earth."

I said, "I guess we'll have to wait and see. Everything in the prophecy that has been predicted has already come to pass and can be identified throughout history. The rise of Christianity, usurping of the old religion, subjugation of women, the rise and split of power between the Vatican in Rome and Constantinople, the coming of Saint Patrick, the binding of old and new in his Celtic Cross or as we know now, the Sword and Shield, the magic surviving in several facets of story form throughout the centuries, the bloodlines to create a human portal for the Light to come through. I think we can safely say that something big is about to happen but for now, I think we should get on with this. I'm feeling a little spooked. It must be getting late and we don't know how much longer we'll have here. Let's get to it."

No more words were spoken. We'd fulfilled our roles to speak, show and hear the tale. Patrice picked up her panel and moved to make one last adjustment on it, first with a single punch from the round-tipped tool and then a few precise taps with a more delicate flat tool. She looked at us with question in her eyes.

'Now?'

We nodded and she placed the panel into the blank spot on the cauldron. It amazed us that the piece fit perfectly into the slot. As though the piece were magnetized, the panel was pulled from Patrice's hand and sealed itself into place with a small blue spark of what appeared to be electric current that soldered the piece around the two sides and bottom.

We sat for a moment waiting and wondered what was next when the bowl itself began to spin in a sunwise direction. Over the mouth of the bowl, a beautiful, cobalt blue color began to illuminate the room as it glowed from within the cauldron. The light took on the shape of a wheel with spokes and spun the bowl faster and faster until the wheel ascended from the bowl developing a column of light up to the ceiling. Myriad sounds and voices filled the room and wind blasted anything not tied down so the room was a blizzard of sound, salt, sage and personal items flying about. Three tendrils of blue light extended from the wheel column and touched each of us on the forehead. I watched as I saw my sisters begin to light with various circles of different colors down their torsos and on the crowns of their heads. I recognized these spinning wheels as the seven chakras of the Hindu religion. They were all open and spinning within us and the light from the wheels rendered my sisters translucent. I could feel my own spinning within me and assumed I appeared the same to them. On the tops of our heads was what appeared to be a halo of light as well. Just as I was beginning to take note of the way my body was feeling with all this activity, I grew frightened as I saw a snake uncoil from the base of my sister's spines and writhe up behind them. I did not see, but felt the same thing happening to me. A consuming female voice filled the room. *"Do not be afraid. The light is within you as is the darkness. It is a part of each of us and can be utilized and productive provided it is honored. Be not afraid of the snake. Be not afraid of the serpent. Be not afraid of the darkness. Be not afraid to use the wheels within you. They are all gifts. Here, the gift of the red."* With that I felt my womb tighten with a primal surge of desire but anger at the same time. *"Here the gift of the orange."* With that I felt an overabundance of emotions, love, anger, empathy, sadness and relief all surging then, in an instant, all were gone as the voice continued to highlight the colors of these wheels within us. *"Here the yellow,"* and I immediately experienced a cooler head. I rationalized what I had just felt and I began to formulate opinions on the experience. Then, *"Here the green."* My heart thrummed and pulled. I felt a bursting of camaraderie for everyone in the room, which instantaneously expanded to everyone in the world and blossomed into recognition that I was an integral part of everyone in the world. *"Here the light blue and here indigo."* Immediately I felt calm and balanced with all of this innate knowledge. I felt right within my skin. I felt the perfect balance between masculine and feminine within me. I knew whatever I opened my mouth to say would be pure and without fear. In this state, I felt the freedom of release from my body as I rose up through the purple wheel in my head and through the corona of pure light above my head.

I thought, *Oh, the eighth Chakra. The eighth spoke in the wheel.* I saw my sisters in spirit light, just as I must have appeared to them. We were androgynous spirits, no longer connected to gender or earthbound. Just as I began to adjust to this phenomenon, we were plunged into the blackest darkness imaginable. Oily, thick, inky, viscous, darkness. I reached for my sisters and had no idea whether I could touch them or even if I had hands in this state. I tried to recall the lesson the voice had just taught us. *Do not be afraid. The light is within you as is the darkness. It is a part of each of us and can be utilized and productive provided it is honored. Be not afraid of the snake. Be not afraid of the serpent. Be not afraid of the darkness. Be not afraid to use the wheels within you. They are all gifts.*

I directed the wheels of my spirit to be calm, without struggle. At the same time, I was aware and knew my sisters were doing the same thing. Then in the absolute darkness, when I'd decided to just trust, and work within the rhythm of the darkness, I saw a small beam of light and with it came the thought: *This is what the very first star must have looked like.* It grew in brilliance until nothing could be seen but the light. It was equally as blinding as the darkness. *Oh! Ha!* I saw the lesson in that and was amused that it was so simple.

Balance is it? Is that it? Balance is the key...to everything? That's it? So simple! There was no answer but in that moment, a band of darkness pushed at the light until we three stood in the light tempered by the darkness and on the other side of the line, we saw and recognized the energies of the three brothers in darkness, illuminated by the light. *Ah,* I thought without surprise. *So there you are. And here we are.* I saw these beings, stripped of any vibrancy in their chakra wheels but for one, which had grown to grotesque proportions. The red wheel, from which the life-force energy springs in the form of a snake or serpent in these men had grown large and twisted. It coiled around the other wheels and choked much of the life and color out of them. This energy in healthy souls is a positive, driving force to couple, to earn, to survive but in these men, the consuming nature had grown to choke out balance in a lustful quest for power and adoration. Greed for power and dominance over the feminine had caused the life force in these three to overwhelm all else. It was amazing to witness the spiritual makeup of the men. It drew my attention with fascination. I wondered where they were in the world and how they had come to be here too.

Upon that thought the serpents uncoiled from these energies and bolted toward us. This aggressive red energy was frighteningly fast and banded together to create one large and overwhelming serpent bearing huge yellow fangs, dead black eyes and sprouted horns of the bull. The head of the serpent bowed low as if preparing to ram and bolted straight for Nora's energy but was momentarily slowed as it entered the light in which we stood. Fear struck my heart at the movement and the light in which we stood flickered, and then went out. I was consumed by images of Nora being ravaged, as this creature finally met its mark after so long.

Far in the distance of what could have been across the room or across the galaxy, another dot of light appeared. I heard a distinct tapping as the light drew closer and I recognized the energy as Mary. The Staff made up of blue light illuminated our fourth sister. She appeared to be using it as a walking stick but stopped her progress toward us at what seemed a great distance away. The Staff, held in her left hand settled on the side of the light. The Mary energy seemed to stand with one foot in the pool of light offered by the Staff and the other in the dark. All attention, even that of the serpent, was drawn and devoted to the distant being as it spoke.

"This is a battle of choice and free will, not one of Power, a challenge of strength of belief in oneself and faith in one another. I can't lend to the strength of either side because none of you had faith in my loyalty. The message I bring with this Staff is that the balance you seek will be maintained. The outcome of this struggle will remain in your hands and hearts by the choices you make. No decision you make will leave the rest of humanity unaffected. We're all connected and will fulfill the contract we have made with one another."

"Contract?"

"Yes. If you are a victim, you have a contract with one who will oppress or dominate. If you make a choice not to be a victim, regardless of what happens to you, you have a contract with the oppressor to be a student in the process of learning. These contracts can be considered Karmic relationships. Some positive, some not, but always designed so that knowledge of and for the soul is the result. Harm may come to the physical being but it must be healed in the spiritual by making the decision as to how the lesson will be learned and how deeply."

We watched as Mary laid down the Staff between the two forces, the men and serpent on one side and we three sisters on the other. The light from the Staff illuminated the space between us and I could no longer see if Mary remained or not. My attention was drawn once again to the serpent and my fear burst and blossomed a second time. Rather than react out of fret for Nora, I consciously quelled my fear. In that moment, I heard a small voice call to me, and my composure shattered. *"Mama?"*

"Luke!"

"Mom, something's happening. I can feel the monster growing. Where are you?"

"Go into your dreams Luke. Go to where you dream. We're in that in-between place. Go there. I know you can. Come and don't be afraid. There's no need to be afraid. The monster won't hurt you." I prayed more fiercely now than I ever had that what I was telling him was true. I had to trust my intuition; it was all I had in this moment.

With the same blind faith I had exhibited as a young child when Nora had given me protection of a paper key, my son just did what I told him without a doubt or a question in his mind. *Faith.*

"Here I am." He said. And when he appeared we all saw his true energetic self as pure light with triple wheels spinning within his core. Lucas was He and She and neither and both all in one. He was innocence and ancient wisdom yet still maintained the countenance of a child. There was my Lucas striding toward us wearing his blue wool blanket as a cloak, fastened at the neck by a bronze brooch bearing the design of a circle with a triangle of stones in the center topped by a single, all-seeing eye. In his hand he carried a bundle of sticks. The Light came to my side and beneath the cloak could be seen billions upon billions of points of light igniting within the framework of its energy. My own cognition swelled with the emotion of pure love for this being.

On another level, I was aware of what was happening with Lucas on the earthly plain as he sat in the back seat of our car while his father battled someone who had intentionally rammed them with his car. Lucas was fine but his father ran the risk of being arrested if he continued to allow himself to be drawn into the conflict. He needed to make a rational choice as to what would be best for Lucas rather than to win the battle over who is right and who is wrong.

I saw also what Mary was experiencing and breathed a sigh of relief to understand that her role in this had come to her unbidden while she was asleep, sunbathing in her yard. This was how she was bathed in fire rather than being consumed by flames. I saw the light and lives of what I thought was all people but in particular my family.

Then the three brothers could be seen asleep on a plane heading to the United States. My instinct was to be afraid that they'd hurt Lucas but I was able to more easily replace that emotion this time with faith. Not an outcome, just faith. I could feel my own existence in the conference room in Denmark as well as Nora and Patrice's. I became aware of what seemed like knowledge of multiple dimensions at once. My eyes, mind and heart were open and aware.

The brother beings in this dimension receded at the light Lucas emanated but the giant serpent didn't. It seemed Nora had seized the opportunity to protect Lucas and herself from the serpent while it was distracted. I watched as her energy took the form of a great raptor and sunk its talons into the serpent, tearing at its flesh with her razor sharp beak. Lucas moved toward the serpent putting a hand of light up to stay the attack. The great hawk eyed the Light and stepped back from its prey. The Light picked up the snake and healed its injuries. He held it in his arms and it was rendered pliant.

Then Lucas told us, "You can't fight it and kill it. You have to understand it and sometimes work with it. It tells us what's wrong so we can heal it. It's really powerful but we can take and use that power if we know how. It demands to be paid attention and if we give it that, before it grows to these proportions, it won't get this far out of control."

"Ophiuchus!" Nora observed. The hidden sign. Look at him! He's the constellation, holding the snake. The return of the thirteenth sign. Does this mean the return of the cycle of the moon?"

All at once I was aware that Lucas had taken on the appearance of the lighted stars in the thirteenth constellation and the cauldron at our feet expanded so that it too opened up to be the ring of the galactic equator, the route through which the sun appears to travel through each constellation. We were literally a part of and a witness to everything.

I recognized the stars that highlighted the thirteen Zodiacal signs. I witnessed this cycle of time as it draws near the end of its revolution. I could see that the Fifth Civilization will be played out in the final age as humanity arrives at the ultimate decision as to whether it will utilize the age of science for the benefit of humanity or the destruction of it. All around me in the spatial dimension, I saw symbols and evidence of every form of spirituality, worship and religion from the most well-known to the most obscure, each giving of light to add to the brilliance of the collective spirit.

"Oh," was all I could muster at the understanding of the concept that any path to the spiritual awakening in a person is the path they should be on. No concept that adheres to the simple quest to harm none is better than another. The harm is when one attempts to claim to be the one and right way for all.

I looked to Lucas again and understood his lesson that one can't eradicate the darkness but must utilize it to bring everything into focus, just as one can't live in complete light. It can be equally blinding as the dark. With a work of art, the beauty can only be seen when the artist fully understands how to master the use of shadow and light in harmony. Humanity is about balance and contrast, light and shadow. By virtue of being human, we are expected to learn by our mistakes, but that can't be done if we exist in perfection. The best we can be as humans, is to truly learn from our mistakes and to honestly try to harm none and help others to their own spiritual best.

We found ourselves, again, sitting on the cold floor of the museum. I found myself in amazement and asking the question aloud, "That's it? Really? That's it? It's that simple?" Then after a fraction of a moment, "And that complex."

The cauldron sitting on the floor in the center just as it had been what seemed like a thousand years ago. In fact if someone had told me that a thousand years had passed, I would have believed them. Travel outside of the body, as an energetic being was such an expansive experience that time seemed irrelevant so that I had no concept of it at all until I'd returned to my heavy, sluggish constraint of a body here on the floor. I knew not much time had passed at all because Cath and Finny, faithful friends, were sitting in a couple of conference chairs staring at us expectantly.

My sisters and I looked to each other without having to ask the question if we'd all experienced the same thing. We knew we had. I understood that the battle we were about to face was not only one waged for humanity but one waged within oneself. In that moment, I strove to commit the lessons gained today to memory and have them become a part of both my conscious and my unconscious way of living. Knowledge is power. Any path to spirituality is the right one for the individual on the path, so long as it does or professes no harm and helps others on their own path. Be honest in self-assessment to be the best I can be. Utilize the darkness harbored within me to learn from my mistakes. I began to understand why we met the three brothers on a spiritual battlefield. Because really, all battles begin there just as soon as one strays off their path but part of the knowledge is to know when to stand up and fight and when to acquiesce, to make the right choices.

I looked at the old men, to my sisters and then to the cauldron. It seemed so inconsequential an artifact now, the vessel through which the message was delivered. Then came the realization that the magic gleaned from the cauldron was most Powerful. We had gained strength in knowledge. Simple knowledge. I was amazed, again at the simplicity of the lesson and the strength it offered. Just then, Faidhe's voice echoed in my head, *Knowledge is Power.* And I understood. I tested my new strength and flashed a thought to Lucas.

Instantly I was in the back seat of our car looking into Lucas's eyes. He saw me and brightened. Once again an eight-year old boy looking small and fragile in our wreck of a car wearing his blue blanket like a Captain America cape, secured with an odd looking clasp, he looked to me for guidance and I told him, *"You know what to do."*

He nodded his head and I watched as a bolt of pure light struck out from his chest and traveled straight to his father's head. In that moment, I watched as Walter, red faced and pulsing with fury, withdrew his argument and took the other person's license and insurance information in silence.

I saw him breathe some, then when he returned the other man's information to him Walter asked, "Do you remember what happened here?" The other man was so taken aback at the question and Walter's subdued demeanor that he impulsively answered with the simple truth.

"Not really." He responded. "I just stepped on the gas even though it was a red light. It was like a bull seeing a red flag. I just stomped on the gas and wanted to crush some steel." The man's face took on a perplexed look revealing he really didn't know what was happening to him or why he admitted the truth.

Walter understood now what had taken place as if a light went on in his head. He turned to check on Lucas locked in the back seat of the car and I knew that he saw me there too. He looked right at me and nodded. I sent a thought to him to allay his confusion. *Do you want to be right or do you want to be happy? What's important here?*

"Okay." He said to the other driver. "I have your information and you have mine. No one's hurt but it looks like you'll need a tow. I can still drive my car so I'll wait until the cops get here and then I'll be off to have my son checked out."

Walter unlocked the car and sat in the back seat with Lucas. "You sure you're alright, Buddy?"

"Yeah Dad, I told you, I'm fine. I saw it coming so no one was hurt."

Walter seemed to understand what Lucas was saying without analyzing it. I thought that was a good thing. He's beginning to accept all this.

"Luke." Walter said.

"Yeah Dad?"

"You see anything unusual?" He asked looking directly at me.

"No Dad. Neither do you. She's here. I see her too."

"Okay then." He said and asked me directly, "Is this...Is everything, okay? Are you still...Ah...?"

"We're all okay." I told him in his thoughts. His eyes grew wide at the sensation of having me speak directly into his mind. *"This is just the beginning though. We have a special boy here and we have to take care with him. Our work over here is finished, I think, or pretty near. I'll let you know when we're planning on coming home. I can't wait to see you."* I chuckled at the silliness of that thought since I was looking directly at him and we all watched as beautiful colors and tinkling sounds emitted from the laughter. *"Well you know what I mean."*

"I do."

"Will you do me a favor?" I asked.

Lucas interrupted. "Mom that's where we were going when we got hit."

I looked back and forth between the two men in my life. *"Where?"*

Walter answered. "Lucas told me we had to take a ride to your sister Mary's house. We're on our way there now."

"Okay. Good. Thanks. I know you don't see eye to eye with her on much, but there are lessons to learn from her. And tell her she might be receiving an unexpected visit from some unpleasant men but we'll be able to handle that now. I don't know what she knows. I think she may have had some pretty graphic dreams today but tell her I'll call her later...It's the right thing to do. We have some talking to do." I turned to Lucas. *"You're gonna leave some light there aren't you?"* I said not needing an answer. I knew he would take care of her. I had faith in him. *"I'll call you both later too."* I said to wrap up.

Habitually, Walter leaned in to kiss me and abruptly pulled back at the odd sensation of an electrical current where we touched. He touched his forefinger to his lips, then ran his tongue over the numbness he felt on his mouth.

"Tingly," he said. "I guess I'll wait until you get home. Too weird." He shook his head and tapped his lips.

"Electric!" I told him switching my eyebrows up and down in mock seduction. He smiled and I hugged Lucas. *"Take care of our boy."* I said and was back at the museum.

Nora and Patrice were inspecting the final panel that had been released from the cauldron, no longer a part of it. On it was the impromptu work Patrice had etched in the form of a bright sun in the exact position the Light had appeared to us in the vision or dimension travel or whatever it could be called.

"Wow." I said. The word was so simple but encapsulated all the amazement and marvel I felt at the symbolism of the work. We all stood in contemplation for a moment then there was nothing left so I suggested, "Should we clean up?"

It took us less than five minutes to right the table and chairs and to clean up the salt, sage and water mess with paper napkins from the sideboard of the conference room ensuring no salt or water remained on the cauldron. As if on cue, Dr. Erland Strykersen knocked politely before keying in the code to open the security door.

"Everything well?" He asked the room in general but was looking directly at Patrice.

In a moment of rare synchronicity, all five of us in the room said at exactly the same time, "Everything's fine." then burst into gales of laughter.

I watched as the room filled with beautiful blooms of the colors and designs of laughter. I think most of us did.

54

Finding Home

We found ourselves back at the hotel room suddenly at a loss for what to do next. We'd come back from the museum in relative silence considering what we'd all just been through and witnessed. I wondered at what Cath and Finny were thinking after so long in waiting for this duty to be fulfilled, to suddenly have lost their primary purpose in life now that the story had been told and we had successfully unleashed the Power of the cauldron.

I went to the bar, got out five glasses and opened a couple of bottles of wine splits supplied in the mini bar from the tiny refrigerator. I poured out the wine and served the others. Raising my glass. "To family."

"To family." They all responded.

We sipped in silence for a minute and Nora was the first to speak asking the men, "So were we alone there, or did you guys know what was happening during our experience?"

"We were able te pick up the gist of yer experience without actually participatin', yes." Finny replied.

"So what was the story with the Hindu chakras?" She asked.

"I think I might be able to field this one." I said. "The Celts came across the continent and populated much of eastern and western Europe through the centuries but they originated in Indo-European culture. Hinduism is one of the oldest religions in the world. Much of the Celtic faith was based and descended from this original system. So, we as spiritual beings are really an amalgam of all the faiths, practiced in earnest and so have adopted the spiritual features to a greater or lesser degree of those faiths. A sort of 'you are what you believe' kind of thing."

"But we're not Hindu or Hindi or whatever you'd call it." Patrice said.

"I get it." Nora interjected. "What we experienced was kind of a map of all the religions in some way. There were halos on us, you know, coronas like you'd see depicted in Judeo-Christian paintings. There was the Cauldron, an artifact from the pre-Celtic faith; there was the astrological aspect to what we saw, the Staff is used in so many faiths, not just our Old Ways and the Christian one, but in some African and Native American religions, and I'll bet if we sat and thought about everything that was detailed around us, we'd be able to come up with a symbol, a reference or something from every religion or spiritual belief system!"

"Okay," Patrice said, contemplating the concept. Her head was nodding as she continued; "I remember a few obvious things, like I saw the Star of David during some part of the whole strange experience. I know that's in the old religion as well as the Jewish faith. You're probably right."

I jumped back into the conversation. "We were in the realm of the spirit but not just *the* realm, as if there's only one. It was about *all* spirit. It's like our map to reach that balance we're trying for. Is it better to be Catholic or Pagan? Well for me, the true map for me to follow is the Old Ways because that's what my path is. But to try to have someone else follow my map just because it's right for me may not bring him or her to the balance they strive for. They have to follow their *own* map to reach their *own* destination. It's all in how it's perceived." *There was that concept again. Perception is the key.* I grew excited at this new understanding. "I've been struggling with this battle my whole life. I was coming from an understanding of the Old Ways as my true path but was told that I was wrong or bad because I couldn't find 'enlightenment' in the Christian faith. Well, that's because I needed to follow a different set of directions...a different map! I found my way back to the Old Ways and Patrice, you were more comfortable with the Christian path, like Nora has found her map in Astrology. None of them are bad or wrong if they lead us to our peace or balance. And achieving your enlightenment, balance, Nirvana, Heaven, self actualization or whatever, is an individual quest. Sometimes you have to leave the Tuath or tribe and their concept of the right path to find your own right path so long as you harm none on any level. Keeping in mind the 'eye for an eye' thing has to be balanced with the 'turn the other cheek' thing. Self-preservation is an equal part of that concept too."

We sipped a little more and thought about our simple discovery that severed forever, for me anyway, the guilt that tortured me so severely and kept me connected to the mores of the Catholic Church despite my absolute knowledge that the Old Ways were the right path for me. I was no longer connected to the shame that came along with not being a part of the majority. I felt free as a bird.

"Ha!" I saw the humor in the statement. "Free as a bird. That's me! Free to be me." The others stared at me, uncomprehending. "We can slip the bonds of "supposed to" and just be "what we are" when we choose the right path for the self. And really there are no coincidences. Nora, remember when you and Laoghaire got back together and on his coronation night he crowned you with ivy and flowers and said that that's how you'd be celebrated as their queen every year?"

"Yeah." She said tentatively, waiting for an explanation.

"Well, you came into this life when?"

"Ah, May First."

"Right!" I wave an arm and spilt a little wine. "Sorry." I said. But, right. You were born on the day of the May Queen. May Day. The day to celebrate who you were back then and what is part of who you are now. You found your path in the Old Ways in the astrological map. And Patrice was crowned as the Mother Mary, in the Catholic Church in the May Procession when we were kids. It's funny, we each found our way to the Goddess in different ways. Patrice found her comfort in the path the church offered. Me, I was troubled by being torn in both directions as you never were Nora, because I was looking for balance between the two instead of looking for it within myself. But now, I've found my path in being me. Free as a bird, the bird that carries the light and knows of the hidden things like it said in the prophecy. I feel like I can be the Black Bird or Raven of the spirit...the free spirit again. Unleashed from the chains of religion and released into the freedom of the spirit!" I felt as though I were soaring with the jubilation of the glow I felt within me.

"What do you think all this meant for Mary?" Patrice asked. "She was Gara and now she's Mary. She tried her hand at dabbling in things that maybe she shouldn't have when we were younger, but where does her path lead?"

We were all quiet again until Finny spoke. "It's perhaps her time te begin te lorn about comin' from a place of I and goin' te a place of we. She came with the Staff te the meditation or whatever ye choose te call it, but as ye depicted in the panel, Patrice, she did not draw near on either side. She delivered a message that was so distinctly her own lesson in the other time. For she was certainly happiest when she allowed herself to let go and leave off of controlling things. And perhaps that was her epiphany of sorts, that the answer to arriving at your own spiritual strength is a matter of choice, not Power or power over others. 'Belief in oneself and have faith in another' is what she said. Well, it could be that her spirit has arrived at that knowledge but her physical being has not quite come te the realization as yet. Plenty of people have the *knowing* of something long before they actually allow themselves te live it."

We three sisters sat with raised eyebrows as we began to recognize the value in that perspective of our other sister. We had hope that she would have faith in herself and allow that final walk toward us to trust us enough to join us in the light to find her own path.

"So how did she get the Staff," Nora asked, "if she wasn't here?"

"It's possible that it wasn't necessary for her to come te the full knowledge of memory as did ye gorls." Cath began. "It may be that ye were ready and needed for the purpose of bringing the cauldron te its task, but that Mary had no true need of comin' te the full memory, she may have delivered her message and carried the Staff without the burden of the memory of who she was in that other time. She did not choose te side with the dark and did not succumb te the allure of its Power so there is evidence that she has partially come from the dark in te the light but has not yet found her comfort there. She may have te develop relationships worth trustin' before she'd completely abandon the hope of whatever the allure is for her: riches, notoriety, control. Ye'll have te detormine what of the story she knows and whether she has raised the Staff or merely delivered a message."

More silent thinking, and head bobbing. My thoughts went to Lucas and Walter. I wanted to know how their visit with Mary had gone. I wanted to know how everything went after the accident. I wanted to know what had happened to the bull-brothers. Although, after Nora chewed on the serpent for a bit and then Lucas had taken the serpent in hand, I didn't think they'd be bothering any of us. I did think they'd be the awful people they'd always been without much hope that they would come into the light. But that was not what I was supposed to think. I corrected myself. I should trust that one day, they might come to find their own way to a place of peace with true introspection. I breathed a sigh at how difficult it was to try to perceive those 'amadans' with a positive perspective.

"I wonder what they'll do in America." No one asked whom I meant. We were all thinking the same thing. A ring of light rose above us as a group and shot out of the area in the blink of an eye. "What was that?" I asked.

Cath's face screwed up into a crinkly smile that made me smile myself. "That gorls, was a true prayer of unadulterated purity. It seems we've learned well, the treasure and power of the lessons taken here today."

I started crying. Partly it was a release of all that we'd been through, and partly because I realized that my entire life was going to change and so was that of my entire family but mostly because I knew how much I was going to miss these dear men I had grown to love so deeply. I didn't have to say it, they all knew but I announced. "I love you all so much...Tomorrow, I'm going home."

We sat with our bare feet up on the heavy coffee table made of lustrous wood and contemplated tomorrow. Nora said, "I think I'll stay on for a while." My mind flashed the congenial face of Eric, the Norwegian. *There are no coincidences.*

"You going to Norway?"

"No, I'll be going home, but I want to get some things settled in my heart before I do. There's some work to be done at home before I'll be free to pursue that other path. First things first and I have to make things right with Will. We owe it to each other to end things right. Maybe I can help him on his path. Then I'll see about that other."

"Good for you." I said.

"Yeah, I think so. I've done all I can for the life I left at home. I think I'm relieved to let that old life go and build something more positive. I bless Will with a full heart and hope he finds his own map, but I think I'll see where my path leads me now that I realize I don't have to stay on in a relationship that is no longer beneficial for either of us." Another spark of light jotted from the crown of her head and off to its destination.

I felt good for Nora and had a little adrenaline rush at the thought of her traveling this new path alone but I knew she was striking out on her own as part of what was necessary for her. She'd been a part of either the family or her marriage her entire life. Now, I thought, she must be feeling free as a bird too.

"I looked at Patrice. "I don't suppose you'll be coming back anytime soon?"

"Oh," she said, "I'll be coming back. I can't leave Marcus, Matt and Jonas home too long at their father's but I think I'll hang around long enough to see some other exhibits at the Museum of Denmark."

"Oh, you mean the one that has dark hair and dimples? I figured as much." I kidded.

She squirmed a little.

I said with a knowing grin on my face. "Don't hurt yourself!" Patrice flushed and buried her smirk in her wine glass.

"I don't plan to." She quipped.

"Cath, Finny," I started, "but couldn't find the words and began to blubber at the idea of saying goodbye to them. They had selflessly kept to their path and led me back to mine. And I loved them for it and for so much more. I didn't know how I would leave them. "I...I can't imagine now..."

I completely broke down and just hugged Cath as I rolled into him on the couch next to me and reached across him to grab Finny's hand.

"There now, lass." Cath comforted as he patted my hair and I soaked his shirt. "It's not the end now, it's your beginning. We've still lornin' and teachin' a plenty te be done."

"We will?" I sniffled.

"For cortain." Finny broke in. "You don't keep the Light under a bushel, as they say. Now as ye've come te the lornin, ye've got te commence with the teachin'. I'm sure there're people a plenty out there who've been as troubled with their own path as ye have with yer own. How can ye not offer direction te those who're lost? There's the real journey, now isn't it?"

"I guess. We'll still talk and see each other?" I asked hopefully.

"How could ye think otherwise?" Cath retorted. "We've not waited the better part of two Civilization fer ye te not stick around te see how the next one torns out!"

It would have been too cruel to have found these two and lost them again so quickly. I breathed a sigh of contentedness with the comfort of knowing these friends would continue to be our mentors. And it was even more of comfort to know that I could just think of either one and be there with them if the need arose.

"Good, then. Let's have some more wine tonight. I have a date with two other guys tomorrow."

———

I hadn't actually gotten on a plane the next day but the day after that on the first flight I could book out of Denmark to get me home. By the time I landed in Boston, I was ready to be home. It seemed the floodgates had opened and once I started crying I just couldn't stop. All I could do was stand and cry as I toggled between trying to hug Walter and bending to hug Lucas. Finally, I took Lucas up in my arms and carried him to stand on a bench so he was my height. I buried my face and breathed in the scent of both of them as all three of us just stood and hugged. It was the scent of home. I felt the thrum of the energy as it surged through us and around us in the reunion.

"I missed you so much." I cried. "I missed you so much. Oh it's so good to be home."

I stopped and looked at the familiar landscape of Walter's face. I had to touch it and re-familiarize myself with the lines and creases. Then to Lucas, I said, we've been through a lot haven't we Spooky?"

"Yeah, but we still have stuff to do too." He said in a more serious tone.

It was strange, but as soon as my feet touched the ground back in America, I knew I wasn't in the magical land of my history. The energy was different and I'd have to readjust but I also could feel a strong undercurrent of change taking place. It was as though, now that my door to the Light had been opened, I began to be able to see, hear, feel and recognize the trends in the energy of things far beyond the perception of just my physical senses.

"Times are changing." I said.

"Yeah, but now we know what to do now. Right?"

"We'll find our way, Baby. We'll definitely find our way. But right now, let's find our way home."

Luke chirped, "You're here, Mom. We *are* home."

He was so right.

55

Times Are Changing

Almost a year has passed since my sisters and I found our paths in Ireland and Denmark. Some things have changed for us in that we no longer depend on one another to reach our Power. We've gained strength in self-reliance; much like our Valkyrie ancestors and we tend to our individual paths and rejoice when they converge to come together in our spiritual journeys.

Patrice has hit her stride in growing her jewelry business well enough to support herself and sons quite comfortably. This boost in popularity for her pieces came with the boost in her confidence in her own talent and abilities, a simple change in her perspective brought her success. Although it was obvious to her that she would not produce the silver panels for the general market, Patrice has rekindled her connection to her magic as she had in her past life, by creating meaningful panels while in a meditative state. The first reintroduction to her magic in this way was the panel created for use in the ritual at the museum. Though that piece was needed to complete the original cauldron to release its magic, it was not the last panel of that prehistoric time, but the first panel for this current time. When the ritual there in the museum had finished, the Cauldron had dropped the final panel and resumed its original appearance. Patrice took back her panel and since, has produced four more, depicting the life of each of the four sisters. She's currently working on one for Lucas as well. We watch to see how our individual depictions and symbols will unfold for us and whether this is the beginning of a new bowl with a new purpose.

Nora went home, as she had planned, to let go of her husband with all the love and forgiveness she could conjure for him. Hers was a true challenge for the lesson we'd learned in the museum basement. She did not accuse, argue, blame or challenge her husband. She simply went home and released him from the contract they had entered into so many years ago. She bathed him in the light of love and gave him nothing to rail against. They parted amicably enough, though I still think he doesn't quite know what happened. They had lived under their contract for so long that he was at a loss when she blessed him and moved on. The last I heard, he continued his old habits with his new girlfriend.

I knew Nora's heart ached for the companionship she'd come to take for granted in her husband, such as it was, but she did not let that force her to fly headlong into something new. She spent much of the last year on her own, reflecting and allowing for healing and bringing herself to the point when she thought she was ready to enter into a relationship in which she would allow herself to trust and let the other person into her heart, to truly get to know her. She apparently felt ready because she'd called the number on the worn out napkin she kept from Eric the Norwegian, and after a few months of communication, arranged for a trip to South Carolina. I felt caution for her at first, but it was just my fear speaking. I sent her all the love and prayers I could so that she would determine honestly if this man is to be part of her path.

Mary, thankfully, never really understood beyond her dream that she had participated in bringing a message to the world. She had remained neutral in our quest on that day; she had not yet stepped toward either of the opposing forces at work. But since then she has made progress toward the light each time we, Patrice, Nora, Walter, Lucas and I welcomed and trusted with our faith that she would come to the light. We prayed for her and it did her a world of good as opposed to blaming her for past injuries she could never really admit having committed. I think it did me a world of good too.

Not long after we returned from our trip to Europe, our father, Patrick (Laoghaire) O'Leary, surrendered to the Otherworld. He had so much knowledge of the world and history stored within him and yet, he never actually came to the understanding of who he had been and the enormous role he played in our upbringing; giving us the foundation to build strong, unique, independent personalities enough to trust our magical selves and come up against the darkness. He gave us the tools to honor the gift of our own spirits. One of those billions of points of light has gone out for having lost this man, but I am comforted in knowing I will see him again when my path leads me to him. Until then, I surround myself in the beauty of his poetry that is so revealing of his heart and with his artwork that allows me to see the world as he did. And I take in all I can of his library so that the knowledge he had in his arsenal will be at my disposal as well so that I can pass it on to my son, when he has need of such things.

Our mother, without our father, is on a journey of her own now, after over a half a century of being coupled with another person she is beginning to determine her own path. It seems that having given up the latter part of her life as Craiche for Laoghaire in the past, she will have the addendum to her life now, after he has passed. It's my sincere hope and prayer that she will be fulfilled in finding her path for herself and enjoys the journey as she follows it.

We 'pushed back the chairs' on this past Winter Solstice at our home in Plymouth. For the first time without our father, we burned the Yule log and welcomed all our ancestors from the recent past and the distant past to 'join in the Frey.' We danced and laughed and ate as the darkness of the longest night of the year waited while we basked in the Light of love and our family. We left an empty seat at our table for any soul who cared to come and sit in the Light. We kept the old traditions and began some new.

I see all these things in my mind's eye now as I stand at the window of a two hundred year old cottage in County Clare, Ireland. Down the driveway I see the husk of a burnt out building that used to be a cottage and small pig farm. I look to the left of that husk and I see an old, ramshackle truck parked inside a barn next to Bridey Flynn's neat farmhouse. I watch as Bridey herself picks early garden cabbage and wraps it into her apron with a broad smile on her face as she watches her two ancient brothers teach a small, sunny-faced boy how to do handspring to back flips around the newly placed circle of stones in what used to be the dooryard of the burnt cottage. I heard the far off laughter of my son, who is turning nine years old today, the Summer Solstice, and wonder at his future but immediately bathe the thought in light. *Faith* I remind myself. *No fear.* This has become my mantra lately. With my right hand, I finger the Celtic cross I wear on a gold chain around my neck and with my left, I reach up to the small golden cauldron with a hooked stirring stick also on the chain. They feel right to me; and what's even more telling is that I wear them both proudly without keeping one religion in the dark, away from scrutiny. I know now, nothing good can come of keeping any true spark of spirituality in the dark.

I reflect on our experience of the day before. The McDonough brothers, Bridey, Lucas, Walter and I came to the landscape I recognized as approaching the Hill of Tara on our way to the Knowth Cairns as part of Lucas's education.

Lucas shouted, "Stop! We have to stop, up there!" He pointed enthusiastically. "It's the last one, Mom. You have to go. It's the last one. Then you can finish the last tale and start the new one.

We did as he said and Cath pulled to where we could safely park. Before we could think about what was next, Lucas was out the car and off toward the horizon.

We all gathered where Lucas was standing a fair distance from anything of note.

"Here." He said. "It's here." He was positively glowing as he looked up toward the sky.

"What's here, Luke?" Walter asked. "What do you see?"

"The Stone. It was here. Before they took it. But when they took it, it wasn't really the Stone anymore 'cause the heart was gone out of it when Faidhe made everything move on."

Walter was bewildered but the rest of us understood. The Stone of Fal no longer held the seat of Kingship of Ireland when the magic had gone under to the Sidhe. I had no idea where the actual Stone was at this point in time but obviously, Lucas seemed to be looking at something he thought was the Stone.

He answered my thought with, "I don't think it's the Stone, Mom. It is the Stone, but like its ghost. It's right here!" He was emphatic as he pointed up at an empty sky.

I had learned not to doubt my son and tried to see with my spirit rather than my eyes and gradually, I began to see a faint, bluish light outlining what must have been a great monolith. As the image became more clear and finite to me, I asked, "Does everyone see it?"

He didn't answer so I looked at Walter and he had the look of amazement on his face. I knew he saw it. He pointed. "Look. What's that?"

We all looked back and within the outline of the Stone, there was a deeper blue light gathering from within the ghost-stone. About five or so feet tall with a hook shape on the top was an ornately carved Staff within the Stone.

I looked at Cath with a question and he shrugged his shoulder.

"I told ye as we thought the Staff would be where Patrick gained great strength. It is the implement of fire and it was borned in the fire all those years ago. To this, I was a witness. So I knew the Power would be most likely here for the takin', when the time is right. So likely, now, the time is right."

"But what about Mary?" Isn't this her task? And aren't we sort of finished with taking on the energy of the implements?"

Finny answered. "Do ye remember the part of the prophecy that we'd shared wi' ye not about yer family comin through and how they'd be known to us but the other of how we'd know who you yerself are and what yer task would be in this world?"

"How could I not? It's burned into my memory." I answered.

"Well then, recite for us a few lines if ye will."

Lucas hopped up and down. "Oh, I know. I know. Raising his hand as if he were in school."

"Wait now, lad. Let yer mother come to it." Cath told him with a gentle voice as though they were dealing with a slow learner.

I recited, "At her birth she will don her name as the mark to be borne, a gift of balance from the heavens above and those below the Sidhe."

"Go on." Finny prodded.

"In her name, she'll carry the Sword of Light and Knowledge to pierce through ignorance."

"Continue."

"In her name, she will keep commune with the secret of wisdom of the dark bird of the heavens as a Staff to carry and spread a message of balance...Oh."

"It's for you, Mom. It's for you! You get to deliver the message with your Sword. Just like Aunt Patrice said you would. Your pen is your sword! Lucas did a few newly learned back flips and laughed out loud. "You told the old story, now you have to tell the new story. That's it. Take it, Mom. Take it."

I looked at all the faces here with me now. Lucas's, jubilant with what he knew would be a surprise. Cath and Finny with expressions that said they also knew this would reveal itself to me in time. Bridey smiled encouragingly and Walter looked as if he didn't know what to think but was resigned that this would be the way of it for us now.

I stepped toward the Stone-light and reached for the Staff. It was easily obtainable as I wrapped my hand around the hilt. From my solar plexus, bubbled up the unexpected words: *From her chest she'll breathe life back into the forgotten and all who meet her will hear the voice of the earthen meadow.* I inhaled and the Staff was absorbed into my middle.

"You did it, Mom. You did it. Now you can tell the story. Now you can tell everyone!" Lucas hugged me tight around the waist.

"Okay, I did it. Now we'll see just what that means."

"It means you write your story." He said as if I should have known this already.

"What story is that, Luke?"

"This one. Our story. What happened before, now and what will happen next. You know, when things really start to change."

"Really?" I blinked at the simplicity. Since I decided not to continue my dissertation after all that had happened I hadn't really thought about what came next. I was completely satisfied to be with my family as we restructured the way we prioritized our lives. I hadn't wanted to think beyond that but now I saw that we had little more than three years before Lucas comes to his 'manhood' at the end of 2012.

"What will I do?" I asked.

"Ye've been collectin' the material fer years now, lass. Ye've filled yer satchel with history. De we have te show you a map?" Cath admonished. "Go and tell it!"

———

The threat of the three brothers has gone to ground and been silent. They neither came to our door nor to Mary's. We don't know if they remain in America or if they've returned to Ireland. We can no longer feel their overt presence but keep watch for them as we look to the future. We also keep watch in our own hearts for those occasions when we might lend strength to them through our fears. It may be that we weaken them with our confidence but will always be connected to them. We are the balancing light to their darkness. But they have so many other hearts to feed upon, so many fearful hearts, so many secrets to fertilize, so many human frailties upon which to capitalize. I know now, it's my new quest to shed light on as many as I can, and share the light of knowledge.

Now, standing at the window in the little cottage with my family around me, I contemplated all that had happened since last year and right up until this new discovery of the Staff just yesterday. Walter came from our bedroom behind me and wrapped his arms around me. "Thinking about the book?" he asked.

"Mm hmm." I answered. I looked down the drive again to Cath, Finny and Bridey, within the Circle of stones, teaching Lucas things he'll need to know for what is coming. A flash of blue light caught my eye and I spied what looked like the familiar form of a woman with her hand on Lucas's shoulder. I drew strength from the sight, knowing that she's still here for him.

"I better get started. Things are already changing fast."

56

Epilog

Inauguration of

The Boy's Club

June 2013

Young boys, tanned and beautiful with bushy blond hair streaked with summer, jump and writhe in good-natured competition. *Of course they're beautiful; look at their parents.* I watch them and feel old despite my own good fortune in a family trait of having a youthful appearance for my age, which at this point was creeping uncomfortably more toward the middle of middle-age rather than the beginning of it. It seems it was only yesterday I was as young as they are now. My sister's boys, all tanned and toned, moved like a ballet in motion on the basketball court behind her Cape Cod home. Watching, I see the man my son will become peeking through in all his pre-pubescent glory: a shadow of a fuzzy moustache, the occasional crackling voice, his developing muscle tone that already has the girls calling on the phone but as pleasing as he is to look at, it's his personality that draws people to him.

Good. I think to myself. *Not doomed to a life of reluctant independence like me.* But that solace isn't enough to uncoil the knot in my gut as I contemplate his future. Quick with a smile and a kind word or joke, he seems to know just how to put people at ease. He knows how to talk to people. He helps them to see themselves in the most positive possible light and they reward him with their friendship. He makes it appear so effortless and for that, I'm pleased and relieved for him. As a kid, friendships came hard for me...still do. Not so for my boy.

Lucas was born into this world with a purpose, a destiny foretold in a prophecy nearly 4000 years ago. It's a simple destiny, really or should I say, unvarnished destiny.

As we drew closer to when he'd come to his maturity at the age of 12 years and a half, we began the countdown to the time when he'd be called to his that destiny, which is a tall order for one so young; to save humanity from itself. Now, at six months past that 12 years and a half mark, how that will take place is still yet to be revealed.

Although Lucas understands that he has a tremendous responsibility, he is still able to be a kid. He amazes me. He makes me so proud. And I suffer quietly, as any mother would, that my son will not be allowed to live a normal childhood and be concerned only with those things important to boys his age: grades, video games, basketball, food, girls and more food.

Instead, he has been in training since his destiny was discovered when he was 8-years old. Training about the unseen. Training in how to use his strength and magical abilities. Training in recognizing astrological concepts and symbology. Training for how to shine light on people's lives to show them the potential in the paths they have chosen for themselves, for good or not so good. He brings the light of truth: Lucas, the bringer of light and knowledge. It all sounds so noble and seemingly impossible now as I look at him shooting baskets with his cousins, Patrice's kids, Jonas, Marcus, and Matt, all legs and arms and shiny white teeth as they play and bump into each other trying to emulate the pro-ball moves they see on television.

I feel a nostalgic pang of empathy for my youngest nephew Mather, 10-years old, as he grows frustrated at his chronological disability and shouts at his brothers.

"You're not fair! That's not fair. I never get to shoot!" As boys will do, his brothers faked passing him the ball and teased him for being so small. As Marcus, the middle brother at 15-years took two long strides toward Mather and adroitly twirled around him, the ball inexplicably flew out of his hands and into Lucas's who pointedly passed the ball to Mather.

"Shoot, Matt. Shoot." Lucas said. "Quick, you'll make it."

Matt looked at his brothers and with a gleam of hope, stuck out his tongue in effort and heaved the ball into the air. The ball should have lobbed an arc far too low to make the basket but inexplicably, it changed course, mid-air, and defied laws of physics. The basketball hovered a bit, and with a second arcing hump, found the hoop and landed directly in the basket to Matt's shouts of triumph.

"I did it! I did it!" He jumped in the air.

Jonas, the oldest of the boys at 17, scowled and looked directly at Lucas. "You can't do that. That's cheating."

"What?" Lucas said, feigning innocence. He reminded me so much of Finny when he did that.

"You did that and you know it. You can't use that on the court and play fair."

"Are you playing for money or something?" Lucas retorted but in a convincing and congenial way. "Look at him." He said, pointing to Matt. "He's half your size. Is it gonna kill you to let him get in the game once in a while?"

Looking at his brother who was still beaming, Jonas acquiesced. "I guess not. Nice shot, squirt." Jonas called to his baby brother. Matt's face lit up with the pleasure of being praised. And just like that, Lucas shone his light and brought the two brothers closer together.

"Thanks." Matt answered in disbelief. Apparently, praise didn't come often from Jonas. After his older brother turned back to the hoop for a hook shot, he turned to Lucas and said more quietly, "Thanks."

"No problem," Lucas said and ruffled Matt's hair. "Marcus never could hold the ball anyway." He teased loud enough so Marcus would catch the good-natured jab.

"Hey!" Marcus called.

I watched as the four boys bantered and did that masculine jousting seemingly required of boys to achieve position in the hierarchy of adolescence. I was glad that they were becoming close. It wasn't always so but so much has happened since the trip to Europe with my sisters, Nora and Patrice five years ago. We recognized the importance of family...our family, and we made strides to bring our children, my son Lucas closer to his cousins, the Roccia brothers when prior to then, they had been more like just acquaintances, seeing one another at family gatherings rather than true kin.

"Five years." Patrice said from behind me as though she'd been reading my mind.

"Hmm?" I questioned, coming back from my thoughts.

"It's been five years since we fitted the last piece of silver into the Gundestrup Cauldron and released the Power of the Old Ones back into the world. Five years since we've been to Europe, since Dad died, since Lucas's strength in magic began to grow, and since my own boys began to show unmistakable signs of their magical heritage. Take your pick. Don't play with me now. Five years and we both know why we're here."

I sighed. I liked the pretense that we were just sisters having a visit while our boys sparred in the ring of youth but I knew better.

"Okay, I know." I said. "Where's Nora?"

"Here," she called as she entered Patrice's bright Cape Cod kitchen with a tray holding three Waterford crystal shot glasses and an aged bottle of Jameson's Whiskey.

As sisters, our closeness at one time acted sort of as a conduit for one another so that as long as we were together, we were much more Powerful than when we were apart. We've lately developed our magical strength on our own as individuals, and considering the battle that may lie ahead for us, that's a good thing but we're quite a formidable force when we're together.

"A wee bit of the sweetness of home." Nora said in a mock Irish accent, her long, curly brown hair cascading over her shoulders as she put the tray down.

The accent sounded light but we all knew this was an important ritual as we gathered to talk about darker things. Nora poured out three healthy shots of the sweet whiskey bottled in Midleton, County Cork, Ireland; the land of our ancestors. It was our way of calling the attention and protection of those ancestors to be in attendance as we discussed our situation and plans for the future. We'd done this many times over the last five years as time had grown closer to when Lucas, would be exactly 12 years and six months old and come to his full potential in his magical ability.

As it was told in prophecy, he would come to his full strength in his magical power to begin to fulfill his destiny. Knowing there would be an equal and opposing force to his goodness and light, we planned for the time when we knew, there would be the ultimate showdown. But as the significant date that was designated by many seers through the civilizations as the crossroads for humanity, December 21, 2012, came and went, we knew we'd see the opening of the Fifth Civilization. We began to understand that our battle, Luke's battle wouldn't be a showdown but a continual pushing back against the growth of the power of that dark opposition. A continual struggle for the soul of humanity.

We held up our glasses.

"To family." Nora said and we repeated.

"To laughter." Patrice announced and again we all repeated.

"To the Light." I toasted and they followed. Then together we raised our glasses high and said in unison, "To life. Slainte!"

We all drank the sweetness and warmth of the fiery liquid and watched as the family trait of red cheeks crept onto our faces just after the whisky warmed our insides. Nora started first.

"Okay, what's the last we heard about the Bull brothers?" Nora inquired.

To the general public, the brothers have been considerably busier than we have due to their public agenda and growing following. Apparently, they have made full use of their astrological attributes and created a cult of zealots willing to go to great lengths to stamp out the 'wickedness of witches.' And apparently witches are any females who will not acquiesce and submit to the power of their masculine dominance. They espouse that women should not be seen in public, should not hold public office, should not hold any position in places of worship and really have no higher purpose than to be calving cows submitting to the will of the bull. Consequently, the cult has a following of men who are insecure and feel emasculated by women in authority, who fear or hate women. The cult has attracted every sociopath looking to take advantage of a network of men who pool resources for heinous operations of trafficking in human sexual slavery all under the guise of a church-like organization.

Starting with the insidious news, I informed Nora and Patrice with what I knew.

"Well they haven't wasted any time setting up shop and becoming a franchise of sorts. They have spawned growth here in the states primarily in places you'd expect: Reno, Las Vegas, New York, Chicago, and for some reason, Vermont has been a warm spot for their bacteria to grow as an easy international highway to Montreal and like cities up there in Canada. There are places in Europe popping up too; London, Sicily, Paris, Greece, Portugal just to name a few but even more scary, they've made inroads in places like Bulgaria, Turkey, Poland and on to the African continent and South America where there was already plenty of machismo as fertile ground for this type of cult to take hold. The cult has no spiritual or religious doctrine so the philosophy dovetails with the harsh and radical faction of the blossoming tides of religion already subjugating women in some regions. They could be anywhere right now and we don't know their exact where-abouts or even if they remained together. I'm still searching on the web but I think Lucas will be the one to tell us exactly where they are. He gets involuntary flashes of insight every now and then as though he's connected with the force of energy they put out."

"Jeeze." Nora whispered.

"In these few short years they've grown so much?" Patrice questioned. "How did that happen? Where did they get the money and funding for such an operation?"

Nora responded. "Remember when I did their chart back when we first learned about them?"

"What about it?" Patrice asked.

"Granted, it was a very unusual chart due to the fact that all three brothers were born at the same time and place but part of what can be seen in their chart is that they have a strong capacity for being intuitive at the very least but also, what they come to believe about the world, they think others should believe the same as they do. It's not just a ruse for control or power they *believe* women are secondary and that it's their divine journey to right the world and inflict what they think the order of things should be on the rest of the world. Trouble is, they're very smart, contrary to their appearance, and they are able to use any intuitions they have about people to their advantage. They're not above blackmail or extortion to meet their ends and then utilize monetary gains to grow their message. They everything as a part of them and already they are growing like a wildfire across the globe. They see, think and feel everything in terms of only what is important to them and their focus would be limited to supporting that subjective perspective. They have no love, no family other than each other and they are like a single mind focused on a single goal with no distractions. I think I told you before that the way their chart is clustered, they have a laser-like focus that borders obsession much like the way it is found in the chart of some serial killers; they are methodical, patient and deadly. In the best possible scenario, these men have the possibility of success in the priesthood, or perhaps as writers who reach a wide audience. But that's at their best, the way they have chosen to be, they are domineering, controlling, surreptitious by avoiding confrontation with deceit and cunning. Instead of priests or writers they have manifested a life for themselves as cult leaders and charismatic speakers. And we all know what power there is in the spoken word."

Nora's words echoed in the kitchen as the sounds of the boy's game filtered into the house from outside. We had been trained in the Power of the Word. We knew that words carry with them energy and something spoken in passion, or with purpose in the right ear, or said enough times or with a certain intention was sure to bring results enough to manifest change, to make the focused intention a reality. We began to feel the weight of the purpose of our meeting today and the silence threatened to allow defeatist thoughts to sneak into the conversation.

Taking a deep breath I said, "Okay, that's what they've been doing. What progress have we made? How are the boys coming in their lessons, Patrice?"

My sister Patrice had married a man whom we suspected also held one of the lines, as there are likely thousands, if not hundreds of thousands of descendants from the original families out there, but history waited for the right combination of the right blood at the right time for the four lines to come together. I thought it was a kind of cosmic backup plan that Patrice had three boys, each with three of the bloodlines, each with less power than my Lucas, but three might have been enough should something have happened to the one. I shuddered at that thought and refocused on the conversation.

Patrice told us, "Mather is willing but hasn't really shown a lot of control in any particular ability yet. He's still so young but seems to be making progress in knowing what people are thinking based on their emotive energy. He doesn't see auras but he can empathically pick up on moods and from there, he can follow the stream of emotions as a sort of key into the mind. There he can ascertain general thoughts not actual mind-reading stuff but general things like he can tell who someone is mad at but maybe not why or the other way around. He's getting better at targeting an individual and next we're going to work on the long distance thing. He says it's easier for him to follow a negative emotion but he doesn't' like to do it. He feels too sad or angry or whatever the emotion he picks up in his subject. He feels what they feel so he hesitates even though it's easier for him, when the mood of the subject is dark."

"Can't blame the little guy." I said. "That'd be a tough row to hoe for an adult never mind a little kid." I said.

Patrice continued. "Jonas is coming along. He practices his skills but I get concerned sometimes that he likes the power of the things he can do more because it's cool than because he understands the battle we may have ahead of us. He talks about showing his friends what he can do."

My eyes grew wide. "Do you think he uses his magic for entertainment?"

Patrice was thoughtful for a minute and answered tentatively. "I don't think so. But he's the oldest of the four boys and he was already twelve years old when all this took place for them. For him, it was like having the newest coolest video game and not being able to show it or play it with his friends. He's only human."

"At least he has his brothers. He's got someone to practice with on a daily basis." I reminded Patrice. "Lucas has no one his own age to work with."

"I know." She answered. "It's just, well, even though Jonas and Marcus are close in age, they're not really close. You know? They're so different. Jonas is so competitive and Marcus has interests that are closer to Lucas's; they both are talented in art and are gifted athletically, they like to discover things in nature. People tend to like them right away. They're so much like Dad, each in their own way, you know? Confident and happy in themselves. I think that's why Marcus and Lucas get along so well despite the age difference. They're more like brothers than Marcus and Jonas. Jonas has a tougher time making friends so I think he thinks a special gift would go a long way in impressing people. But on some level he knows that people would just want to use his talents for things he'd rather not get in to." She thought for a moment and added, "At least I hope he wouldn't allow himself to be used that way."

At the mention of our father, we all sat in contemplation for a moment. I know for my own part, after discovering who we are and what role we have to play in this prophecy business, I couldn't help but lament the fact that as soon as I found out about our heritage and who we all were in earlier times, the opportunity to discuss it all with our father was lost. We came home from our pilgrimage in Ireland and other parts of Europe and were so wrapped up in things necessary for the moment, that the opportunity to speak with our father, an integral part in the origins of all of this long ago, had quietly died in his sleep. It was a bitter pill to swallow for all of us but particularly for Nora. But as a clock chimes it's last call to attention, I think as soon as we found who we are and what we need to do in this present time, our father, Patrick O'Leary, blood kin to King Laoghaire and Saint Patrick, breathed his last. His job here, finished.

Nora, not wanting to dwell on the tragedy that both times she lived and loved this man she'd lost him, returned to the conversation at hand. "So, how is Marcus doing with his training?"

Patrice informed us, "Marcus, is a lot like me. Or he's like I was when I was younger. He doesn't really know he's utilizing his abilities; he just creates these beautiful pieces of art and they eventually prove to be prophetic or at least telling about the subject. He'll do a portrait sketch of someone and add details or symbols to the piece he picks up about them. He just intuits and more often than not, the picture delivers a message about the person. Sometimes it's a hidden trait or secret, other times he'll reveal things that happen shortly after the portrait is done; you know, an injury or trip or new job. Stuff like that. I guess we each got a hint of that artistic gene from Dad and passed it on to our kids." She said, referring to both Marcus and Lucas who each have a natural aptitude for drawing, painting and sculpting.

"Lately though," she continued, "He's been trying some interesting variations to the detailed work I do and he's taken to using a blowtorch to cut and weld metal sculptures. He's done some peculiar pieces recently but the detail is really something."

"What do you mean peculiar?" I asked.

"I'll show you. C'mon." Patrice headed for the basement door. Flapping her hand at us so we'd follow her. At the bottom of the stairs, the basement was illuminated and we saw Pat's workshop that she had set up for her handmade jewelry business. There were halogen lighted magnifying glasses, tools and stones, both precious and semi-precious. There was gold and silver in varying stages of creation. Bolted to the floor in the corner, behind the workbench and stools, was a sturdy looking safe in which Patrice stored her materials and tools except for the pieces in progress on her bench.

Beyond Patrice's work area, an additional bench was set up since the last time I'd been down here. Apparently, this is where Marcus has begun to weld his sculptures. We could see four separate pieces and I understood Patrice's description of them as 'peculiar.' In what appeared to be a set of four figures, each standing about a foot and a half high, he had created figures with human bodies and some with animal's heads like you might see in ancient Egypt or something. One had the head of a bird, one the head of a lion, one was a man and the last had the head of a bull and it made me shudder to recall the O'Tarbh brothers again.

"Wow." I marveled at the detail in Marcus's work. "These are something. Is there some meaning behind the odd figures? Do they represent anything in particular?"

"I don't really know." Patrice responded. "He just works on them when the mood strikes him. Sometimes he'll talk to me when he's working and other times he won't. If he knows why he chose these figures, he hasn't discussed them with me but he did say something in the beginning when he started working on the pieces. He called one of the figures by name when he was talking about it. He said something like, 'I was working on Jonas' and I didn't want to interrupt his train of thought 'cause it's not too often he'll talk about his work with me so I didn't say anything at the time. Like I told you, his work usually reveals the meaning in its own time."

"Maybe we should ask him about them." Nora suggested. "If he has this ability to depict people and their traits through his art, I'd like to know who these guys are. Especially this one." She pointed to the figure with the bull's head and I figured she was thinking the same thing I had about the O'Tarbh brothers.

"Okay," Patrice said. "I will when the right moment arises. He's so private about his work."

"Let's not wait too long though. If there's meaning in the pieces, we should know as soon as possible."

Something nagged at me as we walked back up the stairs. Those figures looked familiar but I couldn't quite place it. Every time I had a glimpse of recognition the answer slipped around a corner in my mind. I wanted a quiet moment to concentrate on it but the conversation already continued and called for my attention. I looked over my shoulder one more time, at the figures on my nephew's workbench before I flipped the switch to turn out the lights as I ascended the stairs.

Names, Pronunciation and Meanings

Names of Prehistoric Characters in Order of Appearance

Faidhe – (Fay or Faith) – Seer

Greenman – Masculine spirit of the woods and growing things

Lon Dubh – (Lon Doov) – Blackbird

Emer – (EH-mer)

Colm – (COL-m) – Dove

Laoghaire – (LAHR-ugh) – Calf herder

Croi – (Cree) – Heart

Cuan – (CEW-an) - Wolf

Morgan – (MOR-gan) Associated with The Morrigan, Irish Goddess of death on the battlefield.

Macha – (MAH-kha) Associated with Morgan and other war Goddesses (portrayed as a male figure in this tale.)

Iarann – (ih-AH-run) Iron

Ethlinn – (ETH-lin)

Craiche – (CRAY-ek)

Faeg – FAY-eg)

Brath – (Braht)

Gara – (GAH-rah)

Briciu – (BRECK-eyoo) – One of the troublemakers of Irish myth.

Triag – (TREE-ahg)

Nemain – (nee-MAIN) – A goddess of war in Irish myth. Means "dreadful" or "venomous")

Clan, Duibhe – (Dew-eev) – Clan, in Darkness

The Seven Chieftains of the Clan, Duibhe:

> Gruama – (groo-AH-ma) Black humored, dismal, gloomy
>
> Sli bain – (SLEE – bayin) The way to reap or cut
>
> Do pib – (Do- peeb) Burning pipes, as in, playing a pipe instrument with skill
>
> Snatsta – SNAH-zha) A glossy cut, as in a fine gem cutter

Bas fill – (BASH-fill) A recurring, returning death

Tha binn – (HAH-bin) I am mountain peak

Daigh – (DAY-ich) Adamant, obstinate

Diog – (DI-och) Ditch

Padraig – (Pad RAY-ig) Patrick - From the Roman name *Patricius*, which meant "nobleman" in Latin. A 5th-century saint, the patron saint of Ireland, adopted this name (his birth name was Sucat, (see Sagart). During his youth he was captured by Irish raiders and enslaved, but after six years of servitude he escaped to his home in Britain. Eventually he became a bishop and went back to Ireland as a missionary, where he succeeded in Christianizing the entire country.

Sagart – (SUH-gart) – Priest

'Lo lani – Royal Hawk (Tahitian)

A'ia'i – Bright like moonlight (Tahitian)

Damhsaigh Cloch – (DAHM-say Clokh) - Dancing Stone

Circle of the winter solstice – Stonehenge

Magda – (MAHG-dah) Bridey's secret foster mother outside the clan of the Duibhe

Sigrdifa – (SIG-urd-ifah) Means, beautiful Victory. Name of one of the seven primary Valkyries of Norse Mythology. She was thought to be the leader of the female warriors who hailed from the Northlands, the origin of the Stone of Falias.

Bryhildr – Name for the leader of the Valkyrie; one wielding much magic.

Dha' Teanga – (Jah TYEN-ga) – Two Tongue

Ri – (Righ) – King

Crionna – (KRIGH-awn-ah) – Advisor

Mananan Mac Lir – Son of the God of the Sea

Sonne – (Sawn) Sun (German)

Vannina – (Van-NEE-nah) Friendly (Swedish)

Svart Fagel – Blackbird

Korp - Raven

Names of Current Day Characters in Order of Appearance

O'Leary – (oh-LEAR-ee) - Descendant of Calf herder

Lenore – (len-ORR) – Light

Lee – (Lee) From a surname derived from Old English *leah* "meadow"...

Kieseling – (KEES-el-ing) From German, Kiesel-enge "Of river stone."

Nora – Honor

Bridey – Short for Bridget

Bridget – (BRIJ-it) – Nickname, Bridey - Goddess of healing and fertility, believed to assist women in labor. Known as a priestess of the goddess prior to conversion to Christianity

Cathbad – (CAT-bad) In Irish mythology, was a seer, Druid and advisor.

Lucas – Bringer of light and knowledge.

Finny – (FIN-ee) – From Fion. Means "fair" or "white" in Gaelic.

McDonough – Clan know for being tinkers in Ireland.

Walter – From a Germanic name meaning "ruler of the army".

Patrice – Noble

Mary – The meaning is not known for certain, but there are several theories including Sea of Bitterness, Rebelliousness.

Sigrid – (SIG-rid) Beautiful Victory. (Swedish)

O'Tarbh – (o-TARV) - Gaelic meaning Of the Bull.

Erland – From old Norse, (orlendr) meaning Foreigner.

Stryker-son – From Denmark meaning Of the Trades, a Tradesman or a Traveler.

Laroccia – Latin meaning The Rock

Terms, Places, Artifacts and Translations

Wheel of the Year – consists of four major fire festivals or solar festivals and four minor moon festivals. Together they create a wheel, which represents the cycle of the Celtic Year. During the Celtic Wheel of the Year, the Solstices and Equinoxes are celebrated in association with the sun and are defined at the moment when the sun reaches the exact moment when the shift between Light and dark takes place; and are therefore solar celebrations. The other four festivals in the Wheel are lunar celebrations. The Celts began the celebration of the Lunar Festivals, Samhian, (dark moon) Imbolc, (new Moon) Beltane, (full moon) and Lughnasadh (old moon) on the eve before. This may be the reason we find some conflicting sources at to whether February 1st or 2nd is the correct date on which Imbolc was and is celebrated. As with most Celtic celebrations, the eve of the date is when the Celts began the process of ritual. The Celts counted each day from sundown to sundown and so the ritual for Imbolc, for example, began on February 1st when the energy or the essence of the day was apparently mounting or waxing rather than dwindling or waning but the recognized date reserved for this festival is February 2nd.

Stone of Fal – Stone brought from Falias, one of four lands of magic, knowledge and learning. The myth is that the stone screams truth of Irish leaders, kings and destiny of the land. It is linked with royalty of the land of the Danann. The stone is the basis for the tale of the Sword and the Stone and is strongly linked with the Arthurian legend.

Sword of Nuada – Basis of protective magic of the Tuatha de Danann. Is linked to Excalibur in Arthurian legend. Suit of swords in the Tarot signifies air, masculine energy, challenge, intellect, double sided situations, opportunity, problems and solving, opening communication, rational thinking, strategy and intelligence.

Staff of Lugh– (wand) Made of Ash, is also linked with Odin who regained youth after hanging on a sacred ash tree for nine days before gaining esoteric wisdom and regaining youth. Also synonymous with the Christ tale, hanging on the tree before resurrection. Suit of wands in the Tarot signifies fire, masculine, positive growth and change through enterprise and distinction, joy, authority, creativity, virility, new beginnings, and action.

Shield of Lugh – Works in unison with the protective magic of the Sword of Nuada. Suit in the Tarot indicated by pentacles signifies earth, feminine, physical or practical self. The five points on the pentacle represent the five races on earth, hence the meaning of all things earthly: money, coin, job, financial material, efforts to get along materially.

Time of the Second Planting – May Day or May 1st.

Cauldron of Dagda or Ceridwen – Linked to the Holy Grail and the Arthurian legend. Dagda's cauldron of plenty overflowed with abundant, delicious meats; no hero left his bowl hungry. Linked with the cornucopia or horn of plenty. Ceridwen's cauldron was said to have contained elixir of knowledge. Suit of cups in the Tarot signifies water, feminine, emotions, feelings, instincts in relation to people.

Firbolg and the Fomorii- Tribes said to have populated Ireland prior to the Tuatha De Danann.

Gundestrup Cauldron – Silver cauldron found in 1891 in a peat bog near Gundestrup in Himmerland, Denmark. Consists of 13 plates made of 97% pure silver, one round, base plate, five long rectangular (interior) plates, seven shorter (exterior) plates, with the eighth one missing.

Bog Men – Two men radiocarbon dated to have lived around 400 B.C. One found in the Croghan Hill Bog near Tullamore, Ireland and the other about 25 miles east in the Clonycavan Bog, near Clonee, Ireland. Both found in 2003.

Old Croghan Man's torso was found with deep cuts under each nipple, piercings through the upper portion of each arm through which a rope was strung. He had a braided leather bracelet on his left wrist. His head and lower extremities had been removed.

Clonycavan man's body was found with a large wound cleaved in the chest and three wounds, as like from an ax to the head.

The Hill T'airg – (TEE-ear-ah) A place that produces or has much to yield. The Hill T'airg is conceived in this story to later be the Hill of Tara where the historical meeting between King Laoghaire and St. Patrick met and the balance between the Old Ways and Christianity was tipped toward the latter in Ireland in the 5th century. (See Padraig)

Baile Laoghaire – Home of the Laoghaire clan, later known as Dun Laoghaire (Fort of the Laoghaire clan) located on the east coast of Ireland just south of Dublin.

Lake of the Ivory Heron – An interpretation of the Gaelic terms (Lough meaning lake - corr, meaning heron - and eabhar meaning ivory), which translates into today's geographical site, Lough Corrib in Galway, just north of Galway Bay; the place where the Tuatha de Danann was said to have first settled in Ireland.

Sidhe – (Shee) When the first Gaels arrived in Ireland, they found that the Tuatha De Danann, the people of the goddess Dana, already populated and had control of the land. The Gaels fought the sons and daughters of the Danu in battle and defeated them, driving them 'underground' where it is said they remain to this day in the hollow hills or **sidhe** mounds. Often the sidhe is used to describe both the mounds and peoples said to live beneath them.

Valkyries – Tribe of warrior women of Norse Mythology

Norns – Land of the Goddesses of destiny, (Urd) Goddess of Fate (Verdandi) Goddess of Present, and (Skuld) Goddess of Future. Norns decided destinies of Gods as well as humankind.

Frey – (Fray) From Norse Myth, the god of crops, fruitfulness, love, peace and prosperity.

The Large Island to the east – The Island to the east of Ireland if England

Inlet between two vast lands – The Straits of Gibraltar between Western Europe and Africa.

Peninsula birthplace of Faidhe and Greenman's child – Rome, Italy

Stronghold for new religion – The Vatican in Rome

Warrior descendant of Faidhe and Greenman's child – Agricola, Roman general whose conquests included Wales, the western coast of Britain into Scotland 72-85 A.D.

One who brings new religion to Ireland and carries Faidhe's staff – Saint Patrick.

Saint Columbkill - Meaning "Dove of the Church" was an outstanding figure among the Gaelic missionary monks who, some of his advocates claim, introduced Christianity to the Kingdom of the Picts during the Early Medieval Period. He was one of the Twelve Apostles of Ireland.

Amadans – (AHM-a dahns) – Imbecile, fool, idiot

Skullduggery – (Skul-DUG-ery) Underhandedness, foul play

Cruinne Cumhacht – (KROO-in Kum-AKT) – Universal Power

Min shatz- My treasure

www.ingramcontent.com/pod-product-compliance
Lightning Source LLC
Chambersburg PA
CBHW080941020726
47505CB00009B/2108